G. A. Henty

The Life of a Knight

e-artnow 2020

G. A. Henty

The Life of a Knight

Historical Novels - Medieval Series: Winning His Spurs, St. George For England, The Lion of St. Mark, At Agincourt & A Knight of the White Cross

e-artnow, 2020
Contact: info@e-artnow.org

ISBN 978-80-273-3950-1

Contents

Winning His Spurs: A Tale of the Crusades	15
Chapter I. The Outlaws.	16
Chapter II. A Rescue.	21
Chapter III. The Capture Of Wortham Hold.	26
Chapter IV. The Crusades.	30
Chapter V. Preparations.	35
Chapter VI. The Lists.	40
Chapter VII. Revenge.	45
Chapter VIII. The Attack.	50
Chapter IX. The Princess Berengaria.	54
Chapter X. Pirates.	60
Chapter XI. In The Holy Land.	65
Chapter XII. The Accolade.	70
Chapter XIII. In The Hands Of The Saracens.	75
Chapter XIV. An Effort For Freedom.	80
Chapter XV. A Hermit's Tale.	85
Chapter XVI. A Fight Of Heroes.	90
Chapter XVII. An Alpine Storm.	95
Chapter XVIII. Sentenced To Death.	100
Chapter XIX. Dresden.	106
Chapter XX. Under The Greenwood.	110
Chapter XXI. The Attempt On The Convent.	116
Chapter XXII. A Dastardly Stratagem.	122
Chapter XXIII. The False And Perjured Knight.	128
Chapter XXIV. The Siege Of Evesham Castle.	133
Chapter XXV. In Search Of The King.	139
Chapter XXVI. King Richard's Return To England.	146
St. George For England: A Tale of Cressy and Poitiers	151
Preface.	152
Chapter I. A Wayfarer.	153
Chapter II. The Hut In The Marshes.	160
Chapter III. A Thwarted Plot.	166
Chapter IV. A Knight's Chain	172
Chapter V. The City Games.	179
Chapter VI. The Melee.	185

Chapter VII. The Young Esquire.	191
Chapter VIII. Off To The Wars.	198
Chapter IX. The Siege Of Hennebon.	205
Chapter X. A Place Of Refuge.	211
Chapter XI. A Stormy Interview.	217
Chapter XII. Jacob Van Artevelde.	223
Chapter XIII. The White Ford.	229
Chapter XIV. Cressy.	235
Chapter XV. The Siege Of A Fortalice.	241
Chapter XVI. A Prisoner.	247
Chapter XVII. The Capture Of Calais.	254
Chapter XVIII. The Black Death.	260
Chapter XIX. By Land And Sea.	266
Chapter XX. Poitiers.	272
Chapter XXI. The Jacquerie.	278
Chapter XXII. Victory And Death.	285
The Lion of St. Mark: A Story of Venice in the Fourteenth Century	293
Preface.	294
Chapter 1: Venice.	295
Chapter 2: A Conspiracy.	302
Chapter 3: On The Grand Canal.	310
Chapter 4: Carried Off.	318
Chapter 5: Finding A Clue.	327
Chapter 6: The Hut On San Nicolo.	336
Chapter 7: On Board A Trader.	345
Chapter 8: An Attack By Pirates.	353
Chapter 9: The Capture Of The Lido.	361
Chapter 10: Recaptured.	370
Chapter 11: The Battle Of Antium.	378
Chapter 12: In Mocenigo's Power.	387
Chapter 13: The Pirates' Raid.	395
Chapter 14: The End Of The Persecutor.	403
Chapter 15: The Battle Of Pola.	411
Chapter 16: The Recapture Of The Pluto.	419
Chapter 17: An Ungrateful Republic.	427
Chapter 18: The Release Of Pisani.	434

Chapter 19: The Siege Of Chioggia.	443
Chapter 20: The Triumph Of Venice.	452
At Agincourt: A Tale of the White Hoods of Paris	459
Preface	460
Chapter I A Feudal Castle	461
Chapter II Troubles In France	469
Chapter III A Siege	476
Chapter IV A Fatal Accident	484
Chapter V Hostages	492
Chapter VI In Paris	500
Chapter VII In The Streets Of Paris	508
Chapter VIII A Riot	515
Chapter IX A Stout Defence	522
Chapter X After The Fray	530
Chapter XI Danger Threatened	537
Chapter XII In Hiding	544
Chapter XIII The Masters Of Paris	552
Chapter XIV Planning Massacre	560
Chapter XV A Rescue	568
Chapter XVI The Escape	575
Chapter XVII A Long Pause	583
Chapter XVIII Katarina	590
Chapter XIX Agincourt	597
Chapter XX Penshurst	605
A Knight of the White Cross: A Tale of the Siege of Rhodes	615
Preface	616
Chapter I The King Maker	617
Chapter II The Battle Of Tewkesbury	625
Chapter III The Grand Master's Page	633
Chapter IV A Professed Knight	641
Chapter V Scourges Of The Sea	649
Chapter VI Knighted	657
Chapter VII A First Command	664
Chapter VIII An Evening At Rhodes	672
Chapter IX With The Galley Slaves	680
Chapter X. A Plot Discovered.	688
Chapter XI In Command Of A Galley	696

Chapter XII The Boy Galley	704
Chapter XIII The First Prizes	711
Chapter XIV The Corsair Fleet	721
Chapter XV A Splendid Exploit	729
Chapter XVI Festivities	736
Chapter XVII Captured	745
Chapter XVIII A Kind Master	754
Chapter XIX Escape	764
Chapter XX Beleaguered	772
Chapter XXI The Fort Of St. Nicholas	780
Chapter XXII The Struggle At The Breach	788
Chapter XXIII The Reward Of Valour	799

Winning His Spurs: A Tale of the Crusades

1882

Chapter I
The Outlaws.

It was a bright morning in the month of August, when a lad of some fifteen years of age, sitting on a low wall, watched party after party of armed men riding up to the castle of the Earl of Evesham. A casual observer glancing at his curling hair and bright open face, as also at the fashion of his dress, would at once have assigned to him a purely Saxon origin; but a keener eye would have detected signs that Norman blood ran also in his veins, for his figure was lither and lighter, his features more straightly and shapely cut, than was common among Saxons. His dress consisted of a tight-fitting jerkin, descending nearly to his knees. The material was a light-blue cloth, while over his shoulder hung a short cloak of a darker hue. His cap was of Saxon fashion, and he wore on one side a little plume of a heron. In a somewhat costly belt hung a light short sword, while across his knees lay a crossbow, in itself almost a sure sign of its bearer being of other than Saxon blood. The boy looked anxiously as party after party rode past towards the castle.

"I would give something," he said, "to know what wind blows these knaves here. From every petty castle in the Earl's feu the retainers seem hurrying here. Is he bent, I wonder, on settling once and for all his quarrels with the Baton of Wortham? or can he be intending to make a clear sweep of the woods? Ah! here comes my gossip Hubert; he may tell me the meaning of this gathering."

Leaping to his feet, the speaker started at a brisk walk to meet a jovial-looking personage coming down from the direction of the castle. The new comer was dressed in the attire of a falconer, and two dogs followed at his heels.

"Ah, Master Cuthbert," he said, "what brings you so near to the castle? It is not often that you favour us with your presence."

"I am happier in the woods, as you well know, and was on my way thither but now, when I paused at the sight of all these troopers flocking in to Evesham. What enterprise has Sir Walter on hand now, think you?"

"The earl keeps his own counsel," said the falconer, "but methinks a shrewd guess might be made at the purport of the gathering. It was but three days since that his foresters were beaten back by the landless men, whom they caught in the very act of cutting up a fat buck. As thou knowest, my lord though easy and well-disposed to all, and not fond of harassing and driving the people as are many of his neighbours, is yet to the full as fanatical anent his forest privileges as the worst of them. They tell me that when the news came in of the poor figure that his foresters cut with broken bows and draggled plumes-for the varlets had soused them in a pond of not over savoury water-he swore a great oath that he would clear the forest of the bands. It may be, indeed, that this gathering is for the purpose of falling in force upon that evil-disposed and most treacherous baron, Sir John of Wortham, who has already begun to harry some of the outlying lands, and has driven off, I hear, many heads of cattle. It is a quarrel which will have to be fought out sooner or later, and the sooner the better, say I. Although I am no man of war, and love looking after my falcons or giving food to my dogs far more than exchanging hard blows, yet would I gladly don the buff and steel coat to aid in levelling the keep of that robber and tyrant, Sir John of Wortham."

"Thanks, good Hubert," said the lad. "I must not stand gossiping here. The news you have told me, as you know, touches me closely, for I would not that harm should come to the forest men."

"Let it not out, I beseech thee, Cuthbert, that the news came from me, for temperate as Sir Walter is at most times, he would, methinks, give me short shift did he know that the wagging of my tongue might have given warning through which the outlaws of the Chase should slip through his fingers."

"Fear not, Hubert; I can be mum when the occasion needs. Can you tell me farther, when the bands now gathering are likely to set forth?"

"In brief breathing space," the falconer replied. "Those who first arrived I left swilling beer, and devouring pies and other provisions cooked for them last night, and from what I hear, they will set forth as soon as the last comer has arrived. Whichever be their quarry, they will try to fall upon it before the news of their arrival is bruited abroad."

With a wave of his hand to the falconer the boy started. Leaving the road, and striking across the slightly undulated country dotted here and there by groups of trees, the lad ran at a brisk trot, without stopping to halt or breathe, until after half an hour's run he arrived at the entrance of a building, whose aspect proclaimed it to be the abode of a Saxon franklin of some importance. It would not be called a castle, but was rather a fortified house, with a few windows looking without, and surrounded by a moat crossed by a drawbridge, and capable of sustaining anything short of a real attack. Erstwood had but lately passed into Norman hands, and was indeed at present owned by a Saxon. Sir William de Lance, the father of the lad who is now entering its portals, was a friend and follower of the Earl of Evesham; and soon after his lord had married Gweneth the heiress of all these fair lands-given to him by the will of the king, to whom by the death of her father she became a ward-Sir William had married Editha, the daughter and heiress of the franklin of Erstwood, a cousin and dear friend of the new Countess of Evesham.

In neither couple could the marriage at first have been called one of inclination on the part of the ladies, but love came after marriage. Although the knights and barons of the Norman invasion would, no doubt, be considered rude and rough in these days of broadcloth and civilization, yet their manners were gentle and polished by the side of those of the rough though kindly Saxon franklins; and although the Saxon maids were doubtless as patriotic as their fathers and mothers, yet the female mind is greatly led by gentle manners and courteous address. Thus then, when bidden or forced to give their hands to the Norman knights, they speedily accepted their lot, and for the most part grew contented and happy enough. In their changed circumstances it was pleasanter to ride by the side of their Norman husbands, surrounded by a gay cavalcade, to hawk and to hunt, than to discharge the quiet duties of mistress of a Saxon farm-house. In many cases, of course, their lot was rendered wretched by the violence and brutality of their lords; but in the majority they were well satisfied with their lot, and these mixed marriages did more to bring the peoples together and weld them in one, than all the laws and decrees of the Norman sovereigns.

This had certainly been the case with Editha, whose marriage with Sir William had been one of the greatest happiness. She had lost him, three years before the story begins, fighting in Normandy, in one of the innumerable wars in which our first Norman kings were constantly involved. On entering the gates of Erstwood, Cuthbert had rushed hastily to the room where his mother was sitting with three or four of her maidens, engaged in work.

"I want to speak to you at once, mother," he said.

"What is it now, my son?" said his mother, who was still young and very comely. Waving her hand to the girls, they left her.

"Mother," he said, when they were alone, "I fear me that Sir Walter is about to make a great raid upon the outlaws. Armed men have been coming in all the morning from the castles round, and if it be not against the Baron de Wortham that these preparations are intended, and methinks it is not, it must needs be against the landless men."

"What would you do, Cuthbert?" his mother asked anxiously. "It will not do for you to be found meddling in these matters. At present you stand well in the favour of the Earl, who loves you for the sake of his wife, to whom you are kin, and of your father, who did him good liegeman's service."

"But, mother, I have many friends in the wood. There is Cnut, their chief, your own first cousin, and many others of our friends, all good men and true, though forced by the cruel Norman laws to refuge in the woods."

"What would you do?" again his mother asked.

"I would take Ronald my pony and ride to warn them of the danger that threatens."

"You had best go on foot, my son. Doubtless men have been set to see that none from the Saxon homesteads carry the warning to the woods. The distance is not beyond your reach, for you have often wandered there, and on foot you can evade the eye of the watchers; but one thing, my son, you must promise, and that is, that in no case, should the Earl and his bands meet with the outlaws, will you take part in any fray or struggle."

"That will I willingly, mother," he said. "I have no cause for offence against the castle or the forest, and my blood and my kin are with both. I would fain save shedding of blood in a quarrel like this. I hope that the time may come when Saxon and Norman may fight side by side, and I maybe there to see."

A few minutes later, having changed his blue doublet for one of more sober and less noticeable colour, Cuthbert started for the great forest, which then stretched to within a mile of Erstwood. In those days a large part of the country was covered with forest, and the policy of the Normans in preserving these woods for the chase, tended to prevent the increase of cultivation.

The farms and cultivated lands were all held by Saxons, who although nominally handed over to the nobles to whom William and his successors had given the fiefs, saw but little of their Norman masters. These stood, indeed, much in the position in which landlords stand to their tenants, payment being made, for the most part, in produce. At the edge of the wood the trees grew comparatively far apart, but as Cuthbert proceeded farther into its recesses, the trees in the virgin forest stood thick and close together. Here and there open glades ran across each other, and in these his sharp eye, accustomed to the forest, could often see the stags starting away at the sound of his footsteps.

It was a full hour's journey before Cuthbert reached the point for which he was bound. Here, in an open space, probably cleared by a storm ages before, and overshadowed by giant trees, was a group of men of all ages and appearances. Some were occupied in stripping the skin off a buck which hung from the bough of one of the trees. Others were roasting portions of the carcass of another deer. A few sat apart, some talking, others busy in making arrows, while a few lay asleep on the greensward. As Cuthbert entered the clearing, several of the party rose to their feet.

"Ah, Cuthbert," shouted a man of almost gigantic stature, who appeared to be one of the leaders of the party, "what brings you here, lad, so early? You are not wont to visit us till even, when you can lay your crossbow at a stag by moonlight."

"No, no, Cousin Cnut," Cuthbert said, "thou canst not say that I have ever broken the forest laws, though I have looked on often and often, whilst you have done so."

"The abettor is as bad as the thief," laughed Cnut, "and if the foresters caught us in the act, I wot they would make but little difference whether it was the shaft of my longbow or the quarrel from thy crossbow which brought down the quarry. But again, lad, why comest thou here? for I see by the sweat on your face and by the heaving of your sides that you have run fast and far."

"I have, Cnut; I have not once stopped for breathing since I left Erstwood. I have come to warn you of danger. The earl is preparing for a raid."

Cnut laughed somewhat disdainfully.

"He has raided here before, and I trow has carried off no game. The landless men of the forest can hold their own against a handful of Norman knights and retainers in their own home."

"Ay," said Cuthbert, "but this will be no common raid. This morning bands from all the holds within miles round are riding in, and at least 500 men-at-arms are likely to do chase today."

"Is it so?" said Cnut, while exclamations of surprise, but not of apprehension, broke from those standing round. "If that be so, lad, you have done us good service indeed. With fair warning we can slip through the fingers of ten times 500 men, but if they came upon us unawares, and hemmed us in it would fare but badly with us, though we should, I doubt not give a good account of them before their battle-axes and maces ended the strife. Have you any idea by which road they will enter the forest, or what are their intentions?"

"I know not," Cuthbert said; "all that I gathered was that the earl intended to sweep the forest, and to put an end to the breaches of the laws, not to say of the rough treatment that his foresters have met with at your hands. You had best, methinks, be off before Sir Walter and his heavily-armed men are here. The forest, large as it is, will scarce hold you both, and methinks you had best shift your quarters to Langholm Chase until the storm has passed."

"To Langholm be it, then," said Cnut, "though I love not the place. Sir John of Wortham is a worse neighbour by far than the earl. Against the latter we bear no malice, he is a good knight and a fair lord; and could he free himself of the Norman notions that the birds of the air, and the beasts of the field, and the fishes of the water, all belong to Normans, and that we Saxons have no share in them, I should have no quarrel with him. He grinds not his neighbours, he is content with a fair tithe of the produce, and as between man and man is a fair judge without favour. The baron is a fiend incarnate; did he not fear that he would lose by so doing, he would gladly cut the throats, or burn, or drown, or hang every Saxon within twenty miles of his hold. He is a disgrace to his order, and some day when our band gathers a little stronger, we will burn his nest about his ears."

"It will be a hard nut to crack," Cuthbert said, laughing. "With such arms as you have in the forest the enterprise would be something akin to scaling the skies."

"Ladders and axes will go far, lad, and the Norman men-at-arms have learned to dread our shafts. But enough of the baron; if we must be his neighbours for a time, so be it."

"You have heard, my mates," he said, turning to his comrades gathered around him, "what Cuthbert tells us. Are you of my opinion, that it is better to move away till the storm is past, than to fight against heavy odds, without much chance of either booty or victory?"

A general chorus proclaimed that the outlaws approved of the proposal for a move to Langholm Chase. The preparations were simple. Bows were taken down from the boughs on which they were hanging, quivers slung across the backs, short cloaks thrown over the shoulders. The deer was hurriedly dismembered, and the joints fastened to a pole slung on the shoulders of two of the men. The drinking-cups, some of which were of silver, looking strangely out of place among the rough horn implements and platters, were bundled together, carried a short distance and dropped among some thick bushes for safety; and then the band started for Wortham.

With a cordial farewell and many thanks to Cuthbert, who declined their invitations to accompany them, the retreat to Langholm commenced.

Cuthbert, not knowing in which direction the bands were likely to approach, remained for a while motionless, intently listening.

In a quarter of an hour he heard the distant note of a bugle.

It was answered in three different directions, and Cuthbert, who knew every path and glade of the forest, was able pretty accurately to surmise those by which the various bands were commencing to enter the wood.

Knowing that they were still a long way off, he advanced as rapidly as he could in the direction in which they were coming. When by the sound of distant voices and the breaking of branches he knew that one at least of the parties was near at hand, he rapidly climbed a thick tree and ensconced himself in the branches, and there watched, secure and hidden from the sharpest eye, the passage of a body of men-at-arms fully a hundred strong, led by Sir Walter himself, accompanied by some half dozen of his knights.

When they had passed, Cuthbert again slipped down the tree and made at all speed for home. He reached it, so far as he knew without having been observed by a single passer-by.

After a brief talk with his mother, he started for the castle, as his appearance there would divert any suspicion that might arise; and it would also appear natural that seeing the movements of so large a body of men, he should go up to gossip with his acquaintances there.

When distant a mile from Evesham, he came upon a small party.

On a white palfrey rode Margaret, the little daughter of the earl. She was accompanied by her nurse and two retainers on foot.

Cuthbert—who was a great favourite with the earl's daughter, for whom he frequently brought pets, such as nests of young owlets, falcons, and other creatures—was about to join the party when from a clump of trees near burst a body of ten mounted men.

Without a word they rode straight at the astonished group. The retainers were cut to the ground before they had thought of drawing a sword in defence.

The nurse was slain by a blow with a battle-axe, and Margaret, snatched from her palfrey, was thrown across the saddle-bow of one of the mounted men, who then with his comrades dashed off at full speed.

Chapter II
A Rescue.

The whole of the startling scene of the abduction of the Earl of Evesham's daughter occupied but a few seconds. Cuthbert was so astounded at the sudden calamity that he remained rooted to the ground at the spot where, fortunately for himself, unnoticed by the assailants, he had stood when they first burst from their concealment.

For a short time he hesitated as to the course he should take.

The men-at-arms who remained in the castle were scarce strong enough to rescue the child, whose captors would no doubt be reinforced by a far stronger party lurking near.

The main body of Sir Walter's followers were deep in the recesses of the forest, and this lay altogether out of the line for Wortham, and there would be no chance whatever of bringing them up in time to cut off the marauders on their way back.

There remained only the outlaws, who by this time would be in Langholm Forest, perhaps within a mile or two of the castle itself.

The road by which the horsemen would travel would be far longer than the direct line across country, and he resolved at once to strain every nerve to reach his friends in time to get them to interpose between the captors of the Lady Margaret and their stronghold.

For an instant he hesitated whether to run back to Erstwood to get a horse; but he decided that it would be as quick to go on foot, and far easier so to find the outlaws.

These thoughts occupied but a few moments, and he at once started at the top of his speed for his long run across the country.

Had Cuthbert been running in a race of hare and hound, he would assuredly have borne away the prize from most boys of his age. At headlong pace he made across the country, every foot of which, as far as the edge of Langholm Chase, he knew by heart.

The distance to the woods was some twelve miles, and in an hour and a half from the moment of his starting Cuthbert was deep within its shades. Where he would be likely to find the outlaws he knew not; and, putting a whistle to his lips, he shrilly blew the signal, which would, he knew, be recognized by any of the band within hearing.

He thought that he heard an answer, but was not certain, and again dashed forward, almost as speedily as if he had but just started.

Five minutes later a man stood in the glade up which he was running. He recognized him at once as one of Cnut's party.

"Where are the band?" he gasped.

"Half a mile or so to the right," replied the man.

Guided by the man, Cuthbert ran at full speed, till, panting and scarce able to speak, he arrived at the spot where Cnut's band were gathered.

In a few words he told them what had happened, and although they had just been chased by the father of the captured child, there was not a moment of hesitation in promising their aid to rescue her from a man whom they regarded as a far more bitter enemy, both of themselves and their race.

"I fear we shall be too late to cut them off," Cnut said, "they have so long a start; but at least we will waste no time in gossiping."

Winding a horn to call together some of the members of the band who had scattered, and leaving one at the meeting-place to give instructions to the rest, Cnut, followed by those assembled there, went off at a swinging trot through the glades towards Wortham Castle.

After a rapid calculation of distances, and allowing for the fact that the baron's men-knowing that Sir Walter's retainers and friends were all deep in the forest, and even if they heard of the outrage could not be on their traces for hours-would take matters quietly, Cnut concluded that they had arrived in time.

Turning off, they made their way along the edge of the wood to the point where the road from Evesham ran through the forest.

Scarcely had the party reached this point when they heard a faint clatter of steel.

"Here they come!" exclaimed Cuthbert.

Cnut gave rapid directions, and the band took up their posts behind the trees, on either side of the path.

"Remember," Cnut said, "above all things be careful not to hit the child, but pierce the horse on which she is riding. The instant he falls, rush forward. We must trust to surprise to give us the victory."

Three minutes later the head of a band of horsemen was seen through the trees. They were some thirty in number, and, closely grouped as they were together, the watchers behind the trees could not see the form of the child carried in their midst.

When they came abreast of the concealed outlaws, Cnut gave a sharp whistle, and fifty arrows flew from tree and bush into the closely gathered party of horsemen. More than half their number fell at once; some, drawing their swords, endeavoured to rush at their concealed foes, while others dashed forward in the hope of riding through the snare into which they had fallen. Cuthbert had levelled his crossbow, but had not fired; he was watching with intense anxiety for a glimpse of the bright-coloured dress of the child. Soon he saw a horseman separate himself from the rest and dash forward at full speed. Several arrows flew by him, and one or two struck the horse on which he rode.

The animal, however, kept on its way.

Cuthbert levelled his crossbow on the low arm of a tree, and as the rider came abreast of him touched the trigger, and the steel-pointed quarrel flew true and strong against the temple of the passing horseman. He fell from his horse like a stone and the well-trained animal at once stood still by the side of his rider.

Cuthbert leapt forward, and to his delight the child at once opened her arms and cried in a joyous tone, —

"Cuthbert!"

The fight was still raging fiercely, and Cuthbert, raising her from the ground, ran with her into the wood, where they remained hidden until the combat ceased, and the last survivors of the Baron's band had ridden past towards the castle.

Then Cuthbert went forward with his charge and joined the band of outlaws, who, absorbed in the fight, had not witnessed the incident of her rescue, and now received them with loud shouts of joy and triumph.

"This is a good day's work indeed for all," Cuthbert said; "it will make of the earl a firm friend instead of a bitter enemy; and I doubt not that better days are dawning for Evesham Forest."

A litter was speedily made with boughs, on this Margaret was placed, and on the shoulders of two stout foresters started for home, Cnut and Cuthbert walking beside, and a few of the band keeping at a short distance behind, as a sort of rear-guard should the Baron attempt to regain his prey.

There was now no cause for speed, and Cuthbert in truth could scarce drag one foot before another, for he had already traversed over twenty miles, the greater portion of the distance at his highest rate of speed.

Cnut offered to have a litter made for him also, but this Cuthbert indignantly refused; however, in the forest they came upon the hut of a small cultivator, who had a rough forest pony, which was borrowed for Cuthbert's use.

It was late in the afternoon before they came in sight of Evesham Castle. From the distance could be seen bodies of armed men galloping towards it, and it was clear that only now the party were returning from the wood, and had learned the news of the disappearance of the Earl's daughter, and of the finding of the bodies of her attendants.

Presently they met one of the mounted retainers riding at headlong speed.

"Have you heard or seen anything," he shouted, as he approached, "of the Lady Margaret? She is missing, and foul play has taken place."

"Here I am, Rudolph," cried the child, sitting up on the rude litter.

The horseman gave a cry of astonishment and pleasure, and without a word wheeled his horse and galloped past back at headlong speed towards the castle.

As Cuthbert and the party approached the gate, the earl himself, surrounded by his knights and followers, rode out hastily from the gate and halted in front of the little party. The litter was lowered, and as he dismounted from his horse his daughter sprang out and leapt into his arms.

For a few minutes the confusion and babble of tongues were too great for anything to be heard, but Cuthbert, as soon as order was somewhat restored, stated what had happened, and the earl was moved to fury at the news of the outrage which had been perpetrated by the Baron of Wortham upon his daughter and at the very gates of his castle, and also at the thought that she should have been saved by the bravery and devotion of the very men against whom he had so lately been vowing vengeance in the depths of the forest.

"This is not a time," he said to Cnut, "for talking or making promises, but be assured that henceforth the deer of Evesham Chase are as free to you and your men as to me. Forest laws or no forest laws, I will no more lift a hand against men to whom I owe so much. Come when you will to the castle, my friends, and let us talk over what can be done to erase your outlawry and restore you to an honest career again."

Cuthbert returned home tired, but delighted with his day's work, and Dame Editha was surprised indeed with the tale of adventure he had to tell. The next morning he went over to the castle, and heard that a grand council had been held the evening before, and that it had been determined to attack Wortham Castle and to raze it to the ground.

Immediately on hearing of his arrival, the earl, after again expressing his gratitude for the rescue of his daughter, asked him if he would go into the forest and invite the outlaws to join their forces with those of the castle to attack the baron.

Cuthbert willingly undertook the mission, as he felt that this alliance would further strengthen the position of the forest men.

When he arrived there was some considerable consultation and discussion between the outlaws as to the expediency of mixing themselves in the quarrels between the Norman barons. However, Cnut persuaded them that as the Baron of Wortham was an enemy and oppressor of all Saxons, it was in fact their own quarrel that they were fighting rather than that of the earl, and they therefore agreed to give their aid, and promised to be at the rendezvous outside the castle to be attacked, soon after dawn next morning. Cuthbert returned with the news, which gave great satisfaction to the earl.

The castle was now a scene of bustle and business; armourers were at work repairing headpieces and breastplates, sharpening swords and battle-axes, while the fletchers prepared sheaves of arrows. In the courtyard a number of men were engaged oiling the catapults, ballistas, and other machines for hurling stones. All were discussing the chances of the assault, for it was no easy matter which they had set themselves to do. Wortham Hold was an extremely strong one, and it needed all and more than all the machines at their disposal to undertake so formidable an operation as a siege.

The garrison, too, were strong and desperate; and the baron, knowing what must follow his outrage of the day before, would have been sure to send off messengers round the country begging his friends to come to his assistance. Cuthbert had begged permission of his mother to ask the earl to allow him to join as a volunteer, but she would not hear of it. Neither would she suffer him to mingle with the foresters. The utmost that he could obtain was that he might go as a spectator, with strict injunctions to keep himself out of the fray, and as far as possible beyond bow-shot of the castle wall.

It was a force of some 400 strong that issued from the wood early next morning to attack the stronghold at Wortham. The force consisted of some ten or twelve knights and barons, some 150 or 160 Norman men-at-arms, a miscellaneous gathering of other retainers, 200 strong, and some eighty of the forest men. These last were not to fight under the earl's banner, but were to act on their own account. There were among them outlaws, escaped serfs, and some men guilty of bloodshed. The earl then could not have suffered these men to fight under his flag until purged in some way of their offences.

This arrangement suited the foresters well.

Their strong point was shooting; and by taking up their own position, and following their own tactics, under the leadership of Cnut, they would be able to do far more execution, and that with less risk to themselves, than if compelled to fight according to the fashion of the Normans.

As they approached the castle a trumpet was blown, and the herald, advancing, demanded its surrender, stigmatized the Baron of Wortham as a false knight and a disgrace to his class, and warned all those within the castle to abstain from giving him aid or countenance, but to submit themselves to the earl, Sir Walter of Evesham, the representative of King Richard.

The reply to the summons was a burst of taunting laughter from the walls; and scarcely had the herald withdrawn, than a flight of arrows showed that the besieged were perfectly ready for the fray.

Indeed, the baron had not been idle. Already the dispute between himself and the earl had come to such a point that it was certain that sooner or later open hostilities would break out.

He had therefore been for some time quietly accumulating a large store of provisions and munitions of war, and strengthening the castle in every way.

The moat had been cleaned out, and filled to the brim with water. Great quantities of heavy stones had been accumulated on the most exposed points of the walls, in readiness to hurl upon any who might try to climb. Huge sheaves of arrows and piles of crossbow bolts, were in readiness, and in all, save the number of men, Wortham had for weeks been prepared for the siege.

On the day when the attempt to carry off the earl's daughter had failed, the baron, seeing that his bold stroke to obtain a hostage which would have enabled him to make his own terms with the earl, had been thwarted, knew that the struggle was inevitable.

Fleet messengers had been sent in all directions. To Gloucester and Hereford, Stafford, and even Oxford, men had ridden, with letters to the baron's friends, beseeching them to march to his assistance.

"I can," he said, "defend my hold for weeks. But it is only by aid from without that I can finally hope to break the power of this braggart earl."

Many of those to whom he addressed his call had speedily complied with his demand, while those at a distance might be expected to reply later to the appeal.

There were many among the barons who considered the mildness of the Earl of Evesham towards the Saxons in his district to be a mistake, and who, although not actually approving of the tyranny and brutality of the Baron of Wortham, yet looked upon his cause to some extent as their own.

The Castle of Wortham stood upon ground but very slightly elevated above the surrounding country. A deep and wide moat ran round it, and this could, by diverting a rivulet, be filled at will.

From the edge of the moat the walls rose high, and with strong flanking towers and battlements.

There were strong works also beyond the moat opposite to the drawbridge; while in the centre of the castle rose the keep, from whose summit the archers, and the machines for casting stones and darts, could command the whole circuit of defence.

As Cuthbert, accompanied by one of the hinds of the farm, took his post high up in a lofty tree, where at his ease he could command a view of the proceedings, he marvelled much in what manner an attack upon so fair a fortress would be commenced.

"It will be straightforward work to attack the outwork," he said, "but that once won, I see not how we are to proceed against the castle itself. The machines that the earl has will scarcely hurl stones strong enough even to knock the mortar from the walls. Ladders are useless where they cannot be planted; and if the garrison are as brave as the castle is strong, methinks that the earl has embarked upon a business that will keep him here till next spring."

There was little time lost in commencing the conflict.

The foresters, skirmishing up near to the castle, and taking advantage of every inequality in the ground, of every bush and tuft of high grass, worked up close to the moat, and then opened a heavy fire with their bows against the men-at-arms on the battlements, and prevented their using the machines against the main force now advancing to the attack upon the outwork.

This was stoutly defended. But the impetuosity of the earl, backed as it was by the gallantry of the knights serving under him, carried all obstacles.

The narrow moat which encircled this work was speedily filled with great bundles of brushwood, which had been prepared the previous night. Across these the assailants rushed.

Some thundered at the gate with their battle-axes, while others placed ladders by which, although several times hurled backwards by the defenders, they finally succeeded in getting a footing on the wall.

Once there, the combat was virtually over.

The defenders were either cut down or taken prisoners, and in two hours after the assault began, the outwork of Wortham Castle was taken.

This, however, was but the commencement of the undertaking, and it had cost more than twenty lives to the assailants.

They were now, indeed, little nearer to capturing the castle than they had been before.

The moat was wide and deep. The drawbridge had been lifted at the instant that the first of the assailants gained a footing upon the wall. And now that the outwork was captured, a storm of arrows, stones, and other missiles was poured into it from the castle walls, and rendered it impossible for any of its new masters, to show themselves above it.

Seeing that any sudden attack was impossible, the earl now directed a strong body to cut down trees, and prepare a movable bridge to throw across the moat.

This would be a work of fully two days; and in the meantime Cuthbert returned to the farm.

Chapter III
The Capture Of Wortham Hold.

Upon his return home, after relating to his mother the events of the morning's conflict, Cuthbert took his way to the cottage inhabited by an old man who had in his youth been a mason.

"Have I not heard, Gurth," he said, "that you helped to build the Castle of Wortham?"

"No, no, young sir," he said; "old as I am, I was a child when the castle was built. My father worked at it, and it cost him, and many others, his life."

"And how was that, prithee?" asked Cuthbert.

"He was, with several others, killed by the baron, the grandfather of the present man, when the work was finished."

"But why was that, Gurth?"

"We were but Saxon swine," said Gurth bitterly, "and a few of us more or less mattered not. We were then serfs of the baron. But my mother fled with me on the news of my father's death. For years we remained far away, with some friends in a forest near Oxford. Then she pined for her native air, and came back and entered the service of the franklin."

"But why should your mother have taken you away?" Cuthbert asked.

"She always believed, Master Cuthbert, that my father was killed by the baron, to prevent him giving any news of the secrets of the castle. He and some others had been kept in the walls for many months, and were engaged in the making of secret passages."

"That is just what I came to ask you, Gurth. I have heard something of this story before, and now that we are attacking Wortham Castle, and the earl has sworn to level it to the ground, it is of importance if possible to find out whether any of the secret passages lead beyond the castle, and if so, where. Almost all the castles have, I have been told, an exit by which the garrison can at will make sorties or escape; and I thought that maybe you might have heard enough to give us some clue as to the existence of such a passage at Wortham."

The old man thought for some time in silence, and then said, —

"I may be mistaken, but methinks a diligent search in the copse near the stream might find the mouth of the outlet."

"What makes you think that this is so, Gurth?"

"I had been with my mother to carry some clothes to my father on the last occasion on which I saw him. As we neared the castle I saw my father and three other of the workmen, together with the baron, coming down from the castle towards the spot. As my mother did not wish to approach while the baron was at hand, we stood within the trees at the edge of the wood, and watched what was being done. The baron came with them down to the bushes, and then they again came out, crossed the river, and one of them cut some willows, peeled them, and erected the white staves in a line towards the castle. They walked for a bit on each side, and seemed to be making calculations. Then they went back into the castle, and I never saw my father again."

"Why did you not go in at once according to your intention?"

"Because my mother said that she thought some important work was on hand, and that maybe the baron would not like that women should know aught of it, for he was of suspicious and evil mind. More than this I know not. The castle had already been finished, and most of the masons discharged. There were, however, a party of serfs kept at work, and also some masons, and rumour had it that they were engaged in making the secret passages. Whether it was so or not I cannot say, but I know that none of that party ever left the castle alive. It was given out that a bad fever had raged there, but none believed it; and the report went about, and was I doubt not true, that all had been killed, to preserve the secret of the passage."

Cuthbert lost no time in making use of the information that he had gained.

Early next morning, at daybreak, he started on his pony to Wortham.

As he did not wish the earl or his followers to know the facts that he had learned until they were proved, he made his way round the camp of the besiegers, and by means of his whistle called one of the foresters to him.

"Where is Cnut?" he asked.

"He is with a party occupied in making ladders."

"Go to him," Cuthbert said, "and tell him to withdraw quietly and make his way here. I have an important matter on which I wish to speak to him,'"

Cnut arrived in a few minutes, somewhat wondering at the message. He brightened greatly when Cuthbert told him what he had learned.

"This is indeed important," he said. "We will lose no time in searching the copse you speak of. You and I, together with two of my most trusty men, with axes to clear away the brush, will do. At present a thing of this sort had best be kept between as few as may be."

They started at once and soon came down upon the stream.

It ran at this point in a little valley, some twenty or thirty feet deep. On the bank not far from the castle grew a small wood, and it was in this that Cuthbert hoped to find the passage spoken of by Gurth.

The trees and brushwood were so thick that it was apparent at once that if the passage had ever existed it had been unused for some years.

The woodmen were obliged to chop down dozens of young saplings to make their way up from the water towards the steeper part of the bank.

The wood was some fifty yards in length, and as it was uncertain at which point the passage had come out, a very minute search had to be made.

"What do you think it would be like, Cnut?" Cuthbert asked.

"Like enough to a rabbit-hole, or more likely still there would be no hole whatever. We must look for moss and greenery, for it is likely that such would have been planted, so as to conceal the door from any passer-by, while yet allowing a party from inside to cut their way through it without difficulty."

After a search of two hours, Cnut decided that the only place in the copse in which it was likely that the entrance to a passage could be hidden, was a spot where the ground was covered thickly with ivy and trailing plants.

"It looks level enough with the rest," Cuthbert said.

"Ay, lad, but we know not what lies behind this thick screen of ivy. Thrust in that staff."

One of the woodmen began to probe with the end of a staff among the ivy. For some time he was met by the solid ground, but presently the butt of the staff went through suddenly, pitching him on his head, amidst a suppressed laugh from his comrades.

"Here it is, if anywhere," said Cnut, and with their billhooks they at once began to clear away the thickly grown creepers.

Five minutes' work was sufficient to show a narrow cut, some two feet wide, in the hill side, at the end of which stood a low door.

"Here it is," said Cnut, with triumph, "and the castle is ours. Thanks, Cuthbert, for your thought and intelligence. It has not been used lately, that is clear," he went on. "These creepers have not been moved for years. Shall we go and tell the earl of our discovery? What think you, Cuthbert?"

"I think we had better not," Cuthbert said. "We might not succeed in getting in, as the passage may have fallen farther along; but I will speak to him and tell him that we have something on hand which may alter his dispositions for fighting to-morrow."

Cuthbert made his way to the earl, who had taken possession of a small cottage a short distance from the castle.

"What can I do for you?" Sir Walter said.

"I want to ask you, sir, not to attack the castle to-morrow until you see a white flag waved from the keep."

"But how on earth is a white flag to be raised from the keep?"

"It may be," Cuthbert said, "that I have some friends inside who will be able to make a diversion in our favour. However sir, it can do no harm if you will wait till then, and may save many lives. At what hour do you mean to attack?"

"The bridges and all other preparations to assist us across the moat will be ready to-night. We will advance then under cover of darkness, and as soon after dawn as may be attack in earnest."

"Very well, sir," Cuthbert said. "I trust that within five minutes after your bugle has sounded, the white flag will make its appearance on the keep, but it cannot do so until after you have commenced an attack, or at least a pretence of an attack."

Two or three hours before daylight Cuthbert accompanied Cnut and twenty-five picked men of the foresters to the copse. They were provided with crowbars, and all carried heavy axes. The door was soon prised open. It opened silently and without a creak.

"It may be," Cnut said, "that the door has not been opened as you say for years, but it is certain," and he placed his torch to the hinges, "that it has been well oiled within the last two or three days. No doubt the baron intended to make his escape this way, should the worst arrive. Now that we have the door open we had better wait quiet until the dawn commences. The earl will blow his bugle as a signal for the advance; it will be another ten minutes before they are fairly engaged, and that will be enough for us to break open any doors that there may be between this and the castle, and to force our way inside."

It seemed a long time waiting before the dawn fairly broke-still longer before the earl's bugle was heard to sound the attack. Then the band, headed by Cnut and two or three of the strongest of the party, entered the passage.

Cuthbert had had some misgivings as to his mother's injunctions to take no part in the fray, and it cannot be said that in accompanying the foresters he obeyed the letter of her instructions. At the same time as he felt sure that the effect of a surprise would be complete and crushing, and that the party would gain the top of the keep without any serious resistance, he considered the risk was so small as to justify him in accompanying the foresters.

The passage was some five feet high, and little more than two feet wide. It was dry and dusty, and save the marks on the ground of a human foot going and returning, doubtless that of the man who had oiled the lock the day before, the passage appeared to have been unused from the time that it left the hands of its builders.

Passing along for some distance they came to another strong oaken door. This, like the last, yielded to the efforts of the crowbars of the foresters, and they again advanced. Presently they came to a flight of steps.

"We must now be near the castle," Cnut said. "In fact, methinks I can hear confused noises ahead."

Mounting the steps, they came to a third door; this was thickly studded with iron, and appeared of very great strength. Fortunately the lock was upon their side, and they were enabled to shoot the bolt; but upon the other side the door was firmly secured by large bolts, and it was fully five minutes before the foresters could succeed in opening it. It was not without a good deal of noise that they at last did so; and several times they paused, fearing that the alarm must have been given in the castle. As, however, the door remained closed, they supposed that the occupants were fully engaged in defending themselves from the attacks of the earl's party.

When the door gave way, they found hanging across in front of them a very thick arras, and pressing this aside they entered a small room in the thickness of the wall of the keep. It contained the merest slit for light, and was clearly unused. Another door, this time unfastened, led into a larger apartment, which was also at present unoccupied. They could hear now the shouts of the combatants without, the loud orders given by the leaders on the walls, the crack, as the stones hurled by the mangonels struck the walls, and the ring of steel as the arrows struck against steel cap and cuirass.

"It is fortunate that all were so well engaged, or they would certainly have heard the noise of our forcing the door, which would have brought all of them upon us. As it is, we are in the heart of the keep. We have now but to make a rush up these winding steps, and methinks we shall find ourselves on the battlements. They will be so surprised, that no real resistance can be offered to us. Now let us advance."

So saying Cnut led the way upstairs, followed by the foresters, Cuthbert, as before, allowing five or six of them to intervene between him and the leader. He carried his short sword and a quarterstaff, a weapon by no means to be despised in the hands of an active and experienced player.

Presently, after mounting some fifty or sixty steps, they issued on the platform of the keep.

Here were gathered some thirty or forty men, who were so busied in shooting with crossbows, and in working machines casting javelins, stones, and other missives upon the besiegers, that they were unaware of the addition to their numbers until the whole of the foresters had gathered on the summit, and at the order of Cnut suddenly fell upon them with a loud shout.

Taken wholly by surprise by the foe, who seemed to have risen from the bowels of the earth by magic, the soldiers of the Baron of Wortham offered but a feeble resistance. Some were cast over the battlement of the keep, some driven down staircases, others cut down, and then Cuthbert, fastening a small white flag he had prepared to his quarter-staff, waved it above the battlements.

Even now the combatants on the outer wall were in ignorance of what had happened in the keep; so great was the din that the struggle which had there taken place had passed unnoticed; and it was not until the fugitives, rushing out into the courtyard, shouted that the keep had been captured, that the besieged became aware of the imminence of the danger.

Hitherto the battle had been going well for the defenders of the castle. The Baron of Wortham was indeed surprised at the feebleness of the assault. The arrows which had fallen in clouds upon the first day's attack upon the castle among his soldiers were now comparatively few and ineffective. The besiegers scarcely appeared to push forward their bridges with any vigour, and it seemed to him that a coldness had fallen upon them, and that some disagreement must have arisen between the foresters and the earl, completely crippling the energy of the attack.

When he heard the words shouted from the courtyard below he could not believe his ears. That the keep behind should have been carried by the enemy appeared to him impossible. With a roar he called upon the bravest of his men to follow, and rushing across the courtyard, rapidly ascended the staircase. The movement was observed from the keep, and Cnut and a few of his men, stationed themselves with their battle-axes at the top of various stairs leading below.

The signal shown by Cuthbert had not passed unobserved. The earl, who had given instructions to his followers to make a mere feint of attacking, now blew the signal for the real onslaught. The bridges were rapidly run across the moat, ladders were planted, and the garrison being paralyzed and confused by the attack in their rear, as well as hindered by the arrows which now flew down upon them from the keep above, offered but a feeble resistance, and the assailants, led by Sir Walter himself, poured over the walls.

Now there was a scene of confusion and desperate strife. The baron had just gained the top of the stairs, and was engaged in a fierce conflict with Cnut and his men, when the news reached him that the wall was carried from without. With an execration he again turned and rushed down the stairs, hoping by a vigorous effort to cast back the foe.

It was, however, all too late: his followers, disheartened and alarmed, fought without method or order in scattered groups of threes and fours. They made their last stand in corners and passages. They knew there was but little hope of mercy from the Saxon foresters, and against these they fought to the last. To the Norman retainers, however, of the earl they offered a less determined resistance, throwing down their arms and surrendering at discretion.

The baron, when fiercely fighting, was slain by an arrow from the keep above, and with his fall the last resistance ceased. A short time was spent in searching the castle, binding the prisoners, and carrying off the valuables that the baron had collected in his raids. Then a light was set to the timbers, the granaries were fired, and in a few minutes the smoke wreathing out of the various loopholes and openings told the country round that the stronghold had fallen, and that they were free from the oppressor at last.

Chapter IV
The Crusades.

Warm thanks and much praise were bestowed upon Cuthbert for his share in the capture of the castle, and the earl, calling the foresters round him, then and there bestowed freedom upon any of them who might have been serfs of his, and called upon all his knights and neighbours to do the same, in return for the good service which they had rendered.

This was willingly done, and a number of Cnut's party who had before borne the stigma of escaped serfs were now free men.

We are too apt to forget, in our sympathy with the Saxons, that fond as they were of freedom for themselves, they were yet severe masters, and kept the mass of the people in a state of serfage. Although their laws provided ample justice as between Saxon man and man, there was no justice for the unhappy serfs, who were either the original inhabitants or captives taken in war, and who were distinguished by a collar of brass or iron round their neck.

Cnut's party had indeed long got rid of these badges, the first act of a serf when he took to the woods being always to file off his collar; but they were liable when caught to be punished, even by death, and were delighted at having achieved their freedom.

"And what can I do for you, Cuthbert?" Sir Walter said, as they rode homewards. "It is to you that I am indebted: in the first place for the rescue of my daughter, in the second for the capture of that castle, which I doubt me much whether we should ever have taken in fair fight had it not been for your aid."

"Thanks, Sir Walter," the lad replied. "At present I need nothing, but should the time come when you may go to the wars, I would fain ride with you as your page, in the hope of some day winning my spurs also in the field."

"So shall it be," the earl said, "and right willingly. But who have we here?"

As he spoke a horseman rode up and presented a paper to the earl.

"This is a notice," the earl said, after perusing it, "that King Richard has determined to take up the cross, and that he calls upon his nobles and barons to join him in the effort to free the holy sepulchre from the infidels. I doubt whether the minds of the people are quite prepared, but I hear that there has been much preaching by friars and monks in some parts, and that many are eager to join in the war."

"Think you that you will go to the war, Sir Walter?" Cuthbert asked.

"I know not as yet; it must much depend upon the king's mood. For myself, I care not so greatly as some do about this question of the Holy Land. There has been blood enough shed already to drown it, and we are no nearer than when the first swarms of pilgrims made their way thither."

On Cuthbert's returning home and telling his mother all that had passed, she shook her head, but said that she could not oppose his wishes to go with the earl when the time should come, and that it was only right he should follow in the footsteps of the good knight his father.

"I have heard much of these Crusades," he said; "canst tell me about them?"

"In truth I know not much, my son; but Father Francis, I doubt not, can tell you all the particulars anent the affair."

The next time that Father Francis, who was the special adviser of Dame Editha, rode over from the convent on his ambling nag, Cuthbert eagerly asked him if he would tell him what he knew of the Crusades.

"Hitherto, my son," he said, "the Crusades have, it must be owned, brought many woes upon Europe. From the early times great swarms of pilgrims were accustomed to go from all parts of Europe to the holy shrines.

"When the followers of the evil prophet took possession of the land, they laid grievous burdens upon the pilgrims, heavily they fined them, persecuted them in every way, and treated them as if indeed they were but the scum of the earth under their feet.

"So terrible were the tales that reached Europe that men came to think that it would be a good deed truly, to wrest the sepulchre of the Lord from the hands of these heathens. Pope Urban was the first to give authority and strength to the movement, and at a vast meeting at Claremont of 30,000 clergy and 4000 barons, it was decided that war must be made against the infidel. From all parts of France men flocked to hear Pope Urban preach there; and when he had finished his oration, the vast multitude, carried away by enthusiasm, swore to win the holy sepulchre or to die.

"Mighty was the throng that gathered for the First Crusade. Monks threw aside their gowns and took to the sword and cuirass; even women and children joined in the throng. What, my son, could be expected from a great army so formed? Without leaders, without discipline, without tactics, without means of getting food, they soon became a scourge of the country through which they passed.

"Passing through Hungary, where they greatly ravaged the fields, they came to Bulgaria. Here the people, struck with astonishment and dismay at this great horde of hungry people who arrived among them like locusts, fell upon them with the sword, and great numbers fell. The first band that passed into that country perished miserably, and of all that huge assembly, it may be said that, numbering, at the start, not less than 250,000 persons, only about 100,000 crossed into Asia Minor. The fate of these was no better than that of those who had perished in Hungary and Bulgaria. After grievous suffering and loss they at last reached Nicaea. There they fell into an ambuscade; and out of the whole of the undisciplined masses who had followed Peter the Hermit, it is doubtful whether 10,000 ever returned home.

"This first attempt to rescue the holy sepulchre was followed by others equally wild, misguided, and unfortunate. Some of them indeed began their evil deeds as soon as they had left their home. The last of these bodies fell upon the Jews, who are indeed enemies of the Christian faith, but who have now, at least, nothing to do with the question of the holy sepulchre. As soon as they entered into Germany the Crusaders put them to death with horrible torture. Plunder and rapine indeed appeared to be the object of the crusaders. On this as well as on most other preceding bands, their misdeeds drew down the vengeance of the people. At an early period of their march, and as soon as they reached Hungary, the people fell upon them, and put the greater portion to the sword.

"Thus, in these irregular expeditions no less than 500,000 people are supposed to have perished. Godfrey de Bouillon was the first who undertook to lead a Crusade according to the military knowledge of the day. With him were his brothers Eustace and Baldwin, the Counts of Anault and St. Paul, and many other nobles and gentlemen, with their retainers, well armed and under good order; and so firm was the discipline of Duke Godfrey that they were allowed to pass freely, by the people of the countries who had opposed the previous bands.

"Through Hungary, Bulgaria, and Thrace he made his way; and though he met with many difficulties from Alexius, the crafty and treacherous Emperor of the Greeks, he at last succeeded in crossing into Asia. There he was joined by many from England, as well as from France and other countries. Duke Robert, the son of our first William, led a strong band of Normans to the war, as did the other great princes of France and Spain.

"The army which crossed the narrow passage of the Hellespont is estimated at no less than 700,000 fighting men. Of these 100,000 were knights clad in complete armour, the remainder were men-at-arms and bowmen.

"Nicaea, the place which had been the scene of the massacre of Peter the Hermit's hosts, was taken after a desperate conflict, lasting for many weeks, and the crusaders afterwards defeated the Turks in a great battle near the town of Dorylaeum. After these successes disputes arose among the leaders, and Count Baldwin, brother of Duke Godfrey, left the main body with about 1500 men, and founded a kingdom for himself in Mesopotamia.

"The main body, slowly and painfully, and suffering from disease, famine, and the heat, made its way south. Antioch, a city of great strength and importance, was besieged, but it proved so strong that it resisted for many months, and was at last only taken by treachery.

"After the capture of this place the sufferings of the crusaders so far from being diminished were redoubled. They themselves during the siege had bought up all the food that could be brought from the surrounding country, while the magazines of the town were found, when an entry was effected, to be entirely deserted. The enemy, aided by a great Persian host, came down, and those who had been the besiegers were now besieged. However, when in the last strait the Christian army sallied out, and inspired with supernatural strength, defeated the Turks and Persians, with a slaughter of 100,000 men. Another slow movement to the south brought them into the Holy Land, and pressing forward, they came at last within sight of Jerusalem itself.

"So fearful had been the losses of the crusaders that of 700,000 who crossed the Hellespont, not more than 40,000 reached the end of the pilgrimage. This fragment of an army, which had appeared before a very strongly fortified town, possessed no means of capturing the place-none of the machines of war necessary for the purpose, no provisions or munitions of any kind. Water was scarce also; and it appeared as if the remnant of the great army of Godfrey de Bouillon had arrived before Jerusalem only to perish there.

"Happily just at this time a further band of crusaders from Genoa, who had reached Jaffa, made their appearance. They were provided with stores, and had skilled workmen capable of making the machines for the siege. On July 14th, 1099, the attack was made, and after resistance gallant and desperate as the assault, the crusaders burst into the city, massacred the whole of the defenders and inhabitants, calculated at 70,000 in number, and so became masters of the holy sepulchre.

"The Sultan of Egypt was meanwhile advancing to the assistance of the Mohammedans of Syria; but Godfrey, with 20,000 of his best men, advanced to meet the vast host, and scattered them as if they had been sheep. Godfrey was now chosen King of Jerusalem, and the rest of his army-save 300 knights and 200 soldiers, who agreed to remain with him-returned to their home. The news of the victory led other armies of crusaders to follow the example of that of Godfrey; but as these were almost as completely without organization or leadership as those of Peter the Hermit, they suffered miserably on their way, and few indeed ever reached the Holy Land. Godfrey died in 1100, and his brother Baldwin succeeded him.

"The history of the last 100 years has been full of fresh efforts to crush the Moslem power, but hitherto it cannot be said that fortune has attended the efforts of the Christians. Had it not been indeed for the devotion of the Knights of St. John and of the Templars, two great companies formed of men who devoted their lives to the holding of the sepulchre against the infidel, our hold of the Holy Land would have been lost.

"Gradually the Saracens have wrested post after post from our hands. Edessa was taken in 1144, and the news of this event created an intense excitement. The holy St. Bernard stirred up all France, and Louis VII. himself took the vow and headed a noble army. The ways of God are not our ways, and although the army of Germany joined that of France, but little results came of this great effort. The Emperor Conrad, with the Germans, was attacked by the Turk Saladin of Iconium, and was defeated with a loss of 60,000 men. The King of France, with his army, was also attacked with fury, and a large portion of his force were slaughtered. Nothing more came of this great effort, and while the first Crusade seemed to show that the men-at-arms of Europe were irresistible, the second on the contrary gave proof that the Turks were equal to the Christian knights. Gradually the Christian hold of the Holy Land was shaken. In 1187, although fighting with extraordinary bravery, the small army of Christian Knights of the Temple and of St. John were annihilated, the King of Jerusalem was made prisoner, and the Christian power was crushed. Then Saladin, who commanded the Turks, advanced against Jerusalem, and forced it to capitulate.

"Such, my boy, is the last sad news which has reached us; and no wonder that it has stirred the hearts of the monarchs of Europe, and that every effort will be again made to recapture the holy sepulchre, and to avenge our brethren who have been murdered by the infidels."

"But, Father Francis, from your story it would seem that Europe has already sacrificed an enormous number of lives to take the holy sepulchre, and that after all the fighting, when she has taken it, it is only to lose it again."

"That is so, my son; but we will trust that in future things will be better managed. The Templars and Hospitallers now number so vast a number of the best lances in Europe, and are grown to be such great powers, that we may believe that when we have again wrested the holy sepulchre from the hands of the infidels they will be able to maintain it against all assaults. Doubtless the great misfortunes which have fallen upon the Christian armies have been a punishment from heaven, because they have not gone to work in the right spirit. It is not enough to take up lance and shield, and to place a red cross upon the shoulder. Those who desire to fight the battle of the Lord must cleanse their hearts, and go forth in the spirit of pilgrims rather than knights. I mean, not that they should trust wholly to spiritual weapons-for in truth the infidel is a foe not to be despised-but I mean, that they should lay aside all thoughts of worldly glory, and rivalry one against another."

"And think you, Father, that such is the spirit with which King Richard and the other kings and nobles now preparing to go to the Holy Land are animated?"

Father Francis hesitated.

"It is not for me, my son, to judge motives, or to speak well or ill the instruments who have been chosen for this great work. It is of all works the most praiseworthy, most holy. It is horrible to think that the holy shrines of Jerusalem should be in the hands of men who believe not in our Redeemer; and I hold it to be the duty of every man who can bear arms, no matter what his rank or his station, to don his armour and to go forth to battle in the cause. Whether success will crown the effort, or whether God wills it otherwise, it is not for man to discuss; it is enough that the work is there, and it is our duty to do it."

"And think you, Father, that it will do good to England?"

"That do I, my son, whether we gain the Holy Land or no. Methinks that it will do good service to the nation that Saxon and Norman should fight together under the holy cross. Hitherto the races have stood far too much apart. They have seen each other's bad qualities rather than good; but methinks that when the Saxon and the Norman stand side by side on the soil of the Holy Land, and shout together for England, it must needs bind them together, and lead them to feel that they are no longer Normans and Saxons, but Englishmen. I intend to preach on the village green at Evesham next Sunday morning on this subject, and as I know you are in communication with the forest men, I would, Cuthbert, that you would persuade them to come in to hear me. You were wondering what could be found for these vagrants. They have many of them long since lost the habits of honest labour. Many of them are still serfs, although most have been freed by the good earl and the knights his followers. Some of those who would fain leave the life in the woods, still cling to it because they think that it would be mean to desert their comrades, who being serfs are still bound to lurk there; but methinks that this is a great opportunity for them. They are valiant men, and the fact that they are fond of drawing an arrow at a buck does not make them one whit the worse Christians. I will do my best to move their hearts, and if they will but agree together to take the cross, they would make a goodly band of footmen to accompany the earl."

"Is the earl going?" Cuthbert asked eagerly.

"I know not for certain," said Father Francis; "but I think from what I hear from his chaplain, Father Eustace, that his mind turns in that direction."

"Then, Father, if he goes, I will go too," Cuthbert exclaimed. "He promised to take me as his page the first time he went to war."

Father Francis shook his head.

"I fear me, Cuthbert, this is far from the spirit in which we a while ago agreed that men should go to the holy war."

Cuthbert hung his head a little.

"Ay, Father Francis, men; but I am a boy," he said, "and after all, boys are fond of adventure for adventure's sake. However, Father," he said, with a smile, "no doubt your eloquence on the green will turn me mightily to the project, for you must allow that the story you have told me this morning is not such as to create any very strong yearning in one's mind to follow the millions of men who have perished in the Holy Land."

"Go to," said Father Francis, smiling, "thou art a pert varlet. I will do my best on Sunday to turn you to a better frame of mind."

Chapter V
Preparations.

Next Sunday a large number of people from some miles round were gathered on the green at Evesham, to hear Father Francis preach on the holy sepulchre. The forest men in their green jerkins mingled with the crowd, and a look of attention and seriousness was on the faces of all, for the news of the loss of the holy sepulchre had really exercised a great effect upon the minds of the people in England as elsewhere.

Those were the days of pilgrimage to holy places, when the belief in the sanctity of places and things was overwhelming, and when men believed that a journey to the holy shrines was sufficient to procure for them a pardon for all their misdeeds. The very word "infidel" in those days was full of horror, and the thought that the holy places of the Christians were in the hands of Moslems, affected all Christians throughout Europe with a feeling of shame as well as of grief.

Among the crowd were many of the Norman retainers from the castle and from many of the holds around, and several knights with the ladies of their family stood a little apart from the edge of the gathering; for it was known that Father Francis would not be alone, but that he would be accompanied by a holy friar who had returned from the East, and who could tell of the cruelties which the Christians had suffered at the hands of the Saracens.

Father Francis, at ordinary times a tranquil preacher, was moved beyond himself by the theme on which he was holding forth. He did not attempt to hide from those who stood around that the task to be undertaken was one of grievous peril and trial; that disease and heat, hunger and thirst, must be dared, as well as the sword of the infidel. But he spoke of the grand nature of the work, of the humiliation to Christians of the desecration of the shrines, and of the glory which awaited those who joined the crusade, whether they lived or whether they died in the Holy Land.

His words had a strong effect upon the simple people who listened to him, but the feelings so aroused were as nought to the enthusiasm which greeted the address of the friar.

Meagre and pale, with a worn, anxious face as one who had suffered much, the friar, holding aloft two pieces of wood from the Mount of Olives tied together in the form of a cross, harangued the crowd. His words poured forth in a fiery stream, kindling the hearts, and stirring at once the devotion and the anger of his listeners.

He told of the holy places, he spoke of the scenes of Holy Writ, which had there been enacted; and then he depicted the men who had died for them. He told of the knights and men-at-arms, each of whom proved himself again and again a match for a score of infidels. He spoke of the holy women, who, fearlessly and bravely, as the knights themselves, had borne their share in the horrors of the siege and in the terrible times which had preceded it.

He told them that this misfortune had befallen Christianity because of the lukewarmness which had come upon them.

"What profited it," he asked, "if the few knights who remained to defend the holy sepulchre were heroes? A few heroes cannot withstand an army. If Christendom after making a mighty effort to capture the holy sepulchre had not fallen away, the conquest which had been made with so vast an expenditure of blood would not have been lost. This is a work in which no mere passing fervour will avail; bravery at first, endurance afterwards, are needed. Many men must determine not only to assist to wrest the holy sepulchre from the hands of the infidels, but to give their lives, so long as they might last, to retaining it. It is scarce to be expected that men with wives and families will take a view like this, indeed it is not to be desired. But there are single men, men of no ties, who can devote their whole lives, as did the Knights of the Orders of the Cross, to this great object. When their life has come to an end, doubtless others will take up the banner that their hands can no longer hold. But for life it is, indeed, that many of humble as well as of princely class must bind themselves to take and defend to death the holy sepulchre."

So, gradually raising the tone of his speech, the friar proceeded; until at length by his intense earnestness, his wild gesticulations, his impassioned words, he drew the whole of his listeners along with him; and when he ceased, a mighty shout of "To the Holy Land!" burst from his hearers.

Falling upon their knees, the crowd begged of him to give them the sign of the cross, and to bestow his blessing upon their swords, and upon their efforts.

Father Francis had prepared, in contemplation of such a movement, a large number of small white crosses of cloth. These he and the friar now fastened to the shoulders of the men as they crowded up to receive it, holding their hands aloft, kissing the cross that the Friar extended to them, and swearing to give their lives, if need be, to rescue the holy shrines from the infidel.

When all had received the holy symbol, Father Francis again ascended the bank from which they had addressed the crowd:

"Now go to your homes, my sons," he said. "Think of the oath that you have taken, and of the course that lies open to you when the time comes. When King Richard is prepared to start, then will you be called upon to fulfil your vows. It may be that all who have sworn may not be called upon to go. It needs that the land here should be tilled, it needs that there should be protectors for the women and children, it needs that this England of ours should flourish, and we cannot give all her sons, however willing they might be to take the cross. But the willingness which you will, I am sure, show to go if needs be, and to redeem your vows, will be sufficient. Some must go and some must stay; these are matters to be decided hereafter; for the time let us separate; you will hear when the hour for action arrives."

A fortnight later the Earl of Evesham, who had been on a long journey to London, returned with full authority to raise and organize a force as his contingent to the holy wars.

All was now bustle and activity in the castle.

Father Francis informed him of the willingness of such of the forest men as he deemed fit to enlist under his banner; and the earl was much gratified at finding that the ranks of heavily-armed retainers whom he would take with him, were to be swollen by the addition of so useful a contingent as that of 100 skilful archers.

Cuthbert was not long in asking for an interview with the earl.

He had indeed great difficulty in persuading Dame Editha that he was old enough to share in the fatigues of so great an expedition, but he had Father Francis on his side; and between the influence of her confessor, and the importunities of her son, the opposition of the good lady fell to the ground.

Cuthbert was already, for his age, well trained to arms. Many of the old soldiers at the castle who had known and loved his father, had been ever ready to give lessons in the use of arms to Cuthbert, who was enthusiastic in his desire to prove as good a knight as his father had been. His friends, the outlaws, had taught him the use of the bow and of the quarter-staff; and Cuthbert, strong and well-built for his age, and having little to do save to wield the sword and the bow, had attained a very considerable amount of skill with each.

He had too, which was unusual, a certain amount of book learning, although this, true to say, had not been acquired so cheerfully or willingly as the skill at arms. Father Francis had, however, taught him to read and to write-accomplishments which were at that time rare, except in the cloister. In those days if a knight had a firm seat in his saddle, a strong arm, a keen eye, and high courage, it was thought to be of little matter whether he could or could not do more than make his mark on the parchment. The whole life of the young was given to acquiring skill in arms; and unless intended for the convent, any idea of education would in the great majority of cases have been considered as preposterous.

To do Cuthbert justice, he had protested with all his might against the proposition of Father Francis to his mother to teach him some clerkly knowledge. He had yielded most unwillingly at last to her entreaties, backed as they were by the sound arguments and good sense of Father Francis.

The Earl of Evesham received Cuthbert's application very graciously.

"Certainly, Cuthbert," he said, "you shall accompany me; first, on account of my promise to you; secondly, because from the readiness you displayed both in the matter of my daughter and of the attack on Wortham, you will be a notable aid and addition to my party; thirdly, from my friendship for your father and Dame Editha."

This point being settled, Cuthbert at once assumed his new duties. There was plenty for him to do—to see that the orders of the earl were properly carried out; to bear messages to the knights who followed the earl's fortunes, at their various holds; to stand by and watch the armourers at work, and the preparation of the stores of arms and missiles which would be necessary for the expedition.

Sometimes he would go round to summon the tenants of the various farms and lands, who held from the earl, to come to the castle; and here Sir Walter would, as far as might be without oppression, beg of them to contribute largely to the expedition.

In these appeals he was in no slight way assisted by Father Francis, who pointed out loudly to the people that those who stayed behind were bound to make as much sacrifice of their worldly goods, as those who went to the war might make of their lives. Life and land are alike at the service of God. Could the land be sold, it would be a good deed to sell it; but as this could not be, they should at least sell all that they could, and pledge their property if they could find lenders, in order to contribute to the needs of their lord, and the fitting out of this great enterprise.

The preparations were at last complete, and a gallant band gathered at the castle ready for starting. It consisted of some 200 men-at-arms led by six knights, and of 100 bowmen dressed in Lincoln green, with quilted jerkins to keep out the arrows of the enemy. All the country from around gathered to see the start. Dame Editha was there, and by her side stood the earl's little daughter. The earl himself was in armour, and beside him rode Cuthbert in the gay attire of a page.

Just at that moment, however, his face did not agree with his costume, for although he strove his best to look bright and smiling, it was a hard task to prevent the tears from filling his eyes at his departure from his mother. The good lady cried unrestrainedly, and Margaret joined in her tears. The people who had gathered round cheered lustily; the trumpets blew a gay fanfaronade; and the squire threw to the wind the earl's colours.

It was no mere pleasure trip on which they were starting, for all knew that, of the preceding crusades, not one in ten of those who had gone so gladly forth had ever returned.

It must not be supposed that the whole of those present were animated by any strong religious feeling. No doubt there existed a desire, which was carefully fanned by the preaching of the priests and monks, to rescue the holy sepulchre from the hands of the Saracens; but a far stronger feeling was to be found in the warlike nature of the people in those days. Knights, men-at-arms, and indeed men of all ranks, were full of a combative spirit. Life in the castle and hut was alike dull and monotonous, and the excitement of war and adventure was greatly looked for, both as a means of obtaining glory and booty, and for the change they afforded to the dreary monotony of life.

There is little to tell of the journey of the Earl of Evesham's band through England to Southampton, at which place they took ship and crossed to France-or rather to Normandy, for in those days Normandy was regarded, as indeed it formed, a part of England.

Cuthbert, as was natural to his age, was full of delight at all the varying scenes through which they passed. The towns were to him an especial source of wonder, for he had never visited any other than that of Worcester, to which he had once or twice been taken on occasions of high festival. Havre was in those days an important place, and being the landing-place of a great portion of the English bands, it was full of bustle and excitement. Every day ships brought in nobles and their followings.

The King of England was already in Normandy hastening the preparations, and each band, as it landed, marched down to the meeting-place on the plains of Vezelay. Already they began to experience a taste of the hardships which they were to endure.

In those days there was no regular supply train for an army, but each division or band supported itself by purchase or pillage, as the case might be, from the surrounding country.

As the English troops were marching through a friendly country, pillage was of course strictly forbidden; but while many of the leaders paid for all they had, it must be owned that among the smaller leaders were many who took anything that they required with or without payment.

The country was eaten up.

The population in those days was sparse, and the movement of so large a number of men along a certain route completely exhausted all the resources of the inhabitants; and although willing to pay for all that his men required, the Earl of Evesham had frequently to lie down on the turf supperless himself.

"If this is the case now," he said to Cuthbert, "what will it be after we have joined the French army? Methinks whatever we may do if we reach the Holy Land, that we have a fair chance of being starved before we sail."

After a long succession of marches they arrived in sight of the great camp at Vezelay. It was indeed rather a canvas town than a camp. Here were gathered nearly 100,000 men, a vast host at any time, but in those days far greater in proportion to the strength of the countries than at present. The tents of the leaders, nobles, and other knights and gentlemen, rose in regular lines, forming streets and squares.

The great mass of troops, however, were contented to sleep in the open air; indeed the difficulties of carriage were so great that it was only the leaders who could carry with them their canvas abodes. Before each tent stood the lance and colours of its owner, and side by side in the centre of the camp stood the royal pavilions of Phillip of France and Richard of England, round which could be seen the gonfalons of all the nobles of Western Europe.

Nothing could be gayer than the aspect of this camp as the party rode into it. They were rather late, and the great body of the host were already assembled.

Cuthbert gazed with delight at the varied colours, the gay dresses, the martial knights, and the air of discipline and order which reigned everywhere.

This was indeed war in its most picturesque form, a form which, as far as beauty is concerned, has been altogether altered, and indeed destroyed, by modern arms.

In those days individual prowess and bravery went for everything. A handful of armoured knights were a match for thousands of footmen, and battles were decided as much by the prowess and bravery of the leader and his immediate following as by that of the great mass of the army.

The earl had the day before sent on a messenger to state that he was coming, and as the party entered the camp they were met by a squire of the camp-marshal, who conducted them to the position allotted to them.

The earl's tent was soon erected, with four or five grouped around it for his knights, one being set aside for his squires and pages.

When this was done, Cuthbert strolled away to look at the varied sights of the camp. A military officer in these days would be scandalized at the scenes which were going on, but the strict, hard military discipline of modern times was then absolutely unknown.

A camp was a moving town, and to it flocked the country people with their goods; smiths and armourers erected their forges; minstrels and troubadours flocked in to sing of former battles, and to raise the spirits of the soldiers by merry lays of love and war; simple countrymen and women came in to bring their presents of fowls or cakes to their friends in camp; knights rode to and fro on their gaily caparisoned horses through the crowd; the newly raised levies, in many cases composed of woodmen and peasants who had not in the course of their lives wandered a league from their birthplaces, gaped in unaffected wonder at the sights around them; while last, but by no means least, the maidens and good wives of the neighbourhood, fond then as now of brave men and gay dresses, thronged the streets of the camp, and joined in, and were the cause of, merry laughter and jest.

Here and there, a little apart from the main stream of traffic, the minstrels would take up their position, and playing a gay air, the soldier lads and lasses would fall to and foot it merrily to the strains. Sometimes there would be a break in the gaiety, and loud shouts, and perhaps fierce oaths, would rise. Then the maidens would fly like startled fawns, and men hasten to the spot; though the quarrel might be purely a private one, yet should it happen between the retainers of two nobles, the friends of each would be sure to strike in, and serious frays would arise before the marshal of the camp with his posse could arrive to interfere. Sometimes indeed these quarrels became so serious and desperate that alliances were broken up and great intentions frustrated by the quarrels of the soldiery.

Here and there, on elevated platforms, or even on the top of a pile of tubs, were friars occupied in haranguing the soldiers, and in inspiring them with enthusiasm for the cause upon which they were embarked. The conduct of their listeners showed easily enough the motives which had brought them to war. Some stood with clasped hands and eager eyes listening to the exhortations of the priests, and ready, as might be seen from their earnest gaze, to suffer martyrdom in the cause. More, however, stood indifferently round, or after listening to a few words walked on with a laugh or a scoff; indeed preaching had already done all that lay in its power. All those who could be moved by exhortations of this kind were there, and upon the rest the discourses and sermons were thrown away.

Several times in the course of his stroll round the camp Cuthbert observed the beginnings of quarrels, which were in each case only checked by the intervention of some knight or other person in authority coming past, and he observed that these in every instance occurred between men of the English and those of the French army.

Between the Saxon contingent of King Richard's army and the French soldiers there could indeed be no quarrel, for the Saxons understood no word of their language; but with the Normans the case was different, for the Norman-French, which was spoken by all the nobles and their retainers in Britain, was as nearly as possible the same as that in use in France.

It seemed, however, to Cuthbert, watching narrowly what was going on, that there existed by no means a good feeling between the men of the different armies; and he thought that this divergence so early in the campaign boded but little good for the final success of the expedition.

When he returned to the tent the earl questioned him as to what he had seen, and Cuthbert frankly acknowledged that it appeared to him that the feeling between the men of the two armies was not good.

"I have been," the earl said, "to the royal camp, and from what I hear, Cuthbert, methinks that there is reason for what you say. King Richard is the most loyal and gallant of kings, but he is haughty, and hasty in speech. The Normans, too, have been somewhat accustomed to conquer our neighbours, and it may well be that the chivalry of France love us not. However, it must be hoped that this feeling will die away, and that we shall emulate each other only in our deeds on the battlefield."

Chapter VI
The Lists.

The third day after the arrival of the Earl of Evesham there was a great banquet given by the King of France to King Richard and his principal nobles.

Among those present was the Earl of Evesham, and Cuthbert as his page followed him to the great tent where the banquet was prepared.

Here, at the top of the tent, on a raised dais, sat the King of France, surrounded by his courtiers.

The Earl of Evesham, having been conducted by the herald to the dais, paid his compliments to the king, and was saluted by him with many flattering words.

The sound of a trumpet was heard, and Richard of England, accompanied by his principal nobles, entered.

It was the first time that Cuthbert had seen the king.

Richard was a man of splendid stature and of enormous strength. His appearance was in some respects rather Saxon than Norman, for his hair was light and his complexion clear and bright. He wore the moustache and pointed beard at that time in fashion; and although his expression was generally that of frankness and good humour, there might be observed in his quick motions and piercing glances signs of the hasty temper and unbridled passion which went far to wreck the success of the enterprise upon which he was embarked.

Richard possessed most of the qualities which make a man a great king and render him the idol of his subjects, especially in a time of semi-civilization, when personal prowess is placed at the summit of all human virtues. In all his dominions there was not one man who in personal conflict was a match for his king.

Except during his fits of passion, King Richard was generous, forgiving, and royal in his moods. He was incapable of bearing malice. Although haughty of his dignity, he was entirely free from any personal pride, and while he would maintain to the death every right and privilege against another monarch, he could laugh and joke with the humblest of his subjects on terms of hearty good fellowship. He was impatient of contradiction, eager to carry out whatever he had determined upon; and nothing enraged him so much as hesitation or procrastination. The delays which were experienced in the course of the Crusade angered him more than all the opposition offered by the Saracens, or than the hardships through which the Christian host had to pass.

At a flourish of trumpets all took their seats at dinner, their places being marked for them by a herald, whose duty it was to regulate nicely the various ranks and dignities.

The Earl of Evesham was placed next to a noble of Brabant. Cuthbert took his place behind his lord and served him with wines and meats, the Brabant being attended by a tall youth, who was indeed on the verge of manhood.

As the dinner went on the buzz of conversation became fast and furious. In those days men drank deep, and quarrels often arose over the cups. From the time that the dinner began, Cuthbert noticed that the manner of Sir de Jacquelin Barras, Count of Brabant, was rude and offensive.

It might be that he was accustomed to live alone with his retainers, and that his manners were rude and coarse to all. It might be that he had a special hostility to the English. At any rate, his remarks were calculated to fire the anger of the earl.

He began the conversation by wondering how a Norman baron could live in a country like England, inhabited by a race but little above pigs.

The earl at once fired up at this, for the Normans were now beginning to feel themselves English, and to resent attacks upon a people for whom their grandfathers had entertained contempt.

He angrily repelled the attack upon them by the Brabant knight, and asserted at once that the Saxons were every bit as civilized, and in some respects superior, to the Normans or French.

The ill-feeling thus begun at starting clearly waxed stronger as dinner went on. The Brabant knight drank deeply, and although his talk was not clearly directed against the English, yet he continued to throw out innuendoes and side attacks, and to talk with a vague boastfulness, which greatly irritated Sir Walter.

Presently, as Cuthbert was about to serve his master with a cup of wine, the tall page pushed suddenly against him, spilling a portion of the wine over his dress.

"What a clumsy child!" he said scoffingly.

"You are a rough and ill-mannered loon," Cuthbert said angrily. "Were you in any other presence I would chastise you as you deserve."

The tall page burst into a mocking laugh.

"Chastise me!" he said. "Why, I could put you in my pocket for a little hop-of-my-thumb as you are."

"I think," said Sir Jacquelin-for the boys' voices both rose loud-to the earl, "you had better send that brat home and order him to be whipped."

"Sir count," said the earl, "your manners are insolent, and were we not engaged upon a Crusade, it would please me much to give you a lesson on that score."

Higher and higher the dispute rose, until some angry word caught the ear of the king.

Amid the general buzz of voices King Phillip rose, and speaking a word to King Richard, moved from the table, thus giving the sign for the breaking up of the feast.

Immediately afterwards a page touched the earl and Sir Jacquelin upon the shoulder, and told them that the kings desired to speak with them in the tent of the King of France.

The two nobles strode through the crowd, regarding each other with eyes much like those of two dogs eager to fly at each other's throat.

"My lords, my lords," said King Phillip when they entered, "this is against all law and reason. For shame, to be brawling at my table. I would not say aught openly, but methinks it is early indeed for the knights and nobles engaged in a common work to fall to words."

"Your Majesty," said the Earl of Evesham, "I regret deeply what has happened. But it seemed, from the time we sat down to the meal, that this lord sought to pass a quarrel upon me, and I now beseech your Majesty that you will permit us to settle our differences in the lists."

King Richard gave a sound of assent, but the King of France shook his head gravely.

"Do you forget," he said, "the mission upon which you are assembled here? Has not every knight and noble in these armies taken a solemn oath to put aside private quarrels and feuds until the holy sepulchre is taken? Shall we at this very going off show that the oath is a mere form of words? Shall we show before the face of Christendom that the knights of the cross are unable to avoid flying at each other's throats, even while on their way to wrest the holy sepulchre from the infidel? No, sirs, you must lay aside your feuds, and must promise me and my good brother here that you will keep the peace between you until this war is over. Whose fault it was that the quarrel began I know not. It may be that my Lord of Brabant was discourteous. It may be that the earl here was too hot. But whichever it be, it matters not."

"The quarrel, sire," said Sir Jacquelin, "arose from a dispute between our pages, who were nigh coming to blows in your Majesty's presence. I desired the earl to chide the insolence of his varlet, and instead of so doing he met my remarks with scorn."

"Pooh, pooh," said King Richard, "there are plenty of grounds for quarrel without two nobles interfering in the squabbles of boys. Let them fight; it will harm no one. By-the-bye, your Majesty," he said, turning to the King of France with a laugh, "if the masters may not fight, there is no reason in the world why the varlets should not. We are sorely dull for want of amusement. Let us have a list to-morrow, and let the pages fight it out for the honour of their masters and their nations."

"It were scarce worth while to have the lists set for two boys to fight," said the King of France.

"Oh, we need not have regular lists," said King Richard. "Leave that matter in my hands. I warrant you that if the cockerels are well plucked, they will make us sport. What say you, gentlemen?"

The Brabant noble at once assented, answering that he was sure that his page would be glad to enter the lists; and the earl gave a similar assent, for he had not noticed how great was the discrepancy between the size of the future combatants.

"That is agreed, then," said King Richard joyously. "I will have a piece of ground marked out on the edge of the camp to-morrow morning. It shall be kept by my men-at-arms, and there shall be a raised place for King Phillip and myself, who will be the judges of the conflict. Will they fight on foot or on horse?"

"On foot, on foot," said the King of France. "It would be a pity that knightly exercises should be brought to scorn by any failure on their part on horseback. On foot at least it will be a fair struggle."

"What arms shall they use?" the Brabant knight asked.

"Oh, swords and battle-axes, of course," said King Richard with a laugh.

"Before you go," King Phillip said, "you must shake hands, and swear to let the quarrel between you drop, at least until after our return. If you still wish to shed each other's blood, I shall offer no hindrance thereto."

The earl and Count Jacquelin touched each other's hands in obedience to the order, went out of the tent together, and strode off without a word in different directions.

"My dear lad," the Earl of Evesham said on entering his tent where his page was waiting him, "this is a serious business. The kings have ordered this little count and myself to put aside our differences till after the Crusade, in accordance with our oath. But as you have no wise pledged yourself in the same fashion, and as their Majesties fell somewhat dull while waiting here, it is determined that the quarrel between me, and between you and the count's page, shall be settled by a fight between you in the presence of the kings."

"Well, sir," Cuthbert said, "I am glad that it should be, seeing the varlet insulted me without cause, and purposely upset the cup over me."

"What is he like?" the earl asked. "Dost think that you are a fair match?"

"I doubt not that we are fair match enough," Cuthbert said. "As you know, sir, I have been well trained to arms of all kinds, both by my father and by the men-at-arms at the castle, and could hold my own against any of your men with light weapons, and have then no fear that this gawky loon, twenty years old though he seems to be, will bring disgrace upon me or discredit upon my nation."

"If thou thinkest so," the earl said, "the matter can go on. But had it been otherwise, I would have gone to the king and protested that the advantage of age was so great that it would be murder to place you in the list together."

"There is," Cuthbert said, "at most no greater difference between us than between a strong man and a weak one, and these, in the ordeal of battle, have to meet in the lists. Indeed I doubt if the difference is so great, for if he be a foot taller than I, methinks that round the shoulders I should have the advantage of him."

"Send hither my armourer," the earl said; "we must choose a proper suit for you. I fear that mine would be of little use; but doubtless there are some smaller suits among my friends."

"The simpler and lighter the better," Cuthbert said. "I'd rather have a light coat of mail and a steel cap, than heavy armour and a helmet that would press me down and a visor through which I could scarcely see. The lighter the better, for after all if my sword cannot keep my head, sooner or later the armour would fail to do so too."

The armourer speedily arrived, and the knights and followers of the earl being called in and the case stated, there was soon found a coat of fine linked mail, which fitted Cuthbert well. As to the steel cap, there was no difficulty whatever.

"You must have a plume at least," the earl said, and took some feathers from his own casque and fastened them in. "Will you want a light sword and battle-axe?"

"No," Cuthbert said, "my arms are pretty well used to those of the men-at-arms. I could wield my father's sword, and that was a heavy one."

The lightest of the earl's weapons were chosen, and it was agreed that all was now ready for the conflict to-morrow.

In the morning there was a slight bustle in the camp.

The news that a fight was to take place between an English and a Brabant page, by the permission of the Kings of England and France, that their Majesties were to be present, and that all was to be conducted on regular rules, caused a stir of excitement and novelty in the camp.

Nowhere is life duller than among a large body of men kept together for any time under canvas, and the thought of a combat of this novel kind excited general interest.

In a meadow at a short distance from the camp, a body of King Richard's men-at-arms marked off an oval space of about an acre. Upon one side of this a tent was pitched for the kings, and a small tent was placed at each end for the combatants. Round the enclosure the men-at-arms formed the ring, and behind them a dense body of spectators gathered, a place being set aside for nobles, and others of gentle blood.

At the hour fixed the Kings of England and France arrived together. King Richard was evidently in a state of high good humour, for he preferred the clash of arms and the sight of combat to any other pleasure.

The King of France, on the other hand, looked grave. He was a far wiser and more politic king than Richard; and although he had consented to the sudden proposal, yet he felt in his heart that the contest was a foolish one, and that it might create bad feeling among the men of the two nationalities whichever way it went. He had reserved to himself the right of throwing down the baton when the combat was to cease, and he determined to avail himself of this right, to put a stop to the conflict before either party was likely to sustain any deadly injury.

When the monarchs had taken their places the trumpeters sounded their trumpets, and the two combatants advanced on foot from their ends of the lists. A murmur of surprise and dissatisfaction broke from the crowd.

"My Lord of Evesham," the king said angrily to the earl, who with Count Jacquelin was standing by the royal party, "thou shouldst have said that the difference between the two was too great to allow the combat to be possible. The Frenchman appears to be big enough to take your page under his arm and walk off with him."

The difference was indeed very striking. The French champion was arrayed in a full suit of knightly armour-of course without the gold spurs which were the distinguishing mark of that rank-and with his helmet and lofty plume of feathers he appeared to tower above Cuthbert, who, in his close-fitting steel cap and link armour, seemed a very dwarf by the side of a giant.

"It is not size, sire, but muscle and pluck will win in a combat like this. Your Majesty need not be afraid that my page will disgrace me. He is of my blood, though the kinship is not close. He is of mixed Saxon and Norman strain, and will, believe me, do no discredit to either."

The king's brow cleared, for in truth he was very proud of his English nationality, and would have been sorely vexed to see the discomfiture of an English champion, even though that champion were a boy.

"Brother Phillip," he said, turning to the king, "I will wager my gold chain against yours on yonder stripling."

"Methinks that it were robbery to take your wager," the King of France said. "The difference between their bulk is disproportionate. However, I will not baulk your wish. My chain against yours."

The rule of the fight was that they were to commence with Swords, but that either could, if he chose, use his battle-axe.

The fight need scarcely be described at length, for the advantage was all one way. Cuthbert was fully a match in strength for his antagonist, although standing nigh a foot shorter. Constant exercise, however, had hardened his muscles into something like steel, while the teaching that he had received had embraced all that was then known of the use of arms.

Science in those days there was but little of; it was a case rather of hard, heavy hitting, than of what we now call swordsmanship.

With the sword Cuthbert gained but slight advantage over his adversary, whose superior height enabled him to rain blows down upon the lad, which he was with difficulty enabled to guard; but when the first paroxysm of his adversary's attack had passed, he took to the offensive, and drove his opponent back step by step. With his sword, however, he was unable to cut through the armour of the Frenchman, but in the course of the encounter, guarding a severe blow aimed at him, his sword was struck from his hand, and he then, seizing his axe, made such play with it that his foe dropped his own sword and took to the same weapon.

In this the superior height and weight of his opponent gave him even a greater advantage than with the sword, and Cuthbert knowing this, used his utmost dexterity and speed to avoid the sweeping blows showered upon him. He himself had been enabled to strike one or two sweeping strokes, always aiming at the same place, the juncture of the visor with the helmet. At last the Frenchman struck him so heavy a blow that it beat down his guard and struck his steel cap from his head, bringing him to the knee. In an instant he was up, and before his foe could be again on guard, he whirled his axe round with all its force, and bringing it just at the point of the visor which he had already weakened with repeated blows, the edge of the axe stove clean through the armour, and the page was struck senseless to the ground.

A great shout broke from the English portion of the soldiery as Cuthbert leant over his prostrate foe, and receiving no answer to the question "Do you yield?" rose to his feet, and signified to the squire who had kept near that his opponent was insensible.

King Richard ordered the pursuivant to lead Cuthbert to the royal enclosure.

"Thou art a brave lad and a lusty," the king said, "and hast borne thee in the fight as well as many a knight would have done. Wert thou older, I would myself dub thee knight; and I doubt not that the occasion will yet come when thou wilt do as good deeds upon the bodies of the Saracens as thou hast upon that long-shanked opponent of thine. Here is a gold chain; take it as a proof that the King of England holds that you have sustained well the honour of his country; and mark me, if at any time you require a boon, bring or send me that chain, and thou shall have it freely. Sir Walter," he said, turning to the earl, "in this lad thou hast a worthy champion, and I trust me that thou wilt give him every chance of distinguishing himself. So soon as thou thinkst him fit for the knightly rank I myself will administer the accolade."

Chapter VII
Revenge.

After his interview with the king, Cuthbert was led to his tent amid the hearty plaudits of the English troops.

His own comrades flocked round him; the men of the greenwood headed by Cnut, were especially jubilant over his victory.

"Who would have thought," said the tall forester, "that the lad who but a short time ago was a child, should now have sustained the honour of the country? We feel proud of you, Cuthbert; and trust us some day or other to follow wherever you may lead, and to do some deed which will attain for you honour and glory, and to show that the men of Evesham are as doughty as any under King Richard's rule."

"You must be wary, Cuthbert," the earl said to him that evening. "Believe me that you and I have made a foe, who, although he may not have the power, has certainly the will to injure us to the death. I marked the eye of Count Jacquelin during the fight, and again when you were led up to the king. There was hatred and fury in his eye. The page too, I hear, is his own nephew, and he will be the laughing-stock of the French camp at having been conquered by one so much younger than himself. It will be well to keep upon your guard, and not go out at night unattended. Keep Cnut near you; he is faithful as a watch-dog, and would give his life, I am sure, for you. I will myself be also upon my guard, for it was after all my quarrel, and the fury of this fierce knight will vent itself upon both of us if the opportunity should come. I hear but a poor account of him among his confreres. They say he is one of those disgraces to the name of knight who are but a mixture of robber and soldier; that he harries all the lands in his neighbourhood; and that he has now only joined the Crusade to avoid the vengeance which the cries of the oppressed people had invoked from his liege lord. I am told indeed that the choice was given him to be outlawed, or to join the Crusades with all the strength he could raise. Naturally he adopted the latter alternative; but he has the instincts of the robber still, and will do us an evil turn, if he have the chance."

Two days later the great army broke up its camp and marched south. After a week's journeying they encamped near a town, and halted there two or three days in order to collect provisions for the next advance; for the supplies which they could obtain in the country districts were wholly insufficient for so great a host of men. Here the armies were to separate, the French marching to Genoa, the English to Marseilles, the town at which they were to take ship.

One evening the earl sent Cuthbert with a message for another English lord, staying in the town at the palace of the bishop, who was a friend of his.

Cnut accompanied Cuthbert, for he now made a point of seldom letting him out of his sight. It was light when they reached the bishop's palace, but here they were delayed for some time, and night had fallen when they sallied out.

The town was quiet, for the inhabitants cared not to show themselves in the streets now that such a large army of fierce men were in the neighbourhood.

The others indeed of the monarchs were stringent, but discipline there was but little of, and the soldiery in those days regarded peaceful citizens as fair game; hence, when they came from the palace the streets of the city were already hushed and quiet, for the orders of the king had been preemptory that no men-at-arms, or others except those on duty, were to be away from their camp after nightfall.

This order had been absolutely necessary, so many were the complaints brought in by country peasants and farmers, of the doings of bands of soldiers.

Cnut and Cuthbert proceeded along the streets unmolested for some distance. Occasionally a solitary passer-by, with hooded cape, hurried past. The moon was half full, and her light was welcome indeed, for in those days the streets were unlighted, and the pavement so bad that passage through the streets after dark was a matter of difficulty, and even of danger.

Here and there before some roadside shrine a lamp dimly burned; before these they paused, and, as good Catholics, Cnut and Cuthbert crossed themselves. Just as they had passed one of these wayside shrines, a sudden shout was heard, and a party of eight or ten men sprang out from a side street and fell upon them.

Cnut and Cuthbert drew their swords and laid about them heartily, but their assailants were too strong. Cnut was stricken to the ground, and Cuthbert, seeing that defence was hopeless, took to his heels and ran for his life. He was already wounded, but happily not so severely as in any way to disable him.

Seeing that it was speed, and speed alone, which now could save him, he flung aside his belt scabbard and as he ran, and with rapid steps flew along the streets, not knowing whither he went, and striving only to keep ahead of his pursuers. They, more encumbered by arms and armour, were unable to keep up with the flying footsteps of a lad clothed in the light attire of a page; but Cuthbert felt that the blood running from his wound was weakening him fast, and that unless he could gain some refuge his course must speedily come to an end. Happily he saw at some little distance ahead of him a man standing by a door. Just as he arrived the door opened, and a glow of light from within fell on the road, showing that the person entering was a monk.

Without a moment's hesitation Cuthbert rushed through the door, shouting "Sanctuary!" and sank almost fainting on the ground.

The monks, accustomed to wild pursuits and scenes of outrage in those warlike days, hastily closed the door, barring it securely. In a moment there was a rush of men against it from without.

One of the monks opened a lattice above the door.

"What mean you," he said, "by this outrage? Know ye not that this is the Monastery of St. John, and that it is sacrilege to lay a hand of violence even against its postern? Begone," he said, "or we'll lodge a complaint before the king."

The assailants, nothing daunted, continued to batter at the door; but at this moment the monks, aroused from their beds, hastened to the spot, and seizing bill and sword-for in those days even monks were obliged at times to depend upon carnal weapons-they opened the door, and flung themselves upon the assailants with such force that the latter, surprised and discomfited, were forced to make a hasty retreat.

The doors were then again barred, and Cuthbert was carried up to a cell in the building, where the leech of the monastery speedily examined his wound, and pronounced, that although his life was not in danger by it, he was greatly weakened by the loss of blood, that the wound was a serious one, and that it would be some time before the patient would recover.

It was two days before Cuthbert was sufficiently restored to be able to speak. His first question to the monk was as to his whereabouts, and how long he had been there. Upon being answered, he entreated that a messenger might be despatched to the camp of the Earl of Evesham, to beg that a litter might be sent for him, and to inquire what had become of Cnut, whom he had last seen stricken down.

The monk replied, "My son, I grieve to tell you that your request cannot be complied with. The army moved away yesternoon, and is now some five-and-twenty miles distant. There is nothing for you but patience, and when restored you can follow the army, and rejoin your master before he embarks at Marseilles. But how is it that a lad so young as you can have incurred the enmity of those who sought your life? For it is clear from the pertinacity with which they urged their attack that their object was not plunder, of which indeed they would get but little from you, but to take your life."

Cuthbert recounted the circumstances which had led to the feud of the Count of Brabant against him, for he doubted not that this truculent knight was at the bottom of the attack.

"After what has happened," the monk said, "you will need have caution when you leave here. The place where you have taken refuge is known to them, and should this wild noble persist in his desire for vengeance against you, he will doubtless leave some of his ruffians to watch the monastery. We will keep a look-out, and note if any strangers are to be seen near the gates; if we find that it is so, we shall consider what is best to be done. We could of course appeal to the mayor for protection against them, and could even have the strangers ejected from the town or cast into prison; but it is not likely that we should succeed in capturing more than the fellow who may be placed on the look-out, and the danger would be in no wise lessened to yourself. But there is time to talk over this matter before you leave. It will be another fortnight at least before you will be able to pursue your journey."

Cuthbert gained strength more rapidly than the monk had expected. He was generously fed, and this and his good constitution soon enabled him to recover from the loss of blood; and at the end of five days he expressed his hope that he could on the following day pursue his journey. The monk who attended him shook his head.

"Thou mightst, under ordinary circumstances, quit us to-morrow, for thou art well enough to take part in the ordinary pursuits of a page; but to journey is a different thing. You may have all sorts of hardships to endure; you may have even to trust for your life to your speed and endurance; and it would be madness for you to go until your strength is fully established. I regret to tell you that we have ascertained beyond a doubt that the monastery is closely watched. We have sent some of the acolytes out, dressed in the garbs of monks, and attended by one of our elder brethren; and in each case, a monk who followed at a distance of fifty yards was able to perceive that they were watched. The town is full of rough men, the hangers-on of the army; some, indeed, are followers of laggard knights, but the greater portion are men who merely pursue the army with a view to gain by its necessities, to buy plunder from the soldiers, and to rob, and, if necessary, to murder should there be a hope of obtaining gold. Among these men your enemies would have little difficulty in recruiting any number, and no appeal that we could make to the mayor would protect you from them when you have left the walls. We must trust to our ingenuity in smuggling you out. After that, it is upon your own strength and shrewdness that you must rely for an escape from any snares that may be laid for you. You will see, then, that at least another three or four days are needed before you can set forth. Your countrymen are so far away that a matter of a few days will make but little difference. They will in any case be delayed for a long time at Marseilles before they embark; and whether you leave now or a month hence, you would be equally in time to join them before their embarkation-that is, supposing that you make your way through the snares which beset you."

Cuthbert saw the justice of the reasoning, and it was another week before he announced himself as feeling absolutely restored to strength again, and capable of bearing as much exertion as he could have done before his attack.

A long consultation was held with the prior and a monk who had acted as his leech, as to the best plan of getting Cuthbert beyond the walls of the city. Many schemes were proposed and rejected. Every monk who ventured beyond the walls had been closely scrutinized, and one or two of short stature had even been jostled in the streets, so as to throw back their hoods and expose a sight of their faces. It was clear, then, that it would be dangerous to trust to a disguise. Cuthbert proposed that he should leave at night, trusting solely to their directions as to the turnings he should take to bring him to the city walls, and that, taking a rope, he should there let himself down, and make the best of his way forward. This, however, the monks would not consent to, assuring him that the watch was so strictly kept round the monastery that he would inevitably be seen.

"No," the prior said, "the method, whatever it is, must be as open as possible; and though I cannot at this moment hit upon a plan, I will think it over to-night, and putting my ideas with those of Father Jerome here, and the sacristan, who has a shrewd head, it will be hard if we cannot between us contrive some plan to evade the watch of those robber villains who beset the convent."

The next morning when the prior came in to see Cuthbert, the latter said, "Good father, I have determined not to endeavour to make off in disguise. I doubt not that your wit could contrive some means by which I should get clear of the walls without observation from the scouts of this villain noble. But once in the country, I should have neither horse nor armour, and should have hard work indeed to make my way down through France, even though none of my enemies were on my track. I will therefore, if it please you, go down boldly to the Mayor, and claim a protection and escort. If he will but grant me a few men-at-arms for one day's ride from the town, I can choose my own route, and riding out in mail can then take my chance of finding my way down to Marseilles."

"I will go down with you, my son," the prior said, "to the mayor. Two of my monks shall accompany us; and assuredly no insult will be offered to you in the street thus accompanied." Shortly afterwards, Cuthbert started as arranged, and soon arrived at the house of the mayor, Sir John de Cahors.

Upon the prior making known to this knight whom he had brought with him, the mayor exclaimed, —

"Pest! young gentleman; you have caused us no small trouble and concern. We have had ridings to and fro concerning you, and furious messages from your fiery king. When in the morning a tall, stalwart knave dressed in green was found, slashed about in various places, lying on the pavement, the townsmen, not knowing who he was, but finding that he still breathed, carried him to the English camp, and he was claimed as a follower of the Earl of Evesham. There was great wrath and anger over this; and an hour later the earl himself came down and stated that his page was missing, and that there was reason to believe that he had been foully murdered, as he had accompanied the man found wounded. Fortunately the bulk of the armies had marched away at early dawn, and the earl had only remained behind in consequence of the absence of his followers. I assured the angry Englishman that I would have a thorough search made in the town; and although in no way satisfied, he rode off after his king with all his force, carrying with him the long-limbed man whom we had picked up. Two days after, a message came back from King Richard himself, saying that unless this missing page were discovered, or if, he being killed, his murderers were not brought to justice and punished, he would assuredly on his return from the Holy Land burn the town over our ears. Your king is not a man who minces matters. However, threatened men live long, especially when the person who threatens is starting for a journey, from which, as like or not, he may never return. However, I have had diligent search made for you. All the houses of bad repute have been examined, and their inhabitants questioned. But there are so many camp-followers and other rabble at present in the town that a hundred men might disappear without our being able to obtain a clue. I doubted not indeed that your body had been thrown in the river, and that we should never hear more of you. I am right glad that you have been restored; not indeed from any fear of the threats of the king your master, but because, from what the Earl of Evesham said, you were a lad likely to come to great fame and honour. The earl left in my charge your horse, and the armour which he said you wore at a tournament lately, in case we should hear aught of you."

Cuthbert gave an exclamation of pleasure. His purse contained but a few pieces of silver, and being without arms except for his short dagger, or means of locomotion, the difficulties of the journey down to Marseilles had sorely puzzled him. But with his good horse between his knees, and his suit of Milan armour on his back, he thought that he might make his way through any dangers which threatened him.

The prior now told the knight that circumstances had occurred, which showed that it was known to the assailants of Cuthbert that he had taken refuge in the convent, over which a strict watch had been kept by Cuthbert's enemies.

"If I could find the varlets, I would hang them over the gates of the town," the knight said wrathfully. "But as at the present moment there are nearly as many rogues as honest men in the place, it would be a wholesale hanging indeed to ensure getting hold of the right people. Moreover, it is not probable that another attempt upon his life will be made inside our walls; and doubtless the main body of this gang are somewhere without, intending to assault him when he continues his journey, and they have left but a spy or two here to inform them as to his movements. I will give you any aid in my power, young sir. The army is by this time nigh Marseilles, and, sooth to say, I have no body of men-at-arms whom I could send as your escort for so long a distance. I have but a small body here, and they are needed, and sorely too, to keep order within the walls."

"I thought, sir," Cuthbert said, "that if you could lend me a party of say four men-at-arms to ride with me for the first day, I could then trust to myself, especially if you could procure me one honest man to act as guide and companion. Doubtless they suppose that I should travel by the main road south; but by going the first day's journey either east or west, and then striking some southward road, I should get a fair start of them, throw all their plans out, and perchance reach Marseilles without interruption."

The knight willingly agreed to furnish four men-at-arms, and a trustworthy guide who would at least take him as far south as Avignon.

"I will," he said, "tell the men-at-arms off to-night. They shall be at the western gate at daybreak with the pass permitting them to ride through. The guide shall be at the convent door half an hour earlier. I will send up to-night your armour and horse. Here is a purse which the Earl of Evesham also left for your use. Is there aught else I can do for you?"

"Nothing, sir," Cuthbert said; "and if I regain the army in safety, I shall have pleasure in reporting to King Richard how kindly and courteously you have treated me."

The arrangements were carried out.

An hour before daybreak Cuthbert was aroused, donned his armour and steel casque, drank a flask of wine, and ate a manchet of bread which the prior himself brought him; and then, with a cordial adieu to the kind monks, issued forth.

The guide had just reached the gate, and together they trotted down the narrow streets to the west gate of the city, where four men-at-arms were awaiting them.

The gates were at once opened, and Cuthbert and his little troop sallied forth.

Chapter VIII
The Attack.

All day they rode with their faces west, and before nightfall had made a journey of over forty miles. Then bestowing a largess upon the men-at-arms, Cuthbert dismissed them, and took up his abode at a hostelry, his guide looking to the two horses.

Cuthbert was pleased with the appearance of the man who had been placed at his disposal. He was a young fellow of two-or-three-and-twenty, with an honest face. He was, he told Cuthbert, the son of a small farmer near Avignon; but having a fancy for trade, he had been apprenticed to a master smith. Having served his apprenticeship, he found that he had mistaken his vocation, and intended to return to the paternal vineyards.

Cuthbert calculated that he would make at least four days' journey to the south before he could meet with any dangers. Doubtless his exit from the convent had been discovered, and the moment the gates of the city were opened the spy would have proceeded south to warn his comrades, and these would doubtless have taken a road which at a distance would again take them on to that by which Cuthbert would be now travelling. As, however, he rode fast, and made long marches each day, he hoped that he might succeed in distancing them. Unfortunately, upon the third day his horse cast his shoe, and no smith could be met with until the end of the day's journey. Consequently, but a short distance could be done, and this at a slow pace. Upon the fifth day after their first start they arrived at a small town.

The next morning, Cuthbert on rising found that his guide did not present himself as usual. Making inquiries, he found that the young man had gone out the evening before, and had not returned. Extremely uneasy at the circumstance, Cuthbert went to the city guard, thinking that perhaps his guide might have got drunk, and been shut up in the cells. No news, however, was to be obtained there, and after waiting some hours, feeling sure that some harm had befallen him, he gave notice to the authorities of his loss, and then, mounting his horse, and leaving some money with the landlord of the hostelry to give to his guide in case the latter should return, he started at mid-day by the southern road.

He felt sure now that he was overtaken, and determined to keep his eyes and faculties thoroughly on watch.

The roads in those days were mere tracks. Here and there a little village was to be met with; but the country was sparsely cultivated, and travelling lonely work. Cuthbert rode fast, carefully avoiding all copses and small woods through which the road ran, by making a circuit round them and coming on to it again on the other side.

His horse was an excellent one, the gift of the earl, and he had little fear, with his light weight, of being overtaken, if he could once leave his enemies behind him.

At length he approached an extensive forest, which stretched for miles on either side.

Half a mile before he reached it the track divided.

He had for some little time eased his horse down to a walk, as he felt that the wood would be the spot where he would in all probability be attacked, and he needed that his steed should be possessed of its utmost vigour.

At the spot where the track branched, a man in the guise of a mendicant was sitting. He begged for alms, and Cuthbert threw him a small coin.

A sudden thought struck him as he heard a rustling in the bushes near.

"Which is the nearest and best road to Avignon?" he said.

"The right-hand road is the best and shortest," the beggar said. "The other makes a long circuit, and leads through several marshes, which your honour will find it hard to pass."

Cuthbert thanked him, and moved forward, still at a walk, along the right-hand road.

When he had gone about 200 yards, and was hidden from the sight of the man he had left-the country being rough, and scattered with clumps of bushes-he halted, and, as he expected, heard the sound of horses' hoofs coming on at full gallop along the other road.

"Your master must have thought me young indeed," he said, "to try and catch me with such a transparent trick as that. I do not suppose that accursed page has more than ten men with him, and doubtless has placed five on each road. This fellow was placed here to see which track I would follow, and has now gone to give the party on the left hand the news that I have taken this way. Had it not been for him I should have had to run the gauntlet with four or five of my enemies. As it is, the path will doubtless be clear."

So saying, he turned his horse, galloped back to the spot where the tracks separated, and then followed the left-hand route.

As he had hoped, he passed through the wood without incident or interruption, and arrived safely that night at a small town, having seen no signs of his enemies.

The next day he started again early, and rode on until mid-day, when he halted at a large village, at which was the only inn between the place from which he started and his destination. He declined the offer of the servant of the inn to take his horse round to the stable, telling the man to hold him outside the door and give him from a sieve a few handfuls of grain.

Then he entered the inn and ate a hearty meal. As he appeared at the door, he saw several men gathered near. With a single spring he threw himself into the saddle, just as a rush forward was made by those standing round. The man next to him sprang upon him, and endeavoured to drag him from the saddle. Cuthbert drew the little dagger called a Misricorde from his belt, and plunged it into his throat. Then seizing the short mace which hung at the saddle bow, he hurled it with all his force full in the face of his enemy, the page of Sir Philip, who was rushing upon him sword in hand. The heavy weapon struck him fairly between the eyes, and with a cry he fell back, his face completely smashed in by the blow, the sword which he held uplifted to strike flying far through the air.

Cuthbert struck his spurs into his horse, and the animal dashed forward with a bound, Cuthbert striking with his long sword at one or two men who made a snatch at the reins. In another minute he was cantering out of the village, convinced that he had killed the leader of his foes, and that he was safe now to pursue the rest of his journey on to Marseilles.

So it turned out.

Without further incident, he travelled through the south of France, and arrived at the great seaport. He speedily discovered the quarters in which the Earl of Evesham's contingent were encamped, and made towards this without delay. As he entered a wild shout of joy was heard, and Cnut ran forward with many gestures of delight.

"My dear Cuthbert, my dear Cuthbert!" he exclaimed. "Can it be true that you have escaped? We all gave you up; and although I did my best, yet had you not survived it I should never have forgiven myself, believing that I might have somehow done better, and have saved you from the cut-throats who attacked us."

"Thanks, thanks, my good Cnut," Cuthbert cried. "I have been through a time of peril, no doubt; but as you see, I am hale and well-better, methinks than you are, for you look pale and ill; and I doubt not that the wound which I received was a mere scratch to that which bore you down. It sounded indeed like the blow of a smith's hammer upon an anvil."

"Fortunately, my steel cap saved my head somewhat," Cnut said, "and the head itself is none of the thinnest; but it tried it sorely, I confess. However, now that you are back I shall, doubt not, soon be as strong as ever I was. I think that fretting for your absence has kept me back more than the inflammation from the wound itself-but there is the Earl at the door of his tent."

Through the foresters and retainers who had at Cnut's shout of joy crowded up, Cuthbert made his way, shaking hands right and left with the men, among whom he was greatly loved, for they regarded him as being in a great degree the cause of their having been freed from outlawry, and restored to civil life again. The earl was really affected. As Cuthbert rode up he held out both arms, and as his page alighted he embraced him as a father.

"My dear Cuthbert!" he exclaimed. "What anxiety have we not suffered. Had you been my own son, I could not have felt more your loss. We did not doubt for an instant that you had fallen into the hands of some of the retainers of that villain Count; and from all we could learn, and from the absence of any dead body by the side of that of Cnut, I imagined that you must have been carried off. It was clear that your chance of life, if you fell into the hands of that evil page, or his equally vile master, was small indeed. The very day that Cnut was brought in, I visited the French camp, and accused him of having been the cause of your disappearance and Cnut's wounds. He affected the greatest astonishment at the charge. He had not, as he said, been out of the camp for two days. My accusation was unfounded and malicious, and I should answer this as well as the previous outrage, when the vow of the Crusaders to keep peace among themselves was at an end. Of course I had no means of proving what I said, or I would have gone direct to the king and charged him with the outrage. As it was I gained nothing by my pains. He has accompanied this French division to Genoa; but when we meet at Sicily, where the two armies are to rendezvous, I will bring the matter before the king, as the fact that his page was certainly concerned in it must be taken as showing that he was the instigator."

"It would, my lord earl, be perhaps better," Cuthbert said, "if I might venture to advise, to leave the matter alone. No doubt the count would say that he had discharged his page after the tournament, and that the latter was only carrying out his private feud with me. We should not be able to disprove the story, and should gain no satisfaction by the matter."

The earl admitted the justice of Cuthbert's reasoning, but reserved to himself the task of punishing the author of the outrage upon the first fitting opportunity.

There was a weary delay at Marseilles before the expedition set sail. This was caused by the fact of the English fleet, which had been ordered to be there upon their arrival, failing to keep the agreement.

The words English fleet badly describe the vessels which were to carry the English contingent to their destination. They were ships belonging to the maritime nations of Italy-the Venetians, Genoese, Pisans, etc.; for England at that time had but few of her own, and these scarcely fitted for the stormy navigation of the Bay of Biscay.

King Richard, impatient as ever of delay, at last lost his temper, and embarked on board a ship with a few of his chosen knights, and set sail by himself for Sicily, the point at which the two armies of the expedition were to re-unite. A few days after his departure, the long-looked-for fleet arrived, and a portion of the English host embarked at once, and set sail for Sicily, where they were to be landed, and the ships were to return to fetch the remaining contingent.

A sea voyage of this kind in those days was a serious matter. Long voyages were rare, and troops were carried very much upon the principle of herrings; that is, were packed as close as they could be, without any reference to their comfort. As the voyages seldom lasted more than twenty-four hours, this did not much matter, but during long voyages the discomforts, or as may be said sufferings, of the troops were considerable. So tightly packed were the galleys in which the English set sail from Marseilles, that there was no walking about. Every man slept where he sat, and considered himself lucky indeed if he could obtain room sufficient to stretch himself at full length. Most slept sitting against bulwarks or other supports. In the cabins, where the knights, their pages and squires, were placed, the crowding was of course less excessive, but even here the amount of space, which a subaltern travelling to India for the first time now-a-days would grumble at, was considered amply sufficient for half-a-dozen knights of distinction. It was a week after sailing, when Cnut touched Cuthbert's arm as he came on deck one morning, and said, —

"Look, look, Cuthbert! that mountain standing up in the water has caught fire on the top. Did you ever see such a thing?"

The soldiers crowded to the side of the vessel, in intense astonishment and no little awe. From the top of a lofty and rugged hill, rising almost straight from the sea, flames were roaring up, smoke hung over the island, and stones were thrown into the air and rattled down the side of the hill, or fell into the sea with a splash.

"That is a fearsome sight," Cnut said, crossing himself.

"It looks as if it was the mouth of purgatory," exclaimed another, standing by.

Cuthbert himself was amazed, for the instruction he had received from Father Francis was of too slight a nature to include the story of volcanoes. A priest, however, who accompanied the ship in the character of leech and confessor, explained the nature of the phenomenon to his astonished listeners, and told them that over on the mainland was a mountain which at times vomited forth such masses of stones and of liquid rock that it had swallowed up and covered many great cities. There was also, he told them, another mountain of the same sort, even more vast, on the island of Sicily itself; but that this had seldom, as far back as man could remember, done any great harm.

Sailing on, in another day they arrived off the coast of Sicily itself, and sailing up the straits between it and the mainland, they landed at Messina. Here a considerable portion of the French army had already arrived, having been brought down from Genoa.

There was no news of the King of England; and, as often happens, the saying "the more haste the less speed," had been verified here.

It was some days later before King Richard arrived, having been driven from his course by tempests, well-nigh cast ashore, and having besides gone through many adventures. Three weeks later, the whole of the army of the Crusaders were gathered around Messina, where it was intended to remain some little time before starting. It was a gay time; and the kings vied with each other in entertainments, joustings, and tournaments. The Italian knights also made a brave show, and it might have been thought that this huge army of men were gathered there simply for amusement and feasting. In the tournaments every effort was made to prevent any feeling of national rivalry, and although parties of knights held their own against all comers, these were most carefully selected to represent several nationalities, and therefore victory, on whichsoever side it fell, excited no feelings of bitterness.

Alone, King Richard was undoubtedly the strongest cavalier of the two armies. Against his ponderous strength no knight could keep his seat; and this was so palpable, that after many victories, King Richard was forced to retire from the lists from want of competitors, and to take his place on the dais with the more peace-loving King of France.

The gaiety of the camp was heightened by the arrival of many nobles and dames from Italy. Here, too, came the Queen of Navarre, bringing with her the beautiful Princess Berengaria.

"Methinks," the Earl of Evesham said to Cuthbert, a fortnight after the arrival of the queen, "that unless my eyes deceive me, the princess is likely to be a cause of trouble."

"In what way?" asked Cuthbert with surprise, for he had been struck with her marvellous beauty, and wondered greatly what mischief so fair a being could do.

"By the way in which our good lord, the king, gazes upon her, methinks that it were like enough that he broke off his engagement with the Princess of France, for the sake of the fair eyes of this damsel."

"That were indeed a misfortune," Cuthbert said gravely, for he saw at once the anger which such a course would excite in the minds of the French king and his knights, who would naturally be indignant in the extreme at the slight put upon their princess. As day after day passed, it became evident to all that the King of England was infatuated by the princess. Again he entered the lists himself, and as some fresh Italian knights and others had arrived, he found fresh opponents, and conspicuously laid the spoils of victory at the feet of the princess, whom he selected as the Queen of Beauty.

All sorts of rumours now became current in camp; violent quarrels between the kings, and bad feeling between the French and English knights, broke out again in consequence, and this more violently than before.

Chapter IX
The Princess Berengaria.

One night it chanced that Cuthbert was late in his return to camp, and his road took him through a portion of the French encampment; the night was dark, and Cuthbert presently completely lost all idea as to his bearings. Presently he nearly ran against a tent; he made his way to the entrance in order to crave directions as to his way-for it was a wet night; the rain was pouring in torrents, and few were about of whom he could demand the way-and, as he was about to draw aside the hangings, he heard words said in a passionate voice which caused him to withdraw his hand suddenly.

"I tell you," said a voice, "I would rather drive a dagger myself into her heart, than allow our own princess to be insulted by this hot-headed island dog."

"It is sad indeed," said another, but in a calmer and smoother tone, "that the success of a great expedition like this, which has for its object the recovery of the holy sepulchre from the infidels, should be wrecked by the headstrong fancies of one man. It is even, as is told by the old Grecian poet, as when Helen caused a great war between peoples of that nation."

"I know nothing," another voice said, "either of Helen or the Greeks, or of their poets. They are a shifty race, and I can believe aught that is bad of them. But touching this princess of Navarre, I agree with our friend, it would be a righteous deed to poniard her, and so to remove the cause of dispute between the two kings, and, indeed, the two nations. This insult laid upon our princess is more than we, as French knights and gentlemen, can brook; and if the king says the word, there is not a gentleman in the army but will be ready to turn his sword against the islanders."

Then the smooth voice spoke again.

"It would, my brethren, be wrong and useless to shed blood; but methinks, that if this apple of discord could be removed, a good work would be done; not, as our friend the count has suggested, by a stab of the dagger; that indeed would be worse than useless. But surely there are scores of religious houses, where this bird might be placed in a cage without a soul knowing where she was, and where she might pass her life in prayer that she may be pardoned for having caused grave hazards of the failure of an enterprise in which all the Christian world is concerned."

The voices of the speakers now fell, and Cuthbert was straining his ear to listen, when he heard footsteps approaching the tent, and he glided away into the darkness.

With great difficulty he recovered the road to the camp, and when he reached his tent he confided to the Earl of Evesham what he had heard.

"This is serious indeed," the earl said, "and bodes no little trouble and danger. It is true that the passion which King Richard has conceived for Berengaria bids fair to wreck the Crusade, by the anger which it has excited in the French king and his nobles; but the disappearance of the princess would no less fatally interfere with it, for the king would be like a raging lion deprived of his whelps, and would certainly move no foot eastward until he had exhausted all the means in his power of tracing his lost lady love. You could not, I suppose, Cuthbert, point out the tent where this conversation took place?"

"I could not," Cuthbert answered; "in the darkness one tent is like another. I think I should recognize the voices of the speakers did I hear them again; indeed, one voice I did recognize, it was that of the Count of Brabant, with whom we had trouble before."

"That is good," the earl said, "because we have at least an object to watch. It would never do to tell the king what you have heard. In the first place, his anger would be so great that it would burst all bounds, and would cause, likely enough, a battle at once between the two armies; nor would it have any good effect, for he of Brabant would of course deny the truth of your assertions, and would declare it was merely a got-up story to discredit him with the king, and so to wipe out the old score now standing between us. No, if we are to succeed, alike in preventing harm happening to the princess, and an open break between the two monarchs, it must be done by keeping a guard over the princess, unsuspected by all, and ourselves frustrating any attempt which may be made."

Cuthbert expressed his willingness to carry out the instructions which the earl might give him; and, much disturbed by the events of the day, both earl and page retired to rest, to think over what plan had best be adopted.

The princess was staying at the palace of the bishop of the town; this he, having another residence a short distance outside the walls, had placed at the disposal of the Queen of Navarre and her suite; and the first step of Cuthbert in the morning was to go into the town, to reconnoitre the position and appearance of the building. It was a large and irregular pile, and communicated with the two monasteries lying alongside of it. It would therefore clearly be a most difficult thing to keep up a complete watch on the exterior of so large a building. There were so many ways in which the princess might be captured and carried off by unscrupulous men, that Cuthbert in vain thought over every plan by which it could be possible to safeguard her. She might be seized upon returning from a tournament or entertainment; but this was improbable, as the queen would always have an escort of knights with her, and no attempt could be successful except at the cost of a public fracas and much loss of blood. Cuthbert regarded as out of the question that an outrage of this kind would be attempted.

The fact that one of the speakers in the tent had used the words "my sons," showed that one priest or monk, at least, was connected with the plot. It was possible that this man might have power in one of the monasteries, or he might be an agent of the bishop himself; and Cuthbert saw that it would be easy enough in the night for a party from one or other of the monasteries to enter by the door of communication with the palace, and carry off the princess without the slightest alarm being given. Once within the walls of the convent, she could be either hidden in the dungeons or secret places, which buildings of that kind were sure to possess, or could be at once carried out by some quiet entrance, and taken into the country, or transferred to some other building in the town.

When Cuthbert joined the earl he told him the observations that he had made, and Sir Walter praised the judgment which he had shown in his conclusions. The earl was of opinion that it would be absolutely necessary to get some clue as to the course which the abductors purposed to take; indeed it was possible that on after-consideration they might drop their plan altogether, for the words which Cuthbert had overheard scarcely betokened a plan completely formed and finally decided upon.

The great point he considered, therefore, was that the tent of his old enemy should be carefully watched, and that an endeavour should be made to hear something of what passed within, which might give a clue to the plan fixed upon. They did not, of course, know whether the tent in which the conversation had been heard by Cuthbert was that of Sir de Jacquelin Barras, or of one of the other persons who had spoken; and Cuthbert suggested that the first thing would be to find out whether the count, after nightfall, was in the habit of going to some other tent, or whether, on the other hand, he remained within, and was visited by others.

It was easy, of course, to discover which was his tent; and Cuthbert soon got its position, and then took Cnut into his counsels.

"The matter is difficult," Cnut said, "and I see no way by which a watch can be kept up by day; but after dark —I have several men in my band who can track a deer, and surely could manage to follow the steps of this baron without being observed. There is little Jack, who is no bigger than a boy of twelve, although he can shoot, and run, and play with the quarter-staff, or, if need be, with the bill, against the best man in the troop. I warrant me that if you show him the tent, he will keep such sharp watch that no one shall enter or depart without his knowing where they go to. On a dark night he will be able to slip among the tents, and to move here and there without being seen. He can creep on his stomach without moving a leaf, and trust me the eyes of these French men-at-arms will look in vain for a glimpse of him."

"You understand, Cnut, all that I want to know is whether the other conspirators in this matter visit his tent, or whether he goes to theirs."

"I understand," Cnut said. "That is the first point to be arrived at."

Three days later Cnut brought news that each night after dark a party of five men met in the tent that was watched; that one of the five always came out when all had assembled, and took his station before the entrance of the tent, so as to be sure that no eavesdropper was near.

Cuthbert smiled, —

"It is a case of locking the door after the horse has gone."

"What is to be done now?" Cnut asked.

"I will talk with the earl before I tell you, Cnut. This matter is too serious for me to take a step without consulting Sir Walter."

That night there was a long talk between the earl and his page as to the best course to be pursued. It was clear that their old enemy was the leading person in the plot, and that the only plan to baffle it with any fair chances of success was to keep a constant eye upon his movements, and also to have three or four of the sturdiest men of the band told off to watch, without being perceived, each time that the princess was in her palace.

The Earl of Evesham left the arrangements entirely in the hands of his page, of whose good sense and sagacity he had a very high opinion.

His own first impulse had been to go before the king and denounce the Count of Brabant. But the ill-will between them was already well known; for not only was there the original dispute at the banquet, but when the two armies had joined at Sicily, King Richard, who had heard from the earl of the attempt at the assassination of Cuthbert, had laid a complaint before King Phillip of the conduct of his subject.

Sir de Jacquelin Barras, however, had denied that he had any finger in the matter.

"He had," he said, "discharged his page after the encounter with Cuthbert, and knew nothing further whatever of his movements."

Although it was morally certain that the page could not have purchased the services of the men who assisted him, from his own purse, or gain them by any means of persuasion, but that they were either the followers of the Count of Brabant, or ruffians hired with his money, as no proof could be obtained, the matter was allowed to drop.

The earl felt, however, that an accusation against the count by him of an intention to commit a high crime, and this merely on the evidence of his page, would appear like an attempt to injure the fair fame of his rival.

Feeling, therefore, that nothing could be done save to watch, he left the matter entirely in the hands of his page, telling him that he could take as many men-at-arms or archers as he might choose and use them in his name.

Cnut entered warmly into Cuthbert's plans; and finally it was arranged between them that six of the archers should nightly keep watch opposite the various entrances of the bishop's palace and of the two monasteries joining. Of course they could not patrol up and down without attracting attention, but they were to take up posts where they could closely observe the entrances, and were either to lie down and feign drunken sleep, or to conceal themselves within the shadow of an arch or other hiding-place.

Down on the sea-shore, Cuthbert made an arrangement with one of the owners of small craft lying there that ten of his men should sleep on board every night, together with some fishermen accustomed to the use of the oar.

Cuthbert himself determined to be always with this party.

Night after night passed, and so long a time went by that Cuthbert began to think the design must have been given up.

However, he resolved to relax none of his watchfulness during the remaining time that the expedition might stop in Sicily.

It was in January, three weeks after the first watch had been set, when one of the men who had been placed to watch the entrance to one of the monasteries, leapt on board the craft and shook Cuthbert by the shoulder.

"A party of some five men," he said, "have just issued out from the monastery. They are bearing a burden-what, I cannot see. They were making in the direction of the water. I whistled to Dick, who was next to me in the lane. He is following them, and I came on to tell you to prepare."

The night was pitch dark, and it was difficult in the extreme to see any one moving at a short distance off.

There were two or three streets that led from the monastery, which stood at the top of the town, towards the sea; and a party coming down might take any of these, according to the position in which the boat they were seeking was placed.

Cuthbert now instantly sent five or six of his men, with instructions to avoid all noise, along the line of the port, with orders to bring in word should any one come down and take boat, or should they hear any noise in the town.

He himself with the sailors loosed the ropes which fastened the boat to shore, got out the oars, and prepared to put off at a moment's notice.

He was of course ignorant whether the abductors would try to carry the princess off by water, or would hide her in one of the convents of the town; but he was inclined to think that the former would be the course adopted; for the king in his wrath would be ready to lay the town in flames, and to search every convent from top to bottom for the princess. Besides, there would be too many aware of the secret.

Cuthbert was not wrong in his supposition.

Soon the man he had sent to the extreme right came running up with the news that a boat had embarked at the farther end, with a party of some ten men on board. As he came along he had warned the others, and in five minutes the whole party were collected in the craft, numbering in all twelve of Cuthbert's men and six sailors. They instantly put out, and rowed in the direction in which the boat would have gone, the boatmen expressing their opinion that probably the party would make for a vessel which was lying anchored at some little distance from shore. The bearings of the position of this ship was known to the boatmen, but the night was so dark that they were quite unable to find it. Orders had been given that no sound or whisper was to be heard on board the boat; and after rowing as far as they could, the boatmen said they were in the direction of the ship.

The boatmen all lay on their oars, and all listened intently. Presently the creaking of a pulley was heard in the still night, at a distance of a few hundred yards. This was enough. It was clear that the vessel was getting up sail. The boat's head was turned in that direction; the crew rowed steadily but noiselessly, and in a few minutes the tall mast of a vessel could be seen faintly against the sky. Just as they perceived the situation, a hail from on board showed that their approach was now observed.

"Stretch to your oars," Cuthbert said, "we must make a dash for it now."

The rowers bent to their work and in a minute the boat ran alongside the craft.

As Cuthbert and his followers scrambled upon the deck, they were attacked by those of the crew and passengers who were standing near; but it was evident at once that the chiefs of the expedition had not heard the hail, and that there was no general plan of defence against them.

It was not until the last of them had gained a footing, and were beginning to fight their way along the vessel, that from below three or four men-at-arms ran up, and one in a tone of authority demanded what was the matter. When he heard the clash of swords and the shouts of the combatants, he put himself at once at the head of the party, and a fierce and obstinate fight now took place.

The assailants had, however, the advantage.

Cuthbert and his men were all lightly clad, and this on the deck of a ship lumbered with ropes and gear, and in the dark, was a great advantage, for the mailed men-at-arms frequently stumbled and fell. The fight lasted for several minutes. Cnut who was armed with a heavy mace, did great service, for with each of his sweeping blows he broke down the guard of an opponent, and generally levelled him to the deck.

The numbers at the beginning of the fight were not unequal, but the men to whom the vessel belonged made but a faint resistance when they perceived that the day was going against them. The men-at-arms, however, consisting of three, who appeared to be the leaders, and of eight pikemen, fought stubbornly and well.

Cuthbert was not long in detecting in the tones of the man who was clearly at the head of affairs the voice of Sir de Jacquelin Barras. To do him justice he fought with extreme bravery, and when almost all his followers were cut down or beaten overboard, he resisted staunchly and well. With a heavy two-handed sword he cleaved a space at the end of the boat, and kept the whole of Cuthbert's party at bay.

At last Cnut, who had been engaged elsewhere, came to the front, and a tough fight ensued between them.

It might have ended badly for the brave forester, for his lack of armour gave an enormous advantage to his opponent. Soon, however, the count's foot slipped on the boards of the deck, and before he could recover himself the mace of Cnut descended with tremendous force upon his head, which was unprotected, as he had taken off his casque on arriving at the ship. Without a word or a cry the count fell forward on the deck, killed as a bullock by a blow of a pole-axe.

While this conflict had been going on, occasionally the loud screams of a woman had been heard below.

Cuthbert, attended by Cnut and two of his followers, now descended.

At the bottom of the steps they found a man-at-arms placed at the door of a cabin. He challenged them as they approached, but being speedily convinced that the vessel was in their hands, and that his employer and party were all conquered, he made a virtue of necessity, and laid down his arms.

"You had better go in alone," Cnut said, "Master Cuthbert. The lady is less likely to be frightened by your appearance than by us, for she must wonder indeed what is going on."

On entering the cabin, which had evidently been fitted up for the use of a lady, Cuthbert saw standing at the other end the princess whom of course he knew well by sight. A lamp was burning in the cabin, and by its light he could see that her face was deadly pale. Her robes were torn and disarranged, and she wore a look at once of grave alarm and surprise upon seeing a handsomely dressed page enter with a deep reverence.

"What means this outrage, young sir? Whoever you be, I warn you that the King of England will revenge this indignity."

"Your Highness," Cuthbert said, "you have no further reason for alarm; the knaves who carried you off from the bishop's palace and conveyed you to this ship are all either killed or in our power. I am the page of the Earl of Evesham, a devoted follower of King Richard. Some of the designs of the bold men came to the ears of my lord, and he ordered me and a band of his followers to keep good guard over the palace and buildings adjoining. We were unable to gather our strength in time to prevent your being taken on board, but we lost no time in putting forth when we found that your abductors had taken boat, and by good fortune arrived here in time; a few minutes later, and the knaves would have succeeded in their object, for the sails were already being hoisted, and the vessel making way, when we arrived. Your abductors are all either killed or thrown overboard, and the vessel's head is now turned towards the shore, and I hope in a few minutes to have the honour of escorting you to the palace."

The princess, with a sigh of much satisfaction and relief, sank on to a couch.

"I am indeed indebted to you, young sir," she said. "Believe me, the Princess Berengaria is not ungrateful, and should it be ever in her power to do aught for your lord, or for yourself, or for those who have accompanied you to rescue her, believe me that she will do it."

"May I be so bold as to ask a boon?" Cuthbert said, dropping on one knee before her.

"It is granted at once, whatever it be, if in my power."

"My boon is, lady," he said, "that you will do your best to assuage the natural anger which the King of England will feel at this bold and most violent attempt. That he should be told, is of course necessary; but, lady, much depends upon the telling, and I am sure that at your request the king would restrain his anger. Were it not for that, I fear that such quarrels and disputes might arise as would bring the two armies to blows, and destroy for ever all hope of the successful termination of our joint enterprise."

"You are a wise and good youth," the princess said, holding out her hand to Cuthbert, which, as in duty bound, he placed to his lips. "Your request is wise and most thoughtful. I will use any poor influence which I may possess"—and Cuthbert could see that the blood came back now to the white face—"to induce King Richard to allow this matter to pass over. There is no reason why he should take up the case. I am no more under his protection than under that of the King of France, and it is to the latter I should appeal, for as I believe the men who abducted me were his subjects."

"The leader of them, madam, was a certain Sir de Jacquelin Barras, a Count of Brabant, with whom my master has had an old feud, and who has been just killed by the leader of our men-at-arms. The others, who have had the most active hand in the matter, have also perished; and it would, I think, be doubtful whether any clue could be obtained to those who were in league with them. The only man in the party who is alive, was placed as a sentry at your door, and as he is but a man-at-arms, we may be sure that he knows nought of the enterprise, but has merely carried out the orders of his master."

The vessel had by this time brought up close to the port. The princess determined to wait on board until the first dawn was seen in the skies, and then under the escort of her deliverers to go back to the palace, before the town was moving. This plan was carried out, and soon after dawn the princess was safe in the palace from which she had been carried a few hours previously.

Chapter X
Pirates.

It was not possible that a matter of this sort could be entirely hushed up. Not many hours passed before rumours were current of events which had taken place, though none knew what those events were.

There were reports that the tire-woman of the Princess Berengaria had in the night discovered that her mistress's couch was unoccupied, that she had found signs of a struggle, and had picked up a dagger on the floor, where it had evidently fallen from the sheath; also it was said, that the princess had returned at daylight escorted by an armed party, and that she was unable to obtain entrance to the palace until one of the ladies of the queen had been fetched down to order the sentries at the gate to allow her to enter.

This was the news which rumour carried through the camp. Few, however, believed it, and none who could have enlightened them opened their lips upon the subject.

It was known, however, that a messenger had come to King Richard early, and that he had at once mounted, and ridden off to the bishop's palace. What had happened there none could say, but there were rumours that his voice had been heard in furious outbursts of passion. He remained there until the afternoon, when he sent for a number of his principal nobles.

When these arrived, they found him standing on a das in the principal hall of the palace, and he there formally introduced to them the Princess Berengaria as his affianced wife. The ceremony of the marriage, he told them, would shortly take place.

This announcement caused a tremendous stir in both armies. The English, who had never been favourable to the alliance with the French princess, were glad to hear that this was broken off, and were well content that the Princess Berengaria should be their future queen, for her beauty, high spirit, and kindness had won all hearts.

On the part of the French, on the other hand, there was great indignation, and for some time it was feared that the armies would come to open blows.

King Phillip, however, although much angered, was politic enough to deprecate any open outbreak. He knew that a dispute now began, would not only at once put a stop to the Crusade, but that it might lead to more serious consequences at home. The fiery bravery of the English king, backed as it would be by the whole strength of his subjects, might render him a very formidable opponent; and the king felt that private grievances must be laid aside where the good of France was concerned.

Still the coldness between the armies increased, their camps were moved further apart, and during the time that they remained in Sicily, there was but little commerce between the two forces.

As soon as the winter had broken, the French monarch broke up his camp, and in March sailed for the Holy Land.

The English had expected that the marriage ceremony of the king and Princess Berengaria would be celebrated before they left Sicily, but this was not the case. There were high joustings and fetês in honour of the princess, but the marriage was delayed. A fortnight after the French had sailed, the English embarked in the 200 ships, which had been prepared, and sailed also on their way to Acre.

It must not be supposed that the attempted abduction of the Princess Berengaria was unimportant in its results to Cuthbert.

After returning from the palace the king, who had heard from her the details of what had taken place, and the names of her rescuers, sent for the Earl of Evesham. The latter had of course learned from Cuthbert all that had happened, and had expressed his high approval of his conduct, and his gratification at the result.

"I learn, Sir Earl," said King Richard, "that it is to you that I am indebted for the rescue of the princess. She tells me, that suspecting some plot, you placed a guard around the bishop's palace, with a strong body on the shore ready to rescue her from the hands of any who might attempt to take her to sea."

"It is as you say, sire," replied the earl; "but the whole merit of the affair rests upon my page, the lad whom you may remember as having fought with and conquered the French page, and of whose conduct you then approved highly. You may also remember that he escaped by some display of bravery and shrewdness the further attempts to assassinate him, and your Majesty was good enough to make a complaint to King Phillip of the conduct of one of his nobles on that head. It seems that some two months since, the lad in coming through the French camp at night missed his way, and accidentally overheard a few words spoken in a voice which he recognized as that of his enemy. The name of your Majesty being mentioned, he deemed it his duty to listen, and thus discovered that a plot was on foot for carrying off the princess. After consultation with me, we agreed upon the course to be adopted, namely, to place sentries round the bishop's palace and the buildings adjoining, who should follow and bring word should she be taken to another place in town, while a band was placed on the shore in readiness to interfere at once to prevent her being carried away by sea. He undertook the management of all details, having with him a trusty squire who commands my Saxon bowmen."

"For your own part I thank you, my lord," the king said, "and, believe me, you shall not find Richard ungrateful. As to your page, he appears brave and wise beyond his years. Were it not that I think that it would not be good for him, and might attract some envy upon the part of others, I would at once make him a knight. He already has my promise that I will do so on the first occasion when he can show his prowess upon the infidels. Bring him to me to-morrow, when the princess will be here with the Queen of Navarre at a banquet. I would fain thank him before her; and, although I have agreed-at the princess's earnest solicitation-to take no further notice of the matter, and to allow it to pass as if it had not been, yet I cannot forgive the treachery which has been used, and, without letting all know exactly what has occurred, would fain by my reception of your page, let men see that something of great import has happened, of the nature of which I doubt not that rumour will give some notion."

Upon the following day, therefore, Cuthbert to his confusion found himself the centre of the royal circle. The king expressed himself to him in the most gracious manner, patting him on the shoulder, and said that he would be one day one of the best and bravest of his knights. The princess and the Queen of Navarre gave him their hands to kiss; and somewhat overwhelmed, he withdrew from the royal presence, the centre of attention, and, in some minds, of envy.

Cnut too did not pass unrewarded.

His Majesty, finding that Cnut was of gentle Saxon blood, gave him a gold chain in token of his favour, and distributed a heavy purse among the men who had followed him.

When the British fleet, numbering 200 ships, set sail from Sicily, it was a grand and martial sight. From the masts were the colours of England and those of the nobles who commanded; while the pennons of the knights, the bright plumes and mantles, the flash of armour and arms, made the decks alive with light and colour.

The king's ship advanced in the van, and round him were the vessels containing his principal followers. The Queen of Navarre and the Princess Berengaria were with the fleet. Strains of music rose from the waters, and never were the circumstances of war exhibited in a more picturesque form.

For two days the expedition sailed on, and then a change of a sudden and disastrous kind took place.

"What is all this bustle about?" Cuthbert said to Cnut. "The sailors are running up the ladders, and all seems confusion."

"Methinks," said Cnut, "that we are about to have a storm. A few minutes ago scarce a cloud was to be seen; now that bank over there has risen half-way up the sky. The sailors are accustomed to these treacherous seas, and the warnings which we have not noticed have no doubt been clear enough to them." With great rapidity the sails of the fleet came down, and in five minutes its whole aspect was changed; but quickly as the sailors had done their work, the storm was even more rapid in its progress. Some of the ships whose crews were slower or less skilful than the others, were caught by the gale before they could get their sails snug, and the great sheets of white canvas were blown from the bolt ropes as if made of paper, and a blackness which could almost be felt, covered the sea, the only light being that given by the frothing waters. There was no longer any thought of order. Each ship had to shift for herself; and each captain to do his best to save those under his charge, without thought of what might befall the others.

In the ship which carried the Earl of Evesham's contingent, order and discipline prevailed. The earl's voice had been heard at the first puff of wind, shouting to the men to go below, save a few who might be of use to haul at ropes. His standard was lowered, the bright flags removed from the sides of the ship, the shields which were hanging over the bulwarks were hurriedly taken below, and when the gale smote them, the ship was trim, and in readiness to receive it. A few square yards of sail alone were all that the captain had thought it prudent to keep spread, and in a minute from the time she was struck the lofty hulk was tearing along through the waters at a tremendous speed. Four of the best hands were placed at the helm; and here the captain took his post.

The danger was now that in the darkness they might run against one of their consorts. Even in the war of the elements they could hear from time to time crashes as of vessels striking against each other, with shouts and cries. Once or twice from the darkness ships emerged, close on one hand or the other; but the steadiness of the captain in each case saved the ship from collision.

As the storm continued, these glimpses of other vessels became more and more rare, and the ship being a very fast sailer, the captain indulged the hope that he was now clear of the rest of the fleet.

He now attempted to lie-to the storm, but the wind was too strong. The ships in those days too, were so high out of the water, and offered in themselves such a target to the wind, that it was useless to adopt any other maneuver than to run before it.

For two days and nights the tempest raged.

"What think you," the earl said to the captain, "of our position? Where are we, and where will the course upon which we are running take us?"

"I cannot say with certainty," the captain said, "for the wind has shifted several times. I had hoped to gain the shelter of Rhodes, but a shift of wind bore us away from there, and I much fear that from the direction in which we have been running we must be very nigh on the coast of Africa."

"Pest!" the earl said. "That would indeed be a speedy end to our Crusade. These Moors are pirates and cut-throats to a man; and even should we avoid the risk of being dashed to pieces, we should end our lives as slaves to one of these black infidels."

Three hours later, the captain's prophecies turned out right. Breakers were seen in various points in front, and with the greatest difficulty the vessel was steered through an opening between them; but in another few minutes she struck heavily, one of her masts went over the side, and she lay fast and immovable. Fortunately, the outside bank of sand acted as a sort of breakwater; had she struck upon this, the good ship would have gone to pieces instantly; but although the waves still struck her with considerable force, the captain had good hope that she would not break up. Darkness came on; the tempest seemed to lull. As there was no immediate danger, and all were exhausted by the tossing which they had received during the last forty-eight hours, the crew of the "Rose" slept soundly.

In the morning the sun rose brilliantly, and there was no sign of the great storm which had scattered the fleet of England. The shore was to be seen at a distance of some four miles, It was low and sandy, with lofty mountains in the distance. Far inland a white town with minaret and dome could be seen.

"Know you where we are?" the earl asked.

"As far as I can tell," the captain said, "we have been driven up the bay called the Little Syrtis—a place full of shoals and shallows, and abounding with pirates of the worst kind."

"Think you that the ship has suffered injury?"

"Whether she has done so or not," the captain said, "I fear greatly that she is fast in the sand, and even the lightening of all her cargo will scarce get her off; but we must try at least."

"It is little time that we shall have to try, Master Captain," Cuthbert, who was standing close, said. "Methinks those two long ships which are putting out from that town will have something to say to that."

"It is too true," the captain said. "Those are the galleys of the Moorish corsairs. They are thirty or forty oars, draw but little water, and will be here like the wind."

"What do you advise?" asked the earl. "The balistas which you have upon the poop can make but a poor resistance to boats that can row around us, and are no doubt furnished with heavy machines. They will quickly perceive that we are aground and defenceless, and will be able to plump their bolts into us until they have knocked the good ship to pieces. However, we will fight to the last. It shall not be said that the Earl of Evesham was taken by infidel dogs and sold as a slave, without striking a blow in his defence."

Cuthbert stood watching the corsairs, which were now rowing towards them at all speed.

"Methinks, my lord," he said, presently, "if I might venture to give an opinion, that we might yet trick the infidel."

"As how, Cuthbert?" the earl said. "Speak out; you know that I have great faith in your sagacity."

"I think, sir," the page said, "that did we send all your men below, leaving only the crew of the vessel on deck, they would take us for a merchant ship which has been wrecked here, and exercise but little care how they approach us. The men on deck might make a show of shooting once or twice with the balistas. The pirates, disdaining such a foe, would row alongside. Once there, we might fasten one or both to our side with grapnels, and then, methinks, that English bill and bow will render us more than a match for Moorish pirates, and one of these craft can scarcely carry more men than we have. I should propose to take one of them by force, and drive the pirates overboard; take possession of, if possible, or beat off, her consort; and then take the most valuable stores from the ship, and make our way as best we can to the north."

"Well thought of!" exclaimed the earl, cordially. "You have indeed imagined a plan which promises well. What think you, captain?"

"I think, my lord," the Genoese said, "that the plan is an excellent one, and promises every success. If your men will all go below, holding their arms in readiness for the signal, mine shall prepare grapnels and ropes, and the first of these craft which comes alongside they will lash so securely to the "Rose" that I warrant me she gets not away."

These preparations were soon made.

The soldiers, who at first had been filled with apprehension at the thought of slavery among the infidels, were now delighted at the prospect of a struggle ending in escape.

The archers prepared their bows and arrows, and stood behind the port-holes in readiness to pour a volley into the enemy; the men-at-arms grasped their pikes and swords; while above, the sailors moved hither and thither as if making preparations for defence, but in reality preparing the grapnels and ropes.

One of the pirates was faster than the other, and soon coming within reach, poured flights of javelins and stones upon the "Rose" from powerful machines, which she carried in her bow.

The crew of the "Rose" replied with their crossbows and arrows from the poop.

The corsair at first did not keep her course direct for the ship, but rowed round her, shooting arrows and casting javelins. Then, apparently satisfied that no great precaution need be observed with a feebly-manned ship in so great a strait as the "Rose," they set up a wild cry of "Allah!" and rowed towards her.

In two minutes the corsair was alongside of the "Rose," and the fierce crew were climbing up her sides. As she came alongside the sailors cast grapnels into her rigging, and fastened her to the "Rose;" and then aloud shout of "Hurrah for England!" was heard; the ports opened, and a volley of arrows was poured upon the astonished corsair; and from the deck above the assailants were thrown back into the galley, and a swarm of heavily armed men leapt down from the ship upon them.

Taken by surprise, and indeed outnumbered, the resistance of the corsairs was but slight. In a close fierce mle like this the light-armed Moors had but little chance with the mail-clad English, whose heavy swords and axes clove their defences at a blow. The fight lasted but three minutes, and then the last of the corsairs was overboard.

The men who rowed the galley had uttered the most piercing cries while this conflict had been raging. They were unable to take any part in it, had they been disposed to do so, for they were all slaves chained to the oars.

Scarcely had the conflict ended when the other galley arrived upon the scene; but seeing what had happened, and that her consort had fallen into the hands of the English, she at once turned her head, and rowed back rapidly to the town from which she had come.

Among the slaves who rowed the galley were many white men, and their cries of joy at their liberation greatly affected those who had thus unexpectedly rescued them. Hammers were soon brought into requisition, the shackles struck off them, and a scene of affecting joy took place. The slaves were of all nationalities, but Italians and Spaniards, French and Greeks, formed the principal part. There was no time, however, to be lost; the arms and munitions of war were hastily removed from the "Rose," together with the most valuable of the stores.

The galley-slaves again took their places, and this time willingly, at the oars, the places of the weakest being supplied by the English, whose want of skill was made up by the alacrity with which they threw their strength into the work; and in an hour from the time that the galley had arrived alongside of the "Rose," her head was turned north, and with sixty oars she was rowing at all speed for the mouth of the bay.

Chapter XI
In The Holy Land.

As soon as the galley which had escaped reached the town from which it had started, it with three others at once set out in pursuit; while from a narrow creek two other galleys made their appearance.

There were a few words of question among the English whether to stop and give battle to these opponents, or to make their way with all speed. The latter counsel prevailed; the earl pointing out that their lives were now scarcely their own, and that they had no right on their way to the holy sepulchre to risk them unnecessarily.

Fortunately they had it in their hands to fight or escape, as they chose; for doubly banked as the oars now were, there was little chance of the enemy's galleys overtaking them. Gradually as they rowed to sea the pursuing vessels became smaller and smaller to view, until at last they were seen to turn about and make again for land.

After some consultation between the earl and the captain of the lost ship, it was determined to make for Rhodes. This had been settled as a halting-point for the fleet, and the earl thought it probable that the greater portion of those scattered by the storm would rendezvous there.

So it proved; after a voyage, which although not very long was tedious, owing to the number of men cramped up in so small a craft, they came within sight of the port of Rhodes, and were greatly pleased at seeing a perfect forest of masts there, showing that at least the greater portion of the fleet had survived the storm.

This was indeed the fact, and a number of other single ships dropped in during the next day or two.

There was great astonishment on the part of the fleet when the long swift galley was seen approaching, and numerous conjectures were offered as to what message the pirates could be bringing-for there was no mistaking the appearance of the long, dangerous-looking craft.

When, upon her approach, the standard of the Earl of Evesham was seen flying on the bow, a great shout of welcome arose from the fleet; and King Richard himself, who happened to be on the deck of the royal ship, shouted to the earl to come on board and tell him what masquerading he was doing there. The earl of course obeyed the order, anchoring near the royal vessel, and going on board in a small boat, taking with him his page and squire.

The king heard with great interest the tale of the adventures of the "Rose"; and when the Earl of Evesham said that it was to Cuthbert that was due the thought of the stratagem by which the galley was captured, and its crew saved from being carried away into hopeless slavery, the king patted the boy on the shoulder with such hearty force as nearly to throw Cuthbert off his feet.

"By St. George!" said the monarch, "you are fated to be a very pink of knights. You seem as thoughtful as you are brave; and whatever your age may be, I declare that the next time your name is brought before me I will call a chapter of knights, and they shall agree that exception shall be made in your favour, and that you shall at once be admitted to the honourable post. You will miss your page, Sir Walter; but I am sure you will not grudge him that."

"No, no, sire," said the earl. "The lad, as I have told your Majesty, is a connexion of mine-distant, it is true, but one of the nearest I have-and it will give me the greatest pleasure to see him rising so rapidly, and on a fair way to distinguish himself highly. I feel already as proud of him as if he were my own son."

The fleet remained some two or three weeks at Rhodes, for many of the vessels were sorely buffeted and injured, masts were carried away as well as bulwarks battered in, and the efforts of the crews and of those of the whole of the artificers of Rhodes were called into requisition. Light sailing craft were sent off in all directions, for the king was in a fever of anxiety. Among the vessels still missing was that which bore the Queen of Navarre and the fair Berengaria.

One day a solitary vessel was seen approaching.

"Another of our lost sheep," the earl said, looking out over the poop.

She proved, however, to be a merchant ship of Greece, and newly come from Cyprus.

Her captain went on board the royal ship, and delivered message to the king, to the effect that two of the vessels had been cast upon the coast of Cyprus, that they had been plundered by the people, the crews ill-treated and made prisoners by the king, and that the Queen of Navarre and the princess were in their hands.

This roused King Richard into one of his furies.

"Before I move a step towards the Holy Land," he said, "I will avenge these injuries upon this faithless and insolent king. I swear that I will make him pay dearly for having laid a hand upon these ladies."

At once the signal was hoisted for all the vessels in a condition to sail to take on board water and provisions, and to prepare to sail for Cyprus; and the next morning at daybreak the fleet sailed out, and made their way towards that island, casting anchor off the harbour of Famagosta.

King Richard sent a messenger on shore to the king, ordering him at once to release the prisoners; to make the most ample compensation to them; to place ships at their service equal to those which had been destroyed; and to pay a handsome sum of money as indemnity.

The King of Cyprus, however, an insolent and haughty despot, sent back a message of defiance. King Richard at once ordered the anchors to be raised, and all to follow the royal ship.

The fleet entered the harbour of Famagosta; the English archers began the fight by sending a flight of arrows into the town. This was answered from the walls by a shower of stones and darts from the machines.

There was no time wasted. The vessels were headed towards the shore, and as the water was deep, many of them were able to run close alongside the rocky wharves. In an instant, regardless of the storm of weapons poured down by the defenders, the English leapt ashore.

The archers kept up so terrible a rain of missiles against the battlements that the defenders could scarcely show themselves for an instant there, and the men-at-arms, placing ladders against them, speedily mounted, and putting aside all opposition, poured into the town. The effeminate Greek soldiers of the monarch could offer no effectual resistance whatever, and he himself fled from the palace and gained the open country, followed by a few adherents. The English gained a considerable booty, for in those days a town taken by assault was always looked upon as the property of the captors. The Queen of Navarre and the princess were rescued.

King Richard, however, was not satisfied with the success he had gained, and was determined to punish this insolent little king. Accordingly the English were set in motion into the interior, and town after town speedily fell, or opened their gates to him. The king, deserted by his troops, and detested by his people for having brought so terrible a scourge upon them by his reckless conduct, now sued for peace; but King Richard would give him no terms except dethronement, and this he was forced to accept. He was deprived of his crown, and banished from the island.

The king now, to the surprise of his barons, announced his intention of at once marrying the Princess Berengaria.

Popular as he was, there was yet some quiet grumbling among his troops; as they said, with justice, they had been waiting nearly six months in the island of Sicily, and the king might well have married there, instead of a fresh delay being caused when so near their place of destination.

However, the king as usual had his own way, and the marriage was solemnized amidst great rejoicing and solemnity.

It was a brilliant scene indeed in the cathedral of Limasol. There were assembled all the principal barons of England, together with a great number of the nobles of Cyprus.

Certainly no better matched pair ever stood at the altar together, for as King Richard was one of the strongest and bravest men of his own or any other time, so Berengaria is admitted to have been one of the loveliest maidens.

The air was rent with the acclamations of the assembled English host and of the numerous inhabitants of Limasol as they emerged from the cathedral. For a fortnight the town was given up to festivity; tournaments, joustings, banquets succeeded each other day after day, and the islanders, who were fond of pleasure, and indeed very wealthy, vied with the English in the entertainments which they gave in honour of the occasion.

The festivities over, the king gave the welcome order to proceed on their voyage. They had now been joined by all the vessels left behind at Rhodes, and it was found that only a few were missing, and that the great storm, terrible as it had been, had inflicted less damage upon the fleet than was at first feared.

Two days' sail brought them within sight of the white walls of Acre, and it was on the 8th of June, 1191, that the fleet sailed into the port of that town. Tremendous acclamations greeted the arrival of the English army by the host assembled on the shores.

Acre had been besieged for two years, but in vain; and even the arrival of the French army under Phillip Augustus had failed to turn the scale. The inhabitants defended themselves with desperate bravery; every assault upon the walls had been repulsed with immense slaughter; and at no great distance off the Sultan Saladin, with a large army, was watching the progress of the siege.

The fame of King Richard and the English was so great, however, that the besiegers had little doubt that his arrival would change the position of things; and even the French, in spite of the bad feeling which had existed in Sicily, joined with the knights and army of the King of Jerusalem in acclaiming the arrival of the English.

Phillip Augustus, the French King, was of a somewhat weak and wavering disposition. It would have been thought that after his dispute with King Richard he would have gladly done all in his power to carry Acre before the arrival of his great rival. To the great disappointment of the French, however, he declared that he would take no step in the general assault until the arrival of Richard; and although the French had given some assistance to the besiegers, the army had really remained passive for many weeks.

Now, however, that the English had arrived, little time was lost; for the moment the dissensions and jealousies between the monarchs were patched up, the two hosts naturally imitated the example of their sovereigns, and French and English worked side by side in throwing up trenches against the walls, in building movable towers for the attack, and in preparing for the great onslaught.

The French were the first to finish their preparations, and they delivered a tremendous assault upon the walls. The besieged, however, did not lose heart, and with the greatest bravery repulsed every attempt. The scaling ladders were hurled backwards, the towers were destroyed by Greek fire; boiling oil was hurled down upon the men who advanced under the shelter of machines to undermine the walls; and after desperate fighting the French fell back, baffled and beaten.

There was some quiet exultation in the English lines at the defeat of the French, for they believed that a better fortune would crown their own efforts. Such, however, to their surprise and mortification, was not the case. When their preparations were completed, they attacked with splendid bravery. They were fighting under the eyes of their king, and in sight of the French army, who had a few days before been baffled; and if bravery and devotion could have carried the walls of Acre, assuredly King Richard's army would have accomplished the task.

It was, however, too great for them, and with vast loss the army fell back to its camp, King Richard raging like a wounded lion. Many of his barons had been killed in the assault, and the pikemen and men-at-arms had suffered heavily. The Earl of Evesham had been wounded; Cuthbert had taken no part in the assault, for the earl, knowing his bravery, had forbidden his doing so, as he foresaw the struggle would be of the most desperate character; and as it was not usual for pages to accompany their lords on the battle-field, Cuthbert could not complain of his being forbidden to take part in the fight.

The earl, however, permitted him to accompany Cnut and the bowmen, who did great service by the accuracy of their aim, preventing by their storm of arrows the men on the battlements from taking steady aim and working their machines, and so saved the Earl of Evesham's troop and those fighting near him from suffering nearly as heavy loss as some of those engaged in other quarters.

But while successful in beating off all assaults, the defenders of Acre were now nearly at the end of their resources. The Emperor Saladin, although he had collected an army of 200,000 men, yet feared to advance and give battle to the crusaders in their own lines-for they had thrown up round their camp strong entrenchments, to prevent the progress of the siege being disturbed by forces from without.

The people of Acre seeing the time pass and no sign of a rescuing force, their provisions being utterly exhausted, and pestilence and fever making frightful ravages in the city, at last determined to surrender.

For over two years they had made a resistance of the most valiant description, and now, despairing of success or rescue, and seeing the hosts of their besiegers increasing day by day, they hoisted a flag upon the walls, and sent a deputation to the kings, asking for terms if they submitted. They would have done well had they submitted upon the arrival of the French and English reinforcements. For the monarchs, annoyed by the defeat of their forces and by the heavy losses they had sustained, and knowing that the besieged were now at their last crust, were not disposed to be merciful.

However, the horrors which then attended the capture of cities in a war in which so little quarter was given on either side, were avoided. The city was to be surrendered; the much-prized relic contained within its walls-said to be a piece of the true Cross which had been captured by the Saracens at the battle of Tiberias, in which they had almost annihilated the Christian armies a few years before-was to be surrendered; the Christian prisoners in their hands were to be given up unharmed; and the inhabitants undertook to pay 200,000 pieces of gold to the kings within forty days, under the condition that the fighting men now taken prisoners were to be put to death should this ransom not be paid.

The conquest of Acre was hailed throughout Christendom as a triumph of the highest importance. It opened again the gates of the Holy Land; and so tremendous was the strength of the fortress, that it was deemed that if this stronghold were unable to resist effectually the arms of the crusaders, and that if Saladin with so great an army did not dare to advance to its rescue, then the rest of the Holy Land would speedily fall under the hands of the invading army.

With the fall of Acre, however, the dissensions between the two kings, which had for a while been allowed to rest while the common work was to be done, broke out again with renewed intensity. The jealousy of Phillip Augustus was raised to the highest point by the general enthusiasm of the combined armies for the valiant King of England, and by the authority which that monarch exercised in the councils. He therefore suddenly announced his intention of returning to France.

This decision at first occasioned the greatest consternation in the ranks of the crusaders; but this feeling was lessened when the king announced that he should leave a large portion of the French army behind, under the command of the Duke of Burgundy. The wiser councillors were satisfied with the change. Although there was a reduction of the total fighting force, yet the fact that it was now centred under one head, and that King Richard would now be in supreme command, was deemed to more than counterbalance the loss of a portion of the French army.

Before starting on the march for Jerusalem, King Richard sullied his reputation by causing all the defenders of Acre to be put to death, their ransom not having arrived at the stipulated time.

Then the allied army set out upon their journey. The fleet cruised along near them, and from it they obtained all that was requisite for their wants, and yet, notwithstanding these advantages, the toil and fatigue were terrible. Roads scarcely existed, and the army marched across the rough and broken country. There was no straggling, but each kept his place; and if unable to do so, fell and died. The blazing sun poured down upon them with an appalling force; the dust which rose when they left the rocks and came upon flat sandy ground, almost smothered them. Water was only obtainable at the halts, and then was frequently altogether insufficient for the wants of the army; while in front, on flank, and in rear hovered clouds of the cavalry of Saladin.

At times King Richard would allow parties of his knights to detach themselves from the force to drive off these enemies. But it was the chase of a lion after a hare. The knights in their heavy armour and powerful steeds were left behind as if standing still, by the fleet Bedouins on their desert coursers; and the pursuers, exhausted and worn out, were always glad to regain the ranks of the army.

These clouds of cavalry belonging to the enemy did not content themselves with merely menacing and cutting off stragglers. At times, when they thought they saw an opening, they would dash in and attack the column desperately, sometimes gaining temporary advantages, killing and wounding many, then fleeing away again into the desert.

Finding that it was impossible to catch these wary horsemen, King Richard ordered his bowmen to march outside his cavalry, so that when the enemy's horse approached within bowshot they should open upon them with arrows; then, should the horsemen persist in charging, the archers were at once to take refuge behind the lines of the knights.

Day after day passed in harassing conflicts. The distance passed over each day was very small, and the sufferings of the men from thirst, heat, and fatigue enormous. Cuthbert could well understand now what he had heard of great armies melting away, for already men began to succumb in large numbers to the terrible heat, and the path traversed by the army was scattered with corpses of those who had fallen victims to sunstroke. Not even at night did the attacks of the enemy cease, and a portion of the harassed force was obliged to keep under arms to repel assaults.

So passed the time until the army arrived at Azotus, and there, to the delight of the crusaders, who only longed to get at their foes, they beheld the whole force of Saladin, 200,000 strong, barring their way. Had it not been for the stern discipline enforced by King Richard, the knights of England and France would have repeated the mistake which had caused the extermination of the Christian force at Tiberias, and would have levelled their lances and charged recklessly into the mass of their enemies. But the king, riding round the flanks and front of the force, gave his orders in the sternest way, with the threat that any man who moved from the ranks should die by his hand.

The army was halted, the leaders gathered round the king, and a hasty consultation was held. Richard insisted upon the fight being conducted upon the same principles as the march-that the line of archers should stand outside the knights, and should gall the advancing force with arrows till the last moment, and then retire among the cavalry, only to sally out again as the Bedouins fell back from the steel wall of horsemen.

Cuthbert had now for the first time donned full armour, and rode behind the Earl of Evesham as his esquire, for the former esquire had been left behind, ill with fever, at Acre.

Chapter XII
The Accolade.

It was now a year since they had left England, and Cuthbert had much grown and widened out in the interval, and had never neglected an opportunity of practising with arms; and the earl was well aware that he should obtain as efficient assistance from him in time of need as he could desire.

This was the first time that Cuthbert, and indeed the great proportion of those present in the Christian host, had seen the enemy in force, and they eagerly watched the vast array. It was picturesque in the extreme, with a variety and brightness of colour rivalling that of the Christian host. In banners and pennons the latter made a braver show; but the floating robes of the infidel showed a far brighter mass of colour than the steel armour of the Christians.

Here were people drawn from widely separated parts of Saladin's dominions. Here were Nubians from the Nile, tall and powerful men, jet black in skin, with lines of red and white paint on their faces, giving a ghastly and wild appearance to them. On their shoulders were skins of lions and other wild animals. They carried short bows, and heavy clubs studded with iron. By them were the Bedouin cavalry, light, sinewy men, brown as berries, with white turbans and garments. Near these were the cavalry from Syria and the plains of Assyria-wild horsemen with semi-barbarous armour and scarlet trappings. Here were the solid lines of the Egyptian infantry, steady troops, upon whom Saladin much relied. Here were other tribes, gathered from afar, each distinguished by its own particular marks. In silence did this vast array view awhile the solid mass of the Christians. Suddenly a strange din of discordant music from thousands of musical instruments-conches and horns, cymbals and drums, arose in wild confusion. Shouts of defiance in a dozen tongues and from 200,000 throats rose wild and shrill upon the air, while clear above all the din were heard the strange vibratory cries of the warriors from the Egyptian highlands.

"One would think," said Cnut grimly to Cuthbert, "that the infidels imagine we are a flock of antelopes to be frightened by an outcry. They would do far better to save their wind for future use. They will want it, methinks, when we get fairly among them. Who would have thought that a number of men, heathen and infidel though they be, could have made so foul an outcry?"

Cuthbert laughed.

"Every one fights according to his own method, Cnut; and I am not sure that there is not something to be said for this outcry, for it is really so wild and fearful that it makes my blood almost curdle in my veins; and were it not that I know the proved valour of our knights and footmen, I should feel shaken by this terrible introduction to the fight."

"I heed it no more," said Cnut, "than the outcry of wild fowl, when one comes upon them suddenly on a lake in winter. It means no more than that; and I reckon that they are trying to encourage themselves fully as much as to frighten us. However, we shall soon see. If they can fight as well as they can scream, they certainly will get no answering shouts from us. The English bulldog fights silently, and bite as hard as he will, you will hear little beyond a low growl. Now, my men," he said, turning to his archers, "methinks the heathen are about to begin in earnest. Keep steady; do not fire until you are sure that they are within range. Draw your bows well to your ears, and straightly and steadily let fly. Never heed the outcry or the rush, keep steady to the last moment. There is shelter behind you, and fierce as the attack may be, you can find a sure refuge behind the line of the knights."

Cnut with his archers formed part of the line outside the array of English knights, and the arrows of the English bowmen fell fast as bands of the Bedouin horse circled round them in the endeavour to draw the Christians on to the attack. For some time Saladin persisted in these tactics. With his immense superiority of force he reckoned that if the Christian chivalry would but charge him, the victory of Tiberias would be repeated. Hemmed in by numbers, borne down by the weight of armour and the effects of the blazing sun, the knights would succumb as much to fatigue as to the force of their foes. King Richard's orders, however, were well obeyed, and at last the Moslem chief, urged by the entreaties of his leading emirs, who felt ashamed that so large a force should hesitate to attack one so vastly inferior in numbers, determined upon taking the initiative, and forming his troops in a semicircle round the Christian army, launched his horsemen to the attack. The instant they came within range, a cloud of arrows from the English archers fell among them, but the speed at which the desert horses covered the ground rendered it impossible for the archers to discharge more than one or two shafts before the enemy were upon them. Quickly as they now slipped back and sought refuge under the lances of the knights, many of them were unable to get back in time, and were cut down by the Saracens. The rest crept between the horses or under their bellies into the rear, and there prepared to sally out again as soon as the enemy retired, The Christian knights sat like a wall of steel upon their horses, their lances were levelled, and, brave as the Bedouin horsemen were, they felt to break this massive line was impossible. The front line, however, charged well up to the points of the lances, against which they hewed with their sharp scimitars, frequently severing the steel top from the ashpole, and then breaking through and engaging in hand-to-hand conflict with the knights. Behind the latter sat their squires, with extra spears and arms ready to hand to their masters; and in close combat, the heavy maces with their spike ends were weapons before which the light clad horsemen went down like reeds before a storm.

Hour after hour the Arab horsemen persisted in their attack, suffering heavily, but determined to conquer if possible. Then Saladin suddenly ordered a retreat, and at seeing their enemy fly, the impetuosity of the crusaders at last broke out. With a shout they dashed after the foe. King Richard, knowing that his followers had already shown a patience far beyond what he could have expected, now headed the onslaught, performing prodigies of valour with his single arm, and riding from point to point to see that all was well.

The early resistance of the infidel host was comparatively slight. The heavy mass of the Christian cavalry, with their levelled lances, swept through the ranks of the light horsemen, and trampled them down like grass beneath their feet; but every moment the resistance became more stubborn.

Saladin, knowing the Christians would sooner or later assume the offensive, had gathered his troops line in line behind the front ranks, and as the force of the crusaders' charge abated, so did the number of foes in their front multiply. Not only this, but upon either side chosen bands swept down, and ere long the Christians were brought to a stand, and all were fighting hand to hand with their enemies. The lances were thrown away now, and with axe and mace each fought for himself.

The Earl of Evesham was one of a group of knights whom King Richard had that day ordered to keep close to his person, and around this group the fight raged most furiously.

Saladin, aware of the extreme personal valour and warlike qualities of King Richard, set the greatest value upon his death or capture, and had ordered a large number of his best troops to devote their whole attention to attacking the King of England. The royal standard carried behind the king was a guide to their onslaught, and great as was the strength and valour of King Richard, he with difficulty was able to keep at bay the hosts that swept around him.

Now that the lance had been abandoned for battle-axe, Cuthbert was able to take an active part in the struggle, his duties consisting mainly in guarding the rear of his master, and preventing his being overthrown by any sudden attack on the flank or from behind.

King Richard was bent not only on defending himself from the attacks of his foes, but on directing the general course of the battle; and from time to time he burst, with his own trusty knights, through the ring of foes, and rode from point to point of the field, calling the knights together, exhorting them to steadiness, and restoring the fight where its fortunes seemed doubtful. At one time the impetuosity of the king led him into extreme danger. He had burst through the enemy surrounding him, and these, by order of their captain, allowed him to pass through their ranks, and then threw themselves together in his rear, to cut him off from the knights who rode behind. The maneuver was successful. The rush of horsemen fairly carried away the Christian knights, and one or two alone were able to make their way through.

Amid the wild confusion that raged, where each man was fighting for his own life, and but little view of what was passing could be obtained through the barred visor, the fact that the king was separated from them was known to but few. Sir Walter himself was engaged fiercely in a hand-to-hand fight with four Bedouins who surrounded him, when Cuthbert shouted, —

"The king, Sir Walter! the king! He is cut off and surrounded! For heaven's sake ride to him. See! the royal standard is down."

With a shout the earl turned, brained one of his foes with a sweep of his heavy axe, and, followed by Cuthbert, dashed to the assistance of the king. The weight of his horse and armour cleft through the crowd, and in a brief space he penetrated to the side of King Richard, who was borne upon by a host of foes. Just as they reached them a Bedouin who had been struck from his horse crawled beneath the noble charger of King Richard, and drove his scimitar deep into its bowels. The animal reared high in its sudden pain, and then fell on the ground, carrying the king, who was unable to disengage himself quickly enough.

In an instant the Earl of Evesham had leapt from his horse and with his broad triangular shield extended sought to cover him from the press of enemies. Cuthbert imitated his lord, and strove to defend the latter from attacks from the rear. For a moment or two the sweep of the earl's heavy axe and Cuthbert's circling sword kept back the foe, but this could not last. King Richard in vain strove to extricate his leg from beneath his fallen steed. Cuthbert saw at a glance that the horse still lived, and with a sudden slash of his sword he struck it on the hind quarter. Goaded by the pain the noble animal made a last effort to rise, but only to fall back dead. The momentary action was, however, sufficient for King Richard, who drew his leg from under it, and with his heavy battle-axe in hand, rose with a shout, and stood by the side of the earl.

In vain did the Bedouins strive to cut down and overpower the two champions; in vain did they urge their horses to ride over them. With each sweep of his axe the king either dismounted a foe or clove in the head of his steed, and a wall of slain around them testified to the tremendous power of their arms. Still, even such warriors as these could not long sustain the conflict. The earl had already received several desperate wounds, and the king himself was bleeding from some severe gashes with the keen-edged scimitars. Cuthbert was already down, when a shout of "St. George!" was heard, and a body of English knights clove through the throng of Saracens and reached the side of King Richard. Close behind these in a mass pressed the British footmen with bill and pike, the enemy giving way foot by foot before their steady discipline.

The king was soon on horseback again, and rallying his troops on, led them for one more great and final charge upon the enemy.

The effect was irresistible. Appalled by the slaughter which they had suffered, and by the tremendous strength and energy of the Christian knights, the Saracens broke and fled; and the last reserves of Saladin gave way as the king, shouting his war-cry of "God help the holy sepulchre!" fell upon them. Once, indeed, the battle still seemed doubtful, for a fresh band of the enemy at that moment arrived and joined in the fray. The crusaders were now, however, inspired with such courage and confidence that they readily obeyed the king's war-cry, gathered in a firm body, and hurled themselves upon this new foe. Then the Saracens finally turned and fled, and the Christian victory was complete.

It was one of the features of this war that however thorough the victories of the Christians, the Saracens very speedily recovered from their effects. A Christian defeat was crushing and entire; the knights died as they stood, and defeat meant annihilation. Upon the other hand, the Saracens and Bedouins when they felt that their efforts to win the battle were unsuccessful, felt no shame or humiliation in scattering like sheep. On their fleet horses and in their light attire they could easily distance the Christians, who never, indeed, dreamt of pursuing them. The day after the fight, the enemy would collect again under their chiefs, and be as ready as before to renew their harassing warfare.

On his return from the field, the king assembled many of his principal knights and leaders, and summoned the Earl of Evesham, with the message that he was to bring his esquire with him. When they reached the tent, the king said, —

"My lords, as some of you may be aware, I have this day had a narrow escape from death. Separated from you in the battle, and attended only by my standard-bearer, I was surrounded by the Saracens. I should doubtless have cleft my way through the infidel dogs, but a foul peasant stabbed my charger from below, and the poor brute fell with me. My standard-bearer was killed, and in another moment my nephew Arthur would have been your king, had it not been that my good lord here, attended by this brave lad, appeared. I have seen a good deal of fighting, but never did I see a braver stand than they made above my body. The Earl of Evesham, as you all know, is one of my bravest knights, and to him I can simply say, 'Thanks; King Richard does not forget a benefit like this.' But such aid as I might well look for from so stout a knight as the Earl of Evesham, I could hardly have expected on the part of a mere boy like this. It is not the first time that I have been under a debt of gratitude to him; for it was his watchfulness and bravery which saved Queen Berengaria from being carried off by the French in Sicily. I deemed him too young then for the order of knighthood-although indeed bravery has no age; still for a private benefit, and that performed against allies, in name at least, I did not wish so far to fly in the face of usage as to make him a knight. I promised him then, however, that the first time he distinguished himself against the infidel he should win his spurs. I think that you will agree with me, my lords, that he has done so. Not only did he stand over me, and with great bravery defend Sir Walter from attacks from behind, but his ready wit saved me, when even his sword and that of Sir Walter would have failed to do so. Penned down under poor Robin, I was powerless to move until our young esquire, in an interval of slashing at his assailants, found time to give a sharp blow together with a shout to Robin. The poor beast tried to rise, and the movement, short as it was, enabled me to draw my leg from under him, and then with my mace I was enabled to make a stand until you arrived at my side. I think, my lords, that you will agree with me that Cuthbert, the son of Sir William de Lance, is fit for the honour of knighthood."

A general chorus of approval arose from the assembly, and the king, bidding Cuthbert kneel before him, drew his sword and laid it across his shoulders, dubbing him Sir Cuthbert de Lance. When he had risen, the great barons of England pressed round to shake his hand, and Cuthbert, who was a modest young fellow, felt almost ashamed at the honours which were bestowed upon him. The usual ceremonies and penances which young knights had to undergo before admission into the body-and which in those days were extremely punctilious, and indeed severe, consisting, among other things, in fasting, in watching the armour at night, in seclusion and religious services-were omitted when the accolade was bestowed for bravery in the field.

The king ordered his armourer at once to make for Cuthbert a suit of the finest armour, and authorized him to carry on his shield a sword raising a royal crown from the ground, in token of the deed for which the honour of knighthood had been bestowed upon him.

Upon his return to the earl's camp the news of his new dignity spread at once among the followers of Sir Walter, and many and hearty were the cheers that went up from the throats of the Saxon foresters, led by Cnut. These humble friends were indeed delighted at his success, for they felt that to him they owed very much; and his kindness of manner and the gaiety of heart which he had shown during the hardships they had undergone since their start, had greatly endeared him to them.

Cuthbert was now to take rank among the knights who followed the banner of the earl. A tent was erected for him, an esquire assigned to him, and the lad as he entered his new abode felt almost bewildered at the change which had taken place in one short day-that he, at the age of sixteen, should have earned the honour of knighthood, and the approval of the King of England, expressed before all the great barons of the realm, was indeed an honour such as he could never have hoped for; and the thought of what his mother would say should the news reach her in her quiet Saxon home, brought the tears into his eyes. He had not gone through the usual religious ceremonies, but he knelt in his tent alone, and prayed that he might be made worthy of the honours bestowed upon him; that he might fulfil the duties of a Christian knight fearlessly and honourably; that his sword might never be raised but for the right; that he might devote himself to the protection of the oppressed, and the honour of God; that his heart might be kept from evil; and that he might carry through life, unstained his new escutcheon.

If the English had thought that their victory would have gained them immunity from the Saracen attacks, they were speedily undeceived. The host, indeed, which had barred their way had broken up; but its fragments were around them, and the harassing attacks began again with a violence and persistency even greater than before. The crusaders, indeed, occupied only the ground upon which they stood. It was death to venture 100 yards from the camp, unless in a strong body; and the smallest efforts to bring in food from the country round were instantly met and repelled. Only in very strong bodies could the knights venture from camp even to forage for their horses, and the fatigues and sufferings of all were in a way relieved by the great victory of Azotus.

Chapter XIII
In The Hands Of The Saracens.

The English had hoped that after one pitched battle they should be able to advance upon Jerusalem, but they had reckoned without the climate and illness.

Although unconquered in the fray, the Christian army was weakened by its sufferings to such an extent that it was virtually brought to a standstill. Even King Richard, with all his impetuosity, dared not venture to cut adrift from the seashore, and to march direct upon Jerusalem; that city was certainly not to be taken without a long siege, and this could only be undertaken by an army strong enough, not only to carry out so great a task, but to meet and defeat the armies which Saladin would bring up to the rescue, and to keep open the line down to Joppa, by which alone provisions, and the engines necessary for the siege, could be brought up. Hence the war resolved itself into a series of expeditions and detached fights.

The British camp was thoroughly fortified, and thence parties of the knights sallied out and engaged in conflicts with the Saracens, with varying success. On several of these expeditions Cuthbert attended the earl, and behaved with a bravery which showed him well worthy of the honours which he had received.

Upon one occasion the news reached camp that a party of knights, who had gone out to guard a number of footmen cutting forage and bringing it into camp, had been surrounded and had taken refuge in a small town, whose gates they had battered in when they saw the approach of an overwhelming host of the enemy. King Richard himself headed a strong force and advanced to their assistance. Their approach was not seen until within a short distance of the enemy, upon whom the crusaders fell with the force of a thunderbolt, and cleft their way through their lines. After a short pause in the little town, they prepared to again cut their way through, joined by the party who had there been besieged. The task was now however, far more difficult; for the footmen would be unable to keep up with the rapid charge of the knights, and it was necessary not only to clear the way, but to keep it open for their exit. King Richard himself and the greater portion of his knights were to lead the charge; another party were to follow behind the footmen, who were ordered to advance at the greatest speed of which they were capable, while their rearguard by charges upon the enemy, kept them at bay. To this latter party Cuthbert was attached.

The Saracens followed their usual tactics, and this time with great success. Dividing as the king with his knights charged them, they suffered these to pass through with but slight resistance, and then closed in upon their track, while another and still more numerous body fell upon the footmen and their guard. Again and again did the knights charge through the ranks of the Moslems, while the billmen stoutly kept together and resisted the onslaughts of the enemy's cavalry. In spite of their bravery, however, the storm of arrows shot by the desert horsemen thinned their ranks with terrible rapidity. Charging up to the very point of the spears, these wild horsemen fired their arrows into the faces of their foe, and although numbers of them fell beneath the more formidable missiles sent by the English archers, their numbers were so overwhelming that the little band melted away. The small party of knights, too, were rapidly thinned, although performing prodigious deeds of valour. The Saracens when dismounted or wounded still fought on foot, their object being always to stab or hough the horses, and so dismount the riders. King Richard and his force, though making the most desperate efforts to return to the assistance of the rearguard, were baffled by the sturdy resistance of the Saracens, and the position of those in the rear was fast becoming hopeless.

One by one the gallant little band of knights fell, and a sea of turbans closed over the fluttering plumes. Cuthbert, after defending himself with extreme bravery for a long time, was at last separated from the small remainder of his comrades by a rush of the enemy's horse, and when fighting desperately he received a heavy blow at the back of the head from the mace of a huge Nubian soldier, and fell senseless to the ground.

When he recovered his consciousness, the first impression upon his mind was the stillness which had succeeded to the din of battle; the shouts and war-cries of the crusaders, the wild yells of the Moslems, were hushed, and in their place was a quiet chatter in many unknown tongues, and the sound of laughter and feasting. Raising his head and looking round, Cuthbert saw that he and some ten of his comrades were lying together in the midst of a Saracen camp, and that he was a prisoner to the infidels. The sun streamed down with tremendous force upon them; there was no shelter; and though all were wounded and parched with thirst, the Saracens of whom they besought water, pointing to their mouths and making signs of their extreme thirst, laughed in their faces, and signified by a gesture that it was scarcely worth the trouble to drink when they were likely so soon to be put to death.

It was late in the afternoon before any change was manifest. Then Cuthbert observed a stir in the camp; the men ran to their horses, leapt on their backs, and with wild cries of "Welcome!" started off at full speed. Evidently some personage was about to arrive, and the fate of the prisoners would be solved. A few words were from time to time exchanged between these, each urging the other to keep up his heart and defy the infidel. One or two had succumbed to their wounds during the afternoon, and only six were able to stand erect when summoned to do so by some of their guard, who made signs to them that a great personage was coming. Soon the shouts of the horsemen and other sounds announced that the great chief was near at hand, and the captives gathered from the swelling shouts of the Arabs that the new arrival was Sultan Suleiman-or Saladin, for he was called by both names-surrounded by a body-guard of splendidly-dressed attendants. The emir, who was himself plainly attired, reined up his horse in front of the captives.

"You are English," he said, in the lingua-franca which was the medium of communication between the Eastern and Western peoples in those days. "You are brave warriors, and I hear that before you were taken you slaughtered numbers of my people. They did wrong to capture you and bring you here to be killed. Your cruel king gives no mercy to those who fall into his hands. You must not expect it here, you who without a pretence of right invade my country, slaughter my people, and defeat my armies. The murder of the prisoners of Acre has closed my heart to all mercy. There, your king put 10,000 prisoners to death in cold blood, a month after the capture of the place, because the money at which he had placed their ransom had not arrived. We Arabs do not carry huge masses of gold about with us; and although I could have had it brought from Egypt, I did not think that so brave a monarch as Richard of England could have committed so cruel an action in cold blood. When we are fresh from battle, and our wounds are warm, and our hearts are full of rage and fury, we kill our prisoners; but to do so weeks after a battle is contrary to the laws alike of your religion and of ours. However, it is King Richard who has sealed your doom, not I. You are knights, and I do not insult you with the offer of turning from your religion and joining me. Should one of you wish to save his life on these conditions, I will, however, promise him a place of position and authority among us."

None of the knights moved to accept the offer, but each, as the eye of the emir ran along the line, answered with an imprecation of contempt and hatred. Saladin waved his hand, and one by one the captives were led aside, walking as proudly to their doom as if they had been going to a feast. Each wrung the hand of the one next to him as he turned, and then without a word followed his captors. There was a dull sound heard, and one by one the heads of the knights rolled in the sand.

Cuthbert happened to be last in the line, and as the executioners laid hands upon him and removed his helmet, the eye of the sultan fell upon him, and he almost started at perceiving the extreme youth of his captive. He held his hand aloft to arrest the movements of the executioners, and signalled for Cuthbert to be brought before him again.

"You are but a boy," he said. "All the knights who have hitherto fallen into my hands have been men of strength and power; how is it that I see a mere youth among their ranks, and wearing the golden spurs of knighthood?"

"King Richard himself made me a knight," Cuthbert said proudly, "after having stood across him when his steed had been foully stabbed at the battle of Azotus, and the whole Moslem host were around him."

"Ah!" said the emir, "were you one of the two who, as I have heard, defended the king for some time against all assaults? It were hard indeed to kill so brave a youth. I doubt me not that at present you are as firmly determined to die a Christian knight as those who have gone before you? But time may change you. At any rate for the present your doom is postponed."

He turned to a gorgeously-dressed noble next to him, and said, —

"Your brother, Ben Abin, is Governor of Jerusalem, and the gardens of the palace are fair. Take this youth to him as a present, and set him to work in his gardens. His life I have spared, in all else Ben Abin will be his master."

Cuthbert heard without emotion the words which changed his fate from death to slavery. Many, he knew, who were captured in these wars were carried away as slaves to different parts of Asia, and it did not seem to him that the change was in any way a boon. However, life is dear, and it was but natural that a thought should leap into his heart that soon either the crusaders might force a way into Jerusalem and there rescue him, or that he himself might in some way escape.

The sultan having thus concluded the subject, turned away, and galloped off surrounded by his body-guard.

Those who had captured the Christians now stripped off the armour of Cuthbert; then he was mounted on a bare-backed steed, and with four Bedouins, with their long lances, riding beside him, started for Jerusalem. After a day of long and rapid riding, the Arabs stopped suddenly, on the crest of a hill, with a shout of joy, and throwing themselves from their horses, bent with their foreheads to the earth at the sight of their holy city. Cuthbert, as he gazed at the stately walls of Jerusalem, and the noble buildings within, felt bitterly that it was not thus that he had hoped to see the holy city. He had dreamt of arriving before it with his comrades, proud and delighted at their success so far, and confident in their power soon to wrest the town before them from the hands of the Moslems. Instead of this he was a slave — a slave to the infidel, perhaps never more to see a white face, save that of some other unfortunate like himself.

Even now in its fallen state no city is so impressive at first sight as Jerusalem; the walls, magnificent in height and strength, and picturesque in their deep embattlements, rising on the edge of a deep valley. Every building has its name and history. Here is the church built by the first crusaders; there the mighty mosque of Suleiman on the site of the Temple; far away on a projecting ridge the great building known as the Tomb of Moses; on the right beyond the houses rise the towers on the Roman walls; the Pool of Bethsaida lies in the hollow; in the centre are the cupolas of the Church of the Holy Sepulchre. Among all the fairest cities of the world, there are none which can compare in stately beauty with Jerusalem. Doubtless it was a fairer city in those days, for long centuries of Turkish possession have reduced many of the former stately palaces to ruins. Then, as now, the banner of the Prophet floated over the high places; but whereas at present the population is poor and squalid, the city in those days contained a far large number of inhabitants, irrespective of the great garrison collected for its defence.

The place from which Cuthbert had his first sight of Jerusalem is that from which the best view is to be obtained-the crest of the Mount of Olives. After a minute or two spent in looking at the city, the Arabs with a shout continued their way down into the valley. Crossing this they ascended the steep road to the walls, brandishing their lances and giving yells of triumph; then riding two upon each side of their prisoner, to protect him from any fanatic who might lay a hand upon him, they passed under the gate known as the Gate of Suleiman into the city.

The populace thronged the streets; and the news brought by the horsemen that a considerable portion of the Christian host had been defeated and slain, passed from mouth to mouth, and was received with yells of exultation. Execrations were heaped upon Cuthbert, who rode along with an air as quiet and composed as if he were the centre of an ovation instead of that of an outburst of hatred.

He would, indeed, speedily have been torn from his guards, had not these shouted that he was placed in their hands by Saladin himself for conduct to the governor. As the emir was as sharp and as ruthless with his own people as with the prisoners who fell into his hands, the name acted as a talisman, and Cuthbert and his escort rode forward without molestation until they reached the entrance to the palace.

Dismounting, Cuthbert was now led before the governor himself, a stern and grave-looking man, sitting cross-legged on a divan surrounded by officers and attendants. He heard in silence the account given him by the escort, bowed his head at the commands of Suleiman, and, without addressing a word to Cuthbert, indicated to two attendants that he was to be removed into the interior of the house. Here the young knight was led to a small dungeon-like room; bread and dates with a cruse of water were placed before him; the door was then closed and locked without, and he found himself alone with his thoughts.

No one came near him that night, and he slept as soundly as he would have done in his tent in the midst of the Christian host. He was resolved to give no cause for ill-treatment or complaint to his captors, to work as willingly, as cheerfully, as was in his power, and to seize the first opportunity to make his escape, regardless of any risk of his life which he might incur in doing so.

In the morning the door opened, and a black slave led him into the garden, which was surrounded by a very high and lofty wall. It was large, and full of trees and flowers, and far more beautiful than any garden that Cuthbert had seen in his native land. There were various other slaves at work; and an Arab, who appeared to be the head of the gardeners, at once appointed to Cuthbert the work assigned to him. A guard of Arabs with bow and spear watched the doings of the slaves.

With one glance round, Cuthbert was assured that escape from this garden, at least, was not to be thought of, and that for the present, patience alone was possible. Dismissing all ideas of that kind from his mind, he set to work with a steady attention to his task. He was very fond of flowers, and soon he became so absorbed in his work as almost to forget that he was a slave. It was not laborious-digging, planting, pruning and training the flowers, and giving them copious draughts of water from a large fountain in the centre of the garden.

The slaves were not permitted to exchange a word with each other. At the end of the day's work they were marched off to separate chambers, or, as they might be called, dungeons. Their food consisted of water, dried dates, and bread, and they had little to complain of in this respect; indeed, the slaves in the gardens of the governor's house at Jerusalem enjoyed an exceptionally favoured existence. The governor himself was absorbed in the cares of the city. The head gardener happened to be a man of unusual humanity, and it was really in his hands that the comfort of the prisoners was placed.

Sometimes in the course of the day, veiled ladies would issue in groups from the palace, attended by black slaves with drawn scimitars. They passed without unveiling across the point where the slaves were at work, and all were forbidden on pain of death to look up, or even to approach the konak or pavilion, where the ladies threw aside their veils, and enjoyed the scent and sight of the flowers, the splash of murmuring waters, and the strains of music touched by skilful hands.

Although Cuthbert wondered in his heart what these strange wrapped-up figures might look like when the veils were thrown back, he certainly did not care about the matter to run any risk of drawing the anger of his guards upon himself by raising his eyes towards them; nor did he ever glance up at the palace, which was also interdicted to the slaves. From the lattice casements during the day the strains of music and merry laughter often came down to the captives; but this, if anything, only added to the bitterness of their position, by reminding them that they were shut off for life from ever hearing the laughter of the loved ones they had left behind.

For upwards of a month Cuthbert remained steadily at work, and during that time no possible plan of escape had occurred to him, and he had indeed resigned himself to wait, either until, as he hoped, the city would be taken by the Christians, or until he himself might be removed from his present post and sent into the country, where, although his lot would doubtless be far harder, some chance of escape might open before him.

One night, long after slumber had fallen upon the city, Cuthbert was startled by hearing his door open. Rising to his feet, he saw a black slave, and an old woman beside him. The latter spoke first in the lingua-franca, —

"My mistress, the wife of the governor, has sent me to ask your story. How is it that, although but a youth, you are already a knight? How is it that you come to be a slave to our people? The sultan himself sent you to her lord. She would fain hear through me how it has happened. She is the kindest of ladies, and the sight of your youth has touched her heart."

With thanks to the unknown lady who had felt an interest in him, Cuthbert briefly related the events which had led to his captivity. The old woman placed on the ground a basket containing some choice fruit and white bread, and then departed with the negro as quietly as she had come, leaving Cuthbert greatly pleased at what had taken place.

"Doubtless," he said to himself, "I shall hear again; and it may be that through the pity of this lady some means of escape may open to me."

Although for some little time no such prospect appeared, yet the visits of the old woman, which were frequently repeated, were of interest to him, and seemed to form a link between him and the world.

After coming regularly every night for a week, she bade the young knight follow her, holding her finger to her lips in sign that caution must be observed. Passing through several passages, he was at length led into a room where a lady of some forty years of age, surrounded by several slaves and younger women, was sitting. Cuthbert felt no scruple in making a deep obeisance to her; the respect shown to women in the days of chivalry was very great, and Cuthbert in bowing almost to the ground before the lady who was really his mistress, did not feel that he was humiliating himself.

"Young slave," she said, "your story has interested us. We have frequently watched from the windows, and have seen how willingly and patiently you have worked; and it seems strange indeed that one so young should have performed such feats of bravery as to win the honour of knighthood from the hand of that greatest of warriors, Richard of England. What is it, we would fain learn from your lips, that stirs up the heart of the Christian world that they should launch their armies against us, who wish but to be left alone, and who have no grudge against them? This city is as holy to us as it is to you; and as we live around it, and all the country for thousands of miles is ours, is it likely that we should allow it to be wrested from us by strangers from a distance?"

This was spoken in some Eastern language of which Cuthbert understood no word, but its purport was translated to him by the old woman who had hitherto acted as his mistress's messenger.

Cuthbert reported the circumstances of the fight at Azotus and endeavoured to explain the feelings which had given rise to the Crusade. He then, at the orders of the lady, related the incidents of his voyage out, and something of his life at home, which was more interesting even than the tale of his adventures to his hearers, as to them the home-life of these fierce Christian warriors was entirely unknown.

After an audience of two hours Cuthbert was conducted back to his cell, his mistress assuring him of her good-will, and promising to do all in her power to make his captivity as light as possible.

Chapter XIV
An Effort For Freedom.

Two or three nights afterwards the old woman again came to Cuthbert, and asked him, in her mistress's name, if in any way he could suggest a method of lightening his captivity, as his extreme youth, and bravery of demeanour, had greatly pleased her.

Cuthbert replied that nothing but freedom could satisfy his longings; that he was comfortable and not overworked, but that he pined to be back again with his friends.

The old woman brought him on the following night a message to the effect that his mistress would willingly grant him his liberty, but as he was sent to her husband by the sultan, it would be impossible to free him openly.

"From what she said," the old woman continued, "if you could see some plan of making your escape, she would in no way throw difficulties in your path; but it must not be known that the harem in any way connived at your escape, for my lord's wrath would be terrible, and he is not a man to be trifled with."

Looking round at the high walls that surrounded the garden, Cuthbert said that he could think of no plan whatever for escaping from such a place; that he had often thought it over, but that it appeared to him to be hopeless. Even should he manage to scale these walls, he would only find himself in the town beyond, and his escape from that would be altogether hopeless. "Only," he said, "if I were transported to some country palace of the governor could I ever hope to make my escape." The next night the messenger brought him the news that his mistress was disposed to favour his escape in the way he had pointed out, and that she would in two or three days ask the governor for permission to pay a visit to their palace beyond the walls, and that with her she would take a number of gardeners-among them Cuthbert-to beautify the place. Cuthbert returned the most lively and hearty thanks to his patroness for her kind intentions, and hope began to rise rapidly in his heart.

It is probable, however, that the black guards of the harem heard something of the intentions of their mistress, and that they feared the anger of the governor should Cuthbert make his escape, and should it be discovered that this was the result of her connivance. Either through this or through some other source the governor obtained an inkling that the white slave sent by the sultan was receiving unusual kindness from the ladies of the harem.

Two nights after Cuthbert had begun to entertain bright hopes of his liberty, the door of the cell was softly opened. He was seized by four slaves, gagged, tied hand and foot, covered with a thick burnous, and carried out from his cell. By the sound of their feet he heard that they were passing into the open air, and guessed that he was being carried through the garden; then a door opened and was closed after them; he was flung across a horse like a bale of goods, a rope or two were placed around him to keep him in that position, and then he felt the animal put in motion, and heard by the trampling of feet that a considerable number of horsemen were around him. For some time they passed over the rough, uneven streets of the city; then there was a pause and exchange of watchword and countersign, a creaking of doors, and a lowering of a drawbridge, and the party issued out into the open country. Not for very long did they continue their way; a halt was called, and Cuthbert was taken off his horse.

On looking round, he found that he was in the middle of a considerable group of men. Those who had brought him were a party of the governor's guards; but he was now delivered over to a large band of Arabs, all of whom were mounted on camels. One of these creatures he was ordered to mount, the bonds being loosed from his arms and feet. An Arab driver, with lance, bows, and arrows, and other weapons, took his seat on the neck of the animal, and then with scarcely a word the caravan marched off, with noiseless step, and with their faces turned southwards.

It seemed to Cuthbert almost as a dream. A few hours before he had been exalted with the hope of freedom; now he was being taken away to a slavery which would probably end but with his life. Although he could not understand any of his captors, the repetition of a name led him to believe that he was being sent to Egypt as a present to some man in high authority there; and he doubted not that the Governor of Jerusalem, fearing that he might escape, and dreading the wrath of the sultan, should he do so, had determined to transfer the troublesome captive to a more secure position and to safer hands.

For three days the journey continued; they had now left the fertile lowlands of Palestine, and their faces were turned west. They were entering upon that sandy waste which stretches between the southern corner of Palestine and the land of Egypt, a distance which can be travelled by camels in three days, but which occupied the Children of Israel forty years.

At first the watch had been very sharply kept over the captive; but now that they had entered the desert the Arabs appeared to consider that there was no chance of an attempt to escape. Cuthbert had in every way endeavoured to ingratiate himself with his guard. He had most willingly obeyed their smallest orders, had shown himself pleased and grateful for the dates which formed the staple of their repasts. He had assumed so innocent and quiet an appearance that the Arabs had marvelled much among themselves, and had concluded that there must have been some mistake in the assertion of the governor's guard who had handed the prisoner over to them, that he was one of the terrible knights of King Richard's army.

Cuthbert's heart had not fallen for a moment. He knew well that if he once reached Cairo all hope of escape was at an end; and it was before reaching that point that he determined if possible to make an effort for freedom. He had noticed particularly the camel which appeared to be the fleetest of the band; it was of lighter build than the rest, and it was with difficulty that its rider had compelled it to accommodate itself to the pace of the others. It was clear from the pains he took with it, by the constant patting and the care bestowed upon its watering and feeding, that its rider was extremely proud of it; and Cuthbert concluded that if an escape was to be made, this was the animal on which he must accomplish it.

Upon arriving at the end of each day's journey the camels were allowed to browse at will, a short cord being tied between one of their hind and one of their fore feet. The Arabs then set to work to collect sticks and to make a fire-not for cooking, for their only food was dried dates and some black bread, which they brought with them-but for warmth, as the nights were damp and somewhat chilly, as they sat round the fire, talked, and told stories. Before finally going off to rest, each went out into the bushes and brought in his camel; these were then arranged in a circle around the Arabs, one of the latter being mounted as sentry to prevent any sudden surprise-not indeed that they had the smallest fear of the Christians, who were far distant; but then, as now, the Arabs of the desert were a plundering race, and were ever ready to drive off each other's camels or horses. Cuthbert determined that if flight was possible it must be undertaken during the interval after the arrival at the halting-place and before the bringing in of the camels. Therefore, each day upon the halt he had pretended great fatigue from the rough motion of the camel, and had, after hastily eating the dates handed to him, thrown himself down, covered himself with his Arab robe, and feigned instant sleep. Thus they had in the three days from starting come to look upon his presence sleeping close to them as a matter of course.

The second day after entering the desert, however, Cuthbert threw himself down by the side of an uprooted shrub of small size and about his own length. He covered himself as usual with his long, dark-blue robe, and pretended to go to sleep. He kept his eyes, however, on the alert through an aperture beneath his cloth, and observed particularly the direction in which the camel upon which he had set his mind wandered into the bushes. The darkness came on a very few minutes after they had halted, and when the Arabs had once settled round their fire, Cuthbert very quietly shifted the robe from himself to the long low bush near him, and then crawled stealthily off into the darkness.

He had no fear of his footfall being heard upon the soft sand, and was soon on his feet, looking for the camels. He was not long in finding them, or in picking out the one which he had selected. The bushes were succulent, and close to the camping ground; indeed, it was for this that the halting-places were always chosen. It was not so easy, however, to climb into the high wooden saddle, and Cuthbert tried several times in vain. Then he repeated in a sharp tone the words which he had heard the Arabs use to order their camels to kneel, striking the animal at the same moment behind the fore-legs with a small switch. The camel immediately obeyed the order to which he was accustomed, and knelt down, making, however, as he did so, the angry grumble which those creatures appear to consider it indispensable to raise when ordered to do anything. Fortunately this noise is so frequently made, and the camels are so given to quarrel among themselves, that although in the still air it might have been heard by the Arabs sitting a short hundred yards away, it attracted no notice, and Cuthbert, climbing into the seat, shook the cord that served as a rein, and the animal, rising, set off at a smooth, steady swing in the direction in which his head was turned-that from which they had that day arrived.

Once fairly away from the camping-ground, Cuthbert, with blows of his stick, increased the speed of the camel to a long shuffling trot, and the fire in the distance soon faded out into the darkness.

Cuthbert trusted to the stars as guides. He was not unarmed, for as he crawled away from his resting-place, he had picked up one of the Arabs' spears and bow and arrows, and a large bag of dates from the spot where they had been placed when their owner dismounted. He was already clad in Eastern garb, and was so sun-burnt and tanned that he had no fear whatever of any one at a distance detecting that he was a white man.

Steering his course by the stars, he rode all night without stopping. He doubted not that he would have at least three hours' start, for the Arabs were sure to have sat that time round the fires before going out to bring in their camels. Even then they would suppose for some time that the animal upon which he was seated had strayed, and no pursuit would be attempted until it was discovered that he himself had made his escape, which might not be for a long time, as the Arabs would not think of looking under the cloth to see if he were there. He hoped, therefore, that he would reach the cultivated land long before he was overtaken. He had little fear but that he should then be able to journey onward without attracting attention.

A solitary Arab when travelling rides straight, and his communications to those whom he meets are confined to the set form of two or three words, "May Allah protect you!" the regular greeting of Moslems when they meet.

When morning broke Cuthbert, even when ascending to the top of a somewhat lofty mound, could see no signs of pursuers in the vast stretch of desert behind him. In front, the ground was already becoming dotted here and there with vegetation, and he doubted not that after a few hours' ride he should be fairly in the confines of cultivated country. He gave his camel a meal of dates, and having eaten some himself, again set the creature in motion. These camels, especially those of good breed, will go on for three or four days with scarcely a halt; and there was no fear of that on which he rode breaking down from fatigue, for the journeys hitherto had been comparatively short.

By mid-day Cuthbert had reached the cultivated lands of Palestine. Here and there over the plain, villages were dotted, and parties of men and camels were to be seen. Cuthbert now arranged his robes carefully in Arab fashion, slung the long spear across his shoulders, and went boldly forward at a slinging trot, having little fear that a passer-by would have any suspicion whatever as to his being other than an Arab bent upon some rapid journey. He soon found that his hopes were justified. Several times he came upon parties of men whom he passed with the salute, and who scarcely raised their eyes as he trotted by them. The plain was an open one, and though cultivated here and there, there were large tracts lying unworked. There was no occasion therefore to keep to the road; so riding across country, and avoiding the villages as far as possible, stopping only at a stream to give his camel water, Cuthbert rode without ceasing until nightfall. Then he halted his camel near a wood, turned it in to feed on the young foliage, and wrapping himself in his burnous was soon asleep, for he ached from head to foot with the jolting motion which had now been continued for so many hours without an interval. He had little fear of being overtaken by the party he had left behind; they would, he was convinced, be many hours behind, and it was extremely improbable that they would hit upon the exact line which he had followed, so that even if they succeeded in coming up to him, they would probably pass him a few miles either to the right or left.

So fatigued was he with his long journey, that the next day he slept until after the sun had risen. He was awakened suddenly by being seized by a party of Arabs, who, roughly shaking him, questioned him as to where he came from, and what he was doing there. He saw at a glance that they were not with the party from which he had escaped, and he pointed to his lips to make signs that he was dumb. The Arabs evidently suspected that something was wrong. They examined the camel, and then the person of their captive. The whiteness of his skin at once showed them that he was a Frank in disguise, and without more ado or questioning, they tied him hand and foot, flung him across the camel, and, mounting their own animals, rode rapidly away.

From the position of the sun, Cuthbert saw that they were making their course nearly due east, and therefore that it could not be their intention to take him to Jerusalem, which was to the north of the line they were following. A long day's journeying, which to Cuthbert seemed interminable, found them on the low spit of sand which runs along by the side of the Dead Sea. Behind, lofty rocks rose almost precipitously, but through a cleft in these the Arabs had made their way. Cuthbert saw at once that they belonged to some desert tribe over whom the authority of Suleiman was but nominal. When summoned for any great effort, these children of the desert would rally to his armies and fight for a short time; but at the first disaster, or whenever they became tired of the discipline and regularity of the army, they would mount their camels and return to the desert, generally managing on the way to abstract from the farms of those on their route either a horse, cattle, or some other objects which would pay them for the labours they had undergone.

They were now near the confines of their own country, and apparently had no fear whatever of pursuit. They soon gathered some of the dead wood cast on the shores of the sea, and with these a fire was speedily lighted, and an earthenware pot was taken down from among their baggage: it was filled with water from a skin, and then grain having been placed in it, it was put among the wood ashes. Cuthbert, who was weary and aching in every limb from the position in which he had been placed on the camel, asked them by signs for permission to bathe in the lake. This was given, principally apparently from curiosity, for but very few Arabs were able to swim; indeed, as a people they object so utterly to water, that the idea of any one bathing for his amusement was to them a matter of ridicule.

Cuthbert, who had never heard of the properties of the Dead Sea, was perfectly astonished upon entering the water to find that instead of wading in it up to the neck before starting to swim, as he was accustomed to do at home, the water soon after he got waist-deep took him off his feet, and a cry of astonishment burst from him as he found himself on rather than in the fluid. The position was so strange and unnatural that with a cry of alarm he scrambled over on to his feet, and made the best of his way to shore, the Arabs indulging in shouts of laughter at his astonishment and alarm. Cuthbert was utterly unable to account for the strange sensations he had experienced; he perceived that the water was horribly salt, and that which had got into his mouth almost choked him. He was, however, unaware that saltness adds to the weight of water, and so to the buoyancy of objects cast into it. The saltness of the fluid he was moreover painfully conscious of by the smarting of the places on his wrists and ankles where the cords had been bound that fastened him to the camel. Goaded, however, by the laughter of the Arabs, he determined once more to try the experiment of entering this strange sheet of water, which from some unaccountable cause appeared to him to refuse to allow anybody to sink in it. This time he swam about for some time, and felt a little refreshed. When he returned to the shore he soon re-attired himself in his Bedouin dress, and seated himself a little distance from his captors, who were now engaged in discussing the materials prepared by themselves. They made signs to Cuthbert that he might partake of their leavings, for which he was not a little grateful, for he felt utterly exhausted and worn out with his cruel ride and prolonged fasting.

The Arabs soon wrapped themselves in their burnouses, and feeling confident that their captive would not attempt to escape from them, in a place where subsistence would be impossible, paid no further attention to him beyond motioning to him to lie down at their side.

Cuthbert, however, determined to make another effort to escape; for although he was utterly ignorant of the place in which he found himself, or of the way back, he thought that anything would be better than to be carried into helpless slavery into the savage country beyond the Jordan. An hour, therefore, after his captors were asleep he stole to his feet, and fearing to arouse them by exciting the wrath of one of the camels by attempting to mount him, he struck up into the hills on foot. All night he wandered, and in the morning found himself at the edge of a strange precipice falling abruptly down to a river, which, some fifty feet wide, ran at its foot. Upon the opposite side the bank rose with equal rapidity, and to Cuthbert's astonishment he saw that the cliffs were honeycombed by caves.

Keeping along the edge for a considerable distance, he came to a spot where it was passable, and made his way down to the river bank. Here he indulged in a long drink of fresh water, and then began to examine the caves which perforated the rocks. These caves Cuthbert knew had formerly been the abode of hermits. It was supposed to be an essentially sacred locality, and between the third and fourth centuries of Christianity some 20,000 monks had lived solitary lives on the banks of that river. Far away he saw the ruins of a great monastery, called Mar Saba, which had for a long time been the abode of a religious community, and which at the present day is still tenanted by a body of monks. Cuthbert made up his mind at once to take refuge in these caves. He speedily picked out one some fifty feet up the face of the rock, and approachable only with the greatest difficulty and by a sure foot. First he made the ascent to discover the size of the grotto, and found that although the entrance was but four feet high and two feet wide, it opened into an area of considerable dimensions. Far in the corner, when his eyes became accustomed to the light, he discovered a circle of ashes, and his conjectures that these caves had been the abode of men were therefore verified. He again descended, and collected a large bundle of grass and rushes for his bed. He discovered growing among the rocks many edible plants, whose seeds were probably sown there centuries before, and gathering some of these he made his way back to the cavern. The grass furnished him with an excellent bed, and he was soon asleep.

Chapter XV
A Hermit's Tale.

The next day he discovered on his excursions plenty of eatable berries on the bushes; and now that he had no longer fear of hunger he resolved to stay for some little time, until his wounds, which had festered badly, had recovered, before making an attempt to rejoin the Christian army.

One day when employed in gathering berries he was surprised by meeting a wild-looking figure, who appeared suddenly from one of the caves. It was that of a very old man, with an extremely long white beard flowing to his waist; his hair, which was utterly unkempt, fell to the same point. He was thin to an extraordinary extent, and Cuthbert wondered how a man could have been reduced to such a state of starvation, with so plentiful a supply of fruit and berries at hand.

The old man looked at Cuthbert attentively, and then made the sign of the cross. Cuthbert gave a cry of joy, and repeated the sign. The old man at once came down from his cavern, and looked at him with surprise and astonishment, and then addressed him in the French language.

"Are you a Christian truly; and if so, whence do you come?"

Cuthbert at once explained that he had been taken prisoner when with King Richard's army, and had effected his escape. He also told the old man that he had been remaining for the last four days in a cave higher up the stream. The hermit-for he was one-beckoned him to follow him, and Cuthbert found himself in a cave precisely similar to that which he himself inhabited. There were no signs of comfort of any kind; a bed-place made of great stones stood in one corner, and Cuthbert, remembering the comforts of his own grassy couch, shuddered at the thought of the intense discomfort of such a sleeping-place. In another corner was an altar, upon which stood a rough crucifix, before which the hermit knelt at once in prayer, Cuthbert following his example. Rising again, the hermit motioned to him to sit down, and then began a conversation with him.

It was so long since the hermit had spoken to any living being, that he had almost lost the use of his tongue, and his sentences were slow and ill-formed. However, Cuthbert was able to understand him, and he to gather the drift of what Cuthbert told him. The old man then showed him, that by touching a stone in the corner of his cave the apparently solid rock opened, and revealed an entrance into an inner cave, which was lit by a ray of light, which penetrated from above.

"This," he said, "was made centuries ago, and was intended as a refuge from the persecutors of that day. The caves were then almost all inhabited by hermits, and although many recked not of their lives, and were quite ready to meet death through the knife of the infidel, others clung to existence, and preferred to pass many years of penance on earth for the sake of atoning for their sins before called upon to appear before their Maker.

"If you are pursued, it will be safer for you to take up your abode here. I am known to all the inhabitants of this country, who look upon me as mad, and respect me accordingly. None ever interfere with me, or with the two or three other hermits, the remains of what was once almost an army, who now alone survive. I can offer you no hospitality beyond that of a refuge; but there is water in the river below, fruits and berries in abundance on the shrubs. What would you have more?"

Cuthbert accepted the invitation with thanks; for he thought that even at the worst the presence of this holy man would be a protection to him from any Arabs who might discover him.

For three or four days he resided with the hermit, who, although he stretched his long lean body upon the hard stones of his bed, and passed many hours of the night kneeling on the stone floor in front of his alter, yet had no objection to Cuthbert making himself as comfortable as he could under the circumstances.

At the end of the fourth day Cuthbert asked him how long he had been there, and how he came to take up his abode in so desolate and fearsome a place. The hermit was silent for a time, and then said, —

"It is long indeed since my thoughts have gone back to the day when I was of the world. I know not whether it would not be a sin to recall them; but I will think the matter over to-night, and if it appears to me that you may derive good from my narrative, I will relate it to you to-morrow."

The next day Cuthbert did not renew the request, leaving it to the hermit to speak should he think fit. It was not until the evening that he alluded to the subject; and then taking his seat on a bank near the edge of the river, he motioned to Cuthbert to sit beside him, and began, —

"My father was a peer of France, and I was brought up at the court. Although it may seem strange to you, looking upon this withered frame, sixty-five years back I was as bold and comely a knight as rode in the train of the king, for I am now past ninety, and for sixty years I have resided here. I was a favourite of the king's, and he loaded me with wealth and honour. He, too, was young, and I joined with him in the mad carousals and feastings of the court. My father resided for the most part at one of his castles in the country, and I, an only son, was left much to myself. I need not tell you that I was as wild and as wicked as all those around me; that I thought little of God, and feared neither Him nor man.

"It chanced that one of the nobles —I need not mention his name-whose castle lay in the same province as that of my father, had a lovely daughter, who, being an only child, would be his heiress. She was considered one of the best matches in France, and reports of her exceeding beauty had reached the court. Although my allowance from my father, and from the estates which the king had give me personally, should have been more than enough for my utmost wants, gambling and riotous living swallowed up my revenue faster than it came in, and I was constantly harassed by debt.

"Talking one night at supper with a number of bold companions, as to the means we should take for restoring our wasted fortunes, some said in jest that the best plan would be for one of us to marry the beauty of Dauphiny. I at once said that I would be the man to do it; the ideas was a wild one, and a roar of laughter greeted my words. Her father was known to be a stern and rigid man, and it was certain that he would not consent to give his daughter to a spendthrift young noble like myself. When the laughter had subsided I repeated my intention gravely, and offered to wager large sums with all around the table that I would succeed.

"On the morrow I packed up a few of my belongings, put in my valise the dress of a wandering troubadour, and taking with me only a trusty servant, started for Dauphiny. It would be tedious to tell you the means I resorted to to obtain the affections of the heiress. I had been well instructed in music and could play on the lute, and knew by heart large numbers of ballads, and could myself, in case of necessity, string verses together with tolerable ease. As a troubadour I arrived at the castle gate, and craved permission to enter to amuse its occupants. Troubadours then, as now, were in high esteem in the south, and I was at once made a welcome guest.

"Days passed, and weeks; still I lingered at the castle, my heart being now as much interested as my pride in the wager which I had undertaken. Suffice it to say, that my songs, and perhaps my appearance-for I cannot be accused of vanity now in saying nature had been bountiful to me-won my way to her heart. Troubadours were licensed folk, and even in her father's presence there was nought unseemly in my singing songs of love. While he took them as the mere compliments of a troubadour, the lady, I saw, read them as serious effusions of my heart.

"It was only occasionally that we met alone; but ere long she confessed that she loved me. Without telling her my real name, I disclosed to her that I was of her own rank, and that I had entered upon the disguise I wore in order to win her love. She was romantic, and was flattered by my devotion. I owned to her that hitherto I had been wild and reckless; and she told me at once that her father destined her for the son of an old friend of his, to whom it appeared she had been affianced while still a baby. She was positive that nothing would move her father. For the man she was to marry she entertained no kind of affection, and indeed had never seen him, as she had been brought up in a convent to the age of fifteen; and just before she had returned thence, he had gone to finish his education at Padua.

"She trembled when I proposed flight; but I assured her that I was certain of the protection of the king, and that he would, I was sure, when the marriage was once celebrated, use his influence with her father to obtain his forgiveness.

"The preparations for her flight were not long in making. I purchased a fleet horse in addition to my own, and ordered my servant to bring it to a point a short distance from the castle gate. I had procured a long rope with which to lower her down from her lattice to the moat below, which was at present dry, intending myself to slide after her. The night chosen was one when I knew that the count was to have guests, and I thought that they would probably, as is the custom, drink heavily, and that there would be less fear of any watch being kept.

"The guests arrived just at nightfall. I had feigned illness, and kept my room. From time to time I heard through the windows of the banqueting hall bursts of laughter. These gradually ceased; and at last, when all was still, I, awaiting some time, stole from my room with a rope in my hand to the apartment occupied by her. A slight tap at the door, as arranged, was at once answered, and I found her ready cloaked and prepared for the enterprise. She trembled from head to foot, but I cheered her to the best of my power, and at last she was in readiness to be lowered. The window was at a considerable height from the ground; but the rope was a long one, and I had no fear of its reaching the bottom. Fastening it round her waist, I began to lower her from the window.

"The night was a windy one, and she swung backwards and forwards as she went down. By what chance it was I know not, —for I had examined the rope and found it secure-but methinks in swaying backwards and forwards it may have caught a sharp stone, maybe it was a punishment from Heaven upon me for robbing a father of his child-but suddenly I felt there was no longer a weight on my arms. A fearful shriek rang through the air, and, looking out, I saw far below a white figure stretched senseless in the mud!

"For a minute I stood paralyzed. But the cry had aroused others, and, turning round, I saw a man at the door with a drawn sword. Wild with grief and despair, and thinking, not of making my escape, or of concealing my part in what had happened, but rushing without an instant's delay to the body of her I loved so well, I drew my sword, and like a madman rushed upon him who barred the door. The combat was brief but furious, and nerved by the madness of despair I broke down his guard and ran him through the body. As he fell back, his face came in the full light of the moon, which streamed through the open door of the passage, and to my utter horror and bewilderment I saw that I had slain my father.

"What happened after that night I know not. I believe that I made my escape from the castle and rushed round to the body of her whose life I had destroyed, and that there finding her dead, I ran wildly across the country. When I came to my senses months had passed, and I was the inmate of an asylum for men bereaved of their senses, kept by noble monks. Here for two years I remained, the world believing that I was dead. None knew that the troubadour whose love had cost the lady her life, who had slain the guest of her father, and had then disappeared, was the unhappy son of that guest. My friends in Paris when they heard of the tragedy of course associated it with me, but they all kept silent. The monks, to whom I confessed the whole story, were shocked indeed, but consoled me in my grief and despair by the assurance that however greatly I had sinned, the death of the lady had been accidental, and that if I were a parricide it was at least unintentionally.

"My repentance was deep and sincere; and after a while, under another name, I joined the army of the crusaders, to expiate my sin by warring for the holy sepulchre. I fought as men fight who have no wish to live; but while all around me fell by sword and disease, death kept aloof from me. When the crusade had failed I determined to turn for ever from the world, and to devote my life to prayer and penance; and so casting aside my armour, I made my way here, and took up my abode in a cave in this valley, where at that time were many thousands of other hermits-for the Saracens, while they gained much money from fines and exactions from pilgrims who came to Jerusalem, and fought stoutly against those who sought to capture that city, were in the main tolerant, and offered no hindrance to the community of men whom they looked upon as mad.

"Here, my son, for more than sixty years have I prayed, with much fasting and penance. I trust now that the end is nearly at hand, and that my long life of mortification may be deemed to have obliterated the evil deeds which I did in my youth. Let my fate be a warning to you. Walk steadily in the right way; indulge not in feasting and evil companionship; and above all, do not enter upon evil deeds, the end of which no man can see."

The hermit was silent, and Cuthbert, seeing that his thoughts had again referred to the past, wandered away, and left him sitting by the river side. Some hours later he returned, and found the hermit kneeling before the altar; and the next morning the latter said, —

"I presume, my son, you do not wish to remain here as a hermit, as I have done? Methinks it were well that we made our arrangements for your return to the Christian host, who will, I hope, ere long be at the gates of Jerusalem."

"I should like nothing better," Cuthbert said. "But ignorant as I am of the nature of the country, it seems to be nigh impossible to penetrate through the hosts of the Saracens to reach the camp of King Richard."

"The matter is difficult and not without danger," the hermit said. "As to the nature of the country, I myself know but little, for my dealings with the natives have been few and simple. There are, however, several Christian communities dwelling among the heathen. They are poor, and are forced to live in little-frequented localities. Their Christianity may be suspected by their neighbours, but as they do no man harm, and carry on their worship in secret, they are little interfered with. There is one community among the hills between this and Jerusalem, and I can give you instructions for reaching this, together with a token which will secure you hospitality there, and they will no doubt do their best to forward you to another station. When you approach the flat country where the armies are maneuvering you must doubtless trust to yourself; but as far as the slopes extend, methinks that our friends will be able to pass you without great difficulty."

Cuthbert's heart rose greatly at the prospect of once again entering upon an active life, and the next evening, with many thanks for his kindness, he knelt before the aged hermit to receive his blessing.

With the instructions given him he had no difficulty in making his way through the mountains, until after some five hours' walk he found himself at a little village situated in a narrow valley.

Going to the door of the principal hut, he knocked, and upon entering showed the owner—who opened the door—a rosette of peculiar beads, and repeated the name of Father Anselm. The peasant at once recognized it, and bade Cuthbert welcome. He knew but a few words of French, although doubtless his ancestors had been of European extraction. In the morning he furnished Cuthbert with the sheepskin and short tunic which formed the dress of a shepherd, and dyeing his limbs and face a deep brown, he himself started with Cuthbert on his journey to the next Christian community.

This was a small one, consisting of two huts only, built almost on the summit of a mountain, the inhabitants living partly on the milk and cheese of their goats, and partly upon the scanty vegetables which grew around the huts.

His welcome was as cordial as that of the night before; and the next morning, his former guide taking leave of him, the peasant in whose house he had slept, again conducted him forward to another community. This was the last station, and stood in a narrow gorge on the face of the hills looking down over the plain, beyond which in the far distance a faint line of blue sea was visible.

This community was far more prosperous and well-to-do than those at which the previous nights had been passed. The head of the village appeared to be a personage of some importance; and although clinging in secret to his Christian faith, he and his belongings had so far adopted the usages of the Mussulmen that apparently no thought of their Christianity entered into the minds of the authorities. He was the owner of two or three horses, and of some extensive vineyards and olive grounds. He was also able to speak French with some degree of fluency.

At considerable length he explained to Cuthbert the exact position of the Christian army, which had moved some distance along the coast since Cuthbert had left it. It was, he said, exposed to constant attacks by the Saracens, who harassed it in every way, and permitted it no repose. He said that the high hopes which had been raised by the defeat of the Saracens at Azotus, had now fallen, and that it was feared the Christians would not be able to force their way forward to Jerusalem. The great portion of their animals had died, and the country was so eaten up by the Saracen hosts, that an advance upon Jerusalem without a large baggage train was next to impossible; and indeed if the Christians were to arrive before that city, they could effect nothing without the aid of the heavy machines necessary for battering the walls or effecting an escalade.

Cuthbert was vastly grieved when he heard of the probable failure of the expedition, and he burned with eagerness to take his part again in the dangers and difficulties which beset the Christian army. His host pointed out to him the extreme difficulty and danger of his crossing the enemy's lines, but at the same time offered to do all in his power to assist him. After two days' stay at the village, and discussing the pros and cons of all possible plans, it was decided that the best chance lay in a bold effort. The host placed at his disposal one of his horses, together with such clothes as would enable him to ride as an Arab chief of rank and station; a long lance was furnished him, a short and heavy mace, and scimitar; a bag of dates was hung at the saddle-bow; and with the sincerest thanks to his protector, and with a promise that should the Christian host win their way to Jerusalem the steed should be returned with ample payment, Cuthbert started on his journey.

Chapter XVI
A Fight Of Heroes.

The horse was a good and spirited one, and when he had once descended to the plains, Cuthbert rode gaily along, exulting in his freedom, and in once again possessing arms to defend himself should it be needed. His appearance was so exactly that of the horsemen who were continually passing and repassing that no observation whatever was attracted by it. Through villages, and even through camps, Cuthbert rode fearlessly, and arrived, without having once been accosted, near the main camp of the Saracens, which extended for miles parallel to the sea. But at a distance of some three leagues beyond, could be seen the white tents of the Christian host, and Cuthbert felt that the time of trial was now at hand.

He dismounted for an hour to allow his steed to rest itself, fed it with dates from his wallet, and gave it a drink of water at the stream. Then, when he felt that it had thoroughly recovered its strength and freshness, he re-mounted, and rode briskly on as before. He passed unchallenged, attracting no more notice than a person now-a-days would do in walking along a crowded street. Without hesitation he passed through the tents and started across the open country. Bands of horsemen were seen here and there, some going, and some coming from the direction of the Christian camp. As it was doubtless supposed that he was on his way to join some band that had gone on in advance, the passage of the solitary horseman excited no comment until he approached within about two miles of the Christian camp. There were now, so far as he could see, no enemies between him and the point he so longed to gain. But at this minute a group of Arab horsemen, gathered, apparently on the look-out against any movement of the Christians, shouted to him "Halt!" demanding whither he was going.

Up to this point Cuthbert had ridden at a gentle canter; but at the challenge he put spurs into his steed and made across the plain at full speed. With a wild yell the Arabs started in pursuit. They lay at first some 200 yards on his right, and he had therefore a considerable start of them. His horse was fairly fresh, for the journey that he had made had only been about fifteen miles-an inconsiderable distance to an Arab steed. For half a mile he did not think that his pursuers gained much upon him, riding as they had done sideways. They had now gathered in his rear, and the nearest was some 150 yards behind him. A quarter of a mile farther he again looked round, and found that two of the Arabs, far better mounted than the others, had come within half the distance which separated them from him when he last glanced back. His horse was straining to the utmost, and he felt that it could do no more; he therefore prepared himself for a desperate fight should his pursuers overtake him. In another quarter of a mile they were but a short distance behind, and an arrow whizzing by Cuthbert's ear told him they had be-taken themselves to their bows.

Half a mile ahead he saw riding towards him a group of Christian knights; but he felt that it was too late for him to hope to reach them, and that his only chance now was to boldly encounter his pursuers. The main body of the Arabs was fully 200 yards behind—a short distance when going at a gallop-which left him but little time to shake off the pursuit of the two immediately behind him.

A sharp stinging pain in his leg told him that it was time to make his effort; and checking his horse, he wheeled suddenly round. The two Arabs with a yell rode at him with pointed lance. With his right hand Cuthbert grasped the short heavy mace which hung at his saddle-bow, and being well practised in the hurling of this weapon-which formed part of the education of a good knight-he cast it with all his force at the chest of the Arab approaching on that side. The point of the spear was within a few yards of his breast as he flung the mace; but his aim was true, for it smote the Saracen full on the chest, and hurled him from his horse as if struck with a thunderbolt. At the same instant Cuthbert threw himself flat on the neck of his steed and the lance of the Arab who came up on the other side passed harmlessly between his shoulders, tearing his clothes as it went. In an instant Cuthbert had wheeled his horse, and before the Arab could turn his steed Cuthbert, coming up from behind, had run him through the body.

Short as the delay had been, the main body of the pursuers were scarcely fifty yards away; but Cuthbert now continued his flight towards the knights, who were galloping forward at full speed; and a moment afterwards glancing back, he saw that his pursuers had turned and were in full flight.

With a shout of joy he rode forward to the party who had viewed with astonishment this conflict between what appeared to be three of the infidels. Even louder than his first shout of exultation was the cry of joy which he raised at seeing among the party to whom he rode up, the Earl of Evesham, who reined in his horse in astonishment, and drew his sword as the supposed enemy galloped towards him.

"My lord, my lord!" Cuthbert said. "Thank heaven I am safe with you again."

The earl lowered his sword in astonishment.

"Am I mad," he said, "or dreaming, or is this really Sir Cuthbert?"

"It is I sure enough," Cuthbert exclaimed, "although truly I look more like a Bedouin soldier than a Christian knight."

"My dear boy!" exclaimed the earl, galloping forward and throwing his arms around Cuthbert's neck, "we thought you were dead. But by what wonderful fortune have you succeeded in escaping?"

In a few words Cuthbert related the principal incidents of his adventures, and he was heartily congratulated by the assembled knights.

There was, however, no time for long explanations. Large bodies of the Saracen horse were already sweeping down, to capture, if possible, this small band of knights who had ventured so far from the camp; and as King Richard's orders were that none should venture upon conflicts except by his orders, the party reluctantly turned their horses and galloped back to the camp.

Great as had been the earl's joy, it was, if possible, exceeded by that of Cnut on discovering in the Arab chief who rode up alongside the earl, the lad he loved so well. Loud and hearty were the cheers which rang out from the earl's camp as the news spread, and Cuthbert was compelled to shake hands with the whole party before entering the earl's tent, to refresh himself and give the narrative of what had happened.

Cuthbert, retiring to his tent with the Earl of Evesham, inquired of him what had taken place during his absence.

"For," he said, "although but a short three days' march from here, I have been as one of the dead, and have heard nothing whatever of what has taken place."

"Nothing could have gone worse," the earl said. "We have had nothing but dissensions and quarrels. First, the king fell out with the Archduke of Austria."

"On what ground did this happen?" Cuthbert asked.

"For once," the earl said, "the king our master was wholly in the wrong, which is not generally the case. We had just taken Ascalon, and were hard at work fortifying the place. King Richard with his usual zeal, in order to encourage the army, seized heavy stones and himself bore them into their place. The Archduke stood near with some of his knights: and it may be that the haughty Austrian looked somewhat superciliously at our king, thus labouring.

"'Why do you not make a show of helping?' King Richard said, going up to him. 'It would encourage the men, and show that the labour upon which we are engaged can be undertaken by all without derogation.'

"To this the Archduke replied, —

"'I am not the son of a mason!'

"Whereupon Richard, whose blood no doubt had been excited by the air of the Austrian, struck him with his hand a fierce blow across the face. We nearly betook ourselves to our swords on both sides; but King Richard himself could have scattered half the Austrians, and these, knowing that against his impetuous valour they could do nothing, simply withdrew from our camp, and sailed the next day for home. Then the king, in order to conciliate some at least of his allies, conferred the crown of Jerusalem upon Conrad of Montferat. No sooner had he done this than Conrad was mysteriously wounded. By whom it was done none knew. Some say that it was by emissaries of the Old Man of the Mountain. Others affirm that it was the jealousy of some of the knights of the holy orders. But be that as it may, he died. Some of the French, ever jealous of the valour of our king, ascribed it to his orders. This monstrous accusation coming to the ears of King Richard, he had hot words with the Duke of Burgundy. In this I blame him not, for it is beyond all reason that a man like the king, whose faults, such as they are, arise from too much openness, and from the want of concealment of such dislikes as he may have, should resort to poison to free himself of a man whom he himself had but a day or two before appointed King of Jerusalem. However it be, the consequences were most unfortunate, for the result of the quarrel was that the Duke of Burgundy and his Frenchmen followed the example of the Austrians, and we were left alone. Before this we had marched upon Jerusalem. But the weather had been so bad, and our train was so insufficient to carry the engines of war, that we had been forced to fall back again. King Richard again advanced, and with much toil we went as far as the village of Bethany."

"Why," Cuthbert exclaimed, "I passed through that village, and it is but three miles from the holy city."

"That is so," the earl said; "and many of us, ascending the hill in front, saw Jerusalem. But even then it was certain that we must again retrace our steps; and when we asked King Richard to come to the crest of the hill to see the holy city, he refused to do so, saying, 'No; those who are not worthy of conquering Jerusalem should not look at it!' This was but a short time since, and we are now retracing our steps to Acre, and are treating with Saladin for a peace."

"Then," Cuthbert said sadly, "all our hopes and efforts are thrown away; all this blood has been shed for nothing; and after the three great powers of Europe have engaged themselves solemnly in the war, we are baffled, and have to fall back before the hordes of the infidels."

"Partly before them," the earl said, "partly as the result of our own jealousies and passions. Had King Richard been a lesser man than he is, we might have conquered Jerusalem. But he is so extraordinary a warrior that his glory throws all others into the shade. He is a good general, perhaps the best in Europe; and had he done nothing but lead, assuredly we should have carried out our purpose. See how ably he maneuvered the army at the fight of Azotus. Never was a more complete defeat than that which he inflicted there upon the Saracens; and although the fact that his generalship achieved this, might have caused some jealousy to the other commanders, this might have died away could he between the battles have been a general, and nothing more. But alas! he is in addition a knight-errant—and such a knight-errant as Europe has never seen before. Wherever there is danger, Richard will plunge into the midst. There are brave men in all the three armies; but the strongest and bravest are as children to King Richard. Alone he can dart into ranks of the infidels, and cut a lane for himself by the strength of his right arm. More than this, when danger has threatened he has snatched up his battle-axe and dashed into the fray without helm or cuirass, performing such prodigies of valour and strength that it has been to his prowess alone that victory was to be ascribed. Hence he is the idol of all the soldiers, whatever their nationality; for he is as ready to rush to the rescue of a French or Austrian knight when pressed as to that of his own men. But the devotion which the whole army felt for him was as gall and wormwood to the haughty Austrian and the indolent Frenchman; and the retirement of the King of France, which left Richard in supreme command, was in every way unfortunate."

Upon the following day the army again marched, and Cuthbert could not but notice the difference, not only in number but in demeanour, from the splendid array which had left Acre a few months before. There was little now of the glory of pennon and banner; the bright helms and cuirasses were rusted and dinted, and none seemed to care aught for bravery of show. The knights and men-at-arms were sunburnt and thin, and seemed but half the weight that they had been when they landed. Fatigue, hardship, and the heat had done their work; disease had swept off vast numbers. But the remains of the army were so formidable in their fighting powers that the Saracens, although following them at a distance in vast numbers, did not venture an attack upon them.

A few days after their arrival at Acre, the king gave orders for the embarcation of the troops. Just as they were preparing to enter the ships a small vessel was seen entering the harbour. It drew up to the shore, and a knight leaped from it, and, inquiring where King Richard was to be found, made his way to the king, who was standing superintending the embarcation of some of the horses.

"The Saracens, sire!" he exclaimed. "The Saracens are besieging Jaffa, and the place must be lost unless assistance arrives in a day or two."

The king leaped on board the nearest ship, shouted to his leading officers to follow him, and gave orders to others to bring down the troops with all possible speed, to waste not a moment, and to see that all was done, and then, in five minutes after the receipt of the news he started for Jaffa. The Earl of Evesham and Cuthbert had been standing near the king when the order was given, and followed him at once on board the bark which he had chosen.

"Ah, my gallant young knight," the king exclaimed, "I am right glad to see you with me. We shall have more fighting before we have done, and I know that that suits your mood as well as my own."

The king's vessel was far in advance of any of the others, when early the following morning it arrived at Jaffa.

"Your eyes are better than mine," the king said to Cuthbert. "Tell me what is that flag flying on the top of the town."

Cuthbert looked at it earnestly.

"I fear, sire, that it is the crescent. We have arrived too late."

"By the holy cross," said King Richard, "that shall not be so; for if the place be taken, we will retake it."

As the vessel neared the shore a monk ran out into the water up to his shoulders, and said to the king that the citadel still held out, and that even now the Saracens might be driven back. Without delay the king leaped into the water, followed by the knights and men-at-arms, and entering the gate, threw himself upon the infidels within, who, busy plundering, had not noticed the arrival of the ship.

The war cry of "St. George! St. George!" which the king always shouted in battle, struck panic among the infidels; and although the king was followed but by five knights and a few men-at-arms, the Saracens, to the number of 3000, fled before him, and all who tarried were smitten down. The king followed them out upon the plain, driving them before him as a lion would drive a flock of sheep, and then returned triumphant into the city.

The next day, some more ships having arrived, King Richard found that in all, including the garrison, he could muster 2000 combatants. The enemy renewed the attack in great numbers, and the assaults upon the walls were continuous and desperate. King Richard, who loved fighting in the plain rather than behind walls, was impatient at this, and at one time so fierce was the attack that he resolved to sally out. Only ten horses remained in the town, and King Richard, mounting one, called upon nine of the knights to mount and sally out with him. The little band of ten warriors charged down upon the host of the Saracens and swept them before them. It was a marvellous sight indeed to see so small a group of horsemen dashing through a crowd of Saracen warriors. These, although at first beaten back, yet rallied, and the ten knights had great difficulty in fighting their way back to the town. When near the walls the Christians again made a stand, and a few knights sallied out from the town on foot and joined them. Among these was Cuthbert, the Earl of Evesham having accompanied King Richard in his charge. In all, seventeen knights were now rallied round the king. So fierce was the charge of the Saracens that the king ordered those on horseback to dismount, and with their horses in the centre, the little body knelt with their lances opposed to the Saracens. Again and again the wild cavalry swept down upon this little force, but in vain did they attempt to break their ranks. The scene was indeed an extraordinary one. At last the king, seeing that the enemy were losing heart, again ordered the knights to mount, and these dashing among the enemy, completed their defeat.

While this had been going on, news came to the king that the Saracens from another side had made their way into Jaffa, and were massacring the Christians. Without an instant's delay he flew to their succour, followed only by two knights and a few archers, the rest being so worn by their exertions as to be unable to move. The Mamelukes, the chosen guard of Saladin, had headed the attack; but even these were driven out from the town, and Richard dashed out from the city in their pursuit. One Saracen emir, distinguished for his stature and strength, ventured to match himself against the king, and rode boldly at him. But with one blow Richard severed his head, and his right shoulder and arm, from his body. Then having, by his single arm, put to rout the Saracens at this point, he dashed through them to the aid of the little band of knights who had remained on the defensive when he left them at the alarm of the city being entered. These were almost sinking with fatigue and wounds; but King Richard opened a way around them by slaying numbers of the enemy, and then charged again alone into the midst of the Mussulman host, and was lost to the sight of his companions. All thought that they would never see him again. But he soon reappeared, his horse covered with blood, but himself unwounded; and the attack of the enemy ceased.

From the hour of daybreak, it is said, Richard had not ceased for a moment to deal out his blows, and the skin of his hand adhered to the handle of his battle-axe. This narration would appear almost fabulous, were it not that it is attested in the chronicles of several eye-witnesses, and for centuries afterwards the Saracen women hushed their babes when fractious by threatening them with Malek-Rik, the name which they gave to King Richard.

Glorious as was the success, it was a sad one, for several of the most devoted of the followers of King Richard were wounded badly, some few to death. Among these last, to the terrible grief of Cuthbert, was his friend and patron, the Earl of Evesham. The king, on taking off his armour, hurried to his tent.

"The glory of this day is marred indeed," he said to the wounded knight, "if I am to lose you, Sir Walter."

"I fear that it must even be so, my lord," the dying earl said. "I am glad that I have seen this day, for never did I think to witness such feats as those which your Majesty has performed; and though the crusade has failed, and the Holy City remains in the hands of the infidel, yet assuredly no shadow of disgrace has fallen upon the English arms, and, indeed, great glory has accrued to us. Whatever may be said of the Great Crusade, it will, at least, be allowed by all men, and for all time, that had the princes and soldiers of other nations done as your Majesty and your followers have done, the holy city would have fallen into our hands within a month of our putting foot upon the soil. Your Majesty, I have a boon to ask."

"You have but to name it, Sir Walter, and it is yours."

"Sir Cuthbert, here," he said, pointing to the young knight, who was sorrowfully kneeling by his bedside, "is as a son to me. The relationship by blood is but slight, but by affection it is as close as though he were mine own. I have, as your Majesty knows, no male heirs, and my daughter is but young, and will now be a royal ward. I beseech your Majesty to bestow her in marriage, when the time comes, upon Sir Cuthbert. They have known each other as children, and the union will bring happiness, methinks, to both, as well as strength and protection to her; and further, if it might be, I would fain that you should bestow upon him my title and dignity."

"It shall be so," the king said. "When your eyes are closed, Sir Walter, Sir Cuthbert shall be Earl of Evesham, and, when the time comes, the husband of your daughter."

Cuthbert was too overwhelmed with grief to feel a shadow of exaltation at the gracious intimation of the king; although, even then, a thought of future happiness in the care of the fair young lady Margaret passed before his mind. For the last time the king gave his hand to his faithful servant, who pressed it to his lips, and a few minutes afterwards breathed his last.

Chapter XVII
An Alpine Storm.

The tremendous exertions which King Richard had made told upon him, and attacks of fever succeeded each other at short intervals. This, however, mattered the less, since negotiations were now proceeding between him and Saladin. It was impossible, with the slight means at his disposal, for Richard further to carry on the crusade alone. Moreover, pressing news had arrived from his mother in England, urging him to return, as his brother John was intriguing against him, and had already assumed all but the kingly title. Saladin was equally desirous of peace. His wild troops were, for the most part, eager to return to their homes, and the defeats which they had suffered, and the, to them, miraculous power of King Richard's arm, had lowered their spirit and made them eager to be away. Therefore he consented without difficulty to the terms proposed. By these, the Christians were to surrender Ascalon, but were to keep Jaffa, Tyre, and the fortresses along the coast. All hostilities were to be suspended on both sides for the space of three years, three months, three weeks, three days, and three hours, when Richard hoped to return again and to recommence the struggle.

Between the sultan and King Richard a feeling approaching that of friendship had sprung up during the campaign. Saladin was himself brave in the extreme, and exposed his life as fearlessly as did his Christian rival, and the two valiant leaders recognized the great qualities of each other. Several times during the campaign, when Richard had been ill, the emir had sent him presents of fruit and other matters, to which Richard had responded in the same spirit. An interview had taken place between them which further cemented their friendship; and when Richard promised to return again at the end of the truce with a far larger army, and to accomplish the rescue of the holy city, the sultan smiled, and said that it appeared that valour alone was not sufficient to conquer in the Holy Land, but that if Jerusalem were to fall into the hands of the Christians, it could fall into no worthier hands than those of Malek-Rik.

So, with many mutual courtesies, the great rivals separated, and, soon after, King Richard and the little remnant of his army embarked on board ship, and set sail for England.

It was on the 11th of October, 1192, that Richard Coeur de Lion left Palestine. Soon after they started, a storm suddenly burst upon them, and dispersed them in various directions. The ship in which Queen Berengaria was carried, arrived safely in Sicily; but that in which King Richard was borne was missing, and none of his fellow-voyagers knew what had become of him.

Sir Cuthbert was in the same vessel as the king, and the bark was driven upon the Island of Corfu. All reached shore in safety, and King Richard then hired three small vessels, in which he sailed to the port of Zara, whence he hoped to reach the domains of his nephew, Otho of Saxony, the son of his sister Matilda. The king had with him now but two of his knights, Baldwin of Bthune, and Cuthbert of Evesham. Cnut was with his feudal chief-for such Cuthbert had now, by his accession to the rank of Earl of Evesham, become-and three or four English archers.

"I fear, my lords," the king said to his knights as he sat in a little room in an inn at Zara, "that my plight is a bad one. I am surrounded by enemies, and, alas! I can no longer mount my steed and ride out as at Jaffa to do battle with them. My brother, John Lackland, is scheming to take my place upon the throne of England. Philip of France, whose mind is far better at such matters than at setting armies in the field, is in league with him. The Emperor Henry has laid claim to the throne of Sicily. Leopold of Austria has not forgiven me the blow I struck him in the face at Ascalon, and the friends of Conrad of Montferat are spreading far and wide the lie that I was the instigator of his murder. Sure never had a poor king so many enemies, and few have ever had so small a following as I have now. What think you, my lords? What course would you advise that I should adopt? If I can reach Saxony, doubtless Otho will aid me. But hence to Dresden is a long journey indeed. I have neither credit nor funds to hire a ship to take us by sea. Nor would such a voyage be a safe one, when so many of my enemies' ships are on the main. I must needs, I think, go in disguise, for my way lies wholly through the country of my enemies."

"Surely," Cuthbert said, "no potentate could for very shame venture to detain your Majesty on your way from the Holy Land, where you have wrought such great deeds. Were I in your place, I would at once proclaim myself, mount my horse, have my banner carried before me, and ride openly on. You have, too, another claim, namely, that of being shipwrecked, and even in war-time nations respect those whom the force of God has thrown upon their shores."

"I fear me, Sir Cuthbert," Sir Baldwin said, "that you overrate the chivalry of our master's enemies. Had we been thrown on the shores of France, Philip perhaps would hesitate to lay hands upon the king; but these petty German princelings have no idea of the observances of true chivalry. They are coarse and brutal in their ways; and though in outward form following the usages of knighthood, they have never been penetrated with its spirit. If the friends of Conrad of Montferat lay hands upon King Richard, I fear that no scruples will prevent them from using their advantage to the utmost. Even their emperor I would not trust. The course which you advise would no doubt be in accordance with the spirit of King Richard; but it would be madness for him to judge other people's spirit by his own, and it would be rushing into the lion's den to proclaim himself here. I should recommend, if I might venture to do so, that his Majesty should assume a false name, and that we should travel in small parties so as to attract no attention, each making his way to Saxony as best he may."

There was silence for a minute or two, and then the king with a sigh, said, —

"I fear that you are right, Sir Baldwin, and that there is no chivalry among these swinish German lords. You shall accompany me. Not, Sir Cuthbert," he observed kindly, noticing a look of disappointment upon the face of the young knight, "that I estimate your fidelity one whit lower than that of my brave friend; but he is the elder and the more versed in European travel, and may manage to bring matters through better than you would do. You will have dangers enough to encounter yourself, more even than I shall, for your brave follower, Cnut, can speak no language but his own, and your archers will be hard to pass as any other than what they are. You must be my messenger to England, should you arrive there without me. Tell my mother and wife where you left me, and that, if I do not come home I have fallen into the hands of one or other of my bitter foes. Bid them bestir themselves to hold England for me against my brother John, and, if needs be, to move the sovereigns of Europe to free me from the hands of my enemies. Should a ransom be needed, I think that my people of England will not grudge their goods for their king."

The following day the king bade farewell to his faithful followers, giving his hand to kiss, not only to Sir Cuthbert, but to Cnut and his archers.

"You have done me brave service," he said, "and I trust may yet have occasion to do it again. These are bad times when Richard of England has nought wherewith to reward his friends. But," he said, taking a gold chain from his neck and breaking it with his strong fingers into five fragments, "that is for you, Cnut, and for your four archers, in remembrance of King Richard."

The men, albeit hardened by many scenes of warfare, yet shed tears plenteously at parting with the king.

"We had better," Cuthbert said to them when they were alone, "delay here for a few days. If we are taken, the news that some Englishmen have been captured making their way north from Zara will spread rapidly, and may cause the enemies of Richard to be on the look-out for him, suspecting that the ship which bore us may also have carried him; for the news that he is missing will spread rapidly through Europe, and will set all his enemies on the alert."

In accordance with this plan, they delayed for another ten days at Zara, and then, hiring a small boat, were landed some thirty miles further along the coast. Cuthbert had obtained for Cnut the dress of a palmer, as in this he would pass almost unquestioned, and his silence might be accounted for on the ground that he had taken a vow of silence. He himself had placed on his coat and armour a red cross, instead of the white cross borne by the English knights, and would now pass as a French knight. Similar changes were made in the dress of his followers, and he determined to pass as a French noble who had been wrecked on his way home, and who was returning through Germany to France. The difficulties in his own case would not be serious, as his French would pass muster anywhere in Germany. The greatest difficulty would be with his attendants; but he saw no way of avoiding this.

Cuthbert's object, when with his little party he separated from King Richard, was to make his way to Verona, thence cross by Trent into Bavaria, and so to journey to Saxony. Fortunately he had, at the storming of Acre, become possessed of a valuable jewel, and this he now sold, and purchased a charger for himself. He had little fear of any trouble in passing through the north of Italy, for this was neutral ground, where knights of all nations met, and where, neither as an English nor a French crusader would he attract either comment or attention.

It was a slow journey across the northern plains, as of course he had to accommodate his pace to that of his men. Cnut and the archers had grumbled much at the change in the colour of the cross upon their jerkins; and, as Cnut said, would have been willing to run greater perils under their true colours than to affect to belong to any other nationality. On their way they passed through Padua, and there stopped a few days. Cuthbert could but feel, in looking at the splendour of this Italian city, the courteous manner of its people, and the university which was even then famous, how far in advance were those stately cities of Italy to Western Europe. His followers were as much surprised as himself at the splendour of the city. Here they experienced no trouble or annoyance whatever, for to the cities of Italy knights of all nations resorted, learned men came to study, philosophers to dispute, and as these brought their attendants with them, you might in the streets of Padua and its sister cities hear every language in Europe spoken.

From Padua they journeyed to Verona, marvelling greatly at the richness of the country. The footmen, however, grumbled at the flatness of the plain, and said that it was as bad as marching in the Holy Land. On their right, however, the slopes of the Alps, thickly clad with forests, reached down nearly to the road, and Cuthbert assured them that they would have plenty of climbing before they had done. At Verona they tarried again, and wondered much at the great amphitheatre, then almost perfect. Cuthbert related to Cnut and the archers, how men had there been set to fight, while the great stone benches round were thronged with men and women looking on at their death struggles, and said that not unfrequently British captives were brought hither and made to contend in the arena. The honest fellows were full of indignation and horror at the thought of men killing themselves to give sport to others. They were used to hard knocks, and thought but little of their life, and would have betaken themselves to their bows and bills without hesitation in case of a quarrel. But to fight in cold blood for amusement seemed to them very terrible.

Cuthbert would then have travelled on to Milan at that time next to Rome the richest city in Europe, but he longed to be back in England, and was the more anxious as he knew that King Richard would be passing through great dangers, and he hoped to meet him at the Court of Saxony. His money, too, was fast running out, and he found that it would be beyond his slender means to extend his journey so far. At Verona, then, they turned their back on the broad plains of Lombardy, and entered the valley of the Trent.

So far no observation whatever had been excited by the passage of the English knight. So many crusaders were upon their way home, many in grievous plight, that the somewhat shabby retinue passed unnoticed. But they were now leaving Italy, and entering a country where German was spoken. Trent, in those days an important city, was then, and is still, the meeting place of Italy and Germany. Both tongues are here spoken; but while the Italian perhaps preponderates, the customs, manners, and mode of thought of the people belong to those of the mountaineers of the Tyrol, rather than of the dwellers on the plains.

"You are choosing a stormy time," the landlord of the hostelry where they put up said to Cuthbert. "The winter is now at hand, and storms sweep across the passes with terrible violence. You had better, at the last village you come to in the valley, obtain the services of a guide, for should a snowstorm come on when you are crossing, the path will be lost, and nothing will remain but a miserable death. By daylight the road is good. It has been cut with much trouble, and loaded mules can pass over without difficulty. Poles have been erected at short distances to mark the way when the snow covers it. But when the snowstorms sweep across the mountains, it is impossible to see ten paces before you, and if the traveller leaves the path he is lost."

"But I suppose," Cuthbert said, "that even in winter travellers pass over?"

"They do," the host said. "The road is as open in winter as in summer, although, of course, the dangers are greater. Still, there is nothing to prevent vigorous men from crossing over when the storms come on. Now, too, with the snow already lying in the upper forests, the wolves are abroad, and should you be attacked by one of those herds, you will find it hard work to defend your lives. Much has been done to render the road safe. At the distance of every league stone houses have been erected, where travellers can find shelter either from the storm or from the attacks of wolves or bears, for these, too, abound in the forests, and in summer there is fine hunting among them. You are, as I see, returning from the Holy Land, and are therefore used to heat rather than cold, so I should advise you before you leave this city to buy some rough cloaks to shield you from the cold. You can obtain them for your followers very cheaply, made of the mountain goat or of sheepskins, and even those of bearskin well dressed are by no means dear."

Obtaining the address of a merchant who kept these things, Cuthbert proceeded thither; and purchased five cloaks of goat-skin with hoods to pull over their heads for his followers, while for himself he obtained one of rather finer material.

Another two days' journey brought them to the foot of the steep ascent, and here they hired the services of a guide. The ascent was long and difficult, and in spite of the praises which the host had bestowed upon the road, it was so steep that Cuthbert was, for the most part, obliged to walk, leading his steed, whose feet slipped on the smooth rock, and as in many places a false step would have thrown them down many hundreds of feet into the valley below, Cuthbert judged it safer to trust himself to his own feet. He disencumbered himself of his helmet and gorget, and placed these upon the horse's back. At nightfall they had attained a very considerable height, and stopped at one of the small refuges of which the landlord had spoken.

"I like not the look of the weather," the guide said in the morning-at least that was what Cuthbert judged him to say, for he could speak no word of the man's language. His actions, however, as he looked towards the sky, and shook his head, spoke for themselves, and Cuthbert, feeling his own powerlessness in a situation so novel to him, felt serious misgivings at the prospect.

The scenery was now very wild. On all sides crags and mountain tops covered with snow glistened in the sun. The woods near the path were free of snow; but higher up they rose black above the white ground. The wind blew keenly, and all rejoiced in the warm cloaks which they had obtained; for even with the protection of these they had found the cold bitter during the night.

"I like not this country," Cnut said. "We grumbled at the heat of Palestine, but I had rather march across the sand there than in this inhospitable frozen region. The woods look as if they might contain spectres. There is a silence which seems to be unnatural, and my courage, like the warmth of my body, is methinks oozing out from my fingers."

Cuthbert laughed.

"I have no doubt that your courage would come again much quicker than the warmth, Cnut, if there were any occasion for it. A brisk walk will set you all right again, and banish these uneasy fancies. To-night we shall be at the highest point, and to-morrow begin to descend towards Germany."

All day the men kept steadily on. The guide from time to time looked apprehensively at the sky; and although in the earlier part of the day Cuthbert's inexperienced eye saw nothing to cause the slightest uneasiness, towards the afternoon the scene changed. Light clouds began to gather on the top of all the hills and to shut the mountain peaks entirely from view. The wind moaned between the gorges and occasionally swept along in such sudden gusts that they could with difficulty retain their feet. The sky became gradually overcast, and frequently light specks of snow, so small as to be scarcely perceptible, were driven along on the blast, making their faces smart by the force with which they struck them.

"It scarcely needs our guide's face," Cuthbert said, "to tell us that a storm is at hand, and that our position is a dangerous one. As for me, I own that I feel better pleased now that the wind is blowing, and the silence is broken, than at the dead stillness which prevailed this morning. After all, methinks that a snowstorm cannot be more dreaded than a sandstorm, and we have faced those before now."

Faster and faster the snow came down, until at last the whole air seemed full of it, and it was with difficulty that they could stagger forward. Where the path led across open places the wind swept away the snow as fast as it fell, but in the hollows the track was already covered; and feeling the difficulty of facing the blinding gale, Cuthbert now understood the urgency with which his host had insisted upon the danger of losing the track. Not a word was spoken among the party as they plodded along. The guide kept ahead, using the greatest caution wherever the path was obliterated by the snow, sometimes even sounding with his iron-shod staff to be sure that they were upon the level rock. In spite of his warm cloak Cuthbert felt that he was becoming chilled to the bone. His horse could with difficulty keep his feet; and Cnut and the archers lagged behind.

"You must keep together, lads," he shouted. "I have heard that in these mountains when sleepiness overpowers the traveller, death is at hand. Therefore, come what may, we must struggle on."

Many times the gale was so violent that they were obliged to pause, and take shelter under the side of a rock or precipice, until the fury of the blast had passed; and Cuthbert eagerly looked out for the next refuge. At last they reached it, and the guide at once entered. It was not that in which he had intended to pass the night, for this lay still higher; but it would have been madness to attempt to go further in the face of such a gale. He signed to Cuthbert that it was necessary at once to collect firewood, and he himself proceeded to light some brands which had been left by previous travellers. Cuthbert gave directions to Cnut and the archers; and these, feeling that life depended upon a good fire being kept up, set to with a will, cutting down shrubs and branches growing in the vicinity of the hut. In half an hour a huge fire blazed in the refuge; and as the warmth thawed their limbs, their tongues were unloosened, and a feeling of comfort again prevailed.

"If this be mountaineering, my lord," Cnut said, "I trust that never again may it be my fortune to venture among the hills. How long, I wonder, do the storms last here? I was grumbling all the way up the hill at the load of provisions which the guide insisted that each of us should bring with him. As it was to be but a three days' journey before we reached a village on the other side, I wondered why he insisted upon our taking food enough to last us at least for a week. But I understand now, and thank him for his foresight; for if this storm goes on, we are assuredly prisoners here for so long as it may continue."

The horse had to be brought into the hut, for it would have been death for it to have remained outside.

"What is that?" Cnut said presently, as a distant howl was heard between the lulls of the storm. The guide muttered some word, which Cuthbert did not understand. But he said to Cnut, "I doubt not that it is wolves. Thank God that we are safe within this refuge, for here not even the most ravenous beasts could make their way."

"Pooh!" Cnut said contemptuously. "Wolves are no bigger than dogs. I have heard my grandfather say that he shot one in the forest, and that it was no bigger than a hound. We should make short work of them."

"I know not," Cuthbert said. "I have heard tales of these animals which show that they must be formidable opponents. They hunt in great packs, and are so furious that they will attack parties of travellers; many of these have perished miserably, horses and men, and nothing but their swords and portions of their saddles have remained to tell where the battle was fought."

Chapter XVIII
Sentenced To Death.

Just before arriving at the refuge, they had passed along a very steep and dangerous path. On one side the rock rose precipitously, ten feet above their heads. On the other, was a fall into the valley below. The road at this point was far wider than usual.

Presently, the howl of a wolf was heard near, and soon the solitary call was succeeded by the howling of great numbers of animals. These speedily surrounded the hut, and so fierce were their cries, that Cnut changed his opinion as to the ease with which they could be defeated, and allowed that he would rather face an army of Saracens than a troop of these ill-conditioned animals. The horse trembled in every limb at the sound of the howling of the wolves; and cold as was the night, in spite of the great fire that blazed on the hearth, his coat became covered with the lather of fear. Even upon the roof above the trampling of the animals could be heard; and through the open slits of the windows which some travellers before them had stuffed with straw, they could hear the fierce breathing and snorting of the savage beasts, who scratched and tore to make an entrance.

"Methinks," Cuthbert said, "that we might launch a few arrows through these loopholes. The roof appears not to be over strong; and should some of them force an entrance, the whole pack might follow."

Dark as was the night, the black bodies were visible against the white snow, and the archers shot several arrows forth, each stretching a wolf dead on the ground. Those killed were at once pounced upon by their comrades, and torn to pieces; and this mark of savageness added to the horror which those within felt of the ferocious animals. Suddenly there was a pause in the howling around the hut, and then Cnut, looking forth from the loophole, declared that the whole body had gone off at full speed along the path by which they had reached the refuge. Almost immediately afterwards a loud shout for help was heard, followed by the renewed howling and yelping of the wolves.

"Good heavens!" Cuthbert exclaimed. "Some traveller coming after us is attacked by these horrible beasts. Let us sally out, Cnut. We cannot hear a Christian torn to pieces by these beasts, without lending him a hand."

In spite of the angry shouts and entreaties of the guide, the door thrust open, and the party, armed with their axes and bows, at once rushed out into the night. The storm had for the moment abated and they had no difficulty in making their way along the track. In fifty yards they came to a bend of the path, and saw, a little distance before them, a black mass of animals, covering the road, and congregated round a figure who stood with his back to the rock. With a shout of encouragement they sprang forward, and in a few moments were in the midst of the savage animals, who turned their rage against them at once. They had fired two or three arrows apiece, as they approached, into them; and now, throwing down their bows, the archers betook themselves to their swords, while Cuthbert with his heavy battle-axe hewed and cut at the wolves as they sprang towards him. In a minute they had cleared their way to the figure, which was that of a knight in complete armour. He leant against the rock completely exhausted, and could only mutter a word of thanks through his closed visor. At a short distance off a number of the wolves were gathered, rending and tearing the horse of the knight; but the rest soon recovering from their surprise, attacked with fury the little party. The thick cloaks of the archers stood them in good stead against the animals' teeth, and standing in a group with their backs to the rock, they hewed and cut vigorously at their assailants. The numbers of these, however, appeared almost innumerable, and fresh stragglers continued to come along the road, and swell their body. As fast as those in front fell, their heads cleft with the axes of the party, fresh ones sprang forward; and Cuthbert saw that in spite of the valour and strength of his men, the situation was well nigh desperate. He himself had been saved from injury by his harness, for he still had on his greaves and leg pieces.

"Keep together," he shouted to his men, "and each lend aid to the other if he sees him pulled down. Strike lustily for life, and hurry not your blows, but let each tell." This latter order he gave perceiving that some of the archers, terrified by this furious army of assailants with gaping mouths and glistening teeth, were striking wildly, and losing their presence of mind.

The combat, although it might have been prolonged, could yet have had but one termination, and the whole party would have fallen. At this moment, however, a gust-of wind, more furious than any which they had before experienced, swept along the gorge, and the very wolves had to crouch on their stomachs to prevent themselves being hurled by its fury into the ravine below. Then even above the storm a deep roar was heard. It grew louder and louder. The wolves, as if struck with terror, leaped to their feet, and scattered on either way along the path at full speed.

"What sound can this be?" Cnut exclaimed in an awestruck voice. "It sounds like thunder; but it is regular and unbroken; and, my lord, surely the earth quakes under our feet!"

Louder and louder grew the roar.

"Throw yourselves down against the wall of rock," Cuthbert shouted, himself setting the example.

A moment afterwards, from above, a mighty mass of rock and snow poured over like a cascade, with a roar and sound which nigh stunned them. For minutes-it seemed for hours to them-the deluge of snow and rock continued. Then, as suddenly as it had begun, it ceased, and a silence as of death reigned over the place.

"Arise," Cuthbert said; "the danger, methinks, is past. It was what men call an avalanche —a torrent of snow slipping down from the higher peaks. We have had a narrow escape indeed."

By this time the knight whom they had rescued was able to speak, and raising his visor, he returned his deepest thanks to those who had come so opportunely to his aid.

"I was well nigh exhausted," he said, "and it was only my armour which saved me from being torn to pieces. A score of them had hold of me; but, fortunately, my mail was of Milan proof, and even the jaws and teeth of these enormous beasts were unable to pierce it."

"The refuge is near at hand," Cuthbert said. "It is but a few yards round yonder point. It is well that we heard your voice. I fear that your horse has fallen a victim."

Assisting the knight, who, in spite of his armour, was sorely bruised and exhausted, they made their way back to the refuge. Cnut and the archers were all bleeding freely from various wounds inflicted upon them in the struggle, breathless and exhausted from their exertions, and thoroughly awe-struck by the tremendous phenomenon of which they had been witnesses, and which they had only escaped from their good fortune in happening to be in a place so formed that the force of the avalanche had swept over their heads The whole of the road, with the exception of a narrow piece four feet in width, had been carried away. Looking upwards, they saw that the forest had been swept clear, not a tree remaining in a wide track as far as they could see up the hill. The great bowlders which had strewn the hill-side, and many of which were as large as houses, had been swept away like straws before the rush of snow, and for a moment they feared that the refuge had also been carried away. Turning the corner, however, they saw to their delight that the limits of the avalanche had not extended so far, the refuges, as they afterwards learned, being so placed as to be sheltered by overhanging cliffs from any catastrophe of this kind.

They found the guide upon his knees, muttering his prayers before a cross, which he had formed of two sticks laid crosswise on the ground before him; and he could scarce believe his eyes when they entered, so certain had he considered it that they were lost. There were no longer any signs of the wolves. The greater portion, indeed, of the pack had been overwhelmed by the avalanche, and the rest, frightened and scared, had fled to their fastnesses in the woods.

The knight now removed his helmet, and discovered a handsome yoking man of some four-or-five-and-twenty years old.

"I am," he said, "Baron Ernest of Kornstein. To whom do I owe my life?"

"In spite of my red cross," Cuthbert said, "I am English. My name is Sir Cuthbert, and I am Earl of Evesham. I am on my return from the Holy Land with my followers; and as we are passing through countries where many of the people are hostile to England, we have thought it as well for a time to drop our nationality. But to you I do not hesitate to tell the truth."

"You do well," the young knight said, "for, truth to say, the people of these parts bear but little love to your countrymen. You have saved my life when I was in the sorest danger. I had given myself up for lost, for even my armour could not have saved me long from these wretches; and my sword and life are at your disposal. You are young indeed," he said, looking with surprise at Cuthbert, who had now thrown back the hood of his cloak, "to have gained the honour of knighthood. You scarce look eighteen years of age, although, doubtless, you are older."

"I am scarce seventeen," Cuthbert said; "but I have had the good fortune to attract the notice of King Richard, and to have received the knighthood from his sword."

"None more worthy," said the young knight, "for although King Richard may be fierce and proud, he is the worthiest knight in Christendom, and resembles the heroes of romance rather than a Christian king."

"He is my lord and master," Cuthbert said, "and I love him beyond all men, and would give my life for his. He is the kindest and best of masters; and although it be true that he brooks no opposition, yet is it only because his own bravery and eagerness render hateful to him the indolence and cowardice of others."

They now took their seats round the fire. The archers, by the advice of the guide, rubbed their wounds with snow, and then applied bandages to them. The wallets were opened, and a hearty supper eaten; and all, wrapping themselves in their fur cloaks, were soon asleep.

For four days the gale continued, keeping the party prisoners in the hut. On the fifth, the force of the wind abated, and the snow ceased to fall. They were forced to take the door off its hinges to open it, for the snow had piled up so high that the chimney alone of the hut remained above its surface. With great difficulty and labour they cleared a way out, and then the guide again placing himself at their head, they proceeded on their way. The air was still and cold, and the sky of a deep, dark blue, which seemed even darker in contrast with the whiteness of the snow. At times they had great difficulty in struggling through the deep drifts; but for the most part the wind had swept the path clear. Where it was deepest, the tops of the posts still showed above the snow, and enabled the guide to direct their footsteps. They were, however, obliged to travel slowly, and it was three days before they gained the village on the northern slope of the mountains, having slept at refuges by the road.

"What are your plans?" the knight asked Sir Cuthbert that night, as they sat by the fire of the hostelry. "I would warn you that the town which you will first arrive at is specially hostile to your people, for the baron, its master, is a relation of Conrad of Montferat, who is said to have been killed by order of your king."

"It is false," Cuthbert said. "King Richard had appointed him King of Jerusalem; and, though he liked him not, thought him the fittest of those there to exercise sovereignty. He was the last man who would have had an enemy assassinated; for so open is he of disposition, that he would have fought hand to hand with the meanest soldier of his army, had he desired to kill him."

"I doubt not that it is so, since you tell me," the knight said courteously. "But the people here have taken that idea into their minds, and it will be hard to disabuse them. You must therefore keep up your disguise as a French knight while passing through this neighbourhood. Another week's journeying, and you will reach the confines of Saxony, and there you will, as you anticipate, be safe. But I would not answer for your life were you discovered here to be of English birth. And now tell me if there is aught that I can do for you. I will myself accompany you into the town, and will introduce you as a French knight, so that no suspicion is likely to lie upon you, and will, further, ride with you to the borders of Saxony. I am well known, and trust that my company will avert all suspicion from you. You have told me that your purse is ill-supplied; you must suffer me to replenish it. One knight need not fear to borrow of another; and I know that when you have returned to your home, you will bestow the sum which I now give you upon some holy shrine in my name, and thus settle matters between us."

Cuthbert without hesitation accepted the offer, and was well pleased at finding his purse replenished, for its emptiness had caused him serious trouble. Cuthbert's steed was led by one of the archers, and he himself walked gaily alongside of Sir Ernest, followed by his retainers. Another long day's march brought them down to Innsbruck, where they remained quietly for a week. Then they journeyed on until they emerged from the mountains, crossed the Bavarian frontier, and arrived at Fussen, a strong city, with well-built walls and defences.

They at once proceeded to the principal hostelry, where the young baron was well known, and where great interest was excited by the news of the narrow escape which he had had from the attack of the wolves. A journey across the Alps was in those days regarded as a very perilous enterprise in the winter season, and the fact that he should have been rescued from such a strait appeared almost miraculous. They stayed for two days quietly in the city, Cuthbert declining the invitation of the young noble to accompany him to the houses of his friends, as he did not wish that any suspicion should be excited as to his nationality, and preferred remaining quiet to having forced upon him the necessity of making false statements. As to his followers, there was no fear of the people among whom they mixed detecting that they were English. To the Bavarian inhabitants, all languages, save their native German, were alike unintelligible; and even had French been commonly spoken, the dialects of that tongue, such as would naturally be spoken by archers and men-at-arms, would have been as Greek to those accustomed only to Norman French.

Upon the third day, however, an incident occurred which upset Cuthbert's calculations, and nearly involved the whole party in ruin. The town was, as the young baron had said, governed by a noble who was a near relation of Conrad of Montferat, and who was the bitter enemy of the English. A great fete had been given in honour of the marriage of his daughter, and upon this day the young pair were to ride in triumph through the city. Great preparations had been made; masques and pageants of various kinds manufactured; and the whole townspeople, dressed in their holiday attire, were gathered in the streets. Cuthbert had gone out, followed by his little band of retainers, and taken their station to see the passing show. First came a large body of knights and men-at-arms, with gay banners and trappings. Then rode the bridegroom, with the bride carried in a litter by his side. After this came several allegorical representations. Among these was the figure of a knight bearing the arms of Austria. Underneath his feet, on the car, lay a figure clad in a royal robe, across whom was thrown a banner with the leopards of England. The knight stood with his foot on this figure.

This representation of the dishonour of England at the hands of Austria elicited great acclamations from the crowd. Cuthbert clenched his teeth and grasped his sword angrily, but had the sense to see the folly of taking any notice of the insult. Not so with Cnut. Furious at the insult offered to the standard of his royal master, Cnut, with a bound, burst through the ranks of the crowd, leaped on to the car, and with a buffet smote the figure representing Austria, into the road, and lifted the flag of England from the ground. A yell of indignation and rage was heard. The infuriated crowd rushed forward. Cnut, with a bound, sprang from the car, and, joining his comrades, burst through those who attempted to impede them, and darted down a by-street.

Cuthbert, for the moment amazed at the action of his follower, had on the instant drawn his sword and joined the archers. In the crowd, however, he was for a second separated from them; and before he could tear himself from the hands of the citizens who had seized him, the men-at-arms accompanying the procession surrounded him, and he was led away by them to the castle, the guards with difficulty protecting him from the enraged populace. Even at this moment Cuthbert experienced a deep sense of satisfaction at the thought that his followers had escaped. But he feared that alone, and unacquainted with the language of the country, they would find it difficult indeed to escape the search which would be made for them, and to manage to find their way back to their country. For himself, he had little hopes of liberty, and scarcely more of life. The hatred of the baron towards the English would now be heightened by the daring act of insult to the arms of Austria, and this would give a pretext for any deed of violence which might be wrought.

Cuthbert was, after a short confinement, brought before the lord baron of the place, in the great hall of the castle.

"Who art thou, sir," the noble exclaimed, "who darest to disturb the marriage procession of my daughter, and to insult the standard of the emperor my master?"

"I am Sir Cuthbert, Earl of Evesham, a baron of England," Cuthbert said fearlessly, "and am travelling homeward from the Holy Land. My garb as a crusader should protect me from all interruption; and the heedless conduct of my retainer was amply justified by the insult offered to the arms of England. There is not one of the knights assembled round you who would not in like manner have avenged an insult offered to those of Austria; and I am ready to do battle in the lists with any who choose to say that the deed was a foul or improper one. In the Holy Land, Austrians and English fought side by side; and it is strange indeed to me that on my return, journeying through the country of the emperor, I should find myself treated as an enemy, and see the arms of King Richard exposed to insult and derision by the burghers of this city."

As Cuthbert had spoken, he threw down his mailed glove, and several of the knights present stepped forward to pick it up. The baron, however, waved them back.

"It is no question," he said, "of honourable fight. This is a follower of the murderer of my good cousin of Montferat, who died under the hands of assassins set upon him by Richard of England."

"It is false!" Cuthbert shouted. "I denounce it as a foul lie, and will maintain it with my life."

"Your life is already forfeited," the baron said, "both by your past connexion with Richard of England and as the insulter of the arms of Austria. You die, and to-morrow at noon your head shall be struck off in the great square before my castle."

Without another word Cuthbert was hurried off to his cell, and there remained, thinking moodily over the events of the day, until nightfall. He had no doubt that his sentence would be carried out, and his anxiety was rather for his followers than for himself. He feared that they would make some effort on his behalf, and would sacrifice their own lives in doing so, without the possibility of assisting him.

The next morning he was led out to the square before the castle. It was a large flagged courtyard. Upon one side was the entrance to the castle, one of whose wings also formed a second side to the square. The side facing this was formed by the wall of the city, and the fourth opened upon a street of the town. This side of the square was densely filled with citizens, while the men-at-arms of the baron and a large number of knights were gathered behind a scaffold erected in the centre. Upon this was a block, and by the side stood a headsman. As Cuthbert was led forward a thrill of pleasure ran through him at perceiving no signs of his followers, who he greatly feared might have been captured in the night, and brought there to share his fate.

As he was led forward, the young noble whose life he had saved advanced to the baron, and dropping on one knee before him, craved the life of Cuthbert, relating the event by which he had saved his life in the passage of the mountains. The baron frowned heavily.

"Though he had saved the life of every noble in Bavaria," he said, "he should die. I have sworn an oath that every Englishman who fell into my hands should expiate the murder of my kinsman; and this fellow is, moreover, guilty of an outrage to the arms of Austria."

The young Sir Ernest drew himself up haughtily.

"My lord baron," he said, "henceforth I renounce all allegiance to you, and I will lay the case before the emperor, our common master, and will cry before him at the outrage which has thus been passed upon a noble gentleman. He has thrown down the glove, and challenged any of your knights, and I myself am equally ready to do battle in his cause."

The baron grew red with passion, and he would have ordered the instant arrest of the young man, but as Sir Ernest was connected by blood with many present, and was indeed one of the most popular among the nobles of the province, the baron simply waved him aside, and ordered Cuthbert to be led to the block. The young Englishman was by the executioner divested of his armour and helmet, and stood in the simple attire worn by men of rank at that time. He looked around, and holding up his hand, conveying alike a farewell and a command to his followers to remain in concealment, he gazed round the crowd, thinking that he might see among them in some disguise or other the features of Cnut, whose tall figure would have rendered him conspicuous in a crowd. He failed, however, to see any signs of him, and turning to the executioner, signified by a gesture that he was ready.

At this instant an arrow from the wall above pierced the brain of the man, and he fell dead in his tracks. A roar of astonishment burst from the crowd. Upon the city wall at this point was a small turret, and on this were five figures. The wall around was deserted, and for the moment these men were masters of the position.

"Seize those insolent varlets!" the baron shouted, shaking his sword with a gesture of fury at them.

His words, however, were arrested, for at the moment another arrow struck him in the throat, and he fell back into the arms of those around him.

Quickly now the arrows of the English archers flew into the courtyard. The confusion which reigned there was indescribable. The citizens with shouts of alarm took to their heels. The men-at-arms were powerless against this rain of missiles, and the knights, hastily closing their visors, shouted contradictory orders, which no one obeyed.

In the confusion no one noticed the prisoner. Seizing a moment when the attention of all was fixed upon the wall, he leaped from the platform, and making his way unnoticed through the excited crowd of men-at-arms, darted down a narrow lane that divided the castle from the wall. He ran along until, 100 yards farther, he came to a staircase by which access to the battlements was obtained. Running lightly up this, he kept along the wall until he reached the turret.

"Thanks, my noble Cnut!" he exclaimed, "and you, my brave fellows. But I fear you have forfeited your lives. There is no escape. In a minute the whole force of the place will recover from their confusion, and be down upon us from both sides."

"We have prepared for that," Cnut said. "Here is a rope hanging down into the moat."

Glancing over, Cuthbert saw that the moat was dry; and after a final discharge of arrows into the crowd, the six men slid one after another down the rope and made their way at full speed across the country.

Chapter XIX
Dresden.

It was some ten minutes before the men-at-arms rallied sufficiently from their surprise to obey orders. Two bodies were then drawn up, and proceeded at a rapid pace towards the staircases leading to the wall, one on each side of the turret in which they believed that the little body of audacious assailants were still lying. Having reached the wall, the soldiers advanced, covering themselves with their shields, for they had learnt the force with which an English clothyard shaft drawn by a strong hand flies. Many had been killed by these missiles passing through and through the cuirass and backpiece.

No reply being obtained to the summons to surrender, they proceeded to break in with their battle-axes the door of the little turret. Rushing in with axe and pike, they were astonished to find the place empty. A glance over the wall showed the rope still hanging, and the manner of the escape became manifest. The fugitives were already out of sight, and the knights, furious at the escape of the men who had bearded them in the heart of the city with such audacity, and had slain the lord baron and several of his knights, gave orders that an instant pursuit should be organized. It was, however, a full half hour before the city gates were thrown open, and a strong troop of knights and mounted men issued out.

Cuthbert had been certain that an instant pursuit would be set on foot, and the moment that he was out of sight of the battlements, he changed the direction in which he had started, and turning at right angles, swept round the city, still keeping at a distance, until he reached the side next the mountains, and then plunged into the woods on the lower slopes of the hills.

"They will," he said, as they halted breathless from their run, "follow the road towards the south, and scour the country for awhile before it occurs to their thick German skulls that we have doubled back on our tracks. Why, what is it, Cnut?"

This exclamation was provoked by the forester throwing himself on his knees before Sir Cuthbert, and imploring his pardon for the dire strait into which his imprudence had drawn him.

"It was a dire strait, certainly, Cnut. But if you got me into it, at least you have extricated me; and never say more about it, for I myself was near committing the imprudence to which you gave way, and I can well understand that your English blood boiled at the sight of the outrage to the flag of England. Now, let us waste no time in talk, but, keeping to the foot of this mountain, make along as far as we can to the west. We must cling to the hills for many days' march before we venture again to try to cross the plains. If possible, we will keep on this way until we reach the confines of the country of the Swiss, who will assuredly give us hospitality, and who will care little for any threats of these German barons, should they hear that we have reached their asylum."

By nightfall they had already travelled many leagues, and making a fire in the wood, Cuthbert asked Cnut for an account of what had taken place on the previous day.

"We ran for life, Sir Cuthbert, and had not noticed that you had been drawn into the fray. Had we done so, we would have remained, and sold our lives with yours; but hoping that you had passed unnoticed in the crowd, and that you would find some means to rejoin us, we kept upon our way. After running down three streets, we passed a place where a courtyard with stables ranged round it was open. There were none about, and we entered, and, taking refuge in a loft, hid ourselves beneath some provender. There we remained all night, and then borrowing some apparel which some of the stablemen had hung up on the walls, we issued into the town. As we neared the great square we saw some men employed in erecting a platform in the midst, and a suspicion that all might not be right, and that you might have fallen into the hands of these German dogs, beset our minds. After much consultation we determined to see what the affair meant, and making our way on to the walls, which, indeed, were entirely deserted, we took refuge in that turret where you saw us. Seeing the crowd gather, and being still more convinced that some misfortune was about to occur, I again went back to the stables, where I had noticed a long rope used by the carters for fastening their loads to the waggons. With this

I returned, for it was clear that if we had to mingle in this business it would be necessary to have a mode of escape. Of the rest you are aware. We saw the knights coming out of the castle, with that portly baron, their lord, at their head. We saw the block and the headsman upon the platform, and were scarcely surprised when you were led out, a prisoner, from the gates. We judged that what did happen would ensue. Seeing that the confusion wrought by a sudden attack from men perched up aloft as we were, commanding the courtyard, and being each of us able to hit a silver mark at the distance of 100 yards, would be great indeed, we judged that you might be able to slip away unobserved, and were sure that your quick wit would seize any opportunity which might offer. Had you not been able to join us, we should have remained in the turret and sold our lives to the last, as, putting aside the question that we could never return to our homes, having let our dear lord die here, we should not, in our ignorance of the language and customs of the country, have ever been able to make our way across it. We knew, however, that before this turret was carried we could show these Germans how five Englishmen, when brought to bay, can sell their lives."

They had not much difficulty in obtaining food in the forest, for game abounded, and they could kill as many deer as seemed fit to them. As Cnut said, it was difficult to believe that they were not back again in the forest near Evesham, so similar was their life to that which they had led three years before. To Cnut and the archers, indeed, it was a pleasanter time than any which they had passed since they had left the shores of England, and they blithely marched along, fearing little any pursuit which might be set on foot, and, indeed, hearing nothing of their enemies. After six days' travel they came upon a rude village, and here Cuthbert learnt from the people-with much difficulty, however, and pantomime, for neither could understand a word spoken by the other-that they were now in one of the Swiss cantons, and therefore secure from all pursuit by the Germans. Without much difficulty Cuthbert engaged one of the young men of the village to act as their guide to Basle, and here, after four days' travelling, they arrived safely. Asking for the residence of the Burgomaster, Cuthbert at once proceeded thither, and stated that he was an English knight on the return from the Crusades; that he had been foully entreated by the Lord of Fussen, who had been killed in a fray by his followers; and that he besought hospitality and refuge from the authorities of Basle.

"We care little," the Burgomaster said, "what quarrel you may have had with your neighbours. All who come hither are free to come and go as they list, and you, as a knight on the return from the Holy Land, have a claim beyond that of an ordinary traveller."

The Burgomaster was himself able to speak French, and summoning several of the councillors of the town, he requested Cuthbert to give a narrative of his adventures; which he did. The councillors agreed with the Burgomaster that Cuthbert must be received hospitably; but the latter saw that there was among many of them considerable doubt as to the expediency of quarrelling with a powerful neighbour. He therefore said to the Burgomaster, —

"I have no intention, honourable sir, of taking up any prolonged residence here. I only ask to be furnished with a charger and arms, and in payment of these I will leave this gold chain, the gift of King Richard himself, as a gage, and will on my return to my country forward to you the value of the arms and horse, trusting that you will return the chain to me."

The Burgomaster, however, said that the city of Basle was not so poor that it need take the gage of an honourable knight, but that the arms and charger he required should be given him in a few hours, and that he might pay the value in London to a Jew merchant there who had relations with one at Basle. Full instructions were given to him, and he resolved to travel down upon the left bank of the Rhine, until he reached Lorraine, and thence to cross into Saxony. The same afternoon the promised horse and arms were provided, and Cuthbert, delighted again to be in harness, and thanking courteously the Burgomaster and council for their kindness, started with his followers on his journey north. These latter had been provided with doublets and other garments suitable to the retinue of a knight, and made a better show than they had done since they first left England.

Leaving Basle, they travelled along the left side of the Rhine by easy stages. The country was much disturbed, owing to the return and disbandment of so many of the troops employed in the Crusades. These, their occupation being gone, scattered over the country, and France and Germany alike were harassed by bands of military robbers. The wild country between the borders of Switzerland and Lorraine was specially vexed, as the mountains of the Vosges afforded shelter, into which the freebooters could not be followed by the troops of the duke.

Upon the evening of the third day they reached a small inn standing in a lonely position near the foot of the mountains.

"I like not the look of this place," Cuthbert said; "but as we hear that there is no other within a distance of another ten miles, we must e'en make the best of it."

The host received them with extreme and even fawning civility, which by no means raised him in the estimation of Cuthbert or Cnut. A rough meal was taken, and they then ascended to the rude accommodation which had been provided. It was one large room, barely furnished. Upon one side straw was thickly littered down-for in those days beds among the common people were unknown. In a sort of alcove at the end was a couch with a rough mattress and coverlet. This Cuthbert took possession of, while his followers stretched themselves upon the straw.

"Methinks," Cnut said, "that it were well that one should keep watch at the door. I like not the look of our host, and we are near the spot where the bands of the robbers are said to be busy."

Towards morning the archer on guard reported that he could hear the sound of many approaching footsteps. All at once sprang to their feet, and betook themselves to their arms. Looking from the window they saw a large party of rough men, whose appearance at once betokened that they were disbanded soldiers—a title almost synonymous in those days with that of robber. With the united strength of the party the truckle bed was carried from the alcove and placed against the door. Cuthbert then threw open the window, and asked in French what they wanted. One of the party, who appeared to be the leader, said that the party had better surrender immediately. He promised them good treatment, and said that the knight would be put to ransom, should it be found that the valuables upon his person were not sufficient to pay the worshipful company present for the trouble which they had taken in waiting upon him. This sally was received with shouts of laughter. Cuthbert replied quietly that he had no valuables upon his person; that if they took him there were none would pay as much as a silver mark for the ransom of them all; and that the only things that they had to give were sharp arrows and heavy blows.

"You talk bravely, young sir," the man said. "But you have to do with men versed in fight, and caring but little either for knocks or for arrows. We have gone through the Crusades, and are therefore held to be absolved from all sin, even that so great as would be incurred in the cutting of your knightly throat."

"But we have gone through the Crusades also," Cuthbert said, "and our persons are sacred. The sin of slitting our weazands, which you speak of, would therefore be so great that even the absolution on which you rely would barely extend to it."

"We know most of those who have served in the Holy Land," the man said more respectfully than he had yet spoken, "and would fain know with whom we speak."

"I am an Englishman, and a follower of King Richard," Cuthbert said, "and am known as Sir Cuthbert of Evesham. As I was the youngest among the knights who fought for the holy sepulchre, it may be that my appearance is known to you?"

"Ah," the other said, "you are he whom they called the Boy Knight, and who was often in the thick of the fray, near to Richard himself. How comes it, Sir Cuthbert, that you are here?"

"The fleet was scattered on its return," Cuthbert replied, "and I landed with my followers, well-nigh penniless, at Zara, and have since made my way across the Tyrol. I have, then, as you may well suppose, neither silver nor gold about my person; and assuredly neither Philip of France nor John of Austria would give a noble for my ransom; and it would be long, methinks, to wait ere John of England would care to ransom one of King Richard's followers."

The brigands spoke for awhile among themselves, and then the leader said,—

"You speak frankly and fairly, Sir Knight, and as you have proved yourself indeed a doughty giver of hard blows, and as I doubt not that the archers with you can shoot as straight and as fast as the rest of the Saxon breed, we will e'en let you go on your way, for your position is but little better than ours, and dog should not rob dog."

"Thanks, good fellow," Cuthbert said. "We trust that in any case we might have made a strong defence against you; but it would be hard if those who have fought together in the Holy Land, should slay each other in this lonely corner of Lorraine."

"Are you seeking adventures or employment, Sir Knight? For if so, myself and comrades here would gladly take service with you; and it may be that with a clump of spears you might obtain engagement, either under the Duke of Lorraine or he of Cleves."

"Thanks for your offer," Cuthbert replied; "but at present my face is turned towards England. King Richard needs all his friends; and there is so little chance of sack or spoil, even should we have-which God forfend-civil war, that I fear I could ill reward the services which you offer me."

The leader and his men shouted an adieu to Cuthbert, and departed for the mountains, leaving the latter well pleased with his escape from a fight of which the result was doubtful.

Journeying on without further adventure, they came to Nancy, and were there kindly received by the duke, who was not at that time upon good terms with Phillip of France, and was therefore well disposed towards the English. Cuthbert inquired from him whether any news had been heard of King Richard? but received as a reply that the duke had heard nothing of him since he sailed from Palestine.

"This is strange," Cuthbert said, "for I myself have journeyed but slowly, and have met with many delays. King Richard should long ere this have reached Saxony; and I fear much that some foul treatment has befallen him. On our way, we found how bitter was the feeling among those related to Conrad of Montferat against him; and the Archduke John is still smarting from the blow which King Richard struck him at Ascalon. But surely they would not be so unknightly as to hinder so great a champion of Christendom as King Richard on his homeward way?"

"The Archduke John is crafty and treacherous," the duke said; "and the emperor himself would, I think, be not sorry Conrad of Montferat, who falsely allege that the death of their kinsman was caused by King Richard. The Archduke John, too, owes him no good-will; and even the emperor is evilly disposed towards him. The king travelled under an assumed name; but it might well be that he would be recognized upon the way. His face was known to all who fought in the East; and his lordly manner and majestic stature could ill be concealed beneath a merchant's garb. Still, lady, as I have been so long in making my way across, it may be that King Richard has been similarly delayed without danger befalling him, and it could hardly be that so important a man as the King of England would be detained, or come to any misfortune, without the news being bruited abroad."

In spite of Cuthbert's reassuring words, the duke and duchess were greatly alarmed at the news of King Richard's disappearance, although indeed consoled to find that their previous fears, that he had been drowned in the storm or captured by the Moorish corsairs, were unfounded.

They now requested from Cuthbert the story of what had befallen him since he left the king; and this he related at some length. The duke was greatly interested, and begged Cuthbert at least to remain at his court until some news might arrive of King Richard.

For a month Cuthbert tarried at the castle of the Duke of Saxony, where he was nobly entertained, and treated as a guest of much honour. Cnut and the archers were delighted at the treatment they received, for never in their lives had they been so royally entertained. Their Saxon tongue was nigh enough akin to the language spoken here to be understood; and their tales of adventure in the Holy Land rendered them as popular among the retainers of the duke as their master became with the duke and duchess.

Chapter XX
Under The Greenwood.

At the end of a month, news came from England that Sir Baldwin of Bthune had returned there, bearing the news that the King had been arrested at Gortz, only two days' journey north of the Adriatic-that he had been recognized, and at once captured. He had offered no resistance, finding indeed that it would be hopeless so to do. Sir Baldwin had been permitted to depart without molestation. He believed that the folk into whose hands he had fallen were retainers of the Archduke John. This news, although sad in itself, was yet in some degree reassuring to the duke and his wife; for they felt that while the followers of Conrad of Montferat would not hesitate to put King Richard to death should he fall into their hands, the Archduke John would not dare to bring upon himself the indignation of Europe by such treatment of his royal captive. Cuthbert at once determined to return to England to see Sir Baldwin, and to ascertain what steps were being taken for the discovery of the prison in which King Richard was confined, and for his release therefrom; and also to establish himself in his new dignity as Earl of Evesham. Therefore, bidding adieu to the duke and duchess, he started north. The duke furnished him with letters of introduction to the princes through whose countries he would travel; and again crossing the Rhine, he journeyed through the territories of the Dukes of Cleves and Brabant, and reached the mouth of the Scheldt without interruption. There taking ship, he sailed for London.

It was a long and stormy passage between the mouth of the Scheldt and London. The vessel in which Cuthbert had shipped was old and somewhat unseaworthy, and several times in the force of the gale all on board gave up hope for their lives. At last, however, they reached the mouth of the Thames, and dropping up with the tide, reached London eight days after their embarcation. The noble charger which the King of Saxony had presented to Cuthbert, had suffered greatly, and he feared at one time, that the poor animal would succumb to the effects of the tempest. However, after entering into smooth water it recovered itself, and on landing near the Tower he found that it was able to support his weight. Cnut and the archers were, like Cuthbert, delighted to have their feet again upon English soil; and although London did not now strike them with the same wonder which it would have done had they first visited it before starting on their journey-for in many respects it was greatly behind some of the continental cities-yet the feeling of home, and the pleasure of being able to understand the conversation of those around them, made the poor fellows almost beside themselves with joy. Beyond the main political incidents, Cuthbert had heard little of what had passed in England since his departure; and putting up at a hostelry, he inquired of the host whether Sir Baldwin of Bthune was in London, or whether he was away on his estates. The landlord did not know. There were, he said, but few nobles at court, and London was never so dull as at present. As Cuthbert did not wish his coming home to be known to John until he had learnt something of the position of affairs, he despatched Cnut to the Tower to inquire privately of some of the officials about the place whether Sir Baldwin was there. Cnut soon returned with the news that he had not been at the court since his return from the Holy Land, and that he was living at his castle down in Dorsetshire. After some hesitation, Cuthbert resolved to set out to see his friend, and after six days' travel he arrived at the castle of the knight.

Sir Baldwin received him with immense joy. He had not heard of him since they parted at Zara, and he feared that a fate similar to that which had befallen King Richard had overtaken Cuthbert, even if he were still alive.

"Have you seen aught of the king, our master?" the good knight inquired.

"Nothing," Cuthbert said. "I know no more than yourself. Indeed, I hoped to have learnt something from you as to the king."

"I was separated from him at Gortz, and while he was taken a prisoner to the archduke, I was allowed to pursue my way. I had many difficulties and dangers, and was some weeks in finding my way back. Nothing was known of the king when I returned. Indeed, I was the first bearer of any definite news concerning him since the day when he sailed from Acre. Three weeks ago, as you may have learnt, the news came that he is now detained in captivity by the emperor who demanded his delivery by the Archduke John, into whose hands he first fell. But where he is, no one exactly knows. The news has created an immense excitement in the kingdom, and all are resolved to sacrifice any of their treasures which may be demanded in order to satisfy the ransom which the recreant emperor has placed upon the king. Shame is it indeed that a Christian sovereign should hold another in captivity. Still more, when that other was returning through his dominions as a crusader coming from the Holy Land, when his person should be safe, even to his deadliest enemy. It has long been suspected that he was in the hands either of the emperor, or of the archduke, and throughout Europe the feeling of indignation has been strong; and I doubt not, now that the truth is known, this feeling will be stronger than ever."

"But, now that it is known," Cuthbert said, "I suppose there will be no delay in ransoming the king."

"There will be no delay in raising the ransom," Sir Baldwin said. "But the kingdom is very impoverished by war, by the exactions of Prince John, and by those of Langley, who held it for King Richard. He was a loyal servant of the king, but an exacting and rapacious prelate. However, I doubt not that the rents of the English nobles will soon be charged with sums sufficient for the ransom; and if this avail not, not one of them will grudge their silver flagons and vessels to melt down to make the total required. But we must not flatter ourselves that he will obtain his liberty so soon as the money is raised. Prince John has long been yearning for sovereignty. He has long exercised the real, if not the nominal, power, and he has been intriguing with the Pope and Phillip of France for their support for his seizing the crown. He will throw every obstacle in the way, as, we may be sure, will Phillip of France, Richard's deadly enemy. And now about yourself, Sir Cuthbert; tell me what has befallen you since we last met."

Cuthbert related the adventures which had befallen him, and heard those of Sir Baldwin.

"You have not, I suppose," the latter remarked, "as yet seen Prince John?"

"No," Cuthbert replied, "I thought it better to come down to ask you to advise me on the position of affairs before I attempted to see him."

"You did well," Sir Baldwin said. "When I arrived, I found that the proper officials, had, according to King Richard's instructions, drawn up the patent conferring upon you the lands and title of Earl of Evesham, before leaving Acre, and had received the king's signature to it. This was attested by several of the nobles who were with us and who returned safely to England. Prince John, however, declared that he should not give any heed to the document; that King Richard's power over this realm had ceased before he made it; and that he should bestow the earldom upon whomsoever he chose. As a matter of fact, it has been given to Sir Rudolph Fleming, a Norman knight and a creature of the prince. The king has also, I hear, promised to him the hand of the young Lady Margaret, when she shall become of marriageable age. At present she is placed in a convent in Worcester. The abbess is, I believe, a friend of the late earl, and the girl had been with her for some time previously. Indeed she went there, I think, when her father left England. This lady was ordered to give up her charge to the guardianship of Sir Rudolph; but she refused to do so, saying that it would not be convenable for a young lady to be under the guardianship of a bachelor knight having no lady at the head of his establishment, and that therefore she should retain her, in spite of the orders of the Prince. Prince John, I hear, flew into a fury at this; but he did not dare to provoke the anger of the whole of the clergy by ordering the convent to be violated. And indeed, not only would the clergy have been indignant, but many of the great nobles would also have taken their part, for there can be no doubt that the contention of the abbess was reasonable; and there is among all the friends of King Richard a very strong feeling of anger at your having been deprived of the earldom. This, however, has, so far, not found much vent in words, for as it was uncertain whether you would ever return to claim your rights, it was worth no one's while to embroil himself unnecessarily with the prince upon such a subject. God knows that there are subjects enough of dispute between John Lackland and the English barons without any fresh ones arising. The whole kingdom is in a state of disturbance. There have been several risings against Prince John's authority; but these have been, so far, suppressed. Now that we know where King Richard is, and hope for his return ere very long, it is probable that peace will be maintained; but should treachery prevail, and King Richard's return be prevented, you may be sure that John will not be permitted to mount the throne without the determined resistance of a large number of the nobles."

"But," Cuthbert said, "John is not the successor to the throne. Prince Arthur of Brittany was named by King Richard from the first as his successor. He is so by blood and by right, and John can have no pretence to the throne so long as he lives."

"That is so," Sir Baldwin said. "But, unhappily, in England at present might makes right, and you may be sure that at King Richard's death, be it when it may, Prince John will make a bold throw for the throne, and, aided as he will be by the pope and by Phillip of France, methinks that his chances are better than those of the young prince. A man's power, in warlike times, is more than a boy's. He can intrigue and promise and threaten, while a boy must be in the hands of partisans. I fear that Prince Arthur will have troubled times indeed before he mounts the throne of England. Should Richard survive until he becomes of age to take the field himself and head armies, he may succeed, for all speak well of him as a boy of singular sweetness of disposition, while Prince John is detested by all save those who flatter and live by him. But enough for the present of politics, Cuthbert; let us now to table. It is long since we two feasted together; and, indeed, such meals as we took in the Holy Land could scarcely have been called feasts. A boar's head and a good roasted capon are worthy all the strange dishes that we had there. I always misdoubted the meat, which seemed to me to smack in flavour of the Saracens, and I never could bring myself to inquire whence that strange food was obtained. A stoup of English ale, too, is worth all the Cyprus wines, especially when the Cyprus wines are half full of the sand of the desert. Pah! it makes my throat dry to think of those horrible meals. So you have brought Cnut and your four archers safely back with you?"

"Yes," Cuthbert said, smiling, "But they were, I can assure you, a heavy weight on me, in spite of their faithfulness and fidelity. Their ignorance of the language brought most of my troubles upon me, and Cnut had something of the nature of a bull in him. There are certain things which he cannot stomach, and when he seeth them he rageth like a wild beast, regardless altogether of safety or convenience."

In the evening, the two knights again talked over the course which Cuthbert should adopt. The elder knight's opinion was that his young friend had best formally claim the title by writing to the king-at-arms, and should also announce his return to Prince John, signing himself "Sir Cuthbert, Earl of Evesham;" but that, in the present state of things, it would be unwise for him to attempt to regain his position, should, as was certain to be the case, Prince John refuse to recognize him.

"You are very young yet," Sir Baldwin said, "not eighteen, I think, and can afford to wait, at any rate, to see whether King Richard returns. Should he come back, he will see all these wrongs are righted; and one of his first cares would assuredly be to cast this usurper out of his stolen dignities. How old is the Lady Margaret?"

"She is fifteen," Cuthbert said. "She was three years younger than I."

"I wish she had been younger," Sir Baldwin said. "At fifteen she is not by custom fairly marriageable; but men can strain these points when they choose; and I fear that the news of your coming will hasten both the prince and Sir Rudolph in their determination to strengthen the claim of this usurper by marriage with the heiress of Evesham. The Lady Margaret and her friends can of course claim that she is a royal ward, and that as such the king alone can dispose of her person and estates. But, unfortunately, force overrides argument."

"But surely," Cuthbert said, "they will never venture to take her by force from the convent?"

"They venture a great many strange things in England now," Sir Baldwin said; "and Worcester is perilously near to Evesham. With a clump of twenty spears, Sir Rudolph might break into the convent and carry off the young lady, and marry her by force; and although the Church might cry out, crying would be of little avail when the deed was done; and a handsome present on the part of Sir Rudolph might go far to shut the mouths of many of the complainants, especially as he will be able to say that he has the king's sanction for what he did."

"Methinks," Cuthbert said, "that if such be the case it would be perilous indeed to wait for King Richard's return. Assuredly Sir Rudolph would not tarry until she attained the age of seventeen, and it may well be that two years may yet pass before King Richard comes back. It seems to me the wiser part will be that I should give Prince John no notice that I am in England. As you say, such notice would be of no avail in recovering my lands and title, but it would put the prince upon his guard; and assuredly he and his minions would press forward their measures to obtain possession of the person of the Lady Margaret; while, on the other hand, no harm can come of my maintaining silence."

"I think that you are right, Sir Cuthbert. It were indeed best that your enemies should suppose you either dead or in some dungeon in the Tyrol. What would you then do?"

"I would return to my old home," Cuthbert said. "My lady mother is, I trust, still alive. But I will not appear at her house, but will take refuge in the forest there. Cnut, and the archers with him, were all at one time outlaws living there, and I doubt not that there are many good men and true still to be found in the woods. Others will assuredly join when they learn that Cnut is there, and that they are wanted to strike a blow for my rights. I shall then bide my time. I will keep a strict watch over the castle and over the convent. As the abbess is a friend and relative of Lady Margaret's, I may obtain an interview with her, and warn her of the dangers that await her, and ask if she be willing to fulfil the promise of her father, and King Richard's will, in accepting me as her husband when due time shall arrive, and whether she will be willing that I should take such steps as I may to deliver her from the persecution of Sir Rudolph. If, as I trust, she assents to this, I will keep a watch over the convent as well as the castle, and can then either attack the latter, or carry her off from the former, as the occasion may appear to warrant. There are plenty of snug cottages round the forest, where she can remain in concealment in the care of some good farmer's wife for months, and we shall be close at hand to watch over her. With the aid of the forest men, Sir Walter took the castle of Sir John of Wortham; and although Evesham is a far grander pile than that, yet methinks it could be carried by a sudden assault; and we know more of war now than we did then. Prince John may deny me the right of being the Earl of Evesham; but methinks before many months I can, if I choose, become its master."

"Be not too hasty in that matter," Sir Baldwin said. "You might capture the castle with the aid of your outlaws; but you could scarcely hold it. The prince has, ere now, with the aid of those faithful to him and his foreign mercenaries, captured stronger holds than that of Evesham; and if you turn his favourite out, you would have a swarm of hornets around you such as the walls of Evesham could not keep out. It would therefore be worse than useless for you to attempt what would be something like an act of rebellion against Prince John's authority, and would give him what now he has no excuse for, a ground for putting a price upon your head-and cutting it off if he got the opportunity. You might now present yourself boldly at court, and although he might refuse to recognize your title of earl, yet, as a knight and a crusader who has distinguished himself greatly in the Holy Land, he dare not interfere with your person, for this would be resented by the whole of the chivalry of England. Still, I agree with you that your best course is to keep your return a secret. You will then be unwatched and unnoticed, and your enemies will take their time in carrying their designs into effect."

Two days later Cuthbert, attended by his faithful retainers, left Sir Baldwin's castle, and travelled by easy stages through Wiltshire and the confines of Gloucestershire up to Worcester. He had been supplied by Sir Baldwin with suitable attire for himself and his followers, and now rode as a simple knight, without arms or cognizance, journeying from one part to another. All the crosses and other crusading signs were laid aside, and there was nothing to attract any attention to him upon his passage. Cuthbert had at first thought of going direct to the convent of Worcester, and asking for an interview with Lady Margaret; but he reflected that it might be possible that some of the myrmidons of Sir Rudolph might be keeping a watch over that building, to see that Lady Margaret was not secretly removed to some other place of refuge, and that the appearance of a knight before its doors would excite comment and suspicion. He therefore avoided the town, and journeyed straight to the forest, where he had so often roamed with Cnut and the outlaws.

Here he found that matters had but little changed since he was last there. Many of those who had fought with him in the Holy Land, and who had returned by sea, had again taken to the forest, joined by many new men whom the exactions of Sir Rudolph had already goaded into revolt. Cnut was received with enthusiasm, and when he presented Cuthbert to them as the rightful heir of Evesham and the well-known friend of the foresters, their enthusiasm knew no bounds. They at once accepted him as their lord and master, and promised to obey his orders, and to lay down their lives, if necessary, in his cause, as they knew that it was he who had formally obtained the pardon of the forest band, and who had fought with them in their attack on Wortham Castle.

To Cuthbert's great delight he heard that his mother was in good health, although she had for some months been grievously fretting over his disappearance and supposed death. Cuthbert hesitated whether he should proceed at once to see her; but he feared that the shock of his appearance might be too much for her, and that her expressions of joy might make the retainers and others aware of his arrival, and the news might in some way reach the ears of those at the castle. He therefore despatched Cnut to see her, and break the news to her cautiously, and to request her to arrange for a time when she would either see Cuthbert at some place at a distance from the house, or would so arrange that the domestics should be absent and that he would have an interview with her there unobserved.

Cnut was absent some hours, and on his return told Cuthbert that he had seen Dame Editha, and that her joy on hearing of her son's safe arrival had caused her no harm, but rather the reverse. The news that King Richard had bestowed upon him the title and lands of Evesham was new to her, and she was astonished indeed to hear of his elevation. Having heard much of the character of the pretending earl, she had great fears for the safety of Cuthbert, should his residence in the neighbourhood get to his ears; and although sure of the fidelity of all her retainers, she feared that in their joy at their young master's return they might let slip some incautious word which would come to the ears of some of those at the castle. She therefore determined to meet him at a distance. She had arranged that upon the following day she would give out that she intended to make a pilgrimage to the shrine of St. Dunstan, which lay at the edge of the forest, to thank him for her recovery from illness, and to pray for the safety of her son.

She would be carried thither in a litter, and her journey would excite no comment whatever. She would take with her four of her most trusted retainers, and would on her arrival at the shrine send them to a distance, in order to pay her devotions undisturbed. Cuthbert was to be near, and the moment he saw them depart, to enter.

This arrangement was carried out, and the joy of Dame Editha at again meeting her son was deep indeed. He had left her a lad of fifteen. He now returned a youth of nearly eighteen, stout and strong beyond his age, and looking far older than he was, from the effect of the hot sun of Syria and of the hardships through which he had gone. That he should win his spurs upon the first opportunity the earl had promised her, and she doubted not that he would soon attain the rank which his father had held. But that he should return to her a belted earl was beyond her wildest thoughts. This, however, was but little in her mind then. It was her son, and not the Earl of Evesham, whom she clasped in her arms.

As the interview must necessarily be a short one, Cuthbert gave her but a slight outline of what had happened since they parted, and the conversation then turned upon the present position, and upon the steps which had best be taken.

"Your peril is, I fear, as great here as when you were fighting the infidels in the Holy Land," she said. "Sir Rudolph has not been here long; but he has proved himself a cruel and ruthless master. He has driven forth many of the old tenants and bestowed their lands upon his own servants and retainers. The forest laws he carries out to the fullest severity, and has hung several men who were caught infringing them. He has laid such heavy burdens on all the tenants that remain that they are fairly ruined, and if he stay here long he will rule over a desert. Did he dream of your presence here, he would carry fire and sword through the forest. It is sad indeed to think that so worthless a knave as this should be a favourite of the ruler of England. But all men say that he is so. Thus were you to attack him, even did you conquer and kill him, you would have the enmity of Prince John to contend with; and he spareth none, man or woman, who stand in his way. It will be a bad day indeed for England should our good King Richard not return. I will, as you wish me, write to my good cousin, the Lady Abbess of St. Anne's, and will ask that you may have an interview with the Lady Margaret, to hear her wishes and opinions concerning the future, and will pray her to do all that she can to aid your suit with the fair young lady, and to keep her at all events safe from the clutches of the tyrant of Evesham."

Three days later, a boy employed as a messenger by Dame Editha brought a note to Cuthbert, saying that she had heard from the Abbess of St. Anne's, who would be glad to receive a visit from Cuthbert. The abbess had asked his mother to accompany him; but this she left for him to decide. Cuthbert sent back a message in reply, that he thought it would be dangerous for her to accompany him, as any spy watching would report her appearance, and inquiries were sure to be set on foot as to her companion. He said that he himself would call at the convent on the following evening after nightfall, and begged her to send word to the abbess to that effect, in order that he might, when he presented himself, be admitted at once.

Chapter XXI
The Attempt On The Convent.

Upon the following evening Cuthbert proceeded to Worcester. He left his horse some little distance outside the town, and entered on foot. Having no apprehension of an attack, he had left all his pieces of armour behind, and was in the quiet garb of a citizen. Cnut attended him-for that worthy follower considered himself as responsible that no harm of any sort should befall his young master. The consequences of his own imprudence in the Tyrol were ever before his mind, and he determined that from henceforth there should be no want of care on his part. He accompanied Cuthbert to within a short distance of the convent, and took up his position in the shade of a house, whence he could watch should any one appear to be observing Cuthbert's entrance.

Upon ringing the bell, Cuthbert told the porteress, as had been arranged, that he had called on a message from Dame Editha, and he was immediately ushered into the parlour of the convent, where, a minute or two later, he was joined by the lady abbess. He had when young been frequently to the convent, and had always been kindly received.

"I am indeed glad to see you, Sir Cuthbert," she said, "though I certainly should not have recognized the lad who used to come here with my cousin, in the stalwart young knight I see before me. You are indeed changed and improved. Who would think that my gossip Editha's son would come to be the Earl of Evesham! The Lady Margaret is eager to see you; but I think that you exaggerate the dangers of her residence here. I cannot think that even a minion of Prince John would dare to violate the sanctity of a convent."

"I fear, good mother," Cuthbert said, "that when ambition and greed are in one scale, reverence for the holy church will not weigh much in the other. Had King Richard been killed upon his way home, or so long as nothing was heard of him, Sir Rudolph might have been content to allow matters to remain as they were, until at least Lady Margaret attained an age which would justify him in demanding that the espousal should be carried out. But the news which has now positively been ascertained, that the king is in the hands of the emperor, and the knowledge that sooner or later his freedom will be obtained, will hasten the friends of the usurper to make the most of their advantage. He knows that the king would at once upon his return annul the nomination of Sir Rudolph to the earldom which had previously been bestowed upon me. But he may well think that if before that time he can secure in marriage the person of the late earl's daughter, no small share of the domains may be allotted to him as her dowry, even if he be obliged to lay by his borrowed honours. You will, unless I am greatly mistaken, hear from him before long."

The abbess looked grave.

"There is much in what you say, Sir Cuthbert; and indeed a certain confirmation is given to it by the fact that only yesterday I received a letter from Sir Rudolph, urging that now the Lady Margaret is past the age of fifteen, and may therefore be considered marriageable, the will of the prince should be carried into effect, and that she should for the present be committed to the charge of the Lady Clara Boulger, who is the wife of a friend and associate of Sir Rudolph. He says that he should not wish to press the marriage until she attains the age of sixteen, but that it were well that his future wife should become accustomed to the outside world, so as to take her place as Castellan of Evesham with a dignity befitting the position. I wrote at once to him saying, that in another year it would, in my poor judgment, be quite time to think about such worldly matters; that at the present the Lady Margaret was receiving an education suitable to her rank; that she was happy here; and that unless constrained by force-of which, I said, I could not suppose that any possibility existed —I should not surrender the Lady Margaret into any hands whatsoever, unless, indeed, I received the commands of her lawful guardian, King Richard."

"You said well, holy mother," Sir Cuthbert said. "But you see the hawks scent the danger from afar, and are moving uneasily already. Whether they consider it so pressing that they will dare to profane the convent, I know not. But I am sure that should they do so, they will not hesitate a moment at the thought of the anger of the church. Prince John has already shown that he is ready, if need be, to oppose the authority of the holy father, and he may well, therefore, despise any local wrath that might be excited by an action which he can himself disavow, and for which, even at the worst, he need only inflict some nominal punishment upon his vassal. Bethink thee, lady, whether it would not be safer to send the Lady Margaret to the care of some person, where she may be concealed from the search of Sir Rudolph."

"I would gladly do so," the abbess said, "did I know of such a person or such a place. But it is difficult indeed for a young lady of rank to be concealed from such sharp searchers as Sir Rudolph would be certain to place upon her track. Your proposal that she should take refuge in the house of some small franklin near the forest, I cannot agree to. In the first place, it would demean her to be so placed; and in the second, we could never be sure that the report of her residence there might not reach the ears of Sir Rudolph. As a last resource, of course such a step would be justifiable, but not until at least overt outrages have been attempted. Now I will call Lady Margaret in."

The young girl entered with an air of frank gladness, but was startled at the alteration which had taken place in her former playfellow, and paused and looked at the abbess, as if inquiring whether this could be really the Cuthbert she had known. Lady Margaret was fifteen in years; but she looked much younger. The quiet seclusion in which she had lived in the convent had kept her from approaching that maturity which as an earl's daughter, brought up in the stir and bustle of a castle, she would doubtless have attained.

"This is indeed Sir Cuthbert," the abbess said, "your old playfellow, and the husband destined for you by your father and by the will of the king."

Struck with a new timidity, the girl advanced, and, according to the custom of the times, held up her cheek to be kissed. Cuthbert was almost as timid as herself.

"I feel, Lady Margaret," he said, "a deep sense of my own unworthiness of the kindness and honour which the dear lord your father bestowed upon me; and were it not that many dangers threaten, and that it were difficult under the circumstances to find one more worthy of you, I would gladly resign you into the hands of such a one were it for your happiness. But believe me that the recollection of your face has animated me in many of the scenes of danger in which I have been placed; and although even in fancy my thoughts scarcely ventured to rise so high, yet I felt as a true knight might feel for the lady of his love."

"I always liked you, Sir Cuthbert," the girl said frankly, "better than any one else next to my father, and gladly submit myself to his will. My own inclinations indeed, so far as is maidenly, go with his. These are troubled times," she said anxiously, "and our holy mother tells me that you fear some danger is overhanging me."

"I trust that the danger may not be imminent," Cuthbert answered. "But knowing the unscrupulous nature of the false Earl of Evesham, I fear that the news that King Richard is found will bestir him to early action. But you can rely, dear lady, on a careful watch being kept over you night and day; and should any attempt be made to carry you away, or to put force upon you, be assured that assistance will be at hand. Even should any attempt succeed, do not lose heart, for rescue will certainly be attempted; and I must be dead, and my faithful followers crushed, before you can become the bride of Sir Rudolph."

Then turning to other subjects, he talked to her of the life he had led since he last saw her. He told her of the last moments of her father, and of the gallant deeds he had done in the Holy Land.

After waiting for two hours, the abbess judged that the time for separation had arrived; and Cuthbert, taking a respectful adieu of his young mistress, and receiving the benediction of the abbess, departed.

He found Cnut on guard at the point where he had left him.

"Have you seen aught to give rise to suspicion?" Cuthbert asked.

"Yes," Cnut said, "the place is undoubtedly watched. Just after you had entered, a man came from that house yonder and went up to the gate, as if he would fain learn by staring at its iron adornments the nature of him who had passed in. Then he re-entered his house, and if I mistake not is still on the watch at that casement. If we stand here for a minute or two, perchance he may come out to see what delays you in this dark corner, in which case I may well give him a clout with my axe which will settle his prying."

"Better not," Cuthbert said. "We can retire round this corner and so avoid his observation; and were his body found slain here, suspicion would be at once excited in the mind of his employer. At present he can have no ground for any report which may make the knight uneasy, for he can but know that a gentleman has entered, and remained for two hours at the convent, and he will in no way connect my visit with the Lady Margaret."

They had just turned the corner which Cuthbert indicated, when a man came up rapidly behind them and almost brushed them as he passed, half-turning round and trying to gaze into their faces. Cnut at once assumed the aspect of an intoxicated person, and stretching forth his foot, with a dexterous shove pushed the stranger into the gutter. The latter rose with a fierce cry of anger; but Cnut with a blow of his heavy fist again stretched him on the ground, this time to remain quiet until they had walked on and passed out of sight.

"A meddling fool," Cnut grumbled. "He will not, methinks, have much to report to Sir Rudolph this time. Had I thought that he had seen your face, I would have cleft his skull with no more hesitation than I send an arrow into the brain of a stag in the forest."

As they journeyed along, Cuthbert informed Cnut of what the abbess had told him; and the latter agreed that a watch must be placed on the convent, and that a force must be kept as near as possible at hand so as to defeat any attempt which might be made.

The next day one of the forest men who had been a peaceable citizen, but who had been charged with using false weights and had been condemned to lose his ears, repaired to Worcester. His person was unknown there, as he had before lived at Gloucester. He hired a house in the square in which the convent was situated, giving out that he desired to open a house of business for the sale of silks, and for articles from the Low Countries. As he paid down earnest-money for the rent, no suspicion whatever was excited. He at once took up his abode there, having with him two stout serving-men, and a 'prentice boy; and from that time two sets of watchers observed without ceasing what passed at the Convent of St. Anne.

At a distance of half a mile from the road leading between Worcester and Evesham, stood a grange, which had for some time been disused, the ground belonging to it having been sequestrated and given to the lord of an adjoining estate, who did not care to have the grange occupied. In this, ten men, headed by Cnut, took up their residence, blocking up the window of the hall with hangings, so that the light of the fire kindled within would not be observed.

Two months passed on without any incident of importance. The feeling between the outlaws in the forest and the retainers of the false Earl of Evesham was becoming much embittered. Several times the foresters of the latter, attempting pursuit of men charged with breaking the game laws, were roughly handled. These on making their report were sent back again, supported by a force of footmen; but these, too, were driven back, and the authority of Sir Rudolph was openly defied.

Gradually it came to his ears that the outlaws were commanded by a man who had been their leader in times gone by, but who had been pardoned, and had, with a large number of his band, taken service in the army of the crusaders; also, that there was present a stranger, whose manner and the deference paid to him by Cnut proclaimed him to be of gentle blood. This news awakened grave uneasiness on the part of Sir Rudolph. The knight caused inquiries to be made, and ascertained that Cnut had been especially attached to the young Cuthbert, and that he had fought under the Earl of Evesham's banner. It seemed possible then that with him had returned the claimant for the earldom; and in that case Sir Rudolph felt that danger menaced him, for the bravery of the Earl of Evesham's adopted son had been widely spoken of by those who had returned from the Holy Land.

Sir Rudolph was a man of forty, tall and dark, with Norman features. He held the Saxons in utter contempt, and treated them as beings solely created to till the land for the benefit of their Norman lords. He was brave and fearless, and altogether free from the superstition of the times. Even the threats of the pope, which although Prince John defied them yet terrified him at heart, were derided by his follower, who feared no one thing in the world, save, perhaps, the return of King Richard from captivity.

No sooner had the suspicion that his rival was in the neighbourhood possessed him, than he determined that one of two things must be carried out: either Sir Cuthbert must be killed, or the Lady Margaret must be carried off and forced to accept him as her husband. First he endeavoured to force Sir Cuthbert to declare himself, and to trust to his own arm to put an end to his rival. To that end he caused a proclamation to be written, and to be affixed to the door of the village church at the fair of Evesham.

Cnut and several of his followers were there, all quietly dressed as yeomen. Seeing a crowd round the door of the church, he pressed forward. Being himself unable to read writing, he asked one of the burgesses what was written upon the paper which caused such excitement.

"It is," the burgess said, "in the nature of a cartel or challenge from our present lord, Sir Rudolf. He says that it having come to his ears that a Saxon serf, calling himself Sir Cuthbert, Earl of Evesham, is lurking in the woods and consorting with outlaws and robbers, he challenges him to appear, saying that he will himself, grievously although he would demean himself by so doing, yet condescend to meet him in the lists with sword and battle-axe, and to prove upon his body the falseness of his averments. Men marvel much," the burgess continued, "at this condescension on the earl's part. We have heard indeed that King Richard, before he sailed for England, did, at the death of the late good earl, bestow his rank and the domains of Evesham upon Sir Cuthbert, the son of the Dame Editha. Whether it be true or not, we cannot say; but it seems strange that such honour should have been bestowed upon one so young. In birth indeed he might aspire to the rank, since his father, Sir Walter, was a brave knight, and the mother, Dame Editha, was of good Saxon blood, and descended from those who held Evesham before the arrival of the Normans."

Cnut's first impulse was to stride forward and to tear down the proclamation. But the remembrance of his solemn determination not in future to act rashly, came across him, and he decided to take no steps until he had reported the facts to his master, and taken his counsel thereon.

Cuthbert received the news with much indignation.

"There is nought that I should like better," he said, "than to try my strength against that of this false traitor. But although I have proved my arm against the Saracens, I think not that it is yet strong enough to cope against a man who, whatsoever be his faults, is said to be a valiant knight. But that would not deter me from attempting the task. It is craftily done on the part of Sir Rudolph. He reckons that if I appear he will kill me; that if I do not appear, I shall be branded as a coward, and my claims brought into disrepute. It may be, too, that it is a mere ruse to discover if I be in the neighbourhood. Some rumours thereof may have reached him, and he has taken this course to determine upon their truth. He has gone too far, and honest men will see in the cartel itself a sign that he misdoubts him that my claims are just; for were I, as he says, a Saxon serf, be sure that he would not condescend to meet me in the lists as he proposes. I trust that the time will come when I may do so. But, at present, I will submit to his insult rather than imperil the success of our plans, and, what is of far greater importance, the safety and happiness of the Lady Margaret, who, did aught befall me, would assuredly fall into his hands."

After some thought, however, Cuthbert drew up an answer to the knight's proclamation. He did not in this speak in his own name, but wrote as if the document were the work of Cnut. It was worded as follows: "I, Cnut, a free Saxon and a leader of bowmen under King Richard in the Holy Land, do hereby pronounce and declare the statements of Sir Rudolph, miscalled the Earl of Evesham, to be false and calumnious. The earldom was, as Rudolph well knows, and as can be proved by many nobles and gentlemen of repute who were present with King Richard, granted to Sir Cuthbert, King Richard's true and faithful follower. When the time shall come, Sir Cuthbert will doubtless be ready to prove his rights. But at present right has no force in England, and until the coming of our good King Richard must remain in abeyance. Until then, I support the title of Sir Cuthbert, and do hereby declare Sir Rudolph a false and perjured knight; and warn him that if he falls into my hands it will fare but badly with him, as I know it will fare but badly with me should I come into his."

At nightfall the cartel of Sir Rudolph was torn down from the church and that of Cnut affixed in its place. The reading thereof caused great astonishment in Evesham, and the rage of Sir Rudolph, when the news came to his ears, was very great. Cuthbert was sure that this affair would quicken the intentions of Sir Rudolph with regard to the Lady Margaret, and he received confirmation of this in a letter which the abbess sent him, saying that she had received another missive from Sir Rudolph, authoritatively demanding in the king's name the instant surrender of Lady Margaret to him. That night forty archers stole, one by one, quietly into Worcester, entering the town before the gates were shut, and so mingling with the citizens that they were unobserved. When it was quite dark they quietly took their way, one by one, to the square in which stood the convent, and were admitted into the shop of Master Nicholas, the silk mercer.

The house was a large one, with its floors overhanging each the one beneath it, as was the custom of the time, and with large casements running the whole width of the house.

The mercer had laid by a goodly store of provisions, and for three days the troop, large as it was, was accommodated there. Cuthbert himself was with them, Cnut remaining at the grange with the ten men originally sent there.

On the third day Sir Rudolph, with a number of knights and men-at-arms, arrived in the town, giving out that he was passing northwards, but he would abide that night at the hostelry. A great many of his men-at-arms did, as those on the watch observed, enter one by one into the town. The people of Worcester were somewhat surprised at this large accompaniment of the earl, but thought no harm. The Abbess of St. Anne's, however, was greatly terrified, as she feared that some evil design might be intended against her. She was, however, reassured in the evening by a message brought by a boy, to the effect that succour would be near, whatsoever happened.

At midnight a sudden uproar was heard in the streets of Worcester.

A party of men fell upon the burgesses guarding the gate of the town, disarmed them, and took possession of it. At the same time those who had put up at the hostelry with Sir Rudolph suddenly mounted their horses, and with a great clatter rode down the streets to the Convent of St. Anne. Numbers of men on foot also joined, and some sixty in all suddenly appeared before the great gate of the convent. With a thundering noise they knocked at the door, and upon the grating being opened Sir Rudolph himself told the porteress who looked through it, that she was to go at once to the abbess and order her to surrender the body of the Lady Margaret to him, in accordance with the order of Prince John; adding, that if within the space of five minutes the order was not complied with, he would burst in the gates of the convent and take her for himself. In another minute a casement opened above, and the abbess herself appeared.

"Rash man," she said to Sir Rudolph, "I warn you against committing the sin of sacrilege. Neither the orders of Prince John nor of any other potentate can over-ride the rights of the holy church; and should you venture to lay the hand of force upon this convent you will be placed under the anathema of the church, and its spiritual terrors will be directed against you."

"I am prepared to risk that, holy mother," Sir Rudolph said, with a laugh. "So long as I am obeying the orders of my prince, I care nought for those of any foreign potentate, be he pope or be he emperor. Three minutes of the time I gave you have elapsed, and unless within two more the Lady Margaret appears at the gate I will batter it down; and you may think yourself lucky if I do not order my men to set light to it and to smoke you out of your hole."

The abbess closed the window, and as she did so the long row of casements in the house of Master Nicholas were opened from top to bottom, and a volley of sixty clothyard arrows was poured into the group closely standing round the gate. Many fell, killed outright, and shouts of rage and pain were heard arising.

Furious at this unexpected attack, Sir Rudolph turned, and commanded those with him to attack the house whence this volley of missiles had come. But even while he spoke another flight of arrows, even more deadly than the last, was poured forth. One of the knights standing by the side of Sir Rudolph fell, shot through the brain. Very many of the common men, undefended by harness, fell shot through and through; and an arrow piercing the joint of the armour of Sir Rudolph, wounded him in the shoulder. In vain the knight stormed and raged and ordered his men to advance. The suddenness of the attack seemed to his superstitious followers a direct answer from heaven to the words of the abbess. Their number was already seriously lessened, and those who were in case to do so at once took flight and scattered through the city, making for the gate, which had already been seized by Sir Rudolph's men.

Finding himself alone with only a few of his knights and principal men-at-arms remaining, while the storm of arrows continued unabated, Sir Rudolph was forced to order his men to retreat, with many fierce threats of the vengeance which he would hereafter take.

Chapter XXII
A Dastardly Stratagem.

The return of Sir Rudolph's party to Evesham was not unmarked by incident, for as they passed along the road, from an ambush in a wood other archers, whose numbers they could not discover, shot hard upon them, and many fell there who had escaped from the square at Worcester. When the list was called upon the arrival at the castle, it was found that no less than thirty of those who had set out were missing, while many others were grievously wounded.

The noise of the tumult in the square of the convent aroused the whole town of Worcester. Alarm bells were rung; and the burgesses, hastily arming themselves, poured into the streets. Directed by the sound, they made their way to the square, and were astonished at finding it entirely deserted, save for some twenty men, lying dead or dying in front of the gate of the convent, pierced with long arrows. They speedily found that Sir Rudolph and his troop had departed; and further inquiry revealed the fact that the burgher guard at one of the gates had been overpowered and were prisoners in the watchroom. These could only say that they were suddenly seized, all being asleep save the one absolutely on guard. They knew nothing more than that a few minutes later there was a great clatter of horsemen and men on foot leaving the city. Unable to find any solution to this singular circumstance, but satisfied that Sir Rudolph had departed, and that no more disturbance was likely to arise that night, the burgesses again betook themselves to their beds, having closed the gates and placed a strong guard over them, determining next morning to sift the affair to the bottom.

In the morning the leading burgesses met in council, and finding none who could give them any information, the mayor and two of the councillors repaired to the convent, where they asked for an interview with the lady abbess. Mightily indignant were they at hearing that Sir Rudolph had attempted to break into the convent, and to carry off a boarder residing there. But the abbess herself could give them no further news. She said that after she retired from the window, she heard great shouts and cries, and that almost immediately afterwards the whole of the party in front hastily retired.

That Sir Rudolph had been attacked by a party of archers was evident; but whence they had shot, or how they had come upon the spot at the time, or whither they had gone, were mysteries that could not be solved. In the search which the authorities made, however, it was discovered that the house of the draper, Master Nicholas, was closed. Finding that summonses to open were unanswered, the door was broken in, and the premises were found in confusion. No goods of any kind were discovered there, but many bales filled with dried leaves, bark of trees, and other worthless matters. Such goods as had been displayed in the window had clearly been carried away. Searching the house, they found signs that a considerable number of men had been concealed there, and although not knowing whence the body of archers could have come, they concluded that those who defeated the attempt of Sir Rudolph must have been hidden in the draper's house. The singularity of this incident gave rise to great excitement; but the indignation against Sir Rudolph was in no way lessened by the fact that his attempt had been defeated, not by the townsmen themselves, but by some unknown force.

After much consultation on the part of the council, it was resolved that a deputation, consisting of the mayor and the five senior councillors, should resort to London, and there demand from the prince redress for the injury put upon their town by Sir Rudolph. These worthy merchants betook themselves to London by easy stages, and upon their arrival there were kept for some days before they could obtain an interview with King John. When they appeared before him and commenced telling their story, the prince fell into sudden rage.

"I have heard of this matter before," he said, "and am mightily angry with the people of Worcester, inasmuch as they have dared to interfere to prevent the carrying out of my commands. The Earl of Evesham has written to me, that thinking to scare the abbess of St. Anne's into a compliance with the commands which I had laid upon her, and to secure the delivery of a contumacious ward of the crown, he had pretended to use force, having, however, no idea of carrying his threats into effect. When, as he doubted not, the abbess was on the point of yielding up the ward, the good knight was suddenly set upon by the rascals of the town, who slew some of his companions and followers, and did grievously ill-treat the remainder. This," said the prince, "you now pretend was done by a party of men of whose presence in the town you had no cognizance. Your good sense must be small, if you think that I should believe such a tale as this. It is your rascaldom at Worcester which interfered to prevent my will being carried out, and I have a goodly mind to order the troop of Sir Charles Everest, which is now marching towards Evesham, to sack the town, as a punishment for its rebellion. As, however, I am willing to believe that you and the better class of burgesses were in ignorance of the doings of the rougher kind, I will extend mercy towards the city, and will merely inflict a fine of 3000 golden marks upon it."

The mayor attempted humbly to explain and to entreat; but the prince was seized with a sudden passion, and threatened if he said more he would at once cast him and his fellows into durance. Therefore, sadly crestfallen at the result of their mission, the mayor and councillors returned to Worcester, where their report caused great consternation. This was heightened by the fact that upon the following day Sir Charles Everest, with 500 mercenaries of the prince, together with Sir Rudolph and his following, and several other barons favourable to the cause of the prince, were heard to be approaching the town.

Worcester was capable of making a stout defence, but seeing that no help was likely to be forthcoming, and fearing the utter ruin of the town should it be taken by storm, the council, after sitting many hours in deliberation, determined to raise the money required to pay the fine inflicted by the prince. The bolder sort were greatly averse to this decision, especially as a letter had been received, signed "Cuthbert, Earl of Evesham," offering, should the townspeople decide to resist the unjust demands of Prince John, to enter the town with 150 archers to take part in its defence. With this force, as the more ardent spirits urged, the defeat of any attempt to carry it by storm would be assured. But the graver men argued that even if defeated for the first time, further attempts would be made, and as it was likely that King Richard would not return for a long time, and that Prince John might become Sovereign of England, sooner or later the town must be taken, and, in any case, its trade would for a long time be destroyed, and great suffering inflicted upon all; therefore, that it was better to pay the fine now than to risk all these evils, and perhaps the infliction of a heavier impost upon them.

The abbess was kept informed by friends in the council of the course of the proceedings. She had in the meantime had another interview with Sir Cuthbert, and had determined, seeing that Prince John openly supported the doings of his minion, it would be better to remove the Lady Margaret to some other place, as no one could say how the affair might terminate; and with 500 mercenaries at his back, Sir Rudolph would be so completely master of the city that he would be able in broad daylight, did he choose, to force the gates of the convent and carry off the king's ward.

Accordingly, two days before the arrival of the force before the walls of Worcester, Lady Margaret left the convent by a postern gate in the rear, late in the evening. She was attended by two of the sisters, both of whom, as well as herself, were dressed as countrywomen. Mules were in readiness outside the city gates, and here Sir Cuthbert, with an escort of archers, was ready to attend them. They travelled all night, and arrived in the morning at a small convent situated five miles from the city of Hereford. The abbess here was a cousin of the Superior of St. Anne's, and had already consented to receive Lady Margaret. Leaving her at the door, and promising that, as far as possible, he would keep watch over her, and that even in the worst she need never despair, Sir Cuthbert left her and returned to the forest.

The band there assembled varied considerably in numbers, for provisions could not be found continually for a large body of men. The forest was indeed very extensive, and the number of deer therein large. Still, for the feeding of 150 men many animals are required and other food. The franklins in the neighbourhood were all hostile to Sir Rudolph, whom they regarded as a cruel tyrant, and did their utmost in the way of supplies for those in the forest. Their resources, however, were limited, and it was found necessary to scatter the force, and for a number of them to take up their residence in places a short distance away, forty only remaining permanently on guard.

Sir Rudolph and his friends entered Worcester, and there received with great hauteur the apologies of the mayor and council, and the assurance that the townspeople were in nowise concerned in the attack made upon him. To this he pretended disbelief. The fine demanded was paid, the principal portion in gold, the rest in bills signed by the leading merchants of the place; for after every effort it had been found impossible to collect such a sum within the city.

The day after he arrived, he again renewed his demand to the abbess for the surrender of the Lady Margaret; this time, however, coming to her attended only by two squires, and by a pursuivant bearing the king's order for the delivery of the damsel. The abbess met him at the gate, and informed him that the Lady Margaret was no longer in her charge.

"Finding," she said, in a fearless tone, "that the holy walls of this convent were insufficient to restrain lawless men, and fearing that these might be tempted to acts of sacrilege, which might bring down upon them the wrath of the church and the destruction of their souls, I have sent her away."

"Whither has she gone?" Sir Rudolph demanded, half mad with passion.

"That I decline to say," the lady abbess replied. "She is in good hands; and when King Richard returns, his ward shall be delivered to him at once."

"Will you take oath upon the Bible that she is not within these walls?" Sir Rudolph exclaimed.

"My word is sufficient," the lady abbess replied calmly. "But should it be necessary, I should be ready to swear upon the relics that she is not here."

A few hours later Sir Rudolph, attended by his own party and by 100 of Sir Charles Everest's mercenaries, returned to his castle.

Three days afterwards, as Cuthbert was sitting at a rude but hearty meal in the forest, surrounded by Cnut and his followers, a hind entered breathless. Cuthbert at once recognized him as one of the servitors of his mother.

"What is it?" he exclaimed, leaping to his feet.

"Terrible news, Master Cuthbert, terrible news!" exclaimed the man. "The wicked earl came down this morning, with fifty of his men, set fire to the house, and all its buildings and stacks, and has carried off the lady, your mother, a prisoner to the castle, on a charge, as he said, of harbouring traitors."

A cry of fury broke from Cnut and his men.

"The false traitor shall bitterly regret this outrage," Cuthbert exclaimed.

He had in the first excitement seized his arms, and his followers snatched up their bows, as if for instant warfare. A few moments' reflection, however, showed to Cuthbert the impossibility of his attacking a fortress like Evesham, garrisoned by a strong body of well-armed men, with only the archers of the forest, without implements necessary for such an assault.

"Send at once, Cnut," he said, "and call in all the band. We cannot take the castle; but we will carry fire and sword round its walls. We will cut off all communication from within or from without. If attacked by large forces, we will retire upon the wood, returning to our posts without the walls as soon as the force is withdrawn. These heavily armed men can move but slowly; while we can run at full speed. There cannot be more than some twenty horsemen in the castle; and methinks with our arrows and pikes we can drive these back if they attempt to fall upon us."

Cnut at once sent off swift-footed messengers to carry out Cuthbert's orders, and on the following day the whole of the band were again assembled in the woods. Just as Cuthbert was setting them in motion, a distant blast of a horn was heard.

"It is," Cuthbert exclaimed, "the note calling for a parley. Do you, Cnut, go forward, and see what is demanded. It is probably a messenger from Sir Rudolph."

After half-an-hour's absence, Cnut returned, bringing with him a pursuivant or herald. The latter advanced at once towards Cuthbert, who, now in his full knightly armour, was evidently the leader of the party.

"I bear to you, Sir Cuthbert, falsely calling yourself Earl of Evesham, a message from Sir Rudolph. He bids me tell you that the traitress, Dame Editha, your mother, is in his hands, and that she has been found guilty of aiding and abetting you in your war against Prince John, the Regent of this kingdom. For that offence she has been condemned to die."

Here he was interrupted by a cry of rage which broke from the assembled foresters. Continuing unmoved, he said, —

"Sir Rudolph, being unwilling to take the life of a woman, however justly forfeited by the law, commands me to say, that if you will deliver yourself up to him by to-morrow at twelve, the Dame Editha shall be allowed to go free. But that if by the time the dial points to noon you have not delivered yourself up, he will hang her over the battlements of the castle."

Cuthbert was very pale, and he waved his hand to restrain the fury which animated the outlaws.

"This man," he said to them, "is a herald, and, as such, is protected by all the laws of chivalry. Whatsoever his message, it is none of his. He is merely the mouthpiece of him who sent him." Then, turning to the herald, he said, "Tell the false knight, your master, on my part, that he is a foul ruffian, perjured to all the vows of knighthood; that this act of visiting upon a woman the enmity he bears her son, will bring upon him the execration of all men; and that the offer which he makes me is as foul and villainous as himself. Nevertheless, knowing his character, and believing that he is capable of keeping his word, tell him that by to-morrow at noon I will be there; that the lady, my mother, is to leave the castle gates as I enter them; and that though by his foul device he may encompass my death, yet that the curse of every good man will light upon him, that he will be shunned as the dog he is, and that assuredly heaven will not suffer that deeds so foul should bring with them the prize he seeks to gain."

The herald bowed, and, escorted by two archers to the edge of the forest, returned to Evesham Castle.

After his departure, an animated council took place. Cnut and the outlaws, burning with indignation, were ready to attempt anything. They would, had Cuthbert given the word, have attacked the castle that very night. But Cuthbert pointed out the absolute impossibility of their carrying so strong a place by such an assault, unprovided with engines for battering down the gates. He said that surprise would be impossible, as the knight would be sure to take every precaution against it; and that in the event of such an attack being attempted, he would possibly carry his threat into execution, and murder Dame Editha before their eyes. Cnut was like a madman, so transported with fury was he; and the archers were also beside themselves. Cuthbert alone retained his calmness. Retiring apart from the others, he paced slowly backwards and forwards among the trees, deliberating upon the best course to be pursued. The archers gathered round the fire and passed the night in long and angry talk, each man agreeing that in the event of their beloved leader being sacrificed by Sir Rudolph, they would one and all give their lives to avenge him by slaying the oppressor whensoever he ventured beyond the castle gates.

After a time, Cuthbert called Cnut to him, and the two talked long and earnestly. Cnut returned to his comrades with a face less despairing than that he had before worn, and sent off at once a messenger with all speed to a franklin near the forest to borrow a stout rope some fifty feet in length, and without telling his comrades what the plans of Sir Cuthbert were, bade them cheer up, for that desperate as the position was, all hope was not yet lost.

"Sir Cuthbert," he said, "has been in grievous straits before now, and has gone through them. Sir Rudolph does not know the nature of the man with whom he has to deal, and we may trick him yet."

At eleven o'clock the next day, from the walls of Evesham Castle a body of archers 150 strong were seen advancing in solid array.

"Think you, Sir Rudolph," one of his friends, Sir Hubert of Gloucester, said to him, "that these varlets think of attacking the castle?"

"They might as well think of scaling heaven," Sir Rudolph said. "Evesham could resist a month's siege by a force well equipped for the purpose; and were it not that good men are wanted for the king's service, and that these villains shoot straight and hard, I would open the gates of the castle and launch our force against them. We are two to one as strong as they, and our knights and mounted men-at-arms could alone scatter that rabble."

Conspicuous upon the battlements a gallows had been erected.

The archers stopped at a distance of a few hundred yards from the castle, and Sir Cuthbert advanced alone to the edge of the moat.

"Sir Rudolph of Eresby, false knight and perjured gentleman," he shouted in a loud voice, "I, Sir Cuthbert of Evesham, do denounce you as foresworn and dishonoured, and do challenge you to meet me here before the castle in sight of your men and mine, and decide our quarrel as heaven may judge with sword and battle-axe."

Sir Rudolph leant over the battlements, and said, —

"It is too late, varlet. I condescended to challenge you before, and you refused. You cannot now claim what you then feared to accept. The sun on the dial approaches noon, and unless you surrender yourself before it reaches the mark, I will keep my word, and the traitress, your mother, shall swing from that beam."

Making a sign to two men-at-arms, these brought forward Dame Editha and so placed her on the battlements that she could be seen from below. Dame Editha was still a very fair woman, although nigh forty years had rolled over her head. No sign of fear appeared upon her face, and in a firm voice she cried to her son, —

"Cuthbert, I beg-nay, I order you to retire. If this unknightly lord venture to carry out his foul threats against me, let him do so. England will ring with the dastardly deed, and he will never dare show his face again where Englishmen congregate. Let him do his worst. I am prepared to die."

A murmur rose from the knights and men-at-arms standing round Sir Rudolph.

Several of his companions had from the first, wild and reckless as they were, protested against Sir Rudolph's course, and it was only upon his solemn assurance that he intended but to frighten Sir Cuthbert into surrender, and had no intention of carrying his threats against the lady into effect, that they had consented to take part in the transaction. Even now, at the fearless words of the Saxon lady several of them hesitated, and Sir Hubert of Gloucester stepped forward to Sir Rudolph.

"Sir knight," he said, "you know that I am your true comrade and the faithful servant of Prince John. Yet in faith would I not that my name should be mixed up in so foul a deed. I repent me that I have for a moment consented to it. But the shame shall not hang upon the escutcheon of Hubert of Gloucester that he stood still when such foul means were tried. I pray you, by our long friendship, and for the sake of your own honour as a knight, to desist from this endeavour. If this lady be guilty, as she well may be, of aiding her son in his assaults upon the soldiers of Prince John, then let her be tried, and doubtless the court will confiscate her estates. But let her son be told that her life is in no danger, and that he is free to go, being assured that harm will not come to her."

"And if I refuse to consent to allow my enemy, who is now almost within my hand, to escape," Sir Rudolph said, "what then?"

"Then," said the knight, "I and my following will at once leave your walls, and will clear ourselves to the brave young knight yonder of all hand in this foul business."

A murmur of agreement from several of those standing round showed that their sentiments were in accordance with those of Sir Hubert.

"I refuse," said Rudolph passionately. "Go, if you will. I am master of my actions, and of this castle."

Without a word, Sir Hubert and two others of the knights present turned, and briefly ordering their men-at-arms to follow them, descended the staircase to the courtyard below. Their horses were brought out, the men fell into rank, and the gates of the castle were thrown open.

"Stand to arms!" Sir Cuthbert shouted to the archers. "They are going to attempt a sortie." And hastily he retired to the main body of his men.

Chapter XXIII
The False And Perjured Knight.

As the band of knights and their retainers issued from the gate, a trumpeter blew a parley, and the three knights advanced alone towards the group of archers.

"Sir Cuthbert de Lance," Sir Hubert said, "in the name of myself and my two friends here we ask your pardon for having so far taken part in this foul action. We did so believing only that Sir Rudolph intended the capture of your lady mother as a threat. Now that we see he was in earnest, we wash our hands of the business; and could we in any way atone for our conduct in having joined him, we would gladly do so, consistently only with our allegiance to the Prince Regent."

Cuthbert bowed courteously.

"Thanks for your words, Sir Hubert. I had always heard yourself and the knights here spoken of as brave and gallant gentlemen, whose sole fault was that they chose to take part with a rebel prince, rather than with the King of England. I rejoice that you have cleared your name of so foul a blot as this would have placed upon it, and I acknowledge that your conduct now is knightly and courteous. But I can no more parley. The sun is within a few minutes of twelve, and I must surrender, to meet such fate as may befall me."

So saying, with a bow he left them, and again advanced to the castle gate.

"Sir Rudolph," he shouted, "the hour is at hand. I call upon you to deliver, outside the gate, the lady, my mother. Whether she wills it or not, I call upon you to place her beyond the gate, and I give you my knightly word that as she leaves it I enter it."

Dame Editha would then have attempted resistance; but she saw that it would be useless. With a pale face she descended the steps, accompanied by the men-at-arms. She knew that any entreaty to Sir Rudolph would be vain, and with the courage of her race she mentally vowed to devote the rest of her life to vengeance for her son.

As the gate opened and she was thrust forth, for a moment she found herself in the arms of her son.

"Courage, mother!" he whispered; "all may yet be well."

Cnut was waiting a few paces behind, and offering his hand to Dame Editha, he led her to the group of archers, while Cuthbert, alone, crossed the drawbridge, and entered the portal, the heavy portcullis falling after him.

Cnut immediately ordering four of his men to escort Dame Editha to the wood with all speed, advanced with his men towards the walls. All had strung their bows and placed their arrows on the ground in front of them in readiness for instant use. Cnut himself, with two others carrying the rope, advanced to the edge of the moat. None observed their doings, for all within the castle were intent upon the proceedings there.

In the courtyard Sir Rudolph had taken his post, with the captain of the mercenaries beside him, and the men-at-arms drawn up in order. He smiled sardonically as Cuthbert entered.

"So, at last," he said, "this farce is drawing to an end. You are in my power, and for the means which I have taken to capture you, I will account to the prince. You are a traitor to him; you have attacked and slaughtered many of my friends; you are an outlaw defying the law; and for each of these offences your head is forfeited."

"I deny," Cuthbert said, standing before him, "your right to be my judge. By my peers only can I be tried. As a knight of England and as rightful lord of this castle, I demand to be brought before a jury of my equals."

"I care nothing for rights or for juries," said Sir Rudolph. "I have the royal order for your execution, and that order I shall put into effect, although all the knights and barons in England objected."

Cuthbert looked round to observe the exact position in which he was standing. He knew, of course, every foot of the castle, and saw that but a short distance behind a single row of armed men was the staircase leading to the battlements.

"False and perjured knight," he said, taking a step forward, "I may die; but I would rather a thousand deaths than such a life as yours will be when this deed is known in England. But I am not yet dead. For myself, I could pardon you; but for the outrage to my mother —" and with a sudden movement he struck Sir Rudolph in the face with all his strength, with his mailed hand.

With the blood gushing from his nostrils, the knight fell backwards, and Sir Cuthbert, with a bound, before the assembly could recover from their astonishment at the deed, burst through the line of men-at-arms, and sprang up the narrow staircase. A score of men-at-arms started in pursuit; but Sir Cuthbert gained the battlements first, and without a moment's hesitation sprang upon them and plunged forward, falling into the moat fifty feet below. Here he would have perished miserably, for in his heavy armour he was of course unable to swim a stroke, and his weight took him at once into the mud of the moat. At its margin, however, Cnut stood awaiting him, with one end of the rope in his hand. In an instant he plunged in, and diving to the bottom, grasped Cuthbert by the body, and twisted the rope round him. The two archers on the bank at once hauled upon it, and in a minute Sir Cuthbert was dragged to the bank.

By this time a crowd of men-at-arms appeared upon the battlements. But as they did so the archers opened a storm of arrows upon them, and quickly compelled them to find shelter. Carried by Cnut and the men with him-for he was insensible-Sir Cuthbert was quickly conveyed to the centre of the outlaws, and these at once in a compact body began their retreat to the wood. Cuthbert quickly recovered consciousness, and was soon able to walk. As he did so, the gates of the castle were thrown open, and a crowd of men-at-arms, consisting of the retainers of the castle and the mercenaries of Prince John, sallied forth. So soon as Cuthbert was able to move, the archers started at a brisk run, several of them carrying Cuthbert's casque and sword, and others assisting him to hurry along. The rear ranks turned as they ran and discharged flights of arrows at the enemy, who, more heavily armed and weighted, gained but slowly upon them.

Had not Sir Rudolph been stunned by the blow dealt him by Cuthbert, he would himself have headed the pursuit, and in that case the foresters would have had to fight hard to make their retreat to their fastness. The officer in command of the mercenaries, however, had no great stomach for the matter. Men were hard to get, and Prince John would not have been pleased to hear that a number of the men whom he had brought with such expense from foreign parts had been killed in a petty fray. Therefore after following for a short time he called them off, and the archers fell back into the forest.

Here they found Dame Editha, and for three days she abode among them, living in a small hut in the centre of the forest. Then she left, to take up her abode, until the troubles were past, with some kin who lived in the south of Gloucestershire.

Although the lady abbess had assured Cuthbert that the retreat of Lady Margaret was not likely to be found out, he himself, knowing how great a stake Sir Rudolph had in the matter, was still far from being easy. It would not be difficult for the latter to learn through his agents that the lady superior of the little convent near Hereford was of kin to her of St. Anne's, and, close as a convent is, yet the gossiping of the servants who go to market was certain to let out an affair so important as the arrival of a young lady to reside under the charge of the superior. Cuthbert was not mistaken as to the acuteness of his enemy. The relationship between the two lady superiors was no secret, and after having searched all the farmhouses and granges near the forest, and being convinced that the lady abbess would have sent her charge rather to a religious house than to that of a franklin, Sir Rudolph sought which of those within the circuit of a few miles would be likely to be the one selected. It was not long before he was enabled to fix upon that near Hereford, and spies going to the spot soon found out from the countrypeople that it was a matter of talk that a young lady of rank had been admitted by the superior. Sir Rudolph hesitated whether to go himself at the head of a strong body of men and openly to take her, or to employ some sort of device. It was not that he himself feared the anathema of the church; but he knew Prince John to be weak and vacillating, at one time ready to defy the thunder of the pope, the next cringing before the spiritual authority. He therefore determined to employ some of his men to burst into the convent and carry off the heiress, arranging that he himself, with some of his men-at-arms, should come upon them in the road, and make a feigned rescue of her, so that, if the lady superior laid her complaint before the pope's legate, he could deny that he had any hand in the matter, and could even take credit for having rescued her from the men who had profaned the convent. That his story would be believed mattered but little. It would be impossible to prove its falsity, and this was all that he cared for.

This course was followed out. Late one evening, the lady superior was alarmed by a violent knocking at the door. In reply to questions asked through the grill, the answer was given, "We are men of the forest, and we are come to carry the Lady Margaret of Evesham off to a secure hiding-place. The lord of Evesham has discovered her whereabouts, and will be here shortly, and we would fain remove her before he arrives."

"From whom have you warrant?" the lady superior said. "I surrender her to no one, save to the lady abbess of St. Anne's. But if you have a written warrant from Sir Cuthbert, the rightful lord of Evesham, I will lay the matter before the Lady Margaret, and will act as it may seem fit to her."

"We have no time for parleying," a rough voice said. "Throw open the gate at once, or we will break it down."

"Ye be no outlaws," the lady superior said, "for the outlaws are men who fear God and respect the church. Were ye what ye say, ye would be provided with the warrants that I mention. I warn you, therefore, that if you use force, you will be excommunicated, and placed under the ban of the church."

The only answer was a thundering assault upon the gate, which soon yielded to the blows. The sisters and novices ran shrieking through the corridors at this rude uproar. The lady superior, however, stood calmly awaiting the giving way of the gate.

"Where is the Lady Margaret?" the leader of the party, who were dressed in rough garb, and had the seeming of a band of outlaws, demanded.

"I will say nothing," she said, "nor do I own that she is here."

"We will soon take means to find out," the man exclaimed. "Unless in five minutes she is delivered to us, we will burn your place to the ground."

The lady abbess was insensible to the threat; but the men rushing in, seized some sisters, who, terrified out of their wits by this irruption, at once gave the information demanded, and the men made their way to the cell where the Lady Margaret slept.

The girl had at once risen when the tumult commenced, doubting not in her mind that this was another attempt upon the part of her enemy to carry her off. When, therefore, she heard heavy footsteps approaching along the gallery-having already hastily attired herself-she opened the door and presented herself.

"If you seek the Lady Margaret of Evesham," she said calmly, "I am she. Do not harm any of the sisters here. I am in your power, and will go with you at once. But I beseech you add not to your other sins that of violence against holy women."

The men, abashed by the calm dignity of this young girl, abstained from laying hands upon her, but merely motioned to her to accompany them. Upon their way they met the man who appeared to be their leader, and he, well pleased that the affair was over, led the way to the courtyard.

"Farewell, my child," the abbess exclaimed. "God will deliver you from the power of these wicked men. Trust in Him, and keep up your courage. Wickedness will not be permitted to triumph upon the earth; and be assured that the matter shall be brought to the ears of the pope's legate, and of Prince John himself."

She could say no more, for the men closing round the weeping girl, hurried her out from the convent. A litter awaited them without, and in this the young lady was placed, and, borne upon the shoulders of four stout men, she started at a fast pace, surrounded closely by the rest of the band.

It was a dark night, and the girl could not see the direction in which she was being taken; but she judged from the turn taken upon leaving the convent, that it was towards Evesham.

They had proceeded some miles, when a trampling of horses was heard, and a body of armed men rode up. For a moment Lady Margaret's heart gave a leap, for she thought that she had been rescued by her friends. There was a loud and angry altercation, a clashing of swords, and a sound of shouting and cries outside the litter. Then it was placed roughly on the ground, and she heard the sound of the footsteps of her first captors hurrying away. Then the horsemen closed round the litter, and the leader dismounted.

"I am happy indeed, Lady Margaret," he said approaching the litter, "to have been able to save you from the power of these villains. Fortunately, word came to me that the outlaws in the forest were about to carry you off, and that they would not hesitate even to desecrate the walls of the convent. Assembling my men-at-arms, I at once rode to your rescue, and am doubly happy to have saved you, first, as a gentleman, secondly, as being the man to whom our gracious prince has assigned you as a wife. I am Sir Rudolph, Earl of Evesham."

As from the first the girl had been convinced that she had fallen into the power of her lawless suitor, this came upon her as no surprise.

"Whether your story is true, Sir Rudolph," she said, "or not, God knows, and I, a poor weak girl, will not pretend to venture to say. It is between you and your conscience. If, as you say, you have saved me from the power of the outlaws, I demand that, as a knight and a gentleman, you return with me at once to the convent from which I was taken by force."

"I cannot do that," Sir Rudolph said. "Fortune has placed you in my hands, and has enabled me to carry out the commands of the prince. Therefore, though I would fain yield to your wishes and so earn your goodwill, which above all things I wish to obtain, yet my duty towards the prince commands me to utilize the advantage which fate has thrown in my hands."

"You must do as you will, Sir Rudolph," the girl said with dignity. "I believe not your tale. You sought before, in person, to carry me off, but failed, and you have now employed other means to do so. The tale of your conduct to Dame Editha has reached my ears, and I hold you a foresworn knight and a dishonoured man, and as such I would rather die than become your wife, although as yet I am but a child, and have no need to talk of weddings for years to come."

"We need not parley here," the knight said coldly. "We shall have plenty of time when at my castle."

The litter was now lifted, placed between two horses, and proceeded rapidly on its journey. Although the hope was but faint, yet until the gates of the castle closed upon them the Lady Margaret still hoped that rescue might reach her. But the secret had been too well kept, and it was not until the following day that the man who had been placed in a cottage near the convent arrived in all haste in the forest, to say that it was only in the morning that he had learnt that the convent had been broken open by men disguised as archers, and the Lady Margaret carried off.

Four days elapsed before Sir Rudolph presented himself before the girl he had captured. So fearfully was his face bruised and disfigured by the blow from the mailed hand of Cuthbert three weeks before, that he did not wish to appear before her under such unfavourable circumstances, and the captive passed the day gazing from her casement in one of the rooms in the upper part of the keep, towards the forest whence she hoped rescue would come.

Within the forest hot discussions were going on as to the best course to pursue. An open attack was out of the question, especially as upon the day following the arrival there of Lady Margaret, 300 more mercenaries had marched in from Worcester, so that the garrison was now raised to 500 men.

"Is there no way," Cnut exclaimed furiously, "by which we might creep into this den, since we cannot burst into it openly?"

"There is a way from the castle," Cuthbert said, "for my dear lord told me of it one day when we were riding together in the Holy Land. He said then that it might be that he should never return, and that it were well that I should know of the existence of this passage, which few beside the earl himself knew of. It is approached by a very heavy slab of stone in the great hall. This is bolted down, and as it stands under the great table passes unnoticed, and appears part of the ordinary floor. He told me the method in which, by touching a spring, the bolts were withdrawn and the stone could be raised. Thence a passage a quarter of a mile long leads to the little chapel standing in the hollow, and which, being hidden among the trees, would be unobserved by any party besieging the castle. This of course was contrived in order that the garrison, or any messenger thereof, might make an exit in case of siege."

"But if we could escape," Cnut asked, "why not enter by this way?"

"The stone is of immense weight and strength," Cuthbert replied, "and could not be loosed from below save with great labour and noise. There are, moreover, several massive doors in the passage, all of which are secured by heavy bolts within. It is therefore out of the question that we could enter the castle by that way. But were we once in, we could easily carry off the lady through this passage."

The large force which Sir Rudolph had collected was not intended merely for the defence of the castle, for the knight considered that with his own garrison he could hold it against a force tenfold that which his rival could collect. But he was determined if possible to crush out the outlaws of the forest, for he felt that so long as this formidable body remained under an enterprising leader like Sir Cuthbert, he would never be safe for a moment, and would be a prisoner in his own castle.

Cuthbert had foreseen that the attack was likely to be made and had strengthened his band to the utmost. He felt, however, that against so large a force of regularly armed men, although he might oppose a stout resistance and kill many, yet that in the end he must be conquered. Cnut, however, suggested to him a happy idea, which he eagerly grasped.

"It would be rare sport," Cnut said, "when this armed force comes out to attack us, if we could turn the tables by slipping in, and taking their castle."

"The very thing," Cuthbert exclaimed. "It is likely that he will use the greater portion of his forces, and that he will not keep above fifty or sixty men, at the outside, in the castle. When they sally out we will at first oppose a stout resistance to them in the wood, gradually falling back. Then, at a given signal, all save twenty men shall retire hastily, and sweeping round, make for the castle. Their absence will not be noticed, for in this thick wood it is difficult to tell whether twenty men or two hundred are opposing you among the bushes; and the twenty who remain must shoot thick and fast to make believe that their numbers are great, retiring sometimes, and leading the enemy on into the heart of the wood."

"But supposing, Sir Cuthbert, that they should have closed the gates and lifted the drawbridge? We could not gain entrance by storming, even if only twenty men held the walls, until long after the main body would have returned."

Cuthbert thought for some time, and then said, "Cnut, you shall undertake this enterprise. You shall fill a cart high with faggots, and in it shall conceal a dozen of your best men. You, dressed as a serf, shall drive the oxen, and when you reach the castle shall say, in answer to the hail of the sentry, that you are bringing in the tribute of wood of your master the franklin of Hopeburn. They will then lower the drawbridge and open the gates; and when you have crossed the bridge and are under the portcullis, spring out suddenly, cut loose the oxen so that they will not draw the cart further in, cut the chains of the drawbridge so that it cannot be drawn off, and hold the gate for a minute or two until we arrive."

"The plan is capital," Cnut exclaimed. "We will do the proud Norman yet. How he will storm when he finds us masters of his castle. What then will you do, Sir Cuthbert?"

"We can hold the castle for weeks," Cuthbert said, "and every day is in our favour. If we find ourselves forced to yield to superior numbers, we can at last retire through the passage I have spoken of, and must then scatter and each shift for himself until these bad days be past."

Chapter XXIV
The Siege Of Evesham Castle.

Upon the day before starting out to head the expedition against the outlaws, Sir Rudolph sent word to the Lady Margaret that she must prepare to become his wife at the end of the week. He had provided two tiring maids for her by ordering two of the franklins to send in their daughters for that purpose, and these mingled their tears with Margaret's at the situation in which they were placed. She replied firmly to the messenger of the knight that no power on earth could oblige her to marry him. He might drive her to the altar; but though he killed her there, her lips should refuse to say the words which would unite them.

The following morning, early, the castle rang with the din of preparation. The great portion of the mercenaries were encamped in tents outside the walls, for, spacious as it was, Evesham could hardly contain 400 men in addition to its usual garrison. The men-at-arms were provided with heavy axes to cut their way through the bushes. Some carried bundles of straw, to fire the wood should it be found practicable to do so; and as it was now summer and the wind was blowing high, Sir Rudolph hoped that the dry grass and bushes would catch, and would do more even than his men-at-arms in clearing the forest of those whom he designated the villains infesting it. They had, too, with them several fierce dogs trained to hunting the deer, and these, the knight hoped, would do good service in tracking the outlaws. He and the knights and the men-at-arms with him were all dismounted, for he felt that horses would in the forest be an encumbrance, and he was determined himself to lead the way to the men-at-arms.

When they reached the forest, they were saluted by a shower of arrows; but as all were clad in mail, these at a distance effected but little harm. As they came closer, however, the clothyard arrows began to pierce the coarse and ill-made armour of the foot soldiers, although the finer armour of the knight kept out the shafts which struck against it. Sir Rudolph and his knights leading the way, they entered the forest, and gradually pressed their invisible foe backwards through the trees. The dogs did good service, going on ahead and attacking the archers; but, one by one, they were soon shot, and the assailants left to their own devices. Several attempts were made to fire the wood. But these failed, the fire burning but a short time and then dying out of itself. In addition to the fighting men, Sir Rudolph had impressed into the service all the serfs of his domain, and these, armed with axes, were directed to cut down the trees as the force proceeded, Sir Rudolph declaring that he would not cease until he had levelled the whole forest, though it might take him months to do so.

The assailants gained ground steadily, the resistance being less severe than Sir Rudolph had anticipated. Several small huts and clearings in the forest which had been used by the outlaws, and round which small crops had been planted, were destroyed, and all seemed to promise well for the success of the enterprise.

It was about two hours after they had left the castle, when a heavy cart filled with faggots was seen approaching its gates. The garrison, who had not the least fear of any attack, paid no attention to it until it reached the edge of the moat. Then the warder, seeing that it contained faggots, lowered the drawbridge without question, raised the portcullis, and opened the gates.

"From whom do you bring this wood?" he asked, as the man driving the oxen began to cross the bridge.

"From the franklin of Hopeburn."

"It is well," said the warder, "for he is in arrear now, and should have sent in the firewood two months since. Take it to the wood-house at the other end of the court."

The heavy-waggon crossed the drawbridge, but as it was entering the gate it came suddenly to a stop. With a blow of his ox goad Cnut levelled the warder to the ground, and cutting the cords of the bullocks, drove them into the yard ahead. As he did so the pile of faggots fell asunder, and twelve men armed with bow and pike leaped out. The men-at-arms standing near, lounging in the courtyard, gave a shout of alarm, and the garrison, surprised at this sudden cry, ran to their arms. At first they were completely panic-stricken. But seeing after a time how small was the number of their assailants, they took heart and advanced against them. The passage was narrow, and the twelve men formed a wall across it. Six of them with their pikes advanced, the other six with bent bows standing behind them and delivering their arrows between their heads. The garrison fought stoutly, and although losing many, were pressing the little band backwards. In vain the assistant-warder tried to lower the portcullis, or to close the gates. The former fell on to the top of the waggon, and was there retained. The gates also were barred by the obstacle. The chains of the drawbridge had at once been cut. Cnut encouraged his followers by his shouts, and armed with a heavy axe, did good service upon the assailants. But four of his party had fallen, and the rest were giving way, when a shout was heard, and over the drawbridge poured Cuthbert and 150 of the outlaws of the forest. Struck with terror at this attack, the garrison drew back, and the foresters poured into the yard. For a few minutes there was a fierce fight; but the defenders of the castle, disheartened and taken by surprise, were either cut down or, throwing down their arms, cried for quarter.

Ten minutes after the waggon had crossed the drawbridge, the castle was safely in possession of Sir Cuthbert. The bridge was raised, the waggon removed, the portcullis lowered, and to the external eye all remained as before.

Cuthbert at once made his way to the chamber where the Lady Margaret was confined, and her joy at her deliverance was great indeed. So unlimited was her faith in Sir Cuthbert that she had never lost confidence; and although it did not seem possible that in the face of such disparity of numbers he could rescue her from the power of Sir Rudolph, yet she had not given up hope. The joy of the farmers' daughters who had been carried off to act as her attendants was little inferior to her own; for once in the power of this reckless baron, the girls had small hopes of ever being allowed to return again to their parents.

The flag of Sir Rudolph was thrown down from the keep, and that of the late earl hoisted in its stead; for Cuthbert himself, although he had assumed the cognizance which King Richard had granted him, had not yet any flag or pennon emblazoned with it.

No words can portray the stupefaction and rage of Sir Rudolph when a man who had managed to slip unobserved from the castle at the time of its capture, bore the news to him in the forest. All opposition there had ceased, and the whole of the troops were engaged in aiding the peasants in cutting wide roads through the trees across the forest, so as to make it penetrable by horsemen in every direction. It was supposed that the outlaws had gradually stolen away through the thickets and taken to the open country, intending to scatter to their homes, or other distant hiding-places; and the news that they had by a ruse captured the castle, came as a thunderclap.

Sir Rudolph's first impulse was to call his men together and to march towards the castle. The drawbridge was up, and the walls bristled with armed men. It was useless to attempt a parley; still more useless to think of attacking the stronghold without the proper machines and appliances. Foaming with rage, Sir Rudolph took possession of a cottage near, camped his men around and prepared for a siege.

There were among the mercenaries many men accustomed to the use of engines of war. Many, too, had aided in making them; and these were at once set to work to construct the various machines in use at that time. Before the invention of gunpowder, castles such as those of the English barons were able to defy any attack by an armed force for a long period. Their walls were so thick that even the balistas, casting huge stones, were unable to breach them except after a very long time. The moats which surrounded them were wide and deep, and any attempt at storming by ladders was therefore extremely difficult; and these buildings were consequently more often captured by famine than by other means. Of provisions, as Sir Rudolph knew, there was a considerable supply at present in the castle, for he had collected a large number of bullocks in order to feed the strong body who had been added to the garrison. The granaries, too, were well stored; and with a groan Sir Rudolph thought of the rich stores of French wines which he had collected in his cellars.

After much deliberation with the knights with him and the captain of the mercenaries, it was agreed in the first instance to attempt to attack the place by filling up a portion of the moat and ascending by scaling ladders. Huge screens of wood were made, and these were placed on waggons; the waggons themselves were filled with bags of earth, and a large number of men getting beneath them shoved the ponderous machines forward to the edge of the moat. The bags of stones and earth were then thrown in, and the waggons pushed backwards to obtain a fresh supply. This operation was of course an exceedingly slow one, a whole day being occupied with each trip of the waggons. They were not unmolested in their advance, for, from the walls, mangonels and other machines hurled great stones down upon the wooden screens, succeeding sometimes, in spite of their thickness, in crashing through them, killing many of the men beneath. The experiment was also tried of throwing balls of Greek fire down upon the wood; but as this was green and freshly felled it would not take fire, but the flames dropping through, with much boiling pitch and other materials, did grievously burn and scald the soldiers working below it. Upon both sides every device was tried. The cross-bow men among the mercenaries kept up a fire upon the walls to hinder the defenders from interfering with the operations, while the archers above shot steadily, and killed many of those who ventured within range of their bows.

After ten days' labour, a portion of the moat some twenty yards in length was filled with bags of earth, and all was ready for the assault. The besiegers had prepared great numbers of strong ladders, and these were brought up under shelter of the screens. Then, all being ready, the trumpets sounded for the assault, and the troops moved forward in a close body, covering themselves with their shields so that no man's head or body was visible, each protecting the one before him with his shield held over him. Thus the body presented the appearance of a great scale-covered animal. In many respects, indeed, the warfare of those days was changed in no way from that of the time of the Romans. In the 1200 years which had elapsed between the siege of Jerusalem and the days of the crusades there had been but little change in arms or armour, and the operations which Titus undertook for the reduction of the Jewish stronghold differed but little from those which a Norman baron employed in besieging his neighbour's castle.

Within Evesham Castle all was contentment and merriment during these days. The garrison had no fear whatever of being unable to repel the assault when it should be delivered. Huge stones had been collected in numbers on the walls, cauldrons of pitch, beneath which fires kept simmering, stood there in readiness. Long poles with hooks with which to seize the ladders and cut them down were laid there; and all that precaution and science could do was prepared.

Cuthbert passed much of the day, when not required upon the walls, chatting with the Lady Margaret, who, attended by her maidens, sat working in her bower. She had learnt to read from the good nuns of the convent-an accomplishment which was by no means general, even among the daughters of nobles; but books were rare, and Evesham boasted but few manuscripts. Here Margaret learnt in full all the details of Cuthbert's adventures since leaving England, and the fondness with which as a child she had regarded the lad grew gradually into the affection of a woman.

The courage of the garrison was high, for although they believed that sooner or later the castle might be carried by the besiegers, they had already been told by Cnut that there was a means of egress unknown to the besiegers, and that when the time came they would be able to escape unharmed. This, while it in no way detracted from their determination to defend the castle to the last, yet rendered their task a far lighter and more agreeable one than it would have been had they seen the gallows standing before them as the end of the siege. As the testudo, as it was called in those days, advanced towards the castle, the machines upon the walls-catapults, mangonels, and arbalasts-poured forth showers of stones and darts upon it, breaking up the array of shields and killing many; and as these openings were made, the archers, seizing their time, poured in volleys of arrows. The mercenaries, however, accustomed to war, advanced steadily, and made good their footing beneath the castle wall, and proceeded to rear their ladders. Here, although free from the action of the machines, they were exposed to the hand missiles, which were scarcely less destructive. In good order, and with firmness, however, they reared the ladders, and mounted to the assault, covering themselves as well as they could with their shields. In vain, however, did they mount. The defenders poured down showers of boiling pitch and oil, which penetrated the crevices of their armour, and caused intolerable torment. Great stones were toppled over from the battlements upon them; and sometimes the ladders, seized by the poles with hooks, were cast backwards, with all upon them, on the throng below. For half-an-hour, encouraged by the shouts of Sir Rudolph and their leaders, the soldiers strove gallantly; but were at last compelled to draw off, having lost nigh 100 men, without one gaining a footing upon the walls.

That evening another council of war was held without. Already some large machines for which Sir Rudolph had sent had arrived. In anticipation of the possibility of failure, two castles upon wheels had been prepared, and between these a huge beam with an iron head was hung. This was upon the following day pushed forward on the newly-formed ground across the moat. Upon the upper part of each tower were armed men who worked machines casting sheaves of arrows and other missiles. Below were those who worked the ram. To each side of the beam were attached numerous cords, and with these it was swung backwards and forwards, giving heavy blows each stroke upon the wall. The machines for casting stones, which had arrived, were also brought in play, and day and night these thundered against the walls; while the ram repeated its ceaseless blows upon the same spot, until the stone crumbled before it.

Very valiantly did the garrison oppose themselves to these efforts. But each day showed the progress made by the besiegers. Their forces had been increased, Prince John having ordered his captain at Gloucester to send another 100 men to the assistance of Sir Rudolph. Other towers had now been prepared. These were larger than the first, and overtopped the castle walls. From the upper story were drawbridges, so formed as to drop from the structures upon the walls, and thus enable the besiegers to rush upon them. The process was facilitated by the fact that the battlements had been shot away by the great stones, and there was a clear space on which the drawbridges could fall. The attack was made with great vigour; but for a long time the besieged maintained their post, and drove back the assailants as they poured out across the drawbridges on to the wall. At last Cuthbert saw that the forces opposed to him were too numerous to be resisted, and gave orders to his men to fall back upon the inner keep.

Making one rush, and clearing the wall of those who had gained a footing, the garrison fell back hastily, and were safely within the massive keep before the enemy had mustered in sufficient numbers upon the wall to interfere with them. The drawbridge was now lowered, and the whole of the assailants gained footing within the castle. They were still far from having achieved a victory. The walls of the keep were massive and strong, and its top far higher than the walls, so that from above a storm of arrows poured down upon all who ventured to show themselves. The keep had no windows low enough down for access to be gained; and those on the floors above were so narrow, and protected by bars, that it seemed scaling the walls alone could an entry be effected. This was far too desperate an enterprise to be attempted, for the keep rose eighty feet above the courtyard. It was upon the door, solid and studded with iron, that the attempt had to be made.

Several efforts were made by Sir Rudolph, who fought with a bravery worthy of a better cause, to assault and batter down the door. Protected by wooden shields from the rain of missiles from above, he and his knights hacked at the door with their battle-axes. But in vain. It had been strengthened by beams behind, and by stones piled up against it. Then fire was tried. Faggots were collected in the forest, and brought; and a huge pile having been heaped against the door, it was lighted. "We could doubtless prolong the siege for some days, Lady Margaret," said Cuthbert, "but the castle is ours; and we wish not, when the time comes that we shall again be masters of it, that it should be a mere heap of ruins. Methinks we have done enough. With but small losses on our side, we have killed great numbers of the enemy, and have held them at bay for a month. Therefore, I think that tonight it will be well for us to leave the place."

Lady Margaret was rejoiced at the news that the time for escape had come, for the perpetual clash of war, the rattling of arrows, the ponderous thud of heavy stones, caused a din very alarming to a young girl; and although the room in which she sat, looking into the inner court of the castle, was not exposed to missiles, she trembled at the thought that brave men were being killed, and that at any moment a shot might strike Cuthbert, and so leave her without a friend or protector.

Content with having destroyed the door, the assailants made no further effort that evening, but prepared in the morning to attack it, pull down the stones filled behind it, and force their way into the keep. There was, with the exception of the main entrance, but one means of exit, a small postern door behind the castle, and throughout the siege a strong body of troops had been posted here, to prevent the garrison making a sortie.

Feeling secure therefore that upon the following day his enemies would fall into his power, Sir Rudolph retired to rest.

An hour before midnight the garrison assembled in the hall. The table was removed, and Cuthbert having pressed the spring, which was at a distance from the stone and could not be discovered without a knowledge of its existence, the stone turned aside by means of a counterpoise, and a flight of steps was seen. Torches had been prepared. Cnut and a chosen band went first; Cuthbert followed, with Lady Margaret and her attendants; and the rest of the archers brought up the rear, a trusty man being left in charge at last with orders to swing back the stone into its place, having first hauled the table over the spot, so that their means of escape should be unknown.

The passage was long and dreary, the walls were damp with wet, and the massive doors so swollen by moisture that it was with the greatest difficulty they could be opened. At last, however, they emerged into the little friary in the wood. It was deserted, the priest who usually dwelt there having fled when the siege began. The stone which there, as in the castle, concealed the exit, was carefully closed, and the party then emerged into the open air. Here Cuthbert bade adieu to his comrades. Cnut had very anxiously begged to be allowed to accompany him and share his fortunes, and Cuthbert had promised him that if at any time he should again take up arms in England, he would summon him to his side, but that at present as he knew not whither his steps would be turned, it would be better that he should be unattended. The archers had all agreed to scatter far and wide through the country, many of them proceeding to Nottingham and joining the bands in the forest of Sherwood.

Cuthbert himself had determined to make his way to the castle of his friend, Sir Baldwin, and to leave the Lady Margaret in his charge. Cnut hurried on at full speed to the house of a franklin, some three miles distant. Here horses were obtained and saddled, and dresses prepared; and when Cuthbert with Lady Margaret arrived there, no time was lost. Dressed as a yeoman, with the Lady Margaret as his sister, he mounted a horse, with her behind him on a pillion. The other damsels also mounted, as it would not have been safe for them to remain near Evesham. They therefore purposed taking refuge in a convent near Gloucester for the present. Bidding a hearty adieu to Cnut, and with thanks to the franklin who had aided them, they set forward on their journey. By morning they had reached the convent, and here the two girls were left, and Cuthbert continued his journey. He left his charge at a convent a day's ride distant from the castle of Sir Baldwin, as he wished to consult the knight first as to the best way of her entering the castle without exciting talk or suspicion.

Sir Baldwin received him with joy. He had heard something of his doings, and the news of the siege of Evesham had been noised abroad. He told him that he was in communication with many other barons, and that ere long they hoped to rise against the tyranny of Prince John, but that at present they were powerless, as many, hoping that King Richard would return ere long, shrank from involving the country in a civil war. When Cuthbert told him that the daughter of his old friend was at a convent but a day's ride distant, and that he sought protection for her, Sir Baldwin instantly offered her hospitality.

"I will," he said, "send my good wife to fetch her. Some here know your presence, and it would be better therefore that she did not arrive for some days, as her coming will then seem to be unconnected with yourself. My wife and I will, a week hence, give out that we are going to fetch a cousin of my wife's to stay here with her; and when we return no suspicion will be excited that she is other than she seems. Should it be otherwise, I need not say that Sir Baldwin of Bthune will defend his castle against any of the minions of Prince John. But I have no fear that her presence here will be discovered. What think you of doing in the meantime?"

"I am thinking," Cuthbert said, "of going east. No news has been obtained of our lord the king save that he is a prisoner in the hands of the emperor; but where confined, or how, we know not. It is my intent to travel to the Tyrol, and to trace his steps from the time that he was captured. Then, when I obtain knowledge of the place where he is kept, I will return, and consult upon the best steps to be taken. My presence in England is now useless. Did the barons raise the standard of King Richard against the prince, I should at once return and join them. But without land or vassals, I can do nothing here, and shall be indeed like a hunted hare, for I know that the false earl will move heaven and earth to capture me."

Sir Baldwin approved of the resolution; but recommended Cuthbert to take every precaution not to fall himself into the hands of the emperor; "for," he said, "if we cannot discover the prison of King Richard, I fear that it would be hopeless indeed ever to attempt to find that in which a simple knight is confined."

Chapter XXV
In Search Of The King.

The following day, with many thanks Cuthbert started from the castle, and in the first place visited the convent, and told Lady Margaret that she would be fetched in a few days by Sir Baldwin and his wife. He took a tender adieu of her, not without many forebodings and tears upon her part; but promising blithely that he would return and lead her back in triumph to her castle, he bade adieu and rode for London.

He had attired himself as a merchant, and took up his abode at a hostelry near Cheapside. Here he remained quietly for some days, and, mixing among the people, learnt that in London as elsewhere the rapacity of Prince John had rendered him hateful to the people, and that they would gladly embrace any opportunity of freeing themselves from his yoke. He was preparing to leave for France, when the news came to him that Prince John had summoned all the barons faithful to him to meet him near London, and had recalled all his mercenaries from different parts of the country, and was gathering a large army; also, that the barons faithful to King Richard, alarmed by the prospect, had raised the royal standard, and that true men were hurrying to their support. This entirely destroyed the plans that he had formed. Taking horse again, and avoiding the main road, by which he might meet the hostile barons on their way to London, he journeyed down to Nottingham. Thence riding boldly into the forest, he sought the outlaws, and was not long ere he found them. At his request he was at once taken before their leader, a man of great renown both for courage and bowmanship, one Robin Hood. This bold outlaw had long held at defiance the Sheriff of Nottingham, and had routed him and all bodies of troops who had been sent against him. With him Cuthbert found many of his own men; and upon hearing that the royal standard had been raised, Robin Hood at once agreed to march with all his men to join the royal force. Messengers were despatched to summon the rest of the forest band from their hiding places, and a week later Cuthbert, accompanied by Robin Hood and 300 archers, set out for the rendezvous. When they arrived there they found that Sir Baldwin had already joined with his retainers, and was by him most warmly received, and introduced to the other barons in the camp, by whom Cuthbert was welcomed as a brother. The news that Prince John's army was approaching was brought in, a fortnight after Cuthbert had joined the camp, and the army in good order moved out to meet the enemy.

The forces were about equal. The battle began by a discharge of arrows; but Robin Hood and his men shot so true and fast that they greatly discomfited the enemy; and King John's mercenaries having but little stomach for the fight, and knowing how unpopular they were in England, and that if defeated small mercy was likely to be shown to them, refused to advance against the ranks of the loyal barons, and falling back declined to join in the fray. Seeing their numbers so weakened by this defection, the barons on the prince's side hesitated, and surrounding the prince advised him to make terms with the barons while there was yet time. Prince John saw that the present was not a favourable time for him, and concealing his fury under a mask of courtesy, he at once acceded to the advice of his followers, and despatched a messenger to the barons with an inquiry as to what they wanted of him. A council was held, and it was determined to demand the dismissal of the mercenaries and their despatch back to their own country; also that John would govern only as his brother's representative; that the laws of the country should be respected; that no taxes should be raised without the assent of the barons; that all men who had taken up arms against his authority should be held free; and that the barons on Prince John's side should return peaceably home and disband their forces. Seeing, under the circumstances, that there was no way before him but to yield to these demands, Prince John accepted the terms. The mercenaries were ordered to march direct to London, and orders were given that ships should be at once prepared to take them across to Normandy, and the barons marched for their homes.

Satisfied, now that the mercenaries were gone, that they could henceforth hold their ground against Prince John, the royal barons also broke up their forces. Robin Hood with his foresters returned to Sherwood; and Cuthbert, bidding adieu to Sir Baldwin, rode back to London, determined to carry out the plan which he had formed. He was the more strengthened in this resolution, inasmuch as in the royal camp he had met a friend from whom he parted last in the Holy Land. This was Blondel, the minstrel of King Richard, whose songs and joyous music had often lightened the evening after days of fighting and toil in Palestine. To him Cuthbert confided his intention, and the minstrel instantly offered to accompany him.

"I shall," he said, "be of assistance to you. Minstrels are like heralds. They are of no nationality, and can pass free where a man at arms would be closely watched and hindered. Moreover, it may be that I might aid you greatly in discovering the prison of the king. So great is the secrecy with which this has been surrounded, that I question if any inquiries you could make would enable you to trace him. My voice, however, can penetrate into places where we cannot enter. I will take with me my lute, and as we journey I will sing outside the walls of each prison we come to one of the songs which I sang in Palestine. King Richard is himself a singer and knows my songs as well as myself. If I sing a verse of some song which I wrote there and which, therefore, would be known only to him, if he hears it he may follow with the next verse, and so enable us to know of his hiding place."

Cuthbert at once saw the advantages which such companionship would bring him, and joyfully accepted the minstrel's offer, agreeing himself to go as serving man to Blondel. The latter accompanied him to London. Here their preparations were soon made, and taking ship in a merchantman bound for the Netherlands, they started without delay upon their adventure.

The minstrels and troubadours were at that time a privileged race in Europe, belonging generally to the south of France, although produced in all lands. They travelled over Europe singing the lays which they themselves had composed, and were treated with all honour at the castles where they chose to alight. It would have been considered as foul a deed to use discourtesy to a minstrel as to insult a herald. Their persons were, indeed, regarded as sacred, and the knights and barons strove to gain their good will by hospitality and presents, as a large proportion of their ballads related to deeds of war; and while they would write lays in honour of those who courteously entertained them, they did not hesitate to heap obloquy upon those who received them discourteously, holding them up to the gibes and scoffs of their fellows. In no way, therefore, would success be so likely to attend the mission of those who set out to discover the hiding place of King Richard as under the guise of a minstrel and his attendant. No questions would be asked them; they could halt where they would, in castle or town, secure of hospitality and welcome. Blondel was himself a native of the south of France, singing his songs in the soft language of Languedoc. Cuthbert's Norman French would pass muster anywhere as being that of a native of France; and although when dressed as a servitor attention might be attracted by his bearing, his youth might render it probable that he was of noble family, but that he had entered the service of the minstrel in order to qualify himself some day for following that career. He carried a long staff, a short sword, and at his back the lute or small harp played upon by the troubadour. Blondel's attire was rich, and suitable to a person of high rank.

They crossed to the Scheldt, and thence travelled by the right bank of the Rhine as far as Mannheim, sometimes journeying by boat, sometimes on foot. They were also hospitably entertained, and were considered to more than repay their hosts by the songs which Blondel sang. At Mannheim they purchased two horses, and then struck east for Vienna. The journey was not without danger, for a large portion of this part of Europe was under no settled government, each petty baron living in his own castle, and holding but slight allegiance to any feudal lord, making war upon his neighbour on his own account, levying blackmail from travellers, and perpetually at variance with the burghers of the towns. The hills were covered with immense forests, which stretched for many leagues in all directions, and these were infested by wolves, bears, and robbers. The latter, however, although men without pity or religion, yet held the troubadours in high esteem, and the travellers without fear entered the gloomy shades of the forest.

They had not gone far when their way was barred by a number of armed men.

"I am a minstrel," Blondel said, "and as such doubt not that your courtesy will be extended to me."

"Of a surety," the leader said, "the gay science is as much loved and respected in the greenwood as in the castle; and moreover, the purses of those who follow it are too light to offer any temptation to us. We would pray you, however, to accompany us to our leader, who will mightily rejoice to see you, for he loves music, and will gladly be your host so long as you will stay with him."

Blondel, without objection, turned his horse's head and accompanied the men, followed by Cuthbert. After half an hour's travelling, they came to a building which had formerly been a shrine, but which was now converted to the robbers' headquarters. The robber chief on hearing from his followers the news that a minstrel had arrived, came forward to meet him, and courteously bade him welcome.

"I am Sir Adelbert, of Rotherheim," he said, "although you see me in so poor a plight. My castle and lands have been taken by my neighbour, with whom for generations my family have been at feud. I was in the Holy Land with the emperor, and on my return found that the baron had taken the opportunity of my absence, storming my castle and seizing my lands. In vain I petitioned the emperor to dispossess this traitorous baron of my lands, which by all the laws of Christendom should have been respected during my absence. The emperor did indeed send a letter to the baron to deliver them up to me; but his power here is but nominal, and the baron contemptuously threw the royal proclamation into the fire, and told the messenger that what he had taken by the sword he would hold the sword; and the emperor, having weightier matters on hand than to set troops in motion to redress the grievances of a simple knight, gave the matter no further thought. I have therefore been driven to the forest, where I live as best I may with my followers, most of whom were retainers upon my estate, and some my comrades in the Holy Land. I make war upon the rich and powerful, and beyond that do harm to no man. But, methinks," he continued, "I know your face, gentle sir."

"It may well be so, Sir Adelbert," the minstrel said, "for I too was in the Holy Land. I followed the train of King Richard, and mayhap at some of the entertainments given by him you have seen my face. My name is Blondel."

"I remember now," the knight said. "It was at Acre that I first saw you, and if I remember rightly you can wield the sword as well as the lute."

"One cannot always be playing and singing," Blondel said, "and in lack of amusement I was forced to do my best against the infidel, who indeed would have but little respected my art had I fallen into his hands. The followers of the prophet hold minstrels but in slight reverence."

"What is the news of King Richard?" the knight said. "I have heard that he was lost on the voyage homewards."

"It is not so," Blondel said. "He landed safely on the coast, and was journeying north with a view of joining his sister at the Court of Saxony, when he was foully seized and imprisoned by the Archduke John."

"That were gross shame indeed," the knight said, "and black treachery on the part of Duke John. And where is the noble king imprisoned?"

"That," said Blondel, "no man knows. On my journey hither I have gathered that the emperor claimed him from the hand of the Archduke, and that he is imprisoned in one of the royal fortresses; but which, I know not. And indeed, sir knight, since you are well disposed towards him, I may tell you that the purport of my journey is to discover if I can the place of his confinement. He was a kind and noble master, and however long my search may be, I will yet obtain news of him."

The knight warmly applauded the troubadour's resolution, and was turning to lead him into his abode, when his eye fell upon Cuthbert.

"Methinks I know the face of your attendant as well as your own; though where I can have seen him I know not. Was he with you in the Holy Land?"

"Yes," Blondel said, "the youth was also there; and doubtless you may have noticed him, for he is indeed of distinguished and of good family."

"Then let him share our repast," the knight said, "if it seems good to you. In these woods there is no rank, and I myself have long dropped my knightly title, and shall not reassume it until I can pay off my score to the Baron of Rotherheim, and take my place again in my castle."

The minstrel and Cuthbert were soon seated at the table with the knight and one or two of his principal companions. A huge venison pasty formed the staple of the repast, but hares and other small game were also upon the table. Nor was the generous wine of the country wanting.

The knight had several times glanced at Cuthbert, and at last exclaimed, "I have it now. This is no attendant, sir minstrel, but that valiant young knight who so often rode near King Richard in battle. He is, as I guess, your companion in this quest; is it not so?"

"It is," Cuthbert replied frankly. "I am like yourself, a disinherited knight, and my history resembles yours. Upon my return to England I found another in possession of the land and titles that belonged to the noble I followed, and which King Richard bestowed upon me. The Earl of Evesham was doubtless known to you, and before his death King Richard, at his request, bestowed upon me as his adopted son—although but a distant connexion—his title and lands and the hand of his daughter. Prince John, who now rules in England, had however granted these things to one of his favourites, and he having taken possession of the land and title, though not, happily, of the lady, closed his door somewhat roughly in my face. I found means, however, to make my mark upon him; but as our quarrel could not be fought out to the end, and as the false knight had the aid of Prince John, I am forced for a while to postpone our settlement, and meeting my good friend the minstrel, agreed to join him in his enterprise to discover our lord the king."

The knight warmly grasped Cuthbert's hand.

"I am glad," he said, "to meet so true and valiant a knight. I have often wondered at the valour with which you, although so young, bore yourself; and there were tales afloat of strange adventures which you had undergone in captivity for a time among the infidels."

At Sir Adelbert's request, Cuthbert related the story of his adventures among the Saracens; and then Blondel, tuning his lute, sang several canzonets which he had composed in the Holy Land, of feats of arms and adventure.

"How far are you," Cuthbert asked presently, when Blondel laid his lute aside, "from the estates which were wrongfully wrested from you?"

"But twenty leagues," the knight said. "My castle was on the Rhine, between Coblentz and Mannheim."

"Does the baron know that you are so near?" Cuthbert asked.

"Methinks that he does not," the knight replied, "but that he deems me to have gone to the court of the emperor to seek for redress—which, he guesses, I shall certainly fail to obtain."

"How many men have you with you?" Cuthbert asked.

"Fifty men, all good and true," the knight said.

"Has it never entered your thoughts to attempt a surprise upon his castle?" Cuthbert said.

The knight was silent for a minute.

"At times," he said at length, "thoughts of so doing have occurred to me; but the castle is strong, and a surprise would be difficult indeed."

"If the baron is lulled in security at present," Cuthbert said, "and deems you afar off, the watch is likely to be relaxed, and with a sudden onslaught you might surely obtain possession. Blondel and myself are not pressed for time, and the delay of a few days can make but little difference. If, therefore, you think we could be of assistance to you in such an attempt, my sword, and I am sure that of my friend, would be at your disposal."

The knight sat for some time in silence.

"Thanks, generous knight," he said at last, "I am sorely tempted to avail myself of your offer; but I fear that the enterprise is hopeless. The aid, however, of your arm and knowledge of war would greatly add to my chances, and if it pleases you we will ride to-morrow to a point where we can obtain a sight of the baron's castle. When you see it, you shall judge yourself how far such an enterprise as you propose is possible."

"Is your own castle intact?" Cuthbert asked.

"The walls are standing," he said; "but a breach has been made in them, and at present it is wholly deserted."

"Do you think," Cuthbert asked, "that if you succeeded in surprising and defeating the garrison of the castle that you could then regain your own, and hold it against your enemy?"

"I think that I could," Sir Adelbert said. "The baron's domains are but little larger than my own. Many of my retainers still live upon the estate, and would; I am sure, gladly join me, if I were to raise my flag. The baron, too, is hated by his neighbours, and could I inflict a crushing blow upon him, methinks it would be so long a time before he could assemble a force, that I might regain my castle and put it in an attitude of defence before he could take the field against me."

"If," Cuthbert said, "we could surprise the castle, it might well be that the baron would fall into your hands, and in that case you might be able to make your own terms with him. How strong a force is he likely to have in his castle?"

"Some fifty or sixty men," the knight replied; "for with such a force he could hold the castle against an attack of ten times their number, and he could in twelve hours call in his retainers, and raise the garrison to 300 or 400 men."

Blondel warmly assented to Cuthbert's scheme, and it was settled that at daybreak they should start to view the Castle of Rotherheim. At early dawn they were in the saddle, and the three rode all day, until towards sunset they stood on the crest of a hill looking down into the valley of the Rhine.

The present aspect of that valley affords but a slight idea of its beauty in those days. The slopes are now clad with vineyards, which, although picturesque in idea, are really, to look at from a distance, no better than so many turnip fields. The vines are planted in rows and trained to short sticks, and as these rows follow the declivities of the hillside, they are run in all directions, and the whole mountain side, from the river far up, is cut up into little patches of green lines. In those days the mountains were clad with forests, which descended nearly to the river side. Here and there, upon craggy points, were situate the fortalices of the barons. Little villages nestled in the woods, or stood by the river bank, and a fairer scene could not be witnessed in Europe.

"That is Rotherheim," the knight said, pointing to a fortress standing on a crag, which rose high above the woods around it; "and that," he said, pointing to another some four miles away, similarly placed, "is my own."

Cuthbert examined closely the fortress of Rotherheim. It was a large building, with towers at the angles, and seemed to rise almost abruptly from the edge of the rock. Inside rose the gables and round turrets of the dwelling-place of the baron; and the only access was by a steep winding path on the river side.

"It is indeed a strong place," Cuthbert said, "and difficult to take by surprise. A watch no doubt is always kept over the entrance, and there we can hope for no success. The only plan will be to scale the wall by means of a ladder; but how the ladder is to be got to so great a height, I own at present passes my comprehension." After much thought, Cuthbert went on, "It might, methinks, be practicable for an archer to approach the walls, and to shoot an arrow over the angle of the castle so that it would pass inside the turret there, and fall in the forest beyond. If to this arrow were attached a light cord, it could be gained by one on the other side, and a stronger cord hauled over. To this could be attached a rope ladder, and so this could be raised to the top of the wall. If a sentinel were anywhere near he might hear the rope pulled across the battlements; but if as we may hope, a watch is kept only over the entrance, the operation might be performed without attracting notice."

The knight was delighted with the project, which seemed perfectly feasible, and it was agreed that the attempt should be made.

"It will need," Sir Adelbert said, "an archer with a strong arm indeed to shoot an arrow with a cord attached to it, however light, over the corner of the castle."

"Methinks," Cuthbert said, "that I can do that, for as a lad I was used to the strong bows of my country. The first thing, however, will be to obtain such a bow; but doubtless one can be purchased in one of the towns, which, if not so strong as those to which I was accustomed, will at any rate suffice for us."

The party bivouacked in the woods for the night, for the horses had already done a very long journey, and needed rest before starting back for the Black Forest. At daybreak, however, they started, and at nightfall rejoined their band. These were delighted when they heard the scheme that had been set on foot, and all avowed their eagerness to join in the attempt to restore their lord to his rights.

Two days later they set out, having already procured from the nearest town a strong bow, some arrows, a very light rope, and a stronger one from a portion of which they manufactured a rope ladder capable of reaching from the top of the wall to the rock below. The journey this time occupied two days, as the men on foot were unable to march at the pace at which the mounted party had traversed the ground. The evening of the second day, however, saw them in sight of the castle. By Cuthbert's advice, Sir Adelbert determined to give them twenty-four hours of rest, in order that they might have their full strength for undertaking the task before them. During the day, Cuthbert, guided by the knight, made his way through the woods to the foot of the rocks on which the castle stood. They were extremely steep, but could be mounted by active men if unopposed from above. Cuthbert measured the height with his eye from the top of the castle wall to the place which he selected as most fitting from which to shoot the arrow, and announced to the knight that he thought there would be no difficulty in discharging an arrow over the angle.

At nightfall the whole party made their way silently through the woods. Three men were sent round to the side of the castle opposite that from which Cuthbert was to shoot. The length of light string was carefully coiled on the ground, so as to unwind with the greatest facility, and so offer as little resistance to the flight of the arrow as might be. Then, all being in readiness, Cuthbert attached the end to an arrow, and drawing the bow to its full compass, let fly the arrow. All held their breath; but no sound followed the discharge. They were sure, therefore, that the arrow had not struck the wall, but that it must have passed clear over it. Half-an-hour elapsed before they felt that the cord was pulled, and knew that the men upon the other side had succeeded in finding the arrow and string attached. The stronger cord was now fastened to that which the arrow had carried, and this gradually disappeared in the darkness. A party now stole up the rock, and posted themselves at the foot of the castle wall. They took with them the coil of rope-ladder and the end of the rope. At length the rope tightened, and to the end they attached the ladder. This again ascended until the end only remained upon the ground, and they knew that it must have reached the top of the wall. They now held fast, and knew that those on the other side, following the instructions given them, would have fastened the rope to a tree upon the opposite side. They were now joined by the rest of the party, and Sir Adelbert leading the way, and followed by Cuthbert and Blondel, began cautiously to ascend the rope ladder.

All this time no sound from the castle proclaimed that their intention was suspected, or that any alarm had been given, and in silence they gained the top of the wall. Here they remained quiet until the whole band were gathered there, and then made their way along until they reached the stairs leading to the courtyard. These they descended, and then, raising his war cry, Sir Adelbert sprang upon the men who, round a fire, were sitting by the gate. These were cut down before they could leap to their feet, and the party then rushed at the entrance to the dwelling-house. The retainers of the castle, aroused by the sudden din, rushed from their sleeping places, but taken completely by surprise, were unable to offer any resistance whatever to the strong force which had, as if by magic, taken possession of the castle. The surprise was complete, and with scarce a blow struck they found themselves in possession. The baron himself was seized as he rose from his bed, and his rage at finding himself in the power of his enemy was so great as for some time to render him speechless. Sir Adelbert briefly dictated to him the conditions upon which only he should desist from using his power to hang him over his own gate. The baron was instantly to issue orders to all his own retainers and tenantry to lend their aid to those of Sir Adelbert in putting the castle of the latter into a state of defence and mending the breach which existed. A sum of money, equal to the revenues of which he had possessed himself, was to be paid at once, and the knight was to retain possession of Rotherheim and of the baron's person until these conditions were all faithfully carried out. The baron had no resource but to assent to these terms, and upon the following day Cuthbert and Blondel departed upon their way, overwhelmed with thanks by Sir Adelbert, and confident that he would now be able to regain and hold the possession of his estate.

Chapter XXVI
King Richard's Return To England.

Journeying onward, Blondel and his companion stopped at many castles, and were everywhere hospitably entertained. Arriving at Vienna they lingered for some time, hoping there to be able to obtain some information of the whereabouts of King Richard. Blondel in his songs artfully introduced allusions to the captive monarch and to the mourning of all Christendom at the imprisonment of its champion. These allusions were always well received, and he found that the great bulk of the nobles of the empire were indignant and ashamed at the conduct of the emperor in imprisoning his illustrious rival. The secret of his prison place, however, appeared to have been so well kept that no information whatever was obtainable.

"We must carry out our original plan," he said at length, "and journey into the Tyrol. In one of the fortresses there he is most likely to be confined."

Leaving the capital they wandered up into the mountains for weeks, visiting one castle after another. It was no easy matter in all cases to get so near to these prisons as to give a hope that their voice might be heard within, or an answer received without. More than once cross-bow bolts were shot at them from the walls when they did not obey the sentinel's challenge and move further away. Generally, however, it was in the day time that they sang. Wandering carelessly up, they would sit down within earshot of the castle, open their wallets, and take out provisions from their store, and then, having eaten and drunk, Blondel would produce his lute and sing, as if for his own pleasure. It needed, however, four visits to each castle before they could be sure that the captive was not there; for the song had to be sung on each side. Sometimes they would cheat themselves with the thought that they heard an answering voice; but it was not until the end of the fourth week, when singing outside the castle of Diernstein, that a full rich voice, when Blondel ceased, sang out the second stanza of the poem. With difficulty Blondel and Cuthbert restrained themselves from an extravagant exhibition of joy. They knew, however, that men on the prison wall were watching them as they sat singing, and Blondel, with a final strain taken from a ballad of a knight who, having discovered the hiding place of his ladylove, prepared to free her from her oppressors, shouldered his lute, and they started on their homeward journey.

There was no delay now. At times they sang indeed at castles; but only when their store was exhausted, for upon these occasions Blondel would be presented with a handsome goblet or other solid token of the owner's approval, and the sale of this at the next city would take them far on their way. They thought it better not to pass through France, as Philip, they knew, was on the watch to prevent any news of King Richard reaching England. They therefore again passed through Brabant, and so by ship to England.

Hearing that Longchamp, Bishop of Ely, one of Richard's vicegerents, was over in Normandy, and rightly deeming him the most earnest of his adherents, they at once recrossed the sea, and found the warlike prelate at Rouen. Greatly delighted was he at hearing that Richard's hiding-place had been discovered. He at once sent across the news to England, and ordered it to be published far and wide, and himself announced it to the barons of Normandy. Then with a gorgeous retinue, including Cuthbert and Blondel, he started for Vienna, and arriving there demanded an interview with the emperor.

The news that it was now certain that Richard was imprisoned in a castle of the emperor, had already spread through Europe, and the bishop had been received everywhere with tokens of sympathy; and so great was the feeling shown by the counts and barons of the empire, that the Emperor Henry felt that he could no longer refuse to treat for the surrender of his captive. Therefore he granted the interview which Longchamp demanded. The English envoy was received by the emperor surrounded by his nobles. The prelate advanced with great dignity.

"I come," he said, "in the name of the people of England to demand the restoration of King Richard, most unjustly and unknightly detained a prisoner in his passage through your dominions."

"King Richard was my foe," the emperor said, "open and secret, and I was justified in detaining one who is alike my enemy and a scourge to Europe as a prisoner, when fortune threw him in my hands. I am, however, willing to put him to a ransom, and will upon the payment of 150,000 marks allow him to go free."

"I deny your right to detain him or to put him to ransom," the bishop said. "But as you have the power, so my denial is useless. England is poor, impoverished with war and by the efforts which she made in the service of our holy religion. Nevertheless, poor as she is, she will raise the sum you demand. There is not an Englishman who will not furnish all he can afford for the rescue of our king. But once again, in the presence of your nobles, I denounce your conduct as base and unkingly."

The emperor could with difficulty restrain his passion; but the sight of the sombre visages of his nobles showed that they shared in no slight degree the feelings which the English envoy had so boldly announced.

"Before, however," the emperor said, "I surrender King Richard, he must be tried by my peers of many and various crimes of which he is accused. Should he be found guilty of these, no gold can purchase his release. Should he, however, be acquitted, then as my word is given so shall it be."

"Although," the prelate said, "I deny your right to try our king, and believe that he himself will refuse to accept your jurisdiction, yet I fear not the result if our lord be left in the hands of the nobles of the empire and not in yours. I can trust their honour and courtesy."

And turning upon his heel, without another word he quitted the apartment.

An hour later the bishop and his following took horse and rode with all speed to the north coast, and thence sailed for England. The news of the amount of ransom filled the people with consternation; but preparations were at once made for collecting the sum demanded. Queen Eleanor was unceasing in her efforts to raise the money for the release of her favourite son. The nobles contributed their jewels and silver; the people gave contributions of goods, for money was so scarce in England that few had the wherewithal to pay in coin. Prince John placed every obstacle in the way of the collection; but the barons had since their successful stand obtained the upper hand, and it was by intrigue only that he could hinder the collection.

In the meantime, popular opinion throughout Europe was strong upon the side of King Richard. The pope himself wrote to the emperor on his behalf. The barons of the empire were indignant at the shame placed upon their country; and the emperor, although he would fain have thrown further delays in the way, was obliged at last to order the first step to be taken.

A solemn diet was ordered to assemble at Worms. Here were collected all the nobles of the empire, and before them King Richard was brought. It was a grand assembly. Upon a raised throne on the dais sat the emperor himself, and beside him and near him were the great feudatories of the empire, and along the sides of the walls were ranged in long rows the lesser barons. When the doors were opened and King Richard entered, the whole assembly, save the emperor, rose in respect to the captive monarch. Although pale from his long confinement, the proud air of Richard was in no way abated, and the eyes that had flashed so fearlessly upon the Saracens looked as sternly down the long lines of the barons of Germany. Of splendid stature and physique, King Richard was unquestionably the finest man of his time. He was handsome, with a frank face, but with a fierce and passionate eye. He wore his moustache with a short beard and closely-cut whisker. His short curly hair was cropped closely to his head, upon which he wore a velvet cap with gold coronet, while a scarlet robe lined with fur fell over his coat of mail, for the emperor had deemed it imprudent to excite the feeling of the assembly in favour of the prisoner by depriving him of the symbols of his rank.

King Richard strode to the place prepared for him, and then turning to the assembly he said, in a voice which rang through the hall, —

"Counts and lords of the Empire of Germany, I, Richard, King of England, do deny your right to try me. I am a king, and can only be tried by my peers and by the pope, who is the head of Christendom. I might refuse to plead, refuse to take any part in this assembly, and appeal to the pope, who alone has power to punish kings. But I will waive my rights. I rely upon the honour and probity of the barons of Germany. I have done no man wrong, and would appear as fearlessly before an assembly of peasants as before a gathering of barons. Such faults as I may have, and none are without them, are not such as those with which I am charged. I have slain many men in anger, but none by treachery. When Richard of England strikes, he strikes in the light of day. He leaves poison and treachery to his enemies, and I hurl back with indignation and scorn in the teeth of him who makes them the charges brought against me."

So saying King Richard took his seat amidst a murmur of applause from the crowded hall.

The trial then commenced. The accusations against Richard were of many kinds. Chief among them was the murder of Conrad of Montferat; but there were charges of having brought the crusade to naught by thwarting the general plans, by his arrogance in refusing to be bound by the decision of the other leaders, and by having made a peace contrary to the interests of the crusaders. The list was a long one; but the evidence adduced was pitiably weak. Beyond the breath of suspicion, no word of real evidence connecting him with the murder of Conrad of Montferat was adduced, and the other charges were supported by no better evidence. Many of the German barons who had been at the crusades themselves came forward to testify to the falsity of these charges, and the fact that Richard had himself placed Conrad of Montferat upon the throne, and had no possible interest in his death, was alone more than sufficient to nullify the vague rumours brought against him. Richard himself in a few scornful words disposed of this accusation. The accusation that he, Richard of England, would stoop to poison a man whom he could have crushed in an instant, was too absurd to be seriously treated.

"I am sure," the king said, "that not one person here believes this idle tale. That I did not always agree with the other leaders is true; but I call upon every one here to say whether, had they listened to me and followed my advice, the crusade would not have had another ending. Even after Phillip of France had withdrawn; even after I had been deserted by John of Austria, I led the troops of the crusaders from every danger and every difficulty to within sight of the walls of Jerusalem. Had I been supported with zeal, the holy city would have been ours; but the apathy, the folly, and the weakness of the leaders brought ruin upon the army. They thought not of conquering Jerusalem, but of thwarting me; and I retort upon them the charge of having sacrificed the success of the crusade. As to the terms of peace, how were they made? I, with some fifty knights and 1000 followers alone remained in the Holy Land. Who else, I ask, so circumstanced, could have obtained any terms whatever from Saladin? It was the weight of my arm alone which saved Jaffa and Acre, and the line of seacoast, to the Cross. And had I followed the example set me by him of Austria and the Frenchman, not one foot of the Holy Land would now remain in Christian hands."

The trial was soon over, and without a single dissentient the King of England was acquitted of all the charges brought against him. But the money was not yet raised, and King Richard was taken back into the heart of Germany. At length, by prodigious exertions, half the amount claimed was collected, and upon the solicitations of the pope and of the counts of his own empire, the emperor consented to release Richard upon, receipt of this sum and his royal promise that the remainder should be made up.

Not as yet, however, were the intrigues at an end. Prince John and King Phillip alike implored the emperor to retain his captive, and offered to him a larger sum than the ransom if he would still hold him in his hands. Popular opinion was, however, too strong. When the news of these negotiations became bruited abroad, the counts of the empire, filled with indignation, protested against this shame and dishonour being brought upon the country. The pope threatened him with excommunication; and at last the emperor, feeling that he would risk his throne did he further insist, was forced to open the prison gates and let the king free. Cuthbert, Blondel, and a few other trusty friends were at hand, and their joy at receiving their long-lost sovereign was indeed intense. Horses had been provided in readiness, and without a moment's delay the king started, for even at the last moment it was feared that the emperor might change his mind. This indeed was the case. The king had not started many hours, when the arrival of fresh messengers from Phillip and John induced the emperor once more to change his intentions, and a body of men were sent in pursuit of the king. The latter fortunately made no stay on the way, but changing horses frequently-for everywhere he was received with honour and attention-he pushed forward for the coast of the North Sea, and arrived there two or three hours only before his oppressors. Fortunately it was night, and taking a boat he embarked without a moment's delay; and when the emissaries of the emperor arrived the boat was already out of sight, and in the darkness pursuit was hopeless.

On landing at Dover, the first to present himself before him was Prince John, who, in the most abject terms besought pardon for the injuries he had inflicted. King Richard waved him contemptuously aside.

"Go," he said, "and may I forget your injuries as speedily as you will forget my pardon."

Then taking horse, he rode on to London, where he was received with the most lively acclamation by his subjects.

The first step of King Richard was to dispossess all the minions of John from the castles and lands which had been taken from his faithful adherents. Some of these resisted; but their fortresses were speedily stormed. Sir Rudolph was not one of these. Immediately the news of King Richard's arrival in England reached him, feeling that all was now lost, he rode to the seacoast, took ship, and passed into France, and Cuthbert, on his arrival at Evesham, found himself undisputed lord of the place. He found that the hiding-place of his mother had not been discovered, and, after a short delay to put matters in train, he, attended by a gallant retinue, rode into Wiltshire to the castle of Sir Baldwin of Bthune. Here he found the Lady Margaret safe and sound, and mightily pleased to see him. She was now seventeen, and offered no objections whatever to the commands of King Richard that she should at once bestow her hand upon the Earl of Evesham. By the king's order, the wedding took place at London, the king himself bestowing the bride upon his faithful follower, whom we may now leave to the enjoyment of the fortune and wife he had so valiantly won.

Attempted Assassination of Sir Walter.

St. George For England: A Tale of Cressy and Poitiers

1885

Preface.

My Dear Lads:

You may be told perhaps that there is no good to be obtained from tales of fighting and bloodshed-that there is no moral to be drawn from such histories. Believe it not. War has its lessons as well as Peace. You will learn from tales like this that determination and enthusiasm can accomplish marvels, that true courage is generally accompanied by magnanimity and gentleness, and that if not in itself the very highest of virtues, it is the parent of almost all the others, since but few of them can be practiced without it. The courage of our forefathers has created the greatest empire in the world around a small and in itself insignificant island; if this empire is ever lost, it will be by the cowardice of their descendants.

At no period of her history did England stand so high in the eyes of Europe as in the time whose events are recorded in this volume. A chivalrous king and an even more chivalrous prince had infected the whole people with their martial spirit, and the result was that their armies were for a time invincible, and the most astonishing successes were gained against numbers which would appear overwhelming. The victories of Cressy and Poitiers may be to some extent accounted for by superior generalship and discipline on the part of the conquerors; but this will not account for the great naval victory over the Spanish fleet off the coast of Sussex, a victory even more surprising and won against greater odds than was that gained in the same waters centuries later over the Spanish Armada. The historical facts of the story are all drawn from Froissart and other contemporary historians, as collated and compared by Mr. James in his carefully written history. They may therefore be relied upon as accurate in every important particular.

Yours sincerely,
G. A. HENTY.

Chapter I
A Wayfarer.

It was a bitterly cold night in the month of November, 1330. The rain was pouring heavily, when a woman, with a child in her arms, entered the little village of Southwark. She had evidently come from a distance, for her dress was travel-stained and muddy. She tottered rather than walked, and when, upon her arrival at the gateway on the southern side of London Bridge, she found that the hour was past and the gates closed for the night, she leaned against the wall with a faint groan of exhaustion and disappointment.

After remaining, as if in doubt, for some time, she feebly made her way into the village. Here were many houses of entertainment, for travelers like herself often arrived too late to enter the gates, and had to abide outside for the night. Moreover, house rent was dear within the walls of the crowded city, and many, whose business brought them to town, found it cheaper to take up their abode in the quiet hostels of Southwark rather than to stay in the more expensive inns within the walls. The lights came out brightly from many of the casements, with sounds of boisterous songs and laughter. The woman passed these without a pause. Presently she stopped before a cottage, from which a feeble light alone showed that it was tenanted.

She knocked at the door. It was opened by a pleasant-faced man of some thirty years old.
"What is it?" he asked.
"I am a wayfarer," the woman answered feebly. "Canst take me and my child in for the night?"
"You have made a mistake," the man said; "this is no inn. Further up the road there are plenty of places where you can find such accommodation as you lack."
"I have passed them," the woman said, "but all seemed full of roisterers. I am wet and weary, and my strength is nigh spent. I can pay thee, good fellow, and I pray you as a Christian to let me come in and sleep before your fire for the night. When the gates are open in the morning I will go; for I have a friend within the city who will, methinks, receive me."

The tone of voice, and the addressing of himself as good fellow, at once convinced the man that the woman before him was no common wayfarer.

"Come in," he said; "Geoffrey Ward is not a man to shut his doors in a woman's face on a night like this, nor does he need payment for such small hospitality. Come hither, Madge!" he shouted; and at his voice a woman came down from the upper chamber. "Sister," he said, "this is a wayfarer who needs shelter for the night; she is wet and weary. Do you take her up to your room and lend her some dry clothing; then make her a cup of warm posset, which she needs sorely. I will fetch an armful of fresh rushes from the shed and strew them here. I will sleep in the smithy. Quick, girl," he said sharply; "she is fainting with cold and fatigue." And as he spoke he caught the woman as she was about to fall, and laid her gently on the ground. "She is of better station than she seems," he said to his sister; "like enough some poor lady whose husband has taken part in the troubles; but that is no business of ours. Quick, Madge, and get these wet things off her; she is soaked to the skin. I will go round to the Green Dragon and will fetch a cup of warm cordial, which I warrant me will put fresh life into her."

So saying, he took down his flat cap from its peg on the wall and went out, while his sister at once proceeded to remove the drenched garments and to rub the cold hands of the guest until she recovered consciousness. When Geoffrey Ward returned, the woman was sitting in a settle by the fireside, dressed in a warm woolen garment belonging to his sister. Madge had thrown fresh wood on the fire, which was blazing brightly now. The woman drank the steaming beverage which her host brought with him. The color came faintly again into her cheeks.

"I thank you, indeed," she said, "for your kindness. Had you not taken me in I think I should have died at your door, for indeed I could go no further; and though I hold not to life, yet would I fain live until I have delivered my boy into the hands of those who will be kind to him, and this will, I trust, be to-morrow."

"Say naught about it," Geoffrey answered. "Madge and I are right glad to have been of service to you. It would be a poor world indeed if one could not give a corner of one's fireside to a fellow-creature on such a night as this, especially when that fellow-creature is a woman with a child. Poor little chap! he looks right well and sturdy, and seems to have taken no ill from his journey."

"Truly, he is well and sturdy," the mother said, looking at him proudly; "indeed. I have been almost wishing to-day that he were lighter by a few pounds, for in truth I am not used to carry him far, and his weight has sorely tried me. His name is Walter, and I trust," she added, looking at the powerful figure of her host, "that he will grow up as straight and as stalwart as yourself." The child, who was about three years old, was indeed an exceedingly fine little fellow, as he sat, in one scanty garment, in his mother's lap, gazing with round eyes at the blazing fire; and the smith thought how pretty a picture the child and mother made. She was a fair, gentle-looking girl some twenty-two years old, and it was easy enough to see now from her delicate features and soft, shapely hands that she had never been accustomed to toil.

"And now," the smith said, "I will e'en say good-night. The hour is late, and I shall be having the watch coming along to know why I keep a fire so long after the curfew. Should you be a stranger in the city, I will gladly act as your guide in the morning to the friends whom you seek, that is, should they be known to me; but if not, we shall doubtless find them without difficulty."

So saying, the smith retired to his bed of rushes in the smithy, and soon afterward the tired visitor, with her baby, lay down on the rushes in front of the fire, for in those days none of the working or artisan class used beds, which were not indeed, for centuries afterward, in usage by the common people.

In the morning Geoffrey Ward found that his guest desired to find one Giles Fletcher, a maker of bows.

"I know him well," the smith said. "There are many who do a larger business, and hold their heads higher, but Giles Fletcher is well esteemed as a good workman, whose wares can be depended upon. It is often said of him that did he take less pains he would thrive more; but he handles each bow that he makes as if he loved it, and finishes and polishes each with his own hand. Therefore he doeth not so much trade as those who are less particular with their wares, for he hath to charge a high price to be able to live. But none who have ever bought his bows have regretted the silver which they cost. Many and many a gross of arrow-heads have I sold him, and he is well-nigh as particular in their make as he is over the spring and temper of his own bows. Many a friendly wrangle have I had with him over their weight and finish, and it is not many who find fault with my handiwork, though I say it myself; and now, madam, I am at your service."

During the night the wayfarer's clothes had been dried. The cloak was of rough quality, such as might have been used by a peasant woman; but the rest, though of somber color, were of good material and fashion. Seeing that her kind entertainers would be hurt by the offer of money, the lady contented herself with thanking Madge warmly, and saying that she hoped to come across the bridge one day with Dame Fletcher; then, under the guidance of Geoffrey, who insisted on carrying the boy, she set out from the smith's cottage. They passed under the outer gate and across the bridge, which later on was covered with a double line of houses and shops, but was now a narrow structure. Over the gateway across the river, upon pikes, were a number of heads and human limbs. The lady shuddered as she looked up.

"It is an ugly sight," the smith said, "and I can see no warrant for such exposure of the dead. There are the heads of Wallace, of three of Robert Bruce's brothers, and of many other valiant Scotsmen who fought against the king's grandfather some twenty years back. But after all they fought for their country, just as Harold and our ancestors against the Normans under William, and I think it a foul shame that men who have done no other harm should be beheaded, still less that their heads and limbs should be stuck up there gibbering at all passers-by. There are over a score of them, and every fresh trouble adds to their number; but pardon me," he said suddenly as a sob from the figure by his side called his attention from the heads on the top of the gateway, "I am rough and heedless in speech, as my sister Madge does often tell me, and it may well be that I have said something which wounded you."

"You meant no ill," the lady replied; "it was my own thoughts and troubles which drew tears from me; say not more about it, I pray you."

They passed under the gateway, with its ghastly burden, and were soon in the crowded streets of London. High overhead the houses extended, each story advancing beyond that below it until the occupiers of the attics could well-nigh shake hands across. They soon left the more crowded streets, and turning to the right, after ten minutes' walking, the smith stopped in front of a bowyer shop near Aldgate.

"This is the shop," he said, "and there is Giles Fletcher himself trying the spring and pull of one of his bows. Here I will leave you, and will one of these days return to inquire if your health has taken aught of harm by the rough buffeting of the storm of yester-even."

So saying he handed the child to its mother, and with a wave of the hand took his leave, not waiting to listen to the renewed thanks which his late guest endeavored to give him.

The shop was open in front, a projecting penthouse sheltered it from the weather; two or three bows lay upon a wide shelf in front, and several large sheaves of arrows tied together stood by the wall. A powerful man of some forty years old was standing in the middle of the shop with a bent bow in his arm, taking aim at a spot in the wall. Through an open door three men could be seen in an inner workshop cutting and shaping the wood for bows. The bowyer looked round as his visitor entered the shop, and then, with a sudden exclamation, lowered the bow.

"Hush, Giles!" the lady exclaimed; "it is I, but name no names; it were best that none knew me here."

The craftsman closed the door of communication into the inner room. "My Lady Alice," he exclaimed in a low tone, "you here, and in such a guise?"

"Surely it is I," the lady sighed, "although sometimes I am well-nigh inclined to ask myself whether it be truly I or not, or whether this be not all a dreadful dream."

"I had heard but vaguely of your troubles," Giles Fletcher said, "but hoped that the rumors were false. Ever since the Duke of Kent was executed the air has been full of rumors. Then came news of the killing of Mortimer and of the imprisonment of the king's mother, and it was said that many who were thought to be of her party had been attacked and slain, and I heard — —" And there he stopped.

"You heard rightly, good Giles, it is all true. A week after the slaying of Mortimer a band of knights and men-at-arms arrived at our castle and demanded admittance in the king's name. Sir Roland refused, for he had news that many were taking up arms, but it was useless. The castle was attacked and, after three days' fighting, was taken. Roland was killed, and I was cast out with my child. Afterward they repented that they had let me go, and searched far and wide for me; but I was hidden in the cottage of a wood-cutter. They were too busy in hunting down others whom they proclaimed to be enemies of the king, as they had wrongfully said of Roland, who had but done his duty faithfully to Queen Isabella, and was assuredly no enemy of her son, although he might well be opposed to the weak and indolent king, his father. However, when the search relaxed I borrowed the cloak of the good man's wife and set out for London, whither I have traveled on foot, believing that you and Bertha would take me in and shelter me in my great need."

"Ay, that will we willingly," Giles said. "Was not Bertha your nurse? and to whom should you come if not to her? But will it please you to mount the stairs? for Bertha will not forgive me if I keep you talking down here. What a joy it will be to her to see you again!"

So saying, Giles led the way to the apartment above. There was a scream of surprise and joy from his wife, and then Giles quietly withdrew downstairs again, leaving the women to cry in each other's arms.

A few days later Geoffrey Ward entered the shop of Giles Fletcher.

"I have brought you twenty score of arrow-heads, Master Giles," he said. "They have been longer in hand than is usual with me, but I have been pressed. And how goes it with the lady whom I brought to your door last week?"

"But sadly, Master Ward, very sadly, as I told you when I came across to thank you again in her name and my own for your kindness to her. She was but in poor plight after her journey; poor thing, she was little accustomed to such wet and hardship, and doubtless they took all the more effect because she was low in spirit and weakened with much grieving. That night she was taken with a sort of fever, hot and cold by turns, and at times off her head. Since then she has lain in a high fever and does not know even my wife; her thoughts ever go back to the storming of the castle, and she cries aloud and begs them to spare her lord's life. It is pitiful to hear her. The leech gives but small hope for her life, and in troth, Master Ward, methinks that God would deal most gently with her were he to take her. Her heart is already in her husband's grave, for she was ever of a most loving and faithful nature. Here there would be little comfort for her-she would fret that her boy would never inherit the lands of his father; and although she knows well enough that she would be always welcome here, and that Bertha would serve her as gladly and faithfully as ever she did when she was her nurse, yet she could not but greatly feel the change. She was tenderly brought up, being, as I told you last week, the only daughter of Sir Harold Broome. Her brother, who but a year ago became lord of Broomecastle at the death of his father, was one of the queen's men, and it was he, I believe, who brought Sir Roland Somers to that side. He was slain on the same night as Mortimer, and his lands, like those of Sir Roland, have been seized by the crown. The child upstairs is by right heir to both estates, seeing that his uncle died unmarried. They will doubtless be conferred upon those who have aided the young king in freeing himself from his mother's domination, for which, indeed, although I lament that Lady Alice should have suffered so sorely in the doing of it, I blame him not at all. He is a noble prince and will make us a great king, and the doings of his mother have been a shame to us all. However, I meddle not in politics. If the poor lady dies, as methinks is well-nigh certain, Bertha and I will bring up the boy as our own. I have talked it over with my wife, and so far she and I are not of one mind. I think it will be best to keep him in ignorance of his birth and lineage, since the knowledge cannot benefit him, and will but render him discontented with his lot and make him disinclined to take to my calling, in which he might otherwise earn a living and rise to be a respected citizen. But Bertha hath notions. You have not taken a wife to yourself, Master Geoffrey, or you would know that women oft have fancies which wander widely from hard facts, and she says she would have him brought up as a man-at-arms, so that he may do valiant deeds, and win back some day the title and honor of his family."

Geoffrey Ward laughed. "Trust a woman for being romantic," he said. "However, Master Fletcher, you need not for the present trouble about the child's calling, even should its mother die. At any rate, whether he follows your trade, or whether the blood in his veins leads him to take to martial deeds, the knowledge of arms may well be of use to him, and I promise you that such skill as I have I will teach him when he grows old enough to wield sword and battle-ax. As you know I may, without boasting, say that he could scarce have a better master, seeing that I have for three years carried away the prize for the best sword-player at the sports. Methinks the boy will grow up into a strong and stalwart man, for he is truly a splendid lad. As to archery, he need not go far to learn it, since your apprentice, Will Parker, last year won the prize as the best marksman in the city bounds. Trust me, if his tastes lie that way we will between us turn him out a rare man-at-arms. But I must stand gossiping no longer; the rumors that we are likely ere long to have war with France have rarely bettered my trade. Since the wars in Scotland men's arms have rusted somewhat, and my two men are hard at work mending armor, and fitting swords to hilts, and forging pike-heads. You see I am a citizen, though I dwell outside the bounds, because house rent is cheaper and I get my charcoal without paying the city dues. So I can work somewhat lower than those in the walls, and I have good custom from many in Kent, who know that my arms are of as good temper as those turned out by any craftsman in the city."

Giles Fletcher's anticipations as to the result of his guest's illness turned out to be well founded. The fever abated, but left her prostrate in strength. For a few weeks she lingered; but she seemed to have little hold of life, and to care not whether she lived or died. So gradually she faded away.

"I know you will take care of my boy as if he were your own, Bertha," she said one day, "and you and your husband will be far better protectors for him than I should have been had I lived. Teach him to be honest and true. It were better, methinks, that he grew up thinking you his father and mother, for otherwise he may grow discontented with his lot; but this I leave with you, and you must speak or keep silent according as you see his disposition and mind. If he is content to settle down to a peaceful life here, say naught to him which would unsettle his mind; but if Walter turn out to have an adventurous disposition, then tell him as much as you think fit of his history, not encouraging him to hope to recover his father's lands and mine, for that can never be, seeing that before that time can come they would have been enjoyed for many years by others; but that he may learn to bear himself bravely and gently, as becomes one of good blood."

A few days later Lady Alice breathed her last, and at her own request was buried quietly and without pomp, as if she had been a child of the bowman, a plain stone, with the name "Dame Alice Somers," marking the grave.

The boy grew and throve until at fourteen years old there was no stronger or sturdier lad of his age within the city bounds. Giles had caused him to be taught to read and write, accomplishments which were common among the citizens, although they were until long afterward rare among the warlike barons. The greater part of his time, however, was spent in sports with lads of his own age in Moorfields beyond the walls. The war with France was now raging, and as was natural, the boys in their games imitated the doings of their elders, and mimic battles, ofttimes growing into earnest, were fought between the lads of the different wards. Walter Fletcher, as he was known among his play-fellows, had by his strength and courage won for himself the proud position of captain of the boys of the ward of Aldgate.

Walter in the Armorer's Forge. —Page 14.

Geoffrey Ward had kept his word, and had already begun to give the lad lessons in the use of arms. When not engaged otherwise Walter would, almost every afternoon, cross London Bridge and would spend hours in the armorer's forge. Geoffrey's business had grown, for the war had caused a great demand for arms, and he had now six men working in the forge. As soon as the boy could handle a light tool Geoffrey allowed him to work, and although not able to wield the heavy sledge, Walter was able to do much of the finer work. Geoffrey encouraged him in this, as, in the first place, the use of the tools greatly strengthened the boy's muscles, and gave him an acquaintance with arms. Moreover, Geoffrey was still a bachelor, and he thought that the boy, whom he as well as Giles had come to love as a son, might, should he not take up the trade of war, prefer the occupation of an armorer to that of a bow maker, in which case he would take him some day as his partner in the forge. After work was over and the men had gone away Geoffrey would give the lad instructions in the use of the arms at which he had been at work, and so quick and strong was he that he rapidly acquired their use, and Geoffrey foresaw that he would one day, should his thoughts turn that way, prove a mighty man-at-arms.

It was the knowledge which he acquired from Geoffrey which had much to do with Walter's position among his comrades. The skill and strength which he had acquired in wielding the hammer, and by practice with the sword, rendered him a formidable opponent with the sticks, which formed the weapons in the mimic battles, and indeed not a few were the complaints which were brought before Giles Fletcher of bruises and hurts caused by him.

"You are too turbulent, Walter," the bowyer said one day when a haberdasher from the ward of Aldersgate came to complain that his son's head had been badly cut by a blow with a club from Walter Fletcher. "You are always getting into trouble, and are becoming the terror of other boys. Why do you not play more quietly? The feuds between the boys of different wards are becoming a serious nuisance, and many injuries have been inflicted. I hear that the matter has been mentioned in the Common Council, and that there is a talk of issuing an order that no boy not yet apprenticed to a trade shall be allowed to carry a club, and that any found doing so shall be publicly whipped."

"I don't want to be turbulent," Walter said; "but if the Aldersgate boys will defy us, what are we to do? I don't hit harder than I can help, and if Jonah Harris would leave his head unguarded I could not help hitting it."

"I tell you it won't do, Walter," Giles said. "You will be getting yourself into sore trouble. You are growing too masterful altogether, and have none of the quiet demeanor and peaceful air which becomes an honest citizen. In another six months you will be apprenticed, and then I hope we shall hear no more of these doings."

"My father is talking of apprenticing me, Master Geoffrey," Walter said that evening. "I hope that you will, as you were good enough to promise, talk with him about apprenticing me to your craft rather than to his. I should never take to the making of bows, though, indeed, I like well to use them; and Will Parker, who is teaching me, says that I show rare promise; but it would never be to my taste to stand all day sawing, and smoothing, and polishing. One bow is to me much like another, though my father holds that there are rare differences between them; but it is a nobler craft to work on iron, and next to using arms the most pleasant thing surely is to make them. One can fancy what good blows the sword will give and what hard knocks the armor will turn aside; but some day, Master Geoffrey, when I have served my time, I mean to follow the army. There is always work there for armorers to do, and sometimes at a pinch they may even get their share of fighting."

Walter did not venture to say that he would prefer to be a man-at-arms, for such a sentiment would be deemed as outrageous in the ears of a quiet city craftsman as would the proposal of the son of such a man nowadays to enlist as a soldier. The armorer smiled; he knew well enough what was in Walter's mind. It had cost Geoffrey himself a hard struggle to settle down to a craft, and he deemed it but natural that with the knightly blood flowing in Walter's veins he should long to distinguish himself in the field. He said nothing of this, however, but renewed his promise to speak to Giles Fletcher, deeming that a few years passed in his forge would be the best preparation which Walter could have for a career as a soldier.

Chapter II
The Hut In The Marshes.

A week later a party of knights and court gallants, riding across the fields without the walls, checked their horses to look at a struggle which was going on between two parties of boys. One, which was apparently the most powerful, had driven the other off from a heap of rubbish which had been carried without the walls. Each party had a flag attached to a stick, and the boys were armed with clubs such as those carried by the apprentice boys. Many of them carried mimic shields made of wood, and had stuffed their flat caps with wool or shavings, the better to protect their heads from blows. The smaller party had just been driven from the heap, and their leader was urging them to make another effort to regain it.

"That is a gallant-looking lad, and a sturdy, my Lord de Vaux," a boy of about ten years of age said. "He bears himself like a young knight, and he has had some hard knocks, for, see, the blood is streaming down his face. One would scarcely expect to see these varlets of the city playing so roughly."

"The citizens have proved themselves sturdy fighters before now, my prince," the other said; "they are ever independent, and hold to their rights even against the king. The contingent which the city sends to the wars bears itself as well as those of any of the barons."

"See!" the boy interrupted, "they are going to charge again. The leader has himself seized the flag and has swung his shield behind him, just as a knight might do if leading the stormers against a place of strength. Let us stop till we see the end of it."

With a shout of "Aldgate! Aldgate!" the leader of the assailants dashed forward, followed by his comrades, and with a rush reached the top of the heap.

"Well done!" the young prince exclaimed, clapping his hands. "See how he lays about him with that club of his. There, he has knocked down the leader of the defenders as if his club had been a battle-ax. Well done, young sir, well done! But his followers waver. The others are too strong for them. Stand, you cowards, rally round your leader!" And in his enthusiasm the young prince urged his horse forward to the scene of conflict.

But the assailants were mastered; few of them could gain the top of the heap, and those who did so were beaten back from it by the defenders. Heavy blows were exchanged, and blood flowed freely from many of their heads and faces, for in those days boys thought less than they do now of hard knocks, and manliness and courage were considered the first of virtues. Their leader, however, still stood his ground on the crest, though hardly pressed on all sides, and used his club both to strike and parry with a skill which aroused the warmest admiration on the part of the prince. In vain his followers attempted to come to his rescue; each time they struggled up the heap they were beaten back again by those on the crest.

"Yield thee prisoner," the assailants of their leader shouted, and the prince in his excitement echoed the cry. The lad, however, heard or heeded them not. He still kept his flag aloft in his left hand. With a sudden spring he struck down one of his opponents, plucked up their flag from the ground, and then fought his way back through his foes to the edge of the battle ground; then a heavy blow struck him on the temple, and, still holding the flags, he rolled senseless to the foot of the heap. The defenders with shouts of triumph were rushing down, when the prince urged his horse forward.

"Cease!" he said authoritatively. "Enough has been done, my young masters, and the sport is becoming a broil."

Hitherto the lads, absorbed in their strife, had paid but little heed to the party of onlookers; but at the word they at once arrested their arms, and, baring their heads, stood still in confusion.

"No harm is done," the prince said, "though your sport is of the roughest; but I fear that your leader is hurt, he moves not; lift his head from the ground." The boy was indeed still insensible. "My lords," the prince said to the knights who had now ridden up, "I fear that this boy is badly hurt; he is a gallant lad, and has the spirit of a true knight in him, citizen's son though he be. My Lord de Vaux, will you bid your squire ride at full speed to the Tower and tell Master Roger, the leech, to come here with all haste, and to bring such nostrums as may be needful for restoring the boy to life?"

The Tower was but half a mile distant, but before Master Roger arrived Walter had already recovered consciousness, and was just sitting up when the leech hurried up to the spot.

"You have arrived too late, Master Roger," the prince said; "but I doubt not that a dose of your cordials may yet be of use, for he is still dazed, and the blow he got would have cracked his skull had it been a thin one."

The leech poured some cordial from a vial into a small silver cup and held it to the boy's lips. It was potent and nigh took his breath away; but when he had drunk it he struggled to his feet, looking ashamed and confused when he saw himself the center of attention of so many knights of the court.

"What is thy name, good lad?" the prince asked.

"I am known as Walter Fletcher."

"You are a brave lad," the prince said, "and if you bear you as well as a man as you did but now, I would wish no better to ride beside me in the day of battle. Should the time ever come when you tire of the peaceable life of a citizen and wish to take service in the wars, go to the Tower and ask boldly for the Prince of Wales, and I will enroll you among my own men-at-arms, and I promise you that you shall have your share of fighting as stark as that of the assault of yon heap. Now, my lords, let us ride on; I crave your pardon for having so long detained you."

Walter was some days before he could again cross London Bridge to inform his friend Geoffrey of the honor which had befallen him of being addressed by the Prince of Wales. During the interval he was forced to lie abed, and he was soundly rated by Master Giles for again getting into mischief. Geoffrey was far more sympathetic, and said: "Well, Walter, although I would not that Gaffer Giles heard me say so, I think you have had a piece of rare good fortune. It may be that you may never have cause to recall the young prince's promise to him; but should you some day decide to embrace the calling of arms, you could wish for nothing better than to ride behind the Prince of Wales. He is, by all accounts, of a most noble and generous disposition, and is said, young as he is, to be already highly skilled in arms. Men say that he will be a wise king and a gallant captain, such a one as a brave soldier might be proud to follow; and as the king will be sure to give him plenty of opportunities of distinguishing himself, those who ride with him may be certain of a chance of doing valorous deeds. I will go across the bridge to-morrow, and will have a talk with Master Fletcher. The sooner you are apprenticed the sooner you will be out of your time; and since Madge married eight years since I have been lonely in the house and shall be glad to have you with me."

Geoffrey Ward found his friend more ready to accede to his request that Walter should be apprenticed to him than he had expected. The bowyer, indeed, was a quiet man, and the high spirits and somewhat turbulent disposition of his young charge gave him so much uneasiness that he was not sorry the responsibility of keeping him in order should be undertaken by Geoffrey. Moreover, he could not but agree with the argument that the promise of the Prince of Wales offered a more favorable opportunity for Walter to enter upon the career of arms, and so, perhaps, some day to win his way back to rank and honors than could have been looked for. Therefore, on the following week Walter was indentured to the armorer, and, as was usual at the time, left his abode in Aldgate and took up his residence with his master. He threw himself with his whole heart into the work, and by the time he was fifteen was on the way to become a skillful craftsman. His frame and muscles developed with labor, and he was now able to swing all save the very heaviest hammers in the shop. He had never abated in his practice at arms, and every day when work was over he and his master had a long bout together with cudgel or quarter-staff, sword or ax. Walter, of course, used light weapons, but so quick was he with them that Geoffrey Ward acknowledged that he needed to put out all his skill to hold his own with his pupil. But it was not alone with Geoffrey that Walter had an opportunity of learning the use of arms. Whenever a soldier, returned from the wars, came to have a weapon repaired by the armorer, he would be sure of an invitation to come in in the evening and take a stoup of ale, and tell of the battles and sieges he had gone through, and in the course of the evening would be asked to have a bout of arms with the young apprentice, whom Geoffrey represented as being eager to learn how to use the sword as well as how to make it.

Thus Walter became accustomed to different styles of fighting, but found that very few, indeed, of their visitors were nearly so well skilled with their arms as his master. Some of the soldiers were mortified at finding themselves unable to hold their own with a boy; others would take their reverses in good part and would come again, bringing with them some comrade known to be particularly skilled with his weapons, to try the temper of the armorer's apprentice. At the age of fifteen Walter had won the prize at the sports, both for the best cudgel play and for the best sword-and-buckler play among the apprentices, to the great disgust of many who had almost reached the age of manhood and were just out of their time.

On Sundays Walter always spent the day with Giles Fletcher and his wife, going to mass with them and walking in the fields, where, after service, the citizens much congregated. Since Walter had gone to work he had taken no part in the fights and frolics of his former comrades; he was, in fact, far too tired at the end of his day's work to have any desire to do aught but to sit and listen to the tales of the wars, of the many old soldiers who pervaded the country. Some of these men were disabled by wounds or long service, but the greater portion were idle scamps, who cared not for the hard blows and sufferings of a campaign, liking better to hang about taverns drinking, at the expense of those to whom they related fabulous tales of the gallant actions they had performed. Many, too, wandered over the country, sometimes in twos or threes, sometimes in larger bands, robbing and often murdering travelers or attacking lonely houses. When in one part or another their ill deeds became too notorious, the sheriffs would call out a posse of men and they would be hunted down like wild beasts. It was not, however, easy to catch them, for great tracts of forests still covered a large portion of the country and afforded them shelter.

In the country round London these pests were very numerous, for here, more than anywhere else, was there a chance of plunder. The swamps on the south side of the river had especially evil reputation. From Southwark to Putney stretched a marshy country over which, at high tides, the river frequently flowed. Here and there were wretched huts, difficult of access and affording good hiding-places for those pursued by justice, since searchers could be seen approaching a long way off, and escape could be made by paths across the swamp known only to the dwellers there, and where heavily armed men dared not follow. Further south, in the wild country round Westerham, where miles of heath and forest stretched away in all directions, was another noted place where the robber vagrants mustered thickly, and the Sheriff of Kent had much trouble with them.

The laws in those days were extremely severe, and death was the penalty of those caught plundering. The extreme severity of the laws, however, operated in favor of its breakers, since the sympathy of the people who had little to lose was with them, and unless caught red-handed in the act they could generally escape, since none save those who had themselves been robbed would say aught that would place the pursuers on their traces, or give testimony which would cost the life of a fellow-creature. The citizens of London were loud in their complaints against the discharged soldiers, for it was upon them that the loss mainly fell, and it was on their petitions to the king that the sheriffs of Middlesex and Hertford, Essex, Surrey, and Kent, were generally stirred up to put down the ill-doers.

Sometimes these hunts were conducted in a wholesale way, and the whole posse of a county would be called out. Then all found within its limits who had not land or visible occupation were collected. Any against whom charges could be brought home were hung without more ado, and the rest were put on board ship and sent across the sea to the army. Sometimes, when they found the country becoming too hot for them, these men would take service with some knight or noble going to the war, anxious to take with him as strong a following as might be, and not too particular as to the character of his soldiers.

Walter, being of an adventurous spirit, was sometimes wont of a summer evening, when his work was done, to wander across the marshes, taking with him his bow and arrows, and often bringing home a wild duck or two which he had shot in the pools. More than once surly men had accosted him, and had threatened to knock him on the head if they again found him wandering that way; but Walter laughed at their threats, and seeing that though but an apprentice lad, he might be able to send an arrow as straight to the mark as another, they were content to leave him alone.

One day when he was well-nigh in the heart of the swamp of Lambeth he saw a figure making his way across. The hour was already late and the night was falling, and the appearance of the man was so different from that of the usual denizens of the swamp that Walter wondered what his business there might be. Scarcely knowing why he did so, Walter threw himself down among some low brushwood and watched the approaching figure. When he came near he recognized the face, and saw, to his surprise, that it was a knight who had but the day before stopped at the armorer's shop to have two rivets put in his hauberk. He had particularly noticed him, because of the arrogant manner in which he spoke. Walter had himself put in the rivets, and had thought, as he buckled on the armor again, how unpleasant a countenance was that of its wearer. He was a tall and powerful man, and would have been handsome had not his eyes been too closely set together; his nose was narrow, and the expression of his face reminded Walter of a hawk. He had now laid aside his helmet, and his figure was covered with a long cloak.

"He is up to no good," Walter said to himself, "for what dealings could a knight honestly have with the ruffians who haunt these swamps? It is assuredly no business of mine, but it may lead to an adventure, and I have had no real fun since I left Aldgate. I will follow and see if I can get to the bottom of the mystery."

When he came close to the spot where Walter was lying the knight paused and looked round as if uncertain of his way. For four or five minutes he stood still, and then gave a shout of "Humphrey!" at the top of his voice. It was answered by a distant "Halloo!" and looking in the direction from which the answer had come, Walter saw a figure appear above some bushes some four hundred yards distant. The knight at once directed his steps in that direction, and Walter crept cautiously after him.

"A pest upon these swamps and quagmires," the knight said angrily as he neared the other. "Why didst not meet me and show me the way through, as before?"

"I thought that as you had come once you would be able to find your way hither again," the man said. "Had I thought that you would have missed it I would have come ten times as far, rather than have had my name shouted all over the country. However, there is no one to hear, did you shout thrice as loud, so no harm is done."

"I thought I saw a figure a short time since," the knight said.

The man looked round in all directions.

"I see none," he said, "and you may have been mistaken, for the light is waning fast. It were ill for any one I caught prying about here. But come in, sir knight; my hovel is not what your lordship is accustomed to, but we may as well talk there as here beneath the sky."

The two men disappeared from Walter's sight. The latter in much surprise crept forward, but until he reached the spot where he had last seen the speakers he was unable to account for their disappearance. Then he saw that the spot, although apparently a mere clump of bushes no higher than the surrounding country, was really an elevated hummock of ground. Any one might have passed close to the bushes without suspecting that aught lay among them. In the center, however, the ground had been cut away, and a low doorway, almost hidden by the bushes, gave access into a half-subterranean hut; the roof was formed of an old boat turned bottom upward, and this had been covered with brown turf. It was an excellent place of concealment, as searchers might have passed within a foot of the bushes without suspecting that aught lay concealed within them.

"A clever hiding-place," Walter thought to himself. "No wonder the posse search these swamps in vain. This is the lowest and wettest part of the swamp, and would be but lightly searched, for none would suspect that there was a human habitation among these brown ditches and stagnant pools."

To his disappointment the lad could hear nothing of the conversation which was going on within the hut. The murmur of voices came to his ear, but no words were audible; however, he remained patiently, thinking that perhaps as they came out a word might be said which would give him a clew to the object of the mysterious interview between a knight and one who was evidently a fugitive from justice.

His patience was rewarded. In the half-hour which he waited the night had fallen, and a thick fog which was rising over the swamps rendered it difficult to discern anything at the distance of a few paces.

"You are quite sure that you can manage it?" a voice said as the two men issued from the hut.

"There is no difficulty in managing it," the other replied, "if the boat is punctual to the hour named. It will be getting dusk then, and if one boat runs into another no one need be surprised. Such accidents will happen."

"They will be here just before nightfall," the other said, "and you will know the boat by the white mantle the lady will wear. The reward will be fifty pieces of gold, of which you have received ten as earnest. You can trust me, and if the job be well done I shall take no count of the earnest-money."

"You may consider it as good as done," the other replied. "If the boat is there the matter is settled. Now I will lead you back across the swamps. I would not give much for your life if you tried to find the way alone. Who would have thought when you got me off from being hung, after that little affair at Bruges, that I should be able to make myself useful to your worship?"

"You may be sure," the knight replied, "that it was just because I foresaw that you might be useful that I opened the doors of your cell that night. It is always handy in times like these to be able to lay one's hand on a man whom you can hang if you choose to open your mouth."

"Did it not strike you, sir knight, that it might enter my mind that it would be very advisable for me to free myself from one who stands toward me in that relation?"

"Certainly it did," the knight replied; "but as I happen to be able to make it for your interest to serve me, that matter did not trouble me. I knew better than to bring money into this swamp of yours, when I might be attacked by half a dozen ruffians like yourself; and I took the precaution of informing Peter, the captain of my men-at-arms, of the spot to which I was going, bidding him, in case I came not back, to set a hue-and-cry on foot and hunt down all who might be found here, with the especial description of your worthy self."

Walter could hear no more; he had taken off his shoes and followed them at a distance, and their voices still acted as a guide to him through the swamp. But he feared to keep too close, as, although the darkness would conceal his figure, he might at any moment tread in a pool or ditch, and so betray his presence. Putting his foot each time to the ground with the greatest caution, he moved quietly after them. They spoke little more, but their heavy footsteps on the swampy ground were a sufficient guidance for him. At last these ceased suddenly. A few words were spoken, and then he heard returning steps. He drew aside a few feet and crouched down, saw a dim figure pass through the mist, and then resumed his way.

The ground was firmer now, and, replacing his shoes, he walked briskly on. As he neared the higher ground along which the road ran he heard two horsemen galloping away in the distance. He now turned his face east, and after an hour's walking he reached the armorer's.

"Why, Walter, you are late," the smith said. "The men are in bed this hour or more, and I myself can scarce keep awake. Where hast thou been, my boy?"

"I have been in the swamps and lost my way," Walter replied.

"It is a bad neighborhood, lad, and worse are the people who live there. If I had my way the whole posse should be called out, and the marshes searched from end to end, and all found there should be knocked on the head and thrown into their own ditches. There would be no fear of any honest man coming to his end thereby; but now to bed, lad. You can tell me all about it to-morrow; but we have a rare day's work before us, and the fire must be alight at daybreak."

On his way back Walter had debated with himself whether to inform his master of what had happened. He was, however, bent upon having an adventure on his own account, and it was a serious thing in those days for an apprentice lad to bring an accusation against a noble. The city would not indeed allow even an apprentice to be overridden, and although Geoffrey Ward's forge stood beyond the city walls it was yet within the liberties, the city allowing its craftsmen to open shops just outside the gates, and to enjoy the same privileges as if dwelling actually within the walls.

On the following afternoon Walter asked leave to cease work an hour earlier than usual, as he wished to go across into the city. The armorer was surprised, since this was the first time that such a thing had happened since the lad had worked for him.

"What are you up to, Walter? —some mischief, I will be bound. Go, lad; you have worked so steadily that you have well earned more than an hour's holiday should you want it."

Walter crossed the bridge, and seeking out four or five of his old companions, begged them to bring their bows and clubs and rejoin him at the stairs by London Bridge. To their laughing inquiries whether he meant to go a-shooting of fish, he told them to ask no questions until they joined him. As soon as work was over the boys gathered at the steps, where Walter had already engaged a boat. There were some mocking inquiries from the watermen standing about as to where they were going shooting. Walter answered with some light chaff, and, two of the party taking oars, they started up the river.

"Now I will tell you what we are bent on," Walter said. "From some words I overheard I believe that some of the ruffians over in the marshes are this evening going to make an attack upon a boat with a lady in it coming down the river. We will be on the spot, and can give them a reception such as they do not expect."

"Do you know who the lady is, Walter?"

"I have not the least idea. I only caught a few words, and may be wrong; still it will do no harm should I be mistaken."

The tide was running down strongly, for there had been a good deal of rain during the preceding week, and all night it had poured heavily. It was fine now, but the stream was running down thick and turbid, and it needed all the boys' efforts to force the wherry against it. They rowed by turns; all were fairly expert at the exercise, for in those days the Thames was at once the great highway and playground of London. To the wharves below the bridge ships brought the rich merchandise of Italy and the Low Countries; while from above, the grain needed for the wants of the great city was floated down in barges from the west.

Passing the Temple, the boys rowed along by the green banks and fields as far as Westminster, which at that time was almost a rival of the city, for here were the abbey and great monastery; here were the king's palace and court, and the houses of many of his nobles. Then they went along by the low shores of Millbank, keeping a sharp lookout for boats going down with the stream. It was already getting dark, for Walter had not allowed for the strength of the stream, and he was full of anxiety lest he should arrive too late.

Chapter III
A Thwarted Plot.

A boat was rowing rapidly down the stream. It had passed the village of Chelsea, and the men were doing their best to reach their destination at Westminster before nightfall. Two men were rowing; in the stern sat a lady with a girl of about eleven years old. A woman, evidently a servant, sat beside the lady, while behind, steering the boat, was an elderly retainer.

"It is getting dark," the lady said; "I would that my Cousin James had not detained us so long at Richmond, and then after all he was unable to accompany us. I like not being out on the river so late."

"No, indeed, my lady," the woman replied; "I have heard tell lately much of the doings of the river pirates. They say that boats are often picked up, stove in and broken, and that none know what had become of their occupants, and that bodies, gashed and hewn, are often found floating in the river."

"How horrible," the girl said; "your tale makes me shiver, Martha; I would you had said nothing about it till we were on land again."

"Do not be afraid, Edith," the lady said cheerfully; "we shall soon be safe at Westminster."

There were now only two or three boats to be seen on the river. They were nearing the end of their journey now, and the great pile of the abbey could be seen through the darkness. A boat with several men in it was seen rowing across the river toward the Lambeth side. It was awkwardly managed.

"Look out!" the steersman of the boat coming down stream shouted; "you will run into us if you don't mind."

An order was given in the other boat, the men strained to their oars, and in an instant the boat ran with a crash into the side of the other, cutting it down to the water's edge. For a minute there was a wild scene of confusion; the women shrieked, the watermen shouted, and, thinking that it was an accident, strove, as the boat sank from under them, to climb into that which had run them down. They were speedily undeceived. One was sunk by a heavy blow with an oar, the other was stabbed with a dagger, while the assailants struck fiercely at the old man and the women.

At this moment, however, a third boat made its appearance on the scene, its occupants uttering loud shouts. As they rowed toward the spot their approach was heralded by a shower of arrows. Two of the ruffians were struck-one fell over mortally wounded, the other sank down into the boat.

"Row, men, row," their leader shouted, "or we shall all be taken."

Again seizing their oars, the rowers started at full speed toward the Lambeth shore. The arrows of their pursuers still fell among them, two more of their number being wounded before they reached the opposite shore. The pursuit was not continued, the new-comers ceasing to row at the spot where the catastrophe had taken place. Walter stood up in the boat and looked round. A floating oar, a stretcher, and a sheep-skin which had served as a cushion alone floated.

Suddenly there was a choking cry heard a few yards down stream, and Walter leaped into the river. A few strokes took him to the side of the girl, and he found, on throwing his arm around her, that she was still clasped in her mother's arms. Seizing them both, Walter shouted to his comrades. They had already turned the boat's head and in a minute were alongside.

It was a difficult task to get the mother and child on board, as the girl refused to loose her hold. It was, however, accomplished, and the child sat still and quiet by Walter's side, while his comrades endeavored to stanch the blood which was flowing from a severe wound in her mother's head. When they had bound it up they rubbed her hands, and by the time they had reached the steps at Westminster the lady opened her eyes. For a moment she looked bewildered, and then, on glancing round, she gave a low cry of delight at seeing her child sitting by Walter's side.

On reaching the steps the boys handed her over to the care of the watermen there, who soon procured a litter and carried her, she being still too weak to walk, to the dwelling of the Earl of Talbot, where she said she was expected. The apprentices rowed back to London Bridge, elated at the success of their enterprise, but regretting much that they had arrived too late to hinder the outrage, or to prevent the escape of its perpetrators.

Walter on his return home related the whole circumstance to his master.

"I would you had told me, Walter," the latter said, "since we might have taken precautions which would have prevented this foul deed from taking place. However, I can understand your wanting to accomplish the adventure without my aid; but we must think now what had best be said and done. As the lady belongs to the court, there is sure to be a fine pother about the matter, and you and all who were there will be examined touching your share of the adventure, and how you came to be upon the spot. The others will, of course, say that they were there under your direction; and we had best think how much of your story you had better tell."

"Why should I not tell it all?" Walter asked indignantly.

"You should never tell a lie, Walter; but in days like these it is safer sometimes not to tell more than is necessary. It is a good rule in life, my boy, to make no more enemies than may be needful. This knight, who is doubtless a great villain, has maybe powerful friends, and it is as well, if it can be avoided, that you should not embroil yourself with these. Many a man has been knocked on the head or stabbed on a dark night, because he could not keep his tongue from wagging. 'Least said, the sooner mended,' is a good proverb; but I will think it over to-night, and tell you in the morning."

When they met again in the workshop the armorer said: "Clean yourself up after breakfast, Walter, and put on your best clothes. I will go with you before the mayor, and then you shall tell him your story. There is sure to be a stir about it before the day is done. As we walk thither we can settle how much of your story it is good to tell."

On their way over the bridge Geoffrey told Walter that he thought he had better tell the whole story exactly as it had occurred, concealing only the fact that he had recognized the knight's face. "You had best, too," he said, "mention naught about the white cloak. If we can catch the man of the hut in the swamp, likely enough the rack will wring from him the name of his employer, and in that case, if you are brought up as a witness against him you will of course say that you recognize his face; but 'tis better that the accusation should not come from you. No great weight would be given to the word of a 'prentice boy as against that of a noble. It is as bad for earthen pots to knock against brass ones as it is for a yeoman in a leathern jerkin to stand up against a knight in full armor."

"But unless the lady knows her enemy she may fall again into his snares."

"I have thought of that," Geoffrey said, "and we will take measures to prevent it."

"But how can we prevent it?" Walter asked, surprised.

"We must find out who this knight may be, which should, methinks, not be difficult. Then we will send to him a message that his share in this night's work is known to several, and that if any harm should ever again be attempted against the lady or her daughter, he shall be denounced before King Edward himself as the author of the wrong. I trust, however, that we may capture the man of the swamp, and that the truth may be wrung from him."

By this time they had arrived at the guildhall, and making their way into the court, Geoffrey demanded private speech with the lord mayor.

"Can you not say in open court what is your business?" the lord mayor asked.

"I fear that if I did it would defeat the ends of justice."

Retiring with the chief magistrate into an inner room, Geoffrey desired Walter to tell his story. This he did, ending by saying that he regretted much that he had not at once told his master what he had heard; but that, although he deemed evil was intended, he did not know that murder was meant, and thought it but concerned the carrying off of some damsel, and that this he had intended, by the aid of his comrades, to prevent.

"You have done well, Master Walter, since that be your name," the magistrate said. "That you might have done better is true, for had you acted otherwise you might have prevented murder from being done. Still one cannot expect old heads upon young shoulders. Give me the names of those who were with you, for I shall doubtless receive a message from Westminster this morning to know if I have heard aught of the affair. In the mean time we must take steps to secure these pirates of the marsh. The ground is across the river, and lies out of my jurisdiction."

"It is for that reason," Geoffrey said, "that I wished that the story should be told to you privately, since the men concerned might well have sent a friend to the court to hear if aught was said which might endanger them."

"I will give you a letter to a magistrate of Surrey, and he will dispatch some constables under your guidance to catch these rascals. I fear there have been many murders performed by them lately besides that in question, and you will be doing a good service to the citizens by aiding in the capture of these men."

"I will go willingly," the smith assented.

"I will at once send off a messenger on horseback," the lord mayor said, after a moment's thought. "It will be quicker. I will tell the justice that if he will come to the meeting of the roads on Kensington Common, at seven this evening, you will be there with your apprentice to act as a guide."

"I will," the armorer said, "and will bring with me two or three of my men who are used to hard blows, for, to tell you the truth, I have no great belief in the valor of constables, and we may meet with a stout resistance."

"So be it," the lord mayor said; "and luck be with you, for these men are the scourges of the river."

That evening the armorer shut up his shop sooner than usual, and accompanied by Walter and four of his workmen, all carrying stout oaken cudgels, with hand-axes in their girdles, started along the lonely road to Kensington. Half an hour after their arrival the magistrate, with ten men, rode up. He was well pleased at the sight of the reënforcement which awaited him, for the river pirates might be expected to make a desperate resistance. Geoffrey advised a halt for a time until it should be well-nigh dark, as the marauders might have spies set to give notice should strangers enter the marsh.

They started before it was quite dark, as Walter doubted whether he should be able to lead them straight to the hut after the night had completely fallen. He felt, however, tolerably sure of his locality, for he had noticed that two trees grew on the edge of the swamp just at the spot where he had left it. He had no difficulty in finding these, and at once led the way. The horses of the magistrate and his followers were left in charge of three of their number.

"You are sure you are going right?" the magistrate said to Walter. "The marsh seems to stretch everywhere, and we might well fall into a quagmire, which would swallow us all up."

"I am sure of my way," Walter answered; "see, yonder clump of bushes, which you can just observe above the marsh, a quarter of a mile away, is the spot where the house of their leader is situated."

With strict injunctions that not a word was to be spoken until the bush was surrounded, and that all were to step noiselessly and with caution, the party moved forward. It was now nearly dark, and as they approached the hut, sounds of laughter and revelry were heard.

"They are celebrating their success in a carouse," Geoffrey said. "We shall catch them nicely in a trap."

When they came close a man who was sitting just at the low mouth of the hut suddenly sprang to his feet and shouted, "Who goes there?" He had apparently been placed as sentry, but had joined in the potations going on inside, and had forgotten to look round from time to time to see that none were approaching.

At his challenge the whole party rushed forward, and as they reached the hut the men from within came scrambling out, sword in hand. For two or three minutes there was a sharp fight, and had the constables been alone they would have been defeated, for they were outnumbered and the pirates were desperate.

The heavy clubs of the armorers decided the fight. One or two of the band alone succeeded in breaking through, the rest were knocked down and bound; not, however, until several severe wounds had been inflicted on their assailants.

When the fray was over, it was found that nine prisoners had been captured. Some of these were stunned by the blows which the smiths had dealt them, and two or three were badly wounded; all were more or less injured in the struggle. When they recovered their senses they were made to get on their feet, and with their hands tied securely behind them, were marched between a double line of their captors off the marsh.

"Thanks for your services," the justice said when they had gained the place where they had left their horses. "Nine of my men shall tie each one of these rascals to their stirrups by halters round their necks, and we will give them a smart run into Richmond, where we will lodge them in the jail. Tomorrow is Sunday; on Monday they will be brought before me, and I shall want the evidence of Master Walter Fletcher and of those who were in the boat with him as to what took place on the river. Methinks the evidence on that score, and the resistance which they offered us this evening, will be sufficient to put a halter round their necks; but from what I have heard by the letter which the lord mayor sent me, there are others higher in rank concerned in the affair; doubtless we shall find means to make these ruffians speak."

Accordingly, at the justice's orders, halters were placed round the necks of the prisoners, the other ends being attached to the saddles, and the party set off at a pace which taxed to the utmost the strength of the wounded men. Geoffrey and his party returned in high spirits to Southwark.

On the Monday Walter went over to Richmond, accompanied by the armorers and by the lads who had been in the boat with him. The nine ruffians, strongly guarded, were brought up in the justice room. Walter first gave his evidence, and related how he had overheard a portion of the conversation which led him to believe that an attack would be made upon the boat coming down the river.

"Can you identify either of the prisoners as being the man whom you saw at the door of the hut?"

"No," Walter said. "When I first saw him I was too far off to make out his face. When he left the hut it was dark."

"Should you know the other man, the one who was addressed as sir knight, if you saw him again?"

"I should," Walter replied. He then gave an account of the attack upon the boat, but said that in the suddenness of the affair and the growing darkness he noticed none of the figures distinctly enough to recognize them again. Two or three of the other apprentices gave similar testimony as to the attack.

A gentleman then presented himself, and gave his name as Sir William de Hertford. He said that he had come at the request of the Lady Alice Vernon, who was still suffering from the effects of the wound and immersion. She had requested him to say that at some future occasion she would appear to testify, but that in the confusion and suddenness of the attack she had noticed no faces in the boat which assailed them, and could identify none concerned in the affair.

The justice who had headed the attack on the hut then gave his evidence as to that affair, the armorer also relating the incidents of the conflict.

"The prisoners will be committed for trial," the justice said. "At present there is no actual proof that any of them were concerned in this murderous outrage beyond the fact that they were taken in the place where it was planned. The suspicion is strong that some at least were engaged in it. Upon the persons of all of them were valuable daggers, chains, and other ornaments, which could not have been come by honestly, and I doubt not that they form part of the gang which has so long been a terror to peaceful travelers alike by the road and river, and it may be that some who have been robbed will be able to identify the articles taken upon them. They are committed for trial: firstly, as having been concerned in the attack upon Dame Alice Vernon; secondly, as being notorious ill-livers and robbers; thirdly, as having resisted lawful arrest by the king's officers. The greatest criminal in the affair is not at present before me, but it may be that from such information as Dame Vernon may be able to furnish, and from such confessions as justice will be able to wring from the prisoners, he will at the trial stand beside his fellows."

Walter returned to town with his companions. On reaching the armorer's they found a retainer of the Earl of Talbot awaiting them, with the message that the Lady Alice Vernon wished the attendance of Walter Fletcher, whose name she had learned from the lord mayor as that of the lad to whom she and her daughter owed their lives, at noon on the following day, at the residence of the Earl of Talbot.

"That is the worst of an adventure," Walter said crossly, after the retainer had departed. "One can't have a bit of excitement without being sent for, and thanked, and stared at. I would rather fight the best swordsman in the city than have to go down to the mansion of Earl Talbot with my cap in my hand."

Geoffrey laughed. "You must indeed have your cap in your hand, Walter; but you need not bear yourself in that spirit. The 'prentice of a London citizen may have just as much honest pride and independence as the proudest earl at Westminster; but carry not independence too far. Remember that if you yourself had received a great service you would be hurt if the donor refused to receive your thanks; and it would be churlish indeed were you to put on sullen looks, or to refuse to accept any present which the lady whose life you have saved may make you. It is strange, indeed, that it should be Dame Vernon, whose husband, Sir Jasper Vernon, received the fiefs of Westerham and Hyde."

"Why should it be curious that it is she?" Walter asked.

"Oh!" Geoffrey said rather confusedly. "I was not thinking-that is —I mean that it is curious because Bertha Fletcher was for years a dependent on the family of Sir Roland Somers, who was killed in the troubles when the king took the reins of government in his hands, and his lands, being forfeit, were given to Sir Jasper Vernon, who aided the king in that affair."

"I wish you would tell me about that," Walter said. "How was it that there was any trouble as to King Edward having kingly authority?"

"It happened in this way," Geoffrey said. "King Edward II., his father, was a weak prince, governed wholly by favorites and unable to hold in check the turbulent barons. His queen, Isabella of France, sister of the French king, a haughty and ambitious woman, determined to snatch the reins of power from the indolent hands of her husband, and after a visit to her brother she returned with an army from Hainault in order to dethrone him. She was accompanied by her eldest son, and after a short struggle the king was dethroned. He had but few friends, and men thought that under the young Edward, who had already given promise of virtue and wisdom, some order might be introduced into the realm. He was crowned Edward III., thus, at the early age of fifteen, usurping the throne of his father. The real power, however, remained with Isabella, who was president of the council of regency, and who, in her turn, was governed by her favorite Mortimer. England soon found that the change which had been made was far from beneficial. The government was by turns weak and oppressive. The employment of foreign troops was regarded with the greatest hostility by the people, and the insolence of Mortimer alienated the great barons. Finally, the murder of the dethroned king excited throughout the kingdom a feeling of horror and loathing against the queen.

"All this feeling, however, was confined to her, Edward, who was but a puppet in her hands, being regarded with affection and pity. Soon after his succession the young king was married to our queen, Philippa of Hainault, who is as good as she is beautiful, and who is loved from one end of the kingdom to the other. I can tell you, the city was a sight to see when she entered with the king. Such pageants and rejoicing were never known. They were so young, he not yet sixteen and she but fourteen, and yet to bear on their shoulders the weight of the state. A braver-looking lad and a fairer girl mine eyes never looked on. It was soon after this that the events arose which led to the war with France, but this is too long a tale for me to tell you now. The Prince of Wales was born on the 15th of June, 1330, two years after the royal marriage.

"So far the king had acquiesced quietly in the authority of his mother, but he now paid a visit to France, and doubtless the barons around him there took advantage of his absence from her tutelage to shake her influence over his mind; and at the same time a rising took place at home against her authority. This was suppressed, and the Earl of Kent, the king's uncle, was arrested and executed by Isabella. This act of severity against his uncle no doubt hastened the prince's determination to shake off the authority of his haughty mother and to assume the reins of government himself. The matter, however, was not easy to accomplish. Mortimer having the whole of the royal revenue at his disposal, had attached to himself by ties of interest a large number of barons, and had in his pay nearly two hundred knights and a large body of men-at-arms. Thus it was no easy matter to arrest him. It was determined that the deed should be done at the meeting of the parliament at Nottingham. Here Mortimer appeared with Isabella in royal pomp. They took up their abode at the castle, while the king and other members of the royal family were obliged to content themselves with an inferior place of residence.

"The gates of the castle were locked at sunset, and the keys brought by the constable, Sir William Eland, and handed to the queen herself. This knight was a loyal and gallant gentleman, and regarded Mortimer with no affection, and when he received the king's commands to assist the barons charged to arrest him he at once agreed to do so. He was aware of the existence of a subterranean communication leading from the interior of the castle to the outer country, and by this, on the night of the 19th of October, 1330, he led nine resolute knights-the Lords Montague, Suffolk, Stafford, Molins, and Clinton, with three brothers of the name of Bohun, and Sir John Nevil-into the heart of the castle. Mortimer was found surrounded by a number of his friends. On the sudden entry of the knights known to be hostile to Mortimer his friends drew their swords, and a short but desperate fight took place. Many were wounded, and Sir Hugh Turpleton and Richard Monmouth were slain. Mortimer was carried to London, and was tried and condemned by parliament, and executed for felony and treason. Several of his followers were executed, and others were attacked in their strongholds and killed; among these was Sir Roland Somers.

"Queen Isabella was confined in Castle Risings, where she still remains a prisoner. Such, Walter, were the troubles which occurred when King Edward first took up the reins of power in this realm; and now, let's to supper, for I can tell you that my walk to Kingston has given me a marvelous appetite. We have three or four hours' work yet before we go to bed, for that Milan harness was promised for the morrow, and the repairs are too delicate for me to intrust it to the men. It is good to assist the law, but this work of attending as a witness makes a grievous break in the time of a busy man. It is a pity, Walter, that your mind is so set on soldiering, for you would have made a marvelous good craftsman. However, I reckon that after you have seen a few years of fighting in France, and have got some of your wild blood let out, you will be glad enough to settle down here with me; as you know, our profits are good and work plentiful; and did I choose I might hold mine head higher than I do among the citizens; and you, if you join me, may well aspire to a place in the common council, ay, and even to an alderman's gown, in which case I may yet be addressing you as the very worshipful my lord mayor."

"Pooh!" Walter laughed; "a fig for your lord mayors! I would a thousand times rather be a simple squire in the following of our young prince."

Chapter IV
A Knight's Chain

The following morning Walter put on the sober russet dress which he wore on Sundays and holidays, for gay colors were not allowed to the apprentices, and set out for Westminster. Although he endeavored to assume an air of carelessness and ease as he approached the dwelling of Earl Talbot, he was very far from feeling comfortable, and wished in his heart that his master had accompanied him on his errand. Half a dozen men-at-arms were standing on the steps of the mansion, who looked with haughty surprise at the young apprentice.

"Dame Alice Vernon has sent to express her desire to have speech with me," he said quietly, "and I would fain know if she can receive me."

"Here, Dikon," one of the men cried to another within the hall. "This is the lad you were sent to fetch yesterday. I wondered much who the city apprentice was who, with such an assured air, marched up to the door; but if what thou sayest be true, that he saved the life of Dame Vernon and her little daughter, he must be a brave lad, and would be more in place among men and soldiers than in serving wares behind the counter of a fat city tradesman."

"I serve behind no counter," Walter said indignantly. "I am an armorer, and mayhap can use arms as well as make them."

There was a laugh among the men at the boy's sturdy self-assertion, and then the man named Dikon said:

"Come along, lad. I will take you to Dame Vernon at once. She is expecting you; and, my faith, it would not be safe to leave you standing here long, for I see you would shortly be engaged in splitting the weasands of my comrades."

There was another roar of laughter from the men, and Walter, somewhat abashed, followed his conductor into the house. Leading him through the hall and along several corridors, whose spaciousness and splendor quite overpowered the young apprentice, he handed him over to a waiting-woman, who ushered him into an apartment where Dame Vernon was reclining on a couch. Her little daughter was sitting upon a low stool beside her, and upon seeing Walter she leaped to her feet, clapping her hands.

"Oh! mother, this is the boy that rescued us out of the river."

The lady looked with some surprise at the lad. She had but a faint remembrance of the events which occurred between the time when she received a blow from the sword of one of her assailants and that when she found herself on a couch in the abode of her kinsman; and when she had been told that she had been saved by a city apprentice, she had pictured to herself a lad of a very different kind to him who now stood before her.

Walter was now nearly sixteen years old. His frame was very powerful and firmly knit. His dark-brown hair was cut short, but, being somewhat longer than was ordinary with the apprentices, fell with a slight wave back on his forehead. His bearing was respectful, and at the same time independent. There was none of that confusion which might be expected on the part of a lad from the city in the presence of a lady of rank. His dark, heavy eyebrows, resolute mouth, and square chin gave an expression of sternness to his face, which was belied by the merry expression of his eyes and the bright smile when he was spoken to.

"I have to thank you, young sir," she said, holding out her hand, which Walter, after the custom of the time, raised to his lips, bending upon one knee as he did so, "for the lives of myself and my daughter, which would surely have been lost had you not jumped over to save us."

"I am glad that I arrived in time to be of aid," Walter said frankly; "but indeed I am rather to be blamed than praised, for had I, when I heard the plotting against the safety of the boat, told my master of it, as I should have done, instead of taking the adventure upon mine own shoulders, doubtless a boat would have been sent up in time to prevent the attack from taking place. Therefore, instead of being praised for having arrived a little too late, I should be rated for not having come there in time."

Dame Vernon smiled.

"Although you may continue to insist that you are to blame, this does not alter the fact that you have saved our lives. Is there any way in which I can be useful to you? Are you discontented with your state? for, in truth, you look as if Nature had intended you for a gallant soldier rather than a city craftsman. Earl Talbot, who is my uncle, would, I am sure, receive you into his following should you so choose it, and I would gladly pay for the canceling of your indentures."

"I thank you, indeed, lady, for your kind offices," Walter said earnestly; "for the present I am well content to remain at my craft, which is that of an armorer, until, at any rate, I have gained such manly strength and vigor as would fit me for a man-at-arms, and my good master, Geoffrey Ward, will, without payment received, let me go when I ask that grace of him."

"Edith, go and look from the window at the boats passing along the river; and now," she went on as the girl had obeyed her orders, "I would fain ask you more about the interview you overheard in the marshes. Sir William de Hertford told me of the evidence that you had given before the justice. It is passing strange that he who incited the other to the deed should have been by him termed 'Sir Knight.' Maybe it was merely a nickname among his fellows."

"Before I speak, lady," Walter said quietly, "I would fain know whether you wish to be assured of the truth. Sometimes, they say, it is wiser to remain in ignorance; at other times forewarned is forearmed. Frankly, I did not tell all I know before the court, deeming that peradventure you might wish to see me, and that I could then tell the whole to your private ear, should you wish to know it, and you could then bid me either keep silence or proclaim all I knew when the trial of these evil-doers comes on."

"You seem to me to be wise beyond your years, young sir," the lady said.

"The wisdom is not mine, lady, but my master's. I took counsel with him, and acted as he advised me."

"I would fain know all," the lady said. "I have already strange suspicions of one from whom assuredly I looked not for such evil designs. It will grieve me to be convinced that the suspicions are well founded; but it will be better to know the truth than to remain in a state of doubt."

"The person, then, was a knight, for I had seen him before when he came in knightly harness into my master's shop to have two rivets put into his hauberk. I liked not his face then, and should have remembered it anywhere. I knew him at once when I saw him. He was a dark-faced knight, handsome, and yet with features which reminded me of a hawk."

Dame Vernon gave a little exclamation, which assured the lad that she recognized the description.

"You may partly know, lady, whether it is he whom you suppose, for he said that he would detain your boat so that it should not come along until dark, and, moreover, he told them that they would know the boat since you would be wrapped in a white mantle."

The lady sat for some time with her face hidden in her hands.

"It is as I feared," she said at last, "and it grieves me to the heart to think that one who, although not so nearly related in blood, I regarded as a brother, should have betrayed me to death. My mind is troubled indeed, and I know not what course I shall take, whether to reveal this dreadful secret or to conceal it."

"I may say, madam," Walter said earnestly, "that should you wish the matter to remain a secret, you may rely upon it that I will tell no more at the trial than I revealed yesterday; but I would remind you that there is a danger that the leader of yon ruffians, who is probably alone acquainted with the name of his employer, may, under the influence of the torture, reveal it."

"That fear is for the present past, since a messenger arrived from Kingston but a few minutes since, saying that yester even, under the threat of torture, the prisoners had pointed out the one among their number who was their chief. This morning, however, it was found that the warder who had charge of them had been bribed; he was missing from his post, and the door of the cell wherein the principal villain had been immured, apart from the others, was opened, and he had escaped."

"Then," Walter said, "it is now open to you to speak or be silent as you will. You will pardon my forwardness if I say that my master, in talking the matter over with me, suggested that this evil knight might be scared from attempting any future enterprise against you were he informed that it was known to several persons that he was the author of this outrage, and that if any further attempts were at any time made against you, the proofs of his crime would be laid before the king."

"Thanks, good lad," the lady said, "for your suggestion. Should I decide to keep the matter secret, I will myself send him a message to that effect, in such guise that he would not know whence it comes. And now, I would fain reward you for what you have done for us; and," she went on, seeing a flush suddenly mount upon the lad's face as he made a half-step backward, "before I saw you, had thought of offering you a purse of gold, which, although it would but poorly reward your services, would yet have proved useful to you when the time came for you to start as a craftsman on your own account; but now that I have seen you, I feel that although there are few who think themselves demeaned by accepting gifts of money in reward for services, you would rather my gratitude took some other form. It can only do that of offering you such good services that I can render with Earl Talbot, should you ever choose the profession of arms; and in the mean time, as a memento of the lives you have saved, you will, I am sure, not refuse this chain," and she took a very handsome one of gold from her neck, "the more so since it was the gift of her majesty, our gracious queen, to myself. She will, I am sure, acquit me of parting with her gift when I tell her that I transferred it to one who had saved the lives of myself and my daughter, and who was too proud to accept other acknowledgment."

Coloring deeply, and with tears in his eyes at the kindness and thoughtful consideration of the lady, Walter knelt on one knee before her, and she placed round his neck the long gold chain which she had been wearing.

"It is a knight's chain," the lady said, smiling, "and was part of the spoil gained by King Edward from the French. Maybe," she added kindly, "it will be worn by a knight again. Stranger things have happened, you know."

Walter flushed again with pleasure.

"Maybe, lady," he said modestly, "even apprentices have their dreams, and men-at-arms may always hope, by deeds of valor, to attain a knight's spurs even though they may not be of noble blood or have served as page and squire to a baron; but whether as a 'prentice or soldier, I hope I shall never do discredit to your gift."

"Edith, come here," Dame Vernon said, "I have done talking now. And what are you going to give this brave knight of ours who saved us from drowning?"

The girl looked thoughtfully at Walter. "I don't think you would care for presents," she said; "and you look as if a sword or a horse would suit you better than a girl's gift. And yet I should like to give you something, such as ladies give their knights who have done brave deeds for them. It must be something quite my own, and you must take it as a keepsake. What shall it be, mamma?"

"Give him the bracelet which your cousin gave you last week," her mother said; "I would rather that you did not keep it, and I know you are not very fond of him."

"I can't bear him," the girl said earnestly, "and I wish he would not kiss me; he always looks as if he were going to bite, and I will gladly give his bracelet to this brave boy."

"Very well, Edith, fetch the bracelet from that coffer in the corner."

The girl went to the coffer and brought out the little bracelet; then she approached Walter.

"You must go down on your knee," she said; "true knights always do that to receive their lady's gifts. Now hold out your hand. There," she went on in a pretty imperious way, "take this gage as a reward of your valor, and act ever as a true knight in the service of your lady."

"Take this gage as a reward of your valor." —Page 62

Bending down she dropped a kiss upon Walter's glowing cheek, and then, half-frightened at her own temerity, ran back to her mother's side.

"And now," Dame Vernon went on, "will you thank your five comrades for their service in the matter, and give them each two gold pieces to spend as they will?"

"He is a noble lad," Dame Vernon had said to herself when Walter had taken his leave. "Would he had been the son of one of the nobles of the court! It might have been then, if he had distinguished himself in war, as he would surely do, that the king might have assigned Edith to him. As her lord and guardian he is certain to give her hand as a reward for valor in the field, and it may well be to a man with whom she would be less happy than with this 'prentice lad; but there, I need not be troubling myself about a matter which is five or six years distant yet. Still, the thought that Edith is a ward of the crown, and that her hand must go where the king wills, often troubles me. However, I have a good friend in the queen, who will, I know, exert what influence she has in getting me a good husband for my child. But even for myself I have some fears, since the king hinted, when last he saw me, that it was time I looked out for another mate, for that the vassals of Westerham and Hyde needed a lord to lead them in the field. However, I hope that my answer that they were always at his service under the leading of my Cousin James will suffice for him. Now, what am I to do in that matter? Who would have thought that he so coveted my lands that he would have slain me and Edith to possess himself of them? His own lands are thrice as broad as mine, though men say that he has dipped deeply into them and owes much money to the Jews. He is powerful and has many friends, and although Earl Talbot would stand by me, yet the unsupported word of an apprentice boy were but poor evidence on which to charge a powerful baron of such a crime as this. It were best, methinks, to say naught about it, but to bury the thought in my own heart.

Nevertheless, I will not fail to take the precaution which the lad advised, and to let Sir James know that there are some who have knowledge of his handiwork. I hear he crosses the seas to-morrow to join the army, and it may be long ere he return. I shall have plenty of time to consider how I had best shape my conduct toward him on his return; but assuredly he shall never be friendly with me again or frighten Edith with his kisses."

"Well, Walter, has it been such a dreadful business as you expected?" the armorer asked the lad when he reëntered the shop. "The great folks have not eaten you, at any rate."

"It has not been dreadful," Walter replied with a smile, "though I own that it was not pleasant when I first arrived at the great mansion; but the lady put me quite at my ease, and she talked to me for some time, and finally she bestowed on me this chain, which our lady, the queen, had herself given her."

"It is a knight's chain and a heavy one," Geoffrey said, examining it, "of Genoese work, I reckon, and worth a large sum. It will buy you harness when you go to the wars."

"I would rather fight in the thickest *mêlée* in a cloth doublet," Walter said indignantly, "than part with a single link of it."

"I did but jest, Walter," Geoffrey said, laughing; "but as you will not sell it, and you cannot wear it, you had best give it me to put aside in my strong coffer until you get of knightly rank."

"Lady Vernon said," the lad replied, "that she hoped one day it might again belong to a knight; and if I live," he added firmly, "it shall."

"Oh! she has been putting these ideas into your head; nice notions truly for a London apprentice! I shall be laying a complaint before the lord mayor against Dame Vernon, for unsettling the mind of my apprentice and setting him above his work. And the little lady, what said she? Did she give you her colors and bid you wear them at a tourney?"

Walter colored hotly.

"Ah! I have touched you," laughed the armorer; "come now, out with the truth. My lad," he added more gravely, "there is no shame in it; you know that I have always encouraged your wishes to be a soldier, and have done my best to render you as good a one as any who draws sword 'neath the king's banner, and assuredly I would not have taken all these pains with you did I think that you were always to wear an iron cap and trail a pike. I too, lad, hope some day to see you a valiant knight, and have reasons that you wot not of for my belief that it will be so. No man rises to rank and fame any the less quickly because he thinks that bright eyes will grow brighter at his success."

"But, Geoffrey, you are talking surely at random. The Lady Edith Vernon is but a child; a very beautiful child," he added reverently, "and such that when she grows up the bravest knight in England might be proud to win. What folly for me, the son of a city bowyer, and as yet but an apprentice, to raise mine eyes so high!"

"The higher one looks the higher one goes," the armorer said sententiously. "You aspire some day to become a knight, you may well aspire also to win the hand of Mistress Edith Vernon. She is five years younger than yourself, and you will be twenty-two when she is seventeen. You have time to make your way yet, and I tell you, though why it matters not, that I would rather you set your heart on winning Mistress Edith Vernon than any other heiress of broad lands in merry England. You have saved her life, and so have made the first step and a long one. Be ever brave, gentle, and honorable, and, I tell you, you need not despair; and now, lad, we have already lost too much time in talking; let us to our work."

That evening Walter recalled to Geoffrey his promise to tell him the causes which had involved England in so long and bloody a war with France.

"It is a tangled skein," Geoffrey said, "and you must follow me carefully. First, with a piece of chalk I will draw upon the wall the pedigree of the royal line of France from Philip downward, and then you will see how it is that our King Edward and Philip of Valois came to be rival claimants to the throne of France.

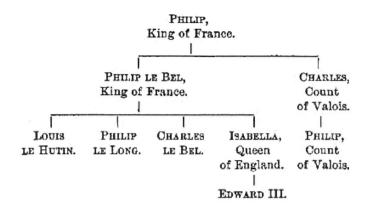

"Now, you see that our King Edward is nephew of Charles le Bel, the last King of France, while Philip of Valois is only nephew of Philip le Bel, the father of Charles. Edward is consequently in the direct line, and had Isabella been a man instead of a woman his right to the throne would be unquestionable. In France, however, there is a law, called the Salic law, which excludes females from the throne; but it is maintained by many learned in the law, that although a female is held to be incompetent to reign because from her sex she cannot lead her armies to battle, yet she no way forfeits otherwise her rights, and that her son is therefore the heir to the throne. If this contention, which is held by all English jurists, and by many in France also, be well founded, Edward is the rightful King of France. Philip of Valois contends that the Salic law not only bars a female from ascending the throne, but also destroys all her rights, and that the succession goes not to her sons, but to the next heir male; in which case, of course, Philip is rightful king. It is not for me to say which view is the right one, but certainly the great majority of those who have been consulted have decided that, according to ancient law and usage, the right lies with Edward. But in these matters 'right is not always might.' Had Isabella married a French noble instead of an English king it is probable that her son's claims to the throne would have been allowed without dispute, but her son is King of England, and the French nobles prefer being ruled by one of themselves to becoming united with England under one king.

"At the time of the death of the last king, Edward was still but a boy under the tuition of his mother, Philip was a man, and upon the spot, therefore he was able to win support by his presence and promises, and so it came that the peers of France declared Philip of Valois to be their rightful monarch. Here in England, at a parliament held at Northampton, the rights of Edward were discussed and asserted, and the Bishops of Worcester and Coventry were dispatched to Paris to protest against the validity of Philip's nomination. As, however, the country was not in a position to enforce the claim of their young king by arms, Philip became firmly seated as King of France, and having shown great energy in at once marching against and repressing the people of Flanders, who were in a state of rebellion against their count, one of the feudatories of the French crown, the nobles were well satisfied with their choice, and no question as to his right was ever henceforth raised in France. As soon as the rebellion in Flanders was crushed, Philip summoned the King of England to do homage for Aquitaine, Ponthieu, and Montreuil, fiefs held absolutely from the crown of France. Such a proceeding placed Edward and his council in a great embarrassment. In case of a refusal the whole of the possessions of the crown in France might be declared forfeited and be seized, while England was in no condition to defend them; on the other hand, the fact of doing homage to Philip of Valois would be a sort of recognition of his right to the throne he had assumed. Had Edward then held the reins of power in his hands, there can be little doubt that he would at once have refused, and would have called out the whole strength of England to enforce his claim. The influence of Isabella and Mortimer was, however, all-powerful, and it was agreed that Edward should do homage as a public act, making a private reservation in secret to his own councilors, taking exception to the right of Philip.

"Edward crossed to France and journeyed to Amiens, where Philip with a brilliant court awaited him, and on the appointed day they appeared together in the cathedral. Here Edward, under certain protestations, did homage for his French estates, leaving certain terms and questions open for the consideration of his council. For some time the matter remained in this shape; but honest men cannot but admit that King Edward did, by his action at the time, acknowledge Philip to be King of France, and that he became his vassal for his estates there; but, as has happened scores of times before, and will no doubt happen scores of times again, vassals, when they become powerful enough, throw off their allegiance to their feudal superiors, and so the time came to King Edward.

"After the death of Mortimer and the imprisonment of Isabella, the king gave rein to his taste for military sports. Tournaments were held at Dartford and other places, one in Westcheape. What a sight was that, to be sure! For three days the king, with fourteen of his knights, held the list against all comers, and in the sight of the citizens and the ladies of the court jousted with knights who came hither from all parts of Europe. I was there each day, and the sight was a grand one, though England was well-nigh thrown into mourning by an accident which took place. The gallery in which the queen and her attendants were viewing the sports had been badly erected, and in the height of the contests it gave way. The queen and her ladies were in great peril, being thrown from a considerable height, and a number of persons were severely injured. The king, who was furious at the danger to which the queen had been exposed, would have hung upon the spot the master workman whose negligence had caused the accident, but the queen went on her knees before him and begged his life of the king. The love of Edward for warlike exercises caused England to be regarded as the most chivalrous court in Europe, and the frequent tournaments aroused to the utmost the spirits of the people and prepared them for the war with France. But of the events of that war I will tell you some other night. It is time now for us to betake us to our beds."

Chapter V
The City Games.

The next evening the armorer, at Walter's request, continued his narrative.

"Soon after the tournament we began to fight again with Scotland. For some years we had had peace with that country, and under the regency a marriage was made between David, King of Scotland, son of Robert the Bruce, with the Princess Joan, sister to our king, and a four years' truce was agreed to."

"But why should we always be fighting with Scotland?" Walter asked.

"That is more than I can tell you, Walter. We were peaceful enough with them until the days of Edward I.; but he set up some claim to the throne of Scotland, the rights of which neither I nor any one else, so far as I know, have ever been able to make out. The fact was he was strong, and thought that he could conquer Scotland. The quarrels between her nobles-most of them were allied by blood with our own and held possessions in both kingdoms-gave Edward an excuse to interfere. Scotland was conquered easily enough, but it was a hard task to hold it. Sir William Wallace kept the country in a turmoil for many years, being joined by all the common people. He inflicted one heavy defeat upon us at Stirling, but receiving no support from the nobles he was defeated at Falkirk, and some years afterward was captured and executed here. His head you may see any day over London Bridge. As he fought only for his country and had ever refused allegiance to our king, it seems to me that his fate was a cruel one. Then, when all appeared quiet, Robert Bruce raised Scotland again and was crowned king. There was war for many years, but at last, at Bannockburn, he inflicted such a defeat upon us as we have never had before. After that there were skirmishes and excursions, but Edward II. was a weak prince, and it seemed that the marriage of David and the Princess Joan would bring about a permanent peace between the two countries; but it was not to be so.

"Many of the English nobles held claims by marriage or grants upon lands in Scotland. They had, of course, been driven from these when the English were turned out by Bruce. By the terms of the marriage treaty in 1328 it was agreed that they should be reinstated. It was a foolish clause, because it was plain that the King of Scotland could not take these lands again from the Scotch nobles who had possession of them, many of them being well-nigh as powerful as himself. At this time Edward Baliol, son of the great rival of Robert Bruce, was in England. He still claimed the throne of Scotland as his right. Round him gathered a number of the English nobles who claimed lands in Scotland. The king offered no hindrance to the gathering of this force, for I doubt not that he was glad to see dissension in Scotland, which might give him some such pretext for interference as that which Edward I. had seized to possess himself of that country. At first Baliol was successful and was crowned at Scone, but he was presently defeated and driven out of Scotland. The Scots now made an eruption across the frontier as a retaliation for Edward's having permitted Baliol to gather a force here for his war against Bruce. King Edward was on the point of starting for Ireland, and he at once hastened north. He defeated the Scots at Halidon Hill, captured Berwick, and placed Baliol upon the throne. Bruce fled to France, where he was supported and encouraged by the French king.

"The ill-feeling between Edward and Philip of Valois had gone on increasing ever since the former had been compelled to take the oath of allegiance to the latter, but outwardly the guise of friendship was kept up, and negotiations went on between the two courts for a marriage between the little Prince of Wales and Joanna, daughter of the French king.

"The aid which Philip gave to Bruce increased the bad feeling, and Edward retaliated for Philip's patronage of Bruce by receiving with the greatest honor and courtesy Robert of Artois, a great feudatory of France, who had been banished by King Philip. For a time, although both countries were preparing for war, peace was not broken, as Edward's hands were full in Scotland, where Baliol having bestowed immense possessions upon the English nobles who had assisted him, the country again rose in favor of Bruce. During the three years that followed King Edward was obliged several times to go to Scotland to support Baliol, who held the crown as his feudal vassal. He was always successful in the field, but directly his army recrossed the frontier the Scotch rose again. In 1330 a new crusade was preached, and in October of that year King Philip solemnly received the cross and collected an immense army nominally for the recovery of Jerusalem. Whether his intentions were honest or not I cannot say, but certainly King Edward considered that Philip's real aim in creating so great an army was to attack England. Whether this was so or not would need a wiser head than mine, Walter, to tell. Certainly Philip of Valois invited Edward to coöperate with him in the crusade. The king in reply stated his belief that the preparations were intended for war in Europe rather than in Asia; but that if the King of France would agree to conclude a firm league of amity between the two countries, to restore the castles and towns of Aquitaine, whose surrender had been frequently promised, but never carried out, and would bind himself by oath to give no assistance, direct or indirect, to Scotland, he would join him in his war for the delivery of the Holy Land.

"I must say that King Edward's demands were reasonable, for it was clear that he could not march away from England with his whole force and leave Baliol unsupported against the assaults of his Scotch enemies, aided by France. Philip was willing to accede to the first two conditions; but in regard to the third positively declined treating until David Bruce should be restored to the throne of his father. Now, had the French king openly supported Bruce from the first, none could have said that his conduct in befriending a dethroned monarch was aught but noble and generous; but he had all along answered Edward's complaints of the aid afforded by Frenchmen to the Bruce by denials that he himself supported him; and this declaration in his favor now certainly seemed to show that he had at last determined openly to throw off the veil, and that his great army was really collected against England. Robert of Artois craftily seized a moment when the king's indignation against Philip was at the highest. At a great banquet held by King Edward, at which all his warlike nobles were present, Robert entered, preceded by two noble maidens carrying a heron, which, as you know, Walter, is considered the most cowardly of birds. Then in loud tones he called upon the knights present each to swear on the bird to perform some deed of chivalrous daring. First he presented it to King Edward himself, giving him to understand that he regarded him but as little braver than the heron for resigning without a blow the fair heritage of France.

"The moment was well chosen, for Edward was smarting under the answer he had just received from Philip. He at once rose and took an oath to enter France in arms; to wait there a month in order to give Philip time to offer him battle, and to accept the combat, even should the French outnumber him ten to one. Every knight present followed the example of the king, and so the war with France, which had been for years a mere question of time, was at last suddenly decided upon. You yourself, Walter, can remember the preparations which were made throughout England: men were enrolled and arms prepared. We armorers were busy night and day, and every man felt that his own honor, as well as that of the country, was concerned in winning for King Edward the heritage of which he had been unlawfully robbed by the King of France.

"On the 17th of March, 1337, at the parliament at Westminster, the king created the little prince, then seven years of age, Duke of Cornwall; and the prince immediately, in exercise of his new dignity, bestowed upon twenty of the most distinguished aspirants the honor of knighthood. Immense supplies were voted by the parliaments held at Nottingham, Westminster, and Northampton. Half the wool shorn in the summer following was granted to the king, with a variety of other taxes, customs, and duties. The revenues of all the foreign priories in England, a hundred and ten in number, were appropriated to the crown. Provisions of bacon, wheat, and oats were granted, and the king pawned his own jewels, and even the crown itself, to hire soldiers and purchase him allies on the Continent. So great did the scarcity of money become in the country that all goods fell to less than half their value. Thus a vast army was raised, and with this King Edward prepared to try his strength with France.

"Philip on his part was making great preparations. While Edward had purchased the assistance of many of the German nobles Philip raised large armaments in the maritime states of Italy. Spain also contributed a number of naval adventurers, and squadrons were fitted out by his vassals on the sea-coasts of Normandy, Brittany, and Picardy. King Edward had crossed over into Belgium, and after vast delays in consequence of the slowness of the German allies, at last prepared to enter France at the end of September, 1339. Such, my lad, is the story, as far as I know, of the beginning of that war with France which is now raging, and whose events you know as well as I do, seeing that they are all of late occurrence. So far, although the English have had the best of it, and have sorely mauled the French both in the north and south, we have not gained any such advantages as would lead to a belief that there is any likelihood of an early termination, or that King Edward will succeed for a long time in winning back his inheritance of the throne of France.

"There is no doubt that the war weighs heavily upon the people at large. The taxes are doubled, and the drain of men is heavy. We armorers, of course, have a busy time of it, and all trades which have to do with the furnishing of an army flourish exceedingly. Moreover, men of metal and valor have an opportunity of showing what they are composed of, and England rings with the tales of martial deeds. There are some, Walter, who think that peace is the greatest of blessings, and in some ways, lad, they are no doubt right; but there are many compensations in war. It brings out the noble qualities; it raises men to think that valor and fortitude and endurance and honor are qualities which are something above the mere huckstering desire for getting money, and for ignoble ease and comfort. Some day it may be that the world will change, and that war may become a thing of the past; but to my mind, boy, I doubt whether men will be any happier or better for it. The priests, no doubt, would tell you otherwise; but then you see I am an armorer, and so perhaps am hardly a fair judge on the matter, seeing that without wars my craft would come to an end."

Walter remained in thought for some time. "It seems to me, Master Geoffrey, that while wars may suit strong and courageous men, women would rejoice were such things to be at an end."

"Women suffer most from wars, no doubt," Geoffrey said, "and yet do you mark that they are more stirred by deeds of valor and chivalry than are we men; that they are ever ready to bestow their love upon those who have won honor and glory in war, even although the next battle may leave them widows. This has been always somewhat of a marvel to me; but I suppose that it is human nature, and that admiration for deeds of valor and bravery is ingrained in the heart of man, and will continue until such times come that the desire for wealth, which is ever on the increase, has so seized all men that they will look with distaste upon everything which can interfere with the making of money, and will regard the man who amasses gold by trading as a higher type than he who does valiant deeds in battle."

"Surely that can never be," Walter said indignantly.

"There is no saying," the armorer answered; "at any rate, Walter, it will matter little to you or to me, for many generations must pass before such a state of things can come about."

Two days later Walter, who had been across into the city, returned in a state of excitement.

"What do you think, Geoffrey? The king, with the Prince of Wales and all his court, are coming to the games next month. They say that the king himself will adjudge the prizes, and there is to be a grand assault-at-arms between ten of the 'prentices with a captain, and an equal number of sons of nobles and knights."

"That will be rare," Geoffrey Ward exclaimed; "but there will be some broken limbs, and maybe worse. These assaults-at-arms seldom end without two or three being killed. However, you youngsters will not hit as hard as trained knights; and if the armor be good, no great damage should be done."

"Do you think that I shall be one of the ten?" Walter asked anxiously.

"Just as if you did not know you would," Geoffrey replied, laughing. "Did you not win the prize for sword-play last year? and twelve months have added much to the strength of your arm, to say nothing of your skill with weapons. If you win this year again-and it will be strange if you do not-you are like enough to be chosen captain. You will have tough fighting, I can tell you, for all these young aspirants to knighthood will do their best to show themselves off before the king and queen. The fight is not to take place on horseback, I hope; for if so, it will be settled as soon as it begins."

"No, it is to be on foot; and the king himself is to give orders as to the fighting."

"You had best get out that helmet and coat of mail of yours," Geoffrey said. "I warrant me that there will be none of finer make or truer metal in the tourney, seeing that I made them specially for you. They are light, and yet strong enough to withstand a blow from the strongest arm. I tried them hard, and will warrant them proof, but you had best see to the rivets and fastenings. They had a rough handling last year, and you have not worn them since. There are some other pieces that I must put in hand at once, seeing that in such a *mêlée* you must be covered from head to foot."

For the next week nothing was talked of in London but the approaching sports, and the workmen were already engaged in the erection of the lists and pavilions in the fields between the walls and Westminster. It was reported that the king would add valuable prizes to those given to the winners by the city, that there would be jousting on horseback by the sons of the court nobles, and that the young Prince of Wales would himself ride.

The king had once before taken part in the city sports, and with ten of the citizens had held his own against an equal number of knights. This was at the commencement of his reign; but the accident to the queen's stand had so angered him that he had not again been present at the sports, and his reappearance now was considered to be an act of approval of the efforts which the city had made to aid him in the war, and as an introduction of the young prince to the citizens.

When the day arrived there was a general flocking out of the citizens to the lists. The scene was a picturesque one; the weather was bright and warm; the fields were green; and Westminster, as well as London, sent out large numbers to the scene. The citizens were all in their best; their garments were for the most part of sober colors-russet, murrey, brown, and gray. Some, indeed, of the younger and wealthier merchants adopted somewhat of the fashion of the court, wearing their shoes long and pointed and their garments parti-colored. The line of division was down the center of the body one leg, arm, and half the body would be blue, the other half russet or brown. The ladies' dresses were similarly divided. Mingling with the citizens, as they strolled to and fro upon the sward, were the courtiers. These wore the brightest colors, and their shoes were so long that the points were looped up to the knees with little gold chains to enable them to walk. The ladies wore head-dresses of prodigious height, culminating in two points; and from these fell, sweeping to the ground, streamers of silk or lighter material. Cloths of gold and silver, rich furs, silks, and velvets were worn both by men and women.

None who saw the nobles of the court walking in garments so tight that they could scarce move, with their long parti-colored hose, their silk hoods buttoned under the chin, their hair braided down their back, would have thought that these were the most warlike and courageous of knights, men whose personal prowess and gallantry were the admiration of Europe. Their hair was generally cut close upon the forehead, and the beard was suffered to grow, but was kept trimmed a moderate length. Many of the ladies had the coat of arms of their family embroidered upon their dresses, giving them the appearance of heralds' tabards. Almost all wore gold or silver girdles, with embroidered pouches, and small daggers.

Thus the appearance of the crowd who moved about among the fields near the lists was varied and brilliant indeed. Their demeanor was quiet, for the London merchants deemed a grave demeanor to belong to their calling and the younger men and apprentices restrained their spirits in the presence of their superiors. For their special amusement, and in order, perhaps, to keep them from jostling too freely against the court gallants and ladies, the city authorities had appointed popular sports such as pleased the rougher classes; and bull-baiting, cock-fighting, wrestling for a ram, pitching the bar, and hand-ball, were held in a field some distance away. Here a large portion of the artisans and apprentices amused themselves until the hour when the king and queen were to arrive at their pavilion and the contests were to commence.

Presently a sound of trumpets was heard, and the royal procession was seen moving up from Westminster. Then the minor sports were abandoned; the crowd gathered round the large fenced-in space, and those who, by virtue of rank or position in the city, had places in the various stands, took their places there.

There was a flourish of trumpets as the king and queen appeared in front of their pavilion, accompanied by the Prince of Wales and many of the nobles of the court, and a shout of welcome arose from the crowd. The shooting at a mark at once began. The preliminary trials had been shot off upon the preceding day, and the six chosen bowmen now took their places.

Walter had not entered for the prizes at archery. He had on previous years shot well; but since he had fully determined to become a man-at-arms he had given up archery, for which, indeed, his work at the forge and his exercises at arms when the fires were out left him but little time. The contest was a close one, and when it was over the winner was led by the city marshal to the royal pavilion, where the queen bestowed upon him a silver arrow, and the king added a purse of money. Then there were several combats with quarter-staff and broadsword between men who had served among the contingents sent by the city to aid the king in his wars. Some good sword-play was shown and many stout blows exchanged, two or three men were badly hurt, and the king and all present were mightily pleased with the stoutness with which they fought.

The apprentices then came forward to compete for the prizes for sword-play. They wore light iron caps and shirts of thickly quilted leather, and fought with blunted swords, for the city fathers deemed wisely that with these weapons they could equally show their skill, and that with sharpened swords not only would severe wounds be given, but bad blood would be created between the apprentices of the various wards. Each ward sent its champion to the contest, and as these fought in pairs, loud was the shouting which rose from their comrades at each blow given or warded, and even the older citizens joined sometimes in the shouting and took a warm interest in the champions of their respective wards.

The iron caps had stout cheek-pieces which defended the sides of the face and neck, for even a blunted sword can deliver a terrible blow if it fall upon the naked flesh. It took a long time to get through the combats; the pairs were drawn by lot and fought until the king decided which was the superior. Some were speedily beaten; at other times the contests were long and severe. It was generally thought by the apprentices that the final contest lay between Walter Fletcher of Aldgate and Ralph Smith of Ludgate. The former was allowed to be superior in the use of his weapon, but the latter was also skillful, was two years older, and greatly superior in strength. He had not taken part in the contest in the preceding year, as he had been laid up with a hurt in his hand which he had got in his employment as a smith, and the lads of Ludgate were confident that he would turn the tables upon the champion of the eastern ward. Both had defeated with ease the various opponents whom they had met, but it chanced that they had not drawn together until the last round, when they remained alone to struggle for the first and second prizes.

The interest in the struggle had increased with each round, and wagers were freely laid upon the result. According to custom the two champions had laid aside their leathern shirts and had donned mail armor, for it was considered that the crowning contest between the two picked young swordsmen of the city would be a severe one, and greater protection to the limbs was needed.

Before taking their places they were led up to the royal pavilion, where they were closely inspected by the king and his nobles.

"You are sure that this man is still an apprentice?" the king asked the lord mayor, who was seated next to him; "he has the appearance of a man-at-arms, and a stout one too; the other is a likely stripling, and is, as I have seen, marvelously dexterous with his sword, but he is but a boy while the other is a grown man."

"He is an apprentice, my liege, although his time will be up in a few days, while the other has yet three years to serve, but he works for an armorer, and is famed through the city, boy as he is, for his skill with weapons."

After a few words to each, exhorting them to do their best in the sight of the queen and her ladies, the king dismissed them.

"I know the young one now!" the Prince of Wales said, clapping his hands as the apprentices turned away to take their places. "My Lord Talbot, I will wager a gold chain with you upon the smaller of the two."

"I will take your wager," the noble answered; "but I am by no means sure that I shall win it, for I have watched your champion closely, and the downright blows which he struck would seem to show that he has the muscle and strength of a man, though still but a boy."

The event justified the Prince of Wales' confidence; at the commencement of the struggle Ralph Smith tried to beat down his opponent by sheer strength as he had done his prior opponents, but to his surprise he found that all his efforts could not break down his opponent's guard. Walter indeed did not appear to take advantage of his superior lightness and activity, but to prefer to prove that in strength as well as skill he was equal to his antagonist. In the latter respect there was no comparison, for as soon as the smith began to relax his rain of blows Walter took the offensive and with a sweeping blow, given with all his strength, broke down his opponent's guard and smote him with such force upon his steel cap that, blunted as the sword was, it clove through the iron, and stretched the smith senseless on the ground. A loud shout broke from the assemblage. The marshal came up to Walter, and removing his helmet, led him to the royal pavilion, while Ralph was carried to a tent near, where a leech attended to his wound.

Chapter VI
The Melee.

"You have won your prize stoutly and well, sir 'prentice," the king said. "I should not have deemed it possible that one of your age could have smitten such a blow, and right glad should I be of a few hundred lads of your mettle to follow me against the French. What is your calling?"

"I am an armorer, my liege," Walter answered.

"An you are as good at mending armor as you are at marring it," the king said, "you will be a rare craftsman one of these days. 'Tis a rare pity so promising a swordsman should be lost to our army. Wouldst like to change your calling, boy, and take to that of arms?"

"It is my hope to do so, sir," Walter answered modestly, "and his grace the Prince of Wales has already promised me that I shall some day ride behind him to the wars."

"Ah! Edward," the king ejaculated, "how is this? Have you been already enlisting a troop for the wars?"

"No, sir," the young prince replied, "but one day, now some four years since, when I was riding with my Lord Talbot and others in the fields near the Tower, I did see this lad lead his play-fellows to the assault of an earthen castle held by others, and he fought so well and gallantly that assuredly no knight could have done better, until he was at last stricken senseless, and when he recovered I told him that should he choose to be a man-at-arms I would enlist him in my following to the wars."

The king laughed.

"I deemed not that the lads of the city indulged in such rough sports; but I wonder not, seeing that the contingent which my good city of London furnishes me is ever one of the best in my army. We shall see the lad at work again to-morrow and will then talk more of it. Now let us bestow upon him the prize that he has so well earned."

Walter bent on one knee, and the queen handed to him a sword of the best Spanish steel, which was the prize given by the city to the victor. The king handed him a heavy purse of gold pieces, saying:

"This may aid in purchasing your freedom."

Walter bowed deeply and murmured some words of thanks, and was then led off by the marshal. After this many of the young nobles of the court jousted on horseback, ran at the ring, and performed other feats of knightly exercise to the great pleasure of the multitude. The marshal on leading Walter away said to him, "You will be captain of the city band to-morrow, and I must therefore tell you what the king purports. He has prepared a surprise for the citizens, and the present show will be different to anything ever before seen in London. Both to show them somewhat of the sieges which are taking place on the borders of France and the Low Countries, in which Sir Walter Manny and many other gallant knights have so greatly distinguished themselves, and as an exercise for the young nobles he has determined that there shall be a castle erected. It will be built of wood, with battlements and towers, with a moat outside. As soon as the lists are over a large number of workmen will commence its erection; the pieces are all sawn and prepared. There will be machines, ladders, and other appliances. The ten champions on either side will fight as knights; you will have a hundred apprentices as men-at-arms, and the court party will have an equal number of young esquires. You, as winner of to-day's tourney, will have the choice of defense or attack. I should advise you to take the defense, since it is easier and requires less knowledge of war, and many of the other party have accompanied their fathers and masters in the field and have seen real sieges carried out."

"Can you show me a plan of the castle," Walter said, "if it be not contrary to the rules, in order that I may think over to-night the plan of fighting to-morrow?"

"Here it is," the marshal said. "You see the walls are two hundred feet long and twelve feet in height, with a tower at the end and one over the gateway in the center six feet high. There is a drawbridge defended by an outwork of palisades six feet high. The moat will be a dry one, seeing that we have no means of filling it with water, but it will be supposed to be full, and must be crossed on planks or bridges. Two small towers on wheels will be provided, which may be run up to the edge of the moat, and will be as high as the top of the towers."

"Surely they cannot make all this before morning?" Walter said.

"They will do so," the marshal replied. "The castle has been put together in the king's courtyard, and the pieces are all numbered. Two hundred carpenters will labor all night at it, besides a party of laborers for the digging of the moat. It will be a rare show, and will delight both the citizens and the ladies of the court, for such a thing has never before been attempted. But the king grudges not the expense which it will cost him, seeing that spectacles of this kind do much to arouse the warlike spirit of the people. Here is a list of the various implements which will be provided, only it is understood that the mangonels and arblasts will not be provided with missiles, seeing that many would assuredly be killed by them. They will be employed, however, to show the nature of the work, and parties of men-at-arms will be told off to serve them. Cross-bows and arrows will be used, but the weapons will be blunted. You will see that there are ladders, planks for making bridges, long hooks for hauling men down from the wall, beams for battering down the gate, axes for cutting down the palisades, and all other weapons. The ten who will serve under you as knights have already been nominated, and the city will furnish them with full armor. For the others, the apprentices of each ward will choose sufficient representatives to make up the hundred who will fight as men-at-arms; these will wear steel caps and breast-pieces, with leather jerkins, and vizors to protect their faces, for even a blunted arrow or a wooden quarrel might well kill if it struck true."

On leaving the marshal Walter joined Giles Fletcher and Geoffrey Ward, who warmly congratulated him upon his success. He informed them of the spectacle which the king had prepared for the amusement of the citizens on the morrow.

"In faith," Geoffrey said, "the idea is a good one, and promises rare sport, but it will be rough, and we may expect many broken limbs, for it will be no joke to be thrown down with a ladder from a wall even twelve feet high, and there will be the depth of the moat besides."

"That will only be two feet," Walter said, "for so it is marked on the plan."

"And which do you mean to take, Walter, the attack or the defense? Methinks the king has erred somewhat in making the forces equal, for assuredly the besiegers should outnumber the besieged by fully three to one to give them a fair chance of success."

"I shall take the assault," Walter answered; "there is more to be done that way than in the defense. When we get home, Geoffrey, we will look at the plans, and see what may be the best manner of assault."

Upon examining the plan that evening they found that the wall was continued at an angle at either end for a distance of some twenty feet back so as to give a postern gate behind each of the corner towers through which a sortie might be made. Geoffrey and Walter talked the matter over, and together contrived a plan of operation for the following day.

"You will have one great advantage," Geoffrey said. "The apprentices are all accustomed to the use of the bow, while the young nobles will know but little of that weapon; therefore your shooting will be far straighter and truer, and even a blunt-headed arrow drawn from the shoulder will hit so smart a blow that those on the wall will have difficulty in withstanding them."

After the talk was ended Walter again crossed London Bridge, and made his way to Ludgate, where he found his late antagonist, whose head had been plastered up and was little the worse for the conflict.

"There is no ill-will between us, I hope," Walter said, holding out his hand.

"None in the world," the young smith said frankly.

He was a good tempered-looking young giant, with closely cropped hair, light-blue eyes, and a pleasant but somewhat heavy face.

"My faith! but what a blow was that you gave me! why, one would think that your muscles were made of steel. I thought that I could hit a good downright blow, seeing that I have been hammering at the anvil for the last seven years; but strike as I would I could not beat down your guard, while mine went down as if it had been a feather before yours. I knew, directly that I had struck the first blow, and felt how firm was your defense, that it was all up with me, knowing that in point of skill I had no chance whatever with you."

"I am glad to see that you bear no malice, Ralph," Walter said, "and hope that we shall be great friends henceforth, that is, if you will take me as such, seeing that you are just out of your apprenticeship, while I am not yet half-through mine. But I have come to talk to you about to-morrow. Have you heard that there is to be a mimic siege?"

"I have heard about it," Ralph said. "The city is talking of nothing else. The news was published at the end of the sports. It will be rare fun, surely."

"It will be pretty rough fun," Walter replied; "and I should not be much surprised if some lives are lost; but this is always so in a tournament; and if knights and nobles are ready to be killed, we apprentices need not fear to hazard our lives. But now as to to-morrow. I, as the winner to-day, am to be the leader of the party, and you, as second, will of course be captain under me. Now I want to explain to you exactly what I propose to do, and to arrange with you as to your share in the business."

The young smith listened attentively to Walter's explanation, and, when he had done, exclaimed admiringly: "Why, Walter, you seem to be made for a general. How did it all come to you, lad? I should never have thought of such a scheme."

"I talked it over with my master," Walter said, "and the idea is his as much as mine. I wonder if it will do?"

"It is sure to do," the smith said enthusiastically. "The castle is as good as taken."

The next day all London poured out to the scene of the sports, and the greatest admiration and wonder were expressed at the castle, which had risen, as if by magic, in the night. It was built at one end of the lists, which had been purposely placed in a hollow, so that a great number of people besides those in the pavilions could obtain a view from the surrounding slopes. The castle was substantially built of heavy timber painted gray, and looked at a little distance as if constructed of stone. A flag floated from the central tower, and the building looked so formidable that the general opinion was freely expressed that the task of the assailants, whoever they might be-for at present this was unknown-was quite impossible. At ten o'clock the king and his court arrived. After they had taken their places the two bands, headed by their leaders, advanced from the lower end of the lists, and drew up in front of the royal pavilion. The leaders took their places in front. Behind them stood the ten chosen followers, all of whom, as well as their chiefs, were incased in full armor. Behind, on one side, were one hundred apprentices, on the other, one hundred esquires, all attired as men-at-arms. The court party were led by Clarence Aylmer, son of the Earl of Pembroke. His companions were all young men of noble family, aspirants for the order of knighthood. They were, for the most part, somewhat older than the apprentices, but as the latter consisted chiefly of young men nearly out of their term the difference was not great. Walter's armor was a suit which the armorer had constructed a year previously for a young knight who had died before the armor could be delivered. Walter had wondered more than once why Geoffrey did not endeavor to sell it elsewhere, for although not so decorated and inlaid as many of the suits of Milan armor, it was constructed of the finest steel, and the armorer had bestowed special care upon its manufacture, as the young knight's father had long been one of his best customers. Early that morning Geoffrey had brought it to his room and had told him to wear it instead of that lent by the city.

"But I fear it will get injured," Walter had urged. "I shall not spare myself, you know, Geoffrey, and the blows will be hard ones."

"The more need for good armor, Walter. These city suits are made for show rather than use. You may be sure that young Pembroke and his band will fight their hardest rather than suffer defeat at the hands of those whom they consider as a band of city varlets."

Before issuing from the tent where he and his companions had put on their mail, Walter carefully fastened in the front of his helmet a tiny gold bracelet. Upon taking their places before the pavilion the king ordered the two leaders to advance, and addressed them and the multitude in the following words:

"Brave leaders, and you, my people, I have contrived the pastime to-day that I may show you on a mimic scale the deeds which my brave soldiers are called upon to perform in France. It is more specially suited for the combatants of to-day, since one party have had but small opportunity of acquiring skill on horseback. Moreover, I wish to teach the lesson that fighting on foot is as honorable as fighting on horseback, for it has now been proved, and sometimes to our cost, in Scotland, that footmen can repulse even the bravest chivalry. To-day each party will fight his best. Remember that, even in the heat of conflict, matters must not be carried to an extreme. Those cut off from their friends will be accounted prisoners, as will those who, being overpowered, throw down their arms. Any wounded on either side will not be accounted as prisoners, but may retire with honor from the field. You," he said, looking at Walter, "as the conqueror of yesterday, have the choice of either the attack or defense; but I should advise you to take the latter, seeing that it is easier to defend a fortress than to assault it. Many of your opponents have already gained credit in real warfare, while you and your following are new to it. Therefore, in order to place the defense on fair terms with the assault, I have ordered that both sides shall be equal in numbers."

"If your liege will permit me," Walter said, bowing, "I would fain take the assault. Methinks that, with my following, I could do better thus than in defense."

The king looked somewhat displeased.

"As you will," he said coldly; "but I fear that this will somewhat mar the effect of the spectacle, seeing that you will have no chance whatever against an equal force, more accustomed to war than your party, and occupying so superior a position. However," he went on, seeing that Walter made no sign of changing his mind, "as you have chosen, so be it; and now it is for you to choose the lady who shall be queen of the tourney and shall deliver the prizes to the victors. Look round you; there are many fair faces, and it is for you to choose among them."

Smiles passed between many of the courtly dames and ladies at the choice that was to be made among them by the apprentice lad; and they thought that he would be sorely puzzled at such a duty. Walter, however, did not hesitate an instant. He ran his eye over the crowd of ladies in the royal gallery, and soon saw the object of his search.

"Since I have your majesty's permission," he said, "I choose, as queen of the tournament, Mistress Edith Vernon."

There was a movement of surprise and a general smile. Perhaps to all who thought that they had a chance of being chosen the selection was a relief, as none could be jealous of the pretty child, who, at the king's order, made her way forward to the front, and took her seat in a chair placed between the king and queen. The girl colored brightly; but she had heard so much of tourneys and jousts that she knew what was her duty. She had been sitting far back on the previous day, and the apprentice, when brought up before the king, was too far below for her to see his features. She now recognized him.

"Sir knights," she said in a loud, clear, childish voice, "you will both do your duty to-day and show yourselves worthy cavaliers. Methinks that, as queen of the tourney, I should be neutral between you, but as one of you carries my gage in his helm, my good wishes must needs go with him; but bright eyes will be fixed on you both, and may well stir you to deeds of valor."

So saying, she resumed her seat with a pretty air of dignity.

"Why, sweetheart," the king said, "how is it that this 'prentice lad knows your name, and how is it that he wears your gage, for I know that the young Pembroke wears the glove of the Earl of Surrey's daughter?"

"He saved my life, sir, mine and my mother's," the child said, "and I told him he should be my true knight, and gave him my bracelet, which you see he wears in his helm."

"I recall somewhat of the story," the king said, "and will question my Lady Vernon further anon; but see, the combatants are filing off to their places."

With flags flying and trumpets blowing young Pembroke led his forces into the castle. Each of his ten knights was followed by an esquire bearing his banner, and each had ten men-at-arms under his immediate order. Two of them, with twenty men, remained in the outwork beyond the drawbridge. The rest took their station on the walls and towers, where a platform had been erected running along three feet below the battlements. The real men-at-arms with the machines of war now advanced, and for a time worked the machines, which made pretense at casting great stones and missiles at the walls. The assailants then moved forward and, unslinging their bows, opened a heavy fire of arrows at the defenders, who, in turn, replied with arrows and cross-bows.

"The 'prentices shoot well," the king said; "by our lady, it would be hot work for the defenders were the shafts but pointed! Even as it is the knocks must be no child's play, for the arrows, although not pointed, are all tipped with iron, without which, indeed, straight shooting would be impossible."

The return fire from the walls was feeble, and the king said, laughing, "So far your knight, fair mistress, has it all his own way. I did not reckon sufficiently upon the superiority of shooting of the London lads, and, indeed, I know not that I ought not in fairness to order some of the defenders off the walls, seeing that in warfare their numbers would be rapidly thinned. See, the assailants are moving up the two towers under shelter of the fire of the archers."

By this time Aylmer, seeing that his followers could make no effectual reply to the arrow fire, had ordered all, save the leaders in full armor, to lie down behind the parapet. The assailants now gathered thickly round each tower, as if they intended to attempt to cross by the bridges, which could be let down from an opening in the tower level with the top of the wall, while archers upon the summit shot fast and thick among the defenders who were gathering to oppose them.

"If the young Pembroke is wise," the king said, "he will make a strong sally now and fall upon one or other of the parties."

As he spoke there was a sudden movement on the part of the assailants, who, leaving the foot of the towers, made a rush at the outwork in the center. The instant they arrived they fell to work with axes upon the palisades. Many were struck down by the blows dealt them by the defenders, but others caught up the axes and in less than a minute several of the palisades were cut down and the assailants poured in. The defenders fought gallantly, but they were overpowered by numbers. Some were struck down, others taken prisoners by main force, and the rest driven across the drawbridge just as the gates were opened and Pembroke, at the head of the defenders, swarmed out to their assistance.

There was a desperate fight on the bridge, and it was well that the armor was stout, and the arms that wielded the weapons had not yet attained their full strength. Several were knocked off the bridge into the moat, and these were, by the rules, obliged at once to retire and take no further part in the contest. Walter and Ralph the smith fought in front of their men, and hard as Pembroke and his followers struggled, they could not drive them back a foot. The court party was galled by the heavy fire of arrows kept up by the apprentices along the side of the moat, and finding all his efforts to regain the earthwork useless, Pembroke withdrew his forces into the castle, and in spite of the efforts of the besiegers managed to close the gates in their faces. The assailants, however, succeeded in severing the chains of the drawbridge before it could be raised.

From the tower above, the defenders now hurled over great stones, which had been specially placed there for the purpose of destroying the drawbridge should the earthwork be carried. The boards were soon splintered, and the drawbridge was pronounced by the Earl of Talbot, who was acting as judge, to be destroyed. The excitement of the spectators was worked up to a great pitch while the conflict was going on, and the citizens cheered lustily at the success of the apprentices.

"That was gallantly done," the king said to Queen Philippa, "and the leader of the assailants is a lad of rare mettle. Not a captain of my army, no, not Sir Walter Manny himself, could have done it more cleverly. You see, by placing his forces at the ends of the wall he drew all the garrison thither to withstand the assaults from them, and thus by his sudden movement he was able to carry the outwork before they could recover from their surprise and come down to its aid. I am curious to know what he will do next. What thinkst thou, Edward?" he asked his son, who was standing by his side.

"He will win the day," the young prince said; "and in faith, although the others are my comrades, I should be glad to see it. He will make a gallant knight, sir, one of these days, and remember he is engaged to follow my banner, so you must not steal him from me. See, my liege, they are taking planks and ladders to the outwork."

"They are doing wrongly, then," the king said, "for even should they bridge the moat where the drawbridge is, they cannot scale the wall there, since the tower defends it, and the ladders are but long enough to reach the lower wall. No, their leader has changed his mind: they are taking the planks along the edge of the moat toward the tower on the left, and will aid the assault by its bridge by a passage of the moat there."

It seemed, indeed, that this was the plan. While some of the assailants kept up the arrow fire on the wall others mounted the tower, while a party prepared to throw a bridge of planks across the moat. The bridge from the tower was now lowered; but a shout of triumph rose from the defenders when it was seen that by some mistake of the carpenters this was too short, and when lowered did not reach within six feet of the wall.

"All the better," the king said, while the prince gave an angry exclamation. "Accidents of this kind will happen, and give an opportunity to a leader to show his resources. Doubtless he will carry planks up to the tower and so connect the bridge and the wall."

This, indeed, was what the assailants tried to do, while a party threw planks across the moat, and rushing over placed ladders against the wall and strove to climb. They strove in vain, however. The ladders were thrown down as fast as they were placed, while the defenders, thickly clustered on the walls, drove back those who tried to cross from the tower.

"I do not see the leader of the assailants," the prince said.

"He has a white plume, but it may have been shorn off," the king said. "Look, the young Pembroke is making a sortie!"

From the sortie gate behind the tower the defenders now poured out, and running down the edge of the moat fell upon the stormers. These, however, received them with great steadiness, and while some continued to attack the rest turned upon the garrison, and, headed by Ralph the smith, drove them gradually back.

"They fight well and steadily," the king said. "One would have thought that they had reckoned on the sortie, so steadily did they receive it."

As only a portion of the garrison had issued out, they were unable to resist long the pressure of the apprentices, who drove them back step by step to the sally-port, and pressing them hard endeavored to force their way in at their heels.

Chapter VII
The Young Esquire.

While the attention of the whole of the spectators and combatants was fixed upon the struggle at the right-hand angle of the castle, a party of twenty 'prentices suddenly leaped to their feet from among the broken palisades of the outwork. Lying perdu there they had escaped the attention of the spectators as well as of the defenders. The reason why the assailants carried the planks and ladders to this spot was now apparent. Only a portion had been taken on to the assault of the right-hand tower; those who now rose to their feet lifted with them planks and ladders, and at a rapid pace ran toward the left angle of the castle, and reached that point before the attention of the few defenders who remained on the wall there was attracted to them, so absorbed were they in the struggle at the other angle. The moment that they saw the new assailants they raised a shout of alarm, but the din of the combat, the shouts of the leaders and men were so loud that their cries were unheard. Two or three then hurried away at full speed to give the alarm, while the others strove to repel the assault. Their efforts were in vain. The planks were flung across the moat, the ladders placed in position, and led by Walter the assailants sprang up and gained a footing on the wall before the alarm was fairly given. A thundering cheer from the spectators greeted the success of the assailants. Springing along the wall they drove before them the few who strove to oppose them, gained the central tower, and Walter, springing up to the top, pulled down the banner of the defenders and placed that of the city in its place. At this moment the defenders, awakened too late to the ruse which had been played upon them, came swarming back along the wall and strove to regain the central tower. In the confusion the assault by the flying tower of the assailants was neglected, and at this point also they gained a footing on the wall. The young nobles of the court, furious at being outwitted, fought desperately to regain their lost laurels. But the king rose from his seat and held up his hand. The trumpeter standing below him sounded the arrest of arms, which was echoed by two others who accompanied Earl Talbot, who had taken his place on horseback close to the walls. At the sound swords dropped and the din abruptly ceased, but the combatants stood glaring at each other, their blood too heated to relinquish the fray readily.

Already much damage had been done. In spite of armor and mail many serious wounds had been inflicted, and some of the combatants had already been carried senseless from the field. Some of the assailants had been much shaken by being thrown backward from the ladders into the moat, one or two were hurt to death; but as few tourneys took place without the loss of several lives, this was considered but a small amount of damage for so stoutly fought a *mêlée*, and the knowledge that many were wounded, and some perhaps dying, in no way damped the enthusiasm of the spectators, who cheered lustily for some minutes at the triumph which the city had obtained.

In the galleries occupied by the ladies and nobles of the court there was a comparative silence. But brave deeds were appreciated in those days, and although the ladies would far rather have seen the victory incline the other way, yet they waved their handkerchiefs and clapped their hands in token of their admiration at the success of an assault which, at the commencement, appeared well-nigh hopeless.

Lord Talbot rode up to the front of the royal pavilion.

"I was about to stop the fight, sire, when you gave the signal. Their blood was up, and many would have been killed had the combat continued. But the castle was fairly won, the central tower was taken and the flag pulled down, a footing had been gained at another point of the wall, and the assailants had forced their way through the sally-port. Further resistance was therefore hopeless, and the castle must be adjudged as fairly and honorably captured."

A renewed shout greeted the judge's decision. The king now ordered the rival hosts to be mustered before him as before the battle, and when this was done Earl Talbot conducted Walter up the broad steps in front of the king's pavilion. Geoffrey Ward, who had, after fastening on

Walter's armor in the tent before the sports began, taken his place among the guards at the foot of the royal pavilion, stepped forward and removed Walter's helmet at the foot of the steps.

"Young sir," the king said, "you have borne yourself right gallantly to-day, and have shown that you possess the qualities which make a great captain. I do my nobles no wrong when I say that not one of them could have better planned and led the assault than you have done. Am I not right, sirs?" and he looked round.

A murmur of assent rose from the knights and nobles, and the king continued: "I thought you vain and presumptuous in undertaking the assault of a fort held by an equal number, many of whom are well accustomed to war, while the lads who followed you were all untrained in strife, but you have proved that your confidence in yourself was not misplaced. The Earl of Talbot has adjudged you victor, and none can doubt what the end of the strife would have been. Take this chain from your king, who is glad to see that his citizens of London are able to hold their own even against those of our court, than whom we may say no braver exist in Europe. Kneel now to the queen of the tourney, who will bestow upon you the chaplet which you have so worthily earned."

Walter bent his knee before Edith Vernon. She rose to her feet, and with an air of pretty dignity placed a chaplet of laurel leaves, wrought in gold and clasped with a valuable ruby, on his head.

"I present to you," she said, "the chaplet of victory, and am proud that my gage should have been worn by one who has borne himself so bravely and well. May a like success rest on all your undertakings, and may you prove a good and valiant knight!"

"Well said, Mistress Edith," Queen Philippa said, smiling. "You may well be proud of your young champion. I too must have my gift," and drawing a ring set with brilliants from her finger she placed it in Walter's hand.

The lad now rose to his feet. "The prince, my son," the king said, "has promised that you shall ride with his men-at-arms when he is old enough to take the field. Should you choose to abandon your craft and do so earlier I doubt not that one of my nobles, the brave Sir Walter Manny, for example, will take you before that time."

"That will I readily enough," Sir Walter said, "and glad to have so promising a youth beneath my banner."

"I would that you had been of gentle blood," the king said.

"That makes no difference, sire," Sir Walter replied. "I will place him among the young gentlemen, my pages and esquires, and am sure that they will receive him as one of themselves."

Geoffrey Ward had hitherto stood at the foot of the steps leading to the royal pavilion, but doffing his cap he now ascended. "Pardon my boldness, sire," he said to the king, "but I would fain tell you what the lad himself has hitherto been ignorant of. He is not, as he supposes, the son of Giles Fletcher, citizen and bowmaker, but is the lawfully born son of Sir Roland Somers, erst of Westerham and Hythe, who was killed in the troubles at the commencement of your majesty's reign. His wife, Dame Alice, brought the child to Giles Fletcher, whose wife had been her nurse, and dying left him in her care. Giles and his wife, if called for, can vouch for the truth of this, and can give you proofs of his birth."

Walter listened with astonishment to Geoffrey's speech. A thrill of pleasure rushed through his veins as he learned that he was of gentle blood and might hope to aspire to a place among the knights of King Edward's court. He understood now the pains which Geoffrey had bestowed in seeing that he was perfected in warlike exercises, and why he and Giles had encouraged rather than repressed his love for martial exercises and his determination to abandon his craft and become a man-at-arms when he reached man's estate.

"Ah! is it so?" the king exclaimed. "I remember Sir Roland Somers, and also that he was slain by Sir Hugh Spencer, who, as I heard on many hands, acted rather on a private quarrel than, as he alleged, in my interest, and there were many who avowed that the charges brought against Sir Roland were unfounded. However, this matter must be inquired into, and my high justicier shall see Master Giles and his wife, hear their evidence, and examine the proofs which they may bring forward. As to the estates, they were granted to Sir Jasper Vernon and cannot be restored. Nevertheless I doubt not that the youth will carve out for himself a fortune with his sword. You are his master, I suppose. I would fain pay you to cancel his apprenticeship. Sir Walter Manny has promised to enroll him among his esquires."

"I will cancel his indentures willingly, my liege," the armorer answered, "and that without payment. The lad has been to me as a son, and seeing his high spirit, and knowing the gentle blood running in his veins, I have done my best so to teach him and so to put him in the way of winning back his father's rank by his sword."

"He hath gone far toward it already," the king said, "and methinks may yet gain some share in his father's inheritance," and he glanced at little Mistress Edith Vernon and then smiled at the queen. "Well, we shall see," he went on. "Under Sir Walter Manny he will have brave chances of distinguishing himself, and when my son takes the field, he shall ride with him. But I am keeping the hosts waiting. Bring hither," he said to Earl Talbot, "Clarence Aylmer."

The young noble was led up to the king. "You have done well, Clarence; though you have been worsted you fought bravely, but you were deceived by a ruse which might have taken in a more experienced captain. I trust that you will be friends with your adversary, who will be known to you henceforth as Walter Somers, son of Sir Roland of that name, and who will ride to the wars, whither you also are shortly bound, under the standard of Sir Walter Manny."

The cloud which had hung over the face of the young noble cleared. It had indeed been a bitter mortification to him that he, the son of one of the proudest of English nobles, should have been worsted by a London apprentice, and it was a relief to him to find that his opponent was one of knightly blood. He turned frankly to Walter and held out his hand. "I greet you as a comrade, sir," he said, "and hope some day that in our rivalry in the field I may do better than I have done to-day."

"That is well spoken," the king said. Then he rose and in a loud voice addressed the combatants, saying that all had borne themselves well and bravely, and that he thanked them, not only for the rare pastime which they had made, but for the courage and boldness which had been displayed on both sides. So saying, he waved his hand as a token that the proceedings were ended, and returned with the court to Westminster; while the crowd of spectators overflowed the lists, those who had friends in the apprentice array being anxious to know how they had fared. That evening there was a banquet given by the lord mayor. Walter was invited to be present, with Giles and Geoffrey, and many complimentary things were said to him, and he was congratulated on the prospects which awaited him. After dinner all the 'prentices who had taken part in the sports filed through the hall and were each presented with a gold piece by the lord mayor, in the name of the corporation, for having so nobly sustained the renown of the city.

After the entertainment was over Walter returned with Geoffrey to the bowyer's house, and there heard from his two friends and Bertha the details of his mother's life from the time that she had been a child, and the story of her arrival with him, and her death. He had still difficulty in believing that it was all true, that Giles and Bertha, whom he had so long regarded as his father and mother, were only his kind guardians, and that he was the scion of two noble families. Very warmly and gratefully he thanked his three friends for the kindness which they had shown to him, and vowed that no change of condition should ever alter his feelings of affection toward them. It was not until the late hour of nine o'clock that he said good-by to his foster-parents, for he was next day to repair to the lodging of Sir Walter Manny, who was to sail again before the week was out for the Low Countries, from which he had only returned for a few days to have private converse with the king on the state of matters there. His friends would have delivered to him his mother's ring and other tokens which she had left, but thought it better to keep these, with the other proofs of his birth, until his claim was established to the satisfaction of the lord justiciaries.

The next morning early, when Walter descended the stairs, he found Ralph Smith waiting for him. His face was strapped up with plaster and he wore his arm in a sling, for his armor had been twice cut through as he led his party in through the sally-port.

"How goes it with you, Ralph?" Walter said. "Not much the worse, I hope, for your hard knocks?"

"Not a whit," Ralph replied cheerfully, "and I shall be all right again before the week is out; but the leech made as much fuss over me as if I had been a girl, just as though one was not accustomed to hard knocks in a smithy. Those I got yesterday were not half so hard as that which you gave me the day before. My head rings yet with the thought of it. But I have not come to talk about myself. Is the story true which they tell of you, Master Walter, that you are not the son of Giles the bowyer, but of a great noble?"

"Not of a great noble, Ralph, but of a gallant knight, which is just as good. My father was killed when I was three years old, and my mother brought me to Bertha, the wife of Giles the bowyer, who had been her nurse in childhood. I had forgotten all that had passed, and deemed myself the son of the good citizen, but since I have heard the truth my memory has awakened somewhat, and I have a dim recollection of a lordly castle and of my father and mother."

"And they say, Walter, that you are going with Sir Walter Manny, with the force which is just sailing to the assistance of Lady de Montford?"

"That is so, Ralph, and the good knight has taken me among his esquires, young as I am, although I might well have looked for nothing better than to commence, for two years at least, as a page, seeing that I am but eighteen now. Now I shall ride with him into the battles and shall have as good a chance as the others of gaining honor and winning my spurs."

"I have made up my mind that I will go with you, Master Walter, if you will take me; each squire has a man-at-arms who serves him, and I will give you good and faithful service if you will take me with you. I spoke to the smith, my master, last night, when I heard the news, and as my apprenticeship is out next week he was willing enough to give me the few days which remain. Once out of my apprenticeship I may count to be a man, and seeing that I am nineteen, and as I may say well grown of my years, methinks I am fit for service as a man-at-arms, and I would rather fight behind you than labor all my life in the smithy."

"I shall be glad indeed, Ralph, to have you with me if such be really your wish, and I do not think that Sir Walter Manny will say nay, for they have been beating up for recruits through the kingdom, and we proved yesterday that you have courage as well as strength. If he will consent I should be glad indeed to have so brave a comrade with me, so we may consider that settled, and if you will come down to Westminster, to Sir Walter Manny's lodging, this afternoon, I will tell you what he says touching the matter. You will, of course, need arms and armor."

"I can provide that," Ralph replied, "seeing that his worshipful the lord mayor bestowed upon me yesterday five gold pieces as the second in command in the sports. I have already a steel cap and breast and back pieces, which I have made for myself in hours of leisure, and warrant will stand as hard a knock as the Frenchmen can give them."

Going across into the city with Geoffrey, Walter purchased, with the contents of the purse which the king had given him, the garments suited for his new position. He was fortunate in obtaining some which fitted him exactly. These had been made for a young esquire of the Earl of Salisbury; but the tailor, when he heard from Geoffrey for whom they were required, and the need for instant dispatch, parted with them to Walter, saying that he for whom they were made could well wait a few days, and that he would set his journeymen to work at once to make some more of similar fit and fashion.

Walter felt strange in his new attire, and by no means relished the tightness of the garments, which was strictly demanded by the fashion of the day. His long hose, one of which was of a deep maroon, the other a bright yellow, came far up above the knee, then came a short pair of trunks of similar colors divided in the middle. The tight-fitting doublet was short and circled at the waist by a buff belt mounted in silver, and was of the same colors as the hose and trunks. On his head was a cap, peaked in front; this was of maroon, with a short erect feather of yellow. The long-pointed shoes matched the rest of the costume. There were three other suits similar in fashion, but different in color; two like the first were of cloth, the third was of white and blue silk, to be worn on grand occasions.

"You look a very pretty figure, Walter," Geoffrey said, "and will be able to hold your own among the young gallants of the court. If you lack somewhat of courtly manners it will matter not at all, since you are leaving so soon for the wars. The dress sets off your figure, which is fully two years in advance of your age, seeing that hard work has widened you out and thickened your muscles. I need not tell you, lad, not to be quarrelsome, for that was never your way; but just at first your companions may try some jests with you, as is always the manner of young men with new-comers, but take them in a good spirit, and be sure that, seeing the strength of arm and skill which you showed yesterday and the day before, none will care to push matters with you unduly."

One of the journeymen accompanied Walter to Westminster to carry up from the boat the valise with his clothes and the armor which he had worn in the sports. Sir Walter received the lad with much kindness and introduced him to his future companions. They were five in number; the eldest was a man of some thirty years old, a Hainaulter, who had accompanied Sir Walter Manny to England at the time when the latter first came over as a young squire in the suit of the Princess Philippa. He was devotedly attached to the knight, his master, and although he might several times have received the rank of knighthood for his bravery in the field, he preferred remaining in his position as esquire and faithful friend of his master.

The other four were between the ages of nineteen and twenty-one, and all belonged to the families of the highest nobility of England, it being deemed a distinguished honor to be received as a squire by the most gallant knight at the court of England. Their duties were, as Walter soon learned, almost nominal, these being discharged almost exclusively by John Mervaux. Two of the young esquires, Richard Coningsby and Edward Clifford, had fought in the *mêlée*, having been among the ten leaders under Clarence Aylmer. They bore no malice for the defeat, but received Walter with cordiality and kindness, as did the other young men. Walter on his arrival acquainted the knight with Ralph's wish to follow him, and requested permission for him to do so. This was readily granted, Sir Walter Manny telling the lad that although esquires were supposed to wait entirely upon themselves, to groom their horses, and keep their armor and arms bright and in good order, yet, in point of fact, young men of good families had the greater part of these duties performed for them by a retainer who rode in the ranks of their master's following as a man-at-arms.

"The other esquires have each one of their father's retainers with them, and I am glad that you should be in the same position. After you have taken your mid-day meal you had best go across to the Earl of Talbot's and inquire for the Lady Vernon, who is still staying with him. She told me at the king's ball last night that she wished to have speech with you, and I promised to acquaint you with her desire. By the way, dost know aught of riding?"

"I have learned to sit on a horse, Sir Walter," the lad answered. "My good friend Geoffrey, the armorer, advised that I should learn, and frequently hired from the horse dealer an animal for my use. I have often backed half-broken horses which were brought up by graziers from Kent and Sussex for use in the wars. Many of them abode at the hostels at Southwark, and willingly enough granted me permission to ride their horses until they were sold. Thus I have had a good deal of practice, and that of a rough kind; and seeing that latterly the horses have, for the most part, found it difficult to fling me when sitting barebacked across them, I think I could keep my seat in the high-peaked saddles on the most vicious, but I have had no practice at tilting, or at the ring, or other knightly exercises."

"That matters not at all," the knight said. "All these knightly exercises which you speak of are good in time of peace, for they give proficiency and steadiness, but in time of war he who can sit firmly in his saddle and wield sword and battle-ax lustily and skillfully is equal to the best; but never fear, when this expedition is over, and we have time for such things, I will see that you are instructed in them. One who has achieved so much martial skill as you have done at so early an age will have little difficulty in acquiring what may be termed the pastime of chivalry."

Ralph arrived just as Walter was setting out. The latter presented him to the knight, who spoke with praise of the gallantry which he had displayed on the previous day, and then handed him over to John Mervaux, with instructions to enroll him as a man-at-arms among his followers, to inform him of his duties, and to place him with those who attended upon the other esquires.

After seeing Ralph disposed of, Walter went across to the Earl of Talbot and was again conducted to the presence of Dame Vernon.

"You have changed since we met last, young sir," she said with a smile, "though it is but a month since. Then you were a 'prentice boy, now you are an esquire of Sir Walter Manny, and on the highway to distinction. That you will win it I am well assured, since one who risked his life to rescue a woman and child whose very names were unknown to him is sure to turn out a noble and valiant knight. I little thought, when my daughter called you her knight, that in so short a time you might become an aspirant to that honor. I hope that you do not look askance at us, now that you know I am in possession of the lands of your parents. Such changes of land, you know, often occur, but now I know who you are, I would that the estates bestowed upon Sir Jasper had belonged to some other than you; however, I trust that you will hold no grudge against us, and that you may win as fair an estate by the strength of your arm and the king's favor."

"Assuredly I feel no grudge, madam," Walter replied, "and since the lands were forfeited, I am pleased that of all people they should have gone to one so kind and so fair as yourself."

"What, learning to be a flatterer already!" Dame Vernon laughed. "You are coming on fast, and I predict great things from you. And now, Edith, lay aside that sampler you are pretending to be so busy upon and speak to this knight of yours."

Edith laid down her work and came forward. She was no longer the dignified little queen of the tournament, but a laughing, bright-faced girl.

"I don't see that you are changed," she said, "except in your dress. You speak softly and naturally, just as you used to do, and not a bit like those little court fops, Uncle Talbot's pages. I am afraid you will not be my knight any more, now that you are going to get great honors at the war; for I heard my Uncle Talbot tell my lady mother that he was sure you would gain great credit for yourself."

"I shall be always your knight," Walter said earnestly; "I told you I should, and I never break my word. That is," he went on, coloring, "if Dame Vernon makes no objection, as she well might."

"If I did not object before, Walter," she said, smiling, "why should I do so now?"

"It is different, my lady; before, it was somewhat of a jest, a sort of childish play on the part of Mistress Edith, though so far as I was concerned it was no play, but sober earnest."

"It needs no permission from me," Dame Vernon replied, "for you to wear my daughter's colors. Any knight may proclaim any lady he chooses the mistress of his heart, and a reigning beauty will often have a dozen young knights who wear her colors. However, I am well content that one who has done me such great service and who has shown such high promise should be the first to wear the gage of my little daughter, and if in after-years your life fulfills the promise of your youth, and you remain true to her gage, there is none among all the youths of the court whom I would so gladly see at her feet. Remember," she said as Walter was about to speak, "her hand will not be at my disposal, but at that of the king. His majesty is wont to bestow the hands of his wards upon those who most distinguish themselves in the field. You have already attracted his royal attention and commendation. Under Sir Walter Manny you will be sure of opportunities of distinguishing yourself, and the king may well be glad some day at once to reward your services and to repair a cruel injustice by bestowing upon you the hand of the heiress of your father's lands. If I mistake not, such a thought has even now crossed his majesty's mind, unless I misinterpreted a glance which yesterday passed between him and our sweet queen. I need not tell you to speak of your hopes to none, but let them spur you to higher exertions and nobler efforts. Loving my little Edith as I do, I naturally consider the prize to be a high one. I have often been troubled by the thought that her hand may be some day given to one by years or temper unsuited for her, and it will be a pleasure to me henceforth to picture her future connected with one who is, I am sure, by heart and nature fitted for her. And now, farewell, young sir. May God protect you in the field, and may you carry in the battle which awaits you the gage of my daughter as fairly and successfully as you did in the mimic fray of yesterday!"

Chapter VIII
Off To The Wars.

Two days later Walter started with Sir Walter Manny, with a large number of knights, squires, men-at-arms, and archers, for the Orwell. Walter was mounted, as were the other squires and men-at-arms, and indeed many of the archers. Ralph Smith, in the attire of a man-at-arms, rode behind.

Walter was in the highest spirits. A brilliant career was open to him under the most favorable circumstances; he had already distinguished himself, and had gained the attention of the highest personages in the realm, his immediate lord was one of the bravest and most chivalrous knights in Europe, and he had to sustain and encourage him the hopes that Lady Vernon had given him of regaining some day the patrimony of his father. It was a satisfaction to him that he was as well born as those who surrounded him, and his purse was as well lined as any in the company. Although he had spent the largess which had been bestowed upon him at the tournament in procuring clothes fitted for his rank, he was yet abundantly supplied with money, for both Geoffrey Ward and Giles Fletcher, having no children of their own and being both well-to-do men, had insisted upon his accepting a sum which would enable him to make a good appearance with the best.

A large number of squires followed the banner of Sir Walter Manny. The records of the time show that the barons were generally accompanied in the field by almost as many squires as men-at-arms. The former were men of good family, sons of knights and nobles, aspirants for the honor of knighthood, and sons of the smaller gentry. Many were there from pure love of a life of excitement and adventure, others in fulfillment of the feudal tenure by which all land was then held, each noble and landowner being obliged to furnish so many knights, squires, men-at-arms, and archers, in accordance with the size of his holding. The squires fought in the field in the front rank of the men-at-arms, save those who, like Walter, were attached to the person of their leader, and who in the field fought behind him or bore his orders to the companies under his banner.

In the field all drew pay, and it may be interesting in the present day to know what were the rates for which our forefathers risked their lives. They were as follows: Each horse archer received 6 deniers, each squire 12 deniers or 1 sol, each knight 2 sols, each knight banneret 4 sols; 20 sols went to the pound, and although the exact value of money in those days relative to that which it bears at the present time is doubtful, it may be placed at twelve times the present value. Therefore each horse archer received an equivalent to 6s. a day, each squire 12s., each knight 24s., and each knight banneret 48s. per day.

Upon their arrival at the Orwell, where many troops from other parts had been gathered, the expedition at once embarked on board the numerous ships which had been collected. As that in which Sir Walter sailed also carried several of his knights there was not room for all his young esquires, and Walter and the three other juniors were told off into another ship. She was a smaller vessel than most of those which composed the expedition, and only carried twelve men-at-arms and as many archers, together with the four young squires, and a knight, Sir John Powis, who was in command of the whole.

"Your craft is but a small one," the knight said to the captain.

"She is small, but she is fast," the latter answered. "She would sail round and round the best part of the fleet. I had her built according to my own fancy. Small though she be, I warrant you she will be one of the first to arrive at Hennebon, and the sooner the better say I, since I am but paid by the trip, and would fain be back again at my regular work. It pays better carrying merchants' goods between London and Holland than taking his majesty's troops over to France."

"Your speed will not be of much avail," Sir John Powis said, "seeing that the fleet will keep together."

"Yes, I know that is the order," the captain answered; "but accidents happen sometimes, you know"—and his eye twinkled. "Vessels get separated from fleets. If they happen to be slow ones, so much the worse for those on board; if they happen to be fast ones, so much the better, seeing that those they carry will arrive long before their comrades, and may be enabled to gain credit and renown while the others are whistling for a wind in mid-ocean. However, we shall see."

The next morning the fleet sailed from the Orwell. It contained 620 men-at-arms, among whom were many of the noblest and bravest of the country, and 6,000 picked archers in the pay of the king. The whole were commanded by Sir Walter. The scene was a very gay one. The banners of the nobles and knights floated from the lofty poops, and the sun shone on bright armor and steel weapons. Walter, who had never seen the sea before, was delighted. The wind was fair, and the vessels glided smoothly along over the sea. At evening the knight and his four young companions gathered in the little cabin, for it was in the first week in March, and the night was cold.

"Will you please tell me, Sir John," Walter said to the knight, "the merits of this quarrel in which we are going to fight? I know that we are going in aid of the Countess of Montford; but why she is in a sore strait I know not."

"The matter is a mixed one, Walter, and it requires a herald to tell you all the subtleties of it. John III., Duke of Brittany, was present with his liege lord, Philip of Valois, in the last war with England, on the border of the Low Country. When the English retired from before Tournay Philip dismissed his nobles. The Duke of Burgundy was taken ill, and died at Caen, in Normandy, on the 30th of April, 1341. Arthur II., his father, had been twice married. By his first wife he had three sons, John, Guy, and Peter. John and Peter left no issue. Guy, who is also dead, left a daughter, Joan. By his second wife, Jolande de Dieux, Duke Arthur had one son, John, Count of Montford. Thus it happened that when Duke John died his half-brother, the Count of Montford, and Joan, daughter of his second brother Guy, were all that survived of the family. These were the rival claimants for the vacant dukedom. In England we have but one law of succession, which rules through the whole land. In France it is different. There the law of succession depends entirely upon the custom of the county, dukedom, or lordship, which is further affected both by the form of grant by which the territory was conveyed to its first feudal possessors and by the mode in which the province had been acquired by the kings of France. This is important, as upon these circumstances alone it depended whether the son or the granddaughter of Arthur II. should inherit the dukedom.

"Joan claimed the duchy as the daughter of the elder brother. The Salic law of France, which barred females from the right of succession, and in virtue of which Philip of Valois succeeded to the throne instead of King Edward, certainly did not obtain in Brittany. Duke John regarded Joan as his heiress, and married her to Charles of Blois, nephew of the King of France, thus strengthening her in her position; and he also induced the provincial parliament of Brittany to acknowledge her husband as his successor in the dukedom. Altogether it would seem that right is upon Joan's side; but, on the other hand, the Count of Montford is the son of Jolande, a great heiress in Brittany. He is an active and energetic noble. The Bretons love not too close a connection with France, and assuredly prefer to be ruled by a duke whom they regard as one of themselves rather than by Charles of Blois, nephew of the French king. Directly Duke John was dead the Count of Montford claimed the inheritance. Assuming the title of duke he rode to Nantes, where the citizens did him homage, and then proceeded to Limoges with a large train of men-at-arms, and there took possession of the immense treasures which the late duke had accumulated in the course of a long and tranquil reign. With these sinews of war at his command he returned to Nantes, where he had left his wife the countess, who was a sister of the Count of Flanders. He immediately invited the nobility of Brittany to a grand banquet, but only one knight of any renown presented himself at the feast, the rest all holding aloof. With the wealth of which he had possessed himself he levied large forces and took the field. He first marched against Brest, where the garrison, commanded by Walter de Clisson, refused to acknowledge him. After three days' hard fighting the place was taken. Rennes was next besieged, and presently surrendered. Other towns fell into his hands, and so far as Brittany was concerned all opposition, except in one or two fortresses, ceased. In the mean while Charles of Blois sought assistance from his uncle the King of France; the Count de Montford, therefore, crossed to England and besought the aid of King Edward, and did homage to him as King of France. Edward, on his part, promised to assist him. The fact that Philip was sure to espouse the opposite side was in itself sufficient to decide him; besides which, the dukes of Brittany have always been in a special way connected with England and bear the English title of Earl of Richmond.

"Believing that his journey, which had been a secret one, was unknown to the King of France, De Montford went boldly to Paris, where he had been summoned by the king to an assembly of peers called to decide upon the succession. He found, however, that Philip had already obtained news of his journey to England. His manner convinced De Montford that it was unsafe to remain in Paris, and he secretly made his escape. Fifteen days afterward the peers gave judgment in favor of Charles of Blois. The Dukes of Normandy, Burgundy, and Bourbon, the Counts of Alençon, Eu, and Guisnes, and many other French nobles, prepared to lead an army into the field to support Charles, and the king added a body of 3,000 Genoese mercenaries in his pay.

"Knowing the storm that was preparing to break upon him, De Montford put every town and castle in a state of defense. He himself, confiding in the affection of the inhabitants of Nantes, remained in that city, while his wife repaired to Rennes.

"The Duke of Normandy advanced from Angiers with an army of 5,000 men-at-arms and a numerous infantry, and after capturing the castle of Chantoceaux marched to Nantes and laid siege to the city. A sortie was made by the besieged, led by Henry de Leon, but, being attacked by the whole of the French army, they were driven back into the town, a great many of the citizens being killed. A warm altercation took place between Henry de Leon and De Montford, who attributed to him the evil result of the sortie. The result was that a large number of the citizens whose friends had been captured by the French conspired to deliver up the place to Charles of Blois, and Henry de Leon also entered into private negotiations with the Duke of Normandy. De Montford, finding that he could rely neither upon the citizens nor the soldiers, surrendered to the duke on condition that his life was spared. He was sent to Paris, where he still remains a prisoner. Winter was coming on, and after putting Nantes in a fresh state of defense and leaving Charles of Blois there, the Duke of Normandy dismissed his forces, engaging them to reassemble in the spring. Had he pushed on at once he would have experienced no resistance, so great was the panic which the surrender of Nantes and the capture of De Montford had caused among the latter's partisans.

"In Rennes especially the deepest despondency was felt. The countess, however, showed the greatest courage and firmness. Showing herself, with her infant in her arms, she appealed to the citizens, and by her courageous bearing inspired them with new hopes. Having restored heart at Rennes she traveled from garrison to garrison throughout the province, and filled all with vigor and resolution. Feeling, however, the hopelessness of her struggle against all France, she dispatched Sir Almeric de Clisson, who had lately joined her party, to England, to ask the aid which the king had promised. He arrived a month since, and, as you see, our brave king has not been long in dispatching us to her aid; and now, youngsters, to bed, for methinks that the sea is rougher than it was and that the wind is getting up."

"Ay, that is it," the captain, who heard the knight's closing words, exclaimed. "We are in for a storm, and a heavy one, or my name is not Timothy Martin, and though with plenty of sea-room the Kitty makes not much ado about a storm more or less, it's a very different thing in the middle of a fleet of lubberly craft, which may run one down at any time. I shall edge out of them as soon as I can, you may be sure."

Before morning a serious gale was blowing, and for the next three or four days Walter and his companions knew nothing of what was going on. Then the storm abated, and they staggered out from their cabin. The sea was still high, but the sun shone brightly overhead. In front of them the land was visible. They looked round, but to their astonishment not a sail was in sight.

"Why, where is the fleet?" Walter exclaimed in astonishment.

"Snug in the Thames, I reckon," the captain said. "Soon after the storm came on one of the sailors pretended he saw the lights of recall on the admiral's ship; but I was too busy to look that way; I had enough to do to look after the safety of the ship. Anyhow, I saw no more of them."

"And what land is that ahead?" Walter asked.

"That is Brittany, young sir, and before nightfall we shall be in the port of Hennebon; as to the others, it may be days and it may be weeks before they arrive."

The lads were not sorry at the chance which had taken them to their destination before their companions and had given them a chance of distinguishing themselves. Late in the afternoon the ship dropped anchor off the castle of Hennebon, and Sir John Powis and his following were conveyed in the ship's boats to shore. The countess received them most graciously, and was delighted at the news that so strong a force was on its way to her aid.

"In the absence of Sir Walter Manny, madam, I place myself and my men at your orders. Our horses will be landed the first thing in the morning, and we will then ride whithersoever you may bid us."

"Thanks, Sir John," the countess replied. "In that case I would that you ride by Rennes, toward which the army of the Duke of Normandy is already advancing. The garrison there is commanded by Sir William of Caddoudal, a good and valiant knight."

The horses were landed on the following morning, and accompanied by the four young squires and the men-at-arms, and followed by the twenty archers on foot, Sir John Powis set out for Rennes. They arrived there, but just in time, for the assailants were closing round the city. They were received with the greatest cordiality by the governor, who assigned apartments to Sir John and the squires, and lodged the men-at-arms and archers near them.

In a day or two the whole of the French army came up, and the siege commenced. Sir John Powis, his own request, was posted with his men for the defense of a portion of the wall which was especially open to the assaults of the enemy. These soon commenced in earnest, and the Genoese and Spanish mercenaries endeavored to carry the place by assault. Sometimes one point would be attacked, at others points far distant. Covered by the fire of the French cross-bowmen, the Spaniards and Germans came on to the assault, carrying ladders, with which they strove to climb the walls, but the defenders plied them so vigorously with quarrels from their cross-bows and flights of arrows that they frequently desisted before reaching the walls. When they pushed on, and strove to ascend, their luck was no better. Great stones were hurled down, and boiling oil poured upon them. The ladders were flung back, and many crushed by the fall, and in none of the assaults did they gain any footing in the town. Machines were used, but these were not sufficiently powerful to batter down the walls, and at the end of April the city was as far from being captured as it was on the day of the commencement of the siege.

Walter bore his full share in the fighting, but he had no opportunity of especially distinguishing himself, although Sir John several times commended him for his coolness when the bolts of the cross-bowmen and the stones from the machines were flying most thickly. But although as yet uninjured by the enemy's attacks, the prospect of the city holding out was not bright. The burghers, who had at first fought valiantly, were soon wearied of the strife, and of the hardships it entailed upon them. The siege had continued but a short time when they began to murmur loudly. The force under the command of the governor was but a small one, and it would have been impossible for him to resist the will of the whole population. For a time his exhortations and entreaties were attended with success, and the burghers returned to their positions on the walls; but each time the difficulty became greater, and it was clear to Caddoudal and Sir John Powis that ere long the citizens would surrender the place in spite of them. The English knight was furious at the cowardliness of the citizens, and proposed to the governor to summon twenty of the leading burghers, and to hang them as a lesson to the others; but the governor shook his head.

"I have but two hundred men on whom I can rely, including your following, Sir John. We could not keep down the inhabitants for an hour; and were we to try to do so, they would open the gates and let in the French. No; I fear that we must await the end."

The following morning Sir John was awoke with the news that in the night Caddoudal had been seized and thrown into prison by the burghers, and that a deputation of citizens had already gone out through the gate to treat with the Duke of Normandy for the surrender of the city.

The English knight was furious, but with his little band he could do nothing, especially as he found that a strong guard of burghers had been placed at the door of the apartments occupied by him and the esquires, and he was informed that he must consider himself a prisoner until the conclusion of the negotiations.

Cowardly and faithless as the burghers of Rennes showed themselves to be, they nevertheless stipulated with the Duke of Normandy, as one of the conditions of the surrender, that Caddoudal, Sir John Powis, and the troops under them should be permitted to pass through the French lines and go whithersoever they would. These terms were accepted. At mid-day the governor was released, and he with his men-at-arms and the band of Englishmen filed out from the city gate, and took their way unmolested through the lines of the French army to Hennebon.

They had been for a month in ignorance of all that had passed outside the walls, and had from day to day been eagerly looking for the arrival of Sir Walter Manny with his army to their relief. Once past the French lines they inquired of the peasantry, and heard to their surprise that the English fleet had not yet arrived.

"We were in luck indeed," Walter said to his companions, "that Captain Timothy Martin was in a hurry to get back to his tradings with the Flemings. Had he not been so we should all this time have been kicking our heels and fretting on board a ship."

On nearing Hennebon, Sir William Caddoudal, with Sir John Powis and the squires, rode forward and met the countess. They were the first bearers of the news of the surrender of Rennes, and the countess was filled with consternation at the intelligence. However, after her first burst of indignation and regret had passed, she put a brave face on it.

"They shall meet with another reception at Hennebon," she said. "This is but a small place, and my garrison here, and the soldiers you have brought, will well-nigh outnumber the burghers; and we need have no fear of such faint-heartedness as that which has given Nantes and Rennes into the hands of my enemy. The English aid cannot tarry long. Until it come we can assuredly hold the place."

All was now bustle in Hennebon. Sir John Powis took charge of a part of the walls, and busied himself with his men in placing the machines in position, and in preparing for defense. The countess, attired in armor, rode through the streets haranguing the townspeople. She urged the men to fight till the last, and bade the women and girls cut short their dresses so that they could the better climb the steps to the top of the walls, and that one and all should carry up stones, chalk, and baskets of lime to be cast down upon the assailants. Animated by her words and gestures, the townspeople set to work, and all vied with each other, from the oldest to the youngest, in carrying up stores of missiles to the walls. Never did Hennebon present such a scene of life and bustle. It seemed like an ant-hill which a passer-by has disturbed.

Absorbed in their work, none had time to think of the dangers which threatened them, and a stranger would rather have thought from their cheerful and animated countenances that they were preparing for a great *fête* than for a siege by an army to which the two chief towns in Brittany had succumbed.

The Citizens Prepare to Defend Hennebon. —Page 140.

Ere long the French army was seen approaching. The soldiers, who had been laboring with the rest, buckled on their armor. The citizens gathered on the walls to hurl down the piles of stones which had been collected, and all prepared for the assault.

"Sir John Powis," the countess said, "I pray you to grant me one of your esquires, who may attend me while I ride about, and may bear my messages for me. He will not be idle, nor will he escape his share of the dangers; for, believe me, I do not intend to hide myself while you and your brave soldiers are fighting for me."

"Willingly, lady," Sir John answered. "Here is Walter Somers, the son of a good knight, and himself brave and prudent beyond his years; he will, I am sure, gladly devote himself to your service."

The French, encouraged by their successes, thought that it would be a comparatively easy task to capture so small a place as Hennebon, and as soon as their camp was pitched they moved forward to the attack.

"Come with me, Master Somers," the countess said. "I will mount to one of the watch-towers, where we may see all that passes."

Walter followed her, and marveled to see the lightness and agility with which the heroic countess, although clad in armor, mounted the rickety ladders to the summit of the watch-tower. The French were pressing forward to the assault; their cross-bowmen opened a heavy fire upon the walls, which was answered by the shafts of the little party of English bowmen. These did much execution, for the English archers shot far harder and straighter than those of France, and it was only the best armor which could keep out their cloth-yard shafts. So small a body, however, could not check the advance of so large a force, and the French swarmed up to the very foot of the walls.

"Well done, my men!" the countess exclaimed, clapping her hands as a shower of heavy rocks fell among the mass of the assailants, who were striving to plant their ladders, crushing many in their fall; "but you are not looking, Master Somers. What is it that you see in yonder camp to withdraw your attention from such a fight?"

"I am thinking, countess, that the French have left their camp altogether unguarded, and that if a body of horse could make a circuit and fall upon it, the camp, with all its stores, might be destroyed before they could get back to save it."

"You are right, young sir," the countess exclaimed, "and it shall be done forthwith."

So saying, she descended the stairs rapidly and mounted her horse, which stood at the foot of the tower; then riding through the town, she collected a party of about three hundred men, bidding all she met mount their horses and join her at the gate on the opposite side to that on which the assault was taking place. Such as had no horses she ordered to take them from those in her own stables. Walter was mounted on one of the best of the count's chargers. Immediately the force was collected, the gate was opened and the countess rode forth at their head. Making a considerable *détour*, the party rode without being observed into the rear of the French camp. Here only a few servants and horse-boys were found; these were at once killed or driven out; then all dismounting, set fire to the tents and stores; and ere the French were aware of what was going on, the whole of their camp was in flames. As soon as the conflagration was perceived, the French commanders drew off their men from the attack, and all ran at full speed toward the camp.

"We cannot regain the town," the countess said; "we will ride to Auray at full speed, and reënter the castle when best we may."

Don Louis of Spain, who with a considerable following was fighting in the French ranks, hearing from the flying camp-followers that the countess herself was at the head of the party which had destroyed the camp, instantly mounted, and with a large number of horsemen set off in hot pursuit. A few of the countess' party who were badly mounted were overtaken and slain, but the rest arrived safely at Auray, when the gates were shut in the face of their pursuers.

The blow was a heavy one for the besiegers, but they at once proceeded to build huts, showing that they had no intention of relinquishing the siege. Spies were sent from Auray, and these reported that the new camp was established on the site of the old one, and that the French evidently intended to renew the attack upon the side on which they had first commenced, leaving the other side almost unwatched.

Accordingly, on the fifth day after leaving the town the countess prepared to return. Except Walter, none were informed of her intention, as she feared that news might be taken to the French camp by friends of Charles of Blois; but as soon as it was nightfall, and the gates were shut, the trumpet sounded to horse. In a few minutes the troop assembled in the market-place, and the countess, accompanied by Walter, placing herself at their head, rode out from the town. The strictest silence was observed. On nearing the town all were directed to dismount, to tear up the horse-cloths, and to muffle the feet of their horses. Then the journey was resumed, and so careless was the watch kept by the French that they passed through the sentries unobserved, and reached in safety the gate from which they had issued. As they neared it they were challenged from the walls, and a shout of joy was heard when Walter replied that the countess herself was present. The gates were opened and the party entered. The news of their return rapidly ran through the town, and the inhabitants, hastily attiring themselves, ran into the streets, filled with joy. Much depression had been felt during her absence, and few had entertained hopes that she would be able to reënter the town. She had brought with her from Auray two hundred men, in addition to the party that had sallied out.

Chapter IX
The Siege Of Hennebon.

The besiegers of Hennebon were greatly discouraged at the success of the enterprise of the countess. They had already attempted several desperate assaults, but had each time been repulsed with very heavy loss. They now sent to Rennes for twelve of the immense machines used in battering walls, which had been left behind there on a false report of the weakness of Hennebon. Pending the arrival of these, Charles of Blois with one division of the army marched away to attack Auray, leaving Don Louis to carry on the siege with a force considered amply sufficient to compel its surrender after the arrival of the battering machines.

In a few days these arrived and were speedily set to work, and immense masses of stone were hurled at the walls.

Walter continued to act as the countess' especial squire. She had informed Sir William Caddoudal and Sir John Powis that it was at his suggestion that she had made the sudden attack upon the French camp, and he had gained great credit thereby.

The effect of the new machines was speedily visible. The walls crumbled under the tremendous blows, and although the archers harassed by their arrows the men working them, the French speedily erected screens which sheltered them from their fire. The spirits of the defenders began to sink rapidly, as they saw that in a very short time great breaches would be made in the walls, and that all the horrors and disasters of a city taken by assault awaited them. The Bishop of Quimper, who was within the walls, entered into secret negotiations with his nephew, Henry de Leon, who had gone over to the enemy after the surrender of Nantes, and was now with the besieging army. The besiegers, delighted to find an ally within the walls who might save them from the heavy losses which an assault would entail upon them, at once embraced his offers, and promised him a large recompense if he would bring over the other commanders and nobles. The wily bishop set to work, and the consequences were soon visible. Open grumbling broke forth at the hardships which were endured, and at the prospect of the wholesale slaughter which would attend a storm when all hope of a successful resistance was at an end.

"I fear, Walter," Sir John said one morning, "that the end is at hand. On all sides submission is spoken of, and all that I can say to keep up their spirits is useless. Upon our own little band we can rely, but I doubt if outside them a single determined man is to be found in the town. In vain do I speak of the arrival of Sir Walter Manny. Nearly ninety days have elapsed since we sailed, and all hope of his coming is gone. I point out to them that contrary winds have been blowing, and that at any moment he may arrive; but they will not hear me. The bishop has gained over the whole of them by his promises that none shall be molested in property or estate should they surrender."

"It is sad to see the countess," Walter replied; "she who has shown such high spirit throughout the siege now does nothing but weep, for she knows that with her and her child in the hands of the French the cause of the count is lost. If she could carry off the child by sea she would not so much care for the fall of the town, but the French ships lie thick round the port, and there is no hope of breaking through."

Two days later the conspiracy came to a head, and the people, assembling round the countess' house, clamored for surrender. The breaches were open and the enemy might pour in at any time and put all to the sword. The countess begged for a little further delay, but in vain, and withdrew to the turret where she had for so many weary weeks watched the horizon, in hopes of seeing the sails of the approaching fleet. Walter was at the time with Sir John Powis on the walls. Presently a large body of French were seen approaching headed by Henry de Leon, who summoned the town to surrender. Many standing on the walls shouted that the gates should be thrown open; but Sir John returned for answer that he must consult the countess, and that upon her answer must depend whether he and his men would defend the breach until the last.

"Come with me, Walter," he said, "we must fain persuade the countess. If she says no, we Englishmen will die in the breach; but though ready to give my life for so brave a lady, I own that it is useless to fight longer. Save our own little band not one in the town will lift a sword again. Such resistance as we can offer will but inflame them to fury, and all the horrors of a sack will be inflicted upon the inhabitants. There she is, poor lady, on the turret, gazing, as usual, seaward."

Suddenly they saw her throw up her arms, and then turning toward the city she cried as she perceived the English knight, "I see them! I see them! The English fleet are coming!"

"Run up, Walter," Sir John exclaimed, "maybe the countess is distraught with her sorrows."

Walter dashed up to the turret, and looking seaward beheld rising over the horizon a number of masts.

"Hurrah! Sir John," he shouted, "we are saved, the English fleet is in sight."

Many others heard the shout, and the tidings ran like lightning through the town. In wild excitement the people ran to the battlements and roofs, and with cheering and clapping of hands hailed the appearance of the still far-distant fleet. The church bells rang out joyfully and the whole town was wild with excitement.

The Bishop of Quimper, finding that his plans were frustrated, gathered around him some of those who had taken a leading part in the intrigue. These, leaving the city by a gate at which they had placed some of their own faction to open it to the French, issued out and made their way to the assailants' camp, to give news of the altered situation. Don Louis at once ordered an attack to be made with his whole force, in hopes of capturing the place before the arrival of the English succor. But, animated by their new hopes, those so lately despondent and ready to yield manned the breaches and repulsed with great slaughter all attempts on the part of the French to carry them. While the struggle was still going on, the countess, aided by the wives of the burghers, busied herself in preparing a sumptuous feast in honor of her deliverers who were fast approaching, their ships impelled by a strong and favorable breeze. The vessels of the French hastily drew off, and the English fleet sailed into the port hailed by the cheers of the inhabitants. The countess herself received Sir Walter Manny on his landing, and the townspeople vied with each other in offering hospitality to the men-at-arms and archers.

"Ah! Sir John Powis," Sir Walter exclaimed, "what, are you here? I had given you up for lost. We thought you had gone down in the gale the night you started."

"We were separated from the fleet, Sir Walter, but the master held on, and we arrived here four days after we put out. We took part in the siege of Rennes, and have since done our best to aid the countess here."

"And their best has been much," the countess said; "not to say how bravely they have fought upon the walls, it is to Sir John and his little band that I owe it that the town was not surrendered days ago. They alone remained steadfast when all others fell away, and it is due to them that I am still able, as mistress of this town, to greet you on your arrival. Next to Sir John himself, my thanks are due to your young esquire, Walter Somers, who has cheered and stood by me, and to whose suggestions I owe it that I was able at the first to sally out and destroy the French camp while they were attacking the walls, and so greatly hindered their measures against the town. And now, sir, will you follow me? I have prepared for you and your knights such a banquet of welcome as our poor means will allow, and my townspeople will see that good fare is set before your soldiers."

That evening there was high feasting in the town, although the crash of the heavy stones cast by the French machines against the walls never ceased. Early the next morning Sir Walter Manny made a survey of the place and of the disposition of the enemy, and proposed to his knights to sally forth at once and destroy the largest of the enemy's machines, which had been brought up close to the walls. In a few minutes the knights were armed and mounted. Three hundred knights and esquires were to take part in the sortie; they were to be followed by a strong body of men-at-arms.

As soon as the gates were opened a number of archers issued out, and taking their place at the edge of the moat, poured a rain of arrows upon the men working the machine and those guarding it. Most of these took to flight at once; the remainder were cut down by the men-at-arms, who at once proceeded to hew the machine in pieces with the axes with which they were provided. Sir Walter himself and his mounted companions dashed forward to the nearer tents of the French camps, cut down all who opposed them, and setting fire to the huts retired toward the city.

By this time the French were thoroughly alarmed, and numbers of knights and men-at-arms dashed after the little body of English cavalry. These could have regained the place in safety, but in the chivalrous spirit of the time they disdained to retire without striking a blow. Turning their horses, therefore, and laying their lances in rest, they charged the pursuing French.

For a few minutes the conflict was desperate and many on both sides were overthrown; then, as large reënforcements were continually arriving to the French, Sir Walter called off his men and retired slowly. On reaching the moat he halted his forces. The knights wheeled and presented a firm face to the enemy, covering the entrance of their followers into the gate. The French chivalry thundered down upon the little body, but were met by a storm of arrows from the archers lining the moat. Many knights were struck through the bars of their vizors or the joints of their mail. The horses, though defended by iron trappings, fell dead under them, or, maddened by pain, dashed wildly through the ranks, carrying confusion with them, and the French commanders, seeing how heavy were their losses, called off their men from the assault. Sir Walter Manny with his party remained without the gate until the enemy had reëntered their camp, and then rode into the town amid the acclamations of the inhabitants, the countess herself meeting her deliverers at the gate and kissing each, one after the other, in token of her gratitude and admiration.

The arrival of the reënforcements and the proof of skill and vigor given by the English leader, together with the terror caused by the terrible effect of the English arrows, shook the resolution of Don Louis and his troops. Deprived of half their force by the absence of Charles of Blois, it was thought prudent by the leaders to withdraw at once, and the third morning after the arrival of Sir Walter Manny the siege was raised, and the French marched to join Charles of Blois before the castle of Auray.

Even with the reënforcements brought by Sir Walter Manny, the forces of the Countess of Montford were still so greatly inferior to those of the divisions of the French army that they could not hope to cope with them in the field until the arrival of the main English army, which the King of England himself was to bring over shortly. Accordingly the French laid siege to and captured many small towns and castles. Charles of Blois continued the siege of Auray, and directed Don Louis with his division to attack the town of Dinan. On his way the Spaniard captured the small fortress of Conquet and put the garrison to the sword. Sir Walter Manny, in spite of the inferiority of his force, sallied out to relieve it, but it was taken before his arrival, and Don Louis had marched away to Dinan, leaving a small garrison in Conquet. It was again captured by Sir Walter, but finding it indefensible he returned with the whole of his force to Hennebon. Don Louis captured Dinan and then besieged Guerande. Here he met with a vigorous resistance, but carried it by storm, and gave it up to be pillaged by his soldiers. He now sent back to Charles of Blois the greater part of the French troops who accompanied him, and embarked with the Genoese and Spanish, 8,000 in number, and sailed to Quimperlé, a rich and populous town in Lower Brittany.

Anchoring in the River Leita he disembarked his troops, and leaving a guard to protect the vessels marched to the interior, plundering and burning, and from time to time dispatching his booty to swell the immense mass which he brought in his ships from the sack of Guerande.

Quimperlé lies but a short distance from Hennebon, and Sir Walter Manny with Almeric de Clisson, a number of English knights, and a body of English archers, in all three thousand men, embarked in the ships in the port, and entering the Leita captured the enemy's fleet and all his treasure. The English then landed, and dividing into three bodies, set out in search of the enemy.

The English columns marched at a short distance apart so as to be able to give each other assistance in case of attack. The news of the English approach soon reached the Spaniards, who were gathered in a solid body, for the enraged country people, armed with clubs and bills, hung on their flanks and cut off any stragglers who left the main body. Don Louis at once moved toward the sea-coast, and coming in sight of one of the English divisions, charged it with his whole force.

The English fought desperately, but the odds of seven to one were too great, and they would have been overpowered had not the other two divisions arrived on the spot and fallen upon the enemy's flanks. After a severe and prolonged struggle the Genoese and Spaniards were completely routed. The armed peasantry slew every fugitive they could overtake, and of the 7,000 men with whom Don Louis commenced the battle only 300 accompanied him in his flight to Rennes, the troops of Sir Walter and De Clisson pursuing him to the very gates of that city. Sir Walter marched back with his force to the ships, but finding the wind unfavorable returned to Hennebon by land, capturing by the way the castle of Goy la Forèt. Their return was joyfully welcomed, not only for the victory which they had achieved, but because the enemy was again drawing near to the town. Auray had fallen. The brave garrison, after existing for some time upon the flesh of their horses, had endeavored to cut their way through the besiegers. Most of them were killed in the attempt, but a few escaped and made their way to Hennebon.

Vannes, an important town, and Carhaix quickly surrendered, and the French force was daily receiving considerable reënforcements. This arose from the fact that large numbers of French nobles and knights had, with their followers, taken part with Alfonso, King of Castile and Leon, in his war with the Moors. This had just terminated with the expulsion of the latter from Spain, and the French knights and nobles on their way home for the most part joined at once in the war which their countrymen were waging in Bretagne.

Seeing the great force which was gathering for a fresh siege of Hennebon, Sir Walter Manny and the Countess of Montford sent an urgent message to King Edward for further support. The king was not yet ready, but at the beginning of August he dispatched a force under the command of the Earl of Northampton and Robert of Artois. It consisted of twenty-seven knights bannerets and 2,000 men-at-arms. Before, however, it could reach Hennebon the second siege of that city had begun. Charles of Blois had approached it with a far larger army than that with which he had on the first occasion sat down before it. Hennebon was, however, much better prepared than at first for resistance. The walls had been repaired, provisions and military stores laid up, and machines constructed. The garrison was very much larger, and was commanded by one of the most gallant knights of the age, and the citizens beheld undaunted the approach of the great French army.

Four days after the French had arrived before Hennebon they were joined by Don Louis, who had been severely wounded in the fight near Quimperlé, and had lain for six weeks at Rennes. Sixteen great engines at once began to cast stones against the walls, but Sir Walter caused sand-bags to be lowered, and so protected the walls from the attack that little damage was done. The garrison, confident in their powers to resist, taunted the assailants from the walls, and specially enraged the Spaniards and Don Louis by allusions to the defeat at Quimperlé.

So furious did the Spanish prince become that he took a step unprecedented in those days of chivalry. He one morning entered the tent of Charles of Blois, where a number of French nobles were gathered, and demanded a boon in requital of all his services. Charles at once assented, when, to his surprise and horror, Prince Louis demanded that two English knights, Sir John Butler and Sir Hubert Frisnoy, who had been captured in the course of the campaign and were kept prisoners at Faouet, should be delivered to him to be executed. "These English," he said, "have pursued, discomforted, and wounded me, and have killed the nephew whom I loved so well, and as I have none other mode of vengeance I will cut off their heads before their companions who lie within those walls."

Charles of Blois and his nobles were struck with amazement and horror at the demand, and used every means in their power to turn the savage prince from his purpose, but in vain. They pointed out to him that his name would be dishonored in all countries where the laws of chivalry prevailed by such a deed, and besought him to choose some other boon. Don Louis refused to yield, and Charles of Blois, finding no alternative between breaking his promise and delivering his prisoners, at last agreed to his request.

The prisoners were sent for, and were informed by Don Louis himself of their approaching end. At first they could not believe that he was in earnest, for such a proceeding was so utterly opposed to the spirit of the times that it seemed impossible to them. Finding that he was in earnest they warned him of the eternal stain which such a deed would bring upon his name. The Spaniard, however, was unmoved either by their words or by the entreaties of the French nobles, but told them that he would give them a few hours to prepare for death, and that they should be executed in sight of the walls after the usual dinner hour of the army.

In those days sieges were not conducted in the strict manner in which they are at present, and non-combatants passed without difficulty to and fro between town and camp. The news, therefore, of what was intended speedily reached the garrison, whom it filled with indignation and horror. A council was immediately called, and Sir Walter Manny proposed a plan, which was instantly adopted.

Without loss of time Almeric de Clisson issued forth from the great gate of Hennebon, accompanied by 300 men-at-arms and 1,000 archers. The latter took post at once along the edge of the ditches. The men-at-arms rode straight for the enemy's camp, which was undefended, the whole army being within their tents at dinner. Dashing into their midst the English and Breton men-at-arms began to overthrow the tents and to spear all that were in them. Not knowing the extent of the danger or the smallness of the attacking force, the French knights sprang up from table, mounted, and rode to encounter the assailants.

For some time these maintained their ground against all assaults until, finding that the whole army was upon them, Almeric de Clisson gave order for his troop to retire slowly upon the town. Fighting every step of the ground and resisting obstinately the repeated onslaught of the French, Clisson approached the gate. Here he was joined by the archers, who with bent bows prepared to resist the advance of the French. As it now appeared that the garrison were prepared to give battle outside the walls, the whole French army prepared to move against them.

In the mean time Sir Walter Manny, with 100 men-at-arms and 500 horse archers, issued by a sally-port on the other side of the town, and with all speed rode round to the rear of the French camp. There he found none to oppose him save servants and camp-followers, and making his way straight to the tent of Charles of Blois, where the two knights were confined, he soon freed them from their bonds. They were mounted without wasting a moment's time upon two spare horses, and turning again the whole party rode back toward Hennebon, and had reached the postern gate before the fugitives from the camp reached the French commanders and told them what had happened.

Seeing that he was now too late, because of De Clisson's sortie, Charles of Blois recalled his army from the attack, in which he could only have suffered heavily from the arrows of the archers and the missiles from the walls. The same day, he learned from some prisoners captured in the sortie, of the undiminished spirit of the garrison, and that Hennebon was amply supplied by provisions brought by sea. His own army was becoming straitened by the scarcity of supplies in the country round; he therefore determined at once to raise the siege, and to besiege some place where he would encounter less serious resistance.

Accordingly next morning he drew off his army and marched to Carhaix.

Shortly afterward the news came that the Earl of Northampton and Robert of Artois, with their force, had sailed, and Don Louis, with the Genoese and other Italian mercenaries, started to intercept them with a large fleet. The fleets met off the island of Guernsey, and a severe engagement took place, which lasted till night. During the darkness a tremendous storm burst upon them and the combatants separated. The English succeeded in making their way to Brittany and landed near Vannes. The Spaniards captured four small ships which had been separated in the storm from their consorts, but did not succeed in regaining the coast of Brittany, being driven south by the storm as far as Spain. The Earl of Northampton at once laid siege to Vannes, and Sir Walter Manny moved with every man that could be spared from Hennebon to assist him.

As it was certain that the French army would press forward with all speed to relieve the town, it was decided to lose no time in battering the walls, but to attempt to carry it at once by assault. The walls, however, were so strong that there seemed little prospect of success attending such an attempt, and a plan was therefore determined upon by which the enemy might be thrown off their guard. The assault commenced at three points in the early morning and was continued all day. No great vigor, however, was shown in these attempts, which were repulsed at all points.

At nightfall the assailants drew off to their camp, and Oliver de Clisson, who commanded the town, suffered his weary troops to quit the walls and to seek for refreshment and repose. The assailants, however, did not disarm, but after a sufficient time had elapsed to allow the garrison to lay aside their armor two strong parties attacked the principal gates of the town, while Sir Walter Manny and the Earl of Oxford moved round to the opposite side with ladders for an escalade. The plan was successful. The garrison, snatching up their arms, hurried to repel their attack upon the gates, every man hastening in that direction. Sir Walter Manny with his party were therefore enabled to mount the walls unobserved and make their way into the town; here they fell upon the defenders in the rear, and the sudden onslaught spread confusion and terror among them. The parties at the gates forced their way in and joined their friends, and the whole of the garrison were killed or taken prisoners, save a few, including Oliver Clisson, who made their escape by sally-ports. Robert of Artois, with the Earl of Stafford, was left with a garrison to hold the town. The Earl of Salisbury, with four thousand men, proceeded to lay siege to Rennes, and Sir Walter Manny hastened back to Hennebon.

Some of Sir Walter's men formed part of the garrison of Vannes, and among these was Sir John Powis with a hundred men-at-arms.

The knight had been so pleased with Walter's coolness and courage at the siege at Hennebon that he requested Sir Walter to leave him with him at Vannes. "It is possible," he said to Walter, "that we may have fighting here. Methinks that Sir Walter would have done better to leave a stronger force. The town is a large one, and the inhabitants ill-disposed toward us. Oliver Clisson and the French nobles will feel their honor wounded at the way in which we outwitted them, and will likely enough make an effort to regain the town. However, Rennes and Hennebon are not far away, and we may look for speedy aid from the Earl of Salisbury and Sir Walter should occasion arise."

Sir John's previsions were speedily verified. Oliver Clisson and his friends were determined to wipe out their defeat and scattered through the country, raising volunteers from among the soldiery in all the neighboring towns and castles, and a month after Vannes was taken they suddenly appeared before the town with an army of 12,000 men, commanded by Beaumanoir, Marshal of Bretagne for Charles of Blois. The same reasons which had induced the Earl of Northampton to decide upon a speedy assault instead of the slow process of breaching the walls, actuated the French in pursuing the same course, and, divided into a number of storming parties, the army advanced at once to the assault on the walls. The little garrison prepared for the defense.

"The outlook is bad, Walter," Sir John Powis said. "These men approach with an air of resolution which shows that they are bent upon success. They outnumber us by twelve to one, and it is likely enough that the citizens may rise and attack us in the rear. They have been ordered to bring the stones for the machines to the walls, but not one has laid his hand to the work. We must do our duty as brave men, my lad, but I doubt me if yonder is not the last sun which we shall see. Furious as the French are at our recent success here, you may be sure that little quarter will be given."

Chapter X
A Place Of Refuge.

The French, excited to the utmost by the exhortations of their commanders, and by their desire to wipe out the disgrace of the easy capture of Vannes by the English, advanced with ardor to the assault, and officers and men vied with each other in the valor which they displayed. In vain did the garrison shower arrows and cross-bow bolts among them, and pour down boiling oil and quicklime upon them as they thronged at the foot of the wall. In vain were the ladders, time after time, hurled back loaded with men upon the mass below. The efforts of the men-at-arms to scale the defenses were seconded by their archers and cross-bowmen, who shot such a storm of bolts that great numbers of the defenders were killed. The assault was made at a score of different points, and the garrison was too weak to defend all with success. Sir John Powis and his party repulsed over and over again the efforts of the assailants against that part of the wall intrusted to them, but at other points the French gained a footing, and swarming up rushed along the walls, slaying all whom they encountered.

"All is lost," Sir John exclaimed; "let us fall back to the castle and die fighting there."

Descending from the wall the party made their way through the streets. The French were already in the town; every house was closed and barred, and from the upper windows the burghers hurled down stones and bricks upon the fugitives, while parties of the French soldiers fell upon them fiercely. Many threw down their arms and cried for quarter, but were instantly slain.

For awhile the streets were a scene of wild confusion; here and there little knots of Englishmen stood together and defended themselves until the last, others ran through the streets chased by their exulting foes, some tried in vain to gain shelter in the houses. Sir John Powis' band was soon broken and scattered, and their leader slain by a heavy stone from a housetop. Walter fought his way blindly forward toward the castle, although he well knew that no refuge would be found there. Ralph Smith kept close beside him, leveling many of his assailants with the tremendous blows of a huge mace. Somehow, Walter hardly knew how, they made their way through their assailants and dashed in at the castle gate. A crowd of their assailants were close upon their heels. Walter glanced round; dashing across the court-yard he ran through some passages into an inner yard, in which, as he knew, was the well. The bucket hung at the windlass.

"Catch hold, Ralph!" he exclaimed; "there is just a chance, and we may as well be drowned as killed." They grasped the rope and jumped off. The bucket began to descend with frightful velocity. Faster and faster it went and yet it seemed a long time before they plunged into the water, which was nigh a hundred feet below the surface. Fortunately the rope was considerably longer than was necessary, and they sank many feet into the water, still retaining their hold. Then clinging to the rope they hauled themselves to the surface.

"We cannot hold on here five minutes," Ralph exclaimed; "my armor is dragging me down."

"We will soon get rid of that," Walter said. "There go our helmets; now I will hold on with one hand and help you to unbuckle your breast and back pieces; you do the same for me."

With great efforts they managed to rid themselves of their armor, and then held on with ease to the rope. They hauled the bucket to the surface and tied a knot in the slack of the rope, so that the bucket hung four feet below the level of the water. Putting their feet in this, they were able to stand with their heads above the surface without difficulty.

"This is a nice fix," Ralph exclaimed. "I think it would have been just as well to have been killed at once. They are sure to find us here, and if they don't we shall die of cold before to-morrow morning."

"I don't think they will find us," Walter said cheerfully. "When they have searched the castle thoroughly it may occur to some of them that we have jumped down the well, but it will be no particular business of any one to look for us, and they will all be too anxious to get at the wine butts to trouble their heads about the matter; besides, it must be a heavy job to wind up this bucket, and it is not likely there will be such urgent need of water that any one will undertake the task."

"But we are no better off if they don't," Ralph remarked, "for we must die here if we are not hauled out. I suppose you don't intend to try and climb that rope. I might do twenty feet or so on a pinch, but I could no more get up to the top there than I could fly."

"We must think it over," Walter rejoined; "where there is a will there's a way, you know. We will take it by turns to watch that little patch of light overhead; if we see any one looking down we must leave the bucket and swim to the side without making the least noise. They may give a few turns of the windlass to see if any one has hold of the rope below; be sure you do not make the slightest splashing or noise, for the sound would be heard above to a certainty."

Ten minutes later they saw two heads appear above, and instantly withdrew their feet from the bucket and made a stroke to the side, which was but four feet distant, being careful as they did so that no motion was imparted to the rope. Then, though it was too dark to see anything, they heard the bucket lifted from the water. A minute later it fell back again with a splash, then all was quiet.

"We are safe now, and can take our place in the bucket. They are satisfied that if we did jump down here we are drowned. And now we must think about climbing up."

"Ay, that will require a good deal of thinking," Ralph grumbled.

For some time there was silence; then Walter said, "The first thing to do is to cut off the slack of the rope; there are some twelve feet of it. Then we will unwind the strands of that. There are five or six large strands as far as I can feel; we will cut them up into lengths of about a couple of feet, and we ought to be able to tie these to the rope in such a way as not to slip down with our weight. If we tie them four feet apart we can go up step by step; I don't see much difficulty about that."

"No," Ralph said much more cheerfully, "I should think that we could manage that."

They at once set to work. The rope was cut up and unraveled, and the strands cut into pieces about two feet long. They then both set to work trying to discover some way of fastening it by which it would not slip down the rope. They made many fruitless attempts; each time that a strand was fastened with a loop large enough for them to pass a leg through, it slid down the rope when their weight was applied to it. At last they succeeded in finding out a knot which would hold. This was done by tying a knot close to one end of a piece of the strand, then sufficient was left to form the loop, and the remainder was wound round the rope in such away that the weight only served to tighten its hold.

"Shall we begin at once?" Ralph said, when success was achieved.

"No, we had better wait until nightfall. The vibration of the rope when our weight once gets on it might be noticed by any one crossing the court-yard."

"Do you think we have sufficient bits of rope?" Ralph asked.

"Just enough, I think," Walter replied; "there were six strands, and each has made six pieces, so we have thirty-six. I know the well is about a hundred feet deep, for the other day I heard some of the soldiers who were drawing water grumbling over the labor required. So if we put them three feet apart it will take thirty-three of them, which will leave three over; but we had better place them a little over a yard so as to make sure."

In a short time the fading brightness of the circle of light far overhead told them that twilight had commenced, and shortly afterward they attached the first strand to the rope some three feet above the water.

"Now," Walter said, "I will go first, at any rate for a time. I must put one leg through the loop, and sit, as it were, while I fasten the one above, as I shall want both hands for the work. You will find it a good deal easier to stand with your foot in the loop. If I get tired I will fasten another loop by the side of that on which I am resting, so you can come up and pass me. There is no hurry. It ought not to take up above an hour, and it will not do for us to get to the top until the place becomes a little quiet. To-night they are sure to be drinking and feasting over their victory until late."

They now set to work, and step by step mounted the rope. They found the work less arduous than they had expected. The rope was dry, and the strands held tightly to it. Two or three times they changed places, resting in turn from their work; but in less than two hours from the time they made the first loop Walter's head and shoulders appeared above the level of the court-yard. He could hear sounds of shouting and singing within the castle, and knew that a great feast was going on. Descending a step or two he held parley with Ralph.

"I think, perhaps, it will be better to sally out at once. Everyone is intent on his own pleasure, and we shall have no difficulty in slipping out of the castle unnoticed. All will be feasting and rioting in the town, and so long as we do not brush against any one so that they may feel our wet garments we are little likely to be noticed; besides, the gates of the town will stand open late, for people from the villages round will have come in to join in the revels."

"I am ready to try it, Master Walter," Ralph replied, "for I ache from head to foot with holding on to this rope. The sooner the better, say I."

In another minute both stood in the court-yard. It was a retired spot, and none were passing. Going along the passage they issued into the main yard. Here great fires were blazing, and groups of men sat round them drinking and shouting. Many lay about in drunken sleep.

"Stay where you are in the shade, Ralph. You had best lie down by the foot of the wall. Any one who passes will think that you are in a drunken sleep. I will creep forward and possess myself of the steel caps of two of these drunkards, and if I can get a couple of cloaks so much the better."

There was no difficulty about the caps, and by dint of unbuckling the cloaks and rolling their wearers gently over, Walter succeeded at last in obtaining two of them. He also picked up a sword for Ralph-his own still hung in its sheath-and then he joined his companion, and the two putting on the steel caps and cloaks walked quietly to the gate. There were none on guard, and they issued unmolested into the town. Here all was revelry. Bonfires blazed in the streets. Hogsheads of wine, with the heads knocked out, stood before many of the houses for all to help themselves who wished. Drunken soldiers reeled along shouting snatches of songs, and the burghers in the highest state of hilarity thronged the ways.

"First of all, Ralph, we will have a drink of wine, for I am chilled to the bone."

"Ay, and so am I," Ralph replied. "I got hot enough climbing that rope, but now the cold has got hold of me again, and my teeth are chattering in my head."

Picking up one of the fallen vessels by a cask they dipped it in and took a long draught of wine; then, turning off from the principal streets, they made their way by quiet lanes down to one of the gates. To their dismay they found that this was closed. The French commanders knew that Sir Walter Manny or Salisbury might ere this be pressing forward to relieve the town, and that, finding that it had fallen, they might attempt to recapture it by a sudden attack. While permitting, therefore, the usual license, after a successful assault, to the main body of their forces, they had placed a certain number of their best troops on the walls, giving them a handsome largess to make up for their loss of the festivities.

At first Walter and his friend feared that their retreat was cut off for the night, but several other people presently arrived, and the officer on guard said, coming out, "You must wait awhile; the last batch have only just gone, and I cannot keep opening and closing the gate; in half an hour I will let you out."

Before that time elapsed some fifty or sixty people, anxious to return to their villages, gathered round the gate.

"Best lay aside your steel cap, Ralph, before we join them," Walter said. "In the dim light of that lamp none will notice that we have no head gear, but if it were to glint upon the steel cap the officer might take us for deserters and question us as to who we are."

Presently the officer came out from the guard-room again. There was a forward movement of the little crowd, and Walter and Ralph closed in to their midst. The gates were opened, and without any question the villagers passed out, and the gates were shut instantly behind them.

213

Walter and his comrade at once started at a brisk pace and walked all night in the direction of Hennebon. Their clothes soon dried, and elated at their escape from danger they struggled on briskly. When morning broke they entered a wood, and lay there till evening, as they feared to continue their journey lest they might fall into the hands of some roving band of French horse. They were, too, dog-tired, and were asleep a few minutes after they lay down. The sun was setting when they awoke, and as soon as it was dark they resumed their journey.

"I don't know what you feel, Master Walter, but I am well-nigh famished. It is thirty-six hours since I swallowed a bit of food, just as the French were moving to the attack. Hard blows I don't mind —I have been used to it; but what with fighting, and being in the water for five or six hours, and climbing up that endless rope, and walking all night on an empty stomach, it does not suit me at all."

"I feel ravenous too, Ralph, but there is no help for it. We shall eat nothing till we are within the walls of Hennebon, and that will be by daylight to-morrow if all goes well. Draw your belt an inch or two tighter, it will help to keep out the wolf."

They kept on all night, and in the morning saw to their delight the towers of Hennebon in the distance. It was well that it was no further, for both were so exhausted from want of food that they could with difficulty drag their legs along.

Upon entering the town Walter made his way at once to the quarters of the leader. Sir Walter had just risen, and was delighted at the sight of his esquire.

"I had given you up for dead," he exclaimed. "By what miracle could you have escaped? Are you alone?"

"I have with me only my faithful follower, Ralph Smith, who is below; but, Sir Walter, for mercy's sake order that some food be placed before us, or we shall have escaped from the French only to die of hunger here. We have tasted naught since the attack on Vannes began. Have any besides us escaped?"

"Lord Stafford contrived, with two or three others, to cut their way out by a postern-gate, bringing with them Robert of Artois, who is grievously wounded. None others, save you and your man-at-arms, have made their way here."

In a few minutes a cold capon, several manchets of bread, and a stoop of wine were placed before Walter, while Ralph's wants were attended to below. When he had satisfied his hunger the young esquire related his adventures to Sir Walter and several other knights and nobles, who had by this time gathered in the room.

"In faith, Master Somers, you have got well out of your scrape," Sir Walter exclaimed. "Had I been in your place I should assuredly have perished, for I would a thousand times rather meet death sword in hand than drop down into the deep hole of that well. And your brains served you shrewdly in devising a method of escape. What say you, gentlemen?"

All present joined in expressions of praise at the lad's coolness and presence of mind.

"You are doing well, young sir," the English leader went on, "and have distinguished yourself on each occasion on which we have been engaged. I shall be proud when the time comes to bestow upon you myself the order of knighthood if our king does not take the matter off my hands."

A little later Robert of Artois died of his wounds and disappointment at the failure of his hopes.

In October King Edward himself set sail with a great army, and landing in Brittany early in November, marched forward through the country and soon reduced Ploermel, Malestrail, Redon, and the rest of the province in the vicinity of Vannes, and then laid siege to that town. As his force was far more than sufficient for the siege, the Earls of Norfolk and Warwick were dispatched in the direction of Nantes to reconnoiter the country and clear it of any small bodies of the enemy they might encounter. In the mean time Edward opened negotiations with many of the Breton lords, who, seeing that such powerful aid had arrived for the cause of the Countess of Montford, were easily persuaded to change sides. Among them were the Lords of Clisson, Moheac, Machecoul, Retz, and many others of less importance.

The Count of Valentinois, who commanded the garrison of Vannes, supported the siege with great courage and fortitude, knowing that Charles of Blois and the King of France were collecting a great army for his relief. Uniting their forces, they advanced toward the town. Before the force of the French, 40,000 strong, the Earl of Norfolk had fallen back and rejoined the king; but even after this junction the French forces exceeded those of Edward fourfold. They advanced toward Vannes and formed a large intrenched camp near that of the English, who thus, while still besieging Vannes, were themselves inclosed by a vastly superior force. The King of France himself arrived at the French camp. The French, although so greatly superior, made no motion toward attacking the English, but appeared bent upon either starving them out or forcing them to attack the strongly intrenched position occupied by the French.

Provisions were indeed running short in the English camp, and the arrival of supplies from England was cut off by a strong fleet under Don Louis, which cruised off the coast and captured all vessels arriving with stores. At this moment two legates, the Cardinal Bishop of Preneste and the Cardinal Bishop of Tusculum, arrived from the pope and strove to mediate between the two sovereigns and to bring about a cessation of hostilities, pointing out to them the scandal and desolation which their rivalry caused in Christendom, the waste of noble lives, the devastation of once happy provinces, and the effusion of innocent blood. Going from camp to camp they exhorted, prayed, and reproached the rival sovereigns, urging that while Christians were shedding each other's blood in vain, the infidels were daily waxing bolder and more insolent. Their arguments would have been but of little use had either of the monarchs felt sure of victory. King Edward, however, felt that his position was growing desperate, for starvation was staring him in the face, and only by a victory over an immensely superior force in a strongly intrenched position could he extricate himself. Upon the part of the French, however, circumstances were occurring which rendered them anxious for a release from their position, for they were not without their share of suffering. While the English army lay on a hill the French camp was pitched on low ground. An unusually wet season had set in with bitterly cold wind. The rain was incessant, a pestilence had destroyed a vast number of their horses, and their encampment was flooded. Their forces were therefore obliged to spread themselves over the neighboring fields, and a sudden attack by the English might have been fatal.

Thus distress pressed upon both commanders, and the pope's legates found their exertions at last crowned with success. A suspension of hostilities was agreed to, and the Dukes of Burgundy and Bourbon on the one side and the Earls of Lancaster, Northampton, and Salisbury on the other met as commissioners and agreed to a convention by which a general truce was to be made from the date of the treaty to the following Michaelmas, and to be prolonged from that day for the full term of three years. It was agreed that the truce should embrace not only the sovereigns, but all the adherents of each of them. The truce was to hold good in Brittany between all parties, and the city of Vannes was to be given into the hand of the cardinals to dispose of as they chose. It was specially provided that in the case of any of the adherents of either party in the duchies of Gascony and Brittany waging war against each other, neither of the monarchs should either directly or indirectly meddle therewith, nor should the truce be at all broken thereby.

Immediately the treaty was signed, on the 19th of January, 1343, the King of France dismissed his army, and Edward sailed for England with the greater part of his troops. The Countess of Montford and her son accompanied him, and the possessions of her husband in Brittany were left to the guardianship of her partisans, with a small but choice body of English troops.

The towns which had fallen into their hands and still remained were Brest, Quimper-Corentin, Quimperlé, Redon, and Guerande; Vannes was handed over to them by the cardinals, and Hennebon, of course, remained in their possession.

Walter returned to England with Sir Walter Manny, and on reaching London was received with delight by his old friends Geoffrey Ward and Giles Fletcher, who were never tired of listening to his tales of the wars. Dame Vernon also received him with great kindness, and congratulated him warmly upon the very favorable account which Sir Walter Manny had given of his zeal and gallantry.

The time now for awhile passed very quietly. Walter and the other young squires practiced diligently, under the instructions of Sir Walter, at knightly exercises. Walter learned to bear himself well on horseback and to tilt in the ring. He was already a skillful swordsman, but he spared no pains to improve himself with his weapons. The court was a gay one, and Walter, as a favored esquire of one of the foremost knights there, was admitted to all that took place. His courtly education, of course, included dancing, and when he went down, as he often did, for a long chat with his old friends, Geoffrey often said, laughing, that he was growing such a fine gentleman that he hardly liked to sit in his presence; but although changed in manner, Walter continued to be, as before, a frank, manly young fellow, and free from the affectations which were so general among the young men of the court.

Chapter XI
A Stormy Interview.

Soon after Walter's return from France Dame Vernon returned to her country estate, and a year passed before he again saw her. During this time the truce which had been established between England and France had remained unbroken. It was certain, however, that ere long the two powers would again come to blows. The King of England had honorably observed the terms of the treaty. Upon his return home he had entirely disbanded his army and had devoted his whole attention to increasing the trade and prosperity of the country. The measures which he took to do this were not always popular with the people of England, for seeing how greatly they excelled the English manufacturers Edward encouraged large numbers of Flemings and other foreign workmen to settle in London, and gave them many privileges to induce them to do so; this the populace strongly resented. There was a strong ill-feeling against the Flemings and serious popular riots took place, for the English traders and workmen considered that these foreigners were taking the bread from their mouths. The king, however, was wiser than his people, he saw that although the English weavers were able to produce coarse cloths, yet that all of the finer sort had to be imported from the Continent. He deemed that in time the Flemings would teach their art to his subjects, and that England would come to vie with the Low Countries in the quality of her produce. Such was indeed afterward the case, and England gained greatly by the importation of the industrious Flemings, just as she afterward profited from the expulsion from France of tens of thousands of Protestant workmen who brought here many of the manufactures of which France had before the monopoly. The relations between England and the Flemings were at this time very close, for the latter regarded England as her protector against the ambition of the King of France.

But while King Edward had laid aside all thought of war, such was not the case with Philip of Valois. He had retired after the signature of the treaty full of rage and humiliation; for hitherto in all their struggles his English rival had had the better of him, and against vastly superior forces had foiled all his efforts and had gained alike glory and military advantage. King Edward had hardly set sail when Philip began to break the terms of truce by inciting the adherents of Charles of Blois to attack those of De Montford, and by rendering assistance to them with money and men. He also left no means untried to detach Flanders from its alliance with England. Several castles and towns in Brittany were wrested from the partisans of De Montford, and King Edward, after many remonstrances at the breaches of the conditions of the truce, began again to make preparations for taking the field. Several brilliant tournaments were held and every means were taken to stir up the warlike spirit of the people.

One day Walter had attended his lord to the palace and was waiting in the anteroom with many other squires and gentlemen, while Sir Walter, with some other noblemen, was closeted with the king, discussing the means to be adopted for raising funds for a renewal of the war with France, when a knight entered whom Walter had not previously seen at court.

"Who is that?" he asked one of his acquaintances; "methinks I know his face, though it passes my memory to say where I have seen it."

"He has been away from England for some two years," his friend answered. "That is Sir James Carnegie; he is a cousin of the late Sir Jasper Vernon; he left somewhat suddenly a short time after Dame Vernon had that narrow escape from drowning that you wot of; he betook himself then to Spain, where he has been fighting the Moors; he is said to be a valiant knight, but otherwise he bears but an indifferent good reputation."

Walter remembered the face now; it was that of the knight he had seen enter the hut of the river pirate on the Lambeth marshes. When released from duty he at once made his way to the lodging of Dame Vernon. Walter was now nineteen, for a year had elapsed since the termination of the French war, and he was in stature and strength the match of most men, while his skill at knightly exercises, as well as with the sword, was recognized as preeminent among all the young esquires of the court.

After the first greeting he said to Dame Vernon: "I think it right to tell you, lady, that I have but now, in the king's anteroom, seen the man who plotted against your life in the hut at Lambeth. His face is a marked one and I could not mistake it. I hear that he is a cousin of yours, one Sir James Carnegie, as you doubtless recognized from my description of him. I came to tell you in order that you might decide what my conduct should be. If you wish it so I will keep the secret in my breast; but if you fear aught from him I will openly accuse him before the king of the crime he attempted, and shall be ready to meet him in the ordeal of battle should he claim it."

"I have seen Sir James," Lady Vernon said. "I had a letter writ in a feigned hand telling him that his handiwork in the plot against my life was known, and warning him that, unless he left England, the proofs thereof would be laid before justice. He at once sailed for Spain, whence he has returned but a few days since. He does not know for certain that I am aware of his plottings against us; but he must have seen by my reception of him when he called that I no longer regard him with the friendship which I formerly entertained. I have received a message from him that he will call upon me this evening, and that he trusts he will find me alone, as he would fain confer with me on private matters. When I have learned his intentions I shall be the better able to judge what course I had best adopt. I would fain, if it may be, let the matter rest. Sir James has powerful interest, and I would not have him for an open enemy if I can avoid it; besides, all the talk and publicity which so grave an accusation against a knight, and he of mine own family, would entail, would be very distasteful to me; but should I find it necessary for the sake of my child, I shall not shrink from it. I trust, however, that it will not come to that; but I shall not hesitate, if need be, to let him know that I am acquainted with his evil designs toward us. I will inform you of as much of our interview as it is necessary that you should know."

That evening Sir James Carnegie called upon Dame Vernon. "I would not notice it the other day, fair cousin," he said, in return for her stiff and ceremonious greeting; "but methinks that you are mightily changed in your bearing toward me. I had looked on my return from my long journeying for something of the sisterly warmth with which you once greeted me, but I find you as cold and hard as if I had been altogether a stranger to you. I would fain know in what way I have forfeited your esteem."

"I do not wish to enter into bygones, Sir James," the lady said, "and would fain let the past sleep if you will let me. Let us, then, turn without more ado to the private matters concerning which you wished to speak with me."

"If such is your mood, fair dame, I must needs fall in with it, though in no way able to understand your allusion to the past, wherein my conscience holds me guiltless of aught which could draw upon me your disfavor. I am your nearest male relative, and as such would fain confer with you touching the future of young Mistress Edith, your daughter. She is now nigh thirteen years of age, and is the heiress of broad lands; is it not time that she were betrothed to one capable of taking care of them for her, and leading your vassals to battle in these troubled times?"

"Thanks, Sir James, for your anxiety about my child," Dame Vernon said coldly. "She is a ward of the king. I am in no way anxious that an early choice should be made for her; but our good Queen Philippa has promised that, when the time shall come, his majesty shall not dispose of her hand without my wishes being in some way consulted; and I have no doubt that when the time shall come that she is of marriageable age-and I would not that this should be before she has gained eighteen years, for I like not the over young marriages which are now in fashion —a knight may be found for her husband capable of taking care of her and her possessions; but may I ask if, in so speaking to me, you have any one in your mind's eye as a suitor for her hand?"

"Your manner is not encouraging, certes; but I had my plan, which would, I hoped, have met with your approval. I am the young lady's cousin, and her nearest male relative; and although we are within the limited degrees, there will be no difficulty in obtaining a dispensation from Rome. I am myself passably well off, and some of the mortgages which I had been forced to lay upon my estates have been cleared off during my absence. I have returned home with some reputation, and with a goodly sum gained in the wars with the Moors. I am older than my cousin, certainly; but as I am still but thirty-two, this would not, I hope, be deemed an obstacle, and methought that you would rather intrust her to your affectionate cousin than to a stranger. The king has received me very graciously, and would, I trust, offer no opposition to my suit were it backed by your good-will."

"I suppose, Sir James," Dame Vernon said, "that I should thank you for the offer which you have made; but I can only reply, that while duly conscious of the high honor you have done my daughter by your offer, I would rather see her in her grave than wedded to you."

The knight leaped from his seat with a fierce exclamation. "This is too much," he exclaimed, "and I have a right to know why such an offer on my part should be answered by disdain, and even insolence."

Dame Alice Reveals Sir James' Villainy. —Page 187.

"You have a right to know," Dame Vernon answered quietly, "and I will tell you. I repeat that I would rather see my child in her grave than wedded to a man who attempted to compass the murder of her and her mother."

"What wild words are these?" Sir James asked sternly. "What accusation is this that you dare to bring against me?"

"I repeat what I said, Sir James," Dame Alice replied quietly. "I know that you plotted with the water pirates of Lambeth to upset our boat as we came down the Thames; that you treacherously delayed us at Richmond in order that we might not reach London before dark; and that by enveloping me in a white cloak you gave a signal by which I might be known to your creatures."

The knight stood for a moment astounded. He was aware that the fact that he had had some share in the outrage was known, and was not surprised that his cousin was acquainted with the secret; but that she should know all the details with which but one besides himself was, as he believed, acquainted, completely stupefied him. He rapidly, however, recovered himself.

"I recall now," he said scornfully, "the evidence which was given before the justices by some ragged city boy, to the effect that he had overheard a few words of a conversation between some ruffian over in the Lambeth marshes and an unknown person; but it is new to me indeed that there was any suspicion that I was the person alluded to, still less that a lady of my own family, in whose affection I believed, should credit so monstrous an accusation."

"I would that I could discredit it, Sir James," Dame Vernon said sadly; "but the proofs were too strong for me. Much more of your conversation than was narrated in court was overheard, and it was at my request that the ragged boy, as you call him, kept silence."

"And is it possible," the knight asked indignantly, "that you believed the word of a fellow like this to the detriment of your kinsman? Why, in any court of law the word of such a one as opposed to that of a knight and gentleman of honor would not be taken for a moment."

"You are mistaken, sir," Dame Vernon said haughtily. "You may remember, in the first place, that the lad who overheard this conversation risked his life to save me and my daughter from the consequences of the attack which he heard planned; in the second place, he was no ragged lad, but the apprentice of a well-known citizen; thirdly-and this is of importance, since he has recognized you since your return, and is ready, should I give him the word, to denounce you-he is no mere apprentice boy, but is of gentle blood, seeing that he is the son of Sir Roland Somers, the former possessor of the lands which I hold, and that he is in high favor with the good knight Sir Walter Manny, whose esquire he now is, and under whom he distinguished himself in the wars in France, and is, as Sir Walter assures me, certain to win his spurs ere long. Thus you see his bare word would be of equal value to your own, besides the fact that his evidence does not rest upon mere assertion; but that the man in the hut promised to do what you actually performed, namely, to delay me at Richmond, and to wrap me in a white cloak in order that I might be recognized by the river pirates."

Sir James was silent. In truth, as he saw, the evidence was overwhelmingly strong against him. After awhile he stammered out, "I cannot deny that I was the man in question; but I swear to you that this boy was mistaken, and that the scoundrel acted altogether beyond my instructions, which were simply that he should board the boat and carry you and your daughter away to a safe place."

"And with what object, sir," Dame Vernon said contemptuously, "was I to be thus taken away?"

"I do not seek to excuse myself," the knight replied calmly, having now recovered his self-possession, "for I own I acted wrongly and basely; but in truth I loved you, and would fain have made you my wife. I knew that you regarded me with only the calm affection of a kinswoman; but I thought that were you in my power you would consent to purchase your freedom with your hand. I know now that I erred greatly. I acknowledge my fault, and that my conduct was base and unknightly, and my only excuse is the great love I bore you."

"And which," the lady said sarcastically, "you have now transferred to my daughter. I congratulate you, Sir James, upon the possession of a ready wit and an invention which does not fail you at a pinch, and of a tongue which repeats unfalteringly any fable which your mind may dictate. You do not, I suppose, expect me to believe the tale. Still, I own that it is a well-devised one, and might, at a pinch, pass muster; but fear not, Sir James. As hitherto I have kept silence as to the author of the outrage committed upon me, so I have no intention of proclaiming the truth now unless you force me to do so. Suffice that both for myself and for my daughter I disclaim the honor of your hand. So long as you offer no molestation to us, and abstain from troubling us in any way, so long will my mouth be sealed; and I would fain bury in my breast the memory of your offense. I will not give the world's tongue occasion to wag by any open breach between kinsfolk, and shall therefore in public salute you as an acquaintance, but under no pretense whatever will I admit you to any future private interview. Now leave me, sir, and I trust that your future life will show that you deeply regret the outrage which in your greed for my husband's lands you were tempted to commit."

Without a word Sir James turned and left the room, white with shame and anger, but with an inward sense of congratulation at the romance which he had, on the spur of the moment, invented, and which would, he felt sure, be accepted by the world as probable, in the event of the share he had in the matter being made public, either upon the denunciation of Dame Vernon or in any other manner.

One determination, however, he made, and swore, to himself, that he would bitterly avenge himself upon the youth whose interference had thwarted his plans, and whose report to his kinswoman had turned her mind against him. He, at any rate, should be put out of the way at the first opportunity, and thus the only witness against himself be removed; for Lady Vernon's own unsupported story would be merely her word against his, and could be treated as the malicious fiction of an angry woman.

The following day Dame Vernon sent for Walter, and informed him exactly what had taken place.

"Between Sir James and me," she said, "there is, you see, a truce. We are enemies, but we agree to lay aside our arms for the time. But, Walter, you must be on your guard. You know as well as I do how dangerous this man is, and how good a cause he has to hate you. I would not have divulged your name had I not known that the frequency of your visits here and the encouragement which I openly give you as the future suitor of my daughter, would be sure to come to his ears, and he would speedily discover that it was you who saved our lives on the Thames and gave your testimony before the justices as to the conversation in the hut on the marshes. Thus I forestalled what he would in a few days have learned."

"I fear him not, lady," Walter said calmly. "I can hold mine own, I hope, against him in arms, and having the patronage and friendship of Sir Walter Manny I am above any petty malice. Nevertheless, I will hold myself on my guard. I will, so far as possible, avoid any snare which he may, as 'tis not unlikely, set for my life, and will, so far as I honorably can, avoid any quarrel with which he may seek to saddle me."

A few days later Walter again met Sir James Carnegie in the king's anteroom, and saw at once, by the fixed look of hate with which he had regarded him, that he had already satisfied himself of his identity. He returned the knight's stare with a cold look of contempt. The knight moved toward him and in a low tone said, "Beware, young sir, I have a heavy reckoning against you, and James Carnegie never forgets debts of that kind!"

"I am warned, Sir James," Walter said calmly, but in the same low tone, "and, believe me, I hold but very lightly the threats of one who does not succeed even when he conspires against the lives of women and children."

Sir James started as if he had been struck. Then with a great effort he recovered his composure, and, repeating the word "Beware!" walked across to the other side of the chamber.

The next day Walter went down the river and had a talk with his friend Geoffrey.

"You must beware, lad," the armorer said when he told him of the return of Sir James Carnegie and the conversation which had taken place between them. "This man is capable of anything, and careth not where he chooseth his instruments. The man of the hut at Lambeth has never been caught since his escape from Richmond Jail-thanks, doubtless, to the gold of his employer-and, for aught we know, may still be lurking in the marshes there, or in the purlieus of the city. He will have a grudge against you as well as his employer, and in him Sir James would find a ready instrument. He is no doubt connected, as before, with a gang of water pirates and robbers, and it is not one sword alone that you would have to encounter. I think not that you are in danger just at present, for he would know that, in case of your murder, the suspicions of Dame Vernon and of any others who may know the motive which he has in getting rid of you would be excited, and he might be accused in having had a share in your death. Still, it would be so hard to prove aught against him that he may be ready to run the risk in order to rid himself of you. Look here, Walter. What think you of this?" and the smith drew out from a coffer a shirt of mail of finer work than Walter had ever before seen.

"Ay, lad, I knew you would be pleased," he said in answer to Walter's exclamation at the fineness of the workmanship. "I bought this a month ago from a Jew merchant who had recently come from Italy. How he got it I know not, but I doubt if it were honestly, or he would have demanded a higher price than I paid him. He told me that it was made by the first armorer in Milan, and was constructed especially for a cardinal of the church, who had made many enemies by his evil deeds and could not sleep for fear of assassination. At his death it came, the Jew said, into his possession. I suppose some rascally attendant took it as a perquisite, and, knowing not of its value, sold it for a few ducats to the Jew. However, it is of the finest workmanship. It is, as you see, double, and each link is made of steel so tough that no dagger or sword point will pierce it. I put it on a block and tried the metal myself, and broke one of my best daggers on it without a single link giving. Take it, lad. You are welcome to it. I bought it with a special eye to you, thinking that you might wear it under your armor in battle without greatly adding to the weight; but for such dangers as threaten you now it is invaluable. It is so light and soft that none will dream that you have it under your doublet, and I warrant me it will hold you safe against the daggers of Sir James' ruffians."

Walter did not like taking a gift so valuable, for his apprenticeship as an armorer had taught him the extreme rarity and costliness of so fine a piece of work. Geoffrey, however, would not hear of his refusal, and insisted on his then and there taking off his doublet and putting it on. It fitted closely to the body, descending just below the hips, and coming well up on the neck, while the arms extended to the wrists.

"There!" the smith said with delight. "Now you are safe against sword or dagger, save for a sweeping blow at the head, and that your sword can be trusted to guard. Never take it off, Walter, save when you sleep; and except when in your own bed, at Sir Walter Manny's, I should advise you to wear it even at night. The weight is nothing, and it will not incommode you. So long as this caitiff knight lives, your life will not be safe. When he is dead you may hang up the shirt of mail with a light heart."

Chapter XII
Jacob Van Artevelde.

King Edward found no difficulty in awakening the war spirit of England anew, for the King of France, by an act of infamous treachery, in spite of the solemn terms of the treaty, excited against himself the indignation not only of England but of all Europe. Oliver de Clisson, with fourteen other nobles of Brittany and Normandy, were arrested by his order, taken to Paris, and without form of trial there decapitated. This act of treachery and injustice aroused disgust and shame among the French nobles, and murmurs and discontent spread throughout the whole country.

In Brittany numbers of the nobles fell off from the cause of Charles of Blois, and King Edward hastened his preparations to avenge the butchery of the adherents of the house of Montford. Philip, however, in defiance of the murmurs of his own subjects, of the indignant remonstrances of Edward, and even those of the pope, who was devoted to his cause, continued the course he had begun, and a number of other nobles were seized and executed. Godfrey of Harcourt alone, warned by the fate of his companions, refused to obey the summons of the king to repair to Paris, and fled to Brabant. His property in France was at once seized by Philip; and Godfrey, finding that the Duke of Brabant would be unable to shield him from Philip's vengeance, fled to the English court, and did homage to Edward.

On the 24th of April, 1345, Edward determined no longer to allow Philip to continue to benefit by his constant violations of the truce, and accordingly sent a defiance to the King of France.

De Montford, who had just succeeded in escaping from his prison in Paris, arrived at this moment in England, and shortly afterward set sail with a small army under the command of the Earl of Northampton for Brittany, while the Earl of Derby took his departure with a larger force for the defense of Guienne.

King Edward set about raising a large army, which he determined to lead himself, but before passing over to France he desired to strengthen his hold of Flanders. The constant intrigues of Philip there had exercised a great effect. The count of that country was already strongly in his interest, and it was only the influence of Jacob van Artevelde which maintained the alliance with England. This man had, by his talent and energy, gained an immense influence over his countrymen; but his commanding position and ability had naturally excited the envy and hatred of many of his fellow-citizens, among whom was the dean of the weavers of Ghent, one Gerard Denis. The weavers were the most powerful body in this city, and had always been noted for their turbulence and faction; and on a Monday in the month of May, 1345, a great battle took place in the market-place between them and the fullers, of whom 1,500 were slain. This victory of the weavers strengthened the power of the party hostile to Artevelde and the English connection; and the former saw that unless he could induce his countrymen to take some irretrievable step in favor of England they would ultimately fall back into the arms of France. Accordingly he invited Edward to pass over with a strong force into Flanders, where he would persuade the Flemings to make the Prince of Wales their duke. King Edward at once accepted the offer, and sailing from Sandwich on the 3d of July arrived in safety at Sluys. His intention had been kept a profound secret, and his arrival created the greatest surprise throughout Flanders. He did not disembark, but received on board a ship with great honor and magnificence the burgomasters of the various towns who appeared to welcome him. The king had brought with him the Prince of Wales, now fifteen years old, who wore a suit of black armor and was therefore called "the Black Prince."

Walter Somers was on board the royal vessel. The Prince of Wales had not forgotten the promise which he had six years before made to him, and had asked Sir Walter Manny to allow him to follow under his banner.

"You are taking my most trusty squire from me, prince," the knight said; "for although I have many brave young fellows in my following, there is not one whom I value so much as Walter Somers. It is but fair, however, that you should have him, since you told me when I first took him that he was to follow your banner when you were old enough to go to the wars. You can rely upon him implicitly. He cares not for the gayeties of which most young men of his age think so much. He is ever ready for duty, and he possesses a wisdom and sagacity which will some day make him a great leader."

Walter was sorry to leave his patron, but the step was of course a great advancement, and excited no little envy among his companions, for among the young esquires of the Prince of Wales were the sons of many of the noblest families of England.

Sir Walter presented him on leaving with a heavy purse. "Your expenses will be large," he said, "among so many young gallants, and you must do credit to me as well as to yourself. The young prince is generous to a fault, and as he holds you in high favor, both from his knowledge of you and from my report, you will, I know, lack nothing when you are once fairly embarked in his service; but it is needful that when you first join you should be provided with many suits of courtly raiment of cloth of gold and silk, which were not needed while you were in the service of a simple knight like myself, but which must be worn by a companion of the heir of England."

Walter had hoped that Sir James Carnegie would have accompanied the forces of either of the Earls of Northampton or Derby, but he found that he had attached himself to the royal army.

Ralph of course followed Walter's fortunes, and was now brilliant in the appointments of the Prince of Wales' chosen body-guard of men-at-arms.

The councils of all the great towns of Flanders assembled at Sluys, and for several days great festivities were held. Then a great assembly was held, and Van Artevelde rose and addressed his countrymen. He set forth to them the virtues of the Prince of Wales, whose courtesy and bearing had so captivated them; he pointed out the obligations which Flanders was under toward King Edward, and the advantages which would arise from a nearer connection with England. With this he contrasted the weakness of their count, the many ills which his adherence to France had brought upon the country, and the danger which menaced them should his power be ever renewed. He then boldly proposed to them that they should at once cast off their allegiance to the count and bestow the vacant coronet upon the Prince of Wales, who, as Duke of Flanders, would undertake the defense and government of the country with the aid of a Flemish council.

This wholly unexpected proposition took the Flemish burghers by surprise. Artevelde had calculated upon his eloquence and influence carrying them away, but his power had diminished, and many of his hearers had already been gained to the cause of France. The burgher councils had for a long time had absolute power in their own towns, and the prospect of a powerful prince at their head foredoomed a curtailment of those powers. When Artevelde ceased, therefore, instead of the enthusiastic shouts with which he hoped his oration would be greeted, a confused murmur arose. At last several got up and said that, greatly attached as they were to the king, much as they admired the noble young prince proposed for their acceptance, they felt themselves unable to give an answer upon an affair of such moment without consulting their fellow-countrymen and learning their opinions. They therefore promised that they would return on a certain day and give a decided answer.

The Flemish burghers then took their leave. Van Artevelde, after a consultation with the king, started at once to use his influence among the various towns.

After leaving the king he bade adieu to the Prince of Wales. "Would you like," the young prince said, "that one of my esquires should ride with you? His presence might show the people how entirely I am with you; and should you have tidings to send me he could ride hither with them. I have one with me who is prudent and wise, and who possesses all the confidence of that wise and valiant knight, Sir Walter de Manny." (Somers)

"I will gladly take him, your royal highness," Van Artevelde said, "and hope to dispatch him to you very shortly with the news that the great towns of Flanders all gladly receive you as their lord."

In a few minutes Walter had mounted his horse, accompanied by Ralph, and, joining Van Artevelde, rode to Bruges. Here and at Ypres Van Artevelde's efforts were crowned with success. His eloquence carried away the people with him, and both these cities agreed to accept the Prince of Wales as their lord; but the hardest task yet remained. Ghent was the largest and most powerful of the Flemish towns, and here his enemies were in the ascendant. Gerard Denis and the weavers had been stirring up the people against him. All kinds of accusations had been spread, and he was accused of robbing and selling his country. The news of the hostile feeling of the population reached Van Artevelde, and he dispatched Walter with the request to the king for a force of five hundred English soldiers as a guard against his enemies.

Had Artevelde asked for a large force Edward would have disembarked his army and marched at their head into Ghent. As the rest of the country was already won there can be little doubt that this step would at once have silenced all opposition, and would have annexed Flanders to the British crown. Van Artevelde, however, believed himself to be stronger than he really was, and thought with a small party of soldiers he could seize his principal opponents, and that the people would then rally round him.

Upon the arrival of the five hundred men he started for Ghent; but as he feared that the gates would be shut if he presented himself with an armed force, he left the soldiers in concealment a short distance from the town and entered it, accompanied only by his usual suit. At his invitation, however, Walter, followed of course by Ralph, rode beside him. No sooner was he within the gates than Van Artevelde saw how strong was the popular feeling against him. He had been accustomed to be received with bows of reverence; now men turned aside as he approached, or scowled at him from their doors.

"Methinks, sir," Walter said, "that it would be wiser did we ride back, and, joining the soldiers, enter at their head, or as that number would be scarce sufficient should so large a town rise in tumult, to send to King Edward for a larger force and await their coming. Even should they shut the gates we can reduce the town, and as all the rest of Flanders is with you, surely a short delay will not matter."

"You know not these Flemings as well as I do," Van Artevelde replied; "they are surly dogs, but they always listen to my voice, and are ready enough to do my bidding. When I once speak to them you will see how they will smooth their backs and do as I ask them."

Walter said no more, but as he saw everywhere lowering brows from window and doorway as they rode through the streets, he had doubts whether the power of Van Artevelde's eloquence would have the magical potency he had expected from it.

When the party arrived at the splendid dwelling of the great demagogue, messengers were instantly sent out to all his friends and retainers. A hundred and forty persons soon assembled, and while Van Artevelde was debating with them as to the best steps to be taken, Walter opened the casement and looked out into the street. It was already crowded with the people, whose silent and quiet demeanor seemed to bode no good. Arms were freely displayed among them, and Walter saw men passing to and fro evidently giving instructions.

"I am sorry to disturb you, Master Artevelde," he said, returning to the room where the council was being held, "but methinks that it would be wise to bar the doors and windows, and to put yourself in a posture of defense, for a great crowd is gathering without, for the most part armed, and as it seems to me with evil intentions."

A glance from the windows confirmed Walter's statements, and the doors and windows were speedily barricaded. Before many minutes had elapsed the tolling of bells in all parts of the town was heard, and down the different streets leading toward the building large bodies of armed men were seen making their way.

"I had rather have to do with a whole French army, Master Walter," Ralph said, as he stood beside him at an upper window looking down upon the crowd, "than with these citizens of Ghent. Look at those men with bloody axes and stained clothes. Doubtless those are the skinners and butchers. Didst ever see such a ferocious band of savages? Listen to their shouts. Death to Van Artevelde! Down with the English alliance! I thought our case was a bad one when the French poured over the walls into Vannes, but methinks it is a hundred times worse now."

"We got out of that scrape, Ralph, and I hope we shall get out of this, but as you say the prospect is black enough. See, the butchers are hammering at the door with their pole-axes. Let us go down and aid in the defense."

"I am ready," Ralph said, "but I shall fight with a lighter heart if you could fix upon some plan for us to adopt when the rabble break in. That they will do so I regard as certain, seeing that the house is not built for purposes of defense, but has numerous broad windows on the ground-floor by which assuredly they will burst their way in."

"Wait a moment then, Ralph; let us run up to the top story and see if there be any means of escape along the roofs."

The house stood detached from the others, but on one side was separated from that next to it only by a narrow lane, and as the upper stories projected beyond those below, the windows were but six feet distant from those on the opposite side of the way.

"See," Walter said, "there is a casement in the room to our left there which is open; let us see if it is tenanted."

Going into the next room they went to the window and opened it. It exactly faced the casement opposite, and so far as they could see the room was unoccupied.

"It were easy to put a plank across," Ralph said.

"We must not do that," Walter answered. "The mob are thick in the lane below-what a roar comes up from their voices! —and a plank would be surely seen, and we should be killed there as well as here. No, we must get on to the sill and spring across; the distance is not great, and the jump would be nothing were it not that the casements are so low. It must be done as lightly and quickly as possible, and we may not then be seen from below. Now leave the door open that we may make no mistake as to the room, and come along, for by the sound the fight is hot below."

Running down the stairs Walter and Ralph joined in the defense. Those in the house knew that they would meet with no mercy from the infuriated crowd, and each fought with the bravery of despair. Although there were many windows to be defended, and at each the mob attacked desperately, the assaults were all repulsed. Many indeed of the defenders were struck down by the pikes and pole-axes, but for a time they beat back the assailants whenever they attempted to enter.

The noise was prodigious. The alarm-bells of the town were all ringing and the shouts of the combatants were drowned in the hoarse roar of the surging crowd without.

Seeing that however valiant was the defense the assailants must in the end prevail, and feeling sure that his enemies would have closed the city gates and thus prevented the English without from coming to his assistance, Van Artevelde ascended to an upper story and attempted to address the crowd. His voice was drowned in the roar. In vain he gesticulated and made motions imploring them to hear him, but all was useless, and the courage of the demagogue deserted him and he burst into tears at the prospect of death. Then he determined to try and make his escape to the sanctuary of a church close by, and was descending the stairs when a mighty crash below, the clashing of steel, shouts, and cries, told that the mob had swept away one of the barricades and were pouring into the house.

"Make for the stairs," Walter shouted, "and defend yourselves there." But the majority of the defenders, bewildered by the inrush of the enemy, terrified at their ferocious aspect and terrible axes, had no thought of continuing the resistance. A few, getting into corners, resisted desperately to the end; others threw down their arms and dropping on their knees cried for mercy, but all were ruthlessly slaughtered.

Keeping close together Walter and Ralph fought their way to the foot of the stairs, and closely pursued by a band of the skinners headed by Gerard Denis, ran up.

Upon the first landing stood a man paralyzed with terror. On seeing him a cry of ferocious triumph rose from the mob. As nothing could be done to aid him Walter and his follower rushed by without stopping. There was a pause in the pursuit, and glancing down from the upper gallery Walter saw Van Artevelde in the hands of the mob, each struggling to take possession of him; then a man armed with a great ax pushed his way among them, and swinging it over his head struck Van Artevelde dead to the floor. His slayer was Gerard Denis himself.

Followed by Ralph, Walter sprang through the open door into the chamber they had marked, and closed the door behind them. Then Walter, saying, "I will go first, Ralph; I can help you in should you miss your spring," mounted on the sill of the casement.

Short as was the distance the leap was extremely difficult, for neither casement was more than three feet high. Walter was therefore obliged to stoop low and to hurl himself head forward across the gulf. He succeeded in the attempt, shooting clear through the casement on to the floor beyond. Instantly he picked himself up and went to Ralph's assistance. The latter, taller and more bulky, had greater difficulty in the task, and only his shoulders arrived through the window. Walter seized him, and aided him at once to scramble in, and they closed the casement behind them.

"It was well we took off our armor, Ralph; its pattern would have been recognized in an instant."

Walter had thrown off his helmet as he bounded up the stairs, and both he and his companion had rid themselves of their heavy armor.

"I would give a good deal," he said, "for two bourgeois jerkins, even were they as foul as those of the skinners. This is a woman's apartment," he added, looking round, "and nothing here will cover my six feet of height, to say nothing of your four inches extra. Let us peep into some of the other rooms. This is, doubtless, the house of some person of importance, and in the upper floor we may find some clothes of servants or retainers."

They were not long in their search. The next room was a large one, and contained a number of pallet beds, and hanging from pegs on the walls were jerkins, mantles, and other garments, evidently belonging to the retainers of the house. Walter and Ralph were not long in transmogrifying their appearance, and had soon the air of two respectable serving-men in a Flemish household.

"But how are we to descend?" Ralph asked. "We can hardly hope to walk down the stairs and make our escape without being seen, especially as the doors will all be barred and bolted, seeing the tumult which is raging outside."

"It all depends whether our means of escape are suspected," Walter replied. "I should scarce think that they would be. The attention of our pursuers was wholly taken up by Van Artevelde, and some minutes must have passed before they followed us. No doubt they will search every place in the house, and all within it will by this time have been slaughtered. But they will scarce organize any special search for us. All will be fully occupied with the exciting events which have taken place, and as the casement by which we entered is closed it is scarcely likely to occur to any one that we have escaped by that means. I will listen first if the house is quiet. If so, we will descend and take refuge in some room below, where there is a better chance of concealment than here. Put the pieces of armor into that closet so that they may not catch the eye of any who may happen to come hither. The day is already closing. In half an hour it will be nightfall. Then we will try and make our way out."

Listening at the top of the stairs they could hear voices below; but as the gallery was quiet and deserted they made their way a floor lower, and seeing an open door entered it. Walter looked from the window.

"There is a back yard below," he said, "with a door opening upon a narrow lane. We are now upon the second story, and but some twenty-five feet above the ground. We will not risk going down through the house, which could scarce be accomplished without detection, but will at once tear up into strips the coverings of the bed, and will make a rope by which we may slip down into the court-yard as soon as it is dark. We must hope that none will come up before that time; but, indeed, all will be so full of the news of the events which have happened that it is scarce likely that any will come above at present."

The linen sheets and coverings were soon cut up and knotted together in a rope. By the time that this was finished the darkness was closing in, and after waiting patiently for a few minutes they lowered the rope and slid down into the yard. Quietly they undid the bolts of the gate and issued into the lane. The mantles were provided with hoods, as few of the lower class of Flemings wore any other head-covering.

Drawing these hoods well over their heads so as to shade their faces, the two sallied out from the lane. They were soon in one of the principal streets, which was crowded with people. Bands of weavers, butchers, skinners, and others were parading the streets shouting and singing in honor of their victory and of the downfall and death of him whom they had but a few days before regarded as the mainstay of Flanders. Many of the better class of burghers stood in groups in the streets and talked in low and rather frightened voices of the consequences which the deed of blood would bring upon the city. On the one hand, Edward might march upon it with his army to avenge the murder of his ally. Upon the other hand, they were now committed to France. Their former ruler would return, and all the imposts and burdens against which they had rebelled would again be laid upon the city.

"What shall we do now?" Ralph asked, "for assuredly there will be no issue by the gates."

"We must possess ourselves of a length of rope, if possible, and make our escape over the wall. How to get one I know not, for the shops are all closed, and even were it not so I could not venture in to purchase any, for my speech would betray us at once. Let us separate, and each see whether he can find what we want. We will meet again at the entrance to this church in an hour's time. One or the other of us may find what we seek."

Walter searched in vain. Wherever he saw the door of a yard open he peered in, but in no case could he see any signs of rope. At the end of the hour he returned to their rendezvous. Ralph was already there.

"I have found nothing, Ralph. Have you had better fortune?"

"That have I, Master Walter, and was back nigh an hour since. Scarce had I left you when in a back street I came upon a quiet hostelry, and in the court-yard were standing half a dozen teams of cattle. Doubtless their owners had brought hay or corn into the city, and when the tumult arose and the gates were closed found themselves unable to escape. The masters were all drinking within, so without more ado I cut off the ropes which served as traces for the oxen, and have them wound round my body under my mantle. There must be twenty yards at least, and as each rope is strong enough to hold double our weight there will be no difficulty in lowering ourselves from the walls."

"You have done well indeed, Ralph," Walter said. "Let us make our way thither at once. Every one is so excited in the city that, as yet, there will be but few guards upon the wall. The sooner, therefore, that we attempt to make our escape the better."

Chapter XIII
The White Ford.

They made their way without interruption to the wall. This they found, as they expected, entirely deserted, although, no doubt, guards had been posted at the gates. The Flemings, however, could have felt no fear of an attack by so small a force as the five hundred English whom they knew to be in the neighborhood.

Walter and his companion soon knotted the ropes together and lowered themselves into the moat. A few strokes took them to the other side, and scrambling out, they made their way across the country to the spot where the English had been posted. They found the Earl of Salisbury, who commanded, in a great state of uneasiness. No message had reached him during the day. He had heard the alarm-bells of the city ring, and a scout who had gone forward returned with the news that the gates were closed and the drawbridges raised, and that a strong body of men manned the walls.

"Your news is indeed bad," he said, when Walter related to him the events which had taken place in the town. "This will altogether derange the king's plans. Now that his ally is killed, I fear that his hopes of acquiring Flanders for England will fall to the ground. It is a thousand pities that he listened to Van Artevelde and allowed him to enter Ghent alone. Had his majesty landed, as he wished, and made a progress through the country, the prince receiving the homage of all the large towns, we could then very well have summoned Ghent as standing alone against all Flanders. The citizens then would, no doubt, have gladly opened their gates and received the prince, and if they had refused we would have made short work of them. However, as it has turned out, it is as well that we did not enter the town with the Fleming, for against so large and turbulent a population we should have had but little chance. And now, Master Somers, we will march at once for Sluys and bear the news to the king, and you shall tell me as we ride thither how you and your man-at-arms managed to escape with whole skins from such a tumult."

The king was much grieved when he heard of the death of Artevelde, and held a council with his chief leaders. At first, in his indignation and grief, he was disposed to march upon Ghent and to take vengeance for the murder of his ally, but after a time calmer counsels prevailed.

The Flemings were still in rebellion against their count, who was the friend of France. Were the English to attack Ghent they would lose the general good-will of the Flemings, and would drive them into the arms of France, while, if matters were left alone, the effect of the popular outburst which had caused the death of Artevelde would die away, and motives of interest and the fear of France would again drive them into the arms of England. The expedition therefore returned to England, and there the king, in a proclamation to his people, avoided all allusion to the death of his ally, but simply stated that he had been waited upon by the councils of all the Flemish towns, and that their faithful obedience to himself, as legitimate King of France, was established upon a firmer basis than ever.

This course had the effect which he had anticipated from it. The people of Flanders perceived the danger and disadvantage which must accrue to their trade from any permanent disagreement with England. They were convinced by the events which soon afterward happened in France that the King of England had more power than Philip of Valois, and could, if he chose, punish severely any breach of faith toward him. They therefore sent over commissioners to express their grief and submission. The death of Artevelde was represented as the act of a frantic mob, and severe fines were imposed upon the leaders of the party who slew him, and although the principal towns expressed their desire still to remain under the rule of the Count of Flanders, they suggested that the ties which bound them to England should be strengthened by the marriage of Louis, eldest son of the count, to one of Edward's daughters. More than this, they offered to create a diversion for the English forces acting in Guienne and Gascony by raising a strong force and expelling the French garrisons still remaining in some parts of the country. This was done. Hugo of Hastings was appointed by the king captain-general in Flanders, and with a force of English and Flemings did good service by expelling the French from Termond and several other towns.

The character of Jacob van Artevelde has had but scant justice done to it by most of the historians of the time. These, living in an age of chivalry, when noble blood and lofty deeds were held in extraordinary respect, had little sympathy with the brewer of Ghent, and deemed it contrary to the fitness of things that the chivalry of France should have been defied and worsted by mere mechanics and artisans. But there can be no doubt that Artevelde was a very great man. He may have been personally ambitious, but he was a true patriot. He had great military talents. He completely remodeled and wonderfully improved the internal administration of the country, and raised its commerce, manufactures, and agriculture to a pitch which they had never before reached. After his death his memory was esteemed and revered by the Flemings, who long submitted to the laws he had made, and preserved his regulations with scrupulous exactitude.

Edward now hastened to get together a great army. Every means were adopted to raise money and to gather stores, and every man between sixteen and sixty south of the Trent was called upon to take up arms and commanded to assemble at Portsmouth in the middle of Lent. A tremendous tempest, however, scattered the fleet collected to carry the expedition, a great many of the ships were lost, and it was not until the middle of July, 1346, that it sailed from England. It consisted of about five hundred ships and ten thousand sailors, and carried four thousand men-at-arms, ten thousand archers, twelve thousand Welsh, and six thousand Irish.

This seems but a small army considering the efforts which had been made; but it was necessary to leave a considerable force behind for the defense of the Scottish frontier, and England had already armies in Guienne and Brittany. Lionel, Edward's second son, was appointed regent during his father's absence. On board Edward's own ship were Godfrey of Harcourt and the Prince of Wales. Walter, as one of the personal squires of the prince, was also on board.

The prince had been greatly interested in the details of Walter's escape from Van Artevelde's house, the king himself expressed his approval of his conduct, and Walter was generally regarded as one of the most promising young aspirants at the court. His modesty and good temper rendered him a general favorite, and many even of the higher nobles noticed him by their friendly attentions, for it was felt that he stood so high in the good-will of the prince that he might some day become a person of great influence with him, and one whose good-will would be valuable.

It was generally supposed, when the fleet started, that Guienne was their destination, but they had not gone far when a signal was made to change the direction in which they were sailing and to make for La Hogue in Normandy. Godfrey of Harcourt had great influence in that province, and his persuasions had much effect in determining the king to direct his course thither. There was the further advantage that the King of France, who was well aware of the coming invasion, would have made his preparations to receive him in Guienne. Furthermore, Normandy was the richest and most prosperous province in France. It had for a long time been untouched by war, and offered great abundance of spoil. It had made itself particularly obnoxious to the English by having recently made an offer to the King of France to fit out an expedition and conquer England with its own resources.

The voyage was short and favorable, and the expedition landed at La Hogue, on the small peninsula of Cotentin, without opposition. Six days were spent at La Hogue disembarking the men, horses, and stores, and baking bread for the use of the army on the march. A detachment advanced and pillaged and burned Barfleur and Cherbourg and a number of small towns and castles.

In accordance with custom, at the commencement of the campaign a court was held, at which the Prince of Wales was dubbed a knight by his father. A similar honor was bestowed upon a number of other young aspirants, among whom was Walter Somers, who had been highly recommended for that honor to the king by Sir Walter Manny.

The force was now formed into three divisions-the one commanded by the king himself, the second by the Earl of Warwick, and the third by Godfrey of Harcourt. The Earl of Arundel acted as lord high constable, and the Earl of Huntingdon, who was in command of the fleet, followed the army along the sea-coast. Valognes, Carentan, and St. Lo were captured without difficulty, and the English army advanced by rapid marches upon Caen, plundering the country for six or seven leagues on each side of the line of march. An immense quantity of booty was obtained.

As soon as the news of Edward's landing in Normandy reached Paris, Philip dispatched the Count d'Eu, Constable of France, with the Count of Tankerville and six hundred men-at-arms, to oppose Edward at Caen. The Bishop of Bayeux had thrown himself into that city, which was already garrisoned by three hundred Genoese. The town was not defensible, and the only chance of resistance was by opposing the passage of the river Horn, which flowed between the suburbs and the city. The bridge was barricaded, strong wooden towers were erected, and such was the confidence of the inhabitants and their leaders that Edward's promise of protection for the person and property of the citizens was rejected with scorn, and the whole male population joined the garrison in the defense of the bridge. Marching through the deserted suburbs the English army attacked the bridge with such vehemence that although the enemy defended the barricades gallantly they were speedily forced, and the English poured into the town. Before the first fury of the attack was over near five thousand persons were slain. The Count of Tankerville, one hundred and forty knights, and as many squires were made prisoners. The plunder was so enormous as to be sufficient to cover the whole expenses of the expedition, and this with the booty which had been previously acquired was placed on board ship and dispatched to England, while the king marched forward with his army. At Lisieux he was met by two cardinals sent by the pope to negotiate a truce; but Edward had learned the fallacy of truces made with King Philip, and declined to enter into negotiations. Finding that Rouen had been placed in a state of defense and could not be taken without a long siege, he left it behind him and marched along the valley of the Eure, gathering rich booty at every step.

But while he was marching forward a great army was gathering in his rear. The Count of Harcourt, brother of Godfrey, called all Normandy to arms. Every feudal lord and vassal answered to the summons, and before Edward reached the banks of the Seine a formidable army had assembled.

The whole of the vassals of France were gathering by the orders of the king at St. Denis. The English fleet had now left the coast, and Edward had only the choice of retreating through Normandy into Brittany or of attempting to force the passage of the Seine, and to fight his way through France to Flanders. He chose the latter alternative, and marched along the left bank of the river toward Paris, seeking in vain to find a passage. The enemy followed him step by step on the opposite bank, and all the bridges were broken down and the fords destroyed.

Edward marched on, burning the towns and ravaging the country until he reached Poissy. The bridge was as usual destroyed, but the piles on which it stood were still standing, and he determined to endeavor to cross here. He accordingly halted for five days, but dispatched troops in all directions, who burned and ravaged to the very gates of Paris. The villages of St. Germain, St. Cloud, Bourg la Reine, and many others within sight of the walls were destroyed, and the capital itself thrown into a state of terror and consternation. Godfrey of Harcourt was the first to cross the river, and with the advance-guard of English fell upon a large body of the burghers of Amiens, and after a severe fight defeated them, killing over five hundred. The king himself with his whole force passed on the 16th of August.

Philip, with his army, quitted St. Denis when he heard that the English army had passed the Seine, and by parallel marches endeavored to interpose between it and the borders of Flanders. As his force was every hour increasing he dispatched messengers to Edward offering him battle within a few days on condition that he would cease to ravage the country; but Edward declined the proposal, saying that Philip himself by breaking down the bridges had avoided a battle as long as he could, but that whenever he was ready to give battle he would accept the challenge. During the whole march the armies were within a few leagues of each other, and constant skirmishes took place between bodies detached from the hosts.

In some of these skirmishes Walter took part, as he and the other newly made knights were burning to distinguish themselves. Every day the progress of the army became more difficult, as the country people everywhere rose against them, and several times attempted to make a stand, but were defeated with great loss. The principal towns were found deserted, and even Poix, which offered great capabilities of defense, had been left unguarded. Upon the English entering, the burghers offered to pay a large ransom to save the town from plunder. The money was to be delivered as soon as the English force had withdrawn, and Walter Somers was ordered by the king to remain behind with a few men-at-arms to receive the ransom.

No sooner had the army departed than the burghers, knowing that the French army was close behind, changed their minds, refused to pay the ransom, and fell upon the little body of men-at-arms. Although taken quite by surprise by this act of treachery Walter instantly rallied his men, although several had been killed at the first onslaught. He, with Ralph and two or three of the stanchest men, covered the retreat of the rest through the streets, making desperate charges upon the body of armed burghers pressing upon them. Ralph fought as usual with a mace of prodigious weight, and the terror of his blows in no slight degree enabled the party to reach the gate in safety, but Walter had no idea of retreating further. He dispatched one of his followers to gallop at full speed to overtake the rear-guard of the army, which was still but two miles distant, while with the rest he formed a line across the gate and resisted all the attempts of the citizens to expel them.

The approach to the gate was narrow, and the overwhelming number of the burghers were therefore of little avail. Walter had dismounted his force and all fought on foot, and although sorely pressed they held their ground until Lords Cobham and Holland, with their followers, rode up. Then the tide of war was turned, the town was plundered and burned, and great numbers of the inhabitants slain. Walter gained great credit for holding the gate, for had he been driven out, the town could have resisted, until the arrival of Louis, all assaults of the English.

The river Somme now barred the passage of Edward. Most of the bridges had been destroyed, and those remaining were so strongly fortified that they could not be forced.

The position of the English was now very critical. On one flank and in front were impassable rivers. The whole country was in arms against them, and on their rear and flank pressed a hostile army fourfold their strength. The country was swampy and thinly populated, and flour and provisions were only obtained with great difficulty. Edward, on finding from the reports of his marshals who had been sent to examine the bridges, that no passage across the river could be found, turned and marched down the river toward the sea, halting for the night at Oisemont.

Here, a great number of peasantry attempted a defense, but were easily defeated and a number of prisoners taken. Late in the evening the Earl of Warwick, who had pushed forward as far as Abbeville and St. Valery, returned with the news that the passages at those places were as strongly guarded as elsewhere, but that he had learned from a peasant that a ford existed somewhere below Abbeville, although the man was himself ignorant of its position.

Edward at once called the prisoners belonging to that part of the country before him, and promised to any one who would tell him where the ford lay his freedom and that of twenty of his companions. A peasant called Gobin Agase stepped forward and offered to show the ford, where at low tide twelve men could cross abreast. It was, he said, called La Blanche Tache.

Edward left Oisemont at midnight and reached the ford at daylight. The river, however, was full and the army had to wait impatiently for low tide. When they arrived there no enemy was to be seen on the opposite bank, but before the water fell sufficiently for a passage to be attempted, Sir Godemar du Fay with twelve thousand men, sent by King Philip, who was aware of the existence of the ford, arrived on the opposite side.

The enterprise was a difficult one indeed, for the water, even at low tide, is deep. Godemar du Fay, however, threw away part of his advantage by advancing into the stream. The English archers lined the banks, and poured showers of arrows into the ranks of the enemy, while the Genoese bowmen on their side were able to give comparatively little assistance to the French.

King Edward shouted to his knights, "Let those who love me follow me," and spurred his horse into the water. Behind him followed his most valiant knights, and Walter, riding close to the Prince of Wales, was one of the foremost.

The French resisted valiantly and a desperate battle took place on the narrow ford, but the impetuosity of the English prevailed, and step by step they drove the French back to the other side of the river. The whole army poured after their leaders, and the French were soon entirely routed and fled, leaving two thousand men-at-arms dead on the field.

King Edward, having now freed himself from the difficulties which had encompassed him on the other side of the river, prepared to choose a ground to give battle to the whole French army.

Louis had advanced slowly, feeling confident that the English would be unable to cross the river, and that he should catch them hemmed in by it. His mortification and surprise on finding, when he approached La Blanche Tache, that twelve thousand men had been insufficient to hold a ford by which but twelve could cross abreast, and that his enemy had escaped from his grasp, were great. The tide had now risen again, and he was obliged to march on to Abbeville and cross the river there.

King Edward now advanced into the forest of Cressy.

Hugh de le Spencer, with a considerable force, was dispatched to Crotoy, which he carried by assault after a severe conflict, in which four thousand of the French men-at-arms were slain. The capture of this city removed all danger of want from the army, for large stores of wine and meal were found there, and Sir Hugh at once sent off a supply to the tired army in the field.

The possession of Crotoy and the mouth of the Somme would have now rendered it easy for the English monarch to have transported his troops to England, and to have returned triumphant after the accomplishment of his extraordinary and most successful march through France. The army, however, was elated by the many great successes it had won, he was now in Ponthieu, which was one of his own fiefs, and he determined to make a stand in spite of the immense superiority of the enemy.

Next morning, then-Friday, the 25th of August, 1346—he dispatched the Earl of Warwick, with Godfrey of Harcourt and Lord Cobham, to examine the ground and choose a site for a battle.

The plan of the fight was drawn out by the king and his councilors, and the king yielded to the Black Prince the chief place of danger and honor, placing with him the Earl of Warwick, Sir John Chandos, and many of his best knights.

The ground which had been chosen for the battle was an irregular slope between the forest of Cressy and the river Maie near the little village of Canchy. The slope looked toward the south and east, from which quarters the enemy was expected to arrive, and some slight defenses were added to the natural advantages of the ground.

On the night of the 25th all the principal leaders of the British host were entertained by King Edward. Next morning mass was celebrated, and the king, the prince, and many knights and nobles received the sacrament, after which the trumpets sounded, and the army marched to take up its position. Its numbers are variously estimated, but the best account puts it at about thirty thousand men, which, considering that thirty-two thousand had crossed the Channel to La Hogue, is probably about the force which would have been present, allowing that two thousand had fallen in the various actions or had died from disease.

The division of the Black Prince consisted of eight hundred men-at-arms, four thousand archers, and six thousand Welsh foot. The archers, as usual, were placed in front, supported by the light troops of Wales and the men-at-arms; on his left was the second division, commanded by the Earls of Arundel and Northampton; its extreme left rested on Canchy and the river, and it was further protected by a deep ditch; this corps was about seven thousand strong.

The king himself took up his position on a knoll of rising ground surmounted by a windmill, and twelve thousand men under his personal command were placed here in reserve.

In the rear of the prince's division an inclosure of stakes was formed; in this, guarded by a small body of archers, were ranged the wagons and baggage of the army, together with all the horses, the king having determined that the knights and men-at-arms on his side should fight on foot.

When the army had taken up its position, the king, mounted on a small palfrey, with a white staff in his hand, rode from rank to rank exhorting his soldiers to do their duty gallantly. It was nearly noon before he had passed through all the lines, and permission was then given to the soldiers to fall out from their ranks and to take refreshments while waiting for the coming of the enemy. This was accordingly done, the men eating and drinking at their ease and lying down in their ranks on the soft grass, with their steel caps and their bows or pikes beside them.

In the mean time the French had, on their side, been preparing for the battle. Philip had crossed the Somme at Abbeville late on Thursday afternoon, and remained there next day, marshaling the large reënforcements which were hourly arriving. His force now considerably exceeded one hundred thousand men, the number with which he had marched from Amiens three days previously.

Friday was the Festival of St. Louis, and that evening Philip gave a splendid banquet to the whole of the nobles of his army.

On the following morning the king, accompanied by his brother the Count D'Alençon, the old King of Bohemia and his son, the King of Rome, the Duke of Lorraine, the Count of Blois, the Count of Flanders, and a great number of other feudal princes, heard mass at the abbey, and then marched with his great army toward Cressy. He moved but slowly in order to give time to all the forces scattered over the neighborhood to come up, and four knights, headed by one of the King of Bohemia's officers, went forward to reconnoiter the English position. They approached within very short distance of the English lines and gained a very exact knowledge of the position, the English taking no measures to interrupt the reconnaissance. They returned with the information they had gathered, and the leader of the party, Le Moyne de Basele, one of the most judicious officers of his time, strongly advised the king to halt his troops, pointing out that as it was evident the English were ready to give battle, and as they were fresh and vigorous, while the French were wearied and hungry, it would be better to encamp and give battle the next morning.

Philip saw the wisdom of the advice and ordered his two marshals, the Lord of St. Venant and Charles de Montmorency, to command a halt. They instantly spurred off, one to the front and the other to the rear, commanding the leaders to halt their banners. Those in advance at once obeyed, but those behind still pressed on, declaring that they would not halt until they were in the front line. All wanted to be first, in order to obtain their share of the honor and glory of defeating the English. Those in front, seeing the others still coming on, again pressed forward, and thus, in spite of the efforts of the king and his marshals, the French nobles with their followers pressed forward in confusion, until, passing through a small wood, they found themselves suddenly in the presence of the English army.

Chapter XIV
Cressy.

The surprise of the French army at finding themselves in the presence of the English was so great that the first line recoiled in confusion. Those marching up from behind imagined that they had been already engaged and repulsed by the English, and the disorder spread through the whole army, and was increased by the common people, who had crowded to the field in immense numbers from the whole country round to see the battle and share in the plunder of the English camp.

From King Edward's position on the rising ground he could see the confusion which prevailed in the French ranks, and small as were his forces, he would probably have obtained an easy victory by ordering a sudden charge upon them. The English, however, being dismounted, but small results would have followed the scattering of the great host of the French. The English army therefore remained immovable, except that the soldiers rose from the ground, and taking their places in the ranks, awaited the onslaught of the enemy.

King Philip himself now arrived on the field, and his hatred for the English led him at once to disregard the advice which had been given him and to order the battle to commence as soon as possible.

The army was divided into four bodies, of which Philip commanded one, the Count D'Alençon the second, the King of Bohemia the third, and the Count of Savoy the fourth. Besides these were a band of fifteen thousand mercenaries, Genoese cross-bowmen, who were now ordered to pass between the ranks of cavalry and to clear the ground of the English archers, who were drawn up in the usual form in which they fought-namely, in very open order, line behind line, the men standing alternately, so that each had ample room to use his bow and to fire over the heads of those in front. The formation was something that of a harrow, and, indeed, exactly resembled that in which the Roman archers fought, and was called by them a quincunx.

The Genoese had marched four leagues beneath a hot sun loaded with their armor and heavy cross-bows, and they remonstrated against the order, urging that they were in no condition to do good service without some repose. The Count D'Alençon, furious at their hesitation, ordered them up, but as they advanced a terrible thunderstorm, with torrents of rain, broke over the armies, and wetting the cords of the cross-bows rendered many of them unserviceable. At length the cross-bowmen were arranged in front, while behind them were the vast body of French cavalry, and the order was given for the battle to begin.

The Genoese advanced with loud shouts, but the English archers paid no attention to the noise, but waited calmly for the attack. At this moment the sun, now approaching the west, shone out brightly between the clouds behind the English, its rays streaming full in the faces of the French. The Genoese were now within distance, and began to discharge their quarrels at their impassive enemies, but as they opened fire the English archers drew their bows from the cases which had protected them from the rain, and stepping forward poured their arrows among the Genoese. The cross-bowmen were smitten as with a storm, numbers were struck in the face and other unprotected parts, and they were instantly thrown into confusion, and casting away their cross-bows they recoiled in disorder among the horsemen behind them.

Philip, passionate and cruel as ever, instead of trying to rally the Genoese, ordered the cavalry behind them to fall upon them, and the men-at-arms at once plunged in among the disordered mass of the cross-bowmen, and a wild scene of carnage and confusion ensued, the English archers continuing to pour their unerring arrows into the midst. The Count D'Alençon, who was behind, separated his division into two bodies, and swept round on one side himself, while the Count of Flanders did the same on the other to attack the Prince of Wales in more regular array. Taking a circuitous route, D'Alençon appeared upon a rising ground on the flank of the archers of the Black Prince, and thus, avoiding their arrows, charged down with his cavalry upon the eight hundred men-at-arms gathered round the Black Prince, while the Count of Flanders attacked on the other flank.

Nobly did the flower of English chivalry withstand the shock of the French, and the prince himself and the highest nobles and simple men-at-arms fought side by side. None gave way a foot.

In vain the French, with impetuous charges, strove to break through the mass of steel. The spear-heads were cleft off with sword and battle-ax, and again and again men and horses recoiled from the unbroken line. Each time the French retired the English ranks were formed anew, and as attack followed attack a pile of dead rose around them. The Count D'Alençon and the Duke of Lorraine were among the first who fell. The young Count of Blois, finding that he could not ride through the wall of steel, dismounted with his knights and fought his way on foot toward the banner of the Prince of Wales. For a time the struggle was desperate, and the young prince, with his household knights, was for a time well-nigh beaten back.

Walter, fighting close beside the prince, parried more than one blow intended for him, and the prince himself slew the Count of Blois, whose followers all fell around him. The Count of Flanders was also slain, and confusion began to reign among the assailants, whose leaders had now all fallen. Philip himself strove to advance with his division into the fight, but the struggle between the Genoese and the men-at-arms was still continuing, and the very multitude of his troops in the narrow and difficult field which the English had chosen for the battle embarrassed his movements.

Charles of Luxembourg, King of the Romans, and afterward Emperor of Germany, son of the old King of Bohemia, with a large body of German and French cavalry, now assailed the English archers, and in spite of their flights of arrows came to close quarters, and cutting their way through them joined in the assault upon the men-at-arms of the Black Prince. Nearly forty thousand men were now pressing round the little body, and the Earls of Northampton and Arundel moved forward with their divisions to his support, while the Earl of Warwick, who was with the prince, dispatched Sir Thomas of Norwich to the king, who still remained with his powerful reserve, to ask for aid.

"Sir Thomas," demanded the king, "is my son killed, overthrown, or wounded beyond help?"

"Not so, sire," replied the knight, "but he is in a rude fight, and much needs your aid."

"Go back, Sir Thomas, to those who sent you, and tell them from me that whatsoever happens they require no aid from me so long as my son is in life. Tell them also that I command them to let the boy win his spurs, for, God willing, the day shall be his, and the honor shall rest with him and those into whose charge I have given him."

The prince and those around him were filled with fresh ardor when they received this message. Each man redoubled his efforts to repel the forces that were incessantly poured down upon them by the French. On all sides these pressed around them, striving desperately, but ever in vain, to break through the solid ranks of the English. The French men-at-arms suffered, moreover, terribly from the attacks of the Welsh infantry. These men, clad in thick leather jerkins, nimble of foot, accustomed to a life of activity, were armed with shortened lances and knives, and mingled fearlessly among the confused mass of French cavalry, creeping beneath the horses' bellies, standing up when they got a chance, and stabbing horses and men with their knives and pikes. Many were trampled upon or struck down, but numbering, as they did, six thousand, they pervaded the whole mass of the enemy, and did terrible execution, adding in no small degree to the confusion caused by the shower of arrows from the archers within the circle of the men-at-arms. The instant a French knight fell, struck from his horse with a battle-ax or arrow, or by the fall of a wounded steed, the half-wild Welsh were upon him and slew him before he could regain his feet.

The slaughter was immense. The Count of Harcourt, with his nephew the Count D'Aumale and his two gallant sons, fell together, and at last Charles of Luxembourg, seeing his banner down, his troops routed, his friends slain, and the day irreparably lost, and being himself severely wounded in three places, turned his horse and fled, casting off his rich emblazoned surcoat to avoid recognition. In the mean time Prince Charles' father, the veteran King of Bohemia, once one of the most famous warriors of Europe, but now old and blind, sat on horseback at a little distance from the fight; the knights around him told him the events as they happened, and the old monarch soon saw that the day was lost. He asked them for tidings of his son Charles of Luxembourg, but they were forced to reply that the banner of the King of the Romans was no longer in sight, but that, doubtless, he was somewhere engaged in the *mêlée*.

"Lords," said the old man, "you are my vassals, my friends, and my companions, and on this day I command and beseech you to lead me forward so far that I may deal one blow of my sword in the battle."

His faithful friends obeyed him, a number of knights arranged themselves around him, and lest they should lose him in the fight they tied their horses together by the bridles and charged down into the fray. Advancing directly against the banner of the Prince of Wales, the blind monarch was carried into the midst of the thickest strife. There the little group of knights fought gallantly, and after the battle was over the bodies of the king and his friends were found lying together, their dead horses still linked by the bridles.

During this terrible battle, which had been raging since three o'clock, Philip had made strenuous efforts to aid his troops engaged in the front by continually sending fresh bodies to the assault. It was now growing dark, terror and confusion had already spread among the French, and many were flying in all directions, and the unremitting showers of English arrows still flew like hail among their ranks. As the king made his way forward, surrounded by his personal attendants, to take part himself in the fight, his followers fell thick around him, and his horse was slain by an arrow. John of Hainault, who had remained by his side during the whole day, mounted him upon a fresh horse and urged him to fly, as the day was lost. Philip, however, persisted, and made his way into the *mêlée*, where he fought for some time with extreme courage, until almost all around him were slain, the royal standard-bearer killed, and himself wounded in two places. John of Hainault then seized his bridle, exclaiming, "Come away, sire, it is full time; do not throw your life away foolishly; if you have lost this day you will win another," and so almost forced the unwilling king from the field. Philip, accompanied by the lords of Montmorency, Beaujeu, Aubigny, and Mansault, with John of Hainault and sixty men-at-arms, rode to the Castle of Broye, and there halted for a few hours. At midnight he again set out, and in the morning arrived safely at Amiens.

The Black Prince held his station until night without yielding a single step to all the efforts of the French. Gradually, however, the assailants became less and less numerous, the banners disappeared, and the shouts of the leaders and the clang of arms died away, and the silence which prevailed over the field at once announced that the victory was complete and the enemy in full flight. An immense number of torches were now lighted through the English lines, and the king, quitting for the first time his station on the hill, came down to embrace his gallant son. Edward and his host rejoiced in a spirit of humility over the victory. No songs of triumph, no feastings or merriment were permitted, but a solemn service of the Church was held, and the king and his soldiers offered their thanks to God for the victory he had given them. The English army lay all night under arms, and a number of scattered parties of the French wandering about in the darkness entered the lines and were slain or taken prisoners.

The dawn of the next morning was thick and foggy, and intelligence coming in that a large body of the enemy were advancing upon them, the Earls of Northampton, Warwick, and Norfolk, with five hundred men-at-arms and two thousand archers, went out to reconnoiter, and came in the misty twilight upon an immense force composed of the citizens of Beauvais, Rouen, and some other towns, led by the Grand Prior of France and the Archbishop of Rouen, who were approaching the field.

By some extraordinary accident they had not met any of the fugitives flying from Cressy, and were ignorant that a battle had been fought. The English charged them at once. Their advance-guard, consisting of burghers, was easily overthrown. The second division, which was composed of men-at-arms, fought bravely, but was unable to withstand the charge of the triumphant English, and was completely broken and defeated. The grand prior was killed and a vast number of his followers slain or captured. During the whole of the morning detached parties from Edward's army scoured the country, dispersing and slaughtering bands of French who still remained together, and toward night the Earl of Northampton returned to the camp with the news that no enemy remained in the vicinity that could offer a show of resistance to the English force.

It is said that a far greater number of French were killed upon the second day than upon the first. This can be accounted for by the fact that on the first day but a small portion of the English army were engaged, and that upon the second the English were fresh and vigorous, and their enemies exhausted and dispirited.

The greater number of the French nobles and knights who fell died in their attempt to break through the Black Prince's array. Besides the King of Bohemia, nine sovereign princes and eighty great nobles were killed, with twelve hundred knights, fifteen hundred men-at-arms, and thirty thousand foot; while on the English side only three knights and a small number of men-at-arms and infantry were killed. The body of the King of Bohemia and those of the other great leaders were carried in solemn pomp to the Abbey of Maintenay. Edward himself and his son accompanied them as mourners.

On the Monday following Edward marched with his army against Calais, and summoned the town to surrender. John of Vienne, who commanded the garrison, refused to comply with the demand. The fortifications of the town were extremely strong and the garrison numerous, and Edward perceived that an assault would be very unlikely to succeed, and would entail great loss, while a repulse would have dimmed the luster of the success which he had gained. He therefore determined to reduce it by famine, and the troops were set to work to build huts. So permanently and strongly were these constructed that it seemed to the enemy that King Edward was determined to remain before Calais even should he have to stay there for ten years.

Proclamations were issued in England and Flanders inviting traders to establish stores and to bring articles of trade of all kinds, and in a short time a complete town sprang up which was named by Edward New-Town the Bold. The English fleet held complete possession of the sea, cutting off the besieged from all succor by ship, and enabling abundant supplies for the army to be brought from England and Flanders. Strong parties were sent out in all directions. The northern provinces of France were scoured, and the army was amply provided with necessaries and even luxuries.

After the first terrible shock caused by the crushing defeat of Cressy, King Philip began at once to take measures for the relief of Calais, and made immense efforts again to put a great army in the field. He endeavored by all means in his power to gain fresh allies. The young Count of Flanders, who at the death of his father at Cressy was sixteen years of age, was naturally even more hostile to the English than the late prince had been, and he strove to win over his subjects to the French alliance, while Philip made them magnificent offers if they would join him. The Flemings, however, remained stanch to the English alliance, and held their prince in duress until he at last consented to marry the daughter of Edward. A week before the date fixed for the nuptials, however, he managed to escape from the vigilance of his guards when out hawking, and fled to the court of France.

In Scotland, Philip was more successful, and David Bruce, instead of employing the time given him by the absence of Edward with his armies in driving out the English garrisons from the strong places they still held in Scotland, raised an army of fifty thousand men and marched across the border into England plundering and ravaging. Queen Philippa, however, raising an army, marched against him, and the Scotch were completely defeated at Neville's Cross, fifteen thousand being killed and their king himself taken prisoner.

Walter's conduct at the battle of Cressy gained him still further the favor of the Black Prince. The valor with which he had fought was conspicuous even on a field where all fought gallantly, and the prince felt that more than once he would have been smitten down had not Walter's sword interposed. Ralph too had fought with reckless bravery, and many French knights and gentlemen had gone down before the tremendous blows of his heavy mace, against which the stoutest armor availed nothing. After the battle the prince offered to make him an esquire in spite of the absence of gentle blood in his veins, but Ralph declined the honor.

"An it please you, Sir Prince," he said, "but I should feel more comfortable among the men-at-arms, my fellows. In the day of battle I trust that I should do no discredit to my squirehood, but at other times I should feel woefully out of my element, and should find naught for my hands to do; therefore, if it so pleases your royal highness, I would far rather remain a simple man-at-arms."

Ralph did not, however, refuse the heavy purse which the prince gave him, although indeed he, as well as all the soldiers, was well supplied with money, so great were the spoils which the army had gathered in its march before Cressy, and which they now swept off in their raids among the northern provinces of France.

One evening Walter was returning from a banquet at the pavilion of the Prince of Wales, with Ralph as usual following at a little distance, when from a corner of the street a man darted suddenly out and struck a dagger with all his force between his shoulders. Well was it for Walter that he had taken Geoffrey's advice, and had never laid aside the shirt of mail, night or day. Fine as was its temper, two or three links of the outer fold were broken, but the point did not penetrate the second fold, and the dagger snapped in the hand of the striker. The force of the sudden blow, however, hurled Walter to the ground. With a loud cry Ralph rushed forward. The man instantly fled. Ralph pursued him but a short distance and then hastened back to Walter.

"Are you hurt, Sir Walter?" he exclaimed.

"In no way, Ralph, thanks to my shirt of mail. Well, indeed, was it for me that I was wearing it or I should assuredly have been a dead man. I had almost begun to forget that I was a threatened man; but I shall be on guard for the future."

"I wish I had followed the fellow," Ralph said. "I would not have slain him could I have helped it, but would have left it for the hangman to extort from him the name of his employer; but, in truth, he struck so hard, and you fell so straight before the blow, that I feared the mail had given way, and that you were sorely wounded if not killed. You have oft told me that I was over-careful of you, but you see that I was not careful enough; however, you may be assured that if another attempt be made those who attempt it shall not get off scot-free. Do you think of laying a complaint before the provost against him you suspect?"

"It would be useless, Ralph. We may have suspicion of the man from whom the blow came, but have no manner of proof. It might have been done by any ruffian camp-follower, who struck the blow only with the hope of carrying off my chain and purse. The camp swarms with such fellows, and we have no clew which could lead to his detection, unless," he added, stooping and picking up a piece of steel which lay at his feet, "this broken dagger may some day furnish us with one. No; we will say naught about it. Sir James Carnegie is not now in camp, having left a week since on business in England. We exchange no words when we meet, but I heard that he had been called away. Fortunately the young prince likes him not, and I therefore have seldom occasion to meet him. I have no doubt that he credits me with the disfavor in which he is held by the prince; but I have never even mentioned his name before him, and the prince's misliking is but the feeling which a noble and generous heart has, as though by instinct, against one who is false and treacherous. At the same time we must grant that this traitor knight is a bold and fearless man-at-arms; he fought well at La Blanche Tache and Cressy, and he is much liked and trusted by my Lord of Northampton, in whose following he mostly rides; 'tis a pity that one so brave should have so foul and treacherous a heart. Here we are at my hut, and you can sleep soundly to-night, Ralph, for there is little fear that the fellow, who has failed to-night, will repeat his attempt for some time. He thinks, no doubt, that he has killed me, for with a blow so strongly struck he would scarce have felt the snapping of the weapon, and is likely enough already on board one of the ships which ply to and fro from England on his way to acquaint his employer that I am removed from his path."

The next morning Walter mentioned to the Black Prince the venture which had befallen him, and the narrow escape he had had of his life. The prince was extremely exasperated, and gave orders that an inquisition should be made through the camp, and that all men found there not being able to give a good account of themselves as having reasonable and lawful calling there should be forthwith put on board ship and sent to England. He questioned Walter closely whether he deemed that this attack was for the purpose of plunder only, or whether he had any reason to believe that he had private enemies.

"There is a knight who is evilly disposed toward me, your highness," Walter said; "but seeing that I have no proof whatever that he had a hand in this affair, however strongly I may suspect it, I would fain, with your leave, avoid mentioning his name."

"But think you that there is any knight in this camp capable of so foul an action?"

"I have had proofs, your highness, that he is capable of such an act; but in this matter my tongue is tied, as the wrong he attempted was not against myself, but against others who have so far forgiven him that they would fain the matter should drop. He owes me ill-will, seeing that I am aware of his conduct, and that it was my intervention which caused his schemes to fail. Should this attempt against me be repeated it can scarce be the effect of chance, but would show premeditated design, and I would then, both in defense of my own life, and because I think that such deeds should not go unpunished, not hesitate to name him to you, and if proof be wanting to defy him to open combat."

"I regret, Sir Walter, that your scruples should hinder you from at once denouncing him; but seeing how grave a matter it is to charge a knight with so foul a crime, I will not lay stress upon you; but be assured that should any repetition of the attempt be made I shall take the matter in hand, and will see that this caitiff knight receives his deserts."

A short time afterward Walter accompanied the prince in an excursion which he made with a portion of the army, sweeping the French provinces as far as the river Somme. Upon their way back they passed through the village of Près, hard by which stood a small castle. It was situate some forty miles from Calais, and standing upon rising ground it commanded a very extensive view over the country.

"What say you, Sir Walter?" the prince said to the young knight who was riding near him. "That castle would make a good advanced post, and a messenger riding in could bring news of any large movements of the enemy." Walter assented.

"Then, Sir Walter, I name you its chatelain. I shall be sorry to lose your good company; but the post is one of peril, and I know that you are ever longing to distinguish yourself. Take forty men-at-arms and sixty archers. With that force you may make shift to resist any attack until help reaches you from camp. You may be sure that I shall not be slack in spurring to your rescue should you be assailed."

Walter received the proposal with delight. He was weary of the monotony of life in New Town, and this post, in which vigilance and activity would be required, was just to his taste; so, taking the force named by the prince, with a store of provision, he drew off from the column and entered the castle.

Chapter XV
The Siege Of A Fortalice.

Walter's first step on assuming the command was to examine thoroughly into the capabilities of defense of the place, to see that the well was in good order, and the supply of water ample, and to send out a foraging party, which, driving in a number of beasts and some cart-loads of forage, would supply his garrison for some time. The castle he found was less strong than it looked. The walls were lightly built, and were incapable of withstanding any heavy battering. The moat was dry, and the flanking towers badly placed, and affording little protection to the faces of the walls; however, the extent of the defenses was small, and Walter felt confident that with the force at his command he could resist any sudden attack, unless made in overwhelming force, so that all the faces of the wall could be assaulted at the same time. He had a large number of great stones brought in to pile against the gate, while others were brought into the central keep, similarly to defend the door should the outer wall be carried. He appointed Ralph as his lieutenant, and every day, leaving him in charge of the castle, rode through the country for many miles round, with twenty men-at-arms, to convince himself that no considerable force of the enemy were approaching. These reconnaissances were not without some danger and excitement, for several times bodies of the country people, armed with scythes, axes, and staves, tried to intercept them on their return to the castle, and once or twice Walter and his men had to fight their way through their opponents. Contrary to the custom of the times, Walter gave orders to his men not to slay any when resistance had ceased.

"They are but doing what we ourselves should do did French garrisons hold our castles at home, and I deem them in no way to be blamed for the efforts which they make to slay us. In self-defense, of course, we must do our best, and must kill in order that we may not ourselves be slain; but when they are once routed, let them go to their homes. Poor people, the miseries which this war has brought upon them are great, and there is no wonder that they hate us."

This leniency on Walter's part was not without good effect. When the country people found that the garrison of the castle of Près did not carry fire and sword through the villages around, that they took only sufficient for their needs, and behaved with courtesy to all, their animosity to a great extent subsided. No longer did the women and children of the little villages fly to the woods when they saw the gleam of Walter's approaching spears, but remained at their avocations, and answered willingly enough the questions which he asked them as to whether they had heard aught of the movements of French troops. So far as possible, Walter refrained from seizing the cattle or stores of grain of the poorer classes, taking such as he needed from the lands of the wealthy proprietors, all of whom had left the country, and were either with the French army or sheltering in Paris. Five of his best mounted men Walter chose as messengers, and one rode each day to New Town with the news which had been gathered, returning on the following day, and then resting his horse for three days before again setting out.

Night and day sentries were placed on the walls, for although Walter heard nothing of any body gathering in his immediate vicinity, a force might at any moment issue from Amiens and appear suddenly before the place. Such was indeed what really took place, and at daybreak one morning Walter was aroused by the news that the sentinels saw a large body of men rapidly approaching. The horse of the messenger next on duty stood, as usual, saddled and bridled in readiness, and without a moment's delay Walter ordered the man to mount and ride to the prince, and to give news that the castle was assailed, but by how large a force he could not as yet say.

The instant the messenger had started through the gates Walter ascended to the walls; he saw at once that the party was a strong one; for although still at some distance, and but dimly seen in the gray morning light, he judged that it must contain at least a thousand men-at-arms. At this moment a call from the sentry on the other side of the castle was heard, and hastening thither, Walter saw that another body nearly as numerous as the first were approaching from the side of Calais, having made a *détour* so as to place themselves between the castle and the army, to which news would naturally be sent of their coming. Walter watched his messenger, who had now ridden half a mile toward the approaching body. Suddenly he saw him turn his horse and ride off at right angles to the road.

"He sees them," he said, "and is going to try to ride round them. I fear that there is but little hope of his escaping, seeing that they are between him and Calais, and that assuredly some among them must be as well or better mounted than himself." As he spoke a party of horsemen were seen to detach themselves from the flank of the French column and to gallop off at full speed to intercept the messenger; the latter diverged more and more from his course, but he was constantly headed off by his pursuers, and at last, seeing the impossibility of getting through them, he again turned his horse's head and galloped off toward the castle, which he reached a few hundred yards only in advance of his foes.

"I could not help it, Sir Walter," he said as he galloped in at the gate. "I found that although Robin is fast, some of those horsemen had the turn of speed of me, and that it was impossible that I could get through; so deeming that I should do more service by coming to strike a blow here than by having my throat cut out in the fields, I made the best of my way back."

"Quite right, Martin!" Walter said. "I should have been grieved had you thrown your life away needlessly. I saw from the first that your escape was cut off. And now, men, each to his place; but first pile up the stones against the gate, and then let each man take a good meal, for it is like enough to be long before we get a chance of doing so again."

Again ascending to the walls, Walter saw that the first body of men-at-arms he had perceived was followed at a distance by a strong force of footmen having with them some large wagons.

"I fear," he said to Ralph, "that they have brought machines with them from Amiens, and in that case they will not be long in effecting a breach, for doubtless they know that the walls are but weak. We shall have to fight stoutly, for it may be days before the news of our leaguer reaches the camp. However, I trust that the prince will, by to-morrow night, when he finds that two days have elapsed without the coming of my usual messenger, suspect that we are besieged and will sally forth to our assistance. And now let us to breakfast, for we shall need all our strength to-day, and you may be sure that the French will lose no time in attacking, seeing that assistance may shortly arrive from Calais."

There were but few preparations to be made. Each man had had his post assigned to him on the walls in case of an attack, and piles of stones had been collected in readiness to cast down upon the heads of those attempting an assault. Caldrons were carried up to the walls and filled with water, and great fires were lighted under them. In half an hour the French infantry had reached the spot, but another two hours elapsed before any hostile movement was made, the leaders of the assailants giving their men that time to rest after their long march. Then a stir was visible among them, and they were seen to form in four columns, each about a thousand strong, which advanced simultaneously against opposite sides of the castle.

As soon as their intentions were manifest Walter divided his little force, and these, gathering in four groups upon the walls, prepared to resist the assault. To four of his most trusty men-at-arms he assigned the command of these parties, he himself and Ralph being thus left free to give their aid where it was most needed.

The assailants were well provided with scaling ladders, and advanced with a number of cross-bowmen in front, who speedily opened a hot fire on the walls. Walter ordered his archers to bide their time, and not to fire a shot till certain that every shaft would tell. They accordingly waited until the French arrived within fifty yards of the wall, when the arrows began to rain among them with deadly effect; scarce one but struck its mark-the face of an enemy. Even the closed visors of the knights and chief men-at-arms did not avail to protect their wearers; the shafts pierced between the bars or penetrated the slits left open for sight, and many fell slain by the first volley. But their numbers were far too great to allow the columns being checked by the fire of so small a number of archers; the front ranks, indeed, pressed forward more eagerly than before, being anxious to reach the foot of the wall, where they would be in comparative shelter from the arrows.

The archers disturbed themselves in no way at the reaching of the wall by the heads of the columns; but continued to shoot fast and true into the mass behind them, and as these were, for the most part, less completely armed than their leaders, numbers fell under the fire of the sixty English bowmen. It was the turn of the men-at-arms now. Immediately the assailants poured into the dry moat and sought to raise their ladders the men-at-arms hurled down the masses of stones piled in readiness, while some poured buckets of boiling water over them. In spite of the loss they were suffering the French raised their ladders, and covering their heads with their shields the leaders strove to gain the walls. As they did so some of the archers took post in the flanking towers, and as with uplifted arms the assailants climbed the ladders, the archers smote them above the joints of their armor beneath the armpits, while the men-at-arms with pike and battle-ax hewed down those who reached the top of the ladders. Walter and Ralph hastened from point to point encouraging the men and joining in the defense where the pressure was hottest; and at last, after two hours of vain effort and suffering great loss, the assailants drew off and the garrison had breathing-time.

"Well done, my men!" Walter said cheeringly; "they have had a lesson which they will remember, and if so be that they have brought with them no machines we may hold out against them for any time."

It was soon manifest, however, that along with the scaling ladders the enemy had brought one of their war-machines. Men were seen dragging massive beams of timber toward the walls, and one of the wagons was drawn forward and upset on its side at a distance of sixty yards from the wall not, however, without those who drew it suffering much from the arrows of the bowmen. Behind the shelter thus formed the French began to put together the machine, whose beams soon raised themselves high above the wagon.

In the mean time groups of men dragged great stones laid upon a sort of hand sledge to the machine, and late in the afternoon it began to cast its missiles against the wall. Against these Walter could do little. He had no sacks, which, filled with earth, he might have lowered to cover the part of the walls assailed, and beyond annoying those working the machines by flights of arrows shot high in the air, so as to descend point downward among them, he could do nothing.

The wall crumbled rapidly beneath the blows of the great stones, and Walter saw that by the following morning a breach would be effected. When night fell he called his men together and asked if any would volunteer to carry news through the enemy to the prince. The enterprise seemed well-nigh hopeless, for the French, as if foreseeing that such an attempt might be made, had encamped in a complete circle round the castle, as was manifest by the position of their fires. Several men stepped forward, and Walter chose three light and active men-archers-to attempt the enterprise. These stripped off their steel caps and breast-pieces, so that they might move more quickly, and when the French fires burned low and all was quiet save the creak of the machine and the dull heavy blows of the stones against the wall, the three men were lowered by ropes at different points, and started on their enterprise. A quarter of an hour later the garrison heard shouts and cries, and knew that a vigilant watch had been set by the French, and that one, if not all, of their friends had fallen into their hands. All night long the machine continued to play.

An hour before daylight, when he deemed that the enemy's vigilance would be relaxed, Walter caused himself with Ralph and twelve of his men-at-arms to be lowered by ropes from the wall. Each rope had a loop at the bottom in which one foot was placed, and knots were tied in order to give a better grasp for the hands. They were lowered at a short distance from the spot at which the machine was at work; all were armed with axes, and they made their way unperceived until within a few yards of the wagon. Then there was a cry of alarm, and in a moment they rushed forward among the enemy. The men working the machine were instantly cut down, and Walter and his party fell upon the machine, cutting the ropes and smashing the wheels and pulleys and hewing away at the timber itself. In a minute or two, however, they were attacked by the enemy, the officer in command having bade a hundred men lie down to sleep close behind the machine in case the garrison should attempt a sortie. Walter called upon

Ralph and four of the men-at-arms to stand beside him while the others continued their work of destruction. The French came up in a tumultuous body, but standing so far apart that they could wield their axes, the English dealt such destruction among their first assailants that these for a time recoiled. As fresh numbers came up, encouraged by their leader they renewed the attack, and in spite of the most tremendous efforts Walter and his party were driven back. By this time, however, so much damage had been done to the machine that it would be some hours before it could be repaired, even if spare ropes and other appliances had been brought with it from Amiens; so that, reënforced by the working party, Walter was again able to hold his ground, and after repulsing a fresh onslaught of the enemy he gave the word for his men to retire at full speed.

The French were so surprised by the sudden disappearance of their foes that it was a moment or two before they started in pursuit, and Walter and his men had gained some thirty yards before the pursuit really commenced.

The night was a dark one, and they considerably increased this advantage before they reached the foot of the wall, where the ropes were hanging.

"Have each of you found his rope?" Walter asked.

As soon as an affirmative answer was given he placed his foot in the loop and shouted to the men above to draw up, and before the enraged enemy could reach the spot the whole party were already some yards above their heads. The archers opened fire upon the French, doing, in spite of the darkness, considerable execution, for the men had snatched up their arms at the sudden alarm, and had joined the fray in such haste that many of them had not had time to put on their steel caps. There was noise and bustle in the enemy's camp, for the whole force were now under arms, and in their anger at the sudden blow which had been struck them, some bodies of men even moved forward toward the walls as if they intended to renew the assault of the previous day; but the showers of arrows with which they were greeted cooled their ardor, and they presently retired out of reach of bow-shot. There was a respite now for the besiegers. No longer every few minutes did a heavy stone strike the walls.

The morning's light enabled the defenders of the castle to see the extent of the damage which the battering machine had effected. None too soon had they put a stop to its work, for had it continued its operations another hour or two would have effected a breach.

Already large portions of the wall facing it had fallen, and other portions were so seriously damaged that a few more blows would have leveled them.

"At any rate," Walter said to Ralph, "we have gained a respite; but even now I fear that if the Black Prince comes not until to-morrow he will arrive too late."

The French, apparently as well aware as the garrison of the necessity for haste, labored at the repair of the machine. Bodies of men started to cut down trees to supply the place of the beams which had been rendered useless. Scarcely had the assault ceased when horsemen were dispatched in various directions to seek for fresh ropes, and by dint of the greatest exertions the machine was placed in position to renew its attack shortly after noon.

By two o'clock several large portions of the damaged wall had fallen, and the *débris* formed a slope by which an assaulting column could rush to the bridge. As soon as this was manifest the French force formed for the assault and rushed forward in solid column.

Walter had made the best preparation possible for the defense. In the courtyard behind the breach his men had since morning been driving a circle of piles, connected by planks fastened to them. These were some five feet high, and along the top and in the face next to the breach sharp-pointed spikes and nails had been driven, rendering it difficult in the extreme for any one to climb over. As the column of the assailants approached Walter placed his archers on the walls on either side of the breach, while he himself, with his men-at-arms, took his station in the gap and faced the coming host. The breach was some ten yards wide, but it was only for about half this width that the mound of broken stones rendered it possible for their enemies to assault, consequently there was but a space of some fifteen feet in width to be defended.

Regardless of the flights of arrows, the French, headed by their knights and squires, advanced to the assault, and clambering up the rough stones attacked the defenders.

Walter, with Ralph and three of his best men-at-arms, stood in the front line and received the first shock of the assault. The roughness and steepness of the mound prevented the French from attacking in regular order, and the very eagerness of the knights and squires who came first in contact with their enemies was a hindrance to them. When the columns were seen gathering for the assault Walter had scattered several barrels full of oil and tar which he found in the cellars over the mound in front of the breach, rendering it greasy and slippery, and causing the assailants to slip and stagger and many to fall as they pressed forward to the assault. Before the fight commenced he had encouraged his soldiers by recalling to them how a mere handful of men had at Cressy withstood for hours the desperate efforts of the whole of the French army to break through their line, and all were prepared to fight to the death.

The struggle was a desperate one. Served by their higher position, and by the difficulties which the French encountered from the slipperiness of the ground and their own fierce ardor to attack, Walter and his little band for a long time resisted every effort. He with his sword and Ralph with his heavy mace did great execution, and they were nobly seconded by their men-at-arms. As fast as one fell another took his place. The breach in front of them was cumbered with dead and red with blood. Still the French poured upward in a wave, and the sheer weight of their numbers and the fatigue caused by the tremendous exertions the defenders were making began to tell. Step by step the English were driven back, and Walter saw that the defense could not much longer be continued. He bade one of his men-at-arms at once order the archers to cease firing, and, leaving the walls, to take refuge in the keep, and thence to open fire upon the French as they poured through the breach.

When he found that this movement had been accomplished Walter bade the men-at-arms fall back gradually. A gap had been left in the wooden fence sufficient for one at a time to pass, and through this the men-at-arms retired one by one to the keep until only Walter and five others were left. With these Walter flung himself suddenly upon the assailants and forced them a few feet down the slope. Then he gave the word, and all sprang back, and leaping down from the wall into the court-yard ran through the barrier, Walter and Ralph being the last to pass as the French with exulting shouts leaped down from the breach.

There was another fierce fight at the barrier. Walter left Ralph to defend this with a few men-at-arms while he saw that all was in readiness for closing the door rapidly in the keep. Then he ran back again. He was but just in time. Ralph indeed could for a long time have held the narrow passage, but the barriers themselves were yielding. The French were pouring in through the breach, and as those behind could not see the nature of the obstacle which arrested the advance of their companions they continued to push forward, and by their weight pressed those in front against the spikes in the barrier. Many perished miserably on these. Others, whose armor protected them from this fate, were crushed to death by the pressure; but this was now so great that the timbers were yielding. Walter, seeing that in another moment they would be leveled, gave the word, sprang back with Ralph and his party, and entered the keep just as with a crash the barrier fell and the French poured in a crowd into the court-yard. Bolting the door the defenders of the keep piled against it the stones which had been laid in readiness.

The door was on the first floor, and was approached by a narrow flight of stone steps, up which but two abreast could advance. In their first fury the French poured up these steps, but from the loop-holes which commanded it the English bowmen shot so hard that their arrows pierced the strongest armor. Smitten through visor and armor, numbers of the bravest of the assailants fell dead. Those who gained the top of the steps were assailed by showers of boiling oil from an upper chamber which projected over the door, and whose floor was pierced for this purpose, while from the top of the keep showers of stones were poured down. After losing great numbers in this desperate effort at assault the French drew off for awhile, while their leaders held council as to the best measures to be taken for the capture of the keep.

After a time Walter from the summit saw several bodies of men detach themselves from the crowd still without the castle and proceed into the country. Two hours later they were seen returning laden with trunks of trees. These were dragged through the breach, and were, in spite of the efforts of the archers and of the men-at-arms with their stones, placed so as to form a sort of penthouse against one side of the keep. Numbers of the soldiers now poured up with sacks and all kinds of vessels which they had gathered from the surrounding villages, filled with earth. This was thrown over the beams until it filled all the crevices between them and formed a covering a foot thick, so that neither boiling oil nor water poured from above could penetrate to injure those working beneath its shelter. When all was ready a strong body armed with picks and crowbars entered the penthouse and began to labor to cut away the wall of the keep itself.

"Their commander knows his business," Walter said, "and the device is an excellent one. We can do nothing, and it only depends upon the strength of the wall how long we can hold out. The masonry is by no means good, and before nightfall, unless aid comes, there will be naught for us but death or surrender."

Chapter XVI
A Prisoner.

As long as it was light an anxious lookout was kept from the top of the keep toward Calais. There was nothing to be done. The besiegers who had entered the walls were ensconced in the various buildings in the court-yard or placed behind walls so as to be out of arrow-shot from above, and were in readiness to repel any sortie which might be made to interfere with the work going on under the penthouse. But no sortie was possible, for to effect this it would be necessary to remove the stones from the door, and before this could be accomplished the besiegers would have rallied in overwhelming force, nor could a sortie have effected anything beyond the slaying of the men actually engaged in the work. The beams of the penthouse were too strong and too heavily weighted with earth to be removed, and the attempt would only have entailed useless slaughter. The penthouse was about forty feet in length, and the assailants were piercing three openings, each of some six feet in width, leaving two strong supporting pillars between them. Anxiously the garrison within listened to the sounds of work, which became louder and louder as the walls crumbled before the stroke of pickax and crowbar.

"I shall hold out until the last moment," Walter said to Ralph, "in hopes of relief, but before they burst in I shall sound a parley. To resist further would be a vain sacrifice of life."

Presently a movement could be seen among the stones, and then almost simultaneously two apertures appeared. The chamber into which the openings were made was a large one, being used as the common room of the garrison. Here twenty archers and the remaining men-at-arms —of whom nearly one-half had fallen in the defense of the breach-were gathered, and the instant the orifices appeared the archers began to send their arrows through them. Then Walter ascended to another chamber, and ordered the trumpeter to sound a parley.

The sound was repeated by the assailants' trumpeter.

"Who commands the force?" Walter asked.

"I, Guy, Count of Evreux."

"I am Sir Walter Somers," the young knight continued. "I wish to ask terms for the garrison."

"You must surrender unconditionally," the count replied from the court-yard. "In ten minutes we shall have completely pierced your walls, and you will be at our mercy."

"You may pierce our walls," Walter replied, "but it will cost you many lives before you force your way in; we will defend the hold from floor to floor, and you know how desperate men can fight. It will cost you scores of lives before you win your way to the summit of this keep; but if I have your knightly word that the lives of all within these walls shall be spared, then will I open the doors and lay down our arms."

A consultation took place between the leaders below. There was truth in Walter's words that very many lives would be sacrificed before the resistance of so gallant a garrison could be overcome. Every minute was of importance, for it was possible that at any moment aid might arrive from Calais, and that the table would be turned upon the besiegers. Therefore, after a short parley among themselves, the count replied:

"You have fought as a gallant knight and gentleman, Sir Walter Somers, and have wrought grievous harm upon my leading. I should grieve that so brave a knight should lose his life in a useless resistance. Therefore I agree to your terms, and swear upon my knightly honor that upon your surrendering yourselves prisoners of war, the lives of all within these walls shall be spared."

Walter at once gave the order. The stones were removed and the door thrown open, and leading his men Walter descended the steps into the court-yard, which was now illuminated with torches, and handed his sword to the Count of Evreux.

"You promised me, count," a tall knight standing by his side said, "that if he were taken alive, the commander of this castle should be my prisoner."

"I did so, Sir Philip Holbeaut. When you proposed this adventure to me, and offered to place your following at my command, I agreed to the request you made me; but mind," he said sternly, "my knightly word has been given for his safety. See that he receives fair and gentle treatment at your hand. I would not that aught should befall so brave a knight."

"I seek him no harm," the knight said angrily; "but I know that he is one of the knights of the Black Prince's own suit, and that his ransom will be freely paid, and as my coffers are low from the expenses of the war, I would fain replenish them at the expense of the English prince."

"I said not that I doubted you, Sir Philip," the count said calmly; "but as the knight surrendered on my word, it was needful that I should warn you to treat him as I myself should do did he remain in my hands, and to give him fair treatment until duly ransomed."

"I should be glad, count," Walter said, "if you will suffer me to take with me as companion in my captivity this man-at-arms. He is strongly attached to me, and we have gone through many perils together; it will lighten my captivity to have him by my side."

"Surely I will do so, Sir Walter, and wish that your boon had been a larger one. The rest I will take back with me to Amiens, there to hold until exchanged for some of those who at various times have fallen into your king's hands. And now to work, men; lose not a moment in stripping the castle of all that you choose to carry away, then apply fire to the storehouses, granaries, and the hold itself. I would not that it remained standing to serve as an outpost for the English."

The horses were brought from the stables. Walter and Ralph took their horses by the bridle, and followed Sir Philip Holbeaut through the now open gates of the castle to the spot where the horses of the besiegers were picketed. The knight and his own men-at-arms, who had at the beginning of the day numbered a hundred and fifty, but who were now scarcely two thirds of that strength, at once mounted with their prisoners, and rode off from the castle. A few minutes later a glare of light burst out from behind them. The count's orders had been obeyed; fire had been applied to the stores of forage, and soon the castle of Près was wrapped in flames.

"I like not our captor's manner," Ralph said to Walter as they rode along side by side.

"I agree with you, Ralph. I believe that the reason which he gave the count for his request was not a true one, though, indeed, I can see no other motive which he could have for seeking to gain possession of me. Sir Philip, although a valiant knight, bears but an indifferent reputation. I have heard that he is a cruel master to his serfs, and that when away fighting in Germany he behaved so cruelly to the peasantry that even the Germans, who are not nice in their modes of warfare, cried out against him. It is an evil fortune that has thrown us into his hands; still, although grasping and avaricious, he can hardly demand for a simple knight any inordinate ransom. The French themselves would cry out did he do so, seeing that so large a number of their own knights are in our hands, and that the king has ample powers of retaliation; however, we need not look on the dark side. It is not likely that our captivity will be a long one, for the prince, who is the soul of generosity, will not haggle over terms, but will pay my ransom as soon as he hears into whose hands I have fallen, while there are scores of men-at-arms prisoners whom he can exchange for you. Doubtless Sir Philip will send you over as soon as he arrives at his castle, with one of his own followers, to treat for my ransom."

After riding for some hours the troop halted their weary horses in a wood, and lighting fires, cooked their food, and then lay down until morning. Sir Philip exchanged but few words with his captive; as, having removed his helm, he sat by the fire, Walter had an opportunity of seeing his countenance. It did not belie his reputation. His face had a heavy and brutal expression which was not decreased by the fashion of his hair, which was cut quite short, and stood up without parting all over his bullet-shaped head; he had a heavy and bristling mustache which was cut short in a line with his lips.

"This is a dungeon for a felon," he exclaimed. —Page 273.]

"It is well," Walter thought to himself, "that it is my ransom rather than my life which is dear to that evil-looking knight; for, assuredly, he is not one to hesitate did fortune throw a foe into his hands."

At daybreak the march was resumed, and was continued until they reached the castle of Sir Philip Holbeaut, which stood on a narrow tongue of land formed by a sharp bend of the Somme.

On entering the castle the knight gave an order to his followers, and the prisoners were at once led to a narrow cell beneath one of the towers. Walter looked round indignantly when he arrived there.

"This is a dungeon for a felon," he exclaimed, "not the apartment for a knight who has been taken captive in fair fight. Tell your master that he is bound to award me honorable treatment, and that unless he removes me instantly from this dungeon to a proper apartment, and treats me with all due respect and courtesy, I will, when I regain my liberty, proclaim him a dishonored knight."

The men-at-arms made no reply; but, locking the door behind them, left the prisoners alone.

"What can this mean, Ralph?" Walter exclaimed. "We are in the lowest dungeon, and below the level of the river. See how damp are the walls, and the floor is thick with slimy mud. The river must run but just below that loop-hole, and in times of flood probably enters here."

Philip of Holbeaut, on dismounting, ascended to an upper chamber, where a man in the dress of a well-to-do citizen was sitting.

"Well, Sir Philip," he exclaimed, rising to his feet as the other entered, "what news?"

"The news is bad," the knight growled. "This famous scheme of yours has cost me fifty of my best men. I would I had had nothing to do with it."

"But this Walter Somers," the other exclaimed, "what of him? He has not escaped, surely! The force which marched from Amiens was large enough to have eaten him and his garrison."

"He has not escaped," the knight replied.

"Then he is killed!" the other said eagerly.

"No; nor is he killed. He is at present a prisoner in a dungeon below, together with a stout knave whom he begged might accompany him until ransomed."

"All is well, then," the other exclaimed. "Never mind the loss of your men. The money which I have promised you for this business will hire you two hundred such knaves; but why didst not knock him on the head at once?"

"It was not so easy to knock him on the head," Sir Philip growled. "It cost us five hundred men to capture the outer walls, and to have fought our way into the keep, held as it was by men who would have contested every foot of the ground, was not a job for which any of us had much stomach, seeing what the first assaults had cost us; so the count took them all to quarter. The rest he carried with him to Amiens; but their leader, according to the promise which he made me, he handed over to me as my share of the day's booty, giving me every charge that he should receive good and knightly treatment."

"Which, no doubt, you will observe," the other said, with an ugly laugh.

"It is a bad business," the knight exclaimed angrily, "and were it not for our friendship in Spain, and the memory of sundry deeds which we did together, not without profit to our purses, I would rather that you were thrown over the battlements into the river than I had taken a step in this business. However, none can say that Philip of Holbeaut ever deserted a friend who had proved true to him, not to mention that the sum which you promised me for my aid in this matter will, at the present time, prove wondrously convenient. Yet I foresee that it will bring me into trouble with the Count of Evreux. Ere many days a demand will come for the fellow to be delivered on ransom."

"And what will you say?" the other asked.

"I shall say what is the truth," the knight replied, "though I may add something that is not wholly so. I shall say that he was drowned in the Somme. I shall add that it happened as he was trying to make his escape, contrary to the parole he had given; but in truth he will be drowned in the dungeon in which I have placed him, which has rid me of many a troublesome prisoner before now. The river is at ordinary times but two feet below the loop-hole; and when its tide is swelled by rain it often rises above the sill, and then there is an end of any one within. They can doubt my word; but there are not many who would care to do so openly; none who would do so for the sake of an unknown English knight. And as for any complaints on the part of the Black Prince, King Philip has shown over and over again how little the complaints of Edward himself move him."

"It were almost better to knock him on the head at once," the other said thoughtfully; "the fellow has as many lives as a cat."

"If he had as many as nine cats," the knight replied, "it would not avail him. But I will have no violence. The water will do your work as well as a poniard, and I will not have it said, even among such ruffians as mine, that I slew a captured knight. The other will pass as an accident, and I care not what my men may think as long as they can say nothing for a surety. The count may storm as much as he will, and may even lay a complaint against me before the king; but in times like the present, even a simple knight who can lead two hundred good fighting men into the field is not to be despised, and the king is likely to be easily satisfied with my replies to any question that may be raised. Indeed, it would seem contrary to reason that I should slay a captive against whom I have no cause of quarrel, and so forfeit the ransom which I should get for him."

"But suppose that a messenger should come offering ransom before the river happens to rise?"

"Then I shall anticipate matters, and shall say that what I know will happen has already taken place. Do not be uneasy, Sir James. You have my word in the matter, and now I have gone so far, I shall carry it through. From the moment when I ordered him into that dungeon his fate was sealed, and in truth, when I gave the order I did so to put an end to the indecision in which my mind had been all night. Once in there he could not be allowed to come out alive, for his report of such treatment would do me more harm among those of my own station in France than any rumors touching his end could do. It is no uncommon affair for one to remove an enemy from one's path; but cruelty to a knightly prisoner would be regarded with horror. Would you like to have a look at him?"

The other hesitated. "No," he replied. "Against him personally I have no great grudge. He has thwarted my plans, and stands now grievously in the way of my making fresh ones; but as he did so from no ill-will toward myself, but as it were by hazard, I have no personal hatred toward him, though I would fain remove him from my path. Besides, I tell you fairly, that even in that dungeon where you have thrown him I shall not feel that he is safe until you send me word that he is dead. He has twice already got out of scrapes when other men would have been killed. Both at Vannes and at Ghent he escaped in a marvelous way; and but a few weeks since, by the accident of his having a coat of mail under his doublet he saved his life from as fair a blow as ever was struck. Therefore I would not that he knew aught of my having a hand in this matter, for if after having seen me he made his escape I could never show my face in England again. I should advise you to bid three or four men always enter his cell together, for he and that man-at-arms who follows him like a shadow are capable of playing any desperate trick to escape."

"That matter is easily enough managed," Sir Philip said grimly, "by no one entering the dungeon at all. The river may be slow of rising, though in sooth the sky looks overcast now, and it is already at its usual winter level; and whether he dies from lack of water or from a too abundant supply matters but little to me; only, as I told you, I will give no orders for him to be killed. Dost remember that Jew we carried off from Seville and kept without water until he agreed to pay us a ransom which made us both rich for six months? That was a rare haul, and I would that rich Jews were plentiful in this country."

"Yes, those were good times," the other said, "although I own that I have not done badly since the war began, having taken a count and three knights prisoners, and put them to ransom, and having reaped a goodly share of plunder from your French burghers, else indeed I could not have offered you so round a sum to settle this little matter for me. There are not many French knights who have earned a count's ransom in the present war. And now I will take horse; here is one-half of the sum I promised you, in gold nobles. I will send you the remainder on the day when I get news from you that the matter is finished."

"Have your money ready in a week's time," the knight replied, taking the bag of gold which the other placed on the table, "for by that time you will hear from me. I hope this will not be the last business which we may do together; there ought to be plenty of good chances in a war like this. Any time that you can send me word of an intended foray by a small party under a commander whose ransom would be a high one I will share what I get with you; and similarly I will let you know of any rich prize who may be pounced upon on the same terms."

"Agreed!" the other said. "We may do a good business together in that way. But you lie too far away. If you move up as near as you can to Calais and let me know your whereabout, so that I could send or ride to you in a few hours, we might work together with no small profit."

"I will take the field as soon as this affair of yours is settled," the knight replied; "and the messenger who brings you the news shall tell you where I may be found. And now, while your horse is being got ready, let us drink a stoop of wine together in memory of old times, though, for myself, these wines of ours are poor and insipid beside the fiery juice of Spain."

While this conversation, upon which their fate so much depended, had been going on, Walter and Ralph had been discussing the situation, and had arrived at a tolerably correct conclusion.

"This conduct on the part of this brutal French knight, Ralph, is so strange that methinks it cannot be the mere outcome of his passions or of hate against me as an Englishman, but of some deeper motive; and we were right in thinking that in bargaining for my person with the Count of Evreux it was more than my ransom which he sought. Had that been his only object he would never have thrown us into this noisome dungeon, for my report of such treatment would bring dishonor upon him in the eyes of every knight and noble in France as well as in England. It must be my life he aims at, although what grudge he can have against me it passes me to imagine. It may be that at Cressy or elsewhere some dear relative of his may have fallen by my sword; and yet were it so, men nourish no grudge for the death of those killed in fair fight. But this boots not at present. It is enough for us that it is my life which he aims at, and I fear, Ralph, that yours must be included with mine, since he would never let a witness escape to carry the foul tale against him. This being so, the agreement on which I surrendered is broken, and I am free to make my escape if I can, and methinks the sooner that be attempted the better. So let us to work to plan how we may best get out of this place. After our escape from that well at Vannes we need not despair about breaking out from this dungeon of Holbeaut."

"We might overpower the guard who brings our food," Ralph said.

"There is that chance," Walter rejoined, "but I think it is a poor one. They may be sure that this dishonorable treatment will have rendered us desperate, and they will take every precaution and come well armed. It may be, too, that they will not come at all, but that they intend us to die of starvation, or perchance to be drowned by the floods, which it is easy to see often make their way in here. No, our escape, if escape there be, must be made through that loop-hole above. Were that bar removed methinks it is wide enough for us to squeeze through. Doubtless such a hazard has not occurred to them, seeing that it is nigh twelve feet above the floor and that a single man could by no possibility reach it, but with two of us there is no difficulty. Now, Ralph, do you stand against the wall. I will climb upon your shoulders and standing there can reach the bar and so haul myself up and look out."

This was soon done, and Walter, seizing the bar, hauled himself up so that he could see through the loop-hole.

"It is as I thought," he said. "The waters of the Somme are but a foot below the level of this window; the river is yellow and swollen, and a few hours' heavy rain would bring it above the level of this sill. Stand steady, Ralph, I am coming down again."

When he reached the ground he said:

"Take off your belt, Ralph; if we buckle that and mine together, passing it round the bar, it will make a loop upon which we can stand at the window and see how best we can loosen the bar. Constantly wet as it is, it is likely that the mortar will have softened, in which case we shall have little difficulty in working it out."

The plan was at once put into execution; the belts were fastened together, and Walter standing on Ralph's shoulders passed one end around the bar and buckled it to the other, thus making a loop some three feet in length; putting a foot in this he was able to stand easily at the loop-hole.

"It is put in with mortar at the top, Ralph, and the mortar has rotted with the wet, but at the bottom lead was poured in when the bar was set and this must be scooped out before it can be moved. Fortunately the knight gave no orders to his men to remove our daggers when we were thrust in here, and these will speedily dig out the lead; but I must come down first, for the strap prevents my working at the foot of the bar. We must tear off a strip of our clothing and make a shift to fasten the strap half-way up the bar so as not to slip down with our weight."

In order to accomplish this Walter had to stand upon Ralph's head to gain additional height. He presently, after several attempts, succeeded in fixing the strap firmly against the bar half-way up, and then placing one knee in the loop and putting an arm through the bar to steady himself, he set to work at the lead. The sharp point of the dagger quickly cut out that near the surface, but further down the hole narrowed and the task was much more difficult. Several times Ralph relieved him at the work, but at last it was accomplished, and the bar was found to move slightly when they shook it. There now remained only to loosen the cement above, and this was a comparatively easy task; it crumbled quickly before the points of their daggers, and the bar was soon free to move.

"Now," Walter said, "we have to find out whether the bar was first put in from below or from above; one hole or the other must be a good deal deeper than the iron, so that it was either shoved up or pushed down until the other end could get under or over the other hole. I should think most likely the hole is below, as if they held up the bar against the top, when the lead was poured in it would fill up the space; so we will first of all try to lift it. I must stand on your head again to enable me to be high enough to try this."

"My head is strong enough, I warrant," Ralph replied, "but I will fold up my jerkin, and put on it, for in truth you hurt me somewhat when you were tying the strap to the bar."

All Walter's efforts did not succeed in raising the bar in the slightest, and he therefore concluded that it had been inserted here and lifted while the space was filled with lead. "It is best so," he said; "we should have to cut away the stone either above or below, and can work much better below. Now I will put my knee in the strap again and set to work. The stone seems greatly softened by the wet, and will yield to our daggers readily enough. It is already getting dark, and as soon as we have finished we can start."

As Walter had discovered, the stone was rotten with the action of the weather, and although as they got deeper it became much harder, it yielded to the constant chipping with their daggers, and in two hours Ralph, who at the moment happened to be engaged, announced to Walter that his dagger found its way under the bottom of the bar. The groove was soon made deep enough for the bar to be moved out; but another hour's work was necessary, somewhat further to enlarge the upper hole, so as to allow the bar to have sufficient play. Fortunately it was only inserted about an inch and a half in the stone, and the amount to be cut away to give it sufficient play was therefore not large. Then at last all was ready for their flight.

Chapter XVII
The Capture Of Calais.

When the bar was once ready for removal the captives delayed not a minute, for although it was now so late that there was little chance of a visit being paid them, it was just possible that such might be the case, and that it might occur to the knight that it would be safer to separate them.

"Now, Ralph, do you go first, since I am lighter and can climb up by means of the strap, which you can hold from above; push the bar out and lay it down quietly in the thickness of the wall. A splash might attract the attention of the sentries, though I doubt whether it would, for the wind is high and the rain falling fast. Unbuckle the strap before you move the bar, as otherwise it might fall and I should have difficulty in handing it to you again. Now, I am steady against the wall."

Ralph seized the bar and with a great effort pushed the bottom from him. It moved through the groove without much difficulty, but it needed a great wrench to free the upper end. However, it was done, and laying it quietly down he pulled himself up and thrust himself through the loop-hole. It was a desperate struggle to get through, for it was only just wide enough for his head to pass, and he was so squarely built that his body with difficulty followed. The wall was four feet wide, and as the loop-hole widened considerably without, there was, when he had once passed through from the inside, space enough for him to kneel down and lower one end of the strap to Walter. The latter speedily climbed up, and getting through the slit with much less trouble than Ralph had experienced-for although in height and width of shoulder he was his equal, he was less in depth than his follower-he joined him in the opening, Ralph sitting with his feet in the water in order to make room for him.

The dungeon was upon the western side of the castle, and consequently the stream would be with them in making for shore. It was pitch-dark, but they knew that the distance they would have to swim could not exceed forty or fifty yards.

"Keep along close by the wall, Ralph. If we once get out in the stream we might lose our way; we will skirt the wall until it ends, then there is a cut, for as you saw when we entered, the moat runs right across this neck. If we keep a bit further down and then land we shall be fairly beyond the outworks."

Ralph slipped down into the water, and followed by Walter swam along at the foot of the wall. They had already been deprived of their armor, but had luckily contrived to retain their daggers in their belts, which they had again girdled on before entering the water. The stream hurried them rapidly along, and they had only to keep themselves afloat. They were soon at the corner of the castle. A few strokes further and they again felt the wall which lined the moat. The stream still swept them along, they felt the masonry come to an end, and bushes and shrubs lined the bank. They were beyond the outer defenses of the castle. Still a little further they proceeded down the stream in order to prevent the possibility of any noise they might make in scrambling up being heard by the sentinels on the outer postern. Then when they felt quite safe they grasped the bushes, and speedily climbed the bank. Looking back at the castle they saw lights still burning there. Short as was the time they had been in the water they were both chilled to the bone, for it was the month of February, and the water was bitterly cold.

"It cannot be more than nine o'clock now," Walter said, "for it is not much more than four hours since darkness fell. They are not likely to visit the dungeon before eight or nine to-morrow, so we can rely upon twelve hours' start, and if we make the best of our time we ought to be far on our way by then, though in truth it is not fast traveling on a night like this through a strange country. I would that the stars were shining. However, the direction of the wind and rain will be a guide to us, and we shall soon strike the road we traveled yesterday, and can follow that till morning."

They were not long before they found the track, and then started at a brisk pace along it. All night they struggled on through wind and rain until the first dawn enabled them to see the objects in the surrounding country; and making for the forest which extended to within a mile of the road, they entered deep into its shelter, and there, utterly exhausted, threw themselves down on the wet ground. After a few hours of uneasy sleep they woke, and taking their place near the edge of the forest watched for the passage of any party which might be in pursuit, but until nightfall none came along.

"They have not discovered our flight," Ralph said at last, "or they would have passed long before this. Sir Philip doubtless imagines that we are drowned. The water was within a few inches of the sill when we started, and must soon have flooded the dungeon; and did he trouble to look in the morning, which is unlikely enough seeing that he would be sure of our fate, he would be unable to descend the stairs, and could not reach to the door, and so discover that the bar had been removed. No; whatever his motive may have been in compassing my death, he is doubtless satisfied that he has attained it, and we need have no further fear of pursuit from him. The rain has ceased, and I think that it will be a fine night; we will walk on, and if we come across a barn will make free to enter it, and stripping off our clothing to dry, will sleep in the hay, and pursue our journey in the morning. From our travel-stained appearance any who may meet us will take us for two wayfarers going to take service in the army at Amiens."

It was not until nearly midnight that they came upon such a place as they sought, then after passing a little village they found a shed standing apart. Entering it they found that it was tenanted by two cows. Groping about they presently came upon a heap of forage, and taking off their outer garments lay down on this, covering themselves thickly with it. The shed was warm and comfortable and they were soon asleep, and awaking at daybreak they found that their clothes had dried somewhat. The sun was not yet up when they started, but it soon rose, and ere noon their garments had dried, and they felt for the first time comfortable. They met but few people on the road, and these passed them with the ordinary salutations.

They had by this time left Amiens on the right, and by nightfall were well on their way toward Calais. Early in the morning they had purchased some bread at a village through which they passed; Walter's Norman-French being easily understood, and exciting no surprise or suspicion. At nightfall they slept in a shed within a mile of the ruins of the castle of Près, and late next evening entered the English encampment at New Town. After going to his tent, where he and Ralph changed their garments and partook of a hearty meal, Walter proceeded to the pavilion of the prince, who hailed his entrance with the greatest surprise.

"Why, Sir Walter," he exclaimed, "what good saint has brought you here? I have but an hour since received a message from the Count of Evreux to the effect that you were a prisoner in the hands of Sir Philip de Holbeaut, with whom I must treat for your ransom. I was purporting to send off a herald to-morrow to ask at what sum he held you; and now you appear in flesh and blood before us! But first, before you tell us your story, I must congratulate you on your gallant defense of the Castle of Près, which is accounted by all as one of the most valiant deeds of the war. When two days passed without a messenger from you coming hither, I feared that you were beleaguered, and started that evening with six hundred men-at-arms. We arrived at daybreak, to find only a smoking ruin. Luckily among the crowd of dead upon the breach we found one of your men-at-arms who still breathed, and after some cordial had been given him, and his wounds stanched, he was able to tell us the story of the siege. But it needed not his tale to tell us how stanchly you had defended the castle, for the hundreds of dead who lay outside of the walls, and still more the mass who piled the breach, and the many who lay in the castle yard spoke for themselves of the valor with which the castle had been defended. As the keep was gutted by fire, and the man could tell us naught of what had happened after he had been stricken down at the breach, we knew not whether you and your brave garrison had perished in the flames. We saw the penthouse beneath which they had labored to cut through the wall, but the work had ceased before the holes were large enough for entry, and we hoped that you might have seen that further resistance was in vain, and have made terms for your lives; indeed we heard from the country people that certain prisoners had been taken to Amiens. I rested one day at Près, and the next rode back here, and forthwith dispatched a herald to the Count of Evreux at Amiens asking for news of the garrison; but now he has returned with word that twenty-four men-at-arms and fifty-eight archers are prisoners in the count's hands, and that he is ready to exchange them against an equal number of French prisoners; but that you, with a man-at-arms, were in the keeping of Sir Philip of Holbeaut, with whom I must treat for your ransom. And now tell me how it is that I see you here. Has your captor, confiding in your knightly word to send him the sum agreed upon, allowed you to return? Tell me the sum and my treasurer shall to-morrow pay it over to a herald, who shall carry it to Holbeaut."

"Thanks, your royal highness, for your generosity," Walter replied, "but there is no ransom to be paid."

And he then proceeded to narrate the incidents of his captivity at Holbeaut and his escape from the castle. His narration was frequently interrupted by exclamations of surprise and indignation from the prince and the knights present.

"Well, this well-nigh passes all belief," the prince exclaimed when he had concluded. "It is an outrage upon all laws of chivalry and honor. What could have induced this caitiff knight, instead of treating you with courtesy and honor until your ransom arrived, to lodge you in a foul dungeon, where, had you not made your escape, your death would have been brought about that very night by the rising water? Could it be, think you, that his brain is distraught by some loss or injury which may have befallen him at our hands during the war and worked him up to a blind passion of hatred against all Englishmen?"

"I think not that, your royal highness," Walter replied. "His manner was cool and deliberate, and altogether free from any signs of madness. Moreover, it would seem that he had specially marked me down beforehand, since, as I have told you, he had bargained with the Count of Evreux for the possession of my person should I escape with life at the capture of the castle. It seems rather as if he must have had some private enmity against me, although what the cause may be I cannot imagine, seeing that I have never, to my knowledge, before met him, and have only heard his name by common report."

"Whatever be the cause," the prince said, "we will have satisfaction for it, and I will beg the king, my father, to write at once to Philip of Valois protesting against the treatment that you have received, and denouncing Sir Philip of Holbeaut as a base and dishonored knight, whom, should he fall into our hands, we will commit at once to the hangman."

Upon the following day Walter was called before the king, and related to him in full the incidents of the siege and of his captivity and escape; and the same day King Edward sent off a letter to Philip of Valois denouncing Sir Philip Holbeaut as a dishonored knight, and threatening retaliation upon the French prisoners in his hands.

A fortnight later an answer was received from the King of France saying that he had inquired into the matter, and had sent a seneschal, who had questioned Sir Philip Holbeaut and some of the men-at-arms in the castle, and that he found that King Edward had been grossly imposed upon by a fictitious tale. Sir Walter Somers had, he found, been treated with all knightly courtesy, and believing him to be an honorable knight and true to his word, but slight watch had been kept over him. He had basely taken advantage of this trust, and with the man-at-arms with him had escaped from the castle in order to avoid payment of his ransom, and had now invented these gross and wicked charges against Sir Philip Holbeaut as a cloak to his own dishonor.

Walter was furious when he heard the contents of this letter, and the king and Black Prince were no less indignant. Although they doubted him not for a moment, Walter begged that Ralph might be brought before them and examined strictly as to what had taken place, in order that they might see that his statements tallied exactly with those he had made.

When this had been done Walter obtained permission from the king to dispatch a cartel to Sir Philip de Holbeaut denouncing him as a perjured and dishonored knight and challenging him to meet him in mortal conflict at any time and place that he might name. At the same time the king dispatched a letter to Philip of Valois saying that the statements of the French knight and his followers were wholly untrue, and begging that a time might be appointed for the meeting of the two knights in the lists.

To this King Philip replied that he had ordered all private quarrels in France to be laid aside during the progress of the war, and that so long as an English foot remained upon French soil he would give no countenance to his knights throwing away the lives which they owed to France in private broils.

"You must wait, Sir Walter, you see," the king said, "until you may perchance meet him in the field of battle. In the mean time, to show how lightly I esteem the foul charge brought against you, and how much I hold and honor the bravery which you showed in defending the castle which my son the prince intrusted to you, as well as upon other occasions, I hereby promote you to the rank of knight banneret."

Events now passed slowly before Calais. Queen Philippa and many of her ladies crossed the Channel and joined her husband, and these added much to the gayety of the life in camp. The garrison at Calais was, it was known, in the sorest straits for the want of food, and at last the news came that the King of France, with a huge army of two hundred thousand men, was moving to its relief. They had gathered at Hesdin, at which rendezvous the king had arrived in the early part of April; but it was not until the 27th of July that the whole army was collected, and marching by slow steps advanced toward the English position.

King Edward had taken every precaution to guard all the approaches to the city. The ground was in most places too soft and sandy to admit of the construction of defensive works; but the fleet was drawn up close inshore to cover the line of sand-hills by the sea with arrows and war machines, while the passages of the marshes, which extended for a considerable distance round the town, were guarded by the Earl of Lancaster and a body of chosen troops, while the other approaches to the city were covered by the English camp.

The French reconnoitering parties found no way open to attack the English unless under grievous disadvantages. The Cardinals of Tusculum, St. John, and St. Paul endeavored to negotiate terms of peace, and commissioners on both sides met. The terms offered by Philip were, however, by no means so favorable as Edward, after his own victorious operations and those of his armies in Brittany and Guienne, had a right to expect, and the negotiations were broken off.

The following day the French king sent in a message to Edward saying that he had examined the ground in every direction in order to advance and give battle, but had found no means of doing so. He therefore summoned the king to come forth from the marshy ground in which he was encamped and to fight in the open plain; and he offered to send four French knights, who, with four English of the same rank, should choose a fair plain in the neighborhood, according to the usages of chivalry. Edward had little over thirty thousand men with him; but the same evening that Philip's challenge was received a body of seventeen thousand Flemings and English, detached from an army which had been doing good service on the borders of Flanders, succeeded in passing round the enemy's host and in effecting a junction with the king's army. Early the next morning, after having consulted with his officers, Edward returned an answer to the French king, saying that he agreed to his proposal, and inclosed a safe-conduct for any four French knights who might be appointed to arrange with the same number of English the place of battle.

The odds were indeed enormous, the French being four to one; but Edward, after the success of Cressy, which had been won by the Black Prince's division, which bore a still smaller proportion to the force engaging it, might well feel confident in the valor of his troops. His envoys, on arriving at the French camp, found that Philip had apparently changed his mind. He declined to discuss the matter with which they were charged, and spoke only of the terms upon which Edward would be willing to raise the siege of Calais. As they had no authority on this subject the English knights returned to their camp, where the news was received with great disappointment, so confident did all feel in their power to defeat the huge host of the French. But even greater was the astonishment the next morning, when, before daylight, the tents of the French were seen in one great flame, and it was found that the king and all his host were retreating at full speed. The Earls of Lancaster and Northampton, with a large body of horse, at once started in pursuit, and harassed the retreating army on its march toward Amiens.

No satisfactory reasons ever have been assigned for this extraordinary step on the part of the French king. He had been for months engaged in collecting a huge army, and he had now an opportunity of fighting the English in a fair field with a force four times as great as their own. The only means indeed of accounting for his conduct is by supposing him affected by temporary aberration of mind, which many other facts in his history render not improbable. The fits of rage so frequently recorded of him border upon madness, and a number of strange actions highly detrimental to his own interests which he committed can only be accounted for as the acts of a diseased mind. This view has been to some extent confirmed by the fact that less than half a century afterward insanity declared itself among his descendants.

A few hours after the departure of the French the French standard was lowered on the walls of Calais, and news was brought to Edward that the governor was upon the battlements and desired to speak with some officers of the besieging army. Sir Walter Manny and Lord Bisset were sent to confer with him, and found that his object was to obtain the best terms he could. The English knights, knowing the determination of the king on the subject, were forced to tell him that no possibility existed of conditions being granted, but that the king demanded their unconditional surrender, reserving to himself entirely the right whom to pardon and whom to put to death.

The governor remonstrated on the severe terms, and said that rather than submit to them he and his soldiers would sally out and die sword in hand. Sir Walter Manny found the king inexorable. The strict laws of war in those days justified the barbarous practice of putting to death the garrison of a town captured under such circumstances. Calais had been for many years a nest of pirates, and vessels issuing from its port had been a scourge to the commerce of England and Flanders, and the king was fully determined to punish it severely. Sir Walter Manny interceded long and boldly, and represented to the king that none of his soldiers would willingly defend a town on his behalf from the day on which he put to death the people of Calais, as beyond doubt the French would retaliate in every succeeding siege. The other nobles and knights joined their entreaties to those of Sir Walter Manny, and the king finally consented to yield in some degree. He demanded that six of the most notable burghers of the town, with bare heads and feet, and with ropes about their necks and the keys of the fortress in their hands, should deliver themselves up for execution. On these conditions he agreed to spare the rest. With these terms Sir Walter Manny returned to Sir John of Vienne.

The governor left the battlements, and proceeding to the market-place ordered the bell to be rung. The famished and despairing citizens gathered, a haggard crowd, to hear their doom. A silence followed the narration of the hard conditions of surrender by the governor, and sobs and cries alone broke the silence which succeeded. Then Eustace St. Pierre, the wealthiest and most distinguished of the citizens, came forward and offered himself as one of the victims, saying, "Sad pity and shame would it be to let all of our fellow-citizens die of famine or the sword when means could be found to save them." John of Aire, James and Peter de Vissant, and another whose name has not come down to us, followed his example, and stripping to their shirts set out for the camp, Sir John of Vienne, who, from a late wound, was unable to walk, riding at their head on horseback. The whole population accompanied them weeping bitterly until they came to the place where Sir Walter Manny was awaiting them. Here the crowd halted, and the knight, promising to do his best to save them, led them to the tent where the king had assembled all his nobles around him. When the tidings came that the burghers of Calais had arrived, Edward issued out with his retinue, accompanied by Queen Philippa and the Black Prince.

"Behold, sire," Sir Walter Manny said, "the representatives of the town of Calais!"

The king made no reply while John of Vienne surrendered his sword and, kneeling with the burghers, said: "Gentle lord and king, behold, we six, who were once the greatest citizens and merchants of Calais, bring you the keys of the town and castle, and give ourselves up to your pleasure, placing ourselves in the state in which you see us by our own free will to save the rest of the people of the city, who have already suffered many ills. We pray you, therefore, to have pity and mercy upon us for the sake of your high nobleness."

All present were greatly affected at this speech, and at the aspect of men who thus offered their lives for their fellow-citizens. The king's countenance alone remained unchanged, and he ordered them to be taken to instant execution. Then Sir Walter Manny and all the nobles with tears besought the king to have mercy, not only for the sake of the citizens, but for that of his own fame, which would be tarnished by so cruel a deed.

"Silence, Sir Walter!" cried the king. "Let the executioner be called. The men of Calais have put to death so many of my subjects that I will also put these men to death."

At this moment Queen Philippa, who had been weeping bitterly, cast herself upon her knees before the king. "Oh, gentle lord," she cried, "since I have repassed the seas to see you I have neither asked nor required anything at your hand; now, then, I pray you humbly, and require as a boon, that for the sake of the Son of Mary, and for love of me, you take these men to mercy."

The king stood for a moment in silence, and then said:

"Ah! lady, I would that you had been otherwhere than here; but you beg of me so earnestly I must not refuse you, though I grant your prayer with pain. I give them to you; take them, and do your will."

Then the queen rose from her knees, and bidding the burghers rise, she caused clothing and food to be given them, and sent them away free.

Sir Walter Manny, with a considerable body of men-at-arms, now took possession of the town of Calais. The anger of the king soon gave way to better feelings; all the citizens, without exception, were fed by his bounty. Such of them as preferred to depart instead of swearing fealty to the English monarch were allowed to carry away what effects they could bear upon their persons, and were conducted in safety to the French town of Guisnes. Eustace de St. Pierre was granted almost all the possessions he had formerly held in Calais, and also a considerable pension; and he and all who were willing to remain were well and kindly treated. The number was large, for the natural indignation which they felt at their base desertion by the French king induced very many of the citizens to remain and become subjects of Edward. The king issued a proclamation inviting English traders and others to come across and take up their residence in Calais, bestowing upon them the houses and lands of the French who had left. Very many accepted the invitation, and Calais henceforth and for some centuries became virtually an English town.

A truce was now, through the exertions of the pope's legates, made between England and France, the terms agreed on being very similar to those of the previous treaty; and when all his arrangements were finished Edward returned with his queen to England, having been absent eighteen months, during which time an almost unbroken success had attended his arms, and the English name had reached a position of respect and honor in the eyes of Europe far beyond that at which it previously stood.

Chapter XVIII
The Black Death.

The court at Westminster during the few months which followed the capture of Calais was the most brilliant in Europe. Tournaments and *fêtes* followed each other in rapid succession, and to these knights came from all parts. So great was the reputation of King Edward that deputies came from Germany, where the throne was now vacant, to offer the crown of that kingdom to him. The king declined the offer, for it would have been impossible indeed for him to have united the German crown with that of England, which he already held, and that of France, which he claimed.

Some months after his return to England the Black Prince asked his father as a boon that the hand of his ward Edith Vernon should be bestowed upon the prince's brave follower Sir Walter Somers, and as Queen Philippa, in the name of the lady's mother, seconded the request, the king at once acceded to it. Edith was now sixteen, an age at which, in those days, a young lady was considered to be marriageable, and the wedding took place with great pomp and ceremony at Westminster, the king himself giving away the bride, and bestowing, as did the prince and Queen Philippa, many costly presents upon the young couple. After taking part in several of the tournaments, Walter went with his bride and Dame Vernon down to their estates, and were received with great rejoicing by the tenantry, the older of whom well remembered Walter's father and mother, and were rejoiced at finding that they were again to become the vassals of one of the old family. Dame Vernon was greatly loved by her tenantry; but the latter had looked forward with some apprehension to the marriage of the young heiress, as the character of the knight upon whom the king might bestow her hand would greatly affect the happiness and well-being of his tenants.

Sir James Carnegie had not returned to England after the fall of Calais; he perceived that he was in grave disfavor with the Black Prince, and guessed, as was the case, that some suspicion had fallen on him in reference to the attack upon Walter in the camp, and to the strange attempt which had been made to destroy him by Sir Philip Holbeaut. He had, therefore, for a time taken service with the Count of Savoy, and was away from England, to the satisfaction of Walter and Dame Vernon, when the marriage took place; for he had given proofs of such a malignity of disposition that both felt that although his succession to the estates was now hopelessly barred, yet that he might at any moment attempt some desperate deed to satisfy his feeling of disappointment and revenge.

In spite of the gayety of the court of King Edward a cloud hung over the kingdom; for it was threatened by a danger far more terrible than any combination of foes —a danger from which no gallantry upon the part of her king or warriors availed anything. With a slow and terrible march the enemy was advancing from the East, where countless hosts had been slain. India, Arabia, Syria, and Armenia had been well-nigh depopulated. In no country which the dread foe had invaded had less than two-thirds of the population been slain; in some nine-tenths had perished. All sorts of portents were reported to have accompanied its appearance in the East, where it was said showers of serpents had fallen, strange and unknown insects had appeared in the atmosphere, and clouds of sulphurous vapor had issued from the earth and enveloped whole provinces and countries. For two or three years the appearance of this scourge had been heralded by strange atmospheric disturbances; heavy rains and unusual floods, storms of thunder and lightning of unheard-of violence, hail-showers of unparalleled duration and severity, had everywhere been experienced, while in Italy and Germany violent earthquake shocks had been felt, and that at places where no tradition existed of previous occurrences of the same kind.

From Asia it had spread to Africa and to Europe, affecting first the sea-shores and creeping inland by the course of the rivers. Greece first felt its ravages, and Italy was not long in experiencing them. In Venice more than one hundred thousand persons perished in a few months, and thence spreading over the whole peninsula, not a town escaped the visitation. At Florence sixty thousand people were carried off, and at Lucca and Genoa, in Sicily, Sardinia, and Corsica it raged with equal violence. France was assailed by way of Provence, and Avignon suffered especially. Of the English college at that place not an individual was left, and one hundred and twenty persons died in a single day in that small city. Paris lost upward of fifty thousand of its inhabitants, while ninety thousand were swept away in Lubeck, and one million two hundred thousand died within a year of its first appearance in Germany.

In England the march of the pestilence westward was viewed with deep apprehension, and the approaching danger was brought home to the people by the death of the Princess Joan, the king's second daughter. She was affianced to Peter, the heir to the throne of Spain; and the bride, who had not yet accomplished her fourteenth year, was sent over to Bordeaux with a considerable train of attendants in order to be united there to her promised husband. Scarcely had she reached Bordeaux when she was attacked by the pestilence and died in a few hours.

A few days later the news spread through the country that the disease had appeared almost simultaneously at several of the seaports in the south-west of England. Thence with great rapidity it spread through the kingdom; proceeding through Gloucestershire and Oxfordshire it broke out in London, and the ravages were no less severe than they had been on the Continent, the very lowest estimate being that two-thirds of the population were swept away. Most of those attacked died within a few hours of the seizure. If they survived for two days they generally rallied, but even then many fell into a state of coma from which they never awoke.

No words can describe the terror and dismay caused by this the most destructive plague of which there is any record in history. No remedies were of the slightest avail against it; flight was impossible, for the loneliest hamlets suffered as severely as crowded towns, and frequently not a single survivor was left. Men met the pestilence in various moods: the brave with fortitude, the pious with resignation, the cowardly and turbulent with outbursts of despair and fury. Among the lower classes the wildest rumors gained credence. Some assigned the pestilence to witchcraft, others declared that the waters of the wells and streams had been poisoned. Serious riots occurred in many places, and great numbers of people fell victims to the fury of the mob under the suspicion of being connected in some way with the ravages of the pestilence. The Jews, ever the objects of popular hostility, engendered by ignorance and superstition, were among the chief sufferers. Bands of marauders wandered through the county plundering the houses left empty by the death of all their occupants, and from end to end death and suffering were universal.

Although all classes had suffered heavily the ravages of the disease were, as is always the case, greater among the poor than among the rich, the unsanitary conditions of their life and their coarser and commoner food rendering them more liable to its influence; no rank, however, was exempted, and no less than three Archbishops of Canterbury were carried off in succession by the pestilence within a year of its appearance.

During the months which succeeded his marriage Sir Walter Somers lived quietly and happily with his wife at Westerham. It was not until late in the year that the plague approached the neighborhood. Walter had determined to await its approach there. He had paid a few short visits to the court, where every effort was made by continuous gayety to keep up the spirits of the people and prevent them from brooding over the approaching pestilence; but when it was at hand Walter and his wife agreed that they would rather share the lot of their tenants, whom their presence and example might support and cheer in their need, than return to face it in London. One morning when they were at breakfast a frightened servant brought in the news that the disease had appeared in the village, that three persons had been taken ill on the previous night, that two had already died, and that several others had sickened.

"The time has come, my children," Dame Vernon said calmly, "the danger so long foreseen is at hand, now let us face it as we agreed to do. It has been proved that flight is useless, since nowhere is there escape from the plague; here, at least, there shall be no repetition of the terrible scenes we have heard of elsewhere, where the living have fled in panic and allowed the stricken to die unattended. We have already agreed that we will set the example to our people by ourselves going down and administering to the sick."

"It is hard," Walter said, rising and pacing up and down the room, "to let Edith go into it."

"Edith will do just the same as you do," his wife said firmly. "Were it possible that all in this house might escape, there might be a motive for turning coward, but seeing that no household is spared, there is, as we agreed, greater danger in flying from the pestilence than facing it firmly."

Walter sighed.

"You are right," he said, "but it wrings my heart to see you place yourself in danger."

"Were we out of danger here, Walter, it might be so," Edith replied gently; "but since there is no more safety in the castle than in the cottage, we must face death whether it pleases us or not, and it were best to do so bravely."

"So be it," Walter said; "may the God of heaven watch over us all! Now, mother, do you and Edith busy yourselves in preparing broths, strengthening drinks, and medicaments. I will go down at once to the village and see how matters stand there and who are in need. We have already urged upon all our people to face the danger bravely, and if die they must, to die bravely like Christians, and not like coward dogs. When you have prepared your soups and cordials come down and meet me in the village, bringing Mabel and Janet, your attendants, to carry the baskets."

Ralph, who was now installed as major-domo in the castle, at once set out with Walter. They found the village in a state of panic. Women were sitting crying despairingly at their doors. Some were engaged in packing their belongings in carts preparatory to flight, some wandered aimlessly about wringing their hands, while others went to the church, whose bells were mournfully tolling the dirge of the departed. Walter's presence soon restored something like order and confidence; his resolute tone cheered the timid and gave hope to the despairing. Sternly he rebuked those preparing to fly, and ordered them instantly to replace their goods in their houses. Then he went to the priest and implored him to cause the tolling of the bell to cease.

"There is enough," he said, "in the real danger present to appall even the bravest, and we need no bell to tell us that death is among us. The dismal tolling is enough to unnerve the stoutest heart, and if we ring for all who die its sounds will never cease while the plague is among us; therefore, father, I implore you to discontinue it. Let there be services held daily in the church, but I beseech you strive in your discourses to cheer the people rather than to depress them, and to dwell more upon the joys that await those who die as Christian men and women than upon the sorrows of those who remain behind. My wife and mother will anon be down in the village and will strive to cheer and comfort the people, and I look to you for aid in this matter."

The priest, who was naturally a timid man, nevertheless nerved himself to carry out Walter's suggestions, and soon the dismal tones of the bell ceased to be heard in the village.

Walter dispatched messengers to all the outlying farms desiring his tenants to meet him that afternoon at the castle in order that measures might be concerted for common aid and assistance. An hour later Dame Vernon and Edith came down and visited all the houses where the plague had made its appearance, distributing their soups, and by cheering and comforting words raising the spirits of the relatives of the sufferers.

The names of all the women ready to aid in the general work of nursing were taken down, and in the afternoon at the meeting at the castle the full arrangements were completed. Work was to be carried on as usual in order to occupy men's minds and prevent them from brooding over the ravages of the plague. Information of any case that occurred was to be sent to the castle, where soups and medicines were to be obtained. Whenever more assistance was required than could be furnished by the inmates of a house another woman was to be sent to aid. Boys were told off as messengers to fetch food and other matters as required from the castle.

So, bravely and firmly, they prepared to meet the pestilence; it spread with terrible severity. Scarce a house which did not lose some of its inmates, while in others whole families were swept away. All day Walter and his wife and Dame Vernon went from house to house, and although they could do nothing to stem the progress of the pestilence, their presence and example supported the survivors and prevented the occurrence of any of the panic and disorder which in most places accompanied it.

The castle was not exempt from the scourge. First some of the domestics were seized, and three men and four women died. Walter himself was attacked, but he took it lightly, and three days after the seizure passed into a state of convalescence. Dame Vernon was next attacked, and expired six hours after the commencement of the seizure. Scarcely was Walter upon his feet than Ralph, who had not for a moment left his bedside, was seized, but he too, after being at death's door for some hours, turned the corner. Lastly Edith sickened.

By this time the scourge had done its worst in the village, and three-fifths of the population had been swept away. All the male retainers in the castle had died, and the one female who survived was nursing her dying mother in the village. Edith's attack was a very severe one. Walter, alone now, for Ralph, although convalescent, had not yet left his bed, sat by his wife's bedside a prey to anxiety and grief; for although she had resisted the first attack she was now, thirty-six hours after it had seized her, fast sinking. Gradually her sight and power of speech faded, and she sank into the state of coma which was the prelude of death, and lay quiet and motionless, seeming as if life had already departed.

Suddenly Walter was surprised by the sound of many heavy feet ascending the stairs. He went out into the anteroom to learn the cause of this strange tumult, when five armed men, one of whom was masked, rushed into the room. Walter caught up his sword from the table.

"Ruffians," he exclaimed, "how dare you thus desecrate the abode of death?"

Without a word the men sprang upon him. For a minute he defended himself against their attacks, but he was still weak, his guard was beaten down, and a blow felled him to the ground.

"Now settle her," the masked man exclaimed, and the band rushed into the adjoining room. They paused, however, at the door at the sight of the lifeless figure on the couch.

"We are saved that trouble," one said, "we have come too late."

The masked figure approached the couch and bent over the figure.

"Yes," he said, "she is dead, and so much the better."

Then he returned with the others to Walter.

"He breathes yet," he said. "He needs a harder blow than that you gave him to finish him. Let him lie here for awhile, while you gather your booty together, then we will carry him off. There is scarcely a soul alive in the country round, and none will note us as we pass. I would not dispatch him here, seeing that his body would be found with wounds upon it, and even in these times some inquiry might be made; therefore it were best to finish him elsewhere. When he is missed it will be supposed that he went mad at the death of his wife, and has wandered out and died, maybe in the woods, or has drowned himself in a pond or stream. Besides, I would that before he dies he should know what hand has struck the blow, and that my vengeance, which he slighted and has twice escaped, has overtaken him at last."

After ransacking the principal rooms and taking all that was valuable, the band of marauders lifted the still insensible body of Walter, and carrying it downstairs flung it across a horse. One of the ruffians mounted behind it, and the others also getting into their saddles the party rode away.

They were mistaken, however, in supposing that the Lady Edith was dead. She was indeed very nigh the gates of death, and had it not been for the disturbance would assuredly have speedily entered them. The voice of her husband raised in anger, the clash of steel, followed by the heavy fall, had awakened her deadened brain. Consciousness had at once returned to her, but as yet no power of movement. As at a great distance she had heard the words of those who entered her chamber, and had understood their import. More and more distinctly she heard their movements about the room as they burst open her caskets and appropriated her jewels, but it was not until silence was restored that the gathering powers of life asserted themselves; then with a sudden rush the blood seemed to course through her veins, her eyes opened, and her tongue was loosed, and with a scream she sprang up and stood by the side of her bed.

Sustained as by a supernatural power she hurried into the next room. A pool of blood on the floor showed her that what she had heard had not been a dream or the fiction of a disordered brain. Snatching up a cloak of her husband's which lay on a couch, she wrapped it round her, and with hurried steps made her way along the passages until she reached the apartment occupied by Ralph. The latter sprang up in bed with a cry of astonishment. He had heard but an hour before from Walter that all hope was gone, and thought for an instant that the appearance was an apparition from the dead. The ghastly pallor of the face, the eyes burning with a strange light, the flowing hair, and disordered appearance of the girl might well have alarmed one living in even less superstitious times, and Ralph began to cross himself hastily and to mutter a prayer, when recalled to himself by the sound of Edith's voice.

"Quick, Ralph!" she said, "arise and clothe yourself. Hasten, for your life. My lord's enemies have fallen upon him and wounded him grievously, even if they have not slain him, and have carried him away. They would have slain me also had they not thought I was already dead. Arise and mount, summon every one still alive in the village, and follow these murderers. I will pull the alarm-bell of the castle."

Ralph sprang from his bed as Edith left. He had heard the sound of many footsteps in the knight's apartments, but had deemed them those of the priest and his acolytes come to administer the last rites of the Church to his dying mistress. Rage and anxiety for his master gave strength to his limbs. He threw on a few clothes and rushed down to the stables, where the horses stood with great piles of forage and pails of water before them, placed there two days before, by Walter, when their last attendant died. Without waiting to saddle it, Ralph sprang upon the back of one of the animals, and taking the halters of four others started at a gallop down to the village.

His news spread like wildfire, for the ringing of the alarm-bell of the castle had drawn all to their doors and prepared them for something strange. Some of the men had already taken their arms and were making their way up to the castle when they met Ralph. There were but five men in the village who had altogether escaped the pestilence; others had survived its attacks, but were still weak. Horses there were in plenty. The five men mounted at once, with three others who, though still weak, were able to ride.

So great was the excitement that seven women who had escaped the disease armed themselves with their husbands' swords and leaped on horseback, declaring that, women though they were, they would strike a blow for their beloved lord, who had been as an angel in the village during the plague. Thus it was scarcely more than ten minutes after the marauders had left the castle before a motley band, fifteen strong, headed by Ralph, rode off in pursuit, while some of the women of the village hurried up to the castle to comfort Edith with the tidings that the pursuit had already commenced. Fortunately a lad in the fields had noticed the five men ride away from the castle, and was able to point out the direction they had taken.

At a furious gallop Ralph and his companions tore across the country. Mile after mile was passed. Once or twice they gained news from laborers in the field of the passage of those before them, and knew that they were on the right track. They had now entered a wild and sparsely inhabited country. It was broken and much undulated, so that although they knew that the band they were pursuing were but a short distance ahead, they had not yet caught sight of them, and they hoped that, having no reason to dread any immediate pursuit, these would soon slacken their pace. This expectation was realized, for on coming over a brow they saw the party halted at a turf-burner's cottage in the hollow below. Three of the men had dismounted; two of them were examining the hoof of one of the horses, which had apparently cast a shoe or trodden upon a stone. Ralph had warned his party to make no sound when they came upon the fugitives. The sound of the horses' hoofs was deadened by the turf, and they were within a hundred yards of the marauders before they were perceived; then Ralph uttered a shout, and brandishing their swords the party rode down at a headlong gallop.

The dismounted men leaped into their saddles and galloped off at full speed, but their pursuers were now close upon them. Ralph and two of his companions, who were mounted upon Walter's best horses, gained upon them at every stride. Two of them were overtaken and run through.

The man who bore Walter before him, finding himself being rapidly overtaken, threw his burden on to the ground just as the leader of the party had checked his horse and was about to deliver a sweeping blow at the insensible body.

With a curse at his follower for ridding himself of it, he again galloped on. The man's act was unavailing to save himself, for he was overtaken and cut down before he had ridden many strides; then Ralph and his party instantly reined up to examine the state of Walter, and the two survivors of the band of murderers continued their flight unmolested.

Chapter XIX
By Land And Sea.

Walter was raised from the ground, water was fetched from the cottage, and the blood washed from his head by Ralph, aided by two of the women. It had at once been seen that he was still living, and Ralph on examining the wound joyfully declared that no great harm was done.

"Had Sir Walter been strong and well," he said, "such a clip as this would not have knocked him from his feet, but he would have answered it with a blow such as I have often seen him give in battle; but he was but barely recovering and was as weak as a girl. He is unconscious from loss of blood and weakness. I warrant me that when he opens his eyes and hears that the Lady Edith had risen from her bed and came to send me to his rescue, joy will soon bring the blood into his cheeks again. Do one of you run to the hut and see if they have any cordial waters; since the plague has been raging there are few houses but have laid in a provision in case the disease should seize them."

The man soon returned with a bottle of cordial water compounded of rosemary, lavender, and other herbs. By this time Walter had opened his eyes. The cordial was poured down his throat, and he was presently able to speak.

"Be of good cheer, Sir Walter," Ralph said; "three of your rascally assailants lie dead, and the other two have fled; but I have better news still for you. Lady Edith, who you told me lay unconscious and dying, has revived. The din of the conflict seems to have reached her ears and recalled her to life, and the dear lady came to my room with the news that you were carried off, and then, while I was throwing on my clothes, roused the village to your assistance by ringing the alarm bell. Rarely frightened I was when she came in, for methought at first it was her spirit."

The good news, as Ralph had predicted, effectually roused Walter, and rising to his feet he declared himself able to mount and ride back at once. Ralph tried to persuade him to wait until they had formed a litter of boughs, but Walter would not allow it.

"I would not tarry an instant," he said, "for Edith will be full of anxiety until I return. Why, Ralph, do you think that I am a baby? Why, you yourself were but this morning unable to walk across the room, and here you have been galloping and fighting on my behalf."

"In faith," Ralph said, smiling, "until now I had forgotten that I had been ill."

"You have saved my life, Ralph, you and my friends here, whom I thank with all my heart for what they have done. I will speak more to them another time, now I must ride home with all speed."

Lady Edith's Last Effort. —Page 321.

Walter now mounted; Ralph took his place on one side of him, and one of his tenants on the other, lest he should be seized with faintness; then at a hand-gallop they started back for the castle.

Several women of the village had, when they left, hurried up to the castle. They found Edith lying insensible by the rope of the alarm-bell, having fainted when she had accomplished her object. They presently brought her round; as she was now suffering only from extreme weakness, she was laid on a couch, and cordials and some soup were given to her. One of the women took her place at the highest window to watch for the return of any belonging to the expedition.

Edith felt hopeful as to the result, for she thought that their assailants would not have troubled to carry away the body of Walter had not life remained in it, and she was sure that Ralph would press them so hotly that sooner or later the abductors would be overtaken.

An hour and a half passed, and then the woman from above ran down with the news that she could see three horsemen galloping together toward the castle, with a number of others following in confused order behind.

"Then they have found my lord," Edith exclaimed joyfully, "for Ralph would assuredly not return so quickly had they not done so. 'Tis a good sign that they are galloping, for had they been bearers of ill news they would have returned more slowly; look out again and see if they are bearing one among them."

The woman, with some of her companions, hastened away, and in two or three minutes ran down with the news that Sir Walter himself was one of the three leading horsemen. In a few minutes Edith was clasped in her husband's arms, and their joy, restored as they were from the dead to each other, was indeed almost beyond words.

The plague now abated fast in Westerham, only two or three more persons being attacked by it.

As soon as Edith was sufficiently recovered to travel Walter proceeded with her to London and there laid before the king and prince a complaint against Sir James Carnegie for his attempt upon their lives. Even in the trance in which she lay Edith had recognized the voice which had once been so familiar to her. Walter, too, was able to testify against him, for the rough jolting on horseback had for awhile restored his consciousness, and he had heard words spoken, before relapsing into insensibility from the continued bleeding of his wound, which enabled him to swear to Sir James Carnegie as one of his abductors.

The king instantly ordered the arrest of the knight, but he could not be found; unavailing search was made in every direction, and as nothing could be heard of him it was concluded that he had left the kingdom. He was proclaimed publicly a false and villainous knight, his estates were confiscated to the crown, and he himself was outlawed. Then Walter and his wife returned home and did their best to assist their tenants in struggling through the difficulties entailed through the plague.

So terrible had been the mortality that throughout England there was a lack of hands for field work, crops rotted in the ground because there were none to harvest them, and men able to work demanded twenty times the wages which had before been paid. So great was the trouble from this source that an ordinance was passed by parliament enacting that severe punishment should be dealt upon all who demanded wages above the standard price, and even more severe penalties inflicted upon those who should consent to pay higher wages. It was, however, many years before England recovered from the terrible blow which had been dealt her from the pestilence.

While Europe had been ravaged by pestilence the adherents of France and England had continued their struggle in Brittany in spite of the terms of the truce, and this time King Edward was the first open aggressor, granting money and assistance to the free companies, who pillaged and plundered in the name of England. The truce expired at the end of 1348, but was continued for short periods. It was, however, evident that both parties were determined ere long to recommence hostilities. The French collected large forces in Artois and Picardy, and Edward himself proceeded to Sandwich to organize there another army for the invasion of France.

Philip determined to strike the first blow, and, before the conclusion of the truce, to regain possession of Calais. This town was commanded by a Lombard officer named Almeric of Pavia. Free communication existed, in consequence of the truce, between Calais and the surrounding country, and Jeffrey de Charny, the Governor of St. Omer, and one of the commissioners especially appointed to maintain the truce, opened communications with the Lombard captain. Deeming that like most mercenaries he would be willing to change sides should his interest to do so be made clear, he offered him a large sum of money to deliver the castle to the French.

The Lombard at once agreed to the project. Jeffrey de Charny arranged to be within a certain distance of the town on the night of the 1st of January, bringing with him sufficient forces to master all opposition if the way was once opened to the interior of the town. It was further agreed that the money was to be paid over by a small party of French who were to be sent forward for the purpose of examining the castle, in order to insure the main body against treachery. As a hostage for the security of the detachment, the son of the governor was to remain in the hands of the French without, until the safe return of the scouting party.

Several weeks elapsed between the conclusion of the agreement and the date fixed for its execution, and in the mean time the Lombard, either from remorse or from a fear of the consequences which might arise from a detection of the plot before its execution, or from the subsequent vengeance of the English king, disclosed the whole transaction to Edward.

The king bade him continue to carry out his arrangements with De Charny, leaving it to him to counteract the plot. Had he issued orders for the rapid assembly of the army the French would have taken alarm. He therefore sent private messengers to a number of knights and gentlemen of Kent and Sussex to meet him with their retainers at Dover on the 31st of December.

Walter was one of those summoned, and although much surprised at the secrecy with which he was charged, and of such a call being made while the truce with France still existed, he repaired to Dover on the day named, accompanied by Ralph and by twenty men, who were all who remained capable of bearing arms on the estate.

He found the king himself with the Black Prince at Dover, where they had arrived that day. Sir Walter Manny was in command of the force, which consisted in all of three hundred men-at-arms and six hundred archers. A number of small boats had been collected, and at mid-day on the 1st of January the little expedition started, and arrived at Calais after nightfall.

In the chivalrous spirit of the times the king determined that Sir Walter Manny should continue in command of the enterprise; he and the Black Prince, disguised as simple knights, fighting under his banner.

In the mean time a considerable force had been collected at St. Omer, where a large number of knights and gentlemen obeyed the summons of Jeffrey de Charny. On the night appointed they marched for Calais, in number five hundred lances and a corresponding number of footmen. They reached the river and bridge of Nieullay a little after midnight, and messengers were sent on to the governor, who was prepared to receive them. On their report De Charny advanced still nearer to the town, leaving the bridge and passages to the river guarded by a large body of cross-bowmen under the command of the Lord de Fiennes and a number of other knights. At a little distance from the castle he was met by Almeric de Pavia, who yielded his son as a hostage according to his promise, calculating, as was the case, that he would be recaptured by the English. Then having received the greater portion of the money agreed upon, he led a party of the French over the castle to satisfy them of his sincerity. Upon receiving their report that all was quiet De Charny detached twelve knights and a hundred men-at-arms to take possession of the castle, while he himself waited at one of the gates of the town with the principal portion of his force.

No sooner had the French entered the castle than the drawbridge was raised. The English soldiers poured out from their places of concealment, and the party which had entered the castle were forced to lay down their arms. In the mean time the Black Prince issued with a small body of troops from a gate near the sea, while De Manny, with the king under his banner, marched by the sally-port which led into the fields. A considerable detachment of the division was dispatched to dislodge the enemy at the bridge of Nieullay, and the rest, joining the party of the Black Prince, advanced rapidly upon the force of Jeffrey de Charny, which, in point of numbers, was double their own strength.

Although taken in turn by surprise, the French prepared steadily for the attack. De Charny ordered them all to dismount and to shorten their lances to pikes five feet in length. The English also dismounted, and rushing forward on foot a furious contest commenced. The ranks of both parties were soon broken in the darkness, and the combatants separating into groups, a number of separate battles raged around the different banners.

For some hours the fight was continued with unabating obstinacy on both sides. The king and the Black Prince fought with immense bravery, their example encouraging even those of their soldiers who were ignorant of the personality of the knights who were everywhere in front of the combat. King Edward himself several times crossed swords with the famous Eustace de Ribaumont, one of the most gallant knights in France. At length toward daybreak the king, with only thirty companions, found himself again opposed to De Ribaumont, with a greatly superior force, and the struggle was renewed between them.

Twice the king was beaten down on one knee by the thundering blows of the French knight, twice he rose and renewed the attack, until De Charny, seeing Sir Walter Manny's banner, beside which Edward fought, defended by so small a force, also bore down to the attack, and in the struggle Edward was separated from his opponent.

The combat now became desperate round the king, and Sir Guy Brian, who bore De Manny's standard, though one of the strongest and most gallant knights of the day, could scarce keep the banner erect. Still Edward fought on, and in the excitement of the moment, forgetting his *incognito*, he accompanied each blow with his customary war-cry—"Edward, St. George! Edward, St. George!" At that battle-cry, which told the French men-at-arms that the King of England was himself opposed to them, they recoiled for a moment. The shout too reached the ears of the Prince of Wales, who had been fighting with another group. Calling his knights around him he fell upon the rear of De Charny's party and quickly cleared a space around the king.

The fight was now everywhere going against the French, and the English redoubling their efforts the victory was soon complete, and scarcely one French knight left the ground alive and free. In the struggle Edward again encountered De Ribaumont, who, separated from him by the charge of De Charny, had not heard the king's war-cry. The conflict between them was a short one. The French knight saw that almost all his companions were dead or captured, his party completely defeated, and all prospects of escape cut off. He therefore soon dropped the point of his sword and surrendered to his unknown adversary. In the mean time the troops which had been dispatched to the bridge of Nieullay had defeated the French forces left to guard the passage and clear the ground toward St. Omer.

Early in the morning Edward entered Calais in triumph, taking with him thirty French nobles as prisoners, while two hundred more remained dead on the field. That evening a great banquet was held, at which the French prisoners were present. The king presided at the banquet, and the French nobles were waited upon by the Black Prince and his knights. After the feast was concluded the king bestowed on De Ribaumont the chaplet of pearls which he wore round his crown, hailing him as the most gallant of the knights who had that day fought, and granting him freedom to return at once to his friends, presenting him with two horses, and a purse to defray his expenses to the nearest French town.

De Charny was afterward ransomed, and after his return to France assembled a body of troops and attacked the castle which Edward had bestowed upon Almeric of Pavia, and capturing the Lombard, carried him to St. Omer, and had him there publicly flayed alive as a punishment for his treachery.

Walter had as usual fought by the side of the Prince of Wales throughout the battle of Calais, and had much distinguished himself for his valor. Ralph was severely wounded in the fight, but was able a month later to rejoin Walter in England.

The battle of Calais and the chivalrous bearing of the king created great enthusiasm and delight in England, and did much to rouse the people from the state of grief into which they had been cast by the ravages of the plague. The king did his utmost to maintain the spirit which had been evoked, and the foundation of the order of the Garter, and the erection of a splendid chapel at Windsor, and its dedication, with great ceremony, to St. George, the patron saint of England, still further raised the renown of the court of Edward throughout Europe as the center of the chivalry of the age.

Notwithstanding many treaties which had taken place, and the near alliance which had been well-nigh carried out between the royal families of England and Spain, Spanish pirates had never ceased to carry on a series of aggressions upon the English vessels trading in the Bay of Biscay. Ships were every day taken, and the crews cruelly butchered in cold blood. Edward's remonstrances proved vain, and when threats of retaliation were held out by Edward, followed by preparations to carry those threats into effect, Pedro the Cruel, who had now succeeded to the throne of Spain, dispatched strong reënforcements to the fleet which had already swept the English Channel.

The great Spanish fleet sailed north, and capturing on its way a number of English merchantmen, put into Sluys, and prepared to sail back in triumph with the prizes and merchandise it had captured. Knowing, however, that Edward was preparing to oppose them, the Spaniards filled up their complement of men, strengthened themselves by all sorts of the war machines then in use, and started on their return for Spain with one of the most powerful armadas that had ever put to sea.

Edward had collected on the coast of Sussex a fleet intended to oppose them, and had summoned all the military forces of the south of England to accompany him; and as soon as he heard that the Spaniards were about to put to sea he set out for Winchelsea, where the fleet was collected.

The queen accompanied him to the sea-coast, and the Black Prince, now in his twentieth year, was appointed to command one of the largest of the English vessels.

The fleet put to sea when they heard that the Spaniards had started, and the hostile fleets were soon in sight of each other. The number of fighting men on board the Spanish ships was ten times those of the English, and their vessels were of vastly superior size and strength. They had, moreover, caused their ships to be fitted at Sluys with large wooden towers, which furnished a commanding position to their cross-bowmen. The wind was direct in their favor, and they could have easily avoided the contest, but, confiding in their enormously superior force, they sailed boldly forward to the attack.

The king himself led the English line, and directing his vessel toward a large Spanish ship, endeavored to run her down. The shock was tremendous, but the enemy's vessel was stronger as well as larger than that of the king; and as the two ships recoiled from each other it was found that the water was rushing into the English vessel, and that she was rapidly sinking. The Spaniard passed on in the confusion, but the king ordered his ship to be instantly laid alongside another which was following her, and to be firmly lashed to her. Then with his knights he sprang on board the Spaniard, and after a short but desperate fight cut down or drove the crew overboard. The royal standard was hoisted on the prize, the sinking English vessel was cast adrift, and the king sailed on to attack another adversary.

The battle now raged on all sides. The English strove to grapple with and board the enemy, while the Spaniards poured upon them a shower of bolts and quarrels from their cross-bows, hurled immense masses of stone from their military engines, and, as they drew alongside, cast into them heavy bars of iron, which pierced holes in the bottom of the ship.

Walter was on board the ship commanded by the Black Prince. This had been steered toward one of the largest and most important of the Spanish vessels. As they approached, the engines poured their missiles into them. Several great holes were torn in the sides of the ship, which was already sinking as she came alongside her foe.

"We must do our best, Sir Walter," the prince exclaimed, "for if we do not capture her speedily our ship will assuredly sink beneath our feet."

The Spaniard stood far higher above the water than the English ship, and the Black Prince and his knights in vain attempted to climb her sides, while the seamen strove with pumps and buckets to keep the vessel afloat. Every effort was in vain. The Spaniard's men-at-arms lined the bulwarks, and repulsed every effort made by the English to climb up them, while those on the towers rained down showers of bolts and arrows and masses of iron and stone. The situation was desperate, when the Earl of Lancaster, passing by in his ship, saw the peril to which the prince was exposed, and, ranging up on the other side of the Spaniard, strove to board her there. The attention of the Spaniards being thus distracted, the prince and his companions made another desperate effort, and succeeded in winning their way on to the deck of the Spanish ship just as their own vessel sank beneath their feet; after a few minutes' desperate fighting the Spanish ship was captured.

The English were now everywhere getting the best of their enemies. Many of the Spanish vessels had been captured or sunk, and after the fight had raged for some hours, the rest began to disperse and seek safety in flight. The English vessel commanded by Count Robert of Namur had toward night engaged a Spanish vessel of more than twice its own strength. His adversaries, seeing that the day was lost, set all sail, but looking upon the little vessel beside them as a prey to be taken possession of at their leisure, they fastened it tightly to their sides by the grappling-irons, and spreading all sail, made away. The count and his men were unable to free themselves, and were being dragged away, when a follower of the count named Hennekin leaped suddenly on board the Spanish ship. With a bound he reached the mast, and with a single blow with his sword cut the halyards which supported the main-sail. The sail fell at once. The Spaniards rushed to the spot to repair the disaster which threatened to delay their ship. The count and his followers, seeing the bulwarks of the Spanish vessel for the moment unguarded, poured in, and after a furious conflict captured the vessel. By this time twenty-four of the enemy's vessels had been taken, the rest were either sunk or in full flight, and Edward at once returned to the English shore.

The fight had taken place within sight of land, and Queen Philippa, from the windows of the abbey, which stood on rising ground, had seen the approach of the vast Spanish fleet, and had watched the conflict until night fell. She remained in suspense as to the result until the king himself, with the Black Prince and Prince John, afterward known as John of Gaunt, who, although but ten years of age, had accompanied the Black Prince in his ship, rode up with the news of the victory.

This great sea-fight was one of the brightest and most honorable in the annals of English history, for not even in the case of that other great Spanish Armada which suffered defeat in English waters were the odds so immense or the victory so thorough and complete. The result of the fight was that after some negotiations a truce of twenty years was concluded with Spain.

Chapter XX
Poitiers.

After the great sea-fight at the end of August, 1350, England had peace for some years. Philip of France had died a week before that battle, and had been succeeded by his son John, Duke of Normandy. Upon the part of both countries there was an indisposition to renew the war, for their power had been vastly crippled by the devastations of the plague. This was followed by great distress and scarcity, owing to the want of labor to till the fields. The truce was therefore continued from time to time; the pope strove to convert the truce into a permanent peace, and on the 28th of August, 1354, a number of the prelates and barons of England, with full power to arrange terms of peace, went to Avignon, where they were met by the French representatives. The powers committed to the English commissioners show that Edward was at this time really desirous of making a permanent peace with France; but the French ambassadors raised numerous and unexpected difficulties, and after lengthened negotiations the conference was broken off.

The truce came to an end in June, 1355, and great preparations were made on both sides for the war. The King of England strained every effort to furnish and equip an army which was to proceed with the Black Prince to Aquitaine, of which province his father had appointed him governor, and in November the prince sailed for Bordeaux with the advance-guard of his force. Sir Walter Somers accompanied him. During the years which had passed since the plague he had resided principally upon his estates, and had the satisfaction of seeing that his tenants escaped the distress which was general through the country. He had been in the habit of repairing to London to take part in the tournaments and other festivities; but both he and Edith preferred the quiet country life to a continued residence at court. Two sons had now been born to him, and fond as he was of the excitement and adventure of war, it was with deep regret that he obeyed the royal summons, and left his house with his retainers, consisting of twenty men-at-arms and thirty archers, to join the prince.

Upon the Black Prince's landing at Bordeaux he was joined by the Gascon lords, the vassals of the English crown, and for three months marched through and ravaged the districts adjoining, the French army, although greatly superior in force, offering no effectual resistance. Many towns were taken, and he returned at Christmas to Bordeaux after a campaign attended by a series of unbroken successes.

The following spring the war recommenced, and a diversion was effected by the Duke of Lancaster, who was in command of Brittany, joining his forces with those of the King of Navarre and many of the nobles of Normandy, while King Edward crossed to Calais and kept a portion of the French army occupied there. The Black Prince, leaving the principal part of his forces under the command of the Earl of Albret to guard the territory already acquired against the attack of the French army under the Count of Armagnac, marched with two thousand picked men-at-arms and six thousand archers into Auvergne, and thence turning into Berry, marched to the gates of Bourges.

The King of France was now thoroughly alarmed, and issued a general call to all his vassals to assemble on the Loire. The Prince of Wales, finding immense bodies of men closing in around him, fell back slowly, capturing and leveling to the ground the strong castle of Romorentin.

The King of France was now hastening forward, accompanied by his four sons, one hundred and forty nobles with banners, twenty thousand men-at-arms, and an immense force of infantry. Vast accessions of forces joined him each day, and on the 17th of September he occupied a position between the Black Prince and Guienne. The first intimation that either the Black Prince or the King of France had of their close proximity to each other was an accidental meeting between a small foraging force of the English and three hundred French horse, under the command of the Counts of Auxerre and Joigny, the Marshal of Burgundy, and the Lord of Chatillon. The French hotly pursued the little English party, and on emerging from some low bushes found themselves in the midst of the English camp, where all were taken prisoners. From them the Black Prince learned that the King of France was within a day's march.

The prince dispatched the Captal de Buch with two hundred men-at-arms to reconnoiter the force and position of the enemy, and these coming upon the rear of the French army just as they were about to enter Poitiers, dashed among them and took some prisoners. The King of France thus first learned that the enemy he was searching for was actually six miles in his rear. The Captal de Buch and his companions returned to the Black Prince, and confirmed the information obtained from the prisoners that the King of France, with an army at least eight times as strong as his own, lay between him and Poitiers.

The position appeared well-nigh desperate, but the prince and his most experienced knights at once reconnoitered the country to choose the best ground upon which to do battle. An excellent position was chosen. It consisted of rising ground commanding the country toward Poitiers, and naturally defended by the hedges of a vineyard. It was only accessible from Poitiers by a sunken road flanked by banks and fences, and but wide enough to admit of four horsemen riding abreast along it. The ground on either side of this hollow way was rough and broken so as to impede the movements even of infantry, and to render the maneuvers of a large body of cavalry nearly impracticable. On the left of the position was a little hamlet called Maupertuis. Here on the night of Saturday, the 17th of September, the prince encamped, and early next morning made his dispositions for the battle. His whole force was dismounted and occupied the high ground; a strong body of archers lined the hedges on either side of the sunken road; the main body of archers were drawn up in their usual formation on the hillside, their front covered by the hedge of the vineyard, while behind them the men-at-arms were drawn up.

The King of France divided his army into three divisions, each consisting of sixteen thousand mounted men-at-arms besides infantry, commanded respectively by the Duke of Orleans, the king's brother, the dauphin, and the king himself. With the two royal princes were the most experienced of the French commanders. In the mean time De Ribaumont, with three other French knights, reconnoitered the English position, and on their return with their report strongly advised that as large bodies of cavalry would be quite useless owing to the nature of the ground, the whole force should dismount, except three hundred picked men destined to break the line of English archers and a small body of German horse to act as a reserve.

Just as the King of France was about to give orders for the advance, the Cardinal of Perigord arrived in his camp, anxious to stop, if possible, the effusion of blood. He hurried to the King of France.

"You have here, sire," he said, "the flower of all the chivalry of your realm assembled against a mere handful of English, and it will be far more honorable and profitable for you to have them in your power without battle than to risk such a noble array in uncertain strife. I pray you, then, in the name of God, to let me ride on to the Prince of Wales, to show him his peril, and to exhort him to peace."

"Willingly, my lord," the king replied; "but above all things be quick."

The cardinal at once hastened to the English camp; he found the Black Prince in the midst of his knights ready for battle, but by no means unwilling to listen to proposals for peace. His position was indeed most perilous. In his face was an enormously superior army, and he was, moreover, threatened by famine; even during the two preceding days his army had suffered from a great scarcity of forage, and its provisions were almost wholly exhausted. The French force was sufficiently numerous to blockade him in his camp, and he knew that did they adopt that course he must surrender unconditionally, since were he forced to sally out and attack the French no valor could compensate for the immense disparity of numbers. He therefore replied at once to the cardinal's application that he was ready to listen to any terms by which his honor and that of his companions would be preserved.

The cardinal returned to the King of France, and with much entreaty succeeded in obtaining a truce until sunrise on the following morning. The soldiers returned to their tents, and the cardinal rode backward and forward between the armies, beseeching the King of France to moderate his demands, and the Black Prince to submit to the evil fortune which had befallen him; but on the one side the king looked upon the victory certain, and on the other the Black

Prince thought that there was at least a hope of success should the French attack him. All, therefore, that the cardinal could obtain from him was an offer to resign all he had captured in his expedition, towns, castles, and prisoners, and to take an oath not to bear arms again against France for seven years. This proposal fell so far short of the demands of the French king that pacification soon appeared hopeless.

Early on the Monday morning the cardinal once more sought the presence of the French king, but found John inflexible; while some of the leaders, who had viewed with the strongest disapproval his efforts to snatch what they regarded as certain victory from their hands, gave him a peremptory warning not to show himself again in their lines.

The prelate then bore the news of his failure to the Prince of Wales. "Fair son," he said, "do the best you can, for you must needs fight, as I can find no means of peace or amnesty with the King of France."

"Be it so, good father," the prince replied; "it is our full resolve to fight, and God will aid the right."

The delay which had occurred had not been without advantages for the British army, although the shortness of provisions was greatly felt. Every effort had been made to strengthen the position. Deep trenches had been dug and palisades erected around it, and the carts and baggage train had all been moved round so as to form a protection on the weakest side of the camp, where also a rampart had been constructed.

Upon a careful examination of the ground it was found that the hill on the right side of the camp was less difficult than had been supposed, and that the dismounted men-at-arms who lay at its foot under the command of the dauphin would find little difficulty in climbing it to the assault. The prince therefore gave orders that three hundred men-at-arms and three hundred mounted archers should make a circuit from the rear round the base of the hill, in order to pour in upon the flank of the dauphin's division as soon as they became disordered in the ascent. The nature of the ground concealed this maneuver from the enemies' view, and the Captal de Buch, who was in command of the party, gained unperceived the cover of a wooded ravine within a few hundred yards of the left flank of the enemy. By the time that all these dispositions were complete the huge French array was moving forward. The Black Prince, surrounded by his knights, viewed them approaching.

"Fair lords," he said, "though we be so few against that mighty power of enemies, let us not be dismayed, for strength and victory lie not in multitudes, but in those to whom God give them. If he will the day be ours, then the highest glory of this world will be given to us. If we die, I have the noble lord, my father, and two fair brothers, and you have each of you many a good friend who will avenge us well; thus, then, I pray you fight well this day, and if it please God and St. George I will also do the part of a good knight."

The prince then chose Sir John Chandos and Sir James Audley to remain by his side during the conflict in order to afford him counsel in case of need. Audley, however, pleaded a vow which he had made long before, to be the first in battle should he ever be engaged under the command of the King of England or any of his children. The prince at once acceded to his request to be allowed to fight in the van, and Audley, accompanied by four chosen squires, took his place in front of the English line of battle. Not far from him, also in advance of the line, was Sir Eustace d'Ambrecicourt on horseback, also eager to distinguish himself.

As Sir James rode off the prince turned to Walter. "As Audley must needs fight as a knight-errant, Sir Walter Somers, do you take your place by my side, for there is no more valiant knight in my army than you have often proved yourself to be."

Three hundred chosen French men-at-arms, mounted on the strongest horses, covered with steel armor, led the way under the command of the Maréchals d'Audeham and De Clermont; while behind them were a large body of German cavalry under the Counts of Nassau, Saarbruck, and Nidau, to support them in their attack on the English archers. On the right was the Duke of Orleans with sixteen thousand men-at-arms; on the left the dauphin and his two brothers with an equal force; while King John himself led on the rear-guard.

When the three hundred *élite* of the French army reached the narrow way between the hedges, knowing that these were lined with archers they charged through at a gallop to fall upon the main body of bowmen covering the front of the English men-at-arms. The moment they were fairly in the hollow road the British archers rose on either side to their feet and poured such a flight of arrows among them that in an instant all was confusion and disarray. Through every joint and crevice of the armor of knights and horses the arrows found their way, and the lane was almost choked with the bodies of men and horses. A considerable number, nevertheless, made their way through and approached the first line of archers beyond.

Here they were met by Sir James Audley, who, with his four squires, plunged into their ranks and overthrew the Maréchal d'Audeham, and then fought his way onward. Regardless of the rest of the battle he pressed ever forward, until at the end of the day, wounded in a hundred places and fainting from loss of blood, he fell from his horse almost at the gates of Poitiers, and was borne from the field by the four faithful squires who had fought beside him throughout the day.

Less fortunate was Sir Eustace d'Ambrecicourt, who spurred headlong upon the German cavalry. A German knight rode out to meet him, and in the shock both were dishorsed, but before Sir Eustace could recover his seat he was borne down to the ground by four others of the enemy, and was bound and carried captive to the rear.

In the mean time the English archers kept up their incessant hail of arrows upon the band under the French marshals. The English men-at-arms passed through the gaps purposely left in the line of archers and drove back the front rank of the enemy upon those following, chasing them headlong down the hollow road again. The few survivors of the French force, galloping back, carried confusion into the advancing division of the dauphin. Before order was restored the Captal de Buch with his six hundred men issued forth from his place of concealment and charged impetuously down on the left flank of the dauphin.

The French, shaken in front by the retreat of their advance-guard, were thrown into extreme confusion by this sudden and unexpected charge. The horse archers with the captal poured their arrows into the mass, while the shafts of the main body of the archers on the hill hailed upon them without ceasing.

The rumor spread among those in the French rear, who were unable to see what was going forward, that the day was already lost, and many began to fly. Sir John Chandos marked the confusion which had set in, and he exclaimed to the prince:

"Now, sir, ride forward, and the day is yours. Let us charge right over upon your adversary, the King of France, for there lies the labor and the feat of the day. Well do I know that his great courage will never let him fly, but, God willing, he shall be well encountered."

"Forward, then, John Chandos," replied the prince. "You shall not see me tread one step back, but ever in advance. Bear on my banner. God and St. George be with us!"

The horses of the English force were all held in readiness by their attendants close in their rear. Every man sprang into his saddle, and with leveled lances the army bore down the hill against the enemy, while the Captal de Buch forced his way through the struggling ranks of the French to join them.

To these two parties were opposed the whole of the German cavalry, the division of the dauphin, now thinned by flight, and a strong force under the Constable de Brienne, Duke of Athens. The first charge of the English was directed against the Germans, the remains of the marshal's forces, and that commanded by the constable. The two bodies of cavalry met with a tremendous shock, raising their respective war-cries, "Denis Mount Joye!" and "St. George Guyenne!" Lances were shivered, and horses and men rolled over, but the German horse were borne down in every direction by the charge of the English chivalry. The Counts of Nassau and Saarbruck were taken, and the rest driven down the hill in utter confusion. The division of the Duke of Orleans, a little further down the hill to the right, were seized with a sudden panic, and sixteen thousand men-at-arms, together with their commander, fled without striking a blow.

Having routed the French and German cavalry in advance, the English now fell upon the dauphin's division. This had been already confused by the attacks of the Captal de Buch, and when its leaders beheld the complete rout of the marshals and the Germans, and saw the victorious force galloping down upon them, the responsibility attached to the charge of the three young princes overcame their firmness. The Lords of Landas, Vaudenay, and St. Venant, thinking the battle lost, hurried the princes from the field, surrounded by eight hundred lances, determined to place them at a secure distance, and then to return and fight beside the king.

The retreat of the princes at once disorganized the force, but though many fled a number of the nobles remained scattered over the field fighting in separate bodies with their own retainers gathered under their banners. Gradually these fell back and took post on the left of the French king's division. The constable and the Duke of Bourbon with a large body of knights and men-at-arms also opposed a firm front to the advance of the English.

The king saw with indignation one of his divisions defeated and the other in coward flight, but his forces were still vastly superior to those of the English, and ordering his men to dismount, he prepared to receive their onset. The English now gathered their forces, which had been scattered in combat, and again advanced to the fight. The archers as usual heralded this advance with showers of arrows, which shook the ranks of the French and opened the way for the cavalry. These dashed in, and the ranks of the two armies became mixed, and each man fought hand to hand. The French king fought on foot with immense valor and bravery, as did his nobles. The Dukes of Bourbon and Athens, the Lords of Landas, Argenton, Chambery, Joinville, and many others stood and died near the king.

Gradually the English drove back their foes. The French forces became cut up into groups or confined into narrow spaces. Knight after knight fell around the king. De Ribaumont fell near him. Jeffrey de Charny, who, as one of the most valiant knights in the army, had been chosen to bear the French standard, the oriflamme, never left his sovereign's side, and as long as the sacred banner floated over his head John would not believe the day was lost. At length, however, Jeffrey de Charny was killed, and the oriflamme fell. John, surrounded on every side by foes who pressed forward to make him prisoner, still kept clear the space immediately around himself and his little son with his battle-ax; but at last he saw that further resistance would only entail the death of both, and he then surrendered to Denis de Montbec, a knight of Artois.

The battle was now virtually over. The French banners and pennons had disappeared, and nothing was seen save the dead and dying, groups of prisoners, and parties of fugitives flying over the country. Chandos now advised the prince to halt. His banner was pitched on the summit of a little mound. The trumpets blew to recall the army from the pursuit, and the prince, taking off his helmet, drank with the little body of knights who accompanied him some wine brought from his former encampment.

The two marshals of the English army, the Earls of Warwick and Suffolk, were among the first to return at the call of the trumpet. Hearing that King John had certainly not left the field of battle, though they knew not whether he was dead or taken, the prince at once dispatched the Earl of Warwick and Lord Cobham to find and protect him if still alive. They soon came upon a mass of men-at-arms, seemingly engaged in an angry quarrel. On riding up they found that the object of strife was the King of France, who had been snatched from the hands of Montbec, and was being claimed by a score of men as his prisoner. The Earl of Warwick and Lord Cobham instantly made their way through the mass, and dismounting, saluted the captive monarch with the deepest reverence, and keeping back the multitude led him to the Prince of Wales. The latter bent his knee before the king, and calling for wine, presented the cup with his own hands to the unfortunate monarch.

The battle was over by noon, but it was evening before all the pursuing parties returned, and the result of the victory was then fully known. With less than eight thousand men the English had conquered far more than sixty thousand. On the English side two thousand men-at-arms and fifteen hundred archers had fallen. Upon the French side eleven thousand men-at-arms, besides an immense number of footmen, had been killed. A king, a prince, an archbishop, thirteen counts, sixty-six barons, and more than two thousand knights were prisoners in the hands of the English, with a number of other soldiers, who raised the number of captives to double that of their conquerors. All the baggage of the French army was taken, and as the barons of France had marched to the field feeling certain of victory, and the rich armor of the prisoners became immediately the property of the captors, immense stores of valuable ornaments of all kinds, especially jeweled baldrics, enriched the meanest soldier among the conquerors.

The helmet which the French king had worn, which bore a small coronet of gold beneath the crest, was delivered to the Prince of Wales, who sent it off at once to his father as the best trophy of the battle he could offer him.

Its receipt was the first intimation which Edward III. received of the great victory.

As the prince had no means of providing for the immense number of prisoners, the greater portion were set at liberty upon their taking an oath to present themselves at Bordeaux by the ensuing Christmas in order either to pay the ransom appointed or to again yield themselves as prisoners.

Immediately the battle was over Edward sent for the gallant Sir James Audley, who was brought to him on his litter by his esquires, and the prince, after warmly congratulating him on the honor that he had that day won as the bravest knight in the army, assigned him an annuity of five hundred marks a year.

No sooner was Audley taken to his own tent than he called round him several of his nearest relations and friends, and then and there made over to his four gallant attendants, without power of recall, the gift which the prince had bestowed upon him. The prince was not to be outdone, however, in liberality, and on hearing that Audley had assigned his present to the brave men who had so gallantly supported him in the fight, he presented Sir James with another annuity of six hundred marks a year.

Chapter XXI
The Jacquerie.

On the evening after the battle of Poitiers, a splendid entertainment was served in the tent of the Prince of Wales to the King of France and all the principal prisoners. John with his son and six of his highest nobles were seated at a table raised above the rest, and the prince himself waited as page upon the French king. John in vain endeavored to persuade the prince to be seated; the latter refused, saying that it was his pleasure as well as his duty to wait upon one who had shown himself to be the best and bravest knight in the French army. The example of the Black Prince was contagious, and the English vied with each other in generous treatment of their prisoners. All were treated as friends, and that night an immense number of knights and squires were admitted to ransom on such terms as had never before been known. The captors simply required their prisoners to declare in good faith what they could afford to pay without pressing themselves too hard, "for they did not wish," they said, "to ransom knights or squires on terms which would prevent them from maintaining their station in society, from serving their lords, or from riding forth in arms to advance their name and honor."

Upon the following morning solemn thanksgivings were offered up on the field of battle for the glorious victory. Then the English army, striking its tents, marched back toward Bordeaux. They were unmolested upon this march, for although the divisions of the dauphin and the Duke of Orleans had now reunited, and were immensely superior in numbers to the English, encumbered as the latter were, moreover, with prisoners and booty, the tremendous defeat which they had suffered, and still more the capture of the king, paralyzed the French commanders, and the English reached Bordeaux without striking another blow.

Not long after they reached that city the Cardinal of Perigord and another legate presented themselves to arrange peace, and these negotiations went on throughout the winter. The prince had received full powers from his father, and his demands were very moderate; but in spite of this no final peace could be arranged, and the result of the conference was the proclamation of a truce, to last for two years from the following Easter.

During the winter immense numbers of the prisoners who had gone at large upon patrol came in and paid their ransoms, as did the higher nobles who had been taken prisoners, and the whole army was greatly enriched. At the end of April the prince returned to England with King John. The procession through the streets of London was a magnificent one, the citizens vying with each other in decorating their houses in honor of the victor of Poitiers, who, simply dressed, rode on a small black horse by the side of his prisoner, who was splendidly attired, and mounted on a superb white charger. The king received his royal prisoner in state in the great hall of his palace at Westminster, and did all in his power to alleviate the sorrows of his condition. The splendid palace of the Savoy, with gardens extending to the Thames, was appointed for his residence, and every means was taken to soften his captivity.

During the absence of the Black Prince in Guienne the king had been warring in Scotland. Here his success had been small, as the Scotch had retreated before him, wasting the country. David Bruce, the rightful king, was a prisoner in England, and Baliol, a descendant of the rival of Robert Bruce, had been placed upon the throne. As Edward passed through Roxburgh he received from Baliol a formal cession of all his rights and titles to the throne of Scotland, and in return for this purely nominal gift he bestowed an annual income upon Baliol, who lived and died a pensioner of England. After Edward's return to England negotiations were carried on with the Scots, and a treaty was signed by which a truce for ten years was established between the two countries, and the liberation of Bruce was granted on a ransom of one hundred thousand marks.

The disorganization into which France had been thrown by the capture of its king increased rather than diminished. Among all classes men strove in the absence of a repressive power to gain advantages and privileges. Serious riots occurred in many parts, and the demagogues of Paris, headed by Stephen Marcel, and Robert le Coq, Bishop of Leon, set at defiance the dauphin and the ministers and lieutenant of the king. Massacre and violence stained the streets of Paris with blood. General law, public order, and private security were all lost. Great bodies of brigands devastated the country, and the whole of France was thrown into confusion. So terrible was the disorder that the inhabitants of every village were obliged to fortify the ends of their streets and keep watch and ward as in the cities. The proprietors of land on the banks of rivers spent the nights in boats moored in the middle of the stream, and in every house and castle throughout the land men remained armed as if against instant attack.

Then arose the terrible insurrection known as the Jacquerie. For centuries the peasantry of France had suffered under a bondage to which there had never been any approach in England. Their lives and liberties were wholly at the mercy of their feudal lords. Hitherto no attempt at resistance had been possible; but the tremendous defeat of the French at Poitiers by a handful of English aroused the hope among the serfs that the moment for vengeance had come. The movement began among a handful of peasants in the neighborhood of St. Leu and Claremont. These declared that they would put to death all the gentlemen in the land. The cry spread through the country. The serfs, armed with pikes, poured out from every village, and a number of the lower classes from the towns joined them. Their first success was an attack upon a small castle. They burned down the gates and slew the knight to whom it belonged, with his wife and children of all ages. Their numbers rapidly increased. Castle after castle was taken and stormed, palaces and houses leveled to the ground; fire, plunder, and massacre swept through the fairest provinces of France. The peasants vied with each other in inventing deaths of fiendish cruelty and outrage upon every man, woman, and child of the better classes who fell into their hands.

Owing to the number of nobles who had fallen at Cressy and Poitiers, and of those still captives in England, very many of their wives and daughters remained unprotected, and these were the especial victims of the fiendish malignity of the peasantry. Separated in many bands, the insurgents marched through the Beauvoisis, Soissonois, and Vermandois; and as they approached, a number of unprotected ladies of the highest families in France fled to Meaux, where they remained under the guard of the young Duke of Orleans and a handful of men-at-arms.

After the conclusion of the peace at Bordeaux, Sir Walter Somers had been dispatched on a mission to some of the German princes, with whom the king was in close relations. The business was not of an onerous nature, but Walter had been detained for some time over it. He spent a pleasant time in Germany, where, as an emissary of the king and one of the victors of Poitiers, the young English knight was made much of. When he set out on his return he joined the Captal de Buch, who, ever thirsting for adventure, had on the conclusion of the truce gone to serve in a campaign in Germany; with him was the French Count de Foix, who had been also serving throughout the campaign.

On entering France from the Rhine the three knights were shocked at the misery and ruin which met their eyes on all sides. Every castle and house throughout the country, of a class superior to those of the peasants, was destroyed, and tales of the most horrible outrages and murders met their ears.

"I regret," the Count de Foix said earnestly, "that I have been away warring in Germany, for it is clear that every true knight is wanted at home to crush down these human wolves."

"Methinks," the captal rejoined, "that France will do well to invite the chivalry of all other countries to assemble and aid to put down this horrible insurrection."

"Ay," the count said bitterly; "but who is to speak in the name of France? The dauphin is powerless, and the virtual government is in the hands of Marcel and other ambitious traitors who hail the doings of the Jacquerie with delight, for these mad peasants are doing their work of destroying the knights and nobles."

The villages through which they passed were deserted save by women, and in the small towns the people of the lower class scowled threateningly at the three knights; but they with their following of forty men-at-arms, of whom five were followers of Walter, fifteen of the captal, and twenty of the Count de Foix, ventured not to proceed beyond evil glances.

"I would," De Foix said, "that these dogs would but lift a hand against us. By St. Stephen, we would teach them a rough lesson!"

His companions were of the same mind, for all were excited to fury by the terrible tales which they heard. All these stories were new to them, for although rumors had reached Germany of the outbreak of a peasant insurrection in France, the movement had but just begun when they started. As far as the frontier they had traveled leisurely, but they had hastened their pace more and more as they learned how sore was the strait of the nobles and gentry of the country, and how grievously every good sword was needed. When they reached Chalons they heard much fuller particulars than had before reached them, and learned that the Duchess of Normandy, the Duchess of Orleans, and near three hundred ladies had sought refuge in Meaux, and that they were there guarded but by a handful of men-at-arms under the Duke of Orleans, while great bands of serfs were pouring in from all parts of the country round to massacre them.

Meaux is eighty miles from Chalons, but the three knights determined to press onward with all speed in hopes of averting the catastrophe. Allowing their horses an hour or two to rest, they rode forward, and pressing on without halt or delay, save such as was absolutely needed by the horses, they arrived at Meaux late the following night, and found to their delight that the insurgents, although swarming in immense numbers round the town, had not yet attacked it.

The arrival of the three knights and their followers was greeted with joy by the ladies. They, with their guard, had taken up their position in the market-house and market-place, which were separated from the rest of the town by the river Marne, which flows through the city. A consultation was at once held, and it being found that the Duke of Orleans had but twenty men-at-arms with him, it was determined that it was impossible to defend the city walls, but that upon the following morning they would endeavor to cut their way with the ladies through the peasant hosts. In the night, however, an uproar was heard in the city. The burghers had risen and had opened the gates to the peasants, who now poured in in thousands. Every hour increased their numbers.

The market-place was besieged in the morning, and an hour or two afterward a large body of the ruffians of Paris, under the command of a brutal grocer named Pierre Gille, arrived to swell their ranks.

The attack on the market-house continued, and the Duke of Orleans held a consultation with the three knights. It was agreed that against such a host of enemies the market-place could not long be defended, and that their best hope lay in sallying out and falling upon the assailants. Accordingly the men-at-arms were drawn up in order, with the banners of the Duke of Orleans and the Count de Foix and the pennons of the captal and Sir Walter Somers displayed, the gates were opened, and with leveled lances the little party rode out. Hitherto nothing had been heard save yells of anticipated triumph and fierce imprecations and threats against the defenders from the immense multitude without; but the appearance of the orderly ranks of the knights and men-at-arms as they issued through the gate struck a silence of fear through the mass.

Without an instant's delay the knights and men-at-arms, with leveled lances, charged into the multitude. A few attempted to fight, but more strove to fly, as the nobles and their followers, throwing away their lances, fell upon them with sword and battle-ax. Jammed up in the narrow streets of a small walled town, overthrowing and impeding each other in their efforts to escape, trampled down by the heavy horses of the men-at-arms, and hewn down by their swords and battle-axes, the insurgents fell in vast numbers. Multitudes succeeded in escaping through the gates into the fields; but here they were followed by the knights and their retainers, who continued charging among them and slaying till utter weariness compelled them to cease from the pursuit and return to Meaux. Not less than seven thousand of the insurgents had been slain by the four knights and fifty men, for ten had been left behind to guard the gates of the market-place.

History has no record of so vast a slaughter by so small a body of men. This terrific punishment put a summary end to the Jacquerie. Already in other parts several bodies had been defeated, and their principal leader, Caillet, with three thousand of his followers, slain near Clermont. But the defeat at Meaux was the crushing blow which put an end to the insurrection.

On their return to the town the knights executed a number of the burghers who had joined the peasants, and the greater part of the town was burned to the ground as a punishment for having opened the gates to the peasants and united with them.

The knights and ladies then started for Paris. On nearing the city they found that it was threatened by the forces of the dauphin. Marcel had strongly fortified the town, and with his ally, the infamous King of Navarre, bade defiance to the royal power. However, the excesses of the demagogue had aroused against him the feeling of all the better class of the inhabitants. The King of Navarre, who was ready at all times to break his oath and betray his companions, marched his army out of the town and took up a position outside the walls. He then secretly negotiated peace with the Duke of Normandy, by which he agreed to yield to their fate Marcel and twelve of the most obnoxious burghers, while at the same time he persuaded Marcel that he was still attached to his interest. Marcel, however, was able to bid higher than the Duke of Normandy, and he entered into a new treaty with the treacherous king, by which he stipulated to deliver the city into his hands during the night. Every one within the walls, except the partisans of Marcel, upon whose doors a mark was to be placed, were to be put to death indiscriminately, and the King of Navarre was to be proclaimed King of France.

Fortunately Pepin des Essarts and John de Charny, two loyal knights who were in Paris, obtained information of a few minutes before the time appointed for its execution. Arming themselves instantly, and collecting a few followers, they rushed to the houses of the chief conspirators, but found them empty, Marcel and his companions having already gone to the gates. Passing by the hotel-de-ville, the knights entered, snatched down the royal banner which was kept there, and unfurling it mounted their horses and rode through the streets, calling all men to arms. They reached the Port St. Antoine just at the moment when Marcel was in the act of opening it in order to give admission to the Navarrese. When he heard the shouts he tried with his friends to make his way into the bastile, but his retreat was intercepted, and a severe and bloody struggle took place between the two parties. Stephen Marcel, however, was himself slain by Sir John de Charny, and almost all his principal companions fell with him. The inhabitants then threw open their gates and the Duke of Normandy entered.

Walter Somers had, with his companions, joined the army of the duke and placed his sword at his disposal; but when the French prince entered Paris without the necessity of fighting, he took leave of him, and with the captal returned to England. Rare, indeed, were the jewels which Walter brought home to his wife, for the three hundred noble ladies rescued at Meaux from dishonor and death had insisted upon bestowing tokens of their regard and gratitude upon the rescuers, and as many of them belonged to the richest as well as the noblest families in France, the presents which Walter thus received from the grateful ladies were of immense value.

He was welcomed by the king and Prince of Wales with great honor, for the battle at Meaux had excited the admiration and astonishment of all Europe. The Jacquerie was considered as a common danger in all civilized countries; for if successful it might have spread far beyond the boundaries of France, and constituted a danger to chivalry, and indeed to society universally.

Thus King Edward gave the highest marks of his satisfaction to the captal and Walter, added considerable grants of land to the estates of the latter, and raised him to the dignity of Baron Somers of Westerham.

It has always been a matter of wonder that King Edward did not take advantage of the utter state of confusion and anarchy which prevailed in France to complete his conquest of that country, which there is no reasonable doubt he could have effected with ease. Civil war and strife prevailed throughout France; famine devastated it; and without leaders or concord, dispirited and impoverished by defeat, France could have offered no resistance to such an army as England could have placed in the field. The only probable supposition is that at heart he doubted whether the acquisition of the crown of France was really desirable, or whether it could be permanently maintained should it be gained. To the monarch of a county prosperous, flourishing, and contented the object of admiration throughout Europe, the union with distracted and divided France could be of no benefit. Of military glory he had gained enough to content any man, and some of the richest provinces of France were already his. Therefore it may well be believed that, feeling secure very many years must elapse before France could again become dangerous, he was well content to let matters continue as they were.

King John still remained a prisoner in his hands, for the princes and nobles of France were too much engaged in broils and civil wars to think of raising the money for his ransom, and Languedoc was the only province of France which made any effort whatever toward so doing. War still raged between the dauphin and the King of Navarre.

At the conclusion of the two years' truce Edward, with the most splendidly equipped army which had ever left England, marched through the length and breadth of France. Nowhere did he meet with any resistance in the field. He marched under the walls of Paris, but took no steps to lay siege to that city, which would have fallen an easy prey to his army had he chosen to capture it. That he did not do so is another proof that he had no desire to add France to the possessions of the English crown. At length, by the efforts of the pope, a peace was agreed upon, by which France yielded all Aquitaine and the town of Calais to England as an absolute possession, and not as a fief of the crown of France; while the English king surrendered all his captures in Normandy and Brittany and abandoned his claim to the crown of France. With great efforts the French raised a portion of the ransom demanded for the king, and John returned to France after four years of captivity.

At the commencement of 1363 Edward the Black Prince was named Prince of Aquitaine, and that province was bestowed upon him as a gift by the king, subject only to liege homage and an annual tribute of one ounce of gold. The prince took with him to his new possessions many of the knights and nobles who had served with him, and offered to Walter a high post in the government of the province if he would accompany him. This Walter begged to be excused from doing. Two girls had now been added to his family, and he was unwilling to leave his happy home unless the needs of war called him to the prince's side. He therefore remained quietly at home.

When King John returned to France, four of the French princes of the blood-royal had been given as hostages for the fulfillment of the treaty of Bretigny. They were permitted to reside at Calais and were at liberty to move about as they would, and even to absent themselves from the town for three days at a time whensoever they might choose. The Duke of Anjou, the king's second son, basely took advantage of this liberty to escape, in direct violation of his oath. The other hostages followed his example.

King John, himself the soul of honor, was intensely mortified at this breach of faith on the part of his sons, and after calling together the States-general at Amiens to obtain the subsidies necessary for paying the remaining portion of his ransom, he himself, with a train of two hundred officers and their followers, crossed to England to make excuses to Edward for the treachery of the princes. Some historians represent the visit as a voluntary returning into captivity; but this was not so. The English king had accepted the hostages in his place and was responsible for their safe-keeping, and had no claim upon the French monarch because they had taken advantage of the excess of confidence with which they had been treated. That the coming of the French king was not in any way regarded as a return into captivity is shown by the fact that he was before starting furnished by Edward with letters of safe-conduct, by which his secure and unobstructed return to his own country was expressly stipulated, and he was received by Edward as an honored guest and friend, and his coming was regarded as an honor and an occasion for festivity by all England.

At the same time that John was in London the King of Cyprus, the King of Denmark, and the King of Scotland were also there, and the meeting of four monarchs in London was the occasion of extraordinary festivities and rejoicing, the king and his royal guests being several times entertained at sumptuous banquets by the lord mayor, the ex-mayor, Henry Pickard, and several of the aldermen.

Six weeks after John's arrival in London he was seized with illness at the palace of the Savoy, and died on the 8th of April, 1364. The dauphin, Charles, now succeeded him as Charles V., and the war between the houses of Navarre and Valois was carried on with greater fury than ever. The armies of Navarre were commanded by the Captal de Buch, who was a distant relation of the king; while those of Charles were headed by the Maréchal de Boucicault and Bertrand du Guesclin, one of the most gallant of the French knights. A great battle was fought near Cocherel. Contrary to the orders of the captal, his army, which consisted principally of adventurers, descended from the strong position he had chosen, and gave battle in the plain. They were completely defeated and the captal himself taken prisoner.

In Brittany John of Montford and Charles of Blois had renewed their struggle, and King Charles, seeing the danger of Brittany falling into the hands of De Montford, who was a close ally of England, interfered in favor of Charles of Blois, and sent Du Guesclin to his assistance.

This was a breach of the treaty of Bretigny, and De Montford at once sent to the Black Prince for assistance. The prince did not treat the conduct of Charles as a breach of the treaty, and took no part himself in the war, but permitted Sir John Chandos, who was a personal friend of De Montford, to go to his aid. De Montford's army, after the arrival of Chandos with a force of two hundred spears, amounted to but sixteen hundred men-at-arms and from eight hundred to nine hundred archers, while Charles of Blois had four thousand men-at-arms and a proportionate number of infantry. De Montford tried to negotiate. He offered to divide the dukedom, and to agree that in case he died childless it should revert to the family of Charles. Charles, however, refused all terms, even to grant his adversary's request to put off the battle until the morrow, so as to avoid violating the Sabbath; and having given orders that all prisoners taken in the battle should be hung, he advanced upon De Montford.

Both forces were divided in four bodies. The first on De Montford's side was commanded by Sir Robert Knolles, the second by Oliver de Clisson, the third by Chandos and De Montford, the fourth by Sir Hugh de Calverley. Du Guesclin led the front division of Charles' army, the Counts of Auxerre and Joigny the second, Charles himself the third, and the Lords of Roye and Rieux the reserve. The ducal arms of Brittany were displayed on both sides.

By slow degrees the two armies closed with each other in deadly strife. Both parties had dismounted and fought on foot with lances shortened to five feet. Du Guesclin and his division attacked that of Knolles. Auxerre fell upon De Clisson, while the divisions of the two rival princes closed with each other. After desperate fighting numbers prevailed. De Montford was driven back, but Calverley advanced to his aid, fell upon the rear of the French, threw them into disorder, and then having rallied De Montford's men, retired to his former position in readiness to give succor again where it might be needed.

In the mean time Clisson had been engaged in a desperate struggle with the Count of Auxerre, but was obtaining no advantage. Clisson himself had received the blow of a battle-ax which had dashed in the visor of his helmet and blinded forever one of his eyes. He was still leading his men, but the enemies' superior numbers were pressing him back, when Chandos, the instant the assistance of Calverley had relieved De Montford's division, perceiving his danger, drew off a few men-at-arms, and with them fell upon the rear of the Count of Auxerre, and dashing all who opposed him to the ground with his battle-ax, cleft his way to the very center of the enemy. Pressed by De Clisson in front and broken by the sudden attack of Chandos in the rear, the French division gave way in every direction. Auxerre was desperately wounded, and he and De Joigny both taken prisoners.

Chandos then returned to De Montford, who had gallantly followed up the advantage gained by the confusion into which Charles' division had been thrown by the attack of Calverley. Charles was routed, he himself struck down and slain by an English soldier, and the division defeated with great slaughter. De Montford's whole force now gathered round Du Guesclin's division, which now alone remained, and after fighting gallantly until all hope was gone, the brave French knight and his companions yielded themselves as prisoners.

The battle of Auray terminated the struggle between the houses of Blois and Montford. More than one thousand French men-at-arms died on the field of battle, among whom were many of the noblest in Brittany. Two counts, twenty-seven lords, and fifteen hundred men-at-arms were made prisoners. De Montford now took possession of the whole of Brittany, and at the suggestion of King Edward himself did homage to Charles V. for the duchy, which he afterward ruled with wisdom.

Chapter XXII
Victory And Death.

While the Black Prince was with difficulty governing his province of Aquitaine, where the mutual jealousies of the English and native officers caused continual difficulties, King Edward turned all his attention to advancing the prosperity of England. He fostered trade, commerce, and learning, was a munificent patron of the two universities, and established such order and regularity in his kingdom that England was the admiration of all Europe. Far different was the state of France. The cessation of the wars with England and the subsequent disbandment of troops had thrown upon their own resources great numbers of men who had been so long engaged in fighting that they had no other trade to turn to. The conclusion of the struggle in Brittany after the battle of Auray and the death of Charles of Blois still further added to the number, and these men gathered in bands, some of which were headed by men of knightly rank, and scattered through France plundering the country and extracting heavy sums from the towns.

These "great companies," as they were called, exceeded fifty thousand men in number, and as almost all were trained soldiers they set the king and his nobles at defiance, and were virtually masters of France. The most tempting offers were made to them to lay down their arms, and the pope sent legates threatening excommunication, but the great companies laughed alike at promises and threats. At last a way of deliverance opened to France. Pedro, named the Cruel, of Castile, had alienated his people by his cruelty, and had defeated and driven into exile his half-brother, Henry of Transtamare, who headed an insurrection against him. Pedro put to death numbers of the nobles of Castile, despoiled the King of Arragon, who had given aid to his brother, plundered and insulted the clergy, and allied himself with the Moors.

His quarrel with the clergy was the cause of his ruin. The pope summoned him to appear before him at Avignon to answer to the crimes laid to his charge. Pedro refused to attend, and the pope at once excommunicated him. The King of Arragon and Henry of Transtamare were then summoned to Avignon, and a treaty of alliance was concluded between them, and the pope declared the throne of Castile vacant owing to the excommunication of Pedro, and appointed Henry to it.

These measures would have troubled Pedro little had it not been that France groaned under the great companies, and the French king and the pontiff at once entered into negotiations with them to support Henry in his war against his brother. It was necessary that a leader in whom the companies should have confidence should be chosen, and Du Guesclin, still a prisoner of Chandos, who had captured him at Auray, was selected, and the pope, the King of France, and Don Henry paid between them the one hundred thousand francs demanded for his ransom. Du Guesclin on his release negotiated with the leaders of the great companies, and as the pope and king promised them large gratuities they agreed to march upon Spain. They were joined by a great number of French knights and men-at-arms.

The expedition was under the nominal command of John of Bourbon, but the real guidance was in the hands of Du Guesclin. As the army marched past Avignon they worked upon the terrors of the pope until he paid them two hundred thousand francs in gold. France was filled with joy at the prospect of a riddance of the free companies which had so long been a prey upon them. They were, too, eager to avenge upon the cruel King of Spain the murder of his queen, who was a princess of France. The same feeling animated the people of Aquitaine, and Calverley, D'Ambrecicourt, Sir Walter Hewitt, Sir John Devereux, Sir John Neville, and several other distinguished knights, with a large train of men-at-arms, joined the adventurers. The great army moved through Arragon, whose king in every way facilitated their progress. As they entered Castile the whole people declared in favor of Henry, and Pedro, deserted by all, fled to Bordeaux and besought aid from the Prince of Wales.

Between Pedro and the English court a firm alliance had existed from the time when the former so nearly married the Princess Joan, and immediately the king heard of the expedition against him he issued orders that no English knights should take part in it. The order, however, came too late. The English knights had already marched into Spain with Du Guesclin. As for the English who formed no inconsiderable portion of the great companies, they had already declined to obey the king when, at the instance of the pope and the King of France, he had ordered them to disband.

On Pedro's arrival at Bordeaux with his three daughters and his son, they were kindly received by the Black Prince, courtesy and kindness to those in misfortune being among the leading characteristics of his nature. Pedro, cruel and ruthless as he was, was a man of great eloquence and insinuating manners, and giving his own version of affairs, he completely won over the prince, who felt himself, moreover, bound in some degree to support him, inasmuch as he, an ally of England, had been dethroned by an army composed partly of English. Pedro made the most magnificent promises to the prince in return for his aid, ceding him the whole of the province of Biscay, and agreeing to pay the British troops engaged in his service when he regained his throne, the Black Prince engaging to pay them in the mean time.

King Edward aided his son by raising an army in England, which sailed for Bordeaux under the command of the prince's brother, John of Gaunt, Duke of Lancaster. Walter formed part of this expedition. The king had issued his writs to him and other barons of the southern counties, and the Black Prince had himself written to ask him to join him, in memory of their former deeds of arms together.

As it was now some years since he had taken the field, Walter did not hesitate, but with thirty retainers, headed by Ralph, joined the army of John of Gaunt.

The Black Prince's first step was to endeavor to recall the Englishmen of the free companies, estimated to amount to at least thirty thousand men. The news that he was taking up arms and would himself command the army caused Calverley and the whole of the other English knights to return at once, and ten thousand of the English men-at-arms with the great companies also left Don Henry and marched to Aquitaine. The road led through the territory of the King of Navarre, and the Black Prince advanced fifty-six thousand florins of gold to pay this grasping and treacherous king for the right of passage of the army.

By Christmas, 1366, the preparations were complete, but the severity of the weather delayed the advance for some weeks. Fresh difficulties were encountered with Charles the Bad, of Navarre, who, having obtained the price for the passage, had now opened negotiations with Don Henry, and the governors of the frontier towns refused to allow Sir Hugh Calverley and the free companions, who formed the advance, to pass. These were not, however, the men to stand on ceremony, and without hesitation they attacked and captured the towns, when the King of Navarre at once apologized for his officers, and renewed his engagements. As, however, the Black Prince had received intelligence that he had formed a plan for attacking the English as they passed through the terrible pass of Roncesvalles, he compelled him to accompany the army. The invitation was couched in language which was friendly, but would yet admit of no denial.

On the 17th of February the English army, thirty thousand strong, reached the pass. It marched in three divisions, the first commanded by the Duke of Lancaster and Lord Chandos, the second by the Black Prince, the third by the King of Majorca and the Count of Armagnac. The divisions crossed over on different days, for the pass was encumbered by snow and the obstacles were immense. Upon the day when the prince's division were passing a storm burst upon them, and it was with the greatest difficulty that they succeeded in crossing. On the 20th of February, however, all arrived safe on the other side of the Pyrenees. Du Guesclin, who, seeing the storm which was approaching from Aquitaine, had returned to France and levied a French army, was nigh at hand, and kept within a few miles of the English army as it advanced, avoiding an engagement until the arrival of Don Henry, who was marching to join him with the great companies and sixty thousand Spanish troops.

Du Guesclin kept up secret communications with the King of Navarre, who was still forced to accompany the English army. The latter accordingly went out from the camp under pretense of hunting and was captured by a detachment of French troops.

On the 1st of April, the Spanish army having joined the French, the Black Prince sent letters to Don Henry, urging him in mild but dignified language to return to obedience, and to resign the throne he had usurped, offering at the same time to act as mediator between him and his brother, and to do all in his power to remove differences and abuses. Henry, confident in his strength, replied haughtily and prepared for battle.

The forces were extremely unequal. The Black Prince had under him thirty thousand men; while under Don Henry were three thousand men-at-arms on mail-clad horses, twenty thousand men-at-arms on horses not so protected, six thousand light cavalry, ten thousand crossbowmen, and sixty thousand foot armed with spear and sword.

The night before the battle the Black Prince lodged in the little village of Navarretta, which had been deserted by its inhabitants. Walter had been his close companion since he started, and occupied the same lodging with him in the village.

"This reminds me," the prince said, "of the day before Cressy. They outnumber us by more than three to one."

"There were greater odds still," Walter replied, "at Poitiers, and I doubt not that we shall make as good an example of them."

"They are more doughty adversaries," the prince replied. "There are nigh twenty thousand English in their ranks-all veterans in war-and they are led by Du Guesclin, who is a host in himself."

"Their very numbers will be a hindrance to them," Walter replied cheerfully; "and never did I see a better army than that which you have under you. I would we were fighting for a better man, for Don Pedro is to my mind treacherous as well as cruel. He promises fairly, but I doubt if when he has gained his end he will keep his promises. He speaks fairly and smoothly, but his deeds are at variance with his words."

"It may be, my lord," the prince replied, "that I am somewhat of your opinion, and that I regret I so quickly committed myself to his cruse. However, he was my father's ally, and having fulfilled all his engagements had a right to demand our assistance. I am a bad hand, Walter, at saying no to those who beseech me."

"It is so, Sir Prince," Walter said bluntly. "Would that your heart had been a less generous one, for your nobleness of disposition is ever involving you in debts which hamper you sorely, and cause more trouble to you than all your enemies!"

"That is true enough," the Black Prince said with a sigh. "Since I was a boy I have ever been harassed with creditors; and though all Aquitaine is mine, I verily believe that there is not a man in my father's dominions who is so harassed and straitened for money as I."

"And yet," Walter said, smiling, "no sooner do you get it than you give it away."

"Ah!" the prince laughed, "I cannot deny it. It is so much pleasanter to give than to pay that I can never find heart to balk myself. I am ever surrounded by suitors. Some have lost estates in my cause, others have rendered brilliant services in the field, some have burdened themselves with debts to put their retainers in arms-all have pleas to urge, and for the life of me I cannot say them nay. I trust, though," he added more seriously, "that Don Pedro will fulfill his promises to pay my army. I have bound myself to my soldiers for their wages, besides advancing large sums to Pedro, and if he keeps not his engagements I shall indeed be in a sore strait."

"There is one thing," Walter said; "if he fail to keep his promises, we will not fail to oblige him to do so. If we win a kingdom for him, we can snatch it from him again."

"We have not won it yet," the prince said.

"We will do so to-morrow," Walter rejoined confidently. "I hope the fortunes of the day may bring me face to face with Du Guesclin. I am thrice as strong as when I fought at Cressy, and I should like to try my hand against this doughty champion."

The next morning the two armies prepared for battle, the Black Prince dividing his army as before. The divisions were commanded as in the passage of the Pyrenees, and each numbered ten thousand men.

Don Henry had also divided his force in three parts. In the first division, commanded by Du Guesclin, were four thousand veteran French knights and men-at-arms with eight thousand foot soldiers; the second was led by the prince's brother, Don Tillo, with sixteen thousand horse; while he himself commanded the third, in which were a multitude of soldiers, making up the gross total of one hundred thousand men.

As on the night preceding the battle of Poitiers, the English army had lain down supperless. Soon after midnight the trumpets sounded, and the troops soon moved forward. At sunrise the prince and his forces reached the summit of a little hill, whence was visible the approaching host of Spain. The first division, under the Duke of Lancaster and Lord Chandos, immediately quickened its pace and charged the division of Du Guesclin, which received it with great steadiness, and a desperate conflict ensued. The Black Prince charged the division of Don Tillo, which gave way at the first attack, and its commander, with two thousand horse, at once fled. The remainder of the division resisted for some time, but was unable to withstand the steady advance of the English, who without much difficulty dispersed and scattered it from the field. The King of Majorca now joined his division with that of the Black Prince, and the two advanced against the great division led by Don Henry.

The Spanish slingers opened upon the advancing force and for a time annoyed them greatly, but when the English archers arrived within bow-shot and opened fire they speedily dispersed the slingers, and the men-at-arms on both sides advanced to the attack. The conflict was long and desperate, and both sides fought with great gallantry and determination. Don Pedro-who, although vicious and cruel, was brave-fought in the ranks as a common soldier, frequently cutting his way into the midst of the Spaniards, and shouting to Don Henry to cross swords with him. Henry on his part fought with great valor, although, as he had the burden of command upon him, he was less able to distinguish himself by acts of personal prowess. Though fighting in the thickest of the press, he never lost his grasp of the general purpose of the battle. Three times, when his troops wavered before the assaults of the Black Prince and his knights, he rallied them and renewed the fight.

While this battle was raging, a not less obstinate fight was proceeding between the divisions of Lancaster and Du Guesclin. For a long time victory was doubtful, and indeed inclined toward the side of the French. The ranks of both parties were broken, and all were fighting in a confused mass, when, in the midst of the *mêlée*, a body of French and Spaniards poured in upon the banner of Chandos. He was struck to the ground, and a gigantic Castilian knight flung himself upon him and strove to slay him as he held him down. Chandos had lost sword and battle-ax, but drawing his dagger, he held with one hand his opponent's sword-arm, and at last, after repeated strokes with his dagger, he found an undefended part of his armor and pierced him with his dagger to the hilt. The Spaniard relaxed his hold, and Chandos, throwing him off, struggled to his feet and rejoined his friends, who had thought him dead. They now fought with more enthusiasm than ever, and at last, driving back the main body of the French knights, isolated a body of some sixty strong, and forced them to surrender. Among these were Du Guesclin himself, the Marshal d'Audenham, and the Bigue de Vilaines.

As these were the leaders of the division, the main body lost spirit and fought feebly, and were soon completely routed by Lancaster and Chandos. These now turned their attention to the other part of the field, where the battle was still raging, and charged down upon the flank of Don Henry's army, which was already wavering. The Spaniards gave way at once on every side, and ere long the whole were scattered in headlong rout, hotly pursued by the English. The greater portion fled toward the town of Najarra, where they had slept the previous night, and here vast quantities were slaughtered by the English and Gascons. A number of prisoners were taken and the palace and town sacked. The pursuit was kept up the whole day, and it was not until evening that the leaders began once more to assemble round the banner of the Prince of Wales. Among the last who arrived was Don Pedro himself. Springing from his charger he grasped the hand of the Prince of Wales, thanking him for his victory, which he felt would restore him to his throne.

"Give thanks and praise to God, and not to me," the prince replied, "for from him, and not from me, you have received victory."

About eight thousand men fell in the battle, the loss of the English, French, and Spaniards being nearly equal; but many thousands of the latter fell in the pursuit, and as many more were drowned in endeavoring to cross the river Ebro. Don Henry escaped after fighting till the last, and reaching the French territory in safety took refuge in the papal court of Avignon.

Upon the morning after the battle Don Pedro requested the Black Prince to give him up all the Castilian prisoners, in order that he might put them to death. The prince, however, was always opposed to cruelty, and asked and obtained as a boon to himself that the lives of all the Spanish prisoners, with the exception of one whose conduct had been marked with peculiar treachery, should be spared, and even induced Pedro to pardon them altogether on their swearing fealty to him. Even Don Sancho, Pedro's brother, who had fought at Najarra under Don Henry, was received and embraced by Pedro at the request of the Prince of Wales. The city of Burgos at once opened its gates, and the rest of the country followed its example, and resumed its allegiance to Pedro, who remounted his throne without further resistance.

As Walter had fought by the side of the Black Prince his desire to cross swords with Du Guesclin was not satisfied; but his valor during the day won for him the warm approbation of the prince. Opposed to them were many of the great companies, and these men, all experienced soldiers and many of them Englishmen, had fought with great stubbornness. Walter had singled out for attack a banner bearing the cognizance of a raven. The leader of this band, who was known as the Knight of the Raven, had won for himself a specially evil notoriety in France by the ferocity of his conduct. Wherever his band went they had swept the country, and the most atrocious tortures had been inflicted on all well-to-do persons who had fallen into their hands, to extract from them the secret of buried hoards or bonds, entailing upon them the loss of their last penny.

The Knight of the Raven himself was said to be as brave as he was cruel, and several nobles who had attempted to oppose his band had been defeated and slain by him. He was known to be English, but his name was a mystery; and the Black Prince and his knights had long wished to encounter a man who was a disgrace alike to chivalry and the English name. When, therefore, Walter saw his banner in the king's division he urged his horse toward it, and, followed by Ralph and some thirty men-at-arms, hewed his way through the crowd until he was close to the banner.

A knight in gray armor spurred forward to meet him, and a desperate conflict took place. Never had Walter crossed swords with a stouter adversary, and his opponent fought with as much vehemence and fury as if the sight of Walter's banner, which Ralph carried behind him, had aroused in him a frenzy of rage and hate. In guarding his head from one of his opponent's sweeping blows Walter's sword shivered at the hilt; but before the Gray Knight could repeat the blow Walter snatched his heavy battle-ax from his saddle. The knight reined back his horse for an instant and imitated his example, and with these heavy weapons the fight was renewed. The Knight of the Raven had lost by the change, for Walter's great strength stood him in good stead, and presently with a tremendous blow he beat down his opponent's ax and cleft through his helmet almost to the chin.

The knight fell dead from his horse, and Walter, with his band, pressing on, carried confusion into the ranks of his followers. When these had been defeated Walter rode back with Ralph to the spot where the Knight of the Raven had fallen.

"Take off his helmet, Ralph. Let me see his face. Methinks I recognized his voice, and he fought as if he knew and hated me."

The end of a Recreant Knight. —Page 386.

Ralph removed the helmet.

"It is as I thought," Walter said; "it is Sir James Carnegie, a recreant and villain knight and foul enemy of mine, a disgrace to his name and rank, but a brave man. So long as he lived I could never say that my life was safe from his machinations. Thank God, there is an end of him and his evil doings!"

Walter was twice wounded in the fight, but upon neither occasion seriously, and he was soon able to take part in the tournaments and games which the Prince of Wales instituted partly to keep his men employed, partly for the amusement of the citizens of Burgos, outside whose walls his army lay encamped.

The prince was now obliged to remind the king of his promise to pay his troops; but nothing was further from the mind of the treacherous monarch than to carry out the promises which he had made in exile. He dared not, however, openly avow his intentions, but trusting to the chapter of accidents, he told the prince that at Burgos he could not collect a sufficient sum; but if the army would march into Leon and take up their quarters near Valladolid, he himself would proceed to Seville, and would as soon as possible collect the money which he had bound himself to furnish. The plan was adopted. Edward marched his troops to Valladolid, and Don Pedro went to Seville.

Some time passed on without the arrival of the promised money, and the prince was impatient to return to Aquitaine. Don Henry had gathered a force in France, secretly assisted by the French king, and had made an inroad into Aquitaine, where he obtained several successes, and was joined by many of the disinterested nobles of that province.

"You were right," the prince said to Walter one day; "this treacherous king, who owes his kingdom to us, intends to break his plighted word. I know not what to do; my men are clamorous for their pay, and I am unable to satisfy them. Don Pedro still sends fair promises, and although I believe in my heart that he has no intention of keeping them, yet I can hardly march against him as an enemy, for, however far from the truth it may be, his pretext that the treasury has been emptied by his brother, and that in the disturbed state of the kingdom no money can be obtained, may yet be urged as valid."

Scarcely had the army encamped before Valladolid when a terrible pestilence attacked the army. For a while all questions of pay were forgotten, and consternation and dismay seized the troops. Neither rank nor station was of avail, and the leaders suffered as severely as the men.

Every day immense numbers died, and so sudden were the attacks, and so great the mortality, that the soldiers believed that Don Pedro had poisoned the wells in order to rid himself of the necessity of fulfilling his obligations.

The Black Prince himself was prostrated and lay for some time between life and death. A splendid constitution enabled him to pull through, but he arose from his bed enfeebled and shattered, and although for some years he lived on, he received his death-blow at Valladolid. His personal strength never came to him again, and even his mind was dulled and the brightness of his intellect dimmed from the effects of the fever. When he recovered sufficiently to inquire into the state of his forces, he was filled with sorrow and dismay. Four-fifths of the number were either dead or so weakened as to be useless for service again. The prince wrote urgently to Don Pedro for the money due; but the king knew that the English were powerless now, and replied that he had not been able to collect the money, but would forward it to Aquitaine, if the prince would return there with his army. Edward knew that he lied, but with only six thousand or seven thousand men, many of whom were enfeebled by disease, he was not in a position to force the claim, or to punish the base and ungrateful king. Again, therefore, he turned his face north.

Charles of Navarre had now allied himself with Don Henry, and refused to allow the remnants of the army to pass through his dominions, although he granted permission to the prince himself and his personal attendants and friends. The southern route was barred by the King of Arragon, also an ally of Don Henry; but with him the prince was more successful. He had a personal interview with the monarch, and so influenced him that he not only obtained permission for his troops to pass through his dominions, but detached him from his alliance with Don Henry and induced him to enter into a friendly treaty with Pedro.

A greater act of magnanimity was never performed. In spite of the base ingratitude with which he had been treated, and the breach of faith which saddled him with enormous liabilities and debts, which weighed him down and imbittered the rest of his life, Edward remained faithful to the cause of his father's ally, and did his best to maintain him in the position which English valor had won for him. He himself with a few companions passed through Navarre, and arrived safely in Bordeaux, where his wife awaited him, and where he was received with rejoicings and festivities in honor of his glorious campaign in Spain.

His health was now irreparably injured. Troubles came thick upon him in Aquitaine, and he had no longer the energy to repress them. Risings took place in all directions, and the King of France renewed the war. In addition to his own troubles from the debts he had incurred and the enemies who rose against him, he was further shaken by the death of his mother Philippa, whom he tenderly loved. His friend Chandos, too, was killed in a skirmish. Unhappily, while thus weakened in mind and body the treachery of the bishop and people of Limoges, who, having bound themselves by innumerable promises to him, surrendered their city to the French, caused him to commit the one act of cruelty which sullied the brightness of an otherwise unspotted career, for at the recapture of the town he bade his soldiers give no quarter.

This act, although common enough at the time, is so opposed to the principles of mercy and humanity which throughout all the previous acts of his life distinguished the conduct of the Black Prince that it cannot be doubted that his brain was affected by the illness which was fast hurrying him to the grave. Shortly afterward he returned to England and busied himself in arranging the affairs of the kingdom, which his father's failing health had permitted to fall into disorder. For the remaining four years of life he lived in seclusion, and sank on the 8th of June, 1376.

Walter, Lord Somers, returned home after the conclusion of the campaign in Spain, and rode no more to the wars.

Giles Fletcher and his wife had died some years before, but the good citizen Geoffrey the armorer, when he grew into years, abandoned his calling and took up his abode at Westerham Castle to the time of his death.

In the wars which afterward occurred with France, Walter was represented in the field by his sons, who well sustained the high reputation which their father had borne as a good and valiant knight. He and his wife lived to a green old age, reverenced and beloved by their tenants and retainers, and died surrounded by their descendants to the fourth generation.

The Lion of St. Mark: A Story of Venice in the Fourteenth Century 1889

Preface.

Of all the chapters of history, there are few more interesting or wonderful than that which tells the story of the rise and progress of Venice. Built upon a few sandy islands in a shallow lagoon, and originally founded by fugitives from the mainland, Venice became one of the greatest and most respected powers of Europe. She was mistress of the sea; conquered and ruled over a considerable territory bordering on the Adriatic; checked the rising power of the Turks; conquered Constantinople; successfully defied all the attacks of her jealous rivals to shake her power; and carried on a trade relatively as great as that of England in the present day. I have laid my story in the time not of the triumphs of Venice, but of her hardest struggle for existence--when she defended herself successfully against the coalition of Hungary, Padua, and Genoa--for never at any time were the virtues of Venice, her steadfastness, her patriotism, and her willingness to make all sacrifice for her independence, more brilliantly shown. The historical portion of the story is drawn from Hazlitt's History of the Republic of Venice, and with it I have woven the adventures of an English boy, endowed with a full share of that energy and pluck which, more than any other qualities, have made the British empire the greatest the world has ever seen.

G. A. Henty.

Chapter 1:
Venice.

"I suppose you never have such nights as these in that misty island of yours, Francisco?"

"Yes, we have," the other said stoutly. "I have seen just as bright nights on the Thames. I have stood down by Paul's Stairs and watched the reflection of the moon on the water, and the lights of the houses on the bridge, and the passing boats, just as we are doing now.

"But," he added honestly, "I must confess that we do not have such still, bright nights very often, while with you they are the rule, though sometimes even here a mist rises up and dims the water, just as it does with us."

"But I have heard you say that the stars are not so bright as we have them here."

"No, I do not think they are, Matteo. I do not remember now, but I do know, when I first came here, I was struck with the brightness of the stars, so I suppose there must have been a difference."

"But you like this better than England? You are glad that your father came out here?"

Francis Hammond did not answer at once.

"I am glad he came out," he said after a pause, "because I have seen many things I should never have seen if I had stayed at home, and I have learned to speak your tongue. But I do not know that I like it better than home. Things are different, you see. There was more fun at home. My father had two or three apprentices, whom I used to play with when the shop was closed, and there were often what you would call tumults, but which were not serious. Sometimes there would be a fight between the apprentices of one ward and another. A shout would be raised of 'Clubs!' and all the 'prentices would catch up their sticks and pour out of the shops, and then there would be a fight till the city guard turned out and separated them. Then there used to be the shooting at the butts, and the shows, and the Mayday revels, and all sorts of things. The people were more merry than you are here, and much more free. You see, the barons, who are the same to us that your great families are to you, had no influence in the city. You are a nation of traders, and so are we; but in London the traders have the power, and are absolute masters inside their own walls, caring nothing for the barons, and not much for the king. If anyone did wrong he got an open and fair trial. There was no fear of secret accusations. Everyone thought and said as he pleased. There was no Lion's Mouth, and no Council of Ten."

"Hush! hush! Francisco," the other said, grasping his arm. "Do not say a word against the council. There is no saying who may be listening."

And he looked nervously round to see if anyone was within earshot.

"There it is, you see," his companion said. "So long as we have a safe conscience, in London we are frightened at nothing, whereas here no one can say with certainty that he may not, before tomorrow morning, be lying in the dungeons of St. Mark, without the slightest idea in the world as to what his crime has been."

"There, there, Francisco," Matteo said uneasily. "Do talk about other things. Your notions may do very well in England, but are not safe to discuss here. Of course there are plenty here who would gladly see a change in some matters, but one cannot have everything; and, after all, when one has so much to be proud of, one need not grumble because everything is not just as one would like."

"Yes, you have much to be proud of," Francis Hammond agreed. "It is marvellous that the people of these scattered islets should be masters of the sea, that their alliance should be coveted by every power in Europe, that they should be the greatest trading community in the world. If I were not English I should like to be Venetian."

The speakers were standing at the edge of the water in front of the Palace of St. Mark. In the piazza behind them a throng of people were walking to and fro, gossiping over the latest news from Constantinople, the last rumour as to the doings of the hated rival of Venice, Genoa, or the purport of the letter which had, as everyone knew, been brought by the Bishop of Treviso from the pope to the seignory.

The moon was shining brightly overhead, and glittering in the waters of the lagoon, which were broken into innumerable little wavelets by the continual crossing and recrossing of the gondolas dotting its surface. There was a constant arrival and departure of boats from the steps, fifty yards to the right of the spot where the speakers were standing; but where they had stationed themselves, about halfway between the landing steps and the canal running down by the side of the ducal palace, there were but few people about.

Francis Hammond was a lad between fifteen and sixteen years old. His father was a merchant of London. He was a man of great enterprise and energy, and had four years before determined to leave his junior partner in charge of the business in London, and to come out himself for a time to Venice, so as to buy the Eastern stuffs in which he dealt at the headquarters of the trade, instead of paying such prices as the agents of the Venetian traders might demand in London.

He had succeeded beyond his expectations. In Venice there were constantly bargains to be purchased from ships returning laden with the spoils of some captured Genoese merchantman, or taken in the sack of some Eastern seaport. The prices, too, asked by the traders with the towns of Syria or the Black Sea, were but a fraction of those charged when these goods arrived in London. It was true that occasionally some of his cargoes were lost on the homeward voyage, captured either by the Genoese or the Moorish pirates; but even allowing for this, the profits of the trade were excellent.

The English merchant occupied a good position in Venice. The promptness of his payments, and the integrity of his dealings, made him generally respected; and the fact that he was engaged in trade was no drawback to his social position, in a city in which, of all others, trade was considered honourable, and where members of even the most aristocratic families were, with scarcely an exception, engaged in commerce. There were many foreign merchants settled in Venice, for from the first the republic had encouraged strangers to take up their residence there, and had granted them several privileges and advantages.

Between Venice and England there had always been good feeling. Although jealous of foreigners, England had granted the Venetians liberty to trade in London, Southampton, and some other towns as far back as the year 1304; and their relations had always been cordial, as there were no grounds for jealousy or rivalry between the two peoples; whereas the interference of France, Germany, Austria, and Hungary in the affairs of Italy, had frequently caused uneasiness to Venice, and had on several occasions embroiled her with one or other of the three last named powers. France had as yet taken a very minor part in the continual wars which were waged between the rival cities of Italy, and during the Crusades there had been a close alliance between her and Venice, the troops of the two nations fighting together at the siege of Constantinople, and causing the temporary overthrow of the Greek Empire of the East.

The rise of Venice had been rapid, and she owed her advancement to a combination of circumstances. In the first place, her insular position rendered her almost impervious to attack, and she had therefore no occasion to keep on foot any army, and was able to throw all her strength on to the sea, where Genoa was her only formidable rival. In the second place, her mercantile spirit, and her extensive trade with the East, brought in a steady influx of wealth, and her gold enabled her to purchase allies, to maintain lengthy struggles without faltering, and to emerge unscathed from wars which exhausted the resources, and crippled the powers, of her rivals.

The third source of her success lay in the spirit of her population. Like Rome in her early days, she was never cast down by reverses. Misfortune only nerved her to further exertions, and after each defeat she rose stronger than before. But the cause which, more than all, contributed to give to Venice her ascendancy among the cities of Italy, was her form of government. Democratic at first, as among all communities, it had gradually assumed the character of a close oligarchy, and although nominally ruled by a council containing a large number of members, her destinies were actually in the hands of the Doge, elected for life, and the Council of Ten, chosen from the great body of the council. Thus she had from the first been free from those factions which were the bane of Genoa and Florence. Some of the great families had from time to time come more prominently to the front than others, but none had attained predominant political power, and beyond a few street tumults of slight importance, Venice had not suffered from the popular tumults and uprisings which played so prominent a part in the history of her rivals.

Thus, undisturbed by discord at home, Venice had been able to give all her attention and all her care to her interests abroad, and her affairs, conducted as they were by her wisest citizens, with a single eye to the benefit of the state, had been distinguished by a rare sagacity. Her object had been single and uniform, to protect her own interests, and to prevent any one city on the mainland attaining such a preponderance as would render her a dangerous neighbour. Hence she was always ready to ally herself with the weaker against the stronger, and to aid with money and men any state struggling against an ambitious neighbour. Acting on this principle she by turns assisted Padua against Verona, and Verona against Padua, or either of them when threatened by the growing power of Milan, and at the end of a war she generally came out with an increased territory, and added importance.

It is probable that no community was ever governed, for hundreds of years, with such uniform wisdom and sagacity as was Venice; but the advantage was not without drawbacks. The vigilance of the Council of Ten in repressing plots, not unfrequently set on foot by the enemies of the republic, resulted in the adoption of a hateful system of espionage. The city was pervaded with spies, and even secret denunciations were attended to, and the slightest expression of discontent against the ruling authorities was severely punished. On the other hand, comparatively slight attention was paid to private crime. Assassinations were of frequent occurrence, and unless the victim happened to be very powerfully connected, no notice was taken when a man was found to be missing from his usual place, and his corpse was discovered floating in the lagoon. Consequently crimes of this kind were, in the great majority of cases, committed with impunity, and even when traced, the authors, if possessed of powerful protectors, seldom suffered any greater punishment than temporary banishment.

After standing for some time on the Piazzetta, the two lads turned and, entering the square of Saint Mark, mingled with the crowd. It was a motley one. Nobles in silks and satins jostled with fishermen of the lagoons. Natives of all the coasts and islands which owned the sway of Venice, Greeks from Constantinople, Tartar merchants from the Crimea, Tyrians, and inhabitants of the islands of the Aegean, were present in considerable numbers; while among the crowd, vendors of fruit and flowers from the mainland, and of fresh water or cooling drinks, sold their wares. The English lad's companion--Matteo Giustiniani--belonged to one of the leading families of Venice, and was able to name to Francis most of the nobles and persons of importance whom they passed.

"There is Pisani," he said. "Of course you know him. What a jolly, good-tempered looking fellow he is! The sailors would do anything for him, and they say he will have command of the next fleet that puts to sea. I wish I was going with him. There is sure to be a fierce fight when he comes across the Genoese. His father was one of our greatest admirals.

"That noble just behind him is Fiofio Dandolo. What a grand family they have been, what a number of great men they have given to the republic! I should like to have seen the grand old Doge who stormed the walls of Constantinople, and divided the Eastern empire among the crusading barons. He was a hero indeed.

"No; I don't know who that young noble in the green velvet cap and plum coloured dress is. O yes, I do, though; it is Ruggiero Mocenigo; he has been away for the last two years at Constantinople; he was banished for having killed Polo Morosini--he declared it was in fair fight, but no one believed him. They had quarrelled a few days before over some question of the precedence of their families, and Morosini was found dead at the top of the steps close to the church of Saint Paolo. Some people heard a cry and ran up just as Mocenigo leapt into his gondola, but as it rowed off their shouts called the attention of one of the city guard boats which happened to be passing, and it was stopped. As his sword was still wet with blood, he could not deny that he was the author of the deed, but, as I said, he declared it was in fair fight. The Morosinis asserted that Polo's sword was undrawn, but the Mocenigo family brought forward a man, who swore that he was one of the first to arrive, and pick up the sword and place it in its scabbard to prevent its being lost. No doubt he lied; but as Mocenigo's influence in the council was greater than that of the Morosini, the story was accepted. However, the public feeling was so strong that they could not do less than sentence Ruggiero to two years' banishment. I suppose that has just expired, and he has returned from Constantinople. He had a bad reputation before this affair took place, but as his connections are so powerful, I suppose he will be received as if nothing had happened. There are plenty of others as bad as he is."

"It's a scandalous thing," Francis Hammond said indignantly, "that, just because they have got powerful connections, men should be allowed to do, almost with impunity, things for which an ordinary man would be hung. There ought to be one law for the rich as well as the poor."

"So there is as far as the state is concerned," his companion replied. "A noble who plots against the state is as certain of a place in the lowest dungeons as a fisherman who has done the same; but in other respects there is naturally some difference."

"Why naturally?" Francis retorted. "You belong to a powerful family, Giustiniani, and my father is only a trader, but I don't see that naturally you have any more right to get me stabbed in the back, than I have to get you put out of the way."

"Naturally perhaps not," Matteo laughed; "but you see it has become a second nature to us here in Venice. But seriously I admit that the present state of things has grown to be a scandal, and that the doings of some of our class ought to be put down with a strong hand."

"Well, I shall say goodnight now," the English boy said. "My father doesn't like my being out after ten. He keeps up his English habits of shutting up early, and has not learned to turn night into day as you do here in Venice."

"The bell has just tolled the hour, Francis," his father said as he entered.

"I didn't think it was quite so late, father; the Piazza is crowded. I really do not think there is one person in Venice who goes to bed so early as we do. It is so pleasant in the moonlight after the heat of the day."

"That is true enough, Francis, but men are meant to sleep at night and to work in the day. I think our fathers carried this too far when they rang the curfew at eight; but ten is quite late enough for any honest man to be about in the streets, and the hours of the early morning are just as pleasant and far more healthy than those of the evening, especially in a place like this where the mists rise from the water, to say nothing of the chance of meeting a band of wild gallants on their way homewards heated with wine, or of getting a stab in the back from some midnight assassin. However, I do not blame Venice for enjoying herself while she can. She will have more serious matters to attend to soon."

"But she is at peace with every one at present, father. I thought when she signed the treaty with Austria after a year's fighting, she was going to have rest for a time."

"That was only the beginning of the trouble, Francis, and the council knew it well; that was why they made such terms with Austria as they did. They knew that Austria was only acting in accord with Hungary, and Padua, and Genoa. The others were not ready to begin, so Austria came on her own account to get what booty and plunder she could. But the storm is gathering, and will burst before long. But do not let us stand talking here any longer. It is high time for you to be in bed."

But though Francis retired to his room, it was more than an hour before he got into bed. His window looked down upon one of the canals running into the Grand Canal. Gondolas lighted by lanterns, or by torches held by servitors, passed constantly backwards and forwards beneath his window, and by leaning out he could see the passing lights of those on the Grand Canal. Snatches of song and laughter came up to him, and sometimes the note of a musical instrument. The air was soft and balmy, and he felt no inclination for sleep.

Francis thought over what his father had said of the probability of war, as he sat at his window, and wished that he were a couple of years older and could take part in the struggle. The Venetian fleet had performed such marvels of valour, that, in the days when military service was almost the sole avenue to distinction and fortune, the desire to take part in a naval expedition, which promised unusual opportunities of gaining credit and renown, was the most natural thing possible for a boy of spirit.

Francis was a well built lad of nearly sixteen. He had, until he left London when about twelve years old, taken his full share in the rough sports which formed so good a training for the youths of England, and in which the citizens of London were in no way behind the rest of the kingdom. He had practised shooting with a light bow and arrows, in company with boys of his own age, in the fields outside the city walls; had engaged in many a rough tussle with light clubs and quarterstaffs; and his whole time--except for an hour or two daily which he had, as the son of a well to do citizen, spent in learning to read and write--had been occupied in games and exercises of one kind or other.

Since his arrival in Venice he had not altogether discontinued his former habits. At his earnest solicitation, his father had permitted him to attend the School of Arms, where the sons of patricians and well-to-do merchants learned the use of sword and dagger, to hurl the javelin, and wield the mace and battleaxe; and was, besides, a frequenter of some of the schools where old soldiers gave private lessons in arms to such as could afford it; and the skill and strength of the English lad excited no slight envy among the young Venetian nobles. Often, too, he would go out to one of the sandy islets, and there setting up a mark, practise with the bow. His muscles too, had gained strength and hardness by rowing. It was his constant habit of an evening, when well away from the crowded canals in the gondola, with Giuseppi, the son and assistant of his father's gondolier, to take an oar, for he had thoroughly mastered the difficult accomplishment of rowing well in a gondola; but he only did this when far out from the city, or when the darkness of evening would prevent his figure from being recognized by any of his acquaintances, for no Venetian of good family would demean himself by handling an oar. Francis, however, accustomed to row upon the Thames, could see no reason why he should not do the same in a gondola, and in time he and his companion could send the boat dancing over the water, at a rate which enabled them to overtake and distance most pair-oared boats.

After breakfast next morning he went down to the steps, where Beppo and Giuseppi, in their black cloth suits with red sashes round their waists, were waiting with the gondola in which Mr. Hammond was going out to Malamocco, to examine a cargo which had the day before arrived from Azoph. Giuseppi jumped ashore.

"I have heard of just the gondola to suit you, Messer Francisco, and you can get her a bargain."

"What is she like, Giuseppi?"

"She belongs to a man out at Lido. She was built for the race two years ago, but her owner fell sick and was unable to start. He has not got strong again, and wants to sell his boat, which is far too light for ordinary work. They say she is almost like an eggshell, and you and I will be able to send her along grandly. She cost four ducats, but he will sell her for two."

"That is capital, Giuseppi. This gondola is all well enough for my father, but she is very heavy. This evening we will row over to Lido and look at her."

A few minutes later Mr. Hammond came down. Beppo and his son took off their jackets, and in their snow white shirts and black trousers, set off by the red scarf and a red ribbon round their broad hats, took their places on the bow and stern. Mr. Hammond sat down on the cushions in the middle of the boat, and with an easy, noiseless motion the gondola glided away from the stairs. Francis, with a little sigh, turned away and strolled off for a couple of hours' work with the preceptor, with whom he had continued his studies since he came to Venice.

This work consisted chiefly of learning various languages, for in those days there was little else to learn. Latin was almost universally spoken by educated men in southern Europe, and Greeks, Italians, Spaniards, and Frenchmen were able to converse in this common medium. French Francis understood, for it was the language in use in the court and among the upper classes in England. Italian he picked up naturally during his residence, and spoke it with the facility of a native. He could now converse freely in Latin, and had some knowledge of German.

At the same school were many lads of good Venetian families, and it was here that he had first made the acquaintance of Matteo Giustiniani, who was now his most intimate friend.

Matteo, like all the young nobles of Venice, was anxious to excel in military exercises, but he had none of the ardour for really hard work which distinguished his friend. He admired the latter's strength and activity, but could not bring himself to imitate him, in the exercises by which that strength was attained, and had often remonstrated with him upon his fondness for rowing.

"It is not seemly, Francisco, for a gentleman to be labouring like a common gondolier. These men are paid for doing it; but what pleasure there can be in standing up working that oar, till you are drenched with perspiration, I cannot understand. I don't mind getting hot in the School of Arms, because one cannot learn to use the sword and dagger without it, but that's quite another thing from tugging at an oar."

"But I like it, Matteo; and see how strong it has made my muscles, not of the arm only, but the leg and back. You often say you envy me my strength, but you might be just as strong if you chose to work as I do. Besides, it is delightful, when you are accustomed to it, to feel the gondola flying away under your stroke."

"I prefer feeling it fly away under some one else's stroke, Francisco. That is pleasant enough, I grant; but the very thought of working as you do throws me into a perspiration. I should like to be as strong as you are, but to work as a gondolier is too high a price to pay for it."

That evening, Francis crossed the lagoon in the gondola with Giuseppi, to inspect the boat he had heard of. It was just what he wanted. In appearance it differed in no way from an ordinary gondola, but it was a mere shell. The timbers and planking were extremely light, and the weight of the boat was little more than a third of that of other craft. She had been built like a working gondola, instead of in the form of those mostly used for racing, because her owner had intended, after the race was over, to plank her inside and strengthen her for everyday work. But the race had never come off, and the boat lay just as she had come from the hands of her builder, except that she had been painted black, like other gondolas, to prevent her planks from opening. When her owner had determined to part with her he had given her a fresh coat of paint, and had put her in the water, that her seams might close up.

"I don't like parting with her," the young fisherman to whom she belonged said. "I tried her once or twice, and she went like the wind, but I got fever in my bones and I am unlikely to race again, and the times are hard, and I must part with her."

Francis and Giuseppi gave her a trial, and were delighted with the speed and ease with which she flew through the water. On their return Francis at once paid the price asked for her. His father made him a handsome allowance, in order that he might be able to mix, without discomfort, with the lads of good family whom he met at his preceptor's and at the schools of arms. But Francis did not care for strolling in the Piazza, or sitting for hours sipping liquors. Still less did he care for dress or finery. Consequently he had always plenty of money to indulge in his own special fancies.

As soon as the bargain was completed, Giuseppi took his place in the old gondola, while Francis took the oar in his new acquisition, and found to his satisfaction that with scarcely an effort he could dart ahead of his companion and leave him far behind. By nightfall the two gondolas were fastened, side by side, behind the gaily painted posts which, in almost all Venetian houses, are driven into the canal close to the steps, and behind which the gondolas belonging to the house lie safe from injury by passing craft.

"I have bought another gondola, father," Francis said the next morning. "She is a very light, fast craft, and I got her cheap."

"I don't see what you wanted another gondola for, Francis. I do not use mine very much, and you are always welcome to take it when I do not want it."

"Yes, father, but you often use it in the evening, and that is just the time when one wants to go out. You very often only take Beppo with you, when you do not go on business, and I often want a boat that I could take with Giuseppi. Besides, your gondola is a very solid one, and I like passing people."

"Young people always want to go fast," Mr. Hammond said. "Why, I can't make out. However, Francis, I am not sorry that you have got a boat of your own, for it has happened several times lately, that when in the evening I have gone down intending to row round to the Piazzetta, I have found the boat gone, and have had to walk. Now I shall be able to rely on finding Beppo asleep in the boat at the steps. In future, since you have a boat of your own, I shall not be so particular as to your being in at ten. I do not so much mind your being out on the water, only you must promise me that you will not be in the streets after that hour. There are frequent broils as the evening gets on, not to mention the danger of cutthroats in unfrequented lanes; but if you will promise me that you will never be about the streets after half past nine, I will give you leave to stay out on the water till a later hour; but when you come in late be careful always to close and bar the door, and do not make more noise than you can help in coming up to your room."

Francis was much pleased with this concession, for the obligation to return at ten o'clock, just when the temperature was most delightful and the Grand Canal at its gayest, had been very irksome to him. As to the prohibition against being in the streets of Venice after half past nine, he felt that no hardship whatever, as he found no amusement in strolling in the crowded Piazza.

Chapter 2:
A Conspiracy.

"Who are those ladies, Matteo?" Francis asked his friend one evening, as the latter, who was sitting with him in his gondola, while Giuseppi rowed them along the Grand Canal, half rose and saluted two girls in a passing gondola.

"They are distant cousins of mine, Maria and Giulia Polani. They only returned a short time since from Corfu. Their father is one of the richest merchants of our city. He has for the last three years been living in Corfu, which is the headquarters of his trade. The family is an old one, and has given doges to Venice. They are two of our richest heiresses, for they have no brothers. Their mother died soon after the birth of Giulia."

"They both look very young," Francis said.

"Maria is about sixteen, her sister two years younger. There will be no lack of suitors for their hands, for although the family is not politically powerful, as it used to be, their wealth would cause them to be gladly received in our very first families."

"Who was the middle-aged lady sitting between them?"

"She is only their duenna," Matteo said carelessly. "She has been with them since they were children, and their father places great confidence in her. And he had need to, for Maria will ere long be receiving bouquets and perfumed notes from many a young gallant."

"I can quite fancy that," Francis said, "for she is very pretty as well as very rich, and, as far as I have observed, the two things do not go very often together. However, no doubt by this time her father has pretty well arranged in his mind whom she is to marry."

"I expect so," agreed Matteo.

"That is the worst of being born of good family. You have got to marry some one of your father's choice, not your own, and that choice is determined simply by the desire to add to the political influence of the family, to strengthen distant ties, or to obtain powerful connections. I suppose it is the same everywhere, Matteo, but I do think that a man or woman ought to have some voice in a matter of such importance to them."

"I think so, too, at the present time," Matteo laughed; "but I don't suppose that I shall be of that opinion when I have a family of sons and daughters to marry.

"This gondola of yours must be a fast one indeed, Francisco, for with only one rower she keeps up with almost all the pair oared boats, and your boy is not exerting himself to the utmost, either."

"She can fly along, I can tell you, Matteo. You shall come out in her some evening when Giuseppi and I both take oars. I have had her ten days now, and we have not come across anything that can hold her for a moment."

"It is always useful," Matteo said, "to have a fast boat. It is invaluable in case you have been getting into a scrape, and have one of the boats of the city watch in chase of you."

"I hope I sha'n't want it for any purpose of that sort," Francis answered, laughing. "I do not think I am likely to give cause to the city watch to chase me."

"I don't think you are, Francisco, but there is never any saying."

"At any rate it is always useful to be able to go fast if necessary, and if we did want to get away, I do not think there are many pair-oared gondolas afloat that would overtake us, though a good four oar might do so. Giuseppi and I are so accustomed to each other's stroke now, that though in a heavy boat we might not be a match for two men, in a light craft like this, where weight does not count for so much, we would not mind entering her for a race against the two best gondoliers on the canals, in an ordinary boat."

A few evenings later, Francis was returning homewards at about half past ten, when, in passing along a quiet canal, the boat was hailed from the shore.

"Shall we take him, Messer Francisco?" Giuseppi asked in a low voice; for more than once they had late in the evening taken a fare.

Francis rowed, like Giuseppi, in his shirt, and in the darkness they were often taken for a pair-oared gondola on the lookout for a fare. Francis had sometimes accepted the offer, because it was an amusement to see where the passenger wished to go--to guess whether he was a lover hastening to keep an appointment, a gambler on a visit to some quiet locality, where high play went on unknown to the authorities, or simply one who had by some error missed his own gondola, and was anxious to return home. It made no difference to him which way he rowed. It was always possible that some adventure was to be met with, and the fare paid was a not unwelcome addition to Giuseppi's funds.

"Yes, we may as well take him," he replied to Giuseppi's question.

"You are in no hurry to get to bed, I suppose?" the man who had hailed them said as the boat drew up against the wall of the canal.

"It does not make much difference to us, if we are well paid, to keep awake," Giuseppi said.

Upon such occasions he was always the spokesman.

"You know San Nicolo?"

"Yes, I know it," Giuseppi said; "but it is a long row--six miles, if it's a foot."

"You will have to wait there for an hour or two, but I will give you half a ducat for your night's work."

"What do you say, partner?" Giuseppi asked Francis.

"We may as well go," the lad replied after a moment's pause.

The row was certainly a long one, but the night was delightful, and the half ducat was a prize for Giuseppi; but what influenced Francis principally in accepting was curiosity. San Nicolo was a little sandy islet lying quite on the outside of the group of islands. It was inhabited only by a few fishermen; and Francis wondered that a man, evidently by his voice and manner of address belonging to the upper class, should want to go to such a place as this at this hour of the night. Certainly no ordinary motives could actuate him.

As the stranger took his place in the boat, Francis saw by the light of the stars that he was masked; but there was nothing very unusual in this, as masks were not unfrequently worn at night by young gallants, when engaged on any frolic in which they wished their identity to be unrecognized. Still it added to the interest of the trip; and dipping his oar in the water he set out at a slow, steady stroke well within his power. He adopted this partly in view of the length of the row before them, partly because the idea struck him that it might be as well that their passenger should not suspect that the boat was other than an ordinary gondola. The passenger, however, was well satisfied with the speed, for they passed two or three other gondolas before issuing from the narrow canals, and starting across the broad stretch of the lagoon.

Not a word was spoken until the gondola neared its destination. Then the passenger said:

"You row well. If you like the job I may employ you again."

"We are always ready to earn money," Francis said, speaking in a gruff voice quite unlike his own.

"Very well. I will let you know, as we return, what night I shall want you again. I suppose you can keep your mouths shut on occasion, and can go without gossiping to your fellows as to any job on which you are employed?"

"We can do that," Francis said. "It's no matter to us where our customers want to go, if they are willing to pay for it; and as to gossiping, there is a saying, 'A silver gag is the best for keeping the mouth closed.'"

A few minutes later the bow of the gondola ran up on the sandy shore of San Nicolo. The stranger made his way forward and leapt out, and with the words, "It may be two hours before I am back," walked rapidly away.

"Why, Messer Francisco," Giuseppi said when their passenger was well out of hearing, "what on earth possessed you to accept a fare to such a place as this? Of course, for myself, I am glad enough to earn half a ducat, which will buy me a new jacket with silver buttons for the next festa; but to make such a journey as this was too much, and it will be very late before we are back. If the padrone knew it he would be very angry."

"I didn't do it to enable you to earn half a ducat, Giuseppi, although I am glad enough you should do so; but I did it because it seemed to promise the chance of an adventure. There must be something in this. A noble--for I have no doubt he is one--would never be coming out to San Nicolo, at this time of night, without some very strong motive. There can be no rich heiress whom he might want to carry off living here, so that can't be what he has come for. I think there must be some secret meeting, for as we came across the lagoon I saw one or two boats in the distance heading in this direction. Anyhow, I mean to try and find out what it all means."

"You had better not, sir," Giuseppi said earnestly. "If there is any plot on foot we had best not get mixed up in it. No one is too high or too low to escape the vengeance of the council, if found plotting against the state; and before now gondolas, staved in and empty, have been found drifting on the lagoons, and the men who rowed them have never been heard of again. Once in the dungeons of Saint Mark it would be of no use to plead that you had entered into the affair simply for the amusement. The fact that you were not a regular boatman would make the matter all the worse, and the maxim that 'dead men tell no tales' is largely acted upon in Venice.

"I think, sir, the best plan will be to row straight back, and leave our fare to find his way home as best he may."

"I mean to find something out about it if I can, Giuseppi. A state secret may be dangerous, but it may be valuable. Anyhow, there can be no great risk in it. On the water I think we can show our heels to anyone who chases us; and once in Venice, we are absolutely safe, for no one would suspect a gondola of Mr. Hammond, the English merchant, of having any connection with a hired craft with its two gondoliers."

"That is true enough, sir; but I don't like it for all that. However, if you have made up your mind to it, there is nothing more to be said."

"Very well. You stay here, and I will go and look round. You had better get the gondola afloat, and be ready to start at the instant, so that, if I should have to run for it, I can jump on board and be off in a moment."

Francis made his way quietly up to the little group of huts inhabited by the fishermen, but in none of them could he see any signs of life--no lights were visible, nor could he hear the murmur of voices. There were, he knew, other buildings scattered about on the island; but he had only the light of the stars to guide him, and, not knowing anything of the exact position of the houses, he thought it better to return to the boat.

"I can find no signs of them, Giuseppi."

"All the better, Messer Francisco. There are some sorts of game, which it is well for the safety of the hunter not to discover. I was very glad, I can tell you, when I heard your whistle, and made out your figure returning at a walk. Now you are back I will take an hour's nap, and I should advise you to do the same."

But Francis had no thought of sleep, and sat down at his end of the gondola, wondering over the adventure, and considering whether or not it would be worth while to follow it up another night. That it was a plot of some sort he had little doubt. There were always in Venice two parties, equally anxious perhaps for the prosperity of the republic, but differing widely as to the means by which that prosperity would be best achieved, and as to the alliances which would, in the long run, prove most beneficial to her. There were also needy and desperate men ready enough to take bribes from any who might offer them, and to intrigue in the interest of Padua or Ferrara, Verona, Milan, or Genoa--whichever might for the time be their paymasters.

Francis was English, but he had been long enough in Venice to feel a pride in the island city, and to be almost as keenly interested in her fortunes as were his companions and friends; and a certain sense of duty, mingled with his natural love of adventure, decided him to follow up the chance which had befallen him, and to endeavour to ascertain the nature of the plot which was, he had little doubt, being hatched at San Nicolo.

In a very few minutes the regular breathing of Giuseppi, who had curled himself up in the bottom of the boat, showed that he had gone to sleep; and he did not stir until, an hour and a half after the return of Francis, the latter heard the fall of footsteps approaching the gondola.

"Wake up, Giuseppi, here comes our fare!"

Francis stood up and stretched himself as the stranger came alongside, as if he too had been fast asleep.

"Take me back to the spot where I hailed you," the fare said briefly, as he stepped into the boat and threw himself back on the cushions, and without a word the lads dipped their oars in the water and the gondola glided away towards Venice.

Just as they reached the mouth of the Grand Canal, and were about to turn into it, a six-oared gondola shot out from under the point, and a voice called out:

"Stop, in the name of the republic, and give an account of yourselves!"

"Row on," the passenger exclaimed, starting up. "Ten ducats if you can set me safely on shore."

Had the lads been real gondoliers, it is probable that even this tempting offer would not have induced them to disregard the order from the galley, for they would have run no slight risk in so doing. But Francis had no desire to be caught, and perhaps imprisoned for a considerable time, until he was able to convince the council that his share of the night's work had been merely the result of a boyish freak. With two strokes of his oar, therefore, he swept the boat's head round, thereby throwing their pursuers directly astern of them; then he and Giuseppi threw their whole weight into the stroke, and the boat danced over the water at a pace very different to that at which it had hitherto proceeded.

But, fast as they went, the galley travelled somewhat faster, the rowers doing their utmost in obedience to the angry orders of their officer; and had the race been continued on a broad stretch of water, it would sooner or later have overhauled the gondola. But Francis was perfectly aware of this, and edged the boat away towards the end of the Piazzetta, and then, shooting her head round, dashed at full speed along the canal by the side of the ducal palace, the galley being at the time some forty yards behind.

"The first to the right," Francis said, and with scarce a pause in their speed, they turned off at right angles up the first canal they came to. Again and again they turned and twisted, regardless of the direction in which the canals took them, their only object being to gain on their pursuers, who lost considerably at each turn, being obliged always to check their speed, before arriving at each angle, to allow the boat to go round.

In ten minutes she was far behind, and they then abated their speed, and turned the boat's head in the direction in which they wished to go.

"By San Paolo," the stranger said, "that was well done! You are masters of your craft, and sent your boat along at a pace which must have astonished those fellows in that lumbering galley. I had no reason to fear them, but I do not care to be interfered with and questioned by these jacks-in-office of the republic."

A few minutes later they reached the place where he embarked, and as he got out he handed the money he had promised to Giuseppi.

"Next Thursday night," he said, "at half past ten."

"It seems a dangerous sort of service, signor," Giuseppi said hesitatingly. "It is no joke to disobey the officers of the republic, and next time we may not be so fortunate."

"It's worth taking a little risk when you are well paid," the other said, turning away, "and it is not likely we shall run against one of the state galleys another night."

"Home, now, Giuseppi," Francis said, "we can talk about it tomorrow. It's the best night's work you ever did in your life, and as I have had a grand excitement we are both contented."

During the next few days Francis debated seriously with himself whether to follow up the adventure; but he finally decided on doing so, feeling convinced that there could be no real danger, even were the boat seized by one of the state galleys; as his story, that he had gone into the matter simply to discover whether any plot was intended against the republic, would finally be believed, as it would be beyond the bounds of probability that a lad of his age could himself have been concerned in such a conspiracy. As to Giuseppi, he offered no remonstrance when Francis told him that he intended to go out to San Nicolo on the following Thursday, for the ten ducats he had received were a sum larger than he could have saved in a couple of years' steady work, and were indeed quite a fortune in his eyes. Another such a sum, and he would be able, when the time came, to buy a gondola of his own, to marry, and set up housekeeping in grand style. As for the danger, if Francis was willing to run it he could do the same; for after all, a few months' imprisonment was the worst that could befall him for his share in the business.

Before the day came Matteo Giustiniani told Francis a piece of news which interested him.

"You remember my cousin Maria Polani, whom we met the other evening on the Grand Canal?"

"Of course I do, Matteo. What of her?"

"Well, what do you think? Ruggiero Mocenigo, whom I pointed out to you on the Piazza-- the man who had been banished for two years--has asked for her hand in marriage."

"He is not going to have it, I hope," Francis said indignantly. "It would be a shame, indeed, to give her to such a man as that."

"That is just what her father thought, Francisco, and he refused Ruggiero pretty curtly, and told him, I believe, he would rather see her in her grave than married to him; and I hear there was a regular scene, and Ruggiero went away swearing Polani should regret his refusal."

"I suppose your cousin does not care much about his threats," Francis said.

"I don't suppose he cares much about them," Matteo replied; "but Ruggiero is very powerfully connected, and may do him damage, not to speak of the chance of his hiring a bravo to stab him on the first opportunity. I know my father advised Polani to be very cautious where he went at night for a time. This fellow, Ruggiero, is a dangerous enemy. If he were to get Polani stabbed, it would be next to impossible to prove that it was his doing, however strong the suspicion might be; for mere suspicion goes for nothing against a man with his influence and connections. He has two near relations on the council, and if he were to burn down Polani's mansion, and to carry off Maria, the chances are against his being punished, if he did but keep out of the way for a few months."

As in England powerful barons were in the habit of waging private wars with each other, and the carrying off a bride by force was no very rare event, this state of things did not appear, to Francis, as outrageous as it would do to an English lad of the present day, but he shook his head.

"Of course one understands, Matteo, that everywhere powerful nobles do things which would be regarded as crimes if done by others; but, elsewhere, people can fortify their houses, and call out and arm their retainers, and stand on their guard. But that here, in a city like this, private feuds should be carried on, and men stabbed when unconscious of danger, seems to me detestable."

"Of course it isn't right," Matteo said carelessly, "but I don't know how you are going to put a stop to it; and after all, our quarrels here only involve a life or two, while in other countries nobles go to war with each other, and hundreds of lives, of people who have nothing to do with the quarrel, may be sacrificed."

This was a light in which Francis had hardly looked upon the matter before, and he was obliged to own that even private assassination, detestable as it was, yet caused much less suffering than feudal war. Still, he was not disposed entirely to give in to his friend's opinion.

"That is true, Matteo; but at the same time, in a war it is fair fighting, while a stab in the back is a cowardly business."

"It is not always fair fighting," Matteo replied. "You hear of castles being surprised, and the people massacred without a chance of resistance; of villages being burned, and the people butchered unresistingly. I don't think there is so much more fairness one way than the other. Polani knows he will have to be careful, and if he likes he can hire bravos to put Ruggiero out of the way, just as Ruggiero can do to remove him. There's a good deal to be said for both sides of the question."

Francis felt this was so, and that although he had an abhorrence of the Venetian method of settling quarrels, he saw that as far as the public were concerned, it was really preferable to the feudal method, of both parties calling out their retainers and going to war with each other, especially as assassinations played no inconsiderable part in the feudal struggles of the time.

On the Thursday night the gondola was in waiting at the agreed spot. Francis had thought it probable that the stranger might this time ask some questions as to where they lived and their usual place of plying for hire, and would endeavour to find out as much as he could about them, as they could not but suspect that he was engaged in some very unusual enterprise. He had therefore warned Giuseppi to be very careful in his replies. He knew that it was not necessary to say more, for Giuseppi had plenty of shrewdness, and would, he was sure, invent some plausible story without the least difficulty, possessing, as he did, plenty of the easy mendacity so general among the lower classes of the races inhabiting countries bordering on the Mediterranean. Their fare came down to the gondola a few minutes after the clock had tolled the half hour.

"I see you are punctual," he said, "which is more than most of you men are."

Francis was rowing the bow oar, and therefore stood with his back to the passenger, and was not likely to be addressed by him, as he would naturally turn to Giuseppi, who stood close behind him. As Francis had expected, as soon as they were out on the lagoon the passenger turned to his companion and began to question him.

"I cannot see your faces," he said; "but by your figures you are both young, are you not?"

"I am but twenty-two," Giuseppi said, "and my brother is a year younger."

"And what are your names?"

"Giovanni and Beppo Morani."

"And is this boat your own?"

"It is, signor. Our father died three years ago, leaving us his boat."

"And where do you usually ply?"

"Anywhere, signor, just as the fancy seizes us. Sometimes one place is good, sometimes another."

"And where do you live?"

"We don't live anywhere, signor. When night comes, and business is over, we tie up the boat to a post, wrap ourselves up, and go to sleep at the bottom. It costs nothing, and we are just as comfortable there as we should be on straw in a room."

"Then you must be saving money."

"Yes; we are laying money by. Some day, I suppose, we shall marry, and our wives must have homes. Besides, sometimes we are lazy and don't work. One must have some pleasure, you know."

"Would you like to enter service?"

"No, signor. We prefer being our own masters; to take a fare or leave it as we please."

"Your boat is a very fast one. You went at a tremendous rate when the galley was after us the other night."

"The boat is like others," Giuseppi said carelessly; "but most men can row fast when the alternative is ten ducats one way or a prison the other."

"Then there would be no place where I could always find you in the daytime if I wanted you?"

"No, signor; there would be no saying where we might be. We have sometimes regular customers, and it would not pay us to disappoint them, even if you paid us five times the ordinary fare. But we could always meet you at night anywhere, when you choose to appoint."

"But how can I appoint," the passenger said irritably, "if I don't know where to find you?"

Giuseppi was silent for a stroke or two.

"If your excellency would write in figures, half past ten or eleven, or whatever time we should meet you, just at the base of the column of the palace--the corner one on the Piazzetta--we should be sure to be there sometime or other during the day, and would look for it."

"You can read and write, then?" the passenger asked.

"I cannot do that, signor," Giuseppi said, "but I can make out figures. That is necessary to us, as how else could we keep time with our customers? We can read the sundials, as everyone else can; but as to reading and writing, that is not for poor lads like us."

307

The stranger was satisfied. Certainly every one could read the sundials; and the gondoliers would, as they said, understand his figures if he wrote them.

"Very well," he said. "It is probable I shall generally know, each time I discharge you, when I shall want you again; but should there be any change, I will make the figures on the base of the column at the corner of the Piazzetta, and that will mean the hour at which you are to meet me that night at the usual place."

Nothing more was said, until the gondola arrived at the same spot at which it had landed the passenger on the previous occasion.

"I shall be back in about the same time as before," the fare said when he alighted.

As he strode away into the darkness, Francis followed him. He was shoeless, for at that time the lower class seldom wore any protection to the feet, unless when going a journey over rough ground. Among the gondoliers shoes were unknown; and Francis himself generally took his off, for coolness and comfort, when out for the evening in his boat.

He kept some distance behind the man he was following, for as there were no hedges or inclosures, he could make out his figure against the sky at a considerable distance. As Francis had expected, he did not make towards the village, but kept along the island at a short distance from the edge of the water.

Presently Francis heard the dip of oars, and a gondola ran up on the sands halfway between himself and the man he was following. He threw himself down on the ground. Two men alighted, and went in the same direction as the one who had gone ahead.

Francis made a detour, so as to avoid being noticed by the gondoliers, and then again followed. After keeping more than a quarter of a mile near the water, the two figures ahead struck inshore. Francis followed them, and in a few minutes they stopped at a black mass, rising above the sand. He heard them knock, and then a low murmur, as if they were answering some question from within. Then they entered, and a door closed.

He moved up to the building. It was a hut of some size, but had a deserted appearance. It stood between two ridges of low sand hills, and the sand had drifted till it was halfway up the walls. There was no garden or inclosure round it, and any passerby would have concluded that it was uninhabited. The shutters were closed, and no gleam of light showed from within.

After stepping carefully round it, Francis took his post round the angle close to the door, and waited. Presently he heard footsteps approaching--three knocks were given on the door, and a voice within asked, "Who is there?"

The reply was, "One who is in distress."

The question came, "What ails you?"

And the answer, "All is wrong within."

Then there was a sound of bars being withdrawn, and the door opened and closed again.

There were four other arrivals. The same questions were asked and answered each time. Then some minutes elapsed without any fresh comers, and Francis thought that the number was probably complete. He lay down on the sand, and with his dagger began to make a hole through the wood, which was old and rotten, and gave him no difficulty in piercing it.

He applied his eye to the orifice, and saw that there were some twelve men seated round a table. Of those facing him he knew three or four by sight; all were men of good family. Two of them belonged to the council, but not to the inner Council of Ten. One, sitting at the top of the table, was speaking; but although Francis applied his ear to the hole he had made, he could hear but a confused murmur, and could not catch the words. He now rose cautiously, scooped up the sand so as to cover the hole in the wall, and swept a little down over the spot where he had been lying, although he had no doubt that the breeze, which would spring up before morning, would soon drift the light shifting sand over it, and obliterate the mark of his recumbent figure. Then he went round to the other side of the hut and bored another hole, so as to obtain a view of the faces of those whose backs had before been towards him.

One of these was Ruggiero Mocenigo. Another was a stranger to Francis, and some difference in the fashion of his garments indicated that he was not a Venetian, but, Francis thought, a

Hungarian. The other three were not nobles. One of them Francis recognized, as being a man of much influence among the fishermen and sailors. The other two were unknown to him.

As upwards of an hour had been spent in making the two holes and taking observations, Francis thought it better now to make his way back to his boat, especially as it was evident that he would gain nothing by remaining longer. Therefore, after taking the same precautions as before, to conceal all signs of his presence, he made his way across the sands back to his gondola.

"Heaven be praised, you are back again!" Giuseppi said, when he heard his low whistle, as he came down to the boat. "I have been in a fever ever since I lost sight of you. Have you succeeded?"

"I have found out that there is certainly a plot of some sort being got up, and I know some of those concerned in it, but I could hear nothing that went on. Still, I have succeeded better than I expected, and I am well satisfied with the night's work."

"I hope you won't come again, Messer Francisco. In the first place, you may not always have the fortune to get away unseen. In the next place, it is a dangerous matter to have to do with conspiracies, whichever side you are on. The way to live long in Venice is to make no enemies."

"Yes, I know that, Giuseppi, and I haven't decided yet what to do in the matter."

A quarter of an hour later, their fare returned to the boat. This time they took a long detour, and, entering Venice by one of the many canals, reached the landing place without adventure. The stranger handed Giuseppi a ducat.

"I do not know when I shall want you again; but I will mark the hour, as agreed, on the pillar. Do not fail to go there every afternoon; and even if you don't see it, you might as well come round here at half past ten of a night. I may want you suddenly."

Before going to sleep that night, Francis thought the matter over seriously, and finally concluded that he would have no more to do with it. No doubt, by crossing over to San Nicolo in the daytime, he might be able to loosen a plank at the back of the hut, or to cut so large an opening that he could hear, as well as see, what was going on within; but supposing he discovered that a plot was on hand in favour of the enemies of Venice, such as Padua or Hungary, what was he to do next? At the best, if he denounced it, and the officers of the republic surrounded the hut when the conspirators were gathered there, arrested them, and found upon them, or in their houses, proofs sufficient to condemn them, his own position would not be enviable. He would gain, indeed, the gratitude of the republic; but as for rewards, he had no need of them. On the other hand, he would draw upon himself the enmity of some eight or ten important families, and all their connections and followers, and his life would be placed in imminent danger. They would be all the more bitter against him, inasmuch as the discovery would not have been made by accident, but by an act of deliberate prying into matters which concerned him in no way, he not being a citizen of the republic.

So far his action in the matter had been a mere boyish freak; and now that he saw it was likely to become an affair of grave importance, involving the lives of many persons, he determined to have nothing further to do with it.

Chapter 3:
On The Grand Canal.

Giuseppi, next morning, heard the announcement of the determination of Francis, to interfere no further in the matter of the conspiracy at San Nicolo, with immense satisfaction. For the last few nights he had scarcely slept, and whenever he dozed off, dreamed either of being tortured in dungeons, or of being murdered in his gondola; and no money could make up for the constant terrors which assailed him. In his waking moments he was more anxious for his employer than for himself, for it was upon him that the vengeance of the conspirators would fall, rather than upon a young gondolier, who was only obeying the orders of his master.

It was, then, with unbounded relief that he heard Francis had decided to go no more out to San Nicolo.

During the next few days Francis went more frequently than usual to the Piazza of Saint Mark, and had no difficulty in recognizing there the various persons he had seen in the hut, and in ascertaining their names and families. One of the citizens he had failed to recognize was a large contractor in the salt works on the mainland. The other was the largest importer of beasts for the supply of meat to the markets of the city.

Francis was well satisfied with the knowledge he had gained. It might never be of any use to him, but it might, on the other hand, be of importance when least expected.

As a matter of precaution he drew up an exact account of the proceedings of the two nights on the lagoons, giving an account of the meeting, and the names of the persons present, and placed it in a drawer in his room. He told Giuseppi what he had done.

"I do not think there is the least chance of our ever being recognized, Giuseppi. There was not enough light for the man to have made out our features. Still there is nothing like taking precautions, and if--I don't think it is likely, mind--but if anything should ever happen to me--if I should be missing, for example, and not return by the following morning--you take that paper out of my drawer and drop it into the Lion's Mouth. Then, if you are questioned, tell the whole story."

"But they will never believe me, Messer Francisco," Giuseppi said in alarm.

"They will believe you, because it will be a confirmation of my story; but I don't think that there is the least chance of our ever hearing anything further about it."

"Why not denounce them at once without putting your name to it," Giuseppi said. "Then they could pounce upon them over there, and find out all about it for themselves?"

"I have thought about it, Giuseppi, but there is something treacherous in secret denunciations. These men have done me no harm, and as a foreigner their political schemes do not greatly concern me. I should not like to think I had sent twelve men to the dungeons and perhaps to death."

"I think it's a pity you ever went there at all, Messer Francisco."

"Well, perhaps it is, Giuseppi; but I never thought it would turn out a serious affair like this. However, I do wish I hadn't gone now; not that I think it really matters, or that we shall ever hear anything more of it. We may, perhaps, some day see the result of this conspiracy, that is, if its objects are such as I guess them to be; namely, to form a party opposed to war with Hungary, Padua, or Genoa."

For some days after this Francis abstained from late excursions in the gondola. It was improbable that he or Giuseppi would be recognized did their late passenger meet them. Still, it was possible that they might be so; and when he went out he sat quietly among the cushions while Giuseppi rowed, as it would be a pair-oared gondola the stranger would be looking for. He was sure that the conspirator would feel uneasy when the boat did not come to the rendezvous, especially when they found that, on three successive days, figures were marked as had been arranged on the column at the corner of the Piazzetta.

Giuseppi learned indeed, a week later, that inquiries had been made among the gondoliers for a boat rowed by two brothers, Giovanni and Beppo; and the inquirer, who was dressed as a retainer of a noble family, had offered five ducats reward for information concerning it. No such names, however, were down upon the register of gondoliers licensed to ply for hire. Giuseppi learned that the search had been conducted quietly but vigorously, and that several young gondoliers who rowed together had been seen and questioned.

The general opinion, among the boatmen, was that some lady must have been carried off, and that her friends were seeking for a clue as to the spot to which she had been taken.

One evening Francis had been strolling on the Piazza with Matteo, and had remained out later than he had done since the night of his last visit to San Nicolo. He took his seat in the gondola, and when Giuseppi asked him if he would go home, said he would first take a turn or two on the Grand Canal as the night was close and sultry.

There was no moon now, and most of the gondolas carried torches. Giuseppi was paddling quietly, when a pair-oared gondola shot past them, and by the light of the torch it carried, Francis recognized the ladies sitting in it to be Maria and Giulia Polani with their duenna; two armed retainers sat behind them. They were, Francis supposed, returning from spending the evening at the house of some of their friends. There were but few boats now passing along the canal.

Polani's gondola was a considerable distance ahead, when Francis heard a sudden shout of, "Mind where you are going!"

Then there was a crash of two gondolas striking each other, followed by an outburst of shouts and cries of alarm, with, Francis thought, the clash of swords.

"Row, Giuseppi!" he exclaimed, leaping from his seat and catching up the other oar; and with swift and powerful strokes the two lads drove the gondola towards the scene of what was either an accident, or an attempt at crime.

They had no doubt which it was when they arrived at the spot. A four-oared gondola lay alongside that of the Polanis, and the gondoliers with their oars, and the two retainers with their swords, had offered a stout resistance to an armed party who were trying to board her from the other craft, but their resistance was well nigh over by the time Francis brought his gondola alongside.

One of the retainers had fallen with a sword thrust through his body, and a gondolier had been knocked overboard by a blow from an oar. The two girls were standing up screaming, and the surviving retainer was being borne backwards by three or four armed men, who were slashing furiously at him.

"Quick, ladies, jump into my boat!" Francis exclaimed as he came alongside, and, leaning over, he dragged them one after the other into his boat, just as their last defender fell.

With a fierce oath the leader of the assailants was about to spring into the gondola, when Francis, snatching up his oar, smote him with all his strength on the head as he was in the act of springing, and he fell with a heavy splash into the water between the boats.

A shout of alarm and rage rose from his followers, but the gondolas were now separated, and in another moment that of Francis was flying along the canal at the top of its speed.

"Calm yourselves, ladies," Francis said. "There is no fear of pursuit. They will stop to pick up the man I knocked into the canal, and by the time they get him on board we shall be out of their reach."

"What will become of the signora?" the eldest girl asked, when they recovered a little from their agitation.

"No harm will befall her, you may be sure," Francis said. "It was evidently an attempt to carry you off, and now that you have escaped they will care nothing for your duenna. She seemed to have lost her head altogether, for as I lifted you into the boat she clung so fast to your garments that I fancy a portion of them were left in her grasp."

"Do you know where to take us? I see you are going in the right direction?" the girl asked.

"To the Palazzo Polani," Francis said. "I have the honour of being a friend of your cousin, Matteo Giustiniani, and being with him one day when you passed in your gondola, he named you to me."

"A friend of Matteo!" the girl repeated in surprise. "Pardon me, signor, I thought you were two passing gondoliers. It was so dark that I could not recognize you; and, you see, it is so unusual to see a gentleman rowing."

"I am English, signora, and we are fond of strong exercise, and so after nightfall, when it cannot shock my friends, I often take an oar myself."

"I thank you, sir, with all my heart, for my sister and myself, for the service you have rendered us. I can hardly understand what has passed, even now it seems like a dream. We were going quietly along home, when a large dark gondola dashed out from one of the side canals, and nearly ran us down. Our gondolier shouted to warn them, but they ran alongside, and then some men jumped on board, and there was a terrible fight, and every moment I expected that the gondola would have been upset. Beppo was knocked overboard, and I saw old Nicolini fall; and then, just as it seemed all over, you appeared suddenly by our side, and dragged us on board this boat before I had time to think."

"I am afraid I was rather rough, signora, but there was no time to stand on ceremony. Here is the palazzo."

The boat was brought up by the side of the steps. Francis leapt ashore and rang the bell, and then assisted the girls to land. In a minute the door was thrown open, and two servitors with torches appeared. There was an exclamation of astonishment as they saw the young ladies alone with a strange attendant.

"I will do myself the honour of calling tomorrow to inquire if you are any the worse for your adventure, signora."

"No, indeed," the eldest girl said. "You must come up with us and see our father. We must tell him what has happened; and he will be angry indeed, did we suffer our rescuer to depart without his having an opportunity of thanking him."

Francis bowed and followed the girls upstairs. They entered a large, very handsomely furnished apartment where a tall man was sitting reading.

"Why, girls," he exclaimed as he rose, "what has happened? you look strangely excited. Where is your duenna? and who is this young gentleman who accompanies you?"

"We have been attacked, father, on our way home," both the girls exclaimed.

"Attacked?" Signor Polani repeated. "Who has dared to venture on such an outrage?"

"We don't know, father," Maria said. "It was a four-oared gondola that ran suddenly into us. We thought it was an accident till a number of men, with their swords drawn, leaped on board. Then Nicolini and Francia drew their swords and tried to defend us, and Beppo and Jacopo both fought bravely too with their oars; but Beppo was knocked overboard, and I am afraid Nicolini and Francia are killed, and in another moment they would have got at us, when this young gentleman came alongside in his gondola, and dragged us on board, for we were too bewildered and frightened to do anything. One of them--he seemed the leader of the party--tried to jump on board, but our protector struck him a terrible blow with his oar, and he fell into the water, and then the gondola made off, and, so far as we could see, they did not chase us."

"It is a scandalous outrage, and I will demand justice at the hands of the council.

"Young sir, you have laid me under an obligation I shall never forget. You have saved my daughter from the worst calamity that could befall her. Who is it to whom I am thus indebted?"

"My name is Francis Hammond. My father is an English merchant who has, for the last four years, established himself here."

"I know him well by repute," Polani said. "I trust I shall know more of him in the future.

"But where is your duenna, girls?"

"She remained behind in the gondola, father; she seemed too frightened to move."

"The lady seemed to have lost her head altogether," Francis said. "As I was lifting your daughters into my gondola, in a very hasty and unceremonious way--for the resistance of your servitors was all but overcome, and there was no time to be lost--she held so tightly to their robes that they were rent in her hands."

Signor Polani struck a gong.

"Let a gondola be manned instantly," he said, "and let six of you take arms and go in search of our boat. Let another man at once summon a leech, for some of those on board are, I fear, grievously wounded, if not killed."

But there was no occasion to carry out the order concerning the boat, for before it was ready to start the missing gondola arrived at the steps, rowed by the remaining gondolier. The duenna was lifted out sobbing hysterically, and the bodies of the two retainers were then landed. One was dead; the other expired a few minutes after being brought ashore.

"You did not observe anything particular about the gondola, Maria, or you, Giulia?"

"No, father, I saw no mark or escutcheon upon it, though they might have been there without my noticing them. I was too frightened to see anything; it came so suddenly upon us."

"It was, as far as I noticed, a plain black gondola," Francis said. "The men concerned in the affair were all dressed in dark clothes, without any distinguishing badges."

"How was it you came to interfere in the fray, young gentleman? Few of our people would have done so, holding it to be a dangerous thing, for a man to mix himself up in a quarrel in which he had no concern."

"I should probably have mixed myself up in it, in any case, when I heard the cry of women," Francis replied; "but, in truth, I recognized the signoras as their gondola passed mine, and knew them to be cousins of my friend Matteo Giustiniani. Therefore when I heard the outcry ahead, I naturally hastened up to do what I could in the matter."

"And well you did it," Polani said heartily. "I trust that the man you felled into the water is he who is the author of this outrage. I do not think I need seek far for him. My suspicions point very strongly in one direction, and tomorrow I will lay the matter before the council and demand reparation."

"And now, signor, if you will permit me I will take my leave," Francis said. "The hour is late, and the signoras will require rest after their fright and emotion."

"I will see you tomorrow, sir. I shall do myself the honour of calling early upon your father, to thank him for the great service you have rendered me."

Signor Polani accompanied Francis to the steps, while two servants held torches while he took his seat in the gondola, and remained standing there until the barque had shot away beyond the circle of light.

"We seem fated to have adventures, Giuseppi."

"We do indeed, Messer Francisco, and this is more to my liking than the last. We arrived just at the nick of time; another half minute and those young ladies would have been carried off. That was a rare blow you dealt their leader. I fancy he never came up again, and that that is why we got away without being chased."

"I am of that opinion myself, Giuseppi."

"If that is the case we shall not have heard the last of it, Messer Francisco. Only someone of a powerful family would venture upon so bold a deed, as to try to carry off ladies of birth on the Grand Canal, and you may find that this adventure has created for you enemies not to be despised."

"I can't help it if it has," Francis said carelessly. "On the other hand, it will gain for me an influential friend in Signor Polani, who is not only one of the richest merchants of Venice, but closely related to a number of the best families of the city."

"His influence will not protect you against the point of a dagger," Giuseppi said. "Your share in this business cannot but become public, and I think that it would be wise to give up our evening excursions at present."

"I don't agree with you, Giuseppi. We don't go about with torches burning, so no one who meets us is likely to recognize us. One gondola in the dark is pretty much like another, and however many enemies I had, I should not be afraid of traversing the canals."

The next morning, at breakfast time, Francis related to his father his adventure of the previous evening.

"It is a mistake, my son, to mix yourself up in broils which do not concern you; but in the present instance it may be that your adventure will turn out to be advantageous to your prospects. Signor Polani is one of the most illustrious merchants of Venice. His name is known everywhere in the East, and there is not a port in the Levant where his galleys do not trade. The friendship of such a man cannot but be most useful to me.

"Upon the other hand, you will probably make some enemies by your interference with the plans of some unscrupulous young noble, and Venice is not a healthy city for those who have powerful enemies; still I think that the advantages will more than balance the risk.

"However, Francis, you must curb your spirit of adventure. You are not the son of a baron or count, and the winning of honour and glory by deeds of arms neither befits you, nor would be of advantage to you in any way. A trader of the city of London should be distinguished for his probity and his attention to business; and methinks that, ere long, it will be well to send you home to take your place in the counting house under the eye of my partner, John Pearson.

"Hitherto I have not checked your love for arms, or your intercourse with youths of far higher rank than your own; but I have been for some time doubting the wisdom of my course in bringing you out here with me, and have regretted that I did not leave you in good hands at home. The events of last night show that the time is fast approaching when you can no longer be considered a boy, and it will be better for you to turn at once into the groove in which you are to travel, than to continue a mode of life which will unfit you for the career of a city trader."

Francis knew too well his duty towards his father to make any reply, but his heart sank at the prospect of settling down in the establishment in London. His life there had not been an unpleasant one, but he knew that he should find it terribly dull, after the freedom and liberty he had enjoyed in Venice. He had never, however, even to himself, indulged the idea that any other career, save that of his father, could be his; and had regarded it as a matter of course that, some day, he would take his place in the shop in Cheapside.

Now that it was suddenly presented to him as something which would shortly take place, a feeling of repugnance towards the life came over him. Not that he dreamt for a moment of trying to induce his father to allow him to seek some other calling. He had been always taught to consider the position of a trader of good standing, of the city of London, as one of the most desirable possible. The line between the noble and the citizen was so strongly marked that no one thought of overstepping it. The citizens of London were as proud of their position and as tenacious of their rights as were the nobles themselves. They were ready enough to take up arms to defend their privileges and to resist oppression, whether it came from king or noble; but few indeed, even of the wilder spirits of the city, ever thought of taking to arms as a profession.

It was true that honour and rank were to be gained, by those who rode in the train of great nobles to the wars, but the nobles drew their following from their own estates, and not from among the dwellers in the cities; and, although the bodies of men-at-arms and archers, furnished by the city to the king in his wars, always did their duty stoutly in the field, they had no opportunity of distinguishing themselves singly. The deeds which attracted attention, and led to honour and rank, were performed by the esquires and candidates for the rank of knighthood, who rode behind the barons into the thick of the French chivalry.

Therefore Francis Hammond had never thought of taking to the profession of arms in his own country; though, when the news arrived in Venice of desperate fighting at sea with the Genoese, he had thought, to himself, that the most glorious thing in life must be to command a well-manned galley, as she advanced to the encounter of an enemy superior in numbers. He had never dreamed that such an aspiration could ever be satisfied--it was merely one of the fancies in which lads so often indulge.

Still, the thought that he was soon to return and take his place in the shop in Chepe was exceedingly unpleasant to him.

Soon after breakfast the bell at the water gate rang loudly, and a minute later the servant entered with the news that Signor Polani was below, and begged an interview. Mr. Hammond at once went down to the steps to receive his visitor, whom he saluted with all ceremony, and conducted upstairs.

"I am known to you by name, no doubt, Signor Hammond, as you are to me," the Venetian said, when the first formal greetings were over. "I am not a man of ceremony, nor, I judge, are you; but even if I were, the present is not an occasion for it. Your son has doubtless told you of the inestimable service, which he rendered to me last night, by saving my daughters, or rather my eldest daughter--for it was doubtless she whom the villains sought--from being borne off by one of the worst and most disreputable of the many bad and disreputable young men of this city."

"I am indeed glad, Signor Polani, that my son was able to be of service to you. I have somewhat blamed myself that I have let him have his own way so much, and permitted him to give himself up to exercises of arms, more befitting the son of a warlike noble than of a peaceful trader; but the quickness and boldness, which the mastery of arms gives, was yesterday of service, and I no longer regret the time he has spent, since it has enabled him to be of aid to the daughters of Signor Polani."

"A mastery of arms is always useful, whether a man be a peace-loving citizen, or one who would carve his way to fame by means of his weapons. We merchants of the Mediterranean might give up our trade, if we were not prepared to defend our ships against the corsairs of Barbary, and the pirates who haunt every inlet and islet of the Levant now, as they have ever done since the days of Rome. Besides, it is the duty of every citizen to defend his native city when attacked. And lastly, there are the private enemies, that every man who rises but in the smallest degree above his fellows is sure to create for himself.

"Moreover, a training in arms, as you say, gives readiness and quickness, it enables the mind to remain calm and steadfast amidst dangers of all sorts, and, methinks, it adds not a little to a man's dignity and self respect to know that he is equal, man to man, to any with whom he may come in contact. Here in Venice we are all soldiers and sailors, and your son will make no worse merchant, but rather the better, for being able to wield sword and dagger.

"Even now," he said with a smile, "he has proved the advantage of his training; for, though I say it not boastfully, Nicholas Polani has it in his power to be of some use to his friends, and foremost among them he will henceforward count your brave son, and, if you will permit him, yourself.

"But you will, I trust, excuse my paying you but a short visit this morning, for I am on my way to lay a complaint before the council. I have already been round to several of my friends, and Phillipo Giustiniani and some six others, nearest related to me, will go with me, being all aggrieved at this outrage to a family nearly connected. I crave you to permit me to take your son with me, in order that he may be at hand, if called upon, to say what he knows of the affair."

"Assuredly it is his duty to go with you if you desire it; although I own I am not sorry that he could see, as he tells me, no badge or cognizance which would enable him to say aught which can lead to the identification of those who would have abducted your daughter. It is but too well known a fact that it is dangerous to make enemies in Venice, for even the most powerful protection does not avail against the stab of a dagger."

"That is true enough," the merchant said. "The frequency of assassinations is a disgrace to our city; nor will it ever be put down until some men of high rank are executed, and the seignory show that they are as jealous of the lives of private citizens, as they are of the honour and well being of the republic."

Francis gladly threw aside his books when he was told that Signor Polani desired him to accompany him, and was soon seated by the side of the merchant in his gondola.

"How old are you, my friend?" the merchant asked him, as the boat threaded the mazes of the canals.

"I am just sixteen, signor."

"No more!" the merchant said in surprise. "I had taken you for well-nigh two years older. I have but just come from the Palazzo Giustiniani, and my young kinsman, Matteo, tells me that in the School of Arms there are none of our young nobles who are your match with rapier or battleaxe."

"I fear, sir," Francis said modestly, "that I have given up more time to the study of arms than befits the son of a sober trader."

"Not at all," the Venetian replied. "We traders have to defend our rights and our liberties, our goods and our ships, just as much as the nobles have to defend their privileges and their castles. Here in Venice there are no such distinctions of rank as there are elsewhere. Certain families, distinguished among the rest by their long standing, wealth, influence, or the services they have rendered to the state, are of senatorial rank, and constitute our nobility; but there are no titles among us. We are all citizens of the republic, with our rights and privileges, which cannot be infringed even by the most powerful; and the poorest citizen has an equal right to make himself as proficient in the arms, which he may be called upon to wield in defence of the state, as the Doge himself. In your country also, I believe, all men are obliged to learn the use of arms, to practise shooting at the butts, and to make themselves efficient, if called upon to take part in the wars of the country. And I have heard that at the jousts, the champions of the city of London have ere now held their own against those of the court."

"They have done so," Francis said; "and yet, I know not why, it is considered unseemly for the sons of well-to-do citizens to be too fond of military exercises."

"The idea is a foolish one," the Venetian said hotly. "I myself have, a score of times, defended my ships against corsairs and pirates, Genoese, and other enemies. I have fought against the Greeks, and been forced to busy myself in more than one serious fray in the streets of Constantinople, Alexandria, and other ports, and have served in the galleys of the state. All men who live by trade must be in favour of peace; but they must also be prepared to defend their goods, and the better able they are to do it, the more the honour to them.

"But here we are at the Piazzetta."

A group of nobles were standing near the landing place, and Signor Polani at once went up to them, and introduced Francis to them as the gentleman who had done his daughter and their kinswoman such good service. Francis was warmly thanked and congratulated by them all.

"Will you wait near the entrance?" Signor Polani said. "I see that my young cousin, Matteo, has accompanied his father, and you will, no doubt, find enough to say to each other while we are with the council."

The gentlemen entered the palace, and Matteo, who had remained respectfully at a short distance from the seniors, at once joined his friend.

"Well, Francis, I congratulate you heartily, though I feel quite jealous of you. It was splendid to think of your dashing up in your gondola, and carrying off my pretty cousins from the clutches of that villain, Ruggiero Mocenigo, just as he was about to lay his hands on them."

"Are you sure it was Ruggiero, Matteo?"

"Oh, there can't be any doubt about it. You know, he had asked for Maria's hand, and when Polani refused him, had gone off muttering threats. You know what his character is. He is capable of any evil action; besides, they say that he has dissipated his patrimony, in gaming and other extravagances at Constantinople, and is deep in the hands of the Jews. If he could have succeeded in carrying off Maria it would more than have mended his fortunes, for she and her sister are acknowledged to be the richest heiresses in Venice. Oh, there is not a shadow of doubt that it's he.

"You won't hear me saying anything against your love of prowling about in that gondola of yours, since it has brought you such a piece of good fortune--for it is a piece of good fortune, Francis, to have rendered such a service to Polani, to say nothing of all the rest of us who are connected with his family. I can tell you that there are scores of young men of good birth in Venice, who would give their right hand to have done what you did."

"I should have considered myself fortunate to have been of service to any girls threatened by violence, though they had only been fishermen's daughters," Francis said; "but I am specially pleased because they are relatives of yours, Matteo."

"To say nothing to their being two of the prettiest girls in Venice," Matteo added slyly.

"That counts for something too, no doubt," Francis said laughing, "though I didn't think of it.

"I wonder," he went on gravely, "whether that was Ruggiero whom I struck down, and whether he came up again to the surface. He has very powerful connections, you know, Matteo; and if I have gained friends, I shall also have gained enemies by the night's work."

"That is so," Matteo agreed. "For your sake, I own that I hope that Ruggiero is at present at the bottom of the canal. He was certainly no credit to his friends; and although they would of course have stood by him, I do not think they will feel, at heart, in any way displeased to know that he will trouble them no longer. But if his men got him out again, I should say you had best be careful, for Ruggiero is about the last man in Venice I should care to have as an enemy. However, we won't look at the unpleasant side of the matter, and will hope that his career has been brought to a close."

"I don't know which way to hope," Francis said gravely. "He will certainly be a dangerous enemy if he is alive; and yet the thought of having killed a man troubles me much."

"It would not trouble me at all if I were in your place," Matteo said. "If you had not killed him, you may be very sure that he would have killed you, and that the deed would have caused him no compunction whatever. It was a fair fight, just as if it had been a hostile galley in mid-sea; and I don't see why the thought of having rid Venice of one of her worst citizens need trouble you in any way."

"You see I have been brought up with rather different ideas to yours, Matteo. My father, as a trader, is adverse to fighting of all kinds--save, of course, in defence of one's country; and although he has not blamed me in any way for the part I took, I can see that he is much disquieted, and indeed speaks of sending me back to England at once."

"Oh, I hope not!" Matteo said earnestly. "Hitherto you and I have been great friends, Francis, but we shall be more in future. All Polani's friends will regard you as one of themselves; and I was even thinking, on my way here, that perhaps you and I might enter the service of the state together, and get appointed to a war galley in a few years."

"My father's hair would stand up at the thought, Matteo; though, for myself, I should like nothing so well. However, that could never have been. Still I am sorry, indeed, at the thought of leaving Venice. I have been very happy here, and I have made friends, and there is always something to do or talk about; and the life in London would be so dull in comparison. But here comes one of the ushers from the palace."

The official came up to them, and asked if either of them was Messer Francisco Hammond, and, finding that he had come to the right person, requested Francis to follow him.

Chapter 4:
Carried Off.

It was with a feeling of considerable discomfort, and some awe, that Francis Hammond followed his conductor to the chamber of the Council. It was a large and stately apartment. The decorations were magnificent, and large pictures, representing events in the wars of Venice, hung round the walls. The ceiling was also superbly painted. The cornices were heavily gilded. Curtains of worked tapestry hung by the windows, and fell behind him as he entered the door.

At a table of horseshoe shape eleven councillors, clad in the long scarlet robes, trimmed with ermine, which were the distinguishing dress of Venetian senators, were seated--the doge himself acting as president. On their heads they wore black velvet caps, flat at the top, and in shape somewhat resembling the flat Scotch bonnet. Signor Polani and his companions were seated in chairs, facing the table.

When Francis entered the gondolier was giving evidence as to the attack upon his boat. Several questions were asked him when he had finished, and he was then told to retire. The usher then brought Francis forward.

"This is Messer Francisco Hammond," he said.

"Tell your story your own way," the doge said.

Francis related the story of the attack on the gondola, and the escape of the ladies in his boat.

"How came you, a foreigner and a youth, to interfere in a fray of this kind?" one of the councillors asked.

"I did not stop to think of my being a stranger, or a youth," Francis replied quietly. "I heard the screams of women in distress, and felt naturally bound to render them what aid I could."

"Did you know who the ladies were?"

"I knew them only by sight. My friend Matteo Giustiniani had pointed them out to me, on one occasion, as being the daughters of Signor Polani, and connections of his. When their gondola had passed mine, a few minutes previously, I recognized their faces by the light of the torches in their boat."

"Were the torches burning brightly?" another of the council asked; "because it may be that this attack was not intended against them, but against some others."

"The light was bright enough for me to recognize their faces at a glance," Francis said, "and also the yellow and white sashes of their gondoliers."

"Did you see any badge or cognizance, either on the gondola or on the persons of the assailants?"

"I did not," Francis said. "They certainly wore none. One of the torches in the Polani gondola had been extinguished in the fray, but the other was still burning, and, had the gondoliers worn coloured sashes or other distinguishing marks, I should have noticed them."

"Should you recognize, were you to see them again, any of the assailants?"

"I should not," Francis said. "They were all masked."

"You say you struck down the one who appeared to be their leader with an oar, as he was about to leap into your boat. How was it the oar was in your hand instead of that of your gondolier?"

"I was myself rowing," Francis said. "In London, rowing is an amusement of which boys of all classes are fond, and since I have been out here with my father I have learned to row a gondola; and sometimes, when I am out of an evening, I take an oar as well as my gondolier, enjoying the exercise and the speed at which the boat goes along. I was not rowing when the signora's boat passed me, but upon hearing the screams, I stood up and took the second oar, to arrive as quickly as possible at the spot. That was how it was that I had it in my hand, when the man was about to leap into the boat."

"Then there is nothing at all, so far as you know, to direct your suspicion against anyone as the author of this attack?"

"There was nothing," Francis said, "either in the gondola itself, or in the attire or persons of those concerned in the fray, which could give me the slightest clue as to their identity."

"At any rate, young gentleman," the doge said, "you appear to have behaved with a promptness, presence of mind, and courage--for it needs courage to interfere in a fray of this sort--beyond your years; and, in the name of the republic, I thank you for having prevented the commission of a grievous crime. You will please to remain here for the present. It may be that, when the person accused of this crime appears before us, you may be able to recognize his figure."

It was with mixed feelings that Francis heard, a minute or two later, the usher announce that Signor Ruggiero Mocenigo was without, awaiting the pleasure of their excellencies.

"Let him enter," the doge said.

The curtains fell back, and Ruggiero Mocenigo entered with a haughty air. He bowed to the council, and stood as if expecting to be questioned.

"You are charged, Ruggiero Mocenigo," the doge said, "with being concerned in an attempt to carry off the daughters of Signor Polani, and of taking part in the killing of three servitors of that gentleman."

"On what grounds am I accused?" Ruggiero said haughtily.

"On the ground that you are a rejected suitor for the elder lady's hand, and that you had uttered threats against her father, who, so far as he knows, has no other enemies."

"This seems somewhat scanty ground for an accusation of such gravity," Ruggiero said sneeringly. "If every suitor who grumbles, when his offer is refused, is to be held responsible for every accident which may take place in the lady's family, methinks that the time of this reverend and illustrious council will be largely occupied."

"You will remember," the doge said sternly, "that your previous conduct gives good ground for suspicion against you. You have already been banished from the state for two years for assassination, and such reports as reached us of your conduct in Constantinople, during your exile, were the reverse of satisfactory. Had it not been so, the prayers of your friends, that your term of banishment might be shortened, would doubtless have produced their effect."

"At any rate," Ruggiero said, "I can, with little difficulty, prove that I had no hand in any attempt upon Signor Polani's daughters last night, seeing that I had friends spending the evening with me, and that we indulged in play until three o'clock this morning--an hour at which, I should imagine, the Signoras Polani would scarcely be abroad."

"At what time did your friends assemble?"

"At nine o'clock," Ruggiero said. "We met by agreement in the Piazza, somewhat before that hour, and proceeded together on foot to my house."

"Who were your companions?"

Ruggiero gave the names of six young men, all connections of his family, and summonses were immediately sent for them to attend before the council.

"In the meantime, Messer Francisco Hammond, you can tell us whether you recognize in the accused one of the assailants last night."

"I cannot recognize him, your excellency," Francis said; "but I can say certainly that he was not the leader of the party, whom I struck with my oar. The blow fell on the temple, and assuredly there would be marks of such a blow remaining today."

As Francis was speaking, Ruggiero looked at him with a cold piercing glance, which expressed the reverse of gratitude for the evidence which he was giving in his favour, and something like a chill ran through him as he resumed his seat behind Signor Polani and his friends.

There was silence for a quarter of an hour. Occasionally the members of the council spoke in low tones to each other, but no word was spoken aloud, until the appearance of the first of the young men who had been summoned. One after another they gave their evidence, and all were unanimous in declaring that they had spent the evening with Ruggiero Mocenigo, and that he did not leave the room, from the moment of his arrival there soon after nine o'clock, until they left him at two in the morning.

"You have heard my witnesses," Ruggiero said, when the last had given his testimony; "and I now ask your excellencies, whether it is right that a gentleman, of good family, should be exposed to a villainous accusation of this kind, on the barest grounds of suspicion?"

"You have heard the evidence which has been given, Signor Polani," the doge said. "Do you withdraw your accusation against Signor Mocenigo?"

"I acknowledge, your excellency," Signor Polani said, rising, "that Ruggiero Mocenigo has proved that he took no personal part in the affair, but I will submit to you that this in no way proves that he is not the author of the attempt. He would know that my first suspicion would fall upon him, and would, therefore, naturally leave the matter to be carried out by others, and would take precautions to enable him to prove, as he has done, that he was not present. I still maintain that the circumstances of the case, his threats to me, and the fact that my daughter will naturally inherit a portion of what wealth I might possess, and that, as I know and can prove, Ruggiero Mocenigo has been lately reduced to borrowing money of the Jews, all point to his being the author of this attempt, which would at once satisfy his anger against me, for having declined the honour of his alliance, and repair his damaged fortunes."

There were a few words of whispered consultation between the councillors, and the doge then said:

"All present will now retire while the council deliberates. Our decision will be made known to the parties concerned, in due time."

On leaving the palace, Signor Polani and his friends walked together across the Piazza, discussing the turn of events.

"He will escape," Polani said. "He has two near relations on the council, and however strong our suspicions may be, there is really no proof against him. I fear that he will go free. I feel as certain as ever that he is the contriver of the attempt; but the precautions he has taken seem to render it impossible to bring the crime home to him. However, it is no use talking about it any more, at present.

"You will, I hope, accompany me home, Signor Francisco, and allow me to present you formally to my daughters. They were too much agitated, last night, to be able to thank you fully for the service you had rendered them.

"Matteo, do you come with us."

Three days passed, and no decision of the council had been announced, when, early in the morning, one of the state messengers brought an order that Francis should be in readiness, at nine o'clock, to accompany him. At that hour a gondola drew up at the steps. It was a covered gondola, with hangings, which prevented any from seeing who were within. Francis took his seat by the side of the official, and the gondola started at once.

"It looks very much as if I was being taken as a prisoner," Francis said to himself. "However, that can hardly be, for even if Ruggiero convinced the council that he was wholly innocent of this affair, no blame could fall on me, for I neither accused nor identified him. However, it is certainly towards the prisons we are going."

The boat, indeed, was passing the Piazzetta without stopping, and turned down the canal behind, to the prisons in rear of the palace. They stopped at the water gate, close to the Bridge of Sighs, and Francis and his conductor entered. They proceeded along two or three passages, until they came to a door where an official was standing. A word was spoken, and they passed in.

The chamber they entered was bare and vaulted, and contained no furniture whatever, but at one end was a low stone slab, upon which something was lying covered with a cloak. Four of the members of the council were standing in a group, talking, when Francis entered. Signor Polani, with two of his friends, stood apart at one side of the chamber. Ruggiero Mocenigo also, with two of his companions, stood on the other side.

Francis thought that the demeanour of Ruggiero was somewhat altered from that which he had assumed at the previous investigation, and that he looked sullen and anxious.

"We have sent for you, Francisco Hammond, in order that you may, if you can, identify a body which was found last night, floating in the Grand Canal."

One of the officials stepped forward and removed the cloak, showing on the stone slab the body of a young man. On the left temple there was an extensive bruise, and the skin was broken.

"Do you recognize that body?"

"I do not recognize the face," Francis said, "and do not know that I ever saw it before."

"The wound upon the temple which you see, is it such as, you would suppose, would be caused by the blow you struck an unknown person, while he was engaged in attacking the gondola of Signor Polani?"

"I cannot say whether it is such a wound as would be caused by a blow with an oar," Francis said; "but it is certainly, as nearly as possible, on the spot where I struck the man, just as he was leaping, sword in hand, into my gondola."

"You stated, at your examination the other day, that it was on the left temple you struck the blow."

"I did so. I said at once that Signor Ruggiero Mocenigo could not have been the man who led the assailants, because had he been so he would assuredly have borne a mark from the blow on the left temple."

"Look at the clothes. Do you see anything there which could lead you to identify him with your assailant?"

"My assailant was dressed in dark clothes, as this one was. There was but one distinguishing mark that I noticed, and this is wanting here. The light of the torch fell upon the handle of a dagger in his girdle. I saw it but for a moment, but I caught the gleam of gems. It was only a passing impression, but I could swear that he carried a small gold or yellow metal-handled dagger, and I believe that it was set with gems, but to this I should not like to swear."

"Produce the dagger found upon the dead man," one of the council said to an official.

And the officer produced a small dagger with a fine steel blade and gold handle, thickly encrusted with gems.

"Is this the dagger?" the senator asked Francis.

"I cannot say that it is the dagger," Francis replied; "but it closely resembles it, if it is not the same."

"You have no doubt, I suppose, seeing that wound on the temple, the dagger found in the girdle, and the fact that the body has evidently only been a few days in the water, that this is the man whom you struck down in the fray on the canal?"

"No, signor, I have no doubt whatever that it is the same person."

"That will do," the council said. "You can retire; and we thank you, in the name of justice, for the evidence you have given."

Francis was led back to the gondola, and conveyed to his father's house. An hour later Signor Polani arrived.

"The matter is finished," he said, "I cannot say satisfactorily to me, for the punishment is wholly inadequate to the offence, but at any rate he has not got off altogether unpunished. After you left, we passed from the prison into the palace, and then the whole council assembled, as before, in the council chamber. I may tell you that the body which was found was that of a cousin and intimate of Ruggiero Mocenigo. The two have been constantly together since the return of the latter from Constantinople. It was found, by inquiry at the house of the young man's father, that he left home on the evening upon which the attack was committed, saying that he was going to the mainland, and might not be expected to return for some days.

"The council took it for granted, from the wound in his head, and the fact that a leech has testified that the body had probably been in the water about three days, that he was the man that was stunned by your blow, and drowned in the canal. Ruggiero urged that the discovery in no way affected him; and that his cousin had, no doubt, attempted to carry off my daughter on his own account. There was eventually a division among the council on this point, but Maria was sent for, and on being questioned, testified that the young man had never spoken to her, and that, indeed, she did not know him even by sight; and the majority thereupon came to the conclusion that he could only have been acting as an instrument of Ruggiero's.

"We were not in the apartment while the deliberation was going on, but when we returned the president announced that, although there was no absolute proof of Ruggiero's complicity in the affair, yet that, considering his application for my daughter's hand, his threats on my refusal to his request, his previous character, and his intimacy with his cousin, the council had no doubt that the attempt had been made at his instigation, and therefore sentenced him to banishment from Venice and the islands for three years."

"I should be better pleased if they had sent him back to Constantinople, or one of the islands of the Levant," Mr. Hammond said. "If he is allowed to take up his abode on the mainland, he may be only two or three miles away, which, in the case of a man of his description, is much too near to be pleasant for those who have incurred his enmity."

"That is true," Signor Polani agreed, "and I myself, and my friends, are indignant that he should not have been banished to a distance, where he at least would have been powerless for fresh mischief. On the other hand, his friends will doubtless consider that he has been hardly treated. However, as far as my daughters are concerned, I will take good care that he shall have no opportunity of repeating his attempt; for I have ordered them, on no account whatever, to be absent from the palazzo after the shades of evening begin to fall, unless I myself am with them; and I shall increase the number of armed retainers in the house, by bringing some of my men on shore from a ship which arrived last night in port. I cannot believe that even Ruggiero would have the insolence to attempt to carry them off from the house by force; but when one has to deal with a man like this, one cannot take too great precautions."

"I have already ordered my son, on no account, to be out after nightfall in the streets. In his gondola I do not mind, for unless the gondoliers wear badges, it is impossible to tell one boat from another after dark. Besides, as he tells me, his boat is so fast that he has no fear whatever of being overtaken, even if recognized and chased. But I shall not feel comfortable so long as he is here, and shall send him back to England on the very first occasion that offers."

"I trust that no such occasion may occur just yet, Signor Hammond. I should be sorry, indeed, for your son to be separated so soon from us. We must talk the matter over together, and perhaps between us we may hit on some plan by which, while he may be out of the reach of the peril he has incurred on behalf of my family, he may yet be neither wasting his time, nor altogether separated from us."

For the next fortnight Francis spent most of his time at the Palazzo Polani. The merchant was evidently sincere in his invitation to him to make his house his home; and if a day passed without the lad paying a visit, would chide him gently for deserting them. He himself was frequently present in the balcony, where the four young people--for Matteo Giustiniani was generally of the party--sat and chatted together, the gouvernante sitting austerely by, with at times a strong expression of disapproval on her countenance at their laughter and merriment, although--as her charges' father approved of the intimacy of the girls with their young cousin and this English lad--she could offer no open objections. In the afternoon, the party generally went for a long row in a four-oared gondola, always returning home upon the approach of evening.

To Francis this time was delightful. He had had no sister of his own; and although he had made the acquaintance of a number of lads in Venice, and had accompanied his father to formal entertainments at the houses of his friends, he had never before been intimate in any of their families. The gaiety and high spirits of the two girls, when they were in the house, amused and pleased him, especially as it was in contrast to the somewhat stiff and dignified demeanour which they assumed when passing through the frequented canals in the gondola.

"I do not like that woman Castaldi," Francis said one evening as, after leaving the palazzo, Giuseppi rowed them towards the Palazzo Giustiniani, where Matteo was to be landed.

"Gouvernantes are not popular, as a class, with young men," Matteo laughed.

"But seriously, Matteo, I don't like her; and I am quite sure that, for some reason or other, she does not like me. I have seen her watching me, as a cat would watch a mouse she is going to spring on."

"Perhaps she has not forgiven you, Francisco, for saving her two charges, and leaving her to the mercy of their assailants."

"I don't know, Matteo. Her conduct appeared to me, at the time, to be very strange. Of course, she might have been paralysed with fright, but it was certainly curious the way she clung to their dresses, and tried to prevent them from leaving the boat."

"You don't really think, Francis, that she wanted them to be captured?"

"I don't know whether I should be justified in saying as much as that, Matteo, and I certainly should not say so to anyone else, but I can't help thinking that such was the case. I don't like her face, and I don't like the woman. She strikes me as being deceitful. She certainly did try to prevent my carrying the girls off and, had not their dresses given way in her hands, she would have done so. Anyhow, it strikes me that Ruggiero must have had some accomplice in the house. How else could he have known of the exact time at which they would be passing along the Grand Canal? For, that the gondola was in waiting to dash out and surprise them, there is no doubt.

"I was asking Signora Giulia, the other day, how it was they were so late, for she says that her father never liked their being out after dusk in Venice, though at Corfu he did not care how late they were upon the water. She replied that she did not quite know how it happened. Her sister had said, some time before, that she thought it was time to be going, but the gouvernante--who was generally very particular--had said that there was no occasion to hurry, as their father knew where they were, and would not be uneasy. She thought the woman must have mistaken the time, and did not know how late it was.

"Of course, this proves nothing. Still I own that, putting all the things together, I have my suspicions."

"It is certainly curious, Francisco, though I can hardly believe it possible that the woman could be treacherous. She has been for some years in the service of the family, and my cousin has every confidence in her."

"That may be, Matteo; but Ruggiero may have promised so highly that he may have persuaded her to aid him. He could have afforded to be generous, if he had been successful."

"There is another thing, by the bye, Francisco, which did not strike me at the time; but now you speak of it, may be another link in the chain. I was laughing at Maria about their screaming, and saying what a noise the three of them must have made, and she said, 'Oh, no! there were only two of us--Giulia and I screamed for aid at the top of our voices; but the signora was as quiet and brave as possible, and did not utter a sound.'"

"That doesn't agree, Matteo, with her being so frightened as to hold the girls tightly, and almost prevent their escape, or with the row she made, sobbing and crying, when she came back. Of course there is not enough to go upon; and I could hardly venture to speak of it to Signor Polani, or to accuse a woman, in whom he has perfect confidence, of such frightful treachery on such vague grounds of suspicion. Still I do suspect her; and I hope, when I go away from Venice, you will, as far as you can, keep an eye upon her."

"I do not know how to do that," Matteo said, laughing; "but I will tell my cousins that we don't like her, and advise them, in future, not on any account to stay out after dusk, even if she gives them permission to do so; and if I learn anything more to justify our suspicions, I will tell my cousin what you and I think, though it won't be a pleasant thing to do. However, Ruggiero is gone now, and I hope we sha'n't hear anything more about him."

"I hope not, Matteo; but I am sure he is not the man to give up the plan he has once formed easily, any more than he is to forgive an injury."

"However, here we are at your steps. We will talk the other matter over another time. Anyhow, I am glad I have told you what I thought, for it has been worrying me. Now that I find you don't think my ideas about her are altogether absurd, I will keep my eyes more open than ever in future. I am convinced she is a bad one, and I only hope we may be able to prove it."

"You have made me very uncomfortable, Francisco," Matteo said as he stepped ashore; "but we will talk about it again tomorrow."

"We shall meet at your cousin's in the evening. Before that time, we had better both think over whether we ought to tell anyone our suspicions, and we can hold a council in the gondola on the way back."

Francis did think the matter over that night. He felt that the fact told him by Giulia, that the gouvernante had herself been the means of their staying out later than usual on the evening of the attack, added great weight to the vague suspicions he had previously entertained; and he determined to let the matter rest no longer, but that the next day he would speak to Signor Polani, even at the risk of offending him by his suspicions of a person who had been, for some years, in his confidence. Accordingly, he went in the morning to the palazzo, but found that Signor Polani was absent, and would not be in until two or three o'clock in the afternoon. He did not see the girls, who, he knew, were going out to spend the day with some friends.

At three o'clock he returned, and found that Polani had just come in.

"Why, Francisco," the merchant said when he entered, "have you forgotten that my daughters will be out all day?"

"No, signor, I have not forgotten that, but I wish to speak to you. I dare say you will laugh at me, but I hope you will not think me meddlesome, or impertinent, for touching upon a subject which concerns you nearly."

"I am sure you will not be meddlesome or impertinent, Francisco," Signor Polani said reassuringly, for he saw that the lad was nervous and anxious. "Tell me what you have to say, and I can promise you beforehand that, whether I agree with you or not in what you may have to say, I shall be in no way vexed, for I shall know you have said it with the best intentions."

"What I have to say, sir, concerns the Signora Castaldi, your daughters' gouvernante. I know, sir, that you repose implicit confidence in her; and your judgment, formed after years of intimate knowledge, is hardly likely to be shaken by what I have to tell you. I spoke to Matteo about it, and, as he is somewhat of my opinion, I have decided that it is, at least, my duty to tell you all the circumstances, and you can then form your own conclusions."

Francis then related the facts known to him. First, that the assailants of the gondola must have had accurate information as to the hour at which they would come along; secondly, that it was at the gouvernante's suggestion that the return had been delayed much later than usual; lastly, that when the attack took place, the gouvernante did not raise her voice to cry for assistance, and that she had, at the last moment, so firmly seized their dresses, that it was only by tearing the girls from her grasp that he had been enabled to get them into the boat.

"There may be nothing in all this," he said when he had concluded. "But at least, sir, I thought that it was right you should know it; and you will believe me, that it is only anxiety as to the safety of your daughters that has led me to speak to you."

"Of that I am quite sure," Signor Polani said cordially, "and you were perfectly right in speaking to me. I own, however, that I do not for a moment think that the circumstances are more than mere coincidences. Signora Castaldi has been with me for upwards of ten years. She has instructed and trained my daughters entirely to my satisfaction. I do not say that she is everything that one could wish, but, then, no one is perfect, and I have every confidence in her fidelity and trustworthiness. I own that the chain you have put together is a strong one, and had she but lately entered my service, and were she a person of whom I knew but little, I should attach great weight to the facts, although taken in themselves they do not amount to much. Doubtless she saw that my daughters were enjoying themselves in the society of my friends, and in her kindness of heart erred, as she certainly did err, in allowing them to stay longer than she should have done.

"Then, as to her not crying out when attacked, women behave differently in cases of danger. Some scream loudly, others are silent, as if paralysed by fear. This would seem to have been her case. Doubtless she instinctively grasped the girls for their protection, and in her fright did not even perceive that a boat had come alongside, or know that you were a friend trying to save them. That someone informed their assailants of the whereabouts of my daughters, and the time they were coming home, is clear; but they might have been seen going to the house, and a swift gondola have been placed on the watch. Had this boat started as soon as they took their seat in the gondola on their return, and hastened, by the narrow canals, to the spot where their accomplices were waiting, they could have warned them in ample time of the approach of the gondola with my daughters.

"I have, as you may believe, thought the matter deeply over, for it was evident to me that the news of my daughters' coming must have reached their assailants beforehand. I was most unwilling to suspect treachery on the part of any of my household, and came to the conclusion that the warning was given in the way I have suggested.

"At the same time, Francisco, I thank you deeply for having mentioned to me the suspicions you have formed, and although I think that you are wholly mistaken, I certainly shall not neglect the warning, but shall watch very closely the conduct of my daughters' gouvernante, and shall take every precaution to put it out of her power to play me false, even while I cannot, for a moment, believe she would be so base and treacherous as to attempt to do so."

"In that case, signor, I shall feel that my mission has not been unsuccessful, however mistaken I may be, and I trust sincerely that I am wholly wrong. I thank you much for the kind way in which you have heard me express suspicions of a person in your confidence."

The gravity with which the merchant had heard Francis' story vanished immediately he left the room, and a smile came over his face.

"Boys are boys all the world over," he said to himself, "and though my young friend has almost the stature of a man, as well as the quickness and courage of one, and has plenty of sense in other matters, he has at once the prejudices and the romantic ideas of a boy. Had Signora Castaldi been young and pretty, no idea that she was treacherous would have ever entered his mind; but what young fellow yet ever liked a gouvernante, who sits by and works at her tambour frame, with a disapproving expression on her face, while he is laughing and talking with a girl of his own age. I should have felt the same when I was a boy. Still, to picture the poor signora as a traitoress, in the pay of that villain Mocenigo, is too absurd. I had the greatest difficulty in keeping my gravity when he was unfolding his story. But he is an excellent lad, nevertheless. A true, honest, brave lad, with a little of the bluffness that they say all his nation possess, but with a heart of gold, unless I am greatly mistaken."

At seven o'clock, Francis was just getting into his gondola to go round again to Signor Polani's, when another gondola came along the canal at the top of its speed, and he recognized at once the badge of the Giustiniani. It stopped suddenly as it came abreast of his own boat, and Matteo, in a state of the highest excitement, jumped from his own boat into that of Francis.

"What is the matter, Matteo? What has happened?"

"I have terrible news, Francisco. My cousins have both disappeared."

"Disappeared!" Francis repeated in astonishment "How have they disappeared?"

"Their father has just been round to see mine. He is half mad with grief and anger. You know they had gone to spend the day at the Persanis?"

"Yes, yes," Francis exclaimed; "but do go on, Matteo. Tell me all about it, quickly."

"Well, it seems that Polani, for some reason or other, thought he would go and fetch them himself, and at five o'clock he arrived there in his gondola, only to find that they had left two hours before. You were right, Francisco, it was that beldam Castaldi. She went with them there in the morning, and left them there, and was to have come in the gondola for them at six. At three o'clock she arrived, saying that their father had met with a serious accident, having fallen down the steps of one of the bridges and broken his leg, and that he had sent her to fetch them at once.

"Of course, they left with her instantly. Polani questioned the lackeys, who had aided them to embark. They said that the gondola was not one of his boats, but was apparently a hired gondola, with a closed cabin. The girls had stopped in surprise as they came down the steps, and Maria said, 'Why, this is not our gondola!'

"Castaldi replied, 'No, no; our own gondolas had both gone off to find and bring a leech, and as your father was urgently wanting you, I hailed the first passing boat. Make haste, dears, your father is longing for you.'

"So they got on board at once, and the gondola rowed swiftly away. That is all I know about it, except that the story was a lie, that their father never sent for them, and that up to a quarter of an hour ago they had not reached home."

Chapter 5:
Finding A Clue.

"This is awful, Matteo," Francis said, when his friend had finished his story. "What is to be done?"

"That is just the thing, Francisco. What is to be done? My cousin has been already to the city magistrates, to tell them what has taken place, and to request their aid in discovering where the girls have been carried to. I believe that he is going to put up a proclamation, announcing that he will give a thousand ducats to whomsoever will bring information which will enable him to recover the girls. That will set every gondolier on the canals on the alert, and some of them must surely have noticed a closed gondola rowed by two men, for at this time of year very few gondolas have their covers on. It seems to be terrible not to be able to do anything, so I came straight off to tell you."

"You had better send your gondola home, Matteo. It may be wanted. We will paddle out to the lagoon and talk it over. Surely there must be something to be done, if we could but think of it.

"This is terrible, indeed, Matteo," he repeated, after they had sat without speaking for some minutes. "One feels quite helpless and bewildered. To think that only yesterday evening we were laughing and chatting with them, and that now they are lost, and in the power of that villain Mocenigo, who you may be sure is at the bottom of it.

"By the way," he said suddenly, "do you know where he has taken up his abode?"

"I heard that he was at Botonda, near Chioggia, a week ago, but whether he is there still I have not the least idea."

"It seems to me that the thing to do is to find him, and keep him in sight. He will probably have them hidden away somewhere, and will not go near them for some time, for he will know that he will be suspected, and perhaps watched."

"But why should he not force Maria to marry him at once?" Matteo said. "You see, when he has once made her his wife he will be safe, for my cousin would be driven then to make terms with him for her sake."

"He may try that," Francis said; "but he must know that Maria has plenty of spirit, and may refuse to marry him, threaten her as he will. He may think that, after she has been kept confined for some time, and finds that there is no hope of escape, except by consenting to be his wife, she may give way. But in any case, it seems to me that the thing to be done is to find Ruggiero, and to watch his movements."

"I have no doubt my cousin has already taken steps in that direction," Matteo said, "and I feel sure that, in this case, he will receive the support of every influential man in Venice, outside the Mocenigo family and their connections. The carrying off of ladies, in broad daylight, will be regarded as a personal injury in every family. The last attempt was different. I do not say it was not bad enough, but it is not like decoying girls from home by a false message. No one could feel safe, if such a deed as this were not severely punished."

"Let us go back again, Matteo. It is no use our thinking of anything until we know what has really been done, and you are sure to be able to learn, at home, what steps have been taken."

On reaching home Matteo learned that Polani, accompanied by two members of the council, had already started in one of the swiftest of the state galleys for the mainland. A council had been hastily summoned, and, upon hearing Polani's narrative, had dispatched two of their number, with an official of the republic, to Botonda. If Ruggiero was found to be still there, he was to be kept a prisoner in the house in which he was staying, under the strictest watch. If he had left, orders were to be sent, to every town in the Venetian dominions on the mainland, for his arrest when discovered, and in that case he was to be sent a prisoner, strongly guarded, to Venice.

Other galleys had been simultaneously dispatched to the various ports, ordering a strict search of every boat arriving or leaving, and directing a minute investigation to be made as to the occupants of every boat that had arrived during the evening or night. The fact that a thousand ducats were offered, for information which would lead to the recovery of the girls, was also to be published far and wide.

The news of the abduction had spread, and the greatest indignation was excited in the city. The sailors from the port of Malamocco came over in great numbers. They regarded this outrage on the family of the great merchant as almost a personal insult. Stones were thrown at the windows of the Palazzo Mocenigo, and an attack would have been made upon it, had not the authorities sent down strong guards to protect it. Persons belonging to that house, and the families connected with it, were assaulted in the streets, and all Venice was in an uproar.

"There is one comfort," Giuseppi said, when he heard from Francis what had taken place. "Just at present, Mocenigo will have enough to think about his own affairs without troubling about you. I have been in a tremble ever since that day, and have dreamed bad dreams every night."

"You are more nervous for me than I am for myself, Giuseppi; but I have been careful too, for although Ruggiero himself was away his friends are here, and active, too, as you see by this successful attempt. But I think that at present they are likely to let matters sleep. Public opinion is greatly excited over the affair, and as, if I were found with a stab in my back, it would, after what has passed, be put down to them, I think they will leave me alone."

"I do hope, father," Francis said at breakfast the next morning, "that there may be no opportunity of sending me back to England, until something is heard of the Polanis."

"I have somewhat changed my mind, Francis, as to that matter. After what Signor Polani said the other day, I feel that it would be foolish for me to adhere to that plan. With his immense trade and business connections he can do almost anything for you, and such an introduction into business is so vastly better than your entering my shop in the city, that it is best, in every way, that you should stay here for the present. Of course, for the time he will be able to think of nothing but his missing daughters; but at any rate, you can remain here until he has leisure to pursue the subject, and to state, further than he did the other day, what he proposes for you. My own business is a good one for a London trader, but it is nothing by the side of the transactions of the merchant princes at Venice, among the very first of whom Signor Polani is reckoned."

Francis was greatly pleased at his father's words. He had, ever since Polani had spoken to him, been pondering the matter in his mind. He knew that to enter business under his protection would be one of the best openings that even Venice could afford; but his father was slow to change his plans, and Francis greatly feared that he would adhere to his original plan.

"I was hoping, father, that you would think favourably of what Signor Polani said, although, of course, I kept silence, knowing that you would do what was best for me. And now I would ask you if you will, until this matter is cleared up, excuse me from my tasks. I should learn nothing did I continue at them, for my mind would be ever running upon Signor Polani's daughters, and I should be altogether too restless to apply myself. It seems to me, too, that I might, as I row here and there in my gondola, obtain some clue as to their place of concealment."

"I do not see how you could do that, Francis, when so many others, far better qualified than yourself, will be on the lookout. Still, as I agree with you that you are not likely to apply your mind diligently to your tasks, and as, indeed, you will shortly be giving them up altogether, I grant your request."

Polani returned in the evening to Venice. Ruggiero Mocenigo had been found. He professed great indignation at the accusation brought against him, of being concerned in the abduction of the ladies, and protested furiously when he heard that, until they were found, he was to consider himself a prisoner. Signor Polani considered that his indignation was feigned, but he had no doubt as to the reality of his anger at finding that he was to be confined to his house under a guard.

Immediately after his return, Polani sent his gondola for Francis. He was pacing up and down the room when the lad arrived.

"Your suspicions have turned out correct, as you see, Francis. Would to Heaven I had acted upon them at once, and then this would not have happened. It seemed to me altogether absurd, when you spoke to me, that the woman I have for years treated as a friend should thus betray me. And yet your warning made me uneasy, so much so that I set off myself to fetch them home at five o'clock, only to find that I was too late. I scarcely know why I have sent for you, Francis, except that as I have found, to my cost, that you were more clear sighted in this matter than I, I want to know what you think now, and whether any plan offering even a chance of success has occurred to you. That they have been carried off by the friends of Mocenigo I have no doubt whatever."

"I fear, signor," Francis said, "that there is little hope of my thinking of anything that has not already occurred to you. It seems to me hardly likely that they can be in the city, although, of course, they may be confined in the house of Mocenigo's agents. Still, they would be sure that you would offer large rewards for their discovery, and would be more likely to take them right away. Besides, I should think that it was Mocenigo's intention to join them, wherever they may be, as soon as he learned that they were in the hands of his accomplices. Your fortunate discovery that they had gone, so soon after they had been carried off, and your going straight to him armed with the order of the council, probably upset his calculations, for it is likely enough that his agents had not arrived at the house, and that he learned from you, for the first time, that his plans had succeeded. Had you arrived two or three hours later, you might have found him gone."

"That is what I calculated, Francisco. His agents had but four hours' start of me. They would, no doubt, carry the girls to the place of concealment chosen, and would then bear the news to him; whereas I, going direct in one of the state gondolas, might reach him before they did, and I feel assured that I did so.

"It was nigh midnight when I arrived, but he was still up, and I doubt not awaiting the arrival of the villains he had employed. My first step was to set a watch round the house, with the order to arrest any who might come and inquire for him. No one, however, came.

"The news, indeed, of the sudden arrival of a state galley, at that hour, had caused some excitement in the place, and his agents might well have heard of it upon their arrival. I agree with you in thinking they are not in the town, but this makes the search all the more difficult. The question is, what ought we to do next?"

"The reward that you have offered will certainly bring you news, signor, if any, save those absolutely concerned, have observed anything suspicious; but I should send to all the fishing villages, on the islets and on the mainland, to publish the news of the reward you have offered. Beyond that, I do not see that anything can be done; and I, too, have thought of nothing else since Matteo brought me the news of their being carried off. It will be of no use, that I can see, going among the fishermen and questioning them, because, with such a reward in view, it is certain that anyone who has anything to tell will come, of his own accord, to do so."

"I know that is the case already, Francisco. The authorities have been busy all day with the matter, and a score of reports as to closed gondolas being seen have reached them; but so far nothing has come of it. Many of these gondolas have been traced to their destinations, but in no case was there anything to justify suspicion. Happily, as long as Mocenigo is in confinement, I feel that no actual harm will happen to the girls; but the villain is as crafty as a fox, and may elude the vigilance of the officer in charge of him. I am going to the council, presently, to urge that he should be brought here as a prisoner; but from what I hear there is little chance of the request being complied with. His friends are already declaiming on the injustice of a man being treated as a criminal, when there is no shadow of proof forthcoming against him; and the disturbances last night have angered many who have no great friendship for him, but who are indignant at the attack of the populace upon the house of a noble. So you see that there is but faint chance that they would bring him hither a prisoner."

"I think, sir, that were I in your case, I should put some trusty men to watch round the house where he is confined; so that in case he should escape the vigilance of his guards they might seize upon him. Everything depends, as you say, upon his being kept in durance."

"I will do so, Francisco, at once. I will send to two of my officers at the port, and tell them to pick out a dozen men on whom they can rely, to proceed to Botonda, and to watch closely everyone who enters or leaves the house, without at the same time making themselves conspicuous. At any rate, they will be handy there in case Mocenigo's friends attempt to rescue him by force, which might be done with success, for the house he occupies stands at a short distance out of the town, and the official in charge of Mocenigo has only eight men with him.

"Yes, your advice is excellent, and I will follow it at once. Should any other idea occur to you, pray let me know it immediately. You saved my daughters once, and although I know there is no reason why it should be so, still, I feel a sort of belief that you may, somehow, be instrumental in their again being brought back to me."

"I will do my best, sir, you may depend upon it," Francis said earnestly. "Were they my own sisters, I could not feel more strongly interested in their behalf."

Francis spent the next week almost entirely in his gondola. Starting soon after daybreak with Giuseppi, he would row across to the villages on the mainland, and make inquiries of all sorts there; or would visit the little groups of fishermen's huts, built here and there on posts among the shallows. He would scan every house as he passed it, with the vague hope that a face might appear at the window, or a hand be waved for assistance. But, during all that time, he had found nothing which seemed to offer the slightest clue, nor were the inquiries set on foot by Signor Polani more successful. Every piece of information which seemed to bear, in the slightest degree, upon the affair was investigated, but in no case was it found of the slightest utility.

One evening he was returning late, tired by the long day's work, and discouraged with his utter want of success, when, just as he had passed under the Ponto Maggiore, the lights on the bridge fell on the faces of the sitters in a gondola coming the other way. They were a man and a woman. The latter was closely veiled. But the night was close and oppressive, and, just at the moment when Francis' eyes fell upon her, she lifted her veil for air. Francis recognized her instantly. For a moment he stopped rowing, and then dipped his oar in as before. Directly the other gondola passed through the bridge behind him, and his own had got beyond the circle of light, he swept it suddenly round.

Giuseppi gave an exclamation of surprise.

"Giuseppi, we have luck at last. Did you notice that gondola we met just now? The woman sitting in it is Castaldi, the woman who betrayed the signoras."

"What shall we do, Messer Francisco?" Giuseppi, who had become almost as interested in the search as his master, asked. "There was only a single gondolier and one other man. If we take them by surprise we can master them."

"That will not do, Giuseppi. The woman would refuse to speak, and though they could force her to do so in the dungeons, the girls would be sure to be removed the moment it was known she was captured. We must follow them, and see where they go to. Let us get well behind them, so that we can just make them out in the distance. If they have a suspicion that they are being followed, they will land her at the first steps and slip away from us."

"They are landing now, signor," Giuseppi exclaimed directly afterwards. "Shall we push on and overtake them on shore?"

"It is too late, Giuseppi. They are a hundred and fifty yards away, and would have mixed in the crowd, and be lost, long before we should get ashore and follow them. Row on fast, but not over towards that side. If the gondola moves off, we will make straight for the steps and try to follow them, though our chance of hitting upon them in the narrow lanes and turnings is slight indeed.

"But if, as I hope, the gondola stops at the steps, most likely they will return to it in time. So we will row in to the bank a hundred yards farther up the canal and wait."

The persons who had been seen in the gondola had disappeared when they came abreast of it, and the gondolier had seated himself in the boat, with the evident intention of waiting. Francis steered his gondola at a distance of a few yards from it as he shot past, but did not abate his speed, and continued to row till they were three or four hundred yards farther up the canal. Then he turned the gondola, and paddled noiselessly back until he could see the outline of the boat he was watching.

An hour elapsed before any movement was visible. Then Francis heard the sound of footsteps, and could just make out the figures of persons descending the steps and entering the gondola. Then the boat moved out into the middle of the canal, where a few boats were still passing to and fro. Francis kept his gondola close by the bank, so as to be in the deep shade of the houses. The boat they were following again passed under the Ponto Maggiore, and for some distance followed the line of the Grand Canal.

"Keep your eye upon it, Giuseppi. It is sure to turn off one way or the other soon, and if it is too far ahead of us when it does so, then it may give us the slip altogether."

But the gondola continued its course the whole length of the canal, and then straight on until, nearly opposite Saint Mark's, it passed close to a larger gondola, with four rowers, coming slowly in the other direction; and it seemed to Francis that the two boats paused when opposite each other, and that a few words were exchanged.

Then the boat they were watching turned out straight into the lagoon. It was rather lighter here than in the canal, bordered on each side by houses, and Francis did not turn the head of his gondola for a minute or two.

"It will be very difficult to keep them in sight out here without their making us out," Giuseppi said.

"Yes, and it is likely enough that they are only going out there in order that they may be quite sure that they are not followed, before striking off to the place they want to go to. They may possibly have made us out, and guess that we are tracking them. They would be sure to keep their eyes and ears open."

"I can only just make them out now, Messer Francisco, and as we shall have the buildings behind us, they will not be able to see us as well as we can see them. I think we can go now."

"We will risk it, at any rate, Giuseppi. I have lost sight of them already, and it will never do to let them give us the slip."

They dipped their oars in the water, and the gondola darted out from the shore. They had not gone fifty strokes when they heard the sound of oars close at hand.

"To the right, Giuseppi, hard!" Francis cried as he glanced over his shoulder.

A sweep with both oars brought the gondola's head, in a moment, almost at right angles to the course that she had been pursuing; and the next sent her dancing on a new line, just as a four-oared gondola swept down upon them, missing their stern by only three or four feet. Had they been less quick in turning, the iron prow would have cut right through their light boat.

Giuseppi burst into a torrent of vituperation at the carelessness of the gondoliers who had so nearly run into them, but Francis silenced him at once.

"Row, Giuseppi. It was done on purpose. It is the gondola the other spoke to."

Their assailant was turning also, and in a few seconds was in pursuit. Francis understood it now. The gondola they had been following had noticed them, and had informed their friends, waiting off Saint Mark's, of the fact. Intent upon watching the receding boat, he had paid no further attention to the four-oared craft, which had made a turn, and lay waiting in readiness to run them down, should they follow in the track of the other boat.

Francis soon saw that the craft behind them was a fast one, and rowed by men who were first-rate gondoliers. Fast as his own boat was flying through the water, the other gained upon them steadily. He was heading now for the entrance to the Grand Canal, for their pursuer, in the wider sweep he had made in turning, was nearer to the Piazza than they were, and cut off their flight in that direction.

"Keep cool, Giuseppi," he said. "They will be up to us in a minute or two. When their bow is within a yard or two of us, and I say, 'Now!' sweep her head straight round towards the lagoon. We can turn quicker than they can. Then let them gain upon us, and we will then turn again."

The gondola in pursuit came up hand over hand. Francis kept looking over his shoulder, and when he saw its bow gliding up within a few feet of her stern he exclaimed "Now!" and, with a sudden turn, the gondola again swept out seaward.

Their pursuer rushed on for a length or two before she could sweep round, while a volley of imprecations and threats burst from three men who were standing up in her with drawn swords. Francis and Giuseppi were now rowing less strongly, and gaining breath for their next effort. When the gondola again came up to them they swept round to the left, and as their pursuers followed they headed for the Grand Canal.

"Make for the steps of Santa Maria church. We will jump out there and trust to our feet."

The two lads put out all their strength now. They were some three boats' lengths ahead before their pursuers were fairly on their track. They were now rowing for life, for they knew that they could hardly succeed in doubling again, and that the gondola behind them was so well handled, that they could not gain on it at the turnings were they to venture into the narrow channels. It was a question of speed alone, and so hard did they row that the gondola in pursuit gained but slowly on them, and they were still two lengths ahead when they dashed up to the steps of the church.

Simultaneously they sprang on shore, leaped up the steps, and dashed off at the top of their speed, hearing, as they did so, a crash as the gondola ran into their light craft. There was a moment's delay, as the men had to step across their boat to gain the shore, and they were fifty yards ahead before they heard the sound of their pursuers' feet on the stone steps; but they were lightly clad and shoeless, and carried nothing to impede their movements, and they had therefore little fear of being overtaken.

After racing on at the top of their speed for a few minutes, they stopped and listened. The sound of their pursuers' footsteps died away in the distance; and, after taking a few turns to put them off their track, they pursued their way at a more leisurely pace.

"They have smashed the gondola," Giuseppi said with a sob, for he was very proud of the light craft.

"Never mind the gondola," Francis said cheerfully. "If they had smashed a hundred it would not matter."

"But the woman has got away and we have learned nothing," Giuseppi said, surprised at his master's cheerfulness.

"I think we have learned something, Giuseppi. I think we have learned everything. I have no doubt the girls are confined in that hut on San Nicolo. I wonder I never thought of it before; but I made so sure that they would be taken somewhere close to where Mocenigo was staying, that it never occurred to me that they might hide them out there. I ought to have known that that was just the thing they would do, for while the search would be keen among the islets near the land, and the villages there, no one would think of looking for them on the seaward islands.

"I have no doubt they are there now. That woman came ashore to report to his friends, and that four-oared boat which has chased us was in waiting off Saint Mark's, to attack any boat that might be following them.

"We will go to Signor Polani at once and tell him what has happened. I suppose it is about one o'clock now, but I have not noticed the hour. It was past eleven before we first met the gondola, and we must have been a good deal more than an hour lying there waiting for them."

A quarter of an hour's walking took them to the palazzo of Polani. They rang twice at the bell at the land entrance, before a face appeared at the little window of the door, and asked who was there.

"I wish to see Signor Polani at once," Francis said.

"The signor retired to rest an hour ago," the man said.

"Never mind that," Francis replied. "I am Francis Hammond, and I have important news to give him."

As soon as the servitor recognized Francis' voice, he unbarred the door.

"Have you news of the ladies?" he asked eagerly.

"I have news which will, I hope, lead to something," Francis replied.

A moment later the voice of Polani himself, who, although he had retired to his room, had not yet gone to sleep, was heard at the top of the grand stairs, inquiring who it was who had come so late; for although men had been arriving all day, with reports from the various islands and villages, he thought that no one would come at this hour unless his news were important.

Francis at once answered:

"It is I, Signor Polani, Francis Hammond. I have news which I think may be of importance, although I may be mistaken. Still, it is certainly news that may lead to something."

The merchant hurried down.

"What is it, Francisco? What have you learned?"

"I have seen the woman Castaldi, and have followed her. I do not know for certain where she was going, for we have been chased by a large gondola, and have narrowly escaped with our lives. Still, I have a clue to their whereabouts."

Francis then related the events of the evening.

"But why did you not run into the boat and give the alarm at once, Francisco? Any gondolas passing would have given their assistance, when you declared who she was, for the affair is the talk of the city. If that woman were in our power we should soon find means to make her speak."

"Yes, signor; but the moment she was known to be in your power, you may be sure that they would remove your daughters from the place where they have been hiding them. I thought, therefore, the best plan would be to track them. No doubt we should have succeeded in doing so, had it not been for the attack upon us by another gondola."

"You are right, no doubt, Francisco. Still, it is unfortunate, for I do not see that we are now any nearer than we were before, except that we know that this woman is in the habit of coming into the city."

"I think we are nearer, sir, for I had an adventure some time ago that may afford a clue to their hiding place."

He then told the merchant how he had, one evening, taken a man out to San Nicolo, and had discovered that a hut in that island was used as a meeting place by various persons, among whom was Ruggiero Mocenigo.

"I might have thought of the place before, signor; but, in fact, it never entered my mind. From the first, we considered it so certain that the men who carried off your daughters would take them to some hiding place where Mocenigo could speedily join them, that San Nicolo never entered my mind. I own that it was very stupid, for it seems now to me that the natural thing for them to do, would be to take them in the very opposite direction to that in which the search for them would be made."

The story had been frequently interrupted by exclamations of surprise by Polani. At its conclusion, he laid his hand on Francis' shoulder.

"My dear boy," he said, "How can I thank you! You seem to me to be born to be the preserver of my daughters. I cannot doubt that your suspicion is correct, and that they are confined in this hut at San Nicolo. How fortunate that you did not denounce this conspiracy--for conspiracy no doubt it is--that you discovered, for, had you done so, some other place would have been selected for the girls' prison."

"I would not be too sanguine, sir. The girls may not be in this hut, still we may come on some clue there which may lead us to them. If not, we will search the islands on that side as closely as we have done those on the mainland."

"Now, shall I send for the gondoliers and set out at once? There are ten or twelve men in the house, and it is hardly likely that they will place a guard over them of anything like this strength, as of course they will be anxious to avoid observation by the islanders."

"I do not think I would do anything tonight, sir," Francis said. "The gondola that chased us will be on the alert. They cannot, of course, suspect in the slightest that we have any clue to the hiding place of your daughters. Still, they might think that, if we were really pursuing the other gondola, and had recognized the woman Castaldi, we might bring the news to you, and that a stir might be made. They may therefore be watching to see if anything comes of it; and if they saw a bustle and gondolas setting out taking the direction of the island, they might set off and get there first, for it is a very fast craft, and remove your daughters before we reach the hut.

"I should say wait till morning. They may be watching your house now, and if, in an hour or two, they see all is quiet, they will no doubt retire with the belief that all danger is at an end. Then, in the morning, I would embark the men in two or three gondolas, but I would not start from your own steps, for no doubt your house is watched. Let the men go out singly, and embark at a distance from here, and not at the same place. Once out upon the lagoon, they should row quietly towards San Nicolo, keeping a considerable distance apart, the men lying down in the bottom as the boats approach the island, so that if anyone is on watch he will have no suspicion.

"As I am the only one that knows the position of the hut, I will be with you in the first gondola. We will not land near the hut, but pass by, and land at the other end of the island. The other gondolas will slowly follow us, and land at the same spot. Then three or four men can go along by the sea face, with orders to watch any boats hauled up upon the shore there, and stop any party making down towards them. The rest of us will walk straight to the hut, and, as it lies among sand hills, I hope we shall be able to get quite close to it before our approach is discovered."

"An excellent plan, Francisco, though I am so impatient that the night will seem endless to me; but certainly your plan is the best. Even if the house is watched, and you were seen to enter, if all remains perfectly quiet they will naturally suppose that the news you brought was not considered of sufficient importance to lead to any action. You will, of course, remain here till morning?"

"I cannot do that, sir, though I will return the first thing. There is, lying on my table, a paper with the particulars and names of the persons I saw meet in this hut, and a request to my father that, if I do not return in the morning, he will at once lay this before the council. I place it there every day when I go out, in order that, if I should be seized and carried off by Mocenigo's people, I should have some means of forcing them to let me go.

"Although I know absolutely nothing of the nature of the conspiracy, they will not know how much I am aware of, or what particulars I may have given in the document; and as I could name to them those present, and among them is the envoy of the King of Hungary, now in the city, they would hardly dare harm me, when they knew that if they did so this affair would be brought before the council."

"It was an excellent precaution, Francisco. Why, you are as prudent and thoughtful as you are courageous!"

"It was not likely to be of much use, sir," Francis said modestly. "I was very much more likely to get a stab in the back than to be carried off. Still, it was just possible that Mocenigo might himself like to see his vengeance carried out, and it was therefore worth my while guarding against it. But, as you see, it will be necessary for me to be back sometime before morning."

"At any rate, Francisco, you had better wait here until morning breaks. Your room is not likely to be entered for some hours after that; so while I am preparing for our expedition, you can go out and make your way to the Grand Canal, hail an early gondola, and be put down at your own steps, when, as you have told me, you can enter the house without disturbing anyone. Then you can remove that paper, and return here in the gondola. We will start at seven. There will be plenty of boats about by that time, and the lagoon will be dotted by the fishermen's craft, so that our gondolas will attract no attention."

"Perhaps that will be the best plan, signor; and, indeed, I should not be sorry for a few hours' sleep, for Giuseppi and I have been in our boat since a very early hour in the morning, and were pretty well tired out before this last adventure began."

Chapter 6:
The Hut On San Nicolo.

At seven o'clock all was in readiness for a start. Signor Polani set out alone in his gondola, and picked up Francis, and four men, at a secluded spot some distance from the house. A messenger had been sent, two hours before, to the captain of one of the merchant ships lying in the port. He at once put ten men into a large boat, and rowed down to within half a mile of the island. Here a grapnel was thrown overboard, most of the men lay down in the bottom, and the captain, according to his instructions, kept a sharp lookout to see that no boat left San Nicolo--his instructions being to overhaul any boat coming out, and to see that no one was concealed on board it.

There he remained until Polani's gondola rowed past him. After it had gone a few hundred yards, the grapnel was got up, the men took to their oars and followed the gondola, keeping so far behind that it would not seem there was any connection between them.

Francis made for the narrow channel which separated San Nicolo from the next island, and then directed the gondola to be run ashore, where a low sand hill, close by, hid them from the sight of anyone on the lookout. A few minutes later the ship's boat arrived.

Francis now led the way direct for the hut, accompanied by Polani and six men, while four sailors advanced, at a distance of a hundred yards on either flank, to cut off anyone making for the water.

"We may as well go fast," he said, "for we can scarcely get there without being seen by a lookout, should there be one on the sand hills, and the distance is so short that there will be no possibility of their carrying your daughters off, before we get there."

"The faster the better," the merchant said. "This suspense is terrible."

Accordingly, the party started at a brisk run. Francis kept his eyes on the spot where he believed the hut lay.

"I see no one anywhere near there," he said, as they came over one of the sand ridges. "Had there been anyone on the watch I think we should see him now."

On they ran, until, passing over one of the sand hills, Francis came to a standstill. The hut lay in the hollow below them.

"There is the house, signor. Now we shall soon know."

They dashed down the short slope, and gathered round the door.

"Within there, open!" the merchant shouted, hammering with the hilt of his sword on the door.

All was silent within.

"Break it down!" he said; and two of the sailors, who had brought axes with them, began to hew away at the door.

A few blows, and it suddenly opened, and two men dressed as fishermen appeared in the doorway.

"What means this attack upon the house of quiet people?" they demanded.

"Bind them securely," Polani said, as he rushed in, followed closely by Francis, while those who followed seized the men.

Polani paused as he crossed the threshold, with a cry of disappointment--the hut was empty. Francis was almost equally disappointed.

"If they are not here, they are near by," Francis said to Polani. "Do not give up hope. I am convinced they are not far off; and if we search we may find a clue. Better keep your men outside. We can search more thoroughly by ourselves."

The merchant told his men, who had seized and were binding the two occupants of the hut, to remain outside. The inside of the hut differed in no way from the ordinary dwelling of fishermen, except that a large table stood in the middle of it, and there were some benches against the walls. Some oars stood in one corner, and some nets were piled close to them. A fire burned in the open hearth, and a pot hung over it, and two others stood on the hearth.

"Let us see what they have got here," Francis said, while the merchant leaned against the table with an air of profound depression, paying no attention to what he was doing.

"A soup," Francis said, lifting the lid from the pot over the fire, "and, by the smell, a good one."

Then he lifted the other pots simmering among the burning brands.

"A ragout of kid and a boiled fish. Signor Polani, this is no fisherman's meal. Either these men expect visitors of a much higher degree than themselves, or your daughters are somewhere close.

"Oh! there is a door."

"It can lead nowhere," Polani said. "The sand is piled up to the roof on that side of the house."

"It is," Francis agreed; "but there may be a lower room there, completely covered with the sand. At any rate, we will see."

He pushed against the door, but it did not give in the slightest.

"It may be the sand," he said. "It may be bolts."

He went to the outside door, and called in the sailors with the hatchets.

"Break open that door," he said.

"There is a space behind," he exclaimed, as the first blow was given. "It is hollow, I swear. It would be a different sound altogether if sand was piled up against it."

A dozen blows and the fastenings gave, and, sword in hand, the merchant and Francis rushed through.

Both gave a shout of delight. They were in a room built out at the back of the hut. It was richly furnished, and hangings of Eastern stuffs covered the walls. A burning lamp hung from the ceiling. Two men stood irresolute with drawn swords, having apparently turned round just as the door gave way; for as it did so, two figures struggled to their feet from a couch behind them, for some shawls had been wrapped round their heads, and with a cry of delight rushed forward to meet their rescuers. Seated at the end of the couch, with bowed down head, was another female figure.

"Maria--Giulia!" the merchant exclaimed, as, dropping his sword, he clasped his daughters in his arms.

Francis, followed by the two sailors with hatchets, advanced towards the men.

"Drop your swords and surrender," he said. "Resistance is useless. There are a dozen men outside."

The men threw their swords down on the ground.

"Lead them outside, and bind them securely," Francis said.

For the next minute or two, few words were spoken. The girls sobbed with delight on their father's breast, while he himself was too moved to do more than murmur words of love and thankfulness. Francis went quietly out and spoke to the captain, who went in to the inner room, touched the sitting figure on the shoulder, and, taking her by the arm, led her outside.

"Come in, Francis," Polani called a minute later.

"My dears, it is not me you must thank for your rescue. It is your English friend here who has again restored you to me. It is to him we owe our happiness, and that you, my child, are saved from the dreadful fate of being forced to be the wife of that villain Mocenigo.

"Embrace him, my dears, as a brother, for he has done more than a brother for you. And now tell me all that has happened since I last saw you."

"You know, father, the message that was brought us, that you had been hurt and wanted us home?"

"Yes, my dears, that I learned soon afterwards. I went at five o'clock to fetch you home, and found that you had gone, and why."

"Well, father, directly we had taken our seats in the cabin of the gondola, our gouvernante closed the doors, and soon afterwards she slid to the two shutters before the windows. We cried out in surprise at finding ourselves in the dark, but she bade us be quiet, in a tone quite different to any in which she had ever spoken to us before. We were both frightened, and tried to push back the shutters and open the door, but they were fastened firmly. I suppose there was some spring which held them. Then we screamed; but I could feel that the inside was all thickly padded. I suppose our voices could not be heard outside. I thought so, because once I thought I heard the gondoliers singing, but it was so faint that I could not be sure. Then the air seemed stiflingly close, and I fainted; and when I came to myself one of the windows was open, and Giulia said she had promised we would not scream, but I think we were beyond the canals then, for I could see nothing but the sky as we passed along. When I was better the windows were almost shut again, so that we could not see out, though a little air could get in; then the gondola went on for a long time.

"At last it stopped, and she said we must be blindfolded. We said we would not submit to it, and she told us unless we let her do it, the men would do it. So we submitted, and she wrapped shawls closely over our heads. Then we were helped ashore, and walked some distance. At last the shawls were taken off our heads, and we found ourselves here, and here we have been ever since."

"You have not been ill treated in any way, my children?" the merchant asked anxiously.

"Not at all, father. Until today, nobody has been into this room besides ourselves and that woman. The door was generally left a little open for air, for you see there are no windows here. She used to go into the next room and come back with our food. We could see men moving about in there, but they were very quiet, and all spoke in low tones.

"You may think how we upbraided our gouvernante for her treachery, and threatened her with your anger. She told us we should never be found, and that I might as well make up my mind to marry Ruggiero Mocenigo, for if I did not consent quietly, means would be found to compel me to do so. I said I would die first, but she used to laugh a cruel laugh, and say he would soon be here with the priest, and that it mattered not whether I said yes or no. The ceremony would be performed, and then Ruggiero would sail away with me to the East, and I should be glad enough then to make peace between him and you. But he never came. I think she became anxious, for she went away twice for three or four hours, and locked us in here when she went.

"That, father, is all we know about it. Where are we?"

"You are at San Nicolo."

"On the island!" Maria exclaimed in surprise. "She told us we were on the mainland. And now, how did you find us?"

"I will tell you as we go home, Maria."

"Yes, that will be better, father. Giulia and I long for a breath of fresh air, and the sight of the blue sky."

"Giulia has not had so much to frighten her as you have," her father said.

"Yes, I have, father; for she said I was to go across the seas with Maria, and that Ruggiero would soon find a husband for me among his friends. I told her she was a wicked woman, over and over again, and we told her that we were sure you would forgive, and even reward her, if she would take us back again to you. When she was away, we thought we would try to make our escape behind, and we made a little hole in the boards; but the sand came pouring in, and we found we were underground, though how we got there we didn't know, for we had not come down any steps. So we had to give up the idea of escape."

"You are partly underground," her father said, "for, as you will see when you get out, the sand has drifted up at the back of the hut to the roof, and has altogether hidden this part of the hut; so that we did not know that there was more than one room, and I should never have thought of breaking into that door, had it not been for Francisco. And now come along, my dears. Let us wait here no longer."

The sailors and servitors broke into a cheer as the girls came out of the hut.

"Shall we put a torch to this place?" Francis asked Polani.

"No, Francisco. It must be searched thoroughly first.

"Captain Lontano, do you order four of your men to remain here, until some of the officials of the state arrive. If anyone comes before that, they must seize them and detain them as prisoners. The state will investigate the matter to the bottom."

Now that they were in the open air, the merchant could see that the close confinement and anxiety had told greatly upon his daughters. Both were pale and hollow eyed, and looked as if they had suffered a long illness. Seeing how shaken they were, he ordered one of the retainers to go to the gondola, and tell the men to row it round to the nearest point to the hut. The party then walked along down to the shore.

In a few minutes the gondola arrived. Polani, his two daughters, and Francis took their places in it. The four men, bound hand and foot, were laid in the bottom of the ship's boat; the gouvernante was made to take her place there also, and the sailors were told to follow closely behind the gondola, which was rowed at a very slow pace.

On the way, Polani told his daughters of the manner in which Francis had discovered the place of concealment.

"Had it not been for him, my dears, we should certainly not have found you, and that villain would have carried out his plans, sooner or later. He would either have given his guards the slip, or, when no evidence was forthcoming against him, they would have been removed. He would then have gone outside the jurisdiction of the republic, obtained a ship with a crew of desperadoes, sailed round to the seaward side of San Nicolo, and carried you off. Nothing could have saved you, and your resistance would, as that woman told you, have been futile."

"We shall be grateful to you all our lives, Francisco," Maria said. "We shall pray for you always, night and morning.

"Shall we not, Giulia?"

"Yes, indeed," the young girl said simply. "We shall love him all our lives."

"Answer for yourself, Giulia," Maria said with a laugh, her spirits returning in the bright sunshine and fresh air. "When Francisco asks for my love, it will be quite soon enough to say what I think about it."

"I should never have courage enough to do that, signora. I know what you would say too well."

"What should I say?" Maria asked.

"You would say I was an impudent boy."

Maria laughed.

"I cannot think of you as a boy any longer, Francisco," she said more gravely. "I have, perhaps, regarded you as a boy till now, though you did save us so bravely before; but you see you are only my own age, and a girl always looks upon a boy of her own age as ever so much younger than she is herself. Besides, too, you have none of the airs of being a man, which some of my cousins have; and never pay compliments or say pretty things, but seem altogether like a younger brother. But I shall think you a boy no more. I know you better now."

"But I am a boy," Francis said, "and I don't want to be thought anything else. In England we keep young longer than they do here, and a boy of my age would not think of speaking to his elders, unless he was first addressed.

"What are you going to do with your prisoners, signor?"

"I shall take them direct to my house, and then go and report the recovery of my daughters, and their capture. Officials will at once be sent, with a gondola, to take them off to the prison. There can be no question now as to the part Mocenigo has played in this business, and no doubt he will be brought here a prisoner at once. Even his nearest connections will not dare to defend conduct so outrageous, especially when public indignation has been so excited.

"You do not know, girls, what a stir has been caused in the city on your account. If it had not been for the citizen guard, I believe the Mocenigo Palace would have been burned down; and Ruggiero's connections have scarcely dared to show their faces in the streets, since you have been missing. You see, every father of a family felt personally grieved, for if the nobles were permitted, with impunity, to carry off the daughters of citizens, who could feel safe?

"When this is all over I shall take you, for a time, back to our home in Corfu. It is not good for girls to be the subject of public talk and attention."

"I shall be very glad, father," Giulia said. "I love our home at Corfu, with its gardens and flowers, far better than the palazzo here. The air is always soft and balmy, while here it is so hot sometimes by day, and so damp and foggy in the evening. I shall be glad to go back again."

"And you, Maria?"

"I shall be very happy there, father, but I like Venice best."

"You are getting to an age to enjoy gaiety, Maria; and it is natural you should do so. However, it will not be necessary for you to be long absent. In a city like Venice there are always fresh subjects for talk, and the most exciting piece of scandal is but a three days' wonder. A few weeks at Corfu will restore your nerves, which cannot but have been shaken by what you have gone through, and you will come back here more disposed than ever to appreciate the gaieties of Venice."

"As long as it is for only a few weeks, father, I shall not care; for you know I am very fond, too, of our beautiful home there. Still, I do like Venice."

They had now reached the steps of the Palazzo Polani. They had not proceeded by way of the Grand Canal, as the merchant was anxious that his daughters should reach their home unrecognized, as, had they been noticed, it would have given rise to no little excitement, and they had had more than enough of this, and needed quiet and repose. Besides, until the prisoners were in the safe custody of the officials of the state, it was in every way desirable that the events of the morning should remain unknown.

Their return home created quite a tumult of joy in the house. The preparations that had been made had been kept a profound secret, as the merchant could not be sure but that some other member of his household was in the pay of Mocenigo. Thus, until the girls alighted at the steps, none in the house were aware that any clue had been obtained as to their hiding place. The women ran down with cries of joy. The men would have shouted and cheered, had not Polani held up his hand.

"The signoras have had more than enough excitement," he said. "They are grateful to you for your goodwill and affection, but for the present they need quiet. They may have more to go through today. I pray you that no word, as to their return, be said outside the house. I would not that the news were whispered in the city, till the seignory decide what is to be done in the matter."

As soon as the girls had gone upstairs to their rooms, the ship's boat came alongside, and the prisoners were carried into the house, glances of indignation and anger being cast at the gouvernante, who had, as soon as she was placed on board the boat, closely veiled herself; and some of the women broke out into threats and imprecations.

"Captain Lontano, the servants will show you a room where your men can guard the prisoners. You had better remain with them yourself. Let no one, except your own men, enter the room."

Giuseppi was on the steps, and Francis stepped up to him and eagerly asked, "What news of the gondola?"

"I found her, stove in and full of water, behind the piles close to the steps. Someone must have pushed her there, to be out of the way of the traffic. She has several holes in her bottom, besides being stove in at the gunwale where the other boat struck her. They must have thrust the ends of their oars through her planks, out of sheer spite, when they found that we had escaped them. Father and I have towed her round to your steps, but I doubt whether she is worth repairing."

"Well, we can't help it, Giuseppi. She has done her work; and if every two ducats I lay out were to bring in as good a harvest, I should have no reason to complain."

Having seen the prisoners safely placed, the merchant returned.

"I think, Francisco, you must go with me. They will be sure to want to question you."

"I shall have to say what were my reasons for thinking your daughters were hid in that hut, signor," Francis said as the gondola rowed towards Saint Mark's; "and I can only do that by telling of that secret meeting. I do not want to denounce a number of people, besides Ruggiero. I have no evidence against them, and do not know what they were plotting, nor have I any wish to create for myself more enemies. It is quite enough to have incurred the enmity of all the connections of the house of Mocenigo."

"That is true enough, Francisco, but I do not see how it is to be avoided. Unfortunately, you did recognize others besides Ruggiero."

"Quite so, signor, and I am not going to tell a lie about it, whatever the consequences may be. Still, I wish I could get out of it."

"I wish you could, Francis, but I do not see any escape for it, especially as you say you did not recognize Ruggiero as the passenger you carried."

"No, signor, I did not. It might have been he, but I cannot say. He was wrapped in a cloak, and I did not see his features."

"It is a pity, Francisco, for had you known him, the statement that, moved by curiosity, you followed him and saw him into that hut, would have been sufficient without your entering into the other matter. Most of my countrymen would not hesitate about telling a lie, to avoid mixing themselves up further in such a matter, for the dangers of making enemies are thoroughly appreciated here; but you are perfectly right, and I like your steady love of the truth, whatever the consequences to yourself; but certainly as soon as the matter is concluded, it will be better for you to quit Venice for a time."

"Are you going to the council direct, signor?"

"No. I am going first to the magistrates, to tell them that I have in my hands five persons, who have been engaged in carrying off my daughters, and beg them to send at once to take them into their custody. Then I shall go before the council, and demand justice upon Mocenigo, against whom we have now conclusive evidence. You will not be wanted at the magistracy. My own evidence, that I found them keeping guard over my daughters, will be quite sufficient for the present, and after that the girls' evidence will be sufficient to convict them, without your name appearing in the affair at all.

"I will try whether I cannot keep your name from appearing before the council also. Yes, I think I might do that; and as a first step, I give you my promise not to name you, unless I find it absolutely necessary. You may as well remain here in the gondola until I return."

It was upwards of an hour before Signor Polani came back to the boat.

"I have succeeded," he said, "in keeping your name out of it. I first of all told my daughters' story, and then said that, having obtained information that Ruggiero, before he was banished from Venice, was in the habit of going sometimes at night to a hut on San Nicolo, I proceeded thither, and found my daughters concealed in the hut whose position had been described to me. Of course, they inquired where I had obtained the information; but I replied that, as they knew, I had offered a large reward which would lead to my daughters' discovery, and that this reward had attracted one in the secret of Mocenigo, but that, for the man's own safety, I had been compelled to promise that I would not divulge his name.

"Some of the council were inclined to insist, but others pointed out that, for the ends of justice, it mattered in no way how I obtained the information. I had, at any rate, gone to the island and found my daughters there; and their evidence, if it was in accordance with what I had stated, was amply sufficient to bring the guilt of the abduction of my daughters home to Ruggiero, against whom other circumstances had already excited suspicion. A galley has already started for the mainland, with orders to bring him back a prisoner, and the girls are to appear to give evidence tomorrow. The woman, Castaldi, is to be interrogated by the council this afternoon, and I have no doubt she will make a full confession, seeing that my daughters' evidence is, in itself, sufficient to prove her guilt, and that it can be proved, from other sources, that it was she who inveigled them away by a false message from me."

"I am glad indeed, signor, that I am not to be called, and that this affair of the conspiracy is not to be brought up. I would, with your permission, now return home. Giuseppi took a message to my father from me, the first thing, explaining my absence; and I told him, when we left your house, to go at once to tell him that your daughters had been recovered, and that I should return before long. Still, he will want to hear from me as to the events of the night."

"Will you also tell him, Francisco, that I will call upon him this afternoon. I have much to say to him."

"I am glad Signor Polani is coming," Mr. Hammond said, when his son gave him the message. "I am quite resolved that you shall quit Venice at once. I do not wish to blame you for what you have done, which, indeed, is likely to have a favourable effect upon your fortunes; but that, at your age, you have mixed yourself up in adventures of this kind, taken part in the affairs of great houses, and drawn upon yourself the enmity of one of the most powerful families of Venice, is altogether strange and improper for a lad of your years, and belonging to the family of a quiet trader. I have been thinking about it all this morning, and am quite resolved that the sooner you are out of Venice the better. If I saw any way of sending you off before nightfall I would do so.

"Signor Polani has, you say, so far concealed from the council the fact that you have been mixed up in this business; but there is no saying how soon it may come out. You know that Venice swarms with spies, and these are likely, before many hours, to learn the fact of your midnight arrival at Polani's house; and as no orders were given for the preparation of this expedition to the island before that time, it will not need much penetration to conclude that you were the bearer of the news that led to the discovery of the maidens. Besides which, you accompanied the expedition, and acted as its guide to the hut. Part of this they will learn from the servants of the house, part of it they may get out from the sailors, who, over their wine cups, are not given to reticence. The council may not have pressed Polani on this point, but, take my word for it, some of them, at least, will endeavour to get to the bottom of it, especially Mocenigo's connections, who will naturally be alarmed at the thought that there is somewhere a traitor among their own ranks.

"The affair has become very serious, Francis, and far beyond the compass of a boyish scrape, and no time must be lost in getting you out of Venice. I have no doubt Polani will see the matter in the same light, for he knows the ways of his countrymen even better than I do."

The interview between the two traders was a long one. At its conclusion Francis was sent for.

"Francis," his father said, "Signor Polani has had the kindness to make me offers of a most generous nature."

"Not at all, Messer Hammond," the Venetian interrupted. "Let there be no mistake upon that score. Your son has rendered me services impossible for me ever to repay adequately. He has laid me under an obligation greater than I can ever discharge. At the same time, fortunately, I am in a position to be able to further his interests in life.

"I have proposed, Francisco, that you shall enter my house at once. You will, of course, for some years learn the business, but you will do so in the position which a son of mine would occupy, and when you come of age, you will take your place as a partner with me.

"Your father will return to England. He informs me that he is now longing to return to his own country, and has for some time been thinking of doing so. I have proposed to him that he shall act as my agent there. Hitherto I have not traded direct with England; in future I shall do so largely. Your father has explained to me somewhat of his transactions, and I see there is good profit to be made on trade with London, by a merchant who has the advantage of the advice and assistance of one, like your father, thoroughly conversant in the trade. Thus, I hope that the arrangement will be largely to our mutual advantage. As to yourself, you will probably be reluctant to establish yourself for life in this country; but there is no reason why, in time, when your father wishes to retire from business, you should not establish yourself in London, in charge of the English branch of our house."

"I am most grateful to you for your offer, signor, which is vastly beyond anything that my ambition could ever have aspired to. I can only say that I will try my best to do justice to your kindness to me."

"I have no fear as to that, Francisco," the merchant said. "You have shown so much thoughtfulness, in this business, that I shall have no fear of entrusting even weighty affairs of business in your hands; and you must remember always that I shall still consider myself your debtor. I thoroughly agree with your father's views as to the necessity for your leaving Venice, as soon as possible. In a few months this matter will have blown over, the angry feelings excited will calm down, and you will then be able to come and go in safety; but at present you were best out of the town, and I have, therefore, arranged with your father that you shall embark tonight on board the Bonito, which sails tomorrow. You will have much to say to your father now, but I hope you will find time to come round, and say goodbye to my daughters, this evening."

"Your adventures, Francis," Mr. Hammond said when the merchant had left them, "have turned out fortunate, indeed. You have an opening now beyond anything we could have hoped for. Signor Polani has expressed himself most warmly. He told me that I need concern myself no further with your future, for that would now be his affair. The arrangement that he has made with me, will enable me to hold my head as high as any in the City, for it will give me almost a monopoly of the Venetian trade; and although he said that he had long been thinking of entering into trade direct with England, there is no doubt that it is his feeling towards you, which has influenced him now in the matter.

"My business here has more than answered my expectations, in one respect, but has fallen short in another. I have bought cheaply, and the business should have been a very profitable one; but my partner in London is either not acting fairly by me, or he is mismanaging matters altogether. This offer, then, of Signor Polani is in every respect acceptable. I shall give up my own business and start anew, and selling, as I shall, on commission, shall run no risk, while the profits will be far larger than I could myself make, for Polani will carry it on on a great scale.

"As for you, you will soon learn the ways of trade, and will be able to come home and join me, and eventually succeed me in the business.

"No fairer prospect could well open to a young man, and if you show yourself as keen in business, as you have been energetic in the pursuits you have adopted, assuredly a great future is open to you, and you may look to be one of the greatest merchants in the city of London. I know not yet what offers Polani may make you here, but I hope that you will not settle in Venice permanently, but will always remember that you are an Englishman, and the son of a London citizen, and that you will never lose your love for your native land.

"And yet, do not hurry home for my sake. Your two brothers will soon have finished their schooling, and will, of course, be apprenticed to me as soon as I return; and if, as I hope, they turn out steady and industrious; they will, by the time they come to man's estate, be of great assistance to me in the business.

"And now, you will be wanting to say goodbye to your friends. Be careful this last evening, for it is just when you are thinking most of other matters, that sudden misfortune is likely to come upon you."

Delighted with his good fortune--rather because it opened up a life of activity, instead of the confinement to business that he had dreaded, than for the pecuniary advantages it offered--Francis ran downstairs and, leaping into his father's gondola, told Beppo to take him to the Palazzo Giustiniani. On the way he told Beppo and his son that the next day he was leaving Venice, and was going to enter the service of Signor Polani.

Giuseppi ceased rowing, and, throwing himself down at the bottom of the gondola, began to sob violently, with the abandonment to his emotions common to his race. Then he suddenly sat up.

"If you are going, I will go too, Messer Francisco. You will want a servant who will be faithful to you. I will ask the padrone to let me go with you.

"You will let me go, will you not, father? I cannot leave our young master, and should pine away, were I obliged to stop here to work a gondola; while he may be wanting my help, for Messer Francisco is sure to get into adventures and dangers. Has he not done it here in Venice? and is he not sure to do it at sea, where there are Genoese and pirates, and perils of all kinds?

"You will take me with you, will you not, Messer Francisco? You will never be so hard hearted as to go away and leave me behind?"

"I shall be very glad to have you with me, Giuseppi, if your father will give you leave to go. I am quite sure that Signor Polani will make no objection. In the first place, he would do it to oblige me, and in the second, I know that it is his intention to do something to your advantage. He has spoken to me about it several times, for you had your share of the danger when we first rescued his daughters, and again when we were chased by that four-oared gondola. He has been too busy with the search for his daughters to give the matter his attention, but I know that he is conscious of his obligation to you, and that he intends to reward you largely. Therefore, I am sure that he will offer no objection to your accompanying me.

"What do you say, Beppo?"

"I do not like to stand in the way of the lad's wishes, Messer Francisco; but, you see, he is of an age now to be very useful to me. If Giuseppi leaves me, I shall have to hire another hand for the gondola, or to take a partner."

"Well, we will talk it over presently," Francis said. "Here we are at the steps of the palazzo, and here comes Matteo himself. It is lucky I was not five minutes later, or I should have missed him."

Chapter 7:
On Board A Trader.

"Have you heard the news, Francisco? My cousins are rescued! I have been out this morning and have only just heard it, and I was on the point of starting to tell you."

"Your news is old, Matteo. I knew it hours ago."

"And I hear," Matteo went on, "that Polani found them in a hut on San Nicolo. My father cannot think how he came to hear of their hiding place. He says Polani would not say how he learned the news. My father supposes he heard it from some member of Ruggiero's household."

Francis hesitated for a moment. He had at first been on the point of telling Matteo of the share he had had in the recovery of the girls; but he thought that although his friend could be trusted not to repeat the news wilfully, he might accidentally say something which would lead to the fact being known, and that as Polani had strongly enjoined the necessity of keeping the secret, and had himself declined to mention, even to the council, the source from which he obtained his information, he would look upon him as a babbler, and unworthy of trust, did he find that Matteo had been let into the secret.

"It does not much matter who it is Polani learned the news from. The great point is, he has found his daughters safe from all injury, and I hear has brought back with him the woman who betrayed them. It is fortunate indeed that he took such prompt measures with Ruggiero, and thus prevented his escaping from the mainland, and making off with the girls, as of course he intended to do."

"My father tells me," Matteo said, "that a state gondola has already been dispatched to bring Ruggiero a prisoner here, and that even his powerful connections will not save him from severe punishment, for public indignation is so great at the attempt, that his friends will not venture to plead on his behalf."

"And now I have my bit of news to tell you, Matteo. Signor Polani has most generously offered me a position in his house, and I am to sail tomorrow in one of his ships for the East."

"I congratulate you, Francisco, for I know, from what you have often said, that you would like this much better than going back to England. But it seems very sudden. You did not know anything about it yesterday, and now you are going to start at once. Why, when can it have been settled? Polani has been absent since daybreak, engaged in this matter of the girls, and has been occupied ever since with the council."

"I have seen him since he returned," Francis replied; "and though it was only absolutely settled this morning, he has had several interviews with my father on the subject. I believe he and my father thought that it was better to get me away as soon as possible, as Ruggiero's friends may put down the disgrace which has befallen him to my interference in his first attempt to carry off the girls."

"Well, I think you are a lucky fellow anyhow, Francisco, and I hope that I may be soon doing something also. I shall speak to my father about it, and ask him to get Polani to let me take some voyages in his vessels, so that I may be fit to become an officer in one of the state galleys, as soon as I am of age. Where are you going now?"

"I am going round to the School of Arms, to say goodbye to our comrades. After that I am going to Signor Polani's to pay my respects to the signoras. Then I shall be at home with my father till it is time to go on board. He will have left here before I return from my voyage, as he is going to wind up his affairs at once and return to England."

"Well, I will accompany you to the school and to my cousin's," Matteo said. "I shall miss you terribly here, and shall certainly do all I can to follow your example, and get afloat. You may have all sorts of adventures, for we shall certainly be at war with Genoa before many weeks are over, and you will have to keep a sharp lookout for their war galleys. Polani's ships are prizes worth taking, and you may have the chance of seeing the inside of a Genoese prison before you return."

After a visit to the School of Arms, the two friends were rowed to Signor Polani's. The merchant himself was out, but they were at once shown up to the room where the girls were sitting.

"My dear cousins," Matteo said as he entered, "I am delighted to see you back safe and well. All Venice is talking of your return. You are the heroines of the day. You do not know what an excitement there has been over your adventure."

"The sooner people get to talk about something else the better, Matteo," Maria said, "for we shall have to be prisoners all day till something else occupies their attention. We have not the least desire to be pointed at, whenever we go out, as the maidens who were carried away. If the Venetians were so interested in us, they had much better have set about discovering where we were hidden away before."

"But everyone did try, I can assure you, Maria. Every place has been ransacked, high and low. Every gondolier has been questioned and cross questioned as to his doings on that day. Every fishing village has been visited. Never was such a search, I do believe. But who could have thought of your being hidden away all the time at San Nicolo! As for me, I have spent most of my time in a gondola, going out and staring up at every house I passed, in hopes of seeing a handkerchief waved from a casement. And so has Francisco; he has been just as busy in the search as anyone, I can assure you."

"Francisco is different," Maria said, not observing the signs Francis was making for her to be silent. "Francisco has got eyes in his head, and a brain in his skull, which is more, it seems, than any of the Venetians have; and had he not brought father to our hiding place, there we should have remained until Ruggiero Mocenigo came and carried us away."

"Francisco brought your father the news!" Matteo exclaimed in astonishment. "Why, was it he who found you out, after all?"

"Did you not know that, Matteo? Of course it was Francisco! As I told you, he has got brains; and if it had not been for him, we should certainly never have been rescued. Giulia and I owe him everything--don't we, Giulia?"

"Forgive me for not telling you, Matteo," Francis said to his astonished friend; "but Signor Polani, and my father, both impressed upon me so strongly that I should keep silent as to my share in the business, that I thought it better not even to mention it to you at present. It was purely the result of an accident."

"It was nothing of the sort," Maria said. "It was the result of your keeping your eyes open and knowing how to put two and two together. I did not know, Francisco, that it was a secret. We have not seen our father since we have returned, and I suppose he thought we should see nobody until he saw us again, and so did not tell us that we were not to mention your name in the affair; but we will be careful in future."

"But how was it, Francisco?" Matteo asked. "Now I know so much as this, I suppose I can be told the rest. I can understand well enough why it was to be kept a secret, and why my cousin is anxious to get you out of Venice at once."

Francis related the manner in which he first became acquainted with the existence of the hut on the island, and the fact of its being frequented by Ruggiero Mocenigo; and how, on catching sight of the gouvernante in a gondola, and seeing her make out across the lagoons, the idea struck him that the girls were confined in the hut.

"It is all very simple, you see, Matteo," he concluded.

"I will never say anything against learning to row a gondola in future," Matteo said, "for it seems to lead to all sorts of adventures; and unless you could have rowed well, you would never have got back to tell the story. But it is certain that it is a good thing you are leaving Venice for a time, for Ruggiero's friends may find out the share you had in it from some of my cousin's servants. You may be sure that they will do their best to discover how he came to be informed of the hiding place, and he is quite right to send you off at once."

"What! are you going away, Francisco?" the two girls exclaimed together.

"I am sailing tomorrow in one of your father's ships, signoras."

"And you are not coming back again?" Maria exclaimed.

"I hope to have the pleasure of seeing you again before very long, signora. I am entering your father's service for good, and shall be backwards and forwards to Venice as the ship comes and goes. My father is returning to England, and Signor Polani has most kindly requested me to make my home with him whenever I am in port."

"That is better," Maria said. "We should have a pretty quarrel with papa if he had let you go away altogether, after what you have done for us--

"Shouldn't we, Giulia?"

But Giulia had walked away to the window, and did not seem to hear the question.

"That will be very pleasant," Maria went on; "for you will be back every two or three months, and I shall take good care that papa does not send the ship off in a hurry again. It will be almost as good as having a brother; and I look upon you almost as a brother now, Francisco--and a very good brother, too. I don't think that man will molest us any more. If I thought there was any chance of it, I should ask papa to keep you for a time, because I should feel confident that you would manage to protect us somehow."

"I do not think there is the slightest chance of more trouble from him," Francis said. "He is sure of a long term of imprisonment for carrying you off."

"That is the least they can do to him, I should think," Maria said indignantly. "I certainly shall not feel comfortable while he is at large."

After half an hour's talk Francis and his friend took their leave.

"You certainly were born with a silver spoon in your mouth," Matteo said as they took their seats in the gondola, "and my cousin does well to get you out of Venice at once, for I can tell you there are scores of young fellows who would feel jealous at your position with my cousins."

"Nonsense!" Francis said, colouring. "How can you talk so absurdly, Matteo? I am only a boy, and it will be years before I could think of marriage. Besides, your cousins are said to be the richest heiresses in Venice; and it is not because I have been able to be of some slight service to them, that I should venture to think of either of them in that way."

"We shall see," Matteo laughed. "Maria is a little too old for you, I grant, but Giulia will do very well; and as you have already come, as Maria says, to be looked upon by them as a brother and protector, there is no saying as to how she may regard you in another two or three years."

"The thing is absurd, Matteo," Francis said impatiently. "Do not talk such nonsense any more."

Matteo lay back in his seat and whistled.

"I will say no more about it at present, Francisco," he said, after a pause; "but I must own that I should be well content to stand as high in the good graces of my pretty cousins as you do."

The next morning Francis spent some time with his father talking over future arrangements.

"I have no doubt that I shall see you sometimes, Francis; for Polani will be sure to give you an opportunity of making a trip to England, from time to time, in one of his ships trading thither. Unless anything unexpected happens, your future appears assured. Polani tells me he shall always regard you in the light of a son; and I have no fear of your doing anything to cause him to forfeit his good opinion of you. Do not be over adventurous, for even in a merchant ship there are many perils to be met with. Pirates swarm in the Mediterranean, in spite of the efforts of Venice to suppress them; and when war is going on, both Venice and Genoa send out numbers of ships whose doings savour strongly of piracy. Remember that the first duty of the captain of a merchant ship is to save his vessel and cargo, and that he should not think of fighting unless he sees no other method of escape open to him.

"It is possible that, after a time, I may send one of your brothers out here, but that will depend upon what I find of their disposition when I get home; for it will be worse than useless to send a lad of a headstrong disposition out to the care of one but a few years older than himself. But this we can talk about when you come over to England, and we see what position you are occupying here.

"I fear that Venice is about to enter upon a period of great difficulty and danger. There can be little doubt that Genoa, Padua, and Hungary are leagued against her; and powerful as she is, and great as are her resources, they will be taxed to the utmost to carry her through the dangers that threaten her. However, I have faith in her future, and believe that she will weather the storm, as she has done many that have preceded it.

"Venice has the rare virtue of endurance--the greatest dangers, the most disastrous defeats, fail to shake her courage, and only arouse her to greater efforts. In this respect she is in the greatest contrast to her rival, Genoa, who always loses heart the moment the tide turns against her. No doubt this is due, in no slight extent, to her oligarchic form of government. The people see the nobles, who rule them, calm and self possessed, however great the danger, and remain confident and tranquil; while in Genoa each misfortune is the signal for a struggle between contending factions. The occasion is seized to throw blame and contumely upon those in power, and the people give way to alternate outbursts of rage and depression.

"I do not say there are no faults in the government of Venice, but taking her altogether there is no government in Europe to compare with it. During the last three hundred years, the history of every other city in Italy, I may say of every other nation in Europe, is one long record of intestine struggle and bloodshed, while in Venice there has not been a single popular tumult worthy of the name. It is to the strength, the firmness, and the moderation of her government that Venice owes her advancement, the respect in which she is held among nations, as much as to the commercial industry of her people.

"She alone among nations could for years have withstood the interdict of the pope, or the misfortunes that have sometimes befallen her. She alone has never felt the foot of the invader, or bent her neck beneath a foreign yoke to preserve her existence. Here, save only in matters of government, all opinions are free, strangers of all nationalities are welcome. It is a grand city and a grand people, Francis, and though I shall be glad to return to England I cannot but feel regret at leaving it.

"And now, my boy, it is time to be going off to your ship. Polani said she would sail at ten o'clock. It is now nine, and it will take you half an hour to get there. I am glad to hear that Giuseppi is going with you. The lad is faithful and attached to you, and may be of service. Your trunk has already been sent on board, so let us be going."

On arriving at the ship, which was lying in the port of Malamocco, they found that she was just ready for sailing. The last bales of goods were being hoisted on board, and the sailors were preparing to loosen the sails.

The Bonito was a large vessel, built for stowage rather than speed. She carried two masts with large square sails, and before the wind would probably proceed at a fair rate; but the art of sailing close hauled was then unknown, and in the event of the wind being unfavourable she would be forced either to anchor or to depend upon her oars, of which she rowed fifteen on either side. As they mounted on to the deck they were greeted by Polani himself.

"I have come off to see the last of your son, Messer Hammond, and to make sure that my orders for his comfort have been carried out.

"Captain Corpadio, this is the young gentleman of whom I have spoken to you, and who is to be treated in all respects as if he were my son. You will instruct him in all matters connected with the navigation of the ship, as well as in the mercantile portion of the business, the best methods of buying and selling, the prices of goods, and the methods of payment.

"This is your cabin, Francisco."

He opened the door of a roomy cabin in the poop of the ship. It was fitted up with every luxury.

"Thank you very much indeed, Signor Polani," Francis said. "The only fault is that it is too comfortable. I would as lief have roughed it as other aspirants have to do."

"There was no occasion, Francisco. When there is rough work to be done, you will, I have no doubt, do it; but as you are going to be a trader, and not a sailor, there is no occasion that you should do so more than is necessary. You will learn to command a ship just as well as if you began by dipping your hands in tar. And it is well that you should learn to do this, for unless a man can sail a vessel himself, he is not well qualified to judge of the merits of men he appoints to be captains; but you must remember that you are going as a representative of my house, and must, therefore, travel in accordance with that condition.

"You will be sorry to hear that bad news has just been received from the mainland. The state galley sent to fetch Ruggiero Mocenigo has arrived with the news that, on the previous night, a strong party of men who are believed to have come from Padua, fell upon the guard and carried off Ruggiero. My sailors came up and fought stoutly, but they were overpowered, and several of them were killed; so Ruggiero is again at large.

"This is a great disappointment to me. Though the villain is not likely to show his face in the Venetian territory again, I shall be anxious until Maria is safely married, and shall lose no time in choosing a husband for her. Unless I am mistaken, her liking is turned in the direction of Rufino, brother of your friend Matteo Giustiniani, and as I like none better among the suitors for her hand, methinks that by the time you return you will find that they are betrothed.

"And now I hear the sailors are heaving the anchor, and therefore, Messer Hammond, it is time we took to our boats."

There was a parting embrace between Francis and his father. Then the merchants descended into their gondolas, and lay waiting alongside until the anchor was up, the great sails shaken out, and the Bonito began to move slowly through the water towards the entrance of the port. Then, with a final wave of the hand, the gondolas rowed off and Francis turned to look at his surroundings. The first object that met his eye was Giuseppi, who was standing near him waving his cap to his father.

"Well, Giuseppi, what do you think of this?"

"I don't know what to think yet, Messer Francisco. It all seems so big and solid one does not feel as if one was on the water. It's more like living in a house. It does not seem as if anything could move her."

"You will find the waves can move her about when we get fairly to sea, Giuseppi, and the time will come when you will think our fast gondola was a steady craft in comparison. How long have you been on board?"

"I came off three hours ago, signor, with the boat that brought the furniture for your cabin. I have been putting that to rights since. A supply of the best wine has been sent off, and extra stores of all sorts, so you need not be afraid of being starved on the voyage."

"I wish he hadn't sent so much," Francis said. "It makes one feel like a milksop. Whose cabin is it I have got?"

"I believe that it is the cabin usually used by the supercargo, who is in charge of the goods and does the trading, but the men say the captain of this ship has been a great many years in Polani's employment, and often sails without a supercargo, being able to manage the trading perfectly well by himself. But the usual cabin is only half the size of yours, and two have been thrown into one to make it light and airy."

"And where do you sleep, Giuseppi?"

"I am going to sleep in the passage outside your door, Messer Francisco."

"Oh, but I sha'n't like that!" Francis said. "You ought to have a better place than that."

Giuseppi laughed.

"Why, Messer Francisco, considering that half my time I slept in the gondola, and the other half on some straw in our kitchen, I shall do capitally. Of course I could sleep in the fo'castle with the crew if I liked, but I should find it hot and stifling there. I chose the place myself, and asked the captain if I could sleep there, and he has given me leave."

In an hour the Bonito had passed through the Malamocco Channel, and was out on the broad sea. The wind was very light, and but just sufficient to keep the great sails bellied out. The sailors were all at work, coiling down ropes, washing the decks, and making everything clean and tidy.

"This is a good start, Messer Hammond," the captain said, coming up to him. "If this wind holds, we shall be able to make our course round the southern point of Greece, and then on to

Candia, which is our first port. I always like a light breeze when I first go out of port, it gives time for everyone to get at home and have things shipshape before we begin to get lively."

"She does not look as if she would ever get lively," Francis said, looking at the heavy vessel.

"She is lively enough in a storm, I can tell you," the captain said, laughing. "When she once begins to roll she does it in earnest, but she is a fine sea boat, and I have no fear of gales. I wish I could say as much of pirates. However, she has always been fortunate, and as we carry a stout crew she could give a good account of herself against any of the small piratical vessels that swarm among the islands, although, of course, if she fell in with two or three of them together it would be awkward."

"How many men do you carry altogether, captain?"

"Just seventy. You see she rows thirty oars, and in case of need we put two men to each oar, and though she doesn't look fast she can get along at a fine rate when the oars are double banked. We have shown them our heels many a time. Our orders are strict. We are never to fight if we can get away by running."

"But I suppose you have to fight sometimes?" Francis asked.

"Yes, I have been in some tough fights several times, though not in the Bonito, which was only built last year. Once in the Lion we were attacked by three pirates. We were at anchor in a bay, and the wind was blowing on the shore, when they suddenly came round the headland, so there was no chance of running, and we had to fight it out. We fought for five hours before they sheered off, pretty well crippled, and one of them in flames, for we carried Greek fire.

"Three or four times they nearly got a footing on deck, but we managed to beat them off somehow. We lost a third of our crew. I don't think there was a man escaped without a wound. I was laid up for three months, after I got home, with a slash on the shoulder, which pretty nigh took off my left arm. However, we saved the ship and the cargo, which was a valuable one, and Messer Polani saw that no one was the worse for his share in the business. There's no more liberal-hearted man in the trade than he is, and whatever may be the scarcity of hands in the port, there is never any difficulty in getting a good crew together for his vessels.

"Of course there are the roughs with the smooths. Some years ago I was in prison for six months, with all my crew, in Azoff. It was the work of those rascally Genoese, who are always doing us a bad turn when they have the chance, even when we are at peace with them. They set the mind of the native khan--that is the prince of the country--against us by some lying stories that we had been engaged in smuggling goods in at another port. And suddenly, in the middle of the night, in marched his soldiers on board my ship, and two other Venetian craft lying in the harbour, and took possession of them, and shut us all up in prison. There we were till Messer Polani got news, and sent out another ship to pay the fine demanded. That was no joke, I can tell you, for the prison was so hot and crowded, and the food so bad, that we got fever, and pretty near half of us died before our ransom came. Then at Constantinople the Genoese stirred the people up against us once or twice, and all the sailors ashore had to fight for their lives. Those Genoese are always doing us mischief."

"But I suppose you do them mischief sometimes, captain. I imagine it isn't all one side."

"Of course, we pay them out when we get a chance," the captain replied. "It isn't likely we are going to stand being always put upon, and not take our chance when it comes. We only want fair trade and no favour, while those rascals want it all to themselves. They know they have no chance with us when it comes to fair trading."

"You know, captain, that the Genoese say just the same things about the Venetians, that the Venetians do about them. So I expect that there are faults on both sides."

The captain laughed.

"I suppose each want to have matters their own way, Messer Hammond, but I don't consider the Genoese have any right to come interfering with us, to the eastward of Italy. They have got France and Spain to trade with, and all the western parts of Italy. Why don't they keep there? Besides, I look upon them as landsmen. Why, we can always lick them at sea in a fair fight."

"Generally, captain. I admit you generally thrash them. Still, you know they have sometimes got the better of you, even when the force was equal."

The captain grunted. He could not deny the fact.

"Sometimes our captains don't do their duty," he said. "They put a lot of young patricians in command of the galleys, men that don't know one end of a ship from the other, and then, of course, we get the worst of it. But I maintain that, properly fought, a Venetian ship is always more than a match for a Genoese."

"I think she generally is, captain, and I hope it will always prove so in the future. You see, though I am English, I have lived long enough in Venice to feel like a Venetian."

"I have never been to England," the captain said, "though a good many Venetian ships go there every year. They tell me it's an island, like Venice, only a deal bigger than any we have got in the Mediterranean. Those who have been there say the sea is mighty stormy, and that, sailing up from Spain, you get tremendous tempests sometimes, with the waves ever so much bigger than we have here, and longer and more regular, but not so trying to the ships as the short sharp gales of these seas."

"I believe that is so, captain, though I don't know anything about it myself. It is some years since I came out, and our voyage was a very calm one."

Three days of quiet sailing, and the Bonito rounded the headlands of the Morea, and shaped her course to Candia. The voyage was a very pleasant one to Francis. Each day the captain brought out the list of cargo, and instructed him in the prices of each description of goods, told him of the various descriptions of merchandise which they would be likely to purchase at the different ports at which they were to touch, and the prices which they would probably have to pay for them. A certain time, too, was devoted each day to the examination of the charts of the various ports and islands, the captain pointing out the marks which were to be observed on entering and leaving the harbours, the best places for anchorage, and the points where shelter could be obtained should high winds come on.

After losing sight of the Morea the weather changed, clouds banked up rapidly in the southwest, and the captain ordered the great sails to be furled.

"We are going to have a serious gale," he said to Francis, "which is unusual at this period of the year. I have thought, for the last two days, we were going to have a change, but I hoped to have reached Candia before the gale burst upon us. I fear that this will drive us off our course."

By evening it was blowing hard, and the sea got up rapidly. The ship speedily justified the remarks of the captain on her power of rolling, and the oars, at which the men had been labouring since the sails were furled, were laid in.

"It is impossible to keep our course," the captain said, "and we must run up among the islands, and anchor under the lee of one of them. I should recommend you to get into your bed as soon as possible. You have not learned to keep your legs in a storm. I see that lad of yours is very ill already, but as you show no signs of suffering thus far, you will probably escape."

It was some time, however, before Francis went below. The scene was novel to him, and he was astonished at the sight of the waves, and at the manner in which they tossed the great ship about, as if she were an eggshell. But when it became quite dark, and he could see nothing but the white crests of the waves and the foam that flew high in the air every time the bluff bows of the ship plunged down into a hollow, he took the captain's advice and retired to his cabin.

He was on deck again early. A gray mist overhung the water. The sea was of a leaden colour, crested with white heads. The waves were far higher than they had been on the previous evening, and as they came racing along behind the Bonito each crest seemed as if it would rise over her stern and overwhelm her. But this apprehension was soon dispelled, as he saw how lightly the vessel rose each time. Although showing but a very small breadth of sail, she was running along at a great rate, leaving a white streak of foam behind her. The captain was standing near the helm, and Francis made his way to him.

"Well, captain, and how are you getting on, and where are we?" he asked, cheerfully.

"We are getting on well enough, Messer Francisco, as you can see for yourself. The Bonito is as good a sea boat as ever floated, and would not care for the wind were it twice as strong as it is. It is not the storm I am thinking about, but the islands. If we were down in the Mediterranean I could turn into my cot and sleep soundly; but here it is another matter. We are somewhere up among the islands, but where, no man can say. The wind has shifted a bit two or three times during the night, and, as we are obliged to run straight before it, there is no calculating to within a few miles where we are. I have tried to edge out to the westward as much as I could, but with this wind blowing and the height of the ship out of water, we sag away to leeward so fast that nothing is gained by it.

"According to my calculation, we cannot be very far from the west coast of Mitylene. If the clouds would but lift, and give us a look round for two minutes, we should know all about it, as I know the outline of every island in the Aegean; and as over on this side you are always in sight of two or three of them, I should know all about it if I could get a view of the land. Now, for aught we know, we may be running straight down upon some rocky coast."

The idea was not a pleasant one, and Francis strained his eyes, gazing through the mist.

"What should we do if we saw land, captain?" he asked presently.

"Get out the oars, row her head round, and try to work either to the right or left, whichever point of land seemed easiest to weather. Of course, if it was the mainland we were being driven on there would be no use, and we should try and row into the teeth of the gale, so as to keep her off land as long as possible, in the hope of the wind dropping. When we got into shallow water we should drop our anchors, and still keep on rowing to lessen the strain upon them. If they gave, there would be an end to the Bonito. But if, as I think, we are driving towards Mitylene, there is a safe harbour on this side of the island, and I shall certainly run into it. It is well sheltered and landlocked."

Two more hours passed, and then there was a startling transformation. The clouds broke suddenly and cleared off, as if by magic, and the sun streamed brightly out. The wind was blowing as strong as ever, but the change in the hue of sky and sea would at once have raised the spirits of the tired crew, had not a long line of land been seen stretching ahead of them at a distance of four or five miles.

"Just as I thought," the captain exclaimed as he saw it. "That is Mitylene, sure enough, and the entrance to the harbour I spoke of lies away there on that beam."

The oars were at once got out, the sail braced up a little, and the Bonito made for the point indicated by the captain, who himself took the helm.

Another half hour and they were close to land. Francis could see no sign of a port, but in a few minutes the Bonito rounded the end of a low island, and a passage opened before her. She passed through this and found herself in still water, in a harbour large enough to hold the fleet of Venice. The anchor was speedily let drop.

"It seems almost bewildering," Francis said, "the hush and quiet here after the turmoil of the storm outside. To whom does Mitylene belong?"

"The Genoese have a trading station and a castle at the other side of the island, but it belongs to Constantinople. The other side of the island is rich and fertile, but this, as you see, is mountainous and barren. The people have not a very good reputation, and if we had been wrecked we should have been plundered, if not murdered.

"You see those two vessels lying close to the shore, near the village? They are pirates when they get a chance, you may be quite sure. In fact, these islands swarm with them. Venice does all she can to keep them down, but the Genoese, and the Hungarians, and the rest of them, keep her so busy that she has no time to take the matter properly in hand, and make a clean sweep of them."

Chapter 8:
An Attack By Pirates.

A boat was lowered, and the captain went ashore with a strong crew, all armed to the teeth. Francis accompanied him. The natives were sullen in their manner, but expressed a willingness to trade, and to exchange hides and wine for cloth.

"We may as well do a little barter," the captain said, as they rowed back towards the ship. "The port is not often visited, and the road across the island is hilly and rough, so they ought to be willing to sell their goods cheaply."

"They did not seem pleased to see us, nevertheless," Francis said.

"No; you see the Genoese have got a footing in the island, and of course they represent us to the natives as being robbers, who would take their island if we got the chance. All round these coasts and islands the people are partisans either of Venice or Genoa. They care very little for Constantinople, although they form part of the empire. Constantinople taxes them heavily, and is too weak to afford them protection. Of course they are Greeks, but the Greeks of the islands have very little in common, beyond their language, with the Greeks of Constantinople. They see, too, that the Turks are increasing in power, and they know that, if they are to be saved from falling into the hands of the Moslem, it is Venice or Genoa who will protect them, and not Constantinople, who will have enough to do to defend herself.

"As to themselves, they would naturally prefer Venice, because Venice is a far better mistress than Genoa; but of course, when the Genoese get a footing, they spread lies as to our tyranny and greed, and so it comes that the people of the islands are divided in their wishes, and that while we are gladly received in some of them, we are regarded with hate and suspicion in others."

Trade at once began, and continued until evening.

"How long do you expect to stay here, captain?" Francis asked.

"That must depend upon the wind. It may go down tomorrow, it may continue to blow strong for days, and it is no use our attempting to work down to Candia until it changes its direction. I should hope, however, that in a day or two we may be off. We are doing little more than wasting our time here."

A strong watch was placed on deck at nightfall.

"Why, surely, captain, there is no fear of an attack! War has not yet been proclaimed with Genoa, although there is little doubt it will be so in a few weeks, or perhaps a few days."

"There is never a real peace between Venice and Genoa in these seas," the captain said, "and as war is now imminent, one cannot be too watchful. State galleys would not be attacked, but merchant vessels are different. Who is to inquire about a merchant ship! Why, if we were attacked and plundered here, who would be any the wiser? We should either have our throats cut, or be sent to rot in the dungeons of Genoa. And not till there was an exchange of prisoners, perhaps years hence, would any in Venice know what had befallen us. When weeks passed, and no news came to Venice of our having reached Candia, it would be supposed that we had been lost in the storm.

"Signor Polani would run his pen through the name of the Bonito, and put her down as a total loss, and there would be an end of it, till those of us who were alive, when the prison doors were opened, made their way back to Venice. No, no, Messer Francisco. In these eastern waters one must always act as if the republic were at war. Why, did not Antonio Doria, in a time of profound peace, attack and seize eight Venetian ships laden with goods, killing two of the merchants on board, and putting the ships at a ransom? As to single vessels missing, and never heard of, their number is innumerable.

"It is all put down to pirates; but trust me, the Genoese are often at the bottom of it. They are robbers, the Genoese. In fair trade we can always beat them, and they know it, and so they are always seeking a pretext for a quarrel with us."

Francis smiled quietly at the bigoted hatred which the captain bore the Genoese, but thought it useless to argue with him. The next morning he came up on deck soon after daybreak.

"I see one of those vessels has taken her departure," he said, as he glanced towards the spot where they had been lying.

"So she has," the captain said. "I had not noticed that before. I wonder what that fellow has gone for? No good, you may be sure. Why, it is blowing hard outside still, as you may see by the rate those light clouds travel. He would never have put to sea without having a motive, and he must have had a strong crew on board, to row out in the teeth of the gale far enough to make off the land. That fellow is up to mischief of some sort."

A few minutes later the captain ordered a boat to be lowered, and rowed out to the rocky islet at the mouth of the harbour, and landing, climbed up the rocks and looked out to sea. In half an hour he returned to the ship.

"It is no use," he said to Francis. "The wind is blowing straight into the passage, and we could not row the Bonito out against it. It was different with that craft that went out yesterday evening, for I have no doubt she started as soon as it became dark. She was low in the water, and would not hold the wind; besides, no doubt they lowered the masts, and with a strong crew might well have swept her out. But with the Bonito, with her high sides and heavy tonnage, it could not be done."

"What do you think she went out for, captain?"

"It is likely enough that she may have gone to one of the other islands, and may return with a dozen other craft, pirates like herself. The news that a Venetian merchant ship, without consorts, is weather bound here, would bring them upon us like bees.

"It is a dangerous thing, this sailing alone. I have talked it over several times with the master. Other merchants generally send their ships in companies of eight or ten, and they are then strong enough to beat off any attack of pirates. Messer Polani always sends his vessels out singly. What he says is this: 'A single ship always travels faster than a convoy, because these must go at the rate of the slowest among them. Then the captain is free to go where he will, without consulting others, according as he gets news where trade is to be done, and when he gets there he can drive his own bargains without the competition of other ships.

"So you see there are advantages both ways. The padrone's ships run greater risks, but, if they get through them safely, they bring home much larger profits than do those of others. As a rule, I prefer sailing singly; but just at the present time I should be well pleased to see half a dozen consorts lying alongside."

Three times during the day the captain paid a visit to the rocky island. On his return for the last time before nightfall he said to Francis:

"The wind is certainly falling. I hope that tomorrow morning we shall be able to get out of this trap. I am convinced that there is danger."

"You see nothing else, do you, captain, beyond the departure of that craft, to make you think that there is danger?"

"Yes, I have seen two things," the captain said. "In the first place, the demeanour of the people has changed. They do not seem more unfriendly than they were before, but as I moved about the place today, it seemed to me that there was a suppressed excitement--people gathered together and talked earnestly, and separated if any of our crew happened to go near them; even laughed when they thought that none of us were looking, and looked serious and sullen if we turned round. I am convinced that they are expecting something to happen.

"I have another reason for suspecting it. I have kept a sharp watch on that high hill behind the village; they tell me there is nothing at the top except some curious stones, that look as if they had once been trees, so there is nothing they can want to go up for. Several times today I have made out the figures of men climbing that hill. When they got to the top they stood for some time as if they were looking out over the sea, and then came down again without doing anything. Now, men do not climb such a hill as that merely for exercise. They went up because they expected to see something, and that something could only be a fleet of pirate boats from the other islands. I would give a year's pay if we could get out of this place this evening, but it cannot be done, and we must wait till tomorrow morning. I will try then, even though I risk being driven on the rocks. However, if they do come tonight they will not catch us asleep."

Orders were issued that the whole crew were to remain in readiness for attack, and that those whose watch was below were to sleep with their arms beside them. The lower ports were all closed, a strong watch was kept on deck, and it was certain that, whatever happened, the Bonito would not be taken by surprise.

Being assured by the captain that it was not probable that any attack would be made before morning, as the pirates, not knowing their exact position, would wait until the first gleam of daylight enabled them to make out where she was lying, and to advance in order against her, Francis lay down on his couch, leaving orders that, if asleep, he was to be called two hours before daybreak. He slept but little, however, getting up frequently and going out to ascertain if any sounds indicated the presence of an enemy.

Upon one of these occasions he found that the person leaning next to him against the bulwark, and gazing towards the mouth of the harbour, was Giuseppi.

"Have you been here long, Giuseppi?"

"Since you were out last, Messer Francisco. I thought I would wait a bit, and listen."

"And have you heard anything?"

"I have heard sounds several times."

"What sort of sounds, Giuseppi?"

"Such a sound as is made when the sails and yards are lowered. I have heard it over and over again when out at night on the lagoons near the port. There is no mistake in the creaking of the blocks as the halyards run through them. I am sure, that since I have been here several vessels have brought up inside the mouth of the harbour. Some of the sailors have heard the same noises, so there cannot be any mistake about it. If the captain likes, I will take a small boat and row out, and find out all about them."

"I will ask the captain, Giuseppi."

The captain, however, said that there would be no use in this being done.

"Whether there are few or whether there are many of them, we must wait till morning before we go out. There will be no working out that channel in the dark, even if we were unopposed."

"But they must have managed to come in," Francis said.

"No doubt some of their comrades in the other barque, or people from the village, show a light out there to guide them in. Besides, the wind is favourable to them and against us. No, young sir, there is nothing to do but to wait. In the morning, if there are but few of them, we will try to break through and gain the sea. If there are many we will fight here, as then all hands will be available for the combat, while if we were rowing, half of them would be occupied with the oars. If your lad were to go as he proposes he might fall into the hands of the enemy, and as the information he could gather would be in any case of no use, it is best he should remain where he is."

The hours seemed long until the first tinge of daylight appeared in the sky. All hands were on deck now, for the news that vessels had been arriving in the port had convinced all that danger really threatened them. It was not until half an hour later that they were able to make out some dark objects, lying in under the shadow of the islet across the mouth of the harbour.

"There they are, Messer Francisco," the captain said. "Ten of them, as far as I can make out; but there may be more, for likely enough some of them are lying side by side. There may, too, be some round a corner, where we cannot see them. Another half hour we shall know all about it."

Francis was half surprised that the captain did not order the oars to be put out and lashed in that position, for it was a recognized plan for preventing a ship from being boarded by an enemy, who could thus only approach her at the lofty poop and forecastle.

"Are you not going to get out the oars to keep them off?"

"No, Messer Francisco. In the first place, our sides are so high out of water that the pirates will have a difficulty in boarding us in any case. In the second place, if we get the oars out and they row full at them, sooner or later they will break them off; and it is all important that we should be able to row. I have been thinking the matter over, and my idea is, as soon as they advance, to get three or four oars at work on either side, so as to move her gradually through the water towards the harbour mouth. The rowers will be charged to let their oars swing alongside whenever any of their craft dash at them. We shall want every oar, as well as our sails, to get away when we are once outside. I do not think we have much chance of finally beating them off if we stop and fight here. But if we can do so for a time, and can manage to creep out of the harbour, all may be well."

When daylight fairly broke they were able to make out their enemy. The vessels were of all sizes, from long, low craft, carrying great sails and long banks of oars, down to boats of a few tons burden. All seemed crowded with men.

"None of them are anything like as high out of the water as the Bonito," the captain said, "and they will find it very difficult to climb up our sides. Still the odds against us are serious, but we shall give them a warmer reception than they expect. They will hardly calculate either on our being so strong handed, or so well prepared for them."

Everything was indeed ready for the combat. Two or three barrels of the compound known as Greek fire had been brought up from the hold, and the cooks had heated cauldrons full of pitch. Thirty men with bows and arrows were on the poop, and the rest, with spears, axes, and swords, stood along the bulwarks.

"We may as well get as near the entrance as we can before the fight begins," the captain said. "Get up the anchor, and as soon as it is aboard, get out four oars on each side."

The anchor had already been hove short, and was soon in its place. Then the oars dipped into the water, and slowly the Bonito moved towards the mouth of the harbour. Scarcely had the oars touched the water, than a bustle was perceived on board the piratical ships. Oars were put out, and in two or three minutes the pirates were under way, advancing at a rapid pace towards the Bonito.

The crew made no reply to the shouts and yells of the pirates, but, in accordance with the orders of the captain, remained in a stooping position, so that the figure of the captain, as he hauled up the flag with the lion of Venice to the masthead, was alone visible to the pirates. As these approached volleys of arrows were shot at the Bonito, but not a shot replied until they were within fifty yards of the ship.

Then the captain gave the word. The archers sprang to their feet, and from their eminence poured their arrows thick and fast on to the crowded decks of the pirates. The captain gave the word to the rowers, and they relinquished their oars, which swung in by the side of the vessel.

A moment later two of the largest craft of the pirates dashed alongside. The instant they did so they were saluted with showers of boiling pitch, while pots full of Greek fire were thrown down upon them. Those who tried to climb up the side of the Bonito were speared with lances or cut down with battleaxes.

The combat was of short duration. Many of those on whom the boiling pitch had fallen jumped overboard in their agony, while others did the same to escape the Greek fire, which they in vain endeavoured to extinguish. The fire quickly spread to the woodwork, and in five minutes after the beginning of the fight, the two craft dropped astern from the Bonito, with the flames already rising fiercely from them.

In the meantime the other vessels had not been idle, and a storm of missiles was poured upon the Bonito. The fate which befell their comrades, however, showed them how formidable was the vessel they had regarded as an easy prey, and when the first assailants of the Bonito dropped astern, none of the others cared to take their places.

"Man the oars again!" the captain ordered, and the Bonito again moved forward, her crew stooping behind the bulwarks, while the archers only rose from time to time to discharge their shafts.

"The thing I am most afraid of," the captain said to Francis, who was standing beside him, "is, that they will ram us with their prows. The Bonito is strongly built, but the chances are that they would knock a hole in her."

"I should think, captain, that if we were to get up some of those bales of cloth, and fasten ropes to them, we might lower them over the side and so break the shock."

"It is worth trying, anyhow," the captain said.

And a score of the sailors were at once sent down to fetch up the bales. Ropes were fastened round these, and they were laid along by the bulwarks in readiness for being lowered instantly. Ten bales were placed on each side, and three men told off to each bale.

By this time they were halfway to the mouth of the harbour, and the preparations were completed just in time, for the small boats suddenly drew aside, and two of the largest of the pirates' craft, each rowed by twenty-four oars, dashed at her, one on each side. The captain shouted the order, and the men all sprang to their feet. It was seen at once that the vessels would both strike about midships. Three bales on either side were raised to the bulwarks, and lowered down with the ropes until close to the water's edge and closely touching each other. Francis sprang on to the bulwark and superintended the operations on one side, while the captain did the same on the other.

"A few feet more astern, lads. That is right. Now, keep the bales touching. You are just in the line."

An instant later the Bonito reeled from the shock of two tremendous blows. The bows of the pirates were stove in, but the thick bales enabled the Bonito to withstand the shock, although her sides creaked, the seams started, and the water flowed in freely. But of this the crew thought little. They were occupied in hurling darts, arrows, and combustibles into the pirates as these backed off, in an already sinking condition.

"Now I think we can go," the captain said, and ordered the whole of the oars to be manned.

They were speedily got out, and the Bonito made her way out through the mouth of the harbour. The pirates, in their lighter boats, rowed round and round her, shooting clouds of arrows, but not venturing to come to close quarters, after the fate which had befallen the four largest vessels of their fleet.

As soon as they were clear of the islet the sails were hoisted. The wind had fallen much during the night, and had worked round to the east, and under sails and oars the Bonito left the island, none of the pirates venturing to follow in pursuit. The oars were soon laid in, and the men, with mallets and chisels, set to work to caulk the seams through which the water was making its way. The casualties were now inquired into, and it was found that six men had been shot dead, and that nine-and-twenty had received wounds more or less severe from the arrows of the pirates.

Francis had been twice wounded while superintending the placing of the bales. One arrow had gone through his right leg, another had struck him in the side and glanced off a rib.

"This won't do, Messer Francisco," the captain said as he assisted Giuseppi to bandage the wounds. "Signor Polani placed you on board to learn something of seamanship and commerce, not to make yourself a target for the arrows of pirates. However, we have to thank you for the saving of the Bonito, for assuredly she would have been stove in, had not the happy thought of hanging those bales overboard struck you. It would be of no use against war galleys, whose beaks are often below the waterline, but against craft like these pirates it acts splendidly, and there is no doubt that you saved the ship from destruction, and us from death, for after the burning of the two first vessels that attacked us, you may be sure they would have shown but little mercy. I can't think how you came to think of it."

"Why, I have read in books, captain, of defenders of walls hanging over trusses of straw, to break the blows of battering rams and machines of the besiegers. Directly you said they were going to ram us it struck me we might do the same, and then I thought that bales of cloth, similar to those you got up on deck to trade with the islanders would be just the thing."

"It was a close shave," the captain said. "I was leaning over, and saw the whole side of the ship bend beneath the blow, and expected to hear the ribs crack beneath me. Fortunately the Bonito was stronger built than her assailants, and their bows crumpled in before her side gave; but my heart was in my mouth for a time, I can tell you."

"So was mine, captain. I hardly felt these two arrows strike me. They must have been shot from one of the other boats. Then I could not help laughing to see the way in which the men at the oars tumbled backwards at the moment when their vessel struck us. It was as if an invisible giant had swept them all off their seats together."

The wind continued favourable until they arrived at Candia, where the captain reported, to the commander of a Venetian war galley lying in the port, the attack that had been made upon him; and the galley at once started for the scene of the action, to destroy any pirates she might find there or among the neighbouring islands, or in the various inlets and bays of the mainland.

Having delivered their letters and landed a portion of their cargo for the use of Polani's agents in the islands, the Bonito proceeded to Cyprus. For some weeks she cruised along the coast of Syria, trading in the various Turkish ports, for Venice, although she had shared in some of the crusades, was now, as she had often been before, on friendly terms with the Turks. Her interests all lay in that direction. She carried on a large trade with them; and in the days when she lay under the interdict of the pope, and all Europe stood aloof from her, she drew her stores of provisions from the Moslem ports, and was thus enabled successfully to resist the pressure which she suffered from the interdict. She foresaw, too, the growing power of the Turks, and perceived that in the future they would triumph over the degenerate Greek empire at Constantinople. She had spent her blood and treasure freely in maintaining that empire; but the weakness and profligacy of its emperors, the intestine quarrels and disturbances which were forever going on, and the ingratitude with which she had always treated Venice, had completely alienated the Venetians from her. Genoa had, indeed, for many years exercised a far more preponderating influence at Constantinople than Venice had done.

Having completed the tour of the Syrian ports, the Bonito sailed north, with the intention of passing the Dardanelles and Bosphorus, and proceeding to Azoph.

When she reached the little island of Tenedos, a few miles from the entrance to the strait, she heard news which compelled the captain to alter his intentions. A revolution had broken out in Constantinople, aided by the Genoese of Pera. The cruel tyrant Calojohannes the 5th had been deposed, and his heir Andronicus, whom he had deprived of sight and thrown into a dungeon, released and placed on the throne.

As a reward for the services she had rendered him, Andronicus issued a decree conferring Tenedos upon Genoa. The news had just arrived when the Bonito entered the port, and the town was in a ferment. There were two or three Venetian warships in the harbour; but the Venetian admiral, being without orders from home as to what part to take in such an emergency, remained neutral. The matter was, however, an important one, for the possession of Tenedos gave its owners the command of the Dardanelles, and a fleet lying there could effectually block the passage.

The people thronged up to the governor's house with shouts of "Down with Genoa!" The governor, being unsupported by any Greek or Genoese troops, bowed to the popular will, and declared that he did not recognize the revolution that had taken place in Constantinople, and refused to submit to the decree of Andronicus. Donato Trono, a Venetian merchant resident in the island, and other Venetians, harangued the people, and pointed out to them that alone they could not hope to resist the united forces of Greece and Genoa, and that their only hope of safety lay in placing themselves under the protection of Venice. The people, seeing the justice of the arguments of the Venetians, and preferring the Venetian rule to that of Genoa, agreed to the proposal. The banner of St. Mark was raised amid great enthusiasm, and the island declared subject to Venice.

A Genoese galley in port immediately set sail, and quickly carried the news to Constantinople, where the emperor at once threw the whole of the Venetian residents into prison. As soon as the news of this reached Tenedos the captain of the Bonito held a consultation with Francis.

"It is evident, Messer Francisco, that we cannot proceed upon our northward voyage. We should be captured and held at Constantinople; and, even did we succeed in passing at night, we should fall into the hands of the Genoese--who are far stronger in the Black Sea than we are--for if Venice accepts the offer of the people of this place, and takes possession of the island, Genoa is sure to declare war.

"I think, then, that we had better make our way back to Venice with what cargo we have on board, and there get fresh orders from the padrone. We have not done badly so far, and it is better to make sure of what we have got than to risk its loss, for at any day we may fall in with the Genoese fleet sailing hither."

Francis quite agreed with the captain's opinion, and the Bonito sailed for the south. They touched, on their way, at several islands, and the news that an early outbreak of hostilities between Genoa and Venice was probable--in which case there would be an almost complete cessation of trade--produced so strong a desire, on the part of the islanders, to lay in a store of goods, that the captain was able to dispose of the rest of his cargo on good terms, and to fill up his ship with the produce of the islands.

Thus the Bonito was deep in the water when she re-entered the port of Venice after an absence of about three months. As soon as the anchor was dropped the captain, accompanied by Francis, hired a gondola, and rowed into the city to give an account to Signor Polani of the success of his voyage, and to lay before him a list of the cargo with which the Bonito was laden. The merchant received them with great cordiality, and embraced Francis with the affection of a father.

"Do you go at once into the salon, Francisco. You will find my daughters expecting you there, for the news came an hour ago that the Bonito was entering port. Of course, we heard from the letters from Candia of your adventures with the pirates, and the gallant way in which the Bonito defeated them.

"You will find, captain, that I have ordered an extra month's pay to be given to all on board.

"The captain did full justice, Francisco, in his account of the matter, to your quickness in suggesting a method by which the effort of the ramming of the enemy was neutralized, and for the courage you showed in carrying out your idea; but we will talk of that afterwards. He and I have business to transact which will occupy us for some time, so the sooner you go the better."

Francis at once took himself off and joined the girls, who received him with the heartiest greeting.

"We were glad indeed, Francis," Maria said, "when our father told us that the Bonito was signalled as entering the port. No letters have come for some time, and we feared that you must have entered the Dardanelles, and reached Constantinople, before the news arrived there of that affair at Tenedos, in which case you would no doubt have been seized and thrown into the dungeons."

"We were at Tenedos when the affair took place," Francis said, "and have had no opportunity since of sending a letter by any ship likely to be here before us. The outbreak made us alter our plans, for, of course, it would not have been safe to have sailed farther when the emperor was so enraged against Venice. I need hardly tell you I was not sorry when we turned our faces again towards Venice. I have enjoyed the voyage very much, and have had plenty to occupy me. Still, three months at a time is long enough, and I was beginning to long for a sight of Venice."

"For a sight of Venice and--" Maria repeated, holding up her finger reprovingly.

"And of you both," Francis said smiling. "I did not think it necessary to put that in, because you must know that you are Venice to me."

"That is much better," Maria said approvingly. "I think you have improved since you have been away. Do you not think so, Giulia?"

"I don't think that sort of nonsense is an improvement," Giulia said gravely. "Any of the young Venetian gallants can say that sort of thing. We do not want flattery from Francisco."

"You should say you do not want it, Giulia," Maria said, laughing. "I like it, I own, even from Francisco. It may not mean anything, but it is pleasant nevertheless; besides, one likes to think that there is just a little truth in it, not much, perhaps, but just a little in what Francisco said, for instance. Of course we are not all Venice to him. Still, just as we are pleased to see him, he is pleased to see us; and why shouldn't he say so in a pretty way? It's all very well for you to set up as being above flattery, Giulia, but you are young yet. I have no doubt you will like it when you get as old as I am."

Giulia shook her head decidedly.

"I always think," she said, "when I hear a man saying flattering things to a girl, that it is the least complimentary thing he can do, for it is treating her as if he considers that she is a fool, otherwise he would never say such outrageous nonsense to her."

"There, Francisco," Maria laughed, "you are fairly warned now. Beware how you venture to pay any compliment to Giulia in future.

"It would be a dull world if every one were to think as you do, Giulia, and to say exactly as they meant. Fancy a young man saying to you: 'I think you are a nice sort of girl, no prettier than the rest, but good tempered and pleasant, and to be desired because your father is rich!' A nice sort of way that would be to be made love to!"

"There is no occasion for them to say anything at all," Giulia said indignantly. "We don't go about saying to them, 'I think you are good looking, and well mannered, and witty;' or, 'I like you because they say you are a brave soldier and a good swordsman.' Why should they say such things to us? I suppose we can tell if anyone likes us without all that nonsense."

"Perhaps so," the elder girl assented; "and yet I maintain it's pleasant, and at any rate it's the custom, and as it's the custom, we must put up with it.

"What do you say, Francisco?"

"I don't know anything about it," Francis said. "Certainly some of the compliments I have heard paid were barefaced falsehoods, and I have wondered how men could make them, and how women could even affect to believe in them; but, on the other hand, I suppose that when people are in love, they really do think the person they are in love with is prettier and more charming, or braver and more handsome, than anyone else in the world, and that though it may be flattery, it is really true in the opinion of the person who utters it."

"And now let us leave the matter alone for the present, Francisco. We are dying to hear all about your adventures, and especially that fight with the pirates. The captain, in his letter, merely said that you were attacked and beat the pirates off, and that you would have been sunk if it hadn't been that, at your suggestion, they lowered bales of cloth over to break the shock; and that so many men were killed and so many wounded; and that you were hit twice by arrows, but the wounds were healing. That's all he said, for papa read that portion of his letter out to us. Now we want a full and particular account of the affair."

Francis gave a full account of the fight, and then related the other incidents of the voyage.

"We know many of the ports you touched at," Maria said when he had finished, "for when we were little girls, papa took us sometimes for voyages in his ships, when the times were peaceful and there was no danger. Now let us order a gondola, and go for a row. Papa is sure to be occupied for ever so long with your captain."

Chapter 9:
The Capture Of The Lido.

Signor Polani told Francis, that evening, that he was much pleased with the report that the captain had given of his eagerness to acquire information both in mercantile and nautical matters, and of the manner in which he had kept the ship's books, and the entries of the sales, and purchases of goods.

"Many young fellows at your age, Francis, when there was no compulsion for them to have taken these matters into their charge, would have thought only of amusement and gaiety when they were in port, and I am glad to see that you have a real interest in them. Whatever the line in life a young man takes up, he will never excel in it unless he goes into it with all his heart, and I am very glad to see that you have thrown yourself so heartily into your new profession. The Bonito made a most satisfactory voyage, far more so than I anticipated, when I found that she would not be able to carry out the programme I had laid down for her; but the rise in the prices in the latter part of your voyage have more than made up for the loss of the trade in the Black Sea; and you have done as much in the three months you were absent, as I should have expected had you been, as I anticipated, six months away.

"You will be some little time before you start again, as I wish to see how matters are going before I send the Bonito out upon another adventure. At present nothing is settled here. That there will be war with Genoa before long is certain, but we would rather postpone it as long as possible, and the senate has not yet arrived at the decision to accept the offer of Tenedos. Negotiations are going on with Genoa and Constantinople, but I have little hope that anything will come of them.

"It is getting late in the season now, and the war will hardly break out until next spring; but I have no doubt the struggle will then begin, and preparations are going on with all speed in the dockyards. We are endeavouring to obtain allies, but the combination is so strong against Venice that we are meeting with little success, and Ferrara is really the only friend on whom we can rely, and she is not in a position to aid us materially, in such a struggle as this will be.

"I am glad to tell you that the affair in which you were concerned, before you sailed, has now completely dropped. Nothing has been heard of Mocenigo since he made his escape.

"A decree of banishment was passed against him, but where he is we know not. That wretched woman was sentenced to four years' imprisonment, but upon my petition she will be released at the end of six months, on her promise that she will not again set foot in the territory of the republic. As Mocenigo has not been brought to trial, there will be no further official inquiry into the matter, and I have not been further questioned as to the source from which I obtained my information as to the girls' hiding place. Your share in the matter is therefore altogether unsuspected, and I do not think that there is any further danger to you from Mocenigo's partisans."

"I should be glad enough to remain in Venice a fortnight or so, sir," Francis said. "But if, at the end of that time, you have any vessel going out, I shall prefer to go in her. Now that my studies are over, I shall very soon get tired of doing nothing. Perhaps in a few years I may care more for the gaieties of Venice, but certainly at present I have no interest in them, and would rather be at sea. Matteo tells me that you have promised he shall make a few voyages in your ships, and that you have told him he shall go in one of them shortly. If so, it would be very pleasant to us both if we can sail together."

"I will arrange it so, Francisco. It would be for the benefit of my cousin--who is a good lad, but harebrained, and without ballast--for you to go with him. I should indeed have proposed it, but the vessel in which I have decided he shall sail will be ready for sea in another ten days or so, and I thought that you would prefer a longer stay in Venice before you again set sail. If, however, it is your wish to be off again so soon, I will arrange for you both to sail together.

"This time you will go officially as my supercargo, since you now understand the duties. The captain of the vessel in which you will sail is a good sailor and a brave man, but he has no aptitude for trade, and I must have sent a supercargo with him. Your decision to go relieves me of this, for which I am not sorry, for men who are at once good supercargos, and honest men, are difficult to get."

The fortnight passed rapidly, and Francis enjoyed his stay at the merchant's greatly, but he was not sorry when, at the end of ten days, Polani told him that the lading of the vessel would begin the next day, and that he had best go on board early and see the cargo shipped, so that he might check off the bales and casks as they were sent on board, and see where each description of goods was stowed away.

"I think, papa, it is too bad of you, sending Francisco away so soon," Maria said, when at their evening meal she learned the news of his early departure.

"It is his own doing," her father said. "It is he who wants to go, not I who send him. I consider that it is entirely your fault."

"Our fault!" the two girls repeated in surprise.

"Certainly. If you had made Venice sufficiently pleasant to him, he would not wish to leave. I am too busy to see about such things, and I left it to you to entertain him. As he is in such a hurry to get away again, it is evident that you have not succeeded in doing so."

"Indeed, Signor Polani, your daughters have been everything that is kind, but I have no taste for assemblies and entertainments. I feel out of place there, amid all the gaily dressed nobles and ladies, and no sooner do I get there, than I begin to wonder how anyone can prefer the heated rooms, and clatter of tongues, to the quiet pleasure of a walk backwards and forwards on the deck of a good ship. Besides, I want to learn my profession, and there is so much to learn in it that I feel I have no time to lose."

"I am right glad to see your eagerness in that direction, Francisco, and I did but jest with my daughters. You have not yet asked me what is the destination of the Lido, for that is the name of your new vessel. This time you are going quite in a new direction. In the spring we are certain to have war with Genoa, and as Parma and Hungary will probably both take side against us, we may find ourselves cut off from the mainland, and, in case of a disaster happening to our fleet, in sore straits for food. I am, therefore, going to gather into my warehouses as much grain as they will hold. This will both be a benefit to the state, and will bring me good profit, for the price of wheat will be high in the city if we are leaguered on the land side.

"The Lido will go down to Sicily, and fill up there with corn. You will have to use care before entering port, for with war now certain, both parties will begin to snap up prizes when they get the chance. So you must keep a sharp lookout for Genoese galleys. If you find the coast is too closely watched, you will go to the Moorish ports. We are friends with them at present, though doubtless, as soon as Genoa and ourselves get to blows, they will be resuming their piratical work. Thus you will, this time, take in a much smaller amount of cargo, as you will have to pay for the most part in gold."

It mattered little to Francis where he voyaged; but Matteo, who had been greatly delighted at the thought of sailing with his friend, was much disappointed when he heard that they were only going to fetch grain from Sicily.

"Why, it is nothing to call a voyage," he said in tones of disgust, when Francis told him the destination of the Lido. "I had hoped we were going to make a long voyage, and touch at all sorts of places, just as you did last time."

"I do not see that it matters much, Matteo; and we shall learn navigation just as well from one course as another. The voyage will not be a long one, unless we meet with unfavourable winds; but there's no saying what may happen, and you may meet with adventure, even on a voyage to Sicily and back."

The trip down to Sicily was quickly made. Francis had worked hard on his first voyage, and was now able to make daily calculations as to the run made, the course steered, and the position of the ship, and found that these tallied closely with those of the captain. Matteo and he shared a large and handsome cabin, and the time passed pleasantly as the vessel ran down the coast of Italy. Once out of the Adriatic a sharp lookout was kept, but the coast of Sicily was made without seeing any sails of a suspicious character.

The lads were struck with surprise and admiration when, on coming on deck in the morning, they saw the great cone of Etna lying ahead of them. Neither of them had ever seen a mountain of any size, and their interest in the scene was heightened by a slight wreath of smoke, which curled up from the summit of the hill.

"It is well worth a voyage, if it were only to see that mountain," Francis said. "What an immense height it is, and how regular in its shape!"

"And yet," Matteo said, "those who have journeyed from Italy into France tell me that there are mountains there beside which Etna is as nothing. These mountains are a continuation of the range of hills which we can see from Venice. Their tops are always covered with snow, and cannot be ascended by man; whereas it is easy, they say, to reach the top of Etna."

"Yes, that looks easy enough," Francis agreed. "It seems such a regular slope, that one could almost ride up; but I dare say, when you are close you would find all sorts of difficult places."

"I should like to try," Matteo said. "What a grand view there would be from the top!

"Is the port we are going to try first, captain, anywhere near the foot of the mountain?"

"No, I am going round the southern part of the island. On this side the ground is less fertile, and we should have difficulty in obtaining a cargo. But even were we to put into a port on this side, you would not be able to climb Mount Etna.

"Sicily has been an unfortunate country. Its great natural wealth has rendered it an object of desire, to all its neighbours. It was the battleground of the Romans and Carthaginians. Pisa, Genoa, and Naples have all contended for its possession; and the Moors frequently make descents upon its coasts. It has seldom enjoyed a peaceful and settled government. The consequence is that general lawlessness prevails in the districts remote from the towns; while in the forests that clothe the side of Mount Etna, there are numerous hordes of bandits who set the authorities at defiance, levy blackmail throughout the surrounding villages, and carry off wealthy inhabitants, and put them to ransom. No one in his senses would think of ascending that mountain, unless he had something like an army with him."

"I should like to try it, all the same," Matteo asserted. "If there are woods all over it, it is not likely one would happen to meet with any of these people. I should like, above all things, to get to the top of that hill."

"It would be harder work than you think, young sir," the captain said. "You have no idea from this distance what the height is, or what a long journey it is to ascend to the top. I have been told that it is a hundred and twenty miles round its foot."

"I don't think you would like it, Matteo, if you were to try it," Francis said laughing. "You know you are as lazy as you can be, and hate exerting yourself. I am sure that, before you got a quarter the distance up that mountain, you would have only one wish, and that would be to be at the bottom again."

"I don't know," Matteo said. "I hate exerting myself uselessly--wasting my strength, as you do, in rowing at an oar, or anything of that sort; but to do anything great, I would not mind exertion, and would go on until I dropped."

"That is all very well, Matteo; but to do anything great, you have got to do small things first. You could never wield a sword for five minutes unless you had practised with it; and you will never succeed in accomplishing any feats requiring great strength and endurance, if you do not practise your muscles on every occasion. You used to grumble at the height when you came up to my room in the old house, and I suppose Etna is something like two hundred times as high."

"That does sound a serious undertaking," Matteo said, laughing; "and I am afraid that I shall never see the view from the top of Etna. Certainly I shall not, if it will be necessary beforehand to be always exercising my muscles by running up the stairs of high houses."

The next day they were off Girgenti, the port at which they hoped to obtain a cargo. They steered in until they encountered a fishing boat, and learned from those on board that there was no Genoese vessel in port, nor, as far as the men knew, any state galleys anywhere in the neighbourhood. Obtaining this news, they sailed boldly into the port and dropped anchor.

Francis, who had received before starting a list of houses with whom Signor Polani was in the habit of doing business, at once rowed ashore, Matteo and Giuseppi accompanying him. His business arrangements were soon completed. The harvest had been a good one, and there was an abundance of corn to be had at a cheap rate. In half an hour he arranged for as large a quantity as the Lido would carry.

The work of loading soon commenced, and in four days the ship was full up to the hatches. Francis went on shore to settle the various accounts, and was just making the last payment when Matteo ran into the office.

"Four Genoese galleys are entering the bay!"

Francis ran out, and saw four Genoese galleys rowing in.

"It is too late to escape. Even were we empty we could not get away; but laden as the Lido is, they could row three feet to her one."

"What shall we do, Francisco?"

Francis stood for half a minute thinking.

"You had better stay here, Matteo. I will row out to the ship, and send most of the men on shore. If they seize the ship, they may not take those on board prisoners; but if they do, there is no reason why they should take us all."

"You had better come on shore too, Francisco, and leave the captain in charge. You can do no good by staying there; and Polani would be more concerned at your capture than he would at the loss of a dozen ships. If you could do any good, it would be different; but as it is, it would be foolish to risk capture."

"I will see," Francis said. "At any rate, do you stop here."

Jumping into a boat, he rowed towards the Lido, which was lying but a cable's length from the shore. As he neared her, he shouted to the men to lower the boats.

"Captain," he said, "I do not know whether there is any danger of being captured by the Genoese. But it is useless to run any unnecessary risk. Therefore send all the crew but three or four men on shore. If the Genoese board us, we have our papers as peaceful traders buying wheat; but if, in spite of that, they capture us, we must take our chance."

"Surely you are not thinking of stopping, Messer Francisco. The padrone would be terribly vexed if you were taken. He specially ordered me, before we started, to see that no unnecessary risk was run, and to prevent you from thrusting yourself into danger. Therefore, as captain of the ship, I must insist that you go on shore."

"I think I ought to stay here," Francis said.

"I do not think so," the captain said firmly, "and I will not suffer it. I have to answer for your safety to the padrone; and if you do not go by yourself, I shall order the men to put you into one of the boats by force. I mean no disrespect; but I know my duty, and that is to prevent you from falling into the hands of the Genoese."

"I will not oblige you to use force, captain," Francis said, smiling, "and will do as you wish me."

In five minutes the men were all--save four, whom the captain had selected--in the boat, and rowing towards shore. Matteo was awaiting them when they landed.

"That is right, Francisco. I was half afraid you would stay on board. I know how obstinate you are whenever you take a thing into your head."

"The captain was more obstinate still, Matteo, and said that unless I came away he would send me on shore by force; but I don't like deserting the ship."

"That is nonsense, Francisco. If the Genoese take her, they take her, and your remaining on board could not do any good. What are you going to do now?"

"We will at once leave the place with the men, Matteo, and retire into the country behind. It is not likely the Genoese would land and seize us here, but they might do so, or the inhabitants, to please Genoa, might seize us and send us on board. At any rate, we shall be safer in the country."

The men had, by the captain's orders, brought their arms ashore on leaving the ship. This was the suggestion of Francis, who said that, were they unarmed, the people might seize them and hand them over to the Genoese. At the head of this party, which was about fifty strong, Francis marched up through the little town and out into the country. He had really but little fear, either that the Genoese would arrest them on shore, or that the people would interfere with them, for they would not care to risk the anger of Venice by interfering in such a matter. He thought it probable, however, that if his men remained in the town, broils would arise between them and any of the Genoese sailors who might land.

As soon as the Genoese galleys came up to the head of the bay, a boat was lowered and rowed to the Lido, at whose masthead the Venetian flag was flying. An officer, followed by six men, climbed up on to the deck.

"Are you the captain of this ship?" the officer asked as the captain approached him.

"I am," the captain said.

"What ship is it?"

"It is the Lido, the property of Messer Polani, a merchant of Venice, and laden with a cargo of wheat."

"Then you are my prisoner," the Genoese said. "I seize this vessel as lawful prize."

"There is peace between the republics," the captain said. "I protest against the seizure of this ship, as an act of piracy."

"We have news that several of our ships have been seized by the Venetians," the officer said; "and we therefore capture this vessel in reprisal. Where are your crew?"

"There are only four on board," the captain said. "We have filled up our cargo, and were going to sail tomorrow, and therefore the rest of the crew were allowed to go on shore; and I do not think it is likely that they will return now," for one of the Genoese sailors had hauled down the flag of Venice, and had replaced it with that of Genoa.

The Genoese officer briefly examined the vessel.

"Whom have you here on board with you?" he asked, struck with the furniture and fittings of Francis' cabin.

"This is the cabin of Matteo Giustiniani, a young noble of Venice, who is making his first voyage, in order to fit himself for entering the service of the state: and of Francisco Hammond, who stands high in the affections of my patron."

The Genoese uttered an angry exclamation. The name of Polani was well known in Genoa as one of the chief merchants of Venice and as belonging to a ducal house, while the family of Giustiniani was even more illustrious; and had these passengers fallen into his hands, a ransom might have been obtained greatly exceeding the value of the Lido and her cargo. Leaving four of his men on board he went off to the galley of the officer commanding the fleet, and presently returned with a large boat full of sailors.

"You and your men can go ashore," he said to the captain. "The admiral does not deem you worth the trouble of carrying to Genoa; but be quick, or you will have to swim to shore."

As the Lido's boats had all gone ashore, the captain hailed a fishing boat which was passing, and with the four sailors was rowed to shore, well content that he had escaped the dungeons of Genoa. He rightly imagined that he and his men were released solely on account of the paucity of their numbers. Had the whole crew been captured, they would have been carried to Genoa; but the admiral did not care to bring in five prisoners only, and preferred taking the ship alone.

Francis, with his party, followed the line of the coast, ascending the hills which rose steeply from the edge of the sea at a short distance from the town. He had brought with him from the town a supply of food sufficient for four or five days, and encamped in a little wood near the edge of the cliff. From this they had a view of the port, and could watch the doings of the Genoese galleys. Fires were lit and meat cooked over them; and just as the meal was prepared the captain and the four sailors joined them, amid a hearty cheer from the crew.

"I have made my protest," the captain said as he took his seat by the side of Francis, "and the padrone can make a complaint before the council if he thinks fit to do so; but there is small chance that he will ever recover the Lido, or the value of her cargo."

"I don't like losing the ship," Francis said. "Of course, it is only a stroke of bad fortune, and we could neither fly nor defend ourselves. Still one hates arriving home with the story that one has lost the ship."

"Yes," the captain agreed. "Messer Polani is a just man, yet no one cares to employ men who are unlucky; and the worst of it is that the last ship I commanded was wrecked. Many men would not have employed me again, although it wasn't my fault. But after this second affair, in a few months' time, I shall get the name of being an unlucky man, and no one in his senses would employ a man who is always losing his ships."

"Do you think that there is any chance of our recapturing it, captain?"

"Not the least in the world," the captain replied. "Even supposing that we could get on board, and overpower the Genoese without being heard, and get her out of the port without being seen, we should not get away. Laden as she is with grain, she will sail very slowly, and the Genoese would overtake her in a few hours; and I needn't tell you that then there would be very little mercy shown to any on board."

"That is true enough," Francis said. "Still, I do not like the idea of losing the Lido."

After the meal was over Francis rose, and asked Matteo to accompany him on a stroll along the cliffs, Giuseppi as usual following them. They walked along until they rounded the head of the bay, and were able to look along the coast for some distance. It was steep and rocky, and worn into a number of slight indentations. In one of these rose a ledge of rocks at a very short distance from the shore.

"How much further are we going, Francis?" Matteo said when they had walked a couple of miles.

"About a quarter of a mile, Matteo. I want to examine that ledge of rocks we saw from the first point."

"What on earth do you want to look at them for, Francis? You certainly are the most curious fellow I ever met. You scoffed at me when I said I should like to go up Mount Etna, and now here you are, dragging me along this cliff, just to look at some rocks of no possible interest to any one."

"That is the point to be inquired into, Matteo. I think it's possible they may prove very interesting."

Matteo shrugged his shoulders, as he often did when he felt too lazy to combat the eccentric ideas of his English friend.

"There we are," Francis said at last, standing on the edge of the cliff and looking down. "Nothing could be better."

"I am glad you think so, Francisco," Matteo said, seating himself on the grass. "I hope you intend to stay some little time to admire them, for I own that I should like a rest before I go back."

Francis stood looking at the rocks. The bay was a shallow one, and was but five or six hundred yards from point to point, the rocks rising nearly in a line between the points, and showing for about two hundred yards above water, and at about the same distance from the cliffs behind them.

"What height do you think those rocks are above the water, Giuseppi?"

"It is difficult to judge, signor, we are so high above them; but I should think in the middle they must be ten or twelve feet."

"I should think it likely they were more than double that, Giuseppi; but we shall see better when we get down to the bottom. I daresay we shall find a place where we can clamber down somewhere."

"My dear Francisco," Matteo said earnestly, "is anything the matter with you? I begin to have doubts of your sanity. What on earth do these rocks matter to you, one way or the other? or what can you care whether they are thirty inches or thirty feet above the water?

"They do not differ from other rocks, as far as I can see. They are very rugged and very rough, and would be very awkward if they lay out at sea instead of in this little bay, where they are in nobody's way. Is it not enough that you have tramped two miles to have a look at them, which means four miles, as we have got to return somehow? And now you talk about climbing down that break-neck cliff to have a look at them close!"

But Francis paid no attention to Matteo's words. He was gazing down into the clear smooth water, which was so transparent that every stone and pebble at the bottom could be seen.

"The water looks extremely shallow, Giuseppi. What do you think?"

"It seems to me, signor, that there is not a foot of water between the rocks and the shore."

"It does look so, Giuseppi; but it is possible that the transparency of the water deceives us, and that there may be ten or twelve feet of water there. However, that is what we must go down and find out. Now the first thing is to look about, and find some point at which we can get down to the beach."

"Well, I will lie down and take a nap till you come back," Matteo said in a tone of resignation. "I have no interest either in these rocks or in the water; and as far as I can protest, I do so against the whole proceeding, which to me savours of madness."

"Don't you understand, you silly fellow, what I am thinking about?" Francis said impatiently.

"Not in the smallest degree, Francisco; but do not trouble to tell me--it makes no matter. You have some idea in your head. Carry it out by all means; only don't ask me to cut my hands, tear my clothes, and put myself into a perspiration by climbing down that cliff."

"My idea is this, Matteo. There is no chance of carrying off the Lido by speed from the Genoese; but if we could get her out of the bay we might bring her round here and lay her behind those rocks, and the Genoese would pass by without dreaming she was there. Half a mile out those rocks would look as if they form part of the cliff, and none would suspect there was a passage behind them."

"That is something like an idea!" Matteo said, jumping to his feet. "Why did you not tell me of it before? You have quite alarmed me. Seriously, I began to think that you had become a little mad, and was wondering whether I had not better go back and fetch the captain and some of his men to look after you.

"Now let us look at your rocks again. Why, man, there is not water enough to float a boat between them and the shore, much less the Lido, which draws nine foot of water now she is loaded."

"I don't know, Matteo. Looking down on water from a height is very deceiving. If it is clear and transparent, there is nothing to enable you to judge its depth. At any rate it is worth trying. Before we go down, we will cut some long stiff rods with which we can measure the depth. But we have first to find a place where we can get down to the water."

After a quarter of an hour's search, they found a point where the descent seemed practicable. A little stream had worn a deep fissure in the face of the rock. Shrubs and bushes had grown up in the crevices and afforded a hold for the hands, and there appeared no great difficulty in getting down. Before starting they cut three stiff slender rods twelve feet in length. They then set to work to make the descent. It was by no means difficult, and in a few minutes they stood by the edge of the water.

"It is a great advantage, the path being so easy," Francis said, "for in case they did discover the ship we could land and climb to the top before they had time to come to shore, and once there we could keep the whole force in those galleys at bay. Now for the main point, the depth of the water."

Matteo shook his head.

"It is useless to take the trouble to undress, Francis," he said, as the latter threw off his jacket. "Giuseppi can wade out to the rocks without wetting his knees."

"Giuseppi can try if he likes," Francis said, "but I will wager he will not get far."

Giuseppi, as convinced as Matteo of the shallowness of the water, stepped into it, but was surprised to find that, before he had gone many paces, the water was up to his waist.

"Well, I wouldn't have believed it if I hadn't seen it," Matteo said when he returned, "but I think he must have got into a deep hole among the rocks. However, we shall soon see," and he too began to undress.

In a few minutes the three lads were swimming out towards the rocks which, as Francis had anticipated, rose from twenty to thirty feet above the level of the sea. The water deepened fast, and for the last thirty or forty yards, they were unable to touch the bottom, even when thrusting down their rods to the fullest depth. They then tried the depth in the passages at the end of the rocks, and found that there was ample water for the Lido. When they ascertained this to their satisfaction they swam back to the shore.

"I shall believe you in future, Francis, even if you assert that the moon is made of cheese. I could have taken an oath that there was not a foot of water between those rocks and the shore."

"I hardly ventured to hope that it was as deep as it is," Francis said, "but I know how deceiving clear water is, when you look down upon it from a height. However, that point is settled."

"But they would see our masts above the rocks, Francisco. They are sure to keep a sharp lookout as they go along."

"We must take the masts out of her," Francis said. "I don't know how it is to be done, but the captain will know, and if that can't be managed we must cut them down. There is no difficulty about that.

"Now we will make our way back again, it will be dark in a couple of hours' time. Everything depends upon whether they have towed the Lido out and anchored her among their galleys. If they have, I fear the scheme is impracticable, but if they let her remain where she is lying, we might get her out without being noticed, for there is no moon."

As they began to ascend the cliff, Francis stopped suddenly.

"We should never be able to find this place in the dark," he said.

"Giuseppi, you must stay here. Do you collect a quantity of dried sticks, and lay them in readiness at that point opposite the ledge. We will show a light as we come along, that is if we succeed in getting the Lido out, and directly you see it set fire to the sticks. The fire will be a guide to us as to the position of the rocks."

"Perhaps I had better take the sticks off to the ledge, Messer Francisco, and light my fire on the rock at the end. The water is deep a few yards out, as we found, so you could sail close to the fire and then round behind the rocks without danger."

"That will be the best way, Giuseppi; but how will you get the sticks off without wetting them?"

"I will make a bundle three or four times as big as I want," Giuseppi said, "and then half of them will be dry. I can put my clothes on them and the tinder. I will answer for the fire, but I would rather have been with you in your adventure."

"There will be no danger there, Giuseppi, so you need not be anxious about us. It has to be done quietly and secretly, and there will be no fighting. These Genoese are too strong to think of that; and if we are discovered in the attempt, or as we make off, we shall take to our boats again and row straight on shore.

"Keep a sharp lookout for us, we will hoist two lights, one above the other, to prevent your mistaking any fishing boat which may be coming along for us.

"Now, Matteo, for a climb. We have no time to lose."

The two lads climbed to the top of the cliff, and then started at a brisk pace along the top, and in half an hour reached the wood.

"We were beginning to wonder what had become of you," the captain said as they joined him.

"We have been settling how to carry off the Lido," Francis said, "and have arranged everything."

The captain laughed.

"If we could fly with her through the air, you might get her away, but I see no other way. I have been thinking it over since you left. With luck we might get her safely out of the bay, but the galleys row four feet to our one, and as they would be sure to send some one way, and some the other, along the coast; they would pick us up again in two or three hours after daylight."

"Nevertheless we have settled it, captain. We have found a place where we can hide her, and the Genoese might search the coast for a month without finding her."

"If that be so it is possible," the captain said eagerly, "and you may be sure you will not find us backward in doing our best."

Francis described the nature and position of the rock which would afford a shelter, and the means by which they had ascertained that there was plenty of water for the Lido behind it.

"It seems plausible," the captain said when he had concluded, "and I am quite ready to make the attempt, if, in your opinion, it can be done. You are Messer Polani's representative, and for my own sake as well as his, I would do anything which promises a chance of recapturing the ship. Besides, as you say, there is little danger in it, for we can take to the boats and make for the shore if discovered.

"The Lido is still lying where we anchored her. They can have no fear of a recapture, for they would know that they could overtake us easily enough. I daresay they intend to sail tomorrow morning, and did not think it worth the trouble to get up the anchor and tow her out to where they are lying."

The details of the expedition were now discussed and arranged, and the men told off to their various duties, and at eleven o'clock at night, when all in the town were fast asleep, the party quitted the bivouac and marched down again to the port.

Chapter 10:
Recaptured.

No one was astir in the streets as the band marched through, and they reached the port without encountering a single person. A small boat was chosen, and in this the captain, Francis, Matteo, and two of the strongest and most powerful of the sailors embarked. It was thought unlikely that, lying, as the Lido did, within a couple of hundred yards of the Genoese galleys, any very vigilant watch would be kept, and not more than two sailors would probably be on deck.

The dark mass of the ship could just be made out from the shore, and when all was ready the two sailors with their oars pushed her off with all their strength, and then stood perfectly quiet.

The impetus was sufficient. The boat moved so slowly through the water, indeed, before they reached the ship, that Francis thought it would be necessary for the men to row a stroke or two; but the boat still moved on, until at last it touched the side of the ship. All had removed their boots before starting, and they now clambered up the sides without making the slightest noise.

Once on deck they stood perfectly quiet, listening. Presently they heard a murmur of voices on the other side of the vessel. Very quietly they crept towards the sound, and at length made out two figures leaning over the bulwarks, talking.

Each man's work had been settled, and there was no confusion. One of the sailors and Francis stole towards one of the men, while the other and Matteo approached the second. The captain stood with his sword bared, in readiness to cut down any other man who might be on deck.

The Genoese did not look round. Francis gave the word, "Now," and in a moment the two sailors seized them from behind with a grasp of iron, while the lads at the same moment passed bandages tightly round their mouths, and before the Genoese were quite aware of what had happened, they were lying, bound hand and foot, gagged upon the deck.

The party now made a search, but found no one else about. They then secured and fastened down the hatch of the forecastle by coiling ropes upon it, quietly opened the door leading to the poop cabins, and entering, seized and bound two officers sleeping there without the slightest noise or resistance.

Then they took a light from the cabin and showed it towards the shore. At the signal the sailors, who had already taken their places in the boats, at once rowed out to the vessel. When all were on board, the boats were fastened alongside, in case it should be necessary to abandon the ship again.

The cable was then cut. One of the sailors had already ascended the shrouds, and poured oil over the blocks through which the halyards ran, so that the sails should ascend noiselessly. The wind was very light, scarcely enough to belly out the sails, but it was fortunately in the right direction, and the Lido began to steal through the water.

Not a word had been spoken since they first started, but Francis now whispered to the captain, "I think I can make out the Genoese ships."

"So can I," the captain said, "but they cannot see us. They are against the skyline, while we are in the shadow of the shore. So far all is perfectly safe, and if this breath of wind will but carry us far enough out to be able to use our oars without their hearing us, we shall certainly get away."

The progress of the Lido was so slow, that it was nearly an hour before the captain said that he thought they were now fairly round the point of the bay, and could use their oars.

"We had better tow," he said; "the sweeps make a noise that can be heard miles away on a calm night like this, whereas, if they are careful, men in a boat can row almost noiselessly."

Ten of the men accordingly took their places in one of the large boats in which they had come on board, and a rope being passed down to them they began rowing at the head of the ship.

"We may as well lower the sails," the captain said, "they are doing no good now. Indeed I think it is a current rather than the wind that has helped us so far."

"I will put two lanterns over the side," Francis said. "We may have gone farther than we think, and it would never do to pass our hiding place."

The men in the boat rowed vigorously, but it was slow work towing the deeply-laden vessel. At last, however, a light burst suddenly up from the shore.

"There is Giuseppi," Francis exclaimed. "We are further out than we thought we were. He must be fully a mile and a half away."

The men in the boat were told to row direct for the light, and some of the sweeps were got out and helped the vessel through the water. As they drew near, they could make out Giuseppi throwing fresh wood on the fire.

"You can steer within ten yards of where he is standing, captain, and directly you are abreast of him, put your helm hard to port. You had better get the sweeps in now, the less way she has on her the better."

"All well?" Giuseppi hailed, as they came within fifty yards of it.

"All well, Giuseppi! There has been no fighting, so you have lost nothing. Put all your wood on the fire, we want as much light as we can to get in."

The flames shot up high, and the captain had no difficulty in rounding the corner of the rocks, and bringing up his vessel behind them. A kedge was dropped, and the men in the boat rowed to the end of the rocks, and brought off Giuseppi.

"I was beginning to be anxious," the lad said, as he joined them on deck, "and when I first saw your signal I took you for a fishing boat. You were so far off that the two lights looked like one, but by dint of gazing I made them out at last, and then lit the fire."

"Now, captain," Francis said, "we have a good deal to do before morning, for I take it it will be no easy matter to get out the masts."

"There would be no difficulty in getting the masts out," the captain answered. "I have only to knock out the wedges, and loosen the stays, and get up a tripod made of three spars to lift them out; but I don't see how they are to be got in again."

"How is that, captain? I should have thought it no more difficult to get a mast in than to take it out."

"Nor would it be so, under ordinary circumstances," the captain replied; "but you see, our hold is full of grain, and as the mast comes out, the hole it leaves will fill up, and there will be no getting it down again to step it on the keel without discharging the cargo."

"Yes, I see that, captain. Then you think we had better cut down the masts; but in that case how are we to raise them?"

"We will cut them off about six feet above the deck, Messer Francisco; then when we want to set sail again, we have only to rear the masts up by the side of the stumps, and lash them securely. Of course they will be six feet shorter than before, but that is of little consequence."

"Then so let it be," Francis said, "the sooner we begin the better."

Just at this moment there was a violent knocking against the hatch of the forecastle.

"I had forgotten all about the sailors," the captain said, laughing. "I suppose the men who were to relieve the watch have woke up, and finding they could not get out, have aroused their comrades."

"Shall we leave them there, or take them out and bind them?" Matteo asked.

"We had better have them up," the captain said. "I don't suppose there are more than twenty of them, and it would be best to bind them, and put them down in the hold with the corn, otherwise they may manage to break out when we are not expecting it, and might give us some trouble."

Accordingly, the sailors gathered round the hatch. The ropes were then removed, and the hatch taken off.

"What fooling are you up to?" one of the Genoese exclaimed, angrily, as they rushed up on deck. "You have nearly stifled us down below putting on the hatch and fastening it."

He stopped abruptly as, on gaining the deck, he saw a crowd of armed figures round him, for a lantern had been placed so as to throw a light upon the spot.

"You are prisoners," the captain said. "It is useless to attempt resistance."

"Help, help, treachery!" one of the Genoese shouted at the top of his voice.

"It is useless for you to shout," the captain said, "you are miles away from your fleet. Now, do you surrender, or are we to attack you?"

Taken by surprise, and unarmed, the Genoese who had gained the deck sullenly replied that they surrendered. They were bound and led away, and the others ordered to come up on deck. There were found to be four-and-twenty in all, and these were soon laid side by side on the grain in the hold, the hatch being left off to give them air. The masts were then cut through, and were with some trouble lowered to the deck.

"There is nothing more to be done now," the captain said, "and I think we can all safely turn in till morning."

He then ordered the under officer to place two men on watch on the rocks, and two men on deck, two men to stand as sentinels over the prisoners, and the rest to lie down. He directed that he should be roused at the earliest streak of daylight.

The lads were soon fast asleep, and could hardly believe that the night was over, when Giuseppi awakened them with the news that day was breaking. They were soon on deck, and found that the crew were already astir. The sentinels on the rock were at once ordered to lie down, so that they could command a view of the sea, without exposing themselves to sight. The boats were drawn up alongside, and everything put in readiness for instant debarkation, and then the party waited for the appearance of the Genoese galleys.

"They will be along in less than an hour," the captain said. "It is light enough now for the watch to have discovered that the Lido is missing, and it will not be many minutes before they are under way. They will calculate that we can have but five or six hours' start at the utmost, and that three hours' rowing will bring them up to us."

"I have no fear whatever of their discovering us as they go along," Francis said. "The only fear is that, after rowing for three or four hours and seeing no sign of us, they will guess that we are hidden somewhere under the cliffs, and will come back along the shore, searching every bay."

"There is a chance of that," the captain agreed, "but I should think only a chance. When the party who come this way find they do not overtake us, they will suppose that we have sailed to the west, and that on their return they will find us in the hands of their comrades; and when these also come back empty handed they will conclude that we have sailed straight out to sea. Of course they may have sent a galley southward also, but will conclude that that has somehow missed us when it returns without news. I hardly think that the idea, that we may be hidden so close to them, will enter their minds, and the only fear I entertain is that some peasant may happen to come to the edge of the cliff and see us lying here, and may take the news back to Girgenti."

"Yes, there is certainly a danger of that," Francis said. "I think, captain, it would be the best plan to land twenty men at once. Giuseppi will show them the way up the cliff, and then they must take their station, at short distances apart, along the edge of the cliff, from point to point of this little bay, with orders to seize any one who may approach and bring him down here. They must, of course, be told to lie down, as a line of sentries along the top of the cliff might attract the attention of somebody on the galleys, and lead to a search."

"Yes, I think that will be a wise precaution," the captain agreed.

"Thomaso, do you take twenty men and post them as you hear Messer Francisco say. Tell them to lie in the bushes and keep out of sight, and on no account to show themselves, unless someone comes along sufficiently near to look over the edge of the cliff."

"Giuseppi," Francis said, "do you act as guide to the party. You will have plenty of time to get to the top and to return before the galleys come along."

A quarter of an hour later the captain, with Matteo and Francis, landed on the ledge, and took the place of the sentries, and in twenty minutes a simultaneous exclamation burst from them, as a Genoese galley was seen rowing rapidly along.

"They have sent only one galley," Francis said. "Of course, they would know that it was sufficiently strong to overpower us without difficulty. I suppose one has gone west, and the others have put out to sea in different directions. That certainly was the best course they could have adopted, and it is very lucky that we did not attempt to escape seaward, for they would assuredly have had us. I suppose, captain, you intend to sail tonight."

"Certainly," the captain replied. "We will get everything in readiness for hoisting the masts as soon as the galley has passed us on its way back. There is no fear of their coming along again later on, for the men will have had an eight hours' row of it; the first part, at any rate, at full speed. Besides, they will not know, until all the galleys return, that we have not been found, so I think it will be quite safe to get up the masts as soon as they have passed. Then directly it is dark we will man our oars and row to the southwest. We shall be far away before morning, even if they look further for us, which they are hardly likely to do."

"How about the prisoners, captain?"

"We have no choice but to take them with us, Messer Francisco. I am sure I do not want to be bothered with them, but we cannot land them before we leave, or they would carry the news to Girgenti in an hour, and we should be caught the first thing in the morning."

It was late in the afternoon before the galley was seen returning, rowing slowly and heavily.

"I expect," the captain said, "they kept up the racing pace at which they started for some four hours. By that time they must have been completely worn out, and no doubt they anchored and waited for some hours for the men to feed and rest themselves, for from the hurry with which they started you may be sure that they did not wait to break their fast.

"I would give a month's pay to be in that harbour this evening. What tempers they must be in when they find, after all their toil, that we have slipped through their fingers, How they will talk the matter over, and discuss which way we went. How the men in each ship will say that the others cannot have used their eyes or exerted themselves, else we must have been overtaken. Messer Francisco, I am indebted to you, not only for having saved the ship, but for giving me a joke, which I shall laugh over whenever I think of it. It will be a grand story to tell over the wine cups, how we cheated a whole Genoese fleet, and carried off the Lido from under their noses. What a tale it will be to relate to a Genoese, when we meet in some port after the war is over; it will be enough to make him dance with rage.

"Now, lads," he went on, turning to the men, "stand to your tackle. The moment that galley gets out of sight round the point, up with the mast."

Ten minutes later the masts were up, stout ropes were lashed round them and the stumps, and wedges driven in to tighten the cords to the utmost. The rigging was of the simplest description, and before dark everything was in readiness for hoisting the sails.

"I don't think they can make us out now," the captain said.

"I don't think they could," Francis agreed; "but we had better wait another quarter of an hour. It would be absurd to run any risk after everything has turned out so well; but the men can get into the boats and tow us out through the channel, then we can hoist the boats on board, and by that time it should be nearly dark enough."

"I think there will be a breeze presently," the captain said, "and from the right direction. However, the men won't mind working hard for a bit. They have had an easy time for the last two days."

The oars were all manned, and the men set to work with hearty goodwill. They were delighted at their escape from the island, for they might have been there some time before they got a passage back; and still more pleased at having tricked the Genoese; and the Lido, heavy laden as she was, moved at a steady pace through the water, under the impulsion of the oars.

For an hour they rowed parallel with the shore, as, had they made out to sea, they might possibly have been seen by one of the galleys, returning late from the search for them. At the end of that time the captain turned her head from shore. As soon as they got well out from under the shelter of the land the breeze made itself felt, and the sails were hoisted.

For a time the men kept on rowing, but the breeze increased rapidly, and the captain ordered the oars to be laid in. A double allowance of wine was served out, and an hour or two spent in song and hilarity; then the watch below was sent down, and Francis and Matteo turned into their cots.

In the morning the breeze was blowing strong. The sails had been taken off the mainmast, but that on the foremast was dragging the Lido through the water at a good rate of speed, and before night they were off Cape Spartivento. The wind held till next morning, when they were abreast of the Gulf of Taranto. Then came a long spell of calms or baffling winds, and it was a fortnight before the campaniles of Venice were seen rising apparently from the water.

"I have been anxious about you," Signor Polani said when Francis arrived. "One of our galleys brought the report that a Genoese fleet was cruising on the coast of Sicily, and as, although war had not yet been openly declared, both parties were making prizes, I was afraid that they might have snapped you up."

"They did snap us up," Francis said smiling. "They caught us in the port of Girgenti, and the standard of Genoa waved over the Lido."

"But how can that be," Polani said, "when you have returned in her? For she was signalled as approaching the port hours ago. You could hardly have persuaded the Genoese by fair words to release a prize that they had once taken."

"Eh, captain?"

"No, that is not the Genoese way, nor ours either," the captain said. "We did better than that, signor. We recaptured her, and carried her off from under their noses."

"You are joking," Polani said, "for they signalled the Lido as returning laden, and a laden ship could never get away from state galleys, however long her start. A fat pig might as soon try to escape from a hunting dog."

"That is so, Messer Polani, and we did not trust to our speed. We tricked them famously, sir. At least, when I say we did, Messer Francisco here did, for the credit is due solely to him. If it had not been for this young gentleman, I and the crew would now have been camping out in the forests of Sicily, without the slightest prospect of being able to make our way home, and the Lido would now be moored in the port of Genoa."

"That is so, Cousin Polani," Matteo said. "It is to Francisco that we owe our escape, and you owe the safety of the Lido and her cargo."

"It was just a happy idea that occurred to me," Francis said, "as it would assuredly have occurred to Captain Pesoro, if he had been with us, or to anyone else, and after I had first suggested it the captain carried out all the arrangements."

"Not at all, Messer Francisco," the captain said obstinately. "I had no part or hand in the business, beyond doing what you suggested, and you would have got the Lido off just as well if I hadn't been there."

"Well, I will judge for myself when I hear," Polani said. "But, as it must be an interesting story, my daughters would like to hear it also. So, come into the next room and tell the tale, and I will order up a flagon of Cyprus wine to moisten your throats."

"First of all," the captain began, after the girls had greeted Francis, and all had taken their seats, "I must tell how the Lido was captured."

And he then related how the Genoese fleet had suddenly appeared before them, and how, seeing the impossibility of escape, he had sent all on shore with the exception of four sailors, and how he had, with them, been released and sent on shore.

"That's the Genoese all over," Polani said. "If they could have sent forty prisoners home they would have done so; but the fact that there were only five on board, when they took the vessel, would seem to them to detract from the credit of the capture."

The captain then told how, fearing that the people of Girgenti might give them all up to the Genoese, or that fights might ensue among the Genoese sailors who landed, he had marched the crew away out of the town.

"Now, captain," Matteo broke in, "I will tell the next bit, because I was with Francis when he found a hiding place."

He then related how Francis had seen the ledge of rocks in the distance, and had dragged him along the cliff two miles to observe them more closely; and how he had come to the conclusion that his companion had lost his senses. Then he described the exact position, and the clearness of the water, and how he had been convinced that there was not depth to float a rowboat inside the rocks; and how they had gone down, swum out, fathomed the water, and then returned to the wood.

The captain then took up the tale again, and completed it to the end.

"There is no doubt you were right, captain," Polani said, "and that it is entirely Francisco's quickness of observation, readiness of plan, and determination to see if his ideas could be carried into effect, which saved the Lido. That he possessed these qualities is not new to me, for I have already greatly benefited by them. If he had not been born a peaceful trader, he would have made a great captain some day; but the qualities which would distinguish a man in war are also useful in peace, and I think it fully as honourable to be a successful merchant, as a successful soldier.

"Henceforth, Francisco, I shall no longer consider you as in leading strings, and shall feel that I can confide important business to you, young as you are."

The next voyage that Francis made was to Jaffa, and this was accomplished without adventure. On his return, he found that Venice was in a state of excitement--war had at last been declared, and every effort was being made to fit out a fleet which could cope with that of Genoa.

The command was entrusted to Vettore Pisani, who was invested in the church of Saint Mark with the supreme command of the fleet by the doge himself, who handed to the admiral the great banner of Venice, with the words:

"You are destined by God to defend with your valour this republic, and to retaliate upon those who have dared to insult her and to rob her of that security which she owes to the virtue of her ancestors. Wherefore, we confide to you this victorious and great standard, which it will be your duty to restore to us unsullied and triumphant."

Carlo Zeno, a noble, who had gained a high reputation in various capacities, was appointed commissioner and captain general of Negropont. The three first divisions of those inscribed in the register, as liable to serve in the navy, were called out, and on the 24th of April Pisani sailed from Venice with fourteen war galleys.

Pisani enjoyed the highest popularity among the people of Venice. His manner was that of a bluff hearty sailor. He was always ready to share in the hardships of his men, and to set them an example of good temper and cheerfulness, as well as of bravery. He was quick tempered, and when in a passion cared nothing whom he struck.

When governor of Candia, he had got into a serious scrape, by striking Pietro Cornaro, an officer of the republic, from whom he happened to differ on some point of routine. He was a relative of the Doge Andrea Contarini, and had been employed not only as an officer in the navy, but as a military engineer and as a diplomatist, and in each capacity had shown equal talent.

He was connected with the Polani family, and was at their house several times before he sailed. Here he heard from his kinsman an account of the manner in which Francisco had saved the Bonito from being rammed by the pirates, and how he had succeeded in getting the Lido out of the hands of the Genoese; and he was so much pleased that he offered to take him with him in his galley, but Polani advised Francis not to accept the offer.

"It is quite true," he said, "that most of our noble families are, like myself, engaged in commerce; and that one day they are trading as merchants and the next fighting under the state; but at present, if you take my advice, you will stick to the peaceful side of the profession; especially as, being an Englishman, you are in no way called upon to serve the state. In another five or six years, if we are then at war, it will be different. I have frequently offered galleys for the service of the state, and you can then take the command of one, and will, I have no doubt, distinguish yourself; but were you to enter now, you might remain in the service of the state for some years, and would be losing your time as a merchant.

"There are countries in which, when a man once takes up the profession of arms, he remains a soldier all his life, and may not only achieve honour but wealth and wide possessions. It is not so in Venice. Here we are all citizens as well as all soldiers if need be. We fight for the state while a war lasts, and then return to our peaceful avocations. Even my kinsman, Pisani, may be admiral of the fleet today, and a week hence may be a private citizen. Therefore, my lad, I think it would be very foolish of you to give up commerce at present to take military service."

"I quite agree with you, signor," Francis said, although, in truth, for a moment he had felt a strong mind to accept the offer of Pisani. "I am just beginning to learn a little of trade, and desire nothing better than to be a successful merchant; though I confess that I should like to take part in such a glorious sea fight as that which is likely to take place soon."

"Yes, and perhaps be killed in the first engagement, Francis, for neither skill nor bravery avail against a bolt from a Genoese crossbow. No, my lad, be content with trade, especially since you have seen already that even the life of a trader has plenty of incident and excitement. What with storms, what with pirates, what with the enemies of the state and the treachery of the native peoples with whom we trade, there is no lack of adventure in the life of a Venetian merchant."

Francis felt that this was true, and that he had in the past six months had fully his share in adventures. His stay on shore this time extended over a month, and it was not until three weeks after Pisani sailed that he again set out.

The notice was a short one. Polani had been sent for to attend the council early in the morning, and on his return he said to Francis:

"You must go down to the port at once, Francis. News has been received from Pisani that he has sailed almost into the port of Genoa, without finding the fleet of Fieschi. The Genoese have been in a terrible state of panic. The Lord of Fiesole, who is our ally, is menacing the city by land; the Stella Company of Condottieri, which is in our pay, is also marching against them; and the news that Pisani was close at hand seems to have frightened them out of their senses. Their first step, as usual, has been to depose their doge and choose another.

"However, that is not the point. Pisani has written asking that some ships with provisions and stores shall be sent out to him. They are to go through the Straits of Messina and up the coast of Italy until he meets them. His force is far too small for him to think of making an attack upon Genoa. He will wait in the neighbourhood of the city for a short time in hopes of Fieschi's fleet returning. If it does not do so he will come down the coast searching for it, and as he does not wish to put in port, he desires the stores mentioned to be sent out to him.

"I have placed the Bonito at their service, and have promised that she shall be ready to sail tomorrow morning, if they will send the stores on board today. Three other merchants placed ships at their disposal, but these may not sail for a day or two. They are particularly anxious that the Bonito shall start at once, as, in addition to provisions, she will carry a store of javelins, arrows, and other missiles of which there was not a sufficiency in the arsenal when Pisani sailed.

"You will have a strong party on board, as speed is required, and the oars must be kept going until you join the fleet. Therefore I shall place the crew of the Lido on board as well as the Bonito's own complement, and this will bring the number up to a hundred men. The captain has had an accident, and will not be able to go in charge, therefore the Lido's captain will command. This time I shall appoint you specifically second in command, as well as my representative. Now get off on board as quickly as you can, for there is enough to keep you at work, till tomorrow morning, to get everything in readiness for a start. You had best run in and say goodbye to my daughters, as it may be that you will not find time to return before sailing. You can send your boy ashore for what things you require. Matteo will accompany you."

A few minutes later, Francis was on his way to the port, leaving Giuseppi to charter a gondola and follow with his trunks. As Polani had said, he was occupied without intermission until the time for sailing next morning. The barges of the state kept coming alongside with stores and provisions from the arsenal; while other boats brought out the ship's stores; and Francis had to take a note of all that came on board.

The captain superintended the setting up of the rigging, and the getting of the ship into working order; while the under officers saw to the hoisting in and storing of the cargo. Gangs of men were at work tarring the sides of the ship, for she had only two days before returned from a trip to Spain; and a number of sailors were unloading the cargo from one hatchway, while her fresh freight was being taken in at the other.

It seemed well nigh impossible that she could be ready to sail at the hour named, but everyone worked with a will, and by daybreak things were almost in order. Polani himself came down to the port as soon as it was light, and expressed satisfaction at the work which had been done; and half an hour afterwards the anchor was weighed.

Just as the sails had been hoisted, Matteo arrived.

"You are only just in time, Matteo," Polani said. "Why did you not come off yesterday and help?"

"I was out," Matteo said, "when your message came, and only returned just in time to go to the entertainment at the ducal palace. I knew I could be of no use on board while they were only getting in the cargo."

"You will never be of any use on board, Matteo, if you go to entertainments when there's work to be done. You could have taken the marks on the bales as they came on board, just as well as another. I suppose you thought that the dirt and dust wouldn't suit a fine gentleman like you! Another time, unless you come on board when sent for, and make yourself as useful as you can, while the ship is fitting out and loading, you will not sail in her. One part of the duty is just as important as the other, and seamanship does not consist solely in strolling up and down the deck, and watching a vessel sail for her destination."

Matteo was abashed at the reproach, but soon recovered his usual spirits after Polani had left, when the vessel was under way.

"My cousin was rather in a sharp mood this morning," he said with a laugh to Francis; "but really I did not think I could be of any good, and the entertainment was a grand one. Everyone was there, and I should have been very sorry to have missed it."

"Everyone to his taste, Matteo. For my part, I would very much rather have been at work here all night watching the cargo got in and checking it off, than have been standing about doing nothing in the palace."

"Doing nothing!" Matteo repeated indignantly. "Why, I was talking to someone the whole time I was there."

"Talking about what, Matteo?"

"The heat, and the music, and the costumes, and the last bit of scandal at the Piazza."

"I don't call that talk. I call it chatter. And now, Matteo, I shall leave you to your own devices, for I am going to turn in and get a sleep for a few hours."

"You look as if you wanted it," Matteo said; "but I think that you stand in even more need of a wash. You are grimy with dust. It is just as well that my cousin Giulia did not come on board with her father this morning, for the sight of your face would have given her quite a shock, and would have dissipated any illusions she may have had that you were a good-looking fellow."

Francis went off to his cabin with a laugh, and took Matteo's advice as to the wash before he turned in. In a few minutes he was asleep, and did not wake until Giuseppi came to say that the midday meal was just ready.

The Bonito made a rapid voyage. The winds were light, and for the most part favourable, and the twenty-four oars were kept going night and day, the men relieving each other every two hours, so that they had six hours' rest between the spells of rowing.

When they rounded the southern point of Italy a sharp lookout was kept for the fleet of Fieschi, but they passed through the straits without catching sight of a single vessel carrying the Genoese flag. The most vigilant watch was now kept for Pisani's galleys, and they always anchored at the close of day, lest they should pass him in the dark.

Occasionally they overhauled a fishing boat, and endeavoured to obtain news of the two squadrons; but beyond the fact that Fieschi had been seen steering north some days before, and that no signs had been seen of Pisani's returning fleet, they could learn nothing.

Chapter 11:
The Battle Of Antium.

"We are running very far north," the captain said on the 29th of May. "We are near Antium now, and are getting into what we may call Genoese waters. If anything has occurred to prevent Pisani carrying out his intention of sailing back along this coast, or if he has passed us on the way up, our position would be a hazardous one, for as soon as he has rowed away the Genoese galleys will be on the move again, and even if we do not fall in with Fieschi, we may be snapped up by one of their cruisers."

"It is rather risky, captain," Francis agreed; "but our orders are distinct. We were to sail north till we met Pisani, and we must do so till we are within sight of the walls of Genoa. If we then see he is not lying off the port, we shall put about and make our way back again."

"Yes, if they give us the chance, Messer Francisco; but long before we are sufficiently near to Genoa to make out whether Pisani is lying off the port, they will see us from the hills, and will send off a galley to bring us in. However, we must take our chance, and if we get into a scrape I shall look to you confidently to get us out again."

"I should advise you not to count on that," Francis said, laughing. "It is not always one gets such a lucky combination of circumstances as we did at Girgenti."

At last, they obtained news from a fishing boat that Fieschi's fleet had passed, going northward, on the previous day, and was now lying in the bay of Antium. As Antium lay but a few miles north, they held a consultation as to the best method to pursue. If they sailed on there was a risk of capture; but that risk did not appear to be very great. The Genoese admiral would not expect to find a Venetian merchant ship so near to Genoa, and they might be able to pass without being interfered with. On the other hand, news might possibly have come of the departure of store ships from Venice for Pisani's fleet, and in that case a strict lookout would certainly be kept, and it would be necessary to keep so far to sea as to be out of sight of the Genoese; but in that case there would be a risk of their missing Pisani's fleet on the way down.

"I think," the captain said, after a long debate, "that we had better anchor here close under the shore tonight. If I am not mistaken, we shall have a gale in the morning. I do not like the look of the sky. Tomorrow we shall see how the weather is, and can then come to a decision."

By morning, as the captain had predicted, the wind was blowing strongly, and a heavy sea was running, and it was agreed to keep along under the lee of the shore until they could obtain a view of the Bay of Antium, and see if the fleet of Fieschi was still there. If so, they would tack and run back some distance, and make straight out to sea, so as to pass along four or five miles from the shore, as it would be unlikely in the extreme that the Genoese admiral would send a galley out to overhaul a passing ship in such weather.

They sailed along till they neared the slight depression known as the Bay of Antium, and then bore farther out to sea. Suddenly a fleet was seen running down the coast at some distance away.

"'Bout ship," the captain cried. "The Genoese have been cruising further north, and are coming down the coast. In such weather as this, the Bonito ought to be able to get away from them."

"It may be Pisani's fleet," Francis said, as the ship was put round.

"It is possible," the captain agreed; "but we cannot run the risk of stopping until we make inquiries."

"No, captain; but, at least, if we run a mile or so out to sea, we should be able to see round the point, and discover whether Fieschi's galleys are there."

The captain assented. The vessel's head was turned from the land. In ten minutes there was a joyous shout on board the Bonito, for the Genoese fleet was seen lying in the bay. The distant fleet must then form that of Pisani.

"See!" Francis exclaimed. "The Genoese have just caught sight of them, and are hoisting sail. They are either going to meet them or to run away. Our vessels are the most numerous; but no, there is not much difference. Pisani has fourteen ships, but some must be lagging behind, or have been lost. How many do you make them out to be, captain?"

"I think there are only nine," the captain answered, "and that is just the number of the Genoese."

"Then Fieschi will fight, if he is not a coward," Matteo said; "but, in that case, why are they making out to sea?"

"Fieschi may not care to be attacked at anchor," the captain replied. "That would give all the advantage to us. Besides, if they were beaten there would be but little chance of any of them escaping. No, he is right to make out to sea, but blowing as it is, it will be next to impossible for him to fight there. Two vessels could hardly get alongside to board in such a sea as this. I expect Fieschi thinks that we shall never attack him in such a storm; but Pisani would fight if it were a hurricane."

It did indeed seem almost impossible to fight in such a sea. The Bonito was rolling, gunwale under. Her sail had been reduced to its smallest proportions, and yet, when the squalls struck her she was laid completely over on her side. But the rival admirals were too anxious to fight to be deterred by the difficulty, and both were bent upon bringing on an action at once.

"I would give anything to be on board one of our galleys," Matteo said. "It is horrible standing here doing nothing, when such a fight as this is going to begin."

"Cannot we edge down towards them, captain?" Francis asked. "I do not mean that we should take part in the fight, for we have but a hundred men, and the galleys must each carry at least three times as many. Still, we might be near enough to see something, and perhaps to give succour to any disabled ship that drops out of the fight."

"I will do so if you like, Messer Francisco," the captain said. "If you will take the responsibility. But if our side gets the worst of it, you must remember that the Bonito may be captured."

"I don't think there's much chance of Pisani being beaten by an enemy no stronger than himself," Francis said; "and even if they should be victorious, the Genoese will certainly have enough on their hands, with repairing damages and securing prisoners, to think of setting off in chase of a ship like ours."

"That is true enough," the captain agreed, for he was indeed as anxious as Francis and Matteo to witness the struggle.

The vessels on both sides were under canvas, for it was impossible to row in such a sea. As soon as they approached each other, both fleets broke up, and the vessels each singling an opponent out, the combat began. It was a singular one, and differed widely from ordinary sea fights of the time, in which the combatants always tried to grapple with their enemies and carry them by boarding. This was almost impossible now, for it seemed that the vessels would be dashed in pieces like eggshells were they to strike each other. Clouds of missiles were poured from one to the other. The archers plied their bows. Great machines hurled javelins and big stones, and the crash of the blows of the latter, against the sides of the ships, sounded even above the noise of the wind and waves, and the shouting of the combatants. As for the cannon with which all the galleys were armed, they were far too cumbrous and unmanageable to be worked in such weather. Sometimes one vessel, lifted on the crest of a wave while its opponent lay in a hollow, swept its decks with terrible effect; while a few seconds later the advantage was on the other side.

For a long time, neither party seemed to gain any advantage. Great numbers were killed on both sides, but victory did not incline either way, until the mast of one of the Venetian galleys was struck by a heavy stone and went over the side. She at once fell out of the line of the battle, her opponent keeping close to her, pouring in volumes of missiles, while the sea, taking her on the broad side, washed numbers of her crew overboard. Her opponent, seeing that she was altogether helpless, left her to be taken possession of afterwards, and made for Pisani's galley, which was distinguished by its flag at the masthead, and was maintaining a desperate conflict with the galley of Fieschi.

The admiral's ship was now swept with missiles from both sides, and when his adversaries saw that his crew was greatly weakened, they prepared to close, in spite of the state of the sea. If Pisani himself could be captured, there would remain but seven Venetian ships to the nine Genoese, and victory was certain.

The captain of the Bonito had lashed together some heavy spars and thrown them overboard, having fastened a strong rope to them, and was riding head to the waves by means of this sea anchor, at a distance of about half a mile from the conflict. A cry of grief and rage had arisen when the crew saw that one of their galleys was disabled, and their excitement became intense when they saw the unequal struggle which Pisani was maintaining.

"They are preparing to board, captain," Francis said. "We must go to the admiral's aid. If his ship is captured, the battle is lost."

"I am ready, Messer Francisco, if you authorize me."

"Certainly I do," Francis said. "The loss or capture of the Bonito is as nothing in comparison to the importance of saving Pisani."

The captain gave the order for the hawser to be cut, and the sail hoisted. A cheer broke from the crew as they saw what was to be done. Their arms had been served out at the beginning of the contest, and they now seized them, and gathered in readiness to take part in the fight.

The two Genoese galleys had thrown their grapnels and made fast, one on each side of Pisani's galley. The bulwarks were stove in and splintered as the vessels rolled, and the rigging of the three ships became entangled. The Genoese sprang on to the deck of Pisani's galley, with shouts of triumph, but they were met by the admiral himself, wielding a mighty battleaxe, and the survivors of his crew.

The combat was still raging when the Bonito sailed swiftly up. Her sails were lowered as she came alongside, and she was lashed to one of the galleys. But this manoeuvre was not performed without loss. As she approached, with the Venetian flag flying at her masthead, the Genoese archers on the poop of the galley, who had hitherto been pouring their missiles among Pisani's men, turned round and opened fire upon this new foe. Their arrows did far more execution here than they had done among the armour clad soldiers of the state. The captain fell dead with an arrow which struck him full in the throat, and ten or twelve of the sailors fell on the deck beside him.

"Pour in one volley," Francis shouted; "then throw down your bows, and take to your axes and follow me."

The instant the vessel was lashed, Francis sprang on to the deck of the galley. Matteo was by his side, Giuseppi just behind, and the whole crew followed. Climbing first upon the poop, they fell upon the archers, who, after a short struggle, were cut down; then, descending again to the waist of the galley, they leaped on to the deck of Pisani's ship, and fell upon the rear of the Genoese.

These were taken completely by surprise. Absorbed in the struggle in which they were engaged, they had noticed neither the approach of the Bonito, nor the struggle on board their own galley, and supposed that another of the Venetian warships had come up to the assistance of their admiral.

Taken then by surprise, and finding themselves thus between two bands of foes, they fought irresolutely, and the crew of the Bonito, with their heavy axes, cut down numbers of them, and fighting their way through the mass, joined the diminished force of Pisani.

The admiral shouted the battle cry of "Saint Mark!" His followers, who had begun to give way to despair, rallied at the arrival of this unlooked-for reinforcement, and the whole fell upon the Genoese with fury. The latter fought stoutly and steadily now, animated by the voice and example of Fieschi himself; but their assurance of victory was gone, and they were gradually beaten back to the deck of their admiral's ship. Here they made desperate efforts to cut the lashings and free the vessel; but the yards had got interlocked and the rigging entangled, and the Venetians sprang on to the deck of the ship, and renewed the conflict there.

For some time the struggle was doubtful. The Genoese had still the advantage in numbers, but they were disheartened at the success, which they had deemed certain, having been so suddenly and unexpectedly snatched from their grasp.

The presence of Pisani, in itself, doubled the strength of the Venetians. He was the most popular of their commanders, and each strove to imitate the example which he set them.

After ten minutes' hard fighting, the result was no longer doubtful. Many of the Genoese ran below. Others threw down their arms, and their admiral, at last, seeing further resistance was hopeless, lowered his sword and surrendered.

No sooner had resistance ceased than Pisani turned to Francis, who had been fighting by his side:

"I thank you, in the name of myself and the republic," he said. "Where you have sprung from, or how you came here, I know not. You seemed to me to have fallen from heaven to our assistance, just at the moment when all was lost. Who are you? I seem to know your face, though I cannot recall where I have seen it."

"I am Francis Hammond, Messer Pisani. I had the honour of seeing you at the house of my patron, Signor Polani, and you were good enough to offer to take me with you to sea."

"Oh, I remember now!" Pisani said. "But how came you here?"

"I came in the Bonito, one of Polani's ships. She is lying outside the farther of the Venetian galleys. We bring from Venice some of the stores for which you sent. We were lying off, watching the battle, until we saw that you were sore beset and in need of help, and could then no longer remain inactive. Our captain was killed by an arrow as we ranged up alongside of the galley, and I am now in command. This is my friend, Matteo Giustiniani, a volunteer on board the Bonito."

"I remember you, Master Matteo," Pisani said, as he shook him by the hand. "I have seen you often at your father's house. I shall have to give him a good account of you, for I saw you fighting bravely.

"But we will talk more of this afterwards. We must set to work to separate the galleys, or we shall have them grinding each other to pieces. Then we must hasten to the assistance of our friends."

The Genoese prisoners were all fastened below, and the Venetians then set to work to cut the lashings and free the rigging of the ships. Francis kept only twenty men on board the Bonito. The remainder were distributed between the two captured Genoese galleys, and the admiral turned his attention to the battle.

But it was already almost over. The sight of the Venetian flag, at the mastheads of the admiral's ship and the other galley, struck dismay into the Genoese. Five of their ships immediately hoisted all canvas and made off, while the other two, surrounded by the Venetian galleys, hauled down their flags.

The battle had been a sanguinary one, and but eight hundred men were found alive on board the four galleys captured. The fight is known in history as the battle of Porto d'Anzo. The struggle had lasted nearly the whole day, and it was growing dark when the Venetian fleet, with their prizes, anchored under shelter of the land.

All night long the work of attending upon the wounded went on, and it was daybreak before the wearied crews lay down for repose. In the afternoon, Pisani hoisted a signal for the captains of the galleys to come on board; and in their presence he formally thanked Francis, in the name of the republic, for the aid he had afforded him at the most critical moment. Had it not been for that aid, he acknowledged that he and his crew must have succumbed, and the victory would assuredly have fallen to the Genoese.

After the meeting was over he took Francis into his cabin, and again offered him a post in his own ship.

"Were your merit properly rewarded," he said, "I would appoint you at once to the command of a galley; but to do so would do you no service, for it would excite against you the jealousy of all the young nobles in the fleet. Besides, you are so young, that although the council at home cannot but acknowledge the vastness of the service you have rendered, they might make your age an excuse for refusing to confirm the appointment; but if you like to come as my third officer, I can promise you that you shall have rapid promotion, and speedily be in command of a galley. We Venetians have no prejudice against foreigners. They hold very high commands, and, indeed, our armies in the field are frequently commanded by foreign captains."

Francis thanked the admiral heartily for his offer, but said that his father's wishes, and his own, led him to adopt the life of a merchant, and that, under the patronage of Messer Polani, his prospects were so good that he would not exchange them, even for a command under the state of Venice.

"You are quite right, lad," the admiral said. "All governments are ungrateful, and republics most of all. Where all are supposed to be equal, there is ever envy and jealousy against one who rises above the rest. The multitude is fickle and easily led; and the first change of fortune, however slight, is seized upon by enemies as a cause of complaint, and the popular hero of today may be an exile tomorrow. Like enough I shall see the inside of a Venetian prison some day."

"Impossible, signor!" Francis exclaimed. "The people would tear to pieces anyone who ventured to malign you."

"Just at present, my lad; just at present. But I know my countrymen. They are not as light hearted and fickle as those of Genoa; but they are easily led, and will shout 'Abasso!' as easily as 'Viva!' Time will show. I was within an ace of being defeated today; and you may not be close at hand to come to my rescue next time. And now to business.

"Tomorrow morning I will set the crews to get out your stores, and distribute them as required, and will place four hundred prisoners in your hold, and you shall carry them to Venice with my despatches announcing the victory. The other four hundred Genoese I shall send, in the galley that was dismasted yesterday, to Candia, to be imprisoned there. I shall send prize crews home in the galleys we have captured; and as soon as they are refitted and manned, and rejoin me, I shall sail in search of Doria and his fleet. I shall first cruise up the Adriatic, in case he may have gone that way to threaten Venice, and I can the more easily receive such reinforcements as may have been prepared for me."

The following day was spent in unloading the vessel. This was accomplished by nightfall. The prisoners were then put on board. Francis at once ordered sail to be set, and the Bonito was started on her homeward voyage.

As soon as the Bonito was signalled in sight, Signor Polani went down to the port to meet her, to ascertain where she had fallen in with the fleet, for there was great anxiety in Venice, as no news had been received from Pisani for more than ten days. The vessel had just passed through the entrance between the islands, when the gondola, with her owner, was seen approaching. Francis went to the gangway to receive him.

"Why, what has happened, Francisco?" Polani asked, as the boat neared the side of the ship. "Half your bulwark is carried away, and the whole side of the ship is scraped and scored. She looks as if she had been rubbing against a rock."

"Not quite so bad as that, Messer Polani. She has been grinding against a Genoese galley."

"Against a Genoese galley!" the merchant repeated in surprise, stopping in his passage up the rope ladder, which had been lowered for him. "Why, how is that? But never mind that now. First tell me what is the news from the fleet?"

"There is great news," Francis replied. "The admiral fell in with Fieschi off Antium. There were nine ships on each side, and the battle took place in a storm. We were victorious, and captured four of the Genoese galleys, with Fieschi himself and eight hundred prisoners. The rest fled. Fieschi is now in my cabin, and four hundred prisoners in the hold."

"This is indeed great news," the merchant said, "and will be an immense relief to Venice. We were getting very anxious, for had Pisani been defeated, there was nothing to prevent the Genoese ravaging our coasts, and even assailing Venice itself. But where is the captain?"

"I regret to say, sir, that he has been killed, as well as twenty-seven of the sailors, and many of the others are more or less severely wounded. I am the bearer of despatches from the admiral to the council."

"Then get into my gondola, and come along at once," Polani said. "I deeply regret the death of the captain and sailors. You shall tell me all about it as we come along. We must not delay a moment in carrying this great news ashore. Have you got the despatches?"

"Yes, signor. I put them into my doublet when I saw you approaching, thinking that you would probably wish me to take them on shore at once."

"And now tell me all about the battle," the merchant said as soon as they had taken their seats in the gondola. "You say there were nine ships on either side. Pisani sailed away with fourteen. Has he lost the remainder?"

"They came up next day," Francis replied. "The fleet was in a port north of Antium when the news came that Fieschi's fleet was there. Five of the galleys had been dismantled, and were under repair, and Pisani would not wait for them to be got into fighting order, as he was afraid lest Fieschi might weigh anchor and escape if he delayed an hour. He learned that the Genoese had nine ships with him, and as he had himself this number ready for sea, he sailed at once.

"The weather was stormy, and the sea very high, when he appeared within sight of Antium. Fieschi sailed boldly out to meet him. The battle lasted all day, for it was next to impossible to board; but in the end, as I say, four Genoese galleys surrendered and the rest fled. It was a terrible sight; for it seemed at every moment as if the waves would hurl the vessels against each other, and so break them into fragments; but in no case did such an accident happen."

"Why, you speak as if you saw it, Francisco! Had you joined the admiral before the battle took place?"

"No, signor. We arrived near Antium on the evening before the fight, and heard of Fieschi's presence there. Therefore we anchored south of the promontory. In the morning we put out, intending to sail well out to sea and so pass the Genoese, who were not likely, in such weather, to put out to question a sail passing in the distance; but as we made off from land we saw Pisani's fleet approaching. Then, as Fieschi put to sea and we saw that the battle was imminent, there was nothing for us to do but to lie to, and wait for the battle to be over, before we delivered our stores, having little doubt that Pisani would be victorious."

"Then had the battle gone the other way," the merchant said, "the Bonito at the present moment would probably be lying a prize in the harbour of Genoa!"

"We did not lose sight of the probability of that, signor, but thought that, if the Genoese should gain a victory, they would be too busy with their prizes and prisoners, if not too crippled, to pursue us, and we reckoned that in such weather the Bonito would be able to sail quite as fast as any of the Genoese."

"And now, tell me about your affairs, Francisco. Where was it you fell in with the Genoese galley, and by what miracle did you get off?"

"It was in the battle, sir. One of the Venetian galleys had dropped out of the fight disabled, and its opponent went to the assistance of their admiral's ship, which was engaged with Pisani. They attempted to board him on both sides, and, seeing that he was in great peril, and that if his ship was taken the battle would be as bad as lost, we thought that you yourself would approve of our going to his assistance. This we did, and engaged one of their galleys; and, as her crew were occupied with the admiral, we took them by surprise, and created such a diversion that he succeeded, with what assistance we could give him, in capturing both his opponents."

"That was done well indeed," Polani said warmly. "It was a risky matter, indeed, for you, with sailors unprotected by armour, to enter into a combat with the iron-clad soldiers of Genoa.

"And so the captain and twenty-seven of the men were killed! You must have had some brisk fighting!"

"The captain, and many of the men, were shot by the Genoese archers as we ranged up alongside their vessel. The others were killed in hand-to-hand fighting."

"And my cousin Matteo, what has become of him?" Polani asked suddenly. "I trust he is not among the killed!"

"He is unharmed," Francis replied. "He fought gallantly, and the admiral, the next day, offered to take him on board his own ship, many of the volunteers serving on board having been killed. Matteo, of course, accepted the offer."

"He would have done better to have stayed on board my ship for another two years," Polani said, "and learned his business. He would have made a far better sailor than he can ever become on board a state galley; but I never expected him to stick to it. He has no earnestness of purpose, and is too particular about his dress to care about the rough life of a real seaman."

"He has plenty of courage, sir, and I have always found him a staunch friend."

"No doubt he has courage," the merchant said. "He comes of good blood and could hardly be a coward. I think he is a good-hearted lad, too, and will, I have no doubt, make a brave commander of a galley; but more than that Matteo is never likely to become."

"Your daughters are well, I hope?" Francis asked.

"Quite well; but you will not find them at home--they sailed three days ago, in the Lido, for Corfu. They are going to stay for a time at my villa there. That affair of last year shook them both, and I thought it better that they should go away for a change--the hot months here are trying, and often unhealthy. I will go over myself next week to be with them."

They were now approaching the Piazzetta, and Polani shouted out, to various acquaintances he met in passing gondolas, the news that Pisani had gained a great victory, and had captured the Genoese admiral with four of his galleys. The gondolas at once changed their course, and accompanied them, to gather further details of the fight. The news was shouted to other passing boats, and by the time they reached the steps of the Piazzetta, a throng was round them.

Those on shore shouted out the news, and it spread rapidly from mouth to mouth. The shopkeepers left their stores, and the loungers on the Piazzetta ran up, and it was with difficulty that Polani and Francis could make their way, through the shouting and excited crowd, to the entrance of the ducal palace.

Polani at once led Francis to the doge, to whom he gave an account of the action. Messengers were immediately despatched to some of the members of the council, for it was to them that the despatches had to be delivered. As soon as a sufficient number to transact the business had arrived at the palace, the doge himself led Francis to the council chamber.

"Is the news that we heard, shouted in the streets as we came thither, true, your highness?" one of the councillors asked as they entered. "That our fleet has gained a victory over the Genoese?"

"I am happy to say that it is quite true; but this young gentleman is the bearer of despatches from the admiral, and these will doubtless give us all particulars."

"Admiral Pisani has chosen a strange messenger for so important a despatch," one of the party hostile to the admiral said. "It is usual to send despatches of this kind by a trusted officer, and I do not think it respectful, either to the council or the republic, to send home the news of a victory by a lad like this."

"The admiral apparently chose this young gentleman because, owing to the death of his captain, he was in command of the ship which Messer Polani placed at the service of the republic, and which was present at the fight. The admiral intended, as I hear, to set out at once in search of the fleet of Doria, and doubtless did not wish to weaken himself by despatching a state galley with the news. But perhaps he may explain the matter in his despatches."

Several other councillors had by this time arrived, and the despatches were opened. The admiral's account of the engagement was brief, for he was fonder of the sword than the pen. He stated that, having obtained news that Fieschi's fleet was at anchor under the promontory of Antium, he sailed thither with nine ships, these being all that were at the moment fit to take to sea; that Fieschi had sailed out to meet him, and that an engagement had taken place in the storm, which prevented the ships from pursuing their usual tactics, and compelled them to fight with missiles at a distance. The despatch then went on:

"We fought all day, and the upshot of it was, we captured four of their galleys, the admiral himself, and eight hundred prisoners. Fortunately it is unnecessary for me to give your seignory the details of the fighting, as these can be furnished you by Messer Francisco Hammond, who will hand you these despatches. He was a witness of the action on the Bonito, which had that morning arrived at Antium with some of the stores you despatched me. I have selected this young gentleman as the bearer of these despatches, because it is to him I entirely owe it that I am not at the present moment a prisoner in Genoa, and to him the republic owes that we yesterday won a victory.

"I was attacked by Fieschi and by another galley, and, in spite of the weather, they cast grapnels on to my ship and boarded me. I had already lost half of my crew by their missiles, and things were going very badly with us, when the Bonito came up to our assistance, and grappled with one of the galleys. Her captain was killed, but Messer Hammond--of whom Polani has so high an opinion that he had appointed him second in command--led his men to my rescue. They boarded the galley and slew those who remained on board, and then, crossing on to my ship, fell upon the rear of the Genoese who were pressing us backwards. His sailors, undefended as they were by armour, fought like demons with their axes, and, led by Messer Hammond, cut their way through the enemy and joined me.

"This reinforcement gave fresh strength and spirit to my men, who had a minute before thought that all was lost. Together we fell upon the Genoese, before they could recover from their surprise, beat them back into their admiral's ship, and following them there forced them to surrender. Messer Hammond fought by my side, and although but a lad in years, he showed himself a sturdy man-at-arms, and behaved with a coolness and bravery beyond praise. I hereby recommend him to your gracious consideration, for assuredly to him it is due that it is I, and not Fieschi, who is writing to announce a victory."

A murmur of surprise from the councillors greeted the reading of this portion of the letter. When it was concluded, the doge was the first to speak.

"You have indeed deserved well of the republic, Messer Hammond, for we know that Admiral Pisani is not one to give undue praise, or to exaggerate in aught.

"This is news to me, signors, as well as to you, for in his narrative to me of the events of the fight, he passed over his own share in it, though Messer Polani, who accompanied him, did say that his ship had taken some part in the fight, and that the captain and twenty-seven men had been killed.

"Now, young sir, as the admiral has referred us to you for a detailed narrative of the battle, we will thank you to tell us all you witnessed, omitting no detail of the occurrences."

Francis accordingly gave a full account of the action, and gave great praise to his crew for the valour with which they had fought against the heavy armed Genoese. When he had concluded the doge said:

"We thank you for your narrative, Messer Hammond, as well as for the great service you have rendered the state. Will you now leave us, as we have much to debate on regarding this and other matters, and to arrange for the reinforcements for which, I see by his letter, the admiral asks.

"Will you ask Messer Polani to remain in attendance for a while, as we wish to consult with him as to ships and other matters? As to yourself, we shall ask you to come before us again shortly."

After Francis had left, the council first voted that five ducats should be given to every man of the crew of the Bonito, and that the widows of those who had been slain should be provided for, at the expense of the state. They deferred the question as to the honours which should be conferred upon Francis, until they had consulted Polani.

State barges were at once sent off to bring in the prisoners from the ship, and preparations made for their accommodation, for Venice always treated prisoners taken in war with the greatest kindness, an example which Genoa was very far from following.

Then Polani was sent for, and the question of stores and ships gone into. Orders were issued for redoubled activity in the arsenal, and it was arranged that several ships, belonging to Polani and others, should be at once purchased for the service of the state.

Then they asked him for his opinion as to the reward which should be given to Francis. Upon the merchant expressing his ignorance of any special service his young friend had rendered, the passage from Pisani's letter relating to him was read out.

"The lad is as modest as he is brave," the merchant said, "for although, of course, he told me that the ship had taken some part in the fight, and had done what it could to assist the admiral, in which service the captain and twenty-seven men had lost their lives, I had no idea of the real nature of the encounter. I feel very proud of the service he has rendered the state, for he has rendered me as a private individual no less important service, and I regard him as my adopted son, and my future partner in my business. Such being the case, signors, he needs no gift of money from the state."

"He has not, of course, being still a minor, taken up his papers of naturalization as a citizen?" the doge said.

"No, your highness, nor is it his intention to do so. I spoke to him on the subject once, and he said that, although he regarded Venice with affection, and would at all times do everything in his power for the state, he could not renounce his birthplace, as an Englishman, by taking an oath of allegiance to another state, and that probably he should after a time return to his native country. I pointed out to him that, although foreigners were given every facility for trade in Venice, it would be a grievous disadvantage to him in the islands, and especially with countries such as Egypt, the Turks, and the Eastern empire, with whom we had treaties; as, unless he were a Venetian, he would be unable to trade with them.

"He fully saw the force of my argument, but persisted in his determination. If you ask my opinion, therefore, signors, and you do not think the honour too great, I would suggest that the highest and most acceptable honour that could be bestowed upon him, would be that which you have at various times conferred upon foreign personages of distinction, namely, to grant him the freedom of Venice, and inscribe his name upon the list of her citizens, without requiring of him the renunciation of his own country, or the taking the oath of allegiance."

"The honour is assuredly a great and exceptional one," the doge said, "but so is the service that he has rendered. He has converted what would have been a defeat into a victory, and has saved Venice from a grave peril.

"Will you retire for a few minutes, signor, and we will then announce to you the result of our deliberations on the matter."

Chapter 12:
In Mocenigo's Power.

It was fully an hour before Polani was recalled to the council chamber. He saw at once, by the flushed and angry faces of some of the council, that the debate had been a hot one. At this he was not surprised, for he knew that the friends and connections of Ruggiero Mocenigo would vehemently oppose the suggestion he had made.

The doge announced the decision.

"The council thank you for your suggestion, Signor Polani, and have resolved, by a majority, to confer upon Messer Francisco Hammond the high honour of placing his name upon the list of the citizens of Venice, without requiring from him the oaths of allegiance to the state. As such an honour has never before been conferred, save upon personages of the highest rank, it will be a proof of the gratitude which Venice feels towards one who has done her such distinguished service. The decree to that effect will be published tomorrow."

The merchant retired, highly gratified. The honour was a great and signal one, and the material advantages considerable. The fact that Francis was a foreigner had been the sole obstacle which had presented itself to him, in associating him with his business, for it would prevent Francis from trading personally with any of the countries in which Venetian citizens enjoyed special advantages.

Francis was immensely gratified, when he heard from the merchant of the honour to be conferred upon him. It was of all others the reward he would have selected, had a free choice been given him, but it was so great and unusual an honour, that he could indeed scarcely credit it when the merchant told him the result of his interviews with the council. The difficulty which his being a foreigner would throw in the way of his career as a merchant in Eastern waters, had been frequently in his mind, and would, he foresaw, greatly lessen his usefulness, but that he should be able to obtain naturalization, without renouncing his allegiance to England, he had never even hoped.

"It is a very high honour, doubtless," Polani said, "but no whit higher than you deserve. Besides, after all, it costs Venice nothing, and money is scarce at present. At any rate, I can congratulate myself as well as you, for I foresaw many difficulties in our way. Although the ships carrying the Venetian flag could enter the ports of all countries trading with us, you would personally be liable to arrest, at any time, on being denounced as not being a native of Venice, which you assuredly would be by my rivals in trade."

The next day a bulletin was published, giving the substance of Pisani's despatch, and announcing that, in token of the gratitude of the republic for the great service he had rendered, Messer Hammond would be at once granted the freedom of Venice, and his name inserted on the list of her citizens.

During these two days the delight of Venice at the news of the victory had been extreme. The houses had been decorated with flags, and the bells of all the churches had peeled out joyously. Crowds assembled round the Polani Palace, and insisted upon Francis making his appearance, when they greeted him with tremendous shouts of applause. Upon the evening of the second day he said to Polani:

"Have you any ship fit for sea, signor, because if so, I pray you to send me away, no matter where. I cannot stand this. Since the decree was published, this morning, I have not had a moment's peace, and it is too absurd, when I did no more than any sailor on board the ship. If it went on, I should very soon be heartily sorry I ever interfered on behalf of the admiral."

The merchant smiled.

"I have half promised to take you with me to the reception at the Persanis' this evening, and have had a dozen requests of a similar nature for every night this week and next."

"Then, if you have no ship ready, signor, I will charter a fishing boat, engage a couple of men, and go off for a fortnight. By the end of that time something fresh will have happened."

"I can send you off, if you really wish it, Francisco, the first thing tomorrow morning. I am despatching a small craft with a message to my agent in Corfu, and with letters for my daughters. They will be delighted to see you, and indeed, I shall be glad to know that you are with them, until I can wind up several affairs which I have in hand, and join them myself. She is fast, and you should be at Corfu in eight-and-forty hours after sailing."

Francis gladly embraced the offer, and started the next morning. The vessel was a small one, designed either to sail or row. Her crew consisted of twenty men, who rowed sixteen sweeps when the wind was light or unfavourable. She was an open boat, except that she was decked at each end, a small cabin being formed aft for the captain, and any passengers there might be on board, while the crew stowed themselves in the little forecastle.

When the boat was halfway across, a sail was seen approaching, and the captain recognized her as one of Polani's vessels.

"In that case," Francis said, "we may as well direct our course so as to pass them within hailing distance. When you approach them, hoist the Polani flag, and signal to them to lay to."

This was done, and the two craft brought up within thirty yards of each other. The captain appeared at the side of the vessel, and doffed his cap when he recognized Francis.

"Have you any news from the East?" the latter asked.

"But little, signor. A few Genoese pirates are among the islands, and are reported to have made some captures, but I have seen none. There is nothing new from Constantinople. No fresh attempt has been made by the emperor to recapture Tenedos."

"Did you touch at Corfu on your way back?"

"I left there yesterday, signor. A strange craft has been reported as having been seen on the coast. She carries no flag, but from her appearance she is judged to be a Moor."

"But we are at peace with the Moors," Francis said, "and it is years since they ventured on any depredations, excepting on their own waters."

"That is so, signor, and I only tell you what was the report at Corfu. She appeared to be a swift craft, rowing a great many oars. Her movements certainly seem mysterious, as she has several times appeared off the coast. Two vessels which sailed from Cyprus, and were to have touched at Corfu, had not arrived there when I left, and they say that several others are overdue. I do not say that has anything to do with the strange galley, but it is the general opinion in Corfu that it has something to do with it, and I am the bearer of letters from the governor to the seignory, praying that two or three war ships may at once be sent down to the island."

"It looks strange, certainly," Francis said; "but I cannot believe that any Moorish pirates would be so daring as to come up into Venetian waters."

"I should not have thought so either, signor; but it may be that, knowing there is war between Venice and Genoa, and that the state galleys of the republics, instead of being scattered over the seas, are now collected in fleets, and thinking only of fighting each other, they might consider it a good opportunity for picking prizes."

"It is a good opportunity, certainly," Francis said; "but they would know that Venice would, sooner or later, reckon with them; and would demand a four-fold indemnity for any losses her merchants may have suffered.

"However, I will not detain you longer. Will you tell Signor Polani that you met us, and that we were making good progress, and hoped to reach Corfu some time tomorrow?"

"This is a curious thing about this galley," the captain of the boat said to Francis, as the men again dipped their oars into the water, and the boat once more proceeded on the way.

"It is much more likely to be a Genoese pirate than a Moor," Francis said. "They may have purposely altered their rig a little, in order to deceive vessels who may sight them. It is very many years since any Moorish craft have been bold enough to commit acts of piracy on this side of Sicily. However, we must hope that we shall not fall in with her, and if we see anything answering to her description we will give it a wide berth. Besides, it is hardly likely they would interfere with so small a craft as ours, for they would be sure we should be carrying no cargo of any great value."

"Twenty Christian slaves would fetch money among the Moors," the captain said. "Let us hope we shall see nothing of them; for we should have no chance of resistance against such a craft, and she would go two feet to our one."

The next morning Francis was aroused by a hurried summons from the captain. Half awake, and wondering what could be the cause of the call, for the boat lay motionless on the water, he hurried out from the little cabin. Day had just broken, the sky was aglow with ruddy light in the east.

"Look there, signor!" the captain said, pointing to the south. "The watch made them out a quarter of an hour since, but, thinking nothing of it, they did not call me. What do you think of that?"

Two vessels were lying in close proximity to each other, at a distance of about two miles from the boat. One of them was a large trader, the other was a long galley rigged quite differently to those of either Venice or Genoa.

"That is the craft they were speaking of," the captain said. "There is no mistaking her. She may be an Egyptian or a Moor, but certainly she comes from the African coast."

"Or is got up in African fashion," Francis said. "She may be, as we agreed yesterday, a Genoese masquerading in that fashion, in order to be able to approach our traders without their suspicions being aroused. She looks as if she has made a captive of that vessel. I imagine she must have come up to her late yesterday evening, and has been at work all night stripping her. I hope she is too busy to attend to us."

The sail had been lowered the instant the captain caught sight of the vessels, for there was scarcely enough wind to fill it, and the men were now rowing steadily.

"I do not think she could have taken much of her cargo out. She is very deep in the water."

"Very deep," Francis agreed. "She seems to me to be deeper than she did three minutes ago."

"She is a great deal deeper than when we first caught sight of her," one of the sailors said. "She stood much higher in the water than the galley did, and now, if anything, the galley stands highest."

"See!" the captain exclaimed suddenly, "the galley is rowing her oars on the port bow, and bringing her head round. She has noticed us, and is going to chase us! We have seen too much.

"Row, men--it is for life! If they overtake us it is a question between death, and slavery among the Moors."

A sudden exclamation from one of the men caused the captain to glance round again at the galley. She was alone now on the water--the trader had sunk!

"Do you take the helm, signor," the captain said. "All hands will help at the oars."

Some of the oars were double banked, and beneath the strength of the twenty men, the boat moved fast through the water. The galley was now rowing all her oars, and in full pursuit. For a quarter of an hour not a word was spoken. Every man on board was doing his utmost. Francis had glanced backwards several times, and at the end of a quarter of an hour, he could see that the distance between the boat and her pursuer had distinctly lessened.

"Is she gaining on us?" the captain asked, for the cabin in the stern hid the galley from the sight of the oarsmen.

"She is gaining," Francis said quietly, "but not rapidly. Row steadily, my lads, and do not despair. When they find how slowly they gain, they may give up the chase and think us not worth the trouble.

"Jacopo," he said to an old sailor who was rowing in the bow, and who already was getting exhausted from the exertion, "do you lay in your oar and come aft. I will take your place."

At the end of an hour the galley was little more than a quarter of a mile away.

"We had better stop," the captain said. "We have no chance of getting away, and the longer the chase the more furious they will be. What do you think, signor?"

"I agree with you," Francis replied. "We have done all that we could. There is no use in rowing longer."

The oars fell motionless in the water, and a few minutes later the long galley came rushing up by their side.

"A fine row you have given us, you dogs!" a man shouted angrily as she came alongside. "If you haven't something on board that will pay us for the chase we have had, it will be the worse for you. What boat is that?"

"It is the Naxos, and belongs to Messer Polani of Venice. We are bound to Corfu, and bear letters from the padrone to his agent there. We have no cargo on board."

"The letters, perhaps, may be worth more than any cargo such a boat would carry. So come on board, and let us see what the excellent Polani says to his agent. Now, make haste all of you, or it will be the worse for you."

It was useless hesitating. The captain, Francis, and the crew stepped on board the galley.

"Just look round her," the captain said to one of his sailors. "If there is anything worth taking, take it, and then knock a hole in her bottom with your axe."

Francis, as he stepped on board the galley, looked round at the crew. They were not Genoese, as he had expected, but a mixture of ruffians from all the ports in the Mediterranean, as he saw at once by their costumes. Some were Greeks from the islands, some Smyrniots, Moors, and Spaniards; but the Moors predominated, nearly half the crew belonging to that race.

Then he looked at the captain, who was eagerly perusing the documents the captain had handed him. As his eye fell upon him, Francis started, for he recognized at once the man whose designs he had twice thwarted, Ruggiero Mocenigo, and felt that he was in deadly peril.

After reading the merchant's communication to his agent, Ruggiero opened the letter addressed to Maria. He had read but a few lines when he suddenly looked up, and then, with an expression of savage pleasure in his face, stepped up to Francis.

"So, Messer Hammond, the good Polani sends you to stay for a while with his daughters! Truly, when I set out in chase this morning of that wretched rowboat, I little deemed that she carried a prize that I valued more than a loaded caravel! It is to you I owe it that I am an exile, instead of being the honoured son-in-law of the wealthy Polani. It was your accursed interference that brought all my misfortunes upon me; but thank Heaven my vengeance has come at last!

"Take them all below," he said, turning to his men. "Put the heaviest irons you have got on this fellow, and fasten them with staples into the deck.

"You thought I was going to hang you, or throw you overboard," he went on, turning to Francis. "Do not flatter yourself that your death will be so easy a one--you shall suffer a thousand torments before you die!"

Francis had not spoken a word since Ruggiero first turned to him, but had stood with a tranquil and almost contemptuous expression upon his face; but every nerve and muscle of his body were strained, and in readiness to spring into action. He had expected that Ruggiero would at once attack him, and was determined to leap upon him, and to sell his life as dearly as possible.

The sailors seized Francis and his companions, and thrust them down into the hold, which was already crowded with upwards of a hundred captives. He was chained with heavy manacles. In obedience to Ruggiero's orders, staples were driven through the links of his chain deep into the deck, so that he was forced to remain in a sitting or lying posture. The captain of the Naxos came and sat beside him.

"Who is this pirate captain, Messer Francisco, who thus knows and has an enmity against you? By his speech he is surely a Venetian. And yet, how comes a Venetian in command of a pirate?"

"That man is Ruggiero Mocenigo--the same who twice attempted to carry off Messer Polani's daughters. The second time he succeeded, and would have been tried for the offence by the state had he not, aided by a band of Paduans, escaped from the keeping of his guard."

"Of course I heard of it, signor. I was away at sea at the time, but I heard how you came up at the moment when the padrone's gondoliers had been overcome, and rescued his daughters. And this is that villain Mocenigo, a disgrace to his name and family!"

"Remember the name, captain, and tell it to each of your men, so that if they ever escape from this slavery, into which, no doubt, he intends to sell you, they may tell it in Venice that Ruggiero Mocenigo is a pirate, and an ally of the Moors. As for me, there is, I think, but small chance of escape; but at any rate, if you ever reach Venice, you will be able to tell the padrone how it was that we never arrived at Corfu, and how I fell into the hands of his old enemy. Still, I do not despair that I may carry the message myself. There is many a slip between the cup and the lip, and Mocenigo may have cause, yet, to regret that he did not make an end of me as soon as he got me into his hands."

"It may be so," the captain said, "and indeed I cannot think that so brave a young gentleman is destined to die, miserably, at the hands of such a scoundrel as this man has shown himself to be. As for death, did it come but speedily and sharply, I would far sooner die than live a Moorish slave. Santa Maria, how they will wonder at home, when the days go on, and the Naxos does not return, and how at last they will give up all hope, thinking that she has gone down in a sudden squall, and never dreaming that we are sold as slaves to the Moors by a countryman!"

"Keep up your heart, captain. Be sure that when the war with Genoa is over, Venice will take the matter in hand. As you know, a vessel has already carried tidings thither of the depredation of a Moorish cruiser, and she will take vengeance on the Moors, and may even force them to liberate the captives they have taken; and besides, you may be sure that the padrone, when he hears of the Moorish galley, and finds we never reached Corfu although the weather continued fine, will guess that we have fallen into her hands, and will never rest till he finds where we have been taken, and will ransom those who survive at whatever price they may put upon them."

"He will do his best, I know. He is a good master to serve. But once a prisoner among the Moors, the hope of one's ever being heard of again is slight. Sometimes, of course, men have been ransomed; but most, as I have heard, can never be found by their friends, however ready they may be to pay any ransom that might be asked. It just depends whether they are sold to a Moor living in a seaport or not. If they are, there would be no great difficulty in hearing of them, but if they are sold into the interior, no inquiries are ever likely to discover them."

"You must hope for the best," Francis said. "Chances of escape may occur, and I have heard that Christian captives, who have been released, say that the Moors are for the most part kind masters."

"I have heard so, too," the captain said; "and anyhow, I would rather be a Moorish slave than lie in a Genoese dungeon. The Genoese are not like us. When we take prisoners we treat them fairly and honourably, while they treat their prisoners worse than dogs. I wish I could do something for you, Messer Francisco. Your case is a deal worse than ours.

"Listen, they are quarrelling up on deck!"

There was indeed a sound of men in hot dispute, a trampling of feet, a clash of steel, and the sound of bodies falling.

"It is not possible that one of our cruisers can have come up, and is boarding the pirate," the captain said, "for no sail was in sight when we were brought here. I looked round the last thing before I left the deck. What can they be fighting about?"

"Likely enough, as to their course. They have probably, from what we heard, taken and sunk several ships, and some may be in favour of returning to dispose of their booty, while others may be for cruising longer. I only hope that scoundrel Ruggiero is among those we heard fall. They are quiet now, and one party or the other has evidently got the best of it. There, they are taking to the oars again."

Several days passed. Sometimes the oars were heard going, but generally the galley was under sail. The sailors brought down food and water, morning and evening, but paid no other attention to the captives. Francis discussed, with some of the other prisoners, the chances of making a sudden rush on to the deck, and overpowering the crew; but all their arms had been taken from them, and the galley, they calculated, contained fully a hundred and fifty men. They noticed, too, when the sailors brought down the food, a party armed and in readiness were assembled round the hatchway.

At all other times the hatchway was nearly closed, being only left sufficiently open to allow a certain amount of air to pass down into the hold, and by the steady tramp of steps, up and down, they knew that two sentries were also on guard above. Most of the prisoners were so overcome with the misfortune which had befallen them, and the prospect of a life in hopeless slavery, that they had no spirit to attempt any enterprise whatever, and there was nothing to do but to wait the termination of the voyage.

At the end of six days there was a bustle on deck, and the chain of the anchor was heard to run out. Two or three hours afterwards the hatchway was taken off. When the rest had ascended, two men came below with hammers, and drew the staples which fastened Francis to the deck.

On going up, he was at first so blinded with the glare of the sunshine--after six days in almost total darkness--that he could scarce see where he was. The ship was lying at anchor in a bay. The shores were low, and a group of houses stood abreast of where the ship was anchored. By their appearance Francis saw at once that he was on the coast of Africa, or of some island near it.

The prisoners were ordered to descend into the boats which lay alongside, some sailors taking their places with them. Ruggiero was not at first to be seen, but just as Francis was preparing to take his place in the boat, he came out from the cabin. One of his arms was in a sling, and his head bandaged.

"Take special care of that prisoner," he said to the men. "Do not take off his chains, and place a sentinel at the door of the place of his confinement. I would rather lose my share of all the spoil we have taken, than he should escape me!"

The shackles had been removed from the rest of the captives, and on landing they were driven into some huts which stood a little apart from the village. Francis was thrust into a small chamber with five or six companions. The next morning the other prisoners were called out, and Francis was left alone by himself all day. On their return in the evening, they told him that all the prisoners had been employed in assisting to get out the cargo, with which the vessel was crammed, and in carrying it to a large storehouse in the village.

"They must have taken a rich booty, indeed," said one of the prisoners, who had already told Francis that he was the captain of the vessel they had seen founder. "I could tell pretty well what all the bales contain, by the manner of packing, and I should say that there were the pick of the cargoes of a dozen ships there. All of us here belong to three ships, except those taken with you; but from the talk of the sailors, I heard that they had already sent off two batches of captives, by another ship which was cruising in company of them. I also learned that the quarrel, which took place just after you were captured, arose from the fact that the captain wished a party to land, to carry off two women from somewhere in the island of Corfu; but the crew insisted on first returning with the booty, urging, that if surprised by a Venetian galley, they might lose all the result of their toil. This was the opinion of the majority, although a few sided with the captain, being induced to do so by the fact that he offered to give up all his share of the booty, if they would do so.

"The captain lost his temper and drew his sword, but he and his party were quickly overpowered. He has kept to his cabin ever since, suffering, they say, more from rage than from his wounds. However, it seems that as soon as we and the cargo have been sold, they are to start for Corfu to carry out the enterprise. We are on an island not very far from Tunis, and a fast-rowing boat started early this morning to the merchants with whom they deal, for it seems that a certain amount of secrecy is observed, in order that if any complaints are made by Venice, the Moorish authorities may disclaim all knowledge of the matter."

Two days later the prisoners captured were again led out, their guards telling them that the merchants who had been expected had arrived. Giuseppi, who had hitherto borne up bravely, was in an agony of grief at being separated from Francis. He threw himself upon the ground, wept, tore his hair, and besought the guards to let him share his master's fate, whatever that might be. He declared that he would kill himself were they separated; and the guards would have been obliged to use force, had not Francis begged Giuseppi not to struggle against fate, but to go quietly, promising again and again that, if he himself regained his freedom, he would not rest until Giuseppi was also set at liberty. At last the lad yielded, and suffered himself to be led away, in a heartbroken state, by the guards.

None of the captives returned to the hut, and Francis now turned his whole thoughts to freeing himself from his chains. He had already revolved in his mind every possible mode of escape. He had tried the strong iron bars of the window, but found that they were so rigidly fixed and embedded in the stonework, that there was no hope of escape in this way; and even could he have got through the window, the weight of his shackles would have crippled him.

He was fastened with two chains, each about two feet six inches long, going from the wrist of the right hand to the left ankle, and from the left hand to the right ankle. Thus he was unable to stand quite upright, and anything like rapid movement was almost impossible. The bottom of the window came within four feet of the ground, and it was only by standing on one leg, and lifting the other as high as he could, that he was able to grasp one of the bars to try its strength.

The news he had heard from his fellow prisoner almost maddened him, and he thought far less of his own fate, than of that of the girls, who would be living in their quiet country retreat in ignorance of danger, until suddenly seized by Mocenigo and his band of pirates.

He had, on the first day, tried whether it was possible to draw his hand through the iron band round his wrist, but had concluded it could not be done, for it was riveted so tightly as to press upon the flesh. Therefore there was no hope of freeing himself in that manner. The only possible means, then, would be to cut through the rivet or chain, and for this a tool would be required.

Suddenly an idea struck him. The guard who brought in his food was a Sicilian, and was evidently of a talkative disposition, for he had several times entered into conversation with the captives. In addition to a long knife, he carried a small stiletto in his girdle, and Francis thought that, if he could obtain this, he might possibly free himself. Accordingly, at the hour when he expected his guard to enter, Francis placed himself at his window, with his face against the bars. When he heard the guard come in, and, as usual, close the door behind him, he turned round and said:

"Who is that damsel there? She is very beautiful, and she passes here frequently. There she is, just going among those trees."

The guard moved to the window and looked out.

"Do you see her just going round that corner there? Ah! She is gone."

The guard was pressing his face against the bars, to look in the direction indicated, and Francis, who was already standing on his left leg, with the right raised so as to give freedom to the hand next to the man, had no difficulty in drawing the stiletto from its sheath, and slipping it into his trousers.

"You were just too late," he said, "but no doubt you often see her."

"I don't see any beautiful damsels about in this wretched place," the man replied. "I suppose she is the daughter of the head man in the village. They say he has some good-looking ones, but he takes pretty good care that they are not about when we are here. I suppose she thought she wouldn't be seen along that path. I will keep a good lookout for her in future."

"Don't frighten her away," Francis said, laughing. "She is the one pleasant thing I have in the day to look at."

After some more talk the man retired, and Francis examined his prize. It was a thin blade of fine steel, and he at once hid it in the earth which formed the floor of the hut.

An hour later the guard opened the door suddenly. It was now dusk, and Francis was sitting quietly in a corner.

"Bring a light, Thomaso," the guard shouted to his comrade outside. "It is getting dark in here."

The other brought a torch, and they carefully examined the floor of the cell.

"What is it that you are searching for?" Francis asked.

"I have dropped my dagger somewhere," the man replied. "I can't think how it fell out."

"When did you see it last?"

"Not since dinner time. I know I had it then. I thought possibly I might have dropped it here, and a dagger is not the sort of plaything one cares about giving to prisoners."

"Chained as I am," Francis said, "a dagger would not be a formidable weapon in my hands."

"No," the man agreed. "It would be useless to you, unless you wanted to stick it into your own ribs."

"I should have to sit down to be able to do even that."

"That is so, lad. It is not for me to question what the captain says, I just do as I am told. But I own it does seem hard, keeping a young fellow like you chained up as if you were a wild beast. If he had got Pisani or Zeno as a prisoner, and wanted to make doubly sure that they would not escape, it would be all well enough, but for a lad like you, with one man always at the door, and the window barred so that a lion couldn't break through, I do think it hard to keep you chained like this; and the worst of it is, we are going to have to stop here to look after you till the captain gets back, and that may be three weeks or a month, who knows!"

"Why don't you keep your mouth shut, Philippo?" the other man growled. "It's always talk, talk with you. We are chosen because the captain can rely upon us."

"He can rely upon anyone," Philippo retorted, "who knows that he will get his throat cut if he fails in his duty."

"Well, come along," the other said, "I don't want to be staying here all night. Your dagger isn't here, that's certain, and as I am off guard at present, I want to be going."

As soon as he was left alone, Francis unearthed the dagger, feeling sure that no fresh visit would be made him that evening. As he had hoped, his first attempt showed him that the iron of the rivet was soft, and the keen dagger at once notched off a small piece of the burred end. Again and again he tried, and each time a small piece of metal flew off. After each cut he examined the edge of the dagger, but it was well tempered, and seemed entirely unaffected.

He now felt certain that, with patience, he should be able to cut off the projecting edges of the rivets, and so be able to free his hands. He, therefore, now examined the fastenings at the ankles. These were more heavy, and on trying them, the iron of the rivet appeared to be much harder than that which kept the manacles together. It was, however, now too dark to see what he was doing, and concealing the dagger again, he lay down with a lighter heart than he had from the moment of his capture.

Even if he found that the lower fastenings of the chain defied all his efforts, he could cut the rivets at the wrists, and so free one end of each chain. He could then tie the chains round his legs, and their weight would not be sufficient to prevent his walking.

Chapter 13:
The Pirates' Raid.

As soon as it was daylight next morning, Francis was up and at work. His experiments of the evening before were at once confirmed. Three or four hours' work would enable him to free his wrists, but he could make no impression on the rivets at his ankles. After a few trials he gave this up as hopeless, for he was afraid, if he continued, he would blunt the edge of the dagger.

For an hour he sat still, thinking, and at last an idea occurred to him. Iron could be ground by rubbing it upon stone, and if he could not cut off the burr of the rivet with the dagger, he might perhaps be able to wear it down, by rubbing it with a stone.

He at once turned to the walls of his cell. These were not built of the unbaked clay so largely used for houses of the poorer class in Northern Egypt, but had evidently been constructed either as a prison, or more probably as a strong room where some merchant kept valuable goods. It was therefore constructed of blocks of hard stone.

It seemed to Francis that this was sandstone, and to test its quality, he sat down in the corner where the guard had, the night before, placed his supply of food and water. First he moistened a portion of the wall, then he took up a link of his chain, and rubbed for some time against it. At last, to his satisfaction, a bright patch showed that the stone was capable of wearing away iron. But in vain did he try to twist his legs so as to rub the rivet against the wall, and he gave up the attempt as impossible.

It was clear, then, that he must have a bit of the stone to rub with. He at once began to dig with the dagger in the earth at the foot of the wall, to see if he could find any such pieces. For a long time he came across no chips, even of the smallest size. As he worked, he was most careful to stamp down the earth which he had moved, scattering over it the sand, of which there was an abundance in the corners of the room, to obliterate all traces of his work.

When breakfast time approached he ceased for a while, but after the meal had been taken, he recommenced the task. He met with little success till he reached the door, but here he was more fortunate. A short distance below the surface were a number of pieces of stone of various sizes, which, he had no doubt, had been cut from the blocks to allow for the fixing of the lintel and doorpost. He chose half a dozen pieces of the handiest sizes, each having a flat surface. Then replacing the earth carefully, he took one of the pieces in his hand, and moistening it with water, set to work.

He made little progress. Still the stone did wear the iron, and he felt sure that, by perseverance, he should succeed in wearing off the burrs. All day he worked without intermission, holding a rag wrapped round the stone to deaden the sound. He worked till his fingers ached so that he could no longer hold it, then rested for an hour or two, and resumed his work. When his guard brought his dinner he asked him when the galley was to sail again.

"It was to have gone today," the man said, "but the captain has been laid up with fever. He has a leech from Tunis attending him, and, weak as he is, he is so bent on going that he would have had himself carried on board the ship, had not the leech said that, in that case, he would not answer for his life, as in the state his blood is in, his wounds would assuredly mortify did he not remain perfectly quiet. So he has agreed to delay for three days."

Francis was unable to work with the stone at night, for in the stillness the sound might be heard; but for some hours he hacked away with the dagger at the rivets on his manacles. The next morning he was at work as soon as the chirrup of the cicadas began, as these, he knew, would completely deaden any sound he might make. By nighttime the rivet ends on the irons round his ankles were worn so thin, that he felt sure that another hour's work would bring them level with the iron, and before he went to sleep the rivets on the wrist were in the same condition.

He learned from his guard, next morning, that the captain was better, that he was to be taken on board in the cool of the evening, and that the vessel would start as soon as the breeze sprang up in the morning. In the afternoon his two guards entered, and bade him follow them. He was conducted to the principal house in the village, and into a room where Ruggiero Mocenigo was lying on a couch.

"I have sent for you," Ruggiero said, "to tell you that I have not forgotten you. My vengeance has been delayed from no fault of mine, but it will be all the sweeter when it comes. I am going to fetch Polani's daughters. I have heard that, since you thrust yourself between me and them, you have been a familiar in the house, that Polani treats you as a member of the family, and that you are in high favour with his daughters. I have kept myself informed of what happened in Venice, and I have noted each of these things down in the account of what I owe you. I am going to fetch Polani's daughters here, and to make Maria my wife, and then I will show her how I treat those who cross my path. It will be a lesson to her, as well as for you. You shall wish yourself dead a thousand times before death comes to you."

"I always knew that you were a villain, Ruggiero Mocenigo," Francis said quietly, "although I hardly thought that a man who had once the honour of being a noble of Venice, would sink to become a pirate and renegade. You may carry Maria Polani off, but you will never succeed through her in obtaining a portion of her father's fortune, for I know that, the first moment her hands are free, she will stab herself to the heart, rather than remain in the power of such a wretch."

Ruggiero snatched up a dagger from a table by his couch as Francis was speaking, but dropped it again.

"Fool," he said. "Am I not going to carry off the two girls? and do you not see that it will tame Maria's spirit effectually, when she knows that if she lays hands on herself, she will but shift the honour of being my wife from herself to her sister?"

As the laugh of anticipated triumph rang in Francis's ears, the latter, in his fury, made a spring forward to throw himself upon the villain, but he had forgotten his chains, and fell headlong on to the floor.

"Guards," Ruggiero shouted, "take this fellow away, and I charge you watch over him securely, and remember that your lives shall answer for his escape."

"There is no need for threats, signor," Philippo said. "You can rely on our vigilance, though, as far as I see, if he had but a child to watch him he would be safe in that cell of his, fettered as he is."

Ruggiero waved his hand impatiently, and the two men withdrew with their prisoner.

"If it were not that I have not touched my share of the booty of our last trip," Philippo said as they left the house, "I would not serve him another day. As it is, as soon as the galley returns, and we get our shares of the money, and of the sum he has promised if this expedition of his is successful, I will be off. I have had enough of this. It is bad enough to be consorting with Moors, without being abused and threatened as if one was a dog."

As soon as he was alone again, Francis set to work, and by the afternoon the ends of the four rivets were worn down level with the iron, and it needed but a pressure to make the rings spring open. Then he waited for the evening before freeing himself, as by some chance he might again be visited, and even if free before nightfall he could not leave the house.

Philippo was later than usual in bringing him his meal, and Francis heard angry words passing between him and his comrade, because he had not returned to relieve him sooner.

"Is everything ready for the start?" Francis asked the man as he entered.

"Yes, the crew are all on board. The boat is to be on shore for the captain at nine o'clock, and as there is a little breeze blowing, I expect they will get up sail and start at once."

After a few minutes' talk the man left, and Francis waited until it became almost dark, then he inserted the dagger between the irons at the point of junction. At the first wrench they flew apart, and his left hand was free. A few minutes' more work and the chains lay on the ground.

Taking them up, he rattled them together loudly. In a minute he heard the guard outside move and come to the door, then the key was inserted in the lock and the door opened.

"What on earth are you doing now?" Philippo asked as he entered.

Francis was standing close to the door, so that as his guard entered he had his back to him, and before the question was finished he sprang upon him, throwing him headlong to the ground with the shock, and before the astonished man could speak he was kneeling upon him, with the point of the dagger at his throat.

"If you make a sound, or utter a cry," he exclaimed, "I will drive this dagger into your throat."

Philippo could feel the point of the dagger against his skin, and remained perfectly quiet.

"I do not want to kill you, Philippo. You have not been harsh to me, and I would spare your life if I could. Hold your hands back above your head, and put your wrists together that I may fasten them. Then I will let you get up."

Philippo held up his hands as requested, and Francis bound them tightly together with a strip of twisted cloth. He then allowed him to rise.

"Now, Philippo, I must gag you. Then I will fasten your hands to a bar well above your head, so that you can't get at the rope with your teeth. I will leave you here till your comrade comes in the morning."

"I would rather that you killed me at once, signor," the man said. "Thomaso will be furious at your having made your escape, for he will certainly come in for a share of the fury of the captain. There are three or four of the crew remaining behind, and no doubt they will keep me locked up till the ship returns, and in that case the captain will be as good as his word. You had better kill me at once."

"But what am I to do, Philippo? I must ensure my own safety. If you will suggest any way by which I can do that, I will."

"I would swear any oath you like, signor, that I will not give the alarm. I will make straight across the island, and get hold of a boat there, so as to be well away before your escape is known in the morning."

"Well, look here, Philippo. I believe you are sincere, and you shall take the oath you hold most sacred."

"You can accompany me, signor, if you will. Keep my hands tied till we are on the other side of the island, and stab me if I give the alarm."

"I will not do that, Philippo. I will trust you altogether; but first take the oath you spoke of."

Philippo swore a terrible oath, that he would abstain from giving the alarm, and would cross the island and make straight for the mainland. Francis at once cut the bonds.

"You will lose your share of the plunder, Philippo, and you will have to keep out of the way to avoid the captain's rage. Therefore I advise you, when you get to Tunis, to embark in the first ship that sails. If you come to Venice, ask for me, and I will make up to you for your loss of booty, and put you in the way of leading an honest life again. But before going, you must first change clothes with me. You can sell mine at Tunis for enough to buy you a dozen suits like yours; but you must divide with me what money you now have in your possession, for I cannot start penniless."

"I thank you for your kindness," the man said. "You had it in your power, with a thrust of the dagger, to make yourself safe, and you abstained. Even were it not for my oath, I should be a treacherous dog, indeed, were I to betray you. I do not know what your plans are, signor, but I pray you to follow my example, and get away from this place before daylight. The people here will all aid in the search for you, and as the island is not large, you will assuredly be discovered. It has for many years been a rendezvous of pirates, a place to which they bring their booty to sell to the traders who come over from the mainland."

"Thank you for your advice, Philippo, and be assured I shall be off the island before daybreak, but I have some work to do first, and cannot therefore accompany you."

"May all the saints bless you, signor, and aid you to get safe away! Assuredly, if I live, I will ere long present myself to you at Venice--not for the money which you so generously promised me, but that I may, with your aid, earn an honest living among Christians."

By this time the exchange of clothes was effected, the six ducats in Philippo's purse--the result of a little private plundering on one of the captured vessels--divided; and then they left the prison room, and Philippo locked the door after them.

"Is there any chance of Thomaso returning speedily?" Francis asked. "Because, if so, he might notice your absence, and so give the alarm before the ship sets sail, in which case we should have the whole crew on our tracks."

"I do not think that he will. He will be likely to be drinking in the wine shop for an hour or two before he returns. But I tell you what I will do, signor. I will resume my place here on guard until he has returned. He will relieve me at midnight, and in the darkness will not notice the change of clothes. There will still be plenty of time for me to cross the island, and get out of sight in the boat, before the alarm is given, which will not be until six o'clock, when I ought to relieve him again. As you say, if the alarm were to be given before the vessel sails, they might start at once to cut us off before we reach the mainland, for they would make sure that we should try to escape in that direction."

"That will be the best plan, Philippo; and now goodbye."

Francis walked down to the shore. There were no boats lying there of a size he could launch unaided, but presently he heard the sound of oars, and a small fishing boat rowed by two men approached.

"Look here, lads," he said. "I want to be put on board the ship. I ought to have been on board three hours ago, but took too much wine, and lay down for an hour or two and overslept myself. Do you think you can row quietly up alongside so that I can slip on board unnoticed? If so I will give you a ducat for your trouble."

"We can do that," the fishermen said. "We have just come from the ship now, and have sold them our catch of today. There were half a dozen other boats lying beside her, bargaining for their fish. Besides they are taking on board firewood and other stores that have been left till the last moment. So jump in and we will soon get you there."

In a few minutes they approached the side of the ship.

"I see you have got half a dozen fish left in your boat now," Francis said.

"They are of no account," one of the men said. "They are good enough for our eating, but not such as they buy on board a ship where money is plentiful. You are heartily welcome to them if you have a fancy for them."

"Thank you," Francis said. "I will take two or three of them, if you can spare them. I want to play a trick with a comrade."

As the fishermen said, there were several boats lying near the vessel, and the men were leaning over the sides bargaining for fish. Handing the fishermen their promised reward, Francis sprang up the ladder to the deck. He was unnoticed, for other men had gone down into the boats for fish.

Mingling with the sailors, he gradually made his way to the hatchway leading into the hold, descended the ladder, and stowed himself away among a quantity of casks, some filled with wine and some with water, at the farther end of the hold; and as he lay there devoutly thanked God that his enterprise had been so far successful.

Men came down from time to time with lanterns, to stow away the lately-arrived stores, but none came near the place where Francis was hidden. The time seemed long before he heard the clank of the capstan, and knew the vessel was being hove up to her anchors. Then, after a while, he heard the creaking of cordage, and much trampling of feet on the deck above, and knew that she was under way. Then he made himself as comfortable as he could, in his cramped position, and went off to sleep.

When he woke in the morning, the light was streaming down the hatch, which was only closed in rough weather, as it was necessary frequently to go down into it for water and stores. Francis had brought the fish with him as a means of subsistence during the voyage, in case he should be unable to obtain provisions, but for this there was no occasion, as there was an abundance of fruit hanging from the beams, while piles of bread were stowed in a partition at one end of the hold. During the day, however, he did not venture to move, and was heartily glad when it again became dark, and he could venture to get out and stretch himself. He appropriated a loaf and some bunches of grapes, took a long drink from a pail placed under the tap of a water butt, and made his way back to his corner. After a hearty meal he went out again for another drink, and then turned in to sleep.

So passed six days. By the rush of water against the outside planks, he could always judge whether the vessel was making brisk way or whether she was lying becalmed. Once or twice, after nightfall, he ventured up on deck, feeling certain that in the darkness there was no fear of his being detected. From conversation he overheard on the seventh evening, he learned that Corfu had been sighted that day. For some hours the vessel's sails had been lowered, and she had remained motionless; but she was now again making for the land, and in the course of another two hours a landing was to be made.

The boats had all been got in readiness, and the men were to muster fully armed. Although, as they understood, the carrying off of two girls was their special object, it was intended that they should gather as much plunder as could be obtained. The island was rich, for many wealthy Venetians had residences there. Therefore, with the exception of a few men left on board to take care of the galley, the whole were to land. A picked boat's crew were to accompany the captain, who was now completely convalescent. The rest were to divide in bands and scatter over the country, pillaging as they went, and setting fire to the houses. It was considered that such consternation would be caused that nothing like resistance could be offered for some time, and by daybreak all hands were to gather at the landing place.

How far this spot was from the town, Francis had no means of learning. There was a store of spare arms in the hold, and Francis, furnishing himself with a sword and large dagger, waited until he heard a great movement overhead, and then went upon deck and joined a gang of men employed in lowering one of the boats. The boat was a large one, rowing sixteen oars and carrying some twenty men seated in the stern. Here Francis took his place with the others. The boat pushed off and waited until four others were launched and filled. Then the order was given, and the boats rowed in a body towards the shore. The men landed and formed under their respective officers, one man remaining in each boat to keep it afloat.

Francis leaped ashore, and while the men were forming up, found no difficulty in slipping away unnoticed. As he did not know where the path was, and was afraid of making a noise, he lay down among the rocks until he heard the word of command to start given. Then he cautiously crept out, and, keeping far enough in the rear to be unseen, followed the sound of their footsteps. By the short time which had elapsed between the landing and the start, he had no doubt they were guided by some persons perfectly acquainted with the locality, probably by some natives of the island among the mixed crew.

Francis had, during his voyage, thought over the course he should pursue on landing; and saw that, ignorant as he was of the country, his only hope was in obtaining a guide who would conduct him to Polani's villa before the arrival of Mocenigo and his band. The fact that the crew were divided into five parties, which were to proceed in different directions, and that he did not know which of them was commanded by the captain, added to the difficulty. Had they kept together he might, after seeing the direction in which they were going, make a detour and get ahead of them. But he might now follow a party going in an entirely wrong direction, and before he could obtain a guide, Mocenigo's band might have gone so far that they could not be overtaken before they reached the villa.

There was nothing to do but to get ahead of all the parties, in the hope of coming upon a habitation before going far. As soon, therefore, as the last band had disappeared, he started at a run. The country was open, with few walls or fences; therefore on leaving the road he was able to run rapidly forwards, and in a few minutes knew that he must be ahead of the pirates. Then he again changed his course so as to strike the road he had left.

After running for about a mile he saw a light ahead of him, and soon arrived at a cottage. He knocked at the door, and then entered. The occupants of the room--a man and woman, a lad, and several children--rose to their feet at the sudden entrance of the stranger.

"Good people," Francis said. "I have just landed from a ship, and am the bearer of important messages to the Signoras Polani. I have lost my way, and it is necessary that I should go on without a moment's delay. Can you tell me how far the villa of Polani is distant?"

"It is about three miles from here," the man said.

"I will give a ducat to your son if he will run on with me at once."

The man looked doubtful. The apparel and general appearance of Francis were not prepossessing. He had been six days a prisoner in the hold without means of washing.

"See," he said, producing a ducat, "here is the money. I will give it you at once if you will order your son to go with me, and to hurry at the top of his speed."

"It's a bargain," the man said.

"Here, Rufo! start at once with the signor."

"Come along, signor," the boy said; and without another word to the parents Francis followed him out, and both set off at a run along the road.

Francis had said nothing about pirates to the peasants, for he knew that, did he do so, such alarm would be caused that they would think of nothing but flight, and he should not be able to obtain a guide. It was improbable that they would be molested. The pirates were bent upon pillaging the villas of the wealthy, and would not risk the raising of an alarm by entering cottages where there was no chance of plunder.

After proceeding a few hundred yards, the lad struck off by a byroad at right angles to that which they had been following, and by the direction he took Francis felt that he must at first have gone far out of his way, and that the party going direct to the villa must have had a considerable start. Still, he reckoned that as he was running at the rate of three feet to every one they would march, he might hope to arrive at the house well before them.

Not a word was spoken as they ran along. The lad was wondering, in his mind, as to what could be the urgent business that could necessitate its being carried at such speed; while Francis felt that every breath was needed for the work he had to do. Only once or twice he spoke, to ask how much further it was to their destination.

The last answer was cheering:

"A few hundred paces farther."

"There are the lights, signor. They have not gone to bed. This is the door."

Francis knocked with the pommel of his sword, keeping up a loud continuous knocking. A minute or two passed, and then a face appeared at the window above.

"Who is it that knocks so loudly at this time of night?"

"It is Francisco Hammond. Open instantly. Danger threatens the signoras. Quick, for your life!"

The servant recognized the voice, and ran down without hesitation and unbarred the fastening; but for a moment he thought he must have been mistaken, as Francis ran into the lighted hall.

"Where are the ladies?" he asked. "Lead me to them instantly."

But as he spoke a door standing by was opened, and Signor Polani himself, with the two girls, appeared. They had been on the point of retiring to rest when the knocking began, and the merchant, with his drawn sword, was standing at the door, when he recognized Francis' voice.

They were about to utter an exclamation of pleasure at seeing him, and of astonishment, not only at his sudden arrival, but at his appearance, when Francis burst out:

"There is no time for a word. You must fly instantly. Ruggiero Mocenigo is close at my heels with a band of twenty pirates."

The girls uttered a cry of alarm, and the merchant exclaimed:

"Can we not defend the house, Francisco? I have eight men here, and we can hold it till assistance comes."

"Ruggiero has a hundred," Francis said, "and all can be brought up in a short time--you must fly. For God's sake, do not delay, signor. They may be here at any moment."

"Come, girls," Polani said.

"And you, too," he went on, turning to the servants, whom the knocking had caused to assemble. "Do you follow us. Resistance would only cost you your lives.

"Here, Maria, take my hand.

"Francisco, do you see to Giulia.

"Close the door after the last of you, and bolt it. It will give us a few minutes, before they break in and discover that we have all gone.

"Which way are the scoundrels coming?"

Francis pointed in the direction from which he had come, and the whole party started at a fast pace in the other direction. They had not been gone five minutes, when a loud and sudden knocking broke on the silence of the night.

"It was a close thing, indeed, Francisco," the merchant said, as they ran along close to each other. "At present I feel as if I was in a dream; but you shall tell us all presently."

They were, by this time, outside the grounds of the villa, and some of the servants, who knew the country, now took the lead. In a few minutes the merchant slackened his pace.

"We are out of danger now," he said. "They will not know in which direction to search for us; and if they scatter in pursuit we could make very short work of any that might come up with us."

"I do not know that you are out of danger," Francis said. "A hundred men landed. Mocenigo, with twenty, took the line to your house, but the rest have scattered over the country in smaller bands, bent on murder and pillage. Therefore, we had best keep on as fast as we can, until well beyond the circle they are likely to sweep--that is, unless the ladies are tired."

"Tired!" Maria repeated. "Why, Giulia and I go for long walks every day, and could run for an hour, if necessary."

"Then come on, my dears," the merchant said. "I am burning to know what this all means; and I am sure you are equally curious; but nothing can be said till you are in safety."

Accordingly, the party again broke into a run. A few minutes later one of the servants, looking back, exclaimed:

"They have fired the house, signor. There are flames issuing from one of the lower windows."

"I expected that," the merchant said, without looking back. "That scoundrel would, in any case, light it in his fury at finding that we have escaped; but he has probably done so, now, in hopes that the light will enable him to discover us. It is well that we are so far ahead, for the blaze will light up the country for a long way round."

"There is a wood a little way ahead, signor," the servant said. "Once through that we shall be hidden from sight, however great the light."

Arrived at the wood, they again broke into a walk. A few hundred yards beyond the wood was some rising ground, from which they could see far over the country.

"Let us stop here," the merchant said. "We are safe now. We have placed two miles between ourselves and those villains."

The villa was now a mass of flames. Exclamations of fury broke from the men servants, while the women cried with anger at the sight of the destruction.

"Do not concern yourselves," the merchant said. "The house can be rebuilt, and I will see that none of you are the poorer for the loss of your belongings.

"Now, girls, let us sit down here and hear from Francisco how it is that he has once again been your saviour."

"Before I begin, signor, tell me whether there are any ships of war in the port, and how far that is distant from us?"

"It is not above six miles on the other side of the island. That is to say, we have been going towards it since we left the villa.

"See," he broke off, "there are flames rising in three or four directions. The rest of those villains are at their work."

"But are there any war galleys in the port?" Francis interrupted.

"Yes. Three ships were sent here, on the report that a Moorish pirate had been cruising in these waters, and that several vessels were missing. When the story first came I did not credit it. The captain of the ship who brought the news told me he had met you about halfway across, and had told you about the supposed pirate. A vessel arrived four days later, and brought letters from my agent, but he said no word about your boat having arrived.

"Then I became uneasy; and when later news came, and still no word of you, I felt sure that something must have befallen you; that possibly the report was true, and that you had fallen into the hands of the pirates. So I at once started, in one of the galleys which the council were despatching in answer to the request of the governor here."

"In that case, signor, there is not a moment to lose. The governor should be informed that the pirate is lying on the opposite coast, and that his crew have landed, and are burning and pillaging. If orders are issued at once, the galleys could get round before morning, and so cut off the retreat of these miscreants."

"You are quite right," Polani said, rising at once. "We will go on without a moment's delay! The girls can follow slowly under the escort of the servants."

"Oh, papa," Maria exclaimed, "you are not going to take Francisco away till we have heard his story! Can you not send forward the servants with a message to the governor?"

"No, my dear. The governor will have gone to bed, and the servants might not be able to obtain admittance to him. I must go myself. It is for your sakes, as well as for my own. We shall never feel a moment's safety, as long as this villain is at large. Francisco's story will keep till tomorrow.

"As to your gratitude and mine, that needs no telling. He cannot but know what we are feeling, at the thought of the almost miraculous escape you have had from falling into the hands of your persecutor.

"Now come along, Francisco.

"One of you men who knows the road had better come with us. Do the rest of you all keep together.

"Two miles further, girls, as you know, is a villa of Carlo Maffene. If you feel tired, you had best stop and ask for shelter there. There is no fear that the pirates will extend their ravages so far. They will keep on the side of the island where they landed, so as to be able to return with their booty before daybreak to the ship."

Chapter 14:
The End Of The Persecutor.

Signor Polani was so well known, that upon his arrival at the governor's house the domestics, upon being aroused, did not hesitate to awaken the governor at once. The latter, as soon as he heard that the pirates had landed and were devastating the other side of the island, and that their ship was lying close in to the coast under the charge of a few sailors only, at once despatched a messenger to the commander of the galleys; ordering them to arouse the crews and make ready to put out to sea instantly. He added that he, himself, should follow his messenger on board in a few minutes, and should accompany them. He then issued orders that the bell should toll to summon the inhabitants to arms; and directed an officer to take the command, and to start with them at once across the island, and to fall upon the pirates while engaged in their work of pillage. They were to take a party with them with litters to carry Polani's daughters to the town, and an apartment was to be assigned to them in his palace, until his return.

While he was issuing this order, refreshments had been placed upon the table, and he pressed Polani and his companions to partake of these before starting.

Francis needed no second invitation. He had been too excited, at the news he had heard on board the ship, to think of eating; and he now remembered that it was a good many hours since he had taken his last meal. He was but a few minutes, however, in satisfying his hunger. By the time he had finished, the governor had seen that his orders had been carried out.

Two hundred armed citizens had already mustered in companies, and were now on the point of setting out, burning with indignation at what they had heard of the depredations which the pirates had committed. After seeing his preparations complete the governor, accompanied by Polani and Francis, made his way down to the port, and was rowed out to the galleys.

Here he found all on the alert. The sails were ready for hoisting, and the men were seated at the benches, ready to aid with oars the light wind which was blowing. The governor now informed the commander of the vessels the reason of the sudden orders for sailing. The news was passed to the captains of the other two vessels, and in a very few minutes the anchors were weighed, and the vessels started on their way.

Francis was closely questioned as to the spot at which the pirate vessel was lying, but could only reply that, beyond the fact that it was some four miles from Polani's villa, he had no idea of the locality.

"But can you not describe to us the nature of the coast?" the commander said.

"That I cannot," Francis replied; "for I was hidden away in the hold of the vessel, and did not come on deck until after it was dark, at which time the land abreast of us was only a dark mass."

"Signor Polani has informed me," the governor said, "that, although your attire does not betoken it, you are a dear friend of his; but he has not yet informed me how it comes that you were upon this pirate ship."

"He has been telling me as we came along," Polani replied; "and a strange story it is. He was on his voyage hither in the Naxos, which, as you doubtless remember, was a little craft of mine, which should have arrived here a month since. As we supposed, it was captured by the pirates, the leader of whom is Ruggiero Mocenigo, who, as of course you know, made his escape from the custody of the officers of the state, they being overpowered by a party of Paduans. The sentence of banishment for life has been passed against him, and, until I heard from my friend here that he was captain of the pirate which has been seen off this island, I knew not what had become of him.

"Those on board the Naxos were taken prisoners, and confined in the pirate's hold, which they found already filled with captives taken from other ships. The pirate at once sailed for Africa, where all the prisoners were sold as slaves to the Moors, my friend here alone excepted, Mocenigo having an old feud with him, and a design to keep him in his hands. Learning that a raid was intended upon Corfu, with the special design of carrying off my daughters, whom Mocenigo had twice previously tried to abduct, Francisco managed to get on board the vessel, and conceal himself in her hold, in order that he might frustrate the design. He managed, in the dark, to mingle with the landing party; and then, separating from them, made his way on ahead, and fortunately was able to obtain a guide to my house, which he reached five minutes only before the arrival of the pirates there."

"Admirable, indeed! And we are all vastly indebted to him, for had it not been for him, we should not have known of the doings of these scoundrels until too late to cut off their retreat; and, once away in their ship again, they might long have preyed upon our commerce, before one of our cruisers happened to fall in with them.

"As for Ruggiero Mocenigo, he is a disgrace to the name of a Venetian; and it is sad to think that one of our most noble families should have to bear the brand of being connected with a man so base and villainous. However, I trust that his power of ill doing has come to an end."

"Is the vessel a fast one, signor?"

"I cannot say whether she sails fast," Francis replied; "but she certainly rows fast."

"I trust that we shall catch her before she gets under way," the commander of the galleys said. "Our vessels are not made for rowing, although we get out oars to help them along in calm weather."

"What course do you propose to take?" the merchant asked.

"When we approach the spot where she is likely to be lying, I shall order the captains of the other two ships to lie off the coast, a couple of miles distant and as far from each other, so that they can cut her off as she makes out to sea. We will follow the coast line, keeping in as close as the water will permit, and in this way we shall most likely come upon her. If we should miss her, I shall at the first dawn of morning join the others in the offing, and keep watch till she appears from under the shadow of the land."

It was now three o'clock in the morning, and an hour later the three vessels parted company, and the galley with the governor and commander of the squadron rowed for the shore. When they came close to the land, the captain ordered the oars to be laid in.

"The breeze is very light," he said; "but it is favourable, and will enable us to creep along the shore. If we continue rowing, those in charge of the ship may hear us coming, and may cut their cables, get up sail, and make out from the land without our seeing them. On a still night, like this, the sound of the sweeps can be heard a very long distance."

Quietly the vessel made her way along the shore. Over the land, the sky was red with the reflection of numerous fires, but this only made the darkness more intense under its shadow, and the lead was kept going in order to prevent them from sailing into shallow water. By the captain's orders strict silence was observed on board the ship, and every eye was strained ahead on the lookout for the pirate vessel.

Presently, all became aware of a confused noise, apparently coming from the land, but at some distance ahead. As they got further on, distant shouts and cries were heard.

"I fancy," the governor said to the captain, "the band from the town have met the pirates, and the latter are retreating to their ship."

"Then the ship can't be far off," the captain said. "Daylight is beginning to break in the east, and we shall soon be able to make her out against the sky--that is, if she is still lying at anchor."

On getting round the next point, the vessel was distinctly visible. The shouting on the shore was now plainly heard, and there could be no doubt that a desperate fight was going on there. It seemed to be close to the water's edge.

"There is a boat rowing off to the ship," one of the sailors said.

"Then get out your oars again. She is not more than half a mile away, and she can hardly get under way before we reach her. Besides, judging from the sound of the fight, the pirates must have lost a good many men, and will not be able to man all the oars even if they gain their ship."

The men sat down to their oars with alacrity. Every sailor on board felt it almost as a personal insult, that pirates should dare to enter the Venetian waters and carry on their depredations there. The glare of the burning houses, too, had fired their indignation to the utmost, and all were eager for the fight.

Three boats were now seen rowing towards the ship.

"Stretch to your oars, men," the captain said. "We must be alongside them, if we can, before they can take to their sweeps."

The pirates had now seen them; and Francis, standing at the bow eagerly watching the vessel, could hear orders shouted to the boats. These pulled rapidly alongside, and he could see the men clambering up in the greatest haste. There was a din of voices. Some men tried to get up the sails, others got out oars, and the utmost confusion evidently prevailed. In obedience to the shouts of the officers, the sails were lowered again, and all betook themselves to the oars; but scarce a stroke had been pulled before the Venetian galley ran up alongside. Grapnels were thrown, and the crew, seizing their weapons, sprang on to the deck of the pirate.

The crew of the latter knew that they had no mercy to expect, and although weakened by the loss of nearly a third of their number in the fighting on shore, sprang from their benches, and rushed to oppose their assailants, with the desperation of despair. They were led by Ruggiero Mocenigo, who, furious at the failure of his schemes, and preferring death to the shame of being carried to Venice as a pirate and a traitor, rushed upon the Venetians with a fury which, at first, carried all before it. Supported by his Moors and renegades he drove back the boarders, and almost succeeded in clearing the deck of his vessel.

He himself engaged hand-to-hand with the commander of the Venetian galley, and at the third thrust ran him through the throat; but the Venetians, although they had yielded to the first onslaught, again poured over the bulwarks of the galley. Polani, burning to punish the man who had so repeatedly tried to injure him, accompanied them, Francis keeping close beside him.

"Ruggiero Mocenigo, traitor and villain, your time has come!"

Ruggiero started at hearing his name thus proclaimed, for on board his own ship he was simply known as the captain; but in the dim light he recognized Polani, and at once crossed swords with him.

"Be not so sure, Polani. Perhaps it is your time that has come."

The two engaged with fury. Polani was still strong and vigorous. His opponent had the advantage of youth and activity. But Polani's weight and strength told, and he was forcing his opponent back, when his foot slipped on the bloodstained deck. He fell forward; and in another moment Ruggiero would have run him through the body; had not the weapon been knocked up by Francis, who, watching every movement of the fight, sprang forward when he saw the merchant slip.

"This time, Ruggiero, my hands are free. How about your vengeance now?"

Ruggiero gave a cry of astonishment, at seeing the lad whom he believed to be lying in chains, five hundred miles away, facing him. For a moment he recoiled, and then with the cry, "I will take it now," sprang forward. But this time he had met an opponent as active and as capable as himself.

For a minute or two they fought on even terms, and then Ruggiero fell suddenly backwards, a crossbow bolt, from one of the Venetians on the poop of the vessel, having struck him full in the forehead.

Without their leader, the spirit of the pirates had fled. They still fought, steadily and desperately, but it was only to sell their lives as dearly as possible; and in five minutes after the fall of Ruggiero the last man was cut down, for no quarter was given to pirates.

Just as the combat concluded, the sound of oars was heard, and the other two galleys came up to the assistance of their consort. They arrived too late to take part in the conflict, but cheered lustily when they heard that the pirate captain, and all his crew, had been killed. Upon learning that the commander of the galley was killed, the captain next in seniority assumed the command.

In a few minutes, the bodies of the pirates were thrown overboard, the wounded were carried below to have their wounds attended to, while the bodies of those who had fallen--thirteen in number--were laid together on the deck, for burial on shore.

"Thanks to you, Francisco, that I am not lying there beside them," the merchant said. "I did not know that you were so close at hand, and as I slipped I felt that my end had come."

"You were getting the better of him up to that point," Francis said. "I was close at hand, in readiness to strike in should I see that my aid was wanted, but up to the moment you slipped, I believed that you would have avenged your wrongs yourself."

"It is well that he fell as he did. It would have been dreadful, indeed, had he been carried to Venice, to bring shame and disgrace upon a noble family. Thank God, his power for mischief is at an end! I have had no peace of mind since the day when you first thwarted his attempt to carry off the girls; nor should I have ever had, until I obtained sure tidings that he was dead. The perseverance with which he has followed his resolve, to make my daughter his wife, is almost beyond belief. Had his mind been turned to other matters, he was capable of attaining greatness, for no obstacle would have barred his way.

"It almost seems as if it were a duel between him and you to the death--his aim to injure me, and yours to defend us. And now it has ended. Maria will breathe more freely when she hears the news, for, gay and light hearted as she is, the dread of that man has weighed heavily upon her."

The governor, who from the poop of the vessel had watched the conflict, now came up, and warmly congratulated Francis upon his bravery.

"I saw you rush forward, just as my friend Polani fell, and engage his assailant. At first I thought you lost, for the villain was counted one of the best swordsmen in Venice, and you are still but a lad; but I saw you did not give way an inch, but held your own against him; and I believe you would have slain him unaided, for you were fighting with greater coolness than he was. Still, I was relieved when I saw him fall, for even then the combat was doubtful, and his men, to do them justice, fought like demons. How comes it that one so young as you should be so skilled with your weapon?"

"This is not the first time that my young friend has done good service to the state," Polani said; "for it was he who led a crew of one of my ships to the aid of Pisani, when his galley was boarded by the Genoese, at the battle of Antium."

"Is this he?" the governor said, in surprise. "I heard, of course, by the account of those who came from Venice a month since, how Pisani was aided, when hard pressed, by the crew of one of your ships, headed by a young Englishman, upon whom the state had conferred the rights of citizenship as a recognition of his services; but I did not dream that the Englishman was but a lad."

"What is your age, young sir?"

"I am just eighteen," Francis replied. "Our people are all fond of strong exercise, and thus it was that I became more skilled, perhaps, than many of my age, in the use of arms."

At nine o'clock the squadron arrived in the port, bringing with them the captured galley. As soon as they were seen approaching, the church bells rang, flags were hung out from the houses, and the whole population assembled at the quay to welcome the victors and to hear the news.

"Do you go on at once, directly we land, Francisco, and set the girls' minds at ease. I must come on with the governor, and he is sure to be detained, and will have much to say before he can make his way through the crowd."

Francis was, on his arrival at the governor's, recognized by the domestics, and at once shown into the room where the girls were awaiting him. The fact that the pirate galley had been captured was already known to them, the news having been brought some hours before, by a horseman, from the other side of the island.

"Where is our father?" Maria exclaimed, as Francis entered alone.

"He is well, and sent me on to relieve your minds."

"Saint Mark be praised!" Maria said. "We have been sorely anxious about you both. A messenger, who brought the news, said that it could be seen from the shore that there was a desperate fight on board the pirate ship, which was attacked by one galley only. We felt sure that it would be the ship that the governor was in, and we knew you were with him; and our father was so enraged at what had happened, that we felt sure he would take part in the fight."

"He did so," Francis said, "and himself engaged hand-to-hand with Mocenigo, and would probably have killed him, had not his foot slipped on the deck. I was, of course, by his side, and occupied the villain until a cross bolt pierced his brain. So there is an end to all your trouble with him."

"Is he really dead?" Maria said. "Oh, Francisco, how thankful I am! He seemed so determined, that I began to think he was sure some day to succeed in carrying me off. Not that I would ever have become his wife, for I had vowed to kill myself before that came about. I should have thought he might have known that he could never have forced me to be his wife."

"I told him the same thing," Francis said, "and he replied that he was not afraid of that, for that he should have your sister in his power also, and that he should warn you that, if you laid hands on yourself, he should make her his wife instead of you."

The girls both gave an exclamation of horror.

"I never thought of that," Maria said; "but he would indeed have disarmed me with such a threat. It would have been horrible for me to have been the wife of such a man; but I think I could have borne it rather than have consigned Giulia to such a fate.

"Oh, here is father!"

"I have got away sooner than I expected," Polani said as he entered. "The governor was good enough to beg me to come on at once to you. You have heard all the news, I suppose, and know that our enemy will persecute you no more."

"We have heard, papa, and also that you yourself fought with him, which was very wrong and very rash of you."

"And did he tell you that had it not been for him I should not be here alive now, girls?"

"No, father. He said that when you slipped he occupied Ruggiero's attention until the cross bolt struck him."

"That is what he did, my dear; but had he not occupied his attention I should have been a dead man. The thrust was aimed at me as I fell, and would have pierced me had he not sprung forward and turned it aside, and then engaged in single combat with Mocenigo, who, with all his faults, was brave and a skillful swordsman; and yet, as the governor himself said, probably Francisco would have slain him, even had not the combat ended as it did.

"And now we must have his story in full. I have not heard much about it yet, and you have heard nothing; and I want to know how he managed to get out of the hands of that man, when he had once fallen into them."

"That is what we want to know, too, father. We know what a sharp watch was kept upon us, and I am sure they must have been much more severe with him."

"They were certainly more severe," Francis said smiling, "for my right hand was chained to my left ankle, and the left hand to to my right ankle--not tightly, you know, but the chain was so short that I could not stand upright. But, on the other hand, I do not think my guards were as vigilant as yours. However, I will tell you the whole story."

The girls listened with rapt attention to the story of the capture, the escape, and of his hiding in the hold of the pirate in order to be able to give them a warning in time.

"Your escape was fortunate, indeed," the merchant said when he had finished. "Fortunate both for you and for us, for I have no doubt that Mocenigo had intended to put you to a lingering death, on his return. As for the girls, nothing could have saved them from the fate he designed for them, save the method which you took of arriving here before him."

"What are we to do for him, father?" Maria exclaimed. "We are not tired of thanking him, but he hates being thanked. If he would only get into some terrible scrape, Giulia and I would set out to rescue him at once; but you see he gets out of his scrapes before we hear of them. It is quite disheartening not to be able to do anything."

Francis laughed merrily.

"It is terrible, is it not, signora? But if I manage to get into any scrape, and have time to summon you to my assistance, be sure I will do so. But, you see, one cannot get into a scrape when one chooses, and I must be content, while I am away, in knowing that I have the good wishes of you and your sister."

"Do not trouble yourself, Maria," her father said. "Some day an opportunity may come for our paying our debts, and in the meantime Francis is content that we should be his debtors."

"And now, what are you going to do, papa?"

"I shall sail with you for Venice tomorrow. The governor will be sending one of the galleys with the news of the capture of the pirate, and doubtless he will give us all a passage in her. I shall order steps to be taken at once for rebuilding the villa, and will get it completed by the spring, before which time you will be off my hands, young lady; and I shall not be altogether sorry, for you have been a very troublesome child lately."

"It has not been my fault," Maria pouted.

"Not at all, my dear. It has been your misfortune, and I am not blaming you at all."

"But the trouble is now over, father!"

"So much the better for Rufino," the merchant said. "It will be good news to him that you are freed from the persecution of Ruggiero. And now, I must leave you, for I have arranged to ride over with the governor to the other side of the island. He has to investigate the damage which took place last evening. I hear that upwards of a score of villas were sacked and destroyed, and that many persons were killed; and while he is doing that I shall see what has to be done at our place. I don't know whether the walls are standing, or whether it will have to be entirely rebuilt, and I must arrange with some builder to to go over from here with me, and take my instructions as to what must be done."

On the following day the party set sail for Venice, where they arrived without adventure. Preparations were at once begun for the marriage of Maria with Rufino Giustiniani, and six weeks later the wedding ceremony took place. Francis did not go to sea until this was over, for when he spoke of a fresh voyage, a short time after their return, Maria declared that she would not be married unless he remained to be present.

"You have got me out of all my scrapes hitherto, Francisco, and you must see me safely through this."

As Signor Polani also declared that it was not to be thought of, that Francis should leave until after the marriage, he was obliged to remain for it. He was glad, however, when it was over, for he found the time on shore more tedious than usual. The girls were taken up with the preparations for the ceremony, and visitors were constantly coming and going, and the house was not like itself.

But even when the marriage was over, he was forced to remain some time longer in Venice. The Genoese fleets were keeping the sea, and Pisani had not, since the battle of Antium, succeeded in coming up with them. The consequence was that commerce was at a standstill, for the risk of capture was so great that the merchants ceased to send their ships to sea.

"The profit would not repay us for the risk, Francisco," the merchant said one day when they were talking over it. "If only one cargo in ten fell into their hands the profit off the other nine would be swept away; but as I see that you are longing to be afloat again, you can, if you like, join one of the state galleys which start next week to reinforce Pisani's fleet.

"The last time Pisani wrote to me he said how glad he should be to have you with him; and after your service at Antium, I have no doubt whatever that I could procure for you a post as second in command in one of the ships. What do you say?"

"I should certainly like it, signor, greatly; but, as you said before, it would be a mere waste of time for me to take service with the state, when I am determined upon the vocation of a merchant."

"I did say that, Francis, and meant it at the time; but at present trade is, as you see, at a standstill, so you would not be losing time, and, in the next place, it is always an advantage, even to a trader, to stand well with the state. Here in Venice all the great merchants are of noble family, and trade is no bar to occupying the highest offices of the state. Many of our doges have been merchants; while merchants are often soldiers, diplomatists, or governors, as the state requires their services.

"You have already, you see, obtained considerable benefit by the action at Antium. I do not say that you would derive any direct benefit, even were you to distinguish yourself again as highly as on that occasion. Still, it is always well to gain the consideration of your fellows, and to be popular with the people. Therefore, if you would like to take service with the state until this affair is decided with Genoa, and the seas are again open to our ships, I think it will be advantageous to you rather than not."

"Then, with your permission I will certainly do so, signor," Francis said. "Of course I should prefer to go as an officer on board one of the ships; but if not, I will go as a volunteer."

"You need not fear about that, Francis. With my influence, and that of the Giustiniani, and the repute you have gained for yourself, you may be sure of an appointment. Rufino would have commanded one of the ships had it not been for his marriage."

Rufino Giustiniani had indeed been most warm in his expressions of gratitude to Francis, to whom the whole family had shown the greatest attention, giving him many presents as a proof of their goodwill and gratitude.

"I am quite jealous of your English friend," Rufino had said one day to Maria. "I do believe, Maria, that you care for him more than you do for me. It is lucky for me that he is not two or three years older."

Maria laughed.

"I do care for him dearly; and if he had been, as you say, older and had fallen in love with me, I can't say how it would have been. You must acknowledge, it would be very hard to say no to a man who keeps on saving you from frightful peril; but then, you see, a girl can't fall in love with a man who does not fall in love with her.

"Francisco is so different from us Venetians. He always says just what he thinks, and never pays anyone even the least bit of a compliment. How can you fall in love with a man like that? Of course you can love him like a brother--and I do love Francisco as if he were my brother--but I don't think we should have got further than that, if he had been ever so old."

"And does Francis never pay you compliments, Giulia?"

"Never!" Giulia said decidedly. "It would be hateful of him if he did."

"But Maria doesn't object to compliments, Giulia. She looks for them as if they were her daily bread--

"Don't you, Maria--

"You will have to learn to put up with them soon, Giulia, for you will be out in society now, and the young men will crowd round your chair, just as they have done round that of this little flirt, your sister."

"I shall have to put up with it, I suppose," Giulia said quietly, "just as one puts up with other annoyances. But I should certainly never get to care for anyone who thinks so little of me, as to believe that I could be pleased by being addressed in such terms."

"From which I gather," Giustiniani said, smiling, "that this English lad's bluntness of speech pleases you more than it does Maria?"

"It pleases Maria, too," Giulia said, "though she may choose to say that it doesn't. And I don't think it quite right to discuss him at all, when we all owe him as much as we do."

Giustiniani glanced at Maria and gave a little significant nod.

"I do not think Giulia regards Francisco in quite the brotherly way that you do, Maria," he whispered presently to her.

"Perhaps not," Maria answered. "You see, she had not fallen in love with you before she met him. But I do not know. Giulia seldom speaks of him when we are alone, and if she did, you don't suppose I should tell you my sister's secrets, sir?"

The day after his conversation with Francis, Polani handed him his nomination as second in command of the Pluto, which he had obtained that morning from the seignory.

"You will be glad to hear that it is in this ship that Matteo also sails," for Matteo had come home for his brother's wedding.

"I am very glad of that," Francis said. "I wish that poor Giuseppi was also here to go with me. I shall miss him terribly. He was a most faithful and devoted follower."

"I have already sent orders, to my agent in Tunis, to spare no pains in discovering to whom the crew of the Naxos were sold. It is unfortunate that so many other captives were sold at the same time, as it will make it so much more difficult to trace our men. Those purchasing are not likely to know more than their first names, and may not even take the trouble to find out those, but may give them the first appellation that comes to hand. Therefore he has to find out who are now the masters of the whole of the captives sold at the same time, and then to pursue his investigations until he discovers the identity of the men he is looking for. Once he has found this, I will promise you there will be no delay. I have ordered him to make the best bargain in each case he can, but that at any rate he is to buy every one of them, whatever it may cost.

"I have sent him the personal descriptions of each man of the boat's crew, as given to me by their friends and relatives here, as this will be an assistance in his search. If, for instance, he hears of a Christian slave named Giuseppi living with a master some hundreds of miles in the interior, the fact that this man is middle aged will show at once that he was not the Giuseppi, age 20, of whom he is in search. I have particularly impressed upon him, in my letter, that we were especially anxious for the rescue of the captain, and the young man Giuseppi, so I hope that by the time you return from the voyage, I may have received some news of them."

Matteo was greatly pleased when he heard that he was going to sail under Francis.

"I would rather that we had both been volunteers," Francis said. "It seems absurd my being appointed second officer, while you as yet have no official position."

"I am not in the least bit in the world jealous, Francisco. With the exception of taking part in the fight at Antium, I have had no experience whatever, while you have been going through all sorts of adventures for the last two years, and always have come out of them marvellously well."

An hour after Matteo left him, a retainer of the family brought Francis a letter from Signor Giustiniani, inviting him to come to his house that evening, as many of Matteo's comrades on board the Pluto would be present. On Francis going to the palace he found assembled, not only the young men who would be Matteo's comrades as volunteers, but also the captain and other officers of the ship; and to them Signor Giustiniani personally presented Francis, while Rufino and Matteo did all they could to ensure the heartiest welcome for him, by telling everyone how greatly they were indebted to him, and how gallantly he had behaved on several occasions.

Many of the young men he already knew as Matteo's friends, and by them he was received with the greatest cordiality; but his reception by the captain, and one or two of the other officers, was much more cool. The captain, whose name was Carlo Bottini, was a distant connection of the Mocenigo family, and was therefore already prejudiced against Francis. The coolness of the other officers was due to the fact that Francis, a foreigner and several years junior to themselves, had been placed in command over their heads.

Chapter 15:
The Battle Of Pola.

The squadron, consisting of four galleys, sailed for Cyprus; where Pisani had just endeavoured, without success, to expel the Genoese from Famagosta. It was towards the end of August that they effected a junction with his fleet. Pisani received Francis with great warmth, and, in the presence of many officers, remarked that he was glad to see that the republic was, at last, appointing men for their merits, and not, as heretofore, allowing family connection and influence to be the chief passport to their favour.

For two months the fleet sailed among the islands of the Levant, and along the shores of Greece, Istria, and Dalmatia; hoping to find the Genoese fleet, but altogether without success. In November, when they were on the coast of Istria, winter set in with extraordinary severity, and the frost was intense. Pisani wrote to his government asking permission to bring the fleet into Venice until the spring. The seignory, however, refused his request, for they feared that, were it known that their fleet had come into port for the winter, the Genoese would take advantage of its absence to seize upon some of the islands belonging to Venice, and to induce the inhabitants of the cities of Istria and Dalmatia, always ready for revolt, to declare against her.

The first indications of the winter were more than verified. The cold was altogether extraordinary; and out of the nineteen galleys of Pisani, only six were fit to take the sea, with their full complement of men, when the spring of 1379 began. Many of the vessels had been disabled by storms. Numbers of the men had died, more had been sent home invalided, and it was only by transferring the men from the other vessels to the six in the best condition, that the crews of the latter were made up to their full strength.

As soon as the terrible frost broke, Pisani received a reinforcement of twelve ships from Venice, these being, for the most part, built and equipped at the cost of his personal friends, Polani having contributed two of the number. With the eighteen sail, Pisani put to sea to prosecute a fresh search for the Genoese admiral, Doria, and his fleet.

The Pluto was one of the six vessels which remained in good condition at the end of the winter, thanks, in no small degree, to the energy and care which Francis had bestowed in looking after the welfare of the crew. In the most bitter weather, he had himself landed with the boats, to see that firewood was cut and brought off in abundance, not only for the officers' cabins, but to warm that portion of the ship inhabited by the men. Knowing that Polani would not grudge any sum which might be required, he obtained from his agents ample supplies of warm clothing and bedding for the men, occupying himself incessantly for their welfare, while the captain and other officers passed their time in their warm and comfortable cabins. Francis induced Matteo, and several of his comrades, to brave the weather as he did, and to exert themselves for the benefit of the men; and the consequence was, that while but few of the other ships retained enough men to raise their sails in case of emergency, the strength of the crew of the Pluto was scarcely impaired at the termination of the winter.

The admiral, on paying a visit of inspection to the ship, was greatly struck with the contrast which the appearance of the crew afforded to that of the other galleys, and warmly complimented the commander on the condition of his men. The captain received the praise as if it was entirely due to himself, and said not a single word of the share which Francis had had in bringing it about. Matteo was most indignant at this injustice towards his friend, and managed that, through a relative serving in the admiral's own ship, a true report of the case should come to Pisani's ears.

Francis was in no way troubled at the captain's appropriation of the praise due to himself. There had not, from the time he sailed, been any cordiality between Francis and the other officers. These had been selected for the position solely from family influence, and none of them were acquainted with the working of a ship.

In those days, not only in Venice but in other countries, naval battles were fought by soldiers rather than sailors. Nobles and knights, with their retainers, embarked on board a ship for the purpose of fighting, and of fighting only, the management of the vessel being carried on entirely by sailors under their own officers. Thus, neither the commander of the force on board the galley, nor any of his officers, with the exception of Francis, knew anything whatever about the management of the ship, nor were capable of giving orders to the crew. Among the latter were some who had sailed with Francis in his first two voyages, and these gave so excellent a report of him to the rest, that they were from the first ready to obey his orders as promptly as those of their own sub-officer.

Francis concerned himself but little with the ill will that was shown him by the officers. He knew that it arose from jealousy, not only of the promotion he, a foreigner and a junior in years, had received over them, but of the fact that he had already received the thanks of the republic for the services he had rendered, and stood high in the favour of the admiral, who never lost an opportunity of showing the interest he had in him. Had the hostility shown itself in any offensive degree Francis would at once have resented it; but Matteo, and some of those on board, who had been his comrades in the fencing rooms, had given such reports of his powers with his weapons, that even those most opposed to him thought it prudent to observe a demeanour of outward politeness towards him.

For three months the search for the Genoese fleet was ineffectual. A trip had been made along the coast of Apulia, and the fleet had returned to Pola with a large convoy of merchant ships loaded with grain, when on the 7th of May Doria appeared off the port, with twenty-five sail.

But Pisani was now by no means anxious to fight. Zeno was away with a portion of the fleet, and although he had received reinforcements, he numbered but twenty-one vessels, and a number of his men were laid up with sickness. The admiral, however, was not free to follow out the dictates of his own opinions. The Venetians had a mischievous habit, which was afterwards adopted by the French republic, of fettering their commanders by sea and land by appointing civilian commissioners, or, as they were termed in Venice, proveditors, who had power to overrule the nominal commander. When, therefore, Pisani assembled a council of war, and informed them of his reasons for wishing to remain on the defensive until the return of Zeno, he was overruled by the proveditors, who not only announced themselves unanimously in favour of battle, but sneered at Pisani's prudence as being the result of cowardice. Pisani in his indignation drew his sword, and would have attacked the proveditors on the spot, had he not been restrained by his captains.

However, the council decided upon instant battle, and Pisani was forced, by the rules of the service, at once to carry their decision into effect. Ascending the poop of his galley, he addressed in a loud voice the crews of the ships gathered around him.

"Remember, my brethren, that those who will now face you, are the same whom you vanquished with so much glory on the Roman shore. Do not let the name of Luciano Doria terrify you. It is not the names of commanders that will decide the conflict, but Venetian hearts and Venetian hands. Let him that loves Saint Mark follow me."

The men received the address with a shout, and as soon as the commanders had regained their galleys, the fleet moved out to attack the enemy. The fight was a furious one, each vessel singling out an opponent and engaging her hand to hand.

Carlo Bottini was killed early in the fight, and Francis succeeded to the command. His galley had grappled with one of the largest of the Genoese vessels, and a desperate conflict went on. Sometimes the Venetians gained a footing on the deck of the Genoese, sometimes they were driven back, and the Genoese in turn poured on board, but no decisive advantage was gained on either side after an hour's fighting. The Genoese crew was numerically much stronger than that of the Pluto, and although Francis, with Matteo and his comrades, headed their men and cheered them on, they could make no impression on the ranks of the enemy.

Suddenly, the Genoese threw off the grapnels that attached the two ships, and hoisting their sails, sheered off. Francis looked round to see the cause of this sudden manoeuvre, and perceived for the first time that the Genoese vessels were all in flight, with the Venetians pressing closely upon them. Sails were at once hoisted, and the Pluto joined in the chase.

But the flight was a feigned one, and it was only designed to throw the Venetian rank into confusion. After sailing for two miles, the Genoese suddenly turned, and fell upon their pursuers as they came up in straggling order.

The result was decisive. Many of the Venetian ships were captured before the rest came up to take part in the battle. Others were hemmed in by numerous foes. Pisani, after fighting until he saw that all was lost, made the signal for the ships to withdraw from the conflict, and he himself, with six galleys, succeeded in fighting his way through the enemy's fleet, and gained a refuge in the port of Parenzo.

All the rest were taken. From seven to eight hundred Venetians perished in the fight, two thousand four hundred were taken prisoners, twelve commanders were killed, and five captured. The Genoese losses were also severe, and Doria himself was among the slain, having been killed by a spear thrust by Donato Zeno, commander of one of the galleys, almost at the moment of victory.

The Pluto had defended herself, for a long time, against the attacks of three of the Genoese galleys, and had repeatedly endeavoured to force her way out of the throng, but the Genoese held her fast with their grapnels, and at last the greater part of her crew were driven down below, and Francis, seeing the uselessness of further resistance, ordered the little group, who were now completely pent in by the Genoese, to lower their weapons. All were more or less severely wounded, and were bleeding from sword cuts and thrusts.

"This is an evil day for Venice," Matteo said, as, having been deprived of their weapons, the prisoners were thrust below. "I heard the Genoese say that only six of our galleys have escaped, all the rest have been taken. We were the last ship to surrender, that's a comfort anyhow."

"Now, Matteo, before you do anything else, let me bind up your wounds. You are bleeding in two or three places."

"And you are bleeding from something like a dozen, Francisco, so you had better let me play the doctor first."

"The captain is always served last, so do as you are told, and strip off your doublet.

"Now, gentlemen," he said, turning to the other officers, "let each of us do what we can to dress the wounds of others. We can expect no care from the Genoese leeches, who will have their hands full, for a long time to come, with their own men. There are some among us who will soon bleed to death, unless their wounds are staunched. Let us, therefore, take the most serious cases first, and so on in rotation until all have been attended to."

It was fortunate for them that in the hold, in which they were confined, there were some casks of water; for, for hours the Genoese paid no attention whatever to their prisoners, and the wounded were beginning to suffer agonies of thirst, when the barrels were fortunately discovered. The head of one was knocked in, and some shallow tubs, used for serving the water to the crew, filled, and the men knelt down and drank by turns from these. Many were too enfeebled by their wounds to rise, and their thirst was assuaged by dipping articles of clothing into the water, and letting the fluid from these run into their mouths.

It was not until next morning that the prisoners were ordered to come on deck. Many had died during the night. Others were too weak to obey the summons. The names of the rest were taken, and not a little surprise was expressed, by the Genoese officers, at the extreme youth of the officer in command of the Pluto.

"I was only the second in command," Francis said in answer to their questions. "Carlo Bottini was in command of the ship, but he was killed at the commencement of the fight."

"But how is it that one so young came to be second? You must belong to some great family to have been thus pushed forward above men so much your senior."

"It was a wise choice nevertheless," the commander of one of the galleys which had been engaged with the Pluto said, "for it is but justice to own that no ship was better handled, or fought, in the Venetian fleet. They were engaged with us first, and for over an hour they fought us on fair terms, yielding no foot of ground, although we had far more men than they carried. I noticed this youth fighting always in the front line with the Venetians, and marvelled at the strength and dexterity with which he used his weapons, and afterwards, when there were three of us around him, he fought like a boar surrounded by hounds. I am sure he is a brave youth, and well worthy the position he held, to whatsoever he owed it."

"I belong to no noble family of Venice," Francis said. "My name is Francis Hammond, and my parents are English."

"You are not a mercenary, I trust?" the Genoese captain asked earnestly.

"I am not," Francis replied. "I am a citizen of Venice, and my name is inscribed in her books, as my comrades will vouch."

"Right glad am I that it is so," the Genoese said, "for Pietro Doria, who is now, by the death of his brother, in chief command, has ordered that every mercenary found among the prisoners shall today be slain."

"It is a brutal order," Francis said fearlessly, "whosoever may have given it! A mercenary taken in fair fight has as much right to be held for ransom or fair exchange as any other prisoner; and if your admiral thus breaks the laws of war, there is not a free lance, from one end of Italy to the other, but will take it up as a personal quarrel."

The Genoese frowned at the boldness with which Francis spoke, but at heart agreed in the sentiments he expressed; for among the Genoese officers, generally, there was a feeling that this brutal execution in cold blood was an impolitic, as well as a disgraceful deed.

The officers were now placed in the fore hold of the ship, the crew being confined in the after hold. Soon afterwards, they knew by the motion of the vessel that sail had been put on her.

"So we are on our way to a Genoese prison, Francisco," Matteo said. "We had a narrow escape of it before, but this time I suppose it is our fate."

"There is certainly no hope of rescue, Matteo. It is too early, as yet, to say whether there is any hope of escape. The prospect looked darker when I was in the hands of Ruggiero, but I managed to get away. Then I was alone and closely guarded, now we have in the ship well nigh two hundred friends; prisoners like ourselves, it is true, but still to be counted on. Then, too, the Genoese are no doubt so elated with their triumph, that they are hardly likely to keep a very vigilant guard over us. Altogether, I should say that the chances are in our favour. Were I sure that the Pluto is sailing alone, I should be very confident that we might retake her, but probably the fifteen captured ships are sailing in company, and would at once come to the aid of their comrades here, directly they saw any signs of a conflict going on, and we could hardly hope to recapture the ship without making some noise over it."

"I should think not," Matteo agreed.

"Then again, Matteo, even if we find it impossible to get at the crew, and with them to recapture the ship, some chance may occur by which you and I may manage to make our escape."

"If you say so, Francisco, I at once believe it. You got us all out of the scrape down at Girgenti. You got Polani's daughters out of a worse scrape when they were captives on San Nicolo; and got yourself out of the worst scrape of all when you escaped from the grip of Ruggiero Mocenigo. Therefore, when you say that there is a fair chance of escape out of this business, I look upon it as almost as good as done."

"It is a long way from that, Matteo," Francis laughed. "Still, I hope we may manage it somehow. I have the greatest horror of a Genoese prison, for it is notorious that they treat their prisoners of war shamefully, and I certainly do not mean to enter one, if there is the slightest chance of avoiding it. But for today, Matteo, I shall not even begin to think about it. In the first place, my head aches with the various thumps it has had; in the second, I feel weak from loss of blood; and in the third, my wounds smart most amazingly."

"So do mine," Matteo agreed. "In addition, I am hungry, for the bread they gave us this morning was not fit for dogs, although I had to eat it, as it was that or nothing."

"And now, Matteo, I shall try to get a few hours' sleep. I did not close my eyes last night, from the pain of my wounds, but I think I might manage to drop off now."

The motion of the vessel aided the effect of the bodily weakness that Francis was feeling, and in spite of the pain of his wounds he soon went off into a sound sleep. Once or twice he woke, but hearing no voices or movement, he supposed his companions were all asleep, and again went off, until a stream of light coming in from the opening of the hatchway thoroughly roused him. Matteo, who was lying by his side, also woke and stretched himself, and there was a general movement among the ten young men who were their comrades in misfortune.

"Here is your breakfast," a voice from above the hatchway said, and a basket containing bread and a bucket of water was lowered by ropes.

"Breakfast!" Matteo said. "Why, it is not two hours since we breakfasted last."

"I suspect it is twenty-two, Matteo. We have had a very long sleep, and I feel all the better of it. Now, let us divide the liberal breakfast our captors have given us; fortunately there is just enough light coming down from those scuttles to enable us to do so fairly."

There was a general laugh, from his comrades, at the cheerful way in which Francis spoke. Only one of them had been an officer on the Pluto. The rest were, like Matteo, volunteers of good families. There was a good deal of light-hearted jesting over their meal. When it was over, Francis said:

"Now let us hold a council of war."

"You are better off than Pisani was, anyhow," one of the young men said, "for you are not hampered with proveditors, and anything that your captaincy may suggest will, you may be sure, receive our assent."

"I am your captain no longer," Francis replied. "We are all prisoners now, and equal, and each one has a free voice and a free vote."

"Then I give my voice and vote at once, Francisco," Matteo said, "to the proposal that you remain our captain, and that we obey you, as cheerfully and willingly as we should if you were on the poop of the Pluto, instead of being in the hold. In the first place, at Carlo's death you became our captain by right, so long as we remain together; and in the second place you have more experience than all of us put together, and a very much better head than most of us, myself included.

"Therefore, comrades, I vote that Messer Francisco Hammond be still regarded as our captain, and obeyed as such."

There was a general chorus of assent, for the energy which Francis had displayed throughout the trying winter, and the manner in which he had led the crew during the desperate fighting, had won for him the regard and the respect of them all.

"Very well, then," Francis said. "If you wish it so I will remain your leader, but we will nevertheless hold our council of war. The question which I shall first present to your consideration is, which is the best way to set about retaking the Pluto?"

There was a burst of laughter among the young men. The matter of fact way in which Francis proposed, what seemed to them an impossibility, amused them immensely.

"I am quite in earnest," Francis went on, when the laughter had subsided. "If it is possibly to be done, I mean to retake the Pluto, and I have very little doubt that it is possible, if we set about it in the right way. In the first place, we may take it as absolutely certain that we very considerably outnumber the Genoese on board. They must have suffered in the battle almost as much as we did, and have had nearly as many killed and wounded. In the second place, if Doria intends to profit by his victory, he must have retained a fair amount of fighting men on board each of his galleys, and, weakened as his force was by the losses of the action, he can spare but a comparatively small force on board each of the fifteen captured galleys. I should think it probable that there are not more than fifty men in charge of the Pluto, and we number fully three times that force. The mere fact that they let down our food to us by ropes, instead of bringing it down, showed a consciousness of weakness."

"What you say is quite true," Paolo Parucchi, the other officer of the Pluto, said; "but they are fifty well-armed men, and we are a hundred and fifty without arms, and shut down in the hold, to which must be added the fact that we are cut off from our men, and our men from us. They are, as it were, without a head to plan, while we are without arms to strike."

A murmur of approval was heard among some of the young men.

"I do not suppose that there are no difficulties in our way," Francis said quietly; "or that we have only, next time the hatch is opened, to say to those above, 'Gentlemen of Genoa, we are more numerous than you are, and we therefore request you to change places with us immediately.' All I have asserted, so far, is that we are sufficiently strong to retake the ship, if we get the opportunity. What we have now to settle, is how that opportunity is to come about.

"To begin with, has anyone a dagger or knife which has escaped the eye of our searchers?"

No one replied.

"I was afraid that nothing had escaped the vigilance of those who appropriated our belongings. As, however, we have no weapons or tools, the next thing is to see what there is, in the hold, which can be turned to account. It is fortunate we are on board the Pluto, instead of being transferred to another ship, as we already know all about her. There are some iron bolts driven in along a beam at the farther end. They have been used, I suppose, at some time or other for hanging the carcasses of animals from. Let us see whether there is any chance of getting some of them out."

The iron pegs, however, were so firmly driven into the beam, that all their efforts failed to move them in the slightest.

"We will give that up for the present," Francis said, "and look round for something more available."

But with the exception of the water casks, the closest search failed to find anything in the hold.

"I do not know whether the iron hoops of a cask would be of any use," Matteo said.

"Certainly they would be of use, if we get them off, Matteo."

"There is no difficulty about that," one of the others said, examining the casks closely. "This is an empty one, and the hoops seem quite loose."

In a few minutes, four iron hoops were taken off the cask.

"After all," Matteo said, "they cannot be of much use. The iron is rust eaten, and they would break in our hands before going into any one."

"They would certainly be useless as daggers, Matteo, but I think that with care they will act as saws. Break off a length of about a foot.

"Now straighten it, and tear a piece off your doublet and wrap it round and round one end, so that you can hold it. Now just try it on the edge of a beam."

"It certainly cuts," Matteo announced after a trial, "but not very fast."

"So that it cuts at all, we may be very well content," Francis said cheerfully. "We have got a week, at least, to work in; and if the wind is not favourable, we may have a month. Let us therefore break the hoops up into pieces of the right length. We must use them carefully, for we may expect to have many breakages."

"What next, captain?"

"Our object will, of course, be to cut through into the main hold, which separates us from the crew. There we shall probably find plenty of weapons. But to use our saws, we must first find a hole in the bulkhead. First of all, then, let there be a strict search made for a knothole, or any other hole through the bulkhead."

It was too dark for eyes to be of much use, but hands were run all over the bulkhead. But no hole, however small, was discovered.

"It is clear, then," Francis said, "that the first thing to do is to cut out some of those iron bolts. Pick out those that are nearest to the lower side of the beam, say three of them. There are twelve of us. That will give four to each bolt, and we can relieve each other every few minutes. Remember, it is patience that is required, and not strength."

The work was at once begun. The young men had, by this time, fully entered into the spirit of the attempt. The quiet and businesslike way, in which their leader set about it, convinced them that he at least had a firm belief that the work was possible; and there was a hope, even if but a remote one, of avoiding the dreaded dungeons of Genoa.

The work was slow, and two or three of the strips of iron were at first broken, by the too great eagerness of their holders; but when it was found that, by using them lightly, the edges gradually cut their way into the wood, the work went on regularly. The Pluto had been hurriedly constructed, and any timbers that were available in the emergency were utilized. Consequently much soft wood, that at other times would never have been found in the state dockyards, was put into her. The beam at which they were working was of soft timber, and a fine dust fell steadily, as the rough iron was sawed backward and forward upon it.

Two cuts were made under each bolt, wide at the base and converging towards it. The saws were kept going the whole day, and although the progress was slow, it was fast enough to encourage them; and just as the light, that came through the scuttle, faded away; three of the young men hung their weight upon one of the bolts, and the wood beneath it, already almost severed, gave; and a suppressed cry of satisfaction announced that one bolt was free.

The pieces of iron were two feet long, and were intended for some other purpose, but had been driven in when, on loading the ship, some strong pegs on which to hang carcasses were required. They were driven about three inches into the beam, and could have been cut out with an ordinary saw in two or three minutes.

"Try the others," Francis said. "As many of you get hold of them as can put your hands on."

The effort was made, and the other two bolts were got out. They had been roughly sharpened at the end, and were fully an inch across.

"They do not make bad weapons," Matteo said.

"It is not as weapons that we want them, Matteo. They will be more useful to us than any weapons, except, indeed, a good axe. We shall want at least three more. Therefore, I propose that we continue our work at once. We will divide into watches now. It will be twelve hours before we get our allowance of bread again, therefore that will give three hours' work, and nine hours' sleep to each. They will be just setting the first watch on deck, and, as we shall hear them changed, it will give us a good idea how the time is passing."

"I am ready to work all night, myself," Matteo said. "At first I had not much faith in what we were doing; but now that we have got three of these irons out, I am ready to go on working until I drop."

"You will find, Matteo, that your arms will ache, so that you cannot hold them up, before the end of the three hours. Sawing like that, with your arms above your head, is most fatiguing; and even the short spells of work we have been having made my arms ache. However, each must do as much as he can in his three hours; and as we are working in the dark, we must work slowly and carefully, or we shall break our tools."

"Fortunately, we can get more hoops off now if we want them," Matteo said. "With these irons we can wrench them off the sound casks, if necessary."

"Yes; I did not think of that, Matteo. You see we are already getting a stock of tools. Another thing is, with the point of the irons we have got off, we can wrench the wood out as fast as we saw it, and the saws will not work so stiffly as they did before. But we must not do that till the morning, for any sound like the breaking of wood might be heard by the watch, when everything is quiet."

Although all worked their best, they made but slight progress in the dark, and each worker was forced to take frequent rests, for the fatigue of working with their arms above their heads was excessive. As soon, however, as the light began to steal down, and the movement above head told them that the crew were at work washing the decks, the points of the irons were used to wrench away the wood between the saw cuts; and the work then proceeded briskly, as they relieved each other every few minutes.

At last, to their intense satisfaction, three more irons were got out.

"If anyone had told me," one of the party said, "that a man's arms could hurt as much as mine do, from working a few hours, I should have disbelieved him."

There was a chorus of assent, for none were accustomed to hard manual labour, and the pain in their arms was excessive.

"Let us have half an hour's rest, Francis, before you issue your next orders. I shall want that, at least, before I feel that I have any power in my arms at all."

"We will have an hour's rest, Matteo, if you like. Before that time they will be sending us down our food, and after we have breakfasted we can set to work again."

"Breakfast!" one of the young men groaned. "I cannot call that black bread and water breakfast. When I think of the breakfasts I have eaten, when I think of the dishes I have refused to eat, because they were not cooked to perfection, I groan over my folly in those days, and my enormous stupidity in ever volunteering to come to sea."

"I should recommend you all," Francis said, "to spend the next hour in rubbing and squeezing the muscles of your neighbours' arms and shoulders. It is the best way for taking out stiffness, and Giuseppi used to give me relief that way, when I was stiff with fencing."

The idea was adopted; and while the rest were at work in the manner he suggested, Francis, taking one of the irons, went to the bulkhead. One by one he tried the planks, from the floor boards to the beams above.

"Well, captain, what is your report?" Matteo asked as he joined the rest.

"My report is a most favourable one," Francis said. "By great good luck, the planks are nailed from the other side against the beams both above and below."

"What difference does that make, Francisco?"

"All the difference in the world. Had they been nailed on this side, there would have been nothing for it but to carry out our original plan--that is, to make holes through the planks with these irons, large enough for the saws to go through, and then to saw the wood out from hole to hole. As it is, I believe that with five minutes' work we could wrench a plank away. We have only to push the points of the irons up, between the beams and the planks, and use them as levers. The nails will be strong, indeed, if those irons, with two of us at each, would not wrench them out."

The young men all leapt to their feet, pains and aches quite forgotten in the excitement of this unexpected news, and six of them seized hold of the irons.

"Gently!" Francis said. "You must remember, there may be people going down there at present, getting up stores. Before we venture to disturb a plank, we must make the hole sufficiently large for us to spy through. This will be a very easy affair, in comparison with making a hole large enough for a saw to go through. Still, you will find it will take some time. However, we had better wait, as we agreed, till we have had our food."

Chapter 16:
The Recapture Of The Pluto.

As soon as the hatch had been removed, and the bread and water lowered down, and they heard heavy weights again laid on the hatch, two of the party took one of the irons and began to bore a hole, while the others proceeded to eat their food. Several times, the workers had to be relieved. The iron penetrated comparatively easily for a short distance, but beyond that the difficulty greatly increased; and it was fully four hours before one of the workers, applying his eye to the hole, said that he could see a gleam of light through.

In another quarter of an hour, the orifice was sufficiently enlarged to enable a view to be obtained of the central hold. It was comparatively light there, for the hatch was off, and they could see two men at work, opening a cask for some stores that were required.

"We must wait till it gets dark now," Francis said. "I do not think that we shall make much noise, for the nails will be likely to draw quietly; but we had better choose the time between nightfall and the hour for the crew to turn in, as there will be a trampling of feet on deck, and talking and singing, which would prevent any slight noise we might make, being heard."

"The difficulty will be to force the ends of the iron down, between the beams and the planks, so as to give us a purchase," Matteo said.

"I think we shall be able to manage that," Francis replied. "The beams are put in in the rough, and if we hunt carefully, I think we shall find a plank where we can get the irons in far enough, between it and the beam, to give us a hold."

After a careful examination, they fixed upon a plank to operate upon, and, leaving one of the irons there, so that they could find it in the dark, they lay down to sleep, or sat talking until it was dark. Before this, a glance, through the peephole, showed them that the hatch had been placed over the hatchway of the next hold, so that there was little fear of anyone coming down, unless something special was required.

"Now I think we can begin," Francis said, at last. "Do you, Paolo Parucchi, take one of the irons, I will take another, Matteo a third. We cannot possibly work more than three at the foot of a plank, though perhaps, when we have fixed them and put on the strain, two or three more hands may get at the irons; but first we will try with three, and, unless the nails have got a wonderfully firm hold, we shall certainly be able to draw them."

It took some time to fix the irons, to the best advantage, between the planks and the beam.

"Are you both ready?" Francis asked at last. "Then pull."

As Francis had anticipated, the levers did their work, and the nails yielded a little.

"It has sprung half an inch," Francis said, feeling. "Now you keep your irons as they are, while I thrust mine down farther. I have got a fresh hold. Do you shift yours."

Again the effort was made, and this time the nails drew fully two inches. Another effort, and the plank was completely free at the lower end.

"Now do you push against it as hard as you can," Francis said, "while I get my iron in between it and the beam above."

The upper nails yielded even more easily than those below.

"No farther," Francis said, when they had fairly started them, "or the plank will be falling with a crash. We must push from the bottom now, until it gives sufficiently far for you to get an iron down each side, to prevent its closing again."

"Now," he said, "push the irons higher up. That is right. Now I will loosen a bit farther at the top, and then you will be able to get your hands in at the bottom to steady it, and prevent its falling when the nails are quite drawn."

Another effort, and the plank was free, and, being drawn in, was laid down. The delight of those who were standing in the dark, and could only judge how matters were going on from Francis's low spoken orders, was extreme.

"Can we get through?"

"No," Francis replied. "It will be necessary to remove another plank first, but perhaps one of the slighter among you might manage to squeeze through, and hold the plank at the back. We shall be able to work with more freedom, if we know that there is no danger of its falling."

In a few minutes, the second plank was laid beside the first.

"What is to be done next?" Matteo asked.

"We must establish a communication with the sailors. I will take a working party of four. Paolo Parucchi, with four others, will relieve me. You, Matteo, will with the rest take the last spell. When we have entered the next compartment, we will put up the planks again, and press the nails in tightly enough to prevent their falling. Should, by some chance, anyone descend into the hold while we are working, we shall be hidden from their view. At the other end there are a number of sacks piled up, and we shall be working behind them."

Francis, and the men he had chosen, made their way to the pile of arms they had observed through their peephole, moving with great precaution, so as to avoid falling over anything. Here, with some trouble, they succeeded in finding a dagger among the heap, and they then felt their way on, until they reached the pile of sacks. These were packed to within a foot of the deck beams, and there was but just room for them to crawl in at the top.

"Whatever you do, do not bump against the beams," Francis said. "Any noise of that sort, from below, would at once excite attention. Now do you be quiet, while I find a spot to begin upon."

Commencing at a junction of two planks, Francis began, with the dagger, to cut a hole of some three or four inches across, but tapering rapidly as it went in. After waiting for some ten minutes, he touched the man lying next to him, placed his hand on the hole he had begun, and then moved aside to allow him to continue the work.

In an hour a hole was made in a two inch plank, and this was soon enlarged until it was an inch in diameter. Lying along the side of the bulkhead, so as to get his ear to the hole, Francis listened, but could hear no sound within. Then he put his mouth to the orifice and asked:

"Are you all asleep there?"

Then he listened again. Some of the men were speaking, and asking each other who it was that had suddenly spoken. No one replied; and some of them gave vent to angry threats, against whoever it might be who had just disturbed them from going off to sleep.

Directly the voices ceased again, Francis said:

"Let us have silence in there. Where is Rinaldo, the boatswain?"

"I am here," a voice replied; "but who is speaking? It sounds like the voice of Messer Hammond."

"It is my voice, Rinaldo. We have worked through from the hold at the other end of the ship, having removed some of the planks of the bulkhead. Now it is for you to do the same. We will pass you some daggers through, when we have made this hole a bit larger. You must choose one of the planks in the corner, as this will be less likely to be observed."

"They will not observe us, Messer Hammond. They never come down here at all, but pass our food down in buckets."

"Nevertheless, begin at the plank next to the side," Francis said. "Possibly someone may come down before you have finished. You will have to remove two planks to get through. I will pass a javelin through. You can set to work with it, and bore holes through the plank close to the floor; and then, with the dagger, cut away the wood between them. When you have done them, set to at the top, close to the beams, and cut the two planks through there. There are sacks of grain piled up against them on this side, so that there is no fear of your being observed from here. The work must be carried on perfectly noiselessly, the men relieving each other every few minutes.

"When the planks are cut through, replace them in their former positions, and wedge some small pieces of wood in, so that there shall be no chance of their falling. You ought to finish the work by tomorrow. When you have done it, take no farther step until you get orders from me. It would not do to rise now, for we may be surrounded by other ships, and if we overpowered the crew, we should at once be attacked and recaptured by them. You will, therefore, remain quiet until you have orders, whether it be one day or ten. All the arms they have taken from us are lying piled here, and when the time comes, we shall have no difficulty in overpowering the Genoese, and shall, I hope, bring the Pluto safely to anchor in the port of Venice before long."

There was a murmur of delight among the sailors, pent up in their close quarters. Francis listened a moment, and heard one of the men say:

"What did I tell you? Didn't I tell you that Messer Hammond got us all out of a scrape before, when our ship was captured by the Genoese, and that I would be bound he would do the same again, if he had but the shadow of a chance."

"You did, Pietro, and you have turned out right. That is the sort of fellow to have for a captain. He is not like one of those dainty young nobles, who don't know one rope's end from another, and who turn up their noses at the thought of dirtying their hands. See how he looked after us through the winter. I wish we could give a cheer for him, but that would never do. But when we are out of this, I will give him the loudest shout I ever gave yet.

"Now then, Rinaldo, let us set to work without a moment's delay. There's a chance we aren't going to rot in the dungeons of Genoa, after all."

Convinced that the work would be carried on in accordance with his orders, Francis withdrew his ear from the hole, and, crawling over the sacks again, made his way to the pile of arms, felt about until he found two javelins, and taking these back, passed them one after the other through the hole.

"We have done our share now," he said to his comrades. "Paolo and his party will find it a comparatively easy task to enlarge the hole sufficiently to pass the daggers through."

The party returned to the other end of the hold, removed the planks, and joined their friends. The next watch had arranged to lie down close to the planks, so that they could be aroused without waking the others.

They were soon on their feet. Francis explained to Parucchi the progress they had made, and the orders that had been given to the sailors as to what they were to do.

"When the hole is large enough, pass these five daggers in to the crew, and then come back again. I will guide you to the spot, and on my return will pick out half a dozen more daggers, in case we want them for further work."

When daylight made its way into the hold, Matteo and his watch woke, and were astonished to find that all their comrades were quietly asleep, and that they had not been awakened. Matteo could not restrain his curiosity, but woke Francis:

"Has anything gone wrong, Francis? It is daylight, and Parucchi's party, as well as yours, are all asleep, while we have not been roused!"

"Everything is going on well, Matteo, and we did not wake you, because there was nothing for you to do. We have already passed in knives and javelins to the sailors, and they are at work cutting through two planks in their bulkhead; after which we shall be able to meet in the next hold, arm ourselves, and fall upon the Genoese when the opportunity offers."

"That is excellent indeed, Francis; but I wish you had let us do our share of the work."

"It did not take us more than two hours, Matteo, to make a hole big enough to pass the javelins through, and I should say Parucchi's party enlarged it sufficiently to hand in the daggers in another hour; so you see, it would have been useless to have aroused you, and the less movement we make after they get quiet at night, the better."

"And how long will the sailors be cutting it through, do you think?"

"I should say they would be ready by this time, Matteo, but certainly they will be finished some time today."

"Then we shall soon be free!" Matteo exclaimed joyfully.

"That will depend, Matteo. We must wait till there is a good opportunity, so that we can recapture the ship without an alarm being given to the other vessels, which are no doubt sailing in company with us. And now, if you have nothing to say, I will go off to sleep again, for there is time for another hour or two. I feel as if I had not quite finished my night's rest, and the days pass so slowly here that it is as well for us to sleep when we feel the least inclination.

"By the way, Matteo, put something into that peephole we made. It is possible that they might see the light through it, and come to examine what it is. It is better to run no risk."

That day the captives were far more restless than they had been since they were taken prisoners. At first there had been a feeling of depression, too great to admit even of conversation with each other. The defeat of their fleet, the danger that threatened Venice, and the prospect of imprisonment in the gloomy dungeons of Genoa, combined to depress them on the first day of their imprisonment. On the second, their success in getting out the bolts had cheered them, and they had something to look forward to and talk about; but still, few of them thought that there was any real prospect of their obtaining their freedom. Now, however, that success seemed to lie ready to hand; now that they could, that very evening, remove the sacks, effect a junction with their crew, arm themselves with the weapons lying in sight, and rush up and overpower the Genoese; it seemed hard to remain longer in confinement. Several of them urged Francis to make the attempt that night, but he refused.

"You reckon only on the foe you see," he said. "The danger lies not from them, but from the foes we cannot see. We must wait for an opportunity."

"But no opportunity may occur," one of them urged.

"That is quite possible," Francis agreed; "but should no special opportunity occur, we shall be none the worse for having waited, for it will always be as open to us to make the attempt as it is tonight. It might succeed--possibly we could overpower the guard on deck before they could give the alarm--but the risk is too great to be run, until we are certain that no other way is open to us. In the daylight the hatch is open; but even could we free our comrades, and unite for a rush, unobserved--which we could hardly hope to do--we should find the whole of the Genoese on deck, and could not possibly overpower them before they had time to give the alarm to other vessels. At night, when we can unite, we cannot gain the deck, for the hatch is not only closed, but would almost certainly be fastened, so that men should not get down to pilfer among the stores."

"But if we cannot attack in the daytime, Messer Hammond, without giving the alarm; and cannot attack at all at night, what are we to do?"

"That is the next point to be seen to," Francis replied. "We must cut, either from this hold or from the other, a way up to the deck above. It may take us some days to do this, but that matters little. We have plenty of time for the work before reaching Genoa. The difficulty is not in the work itself, but in doing it unobserved."

"That is difficult, indeed," Matteo said, "seeing that the Genoese sailors are quartered in the forecastle above the forehold, while the officers will be in the cabins in the poop over us."

"That is so, Matteo, and for that reason, it is clear that it is we, not the sailors, who must cut through the planks above. There are no divisions in the forecastle, and it will be, therefore, absolutely impossible to cut through into it, without being perceived long before a hole is made of a sufficient size to enable us to get out. Here we may succeed better, for fortunately we know the exact plan of the cabins above us, and can choose a spot where we should not be likely to be noticed."

"That is so," Matteo agreed, "and as they will not have as many officers as we had--that is, including the volunteers--some of the cabins will not be occupied. Perhaps, by listening to the footsteps above, we might find out which are vacant."

"I thought of that, Matteo, but I doubt whether it would be well to rely upon that. Many on board ship wear soft shoes, which make but little noise, and it would be fatal to us were we to make a mistake. After thinking it over, I have decided that we had best try to cut a way up into the captain's cabin."

"But that is sure to be occupied, Messer Hammond," Parucchi said.

"Yes, it will be certainly be occupied; but it affords a good opportunity of success. As you know, Parucchi, Carlo Bottini had been a long time at Constantinople and the Eastern ports, and had a somewhat luxurious taste. Do you not remember that, against the stern windows, he had caused to be erected a low wide seat running across the cabin? This he called a divan, and spent no small proportion of his time lolling upon it. If I am right, its height was from ten inches to a foot above the deck, and it was fully four feet wide. It would therefore be quite possible to cut through the two planks at the back, without its being observed by anyone in the cabin."

There was a chorus of assent.

"Of course we must work most cautiously," Francis went on. "The wood must be cut out with clean cuts with the daggers. There must be no sawing or scraping. The beams are two feet apart, and we must cut through two planks close to them. In that way there will be no nails to remove. Of course, we shall not cut quite through until the time arrives for us to make the attempt, but just leave enough to hold the planks together. Half an hour's work will get through that, for if we were to cut through it at once, not only would there be risk of the hole being discovered by anyone sweeping the cabin, but we should be obliged to remain absolutely silent, or we should be heard immediately."

"We can begin at once, can we not?" Matteo asked. "Anything is better than sitting quietly here."

"Certainly, Matteo, if you wish. Two can work at once, one on each line. Choose the two sharpest edged of the daggers, and be sure to cut clean, and not to make a scraping noise or to try to break out pieces of wood. The work must be done in absolute quiet. Indeed, however careful you are, it is possible that some slight sound may be heard above, but, if noticed, it will probably be taken for the rats."

Matteo and another of the young men at once fell to work; but it was not until the evening of the following day that cuts were made as deep as was considered prudent. The depth of wood remaining was tested by thrusting the point of a dagger through, and it was decided that little more than a quarter of an inch remained.

Upon the following day the ship anchored, and remained for two days in some port. Provisions were brought on board and carried down into the hold, and the prisoners had no doubt that they were in harbour on the coast of either Sicily, or the south of Italy. They had not set sail many hours, when the motion of the ship told them that the wind was getting up, and by night the vessel was rolling heavily, the noise made by the dashing of the water against her planks being so great, that those below could scarcely hear each other speak. Their spirits had risen with the increase of the motion, for the opportunity for which they had been waiting was now at hand. In a gale the vessels would keep well apart from each other, to prevent the danger of a collision, and any outcry would be drowned by the noise of the wind and water.

Each night Francis had paid a visit to the sailors forward, to enjoin patience until he should give them the order for making the attempt. They had long since cut through the planks, which were only retained in their place by the pressure of the sacks behind them. He had bade them be in readiness on the first occasion on which rough weather might set in, and knew that they would now be expecting the signal.

As soon, then, as it became dark, and the hatch over the middle hold was closed; the planks were removed, and Francis and his party set to work shifting the sacks, in the corner where the sailors had cut the planks. Each sack was taken up, and placed against the pile further on, without the slightest noise, until at last all were removed that stood in the way of the planks being taken down. These were carried out into the hold.

Francis entered the gap. The sailors had already been informed that the occasion had come, and that they were to remain perfectly quiet until bidden to move.

"All is prepared," he said as he entered. "Rinaldo, do you see that the men come out one by one. As each comes out a weapon will be placed in his hands, and he will be then led to the starboard side of the hold, which is free from encumbrance, and will there stand until he receives orders to move further. Remember that not the slightest noise must be made, for if any stumbled and fell, and the noise were heard above, it might be thought that some of the stores had shifted from their places, and men would be sent below to secure them. The alarm would be given, and a light or other signal shown the other ships, before we could overpower all resistance. After the men are all ranged up as I have directed, they will have to remain there for some little time, while we complete our arrangements."

As soon as the sailors were all armed, and ready for action, Francis entered the after hold, where Matteo and another had been engaged in cutting the planks quite through. They had just completed the task when he reached them, and had quietly removed the two pieces of plank. Francis had already given his orders to his companions, and each knew the order in which they were to ascend.

A dim light streamed down from the hole. Two of his comrades lifted Francis so that his head was above the level of the hole, and he was enabled to see into the cabin. So far as he could tell, it was untenanted, but it was possible that the commander might be on the divan above him. This was not, however, likely, as in the gale that was now blowing he would probably be on deck, directing the working of the ship.

Francis now gave the signal, and the others raised him still further, until he was able to get his weight upon the deck above, and he then crawled along underneath the divan, and lay there quiet until Parucchi and Matteo had both reached the deck. Then he gave the word, and all three rolled out and leaped to their feet, with their daggers in their hands, in readiness to fall upon the captain should he be on the divan.

As they had hoped and expected, the cabin was untenanted. The other volunteers now joined them, the last giving the word to Rinaldo, who soon passed up, followed by the crew, until the cabin was as full as it could contain. There were now assembled some fifty men, closely packed together.

"That is ample," Francis said, "as they will be unarmed and unprepared. We can issue out singly until the alarm is given, and then those that remain must rush out in a body. Simply knock them down with the hilts of your swords. There is no occasion to shed blood, unless in the case of armed resistance; but remember they will have their knives in their girdles, and do not let anyone take you by surprise."

Opening the door, Francis walked along a passage, and then through an outer door into the waist of the ship. The wind was blowing fiercely, but the gale was not so violent as it had appeared to them when confined below. The night was dark, but after a week's confinement below, his eyes were able easily to make out almost every object on deck. There were but few sailors in the waist. The officers would be on the poop, and such of the crew as were not required on duty in the forecastle. Man after man joined him, until some thirty were gathered near the bulwarks. An officer on the poop caught sight of them by the light of the lantern, which was suspended there as a signal to the other vessels.

"What are all you men doing down there?" he challenged. "There is no occasion for you to keep on deck until you are summoned."

"Do you move forward with the men here, Parucchi. Knock down the fellows on deck, and rush into the forecastle and overpower them there, before they can get up their arms. I will summon the rest in a body, and we will overpower the officers."

He ran back to the cabin door, and bade the men follow him. As they poured out there was a scuffle on the deck forward, and the officer shouted out again:

"What is going on there? What does all this mean?"

Francis sprang up the ladder to the poop, followed by his men, and before the officer standing there understood the meaning of this sudden rush of men, or had time to draw his sword, he was knocked down. The captain and three other officers, who were standing by the helm, drew their swords and rushed forward, thinking there was a mutiny among their crew; but Francis shouted out:

"Throw down your weapons, all of you. We have retaken the ship, and resistance is useless, and will only cost you your lives."

The officers stood stupefied with astonishment; and then, seeing that fully twenty armed men were opposed to them, they threw down their swords. Francis ordered four of the sailors to conduct them to the captain's cabin, and remain in guard over them; then with the rest he hurried forward to assist Parucchi's party.

But the work was already done. The Genoese, taken completely by surprise, had at once surrendered, as the armed party rushed in the forecastle, and the ship was already theirs. As soon as the prisoners were secured, the after hatch was thrown off, and those whose turn to crawl up through the hole had not yet arrived came up on deck.

"Rinaldo," Francis said, as soon as the crew had fallen into their places, "send a man aloft, and let him suddenly knock out the light in the lantern."

"But we can lower it down, captain, from the deck."

"Of course we can, Rinaldo, but I don't want it lowered down, I want it put suddenly out."

Rinaldo at once sent a man up, and a minute later the light suddenly disappeared.

"If we were seen to lower it down," Francis said to Matteo, "the suspicions of those who noticed it would be at once aroused, for the only motive for doing so would be concealment; whereas now, if it is missed, it will be supposed that the wind has blown it out. Now we have only to lower our sails, and we can drop unobserved out of the fleet."

"There are sixteen lights, I have just been counting them," Matteo said.

"These are probably the fourteen galleys captured with us, and two galleys as guards, in case, on their way, they should fall in with any of our ships.

"Parucchi, will you at once muster the men, and see that all are armed and in readiness for fighting?

"Matteo, do you and some of your friends assist the lieutenant."

In a few minutes, Parucchi reported that the men were all ready for action.

"Rinaldo, brail up the sails, so that we may drop into the rear of the squadron. Watch the lights of the vessels behind, and steer so that they shall pass us as widely as possible."

This was the order the men were expecting to receive, but they were surprised when, just as the last light was abreast of them, Francis gave the order for the brails to be loosed again.

"Signor Parucchi, do you tell off fifty men. I am going to lay the ship alongside that vessel, and recapture her. They will not see us until we are close on board, and will suppose it is an accident when we run alongside. No doubt they, like the Pluto, have only a complement of fifty men, and we shall overpower them before they are prepared to offer any resistance.

"No doubt they have prisoners below. Immediately we have recaptured her, I shall return on board with the rest, leaving you with your fifty men in charge of her. As soon as you have secured the Genoese, free any prisoners there may be in the hold. I shall keep close to you, and you can hear me, and tell me how many there are."

The Pluto was now edged away, till she was close to the other ship. The crew, exulting in having turned the tables on the Genoese, and at the prospect of recovering another of the lost galleys, clustered in the waist, grasping their arms. The ship was not perceived until she was within her own length of the other. Then there was a sudden hail:

"Where are you coming to? Keep away, or you will be into us. Why don't you show your light?"

Francis shouted back some indistinct answer. Rinaldo pushed down the helm, and a minute later the Pluto ran alongside the other vessel. Half a dozen hands, told off for the work, sprang into her rigging, and lashed the vessels together; while Francis, followed by the crew, climbed the bulwarks and sprang on to the deck of the enemy.

Scarce a blow was struck. The Genoese, astonished at this sudden apparition of armed men on their deck, and being entirely unarmed and unprepared, either ran down below or shouted they surrendered, and in two minutes the Venetians were masters of the vessel.

"Back to the Pluto," Francis shouted. "The vessels will tear their sides out!"

Almost as suddenly as they had invaded the decks of the galley, the Venetians regained their own vessel, leaving the lieutenant with his fifty men on board the prize. The lashings were cut, the Pluto's helm put up, and she sheered away from her prize. Her bulwarks were broken and splintered where she had ground against the other vessel in the sea, and Rinaldo soon reported that some of the seams had opened, and the water was coming in.

"Set the carpenter and some of the hands to work, to caulk the seams as well as they can from the inside, and set a gang to work at the pumps at once. It is unfortunate that it is blowing so hard. If the wind had gone down instead of rising, we would have recaptured the whole fleet, one by one."

The Pluto was kept within a short distance of the captured vessel, and Parucchi presently shouted out that he had freed two hundred prisoners.

"Arm them at once!" Francis shouted back. "Extinguish your light, and board the vessel whose light you see on your starboard bow. I will take the one to port. When you have captured her, lower the sails of both vessels. I will do the same. You will keep a little head sail set, so as to keep them before the wind; but do not show more than you can help. I wish the rest of the fleet to outrun us, as soon as possible."

The Pluto sheered off from the prize, and directed her course towards the vessel nearest to her, which she captured as easily as she had done the preceding. But this time, not only were her bulwarks stove in, but the chain plates were carried away; and the mainmast, no longer supported by its shrouds, fell over the side with a crash.

This vessel had but a hundred prisoners on board. They were wild with astonishment and delight, when they found that their vessel had been recaptured. Francis told them to keep by him through the night, as possibly he might need their assistance.

For some hours the gale increased. The Pluto lay head to it, her mast serving as a floating anchor. As soon as the lights of the Genoese squadron disappeared in the distance, Francis hoisted a lantern on his mainmast, as a signal to the other vessels to keep near him.

As soon as day broke, the galley they had last recaptured was seen, half a mile away, while the two others could be made out some six miles to leeward. The gale died out soon after daybreak, and Francis at once set his crew to work to get the mast on board, and to ship it by its stump.

It was a difficult undertaking, for the vessel was rolling heavily. It was first got alongside, two ropes were passed over it, and it was parbuckled on board. Shears were made of two spars, and the end was placed against the stump, which projected six feet above the deck. By the aid of the shears, it was hoisted erect and lashed to the stump, wedges were driven in to tighten the lashings, and it was then firmly stayed; and by the afternoon it was in readiness for sail to be hoisted again.

By this time Parucchi, with the vessel he had captured, was alongside. The Lion of Saint Mark was hoisted to the mainmast of the Pluto, and three similar banners were run up by the other vessels, the crews shouting and cheering with wild enthusiasm.

Chapter 17:
An Ungrateful Republic.

"It is glorious, Francis," Matteo said, "to think that we should have recaptured four of our ships!"

"It is very good, as far as it goes," Francis replied, "but it might have been a great deal better. If it hadn't been for the storm, we might have picked them all up one by one. Each vessel we took, the stronger we became, and I had calculated upon our capturing the greater number. But in such a sea, I don't think we could possibly capture more than we did."

"I should think not," Matteo said. "I had never dreamt of doing more than recovering the Pluto, and when you first talked about that, it seemed almost like madness. I don't think one of us had the slightest belief in the possibility of the thing, when you first proposed it."

"I thought it was to be managed somehow," Francis said. "It would have been a shame, indeed, if a hundred and fifty men were to be kept prisoners for a fortnight, or three weeks, by a third of their number."

"Well, certainly no one would have thought of making the attempt, if you had not proposed it, Francis. I believe, even if you were to propose our sailing north, and capturing Genoa, there is not a man on board but would follow you willingly, with the firm conviction that you would succeed."

"In that case, Matteo," Francis said, laughing, "it is very lucky for you that I am not at all out of my mind. Signal now to Parucchi to lower his boats, and come on board with our men. We may fall in yet with another Genoese squadron, and may as well have our full complement on board, especially as Parucchi has found two hundred men already on board the vessel we captured."

Parucchi and his men soon transferred themselves to the Pluto, and the four vessels hoisted their sails, and made for the south. They had learned, from their captives, that the squadron had already passed through the Straits of Messina, and that it was at Messina they had stopped and taken in provision two days before. Indeed, when, late in the afternoon, the sky cleared and the sun shone out, they saw the mountains of Calabria on their left.

Learning, from the captives, that no Genoese vessels had been seen in the straits as they passed through, Francis did not hesitate to order the course to be shaped for the straits, instead of sailing round Sicily, as he would have done had there been any chance of falling in with a hostile squadron, in passing between the islands and the mainland.

"I should like to have seen the face of the commander of the Genoese squadron this morning," Matteo said, "when he discovered that four of his vessels were missing. He can hardly have supposed that they were lost, for although the wind was strong, it blew nearly dead aft, and there was nothing of a gale to endanger well-handled ships. I almost wonder that he did not send back the two fully manned galleys he had with him, to search for us."

"Perhaps he did," Francis said; "but he would have been a hundred miles further north by daybreak, and it would have taken him a couple of days to get back to where we were lying."

No hostile sail was seen during the voyage back to Venice. Francis remained in command of the little squadron, for the captains, and many of the superior officers, had been transferred to the galley of the officer in command of the squadron, and Francis happened to be the only second officer on board any of the four ships.

Great care was observed when they approached Venice, as, for aught they knew, Doria's squadron might be blockading the port. The Genoese fleet, however, was still cruising on the coast of Dalmatia, capturing port after port of the Venetian possessions there.

The four vessels passed through the channel of the Lido with their colours flying. When first observed from the watchtower of Venice, they were supposed to form part of the squadron of Zeno, but as soon as they cast anchor, and the news spread that they were four of Pisani's galleys, which had been recaptured from the Genoese, the delight of the population was immense.

The ships were speedily surrounded by a fleet of boats, containing relatives and friends of those taken prisoners at the battle of Polo, and the decks were crowded with persons inquiring after their friends, or embracing with delight those whom they had, an hour before, believed to be either dead or immured in the dungeons of Genoa.

One of the first to appear was Polani, who had early received the news by a swift boat from one of his ships in the port, that the Pluto was one of the vessels entering the harbour.

"What miracle is this, Francis?" he asked, as he warmly embraced his young friend.

"Not a miracle at all, Messer Polani. The Genoese fancied that a guard of fifty men was amply sufficient to keep a hundred and fifty Venetians captives, and we taught them their mistake."

"It wasn't we," Matteo put in, as he shook hands with his kinsman. "We had no more idea of escaping than we had of flying. The whole thing was entirely the work of Francisco here."

"I might have been sure the Genoese would not keep you long, Francisco," Polani said; "and the girls and I might have spared ourselves the pain of fretting for you. But how did it all come about?"

"If you will take me to the Piazza in your gondola, I will tell you all about on the way," Francis replied. "For, absurd as it seems, I am the senior officer of the squadron, and must, I suppose, report to the council what has happened."

"Take me, too, kinsman," Matteo said. "I know Francisco so well that I am quite sure that, of himself, he will never tell the facts of this affair, and will simply say that we broke out, avoiding all mention of his share in it, and how it was that under his orders we recaptured the other ships."

"I think that a very good plan, Matteo; so do you come with us, and you shall tell me all about it, instead of my hearing it from Francis, and I will take care the council know the truth of the matter."

"The admiral got safely back, I hope?" Francis asked. "We saw that his galley, with five others, broke through the Genoese fleet and got safely away, but of course, we knew not whether the brave admiral was himself hurt."

"He arrived here safely," Polani replied; "but knowing the Venetians as you do, you will be scarcely surprised to hear that he has been sentenced to six months' imprisonment, for losing the battle."

"But that is shameful," Francis exclaimed indignantly. "I heard from our captain, who was present at the council, that Pisani was opposed to fighting, and that he was only overruled by the proveditors. It is shameful. I will go on shore and make my report, and then I will come back to you, for I swear that not another blow will I strike on behalf of the republic, as long as Pisani is in prison."

"It is a bad business, my lad," Polani said; "but you know that Pisani, popular as he is with the people, has few friends among the nobles. They are jealous of his fame and popularity, and, to say the truth, he has often irritated them, by his bluntness and his disregard for their opinion and rank. Consequently, they seized upon his defeat as an occasion for accusing him, and it was even a question in the council of taking his life, and he may be considered fortunate in getting off with the sentence of six months' imprisonment.

'I do not think he will have to remain very long in confinement. We may expect the Genoese fleet here in a few days, for the Paduan army is already moving, as we heard last night. No doubt it is going to cooperate with the fleet. Once the danger presses, the populace will demand Pisani's release. There have already been demonstrations, and shouts of 'Viva Pisani!' have been raised in the Piazza.

"At any rate, Francis, let me advise you, most strongly, not to suffer any expression of your feelings concerning him to escape you before the council. I need scarcely say it would do no good to the admiral, and would set the whole of his enemies against you. It is no affair of yours, if the governors of Venice behave ungratefully to one who deserves well at their hands, and you have made more than enough enemies by mingling in my affairs, without drawing upon yourself more foes, by your championship of Pisani."

"I will, of course, follow your counsel," Francis said; "but I will certainly serve the state no more, until Pisani is freed."

Several of the councillors were already assembled, on hearing the strange news that four of the ships, which had been captured by the Genoese, had entered port. Francis, on announcing his errand, was at once shown in to them. Polani accompanied him, explaining his presence to the council by saying:

"I have ventured, signors, to accompany my young friend here, in order that I may give you a much further detail of the affair in which he has been engaged, than you are likely to hear from his own lips. I have just come on shore from his ship, the Pluto, and have heard the story from my kinsman, Matteo Giustiniani."

"We have surely seen this young gentleman before, Messer Polani," one of the council said.

"You have, signor," Polani replied. "You may remember that he greatly distinguished himself at the fight of Antium, was sent home by the admiral with his despatches, and had the honour of receiving, from you, the thanks of the republic and the gift of citizenship."

"I remember now," the councillor said; and a murmur of assent from the others showed that they also recalled the circumstance. "Is he again the bearer of despatches, from the officer in command of the little squadron which, as it seems, has just, by some miracle, entered the port? And how is it that the officer did not present himself in person before us?"

"The officer has presented himself," Polani said. "Messer Hammond is in command of the four ships which have just arrived. Not only is he in command by virtue of senior rank, but it is to him that their recapture from the Genoese is entirely due."

There was a murmur of incredulity from the circle of councillors, but Polani went on quietly.

"It may seem well nigh impossible to you, signors, but what I say is strictly true. If Messer Hammond will first relate to you the broad facts of the recapture of the ships, I will furnish you with such details as he may omit."

Francis then briefly related the events which had led to the capture of the four galleys. He explained that by the death of the captain he, as second officer, succeeded to the command of the Pluto, and that afterwards being captured by the Genoese, Signor Parucchi, the sole other surviving officer, and ten gentlemen belonging to noble families and serving as volunteers on board the Pluto, were confined in one hold of that ship on her voyage as a prize to Genoa, the crew being shut up in the other; that by working at night they had effected a junction with the crew, and choosing a stormy night, when any noise that might be made would not be heard on board the ship, they made their way up to the deck above, through a hole they had cut in the planks, and overpowered the Genoese almost without resistance; that they had then, in the darkness, ran alongside another of the ships and captured her with equal ease; and Parucchi, with a portion of the crew of the Pluto, and the Venetian prisoners on board that ship, had retaken a third; while the Pluto had captured a fourth.

"It may seem to you, signors," Francis concluded, "that we might, in the same way, have recaptured the rest of our ships, and it was a bitter disappointment to me that we failed to do so; but the storm was so high, and the sea so rough, that it was only with the greatest danger and difficulty that ships could lie alongside each other. The bulwarks of all four vessels were greatly damaged, and the Pluto lost her foremast while alongside the last ship we captured, and as the storm was increasing, rather than abating, we were, to our great chagrin, obliged to let the rest escape, since in striving for more we might have lost, not only our lives, but the vessels we had taken."

"This is indeed a most notable achievement, Messer Hammond, and the restoration of four ships and their crews, at the present moment, is of great importance to the republic, threatened as she is with invasion by land and sea.

"Now, Messer Polani, if you will give us the full details of which you spoke, we shall be glad."

Polani then related to the council the full story of the means by which the crew of the Pluto had gained their liberty, showing how the recapture was entirely due to the initiative of Francis, and to the ingenuity with which he overcame all difficulties. He ended by saying:

"My kinsman, Matteo, said that should you doubt whether this account is not tinged by his friendship and partiality for Messer Hammond, Signor Parucchi, and all the gentlemen who were confined with them in the hold, can substantiate the account that he has given. He said that Parucchi's evidence would be all the more valuable, since he and the other officers were in the first place much prejudiced against Messer Hammond, deeming it an indignity that one so young, and a foreigner by birth, should be appointed to the command over the heads of others, Venetian born, of good family, and his seniors in age. The circumstances which I have related to you have, however, completely altered his opinion, and he is as enthusiastic, with respect to Messer Hammond's conduct, as are my kinsman and all on board the ship."

"I remember now," one of the council said, "that we had a letter from the admiral in the spring, and that, when describing how terribly the crews had been diminished and weakened by the severity of the winter, he said that the sole exception was the Pluto, whose crew was kept up to their full strength, and in excellent health, owing entirely to the care and attention that Messer Hammond, the officer second in command, had bestowed upon them."

"Thanks, Messer Polani," the president of the council said, "for the light you have thrown on this matter.

"Messer Hammond, it is difficult to overestimate the services that you have rendered to the state. We shall, at an early day, decide in what manner most fitly to reward them, and in the meantime you will remain in command of the squadron you have brought in."

Francis returned thanks for the promise of the president, but expressed his desire to resign the command of the squadron at once.

"I am in business," he said, "with Messer Polani, and although, for a short time, I abandoned commerce in order to sail under Admiral Pisani, I now, from various reasons, desire, as soon as my successor is appointed, to return to my work with Signor Polani.

"I desire to recommend warmly to your excellencies Signor Parucchi, who is, except myself, the sole remaining officer of the Pluto. He seconded me most admirably in our enterprise, and himself commanded at the recapture of one of the ships. The gentlemen volunteers also worked with the greatest energy and spirit. Matteo Giustiniani has been acting as third officer, and to him also the thanks of the republic are due."

On leaving the ship, Messer Polani had despatched a boat, to carry to his house the news that Francis had returned; and when they came back from the palace they found Giulia anxiously expecting them, and a few minutes later Matteo arrived with his brother Rufino, and Maria. The latter was far more effusive in her greeting of Francis than Giulia had been.

"Matteo has been telling us all about it, Francis, and that he, and everyone else, owed their escape from the dungeons of Genoa entirely to your cleverness."

"Not so much to his cleverness, Maria," Matteo corrected, "although he is wonderful in inventing things, but to his energy, determination, and steadfastness. There was not one of us but regarded a visit to the dungeons of Genoa as a foregone conclusion, and when Francis spoke of our recapturing the Pluto, as if it were the easiest and most natural thing in the world, it was as much as we could do not to laugh in his face. However, he set about it as quietly and calmly as if he were carrying on the regular work of a ship. We gradually caught some of his spirit, and when we began to see that there was a method in his madness, did our best to carry out his orders."

"It is wonderful," Maria said; "and do you know, Francisco, that when we first knew you, after you had rescued us from the attack on the canal, I absolutely thought that, though you were brave and straightforward and honourable, yet that by the side of our own people of your age, you were rather stupid, and ever since then I have been learning how mistaken I was."

Francis laughed.

"I think your estimate of me was correct enough," he said. "You see people are often stupid one way, and sharp another. Matteo will tell you I was far behind most of those in the seminary in learning lessons, and certainly when it came to talking, and bandying jokes, I had no chance at all. I suppose that every lady I have ever spoken to, when I have been with you at entertainments, has thought me exceptionally stupid; and I am sure I am, in most things, only I suppose I have got a fair share of common sense, and a habit of thinking for myself. There was no cleverness at all in anything that Matteo is telling you of.

"It was just the same here as it was when I was in that cell near Tunis. I wanted to get out. I supposed there must be some way out, if I could but discover it, and so I sat down to think how it was to be done; and of course, after trying in my mind every possible scheme, I hit upon the right one. There certainly was nothing clever in that."

"But I have heard nothing about it yet," Giulia said; "and everyone else seems to know how it was done."

"Matteo, do you tell Giulia," Maria ordered. "I have lots of questions to ask Francis."

"By the way, Francis," Messer Polani said, "you will be glad to hear that I have succeeded in getting home your man Giuseppi. He returned two days ago, and I have no doubt is somewhere below waiting to see you."

"I will go and see him at once," Francis said, hurrying away. "I am indeed glad to know that you have rescued him."

Maria laughed, as the door closed behind Francis.

"There, Rufino," she said, turning to him, "you pretend sometimes to be jealous of Francisco Hammond; and there, you see, just when I have said I have lots of questions to ask him, and five minutes after my arrival here to greet him, he races away without a word, directly he hears that his man Giuseppi has returned."

"And he is quite right, Maria," Matteo said indignantly. "Giuseppi would give his life for Francisco, and the two have been together every day for the last six or seven years. I don't doubt the faithful fellow is crying with joy now. Francisco is quite right, not to keep him waiting for a minute."

"Perhaps I cried for joy, too, Master Matteo," Maria said.

"I believe I did see tears in your eyes, Maria; but I put them down to my own account. You would naturally be delighted to know that your brother-in-law was safe and sound, to say nothing of the fact that the family would be spared the expense of sending a thousand ducats or so to ransom him."

"A thousand ducats, Matteo! A thousand soldi would more nearly represent your value, if the Genoese did but know it. But why don't you tell Giulia your adventures, as I ordered you?"

"Because Giulia would very much rather hear them from Francisco's lips, and I have no doubt he will be equally glad to tell her himself, though certainly he is a bad hand at recounting his own doings. However, he shall have the pleasure of telling her of it, and I can fill up the details for her, afterwards."

Two days later, a decree was published by the council stating that, in consideration of the very great service rendered to the state by Francisco Hammond, a citizen of Venice, in recapturing four galleys from the Genoese, the council decreed the settlement upon him, for life, of a pension of three hundred ducats a year.

"You will not want it, Francisco," Messer Polani said, as he brought in the news, "for I intend, at the end of these troubles, to take you as a partner in my business. I told your father that I should do so; and you have not only proved yourself earnest in business, quick at learning, and full of resources, but you have vastly added to the debt of gratitude which first caused me to make the proposition, by again saving my daughters from falling into the hands of their enemy. I told your father that I should regard you in the light of a son, and I do so regard you, and as a son of whom I have every reason to be proud.

"I need no thanks, my lad. I am still, and shall always remain, your debtor. You have very much more than fulfilled my expectations, and I shall be glad to place some of the burden of my business upon your shoulders.

"There is another matter, which I have long had in my mind, but of which I will not speak just at present.

"Thus, then, the three hundred ducats, which you will receive each year from the state, may not be needed by you. Still, you are to be congratulated upon the grant, because being the recipient of a pension, for distinguished services, will add to your weight and influence in the city. And so long as you do not need it--and no man can say what may occur, in the course of years, to hinder the trade of Venice--you can bestow the sum annually upon the poor of the city, and thus increase your popularity."

"I shall be happy to do that, signor," Francis said, "although it seems to me that popularity is of little value in Venice. It has not saved the man whom, a short time since, the people hailed as their father, from unmerited disgrace and imprisonment."

"It has not, Francisco, but it has saved his life. You may take my word for it, that the proposal, absolutely made in the council, for the execution of Pisani, would have been voted had it not been for fear of the people; and it may be that you will yet see, that the voice of the people will bring Pisani from his prison, long before the expiration of his term of imprisonment. Popularity is not to be despised, for it is a great power. That power may be abused, as when one, having gained the ear of the people, leads them astray for his own base ends, and uses the popularity he has gained to attack, and hurl from power, men less eloquent and less gifted in the arts of cajoling the people, but more worthy than himself. But, used rightly, the power of swaying and influencing the people is a great one, and especially valuable in a city like Venice, where private enmities and private feuds are carried to so great an extent. Already your name is in every mouth. Your rescue of Pisani, when sorely beset by the enemy, has been the theme of talk in every house; and this feat, which retrieves, to some extent, the misfortune of Pola, will make your name a household word in Venice."

Immediately after the battle of Pola, the Venetians had entered into negotiations with Hungary, to endeavour to detach that power from the league against them. But the demands of King Louis were too extravagant to be accepted. He demanded the cession of Trieste, the recognition of the suzerainty of his crown on the part of the present doge, and all his successors, an annual tribute of one hundred thousand ducats, and half a million of ready money. This demand was so excessive that, even in their distress, the Venetians refused to accept it, and hastened on their preparations for a struggle for life or death.

Fortunately, the Genoese continued for three months, after their success at Pola, to capture the outlying possessions of Venice, instead of striking at the capital. Towards the end of July, seventeen Genoese vessels appeared off Pelestrina, burned a merchant ship lying there, and spent the day in reconnoitring positions, and in taking soundings of the shallows and canals off Brondolo. They then sailed away for Dalmatia. In less than a week six galleys again hove in sight; and Admiral Giustiniani, who was in supreme command of the forces, issued out from the Lido, with an equal number of ships, to give them battle.

On his way, however, a black object was seen in the water. As they neared it, this was seen to be the head of a swimmer. He was soon picked up, and was found to be a Venetian citizen, named Savadia, who had been captured by the enemy, but had managed to escape, and was swimming towards land to warn his countrymen that the whole Genoese fleet, of forty-seven sail, under Pietro Doria, was close at hand; and that the six ships in the offing were simply a decoy, to tempt the Venetians to come out and give battle.

Giustiniani at once returned to port, and scarcely had he done so, than the whole Genoese fleet made its appearance. They approached the passage of the Lido; but the respite that had been afforded them had enabled the Venetians to make their preparations, and the Genoese found, to their disappointment, that the channels of the Lido and Malamocco were completely closed up with sunken vessels, palisades, and chains; and they sailed away to seek another entry through which they could strike at Venice.

Had the same precautions, that had proved so effective at the Lido and Malamocco passages, been taken at all the other channels; Venice could have defied all the efforts of Doria's fleet.

The city is situated on a group of small islands, rising in the midst of a shallow basin twenty-five miles long and five wide, and separated from the sea by a long sandbank, formed by the sediment brought down by the rivers Piave and Adige. Through this sandbank the sea had pierced several channels. Treporti, the northern of these channels, contained water only for the smallest craft. The next opening was known as the port of Lido, and separated the island of San Nicolo from Malamocco. Five miles farther on is the passage of Malamocco, between that island and Pelestrina. Southwest of Pelestrina lay Brondolo, behind which stood Chioggia, twenty miles distant from Venice. The southern point of Brondolo was only separated by a small channel--called the Canal of Lombardy--from the mainland.

Unfortunately, at Brondolo the channel had not been closed. All preparations had been made for doing so, but the work had been postponed until the last moment, in order that trading vessels might enter and leave the harbour, the Chioggians believing that there was sure to be sufficient warning, of the approach of an enemy, to enable them to close the entrance in time. The sudden appearance of Doria's fleet before Brondolo upset all these calculations, and the Genoese easily carried the position. Little Chioggia, the portion of the town separated from the rest by the Canal of Santa Caterina, was captured without difficulty; but the bridge across the canal was strongly defended by bastions and redoubts, and here Pietro Emo made a brave stand, with his garrison of three thousand five hundred men.

The enemy at once erected his batteries, and, on the 12th of August, the Genoese opened fire. The Venetians replied stoutly, and for three days a heavy cannonade was kept up on both sides. Reinforcements had reached the garrison from Venice, and, hour by hour, swift boats brought the news to the city of the progress of the fight.

So far, all seemed going on well. The Genoese had suffered heavily, and made no impression upon the batteries at the head of the bridge. The days passed in Venice in a state of restless disquietude. It was hoped and believed that Chioggia could successfully defend itself; but if it fell, the consequence would be terrible.

Already the Hungarians had overrun the Venetian possessions on the mainland, the Lord of Padua was in the field with his army, and communication was cut with Ferrara, their sole ally. Should Chioggia fall, the Genoese fleet would enter the lagoons, and would sail, by the great channel through the flats, from Chioggia to Venice; and their light galleys could overrun the whole of the lagoons, and cut off all communication with the mainland, and starvation would rapidly stare the city in the face.

Polani made all preparations for the worst. Many of his valuables were hidden away, in recesses beneath the floors. Others were taken on board one of his ships in the port, and this was held in readiness to convey Giulia and Maria, whose husband had willingly accepted Polani's offer, to endeavour to carry her off by sea with Giulia, in case the Genoese should enter the city.

The merchant made an excursion to Chioggia, with Francis, to see for himself how things were going, and returned somewhat reassured. Francis spent much of his time at the port visiting Polani's ships, talking to the sailors, and expressing to them his opinion, that the Genoese and Paduans would never have dared to lay siege to Chioggia, had they not known that Pisani was no longer in command of the Venetian forces.

"I regard the present state of affairs," he said, over and over again, "as a judgment upon the city, for its base ingratitude to the brave admiral, and I am convinced that things will never come right, until we have him again in command of our fleet.

"Giustiniani is no doubt an able man; but what has he ever done in comparison to what Pisani has accomplished? Why should we place our only hope of safety in the hands of an untried man? I warrant, if Pisani was out and about, you would see Venice as active as a swarm of bees, pouring out against our aggressors. What is being done now? Preparations are being made; but of what kind? Ships are sunk in the channel; but what will be the use of this if Chioggia falls? The canals to that place will be blocked, but that will not prevent the Genoese from passing, in their light boats, from island to island, until they enter Venice itself.

"Do you think all these ships would be lying idly here, if Pisani were in command? Talk to your comrades, talk to the sailors in the port, talk to those on shore when you land, and urge, everywhere, that the cry should be raised for Pisani's release, and restoration to command."

Chapter 18:
The Release Of Pisani.

On the morning of the 17th, the party were sitting at breakfast, when Giulia suddenly sprang to her feet.

"Listen!" she exclaimed.

Her father and Francis looked at her in surprise, but instinctively listened for whatever sound she could have heard. Then a deep, solemn sound boomed through the air.

"It is the bell of the Campanile tolling," the merchant exclaimed. "It is the signal for all citizens to take up arms. Some terrible news has arrived."

Hastily putting on his armour, the merchant started to Saint Mark's, accompanied by Francis, who put on a steel cap, which he preferred to the heavy helmet, and a breastplate. A crowd of citizens were pursuing the same direction. The numbers thickened as they approached the Piazza, which they found on their arrival to be already thronged with people, who were densely packed in front of the palace, awaiting an explanation of the summons.

There was a look of deep anxiety on every face, for all felt that the news must be bad, indeed, which could have necessitated such a call. Presently the doge, accompanied by the council, appeared in the balcony. A complete silence fell upon the multitude, the bell ceased tolling, and not the slightest sound disturbed the stillness. One of the councillors stepped to the front, for the doge, Contarini, was now seventy-two years old, and his voice could hardly have been heard over so wide an area.

"Citizens of the republic, gather, I pray you, all your fortitude and constancy, to hear the news which I have to tell. It is bad news; but there is no reason for repining, still less for despair. If Venice has but confidence in herself, such as she has throughout her history shown, when danger seemed imminent, be assured that we shall weather this storm, as we have done all that have preceded it. Chioggia has fallen!"

An exclamation of pain and grief went up from the crowd. The speaker held up his hand for silence.

"Chioggia, contrary to our hopes and expectations, has fallen; but we are proud to say, it has fallen from no lack of bravery on the part of its defenders. As you know, for six days the brave podesta, Emo, and his troops have repulsed every attack; but yesterday an unforeseen accident occurred. While our soldiers were holding their own, as usual, a Genoese fire ship exploded in the canal behind them. The idea, unfortunately, seized the troops that the bridge was on fire. The Genoese shouted 'The bridge is in flames!' and pressed onward, and our soldiers fell back, in some confusion, towards the bridge. Here Emo, with four brave companions, made a noble stand, and for a time checked the advance of the foe; but he was driven back. There was no time to destroy the communication behind him. The enemy pressed on, and, mingled with our retreating soldiers, entered the town. And so Chioggia was taken. Our loss in killed is said to be eight hundred and sixty men; while the rest of the garrison--four thousand in number--were taken prisoners."

A loud cry of anguish burst from the crowd. Numbers of those present had relatives and friends among the garrison of Chioggia; and to all, the news of this terrible disaster was a profound blow. Venice was open now to invasion. In a few hours, the enemy might appear in her canals.

The council and the nobles endeavoured to dispel the feeling of despair. While some harangued the people from the balconies, others went down and mingled with the crowd, assuring them that all was not yet lost, that already messengers had been despatched to Doria, and the Lord of Padua, asking for terms of peace; and even should these be refused, Venice might yet defend herself until Zeno arrived, with his fleet, to their rescue. The doge himself received deputations of the citizens, and, by his calmness and serenity, did much to allay the first feeling of terror and dismay; and in a few hours the city recovered its wonted aspect of tranquillity.

The next morning the answer to the overtures was received. The Lord of Padua, who was doubtless beginning to feel some misgiving as to the final issue of the struggle, declared that he himself was not unwilling to treat upon certain terms, but that the decision must rest in the hands of his colleague. Doria, believing that Venice was now in his grasp, rejected the idea of terms with scorn.

"By God's faith, my lords of Venice," he cried, "ye shall have no peace from the Lord of Padua, nor from our commune of Genoa, until I have put a bit in the mouths of the horses of your evangelist of Saint Mark. When they have been bridled you shall then, in sooth, have a good peace; and this is our purpose and that of our commune!

"As for these captives, my brethren," he said, pointing to some Genoese prisoners of rank, whom the Venetians had sent with their embassy, in hopes of conciliating the Genoese, "take them back. I want them not; for in a few days I am coming to release, from your prisons, them and the rest."

As soon as the message was received, the bell summoned the popular assembly together, and, in the name of the doge, Pietro Mocenigo described to them the terrible nature of the peril that threatened them, told them that, after the insolent reply of Doria, there was now no hope save in their own exertions, and invited all to rally round the national standard, for the protection of their hearths and homes. The reply of the assembly was unanimous; and shouts were raised:

"Let us arm ourselves! Let us equip and man what galleys are in the arsenal! Let us sally out to the combat! It is better to die in the defence of our country, than to perish here from want."

A universal conscription was at once ordered, new taxes were imposed, and the salaries of the magistrates and civil functionaries suspended. All business came to a standstill, and property fell to a fourth of its former value. The imposts were not found adequate to produce the sums required, and a new loan, at five per cent, was decreed. All subscribed to the utmost of their ability, raising the enormous sum of 6,294,040 lire. A new captain general was elected, and the government nominated Taddeo Giustiniani to the post.

The fortification of the city, with earthworks, was commenced. Lines of defence were drawn from Lido to San Spirito, and two wooden towers constructed at the former point, to guard the pass of San Nicolo. Events succeeded each other with the greatest rapidity, and all these matters were settled within thirty-six hours of the fall of Chioggia. In all respects the people, at first, yielded implicit obedience to the order of the council. They enrolled themselves for service. They subscribed to the loan. They laboured at the outworks. But from the moment the appointment of Taddeo Giustiniani was announced, they grew sullen. It was not that they objected to the new captain general, who was a popular nobleman, but every man felt that something more than this was required, in such an emergency, and that the best man that Venice could produce should be at the helm.

The sailors of the port were the first to move in the matter, and shouts for Vettore Pisani were heard in the streets. Others took up the cry, and soon a large multitude assembled in the Piazza, and with menacing shouts, demanded that Pisani should be freed and appointed. So serious did the tumult become, that the council were summoned in haste. Pisani--so popular with the lower class that they called him their father--was viewed with corresponding dislike and distrust by the nobles, who were at once jealous of his fame and superiority, and were alarmed at a popularity which could have made him, had he chosen it, the master of the state.

It was not, therefore, until after some hours of stormy debate, that they decided to give in to the wishes of the crowd, which was continually growing larger and more threatening; and it was late in the evening before the senators deputed by the council, followed by the exulting populace, hurried to the prison to apprise Pisani that he was free, and that the doge and senate were expecting him. Pisani heard the message without emotion, and placidly replied that he should prefer to pass the night where he was in reflection, and would wait on the seignory in the morning.

At daybreak on Friday, the 19th of August, the senatorial delegates and the people, accompanied by the other officers who had been involved in the disgrace of Pisani, and who had now been freed, reappeared at the gates of the prison. These were immediately opened, and Pisani appeared, with his usual expression of cheerfulness and good humour on his face. He was at once lifted on to the shoulders of some sailors, and borne in triumph to the palace, amid the deafening cheers of the populace. On the staircase he was met by the doge and senators, who saluted him cordially. Mass was heard in the chapel, and Pisani and the council then set to business, and were for some time closeted together.

The crowd waited outside the building, continuing to shout, and when Pisani issued out from the palace, he was seized and carried in triumph to his house in San Fantino. As he was passing the Campanile of Saint Mark, his old pilot, Marino Corbaro, a remarkably able seaman, but a perpetual grumbler against those in authority, met him, and elbowing his way through the crowd, drew close to him, loudly shouting at the same time:

"Now is the time, admiral, for revenging yourself, by seizing the dictatorship of this city. Behold, all are at your service. All are willing, at this very instant, to proclaim you prince, if you choose."

The loyalty of Pisani's nature was so affronted by this offer, that, in a fury of rage, he leaned forward and struck Corbaro a heavy blow with his fist, and then raising his voice shouted to those about him:

"Let none who wish me well say, 'Viva Pisani!' but, 'Viva San Marco!'"

And the populace then shouted, "Viva San Marco and our Father Pisani!"

No sooner had Pisani reached his house than the news was bruited about, that the admiral had been merely appointed governor of Lido, and that Giustiniani remained in command of the navy. The people were furious; and a deputation of 600 waited upon Pisani and said:

"We are yours. Command us as you will."

Pisani told them that it was for the republic, and not for him, to command their services. The deputation then went to the council, and declared, in the name of fifty thousand Venetians, that not a man would embark on the galleys until Pisani received his command, as captain general of all the forces of the republic, by land and sea. The Council of Ten, finding it impossible to resist the popular demand, and terrified at the idea of the tumult that a refusal would arouse, at last agreed to their request.

Fortunately for the republic, the four days which elapsed between the fall of Chioggia, and the appointment of Pisani to the supreme command, had not been utilized by the enemy. Carrara and Doria had always been at variance as to their plans of operations, and, as usual, they differed now. The Lord of Padua urged the necessity for following up their success by an instant attack upon Venice, while Doria insisted upon carrying out his original plan, and trusting as much to starvation as to military operations. He, however, gradually pushed forward two outposts, at Poreja and Malamocco, and on the latter island, at a distance of three miles from Venice, he erected a battery, many of whose shot fell at San Spirito.

Francis had borne his share in the events which had led to the installation of Pisani in the supreme command. He had at first instigated the sailors of Polani to raise a cry in the streets for the restoration of the admiral, and had gone about with two or three of his friends, mingling with knots of persons, and urging that the only hope of the republic lay in the energy and talent of Pisani. Even Matteo had joined him, although Taddeo Giustiniani was his own uncle. But, as the lad said, "what matters it about relationship now? What will become of relationship, if the Genoese and Paduans land here, raze the city to the ground, and scatter us over the face of the earth? No. When it comes to a question of ordinary command, of course I should go with my family; but when Venice is in danger, and only one man can save her, I should vote for him, whoever the other may be."

Polani had also exerted the great influence he possessed among the commercial classes, and had aided the efforts of Francis, by giving leave to the sailors of all his ships in port to go on shore. A few hours after Pisani's release the merchant, accompanied by Francis, called upon him.

"Welcome, my friends," he said heartily.

"Well, you see, Messer Hammond, that I was a true prophet, and that I have had my share of the dungeon. However, we need not talk of that now. I am up to my eyes in business."

"I have no doubt of that, admiral," Polani said. "I have called to offer every ship I have in the harbour, for the defence of the city. I myself will continue to pay their crews, as at present. Use the vessels as you like. Make fire ships of them if you will. I can afford the loss."

"Thanks, my friend," the admiral said. "We shall find a use for them, never fear.

"As for you, Messer Hammond, even in my prison I heard of your gallant feat, in recapturing the Pluto and three other ships from the Genoese, and thus retrieving, to some extent, the losses of Pola. I hope to wipe off the rest of the score before long. I shall find a command for you, in a day or two. Age and rank go for nothing now. I am going to put the best men in the best position.

"I have just appointed that old rascal, Corbaro, vice admiral of the Lido. He is a grumbling old scoundrel, and would have had me get up a revolution today, for which I had to knock him down; but he is one of the best sailors Venice ever turned out, and just the man for the place."

"I would rather act as a general aide-de-camp to you, admiral, than have a separate command, if you will allow me," Francis said. "I am still too young to command, and should be thwarted by rivalry and jealousies. I would, therefore, far rather act under your immediate orders, if you will allow me."

"So be it, then, lad. Come to me tomorrow, and I have no doubt I shall have plenty for you to do. At present, I cannot say what course I may adopt, for in truth, I don't know what position I shall hold. The people do not seem content with my having only the government of Lido; but for myself, I care nothing whether I hold that command, or that of captain general. It is all one to me, so that I can serve the republic. And Giustiniani is an able man, and will no doubt do his business well.

"You do not think so, young man?" he broke off, when Francis shook his head.

"I do not, indeed, sir. He has erected two wooden towers at the mouth of the Lido, which the first stone from a Genoese ballista would knock to splinters; and has put up a fence to San Spirito, which a Genoese soldier in full armour could jump over."

"Well, we shall see, Messer Hammond," the admiral said, smiling. "I fear you have one bad quality among your many good ones, and that is that you are a partisan. But go along now. I have no more time to spare to you."

No sooner had Pisani obtained the supreme command, than he set to work in earnest to provide for the safety of the city, the reorganization of the navy, and the conversion of the new levies into soldiers and sailors. The hulls of forty galleys, which were lying in the arsenals, were taken in hand, and two-thirds of them were equipped and ready for sea in three days.

The population was full of ardour and enthusiasm, and crowded to the offices to register their names for service. The women brought their jewels, to be melted down into money; and all vied with each other in zeal.

Pisani's first task, after seeing the galleys put in hand, was to examine the defences Giustiniani had erected. He at once pronounced the two wooden towers--of which Francis had spoken so disrespectfully--to be utterly useless, and ordered two tall towers, of solid masonry, to be erected in their stead.

Giustiniani was indignant at this condemnation of his work; and he and his friends so worked upon the minds of those who were to carry out the work, that they laid down their tools, and refused to embark upon such useless operations. The news was brought to Pisani by one of his friends, and, starting in his gondola, he was soon upon the spot.

He wasted no time in remonstrating with the workmen on their conduct, but, seizing a trowel, lifted a heavy stone into its place, shouting:

"Let him who loves Saint Mark follow my example!"

The success of the appeal was instantaneous. The workmen grasped their tools. A host of volunteers seized the stones and carried them to their places. When they were exhausted, fresh workmen took their places, and in the incredibly short time of four days, the two castles were finished.

The workmen were next set to level the paling and earthwork, from Lido to San Spirito, and in the course of a fortnight the lofty and massive stone walls were erected. By this time, something like a fleet was at Pisani's disposal. In spite of the conduct of Taddeo Giustiniani, Pisani, with his usual magnanimity, gave him the command of three large ships, mounting the heaviest guns in the arsenal. The light boats were under the command of Giovanni Barberigo. Federigo Cornaro was stationed with a force of galleys at San Spirito. Nicholo Gallieano was charged with the defence of the Lazaretto, San Clemente, Santa Elena, and the neighbourhood; while on the strand between Lido and Malamocco, behind the main wall, were the mercenaries, eight thousand strong, under Jacopo Cavalli. Heavy booms were placed across all the canals by which it was likely that the enemy's fleet might advance.

Francis found his office, under the energetic admiral, no sinecure. He was kept constantly moving from one point to the other, to see that all was going on well, and to report the progress made. The work never ceased, night or day, and for the first week neither Francis, nor his commander, ever went to bed, contenting themselves with such chance sleep as they could snatch.

Having wasted eight precious days, the enemy, on the 24th of August, advanced to the attack. A Genoese force, under Doria's brother, landed upon San Nicolo; while the Paduans attacked San Spirito and Santa Marta. They found the besieged in readiness. Directly the alarm was given, the Venetians flocked to the threatened points, and repulsed the enemy with slaughter.

The latter then attempted to make a junction of their forces, but Cornaro with his galleys occupied the canal, drove back the boats in which they intended to cross, and defeated the attempt. Doria had felt certain that the movement, which was attempted under cover of night, would succeed, and his disappointment was extreme.

The Lord of Padua was so disgusted that he withdrew his troops to the mainland. Doria remained before Venice until the early part of October, but without making another attack. Indeed, the defences had long before become so formidable, that attack was well-nigh hopeless. At the end of that time he destroyed all his works and fell back upon Chioggia, and determined to wait there until Venice was starved into surrender.

The suffering in the city was intense. It was cut off from all access to the mainland behind, but occasionally a ship, laden with provisions from Egypt or Syria, managed to evade the Genoese galleys. These precarious supplies, however, availed but little for the wants of the starving city, eked out though they were by the exertions of the sailors, who occasionally sailed across the lagoon, landed on the mainland, and cut off the supplies sent from Padua and elsewhere to the Genoese camp.

The price of provisions was so enormous, that the bulk of the people were famishing, and even in the houses of the wealthy the pressure was great. The nobility, however, did their utmost for their starving countrymen, and the words of Pietro Mocenigo, speaking in the name of the doge to the popular assembly, were literally carried into effect.

"Let all," he said, "who are pressed by hunger, go to the dwellings of the patricians. There you will find friends and brothers, who will divide with you their last crust."

So desperate, indeed, did the position become, that a motion was made by some members of the council for emigrating from the lagoons, and founding a new home in Candia or Negropont; but this proposal was at once negatived, and the Venetians declared that, sooner than abandon their city, they would bury themselves under her ruins.

So October and November passed. Carlo Zeno had not yet arrived, but by some letters which had been captured with a convoy of provisions, it was learned that he had been achieving the most triumphant success, had swept the seas from Genoa to Constantinople, had captured a Genoese galleon valued at three hundred thousand ducats, and was at Candia.

This intelligence revived the hopes of Venice, and on the 16th of November Luigi Moroceni was despatched to order him, in the name of the government, peremptorily to hasten to the rescue of Venice. Almost at the same time, Giovanni Barberigo, with his light craft, surprised and captured three of the enemy's vessels, killing many of the sailors, and taking a hundred and fifty prisoners. The success was not in itself important, but it raised the hopes of the Venetians, as being the first time they had taken the offensive. Pisani himself had endeavoured to reconnoitre the position of the enemy, but had each time been sharply repulsed, losing ten boats and thirty men upon one occasion, when the doge's nephew, Antonio Gradenigo, was also killed by the enemy; but in spite of this, he advised government to make a great effort to recover Chioggia.

He admitted that the chances of failure were great. Still, he maintained that success was possible, and it was better that the Venetians should die fighting than by hunger.

As the result of his expeditions, he had found that Doria had at least thirty thousand men, fifty great ships, and from seven to eight hundred light craft. Moreover his troops were in high spirits, well fed, and well cared for, and should therefore be, man to man, more than a match for the starving soldiers of Venice. Nevertheless, there was a possibility of success, as Zeno would doubtless arrive by the time the siege had fairly commenced.

After much debate, the council determined that the undertaking should be attempted. To stir the people to the utmost exertion, the senate, on the 1st of December, published a decree that the thirty plebeians, who should most liberally meet the urgent necessities of the state by the proffer of their persons or estates, should, after peace was made, be raised to the rank of nobility, and summoned to the great council; that thirty-five thousand ducats of gold should be distributed annually among those who were not elected, and their heirs, forever; that any foreign merchant, who should display peculiar zeal for the cause of the republic, should be admitted to the full privileges of citizenship; and that, on the other hand, such Venetians as might endeavour to elude a participation in the common burdens, and hardships, should be held by so doing to have forfeited all their civil rights.

Seventy-five candidates came forward. Some offered money, some personal service or the service of their sons and relatives; some presented galleys and offered to pay their crews. Immense efforts were made, and by the 21st of December sixty ships, four hundred boats of all sizes, and thirty-four war galleys were equipped. The doge, although just seventy-three years old, signified his wish to assume the supreme command of the expedition, Pisani acting as his lieutenant and admiral.

During the long weeks the siege continued, Francis saw little of the Polanis, his duties keeping him constantly near Pisani, with whom he took such meals as the time would afford, sleeping in his house, in readiness for instant service. Maria had returned to her father's house, for her husband was in command of the outpost nearest to the enemy, and was therefore constantly away from home. Maria's spirits were higher than ever. She made light of the hardships in the way of food, bantered Francis when he came on his business engagements, and affected to treat him with extreme respect, as the trusted lieutenant of Pisani. Giulia, too, kept up her spirits, and no one would have thought, listening to the lively talk of the two girls with their father and Francis, that Venice was besieged by an overwhelming force, and reduced to the direst straits by hunger.

The greater part of Polani's ships were now in the service of the state. Those which remained, were constantly engaged in running across to the Dalmatian coast, and bringing in cargoes of provisions through the cordon of the Genoese galleys.

The light gondola which, after being repaired, had been lying for two years under cover in Messer Polani's yard, had again been made useful. Giuseppi had returned to his old work, and he and another powerful oarsman made the light boat fly through the water, as Francis carried the orders of the admiral to the various posts. He had also been in it upon several of the reconnoitring expeditions, in the canals leading to Chioggia, and although hotly chased he had, on each occasion, left his pursuers behind. The evening before the expedition was to start Pisani said to him:

"I think you have brought me more news, with that fast little craft of yours, than I have been able to obtain even at the cost of some hard fighting, and a good many lives. I wish that you would make an excursion for me tonight, and find out, if you can, whether the enemy have moved their position since the last time I reconnoitred them. I particularly wish to learn if they have strong forces near the outlets of the channels of Chioggia, and Brondolo, and the Canal of Lombardy. You know my plans, and with such a host of recruits as I shall have with me, it is all important that there should be no failure at first. Veterans can stand defeat, but a reverse is fatal to young troops. Heaven knows, they will have enough to bear, with wet, cold, exposure, and hunger, and success will be necessary to keep up their spirits. Do not push your adventure too far. Run no risk if you can help it. I would not, for much, that harm befell you."

Francis at once accepted the commission, and left the admiral in order to make his preparations.

"Giuseppi," he said, as he took his place in the boat, "I want you to find for me, for service tonight, a gondolier who is a native of Chioggia, and who knows every foot of the country round, and every winding of the canals. He must be intelligent and brave, for the risk will be no slight one."

"I think I know such a man, Messer Francisco; but if he happens to be away, there will be no difficulty in finding another, for there are many fishermen here who escaped before the Genoese captured Chioggia."

"When will you see him?"

"As soon as you have landed me at Messer Polani's."

"Go and fetch him, Giuseppi; and if you can find one or two old fishermen of Chioggia, bring them also with you. I want to gain as much information as possible regarding the country."

"Is it true that the fleet starts tomorrow, Francisco?" Maria asked as he entered. "Everyone says so."

"It is quite true. There will be no further change. The orders have been all issued, and you may rely upon it that we are going to sea."

"And when will you return?"

"That's another matter altogether," Francis laughed. "It may be a week, it may be three months."

"But I thought we were going to fight the Genoese galleys. It does not seem to me that a week is wanted to do that. A day to go to Chioggia, a day to fight, and a day to return. What can you want more than that for?"

"I do not think that we are going to fight the Genoese galleys," Francis answered. "Certainly we shall not do so if we can help it. They are vastly stronger than we are; but I do not know that we need fear them for all that."

"What do you mean, Francisco? You do not mean to fight--they are vastly stronger than you are--and yet you do not fear them. You are not given to speak in riddles; but you have puzzled me this time."

"Well, I will explain myself a little," Francis said; "but you must remember that it is a secret, and not to be whispered to anyone."

"That is right," Maria said. "I love a secret, especially a state secret.

"Giulia, come and sit quite close, so that he can whisper it into our ears, and even the walls shall not hear it.

"Now, sir, explain yourself!"

"I will explain it without telling you," Francis said. "Have you not gone to see African lions, who were very much stronger and fiercer than yourself, and yet you did not fear them?"

"Because they have been in cages," Maria said. "But what has that to do with it?"

"It explains the whole matter," Francis said. "We do not mean to fight the Genoese fleet, if we can help it; but we are going to try to put them in a cage, and then we shall not be afraid of them."

"Do not trifle with us, sir," Maria said sternly. "How can you put Genoese galleys in a cage?"

"We cannot put them in a cage, but we can cage them up," Francis said. "Pisani's intention is, if possible, to close all the entrances to the canals round Chioggia. Thus, not only will the

Genoese galleys be unable to sally out to attack us, but the whole of the Genoese army will be cooped up, and we shall then do to them what they have been doing to us, namely, starve them out!"

"Capital, capital!" Maria said, clapping her hands. "Your Pisani is a grand man, Francisco. And if he can do this for us, there is nothing which we would not do to show our gratitude. But you won't find it easy; besides, in the game of starving out, are we likely to win? The contest will not be even, for they start on it full men and strong, while our people are half starved already."

"I do not regard success as certain," Francis replied; "and Pisani himself acknowledges the chances are very great against us. Still, it is possible; and as nothing else seems possible, we are going to attempt it."

Polani looked grave, when he heard of the mission which Francis was going to undertake. Giulia's bright colour fled at once, and Maria said angrily:

"You have no right to be always running into danger, Francisco. You are not a Venetian, and there is no reason why you should be always running risks greater than those which most Venetians are likely to encounter. You ought to think of us who care for you, if you don't choose to think of yourself."

"I did not volunteer for the service," Francis said. "I was asked by the admiral to undertake it, and even had I wished it, I could hardly have refused. The admiral selected me, not from any merit on my part, but because he knows that my boat is one of the fastest on the lagoons, and that I can easily run away from any of the Genoese rowboats. He particularly ordered me to run no unnecessary risks."

"That is all very well," Maria said; "but you know very well that you will run risks, and put yourself in the way of danger, if there is a chance of doing so.

"You should tell him not to go, father!"

"I cannot do that, Maria; for the service he has undertaken is a very important one to Venice. Everything depends upon the success of Pisani's attempt, and undertaken, as it is, against great odds, it is of the utmost importance that there should be no mistake as to the position of the enemy. Whether Francis was wise or not, in accepting Pisani's offer that he should act as his aide-de-camp, may be doubted; but now that he has undertaken it, he must carry out his orders, especially as it is now too late to make other arrangements, did he draw back.

"If you will come into my room, Francisco, I will give you a chart of the passages around Chioggia. You can study that, and you will then the better understand the information you may receive, from the men you are expecting."

Half an hour later Giuseppi arrived with the gondolier he had spoken of, and two old fishermen, and from their explanations, and a study of the map, Francis gained an exact idea of the localities. From his previous expeditions he had learned where the Genoese were generally posted, and something of the strength of the forces at the various points.

In truth, they kept but a careless watch. Feeling convinced that the Venetians possessed no forces capable of attacking him, and that their surrender must now be a matter of a few days only, Doria took no precautions. His troops were all quartered in the houses of Chioggia, his galleys moored alongside its quays, and the utmost he did was to post small bodies of men, with rowboats, at the entrances to the passages from the sea, and up the lagoons, to give warning of any sudden attempt on the part of Barberigo, with his light flotilla, to make a dash at the galleys, and endeavour to burn them.

Having obtained all the information he could from the old fishermen, Francis dismissed them.

"It is evident," he said to Giuseppi, "that we can hardly hope to succeed in passing the boats at the entrance to the canal seaward, or by going up the lagoon. The only plan that I can see is for us to land on the island of Pelestrina, which is held by us, to carry the boat across it, and to embark in the Malamocco channel. In this way, we should be within their cordon of boats, and can row fearlessly either out to the entrances, or to Chioggia itself. We are not likely to be detected, and if we are, we must make a race of it to Pelestrina."

The gondolier agreed that the scheme was practicable, and Francis ordered Giuseppi and him to remove the burdens, and every bit of wood that could be dispensed with from the gondola, so as to facilitate its transport.

Chapter 19:
The Siege Of Chioggia.

Late in the afternoon, Francis embarked in his gondola, and in an hour and a half landed at Pelestrina. He was well known, to those posted there, as the bearer of Pisani's orders, and as soon as it became dark, Rufino Giustiniani, who was in command, ordered a dozen men to carry the light gondola across the island to the Malamocco channel. While this was being done, Francis went to Rufino's tent, and informed him of what was going on in Venice, and that the whole fleet would set sail on the morrow.

"We heard rumours, from the men who brought our rations, that it was to be so," Rufino said; "but we have heard the same story a dozen times. So, now, it is really true! But what can the admiral be thinking of! Sure he can't intend to attack Doria with this newly-manned fleet and rabble army. He could not hope for victory against such odds!"

"The admiral's intentions are kept a profound secret," Francis said, "and are only known to the doge and the Council of Ten."

"And to yourself," Rufino said laughing.

"The admiral is good enough to honour me with his fullest confidence," Francis said; "and in this matter, it is so important that the nature of the design should be kept wholly secret, that I cannot tell it even to you!"

"You are quite right, Francisco; nor do I wish to know it, though I would wager that Maria, and her pretty sister, have some inkling of what is going on."

Francis laughed.

"The signoras are good enough to treat me as a brother," he said, "and I will not affirm that they have not obtained some slight information."

"I will warrant they have!" Rufino said. "When my wife has made up her mind to get to the bottom of a matter, she will tease and coax till she succeeds.

"Ah, here is Matteo! he has been out posting the sentries for the night."

The two friends had not indulged in a talk for some weeks, though they had occasionally met when Francis paid one of his flying visits to the island.

"I have just seen your boat being carried along," Matteo said, as he entered the tent. "I could not think what it was till I got close; but of course, when I saw Giuseppi, I knew all about it. What are you going to do--scout among the Genoese?"

"I am going to find out as much as I can," Francis said.

"It's a capital idea your bringing the boat across the island," Matteo said. "You are always full of good ideas, Francis. I can't make it out. They never seem to occur to me, and at the present time, especially, the only ideas that come into my mind are as to the comfortable meals I will eat, when this business is over. I never thought I cared much for eating before, but since I have had nothing but bread--and not enough of that--and an occasional fish, I have discovered that I am really fond of good living. My bones ache perpetually with lying on the bare ground, and if I escape from this, without being a cripple for life from rheumatism, I shall consider myself lucky, indeed. You are a fortunate fellow, Francisco; spending your time in the admiral's comfortable palace, or flying about in a smooth-rowing gondola!"

"That is one side of the question certainly," Francis said, laughing; "but there is a good deal of hard work, too, in the way of writing."

"I should not like that," Matteo said. "Still, I think you have the best of it. If the Genoese would come sometimes, and try and drive us off the island, there would be some excitement. But, except when the admiral wishes a reconnaissance, or Barberigo's galleys come down and stir them up, there is really nothing doing here."

"That ought to suit you exactly, Matteo, for never but once did I hear you say you wanted to do anything."

"When was that?" Rufino asked, laughing.

"Matteo conceived a violent desire to climb Mount Etna," Francis said, "and it needed all my arguments to prevent his leaving the ship at Girgenti, while she was loading, and starting to make the ascent."

"He would have repented before he had gone a quarter of the way up," Rufino said.

"I might have repented," Matteo replied stoutly, "but I would have done it, if I had begun. You don't know me yet, Rufino. I have a large store of energy, only at present I have had no opportunity of showing what I am made of."

"And now, how do you intend to proceed, Francisco? Have you any plan?"

"None at all," Francis replied. "I simply want to assure myself that the galleys are all in their usual places, and that the Genoese are making no special preparations against our coming."

"I have seen no unusual stir," Rufino said. "Their ships, as far as one can see their masts, seem all in their usual position. I fancy that, since Barberigo carried off two of them, they have put booms across the channels to prevent sudden attacks. I saw a lot of rowboats busy about something, but I could not make out exactly what they were doing; but still, I fancy they were constructing a boom. Their galleys keep a sharp lookout at night, and you certainly would not have succeeded in passing them, had you not hit upon this plan of carrying your boat over.

"Your greatest danger will be at first. When once you have fairly entered the inner canals, you are not likely to be suspected of being an enemy. They will take you for Chioggian fishermen late. We often make out their returning boats near the town. No doubt Doria is fond of fresh fish. Otherwise you would be detected, for the Genoese boats are, of course, quite different to ours, and even in the dark they would make out that you belonged to the lagoons.

"Ah, here is supper! It is not often that I should have anything to offer you, but one of my men managed to catch three or four fish today, and sold them to me at about their weight in silver. However, I have some good wine from my own cellars, and a man who has good wine, fish, and bread can do royally, whatever this grumbling brother of mine may say."

Half an hour later, a soldier brought the news that the gondola was in the water, and Francis bade adieu to his friends, and started at once.

"Row slowly and quietly," he said, as he took his seat. "Do not let your oars make the slightest splash in the water, until we are well across to the opposite shore. They may have a guard boat lying in the channel."

The light craft made her way noiselessly across the water. Once or twice they heard the sound of oars, as some Genoese galley passed up or down, but none came near enough to perceive them, and they crossed the main channel, and entered one of the numerous passages practicable only for boats of very light draught, without being once hailed. A broad shallow tract of water was now crossed, passable only by craft drawing but a few inches of water; then again they were in a deeper channel, and the lights of Chioggia rose but a short distance ahead.

They paused and listened, now, for they were nearing the ship channel, and here the enemy would, if anywhere, be on the alert. Coming across the water they could hear the sound of voices, and the dull noise made by the movement of men in a boat.

"Those are the galleys watching the boom, I expect," Francis said.

"Now, Philippo, we can move on. I suppose there is plenty of water, across the flats, for us to get into the channel without going near the boom."

"Plenty for us, signor; but if the boom goes right across the channel, heavy rowboats would not be able to pass. There are few shallower places in the lagoons than just about here. It may be that in one or two places even we might touch, but if we do, the bottom is firm enough for us to get out and float the boat over."

But they did not touch any shoal sufficiently shallow to necessitate this. Several times Francis could feel, by the dragging pace, that she was touching the oozy bottom; but each time she passed over without coming to a standstill. At last Philippo said:

"We are in the deep channel now, signor. The boom is right astern of us. The town is only a few hundred yards ahead."

"Then we shall be passing the Genoese galleys, directly," Francis said. "Row slowly as we go, and splash sometimes with the oars. If we go quickly and noiselessly past, they might possibly suspect something, but if we row without an attempt at concealment, they will take us for a fisherman's boat."

Soon the dark mass of Genoese ships, with their forests of masts, rose before them. There were lights in the cabins, and a buzz of talking, laughing, and singing among the crews on board.

"What luck today?" a sailor asked them as they rowed past, twenty or thirty yards from the side of one of the ships.

"Very poor," Giuseppi replied. "I think your ships, and the boats lying about, and the firing, have frightened the fish away from this end of the lagoons."

It was half a mile before they passed the last of the crowd of vessels.

"Would you like me to land here, signor?" Philippo said. "There would be no danger in my doing so. I can make my way, through the streets, to the house of some of my relatives, and find out from them whether there are any fresh movements among the Genoese. I will not enter any house; for aught I know there are soldiers quartered everywhere; but I am sure not to go many yards before I run against someone I know."

"I think it will be a very good plan, Philippo. We will lie under the bank here, and wait your return."

It was not more than twenty minutes before the gondolier was back.

"I have spoken to three men I know, signor. They are agreed that there are no movements among the enemy, and no one seems to have an idea that the Venetians are about to put to sea. Of course, I was cautious not to let drop a word on the subject, and only said we had managed to get through the enemy's cordon to learn the latest news, and I expected to earn a ducat or two by my night's work."

"That is excellent," Francis said. "Now, we will row out to the sea mouths of the channels, to assure ourselves that no ships are lying on guard there, for some are going in or out every day to cruise along the coast. A few may have taken up their station there, without attracting notice among the townspeople."

The opening of the passage known as the Canal of Lombardy was first visited. To gain this, they had to retrace their steps for some distance, and to row through the town of Chioggia, passing several boats and galleys, but without attracting notice. They found the mouth of the canal entirely unguarded, and then returned and rowed out to the mouth of the Brondolo passage. Some blazing fires on the shore showed that there were parties of soldiers here, but no ships were lying anywhere in the channel.

After some consultation they determined that, as no watch seemed to be kept, it would be shorter to row on outside the islands, and to enter by the third passage to be examined, that between Pelestrina and Brondolo. Here, however, the Genoese were more on the alert, as the Pelestrina shore was held by the Venetians. Scarcely had they entered the channel, when a large rowboat shot out from the shadow of the shore and hailed them.

"Stop rowing in that boat! Who are you that are entering so late?"

"Fishermen," Philippo shouted back, but without stopping rowing.

"Stop!" shouted the officer, "till we examine you! It is forbidden to enter the channel after dark."

But the gondoliers rowed steadily on, until ahead of the boat coming out. This fell into their wake, and its angry officer shouted threats against the fugitives, and exhorted his men to row their hardest.

"There are two more boats ahead, signor. They are lying on their oars to cut us off. One is a good deal further out than the other, and I don't think we shall gain Pelestrina."

"Then make for the Brondolo shore till we have passed them," Francis said.

The boat whirled off her course, and made towards the shore. The Genoese galleys ahead at once made towards them; but in spite of the numerous oars they pulled, the craft could not keep up with the racing gondola, and it crossed ahead of them. In another five minutes' rowing, the three galleys were well astern, and the gondola again made out from the shore, her head pointing obliquely towards Pelestrina. The galleys were now fifty yards behind, and although their crews rowed their hardest, the gondola gradually gained upon them, and crossing their bows made over towards Pelestrina.

"We are out of the channel now," Philippo said, "and there will not be water enough for them to follow us much further."

A minute or two later a sudden shout proclaimed that the nearest of their pursuers had touched the ground.

"We can take it easy now," Giuseppi said, "and I am not sorry, for we could not have rowed harder if we had been racing."

A few minutes later, the light craft touched the mud a few yards distant from the shore.

"Is that you, Francisco?" a voice, which Francis recognized as Matteo's, asked.

"All right, Matteo!" he replied. "No one hurt this time."

"I have been on the lookout for you the last hour. I have got a body of my men here, in case you were chased. We heard the shouting and guessed it was you."

"If you have got some men there, Matteo, there is a chance for you to take a prize. A galley rowing twelve or fourteen oars is in the mud, a few hundred yards out. She was chasing us, and ran aground when at full speed, and I imagine they will have some trouble in getting her off. I suppose she draws a couple of feet of water. There! Don't you hear the hubbub they are making?"

"I hear them," Matteo said.

"Come along, lads. The night is cold, and I don't suppose the water is any warmer, but a skirmish will heat our blood."

Matteo, followed by a company of some forty men, at once entered the water, and made in the direction of the sounds. Five minutes later, Francis heard shouts and a clashing of weapons suddenly break out. It lasted but a short time. Matteo and his band soon returned with the prisoners.

"What! Have you waited, Francisco? I thought you would be on the other side of the island by this time."

"I was in no particular hurry, Matteo; and besides, I want my boat; and although two men can lift her easily enough, she would be a heavy weight to carry so far."

"You shall have a dozen, Francisco. It is owing to you we have taken these prisoners, and that I have had my first bit of excitement since I came out here.

"Sergeant, here are a couple of ducats. When you have given the prisoners into safe custody, spend the money in wine for the company.

"The water is bitterly cold, I can tell you, Francisco; but otherwise I am warm enough, for one's feet stick to the mud, and it seems, each step, as if one had fifty pounds of lead on one's shoes. But come along to my brother's tent at once. Your feet must be cold, too, though the water was only a few inches deep where you got out of your boat. A glass of hot wine will do us both good; and it will be an hour before your boat is in the water again. Indeed, I don't see the use of your starting before daybreak."

"Nor do I, Matteo; but I must go, nevertheless. Pisani knows how long it will take me to get to Chioggia and return. He will allow an hour or two for me to reconnoitre, and will then be expecting me back. As it is, I shall be two hours after the time when he will be expecting me, for he knows nothing about the boat being carried across this island, and will make no allowance for that. Moreover, Polani and his daughters will be anxious about me."

"Oh, you flatter yourself they will be lying awake for you," Matteo said, laughing. "Thinking over your dangers! Well, there's nothing like having a good idea of one's self."

Francis joined in the laugh.

"It does sound rather conceited, Matteo; but I know they will be anxious. They took up the idea it was a dangerous service I was going on, and I have no doubt they fidgeted over it. Women are always fancying things, you know."

"I don't know anyone who fidgets about me," Matteo said; "but then, you see, I am not a rescuer of damsels in distress, nor have I received the thanks of the republic for gallant actions."

"Well, you ought to have done," Francis replied. "You had just as much to do with that fight on board Pisani's galley as I had, only it happened I was in command.

"Oh, there is your brother's tent! I see there is a light burning, so I suppose he has not gone to bed yet."

"All the better," Matteo said. "We shall get our hot wine all the quicker. My teeth are chattering so, I hardly dare speak for fear of biting my tongue."

Francis was warmly welcomed by Rufino Giustiniani.

"I need hardly ask you if you have succeeded in reconnoitring their positions, for I know you would not come back before morning had you not carried out your orders.

"Why, Matteo, what have you been doing--wading in the mud, apparently? Why, you are wet up to the waist."

"We have captured an officer, and fourteen men, Rufino. They will be here in a few minutes. Their boat got stuck fast while it was chasing Francisco; so we waded out and took them. They made some resistance, but beyond a few slashes, and two or three thumps from their oars, no harm was done."

"That is right, Matteo. I am glad you have had a skirmish with them at last. Now go in and change your things. I shall have you on my hands with rheumatism."

"I will do that at once, and I hope you will have some hot spiced wine ready, by the time I have changed, for I am nearly frozen."

The embers of a fire, outside the tent, were soon stirred together, and in a few minutes the wine was prepared. In the meantime, Francis had been telling Rufino the incidents of his trip. In half an hour, the message came that the gondola was again in the water, and Francis was soon on his way back to the city.

"I was beginning to be anxious about you," was Pisani's greeting, as, upon being informed of his return, he sprang from the couch, on which he had thrown himself for an hour's sleep, and hurried downstairs. "I reckoned that you might have been back an hour before this, and began to think that you must have got into some scrape. Well, what have you discovered?"

"The Genoese have no idea that you are going to put to sea. Their ships and galleys are, as usual, moored off the quays of Chioggia. The entrance to the Canal of Lombardy, and the Brondolo passage, are both quite open, and there appear to be no troops anywhere near; but between Pelestrina and Brondolo they have rowboats watching the entrance, but no craft of any size. There are a few troops there, but, so far as I could judge by the number of fires, not more than two hundred men or so."

"Your news is excellent, Francisco. I will not ask you more, now. It is three o'clock already, and at five I must be up and doing; so get off to bed as soon as you can. You can give me the details in the morning."

The gondola was still waiting at the steps, and in a few minutes Francis arrived at the Palazzo Polani. A servant was sleeping on a bench in the hall. He started up as Francis entered.

"I have orders to let my master know, as soon as you return, signor."

"You can tell him, at the same time, that I have returned without hurt, and pray him not to disturb himself, as I can tell him what has taken place in the morning."

Polani, however, at once came to Francis' room.

"Thank Heaven you have returned safe to us, my boy!" he said. "I have just knocked at the girls' doors, to tell them of your return, and, by the quickness with which they answered, I am sure that they, like myself, have had no sleep. Have you succeeded in your mission?"

"Perfectly, signor. I have been to Chioggia itself, and to the entrances of the three passages, and have discovered that none of them are guarded by any force that could resist us."

"But how did you manage to pass through their galleys?"

"I landed on this side of Pelestrina, and had the gondola carried across, and launched in the channel inside their cordon; and it was not until we entered the last passage--that by Brondolo--that we were noticed. Then there was a sharp chase for a bit, but we outstripped them, and got safely across to Pelestrina. One of the galleys, in the excitement of the chase, ran fast into the mud; and Matteo, with some of his men, waded out and captured the officer and crew. So there is every prospect of our succeeding tomorrow."

"All that is good," Polani said; "but to me, just at present, I own that the principal thing is that you have got safely back. Now I will not keep you from your bed, for I suppose that you will not be able to lie late in the morning."

Francis certainly did not intend to do so, but the sun was high before he woke. He hurriedly dressed, and went downstairs.

"I have seen the admiral," Polani said as he entered, "and told him that you were sound asleep, and I did not intend to wake you, for that you were looking worn and knocked up. He said: 'Quite right! The lad is so willing and active, that I forget sometimes that he is not an old sea dog like myself, accustomed to sleep with one eye open, and to go without sleep altogether for days if necessary.' So you need not hurry over your breakfast. The girls are dying to hear your adventures."

As he took his breakfast, Francis gave the girls an account of his expedition.

"And so, you saw Rufino!" Maria said. "Did he inquire after me? You told him, I hope, that I was fading away rapidly from grief at his absence."

"I did not venture upon so flagrant an untruth as that," Francis replied.

"Is he very uncomfortable?"

"Not very, signora. He has a good tent, some excellent wine, an allowance of bread, which might be larger, and occasionally fish. As he has also the gift of excellent spirits, I do not think he is greatly to be pitied--except, of course, for his absence from you."

"That, of course," Maria said. "When he does come here, he always tells me a moving tale of his privations, in hopes of exciting pity; but, unfortunately, I cannot help laughing at his tales of hardship. But we were really anxious about you last night, Francisco, and very thankful when we heard you had returned.

"Weren't we, Giulia?"

Giulia nodded.

"Giulia hasn't much to say when you are here, Francisco, but she can chatter about you fast enough when we are alone."

"How can you say so, Maria?" Giulia said reproachfully.

"Well, my dear, there is no harm in that. For aught he knows, you may be saying the most unkind things about him, all the time."

"I am sure he knows that I should not do that," Giulia said indignantly.

"By the way, do you know, Francisco, that all Venice is in a state of excitement! A proclamation has been issued by the doge, this morning, that all should be in their galleys and at their posts at noon, under pain of death. So everyone knows that something is about to be done, at last."

"Then it is time for me to be off," Francis said, rising hastily, "for it is ten o'clock already."

"Take your time, my lad," the merchant said. "There is no hurry, for Pisani told me, privately, that they should not sail until after dark."

It was not, indeed, until nearly eight o'clock in the evening, that the expedition started. At the hour of vespers, the doge, Pisani, and the other leaders of the expedition, attended mass in the church of Saint Mark, and then proceeded to their galleys, where all was now in readiness.

Pisani led the first division, which consisted of fourteen galleys. The doge, assisted by Cavalli, commanded in the centre; and Corbaro brought up the rear, with ten large ships. The night was beautifully bright and calm, a light and favourable breeze was blowing, and all Venice assembled to see the departure of the fleet.

Just after it passed through the passage of the Lido, a thick mist came on. Pisani stamped up and down the deck impatiently.

"If this goes on, it will ruin us," he said. "Instead of arriving in proper order at the mouth of the passages, and occupying them before the Genoese wake up to a sense of their danger, we shall get there one by one, they will take the alarm, and we shall have their whole fleet to deal with. It will be simply ruin to our scheme."

Fortunately, however, the fog speedily lifted. The vessels closed up together, and, in two hours after starting, arrived off the entrances to the channels. Pisani anchored until daylight appeared, and nearly five thousand men were then landed on the Brondolo's shore, easily driving back the small detachment placed there. But the alarm was soon given, and the Genoese poured out in such overwhelming force that the Venetians were driven in disorder to their boats, leaving behind them six hundred killed, drowned, or prisoners.

But Pisani had not supposed that he would be able to hold his position in front of the whole Genoese force, and he had succeeded in his main object. While the fighting had been going on on shore, a party of sailors had managed to moor a great ship, laden with stones, across the channel. As soon as the Genoese had driven the Venetians to their boats, they took possession of this vessel, and, finding that she was aground, they set her on fire, thus unconsciously aiding Pisani's object, for when she had burned to the water's edge she sank.

Barberigo, with his light galleys, now arrived upon the spot, and emptied their loads of stone into the passage around the wreck. The Genoese kept up a heavy fire with their artillery, many of the galleys were sunk, and numbers of the Venetians drowned, or killed by the shot.

Nevertheless, they worked on unflinchingly. As soon as the pile of stones had risen sufficiently for the men to stand upon them, waist deep, they took their places upon it, and packed in order the stones that their comrades handed them, and fixed heavy chains binding the whole together.

The work was terribly severe. The cold was bitter. The men were badly fed, and most of them altogether unaccustomed to hardships. In addition to the fire from the enemy's guns, they were exposed to a rain of arrows, and at the end of two days and nights they were utterly worn out and exhausted, and protested that they could do no more. Pisani, who had himself laboured among them in the thickest of the danger, strove to keep up their spirits by pointing out the importance of their work, and requested the doge to swear on his sword that, old as he was, he would never return to Venice unless Chioggia was conquered.

The doge took the oath, and for the moment the murmuring ceased; and, on the night of the 24th, the channel of Chioggia was entirely choked from shore to shore. On that day, Corbaro succeeded in sinking two hulks in the passage of Brondolo. Doria, who had hitherto believed that the Venetians would attempt nothing serious, now perceived for the first time the object of Pisani, and despatched fourteen great galleys to crush Corbaro, who had with him but four vessels. Pisani at once sailed to his assistance, with ten more ships, and the passage was now so narrow that the Genoese did not venture to attack, and Corbaro completed the operation of blocking up the Brondolo passage. The next day the Canal of Lombardy was similarly blocked; and thus, on the fourth day after leaving Venice, Pisani had accomplished his object, and had shut out the Genoese galleys from the sea.

But the work had been terrible, and the losses great. The soldiers were on half rations. The cold was piercing. They were engaged night and day with the enemy, and were continually wet through, and the labour was tremendous.

A fort had already been begun on the southern shore of the port of Brondolo, facing the convent, which Doria had transformed into a citadel. The new work was christened the Lova, and the heaviest guns in the Venetian arsenal were planted there. One of these, named the Trevisan, discharged stones of a hundred and ninety-five pounds in weight, and the Victory was little smaller. But the science of artillery was then in its youth, and these guns could only be discharged once in twenty-four hours.

But, on the 29th, the Venetians could do no more, and officers, soldiers, and sailors united in the demand that they should return to Venice. Even Pisani felt that the enterprise was beyond him, and that his men, exhausted by cold, hunger, and their incessant exertions, could no longer resist the overwhelming odds brought against him. Still, he maintained a brave front, and once again his cheery words, and unfeigned good temper, and the example set them by the aged doge, had their effect; but the soldiers required a pledge that, if Zeno should not be signalled in sight by New Year's Day, he would raise the siege. If Pisani and the doge would pledge themselves to this, the people agreed to maintain the struggle for the intervening forty-eight hours.

The pledge was given, and the fight continued. Thus, the fate of Venice hung in the balance. If Zeno arrived, not only would she be saved, but she had it in her power to inflict upon Genoa a terrible blow. Should Zeno still tarry, not only would the siege be raised, and the Genoese be at liberty to remove the dams which the Venetians had placed, at such a cost of suffering and blood; but there would be nothing left for Venice but to accept the terms, however onerous, her triumphant foes might dictate, terms which would certainly strip her of all her possessions, and probably involve even her independence.

Never, from her first foundation, had Venice been in such terrible risk. Her very existence trembled in the balance. The 30th passed as the days preceding it. There was but little fighting, for the Genoese knew how terrible were the straits to which Venice was reduced, and learned, from the prisoners they had taken, that in a few days, at the outside, the army besieging them would cease to exist.

At daybreak, on the 31st, men ascended the masts of the ships, and gazed over the sea, in hopes of making out the long-expected sails. But the sea was bare. It was terrible to see the faces of the Venetians, gaunt with famine, broken down by cold and fatigue. Even the most enduring began to despair.

Men spoke no more of Zeno. He had been away for months. Was it likely that he would come just at this moment? They talked rather of their homes. The next day they would return. If they must die, they would die with those they loved, in Venice. They should not mind that. And so the day went on, and as they lay down at night, hungry and cold, they thanked God that it was their last day. Whatever might come would be better than this.

Men were at the mastheads again, before daylight, on the 1st of January. Then, as the first streak of dawn broke, the cry went from masthead to masthead:

"There are ships out at sea!"

The cry was heard on shore. Pisani jumped into a boat with Francis, rowed out to his ship, and climbed the mast.

"Yes, there are ships!" he said. And then, after a pause: "Fifteen of them! Who are they? God grant it be Zeno!"

This was the question everyone on ship and on shore was asking himself, for it was known that the Genoese, too, were expecting reinforcements.

"The wind is scarce strong enough to move them through the water," Pisani said. "Let some light boats go off to reconnoitre. Let us know the best or the worst. If it be Zeno, Venice is saved! If it be the Genoese, I, and those who agree with me that it is better to die fighting, than to perish of hunger, will go out and attack them."

In a few minutes, several fast galleys started for the fleet, which was still so far away that the vessels could scarcely be made out, still less their rig and nationality. It would be some time before the boats would return with the news, and Pisani went ashore, and, with the doge, moved among the men, exhorting them to be steadfast, above all things not to give way to panic, should the newcomers prove to be enemies.

"If all is done in order," he said, "they cannot interfere with our retreat to Venice. They do not know how weak we are, and will not venture to attack so large a fleet. Therefore, when the signal is made that they are Genoese, we will fall back in good order to our boats, and take to our ships, and then either return to Venice, or sail out and give battle, as it may be decided."

The boats, before starting, had been told to hoist white flags should the galleys be Venetian, but to show no signal if they were Genoese. The boats were watched, from the mastheads, until they became specks in the distance. An hour afterwards, the lookout signalled to those on shore that they were returning.

"Go off again, Francisco. I must remain here to keep up the men's hearts, if the news be bad. Take your stand on the poop of my ship, and the moment the lookouts can say, with certainty, whether the boats carry a white flag or not, hoist the Lion of Saint Mark to the masthead, if it be Zeno. If not, run up a blue flag!"

Chapter 20:
The Triumph Of Venice.

Francis rowed off to the ship, got the flags in readiness for hoisting, and stood with the lines in his hand.

"Can you make them out, yet?" he hailed the men at the mastheads.

"They are mere specks yet, signor," the man at the foremast said.

The other did not reply at once, but presently he shouted down:

"Far as they are away, signor, I am almost sure that one or two of them, at least, have something white flying."

There was a murmur of joy from the men on the deck, for Jacopo Zippo was famous for his keenness of sight.

"Silence, men!" Francis said. "Do not let a man shout, or wave his cap, till we are absolutely certain. Remember the agony with which those on shore are watching us, and the awful disappointment it would be, were their hopes raised only to be crushed, afterwards."

Another ten minutes, and Jacopo slid rapidly down by the stays, and stood on the deck with bared head.

"God be praised, signor! I have no longer a doubt. I can tell you, for certain, that white flags are flying from these boats."

"God be praised!" Francis replied.

"Now, up with the Lion!"

The flag was bent to the halyards and Francis hoisted it. As it rose above the bulwark, Pisani, who was standing on a hillock of sand, shouted out at the top of his voice:

"It is Zeno's fleet!"

A shout of joy broke from the troops. Cheer after cheer rent the air, from ship and shore, and then the wildest excitement reigned. Some fell on their knees, to thank God for the rescue thus sent when all seemed lost. Others stood with clasped hands, and streaming eyes, looking towards heaven. Some danced and shouted. Some wept with joy. Men fell on to each other's necks, and embraced. Some threw up their caps. All were wild with joy, and pent-up excitement.

Zeno, who, in ignorance of the terrible straits to which his countrymen were reduced, was making with his fleet direct to Venice, was intercepted by one of the galleys, and at once bore up for Brondolo, and presently dropped anchor near the shore. As he did so, a boat was lowered, and he rowed to the strand, where the Venetians crowded down to greet him. With difficulty, he made his way through the shouting multitude to the spot, a little distance away, where the doge was awaiting him.

Zeno was of medium height, square shouldered and broad chested. His head was manly and handsome, his nose aquiline, his eyes large, dark, and piercingly bright, and shaded by strongly-marked eyebrows. His air was grave and thoughtful, and in strong contrast to that of the merry and buoyant Pisani. His temper was more equable, but his character was as impulsive as that of the admiral. He was now forty-five years of age--ten years the junior of Pisani. Zeno was intended for the church, and was presented by the pope with the reversion of a rich prebendal stall at Patras. On his way to Padua, to complete his studies at the university, he was attacked by robbers, who left him for dead. He recovered, however, and went to Padua. He became an accomplished scholar; but was so fond of gambling that he lost every penny, and was obliged to escape from his creditors by flight. For five years he wandered over Italy, taking part in all sorts of adventures, and then suddenly returned to Venice, and was persuaded by his friends to proceed to Patras, where his stall was now vacant.

When he arrived there, he found the city besieged by the Turks. In spite of his clerical dignity, he placed himself in the front rank of its defenders, and distinguished himself by extreme bravery. He was desperately wounded, and was again believed to be dead. He was even placed in his coffin; but just as it was being nailed down, he showed signs of returning life. He did not stay long at Patras, but travelled in Germany, France, and England.

Soon after he returned to Patras he fought a duel, and thereby forfeited his stall. He now renounced the clerical profession, and married a wealthy heiress. She died shortly afterwards, and he married the daughter of the Admiral Marco Giustiniani.

He now entered upon political life, and soon showed brilliant talents. He was then appointed to the military command of the district of Treviso, which the Paduans were then invading. Here he very greatly distinguished himself, and in numberless engagements was always successful, so that he became known as Zeno the Unconquered.

When Pisani was appointed captain general, in April, 1378, he was appointed governor of Negropont, and soon afterwards received a separate naval command. He had been lost sight of for many months, prior to his appearance so opportunely before Brondolo, and he now confirmed to the doge the news that had been received shortly before. He had captured nearly seventy Genoese vessels, of various sizes, had cruised for some time in sight of Genoa, struck a heavy blow at her commerce, and prevented the despatch of the reinforcements promised to Doria. Among the vessels taken was one which was carrying three hundred thousand ducats from Genoa.

He reported himself ready with his men to take up the brunt of the siege forthwith, and selecting Brondolo as the most dangerous position, at once landed his crews. The stores on board ship were also brought ashore, and proved ample for the present necessities of the army.

In a few days, he sailed with his galleys and recaptured Loredo, driving out the Paduan garrison there. This conquest was all important to Venice, for it opened their communication with Ferrara, and vast stores of provisions were at once sent by their ally to Venice, and the pressure of starvation immediately ceased.

The siege of Brondolo was now pushed on, and on the 22nd of January the great bombard, the Victory, so battered the wall opposite to it that it fell suddenly, crushing beneath its ruins the Genoese commander, Doria.

The change which three weeks had made in the appearance of the Venetian forces was marvellous. Ample food, firing, and shelter had restored their wasted frames, and assurance of victory had taken the place of the courage of despair. A month of toil, hardship, and fighting had converted a mob of recruits into disciplined soldiers, and Zeno and Pisani seemed to have filled all with their own energy and courage. Zeno, indeed, was so rash and fearless that he had innumerable escapes from death.

One evening after dusk his own vessel, having been accidentally torn from its anchorage near the Lova Fort by the force of the wind and currents, was driven across the passage against the enemy's forts, whence showers of missiles were poured into it. One arrow pierced his throat. Dragging it out, he continued to issue his orders for getting the galley off the shore--bade a seaman swim with a line to the moorings, and angrily rebuked those who, believing destruction to be inevitable, entreated him to strike his flag. The sailor reached the moorings, and, with a line he had taken, made fast a strong rope to it, and the vessel was then hauled off into a place of safety. As Zeno hurried along the deck, superintending the operation, he tumbled down an open hatchway, and fell on his back, almost unconscious. In a few moments he would have been suffocated by the blood from the wound in his throat, but with a final effort he managed to roll over on to his face, the wound was thus permitted to bleed freely, and he soon recovered.

On the 28th of February, he was appointed general in chief of the land forces, and the next day drove the Genoese from all their positions on the islands of Brondolo and Little Chioggia, and on the following morning established his headquarters under the ramparts of Chioggia, and directed a destructive fire upon the citadel. As the Genoese fell back across the bridge over the Canal of Santa Caterina, the structure gave way under their weight, and great numbers were drowned. The retreat of the Genoese was indeed so hurried and confused, and they left behind them an immense quantity of arms, accoutrements, and war material, so much so that suits of mail were selling for a few shillings in the Venetian camp.

So completely were the Genoese disheartened, by the change in their position, that many thought that the Venetians could at once have taken Chioggia by assault; but the leaders were determined to risk no failure, and knew that the enemy must yield to hunger. They therefore contented themselves with a rigorous blockade, cutting off all the supplies which the Lord of Padua endeavoured to throw into the city. The Venetians, however, allowed the besieged to send away their women and children, who were taken to Venice and kindly treated there.

The army of Venice had now been vastly increased, by the arrival of the Star Company of Milan, and the Condottieri commanded by Sir John Hawkwood. The dikes, erected across the channels with so much labour, were removed, and the fleet took their part in the siege.

On the 14th of May there was joy in Chioggia, similar to that which the Venetians had felt at the sight of Zeno's fleet, for on that morning the squadron, which Genoa had sent to their assistance under the command of Matteo Maruffo, appeared in sight. This admiral had wasted much valuable time on the way, but had fallen in with and captured, after a most gallant resistance, five Venetian galleys under Giustiniani, who had been despatched to Apulia to fetch grain.

The Genoese fleet drew up in order of battle, and challenged Pisani to come out to engage them. But, impetuous as was the disposition of the admiral, and greatly as he longed to avenge his defeat at Pola, he refused to stir. He knew that Chioggia must, ere long, fall, and he would not risk all the advantages gained, by so many months of toil and effort, upon the hazard of a battle. Day after day Maruffo repeated his challenge, accompanied by such insolent taunts that the blood of the Venetian sailors was so stirred that Pisani could no longer restrain them. After obtaining leave from the doge to go out and give battle, he sailed into the roadstead on the 25th. The two fleets drew up in line of battle, facing each other. Just as the combat was about to commence a strange panic seized the Genoese, and, without exchanging a blow or firing a shot, they fled hastily. Pisani pursued them for some miles, and then returned to his old station.

The grief and despair of the garrison of Chioggia, at the sight of the retreat of their fleet, was in proportion to the joy with which they had hailed its approach. Their supply of fresh water was all but exhausted. Their rations had become so scanty that, from sheer weakness, they were unable, after the first week in June, to work their guns.

Genoa, in despair at the position of her troops, laboured unceasingly to relieve them. Emissaries were sent to tamper with the free companies, and succeeded so far that these would have marched away, had they not been appeased by the promise of a three days' sack of Chioggia, and a month's extra pay at the end of the war. Attempts were made to assassinate Zeno, but these also failed. The Genoese then induced the pope to intercede on their behalf; but the council remembered that when Venice was at the edge of destruction, on the 31st of December, no power had come forward to save her, and refused now to be robbed of the well-earned triumph.

On the 15th of July, Maruffo, who had received reinforcements again made his appearance; but Pisani this time refused to be tempted out. On the 21st a deputation was sent out from Chioggia to ask for terms, and though, on being told that an unconditional surrender alone would be accepted, they returned to the city, yet the following day the Genoese flag was hauled down from the battlements.

On the 24th the doge, accompanied by Pisani and Zeno, made his formal entry into Chioggia. The booty was enormous; and the companies received the promised bounty, and were allowed to pillage for three days. So large was the plunder collected, in this time, by the adventurers, that the share of one of them amounted to five hundred ducats. The republic, however, did not come off altogether without spoil--they obtained nineteen seaworthy galleys, four thousand four hundred and forty prisoners, and a vast amount of valuable stores, the salt alone being computed as worth ninety thousand crowns.

Not even when the triumphant fleet returned, after the conquest of Constantinople, was Venice so wild with delight, as when the doge, accompanied by Pisani and Zeno, entered the city in triumph after the capture of Chioggia. From the danger, more imminent than any that had threatened Venice from her first foundation, they had emerged with a success which would cripple the strength, and lower the pride of Genoa for years. Each citizen felt that he had some share in the triumph, for each had taken his share in the sufferings, the sacrifices, and the efforts of the struggle. There had been no unmanly giving way to despair, no pitiful entreaty for aid in their peril. Venice had relied upon herself, and had come out triumphant.

From every house hung flags and banners, every balcony was hung with tapestry and drapery. The Grand Canal was closely packed with gondolas, which, for once, disregarded the sumptuary law that enforced black as their only hue, and shone in a mass of colour. Gaily dressed ladies sat beneath canopies of silk and velvet; flags floated from every boat, and the rowers were dressed in the bright liveries of their employers. The church bells rang out with a deafening clang, and from roof and balcony, from wharf and river, rang out a mighty shout of welcome and triumph from the crowded mass, as the great state gondola, bearing the doge and the two commanders, made its way, slowly and with difficulty, along the centre of the canal.

Francis was on board one of the gondolas that followed in the wake of that of the doge, and as soon as the grand service in Saint Mark's was over, he slipped off and made his way back to the Palazzo Polani. The merchant and Giulia had both been present at the ceremony, and had just returned when he arrived.

"I guessed you would be off at once, Francisco, directly the ceremony was over. I own that I, myself, would have stayed for a time to see the grand doings in the Piazza, but this child would not hear of our doing so. She said it would be a shame, indeed, if you should arrive home and find no one to greet you."

"So it would have been," Giulia said. "I am sure I should not have liked, when I have been away, even on a visit of pleasure to Corfu, to return and find the house empty; and after the terrible dangers and hardships you have gone through, Francisco, it would have been unkind, indeed, had we not been here. You still look thin and worn."

"I think that is fancy on your part, Giulia. To my eyes he looks as stout as ever I saw him. But certainly he looked as lean and famished as a wolf, when I paid that visit to the camp the day before Zeno's arrival. His clothes hung loose about him, his cheeks were hollow, and his eyes sunken. He would have been a sight for men to stare at, had not every one else been in an equally bad case.

"Well, I thank God there is an end of it, now! Genoa will be glad to make peace on any terms, and the sea will once more be open to our ships. So now, Francisco, you have done with fighting, and will be able to turn your attention to the humbler occupation of a merchant."

"That will I right gladly," Francis said. "I used to think, once, I should like to be a man-at-arms; but I have seen enough of it, and hope I never will draw my sword again, unless it be in conflict with some Moorish rover. I have had many letters from my father, chiding me for mingling in frays in which I have no concern, and shall be able to gladden his heart, by writing to assure him that I have done with fighting."

"It has done you no harm, Francisco, or rather it has done you much good. It has given you the citizenship of Venice, in itself no slight advantage to you as a trader here. It has given you three hundred ducats a year, which, as a mark of honour, is not to be despised. It has won for you a name throughout the republic, and has given you a fame and popularity such as few, if any, citizens of Venice ever attained at your age. Lastly, it has made a man of you. It has given you confidence and self possession. You have acquired the habit of commanding men. You have been placed in positions which have called for the exercise of rare judgment, prudence, and courage; and you have come well through it all. It is but four years since your father left you a lad in my keeping. Now you are a man, whom the highest noble in Venice might be proud of calling his son. You have no reason to regret, therefore, that you have, for a year, taken up soldiering instead of trading, especially as our business was all stopped by the war, and you must have passed your time in inactivity."

In the evening, when the merchant and Francis were alone together, the former said:

"I told you last autumn, Francis, when I informed you that, henceforth, you would enter into my house as a partner in the business, when we again recommenced trade, that I had something else in my mind, but the time to speak of it had not then arrived. I think it has now come. Tell me, my boy, frankly, if there is anything that you would wish to ask of me."

Francis was silent for a moment; then he said:

"You have done so much, Signor Polani. You have heaped kindness upon me, altogether beyond anything I could have hoped for, that, even did I wish for more, I could not ask it."

"Then there is something more you would like, Francisco. Remember that I have told you that I regard you as a son, and therefore I wish you to speak to me, as frankly as if I was really your father."

"I fear, signor, that you will think me audacious, but since you thus urge upon me to speak all that is in my mind, I cannot but tell you the truth. I love your daughter, Giulia, and have done so ever since the first day that my eyes fell on her. It has seemed to me too much, even to hope, that she can ever be mine, and I have been careful in letting no word expressive of my feelings pass my lips. It still seems, to me, beyond the bounds of possibility that I could successfully aspire to the hand of the daughter of one of the noblest families in Venice."

"I am glad you have spoken frankly, dear lad," the merchant said. "Ever since you rescued my daughters from the hands of Mocenigo, it has been on my mind that someday, perhaps, you would be my son-in-law, as well as my son by adoption. I have watched with approval that, as Giulia grew from a child into a young woman, her liking for you seemed to ripen into affection. This afternoon I have spoken to her, and she has acknowledged that she would obey my commands, to regard you as her future husband, with gladness.

"I could not, however, offer my daughter's hand to one who might reject it, or who, if he accepted it, would only do so because he considered the match to be a desirable one, from a business point of view. Now that you have told me you love her, all difficulties are at an end. I am not one of those fathers who would force a marriage upon their daughters, regardless of their feelings. I gave to Maria free choice among her various suitors, and so I would give it to Giulia. Her choice is in accordance with my own secret hopes, and I therefore, freely and gladly, bestow her upon you. You must promise only that you do not carry her away altogether to England, so long as I live. You can, if you like, pay long visits with her from time to time to your native country, but make Venice your headquarters.

"I need say nothing to you about her dowry. I intended that, as my partner, you should take a fourth share of the profits of the business; but as Giulia's husband, I shall now propose that you have a third. This will give you an income equal to that of all but the wealthiest of the nobles of Venice. At my death, my fortune will be divided between my girls."

Francis expressed, in a few words, his joy and gratitude at the merchant's offer. Giulia had inspired him, four years before, with a boyish love, and it had steadily increased until he felt that, however great his success in life as Messer Polani's partner, his happiness would be incomplete unless shared by Giulia. Polani cut short his words by saying:

"My dear boy, I am as pleased that this should be so as you are. I now feel that I have, indeed, gained a son and secured the happiness of my daughter. Go in to her now. You will find her in the embroidery room. I told her that I should speak to you this evening, and she is doubtless in a tremble as to the result, for she told me frankly that, although she loved you, she feared you only regarded her with the affection of a brother, and she implored me, above all, not to give you a hint of her feelings towards you, until I was convinced that you really loved her."

Two months later, the marriage of Francis Hammond and Giulia Polani took place. There were great festivities, and the merchant spent a considerable sum in giving a feast, on the occasion, to all the poor of Venice. Maria told Francis, in confidence, that she had always made up her mind that he would marry Giulia.

"The child was silly enough to fall in love with you from the first, Francisco, and I was sure that you, in your dull English fashion, cared for her. My father confided to me, long since, that he hoped it would come about."

Francis Hammond lived for many years with his wife in Venice, paying occasional visits to England. He was joined, soon after his marriage, by his brother, who, after serving for some years in the business, entered it as a partner, when Messer Polani's increasing years rendered it necessary for him to retire from an active participation in it.

Some months after his marriage, Francis was saddened by the death of Admiral Pisani, who never recovered from the fatigue and hardships he suffered during the siege of Chioggia. He had, with the fleet, recovered most of the places that the Genoese had captured, and after chasing a Genoese fleet to Zara, had a partial engagement with them there. In this, Corbaro, now holding the commission of admiral of the squadron, was killed, and Pisani himself wounded. He was already suffering from fever; and the loss of Corbaro, and the check that the fleet had suffered, increased his malady, and he expired three days later.

Venice made peace with Genoa, but the grudge which she bore to Padua was not wiped out until some years later, when, in 1404, that city was besieged by the Venetians, and forced by famine to surrender in the autumn of the following year; after which Zeno, having been proved to have kept up secret communications with the Lord of Padua, was deprived of his honours and sentenced to a year's imprisonment. Thus, in turn, the two great Venetian commanders suffered disgrace and imprisonment.

As she had been patient and steadfast in her time of distress, Venice was clement in her hour of triumph, and granted far more favourable terms to Padua than that city deserved.

At the death of Messer Polani, Francis returned with his wife and family to England, and established himself in London, where he at once took rank as one of the leading merchants. His fortune, however, was so large, that he had no occasion to continue in commerce, and he did so only to afford him a certain amount of occupation. His brother carried on the business in Venice, and became one of the leading citizens there, in partnership with Matteo Giustiniani. Every two or three years Francis made a voyage with his wife to Venice and spent some months there, and to the end of his life never broke off his close connection with the City of the Waters.

At Agincourt: A Tale of the White Hoods of Paris

1897

Preface

The long and bloody feud between the houses of Orleans and Burgundy-which for many years devastated France, caused a prodigious destruction of life and property, and was not even relaxed in the presence of a common enemy-is very fully recorded in the pages of Monstrellet and other contemporary historians. I have here only attempted to relate the events of the early portion of the struggle-from its commencement up to the astonishing victory of Agincourt, won by a handful of Englishmen over the chivalry of France. Here the two factions, with the exception of the Duke of Burgundy himself, laid aside their differences for the moment, only to renew them while France still lay prostrate at the feet of the English conqueror.

At this distance of time, even with all the records at one's disposal, it is difficult to say which party was most to blame in this disastrous civil war, a war which did more to cripple the power of France than was ever accomplished by English arms. Unquestionably Burgundy was the first to enter upon the struggle, but the terrible vengeance taken by the Armagnacs, —as the Orleanists came to be called, —for the murders committed by the mob of Paris in alliance with him, was of almost unexampled atrocity in civil war, and was mainly responsible for the terrible acts of cruelty afterwards perpetrated upon each other by both parties. I hope some day to devote another volume to the story of this desperate and unnatural struggle.

G. A. HENTY.

Chapter I
A Feudal Castle

"And is it true that our lord and lady sail next week for their estate in France?"

"Ay, it is true enough, and more is the pity; it was a sad day for us all when the king gave the hand of his ward, our lady, to this baron of Artois."

"They say she was willing enough, Peter."

"Ay, ay, all say she loved him, and, being a favourite with the queen, she got her to ask the king to accede to the knight's suit; and no wonder, he is as proper a man as eyes can want to look on-tall and stately, and they say brave. His father and grandfather both were Edward's men, and held their castle for us; his father was a great friend of the Black Prince, and he, too, took a wife from England. Since then things have not gone well with us in France, and they say that our lord has had difficulty in keeping clear of the quarrels that are always going on out there between the great French lords; and, seeing that we have but little power in Artois, he has to hold himself discreetly, and to keep aloof as far as he can from the strife there, and bide his time until the king sends an army to win back his own again. But I doubt not that, although our lady's wishes and the queen's favour may have gone some way with him, the king thought more of the advantage of keeping this French noble,—whose fathers have always been faithful vassals of the crown, and who was himself English on his mother's side,—faithful to us, ready for the time when the royal banner will flutter in the wind again, and blood will flow as it did at Cressy and Poitiers.

"The example of a good knight like Sir Eustace taking the field for us with his retainers might lead others to follow his example; besides, there were several suitors for our lady's hand, and, by giving her to this French baron, there would be less offence and heart-burning than if he had chosen one among her English suitors. And, indeed, I know not that we have suffered much from its being so; it is true that our lord and lady live much on their estates abroad, but at least they are here part of their time, and their castellan does not press us more heavily during their absence than does our lord when at home."

"He is a goodly knight, is Sir Aylmer, a just man and kindly, and, being a cousin of our lady's, they do wisely and well in placing all things in his hands during their absence."

"Ay, we have nought to grumble at, for we might have done worse if we had had an English lord for our master, who might have called us into the field when he chose, and have pressed us to the utmost of his rights whenever he needed money."

The speakers were a man and woman, who were standing looking on at a party of men practising at the butts on the village green at Summerley, one of the hamlets on the estates of Sir Eustace de Villeroy, in Hampshire.

"Well shot!" the man exclaimed, as an archer pierced a white wand at a distance of eighty yards. "They are good shots all, and if our lord and lady have fears of troubles in France, they do right well in taking a band of rare archers with them. There are but five-and-twenty of them, but they are all of the best. When they offered prizes here a month since for the bowmen of Hants and Sussex and Dorset, methought they had some good reason why they should give such high prizes as to bring hither the best men from all three counties, and we were all proud that four of our own men should have held their own so well in such company, and especially that Tom, the miller's son, should have beaten the best of them. He is captain of the band, you know, but almost all the others shoot nigh as well; there is not one of them who cannot send an arrow straight into the face of a foe at a hundred and twenty yards. There were some others as good who would fain have been of the party, but our lady said she would take no married men, and she was right. They go for five years certain, and methinks a man fights all the better when he knows there is no one in England praying for his return, and that if he falls, there is no widow or children to bewail his loss. There are as many stout men-at-arms going too; so the Castle of Villeroy will be a hard nut for anyone to crack, for I hear they can put a hundred and fifty of their vassals there in the field."

"We shall miss Sir Aylmer's son Guy," the woman said; "he is ever down at the village green when there are sports going on. There is not one of his age who can send an arrow so straight to the mark, and not many of the men; and he can hold his own with a quarter-staff too."

"Ay, dame; he is a stout lad, and a hearty one. They say that at the castle he is ever practising with arms, and that though scarce sixteen he can wield a sword and heavy battle-axe as well as any man-at-arms there."

"He is gentle too," the woman said. "Since his mother's death he often comes down with wine and other goodies if anyone is ill, and he speaks as softly as a girl. There is not one on the estate but has a good word for him, nor doubts that he will grow up as worthy a knight as his father, though gentler perhaps in his manner, and less grave in face, for he was ever a merry lad. Since the death of his lady mother two years ago he has gone about sadly, still of late he has gotten over his loss somewhat, and he can laugh heartily again. I wonder his father can bear to part with him."

"Sir Eustace knows well enough that he cannot always keep the boy by his side, dame; and that if a falcon is to soar well, he must try his wings early. He goes as page, does he not?"

"Ay, but more, methinks, as companion to young Henry, who has, they say, been sickly from a child, and, though better now, has scarce the making of a stalwart knight in him. His young brother Charles is a sturdy little chap, and bids fair to take after his father; and little Lady Agnes, who comes between them, is full of fire and spirit."

"Yes; methinks Guy will have a pleasant time of it out there; that is, if there are no fresh troubles. I doubt not that in two or three years he will be one of our lord's esquires, and if he has a chance of displaying his courage and skill, may be back among us a dubbed knight before many years have passed over our heads. France is a rare place for gaining honours, and so it may well be, for I see not that we gain much else by our king's possessions there."

"There was plenty of spoil brought over, dame, after Cressy and Poitiers."

"Ay, but it soon goes; easy come, easy go, you know; and though they say that each man that fought there brought home a goodly share of spoil, I will warrant me the best part went down their throats ere many months had passed."

"'Tis ever so, dame; but I agree with you, and deem that it would be better for England if we did not hold a foot of ground in France, and if English kings and nobles were content to live quietly among their people. We have spent more money than ever we made in these wars, and even were our kings to become indeed, as they claim, kings of France as well as England, the ill would be much greater, as far as I can see, for us all. Still there may be things, dame, that we country folks don't understand, and I suppose that it must be so, else Parliament would not be so willing to vote money always when the kings want it for wars with France. The wars in France don't affect us as much as those with Scotland and Wales. When our kings go to France to fight they take with them only such as are willing to go, men-at-arms and archers; but when we have troubles such as took place but five or six years ago, when Douglas and Percy and the Welsh all joined against us, then the lords call out their vassals and the sheriffs the militia of the county, and we have to go to fight willy-nilly. Our lord had a hundred of us with him to fight for the king at Shrewsbury. Nigh thirty never came back again. That is worse than the French wars, dame."

"Don't I know it, for wasn't my second boy one of those who never came back. Ay, ay, they had better be fighting in France, perhaps, for that lets out the hot blood that might otherwise bring on fighting at home."

"That is so, dame, things are all for the best, though one does not always see it."

A week later all the tenantry gathered in front of the castle to wish God-speed to their lord and lady, and to watch the following by which they were accompanied. First there passed half a dozen mounted men-at-arms, who were to accompany the party but half a day's march and then to return with Sir Aylmer. Next to these rode Sir Eustace and Lady Margaret, still a beautiful woman, a worthy mate of her noble-looking husband. On her other side rode Sir Aylmer; then came John Harpen, Sir Eustace's esquire; beside whom trotted Agnes, a bright, merry-faced girl of twelve. Guy rode with the two boys; then came twenty-four men-at-arms, many of whom had fought well and stoutly at Shrewsbury; while Tom, the miller's son, or, as he was generally called, Long Tom, strode along at the head of twenty-four bowmen, each of whom carried the long English bow and quiver full of cloth-yard arrows, and, in addition, a heavy axe at his leathern girdle.

Behind these were some servitors leading horses carrying provisions for the journey, and valises with the clothes of Sir Eustace, his wife, and children, and a heavy cart drawn by four strong horses with the bundles of extra garments for the men-at-arms and archers, and several large sheaves of spare arrows. The men-at-arms wore iron caps, as also breast and back pieces. On the shoulders and arms of their leathern jerkins iron rings were sewn thickly, forming a sort of chain armour, while permitting perfect freedom of the limbs. The archers also wore steel caps, which, like those of the men-at-arms, came low down on the neck and temples. They had on tough leathern frocks, girded in at the waist, and falling to the knee; some of them had also iron rings sewn on the shoulders. English archers were often clad in green cloth, but Sir Eustace had furnished the garments, and had chosen leather, both as being far more durable, and as offering a certain amount of defence.

The frocks were sleeveless, and each man wore cloth sleeves of a colour according to his fancy. The band was in all respects a well-appointed one. As Sir Eustace wished to avoid exciting comment among his neighbours, he had abstained from taking a larger body of men; and it was partly for this reason that he had decided not to dress the archers in green. But every man had been carefully picked; the men-at-arms were all powerful fellows who had seen service; the archers were little inferior in physique, for strength as well as skill was required in archery, and in choosing the men Sir Eustace had, when there was no great difference in point of skill, selected the most powerful among those who were willing to take service with him.

Guy enjoyed the two days' ride to Southampton greatly. It was the first time that he had been away from home, and his spirits were high at thus starting on a career that would, he hoped, bring him fame and honour. Henry and his brother and sister were also in good glee, although the journey was no novelty to them, for they had made it twice previously. Beyond liking change, as was natural at their age, they cared not whether they were at their English or at their French home, as they spoke both languages with equal fluency, and their life at one castle differed but little from that at the other.

Embarking at Portsmouth in a ship that was carrying military stores to Calais, they coasted along the shores of Sussex and of Kent as far as Dungeness, and then made across to Calais. It was early in April, the weather was exceptionally favourable, and they encountered no rough seas whatever. On the way Sir Eustace related to Guy and his sons the events that had taken place in France, and had led up to the civil war that was raging so furiously there.

"In 1392, the King of France being seized with madness, the Dukes of Burgundy and Orleans in a very short time wrested the power of the state from the hands of his faithful councillors, the Constable de Clisson, La Riviere, and others. De Clisson retired to his estate and castle at Montelhery, the two others were seized and thrown into prison. De Clisson was prosecuted before Parliament as a false and wicked traitor; but the king, acting on the advice of Orleans, who had not then broken with the Dukes of Burgundy and Berri, had, after La Riviere and another had been in prison for a year, stopped the prosecution, and restored their estates to them. Until 1402 the Dukes of Burgundy and Berri were all-powerful, and in 1396 a great number of knights and nobles, led by John, Count of Nevers, the eldest son of the Duke of Burgundy, went to the assistance of the King of Hungary, which country was being invaded by the Turks. They were, however, on the 28th of September, utterly defeated. The greater portion of them were killed; Nevers and the rest were ransomed and brought home.

"In 1402 the king, influenced by his wife, Isobel, and his brother, the Duke of Orleans, who were on terms of the closest alliance, placed the entire government in the hands of the latter, who at once began to abuse it to such an extent, by imposing enormous taxes upon the clergy and the people, that he paved the way for the return of his uncle of Burgundy to power. On the

27th of April, 1404, Philip the Bold of Burgundy died. He was undoubtedly ambitious, but he was also valiant and able, and he had the good of France at heart. He was succeeded by his son John, called the Fearless, from the bravery that he had displayed in the unfortunate Hungarian campaign. The change was disastrous for France. John was violent and utterly unscrupulous, and capable of any deed to gratify either his passions, jealousies, or hatreds. At first he cloaked his designs against Orleans by an appearance of friendship, paid him a visit at his castle near Vincennes, where he was at the time lying ill. When he recovered, the two princes went to mass together, dined at their uncle's, the Duke of Berri, and together entered Paris; and the Parisians fondly hoped that there was an end of the rivalry that had done so much harm. It was, however, but a very short time afterwards that, on the 23d of November, 1407, as the Duke of Orleans was returning from having dined with the queen, and was riding with only two esquires and four or five men on foot carrying torches, twenty armed men sprang out from behind a house and rushed upon him.

"'I am the Duke of Orleans,' the prince cried; but they hurled him from his mule, and as he tried to rise to his feet one blow struck off the hand he raised to protect his head, other blows rained down upon him from axe and sword, and in less than a minute the duke lay dead. The Duke of Burgundy at first affected grief and indignation, but at the council the next day he boldly avowed that Orleans had been killed by his orders. He at once took horse and rode to the frontier of Flanders, which he reached safely, though hotly chased by a party of the Duke of Orleans' knights. The duke's widow, who was in the country at the time, hastened up to Paris with her children, and appealed for justice to the king, who declared that he regarded the deed done to his brother as done to himself. The Dukes of Berri and Bourbon, the Constable and Chancellor, all assured her that she should have justice; but there was no force that could hope to cope with that which Burgundy could bring into the field, and when, two months later, Burgundy entered Paris at the head of a thousand men-at-arms, no attempt was made at resistance, and the murderer was received with acclamations by the fickle populace.

"The king at the time was suffering from one of his terrible fits of insanity, but a great assembly was held, at which princes, councillors, lords, doctors of law, and prominent citizens were present. A monk of the Cordeliers, named John Petit, then spoke for five hours in justification of the duke, and the result was that the poor insane king was induced to sign letters cancelling the penalty of the crime. For four months the duke remained absolute master of Paris, disposing of all posts and honours, and sparing no efforts to render himself popular with the burghers. A serious rebellion breaking out at Liege, and the troops sent against the town being repulsed, he was obliged to leave Paris to put down the revolt. As soon as he had left, the queen and the partisans of Orleans prepared to take advantage of his absence, and two months later Queen Isobel marched with the dauphin, now some thirteen years old, from Melun with three thousand men.

"The Parisians received her with applause, and as soon as she had taken up her quarters at the Louvre, the Dukes of Berri, Bourbon, and Brittany, the Constable, and all the great officers of the court rallied round her. Two days later the Duchess of Orleans arrived with a long train of mourning coaches. A great assembly was held, and the king's advocate announced to them the intention of the king to confer the government upon the queen during his illness, and produced a document signed by the king to that effect. The Duchess of Orleans then came forward, and kneeling before the dauphin, begged for justice for the death of her husband, and that she might be granted an opportunity of refuting the calumnies that John Petit had heaped on the memory of her husband. A week later another great assembly was held, and the justification of the duke was read, refuting all these imputations, and the duchess's advocate demanded that the duke should be forced to make public reparation, and then to be exiled for twenty years. The dauphin replied that he and all the princes of blood royal present held that the charges against the Duke of Orleans had been amply refuted, and that the demands with reference to the Duke of Burgundy should be provided for in course of justice.

"Scarcely had the assembly broken up when it became known that Burgundy and his army was on the way back to Paris. Resistance was out of the question; therefore, taking the young dauphin with her, and accompanied by all the members of the royal family, the queen retired to Tours. Burgundy, unscrupulous as he was, finding that although he might remain master of Paris, he could not hope to rule France, except when acting under the pretence of the king's authority, soon sent an embassy to Tours to endeavour to arrange matters. He was able to effect this with the less difficulty, that the Duchess of Orleans had just died from grief at her husband's death, and at the hopelessness of obtaining vengeance on his murderer. The queen was won to the cause of Burgundy by secret proposals submitted to her for a close league between them, and in March a treaty was concluded, and a meeting took place at Chartres, at which the duke, the king, the queen, the royal princes, and the young Duke of Orleans and his adherents were present.

"The king declared that he pardoned the duke, and the princes of Orleans consented to obey his orders and to lay aside all hatred and thoughts of vengeance, and shortly afterwards Paris welcomed with shouts of joy the return of the king and queen and the apparent reconciliation of all parties. But the truce was a brief one; for the princes and adherents of Orleans might bend before circumstances at the moment, but their feelings were unchanged.

"A head of the party was needed, and the young duke married the daughter of Count Bernard d'Armagnac, one of the most powerful and ambitious nobles of the south of France, who at once,—in concert with the Dukes of Berri and Brittany and other lords,—put himself at the head of the Orleans party. On the 10th of July, 1411, the three princes of Orleans sent a long letter to the king, complaining that no reparation whatever had been made for the murder of their father, and begging him that, as what was done at Chartres was contrary to every principle of law, equity, reason, and justice, the case should be reopened again. They also made complaints against the Duke of Burgundy for his conduct and abuse of power.

"As the king was surrounded by Burgundy's creatures no favourable reply was returned, and a formal challenge or declaration of war was, on the 18th of July, sent by the princes to the Duke of Burgundy, and both parties began at once to make preparation for war.

"Now for my own view of this quarrel. King Henry sent for me a year since, and asked for whom I should hold my castle if Orleans and Burgundy came to blows, adding that Burgundy would be viewed by him with most favour.

"'My father and grandfather ever fought faithfully in the service of England,' I said; 'but for years past now, the line betwixt your majesty's possessions and those of France has been drawn in, and my estates and Castle of Villeroy now lie beyond the line, and I am therefore a vassal of France as well as of your majesty. It being known to all men that even before I became Lord of Summerley, on my marriage with your majesty's ward, Mistress Margaret, I, like my father, held myself to be the liege man of the King of England. I am therefore viewed with much hostility by my neighbours, and right gladly would they seize upon any excuse to lay complaint against me before the king, in order that I might be deprived of my fief and castle.

"'This I would fain hold always for your majesty; and, seeing how it is situated but a few miles across the frontier, it is, I would humbly submit to you, of importance to your majesty that it should be held by one faithful to you-since its possession in the hands of an enemy would greatly hinder any English army marching out from Calais to the invasion of France. It is a place of some strength now; but were it in French hands it might be made very much stronger, and would cost much time and loss of men to besiege. At present your majesty is in alliance with Burgundy, but none can say how the war will go, or what changes will take place; and should the Orleanists gain the upper hand, they will be quick to take advantage of my having fought for Burgundy, and would confiscate my estates and hand them over to one who might be hostile to England, and pledged to make the castle a stronghold that would greatly hinder and bar the advance of an English army upon Paris. Therefore, Sire, I would, not for my own sake but for the sake of your majesty's self and your successors, pray you to let me for a while remain quietly at Summerley until the course of events in France is determined.'

"The king was pleased to see the force of what I urged. As far as I had inclinations in the case, they were towards the cause, not of Burgundy himself, whose murder of Orleans was alike treacherous and indefensible, but of his cause, seeing that Flanders is wholly under his authority, and that in Artois he is well-nigh paramount at present. On the other hand, Amiens and Ponthieu, which lie but a short distance to the south of me, are strongly Orleanist, and I have therefore every motive for standing aloof. So far the fortune of war has been so changeable that one cannot say that the chances incline towards one faction more than the other. Even the Church has failed to bring about the end of the troubles. The Orleanists have been formally placed under interdicts, and cursed by book, bell, and candle. The king's commands have been laid upon all to put aside their quarrels, but both the ban of the Church and the king's commands have been ineffectual. I am as anxious as ever to abstain from taking any part in the trouble, the more so as the alliance between our king and Burgundy has cooled somewhat. But I have received such urgent prayers from my vassals at Villeroy to come among them, since they are now being plundered by both parties, that I feel it is time for me to take up my abode there. When the king stayed at Winchester, a month since, I laid the matter before him. He was pleased to say that what I had urged a year ago had turned out to be as I foretold, and that he would give me leave to go over and establish myself at Villeroy, and to hold myself aloof from both parties until the matter should further ripen. What will come of it I cannot say. The English king seemed to me to be ailing, and I fear that it may not be long before young Henry comes to the throne. He is a wild young prince, but has already shown himself in the Northern war to be full of spirit and courage, and methinks that when he comes to the throne he will not long observe the peaceful policy of his father, but that we shall see the royal standard once again spread to the winds of France."

"But, Sir Eustace," Guy said, when he had concluded, "how do these matters affect you? I thought that by the treaty the west part of Artois was English."

"Ay, lad, it was so settled; but at that time the strength of France had been broken at Poitiers, and the Black Prince and his army were so feared that his terms were willingly accepted in order to secure peace. Much has happened since then: war has been constantly going on, sometimes hotly, sometimes sluggishly; France has had her own troubles, and as the English kings have been more pacific, and England has become weary of bearing the heavy expenses of the war, the treaty has become a dead letter. Gascony, in which province Armagnac is the greatest lord, is altogether lost to England, as is the greater part of Guienne. A great proportion of the people there were always bitterly opposed to the change, and, as you know, even in the time of the Black Prince himself there were great rebellions and troubles; since then town after town and castle after castle has declared for France, and no real efforts have ever been made by the English to win them back again. I, who in England am an English baron, and-so long as things go on as at present—a French noble while in France, am in a perilous position between my two Suzerains. Were an English army to land, I should join them, for I still hold myself to be a vassal of the king of England, as we have been for three generations. As to the French disputes, I fear that sooner or later I shall have to declare in favour of one party or the other, for it will be difficult to stand altogether aloof from these conflicts, because all men, at least all men of condition, are well-nigh forced to take one side or the other. The plea that I am a baron of England will be of no avail, for both sides would turn against me and be glad of an excuse for pillaging and confiscating my estate. At present, then, I must regard myself solely as a French noble, for Villeroy has passed into the hands of France, just as for a while it passed into the hands of England, and if this war goes on we shall have to take a side."

"And to which side do your thoughts incline, Sir Eustace, if I may ask you?"

"I love not either side, Guy, and would fain, if it could be so, that my sword should remain in its sheath. I fear that I shall have to go with Burgundy, for he is all-powerful in Artois; but had I been altogether free to choose, I should have sided with Orleans. In the first place, it is certain that the last duke was foully murdered by Burgundy, who thereby laid the foundation for the present troubles. There were jealousies before, as there have always been between the great nobles, but that act forced almost all to take sides. The Dukes of Berri and Brittany, who had been of the party of the late Duke of Burgundy, were driven by this foul act of his son to range themselves with Orleans. Armagnac is very powerful in the south, Berri's dukedom is in the north, that of Orleans to the north-east. Burgundy's strength lies in his own dukedom, — which has ever been all but independent of France, —in Flanders, in Artois, and in Paris; thus, generally, it is the north and east of France against the south and west. This is broadly the case, but in a civil war provinces and countships, neighbours, ay, and families, become split up into factions, as interest, or family ties, or the desire to increase an estate by annexing another next to it, may influence the minds of men.

"So long as it is but a war between the great dukes and princes of France we smaller men may hope to hold aloof, but, as it goes on, and evil deeds are done on both sides, men's passions become heated, the spirit spreads until every man's hand is against his neighbour, and he who joins not against one or the other finds both ready to oppress and rob him. I should not have cared to bring out an English following with me had we been forced to march any distance through France; but as Villeroy is but a few miles from the frontier, and of that distance well-nigh half is through my own estates, we can reach the castle almost unnoticed. Once there, the fact that I have strengthened my garrison will keep me from attack, for either party would be chary in attacking one who can defend himself stoutly. I was minded to leave your lady and the two younger children in England, but in truth she begged so hard to accompany me that I could not say her nay."

The Castle of Villeroy was somewhat larger than the one in which Guy had been born and brought up. The plan, however, was very similar: there was the central keep, but, whereas at home this was the dwelling-house of the family, it was here used as a storehouse, and the apartments of the count and countess were in the range of buildings that formed an inner court round the keep. In point of luxury the French were in advance of the English, and they had already begun to combine comfort with strength in their buildings. The apartments struck Guy as being wonderfully spacious in comparison to those with which he was accustomed. On the ground floor of one side of the square was the banqueting-hall. Its walls were decorated with arms and armour, the joists that supported the floor above were carved, the windows large and spacious, for, looking as they did into the inner court, there was no occasion for their being mere loopholes. Above the banqueting-hall was a room where Lady Margaret sat with her maids engaged in working at tapestry; here the priest gave such slight instruction as was then considered necessary to Agnes and Charles; Henry had already passed out of his hands.

Next to this room was the knight's sleeping apartment, or closet as it was then called, a room which would now be considered of ridiculously straitened dimensions; and close to it were the still smaller closets of the children. Beyond were a series of guest-chambers. Another side of the court-yard contained the apartments of the castellan, Jean Bouvard, a sturdy soldier of long experience, and those of the other officers of the household; the other two sides were occupied by the chapel, the kitchens, and the offices of the servants and retainers. All these rooms were loopholed on the side looking into the outer court. This was considerably wider and more extensive than the one surrounding the keep. Here were the stables, storehouses for grain and forage, and a building, just erected, for the lodging of the English garrison. All these buildings stood against the outer wall, so that they would afford no shelter to an enemy who had obtained possession of the first defences and was making an attack against the second line. The outer wall was twelve feet in thickness, and thirty feet above the court; outside the height was considerably greater, as there was a moat faced with stone fifteen feet deep entirely surrounding it, and containing seven or eight feet of water.

Walls ran half across the outer court, and, from the end of these, light wooden bridges formed a communication with the wall of the inner court, so that in the event of the outer wall being stormed or the gates being carried by assault, the defenders could retire to the inner defences. The ends of these bridges rested upon irons projecting from the wall, and so arranged that they could be instantly withdrawn when the last of the defenders had crossed over, when the bridges would at once fall into the court-yard below. The inner wall was twelve feet higher than the outer one, and, like it, was provided with a crenellated battlement four feet high; there were projecting turrets at each corner, and one in the middle of each side.

The keep rose twenty feet higher than the wall of the inner court. The lower portions of the cross walls of the outer court were carried on as far as the inner wall, thereby dividing the space into four; strong gates gave communication from one to the other. Into these could be driven the cattle of the tenantry, and one of them contained a number of huts in which the tenants themselves would be lodged. The court-yard facing the entrance was the largest of the areas into which the space between the outer and inner walls was divided, extending the whole width between the outer walls. Here the military exercises were carried on. Along the wall, at each side of the gate, were a range of stables for the use of the horses of guests, with rooms over them for the use of their retainers. There was a strong exterior work defending the approach to the drawbridge on the other side of the moat, and in all respects the castle was well appointed, and to Guy it seemed almost impossible that it could be carried by assault, however numerous the foe.

Chapter II
Troubles In France

As soon as it was heard that the lord and lady had returned, the vassals of Villeroy came in to pay their respects, and presents of fowls, game, and provisions of all kinds poured in. The table in the banqueting-hall was bountifully spread, casks of wine broached, and all who came received entertainment. As French was still spoken a good deal at the English court and among the nobles and barons, and was considered part of the necessary education of all persons of gentle blood, Guy, who had always used it in his conversation with his father, had no difficulty in performing his duty of seeing that the wants of all who came were well attended to. In a few days guests of higher degree came in, the knights and barons of that part of the province; a few of these expressed surprise at the height of the sturdy men-at-arms and archers loitering about the court-yard. Sir Eustace always answered any remarks made on the subject by saying, "Yes, Dame Margaret and I thought that instead of keeping all our retainers doing nothing in our castle in England, where there is at present no use whatever for their services, we might as well bring a couple of score of them over here. I have no wish to take part in any of the troubles that seem likely to disturb France, but there is never any saying what may happen, and at any rate it costs no more to feed these men here than in England."

The English archers and men-at-arms were well satisfied with their quarters and food, and were soon on good terms with their French associates. The garrison, before their arrival, had consisted of fifty men-at-arms, and although these had no means of communicating verbally with the new arrivals, they were not long in striking up such acquaintance as could be gained by friendly gestures and the clinking of wine-cups. Their quarters were beside those of the English, and the whole of the men-at-arms daily performed their exercises in the court-yard together, under the command of the castellan, while the archers marched out across the drawbridge and practised shooting at some butts pitched there. To the French men-at-arms their performances appeared astounding. The French had never taken to archery, but the cross-bow was in use among them, and half of the French men-at-arms had been trained in the use of this weapon, which was considered more valuable in the case of sieges than of warfare in the field. While they were able to send their bolts as far as the bowmen could shoot their arrows, there was no comparison whatever in point of accuracy, and the archers could discharge a score of arrows while the cross-bowmen were winding up their weapons.

"*Pardieu*, master page," Jean Bouvard said one day as he stood with Guy watching the shooting of the archers, "I no longer wonder at the way in which you English defeated us at Cressy and Poitiers. I have heard from my father, who fought at Poitiers, how terrible was the rain of arrows that was poured upon our knights when they charged up the hill against the English, but I had never thought that men could shoot with such skill and strength. It was but yesterday that I set my men-at-arms to try and bend one of these English bows, and not one of them could draw an arrow anywhere near the head with all their efforts; while these men seem to do so with the greatest ease, and the speed with which they can shoot off arrow after arrow well-nigh passes belief. That tall fellow, who is their chief, but now sent twenty arrows into a space no greater than a hand's-breadth, at a hundred and twenty yards, and that so quickly that he scarce seemed to take time to aim at all, and the others are well-nigh as skilful. Yesterday I put up a breastplate such as is worn by our men-at-arms and asked them to shoot at it at eighty yards. They fired a volley together at it. It was riddled like a colander; not one of the five-and-twenty arrows had failed to pierce it."

"Ay, at that distance, Captain, an English archer of fair skill could not miss it, and it needs Milan armour, and that of the best, to keep out their arrows."

"By our Lady," the captain remarked, "I should be sorry to attack a castle defended by them, and our lord has done well indeed to bring them over with him. Your men-at-arms are stalwart fellows. My own men feel well-nigh abashed when they see how these men take up a stone that they themselves can with difficulty lift from the ground, and hurl it twenty yards away; and they whirl their heavy axes round their heads as if they were reeds."

"They are all picked men," Guy said with a laugh. "You must not take it that all Englishmen are of equal strength, though no doubt Sir Eustace could have gathered five hundred as strong had he wished it."

"If that be so," the captain said, "I can well believe that if France and England meet again on a field of battle France shall be beaten as she was before. However, there is one comfort, we shall not be among the defeated; for our lord, and his father and his grandfather before, him, have ever been with England, and Sir Eustace, having an English wife and mother, and being a vassal of the English crown for his estates in England, will assuredly take their part in case of a quarrel. Of course, at present we hold ourselves to be neutrals, and though our lord's leanings towards England give some umbrage to his neighbours, their enmity finds no expression, since for years now there has been no righting to speak of between the two nations. How it will be if Orleans and Burgundy come to blows I know not; but if they do so, methinks our lord will have to declare for one or the other, or he may have both upon him. A man with broad estates, on which many cast covetous eyes, can scarce stand altogether aloof. However, if Villeroy is attacked, methinks that with the following Sir Eustace has brought with him across the sea even Burgundy himself will find that it would cost him so dearly to capture the castle that it were best left alone."

"How about the vassals?"

"They will fight for their lord," Jean Bouvard answered confidently. "You see their fathers and grandfathers fought under the Black Prince, and it is natural that their leanings should be on that side. Then they know that there is no better lord in all Artois than Sir Eustace, and his dame has made herself much beloved among them all. There is no fear that they will disobey our lord's orders whatever they be, and will fight as he bids them, for Orleans or Burgundy, England or France. He has never exercised to the full his rights of seigneur; he has never called upon them for their full quota of work; no man has even been hung on his estate for two generations save for crime committed; no vassal's daughter has ever been carried into the castle. I tell you there is not a man for over fifty miles round who does not envy the vassals of Villeroy, and this would be a happy land indeed were all lords like ours. Were we to hoist the flag on the keep and fire a gun, every man on the estate would muster here before sunset, and would march against the King of France himself did Sir Eustace order them to do so."

"In that case what force could we put on the walls, Captain?"

"Two hundred men besides the garrison, and we have provisions stored away in the keep sufficient for them and their women and children for a three months' siege. Sir Eustace gave me orders yesterday to procure wood of the kind used for arrows, and to lay in a great store of it; also to set the smiths to work to make arrow-heads. I asked him how many, and he said, 'Let them go on at it until further orders. I should like a store sufficient at least for a hundred rounds for each of these English archers, and if we had double that it would be all the better. They can make their own arrows if they have suitable wood.' It seemed to me that two hundred rounds was beyond all necessity, but now when I see that these men can shoot nigh twenty rounds a minute, I can well understand that a great supply for them is needful."

The time passed very pleasantly at Villeroy. Sometimes Guy rode with his lord and lady when they went out hawking or paid visits to neighbouring castles. Regularly every day they practised for two hours in arms, and although well instructed before, Guy gained much additional skill from the teaching of Jean Bouvard, who was a famous swordsman. The latter was surprised at finding that the page was able to draw the English bows as well as the archers, and that, although inferior to Long Tom and three or four of the best shots, he was quite as good a marksman as the majority. Moreover, though of gentle blood he would join with the men in their bouts of quarter-staff, and took no more heed of a broken head than they did.

"*Pardieu*, master page," he said one day when Guy came in from the court-yard to have his head, which was streaming with blood, bound up, "our French pages would marvel indeed if they saw you. They all practise in arms as you do, save with the shooting; but they would consider it would demean them sorely to join in such rough sports with their inferiors, or to run the risk of getting their beauty spoiled by a rough blow. No wonder your knights strike so mightily in battle when they are accustomed to strike so heavily in sport. I saw one of your men-at-arms yesterday bury his axe to the very head in a block of oak; he wagered a stoup of wine that no two of my men-at-arms would get the axe out, and he won fairly, for indeed it took four of the knaves at the handle to tug it out, and then indeed it needed all their strength. No armour ever forged could have withstood such a blow; it would have cracked both the casque and the skull inside like egg-shells. It seemed to me that a thousand such men, with as many archers, could march through France from end to end, if they kept well together, and were well supplied with meat and drink by the way-they would need that, for they are as good trenchermen as they are fighters, and indeed each man amongst them eats as much as three of my fellows."

"Yes, they want to be well fed," Guy laughed, "and they are rarely pleased with the provision that you make for them; surely not one of them ever fed so well before."

"Food does not cost much," the captain said; "we have herds of our own which run half wild on the low ground near the river, which our lords always keep in hand for their own uses, and they multiply so fast that they are all the better for thinning; we sell a few occasionally, but they are so wild that it scarce pays the trouble of driving them to the nearest market, and we are always ready to grant permission to any of the vassals, whose cattle have not done as well as usual, to go out and kill one or two for meat."

"I hear from the Governor of Calais," Sir Eustace said, when he returned from a visit to that town, "that a truce has been agreed upon between England and France for a year; it is France who asked for it, I suppose. Both parties here wanted to be able to fight it out without interference. Here, in Artois, where the Burgundians are most numerous, they will profit, as they will have no fear of England trying to regain some of her lost territory, while in the south it will leave Armagnac and his friends equally free from English incursions from Guienne."

"And how will it affect us, Eustace?" his wife asked.

"That I have not been able fully to determine. At any rate they will have no excuse for attacking us upon the ground that we are partly English, and wholly so in feeling; but upon the other hand, if we are attacked either by Burgundians or Orleanists, we cannot hope, as we should have done before, for aid from Calais, lying as we do some fifteen miles beyond the frontier. Amiens has already declared for Burgundy, in spite of the fact that a royal proclamation has been issued, and sent to every town and bailiwick through France, strictly commanding all persons whatsoever not to interfere, or in any manner to assist the Dukes of Orleans or Burgundy in their quarrels with each other. I hear that the Duke of Burgundy has seized Roye, Nesle, and Ham, and a number of other places, and that both parties are fortifying all their towns. They say, too, that there is news that the king has again been seized with one of his fits of madness. However, that matters little. He has of late been a tool in the hands of Burgundy, and the royal signature has no weight one way or the other. However, now that hostilities have begun, we must lose no time, for at any moment one party or the other may make a sudden attack upon us. Burgundy and Orleans may quarrel, but it is not for love of one or the other that most of the nobles will join in the fray, but merely because it offers them an opportunity for pillaging and plundering, and for paying off old scores against neighbours. Guy, bid John Harpen come hither."

When the esquire entered, Sir Eustace went on:

"Take two men-at-arms, John, and ride round to all the tenants. Warn them that there are plundering bands about, and that either the Burgundians or the Orleanists may swoop down upon us any day. Tell them that they had better send in here all their valuables, and at any rate the best of their cattle and horses, and to have everything prepared for bringing in their wives and families and the rest of their herds at a moment's notice. You can say that if they like they can at once send their wives and families in, with such store of grain and forage as they can transport; the more the better. If the plunderers come, so much the more is saved from destruction; if we are besieged, so much the more food have we here. Those who do not send in their families would do well to keep a cart with two strong horses ready day and night, so that no time would be lost when they get the signal. We shall fire a gun, hoist the flag, and light a bonfire on the keep, so that they may see the smoke by day or the fire by night. Tell Jean Bouvard to come to me."

"There is trouble afoot, Jean, and at any moment we may be attacked. Place two men-at-arms on each of the roads to St. Omer, St. Pol, and Bethune. Post them yourself at the highest points you can find near our boundary. By each have a pile of faggots, well smeared with pitch, and have another pile ready on the keep, and a watch always stationed there. He is to light it at once when he sees smoke or fire from either of the three points. Let the men at the outposts be relieved every four hours. They must, of course, be mounted. Let one of the two remain by the faggots, and let the other ride three or four miles in advance, and so post himself as to see a long distance down the road.

"If he sees a force advancing he must gallop back at full speed to his comrade, and light the fire. Have a gun always loaded on the keep, and have a brazier burning hard by, with an iron in it, so that the piece may be fired the instant smoke is seen. It might be two or three minutes before the beacon would give out smoke enough to be noticed, and every minute may be of the greatest importance to the vassals. As soon as you return from setting the posts see that everything is in readiness here. I myself will make sure that the drawbridge works easily and the portcullis runs freely in its groove. I have already sent off John Harpen to warn the tenants, and doubtless many of them will be in this afternoon. Send Pierre with four men, and tell them to drive up a number of the cattle from the marshes. They need not trouble to hunt them all up today. Let them bring the principal herd, the others we will fetch in to-morrow, or let them range where they are until we have further news."

In a few minutes the castle resounded with the din of preparations under the superintendence of Sir Eustace. The men-at-arms and archers carried up stones from the great pile that had been collected in the court-yard in readiness, to the various points on the walls that would be most exposed to assault. Others were employed in fixing barricades in the court-yard at the rear for the reception of the herd of half-wild cattle. The water was turned from the little rivulet running down to the Somme into the moat. Two or three bullocks were killed to furnish food for the fugitives who might come in, and straw was laid down thickly in the sheds that would be occupied by them. Machines for casting heavy stones were taken from the storehouse and carried up to the walls, and set up there. Large stone troughs placed in the court-yard were filled with water, and before nightfall everything was in readiness.

As Sir Eustace had anticipated, most of the vassals whose farms lay at a distance from the castle came in with their wives and families in the course of the afternoon, bringing carts laden with their household goods, and a considerable number of horses and cattle. Lady Margaret herself saw that they were established as comfortably as possible in the sheds, which were large enough to contain all the women and children on the estate. As for the men, no such provision was necessary, as at this time of the year they could sleep in the open air. Guy was busy all day seeing that the orders of his lord were carried out, and especially watching the operations of putting the ballistas and catapults together on the walls. Cannon, though now in use, had by no means superseded these machines, for they were cumbrous and clumsy, and could only be fired at considerable intervals, and their aim was by no means accurate or their range extensive, as the charge of powder that could be used in them was comparatively small, and the powder itself ill-made and defective in strength.

Guy was struck with the difference of demeanour between the men-at-arms and archers, especially among the English contingent, and that of the fugitives who poured in. What was a terrible blow to the latter was the cause of a scarce concealed gratification among the former. The two months that had been spent at the castle had, to the English, been a somewhat monotonous time, and the prospect of active service and of the giving and taking of blows made their blood course more rapidly through their veins. It was the prospect of fighting rather than of pay that had attracted them to the service of Sir Eustace. Then, as for a century previous and until quite modern days, Frenchmen were regarded as the natural foes of England, and however large a force an English king wished to collect for service in France, he had never any difficulty whatever in obtaining the number he asked for, and they were ready cheerfully to give battle whatever the odds against them. The English archer's confidence in himself and his skill was indeed supreme. Before the shafts of his forefathers the flower of the French chivalry had gone down like rushes before a scythe, and from being a mere accessory to a battle the English archers had become the backbone of the force. Their skill, in fact, had revolutionized warfare, had broken the power of cavalry, and had added to the dignity and value of infantry, who had become, as they have ever since continued to be, the prime factor in warfare. Consequently the English archers and men-at-arms went about their work of preparation with a zest and cheerfulness that showed their satisfaction in it.

"Why, Tom," Guy said to the tall leader of the archers, "you look as pleased as if it were a feast rather than a fray for which you were preparing."

"And so I feel, Master Guy. For what have I been practising with the bow since I was eight years old but that I might, when the time came, send an arrow straight through the bars of a French vizor? In faith, I began to think that I should never have an opportunity of exercising my skill on anything more worthy than a target or peeled wand. Since our kings have given up leading armies across the sea, there was no way but to take service with our lord when I heard that he wanted a small company of archers for the defence of his castle over here, and since we have come it has seemed to us all that we were taking pay and food under false pretences, and that we might as well have stopped at home where, at least, we can compete in all honour and good temper against men as good as ourselves, and with the certainty of winning a few silver pennies, to say nothing of plaudits from the onlookers. 'Tis with our people as with the knights of old; if they win in a tournament they take the armour of the vanquished, the prize from the Queen of Beauty, and many a glance of admiration from bright eyes. It is the same with us; for there is not an English maid but would choose an archer who stands straight and firm, and can carry off a prize when in good company, to a hind who thinks of naught but delving the soil and tending the herd."

Guy laughed. "I suppose it is the same, when you put it so, Long Tom; but there will be none of your English maids to watch your prowess here."

"No, Master Guy; but here we shall fight for our own satisfaction, and prove to ourselves that we are as good men as our fathers were. I know naught of this quarrel. Had Sir Eustace taken us into the field to fight for one or other of these factions concerning which we know nothing, we should doubtless have done our duty and fought manfully. But we are all glad that here we are doing what we came for; we are going to defend the castle against Frenchmen of some sort or other who would do ill to our lord and lady, and we shall fight right heartily and joyfully, and should still do so were it the mad king of France himself who marched against us. Besides, master, we should be less than men if we did not feel for the frightened women and children who, having done no wrong, and caring naught for these factions, are forced to flee from their homes for their lives; so we shall strike in just as we should strike in were we to come upon a band of robbers ill-treating a woman at home.... Think you that they will come, master?" he added eagerly.

"That I cannot say surely, Tom; but Sir Eustace has news that the Burgundians have already seized several towns and placed garrisons there, and that armed bands are traversing the country, burning and pillaging. Whether they will feel strong enough to make an attack on this castle I know not, but belike they will do so, for Sir Eustace, belonging as he does, and as his fathers have done before him, to the English party, neither of the others will feel any good-will towards him, and some of his neighbours may well be glad to take advantage of this troubled time to endeavour to despoil him of his castle and possessions."

"They will want to have good teeth to crack this nut, Master Guy-good teeth and strong; and methinks that those who come to pluck the feathers may well go back without their own.

We have a rare store of shafts ready, and they will find that their cross-bowmen are of little use against picked English archers, even though there be but twenty-five of us in all."

"You know very well, Long Tom, that you would have come over here whether there was any chance of your drawing your bow on a Frenchman or not."

"That is true enough, Master Guy. Our lady wanted some bowmen, and I, who have been born and bred on the estate, was of course bound to go with her. Then you see, Master Guy, haven't I taught you to use the bow and the quarter-staff, and carried you on my shoulder many a score of times when you were a little lad and I was a big boy? It would not have been natural for you to have gone out with a chance of getting into a fight without my being there to draw a shaft when you needed it. Why, Ruth Gregory, whose sworn bachelor you know I am, would have cried shame on me if I had lingered behind. I told her that if I stayed it would be for her sake, and you should have seen how she flouted me, saying that she would have no tall lout hiding behind her petticoats, and that if I stayed, it should not be as her man. And now I must be off to my supper, or I shall find that there is not a morsel left for me."

The gates of the castle were closed that night, but it was not considered necessary to lower the drawbridge. Two sentries were posted at the work beyond the moat, and one above the gate, besides the watcher at the top of the keep. The next day things were got into better order. More barricades were erected for the separation of the cattle; a portion was set aside for horses. The provisions brought in from the farms were stored away in the magazines. The women and children began to settle down more comfortably in their sheds. The best of the horses and cattle were removed into the inner court-yard. The boys were set drawing water and filling the troughs, while some of the farm men were told off to carry the fodder to the animals, most of which, however, were for the time turned out to graze near the castle. Many of the men who had come in had returned to their work on the farms. During the day waggons continued to arrive with stores of grain and forage; boys and girls drove in flocks of geese and turkeys and large numbers of ducks and hens, until the yard in which the sheds were was crowded with them. By nightfall every preparation was complete, and even Jean Bouvard himself could find nothing further to suggest.

"If they are coming," he said to Sir Eustace, "the sooner they come the better, my lord; we have done all that we can do, and had best get it over without more ado."

"I still hope that no one will come, Bouvard, but I agree with you, that if it is to come the sooner the better. But there is no saying, it may be to-morrow, it may be months before we are disturbed. Still, in a war like this, it is likely that all will try and get as much as they can as quickly as possible, for at any moment it may suit Burgundy and Orleans to patch up their quarrel again. Burgundy is astute and cunning, and if he sees that the Orleans princes with Armagnac and the Duke of Bourbon are likely to get the best of it, he will use the king and queen to intervene and stop the fighting. Seeing that this may be so, the rogues who have their eye on their neighbours' goods and possessions will, you may be sure, lose no time in stretching out their hands for them."

A week later came the news that Sir Clugnet de Brabant, who styled himself Admiral of France, had gathered two thousand men from the Orleanist garrisons and, with scaling-ladders and other warlike machines, had attacked the town of Rethel. The inhabitants had, however, notice of their coming, and resisted so stoutly that the Orleanists had been forced to retreat, and had then divided into two parties, each of whom had scoured the country, making prisoners all whom they met, firing the villages and driving off the cattle, and then returned to the town of Ham and to the various garrisons from which they had been drawn. Some of the tenants had returned to their farms, but when the news spread they again took refuge in the castle. It was probable that Artois, where almost all the towns were held by the Burgundian party, would be the next object of attack. The Orleanists remained quiet for eight days only, then the news came that they had moved out again from Ham eight thousand strong, and were marching west.

Two days later several fugitives from the country round arrived at the castle with news that the Orleanists were advancing against Bapaume, and the next morning they heard that they had, after a fierce fight, won their way to the gate of the town. The Burgundian garrison had then sallied out and at first met with success, but had been obliged to retreat within the walls again. The Orleanists, however, considering the place too strong to be captured without a long siege, which might be interrupted by a Burgundian force from Flanders, had drawn off from the place, but were still marching north burning and plundering.

"It is likely enough that they will come this way," Sir Eustace said as he and Jean Bouvard talked the matter over. "Assuredly Arras will be too strong for them to attempt. The straight line would take them to St. Pol, but the castle there is a very strong one also. They may sack and burn Avesne and Auvigni, and then, avoiding both St. Pol and Arras, march between them to Pernes, which is large enough to give them much plunder, but has no force that could resist them. As Pernes is but four miles away, their next call may be here."

"But why should they attack us, Sir Eustace? for here, too, they might reckon upon more hard blows than plunder."

"It will depend upon whom they have with them," Sir Eustace replied. "They say that our neighbour Hugh de Fruges went south ten days ago to join the Duke of Bourbon; his castle is but a small place, and as most of Artois is Burgundian he might be afraid he might be captured. He has never borne me good-will, and might well persuade the duke that were my castle and estates in his possession he might do good service to the cause; and that, moreover, standing as we do within twelve miles of the English frontier, its possession might be very valuable to him should the Orleanists ever have occasion to call in the aid of England, or to oppose their advance should the Burgundians take that step."

"Surely neither of these factions will do that, Sir Eustace."

"Why not, Bouvard? Every time that English armies have passed into France they have done it at the invitation of French nobles who have embroiled themselves with their kings. Burgundy and Orleans, Bourbon and Brittany, each fights for his own hand, and cares little for France as a whole. They may be vassals of the Valois, but they regard themselves as being nearly, if not altogether, their equals, and are always ready to league themselves with each other, or if it needs be with the English, against the throne."

At nine o'clock on the following evening Sir Eustace and his family were startled by the report of the gun on the keep, and, running out, saw the signal-fire beginning to blaze up.

"Above there!" Sir Eustace shouted, "where is the alarm?"

"A fire has just blazed up on the road to St. Pol," the warder replied.

"Blow your horn, then, loudly and urgently."

The news that the Orleanists were marching north from Bapaume had caused the greater portion of the farmers to come in on the previous day, and in a short time those who were nearest to the castle, and who had consequently delayed as long as possible, began to arrive. The garrison were already under arms, and had taken the places assigned to them on the walls. All the tenants had brought their arms in with them, and were now drawn up in the court-yard, where a large bonfire, that had been for some days in readiness, was now blazing. The new-comers, after turning their horses into the inclosure with those already there, joined them. All had been acquainted with the share they were to bear should the place be besieged. They were to be divided into two parties, one of which was to be on duty on the walls with the garrison, the other to be held in reserve, and was-every six hours when matters were quiet-to relieve the party on the walls, or, when an attack took place, to be under arms and ready to hasten to any spot where its aid was required. The men were now inspected by Sir Eustace, additional arms were served out from the armoury to those whose equipment was insufficient, and they were then dismissed to join their wives and families until called to the walls.

Chapter III
A Siege

The two men who had lit the alarm fires had already ridden in. They reported that they had, just as it became dark, seen flames rising from a village three miles from them, and that the man in advance had ridden forward until near enough to see that a great body of men were issuing from the village in the direction of the castle.

Ten of the English men-at-arms, and as many French, were now posted in the outwork at the head of the drawbridge under the command of Jean Bouvard. Sir Eustace placed himself with his squire on the wall above the gate, and four men were stationed at the chains of the drawbridge in readiness to hoist it should the order be given. The English archers were on the wall beside Sir Eustace, as their arrows commanded the ground beyond the outwork. Half an hour after the first alarm was given the tale of the tenants was found to be complete, and the guards on the other two roads had also ridden in. Guy, to his great satisfaction, had been ordered by Sir Eustace to don his armour and to take his place beside him.

It was upwards of an hour before a body of horsemen could be heard approaching. They came at a leisurely pace, for the bonfire on the road and that on the keep had apprised them that their hope of taking the castle by surprise had been frustrated by the disobedience of some of their men, who, in defiance of the strictest orders to the contrary, had set fire to several houses in the village after having plundered them. Sir Eustace, accompanied by his esquire and Guy, descended from the wall and crossed the drawbridge to the outwork. As soon as the horsemen came within bow-shot of the castle they lighted some torches, and three knights, preceded by a trooper carrying a white flag, and two others with torches, came towards the work. When within fifty yards of the postern they halted.

"Is Sieur Eustace de Villeroy present?"

"I am here," Sir Eustace replied, and at his order two men with torches took their place one on each side of him. "Who are you that approach my castle in armed force?"

"I am Sir Clugnet de Brabant, Admiral of France. These are Sir Manessier Guieret and Sir Hugh de Fruges, and we come in the name of the Duke of Orleans to summon you to admit a garrison of his highness's troops."

"I am neither for Orleans nor for Burgundy," Sir Eustace replied. "I am a simple knight, holding my castle and estate as a vassal of the crown, and am ready to obey the orders of the king,—and of him only when he is in a condition of mind to give such orders. Until then I shall hold my castle, and will admit no garrison whether of Orleans or of Burgundy."

"We hold you to be but a false vassal of the crown, and we are told that at heart you are an enemy to France and devoted to England."

"I am a vassal of England for the estates of my wife in that country," Sir Eustace said; "and as at present there is a truce between the two nations, I can serve here the King of France as faithfully as if, in England, I should serve the King of England."

"Nevertheless, Sir Eustace, you will have to receive a garrison of Orleans. I have at my back eight thousand men, and if you compel me to storm this hold of yours I warn you that all within its walls will be put to the sword."

"Thanks for your warning, Sir Knight; and I on my part warn you that, eight thousand though you be, I shall resist you to the death, and that you will not carry eight thousand away. As for Sir Hugh de Fruges, I give him my open defiance. I know it is to him that I owe this raid; and if he be man enough, I challenge him to meet me in the morning on fair ground outside this postern, with lance and battle-axe, to fight to the death. If he conquers, my castle shall be surrendered to him, upon promise of good treatment and a safe-conduct to depart where they will for all within it; but if I slay him, you must give me your knightly oath that you and your following will depart forthwith."

"The conditions would be hardly fair, Sir Eustace," Sir Clugnet said; "and though I doubt not that Sir Hugh would gladly accept them, I cannot permit him to do so. I have brought some eight thousand men here to capture this castle, and hold it for the Duke of Orleans, and I see not why I should march away with them because you may perchance prove a better fighter than Sir Hugh. I am ready, however, to give a safe-conduct to all within the walls if you will surrender."

"That will I not do, Sir Clugnet. I hold this castle neither for Burgundy nor Orleans, and am ready to give pledge that I will not draw sword for either of these princes; but if that will not content you, you must even take my castle if you can, and I give you fair warning that it will cost you dear."

"Then adieu, Sir Knight, until to-morrow morning, when we will talk in other fashion."

"So be it," Sir Eustace replied, "you will not find me backward in returning any courtesies you may pay me."

The knights turned away with their torch-bearers.

"Keep a close watch to-night, Bouvard," Sir Eustace said. "Mark you what the knight said, — adieu till the morning. Had I to deal with a loyal gentleman I could have slept soundly, but with these adventurers it is different. It may be that he truly does not intend to attack till morning, but it is more likely that he used the words in order to throw us off our guard."

"We will keep close ward, Sir Eustace. All the men-at-arms have their cross-bows, and though I say not that they can shoot like these English archers, they can shoot straight enough to do good work should those fellows attempt in force to cross the small moat and attack the gate. But if they come, methinks it will be but to try if we are wakeful; 'tis no light thing to attack even an outwork like this, with this loop from the moat surrounding it, without previous examination of the ground and reconnoitring of the castle."

"They would not attempt to attack the fortress itself," Sir Eustace said; "but if they could seize this outwork by surprise it would mightily aid them in their attack on the fortress; at any rate I will send down five archers, and if any of the enemy crawl up to see how wide the water is here, and how the attempt had best be made, I warrant that they will not return if the archers can but get a sight of them. Post half your men on the wall, and let the others sleep; change them every two hours-we want no sleepy heads in the morning."

By this time the confused sound of a large number of men marching could be made out, and a quarter of an hour later three or four cottages, some five hundred yards away, were fired, and an angry murmur broke from the men as the flames shot up. After sending down the five archers, Sir Eustace returned to his post over the main gate.

"Get cressets and torches in readiness to light if they attack the postern," Sir Eustace said; "we must have light to see how things go, so that we may hoist the drawbridge as soon as our men are upon it, should the enemy get the better of them. Be sure that one is not left behind; it were better that half a dozen of the enemy set foot on the drawbridge than that one of our brave fellows should be sacrificed."

"I should think that there is no fear of their attacking until those flames have burnt down; we should see them against the light," John Harpen said.

"No, there is no fear of their attacking; but the fire would be of advantage if any men were crawling up to spy. Of course they would not cross the slope in a line with the fire, but would work along on either side, reckoning, and with reason, that as our men would have the light in their eyes they would be all the less likely to make out objects crawling along in the shade by the side of the moat. Plant half a dozen bowmen at intervals on the wall, Tom, and tell them to keep a shrewd eye on the ground near the moat, and if they see aught moving there to try it with an arrow."

> There was shouting and noise up by the burning cottages, where the enemy were feasting on the spoils they had taken, and drinking from the wine-barrels that had been brought with them in carts from the last village that they had plundered.
> "I wish we were somewhat stronger, or they somewhat weaker," Sir Eustace said;
>
> "were it so, we would make a sally, and give the knaves a sharp lesson, but with only two hundred men against their eight thousand it would be madness to try it; we

might slay a good many, but might lose a score before we were back in the castle, and it would be a heavy loss to us."

"I was thinking that myself, Sir Eustace," his esquire said. "That is the worst of being on the defence; one sees such chances but cannot avail one's self of them."

In the castle everything was quiet, and all those not on duty were already asleep. Along the wall watchers stood at short intervals peering into the darkness, but the main body there were also stretched on the wall with their arms by their side until required to be up and doing. Now that Sir Eustace was himself at the gate his esquire went round the walls at short intervals to be sure that the men on watch were vigilant. Presently a loud cry was heard from the corner of the moat away to the right.

"Go and see what is doing, Guy," Sir Eustace said, "and bring me news."

Guy ran along to the angle of the wall. Here one of the archers was posted.

"What is it, Dickon?"

"A man crept up to that corner opposite, Master Guy. I could not have sworn to him, it is so pesky dark, but I thought there was something moving there and shot almost at a venture, for I could scarce see the end of my arrow; but it hit there or thereabouts, for I heard him shout. A moment later he was on his feet and running. I could see him more plainly then, so I shot again, and over he went. I fancy that in the morning you will see my arrow sticking up somewhere between his shoulder-blades, though there is no saying precisely, for a nicety of shooting is not to be looked for in the dark."

"You have done very well, Dickon. Keep your eyes open; we may be sure there are more than one of these fellows about."

Guy hurried back with the news.

"That is good," said Sir Eustace, "and it was just as well that the archer did not kill him outright with his first arrow, the cry will show any of his comrades who may be about that they had best keep their distance from the walls."

A minute's silence followed, and then Long Tom said, "There is another has had his lesson, Sir Eustace. I heard a bow twang across there, and as there was no cry you may be sure that the shaft sped straight, and that the man had no time to utter one."

"He may have been missed altogether, Tom."

"Missed altogether! no indeed, Sir Eustace, there is no fear of that. There is not one of the men on the wall who would miss a man whose figure he could make out at fifty yards' distance, and they would scarce see them until they were as close as that. No, my lord, I would wager a month's pay that when morning dawns there is a dead man lying somewhere in front of the outwork."

"Now, Guy, you had best go up to your room and lie down until daylight," Sir Eustace said. "There will be naught doing to-night, and unless I am mistaken, we shall be busy from sunrise till sunset. I shall myself lie down for a couple of hours presently, and then send John Harpen to rest till daylight. Long Tom, see that you yourself and all your men take a short sleep by turns; we shall need your eyes to be open above all others to-morrow."

Guy promptly obeyed the order. Dame Margaret was still up.

"Is everything quiet, Guy?" she asked as she entered,

"So quiet, my lady, that Sir Eustace has ordered me to bed, and he said that he himself should come down for a short sleep presently. Two spies who crawled up have been slain by the archers. Sir Eustace is sure that no attack will be made before morning."

Then he went into his little room and threw himself onto his pallet. During the first few minutes he lifted his head several times fancying that he heard noises; then he fell into a sound sleep and did not awake until the day dawned.

In a few minutes Guy was on the wall. The night had passed quietly; so far as was known no fresh attempt at reconnoitring the works had been made, and as the moon had risen soon after he had gone to bed there was reason to believe that the fact that the two spies had not returned was so strong a proof of the vigilance of the garrison, that the enemy had been content to wait until morning. Just as the sun rose the three knights who had summoned the castle on the preceding evening appeared on the brow of the opposite slope, accompanied by a body of men-at-arms, and rode slowly round the castle. From time to time they halted, and were evidently engaged in a discussion as to the point at which it could be best attacked.

"Shall I shoot, my lord?" Long Tom asked. "They are some two hundred and fifty yards away, but from this height methinks that I could reach them."

"It would be useless," Sir Eustace said; "you could hit them, I doubt not, but you would not pierce their armour at this distance, and it is as well that they should not know how far our bows will carry until we are sure of doing execution when we shoot; besides I would rather that they began the fight. The quarrel is not one of my seeking, and I will leave it to them to open the ball. It is true that they did so last night by sending their spies here, but we have balanced that account. Moreover, if they are to attack, the sooner the better. They may have gained news from Sir Hugh of the coming here of the English archers and the men-at-arms, but if they have not done so we shall have a rare surprise in store for them."

After the knights had made a circuit of the castle they retired, and presently a dense mass of men appeared from behind the brow on which the cottages they had burned had stood.

"They have bundles of faggots, Sir Eustace!" Guy exclaimed.

"So they have, Guy! Your eye is a good one. It seemed to me that the outline was a strange one, but doubtless it is as you say-that each man has a faggot on his shoulder. It is evident that they intend, in the first place, to assault the postern, and have brought the faggots to fill up the ditch."

Then he turned to the gunners at the cannon.

"Lay your pieces so as to bear on them when they come half-way down the hill," he said, "and shoot when they are fairly in the line of fire. Take the same orders, Guy, to the men working the ballistas and mangonels on the wall. Tell them not to loose their machines until after the guns are fired. If the fellows take to flight, tell them not to waste their missiles; if they advance, let them be sure that they are well within range before they shoot."

With loud shouts the enemy came down the slope. When they were half-way down the two guns roared out, and their shot ploughed two lanes in the crowded body. There was a movement of retreat, but the three knights and several others threw themselves in front, waving their swords and shouting, and the Orleanists rallied and moved forward, but at a much slower pace than before. They had gone but a short distance when the arrows of the archers in the outwork and the bolts of the cross-bows worked by the men-at-arms there, began to fall among them. So true was the aim of the archers that scarce a shaft was wasted. At the distance at which they were shooting they did not aim at the knights, whose vizors and coats of mail could not have been pierced, but shot at the commonalty, whose faces and throats were for the most part unprotected. Man after man fell, and the cross-bow bolts also told heavily upon the crowd. They had come down but a short distance farther when Long Tom, and the archers with him on the wall, began to send their arrows thick and fast, and the machines hurled heavy stones with tremendous force among them. A moment later the French broke and fled up the slope again, leaving some fifty of their number stretched on the ground. The knights followed more slowly. When they reached the crest a group of them gathered around Sir Clugnet de Brabant.

"By my faith," the latter said bitterly, "we have reckoned without our host, Sir Knights. We came to shear, but in good sooth we seem more likely to go back shorn. Truly those knaves shoot marvellously; scarce an arrow went astray."

"As I mentioned to you, Sir Clugnet," Sir Hugh de Fruges said, "Sir Eustace brought with him from England five-and-twenty bowmen, and I heard tell from men who had seen them trying their skill at targets that they were in no wise inferior to those with whom we have before had to deal to our cost."

"Truly ye did so, Sir Hugh; but the matter made no impression upon my mind, except as a proof that the knight's inclinations were still with England, and that it were well that his castle were placed in better keeping; but in truth these fellows shoot marvellously, both for strength and trueness of aim. I marked as we came back that of the men we passed lying there, nigh all those who had been struck with arrows were hit in the face or throat, and yet the distance must have been over a hundred and fifty yards."

"I can answer for the force," one of the others said, "for a shaft struck me fairly on the chest, and hurled me to the ground as if it had been the shock of a lance, and it is well my mail was of the best work of Milan; but nevertheless the arrow broke two of the links; if the distance had been shorter, I doubt not that it would have slain me. Well, what shall we do next, gentlemen? For very shame we cannot with eight thousand men march away having accomplished nothing. The question is, where shall our next attack be delivered?"

"Methinks," another knight said, "we delivered our attack too rashly. Had I known that there were English archers there I should have advised waiting until nightfall, and I think that it would be best to do so now. If we take our fellows up while there is light they will suffer so much from the stings of these wasps that they will soon lose heart. The knaves shoot not only straight and strong, but they shoot so fast that though, as you say, there may be but twenty-five of them, the air seemed full of arrows, and had you told us that there were two hundred archers shooting, I should have thought the estimate a reasonable one."

They stood for some time discussing the best method of attack, and as soon as they had settled upon it the men were told to scatter. Some were to go to the farmhouses, and bring up any hides that might be stored there, and to fetch all the hurdles they could lay hands upon; a portion were to go to the woods and cut timber for making mantlets and cover, while two thousand were to remain under arms in case the garrison should make a sortie.

Within the castle all were in high spirits at the easy repulse of the first attack.

"Sir Clugnet must have learned from Sir Hugh of my having English archers and men-at-arms here," Sir Eustace said to his lieutenant, "and yet he advanced as carelessly and confidently as if he had been attacking a place defended only by fat Flemish burghers; however, he has had his lesson, and as it is said he is a good knight, he will doubtless profit by it, and we shall hear no more of him till after the sun has set. Run up to the top of the keep, Guy, and bring me back news what they are doing."

In a few minutes the lad returned. "There are two or three thousand of them, my lord, drawn up in a body beyond the crest; the rest of them are scattering in various directions."

"That is as I expected," Sir Eustace remarked; "they have gone to prepare materials for a regular attack. It may be delivered to-night, or may be delayed for a day or two; however, we shall be ready for them. Jean Bouvard, do you go round the walls and tell all, save a few as sentries, to retire until the watchman blows his horn to warn us if they seem to be gathering for an attack; and do you, Long Tom, give the same orders to your archers. There is no use wasting the men's strength till the work begins in earnest. If Sir Clugnet is wise he will march away at once. He would need heavy machines and cannon to make a breach in our walls, and even had he an abundance of them it would take him some time to do so. If he tries again, you may be sure that it will be the work of Sir Hugh de Fruges, who has no doubt a lively interest in the matter. He is a clever fellow, and will no doubt do his best to work on the feelings of the other knights by representing that it would be disgraceful for so large a force to abandon the enterprise merely because a first hasty attack, delivered without preparation, had been repulsed. The fact that they have made so careful an examination of the castle would seem in itself to show that they intended to renew the attempt in another form if the first onset failed, and, moreover, the scattering of the force afterwards while the knights still remained with a large body here points in the same direction."

Guy on descending from the keep joined Sir Eustace and his wife in their apartments.

"The lad has borne himself bravely," Sir Eustace said approvingly to his wife; "he was standing beside me when their shot was bringing down the dust round our ears, and he neither started nor flinched, though in truth it was far from pleasant, especially as we had nothing to do but to look on. It may be next time we shall have sterner fighting, and I doubt not that he will bear himself well."

"Could I not come up and carry your messages, father?" Henry asked; "I am not strong like Guy, but I could do that."

"He is too young for it yet, Eustace," Dame Margaret broke in.

"Nay, wife," the knight said gently, "the lad is not too young for such service. There will be little danger in it, for his head will not show over the battlements, and it is well that he should learn to hear without fear the whizz of an arrow or the shock of a great stone from a ballista, the clash of arms, and the shouting of men. As he says, he is not yet strong enough to bear arms, but he will learn to brace his nerves and show a bold front in danger; that is a lesson that cannot be learned too young. Yes, Henry, you shall be my messenger. If they try an assault to-night, you shall put on for the first time the steel cap and breastpiece I had made for you in England; there will be no danger of your being hit by crossbow bolt or arrow, but there may be splinters of stone flying when a missile hits the battlement. Take no arms with you, only your dagger; they would be useless to you, and would hamper your movements in getting past the men on the wall, or in running up and down the steps leading to it. Now you had better lie down; both Guy and myself are going to do so. At sunset, if no alarm comes before, you will be called."

"We must not coddle the boy, Margaret," he said as Guy and Henry went off. "I know that he is not physically strong as yet, and sorry I am that it should be so, but he might exert himself more than he does, and he is apt to think too much of his ailments. I was glad when he volunteered to do something, for it is at least as well that he should be able to stand fire even if he cannot learn the use of arms; moreover, it may be that after once bearing a part in a fray he may incline more warmly to warlike exercises than he has hitherto done; it may rouse in him a spirit which has so far been wanting. I have often thought that it would have been better if Agnes had been the boy and he the girl; she has far more courage and fire than he has. You remember when that savage bull chased them, how she saw him first over the stile and got tossed over after him for her pains?"

Dame Margaret nodded. "I am not likely to forget it, Eustace, seeing that her arm was broken and I had to nurse her for six weeks. Do you know that she was up on the top of the keep while the fighting was going on? Of course I was there myself, and she begged so hard to be allowed to remain with me that I had not the heart to say her nay."

"Was Henry there too?"

"Oh, yes; and shouted with the best of them when the enemy fled over the hill. Even Charlie was there, and as excited as either of them. Of course, I had to hold him up sometimes for him to be able to see what was going on; and he looked rather pale at first, when they opened fire, but he soon plucked up when he saw that their shot did no damage near us. You see he is a strong healthy boy; while Henry has always been weak, although I do not think that he lacks courage."

"He ought not, wife; he comes from a fighting stock on either side. But I fear that unless he changes greatly he is cut out rather for a monk than a man-at-arms. And now I will lie down, for you may be sure that I shall not close an eye to-night. Did you note the banner of Hugh de Fruges with the others?"

"Yes, and I felt more uncomfortable after seeing it. He is a crafty man, Eustace."

"He is not a brave one," the knight said scornfully. "I challenged him to meet me outside in a fair field, and the craven did not answer me, and Sir Clugnet had to make speech for him and decline the offer."

"You will need all your vigilance, Eustace. I trust that every man within the walls is faithful to us; but if there be a traitor, be sure that Sir Hugh will endeavour to plot with him, nay, he may already have done so."

"They would have no chance of making communication with him were there a dozen of them, wife. Long Tom and his comrades will take good care that none come near enough for speech."

The day passed away in perfect quiet. From time to time word came down from the look-out that the scattered soldiers were returning laden with a great quantity of young trees, wattles, and doors. Dame Margaret kept watch in her room, and allowed no messengers to enter her husband's apartments.

"If there be need, I will wake him," she said; "but he knows well enough what the French have gone for, and there is naught to do until they advance to the attack."

Guy slept but a short time, and as he frequently started up under the impression that the horn was sounding an alarm, in the afternoon he got up and went down into the courtyard. For some time he wandered about in the quarters occupied by the tenants. These had now settled down; the children were playing about as unconcernedly as if they had been on their fathers' farms; women were washing clothes or preparing the evening meal over little charcoal fires. A certain quantity of meat had been served out to each family, and they were therefore doing better than in their own houses, for meat was a luxury seldom touched by the French peasantry.

Almost all who had entered the castle had brought with them a supply of herbs and vegetables; these, with a handful or two of coarsely-ground meal boiled into broth, constituted their usual fare, and the addition of a portion of meat afforded them great satisfaction. Some of the men were still asleep, in preparation for a long night's work; others were standing about talking in little groups; some were on the walls watching with gloomy faces the smoke wreaths that still rose from what had been their homes. Ducks, geese, and hens walked about unconcernedly looking for any stray grains that had passed unnoticed when they had last been fed, and a chorus of dissatisfied grunting arose from the pigs that had a large pen in the yard next to the huts. These were still smarting under a sense of injury excited not only by their removal from their familiar haunts, but by the fact that most of them had been hastily marked by a clipping of some kind in the ear in order to enable their owners to distinguish them from the others. Boys were carrying buckets of water from a well in the court-yard to the troughs for the cattle and horses, and the men-at-arms were cleaning their armour and polishing their steel caps.

"Well, Tom, I hope we shall get on as well to-night as we did this morning," Guy said to the leader of the archers.

"I hope so, Master Guy, but I would rather fight by day than by night; it is random work when you can neither see your mark nor look straight along your arrow. If we had a moon we should do well enough, but on these dark nights skill does not go for much; still, I doubt not that we shall give a good account of ourselves, for at any rate we shall be able to make them out before they come to close work. The women have been making a great store of torches to-day, and that will help us a bit, though I would that they could be planted fifty yards beyond the moat instead of on the walls, for although they will be of some use to us they will be of even more to the enemy. What think you that their plan will be?"

"I should say that they are intending to march forward covered by mantlets of wattles and hides. They will plant them near the edge of the moat, and throw up some earthworks to shelter them and their machines; no doubt they will use the doors they have fetched from all the farmhouses for the same purpose."

"The doors will be more to the point, certainly," the bowman said. "As to their hides and wattles, at fifty yards I will warrant our arrows go through them as if they were paper; but I cannot say as much about stout oaken doors-that is a target that I have never shot against; I fear that the shock would shiver the shafts. The mantlets too would serve them to some purpose, for we should not know exactly where they were standing behind them. As for their machines, they cannot have many of them."

"They had something like a score of waggons with them, Tom; these would carry the beams for half a dozen big ballistas; besides, they have their cannon."

"I don't make much account of the cannon," the archer said; "they take pretty nearly an hour to load and fire them, and at that rate, however hard a shot may hit, it would be some time before they wrought much damage on the walls. It is the sound more than the danger that makes men afraid of the things, and, for my part, I would not take the trouble of dragging them about. They are all very well on the walls of a castle, though I see not that even there they are of great advantage over the old machines. It is true that they shoot further, but that is of no great use. It is when the enemy come to attack that you want to kill them, and at fifty yards I would kill more men with my shafts in ten minutes than a cannon would do with a week's firing. I wonder they trouble to carry them about with them, save that folks are not accustomed to their noise yet, and might open their gates when they see them, while they would make a stout defence if they had only ballistas and mangonels to deal with. I suppose when they have got the shelters close to the moat they will bring up planks to throw across."

"Yes, no doubt they will try that, Tom; but the moat is over wide for planks, and I think it more likely that they will have provided themselves with sacks, and filled them with earth, so as to make a passage across with them."

"As to the planks not being long enough, Master Guy, they could get over that easy enough. They would only have to send three or four swimmers across the moat, then thrust long beams over for those who had crossed to fix firmly, and then lay short planks across them."

"So they would, Tom; I did not think of that. Well, at any rate, I expect they will manage to get across the moat somehow and plant ladders against the wall."

"And we shall chuck them down again," Tom said.

"They won't care much for that. But as long as they cannot knock a breach in the walls I warrant that we can hold them."

Chapter IV
A Fatal Accident

As soon as the sun had set, the defenders gathered on the walls. Fires had already been lighted there and cauldrons of water and pitch suspended over them, and sacks of quicklime placed in readiness to be emptied; great piles of stone were placed at short intervals.

"As long as they attack at only one or two places," Sir Eustace said to his wife, "I am quite confident that we shall repulse them. If they attack at a dozen they may succeed, as we should only have a couple of archers and six or seven men-at-arms at each point, besides a score or so of the vassals. I have no doubt that these will fight stoutly, for the sight of their burning homes has roused them, and each man is longing to get a blow at those who have wrought them so much damage. Still, thirty men are but a small party to beat back an assault by hundreds. However, if they carry the outside wall they will have the second to deal with, and there we shall stand much thicker together, and they cannot attack from many points, while if we are driven into the keep, we shall be stronger still. Have you seen that the women and children are ready to retire into the keep as soon as the assault begins?"

"I have been round myself and given orders," Dame Margaret said. "I have told them that the inner gate will be closed as soon as fighting begins, and that those who do not come in before that must remain outside, or else mount to the walls and cross the bridges, for that on no account will the gates be opened again."

"That is well, Margaret. I am now about to station two men-at-arms on the inner wall at the end of each of the three bridges, so that they may be ready on the instant to turn the catches and let the bridges fall behind our men as they rush across. The tenants have already driven as many more of their best horses and cattle into the inner court as can find standing room, so that their loss may be as small as possible. If the outer wall is carried, I have no great fear that the second wall will be taken; the plunderers who form the mass of Sir Clugnet's force will have had enough and more than enough of fighting by the time that they capture the outer one. Whatever happens, do not show yourself on the walls to-night, and see that the children do not leave their beds; you can do naught, and will see but little in the dark. To-morrow morning, wife, I will leave you free to go among the soldiers and give them encouragement as may be needed, but for to-night, I pray you stir not out. I will send Henry from time to time to let you know how matters go."

Rapidly the men gathered on the walls; each had had his post assigned to him, and when Sir Eustace made a tour of inspection he was glad to see how confidently each man bore himself, and how well prepared to give the enemy a warm reception. As soon as it became dark, the outwork on the other side of the moat was abandoned, the defenders called into the castle, and the drawbridge raised, for it was evident to Sir Eustace that although it might be maintained in daylight, by the aid of the archers on the wall, it could not resist an attack by overwhelming numbers when deprived of that assistance. Sir Eustace, after inspecting the men's arms, ordered all those on the walls, with the exception of a few who were to remain on watch, to sit down with their backs against the battlement, and to maintain an absolute silence.

"It is by sound rather than sight that we shall be able to judge of their movements," he said. "All sitting down may sleep, if it so pleases them, till they are roused."

The sentries were ten in number, and were all taken from among the archers. Most of these men had been accustomed to the chase, were skilled in woodcraft, and accustomed to listen to the slightest noises that might tell of the movement of a stag and enable them to judge his position. Sir Eustace, for the present, posted himself in his old position over the gate. Jean Bouvard and Guy were with him, while Long Tom moved round and round the walls to gather news from his sentries. Sometimes Guy accompanied him.

"They are moving," Tom the archer said as he stood listening intently on the wall at the rear of the castle. "It is an hour past sundown, and about the time the knaves will be mustering if they intend to make a regular attack on us. If it had been only an escalade there would have been no sound until nearly morning. I thought I heard them on the other side, but I am sure of it now."

"I can hear singing up at their camp," Guy said, "but I don't hear anything else."

"They are keeping that up to deceive us, I expect. But besides the singing there is a sort of rustle. I don't think that they are coming this way at present, or we should hear it plainer. It seems to me that it is spreading all round."

"I will go back and tell Sir Eustace what you think, Tom."

Guy hurried back to the other side of the castle.

"Long Tom thinks, Sir Eustace, that he can hear a stir all round."

"We have noticed it too-at least, all round this side. Tell him not to call the men to their feet until the enemy approaches more closely. I believe that it is the march of a large number of men, and that they are probably moving to the positions assigned to them, but it may be another hour or two before they close in."

In a short time the sound became more distinct; from a rustle it rose to a deep confused murmur, then an occasional clink as of arms striking armour became audible. Most of the men on the walls were now on their feet gazing into the darkness. Presently the sound ceased, first on one side and then on another.

"I fancy they are all at their stations now, Jean Bouvard; we shall soon hear more of them. Do not let your archers shoot, Tom, until they can make them out very distinctly. We may be sure that they will come up with their mantlets, and it would be a waste of arrows to loose at them until they are close to the moat; but of course if separate figures can be distinguished your men will draw on them."

In a quarter of an hour messengers came from various points on the wall saying that there was something moving within sight, and to those at the post over the gate a dark confused mass like a shadow seemed to be slowly coming down towards their outwork.

"Touch off the guns, Jean," Sir Eustace said; "we shall get no further chance of catching them in a body."

The captain stooped, lit two touchfires at the lantern standing in readiness, gave one to a man-at-arms, and went with the other to a cannon. Both the guns had been filled to the muzzle with bits of iron and nails, and had been laid to bear on the slope beyond the outwork. They were fired almost simultaneously, and the sound was followed by yells of pain and dismay. The besiegers, seeing that there was nothing further to gain by concealment, burst into a shout that ran all round the castle, and were answered by one of defiance from the walls. The sound was succeeded by loud orders from the leaders of the various assaulting parties, and the objects before but dimly seen, now approached the walls rapidly. Jean Bouvard hurried away to superintend the defence at other parts.

"You may as well go the other way, Guy, and let me know from time to time how things are getting on. Henry, run down to your mother and tell her that the enemy are moving up to the moat, and that it will be some time before there is any hard fighting; then come back here again."

It was easier to see from the side walls than it had been in front, for in front there was a glow in the sky from the number of fires burning beyond the crest of the slope, and Guy was able to make out what seemed to him a wall extending some fifteen yards, near the edge of the moat. The archers and crossbow-men gathered opposite to it had just begun to shoot. Behind this wall there were other dark masses irregularly placed, and extending back as far as he could see. An occasional cry told that the arrows were doing execution upon the unseen assailants behind the mantlets, and soon the blows of cross-bow bolts against the wall and the sharp tap of arrows told that the enemy had also betaken themselves to their arms. A number of giant torches had been prepared, consisting of sheafs of straw soaked with pitch, and one of these was now lighted and elevated on a pole some fifteen feet above the battlement. Its light was sufficient to enable the scene beyond to be clearly made out. A row of mantlets some eight feet high had been placed by the moat, and others of the same height, and seven or eight feet long, elevated at short intervals behind these, were so placed as to afford shelter to the men coming down to the mantlets in front. They stood in two lines; they were some twenty feet apart, but those in one line alternated with those in the other. Guy soon saw the object of this arrangement. Men were darting to and fro across the interval some six feet wide between the two lines. Thus they had but ten feet to run from the shelter on one side to that on the other, and exposed themselves but for an instant to the aim of the archers. Some of the men carried great bundles of faggots, others had sacks on their shoulders.

"Do not heed the mantlets in front," said Dickon, who was in command of the six archers near Guy, "but pick off those fellows as they come down. Shoot in turn; it is no use wasting two arrows on one man. Don't loose your shaft until a man is within three mantlets from the end; then if one misses, the next can take him when he runs across next time. That is right, Hal," he broke off, as an arrow sped and a man with a sack on his shoulder rolled over. "Now, lads, we ought not to miss them by this light."

Eleven men fell, out of the next twelve who attempted to carry their burdens down. Guy went back to Sir Eustace with the news of the manner in which the attack was being carried on, and of the effect of the archers' defence.

"I have just heard the same from the other side; there is one attack on each side and two behind; Jean Bouvard has posted himself there. I am going round myself now; I do not think there will be any attack made in front. I have sent the archers here to the rear, where they will be more useful; the fellows in the outwork across there have enough to do to shelter themselves."

This Guy could well understand, for although the guns could not be depressed sufficiently to fire down into the *tête du pont*, the mangonels were hurling stones into it, and the men-at-arms shooting cross-bow quarrels whenever a man showed himself. The rear of the outwork was open and afforded no shelter to those who had taken possession of it, and already the greater portion had retired to the other side of the small moat surrounding it, where they lay sheltered by the outwork itself. It was not long before the assailants at the other points, finding that the plan they had formed was defeated by the skill of the archers, poured down in a mass between the two lines of mantlets, each man carrying his burden before him, thus sheltering him to a great extent. Against this method of attack the archers could do little, and now confined themselves to shooting at the men who, having thrown down the fascines or sacks by the edge of the moat, stood for a moment and hesitated before running back to the shelter of the mantlets, and not one in three got off scot-free. Guy on going round the wall found the same state of things at each of the other three points of assault. Numbers of the enemy were falling, but great piles of materials were accumulating at the edge of the moat. After a time a number of knights and men-at-arms, fully protected by armour, came down and began to hurl the sacks and bags into the moat, their operations being covered as much as possible by a storm of missiles shot through holes in the mantlets. In a short time Sir Eustace ordered the archers to desist shooting, for they were obliged, in order to aim at those so much below them, to expose a considerable portion of their bodies, and three were killed by the enemy's missiles.

"We can't prevent them from filling up the moat," he said, "and it is but throwing away life to try to do so."

The archers were accordingly placed in the projecting turrets, where, without being themselves exposed, they could shoot through the loopholes at any point on the face of the walls. It was not long before the moat was bridged at all four points of attack. Ladders were then brought down. This the assailants were able to accomplish without loss, as, instead of carrying them, they were pushed backwards and forwards by men stationed behind the mantlets, and were so zigzagged down to the moat without the defenders being able to offer any opposition. Then rushes were made by parties of knights, the ladders were placed, and the fight began in earnest.

In the great court-yard the leader of the English men-at-arms was placed with twelve of his men as a reserve. They were to be summoned by one, two, three, or four blasts of a horn to the point at which their services were most required. The assaults were obstinate, but the walls were as stoutly defended. Sometimes the ladders were hurled back by poles with an iron fork at the end; buckets of boiling water and tar were poured over on to the assailants as they clambered up, and lime cast over on those waiting to take their turns to ascend; while with spear, axe, and mace the men-at-arms and tenants met the assailants as they endeavoured to get a footing on the wall.

Guy had placed himself with the party to which he had first gone, and, taking a pike from a fallen man, was fighting stoutly. The archers from their turrets kept up a constant flight of arrows on the crowd below. Only once was the horn sounded for the aid of the reserve. Sir Eustace had taken the command at the rear, while Jean Bouvard headed the defence on the side opposite to that at which Guy was fighting. The defenders under Sir Eustace had the hardest work to hold their own, being assaulted at two points. This was evidently the main place of attack, for here Sir Clugnet himself and several of his knights led the assault, and at one time succeeded in gaining a footing on the wall at one point, while Sir Eustace was at the other. Then the knight blew his horn, and at the same time called the archers from the turret nearest to him, while some of the other party on the wall rushed to aid him of their own accord and, pressing through the tenants, opposed themselves to the knights and men-at-arms who had obtained a footing on the wall.

Their strength, and the power with which they wielded their heavy axes, so held the assailants in check that they could not gain space sufficient for others to join them, and when the reserve ran up, so fierce an attack was made upon the knights that several were beaten down and the rest forced to spring over the wall at the risk of life and limb. Sir Clugnet himself was the last to do this, and was carried away insensible. Two or three of his companions were killed by the fall, but the rest, leaping far enough out to alight beyond the solid ground at the foot of the walls, had their fall broken by the yielding mass of materials by which they had crossed the moat. A loud shout of triumph rose from the defenders, and was re-echoed by shouts from the other walls. As soon as the news of the repulse at the rear reached the other parties, and that Sir Clugnet was badly hurt, while several of the knights were killed, the assault ceased at once, and the Orleanists withdrew, followed by derisive cries from the defenders.

"Thanks be to the saints that it is all over," Sir Eustace said, as he opened his vizor; "it was a close thing here, and for a time I feared that the outer wall was lost. However, I think that there is an end of it now, and by the morning we shall find that they have moved off. They must have suffered very heavily; certainly three or four hundred must have fallen, for we must admit that they fought stoutly. You have all done well, my friends, and I thank you heartily. Now, the first thing is to fetch the wounded down to the hall prepared for them. Father Gregory has all in readiness for them there. Guy, go round and find who have fallen, and see them carried reverently down to the court-yard, send me a list of their names, and place two men-at-arms at each point where the assault took place. Tom, do you similarly dispose eight of your archers so that should they send a spy up to see if we sleep, a message can be sent back in the shape of a cloth-yard shaft. Bid all the tenants and retainers leave the wall; a horn will recall them should there be need. I will myself visit them shortly, and thank them for their stout defence. I will send round a cup of spiced wine to each man on the wall as soon as it can be prepared, to that all may slake their thirst after their efforts."

Sir Eustace then made his way down from the wall to his Apartments, where Dame Margaret was awaiting him. She hurried to meet him.

"Wait, wife, till I have removed my helmet, and even then you must be careful how you embrace me, for methinks there is more than one blood-stain on my armour, though happily not of mine own. All has gone well, love, and methinks that we shall hear no more of them; but they fought more stoutly than I had given them credit for, seeing that they were but a mixed rabble, with a small proportion of real men-at-arms among them. I suppose Henry brought you my message to close the inner gates, as they had gained a footing on the walls."

"No, I received no message since the one he brought me half an hour ago, saying that all was going well, and I thought that he was with you. Where can he be, Eustace?" she asked anxiously.

"I know not indeed, Margaret, but will search at once. While I do so will you go to the hall that you have prepared for the wounded, and give what aid you can there? Do not fear for the boy; he turned and ran off when I spoke to him, and as his head reaches not to the top of the battlements no harm can have befallen him, though in truth I cannot think what can have delayed him."

He called to two or three of the men below to take torches, and to accompany him at once, and sent others to the sheds to ask if he had been seen there, then went up to the top of the inner wall and crossed the bridge at the back.

"Have any of you seen aught of my son Henry?" he asked the men there.

"No, my lord," one said in reply. "I marked him by our side just before the French got a footing at the other end of the wall, but I saw him not afterwards."

"He ran towards the steps at the corner there," Sir Eustace said, "with a message from me that the inner doors were to be closed. Come along, men," he said to those with torches, and going to the corner of the wall descended the steps, which were steep and narrow. He took a torch from one of the men and held it over his head. As he neared the bottom he gave a low cry and ran down the last few steps, where, lying at the bottom, was the form of his son. He was stretched at full length, and there was a terrible gash on his forehead. The knight knelt beside him and raised his head, from which the steel cap had fallen; there was a deep stain of blood on the pavement beneath. He placed his hand on the boy's heart and his ear to his lips, and the men with the torches stood silently round. It was but too evident what had happened. In his haste to carry the message Henry's foot had slipped, and he had fallen headforemost down the steep steps, his head coming in contact with the edge of one of them. Without a word Sir Eustace raised the boy gently in his arms. His face was sufficient to tell the men the news; their young lord was dead.

Sir Eustace carried him through the inner gate and up to the boy's own room, and laid him down on his bed, then silently he went out again and crossed the court to the keep. Dame Margaret was seeing to the wounded being laid on the straw in the lower room, and did not notice him until he touched her. She turned sharply round, his face was sufficient to tell her the truth. She gave a low cry and stepped back a pace, and he moved forwards and drew her to him.

"Love," he said tenderly, "God has taken him. He was fitter for heaven than any of us; he was too gentle for this rough world of ours. We shall mourn for him, but with him it is well."

Dame Margaret laid her head on his shoulder, and burst into a passion of tears. Sir Eustace let her weep for a time, then he whispered:

"You must be brave, my love. There will be other mourners here for their dear ones who have died fighting for us; they will need your comfort. A Villeroy could not die better than doing his duty. It was not by man's hand that he fell, but God took him. His foot slipped in running down the stair from the wall, and he must assuredly have died without a pang. Take the priest with you; I will see to the wounded here. Father Gregory," he went on, raising his voice, "Dame Margaret has more need of you at the present moment than have these brave fellows. A grievous misfortune has befallen us. My son is dead; he fell while doing his duty. Do you take her to his room; I give her to your charge for the present. I have my work to do, and will see that your patients are well cared for."

There was a murmur of surprise and regret from the wounded and those who had brought them in. The poor lad had been a general favourite in the castle for his gentle and pleasant ways with all, though many a time the rough soldiers had said among themselves, "'Tis a pity that he was not a girl, and the Lady Agnes a boy. He is more fit for a priest than for a baron in times like these, for assuredly he will never grow into a stout man-at-arms like his father." That a soldier should have been killed in such a fight was to be expected, but that a gentle boy like this should have fallen seemed strange and unnatural, and all sorrowed for him as well as for their lord and lady, and the men forgot for a time the smart of their wounds in their regret at his untimely death.

Sir Eustace went about his work quietly and earnestly, bound up the soldiers' wounds, and saw as far as might be to their comfort. Their number was not large, as it was only in the fight on the wall that aught save their heads had been exposed, and those struck by cross-bow bolts had for the most part fallen as they stood. The eight men brought in had without exception received wounds from the swords of the French knights, and though some of the gashes were broad and deep, none of them were likely to prove fatal. Just as the knight had finished, Guy entered. He had heard the news, which had spread like wildfire through the castle. The lad's eyes were red, for he had been greatly attached to Henry, whose constant companion he had been whenever the family had been at their English home.

"It is a strange fate, lad," Sir Eustace said, laying his hand upon Guy's shoulder. "You who have exposed yourself freely-for I marked you in the fight-have come through scatheless, while Henry, whom I thought to keep out of danger, has fallen. And what is your news?"

"There have been seventeen killed, my lord, besides Jean Bouvard, who was struck in the face by one of the last crossbow bolts shot before they drew off."

"This is bad news indeed. I wondered why he came not to me as soon as we had beaten them off, but I thought not of this. He was a good and trustworthy fellow, and I shall miss him sorely. Seventeen, say you? It is too many; and yet there might have been more. Who are they?"

"Four of our archers, Sir Eustace, one of our English men-at-arms, and six of your French men-at-arms. These were all killed by cross-bow bolts and arrows, Two of your tenants, Pierre Leroix and Jules Beaune, and four of their men fell on the wall when the French gained a footing there; three were, I hear, unmarried men, the other has left a wife and three children."

"They shall be my care," the knight said. "The wives of Leroix and Beaune shall hold their farms free of dues until their eldest sons come of age. Does all seem quiet without?"

"All is quiet, my lord; but as I left the wall but now a knight with a white flag and four torch-bearers was coming down the slope towards the outwork."

"I will go there myself," Sir Eustace said; "'tis likely they do but come to ask for leave to carry off the dead and wounded, which we will gladly let them do, for it will save us much trouble to-morrow."

It was as the knight had supposed, and he at once gave the permission asked for, and in a short time a great number of men with torches came down the slope and for the next two hours were occupied in carrying off their dead and wounded comrades. A close watch was maintained all night, though there was small fear of a renewal of the attack. At daybreak the rear-guard of the enemy could be seen retiring, and a party of men-at-arms, under Sir Eustace himself, on going out to reconnoitre, found that none had remained behind. A mound marked the place where their dead had been buried in one great grave. Many of the mantlets had been removed, and they doubted not that these had been used as litters for the conveyance of the wounded. They afterwards heard that some four hundred and fifty men had been killed, and that over a hundred, too sorely wounded to be able to walk, had been carried away.

In the afternoon Henry was buried beneath the chapel in the castle, while the men-at-arms and others were laid in the inner court-yard. Having learned that the Orleanists, greatly disheartened at their heavy repulse, had marched away to the south, the gates of the castle were opened. A small number of the garrison were retained in the castle, and the rest were sent out to aid the tenants in felling trees and getting up temporary shelters near their former homes until these could be rebuilt as before. For the time their wives and families were to remain in the castle.

All fear of another attack by the Orleanists speedily passed away. Artois was, upon the whole, strongly Burgundian, and an army marching from Flanders speedily brought the whole province over to that side. Nothing was done towards commencing the work of rebuilding the farm-houses, for it was evident that the castle might at any moment be again beleaguered.

Two months passed quietly. Sir Eustace busied himself in seeing that the tenants were comfortably re-established in their temporary homes. The Burgundians had again obtained several advantages, and as Sir Clugnet was known to have marched away with his following to the assistance of the Orleanists, who had of late fared badly, there was no fear of any fresh attack being made upon the castle. One day a messenger rode in from the Governor of Calais, who was personally known to Sir Eustace. The letter that he carried was an important one. After the usual greeting it read: —

> For the love I bear you, Sir Eustace, I write to let you know that there is a change in affairs. It seems that the Duke of Burgundy has but been playing with our King Henry, and that the offer of a marriage was made only in order to obtain assistance and the countenance of the king. Being now, as it would seem, powerful enough to hold his own against his enemies without such aid, the matter has fallen through. I have received a royal order, which has also been sent to the governors of other English towns, and it has been proclaimed everywhere by sound of trumpets, that none of Henry's subjects of whatever rank should in any way interfere between the two factions in France, nor go into France to serve either of them by arms or otherwise under pain of death and confiscation of fortune. But I would tell you for your private ear, that I have news that our king is in correspondence with the Dukes of Berri, Orleans, and Bourbon, and that it is like that he will shortly declare for that party, being grievously offended at the treatment that he has received at the hands of the Duke of Burgundy after having given him loyal help and assistance which had, in no slight degree, assisted him in making good his cause against his enemies.

In a short time, indeed, the English from Calais, and from other places held by them in France, began to make sorties and to carry off much plunder from the country round, and especially took by storm the Castle of Banelinghen near Ardres, notwithstanding the truce that prevailed. The intentions of the King of England were made still more manifest by his writing a letter to the Flemish towns, saying that, having heard that the Duke of Burgundy was gathering an army of Flemings to march into Aquitaine to wage war upon and destroy his subjects, and particularly his very dear and well-beloved cousins the Dukes of Berri, Orleans, and Bourbon, and the Counts of Alençon and Armagnac, and the Lord d'Albreth, he therefore begged them to inform him whether they were willing to conform to the truce concluded between them and England without in any way assisting their lord in his wicked purpose.

The Flemish towns replied that they desired in no way to infringe the truce between the two countries, but that they would serve and assist the King of France, their sovereign lord, and their Count the Duke of Burgundy, as heretofore, to the utmost of their power.

In a short time, indeed, it became known that a solemn treaty had been concluded between the King of England and the Orleanist nobles, they engaging to aid him to recover Guienne and the parts of Aquitaine he had lost, while he promised to put an army in the field to assist them.

The position of Sir Eustace was now very difficult. It was uncertain when the English would move, and it was likely enough that if an army set sail it would land in Guienne, and that Calais would be able to render no assistance, so that he would be exposed to the attacks of the Burgundians. Nor was his position improved when he learned that on the 15th of July the two French factions, urged by the Count of Savoy, the Grand Master of Rhodes, and many others, had agreed to terms of peace between them, and that the Orleanists had formally renounced the English alliance.

At the meeting of the leaders of the party, the Duke of Aquitaine, the king's son, presided. For a time all the differences were patched up. The news, however, came too late to arrest the embarkation of the English. Eight thousand men landed at La Hogue, under the Duke of Clarence, overran a wide extent of country, being reinforced by 800 Gascons, who had, according to the agreement with the Orleanists, been raised to join them. They advanced towards Paris, declaring, however, that they would retire if the Duke of Berri and his party kept their engagement with them, and paid them the two hundred thousand crowns he had agreed to do. The Duke had not, however, the means to pay this amount, and the English therefore continued to ravage the country, while a large force from Calais, under the Earl of Warwick, captured the town of Saumer-au-Bois and the Castle of Ruissault. This, however, was scarcely an invasion, and Sir Eustace, being doubtful whether Henry meditated operations upon a large scale now that he had no longer allies in France, took no part in the matter, but remained quietly in his castle.

Towards the end of March, 1413, a royal herald appeared before the gate. He was at once admitted, and was received with all honour in the great hall by Sir Eustace.

"Sir Eustace de Villeroy." he said, "I come to you in the name of the King of France, your lord and suzerain. He bids me to say that he has heard with satisfaction that you refused entry to your castle to those who demanded it altogether without authority from him; but that, seeing the importance of the castle in case of trouble with England, and that you are a vassal of England for estates in that country, he deems it necessary that its safety should be assured, and therefore calls upon you to send, in proof of your loyalty to and affection for him, your wife and children to Paris, where they shall be cared for in all honour and as becomes their condition; or to receive a garrison of royal troops of such strength as to defend it from any fresh assault that may be made upon it, either on the part of those who before attacked it, or of England. He charges you on your fealty to accept one or other of these conditions, or to be deemed a false vassal, which he cannot believe you are, knowing you to be a brave and worthy knight. Here is a document with the king's signature and seal to the effect which I have delivered to you."

"His Majesty's demands come upon me as a surprise," the knight said gravely, "and I pray you to abide with me till to-morrow, by which time I shall have had leisure to consider the alternative and be ready to give you answer."

"Your request is a reasonable one, Sir Eustace," the herald replied, "and I will await the answer for twenty-four hours."

The herald was then conducted to the guest-chamber, and Sir Eustace went out into the court-yard and for some time busied himself with the usual affairs of his estate and talked to the tenants as to their plans; then he went up on to the wall and there paced moodily backwards and forwards thinking over the summons that he had received. He knew that Margaret had been in the gallery in the hall and had heard the message the herald had delivered, and he wished to think it well over before seeing her. His position was, he felt, a perilous one. The last treaty of peace between France and England had drawn the frontier line more straitly in. After Cressy was fought, but a few miles away, Villeroy had stood within the English line as far as it now stood without it. That Henry, who although now old and averse to war, must yet ere long again renew the war that had so long languished he had little doubt; but he had no hope of succour at present, and felt that though able to withstand any sudden attack like that he had recently repulsed, he could not hope to make a successful defence against a great force provided with battering machines.

The message from the king was indeed but a message from Burgundy, but if Burgundy was all-powerful just at present it had the same effect as if it were the king and not he who had sent the summons. He could see no way of temporizing save that Margaret and the children should go as hostages, and the idea of this was wholly repugnant to him. Were he to admit a French garrison the castle would be virtually lost to him; for once powerless, he could easily be set aside in favour of one of Burgundy's followers. The only alternative then seemed to be that he should altogether forsake the castle and estate so long held by his ancestors, and retire to England, until maybe some day Henry might again place him in possession of it. He regretted now that he had not told Margaret that she had best keep her chamber, for she then would have known nothing of the alternative that she should go as a hostage-an alternative, he foresaw, that she was likely to favour, as by so doing the necessity for making an absolute decision and choosing between France and England would be postponed. At length, still undecided in his mind, he descended from the wall and went up to his wife's apartments.

Chapter V
Hostages

Margaret rose to meet her husband when he entered. She had looked pale in her dress of deep mourning before, but he thought that she looked paler now. She, too, had evidently been thinking over the summons that he had received, and there was an expression of firmness and resolution in her face that seemed to say that she had arrived at a more definite conclusion than he had done.

"'Tis a knotty question, wife," Sir Eustace said. "In the first place, it is clear we cannot hope to defend the castle successfully against an attack by Burgundy. The last was but of the character of a raid, the next would be a serious siege by experienced soldiers provided with all proper means and appliances. Before, it was certain that Sir Clugnet would, if he tarried here, be shortly attacked by the Burgundians, whereas now there would be no prospect of assistance. There is no hope of help from England, for there is no force in Calais that could contend with that which would probably be sent against me; therefore I take it that if attacked the castle must in the end fall, in which case probably its defenders would all be put to the sword. I myself should most likely be killed, the estates forfeited, and you and the children taken prisoners to Paris. Now it seems to me that that is not to be thought of. It remains to decide, therefore, whether we shall abandon the castle and journey to England, or whether we will admit a Burgundian garrison, which will in fact, we may be sure, be the first step towards losing the castle and estate altogether. It seems to me that the first will be the best plan. I see no chance of it at present, but in time Henry may invade France; and as we lie only some seven or eight miles from the frontier he would doubtless recapture Villeroy, and we should again become its masters."

"You have not mentioned the other alternative, Eustace, namely, that I and the children should go to Paris as hostages; and this, it seems to me, is the best of the three to follow. If there were indeed a chance of an English invasion I should not say so, but I think not that there is any such prospect. It is many years since England has done aught in earnest, and during all that time her power in France has been waning. I would not that our children should lose this fair estate when it can well be preserved by some slight sacrifice on my part. Were I and the children to go to Paris it would put an end to all doubts as to your loyalty, and you would hold the castle and estates. The peace now patched up between the parties will not last, and as soon as they are engaged with each other, and have no time to spare to think of attacking you here, I will endeavour to escape with the children and rejoin you. I shall assuredly have no cause for complaint. I shall, of course, have honourable treatment, and apartments fitting to our rank assigned to me. It would be no great hardship, and even were it so it would be worth enduring in order that our son Charles should inherit his father's estate."

"I could not part from you, love."

"Nay, Eustace, as I have said, it cannot be for long; and you must remember that twice when the children were infants I remained in England with them while you were some months here. It would be no worse now. I would take Guy with me; the lad has sense and courage, the children are both fond of him, and I myself could, if occasion arose, take counsel with him. Then I could have two or three stout men-at-arms who might ride in my train in peaceful garb as retainers. As to a maid I can, if I need one, hire her in Paris. Surely, husband, it would be far better so than that we should lose castle and land. There could be little danger to one in Paris at any time, still less to the wife of a vassal of the crown, least of all to a hostage. I shall be but staying at the court. If you peril life and limb, Eustace, in defence of your castle, surely it is not much that I should put myself to the slight inconvenience of a stay in Paris for a while."

"I like it not," the knight said moodily. "I see well enough that what you say is true, and that you should be safe at Charles's court, indeed safer than here. The citizens of Paris are indeed turbulent, whether they shout for Orleans or Burgundy, but what if Henry of England should again lead an army here?"

"But why imagine what is not likely to happen? Long ere Henry comes I may have joined you again; should it be otherwise I might perhaps escape, or at the very worst of all they could but keep me in duress in my chamber. Who ever heard of a woman being ill-treated for the disobedience of her lord? All that they could do would be to make you pay ransom for my return."

"I would rather go as a hostage myself."

"Nay, husband, that could hardly be. Who would then take care of your castle? It is not a hard thing that the king asks, merely that I and the children shall for a time live at his court as a proof that you, his vassal, hold your castle for him. Even if the worst comes to the worst we can but lose castle and land, as we must lose it now if I do not go. Nay, my dear lord, do not wrinkle your brow, we cannot strive against the might of France; and at present we must bow our heads and wait until the storm has passed, and hope for better times. There may be an English war; ere long Henry may again extend his frontiers, and you might again become a vassal of England for these possessions of yours even as your fathers were."

"I see that reason is on your side, Margaret, and yet I cannot bring myself to like the plan."

"Nor do I like it, husband; yet I feel that it were a thousand times better that I should be separated from you for a time than that we should risk another siege. The last has cost us dear enough, another might take you from me."

"Well, well, dear, I suppose you must have your way; indeed I do not see that harm can possibly come to you, and it will at any rate ensure peace for a time and enable us to repair our tenants' losses. I shall send over a message at once to Sir Aylmer, and beg him to choose and send me another fifty archers-with that reinforcement I could make head against any attack save in the greatest force-for there is no saying how things may go. The five-and-twenty did wonders, and with thrice that force I should feel confident that Villeroy could withstand any attack save by an army with an abundance of great machines.

"Well, Margaret, since you have decided for me that you are to go-and indeed I myself plainly see that that alternative is really the best-let us talk over who you had best take with you. I quite approve of your choice of Guy; he is a good lad, and will make a brave knight some day. I shall now make him one of my esquires, and as such he will always be in attendance on you; and assuredly Agnes and Charlie will, as well as yourself, benefit by his presence. He will be able to take them out and look after them, and as he talks French as well as English the lad will be useful to you in many ways. Have you any preference as to the four men-at-arms?"

"Could you spare Tom, the leader of the archers? I should like to have another Englishman with me, and he is very good-tempered and obliging. He is shrewd too, and with his strength and courage I should feel that I could wholly rely upon him in any strait, though indeed I see not that there is any probability of such occurring."

"Certainly you can have him, Margaret, and I shall be glad to know that he is with you. Dickon, who is next under him, can act as captain of the archers while he is away. I have noticed that Tom is picking up the language fast. He is always ready to do little kindnesses to the women and children, and I have often heard him talking with them. He will soon get to speak the language fairly. As to the others have you any choice?"

"No, I think you had better choose them for me, Eustace."

"They had better be French," he said; "it would not do for you to surround yourself entirely by English, although of course it is natural enough that you should have an English squire and servant. I think that you could not do better than take Jules Varey and Albert Bongarde. They are both stout men-at-arms, prudent fellows, and not given to the wine-cup. As a fourth I would say Jean Picard's son; he is a stout fellow too, and I know that, but for his father's hopes that he will one day succeed him as butler, he would have taken service regularly as a man-at-arms. He fought stoutly when the French gained the wall, and I marked him exchanging blows with Sir Clugnet himself, and bearing himself as well as any man there. You could choose no better."

"So be it," she said. "I think, Eustace, that with four such defenders, to say nothing of young Guy, you need not feel uneasy about us."

"I don't think that I shall feel uneasy, Margaret; but I know that I can ill spare you. You have ever been at my side since we were married, save when, after the birth of Agnes and Charles, you were forced to stay in England when I came over here. I felt it a dreary time then, and shall feel it so now; but I doubt not that all will go well with you, though it will be a very different life to that to which you have been accustomed."

"I shall do well enough," Margaret said cheerfully, "and maybe I shall get so fond of court that you will have to take me to that of Henry when we return to England."

"Now you had best begin to make your preparations. I will speak to Guy and the others myself."

Sir Eustace went into the court-yard, where Guy was superintending the issue of provisions for the women.

"This can go on without you," he said; "Gervaise will see to it. I would speak to you. You were at the meeting this morning, Guy, and you heard what the herald of France said. The position is a hard one. I cannot hold the castle against the strength of France, while if we take a Burgundian garrison I should cease to be its master, and it would doubtless soon pass into other hands. Again, if I go to England, it would equally be lost to us. Therefore my wife has resolved, in order to gain time until these disorders are over, to go to Paris with the children as a hostage for me. In no case, as it seems to me, are Dame Margaret and the children likely to be in danger; nevertheless, I am greatly loth for them to go. However, seeing no other way out of the business, I have consented, and we have arranged that you shall accompany her. You will go as my esquire, and I shall install you as such this afternoon. You will take Long Tom, two of the men-at-arms, and Robert Picard, all good men and true; but at the same time the burden and responsibility must rest upon your shoulders. You are young yet for so grave a charge, and yet I feel that I can confide it to you. You will have to be the stay and support of your mistress, you will have to be the companion and friend of my children, and I shall charge the four men-at-arms to take orders from you as from me. Tom will be a valuable fellow. In the first place, he is, I know, much attached to you, besides being shrewd, and a very giant in strength. The other three are all honest varlets, and you can rely upon them in any pinch."

"I will do my best, my lord," Guy said quietly; "and I am grateful to you indeed for the confidence that you show in me, and I shall, I hope, prove worthy of it, and of my father."

The news soon spread through the castle that Dame Margaret was going to Paris. The maids wept at the thought, as did many of the tenants' wives, for since the siege began, her kindness and the pains that she had taken to make them comfortable had endeared her greatly to them. On her previous visits they had seen comparatively little of her; she had been to them simply their lord's English wife, now they knew her as a friend. Nevertheless, their regret at her leaving was softened by the thought that her going to be near the king insured peace for them, and that they would now be able to venture out to the houses that were fast rising on the ruins of their former homes, and to take up their life again as they had left it.

Early next morning the little cortege mustered in the court-yard in readiness for a start. Sir Eustace and his wife had said good-bye to each other in their chamber, and she looked calm and tranquil as she mounted her horse; for, having been accustomed from a child to ride with her father hunting and hawking, she could sit a horse well, and scorned to ride, as did so many ladies, on a pillion. Guy rode by her side, with Agnes on a pillion behind him. Long Tom, with Charlie perched in front of him, followed them, and the three men-at-arms brought up the rear. Charlie was in high spirits; he regarded the trip as a sort of holiday, and had been talking, ever since he got up, of the wonders that he should see in Paris. Agnes better understood the situation, and nothing but the feeling that she ought to emulate the calmness of her mother restrained her from bursting into tears when her father lifted her on to her seat. The herald led the way, followed by his two pursuivants. Dame Margaret checked her horse in the middle of the court-yard, and said in a loud clear voice to the tenants and men-at-arms round: "Adieu, good friends; I trust that I shall not be long away from you. I go to stay for a time at the court in Paris, and I leave you with the surety that you will have peace and rest until I return, and be able to repair the damages you suffered from the attack made upon us by men who regard not the law." She turned and waved her hand to Sir Eustace, who was standing immovable on the steps, and then, touching the horse with her heel, they moved on after the herald.

"Do not fear to speak, Tom," Dame Margaret said, after they had left the castle behind them; "the journey is a long one, and it will go all the quicker for honest talk. What think you of this expedition to Paris?"

"I would as lief go there as anywhere else, my lady. Indeed, men say that it is a fine city, and as I have never seen a bigger town than Southampton, I doubt not that I shall find plenty to interest me at times when you may not require our services."

"I see that you have brought your bow with you."

"Ay, my lady, I could not bring myself to part with it. Sir Eustace told me that I could not carry it, as its length would be a matter of remark, and point me out at once as being an Englishman, seeing that the French archers carry no bows of such length; so I have, even as you see, wrapped it round with straw, and fastened it to the saddle beneath my leg. I have also put fourscore arrows among the valises on the pack-horses."

"There is no chance of your needing them, Tom."

"I trust that it is so," the archer replied; "but, indeed, there is never any saying, and an archer without his bow is but a poor creature,—though, indeed, I trust that I can swing an axe as well as another."

"And much better than most, Tom; still, I hope that neither axe nor bow will be required."

"To that I say amen also; for, although a fray may sometimes be to my taste, I have no desire to be mixed up in a mêlée without some of my stout comrades with me."

"Shall we get to Paris to-night, Lady Mother?" Charlie asked.

"No, indeed; it will be five days, if not six, for I see by the way that we are travelling we are bearing east, and shall sleep at Lille or may be at Tournay; then, doubtless, we shall bear south, and may stop the next night at Cambrai, and make to Noyon on the following day, and thence to Compiègne or to Senlis, and the next day will take us to Paris. It all depends how far and how fast we ride each day. But these matters will be arranged by the herald. Were we to go by the shortest route we should get there more quickly; but Amiens is held by the party to whom the men who attacked our castle belong, and by the way we are travelling we shall keep for some time in Artois, and so escape all risk of trouble on the road."

"I don't care for trouble," Charlie said stoutly; "we have got Long Tom and Robert Picard and the other two, and Guy can fight also."

"That would be all very well, my son," his mother said smiling, "if we were only attacked by half a dozen vagrants, but brave as they all are they could do naught if a large body surprised us; but be assured that there is no fear of that-by the way we are travelling we shall meet with none but friends."

"I should like to be attacked by the vagrants, mother. The last time you made us stay with you when there was fighting going on, except just at the first, but here we should see it all."

"Well, I don't want to see it, Charlie, and I am glad that we are not likely to do so; and you must remember that you and I and Agnes would sorely hamper our friends."

Nevertheless whenever a party of peasants was met upon the road Charlie looked out hopefully and heaved a sigh of disappointment when, after doffing their caps in respect, they passed on quietly. Several times they encountered bodies of knights and men-at-arms, but the presence of the royal herald saved them from all question. At each halting-place Dame Margaret, her children and maid, were lodged in the house of one of the principal citizens, while Guy and the men-at-arms lay at an inn. The troubled state of the times was only manifest by the number of men-at-arms in the streets, and the strict watch kept at the gates of the towns. Many of these were kept shut, and were only opened once an hour to let people pass in and out. This, however, did not affect the travellers, for the gates were opened the moment the emblazonings on the surcoat of the herald could be made out.

"We have assuredly nothing to complain of so far, Guy," Dame Margaret said, as they set out on their last day's journey; "had we been the king's special guests we could not have been more honourably treated, and I have no doubt that although we shall be much less important personages at Paris than as travellers under the royal protection, we shall yet be made comfortable enough, and shall have naught to grieve over save the separation from our lord."

"I cannot doubt that it will be so, lady," Guy replied; "and that at any rate there will be no trouble, unless the Armagnacs lay siege to Paris or there are riots in the city. I heard last night at the inn from some travellers who had just left it, that although the majority of the people there are in favour of Burgundy, yet that much discontent exists on account of the harsh measures of the officers he has appointed, and especially of the conduct of the guild of butchers, who, as it seems, are high in favour with the duke, and rule the city as if it belonged to them."

"It matters little to us, Guy, though it seems strange that the nobles of France and the respectable citizens of Paris should allow themselves to be ruled over by such a scum as that; but it was the same in Flanders, where Von Artevelde, our ally, a great man and the chief among them, was murdered by the butchers who at the time held sway in Ghent, and who were conspicuous for many years in all the tumults in the great towns there."

"I hear, madam, that the king is ill, and can see no one."

"Yes, I have heard the same from the herald. It will be John of Burgundy who will, for the time, be our master."

"I could desire a better," Guy said bluntly; "but we shall at any rate know that his fair words are not to be trusted. For my part, however, I wonder that after the (agreement with) the Duke of Orleans, with whom he had sworn a solemn peace, any man should hold converse with him."

"Unfortunately, Guy, men's interests count for more than their feelings, and a great noble, who has it in his power to grant favours and dispense honours, will find adherents though he has waded through blood. Burgundy, too, as I hear, has winning manners and a soft tongue, and can, when it pleases him, play the part of a frank and honest man. At least it must be owned that the title of 'Fearless' does not misbecome him, for, had it been otherwise, he would have denied all part in the murder of Orleans, instead of openly avowing that it was done by his orders."

They had started at an earlier hour than usual that morning, as the herald had pointed out to Dame Margaret, that it were best to arrive in Paris as early as possible, in order that the question of their lodging might be settled at once. Accordingly, they had been up at daybreak, and arrived in Paris at noon.

"How long will it be, I wonder," Dame Margaret said, as they rode through the gates, "before we shall pass through here again?"

"Not very long I hope, my lady," Guy said; "but be sure that if at any time you wish to leave we shall be able to procure disguises for you all, and to make our way out without difficulty."

"Nay, Guy, you forget that it is only so long as we are here that Villeroy is safe from attack. Whatever happens, nothing, save the news that an English army has landed at Calais, and is about to invade France, would leave me free to attempt an escape. If not released before that, I must then, at all hazards, try to escape, for Sir Eustace, knowing that I am here, would be placed in a sore strait indeed; both by his own inclinations and as a vassal of England, for he would want to join the English as soon as they advanced, and yet would be hindered by the knowledge that I was a hostage here. It would be for me to relieve him of that fear; and the same feeling that induced me to come hither would then take me back to Villeroy."

"Then, madam, I fear that our stay here will be a long one, for Henry has never pushed on the war with France vigorously, and though plenty of cause has been given by the capture of his castles in Guienne, he has never drawn sword either to regain them or to avenge the insults put upon the English flag."

"King Henry is old, Guy; and they say that his son is as full of spirit and as fiery as his father is peaceful and indisposed for war. When the king dies, my lord thinks that it will be but a short time before the English banner will be unfurled in France; and this is one of the reasons why he consented to my becoming an hostage, thinking that no long time is likely to elapse before he will have English backing, and will be able to disregard the threats of France."

"How narrow and sombre are these streets!" Guy said, after a pause, "one seems to draw one's very breath with difficulty."

"They are well-nigh as narrow in London," his mistress replied; "but they are gay enough below. See how crowded they are, and how brilliant are some of the costumes!"

"Some of them indeed, madam, but more are poor and miserable; and as to the faces, they are so scowling and sombre, truly were we not on horseback I should keep my hand tight upon my pouch, though in truth there is nothing in it worth stealing."

"Ay, ay, Master Guy," Long Tom broke in, "methinks that there are a good many heads among these scowling knaves that I would gladly have a chance of cracking had I my quarter-staff in my hand and half a dozen stout fellows here with me. See how insolently they stare!"

"Hush, Tom!" Dame Margaret said, turning round, "if you talk of cracking skulls I shall regret that I brought you with me."

"I am not thinking of doing it, my lady," the archer said apologetically. "I did but say that I should like to do it, and between liking and doing there is often a long distance."

"Sometimes, Tom, but one often leads to the other. You must remember that above all things it behoves us to act prudently here, and to avoid drawing the attention of our foes. We English are not loved in Paris, and the less you open your mouth here the better; for when Burgundians and Armagnacs are ready to cut each other's throats over a name, fellow-countrymen though they be, neither would feel any compunction about killing an Englishman."

After riding for half an hour they entered the court-yard of a large building, where men-at-arms and varlets wearing the cognizance of Burgundy were moving about, a group of nobles were standing on the steps, while some grooms were walking their horses round the court-yard. The herald made his way to the door, and here all alighted.

"Whom have we here, I wonder?" one of the young nobles said to another as they came up. "A royal herald and his pursuivants; a young dame and a very fair one; her daughter, I suppose, also fair; the lady's esquire; and a small boy."

"Hostages, I should say," the other replied, "for the good conduct of the lady's lord, whoever he may be. I know her not, and think that she cannot have been at court for the last ten years, for I could hardly have forgotten her face."

Dame Margaret took the hands of her two children and followed the herald up the steps. She had made a motion of her head to Guy to attend her, and he accordingly followed behind.

"A haughty lady as well as a fair one," the young knight laughed. "She did not so much as glance at us, but held her head as high as if she were going in to rate Burgundy himself. I think that she must be English by her looks, though what an English woman can be doing here in Paris is beyond my understanding, unless it be that she is the wife of a knight of Guienne; in that case she would more likely be with Orleans than here."

"Yes, but you see the herald has brought her. It may be her lord's castle has been captured, and she has come under the safe-conduct of a herald to lay a complaint; but I think with you that she is English. The girl was fair too, though not so fair as her mother, and that curly-headed young esquire is of English stock too."

"He is a stout-looking fellow, De Maupas, and will make a powerful man; he looks as if he could strike a shrewd blow even now. Let us question their knaves, one of whom, by the way, is a veritable giant in point of height."

He beckoned to the four men, and Robert Picard came forward.

"Who is your lady, young man?"

"Dame Margaret de Villeroy, may it please you, sir. She is the wife of Sir Eustace de Villeroy."

"Then we were right, De Maupas, for De Villeroy is, I know, a vassal of England for his wife's estates, and his people have always counted themselves English, because for over a hundred years their castle stood inside the English line."

"He is a stout knight. We heard a month ago how bravely he held his castle against Sir Clugnet de Brabant with 8000 Orleanists, and beat him off with a loss of five knights and 400 men. Sir Clugnet himself was sorely wounded. We all ought to feel mightily obliged to him for the check, which sent them back post-haste out of Artois, where they had already done damage enough, and might have done more had they not been so roughly handled. I wonder what the lady is here for?"

"It may be that he would have fought the Burgundians as stoutly as he fought the Armagnacs," the other said, "and that the duke does not care about having so strong a castle held by so stout a knight within a few miles of the English line."

The other shrugged his shoulders. "The English are sleeping dogs," he said; "there is no Edward and no Black Prince to lead them now."

"No, but you must remember that sleeping dogs wake up sometimes, and even try to bite when they do so; moreover we know of old that these particular dogs can bite hard."

"The sooner they wake up the better, I say, De Maupas. We have a long grudge to wipe off against them, and our men are not likely to repeat the mistakes that cost us so dearly before. Besides, the English have had no real fighting for years, and it seems to me that they have altogether given up any hope of extending their possessions in France."

"One can never tell, De Revelle. For my part I own that I care not that they should again spread their banner on this side of the sea. There can be no doubt that they are stout fighting-men, and seeing how France is divided they might do sore damage did they throw their weight into one side of the scale."

"Methinks that there is no fear of that. The dukes both know well enough that their own followers would not fight side by side with the English; and though they might propose an alliance with the Islanders, it would only be for the purpose of bringing the war to a close by uniting both parties against our old enemy."

In the meantime Dame Margaret had followed her conductor to the great chamber, where John of Burgundy held audience in almost royal state. Several nobles were gathered round him, but at the entrance of the herald these fell back, leaving him standing by himself. An eminently politic man, the duke saw at once by the upright figure and the fearless air with which Dame Margaret entered the hall, that this was a case where courtesy and deference were far more likely to bring about the desired end of winning her husband over to his interests, than any menaces or rough speaking; he therefore advanced two or three steps to meet her.

"My lord duke," the herald said, "this lady, Dame Margaret of Villeroy, has journeyed hither with me in accordance with the wish expressed by His Majesty the king."

"As the king's representative in Paris, lady," the duke said to Margaret, "I thank you for your promptness in thus conceding to his wish."

"His Majesty's wish was naturally a command to me, Sir Duke," Margaret said with quiet dignity. "We, my husband and I, understood that some enemy had been influencing His Majesty's mind against my lord, and in order to assure him of my lord's loyalty as a faithful vassal for the land he holds, I have willingly journeyed here with my children, although in much grief for the loss of my eldest son, who died in the attack lately made upon our castle by a large body of men, of whom we knew naught, save that they did not come in the name of our lord the king."

"I have heard of the attack, lady, and of the gallant and successful defence made by Sir Eustace, and the king was greatly pleased to hear of the heavy check thus inflicted upon the men who had raised the banner of revolt, and were harassing His Majesty's faithful subjects."

"That being so, my lord duke," Margaret said, "'tis strange, after my lord had shown how ready and well prepared he was to protect his castle against ill-doers, that he should have been asked to admit a garrison of strangers to aid him to hold it. Sir Eustace has no desire to meddle with the troubles of the times; he holds his castle as a fief directly from the crown, as his ancestors have held it for two hundred years; he wishes only to dwell in peace and in loyal service to the king."

"Such we have always understood, madam, and gladly would the king have seen Sir Eustace himself at his court. The king will, I trust, shortly be recovered from his malady; until he is so I have-for I was made acquainted with your coming by messenger sent forward by Monjoie-arranged for you to be lodged in all honour at the house of Master Leroux, one of the most worshipful of the citizens of Paris, and provost of the guild of silversmiths. My chamberlain will at once conduct you thither."

"I thank you, my lord duke," Margaret said with a stately reverence, "and trust that when I am received by my lord the king I shall be able to prove to him that Sir Eustace is his faithful vassal, and can be trusted to hold his castle for him against all comers."

"I doubt it not, lady," the duke said courteously. "Sir Victor Pierrepoint, I pray you to see this lady to the entrance. Sir Hugo will already be waiting her there."

Chapter VI
In Paris

"A bold dame and a fair one," John of Burgundy said to the gentlemen round him when Margaret left the chamber. "Methinks that she would be able to hold Villeroy even should Sir Eustace be away."

"That would she," one of the knights said with a laugh. "I doubt not that she would buckle on armour if need were. But we must make some allowance for her heat; it is no pleasant thing to be taken away from her castle and brought hither as a hostage, to be held for how long a time she knows not."

"It was the safest way of securing the castle," the duke said. "Can one doubt that, with her by his side, her husband would open his gates to the English, should they appear before it? He himself is a vassal both of England and France, and should the balance be placed before him, there can be little doubt that her weight would incline him to England. How well these English women keep their youth! One might believe her to be but a few years past twenty, and yet she is the mother of that girl, who is well-nigh as tall as herself."

"And who bids to be as fair, my lord duke."

"And as English, De Porcelet. She would be a difficult eaglet to tame, if I mistake not; and had she been the spokeswoman, methinks she would have answered as haughtily as did her mother. But it might be no bad plan to mate her to a Frenchman. It is true that there is the boy, but the fief might well be bestowed upon her if so mated, on the ground that the boy would likely take after his father and mother and hold Villeroy for England rather than for France. However, she is young yet; in a couple of years, De Porcelet, it will be time for you to urge your suit, if so inclined."

There was a general smile from the circle standing round, but the young knight said gravely, "When the time comes, my lord duke, I may remind you of what you have said. 'Tis a fair young face, honest and good, though at present she must naturally feel with her mother at being thus haled away from her home."

Sir Victor escorted Margaret to the court-yard. As they appeared at the entrance a knight came up and saluted her.

"I am intrusted by the duke with the honour of escorting you to your lodgings," he said; "I am Hugo de Chamfort, the duke's chamberlain."

After assisting her into the saddle he mounted a horse which an attendant brought up and placed himself by her side. Two men-at-arms with their surtouts embroidered with the cognizance of Burgundy led the way, and the rest of the party followed in the same order in which they had come. The distance was short, and beyond a few questions by the knight as to the journey and how she had been cared for on the way, and Margaret's replies, little was said until they reached the house of the provost of the silversmiths. As they rode up to the door Maître Leroux himself came out from the house.

"Welcome, lady," he said, "to my abode. My wife will do all that she can to make you comfortable."

"I am sorry indeed, good sir," Margaret said, "to be thus forced upon your hospitality, and regret the trouble that my stay will impose upon you."

"Say not so, lady," he said, "we deem it an honour that his grace the Duke of Burgundy should have selected us for the honour of entertaining you. The house is large, and we have no family. Chambers are already prepared for yourself, your daughter, and son, while there are others at your disposal for your following."

"I would not trespass too much upon you," she said. "My daughter can sleep with me, and I am sure that my esquire here, Master Guy Aylmer, will gladly share a room with my boy. I can obtain lodgings for my four followers without."

"You will grieve me much if you propose it, lady. There is a large room upstairs unoccupied, and I will place pallets for them there; and as for their meals they can have them apart."

By this time they had mounted a fine flight of stairs, at the top of which Dame Leroux was standing to receive her guests. She was a kindly-looking woman between thirty and forty years of age.

"Welcome, Lady Margaret," she said with a cordiality that made Margaret feel at once that her visit was not regarded as an infliction. "We are quiet people, but will do our best to render your stay here a pleasant one."

"Thanks indeed, mistress!" Margaret replied. "I feared much that my presence would be felt as a burden, and had hardly hoped for so kind a welcome. This is my daughter Agnes, and my son Charles." Then she turned to Sir Hugo: "I pray you to give my thanks to his grace the Duke of Burgundy, and to thank him for having so well bestowed me. I thank you also for your courtesy for having conducted me here."

"I will convey your message to the duke," he said, "who will, I am sure, be pleased to hear of your contentment."

Maître Leroux accompanied the knight downstairs again, and when he had mounted and ridden off he called two servitors, and bade one carry the luggage upstairs, and the other conduct the men to the stables he had taken for the horses.

"After you have seen to their comfort," he said to Robert Picard, "you will return hither; you will find a meal prepared for you, and will be bestowed together in a chamber upstairs."

In the meantime his wife had ushered Dame Margaret into a very handsomely furnished apartment. "This is at your entire service, Lady Margaret," she said. "The bedroom behind it is for yourself, the one next to it for your daughter, unless you would prefer that she should sleep with you."

"I thank you. I was telling your husband that I should prefer that; and my son and esquire can therefore occupy the second room. But I fear greatly that I am disturbing yourself and your husband."

"No, indeed; our sitting-room and bedroom are on the other side of the landing. These are our regular guest-chambers, and your being here will make no change whatever in our arrangements. I only regret that the apartments are not larger."

"Do not apologize, I beg of you, madam. I can assure you that the room is far handsomer than that to which I have been accustomed. You citizens of Paris are far in advance of us in your ideas of comfort and luxury, and the apartments both at Villeroy and in my English home cannot compare with these, except in point of size. I never dreamt that my prison would be so comfortable."

"Say not prison, I pray you, lady. I heard, indeed, that your visit to the court was not altogether one of your own choice; but, believe me, here at least you will be but a guest, and an honoured and welcome one. I will leave you now. If there is aught that you desire, I pray you to ring that bell on the table; refreshments will be quickly served. Had I known the precise hour at which you would come we should have been in readiness for you, but I thought not that you would arrive till evening."

"I hope that you will give me much of your company, mistress," Margaret said warmly. "We know no one in this great city, and shall be glad indeed if, when you can spare time, you will sit with us."

"Well, children, what do you think of this?" she asked when their hostess had left the room.

"It is lovely, mother," Agnes said. "Look at the inlaid cabinets, and the couches and tables, and this great warm rug that covers all the floor, how snug and comfortable it all is. Why, mother, I never saw anything like this."

"You might have seen something like it had you ever been in the house of one of our rich London traders, Agnes; at least so I have heard, though in truth I have never myself been in so luxuriously furnished a room. I only hope that we may stay here for some time. The best of it is that these good people evidently do not regard us as a burden. No doubt they are pleased to oblige the Duke of Burgundy, but, beyond that, their welcome seemed really sincere. Now let us see our bedroom. I suppose that is yours, Charlie, through the door in the corner."

The valises had already been brought to the rooms by another entrance, and Margaret and her daughter were charmed with their bedroom. A large ewer and basin of silver stood on a table which was covered with a white cloth, snowy towels hung beside it; the hangings of the bed were of damask silk, and the floor was almost covered by an Eastern carpet. An exquisitely carved wardrobe stood in one corner.

"It is all lovely!" Agnes said, clapping her hands. "You ought to have your room at home fitted up like this, mother."

"It would take a large slice out of a year's revenue, Agnes," her mother said with a smile, "to furnish a room in this fashion. That wardrobe alone is worth a knight's ransom, and the ewer and basin are fit for a king. I would that your father could see us here; it would ease his anxiety about us. I must ask how I can best despatch a messenger to him."

When they returned to the other apartment they found the table already laid, and in a short time a dainty repast was served. To this Guy sat down with them, for except when there were guests, when his place was behind his lord's chair, he had always been treated as one of the family, and as the son of Sir Aylmer rather than as a page.

"Well, Master Guy, what think you of affairs?"

"They seem well to the eye, mistress, but I would not trust that Duke of Burgundy for an hour. With that long face of his and the hooked nose and his crafty look he resembles little a noble of France. He has an evil face, and one which accords well with the foul murder of the king's brother. However, as I see not that he has aught to gain by holding you here, —save that he thinks it will ensure our lord's keeping his castle for him, —there is no reason why he should not continue to treat you honourably and courteously. We have yet to learn whether Master Leroux is one of his party, or whether he is in favour of Armagnac."

"I should think that he cannot be for Armagnac," she said, "or Duke John would hardly have quartered us upon him. No doubt it was done under the semblance of goodwill, but most men would have considered it a heavy tax, even though, as I expect, we shall not remain here long. Doubtless, however, the trader considers that his complaisance in the matter would be taken by the duke as a sign of his desire to show that at least he is not hostile to him."

When they rose from the table Guy, at his mistress's suggestion, went below and found the four men sitting in the great kitchen, where they had just finished an ample meal.

"You have seen to the horses, Robert?"

"Yes, Master Guy, they are comfortably bestowed, with an abundance of provender."

"I am going out to see how matters stand in the town. Our lady says that at all times two of you must remain here, as it may be necessary to send messages, or should she wish to go out, to escort her, but the other two can be out and about as they please, after first inquiring of me whether there is aught for them to do. You can arrange among yourselves which shall stay in, taking turns off duty. Tom, you had better not go out till after dark. There is something in the cut of your garments which tells that you are not French. Robert will go out with me now, and find a clothier, and bid him send garments here for you to choose from, or if he has none to fit, which may likely enough be, send him to measure you. It might lead to broils and troubles were any of the rabble to notice that you were a stranger."

"That is right enough, Master Guy; and in sooth I have no desire to go out at present, for after riding for the last six days I am well content to sit quiet and take my ease here."

Guy then started with Robert Picard. Except in the streets where the principal merchants dwelt, the town struck him as gloomy and sombre. The palaces of the nobles were veritable fortresses, the streets were ill-paved and evil-smelling, and the people in the poorer quarters had a sinister aspect.

"I should not care to wander about in this district after nightfall, Robert," Guy said to the man-at-arms, who kept close to his elbow.

"Nor I," the man growled. "It is as much as I can do to keep my hands off my dagger now, for methinks that nine out of ten of the fellows loitering about would cut our throats willingly, if they thought that we had but a crown in our pockets."

Presently they found themselves on the quays, and, hailing a boat, rowed up the river a little beyond the walls. Hearing the sound of music they landed, and on seeing a number of people gather round some booths they discharged the boat and went on. They found that it was a sort of fair. Here were sword-players and mountebanks, pedlars who vended their wares at a lower price than those at which they were sold within the limits of the city, booths at which wine and refreshments could be obtained. Here many soldiers were sitting drinking, watching the passers-by, and exchanging ribald jests with each other, and sometimes addressing observations to the wives and daughters of the citizens, amid fits of laughter at the looks of indignation on the part of their husbands or fathers.

"It is evidently a holiday of some sort," Guy remarked, as they found that the fair extended for a considerable distance, and that the crowd was everywhere large. They stopped for a minute or two in front of a booth of more pretensions than the generality. In front of it a man was beating a drum, and a negro walking up and down attired in showy garments. The drum ceased and the latter shouted:

"Those of you who wish to see my master, the famous Elminestres, the most learned doctor in Europe, who can read the stars, cast your horoscope, foretell your future, and cure your ailments, should not lose this opportunity."

The curtains opened behind, and a man dressed in dark garments with a long black cloak spotted with silver stars came forward.

"You have heard, good people, what my slave has said. He speaks with knowledge. I saved his life in the deserts of Africa when he was all but dead with fever, by administering to him one of my wonderful potions; he at once recovered and devoted himself to my service. I have infallible remedies for every disease, therefore do you who are sick come to me and be cured; while for you who do not suffer I can do as much or more, by telling you of your future, what evils to avoid and what chances to grasp."

He stood for a minute silent, his eyes wandering keenly over the spectators. "I see," he said, "one among you who loves a fair maiden standing beside him. At present her parents are unfavourable to his suit, but if he will take my advice he will be able to overcome their objections and to win the damsel. Another I see who has come to Paris with the intention of enlisting in the service of our good duke, and who, I foresee, will attain rank and honour and become a distinguished soldier if he does but act prudently at the critical moment, while if he takes a wrong turn misfortune and death will befall him. I see a youth of gentle blood who will become a brave knight, and will better his condition by marriage. He has many dangers to go through before that, and has at present a serious charge for one so young; but as he has circumspection as well as courage he may pass through them unharmed. To him too I could give advice that may be valuable, more especially as he is a stranger to the land, as are those of whom he is in charge."

"It is wonderful, Master Guy!" Robert Picard whispered in Guy's ear in a tone of astonished awe.

"The knave doubtless saw us ride in this morning, and recognized me again. There is naught of magic in it, but the fellow must be shrewd, or he would not have so quickly drawn his conclusions. I will go in and speak to him presently, for though I believe not his prophecies one jot, a fellow of this sort may be useful. Let us be moving on at present."

They passed two monks, who were scowling angrily at the man, who was just exciting the laughter of the crowd by asserting that there was a holy man present who usually preferred a flask of good wine to saying his vespers.

"Rogues like this should be whipped and branded, Brother Anselmo."

"Ay, ay," the other agreed: "and yet," he added slyly, "it may be that he has not altogether missed his mark this time. We are not the only two monks here," he went on as the other turned upon him angrily, "and it may well be that among them is one who answers to the fellow's lewd description."

On the outskirts of the fair were many people of higher degree. Knights and ladies strolled on the turf exchanging greetings, looking for a minute or two at the gambols of a troupe of performing dogs, or at a bout of cudgel play-where two stout fellows belaboured each other heartily, and showed sufficient skill to earn from the crowd a shower of small pieces of money, when at last they ceased from pure exhaustion. Half an hour later Guy returned to the booth of the doctor, and went in by a side entrance, to which those who wished to consult the learned man had been directed by the negro. The latter was at the entrance, and, observing that Guy's condition was above that of the majority of his master's clients, at once took him into an inner apartment divided from the rest of the tent by a hanging. Over the top of this was stretched a black cloth spotted with silver stars, and similar hangings surrounded it; thus all light was cut off, and the room was dimly illuminated by two lamps. A table with a black cloth stood at the back. On this stood a number of phials and small boxes, together with several retorts and alembics. The doctor was seated on a tripod stool. He rose and was about to address Guy in his usual style, when the latter said:

"So you saw us ride in this morning, Master Doctor, and guessed shrewdly as to our condition and nationality. As to the latter, indeed, it needed no sorcery, for it must have been plain to the dullest that my mistress and her daughter were not of French blood, and though I am much less fair, it was a pretty safe guess to suppose that I also was of their country. I need not tell you that I have not come here either for charms or nostrums, but it seemed to me that being, as you said, strangers here, we might benefit by the advice of one who like yourself notes things quickly, and can form his own conclusions."

The doctor removed his tall conical cap, and placed it on the table.

"You guess rightly," he said with a smile. "I was in the crowd and marked you enter, and a soldier standing next to me observed to a comrade that he had heard that Burgundy had sent the herald to demand the surrender of a castle held by one Sir Eustace, a knight who was known to have friendly leanings towards the English, being a vassal of their king for estates that had come to him with an English wife, and that doubtless this was the lady. When my eye fell on you in the crowd I said: Here is a youth of shrewdness and parts, he is alone and is a foreigner, and maybe I can be of service to him; therefore I shot my shaft, and, as you see, with success. I said to myself: This youth, being a stranger, will know of no one to whom he can turn for information, and I can furnish him with almost any that he may require. I come in contact with the highest and the lowest, for the Parisians are credulous, and after dark there are some of rank and station who come to my doors for filtres and nostrums, or to have their horoscope cast and their futures predicted. You will ask why one who has such clients should condescend to stand at a booth and talk to this rabble; but it has its purpose. Were I known only as one whom men and women visit in secret, I should soon become suspected of black arts, the priests would raise an outcry against me, and one of these days I might be burned. Here, however, I ostensibly earn my living as a mountebank vendor of drugs and nostrums, and therefore no one troubles his head about me."

"There is one thing that you have not told me," Guy said when he ceased speaking. "Having, as you say, good clients besides your gains here, why should you trouble to interest yourself in our affairs?"

"Shrewdly put, young sir. I will be frank with you. I too am a stranger, and sooner or later I may fall into discredit, and the power of the church be too much for me. When I saw your mistress to-day I said to myself: Here is an English lady of rank, with a castle and estate in England; should I have to fly-and I have one very dear to me, for whose sake I value my life-it might be well for me that I should have one friend in England who would act as protectress to her should aught befall me. Your mistress is a stranger here, and in the hands of enemies. I may be of use to her. I know this population of Paris, and can perhaps give her better information of what is going on both at the court and in the gutter than any other man, and may be able to render her assistance when she most needs it; and would ask but in payment that, should I come to England, she will extend her protection to my daughter until I can find a home and place her there. You see I am playing an open game with you."

"I will reply as frankly," Guy said. "When I came in here it was, as I told the man-at-arms my companion, with the thought that one who had noticed us so shrewdly, and had recognized me so quickly in the crowd, was no ordinary mountebank, but a keen, shrewd man who had some motive for thus addressing me, and I see that my view was a right one. As to your proposal I can say naught before I have laid it before my mistress, but for myself I may say at once that it recommends itself to me as excellent. We are, as you say, strangers here, and know of no one from whom we might obtain information as to what is going on. My mistress, if not an actual prisoner, is practically so, being held with her children as hostages for my lord's loyalty to France. She is the kindest of ladies, and should she authorize me to enter into further communication with you, you may be sure that she would execute to the full the undertaking you ask for on behalf of your daughter. Where can I see you again? This is scarce a place I could often resort to without my visits being noticed, if, as is likely enough, the Duke of Burgundy may occasionally set spies to inform him as to what we are doing, and whether my mistress is in communication with any who are regarded as either doubtful or hostile to his faction."

"If you will be in front of Notre Dame this evening at nine o'clock, I will meet you there and conduct you to my abode, where you can visit me free of any fear of observation."

"What name shall I call you?" Guy asked.

"My name is Montepone. I belong to a noble family of Mantua, but mixing myself up with the factions there, I was on the losing side, and unfortunately it happened that in a fray I killed a noble connected with all the ruling families; sentence of death was passed upon me in my absence, my property was confiscated. Nowhere in Italy should I have been safe from the dagger of the assassin, therefore I fled to France, and for ten years have maintained myself by the two arts which so often go together, astrology and buffoonery. I had always been fond of knowledge, and had learned all that could be taught in the grand science of astrology, so that however much I may gull fools here, I have obtained the confidence of many powerful personages by the accuracy of my forecasts. Had Orleans but believed my solemn assurance he would not have ridden through the streets of Paris to his death that night, and in other cases where I have been more trusted I have rendered valuable assistance."

The belief in astrology had never gained much hold upon the mass of the English people, many as were the superstitions that prevailed among them. Guy had never even given the matter a thought. Montepone, however, evidently believed in his powers of foreseeing the future, and such powers did not in themselves seem altogether impossible to the lad; he therefore made no direct reply, but saying that he would not fail to be at the appointed place at nine that evening, took his leave.

"Truly, Master Guy, I began to be uneasy about you," Robert Picard said when he rejoined him, "and was meditating whether I had best enter the tent, and demand what had become of you. It was only the thought that there might have been others before you, and that you had to wait your turn before seeing him, that restrained me. You have not been taking his nostrums, I trust; for they say that some of those men sell powders by which a man can be changed into a wolf."

Guy laughed. "I have taken nothing, Robert, and if I had I should have no fear of such a change happening to me. I have but talked to the man as to how he came to know me, and it is as I thought,—he saw us as we entered. He is a shrewd fellow, and may well be of some use to us."

"I like not chaffering with men who have intercourse with the devil," Picard said, shaking his head gravely; "nothing good comes of it. My mother knew a man who bought a powder that was to cure his wife of jealousy; and indeed it did, for it straightway killed her, and he was hung. I think that I can stand up against mortal man as well as another, but my blood ran cold when I saw you enter yon tent, and I fell into a sweat at your long absence."

"The man is not of that kind, Robert, so you can reassure yourself. I doubt not that the nostrums he sells are perfectly harmless, and that though they may not cure they will certainly not kill."

They made their way back to the house of the provost of the silversmiths.

"Well, what do you think of Paris, Guy?" Dame Margaret asked when he entered.

"It is a fine city, no doubt, lady, but in truth I would rather be in the country than in this wilderness of narrow streets. But indeed I have had somewhat of an adventure, and one which I think may prove of advantage;" and he then related to his mistress his visit to the booth of the supposed doctor.

"Do you think that he is honest, Guy?" she asked when he concluded.

"I think so, madam. He spoke honestly enough, and there was a ring of truth in what he said; nor do I see that he could have had any motive for making my acquaintance save what he stated. His story seemed to me to be a natural one; but I shall be able to judge better when I see him in his own house and with this daughter he speaks of; that is, if your ladyship is willing that I should meet him."

"I am willing enough," she said, "for even if he is a spy of Burgundy's there is nothing that we wish to conceal. I have come here willingly, and have no thought of making my escape, or of mixing myself up in any of the intrigues of the court. Therefore there is no harm that he can do us, while on the other hand you may learn much from him, and will gather in a short time whether he can be trusted. Then by all means go and meet him this evening. But it would be as well to take Tom with you. It does not seem to me at all likely that any plot can be intended, but at any rate it will be well that you should have one with you whom you can thoroughly trust, in case there is any snare set, and to guard you against any lurking cut-throats."

"I will tell him to be in readiness to go with me. It will be his turn to go out with one of the others this evening, and he might not be back in time if I did not warn him."

"What arms shall I take with me?" Long Tom said, when Guy told him of their expedition.

"Nothing but your sword and quarter-staff. I see that many of the beggars and others that one meets in the streets carry long staffs, and yours is not much longer than the generality. You brought it tied up with your bow, so you would do well to carry it, for in a street broil, where there is room to swing it, you could desire no better weapon, in such strong hands as yours, Tom. Besides, you can knock down and disable with it and no great harm is done, whereas if you used your sword there would be dead men; and although by all I hear these are not uncommon objects in the streets of Paris, there might be trouble if the town watch came up, as we are strangers. I shall carry a stout cudgel myself, as well as my sword."

Accordingly at half-past eight they set out. Guy put on a long cloak and a cap such as was worn by the citizens, but strengthened inside by a few bands of steel forming sufficient protection to the head against any ordinary blow. This he had purchased at a stall on his way home. Tom had put on the garments that had been bought for him that afternoon, consisting of a doublet of tanned leather that could be worn under armour or for ordinary use, and was thick enough to afford considerable protection. The streets were already almost deserted; those who were abroad hurried along looking with suspicion at all whom they met, and walking in the middle of the road so as to avoid being taken by surprise by anyone lurking in the doorways or at the corners of alleys. Once or twice men came out and stared at Guy and his companion by the light of the lanterns suspended across the streets, but there was nothing about their appearance to encourage an attack, and the stalwart figure of the archer promised hard blows rather than plunder. Arriving at the square in front of Notre Dame they waited awhile. Here there were still people about, for it was a rendezvous both for roistering young gallants, thieves, and others starting on midnight adventures. After walking backwards and forwards two or three times Guy said, "You had best stand here in the shadow of this buttress while I go and place myself beneath that hanging lamp; seeing that we are together, and he, looking perhaps only for one, may not recognize me."

On reaching the lamp, Guy took off his hat, so that the light should fall on his face, waited for a minute, and then replaced it. As soon as he did so a slightly-built lad came up to him.

"Were you not at the fair by the river to-day, sir, and are you not expecting some one to meet you here?"

"That is so, lad. If you will tell me whom I am expecting I shall know that he has sent you, though, indeed, I looked to meet himself and not a messenger."

"Montepone," the lad said.

"That is right. Why is he not here himself?"

"He received a message before starting that one whose orders he could not neglect would call upon him this evening, and he therefore sent me to the rendezvous. I have been looking anxiously for you, but until now had not seen you."

"I have a companion with me; being a stranger here in Paris, I did not care to be wandering through the streets alone. He is a countryman of mine, and can be trusted."

"It is indeed dangerous to be out alone. It is seldom that I am in the streets after dark, but the doctor came with me and placed me in a corner of the porch, and then returned by himself, telling me to stir not until I saw you; and that should you not come, or should I not be able to make you out, I was to remain until he came for me even if I waited until morning."

"I will fetch my follower," Guy said, "and am ready to accompany you."

The lad was evidently unwilling to be left there for a moment alone, and he walked back with Guy to the buttress where the archer was standing.

"This is our guide, Tom," Guy said, as the archer stepped out to join him; "the person I expected was unable to come himself. Now, lad, I am ready; you see we are well guarded."

The boy nodded, evidently reassured by the bulk of the archer, and was about to step on ahead of them, when Guy said, "You had best walk with us. If you keep in front, it will seem as if you were guiding us, and that would point us out at once as strangers. Is it far to the place you are taking us to?"

"A short quarter of an hour's walk, sir."

Chapter VII
In The Streets Of Paris

They crossed the bridge to the right bank of the river, and followed the stream down for some distance. Passing through some narrow lanes, they presently emerged into a street of higher pretensions, and stopped at the door of a small house wedged in between two of much larger size. The boy took a key from his girdle, opened the door, and entered.

"Stand here a moment, I pray you," he said; "I will fetch a light."

In a few seconds he appeared with a lantern. He shut and barred the door, and then led the way upstairs and showed them into a small but well-furnished room, which was lighted by a hanging lamp. He then went to a buffet, brought out a flask of wine and two goblets, and said: "Will it please you to be seated and to help yourselves to the wine; my master may possibly be detained for some little time before he is able to see you." Then he went out and closed the door behind him.

"It is evident, Tom," Guy said, as he took off his hat and cloak, and seated himself, "that the doctor has a good idea of making himself comfortable. Sit down, we may have to wait some time."

"Do you think that it will be safe to touch the wine, Master Guy? Perchance it may be drugged."

"Why should it be?" Guy asked. "We are not such important personages that anyone can desire to make away with us. I am convinced that the doctor was in earnest when he told me that story that I repeated to you this evening. It is possible that he may not be able to give us as much information as he said, but that he means well by us I am certain; and I think we may be sure that his wine is as good as his apartments are comfortable."

This turned out to be the case; the wine was excellent, and the archer soon laid aside any doubt he might have entertained. From time to time steps could be heard in the apartment above, and it was evident that it was here that the interview between the doctor and his visitor was taking place. Presently a ring was heard below.

"Another visitor," Guy said. Getting up, he slightly drew aside a thick curtain that hung before a casement, a moment later he let it fall again. "There are two men-at-arms standing on the other side of the street and one at the door." He heard the door opened, then the boy's step was heard on the stairs, two or three minutes later there was a movement above and the sound of the footsteps of two men coming down. Presently the outside door closed, two or three minutes elapsed; then the door opened and the Italian entered.

"I regret that I have kept you so long," he said courteously, "but my visitor was not to be got rid of hastily. It was a lady, and there is no hurrying ladies. When a man comes in, I have already ascertained what he desires to know; he listens to my answer and takes his departure. A woman, on the contrary, has a thousand things to ask, and for the most part they are questions quite beyond my power to answer."

"I have, as you see, Signor Montepone, brought my tall countryman with me; as you noticed me, I doubt not for a moment that you also marked him when we entered the city. Knowing nothing of the ways of Paris, but having heard that the streets were very unsafe after dark, I thought it best to bring him with me; and I am indeed glad that I did so, for we met with several very rough-looking characters on our way to Notre Dame, and had I been alone I might have had trouble."

"You did quite right," the Italian said; "I regretted afterwards that I did not myself advise you to bring some one with you, for indeed it is not safe for one man to go abroad alone after dark. And now, will you accompany me upstairs; this tall fellow will doubtless be able to pass the time with that flask of wine until you return."

"He should be able to do so," Guy said with a smile, "for indeed it is the best wine I have tasted, so far as my judgment goes, since I crossed the Channel, and indeed the best I have ever tasted."

"'Tis good wine. I received a cask of it from the grower, a Burgundian noble, who had, as he believed, gained some advantage from following my advice."

The man led the way upstairs. The room he entered there was much larger than that which they had left, extending over the whole floor. It was draped similarly to that in the booth, but was far more handsomely and elaborately got up. The hangings were of heavy cloth sprinkled with stars, the ceiling was blue with gold stars, a planisphere and astrolabe stood in the centre of the room, and a charcoal fire burned in a brazier beside them. A pair of huge bats with outstretched wings hung by wires from the ceiling, their white teeth glistening in the light of four lamps on stands, some six feet high, one in each corner of the room. The floor was covered with a dark Eastern carpet, a large chair with a footstool in front stood at a short distance from the planisphere; at one end was a massive table on which were retorts, glass globes, and a variety of apparatus new to Guy. At the other end of the room there was a frame some eight feet square on which a white sheet was stretched tightly.

"Now, Master Guy," the Italian said, "firstly, I beg you to give me the date of your birth and if possible the hour, for I would for my own information if not for yours, cast your horoscope. I like to know for my own satisfaction, as far as may be, the future of those with whom I have to deal. If I perceive that misfortunes and perhaps death threaten them, it is clearly of no use my entering into relations with them. In your case, of course, it is with your mistress that I am chiefly concerned; still as your fortunes are at present so closely mixed up with hers, I may learn something of much utility to me from your horoscope."

"I was born on the 8th of December, 1394, and shall be therefore seventeen in a fortnight's time. I was born a few minutes after midnight, for I have heard my mother say that the castle bell had sounded but a few minutes before I was born. She said that she had been anxious about it, because an old woman had predicted that if she ever had a child born on the 7th day of the month, it would be in every way unfortunate; so my mother was greatly pleased that I had escaped the consequences predicted."

"And now," the Italian went on, having made a note in his tablets, "what said your lady?"

"She bid me say, sir, that she was very sensible of the advantage that it would be to her to receive news or warning from one so well informed as yourself; and that she on her part promises that she will befriend and protect your daughter should you at any time bring her to her castle in England, or should she come alone with such tokens from you as that she might be known; and this promise my lady vows on the sacraments to keep."

"Then we are in agreement," the Italian said; "and right glad am I to know that should aught befall me, my daughter will be in such good hands. As far as worldly means are concerned her future is assured, for I have laid out much of the money I have received in jewels of value, which will produce a sum that will be an ample dowry for her. Now I can give you some news. The Duke of Berri with the queen came two days since from Melun to Corbeil, and Louis of Bavaria came on here yesterday to the Duke of Aquitaine with a message to Burgundy and to the butchers, asking that they would allow him to attend the queen to Paris, and that she might reside in his house of Nasle. Burgundy was minded to grant her leave, but at a meeting of the chiefs of the guild of butchers this afternoon they resolved to refuse the request; and this evening they have broken every door and window of the Duke of Berri's house, and committed great damages there, so that it should not be habitable; they resolved that Berri should not enter Paris, but that the queen might come. I hear that it has been determined that the king shall be placed in the Louvre, where the citizens of Paris can keep guard over him and prevent any attempt by the Orleanists to carry him away.

"All this will make no difference to your mistress directly; the point of it is that the power of these butchers, with whom go the guild of skinners and others, is so increasing that even the Duke of Burgundy is forced to give in to them. Some of the other guilds and the greater part of the respectable traders are wholly opposed to these men. They themselves may care little whether Orleans or Burgundy sways the court and the king, but this usurpation of the butchers, who have behind them the scum of Paris, is regarded as a danger to the whole city, and the feeling may grow into so hot a rage that there may be serious rioting in the streets. I tell you this that you may be prepared. Assuredly the butchers are not likely to interfere with any save such of the townspeople as they may deem hostile to them, and no harm would intentionally be done to her or to any other hostage of Burgundy. But the provost of the silversmiths is one of those who withstands them to the best of his power, and should matters come to serious rioting his house might be attacked. The leaders of the butchers' guild would be glad to see him killed, and their followers would still more like to have the sacking of his rich magazine of silver goods and the spoiling of his furniture.

"I say not that things are likely to come to that yet, but there is no telling how far they may be carried. It is but a dark cloud in the distance at present, but it may in time burst into a storm that will deluge the streets of Paris with blood. I may tell you that, against you as English there is no strong feeling at present among the Burgundians, for I am informed that the duke has taken several bodies of English archers into his pay, and that at Soissons and other towns he has enlisted a score or two of these men. However, I am sure to gain information long before matters come to any serious point, except a sudden outbreak arise from a street broil. I may tell you that one result of the violence of the butchers to-day may be to cause some breach between them and the Burgundian nobles, who are, I am told, greatly incensed at their refusing to give permission to the Duke of Berri to come here after Burgundy had acceded to his request, and that these fellows should venture to damage the hotel of one of the royal dukes seemed to them to be still more intolerable. The Duke of Burgundy may truckle to these fellows, but his nobles will strongly resent their interference and their arrogant insolence, and the duke may find that if he is to retain their support he will have to throw over that of these turbulent citizens. Moreover, their conduct adds daily to the strength of the Orleanists among the citizens, and if a strong Armagnac force approaches Paris they will be hailed by no small portion of the citizens as deliverers."

"In truth I can well understand, Signor Montepone, that the nobles should revolt against this association with butchers and skinners; 'tis past all bearing that fellows like these should thus meddle in public affairs."

"The populace of Paris has ever been turbulent," the Italian replied. "In this it resembles the cities of Flanders, and the butchers are ever at the bottom of all tumults. Now I will introduce my daughter to you; it is well that you should know her, for in case of need she may serve as a messenger, and it may be that I may some day ask you to present her to your lady."

He opened the door. "Katarina!" he said without raising his voice, and at once a girl came running up from the floor below.

"This is my daughter, Master Aylmer; you have seen her before."

Katarina was a girl of some fourteen years of age. She was dressed in black, and was tall and slight. Her complexion was fairer than that of her father, and she already gave promise of considerable beauty. Guy bowed to her as she made her reverence, while her face lit up with an amused smile.

"Your father says I have seen you before, signora, but in sooth I know not where or how, since it was but this morning that I arrived in Paris."

"We parted but half an hour since, monsieur."

"Parted?" Guy repeated with a puzzled expression on his face. "Surely you are jesting with me."

"Do you not recognize my messenger?" the Italian said with a smile. "My daughter is my assistant. In a business like mine one cannot trust a stranger to do one service, and as a boy she could come and go unmarked when she carries a message to persons of quality. She looks a saucy page in the daytime when she goes on the business, but after nightfall she is dressed as you saw her this evening. As a girl she could not traverse the streets unattended, and I am far too busy to bear her company; but as a boy she can go where she likes, and indeed it is only when we are alone, and there is little chance of my having visitors, that she appears in her proper character."

"You must be very courageous, signora," Guy said; "but, indeed, I can well imagine that you can pass where you will without anyone suspecting you to be a girl, for the thought that this was so never entered my head."

"I am so accustomed to the disguise," she said, "that I feel more comfortable in it than dressed as I now am, and it is much more amusing to be able to go about as I like than to remain all day cooped up here when my father is abroad."

"And now, Master Aylmer, that you have made my daughter's acquaintance, and I have told you what news I have gathered, it needs not that I should detain you longer; the hour is getting late already, and your lady may well be getting anxious at your absence. Can you read?"

"Yes, signor; the priest at my lady's castle in England, of which my father is castellan during my lord's absences, instructed me."

"It is well; for sometimes a note can be slipped into a hand when it would not be safe to deliver a message by word of mouth. From time to time if there be anything new you shall hear from me, but there will be no occasion for you to come hither again unless there is something of importance on which I may desire to have speech with you, or you with me. Remain here, Katarina, until my return; I will see monsieur out, and bar the door after him."

Passing downstairs Guy looked in at the room where he had left the archer. The latter sprung to his feet as he entered with a somewhat dazed expression on his face, for indeed, he had fallen off into a sound sleep.

"We are going now, Tom," Guy said. "I have concluded my business with this gentleman. We will not go back the way we came," he went on, as they issued into the street, "for I am sure we should never find our way through those alleys. Let us keep along here until we come to a broader street leading the way we wish to go; fortunately, with the river to our left, we cannot go very far wrong."

They presently came to a street leading in the desired direction. They had scarcely entered it when they heard ahead of them the sound of a fray. A loud cry arose, and there was a clashing of sword-blades.

"Come on, Tom!" Guy said; "it may be that some gentleman is attacked by these ruffians of the streets."

Starting off at a run, they soon arrived at the scene of combat, the features of which they were able to see by the light of the lamp that hung in the centre of the street. A man was standing in a narrow doorway, which prevented his being attacked except in front, and the step on which he stood gave him a slight advantage over his adversaries. These were nearly a dozen in number, and were evidently, as Guy had supposed, street ruffians of the lowest class. Without hesitation Guy and the archer fell upon them, with a shout of encouragement to the defender of the doorway, who was evidently sorely pressed. Tom's quarter-staff sent two of the men rolling on the ground almost before they realized that they were attacked, while Guy ran another through the body. For a moment the assailants scattered, but then, seeing that they were attacked by only two men, they fell upon them with fury.

Guy defended himself stoutly, but he would have fared badly had it not been for the efforts of Long Tom, whose staff descended with such tremendous force upon the heads of his assailants that it broke down their guard, and sent man after man on to the pavement. Guy himself received a sharp wound in the shoulder, but cut down another of his assailants; and the defender of the door, leaving his post of vantage, now joined them, and in a couple of minutes but four of the assailants remained on their feet, and these, with a shout of dismay, turned and took to their heels. Guy had now opportunely arrived. As the latter took off his hat he saw time to look at the gentleman to whose assistance he had so that the stranger was but a year or two older than himself.

"By our Lady, sir," the young man said, "you arrived at a lucky moment, for I could not much longer have kept these ruffians at bay. I have to thank you for my life, which, assuredly, they would have taken, especially as I had disposed of two of their comrades before you came up. May I ask to whom I am so indebted? I am Count Charles d'Estournel."

"My name is Guy Aylmer, sir; I am the son of Sir James Aylmer, an English knight, and am here as the esquire of Dame Margaret de Villeroy, who arrived but this morning in Paris."

"And who is this stalwart fellow whose staff has done more execution than both our sword-blades?" the young count asked; "verily it rose and fell like a flail on a thrashing-floor."

"He is one of Dame Margaret's retainers, and the captain of a band of archers in her service, but is at present here as one of her men-at-arms."

"In truth I envy her so stout a retainer. Good fellow, I have to thank you much, as well as Monsieur Guy Aylmer, for your assistance."

"One is always glad of an opportunity to stretch one's arms a bit when there is but a good excuse for doing so," the archer said; "and one needs no better chance than when one sees a gentleman attacked by such scum as these ruffians," and he motioned to the men lying stretched on the ground.

"Ah, you are English!" D'Estournel said with a slight smile at Tom's very broken French. "I know all about you now," he went on, turning to Guy. "I was not present today when your lady had audience with Burgundy, but I heard that an English dame had arrived, and that the duke came but badly out of the encounter in words with her. But we had best be moving on or we may have the watch on us, and we should be called upon to account for these ten fellows lying here. I doubt not but half of them are only stunned and will soon make off, the other six will have to be carried away. We have a good account to give of ourselves, but the watch would probably not trouble themselves to ask any questions, and I have no fancy for spending a night locked up in the cage with perhaps a dozen unsavoury malefactors. Which way does your course lie, sir?"

"We are lodged at the house of Maître Leroux, provost of the silversmiths."

"Then you are going in the wrong direction. You return up this street, then turn to your right; his house is in the third street to the left. I shall do myself the honour of calling in the morning to thank you more fully for the service you have rendered me, which, should it ever fall into my power, you can count on my returning. My way now lies in the opposite direction."

After mutual salutes they parted, and Guy followed the directions given to them.

"That was a sharp skirmish, Master Guy," Long Tom said contentedly; "the odds were just enough to make it interesting. Did you escape scatheless?"

"Not altogether, Tom, I had a sword-thrust in my shoulder; but I can do with it until I get back, when I will get you to bandage it for me."

"That will I; I did not get so much as a scratch. A quarter-staff is a rare weapon in a fight like that, for you can keep well out of the reach of their swords. In faith I have not had so pleasant an exercise since that fight Dickon and I had in the market-place at Winchester last Lammas fair."

"I am afraid Dame Margaret will scold us for getting into a fray."

"Had it not been for your wound we need have said nothing about it; but you may be sure that you will have to carry your arm in a sling for a day or two, and she will want to know the ins and outs of the matter."

"I think the affair has been a fortunate one, for it has obtained for me the friendship of a young Burgundian noble. Friendless as we are here, this is no slight matter, and I by no means grudge the amount of blood I have lost for such a gain. There is a light in Dame Margaret's casement; she said that she should sit up till my return, and would herself let me in, for the household would be asleep two hours ago; and as Maître Leroux and his wife have shown themselves so kindly disposed towards us, she should not like the household disturbed at such an hour. I was to whistle a note or two of *Richard Mon Roi*, and she would know that we were without."

He whistled a bar or two of the air, they saw a shadow cross the casement, then the light disappeared, and in a minute they heard the bolts undrawn and the door opened.

"You are late, Guy," she said; "I have been expecting you this hour past. Why, what has happened to you?" she broke off as she saw his face.

"It is but a trifle, lady," he said; "a sword-thrust in the shoulder, and a little blood. Long Tom will bind it up. Our delay was caused partly by the fact that the Italian was engaged, and it was half-an-hour before I could see him. Moreover, we had been kept at the trysting-place, as the guide did not recognize me owing to Tom being with me; and lastly, we were somewhat delayed by the matter that cost me this sword-thrust, which I in no way grudge, since it has gained for us a friend who may be useful."

Tom had by this time barred the door and had gone upstairs. "I am disappointed in you, Guy," Dame Margaret said severely when they entered the room. "I told you to keep yourself free from frays of all kinds, and here you have been engaged in one before we have been twelve hours in Paris."

"I crave your pardon, madam, but it is not in human nature to stand by without drawing a sword on behalf of a young gentleman defending himself against a dozen cut-throats. I am sure that in such a case your ladyship would be the first to bid me draw and strike in. The matter did not last three minutes. Tom disposed of six of them with his quarter-staff, the gentleman had killed two before we arrived, and I managed to dispose of two others, the rest took to their heels. The young gentleman was Count Charles d'Estournel; he is, as it seems, in the Duke of Burgundy's train; and as we undoubtedly saved his life, he may turn out a good and useful friend."

"You are right, Guy; I spoke perhaps too hastily. And now about the other matter."

Guy told her all that had taken place.

"And what is this man like?" she asked when he had concluded.

"Now that I saw him without the astrologer's robe and in his ordinary costume he seemed to me a very proper gentleman," Guy replied. "He is my height or thereabouts, grave in face and of good presence. I have no doubt that he is to be trusted, and he has evidently resolved to do all in his power to aid you, should it be necessary to do so. He would scarce have introduced his daughter to me had it not been so."

"He must be a strange man," Dame Margaret said thoughtfully.

"He is certainly no common man, lady. As I have told you, he believes thoroughly in his science, and but adopts the costume in which I first saw him and the role of a quack vendor of nostrums in order that his real profession may not be known to the public, and so bring him in collision with the church."

"It seems to me, Guy," Dame Margaret said the next morning, "that as you have already made the acquaintance of a young French noble, and may probably meet with others, 'twill be best that, when we have finished our breakfast, you should lose no time in sallying out and providing yourself with suitable attire. Spare not money, for my purse is very full. Get yourself a suit in which you can accompany me fitly if I again see the duke, or, as is possible, have an interview with the queen. Get two others, the one a quiet one, and not likely to attract notice, for your ordinary wear; the other a more handsome one, to wear when you go into the company of the young men of station like this Burgundian noble whom you succoured last night. Your father being a knight, you may well, as the esquire of my lord, hold your head as high as other young esquires of good family in the train of French nobles."

On Agnes and Charlie coming into the room, the latter exclaimed, "Why have you got your arm in a scarf, Guy?"

"He was in a fray last night, Charlie. He and Tom came upon a number of ruffians fighting a young gentleman, so they joined in and helped him, and Guy was wounded in the shoulder."

"Did they beat the bad men, mother?"

"Yes, dear; Guy had taken a sword with him, as it was after dark, and Tom had his quarter-staff."

"Then the others can have had no chance," Charlie said decidedly. "I have often seen Long Tom playing with the quarter-staff, and he could beat anyone in the castle. I warrant he laid about him well. I should have liked to have been there to have seen it, mother."

"It will be a good many years yet, Charlie, before you will be old enough to go out after dark in such a place as Paris."

"But I saw real fighting at the castle, mother, and I am sure I was not afraid even when the cannon made a great noise."

"No, you behaved very well, Charlie; but it is one thing to be standing on the top of a keep and another to be in the streets when a fray is going on all round."

"Did you kill anyone, Guy?" the boy asked eagerly.

"Some of them were wounded," Guy replied, "but I cannot say for certain that anyone was killed."

"They ought to be killed, these bad men who attack people in the street. If I were King of France I would have all their heads chopped off."

"It is not so easy to catch them, Charlie. When the watch come upon them when they are doing such things there is not much mercy shown to them."

As soon as breakfast was over Guy went out, after learning from Maître Leroux the address of a tradesman who generally kept a stock of garments in store, in readiness for those passing through Paris, who might not have time to stop while clothes were specially made for them. He returned in the course of an hour, followed by a boy carrying a wooden case with the clothes that he had bought. He had been fortunate in getting two suits which fitted him perfectly. They had been made for a young knight who had been despatched by the duke to Flanders just after he had been measured for them, and the tailor said that he was glad to sell them, as for aught he knew it might be weeks or even months before the knight returned, and he could make other suits for him at his leisure. Thus he was provided at once with his two best suits; for the other he had been measured, and it was to be sent in a couple of days. On his return he went straight to his room, and attired himself in readiness to receive the visit of Count Charles d'Estournel.

The suit consisted of an orange-coloured doublet coming down to the hips, with puce sleeves; the trousers were blue, and fitting closely to the legs; the shoes were of the great length then in fashion, being some eighteen inches from the heel to the pointed toe. The court suit was similar in make, but more handsome-the doublet, which was of crimson, being embroidered with gold; the closely-fitting trousers were striped with light blue and black; the cap with the suit in which he was now dressed was yellow, that with the court suit crimson, and both were high and conical, resembling a sugar-loaf in shape. From his sword-belt he carried a light straight sword, instead of the heavier one that would be carried in actual warfare, and on the right side was a long dagger.

Charlie clapped his hands as he entered the sitting-room.

"That will do very well, Master Esquire," Dame Margaret said with a smile; "truly you look as well fitted as if they had been made for you, and the colours are well chosen."

Guy told her how he had obtained them.

"You are very fortunate," she said, "and this afternoon, when I mean to take a walk to see the city, I shall feel that I am well escorted with you by my side."

"Shall you take us, mother?" Charlie asked anxiously.

"I intend to do so. You are so accustomed to be in the open air that you would soon pine if confined here, though indeed the air outside is but close and heavy compared with that at home. I have been speaking to Master Leroux while you have been away, and he tells me that a post goes once a week to Lille, and that he will send a letter for me to Sir Eustace under cover to a worthy trader of that town, who will forward it thence to Villeroy by a messenger. Therefore I shall write this morning; my lord will be pleased indeed to learn that we are so comfortably bestowed here, and that there is no cause for any uneasiness on his part."

Chapter VIII
A Riot

While Dame Margaret was speaking to Guy, one of the servitors came up with word that Count Charles d'Estournel was below desiring to speak with Master Guy Aylmer.

"Show the count up. Or no, you had best go down yourself to receive him, Guy. Pray him to come up with you; it will be more fitting."

Guy at once went down.

"So this is my saviour of last night," the count said gaily as Guy joined him. "I could scarce get a view of your face then, as the lamps give such a poor light, and I should hardly have known you again. Besides, you were wrapped up in your cloak. But you told me that you were an esquire, and I see that you carry a sword. I want to take you out to introduce you to some of my friends. Can you accompany me now?"

"I shall do so willingly, Count; but first will you allow me to present you to my lady mistress? She prayed me to bring you up to her apartments."

"That shall I right willingly; those who were present yesterday speak of her as a noble lady."

They went upstairs together.

"My lady, this is Count Charles d'Estournel, who desires me to present him to you."

"I am glad to meet you, Sir Count," Dame Margaret said, holding out her hand, which he raised to his lips, "seeing that my esquire, Master Guy Aylmer, was able to render you some slight service last night. This is my daughter Agnes, and my son Charles."

"The service was by no means a slight one," the young count said, returning a deep salute that Agnes and Charlie made to him, "unless indeed you consider that my life is a valueless one, for assuredly without his aid and that of your tall retainer, my father would have been childless this morning. I was indeed in sore plight when they arrived; my arm was tiring, and I could not have defended myself very much longer against such odds, and as I had exasperated them by killing two of their comrades, I should have received no mercy at their hands. In my surprise at being so suddenly attacked I even forgot to raise a shout for the watch, though it is hardly likely that they would have heard me had I done so; the lazy knaves are never on the spot when they are wanted. However, we gave the ruffians a lesson that those of them who escaped are not likely to forget readily, for out of the fourteen who attacked me we accounted for ten, of whom your retainer levelled no less than six with that staff of his, and I doubt whether any of the other four came off scatheless. I imagine that those levelled by your retainer got up and made off,—that is, if they recovered their senses before the watch came,—but I am sure that the other four will never steal pouch or cut throat in future. 'Tis a shame that these rascals are suffered to interfere with honest men, and it would be far better if the city authorities would turn their attention to ridding the streets of these pests instead of meddling with things that in no way concern them."

"It would no doubt be much wiser," Dame Margaret replied; "but since their betters are ever quarrelling among themselves, we can hardly wonder that the citizens do not attend to their own business."

"No doubt you are right," the young count said with a smile; "but it is the highest who set the bad example, and we their vassals cannot but follow them, though I myself would far rather draw my sword against the enemies of France than against my countrymen. But methinks," and here he laughed, "the example of the wars that England has so often waged with Scotland might well cause you to take a lenient view of our misdoings."

"I cannot gainsay you there, Sir Count, and truly those quarrels have caused more damage to England than your disputes between Burgundy and Orleans have, so far, inflicted on France; but you see I am a sufferer in the one case and not in the other. Even now I am ignorant why I have been brought here. There is a truce at present between England and France, and assuredly there are more English in the service of nobles of Burgundy than in those of Orleans, and at any rate I have seen no reason why there can at present be any doubt at all of the conduct of my lord, who has but lately defended his castle against the followers of Orleans.'"

"So I have heard, madame, and I know that there are some of my friends who think that Duke John has behaved hardly in the matter; but he seldom acts without reason, though it may not be always that one which he assigns for any action." Then, changing the subject, he went on. "I have come to take Master Guy for a walk with me, and to introduce him to some of my friends. My father is absent at present, but on his return he will, I know, hasten to express his gratitude. I trust that you can spare your esquire to go out with me."

"Certainly, so that he does but return in time to escort me for a walk through the streets this afternoon."

"I will be sure to come back, madam," Guy said. "You have but to say the hour at which you will start; but indeed I think that I shall probably be in to dinner at one."

"I cannot see," Guy said, when he had sallied out with the young count, "why they should have called upon Sir Eustace to furnish hostages. As the Duke of Burgundy has English archers in his pay, and France is at truce with England, there seems less reason than at other times to demand sureties of his loyalty, especially as he has shown that he is in no way well disposed to the Armagnacs."

"Between ourselves, Guy, I think that the duke in no way expected that hostages would be given, and that he was by no means well pleased when a messenger arrived from the herald to say that he was returning with your lady and her children. What was his intention I know not, but in times like these it is necessary sometimes to reward faithful followers or to secure doubtful ones, and it may be that he would have been glad to have had the opportunity of finding so fair a castle and estate at his disposal. You know the fable of the wolf and the lamb; a poor excuse is deemed sufficient at all times in France when there is a great noble on one side and a simple knight on the other, and I reckon that the duke did not calculate upon the willingness of your Sir Eustace to permit his wife and children to come here, or upon the dame's willingness to do so, and in no way expected matters to turn out as they have done, for there is now no shadow of excuse for him to meddle with Villeroy. Indeed, I question whether the condition about hostages was of his devising; but it may well be that the king or the queen wished it inserted, and he, thinking that there was no chance of that alternative being accepted, yielded to the wish. Mind, all this is not spoken from my own knowledge, but I did hear that Duke John was much put out when he found that the hostages were coming, and there was some laughter among us at the duke being for once outwitted."

"Then you do not love him overmuch, Count?"

"He is our lord, Guy, and we are bound to fight in his cause, but our vows of fealty do not include the word love. The duke his father was a noble prince, just and honourable, and he was loved as well as honoured. Duke John is a different man altogether. He is brave, as he proved in Hungary, and it may be said that he is wise, but his wisdom is not of the kind that Burgundian nobles love. It might have been wise to remove Orleans from his path, although I doubt it, but it was a dastardly murder all the same; and although we are bound to support him, it alienated not a few. Then he condescends to consort with these sorry knaves the butchers, and others of low estate, to take them into his counsels, and to thrust them upon us, at which, I may tell you, there is grievous discontent. All this is rank treason to the duke, I have no doubt, but it is true nevertheless. Here we are at our first stopping-place. This is as it is kept by a Burgundian master, who has with him two or three of the best swordsmen in France, and here a number of us meet every morning to learn tricks of fence, and to keep ourselves in good exercise, which indeed one sorely needs in this city of Paris, where there is neither hawking nor hunting nor jousting nor any other kind of knightly sport, everyone being too busily in earnest to think of amusement. Several of my best friends are sure to be here, and I want to introduce you to them."

When they entered the salon they found some thirty young knights and nobles gathered. Two or three pairs in helmet and body-armour were fighting with blunted swords, others were vaulting on to a saddle placed on a framework roughly representing a high war-horse; one or two were swinging heavy maces, whirling them round their heads and bringing them down occasionally upon great sand-bags six feet high, while others were seated on benches resting themselves after their exercises. D'Estournel's arrival was greeted with a shout, and several of those disengaged at once came over to him.

"Laggard!" one exclaimed, "what excuse have you to make for coming so late? I noted not that De Jouvaux's wine had mounted into your head last night, and surely the duke cannot have had need of your valuable services this morning?"

"Neither one nor the other befell, D'Estelle. But first let me introduce to you all my friend Guy Aylmer, an English gentleman, the son of a knight of that country, and himself an esquire of Sir Eustace de Villeroy. I am sure you will welcome him when I tell you that he saved my life last night when attacked by a band of cut-throats. Guy, these are my friends Count Pierre d'Estelle, Count Walter de Vesoul, the Sieur John de Perron, and the Knights Louis de Lactre, Sir Reginald Poupart, Sir James Regnier, Sir Thomas d'Autre, and Sir Philip de Noisies."

"I can assure you of our friendship," the first-named of these gentlemen said cordially to Guy, "for indeed you have rendered us all a service in thus saving to us our friend D'Estournel. Tell us how the matter occurred, Charles; in sooth, we shall have to take these ruffians of Paris in hand. So long as they cut each other's throats no great harm is done, but if they take to cutting ours it is time to give them a lesson."

"The matter was simple enough," D'Estournel said. "As you know, it was late before we broke up at De Jouvaux's last night, for I heard it strike half-past ten by the bell of St. Germain as I sallied out. I was making my way home like a peaceful citizen, when two men came out from a narrow lane and stumbled roughly across me. Deeming that they were drunk, I struck one a buffet on the side of his head and stretched him in the gutter."

"That was not like a peaceful citizen, Charles," one of the others broke in.

"Well, hardly, perhaps; but I forgot my character at the moment. However, an instant later there was a shout, and a dozen or so armed men poured out from the lane and fell upon me. I saw at once that I had been taken in a trap. Luckily there was a deep doorway close by, so I sprang into it, and, drawing my sword, put myself in a posture of defence before they were upon me. I ran the first through the body, and that seemed to teach the others some caution. Fortunately the doorway was so deep that only two could assail me at once, and I held my ground for some time pretty fairly, only receiving a few scratches. Presently I saw another opening, and, parrying a thrust, I ran my sword through the fellow's throat. He fell with a loud outcry, which was fortunate, for it came to the ears of my friend here, and brought him and a stout retainer — a prodigiously tall fellow, with a staff longer than himself-to my aid. They were but just in time, for the ruffians, furious at the fall of another of their companions, were pressing me hotly, and slashing so furiously with their swords that it was as much as I could do to parry them, and had no time to thrust back in reply. My friend here ran two of them through, his tall companion levelled six to the ground with his staff, while I did what I could to aid them, and at last the four that remained still on their legs ran off. I believe they thought that the man with the staff was the Evil One himself, who had got tired of aiding them in their villainous enterprises."

"It was a narrow escape indeed, Charles," Count Walter de Vesoul said gravely, "and it was well for you that there was that doorway hard by, or your brave friend would have found but your body when he came along. It is evident, gentlemen, that when we indulge in drinking parties we must go home in couples. Of course, Charles, you must lay a complaint before the duke, and he must let the Parisians know that if they do not keep their cut-throats within bounds we will take to sallying out at night in parties and will cut down every man we find about the streets."

"I will lay my complaint, but I doubt if much good will come of it. The duke will speak to the provost of the butchers, and nothing will be done."

"Then we will take them in hand," the other said angrily. "If the Parisians won't keep order in their streets we will keep it for them. Such doings are intolerable, and we will make up parties to scour the streets at night. Men passing peaceably along we shall not of course molest, but any parties of armed men we find about we will cut down without hesitation."

"I shall be heartily glad to join one of the parties whenever you are disposed, De Vesoul," D'Estournel said. "Perchance I may light on one or more of the four fellows who got away last night. Now I am ready to have a bout with swords."

"We have all had our turn, Charles," the other said.

"Then I must work with the mace," the count said. "My friend here, you see, did not come off as scatheless last night as I did, or else I would have asked him to have a bout with me. He held his own so well against two of them who fell on him together that I doubt not I should find him a sturdy adversary."

"I fear not, Count," Guy said smiling. "I can use my sword, it is true, in English fashion, but I know little of feints and tricks with the sword such as I am told are taught in your schools."

"A little practice here will amend that," D'Estournel said. "These things are well enough in a *salle d'armes*, and are useful when one man is opposed to another in a duel, but in a battle or *mêlée* I fancy that they are of but little use, though indeed I have never yet had the chance of trying. We will introduce you to the master, and I hope that you will come here regularly; it will give real pleasure to all. This salon is kept up by the duke for our benefit, and as you are one of his most pressingly invited guests you are certainly free of it."

They went up in a body to the master. "Maître Baudin," Count Charles said, "I have to introduce to you a gentleman who is our mutual friend, and who last night saved my life in a street brawl. He is at present an esquire of Sir Eustace de Villeroy, and has travelled hither with the knight's dame, who has come at the invitation of the duke. His father is an English knight, and as the friend of us all we trust that you will put him upon the list of your pupils."

"I shall be pleased to do so, Count Charles, the more so since he has done you such service."

"I am afraid that you will, find me a very backward pupil," Guy said. "I have been well taught in English fashion, but as you know, maître, we were more famed for downright hard hitting than for subtlety and skill in arms."

"Downright hard hitting is not to be despised," the master said, "and in a battle it is the chief thing of all; yet science is not to be regarded as useless, since it not only makes sword-play a noble pastime, but in a single combat it enables one who is physically weak to hold his own against a far stronger antagonist."

"That I feel greatly, maître. I shall be glad indeed of lessons in the art, and as soon as my shoulder is healed I shall take great pleasure in attending your school regularly, whenever my lady has no need of my presence. I am now in the position of the weak antagonist you speak of, and am therefore the more anxious to acquire the skill that will enable me to take my part in a conflict with full-grown men."

"You showed last night that you could do that," Count Charles said with a smile.

"Nay, men of that sort do not count," Guy said. "They are but rough swordsmen, and it was only their number that rendered them dangerous. There is little credit in holding one's own against ruffians of that kind."

"Well, I will be lazy this morning," the young count said, "and do without my practice. Will you all come round to my rooms, gentlemen, and drink a glass or two of wine and make the better acquaintance of my friend? He is bound to be back at his lodgings by one, and therefore you need not be afraid that I am leading you into a carouse."

Guy passed an hour in the count's lodgings and then returned to the provost's. The count accompanied him, saying that he had not yet seen his tall friend of the night before, and must personally thank him. Long Tom was called down, he being one of the two who had remained in for the morning.

"I must thank you again for the service that you rendered me last night," the count said frankly, holding out his hand to the archer. "I hope that you will accept this ring in token of my gratitude; I have had it enlarged this morning so that it may fit one of your strong fingers. It may be useful some day to turn into money should you find yourself in a pinch."

"I thank you, sir," Tom said. "I will wear it round my neck, for in truth rings are not for the use of men in my condition. As to gratitude, I feel that it is rather the other way, for my arms were beginning to get stiff for want of use. I only wish that the fray had lasted a bit longer, for I had scarce time to warm to it, and I hope that the next time your lordship gets into trouble I may have the good luck to be near at hand again."

"I hope you may, my friend; assuredly I could want no better helper."

After the count had taken his leave Guy went upstairs and told Lady Margaret how he had spent the morning.

"I am very glad to hear what you say about the fencing school, Guy; it will be good for you to have such training. And indeed 'tis well that you should have some employment, for time would hang but wearily on your hands were you to remain long caged up here. I shall be very glad for you to go. It will make no difference to us whether we take our walk in the morning or in the afternoon."

After dinner they went out. Guy escorted Dame Margaret, Agnes and Charlie followed, Long Tom and Jules Varoy bringing up the rear, both armed with swords and carrying in addition heavy cudgels. First of all they visited the cathedral, where Dame Margaret and her daughter knelt for some time in prayer before one of the shrines; then crossing the bridge again they followed along the broad pavement between the foot of the walls and the river, which served as a market, where hucksters of all sorts plied their trade; then entering the next gate on the wall they walked down the street to the Place de la Bastille, which had been finished but a few years.

"'Tis a gloomy place and a strong one," Dame Margaret said with a shiver as she looked at its frowning towers; "the poor wretches who are once entombed there can have but little hope of escape. Surely there cannot be so many state prisoners as to need for their keeping, a building so large as that. Still, with so turbulent a population as this of Paris, it doubtless needs a strong castle to hold them."

"It seems to me, madame, that, though useful doubtless as a prison, the castle was never really built for that purpose, but as a stronghold to overawe Paris."

"That may be so, Guy; at any rate I am glad that they did not use it as our place of detention instead of the house of Maître Leroux."

"They see well enough, madame, that you are more securely held than bolts and bars could detain you. I imagine that they would like nothing better than for you to get away back to Villeroy, since it would give them an excuse for an attack on the castle."

"Doubtless that is so, Guy; I came freely, and I must stay freely until some change takes place that will leave it open to us to fly. But in sooth it seems to me that nothing short of the arrival of an English army could do that. Were the Armagnacs to get the better of the Burgundians our position would be even worse than it is now."

"That is true enough, madame, for the Burgundians have no cause of hostility whatever to Sir Eustace and you, while we have given the Armagnacs good reasons for ill-will against us. Still, were they to come here it would be open to you to fly, for all Artois is Burgundian; and though the duke might not be able to hold his position here, Artois and Flanders would long be able to sustain themselves, and you would therefore be safe at Villeroy, for they would have other matters to attend to without meddling with those who only ask to be let alone."

On their way back from the Bastille they saw a crowd in the street and heard loud shouts.

"We had best turn off by this side street, madame," Guy said; "doubtless it is a body of the scoundrel butchers at their work of slaying some enemy under the pretext of his being an Orleanist. Do you hear their shouts of 'Paris and Burgundy!'?"

Turning down a side street they made a circuit round the scene of the tumult, and then coming up into the main street again resumed their way. After walking a considerable distance they came to a large building.

"What place is this, Guy?"

"It is the Louvre, madame. It should be the abode of the King of France, but he is only sometimes lodged there; but often stays at one of the hotels of the great lords. These palaces are all fortified buildings. Our country castles are strong, but there is no air of gloom about them; these narrow streets and high houses seem to crush one down."

"We will go back again, Guy; I do not think that I shall often go out in future."

"You can take a boat on the river, madame, and row up or down into the country. They say it is pretty; once fairly away from Paris, there are hills and woods and villages."

"That may be pleasant. If they would but let me go and live in one of those quiet spots I should be as contented as it is possible for me to be away from my husband.

"Nothing can be kinder than are Maître Leroux and his wife, but one cannot but feel that one is a burden upon them. My hope is that when the king comes to his senses I may be able to obtain an interview with him, and even if I cannot have leave to return to Villeroy I may be allowed to take up my abode outside the walls, or at any rate to obtain a quiet lodging for ourselves."

For the next three weeks the time passed quietly. Guy went every morning to the *salle d'armes*, for his wound being on his left shoulder he was able to use his sword arm as soon as it began to heal.

"You underrated your skill," the fencing-master said when he had given him his first lesson. "It is true that you do not know the niceties of sword-playing, but indeed you are so quick of eye and wrist that you can afford to do without them. Still, doubtless after a couple of months' practice here you will be so far improved that he will need to be a good swordsman who holds his own with you."

Guy paid only one visit during this time to the lodgings of the Italian.

"You have not heard from me, Master Aylmer," the latter said, "because indeed there has been nothing of importance to tell you. The Armagnacs are, I hear, collecting a great army, and are likely ere long to march in this direction. The butchers are becoming more and more unpopular and more and more violent; not a day passes but many citizens are killed by them under the pretence that they are Armagnacs, but really because they had expressed themselves as hostile to the doings of these tyrants. I have cast your horoscope, and I find that the conjunction of the planets at your birth was eminently favourable. It seems to me that about this time you will pass through many perilous adventures, but you are destined to escape any dangers that threaten you. You will gain honour and renown, and come to fortune through a marriage. There are other things in your career that are uncertain, since I cannot tell at what date they are likely to occur and whether the planets that were favourable at your birth may again be in the ascendant; but, for as much as I have told you, I have no doubt whatever."

"I thank you for the trouble that you have taken, Count Montepone," for Guy had now learned the rank that the Italian held in his own country, "and can only trust that your predictions will be verified. I would rather win fortune by my own hand than by marriage, though it will not come amiss."

"Whatever way it may happen, you will be knighted," the astrologist said gravely, "after a great battle, and by the hand of a sovereign; though by whom the battle will be fought and who the sovereign may be I cannot say, but methinks that it will be the English king."

"That I can wish more than anything," Guy said warmly. "Fortune is good, but to be knighted by a royal hand would be an honour greater than any other that could befall me."

"Bear your destiny in mind," the Italian said earnestly, "remember that in many cases predictions bring about their own fulfilment; and truly I am rejoiced that I have found that the stars point out so prosperous a future for you."

Guy was not free from the superstition of the time, and although in his English home he had seldom heard astrology mentioned, he had found since he had been in France that many even of the highest rank had an implicit belief in it, and he was convinced that at any rate the count himself believed in the power of the stars. He was gratified, therefore, to be told that his future would be prosperous; and, indeed, the predictions were not so improbable as to excite doubt in themselves. He was already an esquire, and unless he fell in combat or otherwise, it was probable that he would attain the honour of knighthood before many years had passed.

The fact, however, that it was to be bestowed by royal hand added greatly to the value of the honour. Knighthood was common in those days; it was bestowed almost as a matter of course upon young men of good birth, especially if they took up the profession of arms. Every noble had some, while not a few had many knights in their service, discharging what would now be the duties of officers when their levies were called out, and they could themselves bestow the rank upon any man possessing a certain amount of land; but to be knighted by a distinguished leader, or by a sovereign, was a distinction greatly prized, and placed its recipient in quite another category to the knights by service. It was a testimony alike of valour and of birth, and was a proof that its bearer was a warrior of distinction. The prophecy that he would better his fortune by marriage weighed little with him; marriage was a matter that appeared to him at present to be a very remote contingency; at the same time it was pleasant to him to be told that his wife would be an heiress, because this would place him above the need of earning his living by his sword, and would enable him to follow his sovereign, not as one of the train of a powerful noble, but as a free knight.

Chapter IX
A Stout Defence

The Duke of Burgundy had left Paris upon the day after he had received Dame Margaret, and as the king had a lucid interval, the Duke of Aquitaine, his son, was also absent with the army. In Paris there existed a general sense of uneasiness and alarm. The butchers, feeling that their doings had excited a strong reaction against them, and that several of the other guilds, notably that of the carpenters, were combining against them, determined to strike terror into their opponents by attacking some of their leaders. Several of these were openly murdered in the streets, and the houses of others were burnt and sacked. One evening when Guy had returned at nine o'clock from a supper at Count Charles's lodgings, it being the first time he had been out after dark since his first adventure, he had but just gone up to his room, when he heard a loud knocking at the door below. Going to the front window he looked out of the casement.

"Who is it that knocks?" he asked.

"It is I—the lad of Notre Dame."

He recognized the voice and ran down and opened the door.

"What is it, signora?"

"My father bids me tell you, sir, that he but learned the instant before he despatched me that the butchers are going to attack this house this evening, under the pretext that there are English spies here, but really to slay the provost of the silversmiths, and to gratify their followers by the sack of his house. I fear that I am too late, for they were to march from the *abattoirs* at nine, and it is already nearly half-past. Look! I see torches coming up the street."

"It is too late, indeed, to fly, even if we wished to," Guy said. "Dame Margaret and the children retired to bed an hour ago. Will you take this ring," and he took off from his finger one that D'Estournel had given him, "and carry it at once to the lodgings of Count Charles d'Estournel? They are in the house on this side of the Hotel of St. Pol. He is still up, and has some of his friends with him. Tell him from me that this house is being attacked, and beg him to gather a party, if he can, and come to our assistance. Say that we shall defend it until the last."

The girl took the ring and ran off at the top of her speed. The roar of the distant crowd could now be distinctly heard. Guy put up the strong bars of the door and then rushed upstairs. First he knocked at the door of Maître Leroux.

"The butchers are coming to attack your house!" he shouted. "Call up your servants; bid them take to their arms." Then he ran up to the room where his men slept. Long Tom, who had met him at D'Estournel's door and accompanied him home, sprang to his feet from his pallet as Guy entered. "The butchers are about to attack the house, Tom; up all of you and arm yourselves; bring down your bow and arrows. Where do the men-servants sleep?"

"There are five of them in the next room, and the two who serve in the shop are in the chamber beyond," the archer replied, as he hastily buckled on his armour. Guy rushed to the door and awoke the inmates of the rooms, telling them to arm and hasten down to defend the house, which was about to be attacked. A moment later Maître Leroux himself appeared and repeated the order.

"Art sure of what you say, Master Guy?" he asked.

"Look from the window and you will see them approaching," Guy replied, and going to the casement window which was at the front of the house he threw it open. Some four hundred yards away a dense throng was coming along; a score of torches lighted up the scene.

"Resistance is vain," the silversmith said. "It is my life they seek; I will go down to them."

"Resistance will not be in vain," Guy said firmly. "I have already sent for aid, and we shall have a body of Burgundian men-at-arms here to our assistance before long. Your life will not satisfy them; it is the plunder of your shop and house that they long for, and you may be sure that they will put all to the sword if they once break in. Now let us run down and see what we can do to strengthen our defences."

"The shutters and doors are all strong," the provost said as they hurried downstairs, followed by the four men-at-arms and the servants-for in those days men removed but few of their garments as they lay down on their rough pallets.

"In the first place," Guy said, "we must pile everything that we can find below against these doors, so that when they yield we can still make a defence here, before we retire. Are there other stairs than these?"

"No."

"So much the better. As soon as we have blocked the door we will barricade the first landing and defend ourselves there. Jean Bart, do you take the command below for the present. Seize everything that you can lay hands on, logs from the wood-store, sacks of charcoal, cases, everything heavy that you can find, and pile them up against the door. Tom, do you come with us; an arrow or two will check their ardour, and it is not likely they have brought bows or cross-bows with them. Try to parley with them as long as you can, Maître Leroux, every minute is of value."

"What is all this, Guy?" Dame Margaret asked as she entered the apartment. Having been aroused by the noise she had hastily attired herself, and had just come into the front room.

"The butchers are about to attack the house, lady; we are going to defend it. I have sent to D'Estournel, and we may hope for aid before long."

At this moment there was a loud knocking at the door and a hoarse roar of voices from the street. The silversmith went to the casement and opened it, and he and Guy looked out. A shout of fury arose from the street, with cries of "Death to the English spies!" "Death to the Armagnac provost!"

Leroux in vain endeavoured to make his voice heard, and so tell the crowd that his guests were not spies, but had been lodged at his house by the Duke of Burgundy himself. A tall man on horseback, one of several who were evidently leaders of the mob, pressed his way through the crowd to the door and evidently gave some orders, and a din of heavy sledge-hammers and axes beating against it at once mingled with the shouts of the crowd. The horseman crossed again to the other side of the street and shook his fist threateningly at Leroux.

"That is Jacques Legoix," the silversmith said, as he retired from the window; "one of the great leaders of the butchers; his family, and the St. Yons and Taiberts rule the market."

"Tom," Guy said to the archer, who was standing behind him. "Begin by picking off that fellow on horseback opposite."

Tom had already bent his bow and had an arrow in readiness, a moment later the shaft flew and struck the butcher between the eyes, and he fell dead from his horse. A yell of consternation and rage rose from the crowd.

"Now you can distribute a few arrows among those fellows at the door," Guy said.

The archer leant far out of the low casement. "It is awkward shooting, Master Guy," he said quietly, "but I daresay I can make a shift to manage it." Disregarding the furious yells of the crowd, he sent arrow after arrow among the men using the sledges and axes. Many of them had steel caps with projecting rims which sheltered the neck, but as they raised their weapons with both hands over their heads they exposed their chests to the marksman above, and not an arrow that was shot failed to bring down a man. When six had fallen no fresh volunteers came forward to take their places, although another horseman made his way up to them and endeavoured by persuasions and threats to induce them to continue the work. This man was clad in armour, and wore a steel cap in the place of the knightly helmet.

"Who is that fellow?" Guy asked the merchant.

"He is the son of Caboche, the head of the flayers, one of the most pestilent villains in the city."

"Keep your eye on him, Tom, and when you see a chance send an arrow home."

"That armour of his is but common stuff, Master Guy; as soon as I get a chance I will send a shaft through it."

The man with a gesture of anger turned and gave instructions to a number of men, who pushed their way through the crowd, first picking up some of the fallen hammers and axes. The fate of his associate had evidently taught the horseman prudence, for as he moved away he kept his head bent down so as not to expose his face to the aim of the terrible marksman at the window. He halted a short distance away and was evidently haranguing the crowd round him, and in his vehemence raised his arm. The moment he did so Tom's bow twanged. The arrow struck him at the unprotected part under the arm-pit, and he fell headlong from his horse. Maddened with rage the crowd no longer hesitated, and again attacked the door. Just as they did so there was a roar of exultation down the street as twelve men brought up a solid gate that they had beaten in and wrenched from its hinges from a house beyond.

"You can shoot as you like now, Tom. I will go down and see how the men are getting on below; the mob will have the door in sooner or later."

Guy found that the men below had not wasted their time. A great pile of logs, sacks, and other materials was piled against the door, and a short distance behind stood a number of barrels of wine and heavy cases ready to be placed in position.

"Get them upstairs, Jean," Guy said; "they will make a better barricade than the furniture, which we may as well save if possible."

The nine men set to work, and in a very short time a strong barricade was formed across the top of the wide staircase.

"Have you all the cases out of the shop?"

"Yes, we have not left one there, Master Guy. If they are all full of silver there must be enough for a royal banqueting-table."

Some, indeed, of the massive chests were so heavy that it required the efforts of six men to carry them upstairs.

"How do matters go, Guy?" Dame Margaret asked quietly as he re-entered the apartment.

"Very well," he replied. "I don't think the door will hold out much longer; but there is a strong barricade behind it which it will take them some time to force, and another on the landing here that we ought to be able to hold for an hour at least, and before that yields we will have another ready on the landing above."

"I will see to that," she said. "I will take Agnes and Charlie up with me, and then, with the women, I will move out the clothes' and linen chests and build them up there."

"Thank you, madame; I trust long before the barricade here is carried we shall have D'Estournel and his friends to our assistance. Indeed, I doubt whether they will be able to carry it at all; it is as solid and almost as strong as a stone wall, and as there are thirteen or fourteen of us to defend it, it seems to me that nothing short of battering the cases to pieces will enable them to force a way."

"I wish I could do something," Agnes broke in; "it is hard not to be able to help while you are all fighting for us. I wish I had brought my bow with me, you know I can shoot fairly."

"I think that it is just as well that you have not," Guy said with a smile. "I do not doubt your courage for a moment, but if you were placing yourself in danger we should all be anxious about you, and I would much rather know that you were safe with your mother upstairs."

Guy now went to the window. Maître Leroux had been directing his servants in the formation of the barricades.

"I can do nothing to protect the door," the archer said; "they have propped up that gate so as to cover the men who are hammering at it. I have been distributing my arrows among the crowd, and in faith there will be a good many vacancies among the butchers and flayers in the market tomorrow morning. I am just going up to fill my quiver again and bring down a spare armful of arrows."

"Leave those on the landing here, Tom, and bring your full quiver down below. The door will not hold many minutes longer: I could see that it was yielding when I was down there just now. I don't think that we shall be able to make a long defence below, for with their hooked halberts they will be able to pull out the logs, do what we will."

One of the servants now ran in.

"They have broken the door down, sir. It is only kept in place by the things behind it."

Guy ran out, climbed the barricade-which on the landing was four feet high, but as it was built on the edge of the top stair it was nine inches higher on that face-let himself drop on to the stairs, and ran down into the passage.

"I think, Maître Leroux," he said, "that you and your men had better go up at once and station yourselves at the barricade. There is no room here for more than five of us to use our arms, and when we retire we shall have to do so quickly. Will you please fasten a chair on the top step in such a way that we can use it to climb over the barricade without delay? We are like to be hard pressed, and it is no easy matter to get over a five-foot wall speedily with a crowd of armed men pressing hotly on your heels."

The provost told two of his men to pick out a square block of firewood, as nearly as possible the thickness of the height of one of the steps. After trying several they found one that would do, and on placing it on the stair next to the top it formed with the step above it a level platform. On this the chair was placed, a strong rope being attached to it so that it could be pulled up over the barricade when the last of the defenders had entered. By the time this was finished the battle below began in earnest. The infuriated assailants had pulled the doors outwards and were making desperate efforts to climb the pile of logs. This they soon found to be impossible, and began with their halberts to pull them down, and it was not long before they had dislodged sufficient to make a slope up which they could climb. Their work had not been carried on with impunity, for the archer had stationed himself on the top and sent his arrows thick and fast among them.

"In faith, master," he said to Guy, who stood close behind, "methinks that I am doing almost as much harm as good, for I am aiding them mightily in making their slope, which will presently contain as many dead men as logs."

As soon as they deemed the slope climbable the furious assailants charged up. They were met by Guy and the four men-at-arms. Tom had now slung his bow behind him and had betaken himself to his heavy axe, which crashed through the iron caps of the assailants as though they had been eggshells. But in such numbers did they press on that Guy saw that this barricade could not be much longer held.

"Get ready to retire when I give the word!" he shouted to his companions. "Tom, you and Jules Varoy and Robert Picard run first upstairs. When you have climbed the barricade, do you, Tom, take your place on the top. Jean Bart and I will come up last, and you can cover us with your arrows. Tell Maître Leroux to remove the light into the room, so that they will not be able to see what there is to encounter, while these torches here and those held by the crowd will enable you to see well enough to take aim. Now!" he shouted, "fall back!"

Tom and the two men-at-arms sprang up the stairs, Guy and Jean Bart followed more slowly, and halted a few steps from the top.

"All up, master!" Tom shouted, and Jean and Guy were able to cross the barricade before the foremost of their pursuers reached them. There had indeed been confusion below, for several of those who had first climbed the barricade had, instead of pressing hotly in pursuit, run along the hall and through the door into the shop, in their eagerness to be the first to seize upon the plunder. They expected the others to follow their example, but one of their leaders placed himself in their way and threatened to cut them down if they did not first assault the stairs.

"Fools!" he shouted, "do you think that the old fox has wasted the time we have given him? You may be sure that the richest prizes have been carried above."

There was an angry altercation, which was continued until those who had first run into the shop returned with the news that it had been completely stripped of its contents. There was now no longer any hesitation in obeying their leader, and the men poured up the stairs in a mass. Suddenly some torches appeared above, and those in front saw with consternation the obstacle that stood between them and their prey. They had little time for consideration, however, for the arrows from the archer now smote them, and that with a force and rapidity that bewildered them. Five or six of those in front fell shot through the brain.

"Heads down!" a voice shouted. There was no retreat for those in front, for the mass behind pressed them forward, and, instinctively obeying the order, they ran up. But neither helm nor breast-plate availed to keep out the terrible English arrows, which clove their way through the iron as if it had been pasteboard. Stumbling over the bodies of those who had fallen, the front rank of the assailants at last reached the barricade, but here their progress was arrested. A line of men stood behind the smooth wall of massive cases, and those who strove to climb it were smitten with axe or sword, while they themselves could not reach the defenders above them. They could but thrust blindly with pike or halbert, for if a face was raised to direct the aim one of the deadly arrows struck it instantly. In vain they strove by the aid of the halberts to haul down a case from its position, the weight was too great for one man's strength to move, and before several could grasp the handle of the halbert to aid them, the shaft was cut in two by the blow of an axe.

Hopeless as the attempt seemed, it was persevered in, for the crowd below, ignorant of the nature of the obstacle, maddened with fury and with the wine which had been freely served out before starting, still pressed forward, each fearing that the silversmith's treasures would be appropriated before he could obtain his share. For half an hour the fight continued, then there was a roar in the street, and Dame Margaret, who, after seeing the barricade above completed, had come down to her room and was gazing along the street, ran out on to the landing.

"Help is at hand!" she cried, "the knights are coming!"

Then came the loud tramp of horses, mingled with shouts of "Burgundy!" The crowd at the entrance at once turned and ran out, and as the alarm reached those within, they too rushed down, until the stairs were untenanted save by the dead. Bidding the others hold their places lest the assailants should return, Guy ran in and joined Lady Margaret at the window. A fierce conflict was going on in the street, with shouts of "Burgundy!" "A rescue!" "A rescue!"

The knights, who were followed by some fifty men-at-arms, rode into the mob, hewing them down with their swords. The humiliations that they had received from the arrogance and insolence of the butchers had long rankled in their minds, and they now took a heavy vengeance. The windows of all the houses opposite, from which men and women had been peering timidly out, were now crowded; women waving their handkerchiefs to the knights, and men loudly shouting greetings and encouragements. The whole of the traders of Paris were bitterly opposed to the domination of the market guilds, and while they cared but little for the quarrel between the rival dukes, the alliance between Burgundy and the butchers naturally drove them to sympathize with the opposite party. The proof afforded by the charge of the knights upon the mob delighted them, as showing that, allied with them though they might be, the Burgundians were determined no longer to allow the rioting and excesses of the men of the market guilds to continue.

In two or three minutes all was over. The resistance, though fierce, was short, and the mob was driven down the side streets and chased until the trading quarter was cleared of them. As the knights returned Guy went down to the door, to which Maître Leroux had already descended to thank his rescuers for their timely aid.

"I thank you, my lords and knights," the silversmith said, "for the timely succour you have rendered me. I would pray you to enter and to allow me to thank you in more worthy fashion, but indeed the stairs and passage are encumbered with dead."

"Dame Margaret of Villeroy prays me to say that she also desires greatly to thank you," Guy said.

"I feared that we should have been too late," Count Charles replied. "We lost no time when your messenger came, Guy, but it took some time to rouse the men-at-arms and to saddle our horses. You must have made a stout defence indeed, judging by the pile of dead that encumber your passage."

"There are many more inside," Guy said, "and methinks that we could have held out for another hour yet if it had been needed. Indeed, the only thing that I feared was that they might set fire to the lower part of the house."

"I should like to see your defences, Maître Leroux," Count Walter de Vesoul said, "What say you, my friends, shall we mount and see the scene of this battle? Methinks we might well gain something by it, for 'tis no slight thing that an unfortified house should for over an hour defend itself against a mob full a couple of thousand strong. I doubt not, too, that Master Leroux will serve us with a flagon of wine; and, moreover, we should surely pay our respects to this English lady,—who while a hostage of the duke has been thus sorely ill-treated by the scum of Paris,—if she will please receive us at this hour of the evening."

The other knights, of whom there were ten in number, at once dismounted. The silversmith's servants brought torches, and after ordering two of them to broach a cask of wine and to regale the men-at-arms, the provost led the way upstairs.

"Wait a moment, good provost," the Count de Vesoul said, "let us understand the thing from the beginning. I see that the knaves lying here and many of those in the road are pierced by arrows, which, as I note, have in some cases gone through iron cap or breast-piece; how comes that?"

"That is the work of one of my lady's retainers. He is an English archer, and one of the most skilful. He comes from her English estate, and when she chose him as one of the four men-at-arms to accompany her, he begged leave to bring his bow and arrows, and has in truth, as you see, made good use of them."

"That is the same tall fellow who, as I told you, Walter, did me such good service in that fray," said D'Estournel.

"By Saint Anne, Guy, I would that I had a dozen such men among my varlets. Why, there are a round dozen lying outside the door."

"There would have been more," Guy said, "had they not brought up that great gate and used it as a screen while they battered in the door here."

"Then you built the barricade behind it?" Count Walter said as he climbed over the heap of logs.

"Yes, Count, it was built against the door, but when that gave way they pulled it down with halberts until they could climb over it. But, as you see, no small portion of slope on the outside is composed of their bodies. The archer's arrows did good execution as they worked at it, and when they made the assault we-that is to say, Dame Margaret's four retainers and I—held it for some time, then we retired up the stairs and defended that barricade we had built across the top."

The knights picked their way among the bodies that encumbered the stairs.

"By Saint Denis, Charles, this is a strong work indeed!" the count said to D'Estournel, as they reached the top; "no wonder the knaves found it too much for them. What are all these massive cases?"

"They contain the goods from my shop," Maître Leroux said. "Master Aylmer had them carried here while the archer was defending the door, and by so doing not only made, as you see, a stout breast-work, but saved them from being plundered."

"They were well fitted for it," Guy said, "for they are very weighty; and though the fellows tried hard they could not move them with their hooks, and as fast as they strove to do so the provost's men and ours struck off the heads of the halberts with axes; and the work was all the more difficult as our archer had always a shaft fitted to let fly whenever they lifted their heads."

"But how did you manage to get over safely when they won the barricade below?" D'Estournel asked; "it was not an easy feat to climb this wall with a crowd of foemen behind."

Guy explained how they had arranged a chair to form a step. "There was, however," he went on, "no great need for haste. The archer and two others went first, and he took his stand on the top of the chests in readiness to cover the retreat of the fourth man-at-arms and myself. But happily many of the knaves wanted to sack the shop more than to follow us, and there was such confusion below, that we had time to climb over and pull up the chair before they had mustered to the attack."

While they were talking Long Tom and the others had removed one of the chests and made a passage by which they could pass through, and Maître Leroux led them into his private apartments, which were similar to, although larger than, Dame Margaret's. A number of candles had already been lighted, and in a minute Mistress Leroux entered, followed by two of her maids carrying trays with great beakers of wine and a number of silver goblets, and she and the provost then poured out the wine and offered it with further expressions of thanks to the knights.

"Say naught about it, madame," Count Walter said; "it was high time that a check was put on these rough fellows who lord it over Paris and deem themselves its masters. I doubt not that they will raise some outcry and lay their complaint before the duke; but you, I trust, and other worthy citizens, will be beforehand with them, and send off a messenger to him laying complaints against these fellows for attacking, plundering, and burning at their will the houses of those of better repute than themselves. We have come to your help not as officers of the duke, but as knights and gentlemen who feel it a foul wrong that such things should be done. Moreover, as Dame Margaret of Villeroy, a hostage of the duke, was lodged here at his request, it was a matter that nearly touched his honour that her life should be placed in danger by these scurvy knaves, and we shall so represent the matter to the duke."

Just as the knights had drunk their wine, Guy, who had left them on the landing, entered, escorting Dame Margaret and her two children. Count Charles d'Estournel, after saluting her, presented his companions to her, and she thanked each very heartily for the succour they had brought so opportunely.

"In truth, lady," the Count de Vesoul said, "methinks from what we saw that you might even have managed without us, so stoutly were you defended by your esquire and your retainers, aided as they were by those of the provost, though in the end it may be that these must have succumbed to numbers; for I can well imagine that your assailants, after the loss that they have suffered, would have spared no effort to avenge themselves, and might indeed, as a last resource, have fired the house. This they would no doubt have done long before had it not been that by so doing they would have lost all the plunder that they counted on. This stout defence will no doubt teach these fellows some moderation, for they will see that citizens' houses are not to be plundered without hard fighting and much loss. As for ourselves, we shall see the Duke of Burgundy's lieutenant to-morrow morning and lay the matter before him, praying him to issue a proclamation saying that in order to suppress the shameful disorders that have taken place, he gives notice that all who attack the houses of peaceful citizens will henceforth be treated as evildoers and punished accordingly."

After some further conversation the knights prepared to leave.

"I shall do myself the honour, sirs," Maître Leroux said, "of sending to your lodgings to-morrow the cups that you have used, as a small testimony of my gratitude to you, and as a memorial of the events of this evening."

While they were upstairs the men-at-arms and servants had been employed in clearing the stairs, throwing the bodies that had encumbered it out into the street. The men-at-arms of the knights had, after drinking the wine that had been sent out to them, aided in clearing the passage; buckets of water had been thrown down on the stairs, and the servitors by a vigorous use of brooms had removed most of the traces of the fray. The work had just been finished, and Dame Margaret's men had, by Guy's orders, stationed themselves on the landing to do honour to the knights as they set out.

"Ah, my tall friend," D'Estournel said to the archer, "so you have been at work again, and I can see that you are even more doughty with the bow than with that long staff of yours. Well, this time there must have been enough fighting to please even you."

"It has been an indifferent good fight, my lord," Tom said; "but in truth, save for the stand on that pile of logs below, when things were for a time brisk, it has been altogether too one-sided to please me."

"Most people would think that the one-sidedness was all the other way," D'Estournel laughed. "Well, men, you have all done your duty to your lady right well this night, and there is not one of us here who would not gladly have such brave fellows in his service. I see that you are all four wounded."

"They are scarce to be called wounds, Sir Count, seeing that they are but flesh cuts from their halberts which we got in the fray below. These slaughterers can doubtless strike a good blow with a pole-axe, but they are but clumsy varlets with other weapons. But to give them their due, they fought stoutly if with but little skill or discretion."

Several of the others also said a few words of commendation to the men. The provost and Guy escorted the knights to the door below. The latter had ordered twenty of their men-at-arms to remain in the house until morning, after which ten were to stay there until the doors had been repaired and refixed. As soon as the knights had ridden off the silversmith ordered several bundles of rushes to be strewn in the shop for the guard, and a meal of cold meat to be set for their supper. Two of them were posted as sentinels at the door.

"I shall not open the shop to-morrow," he said as he ascended the stairs with Guy, "nor indeed shall I do so until things have settled down. There will be for some time a mighty animosity on the part of these butchers and skinners against me, and it is only reasonable that after such an attack I should close my shop. Those who have dealings with me will know that they can do their business with me in private. And now methinks we will retire to bed; 'tis past midnight, and there is no fear of our being disturbed again. If they send anyone to spy out whether we are on the watch, the sight of the Burgundian soldiers below will suffice to tell them that there is nothing to be done. The first thing tomorrow I will set the carpenters to work to make me an even stronger pair of doors than those that have been spoilt."

Chapter X
After The Fray

On going into Dame Margaret's apartments Guy found that she had again retired to rest, and at once threw himself on his bed without disrobing himself further than taking off his armour, for he felt that it was possible the assailants might return after finding that the Burgundian knights and men-at-arms had ridden away. He had told the men-at-arms to keep watch by turns at the top of the stairs, where the barricade still remained, and to run in to wake him should they hear any disturbance whatever at the door below. He slept but lightly, and several times went out to see that the watch was being well kept, and to look up and down the street to assure himself that all was quiet.

"You did nobly last night, Guy," Dame Margaret said as she met him in the morning; "Sir Eustace himself could have done no better had he been here. When I next write to my lord I shall tell him how well you have protected us, and pray him to send word of it to your father."

"I did my best, lady; but it is to Long Tom that it is chiefly due that our defence was made good. It was his shooting that caused the long delay in breaking open the door, and that enabled us to hold the barricade below, and he also stoutly aided in the defence of the landing."

"Nevertheless, Guy, it was under your direction that all things were done. It is to the leader who directs that the first praise is due rather than to the strongest and bravest of his men-at-arms. It was, too, owing to your interference on behalf of Count Charles d'Estournel that we owe it that succour came to us; it was his friendship for you that prompted him to gather his friends to come to our aid; and it was the warning, short though it was, sent us by that strange Italian that enabled you to send to the count for aid. I must see his daughter and thank her personally for the part she played in the matter. No, Guy, had it not been for you this house would now have been an empty shell, and all of us would have been lying under its ruins. I have been thinking during the night that you must be most careful when you go abroad; you know that the son of that monster Caboche, the leader of the skinners, and doubtless many leaders of the butchers, among them Legoix, were killed, and their friends are certain to endeavour to take vengeance on you. They saw you at the window, they will know that you are my esquire, and will doubtless put down their defeat entirely to you. You cannot be too careful, and, above all, you must not venture out at night save on grave occasion. Agnes," she broke off as the girl entered the room, "you too must thank our brave esquire for having so stoutly defended us."

"I do thank you most heartily, Guy," the girl said, "though I felt it very hard that I could do nothing to help you. It was terrible sitting here and hearing the fight so close to us, and the dreadful shouts and screams of those people, and to have nothing to do but to wait. Not that I was frightened, I felt quite confident that you would beat them, but it was so hard to sit quiet. I should not have minded so much if I could have been standing there to see the brave deeds that were being done."

"Like the queen of a tournament, Agnes," her mother said with a smile. "Yes, indeed, it is one of the hardships of us women. It is only when a castle is besieged and her lord is away that a woman may buckle on armour and set an example to her retainers by showing herself on the wall and risking the enemies' bolts, or even, if necessary, taking her place with her retainers on the breach; at other times she must be passive and wait while men fight."

"If I had only had my bow," Agnes said regretfully, "I could really have done something. You would have let me go out then, mother, would you not?"

"I don't know, dear; no, I don't think I should. It was anxious work enough for me as it was. If you had gone out I must have done so, and then Charlie would have wanted to go too. No; it was much better that we all sat together as we did, waiting quietly for what might come, and praying for those who were fighting for us."

"I was glad that Madame Leroux stayed upstairs with her maid instead of coming down here as you asked her, mother; she looked so scared and white that I do think it would have been worse than listening to the fighting to have had to sit and look at her."

Dame Margaret smiled. "Yes, Agnes, but I think that she was more frightened for her husband than for herself, and I don't suppose that she had ever been in danger before. Indeed, I must say that to look out at that crowd of horrible creatures below, brandishing their weapons, shouting and yelling, was enough to terrify any quiet and peaceable woman. As a knight's wife and daughter it was our duty to be calm and composed and to set an example, but a citizen's wife would not feel the same obligation, and might show her alarm without feeling that she disgraced herself or her husband."

On going out Guy found their host already engaged in a conference with a master carpenter as to the construction of the new doors. They were to be very strong and heavy, made of the best oak, and protected by thick sheets of iron; the hinges were to be of great strength to bear the weight. A smith had also arrived to receive instructions for making and setting very strong iron bars before the shop, the front of which would require to be altered to allow of massive shutters being erected on the inside. Iron gates were also to be fixed before the door.

"That will make something like a fortress of it, Master Aylmer," the silversmith said, "and it will then need heavy battering-rams to break into it. Several others of my craft similarly protect their shops; and certainly no one can blame me, after the attack of last night, for taking every means to defend myself. I intend to enlist a party of ten fighting men to act as a garrison until these troubles are all over."

"I think that you will act wisely in doing so," Guy said. "Your servants all bore themselves bravely last night, but they had no defensive armour and were unaccustomed to the use of weapons. Only I would advise you to be very careful as to the men that you engage, or you may find your guard within as dangerous as the mob without."

"I will take every pains as to that, you may be sure, and will engage none save after a careful inquiry into their characters."

The streets had already been cleared of the slain. All through the night little parties had searched for and carried off their dead, and when at early morning the authorities sent a party down to clear the street there remained but some twenty-five bodies, evidently by their attire belonging to the lowest class, and presumably without friends. That day petitions and complaints were sent to the king by the provosts of the merchants, the gold and silver smiths, the cloth merchants, the carpenters and others, complaining of the tumults caused by the butchers and their allies, and especially of the attack without cause or reason upon the house of Maître Leroux, the worshipful provost of the silversmiths. Several skirmishes occurred in the evening between the two parties, but an order was issued in the name of the king to the Maire and syndics of Paris rebuking them for allowing such disturbances and tumults, and ordering them to keep a portion of the burgher guard always under arms, and to repress such disturbances, and severely punish those taking part in them.

Maître Leroux and his wife paid a formal visit to Dame Margaret early in the day to thank her for the assistance that her retainers had given in defending the house.

"You were good enough to say, madame," the silversmith said, "that you regretted the trouble that your stay here gave us. We assured you then, and truly, that the trouble was as nothing, and that we felt your presence as an honour; now you see it has turned out more. Little did we think when you came here but a few days since that your coming would be the means of preserving our lives and property, yet so it has been, for assuredly if it had not been for your esquire and brave retainers we should have been murdered last night. As it is we have not only saved our lives but our property, and save for the renewal of the doors we shall not have been the losers even in the value of a crown piece. Thus, from being our guests you have become our benefactors; and one good result of what has passed is, that henceforth you will feel that, however long your stay here, and however much we may try to do for you, it will be but a trifle towards the discharge of the heavy obligation under which we feel to you."

After a meeting of the city council that afternoon, a guard of ten men was sent to the silversmith's to relieve the Burgundian men-at-arms. Five of these were to be on duty night and day until the house was made secure by the new doors and iron grill erected in front of the shop. Guy proposed to Dame Margaret that he should give up his visit to the *salle d'armes*, but this she would not hear of.

"I myself and the children will go no more abroad until matters become more settled, but it is on all accounts well that you should go to the school of arms. Already the friends that you have made have been the means of saving our lives, and it is well to keep them. We know not what is before us, but assuredly we need friends. Maître Leroux was telling me this morning that the Armagnacs are fast approaching, and that in a few days they will be within a short distance of Paris. Their approach will assuredly embitter the hostility between the factions here, and should they threaten the town there may be fierce fighting within the walls as well as without. At present, at any rate, there are likely to be no more disturbances such as that of last night, and therefore no occasion for you to remain indoors. Even these butchers, arrogant as they are, will not venture to excite the indignation that would be caused by another attack on this house. That, however, will make it all the more likely that they will seek revenge in other ways, and that the house will be watched at night and any that go out followed and murdered.

"You and Tom the archer are no doubt safe enough from the attack of ordinary street ruffians, but no two men, however strong and valiant, can hope to defend themselves successfully against a score of cut-throats. But I pray you on your way to the school go round and thank, in my name, this Italian and his daughter, and say that I desire much to thank the young lady personally for the immense service she has rendered me and my children. Take the archer with you, for even in the daytime there are street brawls in which a single man who had rendered himself obnoxious could readily be despatched."

"In faith, Master Guy," Long Tom said as they sallied out, "it seems to me that if our stay in Paris is a prolonged one I shall return home rich enough to buy me an estate, for never did money so flow into my pocket. We have been here but a short time, and I have gained as much and more than I should do in a year of hard service. First there was that young French count, the very next morning when he called here he gave me a purse with thirty crowns, telling me pleasantly that it was at the rate of five crowns for each skull I cracked on his behalf. Then this morning Maître Leroux came to me and said, 'Good fellow, it is greatly to your skill and valour that I owe my life, and that of my wife; this will help you to set up housekeeping; when you return home,' and he gave me a purse with a hundred crowns in it; what think you of that, master? The other three also got purses of fifty crowns each. If that is the rate of pay in Paris for a couple of hours' fighting, I do not care how often I take a share in a fray."

"You are doing well indeed, Tom, but you must remember that sooner or later you might go into a fray and lose your life, and with it the chance of buying that estate you speak of."

"We must all take our chances, master, and there is no winning a battle without the risk of the breaking of casques. Are we going to the house we went to the first night we came here, Master Guy? Methinks that this is the street we stopped at."

"Yes, Tom. It was the man who lives here who sent me word that the butchers were going to attack the provost's house, by the same messenger who met us before Notre Dame, and who last night, after warning me, carried my message to Count Charles, praying him to come to our aid."

"Then he did us yeoman service," the archer said warmly, "though I think not that they would have carried the barricade had they fought till morning."

"Perhaps not, though I would not say so for certain, for they might have devised some plan such as they did for covering themselves while they assaulted the door. But even had they not done so they would have been sure before they retired to have fired the house."

"That is what I thought of when they were attacking us," the archer said, "and wondered why they should waste men so freely when a torch would have done their business just as well for them."

"That would have been so, Tom, had they only wished to kill us; but though, no doubt, the leaders desired chiefly the life of the provost, the mob simply fought for plunder. If they had found all the jeweller's store in his shop, they would have fired the house very quickly when they discovered that they could not get at us. But it was the plunder that they wanted, and it was the sight of those chests full of silver-ware that made them venture their lives so freely, in order to have the handling of it. I do not think that I shall be long here, Tom. Do not wait for me at the door, but stroll up and down, keeping a short distance away, so that I can see you when I come out."

A decrepit old woman opened the door, and on Guy giving his name she said that she had orders to admit him if he called. The girl came out dressed in her female attire as he went upstairs.

"Ah, signor," she said, "I am glad indeed to see that you are safe."

"Thanks to you," he said warmly; "we are all your debtors indeed."

"I had but to run a mile or two," she said; "but what was there in that? But indeed I had an anxious time, I so feared that I should be too late. When I had seen the Count d'Estournel and delivered your message to him and had shown him your ring, and he and his friends had declared that they would call up their men and come at once to your aid, I could not go back and wait until this morning to learn if they arrived in time, so I ran to your street again and hid in a doorway and looked out. Just as I got there they broke in the door and I saw some of them rush in. But there was a pause, though they were all pressing to enter. They went in very slowly, and I knew that you must be defending the entrance. At last there was a sudden rush, and I almost cried out. I thought that it was all over. A great many entered and then there was a pause again. The crowd outside became more and more furious; it was dreadful to hear their shouts and to see the waving of torches and weapons.

"They seemed to be almost mad to get in. The crush round the door was terrible, and it was only when two or three horsemen rode in among them shouting, that the press ceased a little. One horseman obtained silence for a moment by holding up his hand. He told them that their friends inside were attacking a barricade, and would soon carry it, and then there would be silver enough for all; but that by pressing forward they did but hamper the efforts of their comrades. It seemed, oh, such a long, long time before I saw the Burgundians coming along, and I could not help throwing my cap up and shouting when they charged into the crowd. I waited until it was all over, and then I ran back home and had a rare scolding for being out so late; but I did not mind that much, after knowing that you were all safe."

At this moment a voice from the landing above said: "Are you going to keep Master Aylmer there all day with your chattering, Katarina?" The girl made a little face and nodded to Guy to go upstairs.

"Katarina is becoming a madcap," the astrologer said, as he led Guy into the room. "I cannot blame her altogether; I have made a boy of her, and I ought not to be shocked at her acting like one. But she gave me a rare fright last night when she did not return until close on midnight. Still, it was natural for her to wish to see how her mission had turned out."

"Her quickness saved all our lives," Guy said. "Had it not been for her carrying my message to the Count d'Estournel we should have been burnt alive before morning."

"It was unfortunate that I sent you the message so late, Master Aylmer. I was busy when a medical student who sometimes gathers news for me in the butchers' quarter came here, and left a missive for me. Had he sent up a message to me that it was urgent, I would have begged the personage I had with me to wait a moment while I read the letter. As it was, it lay downstairs till my visitor departed. When I learned the news I sent off Katarina at once. She had but a short time before come in, and was fortunately still in her boy's dress, so there was no time lost. I went out myself at ten o'clock to see what was going on, and must have been close to her without either of us knowing it. I looked on for a short time; but seeing that nothing could be done, and feeling sure that the house must be taken, —knowing nothing of the chance of the Burgundians coming to the rescue, —I returned here and was surprised to find that Katarina had not returned.

"I did not think that she could have reached the shop and warned you before the mob arrived, and therefore I became greatly alarmed as the time went by without her appearing. Indeed, my only hope was that she must have been looking on at the fight and would return when it was

533

all over, as indeed it turned out; and I should have rated her much more soundly than I did had she not told me how she had fetched the Burgundians and that they had arrived in time. I hear that there is a great stir this morning. The number of men they have lost, and specially the deaths of Legoix and of the young Caboche, have infuriated the butchers and skinners. They have already sent off two of their number to lay their complaint before the Duke of Burgundy of the conduct of some of his knights in attacking them when they were assailing the house of a noted Armagnac. But they feel that they themselves for the moment must remain quiet, as the royal order has emboldened the Maire, supported by the traders' guilds, and notably by the carpenters, who are a very strong body, to call out a portion of the city guard, and to issue an order that all making disturbances, whomsoever they may be and under whatsoever pretext they are acting, will be summarily hung if captured when so engaged.

"In spite of this there will no doubt be troubles; but they will not venture again to attack the house of the silversmith, at any rate until an order comes from the Duke of Burgundy to forbid his knights from interfering in any way with their doings."

"Which I trust he will not send," Guy said; "and I doubt if the knights will obey it if it comes. They are already much enraged at the insolence of the butchers, and the royal proclamation this morning will justify them in aiding to put down disturbances whatsoever may be the duke's orders. And now, Sir Count, I have come hither this morning on behalf of my lady mistress to thank you for sending the news, and still more for the service your daughter rendered in summoning the knights to her assistance. She desires much to return thanks herself to your daughter, and will either call here to see her or would gladly receive her at her lodging should you prefer that."

"I should prefer it, Master Aylmer. Your lady can scarce pass through the streets unnoticed, for her English appearance marks her at once; and as all know she lodges at the silversmith's, she will be more particularly noticed after the events of last night, and her coming here will attract more attention to me than I care for. Therefore I will myself bring Katarina round and will do myself the honour of calling upon your lady. I can wrap the girl up in a cloak so that she shall not attract any observation, for no one knows, save the old woman below, that I have a daughter here; and with so many calling at the house, and among them some reckless young court gallants, I care not that it should be known, if for no other reason than, were it so, it would be soon suspected that the lad who goes so often in and out is the girl in disguise, and I could then no longer trust her in the streets alone."

"You will find my lady in at whatever hour you come, signor, for she has resolved not to go abroad again until order is restored in Paris."

"The decision is a wise one," the Italian said; "though indeed I think not that she would be in any danger, save that which every good-looking woman runs in troubled times like these, when crime is unpunished, and those in authority are far too occupied with their own affairs to trouble their heads about a woman being carried off. But it is different with you and your comrade. The butchers know well enough that it was your work that caused their failure last night. Your appearance at the window was noticed, and it was that tall archer of yours who played such havoc among them. Therefore I advise you to be ever on your guard, and to purchase a mail shirt and wear it under your doublet; for, however watchful you may be, an assassin may steal up behind you and stab you in the back. You may be sure that Caboche and the friends of Legoix will spare no pains to take vengeance upon you."

Guy presently rejoined the archer in the street. "Henceforth, Tom," he said, "you must always put on breast-and-back piece when you go out. I have been warned that our lives will almost surely be attempted, and that I had best put on a mail shirt under my doublet."

"Perhaps it would be best, Master Guy. I fear not three men if they stand up face to face with me, but to be stabbed in the back is a thing that neither strength nor skill can save one from. But as I care not to be always going about in armour I will expend some of my crowns in buying a shirt of mail also. 'Tis better by far than armour, for a man coming up behind could stab one over the line of the back-piece or under the arm, while if you have mail under your coat they will strike at you fair between the shoulders, and it is only by striking high up on the neck that they have any chance with you. A good coat of mail is money well laid out, and will last a lifetime; and even if it cost me all the silversmith's crowns I will have a right good one."

Guy nodded. He was wondering in his own mind how he should be able to procure one. His father had given him a purse on starting, but the money might be needed for emergencies. He certainly could not ask his mistress for such a sum, for she too might have need of the money that she had brought with her. He was still turning it over in his mind when they reached the fencing-school. He was greeted with acclamations as he entered by the young count and his friends.

"Here is our defender of houses," the former exclaimed. "Truly, Guy, you have given a lesson to the butchers that they sorely needed. They say that the king himself, who is in one of his good moods to-day, has interested himself mightily in the fray last night, and that he has expressed a wish to hear of it from the esquire who he has been told commanded the defence. So it is not unlikely that there will be a royal message for you to attend at the palace. Fortunately we had the first say in the matter this morning. My father returned last night, and as he is rather a favourite of his majesty, we got him to go to the king and obtain audience as soon as he arose, to complain of the conduct of the butchers in attacking the house of the provost of the silversmiths, and where, moreover, Dame Villeroy, who had arrived here in obedience to his majesty's own commands, was lodged. The king when he heard it was mightily offended. He said he had not been told of her coming, and that this insult to her touched his honour. He sent at once for the Maire and syndics, and upbraided them bitterly for allowing such tumults to take place, and commanded them to put a stop to them under pain of his severe displeasure.

"That accounts, you see, for the Maire's proclamation this morning. The king desired my father to thank me and the other knights and gentlemen for having put down the riot, and said that he would at once send off a message to the Duke of Burgundy commanding him to pay no attention to any reports the butchers might send to him, but to give them a stern answer that the king was greatly displeased with their conduct, and that if any fresh complaint about them was made he would straightway have all their leaders hung.

"It is one thing to threaten, and another to do, Guy; but at any rate, so long as the duke is away they will see that they had best keep quiet; for when the king is in his right senses and is not swayed by others, he is not to be trifled with.

"You can imagine what an excitement there was last night when that boy you sent arrived. The ring was sent up first, and when I gave orders that he should be admitted he came in well-nigh breathless. There were six or eight of us, and all were on the point of leaving. Thinking that it might be something private, they had taken up their hats and cloaks. The boy, as he came in, said, 'Which of you is Count Charles d'Estournel?' 'I am,' I said. 'You are the bearer of a message from Guy Aylmer?' 'I am, my lord. He prays you hasten to his assistance, for the butchers and skinners are attacking Maître Leroux's house, and had begun to hammer on the door when I was still in the street. If they make their way in, they will surely kill all they find in there. They are shouting, 'Death to the Armagnacs! Death to the English spies!'

"I called upon my comrades to join me, and all were eager to do so. We had long been smarting under the conduct of these ruffians, and moreover I was glad to discharge a part of my debt to you. So each ran to his lodgings and despatched servitors to summon their men-at-arms, and to order the horses to be saddled, and to gather in front of my lodging with all speed. Two or three of my friends who had left earlier were also summoned; but though we used all the speed we could it was more than an hour before all were assembled. The men-at-arms were scattered, and had to be roused; then there was the work of getting the stables open, and we had to force the doors in some places to do it. I was on thorns, as you may well imagine, and had little hope when we started that we should find any of you alive. Delighted indeed we were when, on getting near enough, we could see the crowd were stationary, and guessed at once that you were still holding out-though how you could have kept so large a number at bay was beyond us. We struck heartily and heavily, you may be sure, and chased the wolves back to their dens with a will. I hear that, what with those you slew in the house and street and those we cut down, it is reckoned that a couple of hundred were killed; though as to this none can speak with certainty, seeing that so many bodies were carried away before morning."

"I trust that none of you received wounds, Count Charles?"

"None of us; though several of the men-at-arms had gashes from the rascals' weapons, but naught, I think, that will matter."

At this moment one of the attendants of the salon came in.

"An usher from the palace is here, my lords and gentlemen. He has been to the lodging of Master Guy Aylmer, and has learned that he will most likely be here. If so, he has the king's command to conduct him to the palace, as His Majesty desires to have speech with him."

"I told you so, Guy; my father's story has excited the king's curiosity, and he would fain hear all about it. Make the most of it, for His Majesty loves to be entertained and amused."

"Had I better ask the usher to allow me to go back to my lodging to put on a gayer suit than this?" Guy asked.

"Certainly not; the king loves not to be kept waiting. Fortunately no time has been wasted so far, as this is on the road from the silversmith's to the palace."

The Louvre at that time bore no resemblance to the present building. It was a fortress surrounded by a strong embattled wall, having a lofty tower at each corner and others flanking its gates. On the water-face the towers rose from the edge of the river, so that there was no passage along the quays. The building itself was in the castellated form, though with larger windows than were common in such edifices. Eight turret-shaped buildings rose far above it, each surmounted with very high steeple-like roofs, while in the centre rose another large and almost perpendicular roof, terminating in a square open gallery. The building was further protected by four embattled towers on each side, so that if the outer wall were carried it could still defend itself. In the court-yard between the outer wall and the palace were rows of low barracks, where troops were lodged. Two regiments of the best soldiers of Burgundy were quartered here, as the duke feared that some sudden rising of the Armagnac party might put them in possession of the king's person, in which case the Orleanists would easily persuade him to issue proclamations as hostile to Burgundy as those which were now published in his name against the Orleanists. The Louvre, indeed, differed but slightly from palaces of several of the great nobles within the walls of Paris, as all of these were to some extent fortified, and stood as separate fortresses capable of offering a stout resistance to any attack by the populace.

"I would rather face those villains of last night for another hour than go before the king," Guy said, as he prepared to follow the attendant; "but I trust that good may come of my interview, and that I can interest the king in the case of my mistress."

Joining the usher, who was waiting at the entrance, and who saluted him courteously-for the manner in which the message had been communicated to the usher showed him that the young squire was in no disgrace with the king-Guy walked with him to the Louvre, which was a short half-mile distant. Accompanied as he was by a royal officer, the guard at the gate offered no interruption to his passage, and proceeding across the court-yard he entered the great doorway to the palace, and, preceded by the usher, ascended the grand staircase and followed him along a corridor to the apartments occupied by the king.

Chapter XI
Danger Threatened

On being ushered into the royal apartment Guy was led up to the king, who was seated in a large arm-chair. He was stroking the head of a greyhound, and two or three other dogs lay at his feet. Except two attendants, who stood a short distance behind his chair, no one else was present. The king was pale and fragile-looking; there was an expression of weariness on his face, for in the intervals between his mad fits he had but little rest. He was naturally a kind-hearted man, and the troubles that reigned in France, the constant contention among the great lords, and even among the members of his own family, were a constant source of distress to him. Between the Duke of Burgundy, the queen, his nephew of Orleans, and the other royal dukes he had no peace, and the sense of his inability to remedy matters, and of his position of tutelage in the hands of whoever chanced for the moment to be in the ascendant, in no slight degree contributed to the terrible attacks to which he was subject. At the present moment the Duke of Burgundy was away, and therefore, feeling now comparatively free, he looked up with interest when the usher announced Guy Aylmer.

"You are young, indeed, sir," he said, as Guy made a deep bow, "to be the hero of the story that I heard this morning. I hear that you have been slaying many of the good citizens of Paris!"

"Some have certainly been slain, sire; but I think not that any of them could be considered as good citizens, being engaged, as they were, in attacking the house of the worshipful provost of the silversmiths, Maître Leroux."

"I know him," the king said, "and have bought many rare articles of his handiwork, and more than once when I have needed it have had monies from him on usance. 'Tis a grave scandal that so good a citizen should thus be attacked in my city, but I will see that such doings shall not take place again. And now I would hear from your own lips how you and a few men defended the house so long, and, as I hear, with very heavy loss to those attacking it. I am told that you are English."

"Yes, sire, I have the honour to be an esquire to Sir Eustace de Villeroy, and am here in attendance upon his dame, who, with her two children, have been brought as hostages to Paris under your royal order."

A look of pain passed across the king's face. "Your lord is our vassal for his castle at Villeroy?"

"He is, sire, and is also a vassal of England for the estates of his wife."

"Since England and France are not at present on ill terms," the king said, "he may well discharge both duties without treason to either Henry or myself; but they told me that his vassalage to me has sat but lightly upon him."

"His father and grandfather, sire, were vassals of England, as Villeroy was then within the English bounds, but he is, I am assured, ready faithfully to render any service that your majesty might demand of him, and is willing to submit himself, in all respects, to your will. But since he wishes not to take any part in the troubles between the princes, it seems that both regard him with hostility. Two months since his castle was attacked by some eight thousand men from Ham, led by Sir Clugnet de Brabant. These he repulsed with heavy loss, and deemed that in so doing he was acting in accordance with your majesty's proclamation, and was rendering faithful service to you in holding the castle against your enemies, and he had hoped for your majesty's approbation. He was then deeply grieved when your royal herald summoned him, in your name, either to receive a garrison or to send his wife and children hither as hostages."

"I will see into the matter," the king said earnestly. "And so your mistress was bestowed at the house of Maître Leroux?"

"She was, sire, and is most hospitably entertained by him."

"Now let us hear of this defence. Tell me all that took place; withhold nothing."

Guy related the details of the defence.

"Truly it was well done, young sir, and I owe you thanks for having given so shrewd a lesson to these brawlers, Maître Leroux has good reasons for being thankful to the duke for lodging your lady in his house, for he would doubtless have lost his life had you and your four men not been there. When the Duke of Burgundy returns I will take council with him touching this matter of your mistress. I know that he gave me good reasons at the time for the bringing of her hither, but in the press of matters I do not recall what they were. At any rate, as she is here as my hostage her safety must be ensured, and for the present I will give orders that a guard be placed at the house."

He extended his hand to Guy, who went on one knee to kiss it and then retired.

He took the news back to Dame Margaret.

"I knew well enough that the poor king had nothing to do with the matter," she said. "Were it otherwise I would myself have asked for an audience with him; but I knew that it would be useless, he would but have replied to me as he has to you, that he must consult the duke."

In the afternoon the Italian called with his daughter upon Dame Margaret. The former was now dressed in accordance with his rank as an Italian noble, and the girl, on laying aside her cloak, was also in the costume of a young lady of position. Guy presented the count to his mistress.

"I am greatly indebted to you, Count Montepone," she said, "for the timely warning that you sent us, and still more for the service rendered to us by your daughter in summoning the Burgundian knights to our aid. Truly," she added with a smile, "it is difficult to believe that it was this young lady who was so busy on our behalf. I thank you, maiden, most heartily. And, believe me, should the time ever come when you require a friend; which I hope may never be the case, you will find one in me on whom you can confidently rely.

"This is my daughter Agnes. She is, methinks, but a year or so younger than yourself, though she is as tall or taller, and she will gladly be your friend also."

Katarina replied quietly and composedly, and Guy, as he watched her and Agnes talking together, was surprised at the way in which she adapted herself to circumstances. As a boy she assumed the character so perfectly that no one would suspect her of being aught else. She was a French gamin, with all the shrewdness, impudence, and self-confidence of the class. As he saw her at her father's in female attire something of the boy's nature seemed still to influence her. There was still a touch of sauciness in her manner, and something of defiance, as if she resented his knowledge of her in her other character. Now she had the quiet composure of a young lady of rank. As Dame Margaret had said, she was but little older than Agnes; but though less tall than the English girl, she looked a woman beside her. Guy stood talking with them while Dame Margaret and the count conversed apart. Gradually as they chatted Katarina's manner, which had at first been somewhat stiff, thawed, and Guy left her and Agnes together and went to look through the window.

He could vaguely understand that Katarina at first, knowing that Dame Margaret and Agnes must be aware of her going about as a boy, was standing a little on her dignity. The simple straightforwardness of Agnes and her admiration of the other's boldness and cleverness had disarmed Katarina, and it was not long before they were chatting and laughing in girlish fashion. There was a difference in their laughter, the result of the dissimilar lives they had led. One had ever been a happy, careless child, allowed to roam about in the castle or beyond it almost unattended, and had only to hold herself as became the position of a maiden of rank on special occasions, as when guests were staying in the castle; the other had been for years her father's assistant, engaged in work requiring shrewdness and quickness and not unattended at times with danger. She had been brought into contact with persons of all ranks and conditions, and at times almost forgot her own identity, and was in thought as well as manner the quick-witted messenger of her father. After the latter had chatted for some time with Dame Margaret he beckoned her to him.

"Dame Margaret has promised me to be your protector should aught befall me, child," he said, "and I charge you now in her hearing should anything happen to me to go at once to her castle at Villeroy, and should she not be there to her castle at Summerley, which lies but twelve miles from the English port of Southampton, and there to place yourself under her guardianship, and to submit yourself to her will and guidance wholly and entirely. It would be well indeed for you to have a quiet English home after our troubled life. To Italy you cannot go, our estates are long since confiscated; and did you return there you would find powerful enemies and but lukewarm friends. Besides, there would be but one mode of life open to you, namely, to enter a convent, which would, methinks, be of all others the least suited to your inclinations."

"I can promise you a hearty welcome," Dame Margaret said kindly. "I trust that you may never apply for it; but should, as your father says, aught happen to him, come to me fearlessly, and be assured that you will be treated as one of my own family. We shall ever be mindful of the fact that you saved our lives last night, and that nothing that we can do for you will cancel that obligation."

"I trust that I may never be called upon to ask your hospitality, Lady Margaret," the girl said quietly, "but I thank you with all my heart for proffering it, and I feel assured that I should find a happy home in England."

"'Tis strange how it has all come about," her father said. "'Tis scarce a month since I saw Dame Margaret enter Paris with her children, and the thought occurred to me that it would be well indeed for you were you in the charge of such a lady. Then, as if in answer to my thoughts, I saw her young esquire in the crowd listening to me, and was moved at once to say words that would induce him to call upon me afterwards, when I saw that I might possibly in these troublous times be of use to his mistress. And thus in but a short time what was at first but a passing thought has been realized. It is true that there are among my clients those whose protection I could obtain for you; but France is at present as much torn by factions as is our native Italy, and none can say but, however highly placed and powerful a man may be to-day, he might be in disgrace to-morrow."

Carefully wrapping his daughter up in her cloak again, the Italian took his leave, refusing the offer of Dame Margaret for two of her men-at-arms to accompany them.

"There is no fear of trouble of any sort to-day," he said. "The loss that was suffered last night was so severe that the people will be quiet for a few days, especially as the king, as well as the city authorities, are evidently determined to put a stop to rioting. Moreover, the fact that the Burgundian nobles have, now that the duke is away, taken a strong part against the butchers' faction has for the moment completely cowed them. But, apart from this, it is my special desire to return to my house unnoticed. It is seldom that I am seen going in and out, for I leave home as a rule before my neighbours are about, and do not return till after nightfall. I make no secret of my being a vendor of drugs at the fairs, and there are few can suspect that I have visitors after dark."

"I like your astrologer, Guy," Dame Margaret said when they had left. "Before I saw him I own that I had no great faith in his countship. Any man away from his native country can assume a title without anyone questioning his right to use it, so long as he is content to live in obscurity, and to abstain from attracting the attention of those who would be likely to make inquiries. But I have no doubt that our friend is, as he represents himself, the Count of Montepone, and I believe him to be sincere in the matter of his dealings with us. He tells me that he has received more than one hint that the reports that he deals with the stars and exercises divinations have come to the ears of the church, and it is likely ere long he may be forced to leave Paris, and indeed that he would have done so before now had it not been that some of those who have had dealings with him have exercised their influence to prevent things being pushed further.

"No doubt it is true that, as he asserts, he in no way dabbles in what is called 'black art,' but confines himself to reading the stars; and he owned to me that the success he has obtained in this way is to some extent based upon the information that he obtains from persons of all classes. He is evidently a man whose nature it is to conspire, not so much for the sake of any prospect of gain or advantage, but for the pleasure of conspiring. He has dealings with men of both factions. Among the butchers he is believed to be an agent of the duke, who has assumed the character of a vendor of nostrums simply as a disguise, while among the Armagnacs he is regarded as an agent of Orleans. It is doubtless a dangerous game to play, but it both helps him in his profession of astrologer and gives him influence and power. I asked him why he thus mingled in public affairs. He smiled and said: 'We are always conspiring in Italy; we all belong to factions. I have been brought up in an atmosphere of conspiracy, and it is so natural to me that I could scarce live without it. I am rich: men who trade upon the credulity of fools have plenty of clients. My business of a quack doctor brings me in an income that many a poor nobleman would envy. I travel when I like; I visit alternately all the great towns of France, though Paris has always been my head-quarters.

"'As an astrologer I have a wide reputation. The name of the Count Smarondi-for it is under that title that I practise-is known throughout France, though few know me personally or where I am to be found. Those who desire to consult me can only obtain access to me through some of those whose fortunes I have rightly foretold, and who have absolute faith in me, and even these must first obtain my consent before introducing anyone to me. All this mystery adds both to my reputation and to my fees. Could anyone knock at my door and ask me to calculate his horoscope he would prize it but little; when it is so difficult to obtain an introduction to me, and it is regarded as a matter of favour to be allowed to consult me, people are ready to pay extravagant sums for my advice. And,' he said with a smile, 'the fact that ten days or a fortnight always elapses between the time I am asked to receive a new client and his or her first interview with me, enables me to make such minute inquiries that I can not only gain their complete confidence by my knowledge of certain events in their past, but it will aid me in my divination of their future.

"'I believe in the stars, madame, wholly and implicitly, but the knowledge to be gained from them is general and not particular; but with that general knowledge, and with what I know of men's personal character and habits, of their connections, of their political schemes and personal ambitions, I am able in the majority of cases so to supplement the knowledge I gain from the stars, as to trace their future with an accuracy that seems to them astonishing indeed. For example, madame, had I read in the stars that a dire misfortune impended over you last night, and had I learned that there was a talk among the butchers that the provost of the silversmiths was a strong opponent of theirs, and that steps would shortly be taken to show the Parisians the danger of opposing them, it would have needed no great foresight on my part to tell you that you were threatened with a great danger, and that the danger would probably take the form of an attack by the rabble on the house you occupied. I should naturally put it less plainly. I should tell you to beware of this date, should warn you that I saw threatening faces and raised weapons, and that the sounds of angry shouts demanding blood were in my ears.

"'Any astrologer, madame, who works by proper methods can, from the conjunction of the stars at anyone's birth, calculate whether their aspect will be favourable or unfavourable at any given time, and may foretell danger or death; but it needs a knowledge of human nature, a knowledge of character and habits, and a knowledge of the questioner's surroundings to be able to go much farther than this. That I have had marvellous successes and that my counsels are eagerly sought depends, then, upon the fact that I leave nothing to chance, but that while enveloping myself in a certain amount of mystery I have a police of my own consisting of men of all stations, many, indeed most of whom, do not know me even by sight. They have no idea of the object of my inquiries, and indeed believe that their paymaster is the head of the secret police, or the agent of some powerful minister.'

"You see, Guy, the count spoke with perfect frankness to me. His object naturally was to gain my confidence by showing himself as he is, and to explain why he wished to secure a home for his daughter. He took up his strange profession in the first place as a means of obtaining his living, and perhaps to secure himself from the search of private enemies who would have had him assassinated could he have been found; but he follows it now from his love for an atmosphere of intrigue, and for the power it gives him, because, as he told me, he has already amassed a considerable fortune, and could well retire and live in luxury did he choose. He said frankly that if he did not so interest himself his existence would be simply intolerable to him.

"'I may take my daughter to England,' he said; 'I may stay there until I see her established in life, but when I had done so I should have to return here. Paris is always the centre of intrigues; I would rather live on a crust here than be a prince elsewhere.'

"He certainly succeeded in convincing me wholly of his sincerity, as far as we are concerned. Devoted to intrigue himself, he would fain that his daughter should live her life in peace and tranquillity, and that the money for which he has no use himself should be enjoyed by her. 'I have lost my rank,' he said, 'forfeited it, if you will; but she is the Countess Katarina of Montepone, and I should like to know that she and my descendants after her should live the life that my ancestors lived. It is a weakness, a folly, I know; but we have all our weak points and our follies. At any rate I see that that fancy could not well be carried out in France or in Italy, but it may be in England.' At any rate, after all he has told me I feel that he has it in his power to be a very useful friend and ally to us here; I am convinced that he is truly desirous of being so."

"And how did you like the girl, Agnes?" she said, raising her voice. Agnes had fetched Charlie in, and they were looking together down into the street while their mother was talking to Guy.

"I hardly know, mother; she seemed to be so much older than I am. Sometimes when she talked and laughed, I thought I liked her very much, and then a minute later it seemed to me that I did not understand her one bit. But I do think that she would be very nice when one came to know her thoroughly."

"She has lived so different a life to yourself, Agnes, that it is no wonder that you should feel at first that you have nothing in common with her. That she is very clever I have no doubt, and that she is brave and fearless we know. Can you tell us anything more, Guy?"

"Not very much more, Lady Margaret. I should say that she was very true and loyal. I think that at present she enters into what she has to do in something of the same spirit as her father, and that she thoroughly likes it. I think that she is naturally full of fun and has high spirits, and that she enjoys performing these missions with which she is entrusted as a child enjoys a game, and that the fact that there is a certain amount of danger connected with them is in itself attractive to her. I am glad that you have told me what he said to you about himself, for I could not understand him before. I think I can now, and understanding him one can understand his daughter."

At eight o'clock all retired to bed. They had had little sleep the night before, and the day had been full of events. Guy's last thought was that he was sorry for the king, who seemed to wish to do what was right, but who was a mere puppet in the hands of Burgundy or Queen Isobel, to be used as a lay figure when required by whichever had a temporary ascendency.

For the next fortnight Guy worked hard in the *salle d'armes*, being one of the first to arrive and the last to depart, and after taking a lesson from one or other of the masters he spent the rest of the morning in practising with anyone who desired an adversary. Well trained as he was in English methods of fighting, he mastered with a quickness that surprised his teachers the various thrusts and parries that were new to him. At the end of that time he was able to hold his own with the young Count d'Estournel, who was regarded as an excellent swordsman.

The attendance of the Burgundian nobles had now fallen off a good deal. The Armagnac army had approached Paris, St. Denis had opened its gates to them, and there were frequent skirmishes near the walls of Paris between parties of their knights and the Burgundians. Paris was just at present more quiet. Burgundy was still absent, and the future seemed so uncertain, that both factions in the city held their hands for a time.

The news that a reconciliation between Orleans and Burgundy had been fully effected, and that the great lords would soon enter Paris together, was received with a joy that was modified by recollections of the past. Burgundy and Orleans had once before sworn a solemn friendship, and yet a week or two later Orleans lay dead in the streets of Paris, murdered by the order of Burgundy. Was it likely that the present patching up of the quarrel would have a much longer duration? On the former occasion the quarrel was a personal one between the two great houses, now all France was divided. A vast amount of blood had been shed, there had been cruel massacres, executions, and wrongs, and the men of one faction had come to hate those of the other; and although neither party had dared to put itself in the wrong by refusing to listen to the mediators, it was certain that the reconciliation was a farce, and that it was but a short truce rather than a peace that had been concluded. Nevertheless Paris rejoiced outwardly, and hailed with enthusiasm the entry of the queen, the Dukes of Aquitaine, Burgundy, Berri, and Bourbon.

The Duke of Aquitaine was now acting as regent, though without the title, for the king was again insane. He had married Burgundy's daughter, but it was rumoured that he was by no means disposed to submit himself blindly to the advice of her father. The only effect of the truce between the parties was to add to the power of the Burgundian faction in Paris. But few of the Armagnac party cared to trust themselves in the city that had shown itself so hostile, but most of them retired to their estates, and the great procession that entered the town had been for the most part composed of adherents of Burgundy. Three days after their arrival in the town Guy, on leaving the *salle d'armes*, found Katarina in her boy's attire waiting for him at the corner of the street.

"My father would speak with you, Master Guy," she said shyly, for in the past two months she had always been in her girl's dress when he had met her. "Pray go at once," she said; "I will not accompany you, for I have other matters to attend to."

"Things are not going well," the count said when Guy entered the room; "the Orleanists are discouraged and the butchers triumphant. At a meeting last night they determined that a body of them should wait upon the Dukes of Aquitaine and Burgundy to complain of the conduct of the knights who fell upon them when attacking the silversmith's, and demand in the name of Paris their execution."

"They would never dare do that!" Guy exclaimed indignantly.

"They will assuredly do it, and I see not how they can be refused. The duke has no force that could oppose the Parisians. They might defend the Louvre and one or two of the strongly fortified houses, but the butchers would surround them with twenty thousand men. Burgundy's vassals might come to his assistance, but the gates of Paris would be closed, and it would need nothing short of an army and a long siege before they could enter Paris. When they had done so they might punish the leaders, but Burgundy would thereby lose for ever the support of the city, which is all-important to him. Therefore if you would save your friends you must warn them that it will be necessary for them to make their way out of Paris as quickly and as quietly as may be. In the next place, and principally, you yourself will assuredly be murdered. There was a talk of the meeting demanding your execution and that of your four men; but it was decided that there was no need to do this, as you could all be killed without trouble, and that possibly the Duke of Aquitaine might refuse on the ground that, as your lady had come here under safe-conduct as a royal hostage, you were entitled to protection, and it would be contrary to his honour to give you up.

"There are others who have displeased the Parisians whose lives they will also demand, and there are several women among them; therefore, it is clear that even the sex of your lady will not save her and her children from the fury and longing for revenge, felt by the family of Legoix and by Caboche the skinner. The only question is, where can they be bestowed in safety? I know what you would say, that all this is monstrous, and that it is incredible that the Parisians will dare to take such steps. I can assure you that it is as I say; the peril is most imminent. Probably to-night, but if not, to-morrow the gates of Paris will be closed, and there will be no escape for any whom these people have doomed to death. In the first place, you have to warn your Burgundian friends; that done, you must see to the safety of your four men. The three Frenchmen may, if they disguise themselves, perchance be able to hide in Paris, but your tall archer must leave the city without delay, his height and appearance would betray him in whatever disguise he were clad.

"Now as to your lady and the children, remain where they are they cannot. Doubtless were she to appeal to the Duke of Burgundy for protection he would place her in the Louvre, or in one of the other castles-that is, if she could persuade him of the intentions of the Parisians, which indeed it would be difficult for her to do; but even could she do so she would not be safe, for if he is forced to surrender some of his own knights and ladies of the court to these miscreants, he could not refuse to hand over Lady Margaret. They might, it is true, possibly escape from Paris in disguise, but I know that there is already a watch set at the gates. The only resource that I can see is that she should with her children come hither for a time. This is but a poor place for her, but I think that if anywhere she might be safe with me. No one knows that I have had any dealings whatever with you, and no one connects me in any way with politics. What should a vendor of nostrums have to do with such affairs? Thus, then, they might remain here without their presence being in the slightest degree suspected. At any rate I have as good means as any for learning what is being done at their councils, and should receive the earliest information were it decided that a search should be made here; and should this be done, which I think is most unlikely, I shall have time to remove them to some other place of concealment.

"Lastly, as to yourself, I take it that nothing would induce you to fly with your Burgundian friends while your lady is in hiding in Paris?"

"Assuredly not!" Guy said. "My lord appointed me to take charge of her and watch over her, and as long as I have life I will do so."

"You will not be able to aid her, and your presence may even add to her danger. Still, I will not say that your resolution is not honourable and right. But, at least, you must not stay here, for your detection would almost certainly lead to hers. You, however, can be disguised; I can darken your skin and hair, and, in some soiled garb you may hope to pass without recognition. Where to bestow you I will talk over with my daughter. As soon as it becomes dusk this evening she will present herself at the house-door of Maître Leroux. She will bring with her disguises for your lady, the children, and yourself—I have many of them here-and as soon as it is quite dark she will guide here Dame Margaret with her daughter and son. You had best not sally out with them, but can follow a minute or two later and join them as soon as they turn down a side street. As to the men, you must arrange with them what they had best do. My advice is that they should this afternoon saunter out as if merely going for a walk. They ought to go separately; you can decide what they had best do when outside."

Chapter XII
In Hiding

The news of this terrible danger was so wholly unexpected that Guy for a moment felt almost paralyzed.

"It seems almost incredible that such wickedness could take place!" he exclaimed.

"My information is certain," the count replied. "I do not say that I think your Burgundian friends are in so much danger as some of those of the king's party, as Burgundy's influence with these Parisians goes for something; still, he might not be able to save them if they waited till the demand was made, although he might warn them if he learned that they were to be among those demanded."

"Does the duke, then, know what is intended?"

The count smiled. "We know what followed the last reconciliation," he said, "and can guess pretty shrewdly at what will happen now. *Then* the duke murdered Orleans, *now* he may take measures against the supporters of the present duke. It was certain that the struggle would begin again as soon as the kiss of peace had been exchanged. Last time he boldly avowed his share in the murder; this time, most conveniently for him, the Parisians are ready and eager to do his work for him. Dismiss from your mind all doubt; you can rely upon everything that I have told you as being true. Whether you can convince these young knights is a matter that concerns me not; but remember that if you fail to convince your mistress, her life and those of her children are forfeited; and that, so far as I can see, her only hope of safety is in taking refuge here."

"I thank you with all my heart," Guy said, "and will now set about carrying out your advice. First, I will return to my lady and consult with her, and see what we had best do with the men. As to Count Charles d'Estournel and his friends, I will see them as soon as I have arranged the other matter. Their case is not so pressing, for, at least, when once beyond the gates they will be safe. I will see that my lady and the children shall be ready to accompany your daughter when she comes for them."

"Look well up and down the street before you sally out," the count said; "see that there are but few people about. It is a matter of life and death that no one who knows you shall see you leave this house."

Guy followed his advice, and waited until there was no one within fifty yards of the door, then he went out, crossed the street, took the first turning he came to, and then made his way back to the silversmith's as fast as he could.

"What ails you, Guy?" Dame Margaret said as he entered the room, "you look sorely disturbed, and as pale as if you had received some injury."

"Would that that were all, my lady. I have had news from the Count of Montepone of so strange and grave a nature that I would not tell you it, were it not that he is so much in earnest, and so well convinced of its truth that I cannot doubt it."

He then related what the count had told him, and repeated the offer of shelter he had made.

"This is, indeed, beyond all bounds," she said. "What, is it credible that the Duke of Burgundy and the king's son, the Duke of Aquitaine, can hand over to this murderous mob of Paris noble gentlemen and ladies?"

"As to Burgundy, madame, it seems to me from what the count said that he himself is at the bottom of the affair, though he may not know that the Parisians demand the lives of some of his own knights as well as those of his opponents. As he did not of old hesitate to murder Orleans, the king's own brother, we need credit him with no scruples as to how he would rid himself of others he considers to stand in his way. As to Aquitaine, he is a young man and powerless. There are no Orleanist nobles in the town to whom he might look for aid; and if a king's brother was slain, why not a king's son? It seems to me that he is powerless."

"That may be; but I cannot consent to what the count proposes. What! disguise myself! and hide from this base mob of Paris! It would be an unworthy action."

"It is one that I knew you would shrink from, madame; but pardon me for saying that it is not your own life only, but those of your children that are at stake. When royal princes and dukes are unable to oppose these scoundrel Parisians, women and children may well bend before the storm."

Dame Margaret sat for some time with knitted brows. At last she said: "If it must be, Guy, it must. It goes sorely against the grain; but for the sake of the children I will demean myself, and will take your advice. Now you had best summon the four men-at-arms and talk over their case with them."

Guy went upstairs and fetched the four men down.

"We have sure news, my friends," Dame Margaret said calmly, "that to-night we and many others shall be seized by the mob and slain."

An exclamation of rage broke from the four men.

"There will be many others slain before that comes about," Long Tom said.

"That I doubt not, Tom, but the end would be the same. An offer of refuge has been made to me and the children, and for their sake, unwilling as I am to hide myself from this base mob, I have brought myself to accept it. My brave esquire will stay in Paris in disguise, and do what may be to protect us. I have now called you to talk about yourselves. The gates will speedily be guarded and none allowed to sally out, therefore what is to be done must be done quickly."

"We will all stay and share your fate, madame. You could not think that we should leave you," Robert Picard said, and the others murmured their agreement.

"You would add to my danger without being able to benefit me," she said, "and my anxiety would be all the greater. No, you must obey my commands, which are that you forthwith quit Paris. Beyond that I must leave you to judge your own course. As French men-at-arms none would question you when you were once beyond the gate. You may find it difficult to travel in this disturbed time, but you are shrewd enough to make up some story that will account for your movements, and so may work your way back to Villeroy. The difficulty is greater in the case of your English comrade-his height and that light hair of his and ruddy face would mark him anywhere, and if he goes with you would add to your danger, especially as his tongue would betray him as being English the first time he spoke. However, beyond ordering you to quit Paris, I must leave this matter in your hands and his, and he will doubtless take counsel with my esquire and see if any disguise can be contrived to suit him. I will see you again presently. You had best go with them, Guy, and talk the matter over."

"This thing cannot be done, Master Guy," the archer said doggedly when they reached their apartments; "it is not in reason. What should I say when I got home and told them at Summerley that I saved my own skin and left our dear lady and the children to be murdered without striking a blow on their behalf? The thing is beyond all reason, and I will maintain it to be so."

"I can understand what you say, Tom, for I feel exactly as you do. The question is, how is the matter to be arranged?" Then he broke into French, which the archer by this time understood well enough, though he could speak it but poorly.

"Tom is saying that he will not go, men," he said, "and I doubt not that you feel as he does. At the same time our lady's orders must be carried out in the first place, and you must leave Paris. But I say not that you need travel to any distance; on the contrary, I should say that, if it can be arranged, you must return here in a few days, having so changed your attire and aspect that there is no fear of your being recognized, and bestow yourself in some lodging where I may find you if there be need of your services."

"That is what will be best, Master Guy," Robert Picard said. "We have but to get steel caps of another fashion to pass well enough, and if need be we can alter the fashion of our hair. There are few here who have noticed us, and I consider that there is no chance whatever of our being recognized. There are plenty of men among the cut-throats here who have served for a while, and we can easily enough get up some tale that will pass muster for us three. That matter is simple enough, the question is, what are we to do with Tom? We cannot shorten his stature, nor give his tongue a French twist."

"No, that is really the difficulty. We might dye that hair of his and darken his face, as I am going to do myself. There are tall men in France, and even his inches would not matter so much; the danger lies in his speech."

"I would never open my mouth, Master Guy; if need were I would sooner cut out my tongue with a dagger."

"You might bleed to death in the doing of it, Tom. No; we must think of something better than that. You might perhaps pass as a Fleming, if we cannot devise any other disguise."

"Leave that to me, Master Guy, I shall think of something. I will at any rate hide somewhere near Paris, and the lads here will let me know where they are to be found, and I shall not be long before I join them in some such guise as will pass muster. But it will be necessary that we should know where you will be, so that you can communicate with us."

"That I don't know myself yet; but I will be every evening in front of Notre Dame when the bell strikes nine, and one of you can meet me there and tell me where you are bestowed, so that I can always send for you in case of need. Now I think that you had better lose no time, for we know not at what hour a guard will be placed on the gate. You had better go out in pairs as if merely going for a walk. If you are stopped, as may well happen, return here; but as you come purchase a length of strong rope, so that you may let yourselves down from the wall. Now that peace has been made, there will be but slight watch save at the gates, and you should have no difficulty in evading the sight of any who may be on guard."

"That will be easy enough," Robert Picard said confidently. "We had best not come back here, for there may be a watch set upon the house and they may follow us."

"The only thing that troubles me," Tom said, "is that I must leave my bow behind me."

"You can get another when you get back to Villeroy; there are spare ones there."

"Yes, yes, but that is not the same thing, Master Guy; a man knows his own bow, and when he takes to a fresh one his shooting is spoilt until he gets to know it well. Every bow has its niceties; for rough shooting it makes but little matter, but when it comes to aiming at the slit in a knight's vizor at eighty yards one makes poor shooting with a strange bow."

"Well, you must practise with your new one, that is all, Tom; and if you hide yours here it may be that you will be able to recover it before we start for Villeroy. You must leave your bundles behind, it would look suspicious if you were to attempt to take them with you. I should advise you to put on one suit over the other, it will not add greatly to your bulk. When you are ready to start, come below and our lady will say good-bye to you. Do not give her a hint that you are thinking of staying near Paris; if she asks any questions say that you intend to disguise Tom, and he will travel with you."

A few minutes later there was a tapping at Dame Margaret's door; Guy opened it and the four men entered.

"I wish you good fortunes, my friends," Dame Margaret said. "Here is a letter, Robert, that I have written to my lord telling him that you have all served me faithfully and well, and that I commend you to him. I have told him that you are leaving me by my special orders, and that you would willingly have stopped and shared my danger, but that, as I feel that force would avail nothing and your presence might lead to the discovery of my hiding-place, I bid you go. Here are four purses to pay the expenses of your journey and of any disguises you may find it necessary to adopt. And now farewell. Tarry not an instant, my heart will be lighter when I know that you are beyond the walls."

She held out her hand to them; each in turn knelt and kissed it, the three Frenchmen in silence but with tears running down their cheeks. Tom was the last, and said as he rose:

"I am obeying your orders, Lady Margaret, but never before have I felt, as I feel now, that I am doing a mean and cowardly action. I would rather stay by your side, though I knew that I should be cut in pieces this very night, than leave you thus."

"I doubt it not, Tom. I know well how your inclinations lie, and yet I feel that it is necessary that you should go. If the great nobles cannot withstand this cruel mob of Paris, the arm of a single man can avail nothing, and your presence would bring danger rather than safety to me."

"I feel that, my lady; did I not do so I would not go even at your command. You are my liege lady, and I have a right to give my life for you, and would do it were it not that I see that, as you say, my staying here would bring danger upon you."

As soon as they had gone Dame Margaret said: "Now, Guy, I will detain you no longer; hasten and warn your friends."

Guy hurried away; he found that Count Charles was on the point of mounting to go for a ride with some of his friends.

"Stay a moment I beg of you, Count," Guy said as he hurried up, "I have a matter of most serious import to tell you."

"Wait, my friends," the young count said to Sir Pierre Estelle, Count Walter de Vesoul, and the Sieur John de Perron, who were already mounted; "I shall not detain you many minutes."

"Well, what is it, friend Guy?" he asked as he entered his room.

"I have come to warn you of a great danger, Count. This evening a mob of Parisians, I know not how numerous, but at least of great strength, will demand from Burgundy and the Duke of Aquitaine the surrender to them of you and the others who took part in defeating them the other night, besides other gentlemen, and, as I hear, ladies."

"*Pardieu*! if it be so the duke will give the impudent knaves their answer."

"Ten thousand armed men are not apt to take an answer, Count. You know that many times already the Duke of Burgundy has been overborne by the leaders of these Parisians and forced to do things that must have displeased him, as they displeased you all, therefore I implore you to ride off while you may. Even now it is possible that the gales may be closed, but if so, they are not likely to be strongly guarded. It is evident that your going would at any rate save the duke from grave embarrassment."

"Are you sure that this news is true?" the count asked.

"Absolutely certain. If you would save yourself and your friends I pray you to call upon them at once to mount and ride in a body to one of the gates. You may bid some of your retainers mount and follow you at a short distance, and if you find the gates closed and the fellows will not let you out, call them up and fight your way out. You can stay for to-night at Sèvres, and if you find in the morning that I have not spoken truly you can return and upbraid me as you will. If, however, you find that strange events have happened here, then you had best ride away to Burgundy and stay there until you find that these villainous knaves here have been reduced to order, which methinks it will need an army to undertake."

The count went to the window, opened it, and called his friends below to come up.

"No, no," D'Estelle said laughing; "if we once come up we shall stay there. If you cannot come now, join us at the Lion d'Or at Sèvres, where you will find us eating the dinner that we have sent on to order."

"The matter is urgent," D'Estournel said. "I am not joking with you, but pray you to come up at once."

Seeing that the matter was serious the three knights dismounted and went up. They were at first absolutely incredulous when they heard from Count Charles what Guy had told them.

"That the knaves owe us no good-will I know well enough," Count Walter said, "for they have over and over again laid their complaint against us before the duke; but it is hard to believe that they would dare to demand what Burgundy would never grant."

Guy repeated the arguments that he had used with D'Estournel.

"There is no limit," he said, "to the arrogance of these knaves, and in truth it cannot be denied that they are masters here, and that even the duke cannot altogether withstand them; and you know, moreover, how essential is their goodwill to him. But even should he ever so obstinately refuse their demands they might well take their way without his leave. What can he, with a handful of knights and a few hundred armed men, do against the mob of Paris? I earnestly pray you, gentlemen, to treat the matter as serious. Warn your eight friends without delay; bid your retainers mount and ride to the gate. If it is open, all the better, it is but a party of pleasure bound for Sèvres, and if you learn to-morrow morning that all is quiet here you can return. If it seems better to you, and this may save you much argument, merely ask your friends to mount and ride with you to dine there; if any refuse, say you have a motive that they will learn when they get there, and almost compel them to go with you. I pledge you my honour that you will have no reason to regret having taken my advice."

"Well, what do you say, gentlemen?" Count Walter asked. "As Master Aylmer says, it will at worst be but a carouse, which I hope he will share with us."

"That I would right gladly do," Guy replied, "but I have the safety of my lady and her children to look after, for she too, as well as our four men-at-arms, have incurred the enmity of these butchers. I have sent the men out of the town, and a place of safety has been prepared for her and the children. I shall see them safely bestowed there at nightfall."

"Since you have thought such preparations necessary we will at any rate act on the information that you have given us, and will promise not to blame you unduly should it turn out that the affair you speak of does not come off. Let us lose no time, gentlemen; let us each go to two of our friends and take no denial from them to our invitation to dine with us at Sevres. Let us say nothing to them about bringing their men-at-arms and grooms with them. We can ourselves muster some thirty fighting men, and that should be enough with our own swords to bring these knaves to reason if they keep their gates shut against us."

"As my arrangements are all made," Guy said, "and I have an hour to spare, I shall walk down towards the gate and see what comes of it."

The four gentlemen at once mounted and rode off,—after giving directions to their grooms to order their men-at-arms to mount at once and to wait for them at a spot a quarter of a mile from the gate,—and Guy strolled off in the same direction. In half an hour he had the satisfaction of seeing the men-at-arms ride up and halt as ordered. Walking a little further on he saw that something unusual had happened. Groups of people were standing about talking, and each man who came up from the gate was questioned. Joining one of the groups he soon learned that the excitement was caused by the unusual closing of the gates, no one being allowed either to enter or pass out. None could account for this proceeding. It was certain that it had not been done by the orders either of the Dukes of Aquitaine or Burgundy,—for there were no royal guards or men-at-arms with the duke's cognizance,—but by men of the city, who, as all agreed, must be acting under the orders of the butchers.

"It is a bold deed," one said, "for which they will have to account. It is a usurpation of authority, and one the Duke of Aquitaine, who is now king in all but name, will surely resent hotly."

"How strong is the party?" one of the bystanders asked, putting the question that Guy had on his lips.

"Some forty or fifty, all stout fellows with steel caps and breast-pieces, and well armed."

Guy turned and walked back to the spot where the Burgundian men-at-arms were drawn up. In ten minutes D'Estournel and his party rode up. Guy was glad to see that he had with him the whole of his companions. He at once went up to them.

"The gates are closed, Count, and held by forty or fifty of the townsmen in arms, so you see that my information was correct. Had you not better tell your friends of the truth now, for otherwise they might hesitate to take so grave a step as to attack them?"

D'Estournel nodded, and, riding to the others, said in a low voice: "Gentlemen, we had not intended to let you into this little mystery until we had left Paris, but I find it necessary to do so now. I have learned surely that the rabble of Paris have resolved upon massacring us to-night for the share we took in that little affair at the provost of the silversmiths. To that end they have shut the gates, and hold it with some fifty armed men. It is as well that some of us have brought our men-at-arms here. I can hardly fancy that these rascals will try to prevent us from passing out, seeing that they have no warrant but their own for closing the gates against us, but if they do there is nothing for it but to open them ourselves. Let us ride forward at once, gentlemen, for these fellows may receive a reinforcement at any time."

So saying, he put spurs to his horse, calling upon the men-at-arms to follow. His three companions, who were already in the secret, joined him at once; and the others, after a pause of astonishment and almost incredulity, followed, in no way loath at the chance of another fight with the followers of the butchers. As they approached the gate the townsmen hastily drew up in front of it.

"What means this?" Count Walter de Vesoul said haughtily, as he reined up his horse a few paces from the line. "By what authority do you dare close the gates and thus stand armed before them?"

"By the authority of the city of Paris," the leader of the party said insolently.

"I recognize no such authority while the king and the Duke of Aquitaine, who holds his full powers, are resident here. Clear the way, my man, and open the gates, or I will ride over you."

The butcher answered him with a derisive laugh. "It will cost you your lives if you attempt it," he said.

"Gentlemen, draw your swords and give these rough fellows the lesson they need;" and, setting the example, he rode at the butcher and cut him down. The idea that the Burgundian knights would venture to force a passage in the teeth of the prohibition of the master of the butchers had apparently not so much as entered the minds of the guard, and as soon as the knights and their followers fell upon them, the greater portion of them flung down their arms and fled, a few only fighting stoutly until overpowered. As soon as the skirmish was over the keys were brought out from the guard-room, and the gate unlocked and the massive bars taken down. In the meantime some of the men-at-arms had run up on to the wall, hoisted the portcullis, and lowered the drawbridge across the fosse. As soon as they returned and mounted the party rode through. As they did so, four men ran out from a lane near the wall and followed them; and Guy at once recognized in them the archer and his three companions. Greatly pleased, he returned to the city and informed Dame Margaret of what had taken place.

"No doubt," he said, "when they found the gates shut they remembered what I had said, that I was going to warn Count Charles and his friends, and went back to observe what these were doing; and the sight of their retainers going towards the gate must have told them which way they intended to leave; and they, no doubt, went down and hid up near the gate to watch the conflict, and to take advantage of it, if a chance offered, to get off themselves."

"That is indeed a satisfaction, Guy; and I am glad, too, that your friends got away. There can be no doubt now that the count's information was accurate; the gates having been closed, as he said they would be, vouches for this. Katarina has been here; she was dressed this time as an apprentice in the service of some trader, and brought a large box containing our disguises and yours. For you there is a bottle of dye for your hair, a mixture for darkening your skin, and clothes-the latter such as would be worn by a workman. Charlie is to wear a girl's dress, at which he is mightily offended; nor is Agnes better pleased, for a boy's suit has been sent for her. My disguise is simply a long cloak with a hood, such as is worn by the wives of small traders. Katarina explained that it had been thought better to change the sex of Agnes and Charlie, so that, when a hue and cry is raised for a missing woman, with a girl of fourteen, and a boy of ten, no one should associate the woman with two lads and a little girl, whom they passed in the street, as being the party for which search is being made. And now, Guy, do you not think that we should warn our good host of the danger that threatens, for, doubtless, he also has been marked out as a victim?"

"I will see him at once, and will tell him as much as it is necessary for him to know. Assuredly it is now too late for him to escape beyond the walls, unless he were to take his wife with him, and bring his serving-men to let them down from the walls; but this, I should think, he will not do, he would rather take refuge in the house of some of his friends."

The silversmith listened gravely when Guy told him that he had received sure information that the butchers would that evening make a slaughter of some of their opponents, that they would be in such force that resistance would be hopeless, and that the few royal troops and the followers of Burgundy would be insufficient to make head against them.

"Your news does not surprise me, and though I know not how you came by it, I fear that it is true. The news that the city gates have been all shut and are being guarded by strong parties of the butchers' rabble, shows but too surely that there is danger in the air. In the first place, there is your lady to be thought of; I must endeavour to obtain for her also shelter among my friends."

"We have already arranged for a hiding-place for her and the children, Maître Leroux. I may not name where it is to anyone, but suffice that it is a quiet house where there is little fear of any suspicions resting upon them, and where they will be able to remain until order is restored."

"I fear that that will be a long time," the silversmith said. "The butchers boast that they can place 20,000 men under arms, and indeed the terror excited by them is so great, that very many who hate their doings as much as I do myself have been forced to make a semblance of joining them. Next about your men-at-arms, they are brave fellows and I owe them much."

"They are all safe outside the walls. Some Burgundian knights, indignant that this rabble should dare stop them, cut their way out through the Port St. Denis, and our men took advantage of the gates being open to follow them."

"And as to yourself, Master Aylmer?"

"I have dyes to blacken my hair and a tincture for darkening my face. I have also a disguise by which I may pass as an apprentice to a trader. I shall at all hazards remain in Paris, but what I shall yet do I know not. And now about yourself and Madame Leroux-you will not, I hope, think of defending the house as you did before."

"Certainly not; it would not avail to save our lives, and would assuredly cost those of my servitors and most likely of the women. I have friends, who will, I hope, gladly take us in. Maître Lepelletiere, the Master Carpenter, who has been doing my doors, is an old friend of mine, and after the last attack, urged me to withdraw for a time from the attention of the mob, and offered me refuge in his place. He lives in the Rue des Fosses; which is close to the old inner wall that is now for the most part in ruins. You pass along by the hospital, and when beyond the old wall turn to the right; 'tis the third doorway. There are no houses facing it, but it looks straight upon the wall, the ground between being some thirty or forty yards wide; and doubtless when the house was built, it was before the present wall was erected, and stood on the outer side of the fosse round the old one. There are many others of the same trade who live in that quarter, and as they are for the most part opposed to the butchers, I doubt not that my friend will have no difficulty in obtaining a lodging for you among them should no other have been settled upon."

"Thank you indeed," Guy replied; "the arrangement has been made by others, and I know not for certain what has yet been decided upon, but should not a suitable place have been chosen I will gladly accept your offer."

"And now I must set to work," the silversmith said.

"In what way?" Guy asked in surprise.

"In hiding my wares. In a city like Paris, with its sieges and its tumults, a prudent man having goods of great value will assuredly prepare a place of safety for them. I will set my men to work at once; the business must be finished before it becomes dark, for as soon as it does so we must leave the house and close it."

"I have nothing to do at present, and shall be glad to help your men," Guy said.

He followed the silversmith downstairs. Maître Leroux called his head man.

"We must move, Jacques, and that quickly; you have heard that the gates are shut."

"Yes, master, people are talking of nothing else."

"I have news that there will be trouble to-night, so we must set to work at once to place the chests in safety. First let them clear out the wood-cellar."

This was done in a few minutes by the seven men, then Jacques told the others to go back into the shop and pack up all the silver goods in the chests. As soon as they were gone Jacques looked inquiringly at his master, who nodded. Then he touched a brick in the wall some seven feet above the floor; it sprung back.

"Will you lift me up?" the man said to Guy. The lad did as he was asked, and the man thrust his arm into the orifice. A moment later he asked Guy to set him down.

"Go to the doorway," he said, and hurried across to where Maître Leroux was standing; then kneeling down he pushed his hand under the sill of the doorway and then stood up.

"Do you hear that?" the silversmith said.

"I hear a dull rumbling somewhere," Guy replied. As he spoke he saw half the floor, which was apparently of solid flags, beginning to rise.

"This was done in my father's time," Maître Leroux said, "and it was made for him by Maître Lepelletiere's father with the aid of two or three good smiths, who put the machinery together at his house and were in ignorance where it was intended to be placed."

The trap-door was now raised, and Guy to his astonishment saw a stream of running water three feet below the opening.

"Whence comes this?" he asked in astonishment.

"No wonder you are surprised," the silversmith said; "it was a piece of rare good-luck that my father hit upon it. A map that he had showed him that in the old days, before there were any houses on this side of the river, a narrow branch left the stream some hundred yards above the position of his house, made a circuit and came into it again as much below. He inquired among some old men, and learned that they had heard their grandfathers say that they knew that at some time or other this stream had been built over when Paris began to grow in this direction. After he had contrived this apparatus that you see, which is worked by a heavy counterpoise in the wall, he began to dig, and a foot below the surface came upon an arch of brickwork, so my father concluded that his house was exactly over the old stream.

"On breaking through the crown he discovered, as you see, that the water still flowed through this tunnel, which is some three and a half yards wide and eight feet deep. My men, all of whom are trusty fellows, know of the existence of this hiding-place, but Jacques is the only one besides myself who knows the secret of the opening. Now, Jacques, fetch the chests along as fast as they are ready."

The chests were soon brought up and one by one lowered. Chains were attached from the handle of each to that of the one that followed; they were almost the weight of the water and sank until within an inch or two of the surface. Each was floated down as it was lowered, until twenty great chests had been taken down. Then one more heavy and ponderous than the rest was attached to the train, and a sloping board being placed from the cellar floor to the bottom of the stream, the case was allowed to slide down this until it rested on the bottom several feet beyond the trap-door.

"There you see," the silversmith said, "even if they discovered the trap-door and broke up the floor with sledgehammers, which would be no easy matter, and probed the stream with lances, they would find nothing. As you saw, there is a chain to the end of the last box, which is, as it were, an anchor to the rest; this chain Jacques will now attach to a strong wire, and fasten that to a ring below the water's edge, and a foot beyond the trap-door, so that when danger is past we shall haul up the chain and recover the cases one by one in the order in which they have been sent down."

As soon as Jacques had fastened the wire to the ring he touched another heavy spring under the sill, then pulled hard on the trap-door; this gradually began to sink, and in a minute was in its place again. At the same time the brick that had been pushed in above came out into its place again, dust was then swept into the crack at the edge of the trapdoor, and no one who had not seen the latter raised would have dreamt of its existence.

Chapter XIII
The Masters Of Paris

The trap-door closed, the firewood was carried back again, and Guy went upstairs, where he found that Dame Margaret, Agnes, and Charlie had already put on their disguises. Their faces had been slightly darkened; Agnes had coiled her hair up under a cap, while Dame Margaret's would be completely hidden under the hood. She and Charlie could, have passed very well even in daylight, but Agnes by no means looked her character. Her mother had darkened the skin at the back of her neck as well as on her face, but the girl's evident discomfort and shyness were so unboylike that they would at once be noticed. Guy fetched a short cloak reaching only to his hips from his room and brought it in to her.

"I think that you will be more comfortable in this," he said.

"Yes, indeed," she exclaimed gratefully, as she put it over her shoulders; "I shall not mind now."

It reached nearly down to her knees, and the high collar concealed the back of her head effectually.

"I did not expect that you would be ready so soon," he said, turning to Dame Margaret; "it will not be dark for two hours yet."

"No; but I thought it much better to be prepared to leave at any moment. Mistress Leroux has shown me a door opening from the yard into a very narrow lane behind. She says that it has not been used for years, but she has been down herself with the key and has unlocked it, so that we have only to let a bar down to open it, and if there should be an attack on the front of the house we can escape that way."

"It would be best to leave that way in any case," Guy said, "and thereby you will avoid observation by anyone who may be watching. It is evident that the citizens of this quarter are very anxious and alarmed; looking from the window I have seen them standing in groups, or going in and out of each other's houses. They cannot know what is going to take place, but the closing of the gates by the butchers without any warrant has, of course, shown them that something serious is going to occur."

"You had better disguise yourself at once, Guy."

"I will do so, mistress, but I do not think that there is any fear of disturbance until evening; men who are engaged in work, that may some day bring punishment upon those concerned in it, prefer darkness. Besides, at that time all careful men will be in their houses, and will not dare to come out whatever sounds they may hear."

Maître Leroux presently came up.

"I have been out and trying to gather news. There are all sorts of rumours abroad, but none know aught with certainty. They say that the butchers have stationed guards at the end of all the streets leading to the market quarter, and they allow none to pass in or out. It is reported that Aquitaine has sent an officer to the butchers to demand under what warrant they have closed the gates of the city, and to order them to open them forthwith, and to withdraw the men stationed there. It is said that their answer was that they had acted for the good of the state, and for the safety of the king's person, and that they would presently call upon his highness and explain matters to him. This may be true or merely rumour, but it is generally believed. Everyone is talking of the fight at the gate of St. Denis. Some say that it was forced open by order of the Duke of Burgundy, while others affirm that Caboche, and that mischievous varlet John de Troyes, went in great haste to the duke when they received the news, that he declared to them that he knew nothing whatever of the affair, and that whatever was done was certainly done without his orders. Most of my men have already left; it were better that they should go off one by one than that they should move off together. 'Tis well that my wife bethought her of that back entrance. It has never been used in my time, for the lane is but three feet wide, and the houses beyond are of no very good repute. I talked at one time of having it bricked up, and only refrained from doing so from the thought that it might be useful on some such occasion as this. Your esquire has not gone out, I suppose, Lady Margaret?"

"No, he is putting on his disguise-at least, he is colouring his hair and face, and so altering himself that he would not be known; but he will not put on his full disguise until later."

Guy soon came out. He was in his ordinary garments, but having put on his best suit beneath them he looked broader and bulkier than usual, while his blackened hair and darkened face had made so great a change in his appearance that both Agnes and her mother agreed that they would not have known him.

"You could certainly go anywhere, Guy, and mix with any crowd, and no one would have a suspicion that you were the young Englishman for whom the whole town was searching."

Half an hour before it became dark, Guy went down to the front door. Standing there listening attentively, he presently heard three little knocks given, as by a hand on the door. He opened it a little, Katarina slipped in, and he again fastened it and put up the bar.

"I brought the disguises early," she said, "as I thought they might be required in haste, but my father has learned that it will be eight o'clock before the butchers sally out with their forces from the markets."

"All here are ready and prepared to start at a moment's notice, and have arranged to go out by a door behind, that leads into a narrow lane."

"That is good!" the girl said. "I have been near for the last half-hour and have noticed two or three men hanging about, and by their furtive glances in the direction of the house I have no doubt that they are watching it. I had to wait until there happened to be a group of people before the door, and then slipped in behind them, and got in without, I am sure, their having seen me. I have been uneasy as to how we should leave, for if they saw a party of three or four issuing out together, one of them would be sure to follow."

They were now upstairs. The fact that Agnes was in the same disguise as herself freed Katarina from the shame-facedness that she would otherwise have felt at being seen by Dame Margaret in her present attire.

"You are well disguised," the latter said as she entered. "I no longer wonder that you are able to go about as a boy without suspicion; you look one to the life, while Agnes is so awkward that she would be detected in a moment."

"She has not had the practice that I have had," Katarina said with a laugh; "the awkwardness will soon wear off if she has to dress like this for a short time. As for me, I have learnt all a boy's tricks and ways. I can whistle and shout with any of them, can quarrel, and bluster, be saucy on occasion, and have only once been in trouble."

"How was that, Katarina?"

"A boy who was a bit taller than I ran against me and declared that it was my fault, and gave me a cuff on the head. I might have run away, and of course I ought to have done so, but I was angry, for he really hurt me; so I had to do what any boy would have done, and I flew at him so fiercely, and cuffed and scratched and kicked so savagely that at last he turned and ran. He had hit me too, but I did not feel it at the time, and next morning I was all sorts of colours round the eyes. Father was very angry, but when I asked what else he would have done if he had been cuffed, he could not tell me. I had a very important message to carry that morning for him. At first he said I could not go out in that state; but, as I told him, I had never looked so much like a boy before."

All were glad when it became dark enough for them to make a start. The men and maids had all been sent away, and none remained save Maître Leroux and his wife. They were not in any disguise, but were wrapped up in cloaks, and in the badly-lighted streets could pass unrecognized.

"Do you go out first, Master Aylmer," the silversmith said. "I have no fear of anyone watching behind, for it is not likely that any of them know of this entrance to my house; still, it is as well to make certain. When you get out of the lane you had best stay there until the others have passed on, then you can follow them. We will wait for a few minutes after they have gone, and lock the door behind us. You have not forgotten where you are to find us."

"No, I have the name and house right. Shall I ask for you as Maître Leroux?"

"I have not thought of that. No, it will be better, perhaps, to ask for Philip Sampson; it were just as well that none should know my name there except Lepelletiere and his wife."

As arranged Guy went out first; there was still light enough for him to make his way along the narrow lane without falling over piles of dirt and rubbish that at some points almost blocked it. The street into which it opened was also a very narrow one, and no one was about. In a minute Dame Margaret, walking with Katarina, and with Agnes close behind, holding Charlie's hand, passed him.

"It is all quite clear," he said. Keeping some fifteen yards behind he followed them until they entered a broader street. There were a good many people about here. The nearest way would have been to have crossed the road and passed by another small street facing that from which they had come, but somewhat to his surprise they turned and went along the broader street. He soon acknowledged to himself that this was the wiser course, for there were so many people about that their passage would be unnoticed, while in the narrow lanes some rough fellow might have accosted them. Keeping always in frequented streets they made a long detour before they reached that in which the count resided, and it was with a feeling of great relief that Guy saw them enter the house. He himself, as arranged, did not approach it for another quarter of an hour, then he went and knocked on the door with his hand, which was at once opened by Katarina.

"All is well," she said; "your lady is in the room where you first waited-my father is with her."

As Guy entered the count was just saying: "Yes, it would certainly be best, madame, that your daughter should continue at present in that disguise. In the first place, she will get accustomed to it, and should she have occasion to move again she would be able to do so without attracting notice; in the second place, it would be desirable that, even accidentally, no one should know that there is a young lady of her age here. I have no visitors save on business, but possibly either she or your boy might come out on to the stairs when one is going up or down. It would be unfortunate that he should see them at all, but if it were but a boy he caught sight of he would not at any rate associate them with your party. These precautions may seem to you absurd, but it is often by little accidents that things are discovered when as it seemed everything had been provided against."

"I shall not mind," Agnes said. "When I first went out it seemed dreadful, but when I found that nobody noticed me I began to be accustomed to it, and as your daughter is dressed as a boy too I shall not mind it."

"I shall not like being dressed as a girl," Charlie said sturdily.

The count smiled. "Well, we will see what we can do in your case; anyhow, you must keep on that dress-for a day or two. And now, Guy, about yourself. I have arranged for you to lodge with a man who gets news for me; it is in the butchers' quarter, which is the last place where anyone would think of looking for you. Besides, there you will see all that is going on. I have two other disguises in addition to that I sent you; one is that of a young butcher, another is that of one of the lads who live in misery, who sleep at the market where they can earn a few sous by doing odd jobs, and beg or steal when they can do nothing else. I hear that you have also arranged for a shelter in the quarter between the walls; that too may be very useful, and it will be well for you to go thither to-morrow and arrange so that you can have a place to go to when you choose; it will doubtless be much more pleasant for you there than in the market quarter. Lastly, I have got you a white hood, which may be most useful of all." Guy looked surprised. "Henceforth," the count went on, "white is to be the butchers' colour. All who march this evening are to be so clad, and as soon as it is known to-morrow, you will find three-fourths of the people wearing it, for not to do so will be taken as a sign of hostility to their faction. They will have started by this time, and if it pleases you to put on the butcher's dress and the white hood over it you can mingle in safety with them and see all that is done;

then when they return to their quarter, you can go with them. The house to which you are to go is the third on the left-hand side of the Rue des Couteaux. My man lodges at the top of the house, the room to the left when you mount the stair-his name is Simon Bouclier. The lane is at the back of the butchers' market. The man has no idea who you are. I have simply told him that I will send a young man to help gather news for me of what is going on, that you would work separately, but that he was to do all in his power to aid you, and that at any time if he wanted to send a message to me and could not himself come, he was to intrust it to you, and similarly he was to bring any message that you might want to send to the spot where he meets my messenger. The man works for one of the Thiberts. He does not know who I am, but I think he believes me to be an agent of Burgundy's, and that I collect the information so that he may be privately informed of what is doing. I have encouraged that idea, because it is more likely to keep him truthful to me, since he would think that were he to play me false the duke would see that some harm or other befell him. Therefore, it is as well that you should drop a word as if by accident that will confirm that notion, and will lead him to believe that you too are working under the orders of the duke. This will lull any suspicion that he might feel on seeing, as he must do, that you live in a position far higher than would appear from your garb. And now, if you would see to-night's doings, you had best put on that disguise and the white hood, and be off without delay; you will find the things in the room above."

In a few minutes Guy was ready to start. He could not help looking with disfavour at the greasy and stained garments, and he put them on with an expression of strong disgust. The two suits that he had taken off he made up into a bundle, placed the disguise he had brought with him with them, putting up separately that of which the count had spoken, and which was so ragged and dirty that he inwardly hoped he might never be obliged to assume it; then he went downstairs again. He had strapped round his waist a heavy sword placed beside the clothes, and carried in his hand a short pike. Dame Margaret smiled when he entered, and Katarina laughed aloud at the expression of his face.

"Truly, Guy," the former said, "you might go anywhere in that garb without a soul suspecting you. This journey with me is leading you into strange disguises and adventures, which will give you much matter for talk when we are safely back at Summerley."

"I have left my other disguises above," he said to the count. "The decent one of an apprentice I have placed with my own clothes, and will take them with me to any lodging that I may get among the carpenters, but that beggar suit I will take to Simon Bouclier's the next time I come. I suppose you would not wish me to come here during the day."

"No, unless it is very important; and to that end I think you had better carry the apprentice's disguise also to your lodging in the market. You would not gain favour among the carpenters were you to go among them in the dress you now wear, and your calling upon me here in your apprentice's dress would excite no attention; therefore, if you have need to come here during the day, you had best come as an apprentice."

Guy now went down into the street through which the butchers' force would pass. In a short time he heard a deep dull sound, and soon they came along, a host of armed men.

He fell in unnoticed near the head of the column. Soon after he had joined them they halted, and three or four knights came up and entered into conversation with their leaders. Guy recognized among them Sir Robert de Mailly, Sir Charles de Lens, and several others of the household of the Duke of Burgundy. These talked for some time with the Sieur de Jacqueville, Governor of Paris, who had joined the butchers' faction and was now riding at the head of the column, whereupon the force went no farther, but turned and retraced its steps. Guy wondered greatly where the butchers could be going, but soon found that they were making for the Bastille. After much parley between De Jacqueville and the governor, the latter consented, on the order of the Duke of Burgundy's friends, to hand over to them Sir Peter des Essars and his brother Sir Anthony, who were both supporters of the Orleanists and had come to Paris secretly, and had by the orders of the Duke of Aquitaine been admitted as guests to the Bastille.

These were marched back to the Louvre, the gates of which were opened by the orders of Burgundy's friends, and the two knights were thrown into the prison of the palace. On the way back the houses of a very rich upholsterer and of a cannon-founder of great repute, both of whom had withstood the butchers, were broken into and their owners both murdered. After this the mob marched to the house of Maître Leroux. No reply being given to their summons to open, an attack was made upon the door. While they were engaged in doing this, screens of wattles covered with two or three thicknesses of hides were placed so as to shelter the assailants from the arrows that had proved so deadly on the occasion of their last attack. It was thus evident that the outrage was a planned one. Guy looked on with some amusement until the door gave way under the action of some very heavy sledge-hammers wielded by a party of brawny smiths; the moment it did so the crowd made a tremendous rush.

So great was the pressure that many were thrown down and trampled to death in the doorway. It was not long before several of the windows were thrown open and voices shouted down that the house was deserted. A yell of fury burst from the crowd below, but the pressure at the door was even greater than before. The loss incurred during the first attack had caused all but the bravest and most determined to hang back somewhat; now, however, that it seemed that the silversmith's stores could be ransacked without danger, all were anxious to have a hand in it. Presently one of the leaders appeared at a casement on the first floor and waved his arms for silence. The roar of voices ceased and the man cried:

"Citizens, 'tis of no use to press forward into the house, not only has the traitor and those with him fled from the just vengeance of the people, but he has taken away with him the whole of his silverware."

A yell of disappointment and rage rose, then as it ceased for a moment a voice shouted out:

"They are trying to cheat us, my friends; those who got in first have divided up the spoil and wish us to have no share in it."

This caused a fresh outburst of commotion. At a signal from the leader above a number of well-armed men, who were evidently a sort of body-guard, pressed forward to the door and drove back the crowd with blows from the staves of their pikes. Presently those who had entered began to pour out, and in a quarter of an hour the house was cleared. As soon as it was so the windows were lit up by a lurid light which showed that it had been fired on each floor, and the flames very soon burst out through the casements. Satisfied with having done this the butchers returned to their quarter, and Guy mounted to the chamber of Simon Bouclier. The man had evidently just returned, as he too wore a white hood. He had been carrying a torch in the procession, and this was stuck into a ring on the wall.

"Well, comrade," he said as Guy entered, "I suppose you are the man I was told would come here to-night."

"I am so," Guy said. "I should have been here before, but I joined the procession, as I guessed that you would be there also."

"Yes," the man said; "though I should not have gone had I not thought that more would come of it. What have we done? Captured two knights and killed two bourgeois! Pooh, it did not need five thousand men for that."

"No, but it was just as important as if we had killed a hundred."

"How so?" the other asked.

"Because it has shown the Armagnacs that Paris and Burgundy are as united as ever, and that they will stand no intrigues by the court party."

"That is true. We are all sound here; there were but five thousand out to-night, because that was enough for the work, but there will be four times as many next time we go to the Louvre. To-morrow morning, you know, we are going to pay a visit to the Duke of Aquitaine at his hotel, to teach that young man that he has to do as we and Burgundy order him, or that it will be worse for him."

"So I understand," Guy said carelessly. "As long as all hold together in this quarter everything will go right. My duty principally is to find out if there are any signs of wavering; there are no signs, of course, among the butchers, but some of the others are thought to be but half-hearted."

"The butchers and skinners are all right, never fear," the man said; "and if there are others in the quarter who may not be quite so hot in the matter as we are, they know better than to open their mouths. Of course, in the other quarters there may be a strong party who would thwart us; the smiths and the carpenters and masons are ever jealous of us of the markets, but they have no leaders, and hold not together as we do. Besides, they know that we have Burgundy with us, so whatever they think they are not likely to say much, for if it came to a battle we could sweep them out of the city."

"Yes, yes, I know that there is no fear of that, the great thing is to make sure that some of those who seem to be hottest in the matter, are not taking money from the other party; there are one or two I am specially to observe."

"I understand you, comrade. I myself have never had much confidence in John de Troyes nor his medical students. He is good at talking, no one will deny that; but for myself I would rather that we kept among ourselves and had nothing to do with such cattle, who have no interest in the privileges of the guilds, and who take part with us no one knows why. But I am sleepy; that bundle of fresh rushes in the corner is yours, I got them in the hay-market to-day when I heard that you were coming. You can keep beside me to-morrow morning and I will get you a good place in the ranks. From whence shall I say that you come, as many will ask the question, seeing that your face is strange?"

"You can say I am from Nancy."

"Yes, that will be good enough; that is the right quarter of France for a man to have come from just at present."

Guy was thoroughly fatigued with the long excitement of the day. At eleven in the morning everything had been going on as usual, now Dame Margaret and the two children were in hiding, her four men-at-arms fugitives, and Paris was virtually in a state of insurrection against the royal authority, stirred up thereto by the Duke of Burgundy, who had thus openly leagued himself with the scum of Paris. That what he had seen that evening was but the beginning of a series of crimes, Guy could not doubt; and although this man had expressed his confidence in the power of the market-men to sweep the craftsmen out of Paris, he felt sure from what he had heard, that this could not be done until a fierce and doubtful battle had been fought in the streets. At eight next morning he went out with his companion.

"It is well not to go into a place where we shall meet many till your face is better known," the latter said; and he led the way to a small *trattoir* a quarter of a mile away. Here they sat down and breakfasted, then they returned to the market where the White Hoods were mustering. Simon, who was evidently well known to most of the butchers, took his place near the head of the column, and at nine o'clock it got into motion. When it issued from its own quarters it was evident that its approach excited general apprehension. The streets were deserted as it passed along. None of the casements were opened, and although the traders dared not put up their shutters, none of them appeared at the doors, where their apprentices and workmen gathered to look at the procession. Passing along steadily and in good order, and headed as before by the knights of the Duke of Burgundy's household, they drew up before the palace of the Duke of Aquitaine. Caboche, John de Troyes, and one of the butchers entered the house. The guards having no orders, and seeing how strong was the force that was at their back, did not venture to oppose their entrance, and they pushed on into the private apartments of the duke and informed him that they, on behalf of the good town of Paris and for the welfare of his father and himself, required the delivery to them of certain traitors now in the hotel.

The duke, furious at their insolence, told them that such affairs were not their business, and that there were no traitors in the hotel. In the meantime many of the White Hoods had followed their leaders, Simon and Guy entering with them. They scattered through the apartments and seized the duke's chancellor, the Duke of Bar, a cousin of the king, and twelve other knights and gentlemen, some of whom were in the apartment of the Duke of Aquitaine himself. While this was going on the Dukes of Burgundy and Lorraine arrived, and Aquitaine, turning to the former angrily, said:

"Father-in-law, this insurrection has been caused by your advice; those of your household are the leaders of it; you shall some day repent of this. The state shall not be always governed according to your will and pleasure."

However, in spite of his indignation and remonstrance, the twelve gentlemen were carried away and confined in different prisons; and presently discovering the king's secretary, they killed him and threw the body into the river. They compelled the Duke of Aquitaine himself to leave his palace, and with the king, his father, to take up his abode in the Hôtel de St. Pol. Placing a strong guard round it, so as to prevent them from leaving Paris, the mob then compelled all the nobles and even the prelates, they met, to put on white hoods, and their leaders sent off letters to the chief towns in France to inform them that what they had done was for the welfare of the king and kingdom, and requiring them to give aid should there be any necessity for it; they then published an edict in the name of the king ordering that it should be proclaimed in every bailiwick that no person, under penalty of death and confiscation of goods, should obey any summons from their superior lord to take up arms or to trouble the kingdom. The mad king was made to sign this after the Dukes of Aquitaine, Berri, and Lorraine, and other nobles of the council had put their names to it.

At nine o'clock that evening Guy went to the square before Notre Dame. Here many groups of people were talking over the events of the day. Guy had, as soon as he left the market quarter, taken off his white hood, and before starting he put on his dress as an apprentice. There was no doubt that the opinion of the great majority of those in the square was hostile to the authors of the events of the day, and that the consternation among the citizens was very great. After thus forcing the great nobles to obey their will and outraging the palace of the Duke of Aquitaine, there was no saying to what length they would go, and fears were expressed that ere long they might sack the whole of the better quarters of Paris.

It was so evident, however, that they had the support of the Duke of Burgundy that no one saw any way out of their trouble, and that nothing but the arrival of a powerful army of Orleanists could relieve them from their peril. As Guy had no real expectation of seeing any of his followers, —although the gates had been opened that afternoon after the seizure of the knights, —he attended more to the conversations going on about him than to the matter on which he had come. Presently, however, he saw a rough-looking fellow watching him attentively. He walked close to him, but not recognizing him would have passed on, had not the man taken a step forward and said in a low voice:

"Villeroy!"

"Is it you, Robert? In faith I did not recognize you in that attire."

"And I was not sure that it was you, Master Guy; I should certainly not have known you by your face. Your figure and walk, when a short distance away, attracted my attention, and knowing your disguise was that of an apprentice I made sure it was you. Then as you came closer I doubted, and though I ventured upon saying the name of our lord, I scarce thought that you would reply."

"Where are the others, Robert?"

"They are walking about separately seeking for you. We are to meet on the steps of the cathedral at half-past nine."

"What has become of Tom?"

The man laughed. "If you will come along this way, master, you will see." They went to a quiet corner of the square. As they approached it they heard angry voices, and standing under a lamp Guy saw a tall man of wild and unkempt appearance, with black hair and a begrimed face, and a basket of vegetables strapped to his shoulders, threatening angrily with a staff three or four gamins who were making fun of him. He spoke in a wild, incoherent way, and seemed to be half-witted.

"What are you worrying this poor fellow for?" Robert said angrily to the boys. "If you do not be off, and that quickly, I will lay my cudgel about your shoulders."

This threat was much more efficacious than those of the half-witted man had been, and the boys at once took to their heels. The tall man shuffled towards the new-comers.

"Is it really you, Tom?" Guy said in a low tone.

"It is me, sure enough, Master Guy. I should not know myself, and am not surprised that you do not know me; in faith, my back aches with walking with a stoop, and my legs with shuffling along as if I had scarce the use of them, instead of stepping out manfully. Is all well? We have heard of strange doings-that the butchers have, with the countenance of Burgundy, bearded the Duke of Aquitaine, and even carried off some of his friends from before his face; also that the houses of three of those who had withstood them had been burned, among them that of Maître Leroux; also that two traders had been killed, though which two they were we have not been able to learn."

"All is well, Tom; our lady and her children were safely bestowed, as was also the silversmith and his wife."

"I am right glad of that; they were a worthy couple. And so his house is burned and sacked?"

"Burned, but not sacked, Tom; for he had, before they came, stowed away in a hiding-place where they could not be found all those chests of his, and not a single piece of silver fell into the hands of the butchers."

"That was well done," the archer said, rubbing his hands. "I should like to have seen the dogs' faces when they burst in and found nothing. And my bow, Master Guy?"

"I fear that the flames will not have spared it. I went past the house to-day, and naught but the bare walls are standing."

At this moment the bell of the cathedral struck the half-hour, and Robert Picard said: "Will you stay here, Master Guy? I must go and meet the others, and forthwith bring them to you here."

Chapter XIV
Planning Massacre

In a short time Robert Picard returned with his two companions, and leaving the square, they all went along the quays to a quiet spot. "We cannot be overheard here," Guy said, "and now, in the first place, let me know how you have fared. I knew that you had got safely away, for I was near the gate of St. Denis when the Burgundians fought their way out, and I saw you follow."

"We had no difficulty," Robert Picard said. "We went into the wood, and thence I went across to St. Cloud and bought these garments that you see us in, and we hid away our steel caps and harness in some bushes in the heart of the wood, where they are not likely to be found. Then after a long talk with Tom we agreed that he had best go as a half-witted man with a basket of vegetables for sale, and I went into St. Cloud again, dressed as I now am, and found a little shop where they sold rags and old garments, and got his outfit for a couple of francs, and dear at that. We thought in that way he would not have to say much, and that any confusion of speech would be set down to the fact that his brain was weak. Hearing that the gates were open this afternoon, we came in just before they were closed for the night. We have got a room in a lane which honest folk would not care to pass through even in daylight; 'tis a vile hole, but consorts well with our appearance."

"I will try and find you a better place to-morrow, Robert. I am going to see the people with whom Maître Leroux is in hiding. I hear that they have no sympathy with these butchers, and when I tell them that you are stout fellows and good fighters methinks they will find quarters for you; and you may be able to put on safer disguises than those you wear at present, except that of Tom's, which I think we cannot better. Besides, he can lie there quietly, and need not, except when he chooses, sally out. I myself am lodging at present among the butchers. I hear that Caboche and the Legoix are furious at our having slipped through their fingers, and they declare that, as we cannot have escaped from Paris, they will lay hands on us very soon."

"I should like to lay hands on a few of them myself, Master Guy," Tom said earnestly, "say out in that wood there with a quarter-staff, and to deal with four of them at a time. They have burnt my bow, and I shall not get even with them till I have cracked fully a dozen of their skulls."

"I shall be likely to be near you in the quarter where I hope to get you lodging, Tom, for I too am going to have a room there, though I shall generally live where I now am, as I can there obtain news of all that is going on, and might be able to warn our lady in time if they should get any news that may set them on her track. Heard you aught at St. Cloud of any Orleanist gathering?"

"I heard a good deal of talk about it, but naught for certain; but methinks that ere long they will be stirring again. The news that I have heard of the insolence of the mob here to the Duke of Aquitaine, and of the seizure of their friends who were with him, is like to set them on fire, for they will see that all the promises made by Burgundy meant nothing, and that, with the aid of the Parisians, he is determined to exercise all authority in the state, and to hold Aquitaine as well as the king in his hands."

The next morning Guy went to the house of Maître de Lepelletiere, and inquired for Philip Sampson. Maître Leroux was in.

"I have spoken to my friend about you," he said, after they had talked over the events of the last two days, "and he has arranged for a room for you in a house three doors away; and I have no doubt that your four men can be lodged there also, for 'tis a large house, and is let out, for the most part, as he told me, to journeymen carpenters. But since the troubles began there has been little building, and men who can find no work here have moved away to seek for it in places less afflicted by these troubles. That is one of the reasons why the carpenters have not made a firmer stand against the butchers. I will ask him to come up here. You already know him, as you have spoken with him several times when he was looking after his men putting up the new doors."

The master carpenter soon came in. "I will gladly get a lodging for your men," he said, when Guy had explained the matter to him. "We may come to blows with these market people, and four stout fellows are not to be despised. There will be a meeting of the council of our guild this afternoon, and on my recommendation they will give me the necessary documents, saying that the men-you can give me their names-have received permission to work as carpenters in Paris. They can then put on dresses suitable for craftsmen, and the papers will suffice to satisfy anyone who may inquire as to their business. I think that your tall archer may safely lay aside the disguise you say he has assumed, it might be likely to get him into trouble; the change in the colour of the hair and the darkening of his eyebrows should be quite sufficient disguise, and if he is always when abroad with one of his comrades, he has but to keep his mouth shut, and if questioned the man with him can say that he is dumb."

"That would be excellent," Guy said, "and I am greatly obliged to you. Doubtless, too, they will soon make acquaintance with some of the other workmen, and by mixing with these there will be less suspicion excited than if they always went about together."

"I will tell my foreman to present them to the men who work for me, and they will soon get known in the quarter. Five or six of my men lodge in the house where I took the room for you. It might be useful, too, were I to give you a paper of apprenticeship, and if you were similarly introduced. In that case it might be convenient to exchange the small room that I have taken for you for a larger one; as an apprentice you would ordinarily lodge with your master, and if you did not you would scarce have a room to yourself, but were you to lodge with your four men it would seem natural enough."

"That would be a capital plan, Maître Lepelletiere."

"You see, in that way, too," the carpenter went on, "you would only have to place a plank on your shoulder and then go where you will without exciting the least attention. I will furnish you with a list of the houses where I have men at work, and this again would be an assistance to you. It is my foreman who took the lodging for you; I am expecting him here shortly for orders, and he shall go round with you. As you say that your fellows are dressed at present in rough fashion it will be as well that they should provide themselves with their new disguises before they come here, as, if they were seen in their present guise, it would prejudice them with the others in the house, for craftsmen look down greatly upon the rough element of the street."

"They shall do so," Guy said, "and I will come with them myself this evening."

Guy presently went in with the foreman and arranged for a large attic with a dormer window, at the top of the house. At midday he met Robert Picard and told him the arrangements that had been made, supplying him with money for the purchase of the four dresses. "As soon as it becomes dark," he said, "you had best go to some quiet spot and change them. Bring the clothes you now have on in a bundle, for they may yet prove useful, and meet me at eight o'clock at the corner of the Rue des Fosses."

Guy then went to the Italian's and told Dame Margaret of the arrangements he had made.

"Since you have managed it all so well, Guy, I am glad to hear that the men are all back in Paris. I before wished that they should make straight for Villeroy, but since they are so safely bestowed it were best perhaps that they should be within reach. Long Tom is the only one I shall feel anxious about, for of course he is less easy to disguise than the others."

"He has plenty of shrewdness, my lady, and will, I have no doubt, play his part well. I know that I myself feel very glad that there are four true men upon whom we can rely if any difficulty should arise."

"Some evening, mother," Agnes said, "when I have grown more accustomed to this boy's dress I will go with Katarina to this house so that I can carry a message there, should she happen to be away when there is need for sending one."

Lady Margaret hesitated, but Guy said: "By your leave, my lady, I think that the idea is a very good one, saving that I myself will escort the two ladies there as soon as Mistress Agnes feels confident enough to go."

"In that case I should have no objection, Guy. Under your charge I have no doubt Agnes would be perfectly safe, but I could hardly bring myself to let her go out without escort in so wild a city as this is at present."

The Italian and his daughter presently joined them, and heard with satisfaction where Guy and the four men had obtained a safe lodging.

"Still," he said, "I should advise you sometimes to sleep at your lodging by the market-place. Simon is not the sort of companion you would choose. I have only seen him once, and I was then so disguised that he would not recognize me again-for none of those with whom I have dealings know who I am or where I live-but that once was sufficient to show me that the fellow might be trusted to serve me well as long as he was paid well, especially as he believed that I was an agent of the duke's; still, he is a rough and very unsavoury rascal, and had I been able to think at the moment of anywhere else where you could for the time safely shelter I should not have placed you with him."

"I do not mind," Guy said; "and at any rate with him I have opportunities of seeing what is going on, as, for example, when they insulted the Duke of Aquitaine, and it is certainly well to be able to learn what the intentions of the fellows are. As an Englishman I care naught for one party or the other, but as one of gentle blood it fills me with anger and disgust to see this rabble of butchers and skinners lording it over nobles and dragging knights and gentlemen away to prison; and if it were in my power I would gladly upset their design, were it not that I know that, for my lady's sake, it were well to hold myself altogether aloof from meddling in it."

"You are right," the Italian said gravely. "I myself am careful not to meddle in any way with these affairs. I try to learn what is doing, because such knowledge is useful to me and gains me credit as well as money with those who consult me, and may possibly be the means of saving their lives if they do but take my warning. Thus, having learned what was proposed to be done yesterday morning, I was able to warn a certain knight who visited me the evening before that it might cost him his life were he to remain in Paris twelve hours. He was incredulous at first, for I would give him no clue as to the nature of the danger; however, by a little trick I succeeded in impressing him sufficiently for him to resolve to leave at daybreak. This he did; at least they searched for him in vain at the Duke of Aquitaine's, and therefore I have no doubt that he took my advice, engaged a boat, and made his escape by the river. It was his first A to me, and I doubt not that henceforth he will be a valuable client, and that he will bring many of his friends to me. If I mistake not, I shall have more opportunities of doing such services and of so increasing my reputation ere long."

For a time things went on quietly. Tom and his companions were on friendly terms with the other men in the house, who all believed them to be carpenters who had come to Paris in search of employment. Long Tom was supposed by them to be dumb, and never opened his lips save when alone with his companions, and seldom left the house. The room was altogether unfurnished, but furniture was regarded as by no means a necessity in those days. Five bundles of rushes formed their beds, and Guy, as there was little to learn in the markets, generally slept there. An earthenware pan, in which burned a charcoal fire over which they did what cooking was necessary, a rough gridiron, and a cooking pot were the only purchases that it was necessary to make. Slices of bread formed their platters, and saved them all trouble in the matter of washing up. Washing was roughly performed at a well in the court-yard of the house.

Things had now quieted down so much that a considerable number of great nobles resorted to Paris, for the king had now a lucid interval. Among them were the Dukes of Berri, Burgundy, and Lorraine, with Duke Louis of Bavaria, the queen's brother, with the Counts de Nevers, De Charolais, De St. Pol, the Constable of France, and many other great lords and prelates. The queen was also with her husband.

"There will shortly be trouble again," the Italian said one day to Guy. "Simon told my daughter yesterday evening that the butchers were only biding their time to get as many fish into their net as possible, and that when they would draw it they would obtain a great haul. You have not been down there for some time; it were best that you put on your butcher's garb again and endeavour to find out what is intended."

"I was expecting you," Simon said, when that evening Guy entered his room. "There will be a meeting at midnight in the butchers' hall, and I cannot take you in with me, but I will tell you what happens."

"That will do as well as if I went myself," Guy said, "though in truth I should like well to see one of these councils."

"No one is admitted save those known to be, like myself, thoroughly devoted to the cause."

"That I can well understand, Simon; a traitor might mar all their plans."

"Some time I may take you," Simon said, "for doubtless I could smuggle you in; but to-night —" and he hesitated, "to-night it will be specially important, and they have to be more particular than usual as to who are admitted."

Guy noticed the hesitation, and replied carelessly that one occasion would be as good as another for him, and presently lay down in his corner. He wondered to himself what the business could be that his companion was evidently anxious that he should hear nothing of. He might wish that he should alone have the merit of reporting it, or it might be something that it was deemed the Duke of Burgundy himself, the butchers' friend and ally, would not approve of. At any rate he was determined, if possible, to find it all out; he therefore feigned sleep. At eleven o'clock Simon got up and went down; Guy waited for two or three minutes and then rose and followed. As soon as he was out of the door he made direct for the hall of the butchers' guild. He knew that Simon was not going straight there, as the meeting was not, he said, for an hour, and that he would be stopping to drink at some cabaret with his associates. The hall was but a short distance away.

When Guy approached it he saw that as yet it was not lighted up. On three sides it was surrounded by a garden with high trees; near the front entrance some twenty men were gathered talking together. He, therefore, went round to the back; several trees grew near the wall, and the branches of one of these extended over it. With considerable difficulty Guy succeeded in climbing it, and made his way along the branch and got upon the top of the wall. This was about fourteen feet high, and, lowering himself by his arms, he dropped into the garden and crossed to the building. He took off his white hood and thrust it into his doublet. The windows were six feet from the ground, and were, as usual at this time, closed by wooden shutters on the inside. Putting his fingers on the sill he raised himself up. There was plenty of room for him to stand, and, holding on by the iron bars, he took out his dagger and began to cut a hole in the shutter.

The wood was old, and after half an hour's hard work he succeeded in making a hole three inches long and an inch wide. By the time this was finished the hall had been lighted up with torches, and men were pouring in through the doors at the other end. Across the end next to him was a platform on which was a table. For a time no one came up there, for the members as they entered gathered in groups on the floor and talked earnestly together. After a few minutes ten men came up on to the platform; by this time the body of the hall was full, and the doors at the other end were closed. A man, whom Guy recognized as John de Troyes, stepped forward from the others on the platform and, standing in front of the table, addressed his comrades.

"My friends," he said, "it is time that we were at work again. Paris is becoming infested by enemies of the people, and we must rid ourselves of them. The nobles are assembled for the purpose, as they say, of being present at the marriage of Louis of Bavaria with the widow of Peter de Navarre, but we know well enough that this is but a pretext; they have come to consult how best they can overthrow the power of our Duke of Burgundy and suppress the liberty of this great city. The question is, are we tamely to submit to this?"

A deep shout of "No!" ran through the multitude.

"You are right, we will not submit. Were we to do so we know that it would cost the lives of all those who have made themselves prominent in the defence of the liberties of Paris; they might even go so far as to suppress all our privileges and to dissolve our guilds. In this matter the Duke of Burgundy hesitates and is not inclined to go with us to the full, but we Parisians must judge for ourselves what is necessary to be done. The duke has furnished us with a list of twelve names; these men are all dangerous and obnoxious to the safety of Paris. But there must be a longer list, we must strike at our own enemies as well as at those of the duke, and the council has therefore prepared a list of sixty names, which I will read to you."

Then, taking out a roll of paper, he read a list of lords and gentlemen, and also, to Guy's indignation, the names of several ladies of rank.

"These people," he said when he had finished, "are all obnoxious, and must be cast into prison. They must be tried and condemned."

Even among the greater portion of those present the boldness of a proposal that would array so many powerful families against them created a feeling of doubt and hesitation. The bolder spirits, however, burst into loud applause, and in this the others speedily joined, none liking to appear more lukewarm than the rest. Then up rose Caboche, a big, burly man with a coarse and brutal expression of face.

"I say we want no trials," he cried, striking one hand on the palm of the other. "As to the number, it is well enough as a beginning, but I would it were six hundred instead of sixty. I would that at one blow we could destroy all the nobles, who live upon the people of France. It needs but a good example to be set in Paris for all the great towns in France to follow it. Still, paltry as the number is, it will, as I said, do as a beginning. But there must be no mistake; if trials they must have, it must be by good men and true, who will know what is necessary and do it; and who will not stand upon legal tricks, but will take as evidence the fact that is known to all, that those people are dangerous to Paris and are the enemies of the king and the Duke of Burgundy. Last time we went, we marched with five thousand men; this time we must go with twenty thousand. They must see what force we have at our command, and that Paris is more powerful than any lord or noble even of the highest rank, and that our alliance must be courted and our orders obeyed. The Duke of Burgundy may pretend to frown, but at heart he will know that we are acting in his interest as well as our own; and even if we risk his displeasure, well, let us risk it. He needs us more than we need him. Do what he will, he cannot do without us. He knows well enough that the Orleanists will never either trust or forgive him, and he committed himself so far with us last time that, say what he will, none will believe that he is not with us now. For myself, I am glad that De Jacqueville and his knights will not this time, as last, ride at our head; 'tis best to show them that Paris is independent even of Burgundy, and that what we will we can do."

The hall rang with the loud acclamations, then John de Troyes got up again.

"I agree, we all agree, with every word that our good friend has spoken, and can warrant me that the judges shall be men in whom we can absolutely trust, and that those who enter the prisons will not leave them alive. The day after to-morrow, Thursday, the 11th of May, we shall hold a great assembly, of which we shall give notice to the king and the royal dukes, and shall make our proposals to the Duke of Aquitaine. Now, my friends, let each come forward with a list of the number of his friends who he will engage shall be present on Thursday."

At this point, Guy, seeing that the main business of the meeting had been declared, and that there now remained but to settle the details, got down from his post. With the aid of some ivy he climbed the wall and dropped down beyond it, and made his way back to his lodging. When Simon returned an hour later, Guy was apparently as fast asleep as before. When sleeping at the butchers' quarter he always rose at a very early hour, so that none who might have noticed him in his butcher's attire should see him go out in that of an apprentice, and he was obliged to walk about for some time before he could call at the count's. As soon as he thought that they would be likely to be stirring he knocked at the door. The old woman opened it.

"Is your master up yet?" he asked.

She nodded, and without further question he made his way upstairs to the Italian's chamber.

"You are early, Master Aylmer," the latter said in surprise as he entered. "Have you news of importance?"

"I have indeed, Count," and he at once related all that he had heard through the hole in the shutter.

"The insolence of these people surpasses all bounds," the count said angrily as he walked up and down the room. "Were there any force in the town that could resist them I would warn the Duke of Aquitaine what was intended, but as it is, nothing would be gained by it. You can only remember the eight or ten names that you have given me?"

"That is all; they were names that I was familiar with, while the others were strange to me."

"Two or three of them I can at least save from the grasp of these rascals," he said, "but I will take them all down on my tablets. What need was there for you," he went on after he had done this, "to run such risk as you did-for you would assuredly have been killed without mercy had they caught you spying upon them-when Simon, who you say was present, could have sent me full particulars of all that passed?"

Guy stated his reasons for fancying that upon this occasion Simon did not intend to send a full account.

"I thought so before I started," he said, "but I was well assured of it when I heard that, although Burgundy had given the names of twelve persons whom he desired to be arrested, he would go no further in the matter, and that he had no knowledge of their further pretensions. It seems to me, Count, that, believing as he does that you are an agent of the duke's, he was unwilling to say anything about this matter, as Burgundy might thwart the intentions of the butchers. The man is heart and soul with them, and though he is willing to sell you information that can do no harm to their plans, he will say nothing that might enable Burgundy to thwart them."

"If I thought that Burgundy could, or would do so, I would inform him as well as Aquitaine what is doing; but in the first place he has not the power, and in the second he would not have the will. What are a few score of lives to him, and those mostly of men of the Orleanist faction, in comparison with the support of Paris? I am vexed, too, at this failure of Simon, that is to say, if it be a failure. That we shall know by mid-day. My daughter will meet him in the Place de Grève at eleven, and we shall hear when she comes back how much he has told her. I am going after breakfast to my booth outside the walls, where you first saw me. I must send notes to the three gentlemen whom I know, begging them to see me there."

"Can I take them for you? I have nothing to do, and shall be glad of anything to occupy me."

"I shall be obliged if you will; you are sure to find them in at this hour."

He sat down and wrote three short communications. The wording was identical, but the times fixed for the interview were an hour apart. They ran as follows:

> "My Lord, —Consulting the stars last night I find that danger menaces you. It may be averted if you quit Paris when you receive this, for it seems to me that it is here only that your safety is menaced. Should you wish to consult me before doing so, come, I pray you, to my booth in the fair at two, but come mounted. "

Instead of a signature a cabalistic figure was drawn below it, and then the words were added:

> The bearer can be trusted.

The slips of parchment were then rolled up and sealed; no addresses were put on.

"If they question you," he said, "say nothing, save that I told you that the matter contained in the letter was sure and certain, and that a great risk of life would assuredly be run unless my advice was taken. Deliver them into the hands of those they concern, and trust them to no others, Master Aylmer. If you cannot obtain access to them, say to the varlets that they are to inform their lords that one from the man in the Rue des Essarts desires urgently to see them, and that should be sufficient if the message is given. If they refuse to take it, then I pray you wait outside for a while on the chance of the gentlemen issuing out. This, on which you see I have made one dot, is for the Count de Rennes, who is at present at the Hotel of St. Pol, being in the company of the Duke of Berri; this is for Sir John Rembault, who is at the Louvre, where he is lodging with the governor, who is a relation of his; the third is for the Lord of Roubaix, who is also lodged at the Louvre."

"They shall have them," Guy said as he placed them in his doublet, "if I have to stop till midnight to get speech with them; the matter of waiting a few hours is but a trifle in comparison with the life of a man. I would that I could warn others."

The Italian shook his head. "It could not be done without great danger," he said. "Were you to carry an anonymous letter to others you might be seized and questioned. The three to whom you now carry notes have all reason for knowing that my predictions are not to be despised, but the others would not accept any warning from an unknown person. They might take it for a plot, and you might be interrogated and even put to torture to discover who you are and whence you obtained this information. Things must go on as they are; assuredly this is no time for meddling in other people's affairs. We are only at the beginning of troubles yet, and know not how great they may grow. Moreover, you have no right to run a risk for strangers when your life may be of vital service to your mistress. Should you succeed in handing these three letters to the gentlemen to whom they are written by noon, I shall be glad if you will bring the news to me at my booth, and I shall then be able to tell, you how much information the butcher has sent of the proceedings last night."

Guy went first to the Louvre. As many people were going in and out, no question was asked him, and on reaching the entrance he inquired of some varlets standing there for the lodgings of the Lord de Roubaix and Sir John Rembault.

"I am in the service of the Lord de Roubaix; what would you with him?"

"I am charged with a message for him; I was told to deliver it only to himself."

"From whom do you come? I cannot disturb him with such a message from I know not who."

"That is reasonable," Guy replied, "but if you tell him that I come from the man in the Rue des Essarts I warrant that he will see me. You don't suppose that I am joking with you," he went on as the varlet looked at him suspiciously, "when I should likely be whipped for my pains. If you will give the message to your lord I doubt not that he will give me audience."

"Follow me," the varlet said, and led the way upstairs and through several corridors, then he motioned to him to wait, and entered a room. He returned in a minute.

"My lord will see you," he said, and led the way into the room. "This is the person, my lord," he said, and then retired.

The Lord of Roubaix was a tall man of some forty years of age. Guy bowed deeply and handed to him the roll of parchment. The count broke the seal and read it, and when he had finished looked fixedly at Guy.

"The writer tells me that you are to be trusted?"

"I hope so, my lord."

"Do you know the contents of this letter?"

"I know so much, my lord, that the writer told me to assure you that the matter was urgent, and that he could not be mistaken as to what was written in the letter."

The count stood irresolute for a minute or two; then he said:

"Tell him that I will act upon his advice. He has before now proved to me that his warnings are not to be neglected. You seem by your attire to be an apprentice, young sir, and yet your manner is one of higher degree."

"Disguises are convenient in times like these, my lord," Guy said.

"You are right, lad." He put his hand to his pouch, but Guy drew back with a smile.

"No, my lord, had you offered me gold before you remarked that I was but playing a part, I should have taken it in order to keep up that part; as it is I can refuse it without your considering it strange that I should do so."

The count smiled. "Whoever you are, you are shrewd and bold, young sir. I shall doubtless see you when I return to Paris."

Guy then left, and delivered the other two missives. In each case those who received them simply returned an answer that they would be at the place at the hour named, and he then went beyond the walls, observing as he passed out through the gates that a party of White Hoods had stationed themselves there. However, they interfered with no one passing in or out. On reaching the booth he informed the count of the success of his visits.

"I doubt, however," he said, "whether either of the three gentlemen will be here at the time appointed, for the White Hoods are watching at the gate."

"I think that they will not stop anyone to-day, Master Aylmer. They intend to make a great haul to-morrow, and would not wish to excite suspicion by seizing anyone to-day. Were it known that they had done so, many others who have reason to believe they are obnoxious to Burgundy or to the Parisians, might conceal themselves or make their escape in various disguises. I hear that a request has been made that a deputation of the citizens of Paris shall be received by the Duke of Aquitaine to-morrow morning, and that the great lords may be present to hear the request and complaints of the city."

Chapter XV
A Rescue

Guy had found his mornings hang heavy on his hands, as of course he had been obliged to give up attending the fencing-school. Going down to the river now, he sat there watching the passing boats until nearly one o'clock, and then returned to the fair. Before reaching the booth Katarina joined him.

"I have been watching for you, Monsieur Guy. Father said it was as well that you should not, twice in a day, be seen entering his place. He bade me tell you that the three gentlemen have been to him and will not re-enter Paris."

"Did you see Simon this morning?"

"Yes, he only told me that the market men would have an interview with the Duke of Aquitaine to-morrow, and would demand the arrest of those whom the Duke of Burgundy had pointed out as his enemies. He said that they would go in such force that the duke would be unable to refuse their request. Although it was so early, I think that the man had been drinking. My father, when I told him, said I should go no more to meet him."

"I am very glad to hear it," Guy said. "He is a low scoundrel, and though I say not but that the information obtained from him may have been of some advantage, for indeed it was the means of my being enabled to save our lives and those of my Burgundian friends, I like not the thought of your going to meet him; and I am sure that if he were to take the idea into his thick head that it was not for the advantage of the Duke of Burgundy that the information he had given was being used, he is capable of denouncing you."

"I did not mind meeting him,", the girl said. "I never went into the rough quarters, but always met him in one of the better squares or streets. Still, I am glad that I have not to go again. I think that he had been drinking all night, and with his unwashed face and his bloodshot eyes and his foul attire I was ashamed even in my present dress to speak with him."

"I hope that I have done with him too," Guy said. "Of course, for my mistress's sake, I shall go again if there be aught to be learnt by it, but as it seems he is now no longer to be trusted it is not likely that any advantage is to be gained by visiting him. However, I shall hear what your father thinks this evening."

Upon talking over the matter with the astrologer the latter at once said that he thought that it would be better for him not to go to Simon's again.

"When he finds that my daughter meets him no more he will feel aggrieved. I myself shall go in disguise to-morrow to meet him in the Place de Grève, and tell him that for the present there will be no occasion for him to come to the rendezvous, as the events of the meeting which will have taken place before I see him show that there can be no doubt that the butchers are ready to go all lengths against the Orleanist party; but that if any change should occur, and private information be required, you would go to his lodging again, I shall make no allusion to his having given me none of the names save those furnished by the duke, or remark on the strangeness that, having been at the meeting, he should have heard nothing of the measures proposed against the others; his own conscience will no doubt tell him that his failure is one of the causes of my no longer desiring any messages from him. I have other means of gaining information, as I have one of the medical students who follow that cracked-brained fellow, John de Troyes, in my pay. Hitherto I have not employed him largely, but shall now, if need be, avail myself of his services. But I do not think that I shall have any occasion to do so. After the demand by the Parisians for so many nobles and gentlemen to be arrested, it will be clear to all adhering to Orleans that Paris is no longer a place for them, and even the followers of Burgundy will see that those the duke regarded as his servants have become his masters, and there will be but few persons of quality remaining in Paris, and therefore, save when some citizen wishes to consult me, I shall have little to do here save to carry on my work as a quack outside the gates. Even this I can drop for a time, for the people of Paris will not be inclined for pleasure when at any moment there may be fierce fighting in the streets. I shall be well content to look on for a time. I have been almost too busy of late. And it was but yesterday that I received news from a Carthusian monk,—whom I thought it as well to engage to let me know what is passing,—that there have been debates among some of the higher clergy upon reports received that persons, evidently disguised, call upon me at late hours, and that I practise diabolic arts. A determination has been arrived at that an inquisition shall be made into my doings, my house is to be searched, and myself arrested and tried by the judge for having dealings with the devil. This news much disturbed me; however, when you told me that the Archbishop of Bourges was among those on the list of accused, and also Boisratier, confessor to the queen, it is evident that these good ecclesiastics will have ample matter of another sort to attend to, and are not likely to trouble themselves about sorcery at present."

On the following morning some twelve thousand White Hoods marched to the Hôtel de St. Pol, and the leaders, on being admitted, found all the great lords assembled. After making various propositions they presented a roll to the Duke of Aquitaine containing the names of those they charged with being traitors. He at first refused to take it; but so many of their followers at once poured into the great hall that he was obliged to do so, and to read out the names. Twenty of those mentioned in the list were at once, in spite of the protest of the duke, arrested and carried off; a proclamation was made by sound of trumpet in all the squares of Paris summoning the other forty named to appear within a few days, under penalty of having their property confiscated. A week later the king, having recovered his health, went to the church of Notre Dame, he and all the nobles with him wearing white hoods. Four days later the Parisians rose again, seized the gates, drew up the bridges, placed strong guards at each point, and a cordon of armed men outside the walls all round the city, to prevent any from escaping by letting themselves down from the walls.

Groups of ten armed men were placed in every street, and the sheriffs and other leaders marched a large body of men to the Hôtel de St. Pol and surrounded it by a line three deep. They then entered and found the king, dukes, and nobles all assembled in the great hall.

They then ordered a Carmelite friar, named Eustace, to preach to the king. He took for his text, *"Except the Lord keep the city, the watchman waketh but in vain,"* and upon this discoursed on the bad state of the government of the kingdom, and of the crimes committed. The Chancellor of France demanded of the friar when he had concluded who were those who had incited him thus to speak, and the leaders at once said they had done so, and called up a number of other leaders, who on bended knees declared to the king that Father Eustace had spoken their sentiments; that they had the sincerest love for the king and his family, and that what they had done had been for the welfare of himself and the kingdom. While this was going on, the Duke of Burgundy, at once indignant and alarmed at this insolence of the Parisians, had gone out, and, finding the lines of armed men surrounding the hotel, had earnestly entreated them to retire, saying that it was neither decent nor expedient that the king, who had but just recovered from his illness, should thus see them drawn up in battle array round his abode. Those he addressed replied like the leaders within, that they were there for the good of the kingdom, and then gave him a roll, saying that they should not depart until those written on it were delivered up to them.

With the names of Louis of Bavaria, five knights, an archbishop and priest, were those of nine ladies of high rank, including the eldest daughter of the constable. The duke found that neither his authority nor powers were of the slightest avail, and returning to the queen, showed her the list. She was greatly troubled, and begged him to go with the Duke of Aquitaine and beg the Parisians in her name to wait for eight days, and that she would at the end of that time allow them to arrest her brother. The two dukes went out to the Parisians, but they positively refused to grant the request, and declared that they would go up to the queen's apartments and take those named by force, even in her or the king's presence, unless they were given up. On their return to the queen they found Louis of Bavaria and the king with her. On their report of the Parisians' demands the Duke of Bavaria went out and begged them to take him into custody, and that if he were found guilty they could punish him, but that if found innocent he should be allowed to go back to Bavaria, under a promise not to return to France again. He begged them to be content with taking him a prisoner, and to arrest no others.

They would not, however, abate one jot of their pretensions, and the whole of those demanded were at once brought out, including the ladies. They were put two and two on horseback, each horse escorted by four men-at-arms, and were carried to various prisons. The Duke of Burgundy now, with his usual craft, professed to be well satisfied with what the Parisians had done, and handed over to them the Duke of Bar and the other prisoners confined in the Louvre, for whose security he had solemnly pledged himself. The Parisians then obliged the king to appoint twelve knights, nominated by themselves, and six examiners, to try the prisoners and punish all found guilty, while the dukes were obliged to draw up a statement and send it to the University for their seal of approval of what had been done.

The University, however, to their honour, stood firm; and while king and nobles had quailed before the violence of the crowd, they declared in full council before the king that they would in nowise intermeddle or advise in the business; and that so far from having advised the arrests of the dukes and other prisoners, they were much displeased at what had taken place. The University was a power; its buildings were strong, and the students were numerous, and at all times ready to take part in brawls against the Parisians; and even the butchers, violent as they were, were afraid to take steps against it.

They foresaw, however, that the position taken up by the University might lead some day to an inquiry into their conduct, and therefore obtained from the king an edict declaring that all that had been done was done by his approval and for the security of his person and the state, and that the arrests and imprisonments were therefore to be considered and regarded as having been done for the true honour and profit of the crown, and that he accordingly commanded all his councillors, judges, and officers to proclaim that this was so in all public places. This was signed by the king in council, the Dukes of Berri and Burgundy, and several other nobles and ecclesiastics, by the Chancellor of Burgundy, and other knights attached to the duke.

Many nobles quitted Paris at once, either openly or in disguise, including many of the Burgundian party, who were to the last degree indignant at what was going on; for the mock trials were at once commenced, and many of the prisoners, without regard to sex, were daily either put to death in prison or drowned in the Seine. Some of the bodies were exhibited on gibbets, the heads of others were fixed on lances, and some of them were beheaded in the market-place. During this time Paris remained in a state of terror, bands of armed butchers parading the streets were loud in their threats as to what would be done to all who did not join heartily with them. None of the better class ventured from their houses, and the mob were absolute masters of the city. The leaders, however, maintained for the time a certain degree of order. For the time they were anxious to appear in the light of earnest friends of the king, and as carrying out in his name the punishment of his enemies. But many tumults, murders, and conflagrations occurred in the city, and the country in general soon perceived the real nature of their doings. It was known that the Orleanist forces were marching against the city. The Count d'Eu had left Paris and returned to his estates, where he raised two thousand men-at-arms and marched to Verneuil, where the Dukes of Orleans, Brittany, and Bourbon were assembled, with a number of great lords, among whom were the Counts of Vettus and D'Alençon, the king's sons. The former had made his escape from Paris, and brought letters from the Duke of Aquitaine declaring that he himself, with the king and queen, were prisoners in the hands of the Parisians.

All these nobles met in a great assembly, and letters were written to the king, his great council, and to the Parisians, ordering them to allow the Duke of Aquitaine to go wherever he pleased, and to set at liberty the Dukes of Bar and Bavaria and all other prisoners. Should they refuse to comply, they declared war against the town of Paris, which they declared they would destroy, with all within it except the king and the princes of royal blood. The Parisians compelled the king to send a friendly answer, putting them off with excuses, and in the meantime to despatch commissaries to all the towns and baronies of France assuring them that the trials and executions of the traitors had been fairly conducted and their guilt proved, and calling upon the country to take up arms to aid Paris against various nobles who were traitorously advancing against it.

During this time Guy remained quietly in his lodging with the four retainers, seldom stirring abroad. The men were now regarded by all their neighbours as honest carpenters, and they shared the indignation of the great body of the craft at this usurpation by the market men of the government of France, and at the murders of knights and ladies that were daily taking place. At present, however, the opponents of the butchers dared not resort to arms. So great had been the fear that they excited that most men, however much at heart opposed to them, had been constrained to appear to side with and agree with them, and as there was no means of knowing who could be counted upon to join the carpenters were these to take up arms, the latter could not venture alone to enter the lists against the armed host of the other party.

One evening Guy, who had not been near the Italian's for over a fortnight, received a message from Dame Margaret to say that she wished to speak to him, for that she had determined, if any way of escape could be decided on, to quit Paris, and to endeavour to make her way to Villeroy. He was greatly pleased at the news. He had himself ventured to urge this step on the day after the Duke of Bar and his companions were seized, pointing out that it was evident that the Duke of Burgundy had neither the power nor the inclination to thwart the Parisians, and that although both parties were now nominally hostile to the English, neither were likely, at so critical a time, to give so much as a thought to Villeroy. Dame Margaret had agreed to this, but considered the difficulties of getting out of Paris and traversing the intervening country were so great that she preferred to wait until some change took place in the situation of Paris. But it was now too evident that the changes were entirely for the worse, and that if discovered the butchers would undoubtedly add her and her children to their long list of victims.

His companions were equally glad when Guy told them the news.

"The sooner the better, Master Guy," Long Tom said. "I own that I should like to have a tussle with these rascals before I go; their doings are so wicked that every honest man must want to get one fair blow at them. Still, I don't see any chance of that, for although the good fellows round here grumble under their breath, there does not seem any chance of their doing anything. There is not an hour passes that my heart is not in my mouth if I hear a step on the stairs, thinking that they may have found out where my lady is hidden."

Guy had just turned into the street where the astrologer dwelt when he heard loud voices from a little group in front of him. Four armed men, whose white hoods showed that they were one of the butchers' patrols, were standing round a slight figure.

"It is well you stopped him, comrade," a voice said, that Guy recognized at once as being that of Simon Bouclier. "I know the young fellow; he has been to me many a time on the part of a knave who professed to be an agent of Burgundy's, making inquiries of me as to the doings in our quarter. I have found out since that the duke employed no such agent, and this matter must be inquired into. We will take him with us to the market; they will soon find means of learning all about him and his employer."

Guy felt at once that if Katarina were carried to the butchers, not only would the consequences to herself be terrible, but that she would be forced to make such disclosures as would lead to the arrest of the count, and to the discovery of Dame Margaret. He determined at all hazards to get her out of these men's hands. The girl made a sudden attempt to free herself, slipped from the grasp that one of the men had of her shoulder, dived between two others, and would have been off had not Simon seized her by the arm. Guy sprung forward and threw himself on the butcher, and with such force that Simon rolled over in the gutter.

"Run, run!" he shouted at the same moment to Katarina, who darted down a lane to the left, while he himself ran forward and turned down the first lane to the right with the three men in hot pursuit of him. Young, active, and unencumbered by armour, he gained on them rapidly; but when he neared the end of the lane he saw some five or six White Hoods, whose attention had been called by the shouts of his pursuers, running to meet him. He turned and ran back till close to those who had been following him, and then suddenly sprung into a doorway when they were but three or four paces from him. They were unable to check their speed, and as they passed he brought his sword down on the neck of the one nearest, and as he fell to the ground Guy leapt out and ran up the street again. He had gone but ten paces when he met Simon, who rushed at him furiously with an uplifted axe. Springing aside as the blow descended he delivered a slashing cut on the butcher's cheek, dashed past him, and kept on his way. He took the first turning, and then another, leading, like that in which he had been intercepted, towards the river. His pursuers were fifty yards behind him, but he feared that at any moment their shouts would attract the attention of another patrol. More than once, indeed, he had to alter his direction as he heard sounds of shouts in front of him, but at last, after ten minutes' running, he came down on to the main thoroughfare at the point where the street leading to the bridge across to the island issued from it.

His pursuers were still but a short distance away, for fresh parties who had joined them had taken up the chase, and Guy was no longer running at the speed at which he had started. His great fear was that he should be stopped at the gate at the end of the bridge; but as there was no fear of attack this had been left open, so as not to interfere with the traffic between that quarter of the city on the island and those on the opposite banks. Guy was now again running his hardest, in order to get across far enough ahead of his pursuers to enable him to hide himself, when a strong patrol of some twenty White Hoods issued from the gate at the other side of the bridge. Without a moment's hesitation he climbed the parapet and threw himself over. It would, he knew, be as bad for his mistress were he captured as if Katarina had fallen into their hands, for if caught he felt sure that tortures would be applied to discover who he was and where his mistress was hidden, and he had made up his mind that if he was overtaken he would fight until killed rather than be captured.

When he came to the surface of the water Guy turned on his back and suffered himself to float down until he recovered his breath. When he did so he raised his head and, treading the water, listened attentively. He was now nearly a quarter of a mile below the bridge. There was no sound of shouting behind him, but he felt sure that the pursuit was in no way abandoned. Already torches were flashing on the quay between the wall and the river, and in a short time others appeared on his left. On both sides there were dark spaces where the walls of the great chateaux of the nobles extended down to the water's side, and obliged those pursuing him along the quays to make a detour round them to come down again to the bank. He could hardly succeed in reaching one of these buildings without being seen, for the light of the torches on the opposite shore would be almost certain to betray his movements as soon as he began to swim, and even if he did reach the shore unseen he might at once be handed over to the White Hoods by those in the hotel. He therefore remained floating on his back, and in twenty minutes was beyond the line of the city wall. He could now swim without fear of being discovered, and made for the southern shore.

It was now the middle of June, and the water was fairly warm, but he was glad to be out of it. So far as Guy had heard he had not been caught sight of from the moment that he had sprung from the bridge. It might well be supposed that he had been drowned. Climbing up the bank he gained, after walking a quarter of a mile, the forest that surrounded Paris on all sides. Going some distance into it he threw himself down, after first taking off his doublet and hanging it on a bush to dry. He had escaped the first pressing danger, that of being taken and tortured into confession, and the rest was now comparatively easy. He had but to obtain another disguise of some sort and to re-enter Paris; he would then be in no greater danger than before, for in the sudden attack on Simon, and in the subsequent flight through the ill-lighted streets, he was certain that beyond the fact that he was young and active, and that he was evidently not a noble, no one could have noted any details of his dress, and certainly no one could have had as much as a glance at his face.

He started at daybreak, walked through the woods up to Meudon, and thence to Versailles, which was then little more than a village. By the time that he reached it his clothes had thoroughly dried on him, and being of a dark colour they looked little the worse, save that his tight pantaloons had shrunk considerably. The stalls were just opening when he arrived there, and he presently came upon one where garments of all sorts were hanging. The proprietor's wife, a cheery-looking woman, was standing at the door.

"I have need of some garments, madame," he said.

"You look as if you did," she said with a smile, glancing at his ankles. "I see that you are an apprentice, and for that sort of gear you will have to go to Paris; we deal in country garments."

"That will suit me well enough, madame. The fact is that, as you see, I am an apprentice; but having been badly treated, and having in truth no stomach for the frays and alarms in Paris (where the first man one meets will strike one down, and if he slays you it matters not if he but shout loud enough that he has killed an Orleanist), I have left my master, and have no intention of returning as an apprentice. But I might be stopped and questioned at every place I pass through on my way home did I travel in this 'prentice dress, and I would, therefore, fain buy the attire of a young peasant."

The woman glanced up and down the street.

"Come in," she said. "You know that it is against the law to give shelter to a runaway apprentice, but there are such wild doings in Paris that for my part I can see no harm in assisting anyone to escape, whether he be a noble or an apprentice, and methinks from your speech that you are as like to be the former as the latter. But," she went on, seeing that Guy was about to speak, "tell me naught about it. My husband, who ought to be here, is snoring upstairs, and I can sell what I will; therefore, look round and take your choice of garments, and go into the parlour behind the shop and don them quickly before anyone comes in. As to your own I will pay you what they are worth, for although those pantaloons are all too tight for those strong limbs of yours they may do for a slighter figure."

Guy was soon suited, and in a few minutes left the shop in a peasant's dress, and made his way along the village until beyond the houses. Then he left the road, made a long detour, and returned to Sèvres. Here he first purchased a basket, which he took outside the place and hid in a bush. Then he went down into the market and bargained for vegetables, making three journeys backwards and forwards, and buying each time of different women, until his basket was piled up. Then he got a piece of old rope for two or three sous, slung the basket on his shoulders, crossed the ferry, and made for Paris. He felt strange without his sword, which he had dropped into the water on landing; for although in Paris every one now went armed, a sword would have been out of character with his dress, in the country, and still more so in the disguise in which he had determined to re-enter the town. He passed without question through the gate, and made his way to his lodgings. As he entered Long Tom leapt up with a cry of joy.

"Thank God that you are safe, Master Guy! We have been grievously disturbed for your safety, for the count came here early this morning in disguise to ask if we had heard aught of you. He said that his daughter had returned last night saying that you had rescued her from the hands of the White Hoods, and that beyond the fact that they had followed you in hot pursuit she had no news of you, and that the countess was greatly alarmed as to your safety. The other three men-at-arms started at once to find out if aught could be learned of you. I would fain have gone also, but the count said that I must bide here in case you should come, and that there was trouble enough at present without my running the risk of being discovered. An hour since Robert Picard returned; he had been listening to the talk of the White Hoods, and had learned that one of their number had been killed and another sorely wounded by a man who had rescued a prisoner from the hands of a patrol. He had been chased by a number of them, and finally threw himself off the bridge into the Seine to avoid falling into their hands. The general idea was that he was one of the nobles in disguise, of whom they were in search, and that the capture would have been a very important one.

"All agreed that he could never have come up alive, for there were bands of men with torches along both banks, and no sign of him had been perceived. However, they are searching the river down, and hope to come upon his body either floating or cast ashore. Robert went out again to try and gather more news, leaving me well-nigh distraught here."

"The story is true as far as it goes, Tom. I did catch one of them a back-handed blow just under his helmet as he ran past me, and I doubt not that it finished him; as to the other, I laid his cheek open. It was a hot pursuit, but I should have got away had it not been that a strong patrol came out through the gate at the other end of the bridge just as I was in the middle, and there was no course but to jump for it. I thrust my sword into the sheath, and went over. It added somewhat to my weight in the water, and it sunk my body below the surface, but with the aid of my hands paddling I floated so that only my nose and mouth were above the water; so that it is little wonder that they could not make me out. I landed on the other bank a quarter of a mile beyond the walls, slept in the forest, started this morning from Versailles, where I got rid of my other clothes and bought these. I purchased this basket and the vegetables at Sèvres, then walked boldly in. No one could have seen my face in the darkness, and therefore I am safe from detection, perhaps safer than I was before."

"Well done, Master Guy; they would have killed you assuredly if they had caught you."

"It was not that that I was afraid of-it was of being taken prisoner. You see, if they had captured me and carried me before the butchers in order to inquire who I was before cutting my throat, they might have put me to the torture and forced me to say who I was, and where my mistress was in hiding. I hope if they had, that I should have stood out; but none can say what he will do when he has red-hot pincers taking bits out of his flesh, and his nails, perhaps, being torn out at the roots. So even if I could not have swam a stroke I should have jumped off the bridge."

"You did well, Master Guy," the archer said admiringly; "for indeed they say that the strongest man cannot hold out against these devilish tortures."

At this moment a step was heard on the stairs, and Jules Varoy entered.

"The saints be praised!" he exclaimed as he recognized Guy. "I thought that you were drowned like a rat, Master Guy; and though Tom here told us that you could swim well, I never thought to see you again."

Guy told him in a few words how he had escaped, and begged him to carry the news to his mistress. He was about to give him the address-for up till now he had refrained from doing so, telling them that it was from no doubt of their fidelity, but that if by any chance one of them fell into the hands of the White Hoods they might endeavour to wring from them the secret, and it was therefore best that they should not be burdened with it-but the man stopped him.

"The count told us that he would be at his booth at the fair at eleven o'clock, and that if any of us obtained any news we were to take it to him there. He said that there were several parties of White Hoods in the streets, and that as he went past he heard them say that the boy of whom they were in search was a messenger of some person of importance at court, and that doubtless the man who had rescued him was also in the plot, and that a strict watch was to be kept on the quarter both for the boy and for the man, who was said to be tall and young. Simon, who had been wounded by him, had declared that he knew him to be connected with the boy; that he was a young man with dark hair, and was in the habit of using disguises, sometimes wearing the dress of an apprentice, and at other times that of a butcher's assistant. He said that he was about twenty-three."

Guy smiled. He understood that the butcher, who was a very powerful man, did not like to own that the man who had killed one of his comrades and had severely wounded himself was but a lad.

"As you go, Jules," he said, "will you see Maître Leroux and ask him if he can come hither, for I would consult him on the matter."

Chapter XVI
The Escape

Maître Leroux came in shortly after Jules Varoy had left. He had not, until the man told him, heard of the events of the night before, and Guy had to tell him all about it before anything else was said.

"It was a lucky escape, Master Aylmer, if one can call luck what is due to thought and quickness. Is there anything I can do for you?"

"This black hue that I gave my hair has been of good service to me hitherto, but as it is a youth with black hair that they are now looking for, I would fain change its hue again."

"What dye did you use?"

"It was bought for me at a perfumer's in the Rue Cabot. As you see, it is fading now, and the ducking last night has greatly assisted to wash it out. The shopman said that it was used by court ladies and would last for a long time, but I have already had to renew it four or five times. I would now colour my hair a red or a reddish-brown; if I cannot do that I must crop it quite short. It matters nothing in this disguise whether it is altogether out of the fashion or not. What think you?"

"Doubtless you could get dyes of any shade at the perfumer's you speak of, for he supplies most of the court ladies with dyes and perfumes; and I should say that reddish-brown dye would suit you well, since that differs a good deal from your hair's original colour and still more from what it is at present. I will ask one of Lepelletiere's daughters to fetch it for you. It would be better than cutting it short, though that might not go badly with your present disguise, but should you need to adopt any other it would look strange, since in our days there is scarce anyone but wears his hair down to his shoulders. In the meantime I would have you wash your hair several times with a ley of potash, but not too strong, or it will damage it. I warrant me that will take out the dye altogether; but be sure that you wash it well in pure water afterwards, so as to get rid of the potash, for that might greatly affect the new dye. I will send a boy up with some potash to you at once, so that you may be ready to apply the dye as soon as you get it."

Late in the afternoon Guy sallied out in the disguise in which he had arrived. His hair was a tawny brown. He had left his basket behind him, and carried a heavy cudgel in his hand. He sauntered quietly along, stopping often to stare at the goods on the stalls, and at nobles who rode past followed generally by two or three esquires. No one would doubt that he was a young countryman freshly arrived in Paris.

He had sent a message to the count by Jules Varoy that he would pass along the street in the disguise of a young peasant as the clock struck seven, and that if he saw no White Hoods about he would look up at the casement, return a minute or two afterwards, and then try if the door was unfastened. If so he would come in, while if it were fastened he should consider that it was judged unsafe for him to enter. He caught sight of Katarina's face at the window as he glanced up. There was a patrol of the White Hoods in sight, but it was far down the street, and after going a few yards past the house he crossed the road, and as he returned he pushed at the door. It yielded at once, and with a glance round to see that no one was watching he entered quickly and closed it behind him.

"The Madonna be thanked that you are safe!" Katarina, now in her girl's dress, exclaimed as she seized his hand. "Oh, Monsieur Guy, how I have suffered! It was not until two o'clock that my father returned and told us that you were safe; I should never have forgiven myself if harm had come to you from your noble effort to save me. I heard their shouts as they ran in pursuit of you, and scarce thought it possible that you could escape when there was so many of their patrols about in the street. I cried all night at the thought that you should have thrown away your life to try to save mine, for I knew well enough what would have happened had that evil butcher dragged me to his quarter. After my father had been out early and brought back the news that you had leapt into the Seine we had some little hope, for Dame Margaret declared that she knew that you could swim well. We had no one we could send out, for the old woman is too stupid, and my father now strictly forbids me to stir outside the door. So here we all sat worn with anxiety until my father returned from the booth with the news. He could not come back earlier, and he had no one to send, for the black man must keep outside amusing the people as long as my father is there."

All this was poured out so rapidly that it was said by the time they reached the door upstairs. Dame Margaret silently held out her hands to Guy as he entered, and Agnes kissed him with sisterly affection, while Charlie danced round and round him with boisterous delight.

"I hardly knew how much you were to me and how much I depended upon you, Guy," Dame Margaret said presently, "until I feared that I had lost you. When, as I thought must be the case from what Katarina said, I believed you were killed or a prisoner in the hands of those terrible people, it seemed to me that we were quite left alone, although there still remained the four men. Neither Agnes nor I closed our eyes all night Charlie soon cried himself to sleep, Katarina sat up with us till nigh morning, and we had hard work to console her in any way, so deep was her grief at the thought that it was owing to her that you had run this peril. All night we could hear the count walking up and down in the room above. He had pointed out the peril that might arise to us all if you had fallen into the hands of the butchers, but at the time we could not dwell on that, though there were doubtless grounds for his fears."

"Great grounds, madame. That is what I most feared when I was flying from them, and I was resolved that I would not be taken alive, for had I not gained the bridge I was determined to force them to kill me rather than be captured. It was fortunate, indeed, that I came along when I did, Katarina, for had I not heard what Simon said I should have passed on without giving a thought to the matter. There are too many evil deeds done in Paris to risk one's life to rescue a prisoner from the hands of a patrol of the White Hoods."

"As for me, I did not realize it until it was all over," Katarina said. "I felt too frightened even to think clearly. It was not until the shouts of your pursuers had died away that I could realize what you had saved me from, and the thought made me so faint and weak that I was forced to sit down on a door-step for a time before I could make my way home. As to my father, he turned as pale as death when I came in and told him what had happened."

Shortly afterwards the count, who had been engaged with a person of consequence, came down. He thanked Guy in the warmest terms for the service he had rendered his daughter.

"Never was a woman in greater peril," he said, "and assuredly St. Anthony, my patron saint, must have sent you to her rescue. She is all that I have left now, and it is chiefly for her sake that I have continued to amass money, though I say not that my own fancy for meddling in such intrigues may not take some part in the matter. After this I am resolved of one thing, namely, that she shall take no further part in the business. For the last year I had often told myself that the time had come when I must find another to act as my messenger and agent. It was difficult, however, to find one I could absolutely trust, and I have put the matter off. I shall do so no longer; and indeed there is now the less occasion for it, since, as I have just learned, fresh negotiations have been opened for peace. That it will be a lasting one I have no hope, but the Orleanists are advancing in such force that Burgundy may well feel that the issue of a battle at present may go against him. But even though it last but a short time, there will come so many of the Orleanist nobles here with doubtless strong retinues that Paris will be overawed, and we shall have an end of these riots here. I shall, therefore, have no need to trouble as to what is going on at the markets. As to other matters I can keep myself well informed. I have done services to knights and nobles of one party as well as the other, and shall be able to learn what is being done in both camps. The important point at present is, Lady Margaret, that there is like to be a truce, at any rate for a time. As soon as this is made and the Duke of Aquitaine has gained power to act you may be sure that the leaders of the White Hoods will be punished, and there will be no more closing of gates and examination of those who pass in and out. Therefore, madame, you will then be able to do what is now well-nigh impossible, namely, quit the town. At present the orders are more stringent than ever, none are allowed to leave save with orders signed by John de Troyes, who calls himself keeper of the palace, Caboche, or other leaders and even peasants who come in with market goods must henceforth produce papers signed by the syndics of their villages saying they are the inhabitants of his commune, and therefore quiet and peaceable men going about their business of supplying the city with meat or vegetables, as the case may be. These papers must also be shown on going out again. Until a change takes place, then, there is no hope of your making your way out through the gates with your children; but as soon as the truce is concluded and the Orleanists come in you will be able to pass out without trouble."

It was not, indeed, for another month that the truce was settled, although the terms were virtually agreed upon at Pontois, where the Dukes of Berri and Burgundy met the Dukes of Orleans and Bourbon and the other Orleanist nobles, and the conditions were considered at a council to which the delegates of the University and the municipality of Paris were admitted. The conduct of the insurgents of Paris was now repudiated by the Duke of Burgundy, and the severest, censure passed upon them, in the conditions of the treaty. The greatest alarm was excited in the market quarter, and this was increased when, immediately afterwards, the Dukes of Bar and Bavaria were liberated. On the 12th of August and on the 4th of September the rest of the prisoners still left alive were also set free. The bells of the churches rang a joyful peal. De Jacqueville, John de Troyes, Caboche, and many of the leaders of the butchers at once fled from Paris.

Most of the knights who had been agents for the insurgents in the mock trials also left Paris, and shortly afterwards the duke himself, finding how strongly the tide had set against him, and fearing that he himself might shortly be seized and thrown into prison, went out from Paris under the pretence of hunting, and fled. During this time Guy had remained with the four men-at-arms. As soon as the power of the butchers diminished and the guards were removed from the gates, and all who pleased could enter or leave, Dame Margaret prepared for flight. Along with the Burgundian knights and nobles who returned after the truce was proclaimed came Count Charles d'Estournel, and several of those who had fled with him. Guy met the former riding through the street on the day after his return to Paris. Not caring to accost him there, he followed him and saw him dismount at his former lodging. As soon as he had entered Guy went up to the door.

"What do you want?" one of the count's valets said.

"I want to see your master, fellow," Guy said sharply, "and I will pull your ears for your insolence if you accost me in that style."

The valet stared at him open-mouthed, then thinking that this peasant might be deputed by the terrible butchers to see his lord, he inquired in a changed tone what message he should give to the count.

"Say to him that the man of the street fray wants to see him."

A minute later the young count himself ran downstairs and warmly embraced Guy, to the astonishment of the valet.

"My dear friend," he exclaimed, "I am indeed delighted to see you! Twice have you saved my life, for assuredly had we not got through the Port St. Denis that day not one of us would ever have left Paris alive, and we are all under the deepest obligation to you. But even after our skirmish at the gate we scarcely realized the danger that we had escaped, for we believed that even had the Parisians been insolent enough to demand our arrest for stopping them when engaged in attacking the houses of peaceable citizens, the duke would treat their demand with the scorn that it deserved. However, when next day we heard that some of the officers of his household had headed them when they forced their way into the Duke of Aquitaine's hotel, and carried off the Duke of Bar and others from before his eyes, and that the duke in all things assisted them, we knew that he would not have hesitated to deliver us up to the villains.

"We held a council as to what we should do. We could not affirm that he had failed, as our lord, in giving us protection, for he had not done so, seeing that we had taken the matter in our own hands. Had he actually consented to hand us over to the Parisians, we should have issued a declaration laying the matter before all the great vassals of Burgundy and denouncing him as a false lord. There are many who would have been very glad to have taken up the matter, for his truckling to these knaves has greatly displeased all save the men who are mere creatures of his. However, as we had no proof that he was willing to surrender us to the fury of the mob of Paris, we could do nothing, and the crafty fox called upon my father the next day and expressed his satisfaction that we had all ridden away, though at the same time saying that there was no reason whatever for our having done so, as he should of course have refused to give any satisfaction to the mob of Paris, and he caused several letters to the same effect to be sent to my friends who escaped with me.

"My father was very short with him, and told him that as it seemed the Parisians were the masters of the city, and that he had no power to restrain them, however monstrous their doings, he thought that we had all acted very wisely in going. He himself left Paris the next day, and several other nobles, relations or friends to some of us, took the earliest opportunity also of leaving for their estates. Now that the power of the butchers has been broken and that their leaders have fled, I came back again, chiefly to find out what had become of you, and whether you and your charges have passed through these evil times unharmed."

"We have all been in hiding, and save for an adventure or two have passed the time quietly. Now that the gates are open we are going to make our escape, for you see everything points to the probability that the Orleanists will very shortly be supreme here, and after the defeat Sir Eustace gave Sir Clugnet de Brabant they might be glad still to retain our lady as hostage, though methinks they would treat her more honourably than the Duke of Burgundy has done."

"Possibly they might, but I would not count upon it, for indeed wherever they have taken a town they have treated those who fell into their hands most barbarously. 'Tis true that they have some excuse for it in the treatment of so many knights and ladies here. Indeed it seems to me that France has been seized with madness, and that Heaven's vengeance will fall upon her for the evil things that are being done. And now, can we aid you in any way? The duke was extremely civil when I saw him on my arrival here yesterday. He said that I and my friends were wrong in not having trusted in him to protect us from the demands of the butchers. I told him frankly that as he had in other matters been so overborne by them, and had been unable to save noble knights and ladies from being murdered by them under the pretence of a trial that all men knew was a mockery, it was just as well that we had taken the matter into our own hands without adding it to his other burdens; and that I and my friends felt that we had no reason to regret the step we had taken, and we knew that our feelings were shared by many other nobles and knights in Burgundy.

"He looked darkly at me, but at the present pass he did not care to say anything that would give offence, not only to me, but to my friends, who with their connections are too powerful to be alienated at a time when he may need every lance. I could not, however, well ask from him a free conduct for your people without naming them, but I might get such a pass from his chancellor, and if your former host, Maître Leroux, be still alive, he might doubtless get you one from the municipality. As an additional protection I myself shall certainly ride with you. It is for that that I have returned to Paris. I shall simply say to the chancellor that I am riding to Arras on my own business, and that though in most places I should be known to Burgundians, yet that it would be as well that I should have a pass lest I be met by any rude body of citizens or others who might not know me, and I shall request him to make it out for me personally and for all persons travelling in my train. So that, as far as Flanders at any rate, there should be no difficulty. I only propose that you should also get a document from the city in case of anything befalling us on the way.

"I see not indeed what can befall us; but it is always well in such times as these, when such strange things occur, to provide for all emergencies. I may tell you that Louis de Lactre and Reginald Poupart have arrived with me in Paris bent on the same errand, and anxious like myself to testify their gratitude to you; so that we shall be a strong body, and could if necessary ride through France without any pass at all, since one or other of us is sure to find a friend in every town which we may traverse."

"Truly, I am thankful indeed to you and to your friends, Count. I own that it has been a sore trouble to me as to how we should be able, however we might disguise ourselves, to travel through the country in these disturbed times, without papers of any kind, when bodies of armed men are moving to and fro in all directions, and travellers, whoever they may be, are questioned at every place on the road where they stop."

"Do not speak of thanks, Guy; I twice owe you my life, and assuredly 'tis little enough to furnish you in return with an escort to Artois. Now, tell me all that you have been doing since we left."

Guy gave a short account of all that had happened.

"It has been fortunate for us both," the Count Charles said when he had finished, "that this astrologer should have made your acquaintance; it was his warning that enabled you to save us as well as your lady. I have heard several times of him as one who had wondrous powers of reading the stars, but now I see that it is not only the stars that assist him."

"I can assure you that he himself believes thoroughly in the stars, Count; he says that by them he can read the danger that is threatening any person whose horoscope he has cast. I had not heard much of such things in England, but I cannot doubt that he has great skill in them. To my knowledge he has saved several lives thereby."

"He certainly saved ours, Guy, and should he like to join your party and ride with us he will be heartily welcomed."

"I will return at once," Guy said, "and give my lady the good news. I will not ask you to go with me now, for if the count-for he is really a nobleman though an exile-decides to stay here he would not care to attract the attention of his neighbours by the coming of a noble to his house in daylight. Though I cannot without his permission take you there, I will return here this evening at eight o'clock, if you will be at home at that hour."

"I will be here, and De Lactre and Poupart will be here to meet you. I will go now direct to the chancellor and obtain the pass both in their names and mine, then we shall be ready to start whenever your lady is prepared. We have all brought some spare horses, so that you will have no trouble on that score. Your men-at-arms will, of course, ride with ours. We have brought eight horses, knowing the number of your company; if your Italian and his daughter go with us Lady Agnes and Charles can ride behind some of us."

Dame Margaret, Agnes, and Charlie were delighted indeed when they heard from Guy of his meeting with the young Count d'Estournel, and of the latter's offer to escort them to Artois.

"The saints be praised!" his lady said. "I have spoken little about it, Guy, but I have dreaded this journey far more than any of the dangers here. In times so disturbed I have perceived that we should run innumerable risks, and eager as I am to return to my lord I have doubted whether, with Agnes with me, I should be right in adventuring on such a journey. Now there can be no risk in it, saving only that of falling in with any of the bands of robbers who, as they say, infest the country, and even these would scarce venture to attack so strong a party. We shall be ready to start to-morrow, if Count d'Estournel is prepared to go so soon. We will be veiled as we ride out. It is most unlikely that anyone will recognize us, but 'tis as well for his sake that there should be no risk whatever of this being known. The count is out and will not return until six, therefore it will be best that you should go at once and warn the others that we start to-morrow."

The pleasure of Long Tom and his companions at the news was scarcely less than had been that of Dame Margaret, and they started at once to recover their steel caps and armour from the place where they had been hidden, saying that it would take them all night to clean them up and make them fit for service. Then Guy went in to Maître Lepelletiere and saw the silversmith, who was also sincerely glad at the news he gave him.

"I was but yesterday arranging for a house where I could open my shop again until my own was rebuilt," he said, "for there is an end now of all fear of disturbances, at any rate for the present, and I was heartily greeted by many old friends, who thought that I was dead. I will go down with Lepelletiere this afternoon to the offices of the municipality and ask for a pass for madame—what shall I call her?"

"Call her Picard: it matters not what surname she takes."

"Madame Picard, her daughter and son, and her cousin Jean Bouvray of Paris, to journey to St. Omer. It does not seem to me that the pass is likely to be of any use to you; at the same time it is as well to be fortified with it. Now that the tyranny of the market-men is over they will be glad to give us the pass without question."

On the Italian's return that afternoon Dame Margaret herself told him of the offer the Count d'Estournel had made. He sat silent for a minute or two and then said: "I will talk it over with Katarina; but at present it does not seem to me that I can accept it. I am a restless spirit, and there is a fascination in this work; but I will see you presently."

An hour later he came down with Katarina.

"We have agreed to stay, Lady Margaret," he said gravely, "I cannot bring myself to go. It is true that I might continue my work in London, but as a stranger it would be long before I found clients, while here my reputation is established. Two of the knights I enabled to escape have already returned. One called upon me last night and was full of gratitude, declaring, and rightly, that he should have been, like so many of his friends, murdered in prison had I not warned him. I have eight requests already for interviews from friends of these knights, and as, for a time at any rate, their faction is likely to be triumphant here, I shall have my hands full of business. This is a pleasant life. I love the exercise of my art, to watch how the predictions of the stars come true, to fit things together, and to take my share, though an unseen one, in the politics and events of the day. I have even received an intimation that the queen herself is anxious to consult the stars, and it may be that I shall become a great power here. I would fain that my daughter should go under your protection, though I own that I should miss her sorely. However, she refuses to leave me, and against my better judgment my heart has pleaded for her, and I have decided that she shall remain. She will, however, take no further part in my business, but will be solely my companion and solace. I trust that with such protection as I shall now receive there is no chance of even the Church meddling with me, but should I see danger approaching I will send or bring her to you at once."

"I shall be glad to see her whenever she comes, and shall receive her as a daughter. We owe our lives to your shelter and kindness, and we already love her."

"The shelter and the kindness have already been far more than repaid by the inestimable service your esquire rendered us," the Italian said. "I have since blamed myself bitterly that I neglected to consult the stars concerning her. I have since done so, and found that a most terrible danger threatened her on that day; and had I known it, I would have kept her indoors and would on no account have permitted her to go out. However, I shall not be so careless of her safety in future. I see that, at any rate for some time, her future is unclouded. She herself will bitterly regret your absence, and has already been weeping sorely at the thought of your leaving. Save myself she has never had a friend, poor child, and you and your daughter have become very dear to her."

Dame Margaret had no preparations to make, for in their flight from the silversmith's each had carried a bundle of clothes. Guy brought Count d'Estournel round in the evening, and the arrangements were then completed. It was thought better that they should not mount at the house, as this would be certain to attract considerable observation and remark, but that Count Charles should come round at seven in the morning and escort them to his lodging. There the horses would be in readiness, and they would mount and ride off. Guy then went round to the Rue des Fosses and warned the men of the hour at which they were to assemble at the count's. He found them all hard at work burnishing up their armour.

"We shall make but a poor show, Master Guy, do what we will," Tom said; "and I doubt whether this gear will ever recover its brightness, so deeply has the rust eaten into it. Still, we can pass muster on a journey; and the swords have suffered but little, having been safe in their scabbards. I never thought that I should be so pleased to put on a steel cap again, and I only wish I had my bow slung across my shoulder."

"It will be something for you to look forward to, Tom, and I doubt not that you will find among the spare ones at Villeroy one as good as your own, and that with practice you will soon be able to shoot as truly with it."

Tom shook his head doubtfully. "I hope so, but I doubt whether I shall be suited again till I get home, and Master John the bowyer makes one specially suitable for me, and six inches longer than ordinary. Still, I doubt not that, if it be needed, I shall be able to make shift with one of those at Villeroy."

The evening before the departure of Dame Margaret and her children, Maître Leroux and his wife, with a man bearing a large parcel, had called upon Dame Margaret at the house of the astrologer, whose address Guy had given, the provost that day.

"We could not let you leave, Lady Margaret," his wife said, "without coming to wish you God speed. Our troubles, like yours, are over for the present, and I trust that the butchers will never become masters of Paris again, whatever may happen."

"Maître Lepelletiere," said the silversmith, "is going to organize the whole of his craft, the workmen and apprentices, into an armed body, and the master of the smiths will do the same. I shall endeavour to prevail upon all the traders of my own guild and others to raise such a body among their servitors; and while we have no wish whatever to interfere in the political affairs of state, we shall at least see that the market people of Paris shall not become our masters again. Master Aylmer, I have brought hither for you a slight token of my regard and gratitude for the manner in which you saved not only our property but our lives. Within this package are two suits of armour and arms. One is a serviceable one suitable to your present condition of an esquire; the other is a knightly suit, which I hope you will wear in remembrance of us as soon as you obtain that honour, which I cannot but feel assured will not be far distant. Had you been obliged to leave Paris in disguise I should have made an endeavour to send them to you in England by way of Flanders; but as you will issue out in good company, and without examination or question asked, you can wear the one suit and have the other carried for you."

Guy thanked the silversmith most heartily, for, having lost his armour at the burning of the house, he had felt some uneasiness at the thought of the figure that he would cut riding in the train of the three Burgundian knights. But at the same time his own purse had been exhausted in the purchase of the disguises for himself and the men-at-arms, and that of his mistress greatly reduced by the expenses of the keep of the men, and he had determined not to draw upon her resources for the purchase of armour. His thanks were repeated when, on the package being opened, the beauty of the knightly armour was seen. It was indeed a suit of which any knight might be proud. It was less ornate in its inlaying and chasing than some of the suits worn by nobles, but it was of the finest steel and best make, with every part and accessory complete, and of the highest workmanship and finish.

"It is a princely gift, sir," Guy said as he examined it, "and altogether beyond my poor deserts."

"That is not what I think, Master Aylmer. You have shown all through this business a coolness and courage altogether beyond your years, and which would have done honour to an experienced knight. My store of silver-ware that was saved by your exertions, to say nothing of our lives, was worth very many times the value of this armour, and I am sure that your lady will agree with me that this gift of ours has been well and honourably earned."

"I do indeed, Maître Leroux," Dame Margaret said warmly; "and assure you that I am as pleased as Guy himself at the noble gift you have made him. I myself have said but little to him as to the service that he has rendered here, leaving that until we reach our castle in safety, when Sir Eustace, on hearing from me the story of our doings, will better speak in both our names than I can do."

In the morning Dame Margaret and her children set out for the lodging of D'Estournel, escorted by the count and Guy, followed by a porter carrying the latter's second suit of armour and the valises of Dame Margaret. Guy himself had charge of a casket which the Count de Montepone had that morning handed to Dame Margaret.

"These are gems of value," he said, "In the course of my business I more often receive gifts of jewels than of money. The latter, as I receive it, I hand to a firm here having dealings with a banker of Bruges, who holds it at my disposal. The gems I have hitherto kept; but as it is possible that we may, when we leave Paris, have to travel in disguise, I would fain that they were safely bestowed. I pray you, therefore, to take them with you to your castle in England, and to hold them for us until we come."

Dame Margaret willingly took charge of the casket, which was of steel, strongly bound, and some nine inches square.

"Its weight is not so great as you would think by its appearance," the Italian said, "for it is of the finest steel, and the gems have been taken from their settings. It will, therefore, I hope, be no great inconvenience to you."

At parting, Katarina, who was greatly affected, had given Guy a small box.

"Do not open it until you reach Villeroy," she said; "it is a little remembrance of the girl you saved from deadly peril, and who will never forget what she owes to you."

On reaching the count's lodgings they found the other two knights in readiness. Dame Margaret's four men-at-arms were holding the horses.

"I am glad to see you all again," she said as she came up. "This is a far better ending than our fortunes seemed likely to have at one time, and I thank you all for your faithful service."

"I am only sorry, my lady, that we have had no opportunity of doing aught since we were cooped up," Tom replied; "nothing would have pleased us better than to have had the chance again of striking a stout blow in your defence."

"We may as well mount at once, if it is your pleasure, Dame Margaret," Count d'Estournel said, "for the other men-at-arms are waiting for us outside the gates."

The packages were at once fastened on the two pack-horses that were to accompany them; all then mounted. The three knights with Dame Margaret rode first, then Guy rode with Agnes by his side, and the four men-at-arms came next, Charlie riding before Jules Varoy, who was the lightest of the men-at-arms, while two of the count's servants brought up the rear, leading the sumpter horses.

Chapter XVII
A Long Pause

A quarter of a mile beyond the gate the party was joined by eighteen men-at-arms, all fully armed and ready for any encounter; eight of them fell in behind Dame Margaret's retainers, the other ten took post in rear of the sumpter horses. With such a train as this there was little fear of any trouble with bands of marauders, and as the road lay through a country devoted to Burgundy there was small chance of their encountering an Orleanist force. They travelled by almost the same route by which Dame Margaret had been escorted to Paris. At all the towns through which they passed the Burgundian knights and their following were well entertained, none doubting that they were riding on the business of their duke. One or other of the knights generally rode beside Guy, and except that the heat in the middle of the day was somewhat excessive, the journey was altogether a very pleasant one. From Arras they rode direct to Villeroy. As soon as their coming was observed from the keep the draw-bridge was raised, and as they approached Sir Eustace himself appeared on the wall above it to hear any message the new-comers might have brought him. As they came near, the knights reined back their horses, and Dame Margaret and Agnes rode forward, followed by Guy having Charlie in front of him. As he recognized them Sir Eustace gave a shout of joy, and a moment later the drawbridge began to descend, and as it touched the opposite side Sir Eustace ran across to the outwork, threw open the gate, and fondly embraced his wife and children, who had already dismounted.

"Ah, my love!" he exclaimed, "you cannot tell how I have suffered, and how I have blamed myself for permitting you and the children to leave me. I received your first letter, saying that you were comfortably lodged at Paris, but since then no word has reached me. I of course heard of the dreadful doings there, of the ascendency of the butchers, of the massacres in the streets, and the murders of the knights and ladies. A score of times I have resolved to go myself in search of you, but I knew not how to set about it when there, and I should assuredly have been seized by Burgundy and thrown into prison with others hostile to his plans. But who are these with you?"

"They are three Burgundian knights, who from love and courtesy, and in requital of a service done them by your brave esquire here, have safely brought us out of Paris and escorted us on our way. They are Count Charles d'Estournel, Sir John Poupart, and Sir Louis de Lactre."

Holding his hand she advanced to meet them and introduced them to him.

"Gentlemen," Sir Eustace said, "no words of mine can express the gratitude that I feel to you for the service that you have rendered to my wife and children. Henceforth you may command me to the extent of my life."

"The service was requited before it was rendered, Sir Eustace," Count Charles said; "it has been service for service. In the first place your esquire, with that tall archer of yours, saved my life when attacked by a band of cutthroats in Paris. This to some small extent I repaid when, with my two good friends here and some others, we charged a mob that was besieging the house in which your dame lodged. Then Master Aylmer laid a fresh obligation on us by warning us that the butchers demanded our lives for interfering in that business, whereby we were enabled to cut our way out by the Port St. Denis and so save our skins. We could not rest thus, matters being so uneven, and therefore as soon as the king's party arrived in a sufficient force to put down the tyranny of the butchers, we returned to Paris, with the intention we have carried out-of finding Dame Margaret in her hiding-place, if happily she should have escaped all these perils, and of conducting her to you. And now, having delivered her into your hands, we will take our leave."

"I pray you not to do so, Count," the knight said; "it would mar the pleasure of this day to me, were you, who are its authors, thus to leave me. I pray you, therefore, to enter and accept my hospitality, if only for a day or two."

The knights had previously agreed among themselves that they would return that night to Arras; but they could not resist the earnestness of the invitation, and the whole party crossed the drawbridge and entered the castle, amid the tumultuous greeting of the retainers.

"You have been away but a few months," Sir Eustace said to his wife, as they were crossing the bridge, "though it seems an age to me. You are but little changed by what you have passed through, but Agnes seems to have grown more womanly. Charlie has grown somewhat also, but is scarcely looking so strong!"

"It has been from want of air and exercise; but he has picked up a great deal while we have been on the road, and I, too, feel a different woman. Agnes has shared my anxiety, and has been a great companion for me."

"You have brought all the men back, as well as Guy?"

"You should rather say that Guy has brought us all back, Eustace, for 'tis assuredly wholly due to him that we have escaped the dangers that threatened us."

The knights and men-at-arms dismounted in the courtyard, and Sir Eustace and Dame Margaret devoted themselves at once to making them welcome with all honour. The maids hurried to prepare the guest-chambers, the servitors to get ready a banquet. Guy and his men-at-arms saw to the comfort of the knights' retainers and their horses, and the castle rang with sounds of merriment and laughter to which it had been a stranger for months. After the cup of welcome had been handed round Sir Eustace showed the knights over the castle.

"We heard the details of the siege, Sir Eustace, from your esquire, and it is of interest to us to inspect the defences that Sir Clugnet de Brabant failed to capture, for, foe though he is to Burgundy, it must be owned that he is a very valiant knight, and has captured many towns and strong places. Yes, it is assuredly a strong castle, and with a sufficient garrison might well have defeated all attempts to storm it by foes who did not possess means of battering the walls, but the force you had was quite insufficient when the enemy were strong enough to attack at many points at the same time, and I am surprised that you should have made good your defence against so large a force as that which assailed you.

"But it was doubtless in no slight degree due to your English archers. We saw in Paris what even one of these men could do."

"I am all anxiety to know what took place there," Sir Eustace said, "and I shall pray you after supper to give me an account of what occurred."

"We will tell you as far as we know of the matter, Sir Eustace; but in truth we took but little share in it, there was just one charge on our part and the mob were in flight. Any I can tell you that we did it with thorough good-will, for in truth we were all heartily sick of the arrogance of these butchers, who lorded over all Paris; even our Lord of Burgundy was constrained to put up with their insolence, since their aid was essential to him. But to us, who take no very great heed of politics and leave these matters to the great lords, the thing was well-nigh intolerable; and I can tell you that it was with hearty good-will we seized the opportunity of giving the knaves a lesson."

As soon as the visitors had arrived, mounted men had ridden off to the tenants, and speedily returned with a store of ducks and geese, poultry, wild-fowl, brawn, and fish; the banquet therefore was both abundant and varied. While the guests supped at the upper table, the men-at-arms were no less amply provided for at the lower end of the hall, where all the retainers at the castle feasted royally in honour of the return of their lady and her children. The bowmen were delighted at the return of Long Tom, whom few had expected ever to see again, while the return of Robert Picard and his companions was no less heartily welcomed by their comrades. After the meal was concluded Dame Margaret went round the tables with her husband, saying a few words here and there to the men, who received her with loud shouts as she passed along.

Then the party from the upper table retired to the private apartment of Sir Eustace, leaving the men to sing and carouse unchecked by their presence. When they were comfortably seated and flagons of wine had been placed on the board, the knight requested Count Charles to give him an account of his adventure with the cut-throats and the part he had subsequently played in the events of which he had spoken. D'Estournel gave a lively recital, telling not only of the fray with the White Hoods, but of what they saw when, after the defeat of the mob, they entered the house. "Had the passage and stairs been the breach of a city attacked by assault it could not have been more thickly strewn with dead bodies," the count said; "and indeed for my part I would rather have struggled up a breach, however strongly defended, than have tried to carry the barricade at the top of the stairs, held as it was. I believe that, even had we not arrived, Master Aylmer could have held his ground until morning, except against fire."

"I wonder they did not fire the house," Sir Eustace remarked.

"Doubtless the leaders would have done so as soon as they saw the task they had before them; but you see plunder was with the majority the main object of the attack, while that of the leaders was assuredly to get rid of the provost of the silversmiths, who had powerfully withstood them. The cry that was raised of 'Down with the English spies!' was but a pretext. However, as all the plate-cases with the silverware were in the barricade, there would have been no plunder to gather had they set fire to the house, and it was for this reason that they continued the attack so long; but doubtless in the end, when they were convinced that they could not carry the barricade, they would have resorted to fire."

Then he went on to recount how Guy had warned himself and his friends of the danger that threatened, and how difficult it had been to persuade them that only by flight could their safety be secured; and how at last he and the two knights with him had returned to Paris to escort Dame Margaret.

"Truly, Count, your narrative is a stirring one," Sir Eustace said; "but I know not as yet how Guy managed to gain the information that the house was going to be attacked and so sent to you for aid, or how he afterwards learned that your names were included with those of the Duke of Bar and others whom the butchers compelled the Duke of Aquitaine to hand over to them."

"Dame Margaret or your esquire himself can best tell you that," the count said. "It is a strange story indeed."

"And a long one," Dame Margaret added. "Were I to tell it fully it would last till midnight, but I will tell you how matters befell, and to-morrow will inform you of the details more at length."

She then related briefly the incidents that had occurred from the day of her interview with the Duke of Burgundy to that of her escape, telling of the various disguises that had been used, the manner in which Guy had overheard the councils of the butchers before they surrounded the hotel of the Duke of Aquitaine and dragged away a large number of knights and ladies to prison, and how the four men-at-arms had re-entered Paris after their escape, and remained there in readiness to aid her if required.

Guy himself was not present at the narration, as he had, after staying for a short time in the room, gone down into the banqueting-hall to see that the men's wants were well attended to, and to talk with the English men-at-arms and archers.

"It seems to me," Sir Eustace said when his wife had finished the story, "that my young esquire has comported himself with singular prudence as well as bravery."

"He has been everything to me," Dame Margaret said warmly; "he has been my adviser and my friend. I have learned to confide in him implicitly. It was he who secured for me in the first place the friendship of Count Charles, and then that of his friends. He was instrumental in securing for us the assistance of the Italian who warned and afterwards sheltered us-one of the adventures that I have not yet told, because I did not think that I could do so without saying more than that person would like known; but Guy rendered him a service that in his opinion far more than repaid him for his kindness to us. The messenger he employed was a near relation of his."

And she then related how Guy had rescued this relation from the hands of the butchers, how he had himself been chased, and had killed one and wounded another of his assailants; and how at last he escaped from falling into their hands by leaping from the bridge into the Seine.

"You will understand," she said, "that not only our host but we all should have been sacrificed had not the messenger been rescued. He would have been compelled by threats, and if these failed by tortures, to reveal who his employer was and where he lived, and in that case a search would have been made, we should have been discovered, and our lives as well as that of our host would have paid the penalty."

"It is impossible to speak too highly of the young esquire," Sir John Poupart said warmly. "For a short time we all saw a good deal of him at the fencing-school, to which D'Estournel introduced him. He made great progress, and wonderfully improved his swordsmanship even during the short time he was there, and the best of us found a match in him. He was quiet and modest, and even apart from the service he had rendered to D'Estournel, we all came to like him greatly. He is a fine character, and I trust that ere long he may have an opportunity of winning his spurs, for the courage he has shown in the defence of his charges would assuredly have gained them for him had it been displayed in battle."

The knights were persuaded to stay a few days at the castle, and then rode away with their retainers with mutual expressions of hope that they would meet again in quieter times. Guy had opened the little packet that Katarina had given him at starting. It contained a ring with a diamond of great beauty and value, with the words "With grateful regards."

He showed it to Sir Eustace, who said:

"It is worth a knight's ransom, lad, and more, I should say. Take it not with you to the wars, but leave it at home under safe guardianship, for should it ever be your bad luck to be made a prisoner, I will warrant it would sell for a sufficient sum to pay your ransom. That is a noble suit of armour that the silversmith gave you. Altogether, Guy, you have no reason to regret that you accompanied your lady to Paris. You have gained a familiarity with danger which will assuredly stand you in good stead some day, you have learned some tricks of fence, you have gained the friendship of half a score of nobles and knights; you have earned the lasting gratitude of my dame and myself, you have come back with a suit of armour such as a noble might wear in a tournament, and a ring worth I know not how much money. It is a fair opening of your life, Guy, and your good father will rejoice when I tell him how well you have borne yourself. It may be that it will not be long before you may have opportunities of showing your mettle in a wider field. The English have already made several descents on the coast, and have carried off much spoil and many prisoners, and it may not be long before we hear that Henry is gathering a powerful army and is crossing the seas to maintain his rights, and recover the lands that have during past years been wrested from the crown.

"I propose shortly to return to England. My dame has borne up bravely under her troubles, but both she and Agnes need rest and quiet. It is time, too, that Charlie applied himself to his studies for a time and learnt to read and write well, for methinks that every knight should at least know this much. I shall take John Harpen back with me. Such of the men-at-arms and archers as may wish to return home must wait here until I send you others to take their places, for I propose to leave you here during my absence, as my castellan. It is a post of honour, Guy, but I feel that the castle will be in good hands; and there is, moreover, an advantage in thus leaving you, as, should any message be sent by Burgundian or Orleanist, you will be able to reply that, having been placed here by me to hold the castle in my absence, you can surrender it to no one, and can admit no one to garrison it, until you have sent to me and received my orders on the subject. Thus considerable delay may be obtained.

"Should I receive such a message from you, I shall pass across at once to Calais with such force as I can gather. I trust that no such summons will arrive, for it is clear that the truce now made between the two French factions will be a very short one, and that ere long the trouble will recommence, and, as I think, this time Burgundy will be worsted. The Orleanists are now masters of Paris and of the king's person, while assuredly they have the support of the Duke of Aquitaine, who must long to revenge the indignities that were put upon him by Burgundy and the mob of Paris. They should therefore be much the stronger party, and can, moreover, issue what proclamations they choose in the king's name, as Burgundy has hitherto been doing in his own interest. The duke will therefore be too busy to think of meddling with us. Upon the other hand, if the Orleanists gain the mastery they are the less likely to interfere with us, as I hear that negotiations have just been set on foot again for the marriage of King Henry with Katherine of France. The English raids will therefore be stopped, and the French will be loath to risk the breaking off of the negotiations which might be caused by an assault without reason upon the castle of one who is an English as well as a French vassal, and who might, therefore, obtain aid from the garrison of Calais, by which both nations might be again embroiled."

"If you think well, my lord, to leave me here in command I will assuredly do the best in my power to prove myself worthy of your confidence; but it is a heavy trust for one so young."

"I have thought that over, Guy, but I have no fear that you will fail in any way. Were the garrison wholly a French one I might hesitate, but half the defenders of the castle are Englishmen; and in Tom, the captain of the archers, you have one of whose support at all times you will be confident, while the French garrison will have learned from the three men who went with you that they would as readily follow you as they would a knight of experience. Moreover, good fighters as the English are, they are far more independent and inclined to insubordination than the French, who have never been brought up in the same freedom of thought. Therefore, although I have no doubt that they will respect your authority, I doubt whether, were I to put a Frenchman in command, they would prove so docile, while with the French there will be no difficulty. I might, of course, appoint John Harpen, who is ten years your senior, to the command; but John, though a good esquire, is bluff and rough in his ways, and as obstinate as a mule, and were I to leave him in command he would, I am sure, soon set the garrison by the ears. As an esquire he is wholly trustworthy, but he is altogether unfitted for command, therefore I feel that the choice I have made of you is altogether for the best, and I shall go away confident that the castle is in good hands, and that if attacked it will be as staunchly defended as if I myself were here to direct the operations."

Two days later Sir Eustace with his family started, under the guard of ten English and ten French men-at-arms, for Calais. Before starting he formally appointed Guy as castellan in his absence, and charged the garrison to obey his orders in all things, as if they had been given by himself. He also called in the principal tenants and delivered a similar charge to them. The English men-at-arms were well pleased to be commanded by one whom they had known from childhood, and whose father they had been accustomed to regard as their master during the absences of Sir Eustace and Dame Margaret. The archers had not, like the men-at-arms, been drawn from the Summerley estate, but the devotion of their leader to Guy, and the tales he had told them of what had taken place in Paris rendered them equally satisfied at his choice as their leader. As for the French men-at-arms, bred up in absolute obedience to the will of their lord, they accepted his orders in this as they would have done on any other point. Sir Eustace left Guy instructions that he might make any further addition to the defences that he thought fit, pointing out to him several that he had himself intended to carry out.

"I should have set about these at once," he had said, "but it is only now that the vassals have completed the work of rebuilding their houses, and I would not call upon them for any service until that was completed. I have told them now that such works must be taken in hand, and that, as they saw upon the occasion of the last siege, their safety depends upon the power of the castle to defend itself, I shall expect their services to be readily and loyally rendered, especially as they have been remitted for over six months. It would be well also to employ the garrison on the works-in the first place, because they have long been idle, and idleness is bad for them; and in the second place because the vassals will all work more readily seeing that the garrison are also employed. While so engaged an extra measure of wine can be served to each man, and a small addition of pay. Here are the plans that I have roughly prepared. Beyond the moat I would erect at the centre of each of the three sides a strong work, similar to that across the drawbridge, and the latter I would also have strengthened.

"These works, you see, are open on the side of the moat, so that if carried they would offer the assailants no shelter from arrows from the walls, while being triangular in shape they would be flanked by our fire. Each of these three forts should have a light drawbridge running across the moat to the foot of the wall, thence a ladder should lead to an entrance to be pierced through the wall, some fifteen feet above the level of the moat; by this means the garrison could, if assailed by an overwhelming force, withdraw into the castle. These outposts would render it-so long as they were held-impossible for storming-parties to cross the moat and place ladders, as they did on the last occasion. The first task will, of course, be to quarry stones. As soon as sufficient are prepared for one of these outworks you should proceed to erect it, as it would render one side at least unassailable and diminish the circuit to be defended. As soon as one is finished, with its drawbridge, ladder, and entrance, proceed with the next. I would build the one at the rear first. As you see from this plan, the two walls are to be twenty feet high and each ten yards long, so that they could be defended by some twenty men. After they are built I would further strengthen them by leading ditches from the moat, six feet deep and ten feet wide, round them. The earth from these ditches should be thrown inside the walls, so as to strengthen these and form a platform for the defenders to stand on. If the earth is insufficient for that purpose the moat can be widened somewhat."

"I will see that your wishes are carried out, Sir Eustace; assuredly these little outworks will add greatly to the strength of the castle. Are the bridges to be made to draw up?"

"No; that will hardly be necessary. Let them consist of two beams with planks laid crosswise. They need not be more than four feet wide, and the planks can therefore be easily pulled up as the garrison falls back. I have told the tenants that during the winter, when there is but little for their men to do, they can keep them employed on this work, and that I will pay regular wages to them and for the carts used in bringing in the stones."

Guy was very glad that there was something specific to be done that would give him occupation and keep the men employed. Sir Eustace had informed the garrison of the work that would be required of them, and of the ration of wine and extra pay that would be given, and all were well satisfied with the prospect. For the English especially, having no friends outside, found the time hang very heavy on their hands, and their experience during the last siege had taught them that the additional fortifications, of the nature of which they were ignorant, however, would add to their safety.

As soon, therefore, as Sir Eustace had left, Guy commenced operations. A few men only were kept on guard, and the rest went out daily to prepare the stones under the direction of a master mason, who had been brought from Arras by Sir Eustace. Some fifty of the tenants were also employed on the work, and as the winter closed in this number was doubled.

The quarry lay at a distance of half a mile from the castle, and as fast as the stones were squared and roughly dressed they were taken in carts to the spot where they were to be used. Guy had the foundations for the walls dug in the first place, to a depth below that of the bottom of the moats, and filled up with cement and rubble. The trenches were then dug at a distance of five feet from the foot of the walls. With so many hands the work proceeded briskly, and before springtime the three works were all completed, with their bridges and ladders, passages pierced through the castle wall, and stone steps built inside by which those who passed through could either descend into the court yard or mount to the battlements. At the end of September fifteen archers and men-at-arms arrived from England to take the place of those who had desired to return home, and who on their coming marched away to Calais.

From time to time reports were received of the events happening in Paris. Paris had been strongly occupied by the Orleanists, and a proclamation had at once been issued in the name of the king condemning all that had been done in the city, and denouncing by name all the ringleaders of the late tumults, and such of these as were found in Paris were arrested. Another proclamation was then issued enjoining all parties to keep the peace, to refrain from gathering in armed bodies, and to abstain from the use of expressions against each other that might lead to a breach of the peace.

On the 13th of November, the year being 1413, fresh and more stringent orders were issued by the king against any assemblies of men-in-arms, and at the end of this month the Duke of Burgundy sent to the king a letter of complaint and accusation against his enemies. Those surrounding Charles persuaded him to send no answer whatever to what they considered his insolent letter. Some of the Burgundian knights had still remained in Paris, and on the advice of the Dukes of Berri and Orleans and other princes, the queen caused four knights of the suite of the Duke of Aquitaine to be carried away from the Louvre. This so much enraged the duke that he at first intended to sally out and call upon the populace of Paris to aid him to rescue the prisoners. The princes of the blood, however, restrained him from doing this; but although he pretended to be appeased he sent secret letters to the Duke of Burgundy begging him to come to his assistance.

This served as an excuse for Burgundy to gather all his adherents and to march towards Paris, and as he collected the force he sent letters to all the principal towns saying that at the invitation of his son-in-law, the Duke of Aquitaine, and in consequence of the breach of the peace committed by his enemies, he was forced to take up arms to rescue his beloved daughter and the duke from the hands of those who constrained them. Upon the other hand, letters were written in the king's name to the various towns on the line by which Burgundy would advance from Artois, begging them not to open their gates to him.

The Burgundian army advanced and occupied St. Denis, thence the duke sent detachments to the various gates of Paris in hopes that the populace would rise in his favour. However, the citizens remained quiet, and the duke, being unprovided with the engines and machines necessary for a siege, fell back again, placing strong garrisons in Compiègne and Soissons. Then the Orleanists took the offensive, besieged and captured town after town, and revenged the murder of their friends in Paris by wholesale massacres and atrocities of the worst description. The Burgundians in vain attempted to raise an army of sufficient strength to meet that of the king, who himself accompanied the Orleanist forces in the field. The fact that he was present with them had a powerful influence in preventing many lords who would otherwise have done so from joining Burgundy, for although all knew that the king was but a puppet who could be swayed by those who happened to be round him, even the shadow of the royal authority had great weight, and both parties carried on their operations in the king's name, protesting that any decrees hostile to themselves were not the true expression of his opinion, but the work of ambitious and traitorous persons who surrounded him. After occupying Laon, Peronne, and other places, the king's army entered Artois, captured Bapaume, and advanced against Arras, where Sir John of Luxemburg, who commanded a Burgundian garrison, prepared for the siege by sending away the greater part of the women and children, and destroying all the buildings and suburbs outside the walls.

As soon as it was evident that the Orleanist army was marching against Artois, Guy despatched one of the English soldiers to Summerley to inform his lord that if, as it seemed, the Orleanists intended to subdue all the Burgundian towns and fortresses in the province, it was probable that Villeroy would be besieged. The messenger returned with twenty more archers, and brought a letter from Sir Eustace to Guy saying that Dame Margaret had been ill ever since her return from France, and that she was at present in so dangerous a state that he could not leave her.

"I trust," he said, "that as the negotiations for the marriage of the king with the French princess are still going on, you will not be disturbed. The main body of the French army will likely be engaged on more important enterprises, and if you are attacked it will probably be only by strong plundering detachments; these you need not fear. Should you be besieged strongly, hold out as long as you can. I shall be sure to receive news of it from Calais, and will go at once to the king and pray for his protection, and beg him to write to the King of France declaring that, to his knowledge, I have ever been as loyal a vassal of France as of England. Should you find that the pressure upon you is too great, and that the castle is like to be taken, I authorize you to make surrender on condition that all within the castle are permitted to march away free and unmolested whithersoever they will."

Chapter XVIII
Katarina

As soon as the king's army approached Arras, Guy repeated all the precautions that had before been taken, but as this time there had been long warning, these were carried out more effectually. A considerable number of the cattle and sheep of the tenants were driven to Calais and there sold, the rest, with the horses, were taken into the castle. The crops were hastily got in, for it was near July, and these were thrashed and the grain brought in, with the household furniture and all belongings. A great store of arrows had been long before prepared, and Guy felt confident that he could hold out for a long time. The women and children took up their abode in the castle, and the former were all set to work to make a great number of sacks. A hundred cart-loads of earth were brought in, and this was stored in a corner of the court-yard. The earth was to be employed in filling the sacks, which were to be lowered from the walls so as to form a protection against heavy missiles, should an attempt be made to effect a breach.

A few days after the king's army sat down before Arras, the look-out informed Guy that a horseman, together with a lady and two attendants, were riding towards the castle. Wondering who these visitors could be, Guy crossed the drawbridge to the outwork, where a small party were now stationed. As they rode up, he saw, to his surprise and pleasure, that they were the Count of Montepone and his daughter. He ran out to meet them.

"I am delighted to see you, Count, and you also Mistress Katarina. I regret that Sir Eustace and Dame Margaret are not here to receive you properly."

"We were aware that she was absent," the count said as he dismounted, while Guy assisted Katarina from her saddle. "I received a letter three months since; it came by way of Flanders from Sir Eustace, expressing his thanks for what slight services I had rendered to his wife. He told me that they had crossed over to England, and that you were his castellan here. But I thought that ere this he might have returned."

"I heard from him but a few days ago," Guy said. "He is detained in England by the illness of Dame Margaret, or he would have hastened hither on hearing that the French army was moving north. I need scarcely ask how you are, Mistress Katarina, for you have changed much, and if I may say it without offence, for the better."

The girl flushed a little and laughed, and her father said: "It is nigh three months since we left Paris; the country air has done her good. Since we left she has till now been in disguise again, and has ridden as my page, for I could not leave her behind, nor could I in an army, with so many wild and reckless spirits, take her in the dress of a girl."

By this time they had crossed the drawbridge, the servants leading their horses after them.

"My stay must be a short one," the count said as they entered the banqueting-hall, and Guy gave orders for a repast to be served.

"I hoped that you were come to stay for a time, Count; I would do all in my power to make your visit a pleasant one."

The Italian shook his head. "No, I must ride back tonight. I have come here for a double purpose. In the first place I must send Katarina to England; she is almost a woman now, and can no longer wander about with me in times like these. In the second place, I have come to tell you that I think you need have no fear of an attack upon the castle. That news you gave me, which enabled me to save those three Orleanist nobles, has, added to what I had before done in that way, helped me vastly. One of them is a great favourite with Aquitaine, and the latter took me under his special protection; and he and many other great lords, and I may tell you even the queen herself, consult me frequently. Shortly after you left I moved to a larger house, and as there was no longer any need for me to assume the character of a vendor of medicines I abandoned that altogether, and took handsome apartments, with my negro from the booth to open the door, and two other lackeys.

"My knowledge of the stars has enabled me with some success to predict the events that have taken place, and Aquitaine and the queen have both implicit confidence in me and undertake nothing without my advice. The Duke of Orleans, too, has frequently consulted me. I have used my influence to protect this castle. I have told them that success will attend all their efforts, which it was easy enough to foresee, as Burgundy has no army in the field that can oppose them. But I said that I had described a certain point of danger. It was some time before I revealed what this was, and then said that it appeared to me that the evil in some way started from the west of Arras. I would go no further than this for many days, and then said that it arose from a castle held by one who was not altogether French, and that were an attack made upon it evil would arise. I saw that it would lead to a disturbance, I said, in the negotiations for the marriage, and perhaps the arrival of an English army. More than this I said the stars did not tell me.

"Aquitaine made inquiries and soon found that my description applied to Villeroy, and he and the queen have issued strict orders that no plundering party is to come in this direction, and that on no account is the castle to be interfered with, and I shall take care that their intentions in this matter are not changed. I had the royal orders to accompany the army. This I should have done in any case, but of course I professed a certain reluctance, by saying that I had many clients in Paris. However, I received various rich presents, and was therefore prevailed upon to travel with them."

"I thank you most heartily, Count, for, as you saw on crossing the court-yard, I have already called all the vassals in and made preparations to stand a siege. As to your daughter, I will, if you wish it, appoint two of the tenants' daughters as her attendants, and send an elderly woman as her companion, with an escort under Robert Picard,—one of those who were with me in Paris,—and four other men-at-arms to accompany her to Summerley and hand her over to the charge of Dame Margaret, who will, I trust, be in better health than when Sir Eustace wrote to me. It will be a great relief to our lord and lady to know that their presence is not urgently required here. The escort can start to-morrow at daybreak if you wish that they should do so."

The count hesitated, and Guy went on: "I will appoint the woman and the two maids at once. Mistress Katarina can occupy Dame Margaret's chamber, and the woman and the maids can sleep in those adjoining it."

"That will do well," the count said cordially. "We have ridden twenty miles already, and she could hardly go on to-day, while if she starts at daybreak they may reach Calais to-morrow."

"I will give Picard a letter to the governor, asking him in my lord's name to give honourable entertainment to the young lady, who is under Dame Margaret's protection, and to forward her upon her journey to join them by the first vessel sailing to Southampton, or if there be none sailing thither, to send her at once by ship to Dover, whence they can travel by land. One of the four men-at-arms shall be an Englishman, and he can act as her spokesman by the way."

"That will do most excellently," the count said, "and I thank you heartily. As soon as I have finished my meal I must ride for the camp again. I started early this morning in order not to be observed; in the first place because I did not wish my daughter to be seen in her female dress, and in the second because I would not that any should notice my coming in this direction, and indeed we rode for the first mile backwards along the road to Bapaume, and I shall return by the same way."

"What will the end of these troubles be, Count?"

"As I read the stars there will be peace shortly, and indeed it is clear to me that the Duke of Burgundy must by this time see that if the war goes on he will lose all Artois and perhaps Flanders, and that therefore he must make peace, and perhaps keep it until the royal army has marched away and dispersed; after that we may be sure that the crafty duke will not long remain quiet. I have a trusty emissary in Burgundy's household, and as soon as the duke comes to the conclusion that he must beg for peace I shall have intelligence of it, and shall give early news to the queen and to Aquitaine, who would hail it with gladness; for, seeing that the latter's wife is Burgundy's daughter, he does not wish to press him hard, and would gladly see peace concluded."

An hour later the count rode off with his two followers, after taking an affectionate leave of his daughter, and telling her that it would not be long before he joined her-if only for a time-in England. Before he went Guy had chosen the woman who, with her two daughters, was to accompany Katarina, and had installed them in the private apartments.

"What shall we do with ourselves for the day?" he asked the girl, who was, he saw, shy and ill at ease, now that her father had left. "If you are not tired we might take a ride. We have some hawks here, and now that the harvest has been gathered we shall doubtless find sport with the game-birds."

"I am not at all tired," she said eagerly, "and should like it much."

Calling upon Long Tom and another to accompany them, horses were brought up, and they started and remained out until supper-time, bringing home with them some seven or eight partridges that had been killed by the hawks. Guy suggested that perhaps she would prefer to have the meal served in her own apartments and to retire to bed early. She accepted the offer, and at once went to her room, which she did not leave again that evening. Guy, as he ate alone, wondered to himself at the change that some nine or ten months had made in her.

"I suppose she feels strange and lonely," he said to himself. "She was merry enough when we were out hawking; but directly we got back again she seemed quite unlike herself. I suppose it is because I always used to treat her as if she were a boy, and now that she has grown up into a woman she wants to forget that time."

The town of Arras resisted sturdily. The garrison made frequent sorties, took a good many prisoners, and inflicted heavy loss upon the besiegers before these could gather in sufficient numbers to drive them in again, and all assaults were repulsed with loss. The Castle of Belle Moote, near Arras, also repulsed all the efforts of the king's army to take it. Foraging parties of Orleanists committed terrible devastations in the country round, but gained no advantage in their attacks on any fortified place.

On the 29th of August the Duke of Brabant arrived with some deputies from Flanders to negotiate a peace between Burgundy and the king. They were well received, and an armistice was at once arranged. The French troops were suffering severely from disease, and the failure of all their attempts to capture Arras made them ready to agree willingly upon a peace. This was accordingly concluded on the 4th of September, and the next day the royal army marched away.

Three weeks after Katarina had gone to England, Sir Eustace himself, to Guy's great joy, arrived at the castle, bringing with him his esquire and eight men-at-arms, as well as the three serving-women and their escort. As soon as his pennon was seen Guy leapt on a horse that was standing saddled in the court-yard, and rode to meet them. As he came up he checked his horse in surprise, for his father was riding by the side of Sir Eustace. Recovering himself, however, he doffed his cap to his lord.

"Welcome back, my lord!" he said. "I trust that our dear lady is better."

"Much better, Guy. You see I have brought your father over with me."

Guy bent low to his father.

"I am right glad to see you," the latter said, "and to hear such good accounts of you. Dame Margaret and Mistress Agnes were never tired of singing your praises, and in truth I was not weary of hearing them."

"Are you going to make a long stay, father?"

"I shall stay for some little time, Guy. Our lady is going to be her own castellan for the present. And in truth things are so quiet in England that Summerley could well go on without a garrison, so Sir Eustace suggested that I should accompany him hither, where, however, just at present things have also a peaceful aspect. The young countess arrived safely, Guy, and was heartily welcomed, the more so since, as your letter told me, it is to her father that we owe it that we did not have the king's army battering our walls, or, even if they did not try that, devastating the fields and ruining the farmers."

By this time they were at the gate. Long Tom had the garrison drawn up in the court-yard, and they hailed the return of their lord with hearty cheers, while the retainers of Summerley were no less pleased at seeing Sir John Aylmer. "And now, Guy," said Sir Eustace, "I will tell you why I have come hither. It is partly to see after the estate, to hear the complaints of my vassals and to do what I can for them, and in the next place I wanted to see these fortifications that you have raised, and, thirdly, I shall shortly ride to Paris in the train of the Earl of Dorset, the Lord Grey, Admiral of England, some bishops, and many other knights and nobles, amounting in the whole to 600 horse. They go to treat for the marriage of the princess of France with the English king. I had an audience with the king at Winchester as soon as we heard that the royal army was marching towards Artois, and he gave assurance that he would instruct the governor of Calais to furnish what assistance he could should the castle be attacked, and that he himself would at once on hearing of it send a remonstrance to the King of France, urging that I, as a vassal of his as well as of France, had avoided taking any part in the troubles, and had ever borne myself as a loyal vassal of his Majesty.

"He was at Winchester when the young countess arrived, and I rode over to him to tell him that I had news that it was not probable that Villeroy would be attacked. It was then that his Majesty informed me that the Earl of Dorset with a large body of nobles would ere long cross the Channel for the purpose that I have named, and begged me to ride with them. The king, being disengaged at the time, talked with me long, and questioned me as to the former defence of the castle, and how Dame Margaret had fared when, as he had heard, she was obliged to go as a hostage to Paris. I told him all that had befallen her, at which he seemed greatly interested, and bade me present you to him at the first opportunity.

"'He must be a lad after my own heart,' he said, 'and he shall have an opportunity of winning his spurs as soon as may be, which perchance is not so far away as some folks think.'"

Guy thanked Sir Eustace for having so spoken of him to the English king, and asked: "What do you think he meant by those last words, my lord?"

"That I cannot say, Guy; but it may well be that he thinks that this marriage which has been so long talked of may not take place, and that the negotiations have been continued solely for the purpose of keeping him quiet while France was busied with her own troubles. Moreover, I know that the king has been already enlisting men, that he is impatient at having been put off so often with soft words, and that embassy is intended to bring matters to a head; therefore if, as I gathered from some of my friends at his court, he is eager for fighting, it may be that his ambassadors will demand conditions which he is sure beforehand the King of France will not grant. At any rate I shall ride with Dorset to Paris; whatever the sentiments of the Burgundians or Orleanists may be towards me will matter nothing, riding as I shall do in the train of the earl. I am going to take you with me, as well as John Harpen, for I must do as well as others, and have had to lay out a goodly sum in garments fit for the occasion, for the king is bent upon his embassy making a brave show. Your father will be castellan here in my absence. I shall also take with me Long Tom and four of his archers, and five French men-at-arms. I have brought some Lincoln-green cloth to make fresh suits for the archers, and also material for those for the men-at-arms."

Both Sir Eustace and Sir John Aylmer expressed great satisfaction at the manner in which the new outworks had been erected.

"Assuredly it is a strong castle now, Sir Eustace," Sir John said, "and would stand a long siege even by a great army."

"What is all that earth for in the corner, Guy?" Sir Eustace asked as they re-entered the castle after having made a survey of the new works. "I had that brought in, my lord, to fill sacks, of which I had three hundred made, so that if guns and battering machines were brought against us, we might cover the wall at the place they aimed at with sacks hanging closely together, and so break the force of the stones or the cannon balls."

"Excellently well arranged, Guy. You thought, Sir John, that I was somewhat rash to leave the defence solely to the charge of this son of yours, but you see the lad was ready at all points, and I will warrant me that the castle would have held out under him as long a time as if you and I both had been in command of it."

It was not until January, the year being 1414, that the Earl of Dorset and a great company arrived at Calais. As they passed not far from the castle they were joined by Sir Eustace and his retinue. The king's wishes had been carried out, and the knights and nobles were so grandly attired and their retinues so handsomely appointed that when they rode into Paris the people were astonished at the splendour of the spectacle. A few days after they reached the capital the king gave a great festival in honour of the visitors, and there was a grand tournament at which the king and all the princes of the blood tilted. The English ambassadors were splendidly entertained, but their proposals were considered inadmissible by the French court, for Henry demanded with Katherine the duchy of Normandy, the county of Pontieu, and the duchy of Aquitaine.

No direct refusal was given, but the king said that he would shortly send over an embassy to discuss the conditions. Many handsome presents were made to all the knights and noblemen, and the embassy returned to England. Sir Eustace left them near Villeroy with his party, and stayed two days at the castle. Sir John Aylmer said that he would prefer that Guy should return home with Sir Eustace and that he himself should remain as castellan, for he thought that there was little doubt that war would soon be declared; he said that he himself was too old to take the field on active service, and preferred greatly that Guy should ride with Sir Eustace. Long Tom made a petition to his lord that he too should go to England for a time.

"If there was any immediate chance of fighting here, my lord," he said, "I would most willingly remain, but seeing that at present all is quiet, I would fain return, were it but for a month; for I have a maid waiting for me, and have, methinks, kept her long enough, and would gladly go home and fetch her over here."

The request was at once granted, and Sir Eustace, his two esquires, and the archer rode to Calais, and crossed with the company of the Earl of Dorset.

For some months Guy remained quietly at Summerley. Agnes, though nearly sixteen, was still but a young girl, while Katarina had grown still more womanly during the last six months. The former always treated him as a brother, but the latter was changeable and capricious. Occasionally she would laugh and chat when the three were alone, as she had done of old in Paris, but more often she would tease and laugh at him, while sometimes she would be shy and silent.

"I cannot make out the young countess, my lady," he said to Dame Margaret when Katarina had been teasing him even more than usual. "She was never like this in Paris, and I know not that I have done aught to offend her that she should so often pick up my words, and berate me for a meaning they never had."

"You see, things have changed since then," Dame Margaret said with a smile; "'tis two years since you were in Paris, and Katarina, although but little older than Agnes, is already a young woman. You were then still under seventeen, now you are nineteen, and in growth and stature well-nigh a man. You can hardly expect her to be the same with you as when she was running about Paris in boy's attire, for then you regarded her rather as a comrade than as a girl. I think, perhaps, it is that she a little resents the fact that you knew her in that guise, and therefore feels all the less at her ease with you. Do not trouble about it, the thing will right itself in time; and besides, you will shortly be going off to the war."

In fact, preparations were being already made for it. A French embassy of nobles and knights, with three hundred and fifty horsemen, had come over, and, after passing through London, had gone to Winchester, and there met the king and his great lords. The Archbishop of Bourges, who was their spokesman, at once set forth that the king could not hand over so large a portion of his kingdom, but that he would give with his daughter large estates in France, together with a great sum in ready money. This offer was refused, and preparations for war went on in both countries. France was, indeed, but in poor condition to defend itself, for the Duke of Aquitaine had seriously angered both parties. He had made a pretext to get the great lords to ride out from Paris, he being with them; but he had secretly returned, and had ordered the gates to be closed, had called the citizens to arms, and had resumed the supreme authority of the realm.

Having done this, he sent his wife, Burgundy's daughter, to a castle at a distance, and surrounding himself with young nobles as reckless and dissipated as himself, led a life of disorder, squandering money on his pleasures, and heavily taxing the city for his wants. The Duke of

Burgundy, indignant at the treatment of his daughter, sent an ambassador to demand that she should be taken back, and that all the persons, five hundred in number, who had been exempted from the terms of the treaty, should be allowed to return to Paris. Both requests were refused, and the consequence was that the Duke of Burgundy, with his partisans, returned to his own country in deep anger; he would take no part in the war against the English, although he permitted his vassals to do so.

In July the English levies gathered at Southampton. The king was to have embarked immediately, and a great fleet had been collected for the purpose; but, as he was on the point of sailing, Henry obtained news of a plot against his life on the part of Sir Thomas Grey, Lord Scroop, and Richard, Earl of Cambridge, the king's cousin. As Scroop was in constant attendance upon the king and slept in his room, the conspirators had little doubt that their purpose could be carried out, their intention being to proclaim the Earl of March king, and to summon assistance from Scotland. The three conspirators were tried by a jury and were all found guilty. Grey was beheaded, but his companions claimed to be tried again by their peers. No time was lost in carrying out the trial; all the lords assembled at Southampton were called together, and, after hearing the evidence, at once found the two nobles guilty, and they were immediately beheaded.

Orders were then given for the embarkation. Sir Eustace had brought with him thirty archers and as many men-at-arms, and, as they were waiting on the strand for the boats that were to take them out to the ships to which they had been appointed, the king, who was personally superintending the operations, rode past. Sir Eustace saluted him.

"Is this your following, Sir Eustace?" the king asked.

"It is, my lord king, and would that it were larger. Had we landed at Calais I should have been joined by another fifty stout Englishmen from Villeroy, and should we in our marches pass near it I will draw them to me. Your majesty asked me to present to you my esquire, Guy Aylmer, who, as I had the honour of telling you, showed himself a brave and trusty gentleman, when, during the troubles, he was in Paris with my wife. Step forward, Guy!"

The latter did so, saluted the king, and stood erect in military attitude.

"You have begun well," the king said graciously; "and I hereby request your lord that in the day of battle he will permit you to fight near me, and if you bear yourself as well when fighting for your king as you did when looking after your lady mistress, you shall have your share of honours as well as of blows."

The king then rode on, and Sir Eustace and Guy took their places in a boat where the men had already embarked.

"This is something like, Master Guy," said Long Tom, who was in command of the archers. "It was well indeed that I asked to come home to England when I did, else had I been now mewed up at Villeroy while my lord was fighting the French in the open field. Crecy was the last time an English king commanded an army in battle against France; think you that we shall do as well this time?"

"I trust so, Tom; methinks we ought assuredly not to do worse. It is true that the French have been having more fighting of late than we have, but the nobles are less united now than they were then, and are likely to be just as headstrong and incautious as they were at Crecy. I doubt not that we shall be greatly outnumbered, but numbers go for little unless they are well handled. The Constable d'Albrett is a good soldier, but the nobles, who are his equals in rank, will heed his orders but little when their blood is up and they see us facing them. We may be sure, at any rate, that we shall be well led, for the king has had much experience against the Scotch and Welsh, and has shown himself a good leader as well as a brave fighter. I hope, Tom, that you have by this time come to be well accustomed to your new bow."

"That have I. I have shot fourscore arrows a day with it from the time I reached home, not even omitting my wedding day, and I think that now I make as good shooting with it as I did with my old one. 'Tis a pity we are not going to Calais; if we had been joined by thirty archers there we should have made a brave show, and more than that, they would have done good service, for they are picked men. A few here may be as good, but not many. You see when we last sailed with our lord the times were peaceful, and we were able to gather the best shots for fifty miles round, but now that the king and so many of the nobles are all calling for archers we could not be so particular, and have had to take what we could get; still, I would enlist none who were not fair marksmen."

This conversation took place as they were dropping down Southampton waters. Their destination was known to be Harfleur, which, as it was strongly fortified and garrisoned, was like to offer a sturdy resistance. The fleet was a great one, consisting of from twelve to fourteen hundred sail, which the king had collected from all the ports of England and Ireland, or hired from Holland and Friesland. The army consisted of six thousand five hundred horsemen and twenty-four thousand footmen of all kinds. On the 13th of August the fleet anchored in the mouth of the Seine, three miles from Harfleur. The operation of landing the great army and their horses occupied three days, the French, to the surprise of all, permitting the operation to be carried on without let or hindrance, although the ground was favourable for their attacks, As soon as the landing was effected the army took up its position so as to prevent any supplies from entering the town. They had with them an abundance of machines for battering the walls, and these were speedily planted, and they began their work.

The garrison had been reinforced by four hundred knights and picked men-at-arms, and fought with great determination and valour, making several sorties from the two gates of the town. There were, however, strong bodies of troops always stationed near to guard the engines from such attacks, and the French sorties were not only repulsed, but their knights had much difficulty in winning their way back to the town. The enemy were unable to use their cannon to much effect, for a large supply of gunpowder sent by the French king was, on the day after the English landed, captured on its way into the town. The besiegers lost, however, a good many men from the crossbowmen who manned the walls, although the English archers endeavoured to keep down their shooting by a storm of arrows. The most formidable enemy, however, that the English had to contend with was dysentery, brought on by the damp and unhealthy nature of the ground upon which they were encamped. No less than two thousand men died, and a vastly larger number were so reduced by the malady that they were useless for fighting. The siege, however, was carried on uninterruptedly. The miners who had been brought over drove two galleries under the walls, and the gates were so shattered by stones and cannon-balls that they scarce hung together.

The garrison surrendered after having by the permission of the English king sent a messenger to the King of France, who was at Vernon, to say that unless they were succoured within three days they must surrender, as the town was already at the mercy of the English, and received for answer that no army was as yet gathered that could relieve them.

In addition to the ravages of dysentery the English army had suffered much from want of food. Large bodies of French troops were gathered at Rouen and other places, and when knights and men-at-arms went out to forage, they fell upon them and drove them back. Still a large amount of booty was gathered, together with enough provisions to afford a bare subsistence to the army. A considerable amount of booty was also obtained when Harfleur fell. The greater portion of the inhabitants of the town were forced to leave it, the breaches in the walls were repaired and new gates erected. A portion of the treasure obtained was divided by the king among the troops. The prisoners and the main portion of the booty-which, as Harfleur was the chief port of Normandy, and indeed of all the western part of France, was very great-he sent direct to England, together with the engines of war. The sick and ailing were then embarked on ships, with a considerable fighting force under the Earl of Warwick. They were ordered to touch at Calais, where the fighting-men were to be landed and the sick carried home, and Henry then prepared to march to Calais by land.

Chapter XIX
Agincourt

The English king waited some time for an answer to a challenge he had sent to the Duke of Aquitaine to decide their quarrel by single combat; but Aquitaine cared more for pleasure than for fighting, and sent no answer to the cartel. It was open to Henry to have proceeded by sea to Calais, and it was the advice of his counsellors that he should do so; but the king declared that the French should never say that he was afraid to meet them, and that as the country was his by right he would march wherever he pleased across it; and so, after leaving a thousand archers and five hundred men-at-arms under the command of the Duke of Exeter, he set out on the 6th of October on his adventurous journey.

Accounts differ as to the number that started with him, some French historians put it as high as 17,000, but it is certain that it could not have exceeded nine thousand men, of whom two thousand were men-at-arms and the rest archers. Now, while the siege of Harfleur had been going on, the arrangements for the embarkation of the troops and stores carried out, and the town put in a state of defence, troops had been marching from all points of France at the command of the French king to join him at Rouen, so that here and in Picardy two great armies were already assembled, the latter under the command of the constable.

The English force marched by the sea-shore until it arrived at the river Somme. No great resistance was encountered, but large bodies of the enemy's horse hovered near and cut off all stragglers, and rendered it difficult to obtain food, so that sickness again broke out among the troops. On reaching the Somme Henry followed its left bank up, intending to cross at the ford of La Blanche-Tache, across which Edward the Third had carried his army before fighting at Crecy.

The French, as on the previous occasion, held the ford; but they this time had erected defences on each of the banks, and had strong posts driven into the bed of the river. Still ascending along the river bank the English found every bridge broken and every ford fortified, while a great body of troops marched parallel with them on the right bank of the river. At Pont St. Remy, Ponteau de Mer, and several other points they tried in vain to force a passage. Seven days were spent in these attempts; the troops, suffering terrible hardships, were disheartened at their failure to cross the river, and at finding themselves getting farther and farther from the sea. On the morning of the 19th, however, a ford was discovered which had not been staked. The English vanguard at once made a dash across it, repulsed its defenders on the other bank, and the whole army with its baggage, which was of scanty dimensions, swarmed across the river.

Sir Eustace, with his little force, now reduced to half its number, was, as it happened, in front of the army when the ford was discovered, and, followed by his two esquires and ten mounted men-at-arms, dashed into the river, while the archers, slinging their bows behind them, drew their axes and followed. For a short time there was a desperate conflict, but as reinforcements hurried across, the fight became more even and the French speedily gave way. When the king had crossed he thanked Sir Eustace for his prompt action.

"Had you waited to send back for orders," he said, "the French would have come up in such numbers that the ford would not have been won without heavy loss, whereas by dashing across the moment it was discovered, you took the defenders by surprise and enabled us to get over without the loss of a single man."

The constable, disconcerted at finding that all his plans for keeping the English on the left bank of the river were foiled, fell back to St. Pol in Artois. Henry followed, but without haste. His small force was greatly reduced by sickness, while by this time the whole of the royal army had marched round and joined that of the constable. On the day after the passage had been effected three heralds arrived in the English camp to acquaint the king with the resolution of the constable and of the Dukes of Orleans and Brabant to give his army battle before he reached Calais. Henry replied that fear of them would not induce him to move out of his way or to change the order of his march; he intended to go on straight by the road to Calais, and if the

French attempted to stop him it would be at their peril; he accordingly continued to advance at the same rate as before.

The constable fell back from St. Pol and took up his post between the villages of Ruissanville and Agincourt, where, having received all the reinforcements he expected, he determined to give battle. On the 24th the English crossed the Ternois at Blangi, and soon afterwards came in sight of the enemy's columns. These fell back as he advanced, and towards evening he halted at the village of Maisoncelles, within half a mile of the enemy's position. Fortunately provisions had been obtained during the day's march; these were cooked and served out, and the English lay down to sleep. The king sent for Sir Eustace.

"You know this ground well, I suppose, Sir Eustace," he said, "for your Castle of Villeroy is not many miles distant?"

"'Tis but six miles away," the knight replied. "It is a good ground to fight on, for facing it are fields, and on either flank of these are large woods, so that there will be little space for the enemy to move."

"That is just what I would have," the king said. "Were they but half as strong as they are I should feel less confident that we should defeat them; their numbers will hinder them, and the deep wet ground will hamper their movements. As for ourselves, I would not have a man more with me if I could; the fewer we are the greater the glory if we conquer, while if we are defeated the less the loss to England. Does your young esquire also know the ground, Sir Eustace?"

"Yes, sire; he has, I know, often ridden here when hawking."

"Then let him go with four of my officers, who are about to reconnoitre the ground and see where we had best fight."

Guy was accordingly called up and started with the officers. He first took them up to the wood on the right of the French division, then they moved across its front at a distance of fifty yards only from the French line. The contrast between it and the English camp was great. In the latter all was quiet. The men after a hearty meal had lain down to sleep, heeding little the wet ground and falling rain, exhausted by their long marching, and in good spirits,—desperate though the odds seemed against them,—that they were next day to meet their foes. In the French camp all was noise and confusion. Each body of troops had come on the ground under its own commander, and shouts, orders, and inquiries sounded from all quarters. Many of the Frenchmen never dismounted all the night, thinking it better to remain on horseback than to lie down on wet ground. Great fires were lighted and the soldiers gathered round these, warming themselves and drinking, and calculating the ransoms to be gained by the capture of the king and the great nobles of England. Knights and men-at-arms rode about in search of their divisions, their horses slipping and floundering in the deep clay.

Passing along the line of the French army Guy and the officers proceeded to the wood on the left, and satisfied themselves that neither there nor on the other flank had any large body of men been posted. They then returned and made their report to the king. Guy wrapped himself in his cloak and lay down and slept until the moon rose at three o'clock, when the whole army awoke and prepared for the day's work. The English king ordered the trumpeters and other musicians who had been brought with the army to play merry tunes, and these during the three hours of darkness cheered the spirits of the men and helped them to resist the depressing influence of the cold night air following upon their sleep on the wet ground. The French, on the other hand, had no manner of musical instruments with their army, and all were fatigued and depressed by their long vigil.

The horses had suffered as-much as the men from damp, sleeplessness, and want of forage. There was, however, no want of confidence in the French army-all regarded victory as absolutely certain. As the English had lost by sickness since they left Harfleur fully a thousand men out of the 9,000, and as against these were arrayed at least a hundred thousand-some French historians estimate them at 150,000—comprising most of the chivalry of France, the latter might well regard victory as certain. There were, however, some who were not so confident; among these was the old Duke of Berri, who had fought at Poitiers sixty years before, and remembered how confident the French were on that occasion, and how disastrous was the defeat. His counsel that the English should be allowed to march on unmolested to Calais, had been scouted by the French leaders, but he had so far prevailed that the intention that Charles should place himself at the head of the army was abandoned.

"It would be better," the duke had urged, "to lose the battle than to lose the king and the battle together."

As soon as day broke the English were mustered and formed up, and three masses were celebrated at different points in order that all might hear. When this was done the force was formed up into three central divisions and two wings, but the divisions were placed so close together that they practically formed but one. The whole of the archers were placed in advance of the men-at-arms. Every archer, in addition to his arms, carried a long stake sharpened at both ends, that which was to project above the ground being armed with a sharp tip of iron. When the archers had taken up their positions these stakes were driven obliquely into the ground, each being firmly thrust in with the strength of two or three men. As the archers stood many lines deep, placed in open order and so that each could shoot between the heads of the men in front of him, there were sufficient stakes in front of the line to form a thick and almost impassable *chevaux-de-frise*. The baggage and horses were sent to the rear, near the village of Maisoncelles, under a guard of archers and men-at-arms. When all the arrangements were made, the king rode along the line from rank to rank, saying a few words of encouragement to each group of men. He recounted to them the victories that had been won against odds as great as those they had to encounter, and told them that he had made up his own mind to conquer or die, for that England should never have to pay ransom for him.

The archers he fired especially by reminding them that when the Orleanists had taken Soissons a few months before they had hung up like dogs three hundred English archers belonging to the garrison. He told them that they could expect no mercy, for that, as the French in other sieges had committed horrible atrocities upon their own countrymen and countrywomen, they would assuredly grant no mercy to the English; while the latter on their march had burned no town nor village, and had injured neither man nor woman, so that God would assuredly fight for them against their wicked foes. The king's manner as much as his words aroused the enthusiasm of the soldiers; his expression was calm, confident, and cheerful, he at least evidently felt no doubt of the issue.

The Duke of Berri had most strongly urged on the council that the French should not begin the attack. They had done so at Crecy and Poitiers with disastrous effect, and he urged them to await the assault of the English. The latter, however, had no intention of attacking, for Henry had calculated upon the confusion that would surely arise when the immense French army, crowded up between the two woods, endeavoured to advance. The men were therefore ordered to sit down on the ground, and food and some wine were served, out to them.

The constable was equally determined not to move; the French therefore also sat down, and for some hours the two armies watched each other. The constable had, however, some difficulty in maintaining his resolution. The Duke of Orleans and numbers of the hot-headed young nobles clamoured to be allowed to charge the English. He himself would gladly have waited until joined by large reinforcements under the Duke of Brittany and the Marshal de Loigny, who were both expected to arrive in the course of the day. As an excuse for the delay, rather than from any wish that his overtures should be accepted, he sent heralds to the English camp to offer Henry a free passage if he would restore Harfleur, with all the prisoners that he had made there and on his march, and resign his claims to the throne of France. Henry replied that he maintained the conditions he had laid down by his ambassadors, and that he would accept none others. He had, in fact, no wish to negotiate, for he, too, knew that the French would very shortly be largely reinforced, and that were he to delay his march, even for a day or two, his army would be starved.

Perceiving at last that the constable was determined not to begin the battle, he sent off two detachments from the rear of his army, so that their movements should be concealed from the sight of the French. One of these, composed of archers, was to take post in the wood on the left hand of the French, the other was to move on through the wood, to come down in their rear, and to set on fire some barns and houses there, and so create a panic. He waited until noon, by which time he thought that both detachments would have reached the posts assigned to them, and then gave the orders for the advance. The archers were delighted when their commander, Sir Thomas Erpingham, repeated the order. None of them had put on his armour, and many had thrown off their jerkins so as to have a freer use of their arms either for bow or axe. Each man plucked up his stake, and the whole moved forward in orderly array until within bow-shot of the enemy. Then the archers again stuck their stakes into the ground, and, taking up their position as before, raised a mighty shout as they let fly a volley of arrows into the enemy.

The shout was echoed from the wood on the French left, and the archers there at once plied their bows, and from both flank and front showers of arrows fell among the French. As originally formed up, the latter's van should have been covered by archers and cross-bowmen, but, from the anxiety of the knights and nobles to be first to attack, the footmen had been pushed back to the rear, a position which they were doubtless not sorry to occupy, remembering how at Crecy the cross-bowmen had been trampled down and slain by the French knights, desirous of getting through them to attack the English. Therefore, there stood none between the archers and the French array of knights, and the latter suffered heavily from the rain of arrows. Sir Clugnet de Brabant was the first to take the offensive, and with twelve hundred men-at-arms charged down upon the archers with loud shouts. The horses, however, were stiff and weary from standing so long in order; the deep and slippery ground, and the weight of their heavily-armed riders caused them to stagger and stumble, and the storm of arrows that smote them as soon as they got into motion added to the disorder.

So accurate was the aim of the archers, that most of the arrows struck the knights on their helmets and vizors. Many fell shot through the brain, and so terrible was the rain of arrows that all had to bend down their heads so as to save their faces. Many of the archers, too, shot at the horses; some of these were killed and many wounded, and the latter swerving and turning aside added to the confusion. And when at length Sir Clugnet and the leaders reached the line of stakes in front of the archers, only about a hundred and fifty of the twelve hundred men were behind them.

The horses drew up on reaching the hedge of stakes. Their riders could give them no guidance, for without deigning to move from their order the archers continued to keep up their storm of arrows, which at such close quarters pierced all but the very finest armour, while it was certain death to the knights to raise their heads to get a glance at the situation. The horses, maddened with the pain of the arrows, soon settled the matter. Some turned and rushed off madly, carrying confusion into the ranks of the first division, others galloped off to the right or left, and of the twelve hundred men who charged, three only broke through the line of stakes, and these were instantly killed by the bill-hooks and axes of the archers.

The second line of battle was now in disorder, broken by the fugitive men and horses of Sir Clugnet's party, smitten with the arrows to which they had been exposed as that party melted away, and by those of the English archers in the wood on their flank. The confusion heightened every moment as wounded knights tried to withdraw from the fight, and others from behind struggled to take their places in front. Soon the disorder became terrible. The archers plucked up their stakes and ran forward; the French line recoiled at their approach in order to get into fairer order; and the archers, with loud shouts of victory, slung their bows behind them, dropped the stakes, and with axe and bill-hook rushed at the horsemen. These were too tightly wedged together to use their lances, and as they had retired they had come into newly-ploughed ground, which had been so soaked by the heavy rain that the horses sank in the deep mud to their knees, many almost to their bellies. Into the midst of this helpless crowd of armed men the English archers burst. Embarrassed by their struggling horses, scarcely able to wield their arms in the press, seeing but scantily, and that only in front through the narrow slits of their vizors, the chivalry of France died almost unresistingly.

The Constable of France and many of the highest nobles and most distinguished knights fell, and but few of the first line made their escape: these, passing through the second division, in order to draw up behind, threw this also into some confusion. The Duke de Brabant, who had just arrived on the field, charged down upon the flank of the archers. These met him fearlessly, and he and most of those with him were killed. This fight had, however, given time to the second division to close up their ranks. The archers would have attacked them, but the king caused the signal for them to halt to be sounded, and riding up formed them in order again. The French were unable to take advantage of the moment to try and recover their lost ground, for the horses were knee-deep in the ground, upon which they had all night been trampling, and into which the weight of their own and their riders' armour sunk them deeply.

"Now, my lords," the king said, turning to those around him, "our brave archers have done their share; it is our turn;" and then, as arranged, all dismounted and marched forward against the enemy.

In accordance with his orders, Sir Eustace de Villeroy and Guy were posted close to the king, while John Harpen led the men-at-arms from Summerley. For a time the battle raged fiercely. In the centre fought the king with his nobles and knights; while the archers, who had most of them thrown off their shoes and were able to move lightly over the treacherous ground, threw themselves upon the enemy's flanks, and did dreadful execution there. In the centre, however, the progress of the English was slower. The French knights made the most desperate efforts to attack the king himself, and pressed forward to reach the royal banner. His brother, the Duke of Clarence, was wounded, and would have been killed had not the king himself, with a few of his knights, taken post around him, and kept off the attacks of his foes until he recovered his feet. Almost immediately afterwards a band of eighteen knights, under the banner of the Lord of Croye, who had bound themselves by an oath to take or kill the king, charged down upon him. One of them struck him so heavy a blow on the head with a mace that the king was beaten to his knee, but his knights closed in round him, and every one of his assailants was killed.

The Duke of Alençon next charged down with a strong following; he cut his way to the royal standard, and struck the Duke of York dead with a blow of his battle-axe. Henry sprung forward, but Alençon's weapon again fell, and striking him on the head clipped off a portion of the crown which Henry wore round his helmet. But before the French knight could repeat the stroke Guy Aylmer sprung forward and struck so heavy a blow full on the duke's vizor that he fell from his horse dead. His fall completed the confusion and dismay among the French, and the second division of their army, which had hitherto fought gallantly, now gave way. Many were taken prisoners. The third division, although alone vastly superior in numbers to the English, seeing the destruction of the others, began to draw off. They had moved but a short distance when loud shouts were heard in the English rear. Two or three French knights, with a body of several hundred armed peasants, had suddenly fallen upon the English baggage and horses which had been left at Maisoncelles. Many of the guard had gone off to join in the battle, so that the attack was successful, a portion of the baggage, including the king's own wardrobe, and a great number of horses being captured.

Ignorant of the strength of the attacking party, Henry believed that it was the reinforcements under the Duke of Brittany that had come up. At the same moment the third division of the French, whose leaders were also similarly deceived, halted and faced round. Believing that he was about to be attacked in front and rear by greatly superior forces, Henry gave the order that all prisoners should be killed, and the order was to a great extent executed before the real nature of the attack was discovered and the order countermanded. The third division of the French now continued its retreat, and the battle was over. There remained but to examine the field and see who had fallen.

The king gave at once the name of Agincourt to the battle, as this village possessed a castle, and was therefore the most important of those near which the fight had taken place. Properly the name should have been Azincourt, as this was the French spelling of the village. The loss of the French was terrible, and their chivalry had suffered even more than at Poitiers. Several of the relations of the French king were killed. The Duke of Brabant, the Count de Nevers, the Duke of Bar and his two brothers, the constable, and the Duke of Alençon all perished. No less than a hundred and twenty great lords were killed, and eight thousand nobles, knights, and esquires lost their lives, with some thousands of lower degree, while the Duke of Orleans, the Duke of Bourbon, and many others were taken prisoners.

The accounts of the English loss differ considerably, the highest placing it at sixteen hundred, the lowest at one-fourth of that number. The plunder taken by them in the shape of costly armour, arms, rich garments, and the trappings of horses, was great; but of food there was but little, many of the victors lay down supperless around the village of Maisoncelles.

The knights who had led the peasants to the attack of the baggage-train, instead of joining in the fight, and had thereby caused the unfortunate massacre of so many prisoners, fell into great disgrace among the French for their conduct, and were imprisoned for some years by the Duke of Burgundy.

That evening the English king knighted many esquires and aspirants of noble families, among them Guy Aylmer, who was indeed the first to receive the honour.

"No one fought more bravely than you did, young knight," he said, as Guy rose to his feet after receiving the accolade; "I will see that you have lands to support your new dignity. Twice you were at my side when I was in the greatest danger, and none have won their spurs more fairly."

John Harpen would also have been among those knighted, but he declined the honour, saying that he was not come of gentle blood, and wished for nothing better than to remain his lord's esquire so long as he had strength to follow him in the field.

The next morning the army marched to Calais. The king turned aside with Sir Eustace, and with a strong party rode to Villeroy. Guy had gone on with the men-at-arms at daybreak, and a banquet had been prepared, and twenty cartloads of grain and a hundred bullocks sent off to meet the army on its march.

"'Tis a fine castle, Sir Eustace," the king said as he rode in, "but truly it is perilously situated. If after this I can make good terms with France I will see that the border shall run outside your estates; but if not, methinks that it were best for you to treat with some French noble for its sale, and I will see that you are equally well bestowed in England, for in truth, after fighting for us at Agincourt, you are like to have but little peace here."

"I would gladly do so, my lord king," Sir Eustace replied. "During the last three years it has been a loss rather than a gain to me. I have had to keep a large garrison here; the estate has been wasted, and the houses and barns burned. Had it not been that there was for most of the time a truce between England and France I should have fared worse. And now I may well be attacked as soon as your majesty and the army cross to England."

"You will have a little breathing time," the king said; "they will have enough to do for a while to mourn their losses. I will not leave behind any of your brave fellows who have fought so hard here, but when I arrive at Calais will order two hundred men of the garrison to come over to reinforce you until you can make arrangements to get rid of the castle, if it is not to remain within my territory."

Sir Eustace introduced Sir John Aylmer as the father of the newly-made knight.

"You have a gallant son, Sir John," the king said, "and one who is like to make his way to high distinction. I doubt not that before we have done with the French he will have fresh opportunities of proving his valour."

After the meal was over the king went round the walls.

"'Tis a strong place," he said, "and yet unless aid reached you, you could not resist an army with cannon and machines."

"I have long seen that, your majesty, and have felt that I should have to choose between England and France, for that, when war broke out again, I could not remain a vassal of both countries."

"It shall be my duty to show you that you have not chosen wrongly, Sir Eustace. I cannot promise to maintain you here, for you might be attacked when I have no army with which I could succour you. As soon as I return home and learn which of those who have fallen have left no heirs, and whose lands therefore have come into my gift, I will then make choice of a new estate for you."

The army marched slowly to Calais. It was weakened by sickness and hunger, and every man was borne down by the weight of the booty he carried. On arriving there the king held a council, and it was finally determined to return to England. The force under his command was now but the skeleton of an army. Fresh men and money were required to continue the war, and he accordingly set sail, carrying with him his long train of royal and noble prisoners. The news of the victory created the greatest enthusiasm in England. At Dover the people rushed into the sea and carried the king to shore on their shoulders. At Canterbury and the other towns through which he passed he received an enthusiastic welcome, while his entry into London was a triumph. Every house was decorated, the conduits ran with wine instead of water, and the people were wild with joy and enthusiasm. Great subsidies were granted him by Parliament, and the people in their joy would have submitted to any taxation. However, throughout his reign Henry always showed the greatest moderation; he kept well within constitutional usages, and his pleasant, affable manner secured for him throughout his reign the love and devotion of his subjects.

On his arrival at Calais Guy discovered that among the prisoners was his friend Count Charles d'Estournel.

"I am grieved indeed to see you in this plight," he exclaimed as he met him.

"'Tis unfortunate truly, Aylmer, but it might have been worse; better a prisoner than among the dead at Agincourt," the light-hearted young count said; "but truly it has been an awful business. Who could have dreamt of it? I thought myself that the council were wrong when they refused all the offers of the towns to send bodies of footmen to fight beside us; had they been there, they might have faced those terrible archers of yours, for they at least would have been free to fight when we were all but helpless in that quagmire. I see that you have knightly spurs on, and I congratulate you."

"Now, Count, what can I do to ensure your release at once? Whose prisoner are you?"

"I surrendered to one John Parsons, an esquire, and I shall, of course, as soon as we get to England, send home to raise money for my ransom."

"I know him well," Guy said; "his lord's tent was pitched alongside that of Sir Eustace, before Harfleur, and we saw much of each other, and often rode together on the march. If I gave him my guarantee for your ransom, I doubt not that he will take your pledge, and let you depart at once."

"I should be glad indeed if you would do so, Aylmer."

"At any rate he will take the guarantee of Sir Eustace," Guy said, "which will, I know, be given readily, after the service you rendered to his dame, and it may be that you will have it in your power to do him a service in return." He then told the count of the intention of Sir Eustace to sell the estate, or rather to arrange for its transfer.

"It is held directly from the crown," he said, "but just at present the crown is powerless. Artois is everywhere Burgundian, and it would certainly be greatly to the advantage of Burgundy that it should be held by one of his followers, while it would be to the safety of France that it should be held by a Frenchman, rather than by one who is also a vassal of England."

"I should think that that could be managed," the count said thoughtfully. "I will speak to my father. I am, as you know, his second son, but through my mother, who is a German, I have an estate on the other side of the Rhine. This I would gladly exchange-that is to say, would part with to some German baron-if I could obtain the fief of Villeroy. I have no doubt that Burgundy would not only consent, but would help, for, as you know by the manner in which your lady was made a hostage, he looked with great jealousy on this frontier fortress, which not only gives a way for the English into Artois, but which would, in the hands of an Orleanist, greatly aid an invasion of the province from Pontoise and the west. And, although the court would just at present object to give the fief to a Burgundian, it is powerless to interfere, and when the troubles are over, the duke would doubtless be able to manage it."

Guy had no difficulty in arranging the matter with D'Estournel's captor, to whom Sir Eustace and he both gave their surety that his ransom should be paid; and, before sailing, Guy had the satisfaction of seeing his friend mount and ride for St. Omar with a pass through the English territory from the governor.

Chapter XX
Penshurst

After accompanying the king to London Sir Eustace and Guy rode to Summerley, where Long Tom and his companions had already arrived, having marched thither direct from Dover. There were great rejoicings at the castle. Not only the tenants, but people from a long way round came in to join in welcoming home two of the heroes of Agincourt. The archer had already brought news of Guy having been knighted, and he was warmly, congratulated by Dame Margaret and by Agnes, who received him with her usual sisterly affection. Katarina, also, congratulated him, but it was with less warmth of manner. In the evening, how ever, her mood changed, and she said to him:

"Though I do not say much, you know that I am pleased, Sir Guy."

"I am not sure, Countess Katarina-since we are to be ceremonious to each other-that I do quite know, for since I returned from France last time, I have seldom understood you; one moment you seem to me just as you used to be, at another you hold me at a distance, as if I were well-nigh a stranger."

Katarina shrugged her shoulders. "What would you have, Guy? One can't be always in the same humour."

"You are always in the same humour to Dame Margaret and Agnes," he said; "so far as I can see I am the only one whom you delight to tease."

"Now that you are a belted knight, Sir Guy, I shall not presume to tease you any more, but shall treat you with the respect due to your dignity." Then she swept a deep curtsey, and turning, went off with a merry laugh, while Guy looked after her more puzzled than ever.

That evening he received the news that during the absence of Sir Eustace and himself Sir William Bailey, a young knight whose estates lay near, had asked for the hand of Agnes, and that, although Dame Margaret had been unable to give an answer during her lord's absence, Agnes would willingly submit herself to her father's orders to wed Sir William.

Guy remained for some months quietly at Summerley. The Emperor Sigismund had paid a visit to England, and then to Paris, to endeavour to reconcile the two countries. His mediation failed. Henry offered, as a final settlement, to accept the execution, on the part of France, of the treaty of Trepigny. Nothing, however, came of it, for there was no government in France capable of making a binding treaty. In spite of the disgrace and the slaughter of the nobles at Agincourt there was no abatement of the internal dissensions, and the civil war between Burgundy and Armagnac was still raging, the only change in affairs being that the vicious and incapable Duke of Aquitaine had died, and the queen had once again gone over to the Burgundian faction. Count Charles d'Estournel had carried into effect the mission with which he had charged himself. Burgundy had eagerly embraced the opportunity of attaching to his side the castle and estates of Villeroy, and he and the Count d'Estournel between them raised a sum of money which was paid to Sir Eustace for the relinquishment to Burgundy of the fief, which was then bestowed upon Count Charles.

The sum in no way represented what would now be considered the value of the estate, but in those days, when fiefs reverted to the crown or other feudal superior upon the death of an owner without heirs, or were confiscated upon but slight pretence, the money value was far under the real value of the estate. Sir Eustace was well satisfied, however, with the sum paid him. Had his son Henry lived he had intended that the anomalous position of the lord of Villeroy, being also a vassal of England, should have been got rid of by one of his sons becoming its owner, and a vassal of France, while the other would inherit Summerley, and grow up a vassal of England only. Henry's death had put an end to the possibility of this arrangement, and Charlie would now become, at his father's death, Lord of Summerley and of such other English lands as could be obtained with the money paid for the surrender of the fief of Villeroy.

In the first week of July there were great rejoicings at Summerley over the marriage of Agnes with Sir William Bailey. The king had not forgotten his promise to Sir Eustace, and had raised him to the title of Baron Eustace of Summerley, and had presented him with a royal manor near Winchester. Guy was summoned to court to take part in the festivities that were held during the visit of Sigismund, and the king said to him pleasantly one day:

"I have not forgotten you, Sir Guy; but I have had many to reward, and you know importunate suitors, and those who have powerful connections to keep their claims ever in front, obtain an advantage over those who are content to hold themselves in the back-ground."

"I am in all ways contented, your majesty. I have lived all my life in the household at Summerley, and am so much one of my lord's family that I have no desire to quit it. Moreover, my father has just returned from Villeroy with the garrison of the castle, and it is a great pleasure to me to have his society again."

"I thought that some day you would have married Dame Margaret's fair daughter, after acting as their protector in the troubles in Paris, but I hear that she is betrothed to Sir William Bailey."

"Such an idea never entered my mind, your majesty. She was but a child in those days, not so much in years as in thought, and brought up together as we were I have always regarded her rather in the light of a sister."

Guy's quiet stay at Summerley came to an end suddenly. A fortnight after the marriage of Agnes, Harfleur was besieged by the French by land and water, and the Earl of Dorset, its governor, sent to England for aid. The king sent hasty orders to his vassals of Kent, Surrey, and Hampshire, to march with their retainers to Rye, where a fleet was to gather for their conveyance. A body of archers and men-at-arms were also sent thither by the king, and the Duke of Bedford, his brother, appointed to the command of the expedition. Sir Eustace was suffering somewhat from the effects of a fever, the seeds of which he had contracted in France, and he accordingly sent his contingent, thirty archers and as many men-at-arms, under the command of Guy.

"I had hoped that we had done with Harfleur," Long Tom said as they started on their march to the seaport. "I don't mind fighting, that comes in the way of business, but to see men rotting away like sheep with disease is not to my fancy."

"We shall have no fighting on land, Tom," Guy replied, "at least I expect not. When the French see that the garrison is reinforced they will probably give up the siege, though we may have a fight at sea with the French ships that are blockading the town and preventing provisions from reaching the garrison. Doubtless we shall take a good store of food with us, and the French will know well enough that as we had such hard work in capturing the town, they can have no chance whatever of taking it by assault when defended by us."

Guy and his party had a small ship to themselves, with which he was well content, as, being but a newly-made knight, he would, had he been in a large ship, have been under the orders of any others who chanced to be with him; while he was now free to act as he chose. The voyage was favourable, but when the fleet arrived off the mouth of the Seine they found that the work before them was far more serious than they had expected. In addition to their own fleet, which was itself considerably stronger than the English, the besiegers had hired the aid of some great Genoese vessels, and a number of galleys, caravels, and many high-decked ships from Spain. They occupied a strong position off the town, and could be supported by some of the siege batteries. The English fleet lay to at the mouth of the Seine, and at night the captains of the troops on board the various ships were rowed to Bedford's ship, which displayed a light at the mast-head, so that the fleet could all lie in company round her. Here after much discussion a plan for the battle next day was agreed upon. The enterprise would have been a very hazardous one, but, happily, at daybreak the French ships were seen coming out to give battle. Confident in their superior numbers, and anxious to revenge their defeat at Agincourt, the French commanders were eager to reap the whole glory of victory without the assistance of their allies, whose ships remained anchored in the river.

Bedford at once made the signal to attack them, and a desperate fight ensued. Great as was the slaughter in those days in battles on land, it was far greater in sea-fights. Except to knights and nobles, from whom ransom could be obtained, quarter was never given to prisoners either by land or sea, consequently as soon as soldiers in a land battle saw that fortune was going against them they fled. But on sea there was no escape; every man knew that it was either death or victory, and therefore fought with determination and obstinacy to the end. The two first French ships that arrived were speedily captured, but when the rest came up a desperate battle took place. Guy was on the point of ordering his ship to be laid alongside a French craft little larger than his own, when his eye fell upon a great ship carrying the flag of a French admiral, and at once diverting the course of his vessel, he ran alongside her. The archers were on the bow and stern castles of his ship, and as they came within a short distance of the Frenchman, they sent their arrows thick and fast into the crowded mass on her deck. Two grapnels, to each of which were attached twenty feet of chain, were thrown into the shrouds of the French vessel, and Guy shouted to the men-at-arms in the waist to keep the enemy from boarding by holding the vessels apart by thrusting out light spars and using their spears.

The French had a few cross-bowmen on board, but Guy, running up on to the castle at the bow, where Long Tom himself was posted, bade him direct the fire of his men solely against them, and in a very short time the discharge of missiles from the French ship ceased. In vain the French attempted to bring the ships alongside each other by throwing grapnels; the ropes of these were cut directly they fell, and although many of the English spears were hacked in two, others were at once thrust out, and the spars, being inclined so as to meet the hull of the enemy below the water-line, could not be reached by their axes. The wind was light, and there was no great difference in point of sailing. The English sailors were vigilant, and when the Frenchman brailed up his great sail, so as to fall behind, they at once followed his example. At the end of a quarter of an hour the effect of the arrows of the thirty archers was so great that there was much confusion on board the enemy, and Guy thought that, comparatively small as his force was, an attack might be made. So the spars were suddenly drawn in and the chains hauled upon. The archers caught up their axes and joined the men-at-arms, and as the vessels came together they all leapt with a great shout upon the enemy's deck.

The French knights, whose armour had protected them to some extent from the slaughter that the arrows had effected among the soldiers, fought bravely and rallied their men to resistance; but with shouts of "Agincourt!" the men-at-arms and archers, led by Guy,—who now for the first time fought in his knightly armour,—were irresistible. They had boarded at the enemy's stern so as to get all their foes in front of them, and after clearing the stern castle they poured down into the waist and gradually won their way along it. After ten minutes' hard fighting the French admiral and knights were pent up on the fore castle, and defended the ladder by which it was approached so desperately that Guy ordered Tom, with a dozen of the archers, to betake themselves to the English fore castle and to shoot from there, and in a short time the French leaders lowered their swords and surrendered. The French flag at the stern had been hauled down and that of England hoisted as soon as they boarded, and the latter was now run up to the mast-head amid the loud hurrahs of the English.

The moment the French surrendered, Guy called to his men to cease from slaying and to disarm the prisoners, who were still much more numerous than themselves. The common men he told to take to their boats and row away, while the admiral and knights were conducted to the cabin, and a guard placed over them. As soon as this was done Guy looked round; the battle was still raging and many of the French ships had been captured, but others were defending themselves desperately. Twelve of Guy's men had been killed, and several of the others more or less severely wounded, and seeing that his countrymen did not need his assistance, he ordered the decks to be cleared and the dead bodies thrown overboard. In a quarter of an hour, the last French ship had been taken. There was now breathing time for half an hour, during which the Duke of Bedford, whose ship lay not far from Guy's prize, had himself rowed on board.

"All have done well to-day, Sir Guy Aylmer, but assuredly the feat you have performed surpasses any of the others, seeing that you have captured this great ship with one of the smallest in our fleet. Their crew must have been three or four times as strong as yours, which was, as I know, but sixty strong. Has the Count de Valles fallen?"

"No, my lord duke, he is, with six of his knights, a prisoner in the cabin."

"I will see him later," the duke said; "we are now going to attack the Genoese and Spaniards. Is there aught that I can do for you?"

"Some twenty of my men are dead or disabled," Guy said, "and I must leave ten in charge of this prize. I have suffered the French soldiers, after disarming them and the sailors, to leave in their boats, and ten men will therefore be sufficient to hold her. If your grace can spare me thirty men-at-arms I will go on in my own ship to attack the Genoese."

"I will do so," the duke replied. "I will send ten to keep this ship, and twenty to fill the places of those of your men who have fallen. I can spare ten from my own ship and will borrow twenty from such of the others as can best spare them."

In a few minutes the thirty men came on board, with a sub-officer to take charge of the prize. Guy returned with his own men and twenty new-comers to his vessel, and sailed in with the fleet to attack the great ships of the Genoese and Spaniards at their moorings. As they approached they were received with a heavy cannonade from the enemy's ships and shore batteries, but without replying they sailed on and ranged themselves alongside the enemy, their numbers permitting them to lay a vessel on each side of most of the great caravels. Their task was by no means an easy one, for the sides of these ships were fifteen feet above those of the low English vessels, and they were all crowded with men. Nevertheless, the English succeeded in boarding, forcing their way in through port-holes and windows, clambering up the bows by the carved work, or running out on their yards and swinging themselves by ropes on to the enemy's deck, while the cannon plied them with shot close to the water-line.

Most of the ships were taken by boarding, some were sunk with all on board, a few only escaped by cutting their cables and running up the Seine into shallow water. The loss of life on the part of the French and their allies in this brilliant British victory was enormous. With the exception of those on board the few ships which escaped, and the men sent off in the boats by Guy, the whole of the crews of the French, Genoese, and Spaniards, save only the nobles and knights put to ransom, were killed, drowned, or taken prisoners, and during the three weeks that the English fleet remained off Harfleur, the sailors were horrified by the immense number of dead bodies that were carried up and down by the tide. Harfleur was revictualled and put into a state of defence, and the Duke of Bedford then sailed with his fleet to England, having achieved the greatest naval victory that England had ever won save when Edward the Third, with the Black Prince, completely defeated a great Spanish fleet off the coast of Sussex, with a squadron composed of ships vastly inferior both in size and number to those of the Spaniards, which contained fully ten times the number of fighting men carried by the English vessels.

This great naval victory excited unbounded enthusiasm in England. The king gave a great banquet to the Duke of Bedford and his principal officers, and by the duke's orders Guy attended. Before they sat down to the table the duke presented his officers individually to the king. Guy, as the youngest knight, was the last to be introduced.

"The duke has already spoken to me of the right valiant deeds that you accomplished, Sir Guy Aylmer," the king said as he bowed before him, "and that with but a small craft and only sixty men-at-arms and archers you captured the ship of the French admiral, which he estimates must have carried at least three hundred men. We hereby raise you to the rank of knight-banneret, and appoint you to the fief of Penshurst in Hampshire, now vacant by the death without heirs of the good knight Sir Richard Fulk. And we add thereto, as our own gift, the two royal manors of Stoneham and Piverley lying adjacent to it, and we enjoin you to take for your coat-of-arms a great ship. The fief of Penshurst is a sign of our royal approval of your bravery at Harfleur, the two manors are the debt we owe you for your service at Agincourt. We have ordered our chancellor to make out the deeds, and tomorrow you will receive them from him and take the oaths."

Guy knelt and kissed the hand that the king held out to him, and acknowledged the royal gift in fitting words. On the following day, after taking the oaths for his new possessions, he mounted, and the next day rode into Summerley. Here to his surprise he found the Count of Montepone, who had arrived, by way of Calais and Dover, a few days previously. He was suffering from a severe wound, and when Guy entered rose feebly from a chair by the fire, for it was now October and the weather was cold. His daughter was sitting beside him, and Lady Margaret was also in the room. Lord Eustace and Sir John Aylmer had met Guy as he dismounted below.

"So you have gone through another adventure and come out safely," the count said after Guy had greeted him. "Truly you have changed greatly since you left Paris, well-nigh three years ago. It was well that Maître Leroux had the armour made big for you, for I see that it is now none too large. I too, you see, have been at war; but it was one in which there was small honour, though, as you see, with some risk, for it was a private duel forced upon me by one of the Armagnac knights. Up to that time my predictions had wrought me much profit and no harm. I had told Aquitaine and other lords who consulted me that disaster would happen when the French army met the English. That much I read in the stars. And though, when Henry marched north from Harfleur with so small a following, it seemed to me that victory could scarce attend him against the host of France, I went over my calculations many times and could not find that I had made an error. It was owing greatly to my predictions that the duke readily gave way when the great lords persuaded him not to risk his life in the battle.

"Others whom I had warned went to their death, in some cases because they disbelieved me, in others because they preferred death to the dishonour of drawing back. One of the latter, on the eve of the battle, confided to a hot-headed knight in his following that I had foretold his death; and instead of quarrelling with the stars, the fool seemed to think that I had controlled them, and was responsible for his lord's death. So when in Paris some months since, he publicly insulted me, and being an Italian noble as well as an astrologer, I fought him the next day. I killed him, but not before I received a wound that laid me up for months, and from which I have not yet fairly recovered. While lying in Paris I decided upon taking a step that I had for some time been meditating. I could, when Katarina left Paris with your lady, have well gone with her, with ample means to live in comfort and to furnish her with a fortune not unfitted to her rank as my daughter.

"During the past three years the reputation I gained by my success in saving the lives of several persons of rank, increased so rapidly that money has flowed into my coffers beyond all belief. There was scarcely a noble of the king's party who had not consulted me, and since Agincourt the Duke of Aquitaine and many others took no step whatever without coming to me. But I am weary of the everlasting troubles of which I can see no end, and assuredly the aspect of the stars affords no ground for hope that they will terminate for years; therefore, I have determined to leave France, and to practise my art henceforth solely for my own pleasure, I shall open negotiations with friends in Mantua, to see whether, now that twelve years have elapsed since I had to fly, matters cannot be arranged with my enemies; much can often be done when there are plenty of funds wherewith to smooth away difficulties. Still, that is in the future. My first object in coming to England was to see how my daughter was faring, and to enjoy a period of rest and quiet while my wound was healing, which it has begun to do since I came here. I doubted on my journey, which has been wholly performed in a litter, whether I should arrive here alive."

"And now, father," Katarina said, "let us hear what Sir Guy has been doing since he left; we have been all full of impatience since the news came four days ago that the Duke of Bedford had destroyed a great fleet of French, Spanish, and Genoese ships."

"Guy has had his share of fighting, at any rate," Lord Eustace said, as he entered the room while the girl was speaking, "for fifteen of our men have fallen; and, as Long Tom tells me, they had hot work of it, and gained much credit by capturing single-handed a great French ship."

"Yes, we were fortunate," Guy said, "in falling across the ship of the French admiral, Count de Valles. Our men all fought stoutly, and the archers having cleared the way for us and slain many of their crew, we captured them, and I hold the count and five French knights to ransom."

"That will fill your purse rarely, Guy. But let us hear more of this fighting. De Valles's ship must have been a great one, and if you took it with but your own sixty men it must have been a brilliant action."

Guy then gave a full account of the fight, and of the subsequent capture of one of the Spanish carracks with the aid of another English ship.

"If the Duke of Bedford himself came on board," Lord Eustace said, "and sent you some reinforcements, he must have thought highly of the action; indeed he cannot but have done so, or he would not have come personally on board. Did he speak to the king of it?"

"He did, and much more strongly, it seems to me, than the affair warranted, for at the banquet the day before yesterday his majesty was graciously pleased to appoint me a knight-banneret, and to bestow upon me the estates of Penshurst, adding thereto the royal manors of Stoneham and Piverley."

"A right royal gift!" Lord Eustace said, while exclamations of pleasure broke from the others.

"I congratulate you on your new honour, which you have right worthily earned. Sir John, you may well be proud of this son of yours."

"I am so, indeed," Sir John Aylmer said heartily. "I had hoped well of the lad, but had not deemed that he would mount so rapidly. Sir Richard Fulk had a fine estate, and joined now to the two manors it will be as large as those of Summerley, even with its late additions."

"I am very glad," Dame Margaret said, "that the king has apportioned you an estate so near us, for it is scarce fifteen miles to Penshurst, and it will be but a morning ride for you to come hither."

"Methinks, wife," Lord Eustace said with a smile, "we were somewhat hasty in that matter of Sir William Bailey, for had we but waited Agnes might have done better."

"She chose for herself," Dame Margaret replied with an answering smile. "I say not that in my heart I had not hoped at one time that she and Guy might have come together, for I had learnt to love him almost as if he had been my own, and would most gladly have given Agnes to him had it been your wish as well as theirs; but I have seen for some time past that it was not to be, for they were like brother and sister to each other, and neither had any thought of a still closer relation. Had it not been so I should never have favoured Sir William Bailey's suit, though indeed he is a worthy young man, and Agnes is happy with him. You have not been to your castle yet, Guy?" she asked, suddenly changing the subject.

"No, indeed, Lady Margaret, I rode straight here from London, deeming this, as methinks that I shall always deem it, my home."

"We must make up a party to ride over and see it to-morrow," Lord Eustace said. "We will start early, wife, and you and Katarina can ride with us. Charlie will of course go, and Sir John. We could make a horse-litter for the count, if he thinks he could bear the journey."

"Methinks that I had best stay quietly here," the Italian said. "I have had enough of litters for a time, and the shaking might make my wound angry again."

"Nonsense, child!" he broke off as Katarina whispered that she would stay with him; "I need no nursing now; you shall ride with the rest."

Accordingly the next day the party started early. Charlie was in high spirits; he had grown into a sturdy boy, and was delighted at the good fortune that had befallen Guy, whom he had regarded with boundless admiration since the days in Paris. Katarina was in one of her silent moods, and rode close to Lady Margaret. Long Tom, who was greatly rejoiced on hearing of the honours and estates that had been bestowed on Guy, rode with two of his comrades in the rear of the party. Penshurst was a strong castle, though scarcely equal in size to Summerley; it was, however, a more comfortable habitation, having been altered by the late owner's father, who had travelled in Italy, with a view rather to the accommodation of its inmates than its defence, and had been furnished with many articles of luxury rare in England.

"A comfortable abode truly, Guy!" his father said. "It was well enough two hundred years since, when the country was unsettled, for us to pen ourselves up within walls, but there is little need of it now in England, although in France, where factions are constantly fighting against each other, it is well that every man should hold himself secure from attack. But now that cannon are getting to so great a point of perfection, walls are only useful to repel sudden attacks, and soon crumble when cannon can be brought against them. Me thinks the time will come when walls will be given up altogether, especially in England, where the royal power is so strong that nobles can no longer war with each other."

"However, Guy," Lord Eustace said, "'tis as well at present to have walls, and strong ones; and though I say not that this place is as strong as Villeroy, it is yet strong enough to stand a siege."

Guy spent an hour with the steward, who had been in charge of the castle since the death of Sir Richard Fulk, and who had the day before heard from a royal messenger that Sir Guy had been appointed lord of the estates. The new owner learned from him much about the extent of the feu, the number of tenants, the strength that he would be called upon to furnish in case of war, and the terms on which the vassals held their tenure.

"Your force will be well-nigh doubled," the steward said in conclusion, "since you tell me that the manors of Stoneham and Piverley have also fallen to you."

"'Tis a fair country," Guy said as the talk ended, "and one could wish for no better. I shall return to Summerley to-day, but next Monday I will come over here and take possession, and you can bid the tenants, and those also of the two manors, to come hither and meet me at two o'clock."

"Well, daughter," the Count of Montepone said to Katarina as she was sitting by his couch in the evening, "so you think that Penshurst is a comfortable abode?"

"Yes, father, the rooms are brighter and lighter than these and the walls are all hung with arras and furnished far more comfortably."

"Wouldst thou like to be its mistress, child?"

A bright flush of colour flooded the girl's face.

"Dost mean it, father?" she asked in a voice hardly above a whisper.

"Why not, child? You have seen much of this brave young knight, whom, methinks, any maiden might fall in love with. Art thou not more sensible to his merits than was Mistress Agnes?"

"He saved my life, father."

"That did he, child, and at no small risk to his own: Then do I understand that such a marriage would be to your liking?"

"Yes, father," she said frankly, "but I know not that it would be to Sir Guy's."

"That is for me to find out," he said. "I asked Lady Margaret a few days ago what she thought of the young knight's inclinations, and she told me that she thought indeed he had a great liking for you, but that in truth you were so wayward that you gave him but little chance of showing it."

"How could I let him see that I cared for him, father, when I knew not for certain that he thought aught of me, and moreover, I could not guess what your intentions for me might be."

"I should not have sent you where you would often be in his company, Katarina, unless I had thought the matter over deeply. It was easy to foresee that after the service he had rendered you you would think well of him, and that, thrown together as you would be, it was like enough that you should come to love each other. I had cast your horoscope and his and found that you would both be married about the same time, though I could not say that it would be to each other. I saw enough of him during that time in Paris to see that he was not only brave, but prudent and discreet. I saw, too, from his affection to his mistress, that he would be loyal and honest in all he undertook, that it was likely that he would rise to honour, and that above all I could assuredly trust your happiness to him. He was but a youth and you a girl, but he was bordering upon manhood and you upon womanhood. I marked his manner with his lady's daughter and saw that she would be no rival to you. Had it been otherwise I should have yielded to your prayers, and have kept you with me in France. Matters have turned out according to my expectation. I can give you a dowry that any English noble would think an ample one with his bride; and though Guy is now himself well endowed he will doubtless not object to such an addition as may enable him, if need be, to place in the field a following as large as that which many of the great nobles are bound to furnish to their sovereign. I will speak to him on the subject to-morrow, Katarina."

Accordingly, the next morning at breakfast the count told Guy that there was a matter on which he wished to consult him, and the young knight remained behind when the other members of the family left the room to carry out their avocations.

"Hast thought of a mistress for your new castle, Sir Guy?" the count began abruptly.

Guy started at the sudden question, and did not reply at once.

"I have thought of one, Count," he said; "but although, so far, all that you told me long ago in Paris has come true, and fortune has favoured me wonderfully, in this respect she has not been kind, for the lady cares not for me, and I would not take a wife who came not to me willingly."

"How know you that she cares not for you?" the count asked.

"Because I have eyes and ears, Count. She thinks me but a boy, and a somewhat ill-mannered one. She mocks me when I try to talk to her, shuns being left alone with me, and in all ways shows that she has no inclination towards me, but very much the contrary."

"Have you asked her straightforwardly?" the count inquired with a smile.

"No, I should only be laughed at for my pains, and it would take more courage than is required to capture a great French ship for me to put the matter to her."

"I fancy, Sir Guy, that you are not greatly versed in female ways. A woman defends herself like a beleaguered fortress. She makes sorties and attacks, she endeavours to hide her weakness by her bravados, and when she replies most disdainfully to a summons to capitulate, is perhaps on the eve of surrender. To come to the point, then, are you speaking of my daughter?"

"I am, Sir Count," Guy said frankly. "I love her, but she loves me not, and there is an end of it. 'Tis easy to understand that, beautiful as she is, she should not give a thought to me who, at the best, can only claim to be a stout man-at-arms; as for my present promotion, I know that it goes for nothing in her eyes."

"It may be as you say, Sir Guy; but tell me, as a soldier, before you gave up the siege of a fortress and retired would you not summon it to surrender?"

"I should do so," Guy replied with a smile.

"Then it had better be so in this case, Sir Guy. You say that you would willingly marry my daughter. I would as willingly give her to you. The difficulty then lies with the maiden herself, and it is but fair to you both that you should yourself manfully ask her decision in the matter."

He went out of the room, and returned in a minute leading Katarina. "Sir Guy has a question to ask you, daughter," he said; "I pray you to answer him frankly." He then led her to a seat, placed her there and left the room.

Guy felt a greater inclination to escape by another door than he had ever felt to fly in the hour of danger, but after a pause he said:

"I will put the question, Katarina, since your father would have me do it, though I know well enough beforehand what the answer will be. I desire above all things to have you for a wife, and would give you a true and loyal affection were you willing that it should be so, but I feel only too well that you do not think of me as I do of you. Still, as it is your father's wish that I should take your answer from your lips, and as, above all things, I would leave it in your hands without any constraint from him, I ask you whether you love me as one should love another before plighting her faith to him?"

"Why do you say that you know what my answer will be, Guy? Would you have had me show that I was ready to drop like a ripe peach into your mouth before you opened it? Why should I not love you? Did you not save my life? Were you not kind and good to me even in the days when I was more like a boy than a girl? Have you not since with my humours? I will answer your question as frankly as my father bade me." She rose now. "Take my hand, Guy, for it is yours. I love and honour you, and could wish for no better or happier lot than to be your wife. Had you asked me six months ago I should have said the same, save that I could not have given you my hand until I had my father's consent."

During the next month Guy spent most of his time at Penshurst getting everything in readiness for its mistress. Lord Eustace advanced him the monies that he was to receive for the ransoms of Count de Valles and the five knights, and the week before the wedding he went up with the Count of Montepone to London, and under his advice bought many rich hangings and pieces of rare furniture to beautify the private apartments. The count laid out a still larger sum of money on Eastern carpets and other luxuries, as well as on dresses and other matters for his daughter. On jewels he spent nothing, having already, he said, "a sufficient store for the wife of a royal duke."

On his return Guy called upon the king at his palace at Winchester, and Henry declared that he himself would ride to Summerley to be present at the wedding.

"You stood by me," he said, "in the day of battle, it is but right that I should stand by you on your wedding-day. Her father will, of course, give her away, and it is right that he should do so, seeing that she is no ward of mine; but I will be your best man. I will bring with me but a small train, for I would not inconvenience the Baron of Summerley and his wife, and I will not sleep at the castle; though I do not say that I will not stay to tread a measure with your fair bride."

Two days later a train of waggons was seen approaching Summerley; they were escorted by a body of men-at-arms with two officers of the king. Lord Eustace, in some surprise, rode out to meet them, and was informed that the king had ordered them to pitch a camp near the castle for himself and his knights, and that he intended to tarry there for the night. As soon as the waggons were unloaded the attendants and men-at-arms set to work, and in a short time the royal tent and six smaller ones were erected and fitted with their furniture. Other tents were put up a short distance away for the grooms and attendants. This greatly relieved Lady Margaret, for she had wondered where she could bestow the king and his knights if, at the last moment, he determined to sleep there.

For the next three days the castle was alive with preparations. Oxen and swine were slaughtered, vast quantities of game, geese, and poultry were brought in, two stags from the royal preserves at Winchester were sent over by the king, and the rivers for miles round were netted for fish. At ten o'clock Guy rode in with fifty mounted men, the tenants of Penshurst, Stoneham, and Piverley, and these and all the tenants of Summerley rode out under Lord Eustace and Guy to meet the king. They had gone but a mile when he and his train rode up. He had with him the Earl of Dorset and five of the nobles who had fought at Agincourt and were all personally acquainted with Guy. The church at Summerley was a large one, but it was crowded as it had never been before. The king and his nobles stood on one side of the altar, while Lord Eustace, his wife, Agnes, and Charlie were on the other. Guy's tenants occupied the front seats, while the rest of the church was filled by the tenants of Summerley, their wives and daughters, and the retainers of the castle, among them Long Tom, with his pretty wife beside him. When everything was in order the Count of Montepone entered the church with his daughter, followed by the six prettiest maidens on the Summerley estate.

"In truth, Sir Guy," the king whispered as the bride and her father came up the aisle, "your taste is as good in love as your arms are strong in war, for my eyes never fell on a fairer maid."

After the ceremony there was a great banquet in the hall, while all the tenants, with their wives and families, sat down to long tables spread in the court-yard. After the meal was over and the tables removed, the king and the party in the banqueting-hall went out on the steps and were received with tremendous cheering. Guy first returned thanks for himself and his bride for the welcome that they had given him, and then, to the delight of the people, the king stepped forward.

"Good people," he said, "among whom there are, I know, some who fought stoutly with us at Agincourt, you do well to shout loudly at the marriage of this brave young knight, who was brought up among you, and who has won by his valour great credit, and our royal favour. Methinks that he has won, also, a prize in his eyes even greater than the honours that we have bestowed upon him, and I doubt not that, should occasion occur, he will win yet higher honours in our service."

A great shout of "God bless the king!" went up from the assembly. Then the party returned to the hall, while casks of wine were broached in the court-yard. As Lord Eustace had sent for a party of musicians from Winchester, first some stately dances were performed in the hall, as many as could find room being allowed to come into it to witness them. The king danced the first measure with Katarina, the Earl of Dorset led out Lady Margaret, and Guy danced with Lady Agnes, while the other nobles found partners among the ladies who had come in from the neighbourhood. After a few dances the party adjourned to the court-yard, where games of various kinds, dancing and feasting were kept up until a late hour, when the king and his companions retired to their tents. At an early hour next morning the king and his retinue rode back to Winchester.

Until he signed the marriage contract before going to the church, Guy was altogether ignorant of the dowry that Katarina was to bring, and was astonished at the very large sum of money, besides the long list of jewels, entered in it.

"She will have as much more at my death," the count said quietly; "there is no one else who has the slightest claim upon me."

Consequently, in the course of the wars with France, Guy was able to put a contingent of men-at-arms and archers, far beyond the force his feudal obligations required, in the field. Long Tom was, at his own request, allowed by his lord to exchange his small holding for a larger one at Penshurst, and always led Guy's archers in the wars.

Sir John Aylmer remained at Summerley, refusing Guy's pressing invitation to take up his abode at Penshurst. "No, lad," he said; "Lord Eustace and I have been friends and companions for many years, and Lady Margaret has been very dear to me from her childhood. Both would miss me sorely did I leave them, the more so as Agnes is now away. Moreover, it is best that you and your fair wife should be together also for a time. 'Tis best in all respects. You are but two hours' easy riding from Summerley, and I shall often be over to see you."

Four years after his marriage the king promoted Guy to the rank of Baron of Penshurst, and about the same time the Count of Montepone, who had been for some months in Italy, finding that his enemies at Mantua were still so strong that he was unable to obtain a reversal of the decree of banishment that had been passed against him, returned to Penshurst.

"I have had more than enough of wandering, and would fain settle down here, Guy, if you will give me a chamber for myself, and one for my instruments. I shall need them but little henceforth, but they have become a part of myself and, though no longer for gain, I love to watch the stars, and to ponder on their lessons; and when you ride to the wars I shall be company for Katarina, who has long been used to my society alone, and I promise you that I will no longer employ her as my messenger."

Once established at Penshurst the count employed much of his time in beautifying the castle, spending money freely in adding to the private apartments, and decorating and furnishing them in the Italian style, until they became the wonder and admiration of all who visited them. In time he took upon himself much of the education of Katarina's children, and throughout a long life Guy never ceased to bless the day when he and Dame Margaret were in danger of their lives at the hands of the White Hoods of Paris.

A Knight of the White Cross: A Tale of the Siege of Rhodes

1896

Preface

MY DEAR LADS,

The order of the Knights of St. John, which for some centuries played a very important part in the great struggle between Christianity and Mahomedanism, was, at its origin, a semi-religious body, its members being, like other monks, bound by vows of obedience, chastity, and poverty, and pledged to minister to the wants of the pilgrims who flocked to the Holy Places, to receive them at their great Hospital-or guest house-at Jerusalem, dedicated to St. John the Baptist, and to defend them on their passage to and from the sea, against attack by Moslems. In a comparatively short time the constitution of the order was changed, and the Knights Hospitallers became, like the Templars, a great military Order pledged to defend the Holy Sepulchre, and to war everywhere against the Moslems. The Hospitallers bore a leading share in the struggle which terminated in the triumph of the Moslems, and the capture by them of Jerusalem. The Knights of St. John then established themselves at Acre, but after a valiant defence of that fortress, removed to Crete, and shortly afterwards to Rhodes. There they fortified the town, and withstood two terrible sieges by the Turks. At the end of the second they obtained honourable terms from Sultan Solyman, and retiring to Malta established themselves there in an even stronger fortress than that of Rhodes, and repulsed all the efforts of the Turks to dispossess them. The Order was the great bulwark of Christendom against the invasion of the Turks, and the tale of their long struggle is one of absorbing interest, and of the many eventful episodes none is more full of incident and excitement than the first siege of Rhodes, which I have chosen for the subject of my story.

Yours truly,
G. A. Henty

Chapter I
The King Maker

A stately lady was looking out of the window of an apartment in the Royal Chateau of Amboise, in the month of June, 1470. She was still handsome, though many years of anxiety, misfortune, and trouble, had left their traces on her face. In the room behind her, a knight was talking to a lady sitting at a tambour frame; a lad of seventeen was standing at another window stroking a hawk that sat on his wrist, while a boy of nine was seated at a table examining the pages of an illuminated missal.

"What will come of it, Eleanor?" the lady at the window said, turning suddenly and impatiently from it. "It seems past belief that I am to meet as a friend this haughty earl, who has for fifteen years been the bitterest enemy of my House. It appears almost impossible."

"'Tis strange indeed, my Queen; but so many strange things have befallen your Majesty that you should be the last to wonder at this. At any rate, as you said but yesterday, naught but good can come of it. He has done his worst against you, and one can scarce doubt that if he chooses he has power to do as much good for you, as in past times he has done you evil. 'Tis certain that his coming here shows he is in earnest, for his presence,—which is sure sooner or later to come to the ears of the Usurper,—will cause him to fall into the deepest disgrace."

"And yet it seemed," the queen said, "that by marrying his daughter to Clarence he had bound himself more firmly than ever to the side of York."

"Ay, madam," the knight said. "But Clarence himself is said to be alike unprincipled and ambitious, and it may well be that Warwick intended to set him up against Edward; had he not done so, such an alliance would not necessarily strengthen his position at Court."

"Methinks your supposition is the true one, Sir Thomas," the queen said. "Edward cares not sufficiently for his brother to bestow much favour upon the father of the prince's wife. Thus, he would gain but little by the marriage unless he were to place Clarence on the throne. Then he would again become the real ruler of England, as he was until Edward married Elizabeth Woodville, and the House of Rivers rose to the first place in the royal favour, and eclipsed the Star of Warwick. It is no wonder the proud Earl chafes under the ingratitude of the man who owes his throne to him, and that he is ready to dare everything so that he can but prove to him that he is not to be slighted with impunity. But why come to me, when he has Clarence as his puppet?"

"He may have convinced himself, madam, that Clarence is even less to be trusted than Edward, or he may perceive that but few of the Yorkists would follow him were he to declare against the Usurper, while assuredly your adherents would stand aloof altogether from such a struggle. Powerful as he is, Warwick could not alone withstand the united forces of all the nobles pledged to the support of the House of York. Thence, as I take it, does it happen that he has resolved to throw in his lot with Lancaster, if your Majesty will but forgive the evil he has done your House and accept him as your ally. No doubt he will have terms to make and conditions to lay down."

"He may make what conditions he chooses," Queen Margaret said passionately, "so that he does but aid me to take vengeance on that false traitor; to place my husband again on the throne; and to obtain for my son his rightful heritage."

As she spoke a trumpet sounded in the courtyard below.

"He has come," she exclaimed. "Once again, after years of misery and humiliation, I can hope."

"We had best retire, madam," Sir Thomas Tresham said. "He will speak more freely to your Majesty if there are no witnesses. Come, Gervaise, it is time that you practised your exercises." And Sir Thomas, with his wife and child, quitted the room, leaving Queen Margaret with her son to meet the man who had been the bitterest foe of her House, the author of her direst misfortunes.

For two hours the Earl of Warwick was closeted with the queen; then he took horse and rode away. As soon as he did so, a servant informed Sir Thomas and his wife that the queen desired their presence. Margaret was standing radiant when they entered.

"Congratulate me, my friends," she said. "The Star of Lancaster has risen again. Warwick has placed all his power and influence at our disposal. We have both forgiven all the past: I the countless injuries he has inflicted on my House, he the execution of his father and so many of his friends. We have both laid aside all our grievances, and we stand united by our hate for Edward. There is but one condition, and this I accepted gladly-namely, that my son should marry his daughter Anne. This will be another bond between us; and by all reports Anne is a charming young lady. Edward has gladly agreed to the match; he could make no alliance, even with the proudest princess in Europe, which would so aid him, and so strengthen his throne."

"God grant that your hopes may be fulfilled, madam," the knight said earnestly, "and that peace may be given to our distracted country! The Usurper has rendered himself unpopular by his extravagance and by the exactions of his tax collectors, and I believe that England will gladly welcome the return of its lawful king to power. When does Warwick propose to begin?"

"He will at once get a fleet together. Louis, who has privately brought about this meeting, will of course throw no impediment in his way; but, on the other hand, the Duke of Burgundy will do all in his power to thwart the enterprise, and will, as soon as he learns of it, warn Edward. I feel new life in me, Eleanor. After fretting powerless for years, I seem to be a different woman now that there is a prospect of action. I am rejoiced at the thought that at last I shall be able to reward those who have ventured and suffered so much in the cause of Lancaster."

"My hope is, madam, that this enterprise will be the final one,—that, once successful, our dear land will be no longer deluged with blood, and that never again shall I be forced to draw my sword against my countrymen."

"'Tis a good and pious wish, Sir Thomas, and heartily do I join in it. My married life has been one long round of trouble, and none more than I have cause to wish for peace."

"There is the more hope for it, madam, that these wars have greatly diminished the number of powerful barons. It is they who are the authors of this struggle; their rivalries and their ambitions are the ruin of England. Save for their retainers there would be no armies to place in the field; the mass of people stand aloof altogether, desiring only to live in peace and quiet. 'Tis the same here in France; 'tis the powerful vassals of the king that are ever causing trouble."

"'Tis so indeed, Sir Thomas. But without his feudal lords how could a king place an army in the field, when his dominions were threatened by a powerful neighbour?"

"Then it would be the people's business to fight, madam, and I doubt not that they would do so in defence of their hearths and homes. Besides, the neighbour would no longer have the power of invasion were he also without great vassals. These great barons stand between the king and his subjects; and a monarch would be a king indeed were he able to rule without their constant dictation, and undisturbed by their rivalry and ambitions."

"That would be a good time indeed, Sir Thomas," the queen said, with a smile; "but methinks there is but little chance of its coming about, for at present it seems to me that the vassals are better able to make or unmake kings, than kings are able to deprive the great vassals of power; and never since Norman William set foot in England were they more powerful than they are at present. What does my chance of recovering our throne rest upon? Not upon our right, but on the quarrel between Warwick and the House of Rivers. We are but puppets that the great lords play against each other. Did it depend upon my will, it should be as you say; I would crush them all at a blow. Then only should I feel really a queen. But that is but a dream that can never be carried out."

"Not in our time, madam. But perhaps it may come sooner than we expect; and this long war, which has destroyed many great families and weakened others, may greatly hasten its arrival. I presume until Warwick is ready to move naught will be done, your Majesty?"

"That is not settled yet. Warwick spoke somewhat of causing a rising in the north before he set sail, so that a portion at least of Edward's power may be up there when we make our landing."

"It would be a prudent step, madam. If we can but gain possession of London, the matter would be half finished. The citizens are ever ready to take sides with those whom they regard as likely to win, and just as they shout at present 'Long live King Edward!' so would they shout 'Long live King Henry!' did you enter the town."

"This may perhaps change the thought that you have entertained, Sir Thomas, of making your son a Knight of St. John."

"I have not thought the matter over, madam. If there were quiet in the land I should, were it not for my vow, be well content that he should settle down in peace at my old hall; but if I see that there is still trouble and bloodshed ahead, I would in any case far rather that he should enter the Order, and spend his life in fighting the infidel than in strife with Englishmen. My good friend, the Grand Prior of the Order in England, has promised that he will take him as his page, and at any rate in the House of St. John's he will pass his youth in security whatsoever fate may befall me. The child himself already bids fair to do honour to our name, and to become a worthy member of the Order. He is fond of study, and under my daily tuition is making good progress in the use of his weapons."

"That is he," the prince said, speaking for the first time, "It was but yesterday in the great hall downstairs he stood up with blunted swords against young Victor de Paulliac, who is nigh three years his senior. It was amusing to see how the little knaves fought against each other; and by my faith Gervaise held his own staunchly, in spite of Victor's superior height and weight. If he join the Order, Sir Thomas, I warrant me he will cleave many an infidel's skull, and will do honour to the langue of England."

"I hope so, prince," the knight said gravely. "The Moslems ever gain in power, and it may well be that the Knights of St. John will be hardly pressed to hold their own. If the boy joins them it will be my wish that he shall as early as possible repair to Rhodes. I do not wish him to become one of the drones who live in sloth at their commanderies in England, and take no part in the noble struggle of the Order with the Moslem host, who have captured Constantinople and now threaten all Europe. We were childless some years after our marriage, and Eleanor and I vowed that were a son born to us he should join the Order of the White Cross, and dedicate his life to the defence of Christian Europe against the infidel. Our prayers for a son were granted, and Gervaise will enter the Order as soon as his age will permit him. That is why I rejoice at the grand prior's offer to take him as his page, for he will dwell in the hospital safely until old enough to take the first steps towards becoming a knight of the Order."

"I would that I had been born the son of a baron like yourself," the prince said earnestly, "and that I were free to choose my own career. Assuredly in that case I too would have joined the noble Order and have spent my life in fighting in so grand a cause, free from all the quarrels and disputes and enmities that rend England. Even should I some day gain a throne, surely my lot is not to be envied. Yet, as I have been born to the rank, I must try for it, and I trust to do so worthily and bravely. But who can say what the end will be? Warwick has ever been our foe, and though my royal mother may use him in order to free my father, and place him on the throne, she must know well enough that he but uses us for his own ends alone, and that he will ever stand beside the throne and be the real ruler of England."

"For a time, Edward," the queen broke in. "We have shown that we can wait, and now it seems that our great hope is likely to be fulfilled. After that, the rest will be easy. There are other nobles, well nigh as powerful as he, who look with jealousy upon the way in which he lords it, and be assured that they will look with a still less friendly eye upon him when he stands, as you say, beside the throne, once your father is again seated there. We can afford to bide our time, and assuredly it will not be long before a party is formed against Warwick. Until then we must bear everything. Our interests are the same. If he is content to remain a prop to the throne, and not to eclipse it, the memory of the past will not stand between us, and I shall regard him as the weapon that has beaten down the House of York and restored us to our own, and shall give him my confidence and friendship. If, on the other hand, he assumes too much, and tries to lord it over us, I shall seek other support and gather a party which even he will be unable successfully to withstand. I should have thought, Edward, that you would be even more glad than I that this long time of weary waiting for action is over, and that once again the banner of Lancaster will be spread to the winds."

"I shall be that, mother. Rather would I meet death in the field than live cooped up here, a pensioner of France. But I own that I should feel more joy at the prospect if the people of England had declared in our favour, instead of its being Warwick-whom you have always taught me to fear and hate-who thus comes to offer to place my father again on the throne, and whose goodwill towards us is simply the result of pique and displeasure because he is no longer first in the favour of Edward. It does not seem to me that a throne won by the aid of a traitor can be a stable one."

"You are a foolish boy," the queen said angrily. "Do you not see that by marrying Warwick's daughter you will attach him firmly to us?"

"Marriages do not count for much, mother. Another of Warwick's daughters married Clarence, Edward's brother, and yet he purposes to dethrone Edward."

The queen gave an angry gesture and said, "You have my permission to retire, Edward. I am in no mood to listen to auguries of evil at the present moment."

The prince hesitated for a moment as if about to speak, but with an effort controlled himself, and bowing deeply to his mother, left the room.

"Edward is in a perverse humour," the queen said in a tone of much vexation to Sir Thomas Tresham, when Gervaise had left the room. "However, I know he will bear himself well when the hour of trial comes."

"That I can warrant he will, madam; he has a noble character, frank and fearless, and yet thoughtful beyond his years. He will make, I believe, a noble king, and may well gather round him all parties in the state. But your Majesty must make excuses for his humour. Young people are strong in their likes and dislikes. He has never heard you speak aught but ill of Warwick, and he knows how much harm the Earl has done to your House. The question of expediency does not weigh with the young as with their elders. While you see how great are the benefits that will accrue from an alliance with Warwick, and are ready to lay aside the hatred of years and to forget the wrongs you have suffered, the young prince is unable so quickly to forget that enmity against the Earl that he has learnt from you."

"You are right, Sir Thomas, and I cannot blame Edward that he is unable, as I am, to forget the past. What steps would you advise that I myself should take? Shall I remain passive here, or shall I do what I can to rouse our partisans in England?"

"I should say the latter, madam. Of course it will not do to trust to letters, for were one of these to fall into the wrong hands it might cause the ruin of Warwick's expedition; but I should say that a cautious message sent by word of mouth to some of our old adherents would be of great use. I myself will, if your Majesty chooses to entrust me with the mission, undertake to carry it out. I should take ship and land in the west, and would travel in the guise of a simple country gentleman, and call upon your adherents in all the western counties. It would be needful first to make out a list of the nobles who have shown themselves devoted to your cause, and I should bid these hold themselves and their retainers in readiness to take the field suddenly. I should say no word of Warwick, but merely hint that you will not land alone, but with a powerful array, and that all the chances are in your favour."

"But it would be a dangerous mission, Sir Thomas."

"Not greatly so, madam. My own estates lie in Sussex, and there would be but little chance of my recognition, save by your own adherents, who may have seen me among the leaders of your troops in battle; and even that is improbable. At present Edward deems himself so securely seated on the throne that men can travel hither and thither through the country without being questioned, and the Lancastrians live quietly with the Yorkists. Unless I were so unfortunate as to meet a Yorkist noble who knew that I was a banished man and one who had the honour of being in your Majesty's confidence, I do not think that any danger could possibly arise. What say you, wife?"

"I cannot think that there is no danger," Lady Tresham said; "but even so I would not say a word to hinder you from doing service to the cause. I know of no one else who could perform the mission. You have left my side to go into battle before now, and I cannot think that the danger of such an expedition can be as great as that which you would undergo in the field. Therefore, my dear lord, I would say no word now to stay you."

She spoke bravely and unfalteringly, but her face had paled when Sir Thomas first made the proposal, and the colour had not yet come back to her cheeks.

"Bravely spoken, dame," the queen said warmly. "Well, Sir Thomas, I accept your offer, and trust that you will not be long separated from your wife and son, who will of course journey with me when I go to England, where doubtless you will be able to rejoin us a few days after we land. Now let us talk over the noblemen and gentlemen in the west, upon whom we can rely, if not to join our banner as soon as it is spread, at least to say no word that will betray you."

Two days later Sir Thomas Tresham started on his journey, while the queen remained at Amboise eagerly awaiting the news that Warwick had collected a fleet, and was ready to set sail. Up to this point the Duke of Clarence had sided with Warwick against his brother, and had passed over with him to France, believing, no doubt, that if the Earl should succeed in dethroning Edward, he intended to place him, his son-in-law, upon the throne. He was rudely awakened from this delusion by Charles of Burgundy, who, being in all but open rebellion against his suzerain, the King of France, kept himself intimately acquainted with all that was going on. He despatched a female emissary to Clarence to inform him of the league Warwick had made with the Lancastrians, and the intended marriage between his daughter Anne and the young prince; imploring him to be reconciled with his brother and to break off his alliance with the Earl, who was on the point of waging war against the House of York.

Clarence took the advice, and went over to England, where he made his peace with Edward, the more easily because the king, who was entirely given up to pleasure, treated with contempt the warnings the Duke of Burgundy sent him of the intended invasion by Warwick. And yet a moment's serious reflection should have shown him that his position was precarious. The crushing exactions of the tax gatherers, in order to provide the means for Edward's lavish expenditure, had already caused very serious insurrections in various parts of the country, and his unpopularity was deep and general. In one of these risings the royal troops had suffered a crushing defeat. The Earl Rivers, the father, and Sir John Woodville, one of the brothers, of the queen had, with the Earl of Devon, been captured by the rebels, and the three had been beheaded, and the throne had only been saved by the intervention of Warwick.

Thus, then, Edward had every reason for fearing the result should the Earl appear in arms against him. He took, however, no measures whatever to prepare for the coming storm, and although the Duke of Burgundy despatched a fleet to blockade Harfleur, where Warwick was fitting out his expedition, and actually sent the name of the port at which the Earl intended to land if his fleet managed to escape from Harfleur, Edward continued carelessly to spend his time in pleasure and dissipation, bestowing his full confidence upon the Archbishop of York and the Marquis of Montague, both brothers of the Earl of Warwick.

The elements favoured his enemies, for early in September the Duke of Burgundy's Fleet, off Harfleur, was dispersed by a storm, and Warwick, as soon as the gale abated, set sail, and on the 13th landed on the Devonshire coast. His force was a considerable one, for the French king had furnished him both with money and men; on effecting his landing he found no army assembled to oppose him. A few hours after his disembarkation, he was joined by Sir Thomas Tresham, who gave him the good news that the whole of the west was ready to rise, and that in a few days all the great landowners would join him with their retainers. This turned out to be the case, and Warwick, with a great array, marched eastward. Kent had already risen, and London declared for King Henry. Warwick, therefore, instead of marching thither, moved towards Lincolnshire, where Edward was with his army, having gone north to repress an insurrection that had broken out there at the instigation of Warwick.

Lord Montague now threw off the mask, and declared for King Henry. Most of the soldiers followed him, and Edward, finding it hopeless to oppose Warwick's force, which was now within a short march of him, took ship with a few friends who remained faithful, and sailed for Holland. Warwick returned to London, where he took King Henry from the dungeon in the Tower, into which he himself had, five years before, thrown him, and proclaimed him king.

On the day that this took place Dame Tresham arrived in London with her son. The queen had found that she could not for the present cross, as she was waiting for a large French force which was to accompany her. As it was uncertain how long the delay might last, she counselled her friend to join her husband. The revolution had been accomplished without the loss of a single life, with the exception of that of the Earl of Worcester, who was hated for his cruelty by the people. Edward's principal friends took refuge in various religious houses. The queen, her three daughters, and her mother, fled to the sanctuary at Westminster. All these were left unmolested, nor was any step taken against the other adherents of the House of York. Warwick was now virtually King of England. The king, whose intellect had always been weak, was now almost an imbecile, and Margaret of Anjou was still detained in France. Sir Thomas Tresham went down to his estates in Kent, and there lived quietly for some months. The Duke of Clarence had joined Warwick as soon as he saw that his brother's cause was lost; and as the Duke had no knowledge of his changed feelings towards him, he was heartily welcomed. An act of settlement was passed by Parliament entailing the Crown on Henry's son Edward, Prince of Wales, and in case of that prince's death without issue, on the Duke of Clarence. On the 12th of March following (1471) Edward suddenly appeared with a fleet with which he had been secretly supplied by the Duke of Burgundy, and, sailing north, landed in the Humber. He found the northern population by no means disposed to aid him, but upon his taking a solemn oath that he had no designs whatever upon the throne, but simply claimed to be restored to his rights and dignities as Duke of York, he was joined by a sufficient force to enable him to cross the Trent. As he marched south his army speedily swelled, and he was joined by many great lords.

Warwick had summoned Henry's adherents to the field, and marched north to meet him. When the armies approached each other, the Duke of Clarence, who commanded a portion of Henry's army, went over with his whole force to Edward, and Warwick, being no longer in a position to give battle, was obliged to draw off and allow Edward to march unopposed towards London. The citizens, with their usual fickleness, received him with the same outburst of enthusiasm with which, five months before, they had greeted the entry of Warwick. The unfortunate King Henry was again thrown into his dungeon in the Tower, and Edward found himself once more King of England.

Sir Thomas Tresham, as soon as he heard of the landing of Edward, had hastened up to London. In his uncertainty how matters would go, he brought his wife and son up with him, and left them in lodgings, while he marched north with Warwick. As soon as the defection of Clarence opened the road to London, he left the Earl, promising to return in a few days, and rode to town, arriving there two days before Edward's entry, and, purchasing another horse, took his wife and son down to St. Albans, where leaving them, he rejoined Warwick. In a few days the latter had gathered sufficient forces to enable him to risk the fortunes of a battle, and, marching south, he encamped with his army on the common north of Barnet. Edward had come out to meet him, and the two armies slept on Easter Eve within two miles of each other.

Late in the evening Clarence sent a messenger to the Earl, offering to mediate, but the offer was indignantly refused by Warwick.

In the darkness, neither party was aware of the other's precise position. Warwick was much stronger than the king in artillery, and had placed it on his right wing. The king, in his ignorance of the enemy's position, had placed his troops considerably more to the right than those of Warwick's army. The latter, believing that Edward's line was facing his, kept up a heavy cannonade all night upon where he supposed Edward's left to be —a cannonade which was thus entirely futile.

In the morning (April 14th) a heavy mist covered the country and prevented either force from seeing the other's dispositions. Warwick took the command of his left wing, having with him the Duke of Exeter. Somerset was in command of his centre, and Montague and Oxford of his right.

Edward placed himself in the centre of his array, the Duke of Gloucester commanded on his right, and Lord Hastings on his left.

Desirous, from his inferiority in artillery, to fight out the battle hand to hand, Edward, at six o'clock in the morning, ordered his trumpets to blow, and, after firing a few shots, advanced through the mist to attack the enemy. His misconception as to Warwick's position, which had saved his troops from the effects of the cannonade during the night, was now disadvantageous to him, for the Earl's right so greatly outflanked his left that when they came into contact Hastings found himself nearly surrounded by a vastly superior force. His wing fought valiantly, but was at length broken by Oxford's superior numbers, and driven out of the field. The mist prevented the rest of the armies from knowing what had happened on the king's left. Edward himself led the charge on Warwick's centre, and having his best troops under his command, pressed forward with such force and vehemence that he pierced Somerset's lines and threw them into confusion.

Just as Warwick's right had outflanked the king's left, so his own left was outflanked by Gloucester. Warwick's troops fought with great bravery, and, in spite of the disaster to his centre, were holding their ground until Oxford, returning from his pursuit of the king's left, came back through the mist. The king's emblem was a sun, that of Oxford a star with streaming rays. In the dim light this was mistaken by Warwick's men for the king's device, and believing that Oxford was far away on the right, they received him with a discharge of arrows. This was at once returned, and a conflict took place. At last the mistake was discovered, but the confusion caused was irreparable. Warwick and Oxford each suspected the other of treachery, and the king's right still pressing on, the confusion increased, and the battle, which had been so nearly won by the Earl, soon became a complete defeat, and by ten in the morning Warwick's army was in full flight.

Accounts differ as to the strength of the forces engaged, but it is probable that there was no great inequality, and that each party brought some fifteen thousand men into the field. The number of slain is also very uncertain, some historians placing the total at ten thousand, others as low as one thousand; but from the number of nobles who fell, the former computation is probably nearest to the truth. Warwick, his brother Montague, and many other nobles and gentlemen, were killed, the only great nobles on his side who escaped being the Earls of Somerset and Oxford; many were also killed on Edward's side, and the slaughter among the ordinary fighting men was greater than usual.

Hitherto in the battles that had been fought during the civil war; while the leaders taken on the field were frequently executed, the common soldiers were permitted to return to their homes, as they had only been acting under the orders of their feudal superiors, and were not considered responsible for their acts. At Barnet, however, Edward, smarting from the humiliation he had suffered by his enforced flight from England, owing to the whole country declaring for his rival, gave orders that no quarter was to be granted. It was an anxious day at St. Albans, where many ladies whose husbands were with Warwick's army had, like Dame Tresham, taken up their quarters. It was but a few miles from the field of battle. In the event of victory they could at once join their husbands, while in case of defeat they could take refuge in the sanctuary of the abbey. Messengers the night before had brought the news that the battle would begin at the dawn of day, and with intense anxiety they waited for the news.

Dame Tresham and her son attended early mass at the abbey, and had returned to their lodgings, when Sir Thomas rode up at full speed. His armour was dinted and his plume shorn away from his helmet. As he entered the house he was met by his wife, who had run downstairs as she heard his horse stop at the door. A glance at his face was sufficient to tell the news.

"We have lost the day," he said. "Warwick and Montague are both killed. All is lost here for the present. Which will you do, my love, ride with me to the West, where Queen Margaret will speedily land, if indeed she has not landed already, or take sanctuary here with the boy?"

"I will go with you," she said. "I would vastly rather do so."

"I will tell you more on the road," he said. "There is no time to be lost now."

The woman of the house was called, and at once set her son to saddle the other horse and to give a feed to that of the knight. Dame Tresham busied herself with packing the saddlebags while her husband partook of a hasty meal; and ten minutes after his arrival they set off, Gervaise riding behind his father, while the latter led the horse on which his wife was mounted. A thick mist hung over the country.

"This mist told against us in the battle, wife, for as we advanced our forces fell into confusion, and more than once friend attacked friend, believing that he was an enemy. However, it has proved an advantage to us now, for it has enabled great numbers to escape who might otherwise have been followed and cut down. I was very fortunate. I had left my horse at a little farmhouse two miles in the rear of our camp, and in the fog had but small hope of finding it; but soon after leaving the battlefield, I came upon a rustic hurrying in the same direction as myself, and upon questioning him it turned out that he was a hand on the very farm at which I had left the horse. He had, with two or three others, stolen out after midnight to see the battle, and was now making his way home again, having seen indeed but little, but having learned from fugitives that we had been defeated. He guided me to the farmhouse, which otherwise I should assuredly never have reached. His master was favourable to our party, and let the man take one of the cart horses, on which he rode as my guide until he had placed me upon the high road to St. Albans, and I was then able to gallop on at full speed."

"And Warwick and his brother Montague are both killed?"

"Both. The great Earl will make and unmake no more kings. He has been a curse to England, with his boundless ambition, his vast possessions, and his readiness to change sides and to embroil the country in civil war for purely personal ends. The great nobles are a curse to the country, wife. They are, it is true, a check upon kingly ill doing and oppression; but were they, with their great arrays of retainers and feudal followers, out of the way, methinks that the citizens and yeomen would be able to hold their own against any king."

"Was the battle a hard fought one?"

"I know but little of what passed, except near the standard of Warwick himself. There the fighting was fierce indeed, for it was against the Earl that the king finally directed his chief onslaught. Doubtless he was actuated both by a deep personal resentment against the Earl for the part he had played and the humiliation he had inflicted upon him, and also by the knowledge that a defeat of Warwick personally would be the heaviest blow that he could inflict upon the cause of Lancaster."

"Then do you think the cause is lost?"

"I say not that. Pembroke has a strong force in Wales, and if the West rises, and Queen Margaret on landing can join him, we may yet prevail; but I fear that the news of the field of Barnet will deter many from joining us. Men may risk lands and lives for a cause which seems to offer a fair prospect of success, but they can hardly be blamed for holding back when they see that the chances are all against them. Moreover, as a Frenchwoman, it cannot be denied that Margaret has never been popular in England, and her arrival here, aided by French gold and surrounded by Frenchmen, will tell against her with the country people. I went as far as I could on the day before I left Amboise, urging her on no account to come hither until matters were settled. It would have been infinitely better had the young prince come alone, and landed in the West without a single follower. The people would have admired his trust in them, and would, I am sure, have gathered strongly round his banner. However, we must still hope for the best. Fortune was against us today: it may be with us next time we give battle. And with parties so equally divided throughout the country a signal victory would bring such vast numbers to our banners that Edward would again find it necessary to cross the seas."

Chapter II
The Battle Of Tewkesbury

Riding fast, Sir Thomas Tresham crossed the Thames at Reading before any news of the battle of Barnet had arrived there. On the third day after leaving St. Albans he reached Westbury, and there heard that the news had been received of the queen's landing at Plymouth on the very day on which her friends had been defeated at Barnet, and that she had already been joined by the Duke of Somerset, the Earl of Devon, and others, and that Exeter had been named as the point of rendezvous for her friends. As the Lancastrians were in the majority in Wiltshire and Somerset, there was no longer any fear of arrest by partisans of York, and after resting for a day Sir Thomas Tresham rode quietly on to Exeter, where the queen had already arrived.

The battle of Barnet had not, in reality, greatly weakened the Lancastrian cause. The Earl of Warwick was so detested by the adherents of the Red Rose that comparatively few of them had joined him, and the fight was rather between the two sections of Yorkists than between York and Lancaster. The Earl's death had broken up his party, and York and Lancaster were now face to face with each other, without his disturbing influence on either side. Among those who had joined the queen was Tresham's great friend, the Grand Prior of St. John's. Sir Thomas took up his lodgings in the house where he had established himself. The queen was greatly pleased at the arrival of Dame Tresham, and at her earnest request the latter shared her apartments, while Gervaise remained with his father.

"So this is the young Knight of St. John," the prior said, on the evening of the arrival of Sir Thomas. "I would, Tresham, that I were at present at Rhodes, doing battle with the infidels, rather than engaged in this warfare against Englishmen and fellow Christians."

"I can well understand that," Sir Thomas said.

"I could not hold aloof here, Tresham. The vows of our Order by no means hinder us from taking part in the affairs of our own country. The rule of the Order is indeed against it, but the rule is constantly broken. Were it otherwise there could be no commanderies in this or any other country; we should have, on entering the Order, to abandon our nationality, and to form part of one community in the East. The Order is true to its oaths. We cannot defend the Holy Sepulchre, for that, for the present, is hopelessly lost; but we can and do wage war with the infidel. For this funds are necessary as well as swords, and our commanderies throughout Europe supply the funds by which the struggle is maintained, and, when it is needed, send out contingents to help those fighting in the East. It was from the neglect of this cardinal point that the Templars fell. Their commanderies amassed wealth and wide possessions, but unlike us the knights abstained altogether from fulfilling their vows, and ceased to resist the infidel. Therefore they were suppressed, and, with the general approval of Europe, a portion of their possessions was handed over to the knights of St. John. However, as I understand, it is your wish that as soon as the boy comes of age to wield arms he shall go to Rhodes and become an active member of the Order. This is indeed the rule with all neophytes, but having served a certain time they are then permitted to return and join one of the commanderies in their native countries."

"I do not wish that for Gervaise," his father said; "at least, I wish him to remain at Rhodes until all the civil troubles are absolutely at an end here. My life has been ruined by them. Loving retirement and quiet, and longing for nothing so much as a life among my tenantry, I have almost from a boy been actively engaged in warfare or have been away as an exile. Here every one of gentle blood has been more or less mixed up in these civil broils. To few of us does it personally matter whether a member of the House of York or Lancaster sits on the throne, and yet we have been almost compelled to take sides with one or the other; and now, in my middle age I am on the eve of another battle in which I risk my life and fortune. If we win I gain naught but the satisfaction of seeing young Edward made King of England. If we lose I am going into exile again, or I may leave my wife a widow, and my child penniless."

"It is too true, Tresham; and as I am as likely to fall as you are, the child might be left without a protector as well as fatherless. However, against that I will provide. I will write a letter to Peter D'Aubusson, who is the real governor of Rhodes, for the Grand Master Orsini is so old that his rule is little more than nominal. At his death D'Aubusson is certain to be elected Grand Master. He is a dear friend of mine. We entered the Order the same year, and were comrades in many a fight with the Moslems, and I am quite sure that when I tell him that it is my last request of him, he will, in memory of our long friendship, appoint your son as one of the Grand Master's pages. As you know, no one, however high his rank, is accepted as a novice before the age of sixteen. After a year's probation he is received into the body of the Order as a professed knight, and must go out and serve for a time in Rhodes. After three years of active service he must reside two more at the convent, and can then be made a commander. There is but one exception to the rule-namely, that the pages of the grand master are entitled to the privilege of admission at the age of twelve, so that they become professed knights at thirteen. Your son is now but nine, you say, and we must remember that D'Aubusson is not yet Grand Master, and Orsini may live for some years yet. D'Aubusson, however, can doubtless get him to appoint the boy as one of his pages. But, in any case, there are three years yet to be passed before he can go out. Doubtless these he will spend under his mother's care; but as it is as well to provide against everything, I will furnish your dame with a letter to the knight who will probably succeed me as Grand Prior of the English langue, asking him to see to the care and education of the boy up to the time when he can proceed to Rhodes. We may hope, my dear Tresham, that there will be no occasion to use such documents, and that you and I may both be able personally to watch over his career. Still, it is as well to take every precaution. I shall, of course, give D'Aubusson full particulars about you, your vow, and your wishes."

"I thank you greatly, old friend," Sir Thomas said. "It has taken a load off my mind. I shall leave him here with his mother when we march forward, and bid her, if ill befalls me, cross again to France, and then to keep Gervaise with her until she can bring herself to part with him. She has her jewels and a considerable sum of money which I accepted from the man who has been enjoying my estates for the last five years, in lieu of the monies that he had received during that time. Therefore, she will not lack means for some years to come. Besides, Queen Margaret has a real affection for her, and will, doubtless, be glad to have her with her again in exile."

"When I am old enough," Gervaise said, suddenly looking up from a missal of the Grand Prior's which he had been examining, "I will chop off the head of the Duke of York, and bring mother back to England."

"You will be a valiant champion no doubt, my boy," the prior said, laughing. "But that is just what your father does not want. Chop off the heads of as many infidels as you will, but leave Englishmen alone, be they dukes or commoners. It is a far more glorious career to be aiding to defend Europe against the Moslem than to be engaged in wars with your own countrymen. If the great lords will fight, let them fight it out themselves without our aid; but I hope that long before you become a man even they will be tired of these perpetual broils, and that some agreement may be arrived at, and peace reign in this unhappy land."

"Besides, Gervaise," his father added, "you must bear in mind always that my earnest wish and hope is that you will become a champion of the Cross. I took a solemn vow before you were born that if a son were granted to me I would dedicate him to the service of the Cross, and if I am taken from you, you must still try to carry that oath into effect. I trust that, at any rate for some years after you attain manhood, you will expend your whole strength and powers in the defence of Christianity, and as a worthy knight of the Order of St. John. Too many of the knights, after serving for three years against the infidels, return to their native countries and pass the rest of their lives in slothful ease at their commanderies, save perhaps when at any great crisis they go out for a while and join in the struggle. Such is not the life I should wish you to lead. At the death of your mother and myself, you will have no family ties in England-nothing to recall you here. If the House of York succeeds in establishing itself firmly on the throne, my estates will be forfeited. Therefore, regard Rhodes as your permanent home, and devote your life to the Order. Beginning so young, you may hope to distinguish yourself-to gain high rank in it; but remember that though these are my wishes, they are not my orders, and that your career must be in your own hands."

"I will be a brave knight, father," the boy said firmly.

"That is right, my boy. Now go upstairs to your bed; it is already late. I do not regret my vow," he went on, after Gervaise had left the room, "though I regret that he is my only son. It is singular that men should care about what comes after them, but I suppose it is human nature. I should have liked to think that my descendants would sit in the old house, and that men of my race and name would long own the estates. But doubtless it is all for the best; for at least I can view the permanent loss of my estates, in case the Yorkists triumph, without any poignant regret."

"Doubtless it is for the best, Tresham, and you must remember that things may not, even now, turn out as you think. A knight who has done a brave service does not find much difficulty in obtaining from the Pope a dispensation from his vows. Numbers of knights have so left the Order and have married and perpetuated their name. It is almost a necessity that it should be so, for otherwise many princes and barons would object to their sons entering the Order. Its object is to keep back the irruption of the Moslems, and when men have done their share of hard work no regret need be felt if they desire to leave the Order. Our founder had no thought of covering Europe with monasteries, and beyond the fact that it is necessary there should be men to administer our manors and estates, I see no reason why any should not freely leave when they reach the age of thirty or thirty-five, and indeed believe that it would strengthen rather than weaken us were the vows, taken at the age of seventeen, to be for fifteen years only."

"There is something in that," the knight said thoughtfully. "However, that is far in the distance, and concerns me but little; still, I agree with you, for I see no advantage in men, after their time of usefulness to the Order is past, being bound to settle down to a monastic life if by nature and habit unsuited for it. There are some spirits who, after long years of warfare, are well content so to do, but there are assuredly others to whom a life of forced inactivity, after a youth and manhood spent in action, must be well nigh unendurable. And now tell me frankly what you think of our chances here."

"Everything depends upon time. Promises of aid have come in from all quarters, and if Edward delays we shall soon be at the head of an overwhelming force. But Edward, with all his faults and vices, is an able and energetic leader, and must be well aware that if he is to strike successfully he must strike soon. We must hope that he will not be able to do this. He cannot tell whether we intend to march direct to London, or to join Pembroke in Wales, or to march north, and until he divines our purpose, he will hardly dare to move lest we should, by some rapid movement, interpose between himself and London. If he gives us a month, our success is certain. If he can give battle in a fortnight, no one can say how the matter will end."

Edward, indeed, was losing no time. He stayed but a few days in London after his victory at Barnet, and on the 19th of April left for Windsor, ordering all his forces to join him there. The Lancastrians had endeavoured to puzzle him as to their intended movements by sending parties out in various directions; but as soon as he had gathered a force, numerically small, but composed of veteran soldiers, he hurried west, determined to bring on a battle at the earliest opportunity. The queen's advisers determined to move first to Wells, as from that point they could either go north or march upon London. Edward entered Abingdon on the 27th, and then, finding the Lancastrians still at Wells, marched to the northwest, by which means he hoped to intercept them if they moved north, while he would be able to fall back and bar their road to London if they advanced in that direction. He therefore moved to Cirencester, and waited there for news until he learned that they had visited Bristol and there obtained reinforcements of men and supplies of money and cannon, and had then started on the high road to Gloucester.

He at once sent off messengers to the son of Lord Beauchamp, who held the Castle of Gloucester for him, assuring him that he was following at full speed, and would come to his aid forthwith. The messengers arrived in time, and when the queen, after a long march, arrived before Gloucester, she found the gates shut in her face. The governor had taken steps to prevent her numerous adherents in the town from rising on her behalf, and, manning the walls, refused to surrender. Knowing that Edward was coming up rapidly, it was evident that there was no time to spare in an attempt to take the town, and the queen's army therefore pressed on, without waiting, to Tewkesbury. Once across the river they would speedily be joined by the Earl of Pembroke, and Edward would be forced to fall back at once.

By the time they reached the river, however, they were thoroughly exhausted. They had marched thirty-six miles without rest, along bad roads and through woods, and were unable to go farther. The queen urged that the river should be crossed, but the leaders of the force were of opinion that it was better to halt. Edward would be able to follow them across the river, and were he to attack them when in disorder, and still further wearied by the operation of making the passage, he would certainly crush them. Moreover, a further retreat would discourage the soldiers, and as a battle must now be fought, it was better to fight where they were, especially as they could choose a strong position. The queen gave way, and the army encamped on a large field in front of the town. The position was well calculated for defence, for the country around was so broken and intercepted with lanes and deep hedges and ditches, that it was extremely difficult of approach.

In the evening Edward came up, his men having also marched some six-and-thirty miles, and encamped for the night within three miles of the Lancastrian position. The queen's troops felt confident of victory. In point of numbers they were superior to their antagonists, and had the advantage of a strong position. Sir Thomas Tresham had, as he proposed, left his wife and son at Exeter when the force marched away.

"Do not be despondent, love," he said to his weeping wife, as he bade her goodbye. "Everything is in our favour, and there is a good hope of a happy termination to this long struggle. But, win or lose, be assured it is the last time I will draw my sword. I have proved my fidelity to the House of Lancaster; I have risked life and fortune in their cause; but I feel that I have done my share and more, and whichever way Providence may now decide the issue of the struggle, I will accept it. If we lose, and I come scatheless through the fight, I will ride hither, and we will embark at Plymouth for France, and there live quietly until the time comes when Edward may feel himself seated with sufficient firmness on the throne to forgive past offences and to grant an amnesty to all who have fought against him. In any other case, dear, you know my wishes, and I bid you carry them out within twenty-four hours of your receiving news of a defeat, without waiting longer for my appearance."

As soon as it was light, Edward advanced to the attack. The Duke of Gloucester was in command of the vanguard. He himself led the centre, while the rear was commanded by the Marquis of Dorset and Lord Hastings. The most advanced division of Lancastrians was commanded by the Duke of Somerset and his brother. The Grand Prior of the Order of St. John and Lord Wenlock were stationed in the centre, the Earl of Devon with the reserve. Refreshed by their rest, the queen's troops were in good spirits. While awaiting the attack, she and the prince rode among the ranks, encouraging the men with fiery speeches, and promising large rewards to all in case of victory.

Gloucester made his advance with great difficulty. The obstacles to his progress were so many and serious that his division was brought to a halt before it came into contact with the defenders. He therefore brought up his artillery and opened a heavy cannonade upon Somerset's position, supporting his guns with flights of arrows, and inflicting such heavy loss upon him that the duke felt compelled to take the offensive.

Having foreseen that he might be obliged to do so, he had, early in the morning, carefully examined the ground in front of him, and had found some lanes by which he could make a flank attack on the enemy. Moving his force down these lanes, where the trees and hedges completely hid his advance from the Yorkists, he fell suddenly upon Edward's centre, which, taken by surprise at the unexpected attack, was driven in confusion up the hill behind it. Somerset was quick to take advantage of his success, and wheeling his men round fell upon the Duke of Gloucester's division, and was equally successful in his attack upon it. Had the centre, under Lord Wenlock, moved forward at once to his support, the victory would have been assured; but Wenlock lay inactive, and Somerset was now engaged in conflict with the whole of Edward's force. But even under these circumstances he still gained ground, when suddenly the whole aspect of the battle was changed.

Before it began Edward had sent two hundred spearmen to watch a wood near the defenders' lines, as he thought that the Lancastrians might place a force there to take him in flank as he attacked their front. He ordered them, if they found the wood unoccupied, to join in the fight as opportunity might offer. The wood was unoccupied, and the spearmen, seeing the two divisions of their army driven backwards, and being thereby cut off from their friends, issued from the wood and, charging down in a body, fell suddenly upon Somerset's rear.

Astounded and confused by an attack from such a quarter, and believing that it was an act of treachery by one of their own commanders, Somerset's men, who had hitherto been fighting with the greatest bravery, fell into confusion. Edward's quick eye soon grasped the opportunity, and rallying his troops he charged impetuously down upon the Lancastrians, seconded hotly by Gloucester and his division.

The disorder in Somerset's lines speedily grew into a panic, and the division broke up and fled through the lanes to the right and left. Somerset, after in vain trying to stop the panic, rode furiously back into the camp, followed by his principal officers, and riding up to Lord Wenlock he cleft his head in two with a battleaxe. His resentment, although justified by the inactivity of this nobleman at such a crisis, was yet disastrous, as it left the centre without a leader, and threw it into a state of disorganization, as many must have supposed that Somerset had turned traitor and gone over to the enemy. Before any disposition could be made, Edward and Gloucester poured their forces into the camp, and the Lancastrians at once broke and fled. Many of their leaders took refuge in the church, an asylum which they deemed inviolable, and which the Lancastrians had honourably respected in their hour of triumph.

Among them were the Duke of Somerset, the Grand Prior of the Order of St. John, Sir Humphrey Audely, Sir Gervis of Clifton, Sir William Gainsby, Sir William Cary, Sir Henry Rose, Sir Thomas Tresham, and seven esquires. Margaret of Anjou fell into the hands of the victors. As to the fate of the young prince, accounts differ. Some authorities say that he was overtaken and slain on the field, but the majority related that he was captured and taken before Edward, who asked him, "What brought you to England?" On his replying boldly, "My father's crown and mine own inheritance," Edward struck him in the mouth with his gauntlet, and his attendants, or some say his brothers, at once despatched the youth with their swords.

The king, with Gloucester and Clarence, then went to the church at Tewkesbury, where the knights had taken refuge, burst open the doors, and entered it. A priest, bearing the holy vessels, threw himself before the king, and would not move until he promised to pardon all who had taken sanctuary there. The king then retired, and trusting in the royal word, the gentlemen made no attempt to escape, although it is said that they could easily have done so. Two days later a party of soldiers by the king's orders broke into the church, dragged them from the foot of the altar, and beheaded them outside.

The news of the issue of the fatal battle of Tewkesbury, the capture of the queen, and the death of the prince, was borne to Exeter by fugitives on the following day. Beyond the fact that the Earl of Devon and other nobles were known to have been killed, and Somerset with a party of knights had taken sanctuary, they could give no details as to the fate of individuals. In the deepest distress at the utter ruin of the cause, and in ignorance of the fate of her husband, who she could only hope was one of those who had gained sanctuary, Dame Tresham prepared for flight. This accomplished, she had only to wait, and sit in tearless anguish at the window, listening intently whenever a horseman rode past. All night her watch continued. Gervaise, who had cried himself to sleep, lay on a couch beside her. Morning dawned, and she then knew that her husband would not come, for had he escaped from the field he would long ere this have been with her. The messenger with the news had arrived at eight the previous morning, and, faithful to her husband's wishes, at that hour she ordered the horses to be brought round, and, joining a party of gentlemen who were also making for the coast, rode with them to Plymouth. Arrangements were at once made with the captain of a small ship in the port, and two days later they landed at Honfleur, where Sir Thomas had enjoined his wife to wait until she heard from him or obtained sure news of his fate.

A week after her arrival the news was brought by other fugitives of the violation of the sanctuary by the king, and the murder of Somerset and the gentlemen with him, of whom Sir Thomas Tresham was known to have been one.

The blow proved fatal to Dame Tresham. She had gone through many trials and misfortunes, and had ever borne them bravely, but the loss of her husband completely broke her down. Save to see his wishes concerning their son carried out, she had no longer any interest in life or any wish to live. But until the future of Gervaise was assured, her mission was unfulfilled. His education was her sole care; his mornings were spent at a monastery, where the monks instructed the sons of such of the nobles and gentry of the neighbourhood as cared that they should be able to read and write. In the afternoon he had the best masters in the town in military exercises. His evenings he spent with his mother, who strove to instill in him the virtues of patience, mercy to the vanquished, and valour, by stories of the great characters of history. She herself spent her days in pious exercises, in attending the services of the Church, and in acts of charity and kindness to her poorer neighbours. But her strength failed rapidly, and she was but a shadow of her former self when, two years and a half after her arrival at Honfleur, she felt that if she was herself to hand Gervaise over to the Order of St. John, she must no longer delay. Accordingly she took ship to London, and landing there made her way with him to the dwelling of the Order at Clerkenwell. It was in process of rebuilding, for in 1381 it had been first plundered and then burned by the insurgents under Wat Tyler. During the ninety years that had elapsed since that event the work of rebuilding had proceeded steadily, each grand prior making additions to the pile which, although not yet fully completed, was already one of the grandest and stateliest abodes in England.

On inquiring for the grand prior, and stating that she had a letter of importance for him, Dame Tresham and her son were shown up to his apartment, and on entering were kindly and courteously received by him when informed that she was the widow of the late Sir Thomas Tresham.

"I am the bearer of a letter for you, given into my hand by my husband's dear friend your predecessor," she said, "a few days before his murder at Tewkesbury. It relates to my son here."

The grand prior opened the letter and read it.

"Assuredly, madam, I will carry out the wishes here expressed," he said. "They are, that I should forward at once the letter he has given you to Sir Peter D'Aubusson, and that until an answer is received from him, I should take care of the boy here, and see that he is instructed in all that is needful for a future knight of our Order. I grieve to see that you yourself are looking so ill."

"My course is well nigh run," she said. "I have, methinks, but a few days to live. I am thankful that it has been permitted to me to carry out my husband's wishes, and to place my boy in your hands. That done, my work on earth is finished, and glad indeed am I that the time is at hand when I can rejoin my dear husband."

"We have a building here where we can lodge ladies in distress or need, Dame Tresham, and trust that you will take up your abode there."

"I shall indeed be thankful to do so," she replied. "I know no one in London, and few would care to lodge a dying woman."

"We are Hospitallers," the grand prior said. "That was our sole mission when we were first founded, and before we became a military order, and it is still a part of our sworn duty to aid the distressed."

A few minutes later Dame Tresham was conducted to a comfortable apartment, and was given into the charge of a female attendant. The next day she had another interview with the grand prior, to whom she handed over her jewels and remaining money. This she prayed him to devote to the furnishing of the necessary outfit for Gervaise. She spent the rest of the day in the church of the hospital, had a long talk with her son in the evening, giving him her last charges as to his future life and conduct, and that night, as if she had now fulfilled her last duty on earth, she passed away, and was found by her attendant lying with a look of joy and peacefulness on her dead face.

Gervaise's grief was for a time excessive. He was nearly twelve years old, and had never until now been separated from her even for a day. She had often spoken to him of her end being near, but until the blow came he had never quite understood that it could be so. She had, on the night before her death, told him that he must not grieve overmuch for her, for that in any case they must have soon been sundered, and that it was far better that he should think of her as at rest, and happy, than as leading a lonely and sorrowful life.

The grand prior, however, wisely gave him but little time to dwell upon his loss, but as soon as her funeral had taken place, handed him over to the knights who had the charge of the novices on probation, and instructed them in their military exercises, and of the chaplain who taught them such learning as was considered requisite for a knight of the Order.

The knights were surprised at the proficiency the lad had already attained in the use of his weapons.

"By St. Agatha," one of them exclaimed, after the conclusion of his first lesson, "you have had good teachers, lad, and have availed yourself rarely of them. If you go on like this you will become a distinguished knight of our Order. With a few more years to strengthen your arms I warrant me you will bear your part well in your first tussle with the Moslem corsairs."

It fortunately happened that a party of knights were starting for Rhodes a few days after the admission of Gervaise to the Hospital, and the letter to Sir Peter D'Aubusson was committed to their charge. They were to proceed to Bordeaux by ship, then to journey by land to Marseilles, and thence, being joined by some French knights, to sail direct to Rhodes. Two months later an answer was received. D'Aubusson wrote to the grand prior saying that he would gladly carry out the last wishes of his dead friend, and that he had already obtained from the grand master the appointment of Gervaise Tresham as one of his pages, and begged that he might be sent out with the next party of knights leaving England. It was three months before such an opportunity occurred. During that time Gervaise remained at the house of St. John's studying diligently, and continuing his military exercises. These were severe; for the scions of noble houses, who hoped some day to distinguish themselves as knights, were put through many gymnastic exercises-were taught to spring on to a horse when clad in full armour, to wield heavy battleaxes, to run and climb, and to prepare themselves for all the possibilities of the mode of fighting of the day.

Gervaise gained the encomiums, not only of his special preceptor, but of the various knights in the house, and of the grand prior himself, both for his strength and activity, and for the earnestness with which he worked. When the time approached for his leaving England, the grand prior ordered for him the outfit which would be necessary in his position as a page of the grand master. The dresses were numerous and rich, for although the knights of St. John wore over their armour the simple mantle of their order, which was a sleeveless garment of black relieved only by a white cross on the chest, they indulged in the finest and most costly armour, and in rich garments beneath their black mantles when not in armour.

"I am well pleased with you, Gervaise," the grand prior said, on the evening before he was to leave, "and I see in you the making of a valiant knight of the Order. Maintain the same spirit you have shown here; be obedient and reverent to your superiors; give your whole mind to your duties; strive earnestly during the three or four years that your pagedom will last, to perfect yourself in military exercises, that when the time comes for you to buckle on armour you will be able to bear yourself worthily. Remember that you will have to win your knighthood, for the

Order does not bestow this honour, and you must remain a professed knight until you receive it at the hands of some distinguished warrior. Ever bear in mind that you are a soldier of the Cross. Avoid luxury, live simply and modestly; be not led away by others, upon whom their vows may sit but lightly; keep ever in your mind that you have joined the Order neither to gain fame nor personal advantage, but simply that you may devote the strength and the intelligence that God has given you to protect Christendom from the advance of the infidel. I shall hear of you from time to time from D'Aubusson, and feel sure that the expectations I have formed of you will be fulfilled."

Chapter III
The Grand Master's Page

The grand prior had, in accordance with Dame Tresham's request, sent the steward of the house to one of the principal jewellers of the city who, as the Order were excellent customers, paid a good price for her jewels. After the payment for the numerous dresses required for the service as a page to the grand master, the grand prior handed the balance of the money Dame Tresham had brought with her, and that obtained by the sale of her jewels, to one of the knights under whose charge Gervaise was to travel, to be given by him to D'Aubusson for the necessities of Gervaise as a page. During their term of service the pages received no remuneration, all their expenses being paid by their families. Nevertheless, the post was considered so honourable, and of such great advantage to those entering the Order, that the appointments were eagerly sought after.

The head of the party was Sir Guy Redcar, who had been a commander in England, but who was now relinquishing that post in order to take a high office in the convent at the Island. With him were four lads between seventeen and twenty who were going out as professed knights, having served their year of probation as novices at the grand priory. With these Gervaise was already acquainted, as they had lived, studied, and performed their military exercises together. The three eldest of these Gervaise liked much, but the youngest of the party, Robert Rivers, a relation of the queen, had always shown a very different spirit from the others. He was jealous that a member of one of the defeated and disinherited Lancastrian families should obtain a post of such honour and advantage as that of page to the grand master, and that thus, although five years younger, Gervaise should enter the Order on an equality with him.

In point of strength and stature he was, of course, greatly superior to Gervaise; but he had been spoilt from his childhood, was averse to exercise, and dull at learning, and while Gervaise was frequently commended by his instructors, he himself was constantly reproved, and it had been more than once a question whether he should be received as a professed knight at the termination of his year of novitiate. Thus, while the other lads treated Gervaise kindly, and indeed made rather a pet of him, Robert Rivers ignored him as much as possible, and if obliged to speak to him did so with a pointed rudeness that more than once brought upon him a sharp reproof from his companions. Gervaise himself was but little affected by Robert's manner. He was of an exceptionally good tempered nature, and, indeed, was so occupied with his work and so anxious to satisfy his teachers, that Robert's ill humour passed almost unnoticed.

The journey was performed without incident. During their passage across the south of France, Gervaise's perfect knowledge of the language gained for him a great advantage over his companions, and enabled him to be of much use to Sir Guy. They had fine weather during their passage up the Mediterranean, and in the day their leader gave them their first lessons in the management and discipline of a ship.

"You will be nearly as much at sea as you are on land for the five years you must stay at the convent," he said; "and it is essential to the education of a knight of our Order to know all things connected with the management of a ship, even to its building. We construct our own galleys at Rhodes, using, of course, the labour of slaves, but under our own superintendence; and it is even more essential to us to know how to fight on sea than on land. There is, too, you see, a rivalry among ourselves, for each langue has its duties, and each strives to perform more gallant deeds and to bring in more rich prizes than the others. We of England are among the smallest of the langues, and yet methinks we do a fair portion of the work, and gain fully our share of honour. There is no fear of your having much time on your hands, for it is quite certain that there will soon be open war between Mahomet and the Order. In spite of the nominal truce, constant skirmishes are taking place, so that, in addition to our fights with pirates, we have sometimes encounters with the sultan's galleys.

"Seven years ago, a number of our Order took part in the defence of Lesbos, and lost their lives at its capture, and we have sure information that Mahomet is preparing for an attack on the Island. No doubt he thinks it will be an easy conquest, for in '57 he succeeded in landing eighteen thousand men on the Island, and in ravaging a large district, carrying off much booty. Since then, however, the defences of Rhodes have been greatly strengthened. Zacosta, our last grand master, laboured diligently to increase the fortifications, and, specially, built on one side of the entrance to the harbour a strong tower, called Fort St. Nicholas. Orsini has carried on the works, which have been directed by D'Aubusson, who is captain general of the forces of the Island, and who has deepened the ditches and built a wall on the sea front of the town six hundred feet in length and twenty feet in height, money being found by the grand master from his private purse.

"At present we are not sure whether the great armament that Mahomet is preparing is intended for the capture of Negropont, which belongs to Venice, or of Rhodes. Unfortunately Venice and Rhodes are not good friends. In the course of our war with Egypt in '58 we captured from some Venetian vessels, in which they were travelling, several Egyptian merchants with a great store of goods. The Venetians protested that as the ships were theirs we had no right to interfere with our enemies who were travelling in them, and, without giving time for the question to be discussed, at once attacked our galleys, and sent a fleet against Rhodes. They landed on the Island, and not only pillaged the district of Halki, but, a number of natives having sought shelter in a cave, the Venetians blocked up the entrance with brushwood, set it on fire, and suffocated them all.

"Shortly afterwards, another and larger fleet appeared off Rhodes, and demanded the restitution of the Egyptians and their merchandise. There was a great division of opinion in the council; but, seeing the great danger that threatened us both from the Turks at Constantinople and the Venetians, and that it was madness at such a time to engage in war with a Christian power, the grand master persuaded the council to accede to their request. There has never been any friendly feeling between Venice and ourselves since that time. Still, I trust that our common danger will reunite us, and that whether Negropont or Rhodes is attacked by the Moslems, we shall render loyal aid to each other."

There was great excitement among Gervaise and his companions when it was announced that Rhodes was in sight, and as they approached the town they gazed with admiration at the castle with its stately buildings, the palace of the grand master and the Hospital of St. John, rising above the lower town, the massive walls strengthened by projecting bastions, and the fortifications of the ports. Of these there were two, with separate entrances, divided from each other by a narrow tongue of land. At its extremity stood Fort St. Nicholas, which was connected by a strong wall running along the promontory to the town. The inner port, as it was called, was of greater importance, as it adjoined the town itself. It was defended in the first place by Fort St. Nicholas, and at the inner entrance stood the towers of St. John and St. Michael, one on either side. Into this the vessel was steered. There were many craft lying there, among them eight or ten of the galleys of the Order.

"We will go first to the house of our langue," Sir Guy said, "and tell them to send down slaves to fetch up our baggage; then I will take you, Gervaise, to Sir Peter D'Aubusson, and hand you over to his care."

On landing, Gervaise was surprised at the number of slaves who were labouring at the public works, and who formed no small proportion of the population in the streets. Their condition was pitiable. They were, of course, enemies of Christianity, and numbers of them had been pirates; but he could not help pitying their condition as they worked in the full heat of the sun under the vigilant eyes of numbers of overseers, who carried heavy whips, in addition to their arms. Their progress to the upper city was slow, for on their way they met many knights, of whom several were acquainted with Sir Guy; and each, after greeting him, demanded the latest news from England, and in return gave him particulars of the state of things at Rhodes.

At last they arrived at the house of the English langue. The Order was divided into langues or nationalities. Of these there were eight-Provence, Auvergne, France, Italy, Germany, England, Aragon, and Castile and Portugal. The French element was by far the strongest. The Order had been founded in that country, and as it possessed no less than three langues, and held the greater part of the high official positions in the Order, it was only kept in check by the other langues acting together to demand their fair share of dignities. The grand master's authority was considerable, but it was checked by the council, which was composed of the bailiffs and knights of the highest order, known as Grand Crosses. Each langue had its bailiff elected by itself: these resided constantly at Rhodes. Each of these bailiffs held a high office; thus the Bailiff of Provence was always the grand commander of the Order. He controlled the expenditure, superintended the stores, and was governor of the arsenal. The Bailiff of Auvergne was the commander-in-chief of all the forces, army and navy. The Bailiff of France was the grand hospitaller, with the supreme direction of the hospitals and infirmaries of the Order, a hospital in those days signifying a guest house. The Bailiff of Italy was the grand admiral, and the Bailiff of England was chief of the light cavalry. Thus the difficulties and jealousies that would have arisen at every vacancy were avoided.

In the early days of the Order, when Jerusalem was in the hands of the Christians, the care of the hospitals was its chief and most important function. Innumerable pilgrims visited Jerusalem, and these were entertained at the immense guest house of the Order. But with the loss of Jerusalem and the expulsion of the Christians from Palestine, that function had become of very secondary importance although there was still a guest house and infirmary at Rhodes, where strangers and the sick were carefully attended by the knights. No longer did these ride out to battle on their war horses. It was on the sea that the foe was to be met, and the knights were now sailors rather than soldiers. They dwelt at the houses of their respective langues; here they ate at a common table, which was supplied by the bailiff, who drew rations for each knight, and received, in addition, a yearly sum for the supply of such luxuries as were not included in the rations. The average number of knights residing in each of these langues averaged from a hundred to a hundred and fifty.

It was not until some hours after his arrival that Sir Guy could find time to take Gervaise across to the house of the langue of Auvergne, to which D'Aubusson belonged. It was a larger and more stately pile than that of the English langue, but the arrangements were similar in all these buildings. In the English house Gervaise had not felt strange, as he had the companionship of his fellow voyagers; but as he followed Sir Guy through the spacious halls of the langue of Auvergne, where no familiar face met his, he felt more lonely than he had done since he entered the house at Clerkenwell.

On sending in his name Sir Guy was at once conducted to the chamber occupied by D'Aubusson. The knight was seated at his table, examining some plans. The room was furnished with monastic simplicity, save that the walls were hung with rich silks and curtains captured from Turkish galleys.

"Welcome back to us, Sir Guy," D'Aubusson said, rising, and warmly shaking his visitor's hand. "I have been looking for your coming, for we need men with clear heads. Of strong arms and valiant spirits we have no lack; but men of judgment and discretion, who can be trusted to look at matters calmly and not to be carried away by passion, are welcome indeed to us. I was expecting you about this time, and when I heard that a ship had arrived from Marseilles I made inquiries, and was glad to find that you were on board."

"I am heartily glad to be back, D'Aubusson; I am sick of the dull life of a commandery, and rejoice at the prospect of stirring times again. This lad is young Tresham, who has come out in my charge, and for whom you have been good enough to obtain the post of page to the grand master."

"And no slight business was it to do so," D'Aubusson said with a smile. "It happened there was a vacancy when the letter concerning him arrived, and had it been one of the highest offices in the Order there could not have been a keener contention for it. Every bailiff had his candidate ready; but I seldom ask for anything for members of my langue, and when I told the other bailiffs that it was to me a matter of honour to carry out the last request of my dead friend, they all gave way. You see, I am placed in a position of some little difficulty. The grand master is so enfeebled and crippled that he leaves matters almost entirely in my hands, and it would be an abuse of my position, and would excite no little jealousy, were I to use the power I possess to nominate friends of my own to appointments. It is only by the most rigid impartiality, and by dividing as fairly as possible all offices between the eight langues, that all continue to give me their support. As you know, we have had great difficulties and heartburnings here; but happily they have to a great extent been set at rest by forming a new langue of Castile and Portugal out of that of Aragon. This has given one more vote to the smaller langues, and has so balanced the power that of late the jealousies between us have greatly subsided, and all are working well together in face of the common danger. Well, young sir, and how like you the prospect of your pageship?"

"I like it greatly, sir, but shall like still more the time when I can buckle on armour and take a share of the fighting with the infidels. I would fain, sir, offer to you my deep and humble thanks for the great kindness you have shown me in procuring me the appointment of page to the grand master."

The knight smiled kindly. "There are the less thanks due, lad, inasmuch as I did it not for you, but for the dear friend who wrote to me on your behalf. However, I trust that you will do credit to my nomination by your conduct here."

"There is a letter from our grand prior which I have brought to you," Sir Guy said. "He commended the lad to me warmly, and seems to be greatly pleased with his conduct."

D'Aubusson cut the silken string that bound the missive together, and read the letter.

"He does indeed speak warmly," he said, as he laid it down on the table.

"He tells me that the lad, young as he was, had been well trained when he came, and that he worked with great diligence during the five months he was in the House, and displayed such skill and strength for his age, as to surprise his preceptors, who prophesied that he would turn out a stout swordsman, and would be a credit to the Order."

"He is well furnished with garments both for ordinary and state occasions," Sir Guy said; "and in this packet are some sixty gold crowns, which are the last remains of his patrimony, and which I was to hand to you in order to pay the necessary expenses during his pageship."

"He could have done without that," D'Aubusson said. "Recommended to me as he is, I would have seen that he lacked nothing, but was provided with all necessaries for his position. I will in the future take care that in all things he is on a par with his companions." He touched a bell on the table, and a servitor entered.

"Tell Richard de Deauville to come here," he said.

A minute later the hangings at the door were pushed aside, and a lad about a year older than Gervaise appeared, and, bowing deeply to the knight, stood in a respectful attitude, awaiting his orders.

"Deauville, take this youth, Gervaise Tresham to your room. He is appointed one of the pages of the grand master. He is English, but he speaks French as well as you do, having lived in France for some years. Take him to your apartment and treat him kindly and well, seeing that he is a stranger and new to all here. Tomorrow he will go to the palace."

Gervaise bowed deeply to the two knights, and then followed the page.

"I suppose you arrived in that ship which came in today," the latter said, as soon as they had left the room. "You are in luck indeed to have obtained a pageship at the grand master's. You begin to count your time at once, while we do not begin to count ours until we are seventeen. Still, good luck may befall us yet, for if the grand master dies, Sir Peter is sure to be chosen to succeed him. Then, you see, we too shall be pages of the grand master."

"How many are there of you?"

"Only De Lille and myself. Of course D'Aubusson will take on the grand master's present pages; but as there are five vacancies on an average every year, he will be able to find room for us among the number."

"Why, how many pages has the grand master?" Gervaise asked, in surprise.

"Sixteen of them, so you may guess the duties are easy enough, as only two are generally employed, except, of course on solemn occasions."

"Are there any other English besides myself?"

The boy shook his head. "There are eight belonging to the French langues; the others are Spaniards, Italians, or Germans. There, this is our room and this is De Lille. De Lille, this is the grand master's new page, Master Gervaise Tresham, and our lord says we are to treat him kindly and entertain him well until tomorrow, when he will go to the palace. He speaks our language, and has been some years in France."

"How came you to be there?" De Lille asked Gervaise.

"My father was a Lancastrian, and my mother a great friend of our Queen Margaret of Anjou, and they were with her all the time she was in exile."

"How quarrelsome you English are!" De Lille said. "You seem to be always fighting among yourselves."

"I don't think," Gervaise said, with a smile, "there is any love lost between Louis of France and the Duke of Burgundy, to say nothing of other great lords."

"No; you are right there. But though we talk a great deal about fighting, it is only occasionally that we engage in it."

The pages' room was a small one. It contained two pallets, which served as seats by day, and two wooden chests, in which they kept their clothes.

Their conversation was interrupted by the ringing of a bell.

"That is supper," De Lille said, jumping up. "We will leave you here while we go down to stand behind our lord's chair. When the meal is over we will bring a pasty or something else good, and a measure of wine, and have our supper together up here; and we will tell the servitors to bring up another pallet for you. Of course, you can go down with us if you like."

"Thank you, I would much rather stay here. Every one would be strange to me, and having nothing to do I should feel in the way."

The boys nodded, and taking their caps ran off, while Gervaise, tired by the excitement of the day, lay down on the bed which a servant brought up a few minutes after they had left him, and slept soundly until their return.

"I think I have been asleep," he said, starting up when they entered the room again.

"You look as if you had, anyhow," De Lille laughed. "It was the best thing you could do. We have brought up supper. We generally sit down and eat after the knights have done, but this is much better, as you are here." They sat down on the beds, carved the pasty with their daggers, and after they had finished Gervaise gladly accepted the proposal of the others to take a walk round the walls.

They started from the corner of the castle looking down upon the spit of land dividing the two ports.

"You see," De Lille said, "there is a row of small islands across the mouth of the outer port, and the guns of St. Nicholas, and those on this wall, would prevent any hostile fleet from entering."

"I hardly see what use that port is, for it lies altogether outside the town, and vessels could not unload there."

"No. Still, it forms a useful place of refuge. In case a great fleet came to attack us, our galleys would lay up in the inner port, which would be cleared of all the merchant craft, as these would hamper the defence; they would, therefore, be sent round into the outer port, where they would be safe from any attack by sea, although they would doubtless be burnt did an army besiege the town."

Passing along the walls of the grand master's palace, which was a strongly fortified building, and formed a citadel that could be defended after the lower town and the rest of the castle had been taken, they came to the western angle of the fortifications.

"You must know that each langue has charge of a separate part of the wall. From the foot of the mole of St. Nicholas to the grand master's palace it is in charge of France. On the line where we now are, between the palace and the gate of St. George, it is held by Germany. From that gate to the Spanish tower Auvergne is posted. England takes the wall between the Spanish tower and that of St. Mary. You defend only the lower storey of that tower, the upper part being held by Aragon, whose charge extends up to the gate of St. John. Thence to the tower of Italy-behind which lies the Jews' quarter-Provence is in charge, while the sea front thence to the mole of St. Nicholas, is held by Italy and Castile, each taking half. Not only have the langues the charge of defending each its portion of the wall, but of keeping it in order at all times; and I may say that nowhere is the wall better kept or more fairly decorated with carvings than where England holds."

"You have not told me who defends the palace itself."

"That is in charge of a force composed of equal numbers of picked knights from each langue."

Gervaise leant on the battlement and looked with admiration at the scene beyond. The land side was surrounded by hills, the ground rising very gradually from the foot of the walls. Every yard of ground was cultivated, and was covered with brilliant vegetation. Groves and orchards occurred thickly, while the slopes were dotted with chapels, summer houses-in which the natives of the city spent most of their time in the hot season-and other rustic buildings.

"What a rich and beautiful country!" he said.

"It is very pleasant to look at," De Lille agreed. "But all this would be a sore disadvantage to us if the Turks were besieging us, for the groves and orchards would conceal their approaches, the walls and buildings would give them shelter, and our cannon would be of little use until they reached the farther side of the ditch. If the Turks come, I hear it is decided to level all the buildings and walls, and to chop down every tree."

"If they were to plant their cannon on the hills they would do us much harm," Gervaise remarked.

"The Turks are clumsy gunners they say," Deauville replied, "and they would but waste their powder and ball at that distance, without making a breach in our walls."

"Even if they did, they could surely scarce pass that deep fosse," Gervaise said, looking down into the tremendous cutting in the solid rock that ran round the whole circuit of the walls; it was from forty to sixty feet deep, and from ninety to a hundred and forty feet wide. It was from this great cutting that the stones for the construction of the walls, towers, and buildings of the town had been taken, the work having been going on ever since the knights established themselves at Rhodes, and being performed by a host of captives taken in war, together with labour hired from neighboring islands. Upon this immense work the Order had expended no small proportion of their revenue since their capture of the island in 1310, and the result was a fortress that, under the conditions of warfare of that age, seemed almost impregnable; and this without any natural advantage of position.

In addition to the five great towers or bastions, the wall was strengthened by square towers at short intervals. On looking down from the wall upon which the three pages were standing, on to the lower town, the view was a singular one. The houses were all built of stone, with flat roofs, after the manner of most Eastern cities. The streets were very narrow, and were crossed at frequent intervals by broad stone arches. These had the effect, not only of giving shelter from an enemy's fire, but of affording means by which troops could march rapidly across the town upon the roofs of the houses to reinforce the defenders of the wall, wherever pressed by the enemy. Thus the town from above presented the appearance of a great pavement, broken only by dark and frequently interrupted lines.

"How different to the towns at home!" Gervaise exclaimed, as, after gazing long upon the beautiful country outside the walls, he turned and looked inward. "One would hardly know that it was a town at all."

"Yes, it is rather different to the view from the top of the tower of Notre Dame, which I ascended while I was staying in Paris. But this sort of building is best here; the thickness of the stone roofs keeps out the heat of the sun, and it is only when it is almost overhead that it shines down into the narrow streets. As you can see by the number of the people on the roofs, they use them as a resort in the evening. Then carpets are spread, and they receive visitors, and can talk to their neighbours over the low walls that separate the roofs. You can trace the divisions. Some of the house roofs are larger than others, but all are upon the same level; this being the regulation, in order that there might be free passage everywhere for the troops."

By the time they had made the circuit of the walls darkness had fallen, and concealed the martial features of the scene. Lights twinkled everywhere upon the stone terraces; the sound of lutes and other musical instruments came up softly on the still air, with the hum of talk and laughter. The sea lay as smooth as a mirror, and reflected the light of the stars, and the black hulls of the galleys and ships in the harbour lay still and motionless.

Greatly pleased with his first experience of the city that was to be his future home, Gervaise returned, with his companions, to the auberge of Auvergne.

The next morning the bailiff D'Aubusson bade Gervaise accompany him to the palace of the grand master. Here he introduced him to Orsini, an old and feeble man, who, after a few kind words, handed him over to the chamberlain, who, in turn, led him to the official who was in charge of the pages. That officer took him down to the courtyard, where four young knights were engaged in superintending the military exercises of the pages. The scene was exactly the same as that to which Gervaise had been accustomed at the House in London. Some of the lads were fighting with blunted swords, others were swinging heavy bars of iron, climbing ropes, or vaulting on to the back of a wooden horse. All paused as the official entered with his charge.

"This is your new comrade, boys," he said —"Master Gervaise Tresham, a member of the English langue. Be good comrades to him. By the reports I hear I am sure that you will find him a worthy companion."

The pages had been prepared to like the newcomer, for it was well known that he owed his appointment to the bailiff of Auvergne, who was the most popular of the officials of the Order, and who was already regarded as the grand master. His appearance confirmed their anticipation. His fair complexion and nut brown hair tinged with gold, cut somewhat short, but with a natural wave, contrasted with their darker locks and faces bronzed by the sun. There was an honest and frank look in his grey eyes, and an expression of good temper on his face, though the square chin and firm lips spoke of earnestness and resolution of purpose. The official took him round the circle and presented him first to the knights and then to each of his comrades.

"You may as well join them in their exercises. In that way you will sooner become at home with them."

Gervaise at once laid down his mantle, removed his doublet, and then joined the others. There was but one half hour remaining before they broke off to go to dinner, which was at half past ten, but the time sufficed to show the young pages that this English lad was the equal of all-except two or three of the oldest-both in strength and in knowledge of arms. He could climb the rope with any of them, could vault on to the wooden horse with a heavy cuirass and backpiece on him, and held his own in a bout with swords against Conrad von Berghoff, who was considered the best swordplayer among them. As soon as the exercises were over all proceeded to the bath, and then to dinner. The meal was a simple one, but Gervaise enjoyed it thoroughly, for the table was loaded with an abundance of fruits of kinds altogether novel to him, and which he found delicious.

The official in charge of them sat at the head of the table, and the meal was eaten in silence. After it was over and they had retired to their own rooms discipline was at an end, and they were free to amuse themselves as they liked. There were many questions to be asked and answered, but his display of strength and skill in the courtyard saved Gervaise from a good deal of the teasing to which a newcomer among a party of boys is always exposed.

He, on his part, learnt that the duties of the pages were very light. Two only were on duty each day, being in constant attendance on the grand master, and accompanying him wherever he went. When he dined in public four of them waited on him at table, and one of them performed the duties of taster. If he returned to the palace after dark, six others lined the staircase with torches. On occasions of state ceremony, and at the numerous religious festivals, all were in attendance. By this time Gervaise's trunks had been brought over from the English auberge, where they had been conveyed from the ship, and his garments were taken out and inspected by his comrades, who all admitted that they were, in point of beauty of colour and material, and in fashion, equal to their own.

"You will have to get one more suit, Gervaise," one of the lads said. "At one or two of the grand ceremonies every year we are all dressed alike; that is the rule. On other occasions we wear what we choose, so that our garments are handsome, and I think it looks a good deal better than when we are dressed alike; though no doubt in religious processions that is more appropriate. De Ribaumont, our governor, will give orders for the supply of your state costume. He is a good fellow. Of course, he has to be rather strict with us; but so long as there is nothing done that he considers discreditable to our position, he lets us do pretty nearly as we like.

"We have four hours a day at our military exercises, and two hours with the sub-chaplain, who teaches us our books and religious duties. The rest of our time we can use as we like, except that every day eight of us ride for two hours and practise with the lance; for although it is at sea we fight the Moslems, we are expected to become finished knights in all matters. These eight horses are kept for our service, and such as choose may at other times ride them. On Saturdays we are free from all our exercises; then some of us generally go on horseback for long excursions on the island, while others take boats and go out on the sea; one afternoon in the week we all make a trip in a galley, to learn our duties on board."

Chapter IV
A Professed Knight

Gervaise was soon quite at home in the palace of the grand master, and his companions were, like other boys, of varying characters; but as all were of noble families, were strongly impressed with the importance of the Order and the honour of their own position, and were constantly in contact with stately knights and grave officials, their manners conformed to those of their elders; and even among themselves there was no rough fun, or loud disputes, but a certain courtesy of manner that was in accordance with their surroundings. This came naturally to Gervaise, brought up as he had been by his father and mother, and having at frequent intervals stayed with them for months at the various royal castles in which Margaret of Anjou and her son had been assigned apartments during their exile. Even at St. John's house the novices with whom he lived were all a good deal older than himself, and the discipline of the house was much more strict than that at Rhodes.

He enjoyed both his exercises with the knights and the time spent with the sub-chaplain, no small proportion of the hours of study being occupied in listening to stories of chivalry; it being considered one of the most important parts of a knight's education that he should have a thorough acquaintance, not only with the laws of chivalry, but with the brave deeds both of former and of living knights, with the relations of the noble houses of Europe to each other, especially of the many great families whose members were connected with the Order of St. John.

These matters formed, indeed, the main subject of their studies. All were taught to read and write, but this was considered sufficient in the way of actual instruction. The rules of the Order had to be committed to memory. Beyond this their reading consisted largely of the lives of saints, especially of those who distinguished themselves by their charity or their devotion to their vows of poverty, to both of which the members of the Order were pledged. Gervaise, however, could see around him no signs whatever of poverty on their part. It was true that they all lived and fed together in the auberges of their respective langues, and that they possessed no houses or establishments of their own; but the magnificence of their armour and attire, and the lavish expenditure of some upon their pleasures, contrasted strangely with the poverty to which they had vowed themselves. It was true that in many cases the means to support the expenditure was derived from the shares the knights received of the plunder acquired in their captures of Moslem ships; but undoubtedly many must have possessed large private means; the bailiffs, for example, although only required by the rules to place before the knights at their auberges the rations they received for them, with such luxuries as could be purchased by their yearly allowance for that purpose, expended annually very large sums in addition, and supplied their tables with every dainty, in order to gain popularity and goodwill among the members of the langue.

Not only did the post of bailiff confer upon its owner a very high position at Rhodes, but it was a stepping stone to the most lucrative offices in their langues. The bailiffs at Rhodes had the right of claiming any of the grand priories or bailiwicks at home that might fall vacant, and the grand master was frequently chosen from among their number, as, by being present at Rhodes, they had many advantages in the way of making themselves popular among the electors. The emoluments of some of these provincial bailiwicks were large; and as the bailiffs at Rhodes were generally elected by seniority-although younger knights who had greatly distinguished themselves were sometimes chosen-they were usually glad to resign the heavy work and responsibility of their position at Rhodes, and to retire to the far easier position of a provincial bailiff. In the majority of cases, doubtless, the fortunes of the high officials were obtained from the money amassed when in possession of rich commanderies at home; but even this was assuredly incompatible with their vows of poverty.

His hours of leisure Gervaise spent either on the water or in the saddle, and his love of exercise of all sorts excited the wonder and even the amusement of his companions, who for the most part preferred spending the time at their disposal in sleep, in idly looking out from a shaded room at what was going on outside, or in visits to friends and relations at the auberges of the langues to which they belonged. The natural consequence was, that by the time he reached the end of his three years' pageship, Gervaise was indisputably superior in strength, activity, and skill in military exercises, to any of his companions. The majority of these, after completing their time, returned to the headquarters of their langue at home, to pass their time there, until of an age to be eligible for the charge of a commandery obtained for them by family influence, which had no small share in the granting of these appointments. As it was known, however, that Gervaise intended to remain permanently in the Island, his progress was watched with particular attention by his instructors; and, seeing his own earnestness in the matter, they took special pains with his training. The bailiff of Auvergne continued to take much interest in him, inquiring often from the officers in charge of the pages, and from his instructors, of his conduct and progress, and occasionally sending for him to his auberge and talking with him as to his life and progress. Just before his pageship terminated, he said to him, "I was rather puzzled at first, Gervaise, as to what we should do with you when your term of office concluded, but I am so no longer, for, although you are some two years younger than the professed knights who come out here, you are better fitted than the majority to take your place in the naval expeditions, and to fight the Moslem pirates. I will see that you have your share of these adventures. All young knights are, as you know, obliged to make three voyages, but beyond that many of them do not care to share in the rough life at sea, and prefer the bustle, and, I grieve to say, the gaiety and pleasures of this city. For one, then, really eager to distinguish himself, the opportunities are frequent. When danger threatens, or heavy engagements are expected, every knight is desirous of bearing his part in the fray; but this is not the case when the work to be done consists of scouring the sea for weeks, without perchance coming across a single pirate. Of course, as soon as your pageship is over you will go to the English auberge, but I shall still keep my eye upon you, and shall do my best to help you to achieve distinction; and I shall take upon myself the providing of your arms and armour as a knight."

Accordingly, on the day on which his duties as a page terminated, two servitors of the auberge of Auvergne brought across to the palace a suit of fine armour and a sword, a battleaxe, a lance, and a dagger; also three complete suits of clothes, two of them for ordinary wear, and one for state occasions. The next day Gervaise took the oaths of the Order in the Church of St. John. The aged master himself received the vows, and formally inducted him as a professed knight of the Order, Peter D'Aubusson and the bailiff of the English langue acting as his sponsors, vouching that he was of noble blood and in all ways fitted to become a knight of Justice, this being the official title of the professed knights of the Order. Ten newly arrived novices were inducted at the same time, and the ceremony was a stately one, attended by a number of the knights from each langue, all in full armour.

The ceremony over, Gervaise bore the title of Sir Gervaise Tresham; but this was an honorary rather than a real title, as the Order did not profess to bestow the honour of knighthood, and it was usual for its members to receive the accolade at the hands of secular knights. At the conclusion of the ceremony, he returned with the bailiff of the English langue to the auberge, and took up his quarters there. By his frequent visits he was well known to all the members, and in a day or two felt as much at home as he had done in the pages' room in the palace. A week was given to him before he was assigned to any special duty, and he was glad when he was told off as one of the knights who were to take their turn in superintending the work of the slaves employed in strengthening the fortifications, although he would rather that any other employment should have been assigned to him, because he felt deep pity for the unfortunate men who were engaged in the work.

He knew well enough that if he himself were ever made prisoner by the Turks, his lot would be as hard and as hopeless as that of the Moslem captives; but this, although he often repeated it to himself in order to abate his feeling of commiseration, was but a poor satisfaction. He saw one side of the picture, and the other was hidden from him; and although he told himself that after slaving in a Turkish galley he would feel a satisfaction at seeing those who had been his tyrants suffering the same fate, he was well aware that this would not be the case, and that his own sufferings would only make him sympathise more deeply with those of others. He had found, soon after his arrival on the Island, that it was best to keep his feelings on this subject to himself. While the knights were bound, in accordance with their vows, to relieve sufferings of any kind among Christians, they seemed to regard their captives rather in the light of brute beasts than human beings. The slaves were struck on the smallest provocation, and even the killing of a slave was considered a very venial offence, and punished only because the slave was of value to the Order.

It was true that edicts were from time to time published by the council, enjoining fair treatment of slaves, and it was specially ordered that those employed as servants in the auberges were not to be struck. The lot of these servants was, indeed, very much easier than that of those engaged on the public works, and such occupation was therefore considered a privilege, the servants being for the most part selected from among the captives of superior rank.

For the next six months Gervaise worked at various duties in the town. He was employed for a fortnight in the infirmary, then for a while he was transferred to the galleys; but for the most part he was with the slaves working on the fortifications. At the end of that time he was, to his great delight, informed by the bailiff that he was one of the six knights of the langue told off to join a galley that was on the point of sailing. Among those going in her was Sir Ralph Harcourt, one of his companions on the journey from England.

"So you are to go with us, Gervaise," the young knight said, "to try your luck for the first time against the infidels. This is my third voyage, and I hope that it will be more fortunate than its predecessors, for, beyond picking up two or three small craft, which did not venture upon resistance, we gained neither honour nor booty. I regard you as having specially good fortune, and besides being glad that we shall be together, I expect that you will bring good luck to us, and that we shall meet with foes worth contending with. The corsairs have been very active of late, and have captured many prizes, while, on the other hand, our galleys have been unfortunate, and have but seldom come upon the miscreants."

"How many knights will there be on board?"

"Forty. Aragon, like us, furnishes five, Germany ten, Portugal five, Auvergne ten, and Provence five. We shall be commanded by Sir Louis Ricord, a knight of Auvergne, and we could wish no better, for he has proved himself a good seaman and a brave captain. Two other galleys are to start with us. We are to cruise separately unless one gets news of a force so superior that he will need aid to attack it, when he will meet the others at a rendezvous agreed upon, and we shall work together."

"Who are the other three Englishmen?"

"John Boswell, Marmaduke Lumley, and Adam Tedbond—all, as you know, brave knights and good companions."

That evening Gervaise received a message from D'Aubusson, requesting him to call at his auberge.

"So you are going to sea, Sir Gervaise? I hear from your bailiff that you have been working to his satisfaction in the town."

"Yes, sir. I shall indeed be glad to change it for a life at sea. In truth, it is grievous to me to witness the sufferings of the slaves, and I would rather do any other work."

"They are far better off than the Christians who fall into the hands of the Turks," the bailiff said; "and, moreover, it is because their countrymen are preparing to attack us that we are forced to use their labour in strengthening our fortifications. They have naught to complain of in the way of food. Still, I would myself gladly see their lot alleviated; but we could not afford to keep so great a number of captives in idleness; they must work for their living. Had it not been for their labour we could never have built and fortified the city. After all, they are little worse off than our serfs at home; they build our castles and till our land."

"It may be so, sir; but with us in England men are free, and it was, when I first came, strange to me to see them working under the fear of the whip. It is necessary, I know, that such work should be done, but I own that I shall be glad to be away from the sight of the poor wretches, pirates and enemies of the faith though they be."

"I can understand your feelings, and I too felt somewhat the same when I first came here. Nevertheless, there is work that must be done if the Order is not to be crushed by the infidels. Here are captives, for the most part malefactors, who have to be fed; and there is no injustice in their having, like all men, to give work for food. I have learnt to see this and recognise the necessity, though I would that the work could be obtained without the use of harshness and severity. We ourselves are prepared at any moment to sacrifice our lives for the good of the Order and for the great cause, and it would be wrong, nay, sinful, not to use the means that have been placed ready to our hand. Now, Sir Gervaise, I wish you a pleasant voyage. You will find the life somewhat hard, after your three years' residence at the palace, but this I know you will not mind. I have specially commended you to Ricord as one in whom I am personally interested, and from whom I hope great things in the future. Be brave; be resolute. From what you have said I need not say-be merciful. Fulfill all orders promptly and without question; bear yourself courteously to all; above all things, remember that you are a soldier, not only of the Order, but of the Cross."

The next day Gervaise embarked with his companions on board the galley. It was a long, low boat, similar to those in use by the Venetians and Genoese. It was rowed by fifty slaves, who slept at night on or beneath the benches they sat on by day. The knights occupied the great cabins in the poop. There were two tiers of these; the upper one contained the little cabin of the commander, while the rest of the space on this deck, and that below it, was used by the knights in common. In the upper cabin they took their meals, and a third of their number slept there, the remainder in the cabin below. A fourth of their number were, however, always on guard, lest any attempt at a rising or escape should be made by the galley slaves.

On leaving the harbour the galley, with its two consorts, rowed north, and Gervaise learnt that they were to cruise between the mainland and the islands. Some of these were in the hands of the Turks, while others were still occupied by Greeks.

Except when there was a formal and actual state of war, the Moslem and Christian islands remained in a state of neutrality, trading with each other and avoiding all unfriendly proceedings that would lead to struggles which would be fatal to the prosperity of both. The Archipelago, and indeed the whole of the eastern portion of the Mediterranean, was infested by pirates, fitted out, for the most part, on the mainland. These, when in force, openly kept the sea, attacking the Christian merchant ships, but when cruising alone they hid in unfrequented bays, or behind uninhabited islets, until they could pounce upon a passing ship whose size promised an easy capture. The Order of St. John furnished a maritime police, earning thereby the deep gratitude of Spain, France, and Italy. They were aided occasionally by the Venetians, but these, being frequently engaged in quarrels with their neighbours, did but a small share of this work, only sending their fleets to sea when danger threatened some of their possessions in the Levant.

"This is delightful, Ralph," Gervaise said, as they stood together on the poop, looking back at the receding city.

"What a pleasant change it is from standing in the broiling sun watching those poor wretches toiling at the fortifications! There is only one drawback to my pleasure. I wish that we carried sails, and were moved along by the breeze, instead of by the exertions of the slaves."

"Much chance we should have of catching a pirate under such circumstances!" Ralph said, laughing. "You might as well set a tortoise to catch a hare."

"I don't say that we should not be obliged to carry rowers, Ralph; but all the prizes that have been brought in since I have been at Rhodes carry masts and sails, as well as oars, and, as I understand, for the most part cruise about under sail, and only use the oars when chasing or fleeing."

"That is so; because, you see, in most cases the crew themselves have to row, and I have no doubt if we had no slaves to do the work we should soon take to masts and sails also; but for speed the rowing galleys are the best, for unless a brisk wind were blowing, the mast and sails would but check her progress when the oars were out, and at any rate constrain her to travel only before the wind. I know your weakness about the slaves, Gervaise; but as we could neither build our fortifications nor row our galleys without them, I cannot go as far as you do in the matter, though I own that I am sometimes sorry for them. But you must remember that it is the fault of their people, and not of ours, that they are here."

"All that is true enough, Ralph, and I cannot gainsay you. Still I would rather that we were gliding along with sails instead of being rowed by slaves."

"At any rate, Gervaise, you will not see them ill treated, for I myself heard Ricord, just before we were starting, tell the slave overseers that so long as the rowers did fair work they were not to use their whips, and that only if we were in chase of a pirate were they to be urged to their utmost exertions."

"I am right glad to hear it, Ralph, and shall be able to enjoy the voyage all the more, now you have told me that such orders have been issued."

For a fortnight they cruised about among the islands. Several times boats rowed out from the shore to the galley with complaints of outrages by pirates under a notorious corsair named Hassan Ali, who had landed, burnt villages, killed many of the inhabitants, and carried off the rest as slaves; but no one could give any clue to aid them in their search for the corsairs. The time passed very pleasantly. There was no occasion for speed; often they lay all day in some bay, where they could approach near enough to the shore to lie in the shade of trees, while two or three of the knights ascended a hill and kept watch there for the appearance of any vessels of a suspicious character. One morning, after passing the night at anchor, Harcourt and Gervaise were despatched just before sunrise to take a look round before the galley got under way. From the top of the hill they had an uninterrupted view of the sea, studded with islands on all sides of them. Beyond a few fishing boats, looking like black specks on the glassy surface, no craft were in sight. They were about to return to the galley when, taking a last look round, Gervaise suddenly exclaimed, "Look, Ralph! There is smoke ascending from that island to the southwest. There was none just now."

"You mean from that bay, Gervaise? Yes, I see it; it is not more than a light mist."

"It is growing thicker," Gervaise said, "and spreading. Maybe it is but a hut that has accidentally caught fire, but it seems to me that the smoke is rising from several points."

"I think you are right, Gervaise. Let us hurry down with the news. It may be that it is a village which has been attacked by pirates who have landed on the other side of the island during the night, for I can see no ships in the bay."

A few minutes' run and they stood on the shore.

"Quick, men!" Ralph said to the rowers of the boat that had brought them ashore. "Row your hardest."

The slaves bent to their oars, and they were soon alongside the galley, which lay two or three hundred yards from the shore. Those on board had noticed the young knights running down the hill, and, marking the speed at which the boat was rowing, concluded at once that they must have observed one of the pirate's ships.

"Do you see anything of them, Sir Ralph?" the commander shouted, as they came close.

"We have seen no ships, Sir Louis, but there is smoke coming up from a bay in an island four or five miles away to the southwest. It seems to us that it is far too extensive a fire to be the result of an accident, for there was no smoke until within two or three minutes of the time we left, and before we started it was rising from several points, and we both think that it must come from a village that has been attacked by pirates."

The commander rapidly issued his orders, and in two or three minutes the anchor was weighed, the boat hoisted on deck, and the oars in motion.

"Stretch to your oars!" Ricord shouted to the slaves. "Hitherto we have exacted no toil from you, but you have to work now, and woe be to him who does not put out his full strength."

Grateful for the unusual leniency with which they had been treated, the slaves bent to their oars, and the galley sped rapidly through the water. On rounding the end of the island there was an exclamation of satisfaction from the knights as they saw wreaths of white smoke rising from the distant island.

"There can be no doubt that it is a village in flames," Sir Louis said; "and from the suddenness with which it broke out, it is clear that it must have been fired at several points. You say you saw no craft near?" he asked, turning to Harcourt.

"There were none there, or from the top of the hill we should assuredly have made them out, Sir Louis."

"Then the pirates-if this be, as I hope, their work-must have landed at some other point on the island, and if they catch sight of us they may make for their ship and slip away, unobserved by us. Instead of rowing direct, therefore, we will make for that islet to the right, and row round behind it. There are two others almost adjoining it. Once past these, 'tis not more than half a mile to that island stretching away south. Once round that, we shall be beyond the one from which we see the smoke rising, and can come down on its southern side. The course will be double the distance that it would be if we took a straight line, but except when we cross from island to island we shall not be exposed to their view, and may fall upon their ships before the crews have returned from their work of plunder."

The knights fully agreed, and orders were given to the helmsman accordingly.

"We must not over fatigue the rowers," the commander said. "We may have a long chase if they have started before we get round."

He therefore gave orders to the slaves that, while they were to exert themselves to the utmost when crossing the open sea, they were to relax their efforts and to row within their strength while coasting along behind the islands. On board, everything was made in readiness for a fight: the knights buckled on their armour, the cooks set cauldrons of pitch over the fire, the cannoneers loaded her eight guns. It was an hour and a half after their start before they rounded the end of the last island. It extended a little farther to the south than did that to which they were making, and as they rounded the point, eager looks were cast in search of the pirate ships. No craft were, however, to be seen.

"They must be in some bay or inlet," the commander said; "they can hardly have left, for it would have taken them half an hour at least to cross the island with their booty and captives, and even if they made straight away after having fired the village, their ship could have gone no great distance, for we must have seen her if she put to sea-unless indeed they were anchored on the east of the island, and have sailed in that direction."

"Keep them rowing along steadily," he said to the overseers of the slaves; "but do not press them too hard. We may have a chase yet, and need all their strength, for most of these pirates are fast craft, and if they should get a start of three or four miles, it will be a long row before we catch them."

They made straight for the island, and on nearing it coasted along its southern side. It was some three miles long, the shore being for the most part steep, but here and there falling gradually to the water's edge. Two or three little clusters of houses could be seen as they rowed along; one of these was on fire.

"That is good," Sir Louis exclaimed, as, on turning a point, they saw the flames. "That cannot have been lighted long, and we are pretty certain to come upon the vessels before the marauders have set sail."

Several inlets and small bays were passed, but all were empty. A few fishing boats lay on the shore, but there were no signs of life, as no doubt the people would, long since, have taken alarm and sought shelter in the woods. There was a sharp point just before they reached the southeastern extremity of the island, and as the galley shot past this, a shout of exultation rose from the knights, for, near the mouth of an inlet that now opened to their view, there lay four long, low vessels, above each of which floated the Moslem flag. A number of men were gathered on the shore near the ships, and heavily laden boats were passing to and fro.

A yell of rage and alarm rose from the ships as the galley came into view. There was a stir and movement on the shore, and numbers of men leapt into the boats there, and started for the ships. These were some quarter of a mile away when first seen, and half that distance had been traversed when a puff of smoke shot out from the side of one of them, followed almost immediately by a general discharge of their cannon. One ball tore along the waist of the galley, killing six of the rowers, and several oars on both sides were broken. Two balls passed through the cabins in the poop. But there was no pause in the advance of the galley. The whips of the slave masters cracked, and the rowers whose oars were intact strained at them. There was no reply from the guns, but the knights raised loud the war cry of the Order, a war cry that was never heard without striking a thrill of apprehension among their Moslem foes.

As they neared the pirate ships, the helm was put down, and the galley brought up alongside the largest of them and a broadside poured into her; then the knights, headed by their commander, leapt on to her deck.

Although a number of the crew had not yet come off from shore, the Moslems still outnumbered their assailants, and, knowing that their consorts would soon come to their aid, they threw themselves in a body on the Christians. But in a hand-to-hand conflict like this, the knights of the Hospital were irresistible. Protected by their armour and long shields from the blows of their enemies' scimitars and daggers, their long, cross handled swords fell with irresistible force on turbaned head and coat-of-mail, and, maintaining regular order and advancing like a wall of steel along the deck, they drove the Moslems before them, and the combat would soon have terminated had not a shout been raised by one of the overseers of the slaves. One of the other ships had rowed alongside the galley, and the crew were already leaping on board it. At the same moment another ship came up alongside that they had boarded, while the fourth was maneuvering to bring up under her stern.

"Sir John Boswell," Sir Louis shouted, "do you and your countrymen, with the knights of Spain, finish with these miscreants; knights of Germany and Provence keep back the boarders; knights of Auvergne follow me," and he leapt down into the galley.

The English and Spanish knights redoubled their exertions. The Moslems endeavoured to rally, seeing that help was at hand, and that but a small body were now opposed to them, but their numbers availed little. The ten knights kept their line, and, hewing their way forward, pressed them so hotly that the Turks broke and sprang over the bulwarks into the sea. Then the knights looked round. A fierce fight was going on between those of Germany and Provence and the enemy, who strove desperately to board from the ship alongside. The other vessel was now almost touching the stern, and her crew were swarming to her side in readiness to leap on board as soon as the vessels touched.

"We will keep them at bay there," Sir John Boswell shouted. "Do you, Don Pedro, and your comrades, aid Ricord. When his foes are finished with, you can come back to help us."

Then, with the four English knights, he ran along the deck, and reached the stern just in time to hurl backwards the Moslems, who had already obtained a footing. For a time the five knights kept back the surging mass of their foes. The deck was wide enough for each to have fair play for his sword, and in vain the pirates strove to obtain a footing.

At last Sir Marmaduke Lumley fell, severely wounded by an arrow from a Moslem marksman, and before the others could close the gap a score of pirates leapt on to the deck.

"Fall back, comrades, fall back; but keep together!" Sir John Boswell shouted, as he cleft the skull of one of the pirate officers who sprang at him. "Sir Louis will soon finish his work, and be here to our aid. Ah!" he exclaimed, looking over his shoulder, as he retired a step, "Provence and Germany are overmatched too."

This was indeed the case. Stoutly as they fought the knights were unable to guard the whole of the line of bulwark, and the Moslems had already obtained a footing on the deck. The discipline of the knights stood them in good stead. Drawing closely together as they retreated, they made a stand on the opposite side of the deck, and were here joined by Sir John Boswell and his companions. They now formed a semicircle, each flank resting on the bulwark, and the pirates in vain endeavoured to break their line. Again and again they flung themselves upon the knights, only to be beaten off with heavy loss. At length a loud cheer arose from the galley, and Sir Louis Ricord, with the knights of Auvergne and Spain having cleared the galley of their foes, and carried the pirate that had grappled with her, sprang on to the deck of the ship, and fell upon the throng that were attacking the knights there, oblivious of what was going on elsewhere. At once the English knights and their comrades took the offensive, and fell upon their assailants who, at the sight of the reinforcement, for a moment stood irresolute. For a short time there was a fierce struggle; then the pirates sprang back to their two ships, and endeavoured to cast off the grapnels. But the knights followed hotly upon them, and, panic stricken now, the pirates sprang overboard. Many were drowned, but the greater part managed to swim to shore.

Chapter V
Scourges Of The Sea

Breathless and faint from their tremendous exertions, the knights removed their helmets.

"By St. Mary," Sir Louis said, "this has been as hard a fight as I have ever been engaged in, and well may we be content with our victory! Well fought, my brave comrades! Each of these vessels must have carried twice our number at least, and we have captured four of them; but I fear the cost has been heavy."

Seven knights had fallen, struck down by sword, arrow, or thrust of spear. Of the rest but few had escaped unwounded, for, strong as was their armour, the keen Damascus blades of the Moslems had in many cases cut clean through it, and their daggers had found entry at points where the armour joined; and, now that the fight was over, several of the knights sank exhausted on the deck from loss of blood.

But the dressing of wounds formed part of a knight of St. John's training. Those who were unwounded unbuckled the armour and bandaged the wounds. Others fetched wine and water from the galley. The chains of the galley slaves were removed, and these were set to clear the decks of the Moslem corpses. The anchors were dropped, for what little wind there was drifted them towards the shore. They had learned from a dying pirate that the vessels were part of the fleet of Hassan Ali, a fact that added to the satisfaction felt by the knights at their capture, as this man was one of the most dreaded pirates of the Levant. They learnt that he himself had not been present, the expedition being under the command of one of his lieutenants, who had fallen in the fight.

"Now, comrades, let us in the first place take food; we have not broken our fast this morning. Then let us consider what had best be done, for indeed we have got as much in our hands as we can manage; but let us leave that till we eat and drink, for we are faint from want of food and from our exertions. But we shall have to eat what comes to hand, and that without cooking, for our servants all joined the pirates when they boarded us, and are either dead or are ashore there."

A meal was made of bread and fruit, and this with wine sufficed to recruit their energies.

"It seems to me, comrades," Sir Louis said, when all had finished, "that the first thing is to search the holds of these vessels and see what valuables are stored there. These may be all carried on board one ship, and the others must be burnt, for it is clear that, as there are four of them, we cannot take them to Rhodes; and even with one and our galley we should fare but ill, if we fell in with two or three more of Hassan's ships."

"But how about the pirates on shore, Sir Louis?" a knight asked. "There were very many who could not get off to their ships during the fight, and scores must have swum ashore. I should say that there must be full two hundred, and it will be a grievous thing for the islanders if we leave them there."

"It is certain," the commander said, "that we are not strong enough to attack them, for were we to land, a party would have to be left on board, or the pirates might elude our search, seize some fishing boats, and regain possession. Certainly, we are in no position to divide our forces."

"Methinks," Sir John Boswell said, "that the best plan would be to send a boat, manned with ten galley slaves, taking two or three of us to the rendezvous, to fetch hither the other two galleys. With their aid we might take all the four ships safe into port, after first clearing the island of these pirates. It is but forty miles away, and eight hours' rowing would take us there."

There was a general murmur of assent, for all wished that the trophies of their bravery should, if possible, be carried to Rhodes.

"That will certainly be the best plan, Sir John, though it may detain us here for two or three days, or even more, for it is quite uncertain when the other two galleys may put in at the rendezvous. Will you yourself undertake the mission?"

"With pleasure."

"How many will you take with you?"

"Two will be sufficient, for we shall have no fighting to do, as we shall have to trust to our speed if we fall in with an enemy. I will take, with your permission, Sir Ralph Harcourt and Sir Gervaise Tresham, both of whom have today fought with distinguished bravery. Indeed, I owe my life to them, for more than once, when I was hotly pressed, they freed me from my assailants. Truly none bore themselves better in the fray than they did."

Three or four others joined in hearty commendations of the two young knights.

"Indeed," one said, "I was greatly surprised to see how Tresham bore himself. He is but a lad, with scarce, one would think, strength to hold his own in such a fray. It chanced that he was next to me in the circle, and for a time I kept my eye on him, thinking he might require my aid; but I soon saw that I need not trouble myself on his account, for he wielded his weapon as doughtily as the best knight of the Order could have done, and one of the proofs is that, while most of us bear marks of the conflict, he has escaped without scratch. I trust, Sir Louis, that when you give an account of the fighting you will specially mention that this, the youngest knight of the Order, bore himself as stoutly as any of them. I say this, Sir John, because, not being of your langue, I can speak more warmly than you can do of his skill and bravery."

"I thank you, De Boysey," Sir John Boswell said, "and I am proud that my young countryman should have so gained your approbation. And now," he went on, "while the galley slaves are getting a meal—which they have right well earned today—I should like to see what there is under the hatches of these ships, so that I can give our comrades in the other galleys some idea of the value of this booty we have taken."

They rose from the table, and, going on board the prizes, lifted the hatches.

"Beware!" De Boysey exclaimed, looking down into the hold, when the first hatch was taken off. "There are people below."

A chorus of cries followed his exclamation.

"They are the voices of women and children," Sir Louis exclaimed. "They must be captives."

This turned out to be so. In the holds of the four ships were found over a hundred and fifty women and children; these had been brought on board in the first boat loads by the pirates, and when the Christian galley had been seen coming round the point, had been thrust below, and the hatches thrown over them. They had heard the din of battle above, but knew not how the conflict had terminated, and, being afraid to cry out, had remained silent until, on the hatch being lifted, they had seen the figures of Christian knights standing in the bright sunshine. All had come from the village on the other side of the island. They related how the pirates had suddenly burst upon them, had slaughtered all the men, set fire to the village, and had driven them before them across the island to the ships. The poor creatures were delighted at their escape from slavery, but at the same time were full of grief at the loss of husbands, fathers, and sons.

Some laughed, others cried; while some thanked God for their rescue others heaped imprecations upon the authors of their misfortunes.

The knights explained to them that for a short time they must remain on board, as half the pirates were still on shore, but that aid would soon arrive that would enable them to clear the island.

Half an hour later Sir John Boswell, with the two young knights, started in a rowing boat, manned by ten of the galley slaves. The wind had sprung up since the fight ceased, and as it was nearly astern, they anticipated that they would make a good passage, and be at the little islet, named as the place of rendezvous, before nightfall.

Among the many bales of rich merchandise in the hold of the pirate vessels an abundance of wine had been discovered, and of this a tankard had been given to each of the slaves, by Sir Louis's orders, as a token of satisfaction at their work in the morning.

They had gone some two miles when, from one of the inlets in the island they had left a large fishing boat was seen to issue out.

"By St. George!" Sir John exclaimed, "that boat must be full of pirates. And if they see us, which they cannot help doing, and take it in their heads to chase us, we shall have a hard time of it."

The fishing boat for a few minutes kept along the coast, and then suddenly her course was altered, and her head directed towards their boat.

"Now stretch to your oars," Sir John, who spoke some Turkish, said to the slaves. "Keep ahead of that boat, and I promise you, on my honour as a Christian knight, that I will myself purchase your freedom as soon as we get to Rhodes."

With a shout of delight, the galley slaves bent to their oars, and the boat flew along at a greatly increased speed.

"There is but small chance of our getting away," Sir John said quietly. "At present we must be rowing as fast as they sail; but wind never tires, while there are limits to the powers of muscle and bone. If those fellows follow us-and I doubt not that they will, for they must be thirsting for vengeance-they will overtake us long before we get to the rendezvous; and even did we reach it, the chances are that we should not find either of the galleys there. We must hold on as long as we can, and as a last resource must run ashore. Unfortunately there are no large islands on our way. Nor have we any hope of assistance from our friends behind. The inlet looks east, and they will know nothing of our danger; nor, if they did, could they help us. The galley is short handed now, and there are the captured ships to look after, and the captives we rescued. We have only ourselves to depend on."

At the end of an hour's rowing the boat astern had gained little; but the exertions of the rowers were telling severely upon them. They were still doing their best, but their breath came in short gasps, the rowing was getting short and unsteady, and there was a sensible decrease in the speed of the boat. Three miles ahead of them was an islet about half a mile in diameter. In some parts it was covered with foliage, but elsewhere it was bare rock.

"That must be our goal," Sir John said. "They will be close to us by the time we get there." Then he said to the rowers, "Stop for a minute to get breath. We will land at that islet ahead, and I shall hold to my promise if we get there in time. Those of you who like can remain in the boat until your countrymen come up; those who choose can leave the boat and hide yourselves as best you may. I leave the choice to yourselves. If we are overtaken and fall, I cannot keep my promise, and it will be best then for you to remain in the boat."

For three or four minutes the slaves bent forward over their oars; but as soon as Sir John gave the word they straightened themselves up and began rowing again. The rest had done them good, and they again fell into a long, steady stroke.

"Shall we buckle on our armour again?" Sir Ralph Harcourt asked; for they had not put it on when they left the ship, as the heat was very great.

"I think we had better don our mail shirts only. In climbing about that rock ahead of us, the less weight we carry the better, and with this heat I would rather fight unprotected than in casque and armour. Besides, there can be little doubt that, if they come upon us, it will be our last battle. That craft behind is crowded with men, and, armour or no armour, it will come to the same in the end. If it were not that we have a mission to fulfil, and that it is of all things important to send the galleys to aid our friends, I would say let us choose a spot at the foot of the rocks there, where they cannot attack us in the rear, and there fight it out as becomes knights of the Cross; but as it is our duty above all things to carry this message, we must strive to preserve our lives, and must, if we can, conceal ourselves from these paynims."

"What are you going to do?" Sir John asked the slaves, when they were within a quarter of a mile of the islet. "I should think, after we have left the boat, it will be best for you to sit quietly on your benches till our pursuers arrive."

"They would cut our throats at once, Sir Knight; they will be furious at our having given them so long a chase. Hassan Ali's men care little whom they slay, and, irritated by their misfortune, it will be naught to them whether we are Moslem or Christian. I, for one, shall take to the woods, and hide."

There was a chorus of assent among the other rowers.

"I trust that you may escape," the knight said. "It is for us they will be hunting, and if they catch and slay us they will not trouble to search the island further."

"It seems to me, Sir John," Gervaise said, "that with the aid of these good fellows we may yet have a chance of escape."

"What is your plan, Sir Gervaise?"

"I think, Sir John, that if, when we land, we climb straight up that hill, in full sight of the shore, the pirates, when they see us, will follow at once. The slaves should, therefore, be safe for a time if they hide in that wood to the left of the spot we are making for. Will you tell them to keep down by the water's edge among the bushes, and that after crossing that crest, we will try to make a dash round, so as to join them there. 'Tis probable that most of the pirates will start in pursuit of us, and if we and the slaves make a rush for the shore we may seize our boat, push off, and capture their craft, if there are but a few left on board, knock out a plank and scuttle her, and then row away."

"By St. George, your plan is a good one, Tresham! A right good scheme, and we will try it."

He at once translated what Gervaise had said to the rowers, by whom it was received with short exclamations of approval, for they were too breathless and exhausted for talk. Already they could hear the yells of the pirates, who, as the boat ran up on the beach were but a quarter of a mile behind.

"Now, away for that wood!" Sir John cried, as he leapt ashore. "Now, comrades, for a climb up the hill!"

It was a steep ascent, and more than once one had to be helped up by the others, and then in turn to assist them to get up beside him. Louder and louder rose the shouts of the pirates, but the knights did not glance back until they reached the top of the hill; then they turned and looked round. A swarm of men were climbing after them, and were already halfway up the cliff.

"Heave them down!" Sir John exclaimed, pointing to some loose rocks, and set the example by lifting a great stone and hurling it over the edge. Harcourt and Gervaise at once did the same, and twenty or thirty rocks were speedily sent rolling down the steep ascent, and yells, shouts, and cries were heard below.

"That will check them a bit. Now let us be off," Sir John Boswell said, and they at once started. After crossing a hundred yards of bare rock they stood at the edge of another slope into a deep valley, beyond which rose the central hill of the island. The valley ran right across, and was filled with trees extending to the sea at either end. Running rapidly down, the knights were within the shelter of the wood before the Moslems had reached the brow behind them. A minute later they heard the shouts of their enemies. Once in the wood they turned to the left, and in a few minutes stood on the sea shore. It was a little bay some two hundred yards across, and at either point the cliffs rose abruptly from the water.

"We shall have to swim round the point," Sir John said.

"Take off your mail shirts. We will make our way along the rocks as far as we can, and then drop them into the sea, otherwise they will know that we have taken to the water."

They hurried along the rocks, and were able to make their way to within fifty yards of the point; then, throwing their mail shirts into the sea, they plunged in. All knew the importance of getting round before any of the pirates, who would be searching the valley, came down on the shore, and they swam their hardest until they rounded the corner. The wood rang with the shouts of their pursuers, but no yell had risen from the water's edge. A hundred yards farther, and they were able to land, and were in a short time in the shelter of the trees that fringed the water to the point where they had left the boat. There was no longer any occasion for speed, and they made their way through the thick bushes and undergrowth quietly, until they recovered breath after their exertions. They had gone a few hundreds yards when from the bushes the slaves suddenly rose up.

"All has gone well," Sir John said to them in their own language. "The pirates are searching for us on the other side of the hill. There are not likely to be many of them left here. We shall soon be in possession of our boat again."

Followed by the slaves, they made their way forward until they stood at the edge of the wood. Five or six pirates were standing on the shore.

"I expect they have been left there," Harcourt said, "to prevent the slaves from carrying off the boat. They must have seen them run into the wood. They won't reckon on our being with them."

Drawing their swords, the three knights rushed out, followed by the slaves. They had but a hundred yards to run. The pirates, on seeing them, raised a yell and drew their scimitars; but the sight of the knights rushing upon them, when they had expected but a few unarmed rowers, was too much for their courage, and when their assailants were still fifty yards away they turned and fled. The fishing craft had been run ashore but a few yards from their boat.

"Get her afloat, Harcourt, and bring her to the stern of the fisherman. Now, Tresham, follow me."

Sir John Boswell climbed up on to the fishing boat, which was a craft of some fifteen tons burden. She was entirely deserted, but the sail still hung from the yard, and a fire was burning on a stone hearth, raised on some logs of wood in the centre of the deck.

"Look for something to stave in a plank, Tresham."

Gervaise leapt down into the hold. There were some nets and spare sails lying there, but nothing that would answer the purpose. He examined the planks. The boat was very strongly and roughly built.

"There is nothing here, Sir John, that will do, and nothing short of a heavy sledge hammer would suffice to smash one of these planks."

"There are a lot of them coming down the hill, Tresham. We have not many minutes to spare, but we must disable the craft. They will soon be after us again; they have run her hard and fast here, but when they all come back they will soon get her off. Let us try one of these sweeps."

He lifted one of the heavy oars, and holding it upright he and Gervaise together tried to drive the handle through the bottom. Again and again they raised it and drove it down; but the plank was too strong, and too securely fastened to the timbers.

"We must give it up," the knight said, with a sigh. "Fortune has befriended us so far, Tresham, but she has deserted us at last. Another three minutes, and we shall have thirty or forty of them upon us."

At this moment the lad's eye fell upon the fire.

"We shall manage yet," he exclaimed, and, seizing a blazing brand, he jumped below and set fire to the sails stowed there; they were as dry as tinder, and the flame shot up at once.

"That is good, Tresham," the knight said; "but they will put it out before it has caught the boat."

"Not before it has burnt the sails," Gervaise replied. "Now for this one," and he applied the brand to the lower edge of the great sail. Without a word Sir John seized another brand, and fired the sail on the other side of the deck. The flames flashed up, and a wild yell of rage and alarm broke from the pirates, who were now rushing down towards the beach.

"Now to the boat, Tresham; we have no time to lose if we would avoid being pounded with stones."

They dropped over the stern into the boat. The galley slaves dipped their oars into the water, and she shot away just as the foremost of the pirates reached the edge of the water. A few stones were thrown; but the pirates were so anxious about the craft, by which alone they could escape from the island, that the majority at once climbed on board.

At a word from the knight, the slaves stopped rowing a hundred yards from the shore. The sail was already consumed, and the yard and the upper part of the mast were in flames. A dense smoke was rising from the hold, and the pirates were throwing buckets of water down into it. In a few minutes the smoke decreased.

"I thought that they would be able to put it out; but, as far as we are concerned, it matters little. They have lost their sails, and as I saw but four sweeps, we can travel five miles to their one. If we find the galleys we will look in here on our way back, and if they have not left we will fire that craft more effectually, and then the pirates will be trapped, and we can leave them till we have fetched off Sir Louis and his prizes, and then have a grand hunt here. We took no prisoners before, and a hundred slaves will be a useful addition to our wall builders. Now, Tresham, I have to thank you warmly, for Harcourt and I doubly owe our lives to you. It was thanks to your quickness of wit that we regained our boat, for I would not have given a ducat for our chances had you not thought of that scheme. In the second place, we should assuredly have been overtaken again had it not been for your happy thought of crippling them by burning their sails. By St. George, Harcourt, this young countryman of ours is as quick and as ready of wit as he has shown himself a brave and gallant fighter! We have no lack of sturdy fighters; but the wit to devise and to seize upon the right thing in the moment of danger is vastly more rare. As for myself, I have no shame that this lad, who is young enough to be my son, should have thus, twice in a single hour, pointed out the way to safety. With sword and battleaxe I can, I trust, hold my own with any man; but my brain is dull when it comes to hatching schemes. If we live, we shall see Sir Gervaise one of the most distinguished knights of the Order."

"While I feel gratified indeed, as I may well be by your commendation, Sir John, I must, under your favour, say that you have given me a far greater degree of credit than is my due. There was the fire, and there was the sail, and the thought that the one would destroy the other was simply a natural one, which might have occurred to a child. As to the plan about the boat, seeing that there was the hill and the wood, it flashed upon me at once that we might make a circuit and come back to her."

"Just so, lad; but those thoughts did not flash upon my mind, nor upon that of Harcourt. It is just because those sort of ideas do flash upon the minds of some men, and not of others, that the first rise to the rank of distinguished commanders, while the others remain simple knights who would play their part in a charge or in the defence of a breach, but would be of no account as leaders.

"Now row along steadily, men," he went on, speaking to the slaves. "We are still in good time, for it was not an hour from the moment we touched the island to our departure from it, and much of that time we have gained by the speed with which you rowed before. At any rate, we shall make out the island before sunset, and whether we arrive there a little sooner or later matters little. Harcourt, hand me that wineskin and a goblet. A draught will do us good after our climb and swim, and these good fellows will be none the worse for a cup also."

Inspired with the hope of freedom, the slaves rowed steadily, and the sun had just set when they entered a little inlet in the rocky isle that was their place of rendezvous.

"Thanks be to the saints!" Sir John exclaimed, as they reached the entrance. "There is Santoval's galley."

There was a stir on board the galley as the boat was seen approaching. The knights had put on their armour, which they had found still lying in the boat, the pirates, in their haste to pursue, having left her unexamined, while those who had remained on guard had abstained from touching anything until the return of their captain and comrades.

"Whence come you, Sir John, and what is the news? No misfortune has befallen Ricord's galley, I hope?" the Spanish knight in command shouted, as the boat came near enough for him to recognize the features of its occupants.

"All is well," Sir John shouted back; "but we have taken more prizes than we can manage, though not without hard fighting. Seven knights have fallen, and at least ten others will not be able to buckle their armour on again for some time to come, so I have been sent here to beg your assistance; and it is well that it should be given speedily, for if more pirate vessels come up before you join, Ricord and his companions will be in a sorry plight."

By this time the boat had reached the side of the galley, and as Sir John and his two companions stepped on board, the knights crowded round to hear the details of the news. Exclamations of approval and satisfaction arose when Sir John related the incidents of the fight, and told them that the four vessels that had fallen into their hands formed part of Hassan Ali's fleet.

"That is good news indeed, Boswell," Don Santoval said; "and I would I had been there to take part in so gallant a fight. It is well you found us here, for with four prizes on hand, and with half his strength dead or disabled, Ricord must be in sore need of aid. We will start tomorrow morning at daybreak. As all the ships were taken, there is little fear of any of the other pirates hearing news of what has happened."

"I don't know," Sir John replied. "There were, as I told you, some two hundred pirates left on the island. About half those, we know, seized a fishing boat and escaped, for they chased us, and we have had as narrow an escape from death as has ever fallen to my lot, though I have been in over a score of hard fought battles. The rest may well have taken another fishing boat and made off also, for we saw several craft along the shores of the island. If so, they may have made for Hassan Ali's rendezvous, wherever that may be, just as I made here, and by this time some of his ships may be on the way there."

"By St. Anthony, this alters the situation gravely!" Don Santoval said. "Fellow knights, we must lose no time in going to Ricord's assistance. The slaves have had a long row today, but they must start on another. Let them have a good meal to strengthen them, and a cup of wine each. Whatever their scruples at other times, they never refuse wine when there is heavy work to be done, knowing full well that a draught of it helps them mightily in their labours. Your men must have rowed well, Sir John, to have brought you here so quickly?"

"I have promised them their freedom," Sir John said; "and they shall have it, even if I have to pay their value into the treasury. As I told you, we were hotly pursued, for the craft with her sail went faster than we with our oars; and, knowing the importance of bringing the news here, I encouraged them by promising them their freedom, should we get away. Not only did they row right manfully, but they proved faithful in our extremity, and, when all seemed lost, stuck to us instead of deserting and joining the pirates."

"But how did you get away, Sir John, if their craft outsailed you?"

"I owe my life entirely to the quick wit of my young countryman, Sir Gervaise Tresham here." And Sir John then related the incidents of their adventure on the island, his narrative eliciting warm expressions of approval from the knights.

"Of course, you will go with us, Boswell?" Don Santoval said, when the master of the slaves announced that these had eaten their meal, and were ready.

"I must do so," Sir John replied. "I want you, on your way, to look in at that island where we had so narrow an escape, and if we find their craft still there we can destroy it. The place is directly in our course; we shall, therefore, lose but little time in looking in. Of course, they may have gone as soon as they got their vessel afloat, but it is hardly likely. They would have no idea of my returning with a galley so soon, and will probably set to to make a dozen more oars before they start, for she had but four on board, which will scarce suffice to send her a mile an hour through the water. Therefore, I fancy they will not put off until tomorrow morning. If that is so, and we destroy their craft, they will be trapped in the islet, and on our return we can capture them all. I think of leaving Harcourt and Tresham in the boat, in order that when Piccolomini's galley comes in, they may direct him also to join us."

"He may be in at any moment; we met him three days since. He had captured a pirate, and sent her off under charge of ten of his knights. We agreed to meet him this evening; and as he is not here, he will probably be in the first thing in the morning."

Gervaise and Harcourt took their places in the boat again. The galley got up its anchor and started. Just as she reached the mouth of the inlet another galley rounded the point and nearly ran into her.

"I am going to Ricord's assistance, Piccolomini," Don Santoval shouted.

"Is it urgent?" the commander of the galley shouted back. "We have had a very long row, and can go no farther, unless his strait is a very sore one."

655

"No. Come on in the morning. You will hear all the news from a boat lying two hundred yards astern. Two young English knights are waiting in her to give you the news. Ricord has made a fine capture. Row on, men." And the galley proceeded on her way, while the newcomer proceeded up the harbour.

Harcourt and Gervaise at once went on board, and the former gave the Italian commander an account of the battle that had taken place, and the capture of the four pirate vessels. After the exclamations of satisfaction by the knights had ceased, he recounted their own adventures, which were heard with lively interest.

"I hope indeed that Santoval will burn that fishing boat, and that we shall capture the pirates," the commander said. "We have need of more slaves to carry out the works at Rhodes. Now, let us to supper, gentlemen, and then to sleep. In six hours we will be off again, for if some more of these villains have escaped and carried the news to Hassan Ali, our swords may be sorely needed by Ricord and Santoval tomorrow."

Chapter VI
Knighted

At three in the morning all on board the galley were astir. A ration of bread and meat was served out to the slaves, and the boat was soon afterwards under way. The rowers of the English knight's boat had been warmly commended by the commander and placed in charge of the overseer, with instructions that they were to be treated as free men. As soon as the galley slaves set to work, however, they seated themselves on the benches and double banked some of the oars, anxious to please the knights. With the exception of those whose turn it was to be on watch, most of the knights slept until daybreak.

"At the rate we are rowing, Gervaise," Harcourt said, as they went up on to the poop together, "it will not take us very long to join our friends. We are going through the water at fully six miles an hour; and as we have already been two hours under way, in another three we shall be there."

An hour and a half later they passed the island where they had landed. The two young knights pointed out to the others the valley into which they had descended, and the point round which they had swum. In a few minutes they caught sight of the landing place.

"Look, Gervaise, there is something black showing just above the water."

"I see it. I think it is a line of timbers. There were certainly no rocks there when we ran ashore."

"Then Santoval must have found the craft still there and burnt her," one of the knights standing by remarked, "and the pirates are caged up. It will take them some time to make a raft that will carry them to the next island, and before they can do that we shall be back again. I shall be sorry if they escape, for they are as ruthless a set of villains as sail the seas."

The galley had traversed half the remaining distance when the sound of a gun was faintly heard. For a moment there was an absolute hush on the poop; then three or four shots in rapid succession were heard.

"Some more pirate ships must have come up," the commander exclaimed. Then he shouted down to the slaves, "Row, men—row for your lives! Overseer, do not spare your lash if any hang back from their work."

The galley had been travelling fast before, but her speed greatly increased as the slaves rowed their hardest. Fast as she was travelling, the impatience of the knights was extreme. They walked up and down the deck, making vows of candles that should be burnt at the shrine of St. John if they arrived in time to take a share in the fight, stopping at times to listen to the sound of artillery, which was now so frequent as to show that a severe engagement was being fought. Many of the younger knights ran down to the waist and double banked the oars, and in a shorter time than it seemed possible the galley arrived at the mouth of the bay.

A desperate fight was going on. Ricord's ship lay, idle and deserted, at anchor. Five pirate crafts surrounded Santoval's galley. Two of them were alongside of her; the others were raking her fore and aft with their shot. The young knights left the oars, sprang up to the poop and joined in the shout of encouragement raised by the others, and then, resuming their helmets and armour, stood ready to leap on board an enemy as soon as they reached her. Piccolomini directed the helmsman to lay him alongside one of the ships grappling with Santoval. As they came up, their galley's cannon poured their fire into her, and a moment later the knights sprang on board.

In the din of battle their shout had been unheard. The pirates thronging the other side of their ship were intent only on overcoming the resistance of the knights, and even the discharge of cannon had not called their attention to their foe, until the latter, shouting the war cry of the Order, fell suddenly upon them. A panic at once seized them. Some were cut down almost unresistingly, but the great majority, running to the bow or stern, threw themselves overboard and swam to the other ships. The pirate ship on the other side of Santoval's galley instantly threw off the grapnels and thrust off from her side, and, immediately hauling in the sheets of the big sail, began at once to draw away, while her three consorts made for the mouth of the bay.

"Back to your galley, comrades," Piccolomini shouted, "or with this brisk wind they will escape us."

The knights at once crossed on to their own craft, the oars were got out, and the chase began. A minute or two later Don Santoval followed them, but soon gave up, as so large a number of the oars had been broken when the two pirate ships ran alongside him, that it would have been hopeless to pursue. The wind was blowing freshly, and was rapidly increasing in strength, so that, in spite of the efforts of the galley slaves, the pirates gradually drew away, running straight before the wind, and aiding the effects of the sails with oars. Seeing the hopelessness of the chase, Piccolomini abandoned it, after rowing for two miles, and returned to the island. The other two galleys were lying beside each other, and Piccolomini had his craft steered alongside them.

"Thanks, Piccolomini, for arriving so opportunely," Santoval, who was seated on the deck leaning against the bulwarks, said, as his fellow commander leapt on board, and came towards him.

"Would that I had arrived sooner, Santoval, for I see that you have been grievously wounded!"

"Ay. One of the paynims' cannonballs has carried off both my legs below the knee. The leech has been searing the wounds with a hot iron, and says that he thinks I shall get over it; but if so I fear that my fighting days are past, unless, indeed, I fight seated on a chair. However, I ought not to grumble. I have lost many brave comrades, and others are wounded more sorely than I am."

Sir Louis Ricord now joined them. He embraced Piccolomini warmly.

"I never heard a more welcome shout, Piccolomini, than that which you gave when you fell upon the Moslems, for in truth the issue of the conflict was doubtful. I was delighted when this morning at daybreak Santoval's galley rowed in. We had all kept watch during the night, thinking the pirates might obtain boats and make an attack upon us; and, with but twenty of us fit to wield a sword, our position would have been a bad one, and at any rate they might have recaptured the prizes. We agreed that Santoval and his knights should land at once. This they did. Sir John Boswell had of course told me how his boat had been chased by a fishing craft, manned by a large number of the pirates, and that he feared the rest might similarly have escaped, and might have gone to bring some more of Hassan Ali's ships upon us.

"As soon as Santoval landed, some of the natives came down and told him that there was not a pirate remaining there, the rest having started in another boat a few minutes after the one that had chased Boswell. Santoval left two of his men with orders to ascend to the highest spot on the island, and to keep watch, and then brought the rest off to his galley. Our first step was, of course, to send all the women and children ashore. Then we consulted as to what had best be done if the pirates should come back in force. We hoped, at any rate, that this would not happen until you arrived. We expected that you would be here before noon; but we decided that, should they get here before you, we from our galley would embark on Santoval's, as it was better to fight in one strongly manned boat than to divide our forces.

"It was scarce half an hour after Santoval came down before the men left on the lookout appeared on the beach. On fetching them off, they told us that as soon as they reached the top of the hill they saw five vessels approaching with sails and oars, and that they would be here in half an hour at the outside. We at once abandoned my galley, brought the rowers and the wounded here, and prepared for the fight. As you saw, they ran their two biggest ships alongside us, and for two hours the fight went on. They were crowded with men, who in vain strove to get a footing on our decks. Had we only had these two to deal with, we should have had nothing to fear, heavily manned though they were; but the other three kept sailing backwards and forwards, discharging their guns into us as they passed, firing not only shot, but bags of bullets.

"Their gunners were skilful, and, as you see, they have completely riddled our poop. Twenty knights have been killed, and eleven others are sorely wounded. Scarce one has escaped unscathed. You may guess, then, how welcome was your aid, which we had not expected for another three hours. We were on the point of abandoning the waist and gathering on the poop, which we could still have defended for a considerable time, when, as if dropped from the skies, you fell upon the pirates, and turned the tables. How is it that you were here so early?"

"We started at three o'clock, instead of waiting for daybreak. It seemed, from the story of the two young knights, that it was possible you might be attacked early, and, crippled as your command was, and with four prizes on your hands, I deemed it best to come on as soon as the rowers had had a few hours' rest."

"It is well that you did so; it would have been a grievous affair had two of our galleys been captured by the pirates. It would have been a blow to the prestige of the Order, and would have brought such strength to Hassan Ali and other pirate leaders that nothing short of sending out a fleet would have recovered our ascendancy; and as every ducat we can spare has to be spent on the fortifications, it would have been a misfortune indeed had we been obliged to fit out such an expedition at present."

"Who have fallen, Sir Louis?"

"Five more of the knights of my galley-Pierre des Vignes, Raoul de Montpelier, Ernest Schmidt, Raymond Garcia, and Albert Schenck. Here is the list of the knights of Santoval's galley."

"'Tis a long list, and a sad one," Piccolomini said, after reading the names. "With the seven who fell in your first fight, twenty-seven knights have fallen, all brave comrades. Truly, we can ill spare such a loss. It is true there are five prizes to show for it, and we have struck Hassan Ali a blow that will resound through the Levant; but the cost is heavy."

"It is indeed," Ricord agreed. "The four vessels are well filled with rich spoil that the scoundrels had gathered, and I doubt not the one you captured is equally rich. Still, had they been ten times as valuable, the booty would be dearly purchased at such a price."

There was now a consultation among the leaders, and it was agreed that six knights should be placed in each of the captured ships, with ten of the galley slaves to work the sails, the others being equally divided between the three galleys. They were, in the first place, to row to the island where the pirates were imprisoned, and to slay or capture the whole of them; afterwards they were to make direct for Rhodes; with so numerous a fleet there was no fear of their being attacked. The arrangements took but a short time to complete. An hour later they left the port, the three galleys rowing ahead, while the five prizes, under easy sail, followed them.

Sir John Boswell had been wounded, but not so seriously as to altogether disable him, and he was in command of one of the prizes, having Sir Adam Tedbond, Harcourt, Gervaise, and a German knight, with him. Sir Marmaduke Lumley, who, after the first fight was over, was found, to the surprise and pleasure of his comrades, to be still living, was, with the rest of the wounded, on board one of the galleys. Two of the pirates had fallen dead across him, and in the ardour of their attack on the knights, he had lain there unnoticed until the return of Sir Louis and his comrades had driven the pirates overboard. The leech was of opinion that he might yet recover from his wound.

On arriving at the island, sixty of the knights disembarked. The woods near the shore were first searched, but were found untenanted. They were about to advance up the hill when a man appeared on the crest above them waving a white flag. He was told to come down, and on his arrival said that he was sent by his companions to offer to surrender, on the promise that their lives should be spared. The knights were well pleased to be saved the trouble of a long search through the woods, and the messenger left at once to acquaint the pirates that their terms were accepted. In a short time some eighty men made their way down the hill. On reaching the beach they were disarmed, divided equally between the galleys, and distributed among the rowers, filling up the places of those who had been killed by the fire of the Moslems, and of the men drafted into the prizes. They begged for food and water before they began work, and, on being questioned, admitted that their surrender was due principally to the fact that they had been unable to find food of any sort on the island, and that after searching all over it no spring of water could be discovered.

"In that case," Sir John Boswell said, "I have no doubt they have all surrendered. I before thought it probable that a good many of them would have remained hidden, trusting to be able to make a raft after we had left, and so get away, believing rightly enough that we should be disinclined to search every foot of the island for them. As it is, I doubt not, all are here."

The little fleet anchored that night at the rendezvous, and after two more days' rowing reached Rhodes, where the appearance of the three galleys, followed by their five prizes, was greeted with great acclamation. The news, however, that twenty-seven knights had fallen, and that thirteen or fourteen others were very gravely wounded, damped the satisfaction that every one had at first felt. D'Aubusson came down as soon as they reached the mole, and was greatly affected when he received Ricord's report.

"It is an unfortunate loss indeed, Sir Louis," he said, "though it may be that the victory is not too dearly purchased. I do not speak of the captured ships, nor of the spoil they contain, nor even of the slaves you have brought us, welcome though all may be, but of the effect that the defeat and capture of these craft of Hassan Ali's will have. It is plain that the preparations the sultan is making, and the belief that Rhodes is doomed, have so encouraged the infidels that they are becoming really formidable at sea. This blow will show them that the Order has yet power to sweep the sea of pirates. Since, however, this adventure has taught us that a single leader like Hassan sails with at least nine ships under his orders, it is clear that in future our galleys must not adventure singly among the islands. It was fortunate indeed that first Santoval, and then Piccolomini, arrived to your assistance. How was it that they happened to come up so opportunely?"

"Sir John Boswell, with Ralph Harcourt and Gervaise Tresham; went in a boat to the rendezvous we had arranged, and reached it after an adventure, which I will leave Sir John to tell himself. I may say that the two young knights named had in our encounter both obtained very high credit amongst us all for the valour with which they fought. No one bore himself more stoutly, and I am glad to take this early opportunity of bringing their conduct before your notice. As you will learn from Sir John, Gervaise Tresham afterwards showed a quickness of wit that was the means of saving the lives of those with him, and I may say also of all with me, for had they failed to reach the rendezvous we should have fallen easy victims to the five ships Hassan Ali brought against us."

Sending for Sir John Boswell, the grand prior heard from him the details of his adventure in the boat.

"I am right glad to hear you speak so warmly of Tresham, Sir John, for I regard him as my special protege, and am pleased indeed to find that at this outset of his career he has proved himself not only a brave knight, but full of resource, and quick at invention. I think, Sir John, that these two young knights have shown themselves well worthy of receiving the honour of secular knighthood."

"Assuredly they have," Sir John agreed.

"Then, Sir John, will you bestow it upon them? The Order, as an Order, does not bestow the honour, but its members do not forfeit their right as knights to bestow it individually, and none among us are more worthy of admitting them to your rank than yourself."

"I would gladly do it, Sir Peter; but the honour would come far better from yourself, and would not only be more highly prized by them, but would be of greater value in the eyes of others. I am but a simple knight commander of the Order, and my name would scarce be known beyond its ranks. But to be knighted by one whose name is known and honoured throughout Europe would give them a standing wherever they went, and place them on a level with the best."

"If that is your opinion, Boswell, I will myself undertake it, and will do it at once; it were better done here than at a conclave of the Order-now, when they are fresh from the battle. Let the knights be summoned from the other galleys at once."

In a few minutes the whole of the knights were assembled on the poop of the galley.

"Friends, and brother knights," D'Aubusson said. "First, in the name of the Order, I have to thank you all most heartily for the brave deeds that you have performed, and for the fresh honour you have won for it. Every man has, as I learn from the three commanders, borne himself as a true and valiant knight, ready to give his life in the cause of the Order and of humanity. Two names have been specially brought before me by commander Ricord, and by the good knight Sir John Boswell; they are those of two young companions who, though knights of our Order, have not yet received secular knighthood, and this, in the opinion of these two knights, they have right worthily won. Sir Ralph Harcourt and Sir Gervaise Tresham, step forward."

The two young knights, colouring with pleasure at this unexpected honour, removed their helmets, and stood with bowed heads before the grand prior. D'Aubusson went on, turning to the knights around him, "I am about, comrades, to undertake the office of knighting them. Sir Louis Ricord and Sir John Boswell stand as their sponsors. But before I proceed I would ask you all whether you, too, approve, and hold that Sir Ralph Harcourt and Sir Gervaise Tresham have proved themselves worthy of the honour of secular knighthood at my hands?"

There was a general reply in the affirmative, the answer of the survivors of Ricord's crew being specially emphatic. The grand prior drew his sword, and the two young knights knelt before him, their sponsors standing beside them.

"Sir Ralph Harcourt, you have now been four years a knight of this Order, but hitherto you have had no opportunity of drawing sword against the infidels. Now that the chance has come, you have proved yourself a true and valiant brother of the Order, and well worthy of the secular accolade. It is in that capacity that I now knight you. It is not the grand prior of Auvergne, but Sir Peter D'Aubusson, of the grand cross of St. Louis, who now bestows upon you the honour of secular knighthood." He touched him lightly with the sword. He then turned to Gervaise.

"You, Sir Gervaise Tresham, are young indeed to receive the honour of secular knighthood; but valour is of no age, and in the opinion of your commanders, and in that of your comrades, you have proved yourself worthy of the honour. You have shown too, that, as Sir John Boswell has related to me, you are not only brave in action, but able, in the moment of danger, to plan and to execute. You were, he tells me, the means of saving his life and that of your comrade, and, by thus enabling him to bear to the place of rendezvous the news of Sir Louis's danger, were also the means of saving the lives of Sir Louis and his companions, and of bringing home in safety the prizes he had taken. With such a beginning it is easy to foresee that you will win for yourself some day a distinguished position in the ranks of the Order, and are most worthy of the honour I now bestow upon you." And he touched him with his sword.

The two young knights rose to their feet, bowed deeply to D'Aubusson, and then retired, with their sponsors. They were at once surrounded by the knights, who shook them by the hand, and warmly congratulated them upon the honour that had befallen them, receiving equally warm congratulations on their arrival at the auberge of the langue.

The five prizes turned out, when their cargoes were landed, to be much more valuable than the cursory examination made by the knights had warranted them in expecting. They contained, indeed, an accumulation of the most valuable contents of the prizes taken by the pirates for a long time previously; and as these desperadoes preyed upon Turkish commerce as well as Christian, the goods consisted largely of Eastern manufactures of all kinds. Costly robes, delicate embroidery, superb carpets, shawls, goldsmiths' work, and no small amount of jewels, were among the spoil collected, and the bulk of the merchandise captured was, two days later, despatched in galleys to Genoa and Marseilles, to be sold for the benefit of the Order.

D'Aubusson without hesitation carried out Sir John Boswell's promise to the slaves who had rowed his boat. They were not only set at liberty, but were each presented with a sum of money, and were placed on board a galley, and landed on the mainland.

The English knights were all proud of the honour that had been won by their young countrymen, the only exception being Robert Rivers, who was devoured with jealousy at their advancement. He did not openly display his feelings, for the reports not only of Sir John Boswell, but of the other two English knights, were so strong that he dared not express his discontent. He himself had twice been engaged with pirates, but had gained no particular credit, and indeed had, in the opinion of his comrades, been somewhat slack in the fray. He was no favourite in the auberge, though he spared no pains to ingratiate himself with the senior knights, and had a short time before been very severely reprimanded by the bailiff for striking one of the servants.

"I have more than once had to reprove you for your manners to the servants," the bailiff said. "You will now be punished by the septaine; you will fast for seven days, on Wednesday and Friday you will receive bread and water only, and will be confined to the auberge for that period. The next time that I have reason to complain of you, I shall bring the matter before the grand master, and represent to him that it were best to send you home, since you cannot comport yourself to the servants of the auberge as befits a knight of the Order. We have always borne the reputation of being specially kind to our servants, and it is intolerable that one, who has been but a short time only a professed knight, should behave with a hauteur and insolence that not even the oldest among us would permit himself. There is not one of the servants here who was not in his own country of a rank and station equal, if not superior, to your own; and though misfortune has fallen upon them, they are to be pitied rather than condemned for it. In future, you are to give no order whatever to the servants, nor to address them, save when at meals you require anything. If you have any complaints to make of their conduct to you, you will make them to me, and I will inquire into the matter; and if I find they have failed in their duty they will be punished. I shall keep my eye upon you in the future. There are other faults that I have observed in you. More than once I have heard you address Sir Gervaise Tresham in a manner which, were not duelling forbidden by our rules, might bring about bloodshed; and from what I have seen when I have been watching the exercises, he is as much your superior in arms as he is in manner and disposition."

This reproof had greatly subdued Robert Rivers; and as he felt that any display of his jealousy of Gervaise would be resented by the other knights, and might result in serious consequences to himself, he abstained from any exhibition of it when they returned to the auberge, although he could not bring himself to join in the congratulations offered to them. The next day, however, when he was talking to Ralph Harcourt, he remarked, "From what I hear, Harcourt, D'Aubusson praised young Tresham very highly. It seems to me that there was nothing at all out of the way in what he did, and it was very unfair that he should be selected for higher praise than yourself."

"It was not unfair at all," Ralph said warmly, for he was of a generous nature, and incapable of the base feeling of envy. "Tresham did a great deal more than I did. When we saw the pirate boat gaining so fast upon us, it seemed to Sir John Boswell, as well as to myself, that there was scarce a chance of escape, and that all we could do was to choose a spot on which to make a stand, and then to sell our lives as dearly as we could. I could see that Sir John was scanning the hill for a spot where we could best defend ourselves. As to hiding on so small an island, with a hundred men eager for our blood searching for us, it was well nigh impossible. It was Tresham's suggestion alone that saved our lives and enabled us to fetch succour to Sir Louis. Sir John, who is an old and tried soldier, said that for quickness and merit of conception, the oldest knight in the Order could not have done better; and he is not one to praise unduly. I am four years older than Gervaise Tresham, but I tell you that were he named tomorrow commander of a galley, I would willingly serve under him."

"Well, well, you need not be angry, Harcourt, I have nothing to say against Tresham. No doubt he had a happy thought, which turned out well; but I cannot see that there was anything wonderful in it, and it seemed to me unfair that one who is a mere boy should receive higher praise than yourself, who, as I heard Sir John and Sir Adam Tedbond say last night at the refectory, bore yourself right gallantly."

"I did my best," Ralph said shortly; "but there was small credit in that when we were fighting for our lives. The most cowardly beast will fight under such circumstances. When you see a Moslem rushing at you, scimitar in hand, and know that if you do not cut him down he will cut you down, you naturally strike as hard and as quickly as you can. You have never liked Gervaise, Rivers. I am sure I don't know why, but you always speak in a contemptuous sort of tone about him. True, it does him no harm, but it certainly does you no good. For what reason should you feel a contempt for him? Although so much younger, he is a better swordsman and a better rider than you are. He is liked by every one in the auberge, which is more than can be said of yourself; he is always good tempered, and is quiet and unassuming. What on earth do you always set yourself against him for?"

"I do not know that I do set myself against him," Rivers said sullenly. "I own to having no great liking for him, which is natural enough, seeing that his father was a Lancastrian, while we are Yorkists; but it is not pleasant to see so much made of a boy, merely because D'Aubusson has favoured him."

"I am certain," Harcourt said hotly, "that such an idea has never occurred to any one but yourself. Sir Peter is a great man and will soon be our grand master, but at present he is but grand prior of the langue of Auvergne, and whether he favours Tresham or not is a matter that concerns none of us. Gervaise is liked by us for his own good qualities. He bears himself, as a young knight should do, respectfully towards his seniors, and is ever ready to do a service to any one. No one has ever seen him out of temper; he is always kind and considerate to the servants, and when in command of parties of slaves at the public works never says a harsh word to them, but treats them as if they were human beings, and not brute beasts. Besides, though he is more skilful than any of us with his sword, or indeed at any of the military exercises, he is unassuming, and has no particle of pride or arrogance. It is for all these things that he is liked, and the friendship of D'Aubusson has naught whatever to do with it. It is not only D'Aubusson who has prophesied that he will rise to a distinguished rank in the Order. Boswell and Ricord both said the same, and I for one thoroughly believe it. Is there one among us under the age of twenty-and I might go farther-who has already won such credit for himself? One who when but sixteen can make his mark in an Order like ours is certain to rise to high office, and you and I may, before many years are over, be proud to serve under him."

"That I will never do," Rivers said fiercely. "I would rather go and bury myself for life in the smallest commandery in England."

"That may be," Harcourt retorted, his temper also roused, "But possibly you might prefer that to fighting under any other leader."

"That is a reflection on my courage, Sir Ralph Harcourt, I shall lay this matter before the bailiff."

"You can do as you like," Harcourt said disdainfully, "But I don't think you will benefit by your pains."

When his temper cooled down Rivers acknowledged to himself the truth of what Harcourt said. He was not in the favour of the bailiff, while both Harcourt and Tresham stood at the present moment high in his estimation. Any complaint would lead to an inquiry into the matter that had led to the former's words, and even if Harcourt were reprimanded for using them, he himself would assuredly not gain in the estimation of the knights. Harcourt himself thought no more of the matter, though he laughingly told Gervaise that Rivers was by no means gratified at their both attaining the honour of secular knighthood, which virtually placed them over his head.

"He is not a nice fellow," Gervaise said. "But naturally it must be galling to him, and to a good many others who have not yet had the chance of distinguishing themselves. I think it is very good of them that they are all so kind and cordial. Of course it is otherwise with you, who are as old as most of the other professed knights serving here; but with me it is quite different, and as Rivers, somehow, has never been very friendly with me, of course it is doubly galling to him. I hope he will soon get an opportunity of winning his spurs too."

"That is just like you, Tresham. If I were in your place, I should have no good wishes for a fellow who has never lost an opportunity of annoying me, and that without the smallest cause of offence on my part."

"I am sure you would not wish him ill, Harcourt. You would make allowance for him just as I do, and feel that if he had had the same opportunities he would have obtained the same credit and honours."

Chapter VII
A First Command

The first news that the knights heard on their return from their expedition was that the Grand Master Orsini was seriously ill, and that, at his advanced age, the doctors feared there was little hope of his rallying. Gervaise felt a keen regret on hearing that the kind and gentle old man, who had been for three years his master, was at the point of death. Nevertheless, it was generally felt among the knights that, in view of the dangers that threatened Rhodes, it was for the good of the Order that a strong and capable man, whom all respected, and who possessed their entire confidence, should at such a time be invested with absolute power.

D'Aubusson had, indeed, for some years been the real head of the community, but every question had, if only as a matter of form, to be referred to the grand master, in order to obtain his approval and signature. In the state of feebleness to which he had for some months past fallen, much time was frequently lost before he could be made to understand the questions referred to him. Moreover, orders of D'Aubusson could be appealed against, his views thwarted, and his authority questioned; and it was therefore felt that, much as they all respected the old grand master, it would be an advantage to the Order when the supreme authority passed into the hands of D'Aubusson.

Four days after the return of the expedition Orsini died. A few hours later the grand council was convened, and D'Aubusson unanimously elected grand master of the Order. The ceremony of the funeral of his predecessor was an imposing one. Every knight of the Order in Rhodes was present, together with a number of the leading natives of the Island; and although Gervaise had, since his arrival on the Island, seen many stately ceremonies, this far surpassed anything he had previously beheld.

Gervaise had, at one of his first interviews with D'Aubusson after his arrival at the Island, been advised by him to acquire some knowledge of Turkish.

"There are but few knights of the Order who speak the language," he said. "As a rule, while young men are ready to devote any amount of time to acquiring dexterity in all martial exercises, they will bestow no labour in obtaining knowledge that may be fully as useful to them as skill in arms. In our dealings with the Turks, one or other party has to employ an interpreter, and it is often by no means certain that these men convey the full meaning of the speeches they translate. Again, we have large numbers of Turkish slaves, and it is highly to be desired that the knights should be able to give their orders to these men in their own language. Lastly, a knight who has been taken prisoner by the Turks-and even the bravest might meet with such a misfortune-would find it an alleviation of his lot, and might be able to plan and carry out his escape, did he speak Turkish well. I should strongly counsel you to acquire a knowledge of the tongue."

Gervaise had intended to follow the advice of the grand prior, but the duties of his office as page, and the time required for his military exercises and his studies with the chaplain, had rendered it well nigh impossible, during the first three years, to turn his attention to learning Turkish. As soon as his pageship was at an end, and he found that his duties included supervision of Turkish slaves, he felt the want of a knowledge of the language, and from that time devoted an hour a day to its study, employing one of the servants of the auberge, who was a man of rank and education at home, to instruct him.

While he conscientiously spent this amount of time at the work, it was the most disagreeable portion of this day's labour. The events, however, that had taken place during the expedition had impressed him greatly with the utility of a knowledge of Turkish, for had it not been for Sir John Boswell's possessing some acquaintance with the language, it would have been impossible to communicate with the rowers of their boat, or to have arranged the plan by which they had escaped the pirates. He had then and there determined that as soon as he returned to Rhodes he would take the matter up in a very different spirit to that in which he before approached it. He had on the way home spoken to Sir John, who had highly approved of the determination.

"I myself, when I was a young knight of eighteen, was taken captive, twenty-six years ago, at the time when the Egyptian fleet appeared before Rhodes. Our galleys advanced to attack them, but under cover of night they retired, and proceeding to the mainland took shelter under the guns of a Turkish fort. We attacked them there; it was a desperate engagement, but without any decisive advantage on either side. We lost no less than sixty knights, the Egyptians seven hundred men; and their fleet returned to Egypt. I and three others who were left wounded on the deck of one of their ships we had boarded, but failed to capture, were carried to Egypt, and remained there captive for six months, when we were ransomed by the Order.

"During that time I learnt enough of their language, which is akin to Turkish, to be able to make myself understood and to understand what was said to me. I have kept up that much for intercourse with the slaves and servants at Rhodes, and have found it very useful. I consider, then, that you will do well to acquire their tongue; it will be useful not only to yourself, but to others, and when we get back I will, if you like, ask the bailiff to free you from all duty in order that you may devote yourself to it."

The head of the langue at once granted Sir John's request.

"I would," he said, "that more of our young knights would give a portion of their time to study; but most of them look to returning home when their term of service here has expired. Many think only of amusement, and all imagine that advancement is best achieved by valour. Tresham has already distinguished himself very greatly; so much so, that I think it would be well if he did not go on another expedition for a time, but stayed here while others have the opportunity of doing the same. Were we to send him out with the next galleys that start, I should be accused of favouritism, and the lad, who is now deservedly popular with all, would be regarded with envy, and possibly even with dislike.

"At the same time, after what he has done I should have difficulty in refusing, were he to volunteer to sail in the next galley that sets out. The desire, then, on his part to learn Turkish is in all ways opportune. It will, too, in the long run be of great advantage to him in the Order, will give him weight, and bring him into prominence. I do not think there are six in the Order who can fairly translate a Turkish document; there are but two who could write a reply in the same language. Inform him, then, that from the present time he will be excused from all work, except, of course, to join in ceremonials when all are required to be present; and if you, Sir John, will pick out from among the servitors here one who is well instructed and educated, and capable of writing as well as reading his language, I will similarly relieve him of all other work, and place him at the disposal of young Tresham. Tell the lad that I hope he will persevere until he obtains a complete knowledge of the tongue. You can mention to him what I have said as to my opinion of the advantage the knowledge of it will be to him in the Order."

Gervaise accordingly devoted himself to study. His instructor was a Turk of fine presence. He had been a large landowner in Syria, and held a high official position in the province, but had been captured in a galley on his way to Constantinople, whither he was proceeding on an official mission. He was delighted with his new post. Gervaise, both as the youngest member of the community, and from the kind manner in which he always spoke to the servants, —all of whom had acquired some knowledge of English, —was a general favourite among them, and the Turk was glad that he was to be thrown with him. Still more he rejoiced at being appointed his instructor, as it relieved him from all menial work which, although preferable to that to which the bulk of the slaves were condemned, yet galled his spirit infinitely.

Now that he had entered upon the work with the approbation of his superior, and a conviction of its great utility, Gervaise set to work with the same zeal and ardour which he had exhibited in his military exercises. During the heat of the day he sat in the shade reading and writing with his instructor. In the cool of the morning and afternoon he walked with him on the walls, or in the country beyond them. After sunset he sat with him in an unfrequented corner of the roof, all the time conversing with him, either of his own country, or that of his instructor.

At first this was difficult, and he had to eke out the Turkish words he had acquired with English; but it was not long before there was no necessity for this. His intercourse for ten or twelve hours a day with this Turk, and the pains taken by his instructor, caused him to acquire the language with extreme rapidity. Of course, he had to put up with a great deal of banter from the younger knights upon his passion for study. Sometimes they pretended that his mania, as they considered it, arose from the fact that he was determined to become a renegade, and was fitting himself for a high position in the Turkish army. At other times they insisted that his intention was to become a Turkish dervish, or to win a great Turkish heiress and settle in Syria. But as he always bore their banter good temperedly, and was ready occasionally to join them in the sport when assaults-at-arms were carried on, they soon became tired of making fun of him.

After nine months' constant work, the young knight's studies were abruptly stopped by the receipt of a letter from the Pasha of Syria, offering a considerable sum for the ransom of his instructor. The request was at once acceded to, as it was the policy of the knights to accept ransoms for their prisoners, both because the sums so gained were useful, and because they were themselves compelled sometimes to pay ransom for members of the Order. Suleiman Ali was, it was arranged, to be put on board an Egyptian craft bound for Acre, a safe conduct having been sent for the vessel and her crew, and for a knight, who was to receive the ransom from the pasha.

"At any rate, Sir Gervaise," the Turk said, when the young knight expressed great regret at his leaving them, "our position as instructor and pupil would have come to an end shortly. For the last three months there has been but little teaching between us; we have talked, and that has been all, save that for a short time each day you read and wrote. But there has been little to teach. You speak the native language now as fluently as I do, and would pass anywhere as a Syrian, especially as there are slight differences of speech in the various provinces. I believe that in Syria you would not be suspected of being anything but a native, and assuredly you would be taken for a Syrian elsewhere. You have learnt enough, and it would be but a waste of time for you, a knight and a soldier, to spend another day in study."

On the following day Gervaise was, to his surprise, sent for by the grand master. Except on the occasion of a few public ceremonies, he had not seen D'Aubusson since he had been elected to his present high dignity, and the summons to attend at the palace therefore came unexpectedly.

"We have become quite strangers, Tresham," the grand master said cordially when he entered. "I have not forgotten you, and have several times questioned your bailiff concerning you. He tells me that you have become quite an anchorite, and that, save at your meals and for an occasional bout-at-arms, you are seldom to be seen. I was glad to hear of your devotion to study, and thought it better to leave you undisturbed at it. Yesterday evening I sent for your instructor. He is a man of influence in Syria, and I wished to learn how he was affected towards us, now that he is about to return there. We talked for some time, and I then asked him what progress you had made, and was surprised and pleased to find that in his opinion you could pass anywhere as a native, and that you were perfectly capable of drawing up and writing any document I might desire to send to the sultan or any of his generals. This is far more than I had expected, and shows how earnestly you must have worked. Your knowledge may prove of much assistance to the Order, and believe me, the time you have spent in acquiring it may prove of much greater advantage to you in your career than if you had occupied it in performing even the most valiant deeds, and that at some future time it will ensure your appointment to a responsible office here. It was partly to assure you of my approbation that I sent for you, partly to inform you that I have appointed you to proceed with Suleiman Ali as the knight in charge of the vessel, and to receive the ransom agreed on, upon your handing him over. The office is an honourable one and one of trust, and it is the first fruits of the advantages you will gain by your knowledge of Turkish. No, do not thank me. I am selecting you because you are better fitted than any knight I can spare for the mission, and also, I may say, because the choice will be pleasing to Suleiman Ali, whose goodwill I am desirous of gaining. Before now Turkish provinces have thrown off their allegiance to the sultan. They have, I must admit, been usually reconquered, but such might not be always the case; and if such an event happened in Syria, this man's influence and goodwill might be of great advantage to us, as it might well suit us to ally ourselves with Syria against Constantinople. I am glad to say that I found him at least as well disposed as any man could be who had been some years in slavery. He admitted that, for a slave, he had been kindly and gently treated, and added that any unpleasant memories he might have retained had been obliterated by the nine months of pleasant companionship spent with you."

When Gervaise returned to dinner at the auberge, and informed Ralph Harcourt and the other young knights that he had been appointed to take charge of the vessel in which Suleiman Ali was to be conveyed to Acre, the statement was at first received with incredulity. It seemed incredible that the youngest knight in the langue should be chosen for such a mission, involving as it did a separate command. Even the older knights, when the news was passed down the table, were surprised.

"I must say that I am astonished at the grand master's choice. Sir Gervaise Tresham doubtless distinguished himself greatly some months since, but from that time he has not been out with the galleys, or, indeed, done anything that would seem to recommend him for so marked a favour as a separate command."

"I don't know, Wingate," Sir John Boswell said. "It seems to me that when a young knight of seventeen eschews all pleasure, refrains from volunteering for service at sea, and spends his whole time in study, he does distinguish himself, and that very greatly. Of the three or four hundred young knights here I doubt if one other would have so acted. Certainly, none to my knowledge have done so. Yet I do not suppose that D'Aubusson selected him for this duty as a reward for so much self denial and study, but because by that self denial and study he is more fitted for it than any of us here, save some three or four knights in the other langues, all of whom are in too high a position to be employed in so unimportant a duty. He can speak Turkish-not a few score of words and sentences such as I can, but, as Suleiman Ali tells me, like a native. Were one of us chosen for this mission, it would be necessary to send an interpreter with him; and every one knows how hard it is to do business in that manner. It seems to me that the grand master has acted wisely in putting aside all question of seniority, and employing the knight who is better suited than any other for it."

"You are right, Boswell," the bailiff said. "I really have been astonished at the manner in which Tresham has given himself up to study. It would have been a natural thing had he, after gaining so much credit, been anxious and eager to gain more. When you spoke to me about his determination to learn Turkish, I thought he would speedily tire of it, and that when the next galley sailed, his name would be among the list of volunteers for the service. I am sure, comrades, that there are few, if any, among us who would not infinitely prefer fighting the Moslems to spending our whole time in learning their language; and I for one consider the fact that he has for nine months laboured so incessantly and assiduously that he has come, as Boswell says, to speak it like a native, is even more to his credit than the deed for which he was knighted."

This conversation took place at the upper end of the table, and was not heard at the lower end where the younger knights were seated.

"I am not chosen from favour," Gervaise said hotly, to one of his companions who had asserted that this was so. "I am simply chosen because I can speak Turkish."

"How much Turkish can you speak?" one of them laughed. Gervaise turned to the Turkish servant behind them, and said, in his language, "Hassan, Sir Giles Trevor wishes to know how well I speak Turkish. You have heard me talking with Suleiman Ali. Will you give him your opinion about it?"

The man turned gravely to Sir Giles Trevor.

"My lord," he said, in English, "Sir Gervaise Tresham, he speaks Turkish same as I do. If he dress up in Turk clothes I suppose him Turk, not know he Christian by his speech."

Exclamations of surprise broke from the young knights.

"Well, you have earned the appointment, Tresham," Ralph Harcourt said heartily. "You always told me when I asked you that you were getting on, but I had not the least idea that you were getting on like this. And can you read and write the Turkish language?"

"Well enough for practical purposes, Ralph. At any rate, I wrote a complimentary letter this morning from the grand master to the governor of Syria, and the bailiff of Spain, who was, as you know, for ten years a prisoner among the Turks, read it through at D'Aubusson's request, to see that there was no error in it, and was good enough to pass it without alteration."

"I would give a good deal," Sir Giles Trevor said, "if I could follow your example, and shut myself up for nine months with an infidel to study his language; but I could not do it if my life depended on it. I should throw myself off the wall at the end of the first fortnight."

"I don't pretend that I can do what Tresham has done," Ralph Harcourt said. "I always hated our lessons with the chaplain, who gave me the character of having the thickest head of any of his pupils; but I vow" —and he kissed the handle of his dagger— "I will spend half an hour a day in trying to learn something of Turkish. Of course, I know that such time will not be enough to learn a great deal; but if one could get up just enough to be able to give orders to the slaves, to question the captain of a vessel one has captured, and to make them understand a little, if by bad luck one fell into their hands, it would be quite enough for me. I am sure sometimes one is quite at a loss how to pass the hours when the sun is at its hottest, and if one tried one ought to be able to pick up a little without much trouble. Look at the servants; there is not one of them but speaks a little English. And if an infidel can learn enough English to get on with, without any regular study, I can't see why we shouldn't be able to learn enough Turkish in the same way."

Two or three of the other young knights declared that they too would devote a short time during the heat of the day to learning Turkish, and they agreed to begin together forthwith with one of the servants, who spoke English most fluently. Robert Rivers was not present, for he had returned to England six months before, to take up his residence at the House in Clerkenwell, in order that he might bring to bear the interest of his many powerful friends to secure for him an appointment as commander of one of the estates of the Order in England. His departure had caused general satisfaction among the other knights, whom his arrogance and ill temper had frequently irritated. Gervaise especially was glad at his leaving the Island, for after he received the honour of knighthood, Rivers made a point of always addressing him with an affectation of deference and respect that often tried his temper to the utmost.

"It is well that Rivers has gone," Ralph said, laughing, "for I don't know how he would have supported the chagrin your appointment would have given him. He was devoured with jealousy as it was, but this would have been a trial beyond bearing."

"I am heartily glad he has gone," Gervaise said gravely. "I have put up with a great deal from him, but I don't think I could have stood much more. If our vows had not forbidden our fighting I should have called him to account long ago; but the only thing else to do was for me to lodge a formal complaint before the bailiff, of his continually offensive bearing and manner, which I could not bring myself to do, and indeed there was no special matter that would have seemed to justify me, no single speech that in itself would warrant such grave action on my part. I used to wish over and over again that we could but meet in some quiet spot in England, both unarmed, and could there settle the matter in good English fashion, with our fists, or even with a couple of quarterstaffs."

The others laughed.

"That would be a very unknightly form of contest."

"I care not for that," Gervaise replied. "It would be a very satisfactory one anyhow, and quite serious enough for the occasion. His sneers and petty insults were not sufficient to justify the drawing of blood, and there has been enough of that shed for the last twenty years in England without two brother knights betaking themselves to their swords against each other. But a sound thrashing would have done neither of us harm, and if it had fallen to his lot to get the largest share of it, it might have done him some good."

"He thinks he is sure of an appointment," one of the others said, "but he has been so frequently in trouble here that it is likely that the official report, which is always sent home to the grand prior when the knights return to England, will be so unfavourable that even the most powerful influence will fail to obtain him a post. If so, we may have him back here again, especially if the Turks carry out their threat of assailing us, for an appeal will be made to all the grand priors for knights to aid in the defence."

That evening Gervaise went again to the palace to receive final instructions.

"The craft in which you are to travel is an Egyptian trader. As at present war has not been formally declared between us and the sultan, peaceful traders, as you know, carry on their avocations unmolested either by the warships of the Turks or by ours; they do not enter our ports without a special permit, and the crews are never allowed to land, in order that no detailed account of our fortifications may be taken to the sultan. Moreover, brawls might arise between them and the native population, or they might aid slaves to escape. However, you will be altogether safe from interference from Turkish war vessels, and if overhauled by one of them the safe conduct will be sufficient to prevent interference with you. But it is not so with pirates. They will plunder their own countrymen as readily as they will Christians, and the safe guard of the governor of Syria will be of no use whatever to you. In this consists the danger of your mission. I cannot send one of our war galleys on such an errand, and if there are not enough knights on board to beat off any pirate, the fewer there are the better. I hear that the craft is a fast sailor, and as the crew will be as anxious to avoid pirates as you, they will do their best to escape. I leave it to you to take any route. You can either sail hence direct for Acre, or you can coast along the shores of Anatolia and Syria, lying up at night in bays.

"Should you be overtaken I do not think it would be of any use for you to disguise yourself, for some of the crew would be sure to denounce you. Should the worst happen, and you are captured by pirates, you will of course in the first place show them your safe conduct, and if I find that you do not return I shall send at once to the governor of Syria, complaining of your capture when furnished with his safeguard, and requesting him to order a search for you to be made at every port on the coast, with instructions that you are to be at once released, and either sent to him for return hither, or placed on board a craft bound for any Christian port; while you, on your part, will endeavour to acquaint the Turkish authorities with the fact that you have been seized while travelling with a safe conduct from the governor of Syria.

"But, more than from any efforts on your part or mine, I rely upon Suleiman Ali, who will, I am sure, as soon as he is set on shore, lose no time in acquainting the pasha of your capture, and in calling upon him to interfere in your favour. In that case, the worst that could befall you would be a temporary detention, unless, indeed, the pirates should take you to Egypt. As that country is friendly with us at present, since Egypt dreads the ever increasing power of the Turks, it will be but a question of ransom, for I have secret agents there who will inform me without delay of the arrival of a Christian captive."

"I understand, sir, and will do my best in the matter. If I am captured I trust that an opportunity of escape will soon present itself, for I should, if taken, conceal from my captors the fact that I understand their language, and should thus, if I could evade my guard, have every chance of escaping, as in a native dress I could meet and converse with those hunting for me, without their having a suspicion of my being the white slave for whom they were in search."

"Once at Acre you will be safe. But do not land unless it is absolutely necessary, for you might fall a victim to the fanaticism of its inhabitants, and no knight has ever set foot on shore there since the ill fated day when the Moslems wrested it from us, bathed the ruined walls with the best blood of our Order and the Templars', and destroyed the last hope of our ever recovering the Holy Sepulchre."

The next morning at daybreak Gervaise and Suleiman Ali went on board the Egyptian trader, and sailed for Acre. The current of opinion had changed at the auberge when the knights came to think over the mission on which Gervaise was about to start, and the slight feeling of jealousy with which the younger knights had received the news was entirely dissipated. While it did not seem to them that there was any chance of his distinguishing himself, they perceived, as they thought it over, the considerable danger there was of capture by pirates, and Ralph and some of his companions came down to the mole to see him off, with feelings in which envy bore no part whatever.

"I see now, Gervaise, that it is truly no holiday excursion on which you are starting. I should envy you greatly were you going in command of an armed galley, prepared to beat off any craft that might try to overhaul you; but, going alone as you are, it is a very different thing. Should pirates meet you, you could offer no resistance, and your position would be a perilous one indeed. However, I think you are born to good luck, and am confident that your patron saint will look after you, and therefore expect to see you back here in a fortnight's time at the outside."

"I hope so with all my heart, Ralph. It will be no fault of mine if I tarry."

"Will you keep the open sea, or skirt the land, Tresham?" one of the others asked.

"I shall keep the open sea. The grand master left me to choose my course; but I think there is more danger by the coast-where pirates may be hiding in unfrequented bays, in readiness to pounce upon a passing craft-than in the open sea, where we should have at least the advantage that we could not be taken by surprise, and might make a race of it. But the sun will be up in a few minutes, and my orders were to set out at sunrise, so I must say goodbye at once."

As soon as the vessel was under way, Gervaise took a seat on the poop by the side of Suleiman Ali, and related to him the conversation he had had with the grand master.

"The risk that you will run has not escaped me," the Turk said, "and indeed, I now regret that you were chosen as my escort. I almost wish that my son had not purchased my freedom at the present time, since it involves the risk of you losing yours. There is no doubt that the sea swarms with pirates; the sultan is too busy with his own struggles for Empire to bestow any attention upon so small a matter. The pashas and the officers of the ports have not the power, even had they the will, to put down piracy in their districts, and indeed are, as often as not, participators in the spoils. Your Order, which, years back, scoured the seas so hotly that piracy well nigh ceased, have now for forty years been obliged to turn their attention chiefly to their own defence. They possess a comparatively small fleet of galleys, and their wealth is expended on their fortress.

"What with Egypt and the sultan their hands are too full for them to act as the police of the sea, and the consequence is that from every port, bay, and inlet, pirate craft set out-some mere rowboats, some, like those under the command of Hassan Ali, veritable fleets. Thus the humblest coasters and the largest merchant craft go alike in fear of them, and I would that the sultan and Egypt and your Order would for two or three years put aside their differences, and confine their efforts to sweeping the seas of these pests, to storming their strongholds, and to inflicting such punishment upon them as that, for a very long time to come, peaceful merchants might carry on their trade without fear.

"I heard you tell the captain that he was to steer straight for Acre, and I think you are right in avoiding the coast, where the most harmless looking fishing boat may carry a crowd of pirates hidden in her hold. At the same time, if you will take my advice you will head much more to the south, so as to be out of the regular track of ships making from Constantinople or the islands to Acre. You may meet pirates anywhere, but they are assuredly thicker along the more frequented routes. The safest plan of all would probably be to bear south, and strike the Egyptian coast well to the east of the mouth of the Nile. Thence, till you get to Palestine, the country is utterly barren and uninhabited, while, running up the coast to Palestine, there are, save at Jaffa, no ports to speak of until you arrive at Acre; and besides, the inhabitants there, even if pirates, would not venture to disregard the pasha's safe conduct. I do not by any means say that such a course would be absolutely safe. You may meet with vessels on your way south, and doubtless some of them cruise off the barren coast I speak of, to intercept traders to and from Egypt and Acre, and other Syrian ports; for the trade carried on is considerable, and, although of the same religion, the Turks are disposed to view the Egyptians as enemies rather than as friends, and would have even less hesitation in plundering them than in robbing their own countrymen."

"I think that your suggestion is a good one, and will follow it, at any rate. The course is a good deal longer, but that is comparatively of little moment. The great thing is to carry you safely to Acre."

"And to get back with equal safety," Suleiman said, with a smile.

"That is quite as important in my eyes; in fact, of the two, I would far rather that we were captured on our voyage thither, for in that case I might be able to arrange for the ransom of both of us."

Chapter VIII
An Evening At Rhodes

Suleiman Ali's advice was carried out. It added considerably to the length of the voyage; but they saw only one doubtful craft. She was lying close inshore under the shadow of the sand hills, and they did not see her until she hoisted her sails and shot out from the land. They were, however, three miles distant from the land at the time, and the wind was blowing from the north; consequently the pirate was dead to leeward. Every sail was set at once on board the trader, and, being a fast sailor, she maintained her position until nightfall. The wind then dropped, and just as the light faded they could see that the vessel behind them had put out her sweeps. The trader kept up her sails until certain that she could be no longer seen; then the canvas was lowered, and the crew took to the boats and towed her due north.

The night was fortunately a dark one, and those watching anxiously from the deck of the trader were unable to discern her pursuer as she passed behind them. As soon as they were well assured that she must have gone on, the boats were got in, the sails hoisted again, and, taking advantage of every light flaw of wind, they proceeded on their course. In the morning the sails of the galley could be seen on the horizon, but the distance was too great for her to take up the pursuit again with any chance of success, and the trader continued her course to Acre without seeing more of her.

As soon as the trader entered the port, the Egyptian captain went on shore, taking with him a copy of the safe conduct and the letter from the grand master to the pasha. Going to the residence of the governor, he handed these to him, saying that he had on board Aga Suleiman Ali, and a knight who was charged to deliver him up on payment of the ransom.

"I have been expecting you," the governor said. "I have received a letter from the pasha, stating that he had written to the grand master respecting the ransom of the aga, and sending me the amount which Suleiman's son had offered. The young man was not of age when his father was captured, but he is so now, and was therefore able to raise the sum required. I will go down to the port with you myself, hand over the ransom, and welcome Suleiman, whom I know well, back from his captivity."

The transfer was speedily made; a heavy purse was handed to Gervaise, and Suleiman was a free man.

"Send me word, if you can, when you return to Rhodes," the latter said, as he bade farewell to the young knight. "I shall be anxious until I hear. Fortune was with us as we sailed hither, but it may desert you on your return. Should aught befall you, tell your captors that if they bring you to me I will pay any ransom that they could, in fairness, require. Should they refuse to do this, send, if possible, a messenger to me, and on receipt of your message I will send a trusty man to purchase your freedom. You have treated me as a friend and an equal, and a friend I shall always remain."

The vessel was to remain four days in port, to discharge her cargo and take in another, and Suleiman had talked of remaining at Acre until she sailed, but Gervaise protested strongly against this.

"You have your family, from whom you have been so long separated, awaiting your return with anxiety, and I pray you to make no stay on my account. I am well content to remain on board here, and to look at the city which has so often been the theatre of great deeds-which Richard the Lion Heart captured, and which so many of the Hospitallers died to defend. I was charged by the grand master not to land, and indeed I feel myself that it would be an act of folly to do so. There are doubtless many on shore who have relatives and friends now working as slaves among us, and some of these might well seek to avenge them by slaying one of the Order. I feel your kindness, but it would be a pain to me to know that you were lingering here on my account, when you must be longing to embrace your children."

The four days passed rapidly. Gervaise had, at the suggestion of the governor, laid aside the mantle and insignia of the Order.

"If you do not do so," he said, "I must place a strong guard of soldiers on board, in order to ensure that the pasha's safeguard is not violated. Sailors are a turbulent race, and were you recognised here they might make a tumult, and slay you before a word of what was going on reached me. In any case I shall place two soldiers on board until you leave the port."

On the morning of the fifth day the sails were got up, and the vessel sailed out from the port. Fortune again favoured them, and they reached Rhodes without any adventure. Gervaise went at once to the palace, and handed over the purse of gold to the treasurer. He then sent up his name to the grand master, and was immediately conducted to his room.

"I am glad to see you back, Tresham. I have been uneasy about you. Have you fulfilled your mission without adventure?"

"Without any adventure, sir, save that we were once chased by a pirate on our way east, but escaped in the darkness. Save for that, the voyage has been wholly uneventful. I have received the ransom, and handed the purse to your treasurer."

"I am glad that your first command has turned out so well. I will see that you do not lack employment; and the fact that you are able to act as interpreter will ensure you a welcome on any galley. At present, however, it is not my intention to send out many cruisers. Every life now is precious, and no amount of spoil that can be brought in will counter balance the loss of those who fall. However, I may find some mission on which you can be employed. I know that you love an active life; and as, for nine months, you have put a rein on your inclinations, and have devoted yourself wholly to study, so that you might be of greater use to the Order, you have a good right to any employment in which your knowledge can be utilised."

On his arrival at the auberge, Gervaise was very heartily greeted by the younger knights.

"I told you you were born lucky, Gervaise," Ralph Harcourt said. "There has been more than one wager made that you would be captured; but I, for my part, was confident that your good fortune would not desert you. Still, though not surprised, we are delighted to see you again. Now tell us about your voyage."

Gervaise gave a brief account of the adventure with the pirate, and then described the visit of the governor to the ship.

"Did he say anything to you?"

"He was courteous and solemn; just the sort of man you would fancy a Turkish governor should be. He looked a little surprised when I accosted him in Turkish, but asked no questions at the time, though I daresay he inquired afterwards of Suleiman how I came to speak the language. The only time he actually said anything was when he requested that I would not wear the mantle of the Order while in port, as sailors were a turbulent race, and it might lead to an attack upon me; and as he was responsible to the pasha that his safe conduct should be respected, it would be necessary, if I declined to follow his advice, to keep a strong body of soldiers on board. As this would have been a horrible nuisance, especially as I wanted to enjoy in quiet the view of the city, with its castle and walls, I acceded at once to his request, which seemed to me a reasonable one. He did send two soldiers on board, but they remained down in the waist, and did not interfere with my pleasure in any way."

"Next to Jerusalem, how I should like to see Acre!" Ralph Harcourt exclaimed. "It is, of all other cities, the most closely connected with our Order. We helped to win it, and we were the last to defend it. We have heard so much about the fortress, and it has been so often described to me, that I know the situation of every bastion-at least, as it was when we left it, though I know not what changes the Turks may since have made."

"That I know not, Ralph. Of course, I only saw the seafront, and it was upon the land side that the attack was made. We know that the breaches were all repaired long ago, and it is said that the place is stronger than ever. From the port all was solid and massive. It is indeed a grand and stately fortress. Here we have done all that was possible to make Rhodes impregnable, but nature did nothing for us; there nature has done everything, and the castle looks as if it could defy the assaults of an army, however large. And indeed, it was not wrested from us by force. The knights, when the city walls were stormed and the town filled with their foes fought their way down to the water's edge and embarked there, for they were reduced to a mere handful; and however strong a castle may be, it needs hands to defend it. Still, it well nigh moved me to tears to see the Turkish banner waving over it, and to think how many tens of thousands of Christian soldiers had died in the effort to retain the holy places, and had died in vain."

"I wonder whether the Turks will ever be forced to relinquish their hold of the holy places?"

"Who can tell, Sir Giles?" the bailiff, who had come up to the group unobserved, said quietly. "Certainly not in our time-not until the Moslem power, which threatens not only us, but all Europe, has crumbled to dust. So long as Acre remains in their power there is no hope. I say not but that by a mighty effort of all Christendom, Palestine might be wrested from the infidels, as it was wrested before; but the past shows us that while men or nations can be stirred to enthusiasm for a time, the fire does not last long, and once again the faithful few would be overwhelmed by the odds that would be brought against them, while Europe looked on impassive, if not indifferent. No, knights; the utmost that can be hoped for, is that the tide of Moslem invasion westward may be stayed. At present we are the bulwark, and as long as the standard of our Order waves over Rhodes so long is Europe safe by sea. But I foresee that this cannot last: the strongest defences, the stoutest hearts, and the bravest of hearts, cannot in the long run prevail against overpowering numbers. As at Acre, we may repel assault after assault, we may cause army after army to betake themselves again to their ships; but, as a rock is overwhelmed by the rising tide, so must Rhodes succumb at last, if left by Europe to bear alone the brunt of Moslem invasion. All that men can do we shall do. As long as it is possible to resist, we shall resist. When further resistance becomes impossible, we shall, I trust, act as we did before.

"We were driven from Palestine, only to fortify ourselves at Rhodes. If we are driven from Rhodes, we shall, I feel assured, find a home elsewhere, and again commence our labours. The nearer we are to Europe the more hope there is that Christendom will aid us, for they will more generally understand that our defeat would mean the laying open of the shores of the Mediterranean, from Turkey to Gibraltar, to the invasion of the Moslems. However, comrades, this is all in the future. Our share is but in the present, and I trust the flag of the Order will float over Rhodes as long, at least, as the lifetime of the youngest of us, and that we may bequeath the duty of upholding the Cross untarnished to those who come after us; and we can then leave the issue in God's hands."

All listened respectfully to the words of their leader, although his opinion fell like cold water upon the fiery zeal and high hopes of his hearers. The possibility of their losing Rhodes had never once entered into the minds of the majority of them. It was likely that ere long they might be called upon to stand a siege, but, acquainted as they were with the strength of the place-its deep and seemingly impassable moat, its massive walls, and protecting towers and bastions-it had seemed to them that Rhodes was capable of withstanding all assaults, however numerous the foe, however oft repeated the invasion. The bailiff was, as all knew, a man of dauntless courage, of wide experience and great judgment, and that he should believe that Rhodes would, although not in their time, inevitably fall, brought home to them for the first time the fact that their fortress was but an outpost of Europe, and one placed so distant from it that Christendom, in the hour of peril, might be unable to furnish them with aid. As the bailiff walked away, there was silence for a short time, and then Sir Giles Trevor said cheerfully, "Well, if it lasts our time we need not trouble our heads as to what will take place afterwards. As the bailiff says, our duty is with the present, and as we all mean to drive the Turks back when they come, I do not see that there is any occasion for us to take it to heart, even if it be fated that the Moslems shall one day walk over our tombs. If Christendom chooses to be supine, let Christendom suffer, say I. At any rate, I am not going to weep for what may take place after I am turned into dust."

"That sounds all very well, Sir Giles," Ralph Harcourt said, "and I have no argument to advance against it, though I am sure there is much to be said; but if the bailiff, or the chaplain, or indeed any of the elders, had heard you say so, I have no doubt you would have had a fitting reply."

Sir Giles tossed his head mockingly. "I shall fight neither better nor worse, friend Harcourt, because it may be that someday the Moslems are, as the bailiff seems to think, destined to lord it here. I have only promised and vowed to do my best against the Moslems, and that vow only holds good as long as I am in the flesh; beyond that I have no concern. But what are we staying here for, wasting our time? It is the hour for those of us who are going, to be starting for the ball given by Signor Succhi; as he is one of the richest merchants in the town, it will be a gay one, and there is no lack of fair faces in Rhodes. It is a grievous pity that our elders all set their will against even the younger members of the community joining in a dance. It was not one of the things I swore to give up. However, here in Rhodes there is no flying in the face of rules."

Three or four of the other young knights were also going.

"What are you thinking of doing, Gervaise?" Harcourt asked.

"I have nothing particular to do, Ralph, except that, first of all, I must write a letter to Suleiman Ali and hand it to the bailiff, praying him to send it off by the first vessel that may put in here on her way to Acre. If I do not do it now it may be neglected, and I promised to write directly I got here. I will not be half an hour, and after that I shall be ready to do anything you like."

In less than that time, indeed, he rejoined Ralph. "Now what shall we do with ourselves? What do you say to a stroll through the streets? I am never tired of that."

"I like better to go by way of the roofs, Gervaise. The streets are badly lit, and although they are busy enough in some quarters, they are so narrow that one gets jostled and pushed. On the terraces everything is quiet. You have plenty of light and music, and it is pleasant to see families sitting together and enjoying themselves; and if one is disposed for a cup of wine or of cool sherbet, they are delighted to give it, for they all are pleased when one of us joins a group. I have quite a number of acquaintances I have made in this way while you have been working away at your Turkish."

"Very well," Gervaise said. "If such is your fancy, Ralph, let us take one of the paths across the roofs. I might walk there twenty years by myself without making an acquaintance, and I do not pledge myself to join in these intimacies of yours. However, I shall be quite content to amuse myself by looking on at the scene in general, while you are paying your visits and drinking your sherbet."

"There are plenty of fair girls among the Rhodians," Ralph said, with a smile; "and though we are pledged to celibacy we are in no way bound to abstain from admiration."

Gervaise laughed.

"Admire as much as you like, Ralph, but do not expect me to do so. I have scarcely as much as spoken to a woman since I entered the House in London, and I should have no idea what to say to a young girl."

"But it is part of the education of a true knight to be courteous to women. It is one of the great duties of chivalry. And you must remember that we are secular knights, as well knights of the Order."

"The work of the Order is quite sufficient for me at present, Ralph. In time I may come to like the society of women, to admire their beauty, and possibly even to wear the colour of some one, for that seems to be the fashion; though why we, who are bound to celibacy, should admire one woman more than another I cannot understand."

They had by this time descended from the castle, and were taking their way along one of the broad paths that led over the flat roofs of the houses by means of the bridges thrown across the streets.

"These are some acquaintances of mine," Ralph said, stopping at one of the walls, some three feet high, that bordered the path.

Beyond was an enclosure of some fifty feet square. Clumps of shrubs and flowers, surrounded by stonework some eight or ten inches high enclosing the earth in which they grew, were scattered here and there. Lamps were hung to cords stretched above it, while others were arranged among the flowers. In the centre a large carpet was spread, and on this some eight or ten persons were seated on cushions. A girl was playing a lute, and another singing to her accompaniment. She stopped abruptly when her eye fell upon the figures of the two young knights.

"There is Sir Ralph Harcourt, father!" she exclaimed in Italian, which was the language most used on the Island, and spoken with more or less fluency by all the knights, among whom it served as a general medium of communication. "Are you waiting to be invited in, Sir Knight?" she went on saucily. "I thought that by this time you would know you were welcome."

"Your tongue runs too fast, child," her father said, as he rose and walked across to Ralph. "You are welcome, Sir Ralph, very welcome. I pray you enter and join us."

"I will do so with pleasure, Signor Vrados, if you will also extend your hospitality to my friend Sir Gervaise Tresham."

"Most gladly," the merchant said. "I pray him to enter."

The two knights passed through the gate in the wall. All rose to their feet as they went up to the carpet, and greeted Ralph with a warmth which showed that he was a favourite. He introduced Gervaise to them.

"I wonder that I do not know your face, Sir Knight," the merchant's wife said. "I thought I knew all the knights of the Order by sight, from seeing them either at the public ceremonies, or observing them pass in the streets."

"For the last nine months Sir Gervaise has been an anchorite. He has been learning Turkish, and has so devoted himself to the study that even I have scarce caught sight of him, save at meals. As for walking in the streets, it is the last thing he would think of doing. I consider myself a good and conscientious young knight, but I am as nothing in that respect to my friend. I used to look upon him as my little brother, for we were at the House of the Order in London together. He is four years younger than I am, and you know four years between boys makes an immense difference. Now the tables are turned, and I quite look up to him."

"You will believe as much as you like, Signora, of what Sir Ralph says," Gervaise laughed. "As you have, he says, known him for some time, you must by this time have learnt that his word is not to be taken literally."

"We learned that quite early in our acquaintance," the girl who had first noticed them said, with an affectation of gravity. "I always tell him that I cannot believe anything he says, and I am grateful to you, Sir Knight, for having thus borne evidence to the quickness of my perception."

By this time the servants had brought some more cushions, and on these Ralph and Gervaise seated themselves. Wine, sherbet, and cakes, were then handed round. The master of the house placed Gervaise on his right hand, as a stranger.

"You have been among our islands, Sir Gervaise? But indeed, I need not ask that, since I know that you and Sir Ralph were knighted together for your valour in that affair with the ships of Hassan Ali. We come from Lesbos. It is now eighty years since my family settled in Rhodes, and we have seen it grow from a small place to a great fortress."

"'Tis a wonderful place," Gervaise said. "I know nothing of the fortresses of Europe, but it seems to me that no other can well be stronger than this-that is, among places with no natural advantages."

"The knights have always had an abundance of slaves," the merchant said; "so many that they have not only had sufficient for their work here, but have been able to sell numbers to European potentates. Yes, Rhodes is wonderfully strong. That great fosse would seem as if it could defy the efforts of an army to cross; and yet the past has shown that even the strongest defences, held with the greatest bravery, can be carried by generals with immense armies, and careless how they sacrifice them so that they do but succeed. Look at Acre, for example."

"I was looking at it five days ago," Gervaise said, "and thinking that it was beyond the might of man to take."

"Do you mean that you were at Acre?" the merchant asked, with surprise.

"Yes. I went there to hand over a captive who had been ransomed. Of course I had a safe conduct, and I was glad indeed of the opportunity of seeing so famous a fortress."

"You were fortunate indeed, Sir Knight, and it was, if you will pardon my saying so, singular that so young a knight should have been chosen. Assuredly, even the senior knights of the Order would rejoice at the opportunity of beholding a fortress so intimately connected with the past history of the Order."

"It was due entirely to my being able to speak Turkish," Gervaise said. "As my friend Sir Ralph was mentioning, I have been studying hard, and can now speak the language fluently; and as this was a necessity on such a mission, and the few knights who can so speak it are all in high office, and could hardly be asked to undertake so unimportant a service, I was selected."

"And you really speak Turkish well? It is an accomplishment that few, save Greeks subject to Turkey, possess. Do you intend, may I ask, to make Rhodes your home? I ask because I suppose you would not have taken this labour had you intended shortly to return to England."

"Yes; I hope to remain here permanently. I know that the first step towards promotion here is generally a commandery at home, but I did not enter the Order with any idea of gaining office or dignity. I desire simply to be a knight of the Cross, and to spend my life in doing faithful service to the Order."

"A worthy ambition indeed, and one that, so far as my experience goes, very few knights entertain. I see yearly scores of young knights depart, no small proportion of whom never place foot on Rhodes again, although doubtless many of them will hasten back again as soon as the danger of an assault from the Turks becomes imminent. You see, we who dwell here under the protection of the Order naturally talk over these things among ourselves; and although, in the matter of fortifications, all will admit that enormous efforts have been made to render the town secure, it is clear that in the matter of knights to defend them there is very much left to be desired. It is all very well to say that the knights from all parts of Europe would flock hither to defend it; but the journey would be a long one, and would occupy much time, and they would probably not receive news that the Turks had sailed until the place was already invested. Then it would be difficult, if not altogether impossible, for ships with reinforcements to make their way through the Turkish fleet, and to enter the port. To man the walls properly would need a force five times as numerous as that which is now here. I recognise the valour of your knights; they have accomplished wonders. But even they cannot accomplish impossibilities. For a time they could hold the walls; but as their number became reduced by the fire of the Turkish cannon and the battles at the breaches, they would at last be too weak any longer to repel the onslaughts of foes with an almost unlimited supply of soldiers."

"That is true enough," Gervaise admitted; "and to my mind it is shocking that four-fifths at least of the Order, pledged to oppose the infidels, should be occupied with the inglorious work of looking after the manors and estates of the society throughout Europe, while one-fifth, at most, are here performing the duties to which all are sworn. Of the revenues of the estates themselves, a mere fraction finds its way hither. Still, I trust that the greater part of the knights will hasten here as soon as danger becomes imminent, without waiting for the news that the Turkish armament has actually set forth."

For an hour the two young knights remained on the roof, Gervaise talking quietly with the merchant, while his companion laughed and chatted with the ladies and friends of their host. After they had left, with the promise that it would not be long before they repeated their visit, Ralph bantered Gervaise on preferring the society of the merchant to that of his daughters.

"I found him a pleasant and very well informed man, Ralph, and enjoyed my talk with him just as you enjoyed talking nonsense to his daughters and listening to their songs. Who was the man sitting next to the eldest daughter?"

"He doesn't belong to Rhodes, but is a Greek from one of the islands, though I did not catch from which. I don't know whether he is a relative of the family, or a business connection of the merchant's, or a stranger who has brought a letter of introduction to him. Nothing was said on that head; why do you ask?"

"I don't like the man's face; he is a handsome fellow, but has a crafty expression. He did not say much, but it seemed to me that at times, when he appeared to be sitting carelessly sipping his sherbet, he was really trying to listen to what Vrados was saying to me. He could not do so, for we were on the other side of the circle, and were speaking in somewhat low tones, while the rest of you were chatting and laughing."

"What should he want to listen for, most sapient knight?"

"That I can't tell, Ralph; but I am certain that he was trying to listen."

"Well, as you were no doubt both talking more sensibly than most of us," Ralph laughed, "he certainly showed his discernment."

"I daresay I am wrong," Gervaise said quietly; "but you know we have our spies at Constantinople, and probably the sultan has his spies here; and the idea occurred to me that perhaps this man might be one of them."

"Well, I am bound to say, Gervaise," Ralph said, a little irritably, "I have never heard so grave an accusation brought on such insufficient evidence-or rather, as far as I can see, without a shadow of evidence of any kind. We drop in upon a man who is one of our most respected merchants, whose family has been established here many years, whose interests must be the same as those of the Order; and because a guest of his does not care to take any active part in my joking with the girls, and because you imagine that there is a cunning expression on his face, you must straightway take it into your head that he must be a spy."

"Excuse me, Ralph, I simply said that the idea occurred to me that he might be a spy, which is a very different thing to my accusing him of being one. I am ready to admit that the chances are infinitely greater that he is an honest trader or a relation of the merchant, and that his presence here is perfectly legitimate and natural, than that he should be a spy. Still, there is a chance, if it be but one out of a thousand, that he may be the latter. I don't think that I am at all of a suspicious nature, but I really should like to learn a little about this man. I do not mean that I am going to try to do so. It would be an unworthy action to pry into another's business, when it is no concern of one's own. Still, I should like to know why he is here."

Ralph shrugged his shoulders.

"This comes of living the life of a hermit, Gervaise. Other people meet and talk, and enjoy what society there is in the city, without troubling their heads for a moment as to where people come from or what their business is here, still less whether they are spies. Such ideas do not so much as occur to them, and I must say that I think the sooner you fall into the ways of other people the better."

"There is no harm done," Gervaise said composedly. "I am not thinking of asking our bailiff to order him to be arrested on suspicion. I only remarked that I did not like the man's face, nor the way in which, while he pretended to be thinking of nothing, he was trying to overhear what we were saying. I am quite willing to admit that I have made a mistake, not in devoting myself to Turkish, but in going to the merchant's with you this evening. I have had no experience whatever of what you call society, and, so far from it giving me pleasure to talk to strangers, especially to women, it seems to me that such talk is annoying to me, at any rate at present. When I get to your age, possibly my ideas may change. I don't for a moment wish to judge you or others; you apparently enjoy it, and it is a distraction from our serious work. I say simply that it is an amusement which I do not understand. You must remember that I entered the Order in consequence of a solemn vow of my dead father, that I regard the profession we make as a very serious one, and that my present intention is to devote my life entirely to the Order and to an active fulfilment of its vows."

"That is all right, Gervaise," Ralph said good temperedly. "Only I think it would be a pity if you were to turn out a fanatic. Jerusalem and Palestine are lost, and you admit that there is really very little chance of our ever regaining them. Our duties, therefore, are changed, and we are now an army of knights, pledged to war against the infidels, in the same way as knights and nobles at home are ever ready to engage in a war with France. The vow of poverty is long since obsolete. Many of our chief officials are men of great wealth, and indeed, a grand master, or the bailiff of a langue, is expected to spend, and does spend, a sum vastly exceeding his allowance from the Order. The great body of knights are equally lax as to some of their other vows, and carry this to a length that, as you know, has caused grave scandal. But I see not that it is in any way incumbent on us to give up all the pleasures of life. We are a military Order, and are all ready to fight in defence of Rhodes, as in bygone days we were ready to fight in defence of the Holy Sepulchre. Kings and great nobles have endowed us with a large number of estates, in order to maintain us as an army against Islam; and as such we do our duty. But to affect asceticism is out of date and ridiculous."

"I have certainly no wish to be an ascetic, Ralph. I should have no objection to hold estates, if I had them to hold. But I think that at present, with the great danger hanging over us, it would be better if, in the first place, we were all to spend less time in idleness or amusement, and to devote all our energies to the cause. I mean not only by fighting when the time comes for fighting, but by endeavouring in every way to ward off danger."

"When I see danger, I will do my best to ward it off, Gervaise; but I cannot go about with my nose in the air, snuffing danger like a hunting dog in pursuit of game. At any rate, I will not bother you to accompany me on my visits in future."

Chapter IX
With The Galley Slaves

Gervaise, on consideration, was obliged to own to himself that Ralph was right in saying that he had no ground whatever for suspicion against the Greek he had met at Signor Vrados's; and he could see no means of following the matter up. It would not, he felt, be honourable to go again to the merchant's house, and to avail himself of his hospitality, while watching his guest. He determined to dismiss the matter from his mind, and had, indeed, altogether done so when, a week later, it suddenly recurred to his memory.

A party of slaves, under the escort of overseers and in charge of a knight who had been with them at their work on the fortifications, were passing along the street on their way back to barracks. It was already dusk, and as Gervaise was going the same way as they were, he stood aside in a doorway to let them pass. He was on the point of stepping out to follow them, when he saw a man, who had been standing in the shadow of the wall, fall in with their ranks, and, as he walked engaged in an earnest conversation with one of the slaves. He kept beside him for a hundred yards or so, then passed something into the slave's hand, and turned abruptly down a side opening. There were but few people about, and in the growing darkness the action of the man passed unobserved by the overseers. Gervaise, thinking the occurrence a strange one, turned down the same lane as the man.

He slackened his pace until the latter was fifty yards ahead, so that he would not, had he looked round, have been able to perceive that it was a knight who was behind him. After passing through several streets, the man turned into a refreshment house. The door stood open, and as the place was brightly lit up, Gervaise, pausing outside, was able to see what was going on inside. The man he had followed was on the point of seating himself at one of the tables, and as he did so Gervaise recognised him as the Greek he had met at the merchant's house. He at once walked on a short distance, and then paused to think.

The vague suspicions he had before entertained as to the man now recurred with double force; he was certainly in communication with one or more of the slaves, and such communication, so secretly effected, could be for no good purpose. So far, however, there was nothing he could tax the man with. He would probably deny altogether that he had spoken to any of the slaves, and Gervaise could not point out the one he had conversed with. At any rate, nothing could be done now, and he required time to think what steps he could take to follow up the matter. He resolved, however, to wait and follow the Greek when he came out. After a few minutes he again repassed the door, and saw that the man was engaged in earnest conversation with another. After considering for a time, Gervaise thought that it would be best for him to follow this other man when he left, and ascertain who he was, rather than to keep a watch on the movements of the Greek, who, as likely as not, would now return to the merchant's.

He walked several times up and down the street, until at last he saw the two men issue out together. They stopped for a moment outside, and then, after exchanging a few words, separated, the Greek going in the direction of the quarter in which lay the house of Vrados, while the other walked towards Gervaise. The latter passed him carelessly, but when the man had gone nearly to the end of the street, he turned and followed him. He could see at once that he was a lay brother of the Order. This class consisted of men of an inferior social position to the knights; they filled many of the minor offices, but were not eligible for promotion. Following for ten minutes, Gervaise saw him approach one of the barracks, or prisons, occupied by the slaves. He knocked at the door, and, upon its being opened, at once entered.

The matter had now assumed a much more serious aspect. This young Greek, a stranger to Rhodes, was in communication not only with some of the slaves, but with a prison official, and the matter appeared so grave to Gervaise that, after some deliberation, he thought it was too important for him to endeavour to follow out alone, and that it was necessary to lay it before the bailiff. Accordingly, after the evening meal he went up to Sir John Kendall, and asked if he could confer with him alone on a matter over which he was somewhat troubled. The bailiff assented at once, and Gervaise followed him to his private apartment.

"Now, what is this matter, Sir Gervaise?" he asked pleasantly. "Nothing serious, I trust?"

"I don't know, Sir John. That is a matter for your consideration; but it seems to me of such importance that it ought to be brought to your knowledge."

The face of the bailiff grew more grave, and, seating himself in a chair, he motioned to Gervaise to do the same.

"Now, let me hear what it is," he said.

Gervaise told his story simply. A slight smile passed across the bailiff's face as he mentioned that he had met the Greek on the roof of the house of Signor Vrados, and had not liked the expression of his face.

"Vrados has some fair daughters, has he not?" he asked.

"Yes, sir; but I know little of them. That is the only visit that I ever paid there, or, indeed, to the house of any one in the town."

Sir John's face grew grave again as Gervaise recounted how he had seen the man enter into communication with a slave; and he frowned heavily when he heard of his meeting afterwards with one of the prison officers.

"In truth, Sir Gervaise," he said, after a pause, "this seems to be a right serious matter, and you have done wisely in informing me of what you have seen. Assuredly there is mischief of some sort in the wind. The question is how to get to the bottom of it. Of course, the grand master might order the arrest of this Greek and of the prison officer, but you may be sure that neither would commit himself unless torture were applied; and I, for one, have no belief in what any man says under such circumstances. The most honest man may own himself a traitor when racked with torture, and may denounce innocent men. It is at best a clumsy device. What think you of the matter?"

"I have hardly thought it over yet, Sir John; and certainly no plan has yet occurred to me."

"Well, think it over, Sir Gervaise. It is not likely that a few days will make any difference. But I will take measures to see that this Greek does not sail away from the Island at present, and will speak to the port master about it. I will myself give the matter consideration, but as you have shown yourself so quick witted in following up the matter so far, I rely upon you more than myself to carry it farther. There may possibly be some simple explanation of the matter. He may come from an island where the Turks are masters, and has, perhaps, brought a message from some relatives of a slave; as to the talk with the prison officer, it may be wholly innocent. If we should find that it is so we will keep this matter to ourselves, if possible, or we shall get finely laughed at by our comrades for having run upon a false scent. If, on the other hand, the matter should turn out to be serious, you will assuredly get great credit for having discovered it. Therefore, turn it over in your mind tonight, and see if you can arrive at some scheme for seeing further into it before we take any steps."

In the morning Gervaise again called upon Sir John Kendall.

"Well, Sir Gervaise, I hope that you have hit upon some scheme for getting to the bottom of this matter. I confess that I myself, though I have had a sleepless night over it, have not been able to see any method of getting to the root of the affair, save by the application of torture."

"I do not know whether the plan I have thought of will commend itself to your opinion, sir, but I have worked out a scheme which will, I think, enable us to get to the bottom of the matter. I believe that a galley is expected back from a cruise today or tomorrow. Now, sir, my idea is that I should go on board a small craft, under the command of a knight upon whose discretion and silence you can rely, such as, for example, Sir John Boswell, and that we should intercept the galley. Before we board her I should disguise myself as a Turkish slave, and as such Sir John should hand me over to the officer in command of the galley, giving him a letter of private instructions from you as to my disposal. If they have other slaves on board I would ask that I should be kept apart from them, as well as from the rowers of the galley. On being landed I should be sent to the prison where I saw the officer enter last night, and the slaves and rowers should be distributed among the other prisons. Thus, then, the slaves I should be placed with would only know that I had arrived in the galley with other slaves captured by it. I have no doubt I should be able to maintain my assumed character, and should in a short time be taken into the confidence of the others, and should learn what is going on. It would be well, of course, that none of the officials of the prison should be informed as to my true character, for others, besides the one I saw, may have been bribed to participate in whatever plot is going on."

"And do you mean to say, Sir Gervaise, that you, a knight of the Order, are willing to submit to the indignity of being treated as a slave? To keep up the disguise long enough to be taken into the confidence of the plotters, you might have to stay there for some time; and if the prison officials believe you to be but an ordinary slave, you will be put to work either on the walls or in one of the galleys."

"I am ready to do anything for the benefit of the Order, and the safety of Rhodes, that will meet with your approval," Gervaise replied. "It will no doubt be unpleasant, but we did not enter the Order to do pleasant things, but to perform certain duties, and those duties necessarily involve a certain amount of sacrifice."

"Do you think you would be able to maintain the character? Because you must remember that if detected you might be torn in pieces by the slaves, before the officers could interfere to protect you."

"I feel sure that I can do so, Sir John."

"What story would you tell them?"

"I would say that I had come from Syria, and sailed from Acre in a trader, which is perfectly true, and also that I was taken off the ship I was on by a galley-which would not be altogether false, as I crossed one as I landed. I think there would be very little questioning, for I should pretend to be in a state of sullen despair, and give such short answers to questions that I should soon be left alone."

"The scheme is a good one, Sir Gervaise, though full of danger and difficulty. If you are ready to render this great service to the Order, I willingly accept the sacrifice you offer to make. I will send one of my slaves down into the town to buy garments suitable for you, and also stains for your skin. It will, of course, be necessary for you to shave a portion of your head in Turkish fashion. I will also see Sir John Boswell, and ask him to arrange for a craft to be ready to start at noon. The galley is not expected in until evening, but of course she may arrive at any moment now. Come here again in an hour's time, and I will have the clothes ready for you."

"May I suggest, sir, that they should be those appropriate to a small merchant? This might seem to account for my not being placed with the other slaves who may be on board the galley, as it would be supposed that I was set apart in order that I should be sent to one of the auberges as a servant; and my afterwards being herded with the others would be explained by its being found that there was no opening for me in such a capacity. I should think there would be no difficulty in obtaining such a suit, as garments of all kinds are brought here in prizes, and are bought up by some of the Greek merchants, who afterwards find opportunities of despatching them by craft trading among the islands."

Just before noon Gervaise walked down to the port with Sir John Boswell, a servant following with a bundle.

"It seems to me a hare brained scheme, lad," Sir John, who had just joined him, said, as they issued from the auberge; "though I own, from what the bailiff tells me, that there must be some treacherous plot on hand, and when that is the case it is necessary that it should be probed to the bottom. But for a knight to go in the disguise of an infidel slave seems to me to be beyond all bounds."

"If one is ready to give one's life for the Order, Sir John, surely one need not mind a few weeks' inconvenience. I shall, at any rate, be no worse off than you were when serving as a Turkish slave."

"Well, no, I don't know that you will," Sir John replied doubtfully. "But that was from necessity, and not from choice; and it is, moreover, an accident we are all exposed to."

"It is surely better to do a thing of one's own free will than because one is forced to do it, Sir John?"

The knight was silent. He was a stout fighting man, but unused to argument.

"Well," he said, after a long pause, "I can only hope that it will turn out all right, and promise that if you are strangled in prison, I will see that every slave who had a hand in it shall be strung up. I have told Kendall frankly that if I were in his place I would not permit you to try such a venture. However, as I could think of no other plan by which there would be a chance of getting to the bottom of this matter, my words had no effect with him. I should not have so much cared if the officers of the gaol knew who you were; but I can see that if there is treachery at work this would defeat your object altogether. What do you suppose this rascal Greek can be intending?"

"That I cannot say, Sir John. He may be trying to get an exact plan of the fortifications, or he may be arranging some plan of communication by which, in case of siege, news of our condition and of the state of our defences may be conveyed to the Turkish commander."

By this time they had reached the port, and embarked at once on a trading vessel belonging to one of the merchants, from whom Sir John had readily obtained her use for a day or two. Her sails were hoisted at once, and she rowed out from the port. Having proceeded some three or four miles, they lowered her sails, and lay to in the course a galley making for the port would take. A sailor was sent up to the masthead to keep a lookout. Late in the afternoon he called down that he could make out a black speck some twelve miles away. She carried no sails, and he judged her to be a galley.

"It will be dark before she comes along," Sir John Boswell said. "You can hoist your sails, captain, and return to within half a mile of the port, or she may pass us beyond hailing distance."

Gervaise at once retired to the cabin that had been set aside for their use, and proceeded to disguise himself. An hour later Sir John came down. He looked at Gervaise critically.

"You are all right as far as appearances go. I should take you anywhere for a young Turk. Your clothes are not too new, and are in accordance with the tale you are going to tell, which is that you are the son of a Syrian trader. If, as Suleiman says, you speak Turkish well enough to pose as a native, I think you ought to be able to pass muster. How long will that dye last? Because if it begins to fade they will soon suspect you."

"It will last a fortnight; at least, so Sir John Kendall says. But he has arranged that if at the end of ten days I have not succeeded in finding out anything, he will send down to the prison, and under the pretence that he wants to ask me some questions about what ransom my father would be likely to pay for me, he will have me up to the auberge, and there I can dye myself afresh."

"How are you to communicate with him in case of need?"

"His servant Ahmet, who got the things for me, is to come down every morning, and to be near the door of the prison at the hour when the slaves are taken out to work. If I have aught to communicate I am to nod twice, and Sir John Kendall will send down that evening to fetch me, instead of waiting until it is time for me to renew my dye."

"What is going to be said to Harcourt and the others to account for your absence?"

"The bailiff will merely say that he has suddenly sent me away by ship, on a private mission. They may wonder, perhaps, but none of them will venture to ask him its nature."

"Well, I must say that you seem to have made all your arrangements carefully, Tresham, and I hope it will turn out well. I was against the scheme at first, but I own that I do not see now why it should not succeed; and if there is any plot really on hand, you may be able to get to the bottom of it."

It was an hour after darkness had completely fallen when the regular beat of oars was heard. The ship's boat was already in the water, and Gervaise, wrapped up in his mantle, followed Sir John out of his cabin and descended with him into the boat, which was at once rowed towards the approaching galley. Sir John hailed it as it came along.

"Who is it calls?" a voice said.

"It is I—Sir John Boswell. Pray take me on board, Sir Almeric. It is a somewhat special matter."

The order was given, the galley slaves ceased rowing, and the boat ran alongside. Gervaise unclasped his mantle and gave it to Sir John, and then followed him on board.

"I congratulate you on your return, and on your good fortune in having, as your letter stated, made a prosperous voyage," Sir John said, as he shook hands with the commander of the galley.

"I would speak a word with you aside," he added in a low voice.

Sir Almeric moved with him a few paces from the other knights.

"I am sent here by our bailiff, Sir Almeric. I have a Turkish prisoner here with me who is to be landed with those you have taken. There are special reasons for this, which I need not now enter into. Will you let him sit down here by the helm? My instructions are that he is not to mingle with the other slaves; and as there are reasons why it is wished that his coming on board in this manner shall not be known to them, I myself am to take him up to one of the prisons, or at least to hand him over to the officer sent down from that prison to take up the captives allotted to it. The matter is of more importance than it seems to be, or, as you may imagine, I should not be charged to intercept you on such an errand."

"Of course, I don't understand anything about it, Sir John, but will do as you ask me."

He went to where Gervaise had crouched down by the bulwark, beckoned him to follow, and, walking aft, motioned to him to sit down there. Then he returned to Sir John, and joined the other knights, who were all too anxious to learn the latest news-who had left the island, and who had come to it since they sailed-to interest themselves in any way with the figure who had gone aft, supposing him, indeed, to be Sir John's servant, the lantern suspended over the poop giving too feeble a light for his costume to be noted.

A quarter of an hour later they anchored in the harbour. Some of the knights at once went ashore to their respective auberges, but Sir Almeric and a few others remained on board until relieved of their charge in the morning, an account being sent on shore of the number of captives that had been brought in. No thought was given to Gervaise, who slept curled up on the poop. Sir John Boswell passed the night on board. In the morning an officer came off with a list of the prisons to which the slaves were to be sent. Sir John Kendall had seen the officer charged with the distribution, who had, at his request, not included the prison of St. Pelagius in the list.

A message, however, had been sent to that prison, as well as to the others, for an officer to attend at the landing stage. In the morning Sir John went ashore in one of the boats conveying the slaves, of whom some forty had been captured. Gervaise followed him into the boat, and took his seat by the others, who were too dispirited at the fate which had befallen them to pay any attention to him.

When he landed, Sir John asked which was the officer from St. Pelagius. One stepped forward.

"This is the only slave for you," he said, pointing to Gervaise. "He is of a better class than the rest, and in the future may be he will do for a servitor at one of the auberges, but none have at present occasion for one, and so he is to go to you. He says that his father is a merchant, and will be ready to pay a ransom for him; but they all say that, and we must not heed it overmuch. As he seems a smart young fellow, it may be that he will be sent to one of the auberges later on; but at present, at any rate, you can put him with the rest, and send him out with the gangs."

"He is a well built young fellow, Sir John," the officer remarked, "and should make a good rower in a galley. I will put him in the crew of the St. Elmo. Follow me," he said, in Turkish, to Gervaise, and then led the way up to the prison. On entering he crossed a courtyard to a door which was standing open. Within was a vaulted room, some forty feet long by twenty wide; along each side there were rushes strewn thickly.

"The others have just started to their work," he said, "so that for today you can sleep."

After he had left, Gervaise looked with some disgust at the rushes, that had evidently been for weeks unchanged.

"I would rather have the bare stones, if they were clean," he muttered to himself. "However, it can't be helped."

He presently strolled out into the courtyard, where some other slaves, disabled by illness or injuries, were seated in the sun. Gervaise walked across to them, and they looked listlessly up at him as he approached.

"You are a newcomer," one said, as he came up. "I saw you brought in, but it didn't need that. By the time you have been here a week or two, your clothes will be like ours," and he pointed to his ragged garments. "When did you arrive? Are there no others coming up here?"

"The galley came in last night," Gervaise said, "but they did not land us until this morning. I wish they had killed me rather than that I should have been brought here to work as a slave."

"One always thinks so at first," the man said. "But somehow one clings to life. We shall die when Allah wills it, and not before."

"What is the matter with your foot?" Gervaise asked.

"I was with the gang quarrying stones, and a mass of rock fell upon it. I have been in the infirmary for weeks, and I own that the Christian dogs treated me well. A slave has his value, you see. I am nearly cured now, but I shall never walk well again. I expect they will put me in one of their accursed galleys."

"How long have you been here?"

"Seven years; it seems a lifetime. However, there is hope yet. They don't tell us much, but we hear things sometimes, and they say that the sultan is going to sweep them out of Rhodes as they were swept out of Acre. When will it be?"

"I know not. I am from Syria, but even there they are making preparations. The sultan has had troubles in the East, and that has delayed him, but he will be here before long, and then we shall see. It will be our turn then."

"It will, indeed!" one of the others exclaimed. "Oh, to see these dogs brought down, and suffering as we have suffered, toiling at oars in one of our galleys, or at the fortifications of one of our castles! It will make amends for all our suffering. Had you a hard fight with them?"

"No. We were but a small craft, and it was vain to attempt resistance. I would gladly have fought, but the sailors said it would only throw away their lives. There was but little on board, and they allowed the vessel to go free with those of the sailors who were too old to be made useful for hard work."

No further questions were asked. The men seemed to have no interest save in their own misery, and Gervaise soon left them, and, sitting down in a shady corner, presently dropped off to sleep.

In the evening all came in from their various work. The officer man who had brought Gervaise in went up to the overseer of the galley slaves and informed him that he had told off the new slave-pointing to Gervaise-to his gang.

"He was brought in by the galley that arrived last night," he said; "he was the only slave sent up here. I hear that he had been set aside to be appointed a servitor, but there are no vacancies, so they sent him here till one should occur; and I was ordered to make him useful in other ways in the meantime."

"I am two or three hands short," the overseer said. "I wish now I had sent in an application yesterday, for if I had done so, no doubt they would have sent me some more men. However, this fellow will make up an even number, and he is strong and active, though at present he looks sulky enough under his bad fortune."

A few of the slaves spoke to Gervaise as they were waiting for food to be brought them, but the majority dropped upon the rushes, too exhausted with toil and heat to feel an interest in anything. The food consisted of rye bread, with thin broth, brought in a great iron vessel. Each slave had a horn, which was used for soup or water, and which, when done with, he had, by the rule enforced among themselves, to take out to the fountain in the courtyard and wash, before it was added to the pile in the corner of the room.

The cool of the evening aided the meal in restoring the energies of the slaves. Several gathered round Gervaise, and asked questions as to what he knew of the prospects of an early invasion of Rhodes; but as soon as the officer left the room, closing and locking the door after him, the slaves became for the most part silent. A few men sat in groups together, talking in undertones, but the greater number threw themselves down on the rushes, either to sleep or to think alone. Gervaise was struck by the manner in which most of them lay, without making the slightest movement, so long as there was light to enable him to make out their figures. He himself addressed two or three of them, as they lay with their eyes wide open, asking questions with reference to the work; but in no case did he receive any reply. The men seemed altogether unconscious of being addressed, being absorbed in the thought of their far distant homes and families which they might never see again.

Gervaise walked a few times up and down the room, and as he approached a silence fell each time upon the groups of men talking together. More than once a figure rose soon afterwards from the ground, and, as he came along again, asked him a few questions about himself. As soon as it was dark, he lay down in a vacant space on the rushes. Shortly afterwards talking ceased altogether, and there was quiet in the vaulted room. With the first gleam of daylight they were astir, and, when the doors were opened, poured out into the courtyard, where all had a wash at the fountain. Half an hour later, a meal, precisely similar to that of the previous evening, was served out; then the overseers called over the muster roll, the gangs were made up, and each, under its officer, started for its work.

Gervaise, with the men of his room, proceeded down to the port, and at once took their seats on the benches of the galley, one foot being chained to a ring in the deck, the other to that of a companion at the oar. The slaves were more cheerful now. As there was no work to do at present, they were allowed to talk, and an occasional laugh was heard, for the sun and brightness of the day cheered them. Many, after years of captivity, had grown altogether reckless, and it was among these that there was most talking; the younger men seemed, for the most part, silent and moody.

"You will get accustomed to it," the man next to Gervaise said cheeringly. "When I first came here, it seemed to me that I could not support the life for a month-that the fate was too dreadful to be borne, and that death would be most welcome; but, like the rest, I became accustomed to it in time. After all, the work is no harder than one would do at home. There is no stint of food, and it is no worse than one would have, were one labouring in the fields. Were it not for the loss of those we love, it would be nothing; and in time one gets over even that. I have long ago told myself that if they are not dead, at least they are dead to me. They have their livings to get, and cannot be always mourning, and I have tried to forget them, as they must have forgotten me."

"Do you work hard?" Gervaise asked.

"No. We who are in the galleys are regarded by the others with envy. Sometimes-often, indeed-we have naught to do all day. We bask in the sun, we talk, we sleep, we forget that we are slaves. But, generally, we go out for an hour or two's exercise; that is well enough, and keeps us strong and in health. Only when we are away on voyages is the work hard. Sometimes we row from morning to night; but it is only when they are in chase of another craft that we have really to exert ourselves greatly. Then it is terrible. We may be doing our best, our very best, and yet to the impatient knights it seems that we might do more. Then they shout to the overseer, and he lays his whip on our backs without mercy. Then we row until sometimes we drop, senseless, off the benches. But this, you understand, is not very often; and though the work on a cruise is long, it is not beyond our strength. Besides, when we are away in the galley there is always hope. The galley may meet with four or five of our ships, and be captured, or a storm may arise and dash her upon the shore; and though many would lose their lives, some might escape, and each man, in thinking of it, believes that he will be one of the fortunate ones.

"Take my advice: always look cheerful if you can; always put your hand on the oar when the order is given, and row as if you were glad to be at work again; and always make a show, as if you were working your hardest. Never complain when you are struck unjustly, and always speak respectfully to the overseer. In that way you will find your life much easier than you would think. You will be chosen for small boat service; and that is a great thing, as we are not chained in the small boats. Some men are foolish and obstinate, but, so far from doing any good, this only brings trouble on themselves; they come in for punishment daily, they are closely watched, and their lives made hells for them. Even as a help to escape it pays best to be cheerful and alert. We all think of escape, you know, though it is seldom indeed that a chance ever comes to any of us. It is the one thing except death to look forward to, and there is not a man among us who does not think of it scores of times a day; but, small as the chance is, it is greatest for those who behave best. For instance, it is they only who man small boats; and when a small boat rows ashore, it is always possible that the guard may be careless-that he will keep the boat at the landing place, instead of pushing off at once into deep water, as he ought to do-and that in this way a chance will, sooner or later, come for springing ashore and making a dash for liberty."

Chapter X
A Plot Discovered.

The conversation between Gervaise and his fellow slave was interrupted by the arrival at the side of the quay of a party of knights. Silence instantly fell upon the slaves; all straightened themselves up to the oars, and prepared for a start. Among the knights who took their places on the poop Gervaise saw with amusement his friend Ralph. He had no fear of a recognition, for the darkly stained skin and the black hair had so completely altered him that when he had looked at himself in a mirror, after the application of the dye, he was surprised to find that he would not have known it to be his own face. Ralph was in command of the party, which consisted of young knights who had but recently arrived at Rhodes; and as it was the first time he had been appointed as instructor, Gervaise saw that he was greatly pleased at what he rightly regarded as promotion.

The galley at once pushed off from the wharf, and rowed out of the port. The work was hard; but as the slaves were not pressed to any extraordinary exertions, Gervaise did not find it excessive. He congratulated himself, however, that the stain was, as he had been assured, indelible, save by time, for after a few minutes' exercise he was bathed in perspiration. As the galley had been taken out only that instruction might be given to the young knights, the work was frequently broken.

Sometimes they went ahead at full speed for a few hundred yards, as if to chase an adversary; then they would swerve aside, the slaves on one side rowing, while those on the other backed, so as to make a rapid turn. Then she lay for a minute or two immovable, and then backed water, or turned to avoid the attack of an imaginary foe. Then for an hour she lay quiet, while the knights, divesting themselves of their mantles and armour, worked one of the guns on the poop, aiming at a floating barrel moored for the purpose a mile out at sea. At eleven o'clock they returned to the port. Bread and water were served out to the slaves, and they were then permitted to lie down and sleep, the galley being moored under the shadow of the wall.

At four o'clock another party of knights came down, and the work was similar to that which had been performed in the morning. At seven o'clock the slaves were taken back to their barracks.

"Well, what do you think of your work?" one of the slaves asked Gervaise, as they ate their evening meal.

"It would not be so bad if it was all like that."

"No. But I can tell you that when you have to row from sunrise to sunset, with perhaps but one or two pauses for a few minutes, it is a different thing altogether, especially if the galley is carrying despatches, and speed is necessary. Then you get so worn out and exhausted, that you can scarce move an oar through the water, until you are wakened up by a smart as if a red hot iron had been laid across your shoulders. It is terrible work then. The whip cracks every minute across some one's back; you are blinded by exhaustion and rage, and you feel that you would give the world if you could but burst your chain, rush on your taskmasters, and strike, if only one blow, before you are killed."

"It must be terrible," Gervaise said. "And do you never get loose, and fall upon them?"

The man shook his head.

"The chains are too strong, and the watch too vigilant," he said. "Since I came here I have heard tales of crews having freed themselves in the night, and fallen upon the Christians, but for my part I do not believe in them. I have thought, as I suppose every one of us has thought, how such a thing could be done; but as far as I know no one has hit on a plan yet. Now and then men have managed to become possessed of a file, and have, by long and patient work, sawn through a chain, and have, when a galley has been lying near our own shore, sprung overboard and escaped; but for every attempt that succeeds there must be twenty failures, for the chains are frequently examined, and woe be to the man who is found to have been tampering with his.

But as to a whole gang getting free at once, it is altogether impossible, unless the key of the pad locks could be stolen from an overseer, or the man bribed into aiding us."

"And that, I suppose, is impossible?" Gervaise said.

"Certainly, impossible for us who have no money to bribe them with, but easy enough if any one outside, with ample means, were to set about it. These overseers are, many of them, sons of Turkish mothers, and have no sympathy, save that caused by interest, with one parent more than another. Of course, they are brought up Christians, and taught to hold Moslems in abhorrence, but I think many of them, if they had their free choice, would cross to the mainland. Here they have no chance of ever being aught but what they are-overseers of slaves, or small prison officials. They are despised by these haughty knights, and hated by us, while were they to reach the mainland and adopt their mothers' religion, everything would be open to them. All followers of the Prophet have an equal chance, and one may be a soldier today, a bey tomorrow, and a pasha a year hence, if he be brave, or astute, or capable in any way beyond his fellows. Men like these warders would be sure to make their way.

"They cannot have gathered much during their service, therefore the offer of a large sum of money would find plenty among them eager to earn it. But, you see, they are but the inferiors. On our voyages on board the galley, the knights inspect our fetters twice a day, and the keys are kept in the commander's cabin. For an hour or two, when we are not on a long passage, the padlocks are unfastened, in order that we may jump over and bathe, and exercise our limbs; but at this time the knights are always on guard, and as we are without arms we are altogether powerless. It is the same thing here. The senior warders, who all belong to the Order, although of an inferior grade, come round, as you have seen, to examine our fetters, and themselves lock and bar the doors. If one or two of these could be corrupted, escape would be easy enough."

"But is it impossible to do this?" Gervaise asked eagerly. "My father has money, and would I know be ready, if I could communicate with him, to pay a handsome sum, if sure that it would result in my obtaining my freedom."

The man nodded significantly.

"There may be other means of doing it," he said. "Perhaps it will not be long before you hear of it. You seem a stout fellow, and full of spirit, but, as yet, anything that may be going on is known but to a few, and will go no further until the time comes that all may be told. I think not so badly of men of our faith as to believe that any one would betray the secret for the sake of obtaining his own freedom and a big reward; but secrets, when known by many, are apt to leak out. A muttered word or two in sleep, or the ravings of one down with fever, might afford ground for suspicion, and torture would soon do the rest. I myself know nothing of the secret, but I do know that there is something going on which, if successful, will give us our freedom. I am content to know no more until the time comes; but there are few, save those engaged in the matter, that know as much as this, and you can see that it is better it should be so. Look at that man opposite; he has been here fifteen years; he seldom speaks; he does his work, but it is as a brute beast-despair has well nigh turned him into one. Think you that if such a man as that were to know that there is hope, he would not be so changed that even the dullest would observe it? I see you are a brisk young fellow, and I say to you, keep up your courage. The time is nearer than you think when you will be free from these accursed shackles."

Each morning, as he went out to work with his gang, Gervaise saw the servant from the auberge standing near; but he made no sign. He was satisfied that his suspicions had been justified, and that he was not leading this life in vain, but he thought it better to wait until the week passed, and he was taken away to have his colour renewed, than to make a sign that might possibly rouse the suspicions of his comrades. On the eighth morning, when the door of the room was unlocked, the overseer said —"Number 36, you will remain here. You are wanted for other work."

After the gang had left the prison, the overseer returned.

"I am to take you up to the English auberge. The knight who handed you over to me when you landed, told me that you might be wanted as a servitor; and as it is he who has sent down, it may be that a vacancy has occurred. If so, you are in luck, for the servitors have a vastly better time of it than the galley slaves, and the English auberge has the best reputation in that respect. Come along with me."

The English auberge was one of the most handsome of the buildings standing in the great street of the Knights. Its architecture was Gothic in its character, and, although the langue was one of the smallest of those represented at Rhodes, it vied with any of them in the splendour of its appointments. Sir John Boswell was standing in the interior courtyard.

"Wait here for a few minutes," he said to the overseer. "The bailiff will himself question the slave as to his accomplishments; but I fancy he will not be considered of sufficient age for the post that is vacant. However, if this should not be so, I shall no doubt find a post to fit him ere long, for he seems a smart young fellow, and, what is better, a willing one, and bears himself well under his misfortunes."

Then he motioned to Gervaise to follow him to the bailiff's apartments.

"Well, Sir Gervaise," Sir John Kendall exclaimed, as the door closed behind him, "have you found aught to justify this cruel penance you have undertaken?"

"As to the penance, Sir John, it has been nothing unsupportable. The exercise is hard enough, but none too hard for one in good health and strength, and, save for the filth of the chamber in which we are shut up at night, and the foul state of the rushes on which we lie, I should have naught to complain of. No, I have as yet heard nothing of a surety-and yet enough to show me that my suspicions were justified, and that there is a plot of some sort on foot," and he related to the two knights the conversation he had had with the galley slave.

"By St. George!" the bailiff said, "you have indeed been justified in your surmises, and I am glad that I attached sufficient importance to your suspicions to let you undertake this strange enterprise. What think you, Sir John Boswell?"

"I think with you, that Sir Gervaise has fully justified his insistence in this matter, which I own I considered to be hare brained folly. What is to be done next, Sir Gervaise?"

"That is what I have been turning over in my mind. You see, I may have little warning of what is going to take place. I may not hear of it until we are locked up for the night and the affair is on the point of taking place, and it will, of course, be most needful that I shall be able to communicate with you speedily."

"That, of course, is of vital importance," the bailiff said. "But how is it to be managed?"

"That is what I cannot exactly see, Sir John. An armed guard remains in our room all night. But, in the first place, he might be himself in the plot, and if not, the slaves would almost certainly overpower him and kill him, as a preliminary to the work of knocking off their chains."

"Is there a window to the room? At least, of course there is a window, but is it within your reach?"

"There are six small loopholes-one on each side of the door, and two in each of the side walls; they are but four inches across and three feet in length, and there are two crossbars to each; they are four feet from the floor."

"At any rate, they are large enough for your arm to pass through, Sir Gervaise, and you might drop a strip of cloth out."

"Certainly I could, Sir John. I could easily hide a piece of white cotton a yard or so long in my clothes, scanty as these are, and could certainly manage, unobserved, to drop it outside the window."

"Then the rest is for us to contrive, Boswell. We must have some one posted in the yard of the prison, with instructions to go every ten minutes throughout the night to see if a strip of white cotton has been dropped out. When he finds it he must go at once to William Neave, the governor. He is a sturdy Englishman, and there is no fear of his having been bribed to turn traitor; but it were well to take no one into our confidence. I think we cannot do better than employ Ahmet on this business, as he already knows that Sir Gervaise is masquerading there. We will have William Neave up here presently. Tell him that for certain reasons we wish Ahmet to pass the night for the present in the prison, and arrange with him on what excuse we can best bestow him there without exciting suspicion. At any rate, Sir Gervaise, that is our affair."

He went to a closet and took out a white mantle, tore a strip off the bottom, and gave it to Gervaise.

"It would be best not to keep you here any longer," he said, "so renew your stain while I speak. As soon as you learn the details of the plot, you will drop this out from the loophole on the right hand side of the door; that is to say, the one on your right, standing inside. If the affair is not to come off at once, it were best for you to proceed as before. Ahmet will be outside when you go out with your gang, and on your nodding to him we will make some excuse to take you away on your return. I say this because if you see that the affair, whatever it is, is not imminent, you might think it better to remain with them longer, so as to learn their plans more fully, instead of having the thing put a stop to at once."

"I understand, Sir John; but, as I have said, I do not think we should all be told until the blow is ready to be struck, as they would be afraid that some one might inform against them, if time and opportunity were granted them."

"I think so too, Sir Gervaise. This afternoon we will call upon the grand master, for we have no means of knowing how serious or how extended this plot may be; it may include only the crew of a single galley, and, on the other hand, the whole of the slaves may be implicated in it. It is evident, therefore, that the matter is too serious to be kept any longer from his knowledge."

Three more days passed. On the third evening, after the allowance of broth and bread had been consumed, and the door was closed and locked upon them for the night, three or four of the galley slaves, after talking eagerly together, beckoned to the others to gather round them at the end of the room farthest from the door. Two of them took up arms full of the bedding, and stuffed it into the side windows. Gervaise saw, in the dim light, a look of intense excitement on the faces of the slaves. It had been vaguely known among them that a plot was in hand, although but few had been admitted into the confidence of the leaders. Hitherto all had feared that it concerned only a small number, but the preparations now made to insure that they should not be overheard, showed that, whatever the plan might be, all were to share in it.

"Thanks be to Allah, the All Powerful," one of the men began, "my lips are unsealed, and I can tell you the great news that our hour for escape from bondage is at hand! We need not fear the warder there," he went on, as several eyes were turned apprehensively towards the guard, who, with his spear beside him, was leaning carelessly against the wall at the farther end, looking through the window into the courtyard; "he is with us. You must know that for the last two months an agent from Constantinople has been on the Island, and has been engaged in arranging this affair. Two of our taskmasters belonging to the Order have been bribed by large sums of money, and several of the overseers, who are half of our blood, have eagerly embraced the prospect of returning to their mothers' country, and of avowing openly their belief in our religion. These, again, have bought over many of the guards, ours included, and tonight all will be ready for action. Those not of our party will be killed without ceremony. Duplicate keys have been made of all the padlocks of the fetters; the guards who are with us have each one of them, the others will have been slipped into the hands of one man in each gang as they returned tonight from work. The overseers who are in the plot will, at midnight, go quietly round and unlock the doors, and remove the bars from the outside. We have, therefore, only to overcome the eight or ten men who patrol the prison; and as we shall have the arms of the guards, some thirty in number, we shall make quick work of them.

"The two guards at the outside gates must, of course, be killed. Duplicates of the keys have been made, and will be hidden in a spot known to some of our party, close to the gate. Thus we have but to issue out and rush down, in a body, to the port. I and another are to take the arms of our guard, and two others are told off in each room to do the same. That will give us sixty armed men. We shall make very short work of the guards at the gate leading into the port. Then twenty of us are to run along the mole to Fort St. Nicholas, twenty to the Tower of St. Michael, and twenty to that of St. John. There will be, at the most, but three or four men keeping watch at each fort, and thus we shall have in our possession the three forts commanding the entrance to the harbour. There are, as you know, six galleys manned by crews from our prison there. The crew of each galley will embark upon it, and man the oars; the rest will divide themselves among the galleys. Before starting, we shall seize and set fire to all other galleys and ships in the port. The gangs in four of the rooms have been told off specially for this duty. Before firing them, they are to take out such provisions as they may find, and transport them to the galleys. We who take the forts are provided with hammers and long nails, to drive down the vent holes of the cannon; when we have done this, we are to wait until one of the galleys fetches us off. Ten minutes should be ample time for all there is to be done, and even if the alarm is given at once, we shall be away long before the knights can be aroused from sleep, buckle on their armour, and get down to the port."

Exclamations of delight and approbation burst from his hearers.

"Then it is only we of this prison who are in the plot?" one said.

"Yes. In the first place, it would have been too dangerous to attempt to free all. In the second, the galleys would not carry them; we shall be closely packed as it is, for there are over a thousand here. I hear that there was a talk of freeing all, and that we, instead of embarking at first, should make for the other prisons, burst open the doors, and rescue the others; but by the time we could do so the knights would be all in arms, and our enterprise would fail altogether, for as but a small proportion of us can obtain weapons, we could not hope to overcome them. Were it not for the strong wall that separates their quarter from the town, we might make straight for their houses and slay them before the alarm could be given. As it is, that would be impossible, and therefore the plan will be carried out as I have told you. The loss of all their galleys and of over one thousand slaves will be a heavy blow for them. Great pains have been taken to prevent confusion when we reach the port. The men in each room have been instructed as to the galleys on which they are to embark. As for you, you know precisely what is to be done; you will simply take your places, and then wait until all are on board. No galley is to push out from the wharf until the last man of those employed in burning the ships has returned, with the provisions found in them. Then the order will be given by the man who has arranged all this, and the six galleys will put out together.

"One is to row to each of the forts to carry off the party that will have been engaged in silencing its cannon. Our galley is to row to St. Nicholas, and take off the twenty men I shall lead there. There is no possibility of failure. Everything has, you see, been arranged. One of the overseers who is in the plot walked by my side as we returned from the port, and gave me the instructions, and all the others will have been told in the same way, or else by the guards in charge of them." The gang now broke up into little groups, talking excitedly over the unlooked for news, and exulting over the speedy advent of liberty. Gervaise strolled carelessly to the window, and dropped out the white strip of stuff. It was now quite dark, and there was no fear of any one observing the movement. Then he joined the others. After an hour and a half had passed he heard footsteps approaching the door. There was a pause; then the outside bars were taken down, and a key turned in the lock. A deep silence fell on the slaves. Then a voice called, "Number 36!"

"What is it?" replied Gervaise, without raising himself from his seat on the bedding. "I have done my share of work today, and earned my night's sleep."

"It is a knight from the English auberge; he has come to fetch you. It seems that you are to go there as a servitor."

"What a cursed fortune," Gervaise muttered, in Turkish, "just when a road to freedom is open! I have a good mind to say I am ill, and cannot go till the morning."

"No, no!" one of the others exclaimed. "They would only drag you out, and when they saw that there was naught the matter with you, would suspect that there must be some reason why you did not want to go, when, as every one knows, the position of the servitors is in every way preferable to ours."

"Now then, why are you delaying?" a voice said sharply, and a warder entered with a lighted torch. "Get up, you lazy hound! It will be worse for you if I have to speak again."

"I am coming," Gervaise grumbled. "I was just asleep."

He rose, as if reluctantly, and went forward. The warder gave him an angry push, followed him out, and locked and barred the door after him.

"I suppose this is the right man?" Sir John Boswell said.

"This is Number 36, Sir Knight, the same who was taken over to your auberge the other day," and he held the light close to Gervaise's face.

"Yes, that is the man. Follow me," he added, in Turkish. The gate of the courtyard was unbarred, and they passed out unquestioned. Sir John strolled on ahead. Gervaise followed him a pace or two behind. Not until they had passed through the gate of the castle did Sir John turn.

"I have not spoken to you," he said, "as we may have been watched. Keep your news until we reach the auberge."

Upon entering it they went up at once to Sir John Kendall's apartments.

"Well, Sir Gervaise, the strip of cotton was brought to us safely. What is your news?"

"It is very serious, Sir John, and I have been in terrible anxiety since I dropped it out, lest it should not come to hand in time. As it is, you have till midnight to make your preparations." He then repeated the statement made by the galley slave.

"By my faith," Sir John Kendall exclaimed, "this is a pretty plot indeed! And had it succeeded, as it certainly would have done but for your vigilance, it would have been a heavy blow to us. The burning of all our galleys would have crippled us sorely, and the loss of over a thousand slaves would have been a serious one indeed, when we so urgently require them for completing our defences. Get rid of those clothes at once, Sir Gervaise, and don your own. We must go straight to the grand master. You will find your clothes and armour in the next room. I had them taken there as soon as your token was brought me."

In a few minutes Gervaise returned in his usual attire, and with his armour buckled on. The two knights were already in their coats of mail, and leaving the auberge they went to the grand master's palace. A servitor had already been sent to D'Aubusson to inform him that they were coming, and he advanced to meet them as they entered.

"Welcome, Sir Gervaise!" he said. "Whether your news be good or bad, whether you have found that it is a general rising of the slaves that is intended, or a plot by which a handful of slaves may seize a boat and escape, the gratitude of the Order is no less due to you for the hardships and humiliations you have undergone on its behalf."

"It concerns but one prison: that of St. Pelagius."

"The largest of them," the grand master put in.

"The whole of the slaves there are to be liberated at twelve o'clock tonight, are to seize the three water towers and to spike the guns, to burn all the shipping in the harbour, to make off with six galleys, and destroy the rest."

"By St. John!" D'Aubusson exclaimed, "this is indeed a serious matter. But tell me all about it. There must be treachery indeed at work for such a scheme to be carried out."

Gervaise now told him all the details he had learned.

"So two of the Order, though but of the inferior grade, are in the plot?" the grand master said; "and several of the overseers? One of the villains is, of course, the man you saw this Greek talking with. We must get hold of the other if we can. As to the slaves, now that we have warning, there is an end of the matter, though without such warning they would surely have succeeded, for the plans are well laid, and they would have been at sea before we could have gathered in any force at the port. If it were not that it would cost the lives of many of the warders and of the prison guards, I should say we ought to take post outside the gate, for we should then catch the traitors who are to accompany them. As it is, we must be beforehand with them. A hundred men will be more than ample for our purpose. Do you take fifty of your knights, Sir John Kendall, and I will draw fifty of those of Auvergne. At eleven o'clock we will meet at the gate leading down into the town, and will march to the private entrance of the governor's house. I will go in first with a few of you, tell him what we have discovered, and post guards to prevent any one from leaving his house. Then, having admitted the others, we will go quietly out and place a party at each door of the overseers' house, with orders to seize any who may come out. The rest, in small parties, will then go round the prison, and, entering each room, show the slaves that their plot has been discovered. This we must do to save the lives of the guards who may be faithful to their trust. As to the higher officials engaged in the affair, we must obtain their names from the overseers or slaves. It is not likely that the two traitors will quit their houses, as they will leave the matter in the hands of the overseers, who, as you say, intend to first open the doors, and then to accompany the slaves in their escape. Do not warn the knights until it is nearly time to start, Sir John. The less stir made the better, for no one can say whether they may not have suborned some of the servitors to send instant news of any unusual movements in any of the auberges."

At half past ten Sir John Kendall went round among the knights and bade fifty of them arm themselves quietly, and proceed, one by one, down to the gate, and there await orders. Up to this time Gervaise had remained in the bailiff's room, so as to avoid the questioning that would take place, and he went down to the gate with the bailiff and Sir John Boswell.

The knights assembled rapidly. None were aware of the reason for which they had been called out at such an hour, and there was a buzz of talk and conjecture until Sir John Kendall arrived. He was followed by four of the servants, who at once lighted the torches they carried, when he proceeded to go through the roll, and found that the muster was complete. Many of the knights had gazed in some surprise at Gervaise, whose dark complexion altogether concealed his identity, and it was supposed that he must be some newly arrived knight, though none had heard that any ship had entered the harbour that day.

Two or three minutes later fifty knights of the langue of Auvergne came down, headed by the grand master himself, whose appearance greatly heightened the surprise of the English knights. The torches were now extinguished, the gate thrown open, and the party descended into the town. Gervaise had purposely fallen in by the side of Harcourt.

"You are but newly arrived, Sir Knight?" the latter said, as they moved off.

"Not so very newly, Ralph," Gervaise replied.

"What! is it you, Gervaise?" Harcourt exclaimed, with a start of surprise. "Why, I did not know you, though I looked hard at you in the torch light. What have you done with yourself? Where have you been? Do you know what all this is about?"

"I cannot tell you now, Ralph. You must be content to know that I have been in prison, and working in the galleys."

"The saints defend us! Why, what on earth had you done to entail such punishment as that? It is an outrage. The grand master and the council have the right to expel a knight from the Order after due trial and investigation, but not to condemn him to such penalties as the galleys. It is an outrage upon the whole Order, and I would say so to the grand master himself."

"There was no outrage in it, Ralph. Wait until you hear the whole story. That I have not disgraced you, you may judge from the fact that I am in the armour and mantle of the Order, and that, as you saw, I came down with Sir John Kendall himself."

There were no people about in the streets, though the lights still burned on a few of the roofs. For a short distance the knights marched down towards the port, and then turned down a street to the right. After a few minutes' marching they halted under a high wall which all knew to be that of the prison of St. Pelagius. Six knights were posted at the main entrance, with orders that none should be allowed to leave the prison, and that any persons who came up to the gate were to be at once seized and made prisoners.

The rest marched on to a small door leading into the governor's house. Here they were halted, and told to wait till called in; six knights of England, and as many of Auvergne, being told off to accompany the grand master and Sir John Kendall. A note had been sent to the governor, informing him that the grand master intended to visit the prison at eleven o'clock, but that the matter was to be kept an absolute secret; and that the governor himself was to be down at the gate to admit him.

Chapter XI
In Command Of A Galley

William Neave, the governor of the prison, looked astonished indeed when, upon his opening the door, the grand master and the bailiff of the English langue, with the twelve knights behind them, entered. He had been puzzled when, four days before, he had received an order from the grand master that Ahmet, a servitor in the auberge of the English langue, should be permitted to pass the night in his house, with authority to move freely and without question, at any hour, in the courtyard of the gaol, and to depart at any hour, secretly and without observation, by the private gate. Still more had he been surprised when he received the message that the grand master would pay him a secret visit at eleven o'clock at night.

"Let no word be spoken until we are in your apartments," D'Aubusson said in a low voice, as he entered. "But first lead four of these knights and post them so that none can enter the gaol from the house. If there are more than four doors or windows on that side, you must post a larger number. It is imperative that there shall be no communication whatever between your servants and the gaol."

As soon as this was done, the rest of the party were taken to the governor's rooms.

"I can now explain to you all," the grand master said, "the reason of our presence here. I have learned that at twelve tonight there will be a general rising of the slaves in this prison, and that, aided by treachery, they will free themselves from their fetters, overpower and slay such of the guards in their rooms as have not been bribed, throw open the gates, make their way down to the port, burn all the shipping there, and make off in the six galleys manned by them, having first overpowered the sentries in the three forts commanding the entrance, and spiked the guns."

Exclamations of astonishment burst from the knights, who now, for the first time, learnt the reason of their being called out. The governor listened with an expression of stupefaction.

"With all deference to your Highness," he said hesitatingly, "it seems to me that some one must have been deceiving you with this tale. It is altogether incredible that such a plot should have been hatched without a whisper of the matter coming to my ears. It could only be possible were there, not one but many, traitors among the officials; if this is so, then indeed am I a dull ass, and unfit for my duty here, of which I shall pray you to relieve me, and to order such punishment as the council may deem just to be allotted to me for having so signally been hoodwinked."

"My news is sure," the grand master said; "but I deem not that you are in any way to blame in the matter. The plot has been matured, not as a consequence of any laxity of discipline in the prison, but from deliberate treachery, against which no mortal being can guard. The traitors are two of the officials who, being members of the Order, none would suspect of connivance in such a deed. With them are several—I know not how many-under officials, warders, and guards; all these have been bribed by an emissary from Constantinople, now in the town, and who is doubtless furnished with large means. It is well, indeed, for the Order, that this terrible act of treachery has been discovered in time to prevent the plot from coming to a head, for the loss of all our galleys, to say nothing of the disgrace of having been thus bearded by slaves, would be a very heavy blow to it.

"Now that the house is safely guarded, William Neave, you can admit the rest of the knights, who are waiting outside. Then you will, in the first place, conduct a party, and post them so that they may arrest, as they come out to perform their share of the work, all officials, warders, and guards, of whatever rank. When you have posted knights to carry out this-and I need not say that the operation must be performed as silently as possible, for it is above all things necessary that the men concerned shall have no suspicion that their plot has been discovered-you will conduct other parties to the various rooms occupied by the slaves. The guards on duty inside will be made prisoners. The doors will then be locked and barred as before. The appearance of the knights and the arrest of the guards will be sufficient to show the slaves that their plot has been discovered, and there will be no fear of their making any attempt to carry it into execution.

I will myself post the main body of the knights in the courtyard. The arrest of the guards is to be carried out at once, as all those not concerned in the plot would be killed when the hour comes for the rising. Therefore this part of the business must be carried out immediately. I should not, however, lead the guards away to a cell, for the less tramping of feet the better. Therefore I shall place two knights in each room, and beg them to remain inside in charge until the traitors outside are secured."

The knights outside were now marched up. The grand master ordered half those of Auvergne to go round to the main gate, which would be opened for them by the governor; they were to enter quietly, and remain in a body close to it until they received further orders. Sir John Kendall told off the rest of the knights to the various duties of watching the houses occupied by the officials and warders, and of entering the prison rooms and remaining in them on guard. The governor, with his private servants, bearing a supply of torches, was to lead them to the various cells, and unlock the doors. The knights were enjoined to move as noiselessly as possible, and to avoid all clashing of arms against armour.

The governor produced a number of cloths intended to be served out to the slaves. Strips of these were cut off and wrapped round the feet of the English knights, so as to deaden the sound of their boots on the stone pavement. Then, accompanied by the grand master and Sir John Kendall, he went the round of the cells.

In some of these the slaves were found standing up in an attitude of eager expectation, which, as the door opened, and the light of the torches showed a party of knights, changed into one of terror and consternation. Scarce a word was spoken. The guard was ordered to lay down his arms, and to take one of the torches. Two knights placed themselves, one on each side of him, with drawn swords. The door was again locked and barred, and the party proceeded to the next cell. In less than a quarter of an hour this part of the work was finished, and D'Aubusson, Sir John Kendall, and the governor, then took up their station with a party of knights who, concealed behind a buttress, were watching the doors of the officials' houses.

Ten minutes later one of these doors was heard to open, and five dark figures came noiselessly out. They were allowed to go a short distance, in order to see if any others followed; but as no others came out, the governor stepped forward.

"Whither are you going, at this time of night?" he asked. There was a momentary pause, a few hasty words were exchanged, then the five men rushed towards him with bared swords or knives; but before they reached him the knights poured out from their hiding place.

"We are betrayed," one of the men shouted in Turkish. "Fight to the last. Better be killed than tortured and executed." With a yell of fury and despair, they rushed upon the knights. So desperate was their attack that the latter were forced to use their swords, which indeed, burning with rage at the treachery of these men, they were not backward in doing, and in less than a minute the five traitors lay, with cloven heads, dead on the pavement.

"It is as well so," D'Aubusson said, looking sternly down upon them; "perhaps better so, since it has saved us the scandal of their trial. We might have learned more from them, but we have learnt enough, since, doubtless, they have no accomplices among the warders, or they would have been with them. Now we will deal with the arch traitors. There is no need for further concealment; the noise of this fray will assuredly have been heard by them, for they will be listening for the sounds that would tell them the slaves had been liberated."

Followed by the knights, he went to the door of the house occupied by the overseers, all of whom were members of the lower branch of the Order. It was indeed evident that an alarm had been given there, for lights appeared at the windows. As they opened the door and entered the hall, several half-dressed men rushed down the stairs with drawn swords, two of them carrying torches in their left hands. As the light fell upon the figures of the grand master and the knights, they paused in astonishment.

"There is treachery at work in the prison," D'Aubusson said quietly. "I pray you to collect your comrades and to assemble here at once."

In a minute or two some twenty officials were gathered in the hall.

"Are all here?" D'Aubusson asked the governor.

The latter counted the men.

"There are two short," he said—"Pietro Romano and Karl Schumann. They occupy the same room. Go and fetch them down, four of you."

The four men nearest to the stairs at once went up with two torches. They returned in a minute.

"The door is fastened on the inside, and we can obtain no response."

"Fetch an axe and break it in," the grand master ordered. "Sir John Boswell, do you, with some other knights, take post without; they may attempt to escape by the window, though, as we hold the gates, it would avail them little. Sir Gervaise Tresham, do you follow us."

Gervaise, who had been placed with the party watching the house, followed the grand master and governor upstairs. A few blows with an axe splintered the door; its fastenings gave way, and they entered the room. The window was open, and two figures lay prostrate on the ground near it.

"I half expected this," the grand master said. "They were listening there. The conflict in the yard told them that the plot had been discovered, and as they saw us approaching the house, they dared not meet the punishment of their crimes, and have fallen by their own daggers. Put a torch close to their faces. Sir Gervaise, do you recognise in either of these men the official you saw in conversation with the Greek?"

Gervaise stepped forward and examined the men's faces.

"This is the man," he said, pointing to one of them. "I marked him so closely that I cannot be mistaken."

"That is Pietro Romano," the governor said; "he was an able officer, but discontented with his position and given to quarrelling with his comrades."

"Have a hole dug and bury them in the prison," D'Aubusson said; "they have been false to their vows, and false to their religion. They have chosen their own mode of death; let them be buried like dogs, as they are. But let a careful search be made of their garments and of this room. It may be that they have some documents concealed which may be of use to us."

The grand master then descended to the hall.

"Members of the Order," he said to the overseers, "your guilty companions have met death by their own hands, as the others concerned in this plot have met theirs by the swords of the knights. It were well that this matter were not spoken of outside the prison. The attempt has been detected, and has failed; but were it talked of, it might incite others to repeat the attempt, and possibly with better success. Now," he went on, turning to the governor, "our work is done here. Call up the other warders. Let them take the men now prisoners in the rooms, and place them in a dungeon. Let fresh men be placed on guard, and let all the knights gather in the courtyard."

When this was done, and all the knights again assembled, D'Aubusson said, "Our work is nearly done, brothers. The traitors are all dead, and the revolt is at an end. It remains but to capture the author of this attempt; but I believe he is already in our hands. I have given an accurate description of him to Da Veschi, who has taken four knights with him, and they probably will catch him down at the port; if not, he will be arrested the first thing in the morning. As to the slaves, they will be so utterly cowed by the discovery, that there will be no fear of their repeating the attempt. I have ordered the officials of the prison to say naught in the town of what has taken place. There can, however, be no concealment among ourselves. I shall, of course, lay the whole matter before the council. The fact that a strong body of knights has, at so late an hour, started on some unknown mission is, of course, already known in the auberges of Auvergne and England. No concealment of the facts is therefore possible. It is the most serious attempt at a revolt of the slaves that has ever taken place, and will be a warning to us that more vigilance must be exercised. As it is, we have only been saved from the loss of our galleys and slaves by the acuteness of one of the youngest of our knights, who, in the first place, noted a suspicious occurrence which would have been passed by without attracting a moment's thought by ninety-nine out of a hundred men. He laid the matter before his bailiff, Sir John Kendall, who accepted his offer to disguise himself as a slave, to enter the prison under circumstances that would excite no suspicions among the others, and to live and work among them in order to ascertain whether there was any plot on hand. This task—a painful one, as you may imagine-he carried out, and for two weeks he rowed as a galley slave. His lot was as hard as that of the others, for, as he had reason to believe that some of the officials were concerned in the plot, it was necessary that all should be kept in ignorance that he was other than he seemed to be. Thanks to his perfect knowledge of Turkish, he was able to carry his mission through with complete success, and to obtain full particulars of the plot we have tonight crushed. The knight who has performed this inestimable service is Sir Gervaise Tresham, of the English langue. The action he has performed will be noted in the annals of the Order as an example of intelligence and of the extreme of self sacrifice, as well as of courage; for his life would have been assuredly forfeited had the slaves entertained the slightest suspicion of his real character."

There was a murmur of acclamation among the knights. Not one of them but would have freely risked his life in the service of the Order, but there were few who would not have shrunk from the idea of living as a slave among the slaves, sharing their tasks, and subject to the orders of men of inferior rank and often brutal manners.

The knights now returned to their auberges. It was past midnight, but at the English house the lamps and flambeaux were lighted in the great hall. The servitors were called up, wine placed on the table, and the knights discussed the incidents of the evening.

When the meal had concluded, Sir John Kendall said, "Brother knights, when the grand master bestowed the honour of secular knighthood upon this young comrade of ours, he predicted that he would rise to high distinction in the Order. I think you will all agree with me that the prediction is already in a fair way of being fulfilled, and that the services he has rendered to the Order justify us, his comrades of the English langue, in feeling proud of him. I drink, brothers, to his health."

A loud shout rose from the assembled knights, for upon the return of the party who had been away, the rest of those at the auberge had hastily robed themselves and descended to the hall to gather the news. When the shout had died away, and the wine cups were emptied, Gervaise, who was sitting on Sir John Kendall's right hand, would gladly have retained his seat, but the bailiff told him that he must say a few words, and after standing in embarrassed silence for a minute he said, "Sir John Kendall, and brother knights, I can only say that I am very sensible of the kindness with which you have been pleased to regard what seems to me after all to have been a very ordinary affair. I saw a man, whom I knew to be a stranger in the Island, speaking surreptitiously to a slave, and afterwards saw him conversing with a prison officer. That naturally struck me as curious, and I followed the officer, to see to which prison he belonged. Any one would have thought, as I did, that such a thing was strange, if not suspicious, and the only way to find out whether there was anything in it was to mix with the slaves; as I spoke Turkish well enough to do so I asked Sir John Kendall's permission to disguise myself. He gave me every assistance, and I shared their lot for a fortnight. There was no very great hardship in that-certainly nothing to merit the praise that Sir John Kendall has been kind enough to bestow on me. Nevertheless, I am very glad to have gained your good opinion and very grateful to him and to you for drinking to my health."

Then he sat down abruptly.

Sir John Kendall now rose, and the knights, following his example, betook themselves to their dormitories.

The next morning notices were sent by the grand master to the bailiffs of the auberges, and the knights of the grand cross who happened to be in the Island, to assemble in council. Messages were also sent to Gervaise, requesting him to repair at the same hour to the palace, as the council would probably require his attendance.

"Oh dear! I wish this was all over," he said to Ralph, as the latter assisted him to buckle on his armour.

"I don't see anything to sigh about," Ralph said. "I think that you are the most fortunate fellow in the world. I do not say that you have not well deserved it, because it is the tremendous way you worked at Turkish and gave up everything else that has enabled you to do this. Still, there was luck in your noticing that villain talking to the galley slaves, and then to one of the officers of the prison. Of course, as the grand master said last night, it isn't one in a thousand who would have thought anything more about it, and I am sure I shouldn't; so that, and all the rest, is entirely your own doing. Still, it was a piece of luck that you noticed him talking with a slave. Don't think I envy you, Gervaise; I don't a bit, and I feel as much as any one that you have well deserved the honour you have obtained. Still, you know, it is a sort of consolation to me that luck had a little-just a little-to do with it."

"In my opinion luck had everything to do with it," Gervaise said heartily, "and I feel downright ashamed at there being such a fuss made over it. It was bad enough before, merely because I had hit on a plan for our escape from those pirates, but this is worse, and I feel horribly nervous at the thought of having to appear before the grand master and the council."

"Well, that brown dye will hide your blushes, Gervaise. I can only say I wish that I was in your place. By-the-bye, have you heard that they caught that rascal Greek last night?"

"No, I have not heard anything about it."

"Yes. The knights hid themselves behind a pile of goods on the wharf. There was no one about, so far as they could see, but soon after twelve they saw a figure come up on to the deck of a fishing boat moored by the quay. It was the Greek; he stood there for a minute or two listening, and then went down again; he did this five or six times, and at one o'clock they saw him throw up his arms, as if in despair; he stepped ashore, and was about to make his way up into the town when they rushed out and seized him. There is no doubt as to what his fate will be. I am sorry to say that I hear my friend Vrados has been arrested; but there can be no doubt about his loyalty, and he will assuredly be able to explain to the satisfaction of the council how this man became a resident at his house."

"I am sorry I met him there, Ralph. It is a very unpleasant thing to have gone to a house, to have been received kindly, and then to be the means of bringing trouble upon it."

"Yes. I feel that a little myself, because I took you there; and yet I cannot regret it, for if you had not seen him and taken an objection to him, you might not have noticed him particularly when he spoke to one of the galley slaves. It is certainly curious that you should have doubted the man, for I have met him there several times, and even after your visit with me I could see nothing in him to justify your dislike."

Gervaise went up to the palace, and while waiting in the great hall until summoned before the council he was warmly accosted by several knights,—some of whom were quite strangers to him,—who all joined in congratulating him on the immense service he had done to the Order. It was upwards of an hour before he was called in.

"The council have received, Sir Gervaise Tresham," the grand master said, "full details from Sir John Kendall of the manner in which you first discovered, and have since followed up the daring plot by which the slaves at St. Pelagius were to have risen, slain the guards who were faithful, spiked the cannon in the three water forts, burnt the merchant shipping, carried off six galleys and burnt the rest, and in their name I thank you for having saved the Order from a great calamity. The members of the council agree with me that you have shown an amount of discernment of the highest kind, and that you are worthy of exceptional favour and reward for your conduct. I therefore in my own name appoint you to the commandery of our manor of Maltby in Lincolnshire, which, having fallen vacant, is in my gift; and I release it from the usual payment of the first year's revenue. Knowing that you desire to establish yourself here, the council have, at my request, decided to make an exception to the general rule that a knight, on promotion to a commandery, must return and take charge of it in two years from the time the grant is made to him. The commandery will therefore be administered by the senior of the knights attached to it.

"The council, on their part, have requested the bailiff of Auvergne, as grand master of the Fleet, to appoint you to the command of the galley now building, and approaching completion. This he has consented to do, feeling, as we all feel, that although such an appointment is unprecedented for a young knight, yet in the present case such an exception may well be made. I may add that the Admiral has-in order that no knight greatly your senior should be placed under your command-determined that he will appoint to it only young knights, who will, we are assured, gladly serve under one who has so distinguished himself, feeling certain that, under his command, they will have ample opportunities against the infidels to prove themselves worthy of the Order. I may add, also, that the bailiffs of all the langues promise that they will select from among the young knights such as may seem best fitted for such service, by their skill in warlike exercises, by their ready obedience to orders, and good conduct. And I foresee that the spirit of emulation, and the desire to show that, though still but professed knights, they are capable of performing as valiant deeds as their elders, will make the galley under your command one of the most successful in the Order.

"As you are aware, it is a stringent rule, which even in so exceptional a case we should not be justified in breaking, that a knight must reside in the Island for five years previous to being promoted to a commandery. It is now two months more than that time since you were received as page to the late grand master, and in promoting you to a commandery I have not, therefore, broken the rule. You may retire, Sir Gervaise."

Gervaise, overwhelmed by the unlooked for honours thus bestowed upon him, bowed deeply to the grand master and the members of the council, and then retired from the chamber. He passed out of the palace by a side door, so as to avoid being accosted by the knights in the great hall, and took his way out on to the ramparts, where he walked up and down for a considerable time before returning to the auberge. He felt no hilarity at his promotion. He had never entertained any ambition for rising to high office in the Order, but had hoped only to perform his duty as a true knight, to fight against the infidels, and some day, if need be, to die for the Order. The commandery was, he knew, a rich one, and as its chief he would draw a considerable revenue from the estate. This afforded him no pleasure whatever, except inasmuch as it would enable him, in his new command of the galley, to keep a handsome table, and to entertain well the knights who served under him.

It seemed to him, however, that the reward and honours were so far beyond his deserts that he felt almost humiliated by their bestowal. The responsibility, too, was great. Would these young knights, the youngest of whom could be but a year his junior, serve willingly under his orders? And, above all, would they be able to emulate the deeds of experienced warriors, and would the galley worthily maintain the fame of the Order?

At the end of two hours he was joined by Ralph Harcourt.

"I have been looking for you everywhere, Gervaise. You seemed to have disappeared mysteriously. None had marked you leave the council chamber, or knew where you had gone; and after searching everywhere I remembered your fondness for walks upon the walls, so I climbed to the top of St. John's tower and thence espied you. Well, I congratulate you most heartily on the honours that have fallen to your share, especially that of the command of a new galley."

"It is too much altogether, Ralph. I feel ashamed at being thus thrust into a post that ought to be given to a knight of age and experience. How can I expect a number of young knights, of whom well nigh all must be my seniors in age, to obey me as they would an older man?"

"What has age to do with it?" Ralph said. "You have shown that you have a head to think, and, as you before proved, you have an arm to strike. Why, every young knight in the Order must feel proud that one of their own age has gained such honour. It raises them all in their own esteem, and you will see that you will get the pick among all the professed knights, and of a good many who have finished their profession, and are serving here in the hope of some day getting promotion to a commandery. Not such an one as you have got; that, in the ordinary course of things, does not fall to a knight until he is well on in years, and has served in many commanderies of smaller value. I can tell you, directly Sir John Kendall came back and told us that you had been appointed commander of the new galley, and that it was to be manned wholly by young knights, there was not one of those serving their profession in the auberge who did not beg Sir John to put down his name for it; and ten or twelve others, myself among them, who have obtained full knighthood also."

"You don't mean to say that you have put down your name to serve under me, Ralph? It would be monstrous."

"I see nothing monstrous in it, Gervaise. As I said just now, years have nothing to do with it, and, putting aside our friendship, I would rather serve under you than under many knights old enough to be your father. I don't know whether I shall have the luck to be one of the chosen, as Sir John said that there were to be only seven from each langue, which will make forty-nine —with yourself fifty. If I am chosen-and, knowing our friendship, I hope that the bailiff will let me go with you-it is likely enough I may be named your lieutenant, as I shall be the only one beside yourself who is a secular knight, and am, therefore, superior in rank to the rest."

"That would be pleasant indeed, Ralph, though I would rather that you had been made commander and I lieutenant; but at any rate, with you to support me, I shall feel less oppressed by the thought of my responsibility."

As Ralph had declared would be the case, the young knights in the other auberges were as anxious as those of England to be enrolled among the crew of the new galley, and the bailiffs had some trouble in choosing among the aspirants. Very few were selected outside the rank of professed knights, and as great pains were taken to comply with the grand master's wishes that only young knights of good conduct and disposition, and distinguished by their proficiency in warlike exercises, should be chosen, the crew was in every way a picked one. Most of them had made one or two of the three months' voyages in the galleys, though comparatively few had had the good fortune to be absolutely engaged with the Moslem pirates.

To the great satisfaction of himself and Gervaise, Ralph Harcourt was nominated lieutenant of the galley. The fact that so many had volunteered impressed all those who were chosen with the sense that it was at once an honour and a piece of good fortune to be selected, and all were determined that the boy galley, as the elder knights laughingly termed it, should do honour to the Order.

It was a fortnight before she was launched. Gervaise had heard, with great satisfaction, that it had been decided by the council that no punishment should be inflicted upon the slaves for their share in the intended rising at St. Pelagius. All were guilty, and there was no means of saying who had taken prominent parts in the plot. The council felt that it was but natural that they should grasp at the prospect of freedom, for they themselves would have done the same had they been captives of the infidels. Even the warders and guards were allowed to go unpunished, although their offence was a much more serious one. Those who could have named the men who had accepted bribes were dead, and the lesson had been so severe a one that there was no probability of any again turning traitors. The author of the rising had been publicly executed. Seeing the hopelessness of denial, he had boldly avowed his share in the matter, and had acknowledged that he was acting as agent for the sultan, and had been supplied with ample funds before leaving Constantinople.

He declared that he was absolutely unable to give any names whatever of those concerned in the plot, save those of the two overseers, as these had undertaken the work of suborning the warders and guards, though he admitted that he had on several occasions spoken to slaves as the gangs were on their way back to the prison, and had told them to be prepared to take part in a plan that was on foot for their rescue from slavery. The torture had not been, as was then the usual custom, applied to extort information; partly because his story was probable, still more because the grand master and council did not wish that more publicity should be given to the affair, and were glad that it should be allowed to drop without any further trial of the delinquents. In the city generally it was only known that a plot had been discovered for the liberation and escape of some of the slaves; and, outside the members of the Order, none were aware of its extent and dangerous character. To the satisfaction of Gervaise and Ralph, Vrados was able to produce letters and documents that satisfied the council that he had been deceived as to the character of the Greek, and was wholly innocent in the matter.

Chapter XII
The Boy Galley

Among those most pleased at the appointment of Gervaise to the command of the galley was Sir John Boswell. Ever since the adventure with the pirates, the knight had exhibited an almost fatherly interest in him; had encouraged him in his studies, ridden with him on such occasions as he had permitted himself a short holiday, and had, whenever they were together, related to him stories of war, sieges, battles, and escapes, from which he thought the young knight might gain lessons for his future guidance.

"I doubt, Gervaise," he said one day, as they were riding quietly along the road, "whether our plan of life is altogether the best. We were founded, you know, simply as a body of monks, bound to devote ourselves solely to the care of the sick, and to give hospitality to pilgrims in Palestine. Now this was monkish work, and men who devoted themselves solely to such a life of charity as that in our Hospital at Jerusalem, might well renounce all human pleasures; but when the great change was made by Master Raymond du Puy, and from a nursing body we became a brotherhood in arms, it seems to me that the vows of celibacy were no longer needful or desirable. The crusaders were, many of them, married men, but they fought no worse for that. It would have been far better, methinks, had we been converted into an Order pledged to resist the infidel, but without the vows of poverty and of celibacy, which have never been seriously regarded.

"The garrison here might be composed, as indeed it is now, principally of young knights, of those who have not cared to marry, and of the officers of the Order whose wives and families might dwell here with them. This would have many advantages. Among others, the presence of so many ladies of rank would have the excellent effect of discountenancing and repressing extravagances and dissolute habits, which are but too common, and are a shame to the Order. Knights possessing commanderies throughout Europe would be no worse stewards for being married men, and scandals, such as contributed largely to the downfall of the Templars, would be avoided.

"The sole vow necessary, so far as I can see, would be that knights should remain unmarried and disposable at all times for service until ten years after making their profession, and that afterwards they should ever be ready to obey the summons to arms, on occasions when the safety of Rhodes, or the invasion of any Christian country by the Moslems, rendered their services needful, when they would come out just as the knights of Richard the Lion Heart went out as crusaders. I have spent half my life since I joined the Order in commanderies at home, and a dull life it was, and I was glad enough to resign my last command and come out here. Had I been able to marry, I might now have had a son of your age, whose career I could watch and feel a pride in. My life would have been far happier in England, and in all respects I should be a better man than I am now. Methinks it would strengthen rather than weaken the Order. As a fighting body we should be in no way inferior to what we are now, and we should be more liked and more respected throughout Europe, for naturally the sight of so many men leading a luxurious life in commanderies causes a feeling against them."

"But I suppose, Sir John, that there is no great difficulty in obtaining a dispensation from our vows?"

"In this, as in all other matters, everything depends upon interest or money. Of course, dispensations are not common; but doubtless any knight when he had served his term of active service could, especially if his request were backed by the grand master, obtain from the Pope a dispensation of his vows. If he had a commandery it would make a vacancy, and give the grand prior, or the grand master, or the council, in whosoever's gift it might be, an opportunity of rewarding services or of gratifying some powerful family."

"I agree with you that it would have been much better, Sir John. I can understand that monks, ever living a quiet life apart from the world, should be content so to continue; but among a body of warlike knights there must be many who, in time, must come to regret the vows they took when boys. The cadet of a noble family might, by the death of elder brothers, come to be the head of a great family, the ruler over wide domains. Surely it would be desirable that such a man should be able to marry and have heirs."

"Doubtless it could be managed in such cases, Gervaise, but it is a pity that it should have to be managed. I can see no reason in the world why a knight, after doing ten years of service here, should not be free to marry, providing he takes a vow to render full service to the Order whenever called upon to do so. Already the vow of poverty is everywhere broken. Already, in defiance of their oaths, too many knights lead idle and dissolute lives. Already, knights, when in their own countries, disregard the rule that they shall draw sword in no cause save that of the Holy Sepulchre, and, like other knights and nobles, take part in civil strife or foreign wars. All this is a scandal, and it were better by far to do away with all oaths, save that of obedience and willingness to war with the infidel, than to make vows that all men know are constantly and shamelessly broken.

"I am fond of you, Gervaise. I am proud of you, as one who has brought honour to our langue, and who, in time, will bring more honour. I am glad that, so far as there can be between a young knight and one of middle age, there is a friendship between us. But see what greater pleasure it would give to my life were you my son, for whom I could lay by such funds as I could well spare, instead of spending all my appointments on myself, and having neither kith nor kin to give a sigh of regret when the news comes that I have fallen in some engagement with the infidels. I often think of all these things, and sometimes talk them over with comrades, and there are few who do not hold, with me, that it would be far better that we should become a purely military Order, like some of the military Orders in the courts of the European sovereigns, than remain as we are, half monk, half soldier —a mixture that, so far as I can see, accords but badly with either morality or public repute.

"However, I see no chance of such a change coming, and we must be content to observe our vows as well as may be, so long as we are willing to remain monks and try to obtain dispensation from our vows should we desire to alter our mode of life. We ought either to have remained monks pure and simple, spending our lives in deeds of charity, a life which suits many men, and against which I should be the last to say anything, or else soldiers pure and simple, as were the crusaders, who wrested the Holy Sepulchre from the hands of the infidels. At present, Gervaise, your vocation lies wholly in the way of fighting, but it may be that the time will come when you may have other aims and ambitions, and when the vows of the Order will gall you."

"I hope not, Sir John," Gervaise said earnestly.

"You are young yet," the knight replied, with an indulgent smile. "Some day you may think differently. Now," he went on, changing the subject abruptly, "when will your galley be ready?"

"This is my last ride, Sir John. The shipwrights will have finished tomorrow, and the next day we shall take possession of her, and begin to practise, so that each man shall know his duties, and the galley slaves learn to row well, before we have orders to sail. I wish you were going with us, Sir John."

"I should like it, lad, in many respects. It does one good to see the enthusiasm of young men, and doubtless you will be a merry party. But, on the other hand, unless I mistake, you will be undertaking wild adventures, and my time for these is well nigh passed. When the Turk comes here, if he ever comes-and of that I have little doubt —I shall be ready to take my full share of the fighting; but I shall seek adventures no longer, and shall go no more to sea. Next only to the bailiff, I am the senior of our auberge, and-but this is between ourselves, lad-am likely to succeed to the grand priory of England when it becomes vacant, and if not I shall, as the grand master has told me, have the offer of the next high office vacant in the palace."

Two days later Gervaise and his company of young knights went down to the port to take part in the launch of the new galley. This was the occasion of a solemn ceremony, the grand master and a large number of knights being present. A religious service first took place on her poop, and she was named by the grand master the Santa Barbara. When the ceremony was over, Gervaise was solemnly invested with the command of the galley by the grand marshal of the navy; then the shores were struck away, and the galley glided into the water, amid the firing of guns, the blowing of trumpets, and the cheers of the spectators who had gathered at the port to witness the ceremony.

The next morning a gang of galley slaves were marched down. A third of these had been drawn from the crews of other galleys, their places being supplied by new hands. The remainder were taken from the men employed on the fortifications. Three weeks were occupied in teaching the rowers their work, and getting them well together. They were a fine crew, for the governor of St. Pelagius, grateful to Gervaise for the discovery of the plot, had ordered the overseers to pick out from the various gangs men specially suited by age and strength for the work.

The dye by this time had entirely worn off his face, and although his hair was still several shades darker than of old, it differed even more widely from the ebon hue that it had been when he was in prison. Thus, although he recognised three or four men upon the benches who had been fellow occupants of his cell, he had no fear whatever of their detecting in the commander of the galley their late companion in misfortune.

Only a portion of the knights had been out each day while the crew were learning to row, as there was but little for them to learn. The galley carried no sails, and the knights were soldiers rather than sailors, and fought on the deck of their ship, as if defending a breach, or storming one held by the enemy. Moreover, as all of them had already made one or more voyages, they were accustomed to such duties as they would have to discharge on board.

All were glad when an order was published for the galley to sail. On the eve of departure Gervaise was sent for by the grand master. The general of the galleys was with him when Gervaise entered the room. The bailiff of Auvergne always held the position of grand marshal, and the bailiff of Italy that of second in command, with the title of grand admiral. These officials, however, as heads of their respective langues, had many other duties to perform, and it was only on great occasions that they took any practical share in the work of which they were nominally heads. The real control in all naval questions rested with the general of the galleys, who was elected by the council, but on the nomination of the grand master.

His power when at sea with the fleet was absolute. He could suspend any officer from duty, and had unquestioned power of life and death over the crews. He had been frequently on board the galley since she had been launched, and had been pleased with the attention paid by Gervaise to his duties, and with the ready manner in which the young knights carried out his orders.

"Sir Gervaise Tresham," he said, "it is usual, as you know, to appoint each galley to a certain cruising ground, to which it is confined during its three months' absence. At present there is a galley on each of these stations, and as the last relief took place but a month since, it is better that they should remain at the stations allotted to them. I have therefore, after consultation with his Highness the grand master, decided to give you a free hand. You are as likely to meet with pirates in one quarter as in another, and you will pick up from vessels you may overhaul news of their doings, which will enable you to direct your course to the point where you will be most useful."

"In the first place, however, you will proceed to the coast of Tunis. Visconti's galley is already there, but the coast swarms with corsairs, and we have had many complaints as to their depredations. The Court of Spain has twice represented to us lately that the pirates have grown so bold that vessels have been carried off, even when coasting from one Spanish port to another. Visconti is specially watching the coast near Tunis, and you will therefore perhaps do better to proceed farther west, for every village from Tunis to Tangier is little better than a nest of pirates. I should imagine that you will find ample employment there during your three months' cruise. When I say that you are free to choose your own cruising ground, I do not mean that you should go up the Levant, or to the east of the Mediterranean, but that you are not bound to keep close along the African coast, but may, should you obtain any information to warrant your doing so, seek the pirates along the shores of Spain, Sardinia, Corsica, or Sicily.

"I need not warn you to act with prudence as well as courage, for you have proved that you possess both qualities. Do not allow yourself to be carried away by the impetuosity of your knights; it is more often the duty of a commander to restrain than to encourage his crew, and with such young blood as you have under your command the necessity will be greater than usual. Be kind to your slaves, but be ever watchful; yet this I need not tell you. Maintain a strict but not over severe discipline. You are all knights and comrades of the Order, and equals when on shore, but on board you are the captain and they are your soldiers. I have this afternoon had a meeting of your knights, and have urged upon them very strongly that, having volunteered to serve under you, they must obey your orders as promptly and willingly as if you were the senior knight of the Order, and that it behooves them specially upon the present occasion, when the crew is composed entirely of young knights, to show themselves worthy of the honour that has been done to them by entrusting a galley of the Order to their charge. I told them I should regard your report of their individual conduct with the same attention and respect with which I should that of any other commander, and that they might greatly make or mar their future prospects in the Order by their conduct during the cruise. I am convinced, from what I know of you, that you will exercise no undue harshness, but will act with tact and discretion, as well as firmness."

"I will try to do so, your Excellency. I feel that it is a heavy responsibility and will spare no pains to justify the unmerited honour that has been bestowed upon me."

"You have seen that the taking in of stores is complete, and that nothing is wanting for the voyage?"

"Yes, sir. I stood by while the overseer of stores checked off every sack and barrel as it came on board. The water is to be brought off this evening, and as I was unable to be present, Sir Ralph Harcourt is there to count the barrels and see that all are full."

"Goodbye, Sir Gervaise," the grand master said, as the interview terminated.

"Hitherto you have given me, from the time you reached the Island, naught but reason for satisfaction at my nomination of you as page, and I have no fear that you will fail this time. Remember that valour, however great, cannot prevail against overpowering odds. You had a lesson of that when you served under Ricord, though finally the affair turned out well. I do not say, don't attempt desperate undertakings, but don't attempt impossible ones. Be careful of the lives of your knights. Remember that ere long every sword may be of the utmost consequence in the defence of Rhodes, and that even the capture of pirates may be too dearly purchased; but that, at the same time, the honour of the flag of the Order must be upheld at all hazards. Ah!" he broke off, seeing a slight smile on the young knight's face, "you think my orders contradictory? It may be so; but you know what I mean, and I fear not that you will blunder in carrying them out. Be prudent, and yet not over prudent. I mean, be not rash, unless there are such benefits to be obtained as would justify great risk in obtaining them."

On returning to the auberge, Gervaise had a long chat with Ralph.

"I think the admiral's talk with us this afternoon had an excellent effect, Gervaise. I do not say that every one was not before disposed to obey you in all things, willingly and cheerfully; but he put it so strongly to them that they had volunteered specially for service in this galley, knowing well who was to be its commander, and the circumstance that the crew was to consist solely of young knights, and had therefore specially pledged their honour so to act that the enterprise should be in all respects a successful one. To render it so, obedience was even a greater necessity than valour. This was the most important of all the vows taken by the knights of the Order, and it was only by the strictest and most unquestioning obedience on the part of all to the orders of their superiors, that the work of a vast community could be carried on. Passing over the fact that you were their superior in rank, both as being a secular knight and a knight commander of the Order, you had been specially appointed by the grand master and council, as well as by himself, and that they bestowed upon you while at sea, and in the absence of any officers of superior rank, their full powers and authority. You were, in fact, their representative and agent, and therefore to be regarded with the same deference and respect that would be due to the oldest knight similarly placed. 'Lastly,' he said, in a less serious tone, 'you must remember that this is an experiment, and, as some think, a somewhat rash one. Never before did a galley, manned entirely from among the youngest of our knights, put to sea; and you may be sure that, unless successful, the experiment is not likely to be ever repeated. You have been selected from among many other candidates, and you have not only to justify the choice, but to uphold the reputation and honour of the young knights of your Order, by all of whom your doings will be regarded with special interest, as reflecting credit not only upon yourselves individually, but as representatives and champions of them all.'

"I could see that his words had a great effect. He had placed me beside him, and I marked their faces as he spoke. Each face lit up at his appeal, and I do not think there was one but silently registered a vow to do all in his power to prove himself worthy of the confidence placed in him and his companions by the grand master and admiral. I had before no shadow of fear that everything would not go well. I knew almost all of them personally, and if I myself had had the selection from among the whole body of knights in the convent, I could not have made a choice that would have suited me better. It seems to me that in each auberge the bailiff has endeavoured to pick out the seven young knights whom he considered would most worthily support the honour of the langue. Still, confident as I was before, I feel more so now, after the admiral's address to us."

"I had no fear either, Ralph, though doubtless the admiral's words will carry great weight with them. It was thoughtlessness rather than anything else that I dreaded; but now that the admiral himself has spoken to them, there is no fear that anything will occur to give us trouble. I have particularly noticed that when we have been on board, and have been laughing and chatting together before we got under way, their manner changed directly the first order was given, and that all the commands were carried out with as much goodwill and alacrity as if they were under Ricord himself."

On the following morning the knights all went on board the Santa Barbara. Their baggage was carried down by slaves, and by the personal servants from each auberge who were to go as their attendants during the voyage. The grand master had advanced Gervaise a sum equal to half a year's income of his commandery, and with this he had purchased a stock of the best wines, and various other luxuries, to supplement the rations supplied from the funds of the Order to knights when at sea. Gervaise had to go round early to the admiral to sign the receipt for stores and to receive his final orders in writing. All were, therefore, on board before him and, when he arrived, were drawn up in military order to receive him.

Every knight was in full armour, and as, at a word from Ralph, they drew their swords and saluted the young commander, Gervaise felt with a thrill of pleasure and of confidence that with such a following he need not fear any encounter with a pirate force, unless in overwhelming numbers.

The young knights were all, with the exception only of Ralph Harcourt, between the ages of seventeen and nineteen, and their young faces, free in most cases even from the suspicion of a moustache, looked almost those of boys. But there was no mistaking the ardour and enthusiasm in their faces, and the lack of breadth and weight, that years alone would give to them, was compensated by skill in their weapons, acquired by long and severe training, and by the activity and tireless energy of youth.

"Knights and comrades," Gervaise said as, after walking through the double line to the end of the poop he turned and faced them, "I am proud indeed to command so gallant a body of knights. The success of our expedition depends upon you rather than upon me, and as I feel assured of your warm cooperation I have no fear as to what the result will be, if Dame Fortune will but favour us by throwing in our way some of those scourges of the sea in search of whom we are about to set out. Many of us have already encountered them, and, fighting side by side with older knights, have borne our share of the work, while those who have not done so will, I am sure, do equally well when the opportunity arrives. We shall not this voyage have the encouragement and confidence inspired by the presence of those who have long and valiantly borne the standard of the Order; but, on the other hand, we have to show that we are worthy of the confidence reposed in us, and that the young knights of the Order can be trusted to emulate the deeds of those who have rendered the name of the Hospitallers a terror to the infidel."

A shout of approbation greeted the close of his address. Gervaise then walked forward to the end of the poop, and looked down upon the slaves, who, with their oars out, were awaiting the order to row.

"Men," he said in Turkish, "it is my desire that, while it is necessary that you should do your work, your lot shall be no heavier than can be avoided. You will not be taxed beyond your powers, save when the enemy is in sight, or there is supreme need for haste, but then you must be called upon for your utmost exertions. I wish your work to be willing. I abhor the use of the lash, and so long as each man does his fair quota of work, I have given the strictest orders that it shall never be used. I have, at my own cost, made provision that your daily rations shall be improved while under my command. Meat will be served out to you daily, when it can be obtained, and for those of you who hold that the strict tenets of your religion may be relaxed while engaged in such severe labour, a ration of wine will also be served out; and such other indulgences as are compatible with the discipline and safety of the ship, will also be granted to you."

There was a murmur of gratitude among the slaves. Gervaise then gave the order to row, and the galley started on her voyage. The knights had now fallen out from their ranks, and were soon laughing and talking gaily. Being all of noble families and knightly rank, there was, except when on actual duty, a tone of perfect equality and good fellowship prevailing among them. French was the common language, for as the Order was of French foundation, and three of the seven langues belonged to that country, most of the high dignitaries being chosen from their ranks, it was natural that the French language should be the general medium of communication between them.

Until noon the slaves rowed steadily and well. Work was then stopped, for there was scarce a breath of wind stirring the water. Even under the awning that had, as the sun gained power, been erected over the poop, the heat was oppressive. The knights had all divested themselves of their armour, and most of them retired below for a siesta. As soon as the slaves stopped rowing, an awning, which Gervaise had purchased, and which was rolled up under the break of the poop, was, to their astonishment, drawn over them.

"Don't you think you are spoiling your slaves, Sir Gervaise?" one of the Spanish knights asked doubtfully.

"On the contrary, Sir Pedro, I hope that I am improving them. You have not worked as a galley slave, but I have, and I can assure you that I used to feel the hours when we were lying broiling in the sun, doing nothing, much more trying than those during which I was at work. I used to be quite giddy and sick with the heat, and on getting out the oars again had scarce strength to work them. But this is not the most important point. In port the slaves always sleep in the prison, but at sea they must rest on their benches; and to do so with clothes soaked with the heavy dew must be a severe trial, and most prejudicial to the health. The awning cost but a few ducats, and I reckon that, putting aside the comfort to the slaves, it will be very speedily repaid by their better health and capacity for labour. When away in the galley with Sir Louis Ricord, I used to feel the greatest pity for the unfortunate wretches when at daybreak, in their drenched clothes, and shivering with cold and wet, they rose to commence their work. I then took a vow that if ever I should come to command a galley I would provide an awning for the slaves."

Two or three of the knights standing by expressed their warm approval of what Gervaise said. There was, in those days, but little of that sentiment of humanity that is now prevalent, and slaves were everywhere regarded as mere beasts of burden rather than as human beings. When, however, they had the question put to them, as Gervaise had done, they were ready to give a hearty agreement, although it was the utilitarian rather than the humanitarian side of the question that recommended it to them. After three hours' rest the journey was renewed, and just at nightfall the galley anchored off an islet lying to the north of Carpathos.

While the servants were laying the tables along the poop for the evening meal, Gervaise went down to see that his orders were carried out regarding the food for the slaves. They were already eating their bread and meat with an air of satisfaction that showed how warmly they appreciated the unusual indulgence, while there were few indeed who did not hold up their drinking horns as a servant passed along between the benches with a skin of wine. Gervaise spoke to many of them.

"Ah, my lord," one of them said, "if we were always treated like this, slavery would be endurable. For ten years have I rowed in Christian galleys, but never before has an awning been spread to keep off the sun or the dew. We shall not forget your kindness, my lord, and will row our hardest right cheerfully when you call upon us for an effort."

There was a murmur of assent from the galley slaves around.

"May Allah be merciful to you, as you are merciful to us!" another slave exclaimed. "The blessing of those whom you regard as infidels can at least do you no harm."

"On the contrary, it can do me good," Gervaise said. "The God you Moslems and we Christians worship is, I believe, the same, though under another name."

Gervaise had, indeed, during his long conversations with Suleiman Ali, often discussed with him the matter of his faith, and had come, in consequence, to regard it in a very different light to that in which it was viewed by his companions. There was faith in one God at the bottom of both Mohammedanism and Christianity. The Mohammedans held in reverence the lawgivers and prophets of the Old Testament, and even regarded Christ Himself as being a prophet. They had been grievously led away by Mahomet, whom Gervaise regarded as a false teacher; but as he had seen innumerable instances of the fidelity of the Moslems to their creed, and the punctuality and devotion with which the slaves said their daily prayers, exposed though they were to the scorn and even the anger of their taskmasters, he had quite lost, during his nine months of constant association with Suleiman Ali, the bigoted hatred of Mohammedanism so universal at the time. He regarded Moslems as foes to be opposed to the death; but he felt that it was unfair to hate them for being hostile to Christianity, of which they knew nothing.

Chapter XIII
The First Prizes

After leaving the slaves, Gervaise joined his companions on the poop. They were engaged in an animated discussion as to whether it was advisable to grant indulgences to slaves. The majority approved of the steps Gervaise had taken, but some asserted that these concessions would only lead them to look for more, and would create discontent among the crews of other galleys not so favoured.

"Well, comrades," said Gervaise, "I think that so far I am better qualified than any of you to give an opinion; but it may be that it will fall to the lot of some of you to be a slave in Turkish hands. In that case, I can affirm with certainty, that you will keenly appreciate any alleviation, however small, of your lot. You must remember that the one feeling of the slave is dull despair. Death is the only relief he has to look forward to. Do you think that a man so feeling can do his best, either at an oar or at any other kind of work? I am sure it would not be so in my case. But if you brighten his life a little, and show him that he is not regarded as merely a brute beast, and that you take some interest in him, he will work in a different spirit. Even viewed from a merely monetary point of view it must pay well to render him as content as possible with his lot. You know how great is the mortality among the slaves-how they pine away and die from no material malady that can be detected, but simply from hopelessness and weariness of life, aided, undoubtedly, in the case of the galley slaves, by sleeping in the damp night air after an exposure all day to the full heat of the sun. This brings an answer to your second objection. Undoubtedly it might cause discontent among the slaves of other galleys when they hear that others are treated better than themselves. But I hope that if, on our return, we bring back all our slaves in good condition and health, the contrast between their appearance and that of the slaves in most other galleys will be so marked that the admiral may consider it would be well to order awnings to be fixed to all the vessels of the Order, and even to grant to all slaves, when away on voyages, the little indulgences I have given them here. The expense would be very trifling, and it would certainly add a great deal to the average life of a slave, and would render him capable of better work. There is another advantage. If the Turks learn that their countrymen in our hands are treated with a certain amount of kindness and consideration, it might lead them to act similarly to those of our Order who may be unfortunate enough to fall into their hands."

"There is a great deal in what you say, Sir Gervaise," one of the knights, who had before taken the opposite point of view, said. "There is no reason why our galley should not be a model one, and though, like enough, the seniors will laugh at our making innovations, D'Aubusson is a reformer, and will certainly support anything that he sees to be beneficial, from whatever quarter it comes."

Supper was now served, and the young knights were well pleased with the entertainment provided for them. It was the principal meal of the day. Their fast was broken by a glass of wine, a manchet of bread, and fruit soon after rising. At eleven o'clock they sat down to a more substantial meal; but in that climate the heat was at that hour considerable, and as there were duties to be performed, there was no sitting long at table. At supper the day's work was over, their appetite was sharpened by the cool evening breeze, and the meal was hearty and prolonged. After it was concluded, several of the knights brought up from below viols and other instruments of music; for the ability to accompany the voice with such an instrument was considered an essential part of the education of a knight.

For some hours the songs and romances, so popular at the time, were sung in the various languages represented on board; then the knights, one by one, went down to their sleeping places, until only the seven knights of the langue of Auvergne, who were to watch the first night, remained on deck. Five of these wrapped themselves in their mantles and lay down on the benches. One of the others descended to the waist, walked along the plank between the lines of sleeping slaves, and took up his place in the bow, while the other paced up and down the poop, the fall of his footsteps being the only sound to break the silence that reigned throughout the ship.

In the morning, as soon as the knights had all taken a plunge in the sea, the oars were got out, and the galley proceeded on her way. Passing through the islands and skirting the southern shore of Greece, she continued her course west. Malta was sighted, but they did not put in there. Pantellaria was passed, and in a fortnight after leaving Rhodes, Cape Bon, at the entrance to the bay of Tunis, was sighted. Until Greece was left behind them, the nights had generally been spent in small ports, where supplies of fresh meat, fish, and fruit, were obtainable. So far no incident had marked the voyage. The weather had continued fine, and they had heard nothing, from ships they had fallen in with, of any Moslem pirates having been seen. A few hours, however, after sighting the coast of Africa, a dark object was seen ahead.

"It is a ship of some sort," Ralph said; "but her masts have gone. It may be that she is a merchantman that has been captured and sacked by the Moorish pirates."

Orders were given to the rowers to quicken their pace, and in little over an hour they were alongside the hull. As soon as the vessels were close enough for those on the poop of the galley to look down on to the deck of the other craft, it was seen that Ralph's suppositions were correct. Two bodies lay stretched upon it. One was crushed under the fallen mast; the other lay huddled up in a heap, a cannon ball having almost torn him asunder. The knights leapt on to the deck as soon as the galley ran alongside. Gervaise made first for the man lying beneath the mast; as he came up to him, the sailor opened his eyes and murmured, "Water!" Gervaise called out to one of the servants to bring water from the galley, and, as soon as it came, poured some between the man's lips, and the knights by their united efforts lifted the mast from across his body. It was evident, however, that he had but a short time to live, and the dew of death was on his face. After a few minutes he rallied a little, and looked gratefully at his rescuers.

"You have been attacked by pirates," Gervaise said. "Was there one galley, or two?"

"Three galleys," the man replied in a faint whisper.

"Do you know where they were from?"

"Tripoli."

"How long ago?"

"It was about three hours after sunrise when we saw them coming up," the man said, his voice gaining in strength, as some wine they gave him took effect. "It was useless to fight, and I hauled down our flag, but in spite of that one of the pirates fired a broadside, and one of the shot hit the mast and brought it down, and I was crushed under it. They boarded us, took off all the crew as captives, and emptied the hold; I knew that I was done for, and begged them to kill me; but they paid no attention. I know a little of their language, and as I lay there I caught something of what they were saying; they are bound for the Island of Sardinia, where they have a rendezvous, and are to join a great gathering of their consorts. I don't know the name of the place, but it is on the east coast. More water!"

Gervaise knelt to pour some water between his lips, when he gave a sudden cry, a shudder ran through his frame, and he was dead.

"Let us return on board, gentlemen," Gervaise said, rising to his feet. "We can do nothing here."

As soon as he regained the deck of the galley, he signed to Ralph to follow him below.

"Now, Ralph," he said, "this is one of those cases in which we have to decide whether we ought or ought not to be prudent. From what that poor fellow said, the pirates have about five hours' start of us, and as they can have no idea that they are pursued, we can doubtless overtake them before they reach Sardinia. The question is, ought we to pursue them at once, or ought we to coast along until we find Visconti's galley? Three of these Tripoli pirates, crowded as they always are with men, would prove serious opponents, yet we might engage them with a fair hope of victory. But we may be seriously disabled in the fight, and should be, perhaps, unable to carry the news to Genoa that there are many pirate ships gathering on the coast of Sardinia to prey upon their commerce."

"We might be days, or even weeks, before we light upon Visconti's galley, Gervaise, and even when we found it, he might not consider himself justified in leaving the coast where he is stationed. Besides, while we are spending our time looking for him, the pirates will be committing terrible depredations. It must be a big expedition, under some notorious pirate, or they would never venture so far north."

"Then you think that I should be justified in pursuing them alone. It is a fearful responsibility to have to decide."

"I think so, Gervaise. There is no saying what misfortunes might happen if we did not venture to do so."

"Very well then, so be it. But before deciding finally on so grave a matter, I will lay it before the company."

"There is no doubt as to what their decision will be," Ralph said, with a smile.

"Perhaps not, Ralph; but as they will be called upon to risk their lives in a dangerous enterprise, it is as well that they should have a say in the matter."

When they returned on to the poop, there was an expression of eagerness and excitement on the faces of the young knights which showed how anxiously they had been awaiting the result of the conference below. Gervaise stepped on to a bench, and motioned to them to close up round him.

"Comrades," he said, "although the responsibility of whatever course may be taken must rest upon my shoulders, yet I think it but right that, as a general before a battle often calls a council of war to assist him with its advice, so I should lay before you the two courses open to us, and ask your opinion upon them. Sir Ralph Harcourt and I are of one mind in the matter, but as the decision is a grave one we should be loath to act upon it without your concurrence."

He then repeated the alternatives as he had laid them before Ralph. "Now," he went on, "as you see, there is grave danger, and much risk in the one course; but if successful its advantages are obvious. On the other hand, the second plan is more sure, more prudent, and more in accordance with the instructions I have received. I ask you to let me know frankly your opinion on the subject. If your view agrees with ours, although it will not relieve me from the responsibility of deciding, it will at least, in the event of things turning out badly, be a satisfaction to know that the course had your approval, and that it was your desire, as well as ours, that we should undertake it. First, then, let all who are in favour of following the pirates go to the starboard side of the deck, while those who are in favour of joining Visconti, and laying this serious matter we have discovered before him, move to the larboard side."

There was a rush of the knights to the right, and not one moved to the other side.

"Your decision is the same as ours," Gervaise said. "To the north, then! If there is great peril in the adventure, there is also great honour to be gained."

The knights gave a shout of satisfaction at finding that their choice was also that of the officers.

"Lay her head to the north," Gervaise said to the pilot. Then he went to the end of the poop, and ordered the slaves to row on. "Row a long, steady stroke, such as you can maintain for many hours. We have a long journey before us, and there is need for haste. Now is the time for willing work."

The oars dipped into the water, and the galley was soon moving along at a much faster pace than that at which they had performed the journey from Rhodes. The slaves had not, from their benches, been able to see what had passed on board the dismantled vessel, but from the order and the change of course, they had no doubt that the knights had obtained some clue to the direction taken by the corsairs who had captured and sacked the ship.

"There is but little wind," Gervaise said to Ralph, "and their sails will be of slight use to them; therefore we shall go fully three feet to their two. It is quite possible that we may not catch sight of them, for we cannot tell exactly the course they will take. We shall steer for Cape Carbonara, which is some hundred and thirty miles distant. If we do not see them by the time we get there, we shall be sure that we have passed them on the way, unless, indeed, a strong wind should spring up from the south. However, I hope that we shall catch sight of them before that, for we shall be able from our lookout to discover their masts and sails some eight or ten miles away, while they will not be able to see us until we are within half that distance. They cannot be more than twenty miles away now, for the light breeze will aid them but little, and as they will see no occasion for haste, they will not be rowing at their full power, with so long a passage before them."

Already, indeed, one of the knights had perched himself on the seat at the top of a low mast some fifteen feet above the poop, that served as a lookout.

"You can see nothing yet, I suppose, Cairoli?"

"No; the line of sea is clear all round."

It was indeed some four hours before the knight on the lookout cried that he could make out three dark specks on the horizon. Gervaise at once ascended to the lookout, by the ladder that was fixed against the post.

"They are making to the left of the course we are taking. Turn her head rather more to the west. That will do. They are directly ahead now." He then came down to the deck again. "I would that we had seven or eight more hours of daylight, Ralph, instead of but three at the outside. However, as we know the course they are taking, we are not likely to miss them, for as we shall not be near enough for them to make us out before the sun sets, there will be no chance of their changing it. Do you think they will row all night?"

"I should not think so. If the land were nearer they might keep on until they make it, but as they have had no wind since daylight, they will lie on their oars until morning. You see, at sunset they will still be some eighty miles from Cape Carbonara, and the slaves could not possibly row that distance without rest; so that if we keep on we may take them by surprise."

"That is what I have been thinking, Ralph, but it would be well not to attack them until nearly daybreak. We should capture one galley easily enough; but the others, being ignorant of our force, might make off in different directions, and we might lose both of them. If, on the other hand, we could fall upon them a short time before daylight, we should be able to keep them in sight, and, even if they separated, they would soon come together and continue their course, or, as I hope, when they see that we are alone, bear up and fight us. I think that our best plan will be to row on until it is dark, then give the slaves six hours' rest, and after that go on quietly. If we can make them out, which we may do if they have lights on board, we will stop, and wait until it is the hour to attack them. If we miss them, we will row on to Sardinia and lie up, as we proposed, until they come along."

"I think that will be a very good plan, Gervaise."

Before sunset the three pirate ships could be clearly made out from the deck, but the pilot judged them to be fully ten miles away. Half an hour later the slaves were told to cease rowing. Gervaise had ordered the cooks to prepare them a good meal, and this was at once served, together with a full ration of wine. As soon as they had consumed it, they were told to lie down and sleep, as at one o'clock the galley would be again under way.

The knights' supper was served below, as lights on the poop might be made out, should a lookout be placed by the corsairs in their tops.

"We had better follow the example of the galley slaves," Gervaise said, rising as soon as the meal was finished, "and, with the exception of Spain, who is on watch, turn in to sleep till we are off again. All of you will, of course, don your armour on rising."

At the appointed hour the galley was again under way. There was not a breath of air, and before starting, pieces of cloth were wrapped round the oars at the rowlocks to deaden the sound, which might otherwise have been heard at a considerable distance on so still a night. After an hour and a half's rowing, the knight on the lookout said that he could see a light some distance ahead. The pilot, an experienced old sailor, joined him, and speedily descended to the poop again.

"It is a ship's light," he said. "I should say that it was a lantern on board the ship of the captain of the expedition, and is shown to enable the other two to keep near him. I cannot say how far it is away, for I do not know at what height it hangs above the water; but I should imagine, from the feebleness of the light, that it must be some two miles distant."

As soon as the light had been noticed, the slaves had been ordered to cease rowing, and they were now told that they would not be required again for fully two hours. When the first gleam of dawn appeared in the east they were called to their work again. The lantern was still burning, and, in a quarter of an hour, the knights on the poop were able, in the broadening light, to make out three shadowy forms some two miles ahead of them. They decreased this distance by more than half before they could discern any signs of life or motion on board. Then a sudden stir was apparent; they could hear shouts from one vessel to another, oars were thrust out, and an effort made to get the heads of the ships in the same direction, so as to catch the light breeze that had just sprung up.

The moment he saw that the galley was discovered, Gervaise shouted down to the slaves to row their hardest, and told the pilot to steer for the ship farthest to the east. She was some four or five hundred yards from her nearest consort, and the same distance separated that vessel from the third craft.

"We shall have time to carry her, Ralph, before the others come to her assistance, and they will only arrive one at a time. If we were to lie alongside the middle craft, which is probably that of the chief, as it is she that has the light burning, we might have the other two upon us before we had done with her, for she is evidently the largest, and most likely the strongest handed, of them."

The leader of the pirates evidently saw that there was no chance of evading the fight. A flag was run up to the masthead of his ship, and the three vessels began to endeavour to turn, so as to meet the galley. The operation, however, took some time. In the confusion, orders were misunderstood, and instead of all the slaves on one side rowing whilst those on the other side backed, all order was lost, and long before the craft for which the galley was making had got round, the latter was upon her.

"Shall I ram her, Sir Gervaise?" the pilot asked.

"No; we might damage ourselves; besides, I do not want to sink her. Sheer away the oars on one side!"

The galley carried eight guns-three on each side of the poop, and two forward; and these had been loaded with small pieces of iron. A few shots had been fired by the pirates, but, owing to the confusion that prevailed on board, the guns were discharged so hurriedly that the shot either flew overhead or passed wide of the galley. Excited as the young knights were, and eager for the fray, a general laugh broke out as the galley swept along by the pirate ship, breaking many of her oars, and hurling all the slaves who manned them backwards off their benches. A moment later the guns poured their iron contents among the pirates who clustered thickly on the forecastle and poop, and as the vessels grated together the knights sprang on board the corsair.

The members of the English langue had each been provided with short pieces of rope, and before joining their companions in the fray they lashed the vessels together, side by side. The fight was a very short one. France and Auvergne, led by Ralph Harcourt, boarded at the bow, the other five langues at the poop; and so impetuous was their onset that the pirates, who had still scarce recovered from their surprise at being hastily aroused from sleep to repel the attack of the foe who had so suddenly sprung out from the darkness upon them, offered but a feeble resistance. Many threw themselves overboard, and swam to the ship nearest to them; others were cut down; and the rest flung away their arms, and cried for quarter.

All who did so were, without the loss of a minute's time, thrown down into the hold of their ship, and the hatches secured over them. It had before been arranged that Ralph should take the command of the corsair, having with him France, Auvergne, and Germany. As soon, therefore, as the captives were fastened below, Gervaise called the knights of the other four langues back to the deck of the galley. The lashings were cast off, she was pushed from the side of the prize, and the oars were got out. There was no time to be lost, for the largest of the three pirate ships, which had, directly it was seen that her consort was captured, poured two heavy broadsides into the prize, was now approaching-rowing but slowly, however, for the third vessel to come up.

She was but a hundred yards away when the galley swept round the bow of the prize and advanced to meet her. As she did so, Ralph discharged the eight guns of the prize, which he had at once reloaded, into the bow of the corsair, the shot raking the crowded deck from end to end. When but a few yards distant, the two bow guns of the galley poured in a shower of missiles, and a moment later she ran alongside the pirate, the poop guns, as before, preparing the way for the boarders. But no sooner had they leapt on deck than they were met by the pirates, headed by their captain.

Gervaise had specially charged the knights not to allow themselves to be carried away by their ardour. "We are sure to be greatly outnumbered, and, when we first spring on board, we must cut our way across the deck, and then form ourselves in a double or treble line across it, and, so fighting, gradually force them before us."

This, in spite of the efforts of the pirates, was accomplished, and, once formed, the corsairs strove in vain to break through the wall of steel. For a time, however, no forward movement could be made, so furious were the attacks upon them, led by the pirate chief. Several times breaches were made in the front rank, but the knights behind each time bore back the assault, and restored the line. The knights had won their way half along the poop when a yell of exultation rose from the corsairs as the third of their vessels rowed up on the other side of the galley, and her crew sprang on board it. Gervaise called the knights of the second line from their places, and ranged them along the bulwark, to prevent the Moors from boarding from the poop of the galley.

Then for a moment he looked round. The prize was creeping up, and was a length or two away, coming up alongside. Its approach was also noticed by the pirates, who, with wild shouts, flung themselves upon their opponents. Gervaise sprang forward to take the place of a young Italian knight, who staggered back, with his helmet cleft by a heavy blow from the keen yataghan of the pirate captain. The corsair, shouting his war cry of "Allah!" sprang with the bound of a wild cat upon Gervaise; his weapon descended on his uplifted guard, and shore right through the stout blade. With a shout of triumph, the corsair raised his arm to repeat the blow; but Gervaise in turn sprang forward, and struck with all his force with the pommel of his sword on the forehead of his opponent. The latter fell as if shot, his weapon dropping from his hand beside him.

Dismayed at the fall of their leader, his followers recoiled for a moment. Another tall pirate sprang forward to take his place, and, shouting to them to follow, was about to throw himself upon Gervaise, when a gun crashed out close alongside. A storm of iron swept away the front line of Moors, and the shout of "St. John!" "St. John!" rose above the din. It was one of the bow guns of the prize, and as she swept along gun after gun poured its contents among the pirates.

"Do you clear the galley, Ralph. We can manage here now," Gervaise said, as Ralph leapt on board. The latter, followed by his party of knights, rushed across the poop, and sprang on to the galley among the pirates, who had been striving in vain to break through the line of defenders. Gervaise called to his party to follow him, and, taking the offensive, fell upon the remnant of the corsairs who still held the forward end of the poop.

The discharge of the cannon at such close quarters had wrought terrible havoc among them, and the pirates, with but slight resistance, turned, and either ran down the ladder or leapt into the water. The knights followed them forward among the benches of the rowers, who cheered loudly in many tongues as they passed them. At the forecastle the Moors made another stand, but the knights forced their way up, and in two minutes all was over.

"Now to the aid of our comrades!" Gervaise shouted, as the last of the corsairs was struck down.

Ralph's party had indeed cleared the poop of the galley, but they in vain endeavoured to climb up on to that of the third pirate ship, whose superior height gave a great advantage to its defenders. Gervaise leapt down on to the bow of the galley, followed by the knights, and then ran aft until he could climb into the waist of the pirate. So intent were the corsairs upon defending the poop that they did not see what was going on elsewhere, and Gervaise had obtained a fair footing before he was noticed. Then a number of men ran down and attacked his party. But it was too late, for the whole of the knights had, by this time, leaped on board. Their assailants were forced back, and, pressing close upon them, the knights gained the poop before the main body of the pirates were aware of their coming.

Warned by the shouts and shrieks of their comrades that they had been taken in the rear, the Moslems who were defending the side of the poop wavered for a moment. Ralph took advantage of their hesitation, and sprang on board, his companions pouring in after him. There was a stern and desperate fight. The Moslems fought with the fury of despair, disdaining to ask or accept quarter. A few leapt overboard, preferring death by drowning to that by the swords of the Christians; but the great majority died fighting to the last. A shout of triumph rose from the knights as the last of the Moslems fell.

The first impulse of all of them was to take off their helmets in order to breathe the fresh air, and for a while they all stood panting from their exertions.

"Nobly and gallantly done, comrades!" Gervaise exclaimed. "This is indeed a victory of which we have all a right to be proud. Now, the first thing is to free the slaves of their shackles; there are many white faces among them. Let our langue look after the wounded, while the released captives clear the decks of the bodies of the fallen pirates."

It took an hour's hard work to knock off the chains of the slaves. The greater portion of them were Christians-Greeks, Italians, Spaniards, and French, who had been captured in various raids by the corsairs; and among them were the crew of the ship that had been overhauled by the galley on the previous day. Besides these, there were a few Moslems who had been sentenced to labour in the galleys for various crimes.

Among the Christians, the joy at their liberation was intense. Some laughed, some cried, others were too overcome to speak coherently. Among the rest were found, to the intense pleasure of their rescuers, three knights of the Order who had for years been missing. They had been taken prisoners on an island at which the galley to which they belonged had touched. Many of the knights had landed, and three of them, all belonging to the langue of Italy, had wandered away from the rest, and had not returned. A search had been made for them, and it was discovered that a struggle had taken place. As there were no marks of blood, it was supposed that they were suddenly pounced upon by a party of hidden marauders, who had been watching them from some hiding place, and had thrown themselves upon the knights before they had had time to draw their swords. Following the trail by bushes broken down, and plants crushed under foot, it was found to lead to a creek on the other side of the island. Here there were signs that a craft had been anchored, as there were the ashes of fires, fragments of food, and other matters, scattered about on the shore. Hours had passed before the knights had been missed, and therefore the craft in which they had been carried off was long out of sight. Letters were written by the grand master to the Pasha of Syria, to the Emperor of Egypt, and to the Bey of Tunis, offering to ransom the knights, but all replied that they were unaware of any such captives having been landed.

An attempt had then been made to ascertain whether they had been carried to Tripoli; but the bey had little authority over the various tribesmen along the coast, and only replied that no such captives had been sold in the city. Thus all hope of ransoming them had died away, and their names were inscribed in the list of those who had fallen into the hands of the infidels, but of whose subsequent fate no clue could be obtained.

All were greatly emaciated, and their faces showed signs of the sufferings they had undergone. The young knights were all familiar with their names, but personally none had known them, for they had been carried off two or three months before Gervaise and Ralph Harcourt had arrived at Rhodes.

All three had struggled desperately to break their chains while the fight was going on, and had, as soon as the contest was decided, risen to their feet and shouted the battle cry of the Order; then, overcome by their emotions, they sank down upon their benches, and remained as if in a stupor until the knights, who had hurried first to them, struck off their fetters. Then the three men grasped each other's hands, while tears streamed down their cheeks.

"It is no dream, comrades," one of them said, in a hoarse voice. "We are free again. Let us first return thanks to God for our release, and then we can thank these our brothers."

The three knights knelt at the benches where they had toiled and suffered, and hid their faces in their hands. No sounds came from their lips, but their stifled sobs and the heaving of their naked shoulders, seamed and scarred by the strokes of their taskmasters' whips, told the young knights, who stood unhelmeted and silent around, how deep was their emotion. Then they rose.

"I am Fabricius Caretto," one said; "this is Giacomo Da Vinci; this Pietro Forzi: all knight commanders of the Order, and now for six years prisoners in the hands of these corsairs. Assuredly no one would know us, so changed are we." He looked round inquiringly for a familiar face. "Your commander must surely be a comrade of ours?"

"We know all your names," Gervaise said, coming forward, "though none of us reached the convent until after your capture. I have the honour to command this galley. My name is Gervaise Tresham, and I have for my lieutenant Sir Ralph Harcourt. All of us, glad as we are at the capture we have effected of these three corsairs, are still more pleased that we should have been the means of rescuing three noble knights of our Order from captivity. Now, I pray you first of all to accompany me on board the galley, where we will do all we can to make you forget the sufferings you have gone through. After you have bathed, and reclad yourselves, I will present to you the knights my comrades, amongst whom are seven of your own langue. Three of these I will tell off to see to your comfort, for, as you will understand, I have my hands full indeed at present."

"First, before all things, Sir Knight, let me express to you all our deep gratitude and our admiration of the gallant deed that you have accomplished in thus, single handed, capturing three vessels belonging to the fiercest and most dreaded of the corsairs of Tripoli. God bless you all, sirs"—and his voice broke again—"for the deed you have done, and for bringing us out of this living hell!"

Gervaise called to three of the Italian knights, and, followed by them and the released captives, led the way to the galley. Here he left them in charge of their countrymen. "Give them each a draught of old Cyprus, and something to eat," he said aside to one of the knights; "they sorely need refreshment before aught else, for, as you see, they are well nigh dazed with this unlooked for change. I will put out clothes enough for one of them; the others you must supply for the present from your stores. Now I must be off."

There was indeed much to be done. Four of the knights were told off to attend upon the most urgent cases among their own wounded. Only two of their number had been killed outright, but there were four serious cases among the wounded, while eight or ten others had received wounds that required bandaging and attending to. As fast as the slaves' fetters were struck off, food and wine were given to them, together with such garments as could be found at the moment. Then the bodies of the fallen pirates were thrown overboard, while the wounded were attended to, and the released Christians were divided equally between the three prizes. To each of these the knights of one of the langues were told off, the seniors being appointed to the command. There were in all some ninety Christian captives on board the three ships. Thus each vessel had a complement of seven knights and thirty Christians, and to these were added ten of the thirty Moslems found at the oars, and fifteen of the pirates to whom quarter had been given.

It was past noon before all these arrangements had been made, and during the time so occupied, the ships lay idly side by side, drifting slowly before the wind, the sails having been lowered as soon as the struggle was over. Up to this time, the knights had been too busily engaged to think of food, but they were right glad when they were summoned to a meal on board the galley.

Gervaise found the three knights in the cabin, dressed in the usual attire of the Order. They presented a very different appearance, indeed, to that which they wore when he had first seen them. They had bathed, and combed their matted hair, which was alone sufficient to transform them, but the feeling that they were once more free men, and knights of an honoured Order, had done even more to effect the change; and although they looked thin and worn, the martial bearing had come back naturally as they donned their knightly robes and buckled on swords.

"I am glad to see that you are better," Gervaise said, as he went up to greet them. "Twenty years seem to have dropped off your shoulders since this morning."

"We are not the same men, Sir Gervaise. We were slaves, and are now free. We were Christian dogs; now we are Christian knights. We were subject to scoffs and blows; now, thank God, we have swords to strike with, and though as yet our arms may not have regained their full strength, we could at least bear a share in a fray. Our comrades have been telling us somewhat of how this wonderful thing has come about, and have been explaining what at first filled us with surprise, that a galley should be manned solely by young knights, of whom their commander is one of the youngest. We can testify, at least, that had the grand master been himself in command, and his crew composed of veteran knights, he could have done no better."

"We were fortunate in taking them so much by surprise that the first of their ships fell into our hands before her consorts could come to her assistance; and her guns did us good service in our struggle with the others."

"The matter was well arranged, as well as gallantly fought," one of the other knights said. "Had you first fallen foul of the chief's galley, it would have gone hard with you, for his crew were so strong that you could scarce have overcome them before the other two vessels came up to his assistance."

"Now let us to our meal," Gervaise said.

The three knights were placed at the head of the table by him, and it was pleasant to see how they enjoyed their food.

"I can scarce persuade myself that I am not dreaming," Caretto said. "Sometimes, when lying at night, wet through with the damp air, I have wondered to myself whether I could ever have lived thus, and whether I should ever exchange my hard bread and water for what seemed to me fabulous luxuries, though at the time one had taken them as a matter of course. You cannot tell how strange it feels to me to come back to the old life again."

"You will soon be accustomed to it," Gervaise said, with a smile, "and then you will look upon your captivity as a dream, just as you then regarded your past life."

"I suppose, Sir Gervaise," Pietro Forzi said, "that you will sail direct for Rhodes with your prizes?"

"No indeed," Gervaise replied. "At the same time that we learned, from a dying man left on board the ship the pirates captured yesterday, of the course they had taken, and were so enabled to follow them, we also learned that they were on their way to join a corsair fleet that was collecting at some point on the eastern side of Sardinia, with the intention of sweeping the coast of Italy. It was this, rather than the capture of these three vessels, that induced us to disobey the general instructions we had been given to cruise along the northern coast of Africa, and determined us to push north to give warning along the coast from Naples to Genoa of the danger that threatened, and, if possible, to enable Genoa to fit out her galleys to encounter the corsairs. That duty has still to be fulfilled, though I fear that Genoa will be able to do little, for of late she has been engaged in a long civil struggle between her great families, and has taken but a small part in maritime affairs. However, we can at least warn her, as well as Naples, Pisa, and other towns, and may possibly find some opportunity for ourselves striking another blow against the pirates."

"If so, certainly we shall be glad to accompany you, if you will allow us to serve under you; for nothing would please us so much as the opportunity of paying off a small share of the vengeance we owe them. But of course, if you would rather, we will sail for Rhodes in the prizes."

"I am not thinking of sending them to Rhodes at present," Gervaise said. "It seems to me that we may be able, in some way, to utilise them to advantage. They have their sails, and rowers for the oars. There will be, in each, besides seven knights of the Order, thirty men who, like yourselves, must feel willing to strike a blow at their late oppressors. I need hardly say that I shall be glad indeed to have the company and aid of three such well known knights of the Order, and would, could I do so, gladly resign my command into your experienced hands. But this I cannot do, and, anticipating that you would be willing to join us in this expedition, I have been thinking how I could best utilise your aid. I have thought that, if you would accept the positions, I would appoint one of you to each of the prizes, to act, not as its commander, but as the leader of the band of released captives. Most of them are sailors, of course, and with them you could work the guns and give effective aid to the little party of knights in any actual fight."

The three knights all exclaimed that they would gladly accept the posts he offered them.

"The idea is a capital one, Sir Gervaise; and, as long as it does not come to close fighting, the three ships should be able to render efficient aid to your galley in any encounter. They will be, at any rate, a match for their own number of pirate ships," Caretto said.

As soon as the meal concluded, the Moslem captives were questioned one by one as to the rendezvous at which the pirate fleet was to assemble; all, however, protested that the place was known only to the three commanders, all of whom had fallen in the fight.

Chapter XIV
The Corsair Fleet

An hour later all was ready for a start. The knights of the langues of France, Germany, and Spain went on board their respective ships, as did the three parties of released captives, with the knights who were to command them, while the rowers took their seats on the benches, shackled with the chains that had recently held the Christians. The wind was from the south, and with sails and oars the prizes were able to keep fairly abreast of the galley. With a few short intervals of rest, the slaves continued their work all night, until, shortly before daybreak, land was seen ahead, and the pilot at once pronounced it to be Cape Carbonara.

"A good landfall, Gervaise," Ralph said. "The pilot has done right well. I suppose you mean to anchor when you get there?"

"Certainly, Ralph. The slaves will have rowed nearly eighteen hours, with only two hours' rest. They must have some hours, at least, of sleep before we go on. As you and I have been up all night, we will turn in also. We will send a boat ashore to try and find out from the natives they may come across whether any vessels, bearing the appearance of Moorish corsairs, have been seen passing up the coast, and also to find out what bays and inlets there are where they would be likely to anchor. Some of the Italian knights had best go with the boat, for though I believe these people speak a different dialect to those of the mainland, they would have more chance of understanding them than any of the others."

The sun had risen when the little fleet came to an anchor close to the cape. A boat was at once prepared to go ashore, and Gervaise begged Fabricius Caretto, the senior of the rescued Italian knights, to endeavour to find out whether a swift sailing craft of some kind could be hired. If so, he was to secure her on any terms, and come off in her at once to the galley.

Gervaise had already talked the matter over with Ralph, and they agreed that a strongly manned craft of this kind would go faster than any of those they had taken, and that, moreover, it would be a pity to weaken their force by sending one of the prizes away. Having seen them off, Gervaise retired to the cabin and threw himself down for a short sleep, leaving the knights who had been off watch during the night, to see that all went well. In two hours he was roused. A native craft had come alongside with Sir Fabricius Caretto.

"I think she is just the craft for us," the knight said, as Gervaise came on deck. "She belongs to a large fishing village just round the point to the left. There were several boats there, but the villagers all said that this was the speediest vessel anywhere along the coast. She belongs to two brothers, who, with four men, constitute her regular crew; but I have arranged for twelve others to go in her, in order that they may row her along at a good pace if the wind falls light."

"Are your companions come off yet?"

"No; but we can hoist a flag for their recall."

"Do so. I shall be greatly obliged if you will undertake this mission to the seaports. It needs one of name and rank to speak with the nobles and officials authoritatively."

"I will gladly do so, Sir Gervaise. Give me your instructions, and you can rely upon my carrying them out."

"I thank you greatly, Sir Fabricius, and shall be glad if you will take with you any two of the knights you may select. I have to write letters for you to deliver to the authorities at Naples, Pisa, and Genoa. I shall write but briefly, and leave you to explain matters more fully. I shall merely say that I have intelligence of the arrival here of a fleet of Moorish corsairs, of whose strength I am ignorant, but that assuredly their intention is to make a raid on the commerce of the coast, and perhaps to land at unprotected places. At Ostia, after warning the authorities to send orders along the coast for the inhabitants to be on their guard, pray them to carry word at once to Rome, and request his Holiness the Pope to order some armed galleys to put to sea as soon as possible. Beg them at Naples and Pisa to do the same thing. But of course it is from Genoa that we must hope for the most assistance."

"In each place you will, if possible, see the syndic himself, and such of his council as can be got quickly together. The moment you have done all you can at Genoa sail for the Island of Madalena, which lies off the northeastern point of the island. There you will either find us, or a boat with a message where to direct your course. I think perhaps it will be best to omit Naples-it will save you fully a day, if not two, to do so. Pray them at Ostia to send off news down the coast, or to request the papal authorities to despatch mounted messengers. 'Tis likely that, at first, at any rate, the corsairs will try the narrower waters to the north. From here to Ostia is nigh two hundred miles, and if the wind is brisk you may arrive there tomorrow afternoon, and start again at night, arriving at Pisa before noon on the following day; while, allowing for four or five hours to ascend the river there, you may be at Genoa next morning.

"Three hours should suffice to gather from the authorities what force they can despatch, and as soon as you have learned this, embark again and sail south. You may reach Madalena in two days. Thus, at the earliest, it must be from six to seven days before you can bring us the news there; if you meet with calms or foul winds you may be well nigh double that time. If at Ostia you can get a faster craft than this, hire it, or take a relay of fresh rowers. I will furnish you with means when I give you the letters."

In less than half an hour Gervaise was on deck again. The boat had returned with the other Italian knights. An ample store of provisions had been placed on board the Sperondra, both for the crew and for the three knights, and, without a minute's delay, these took their places on board, the great sails were hoisted, and the craft glided rapidly away.

"The villagers spoke truly as to her speed," Ralph said, as they looked after her. "Even with this light wind, she is running fully six miles an hour, and as, by the look of the sky, there will be more of it soon, she will make the run to Ostia well within the time we calculated."

Gervaise now questioned the other Italian knights as to what information they had gained.

They said the peasants had told them that several strange craft, using both oars and sails, had been noticed passing northwards, and that so strong was the opinion that these were either Algerines or Tunisians that, for the last three or four days, none of the fishing craft had ventured to put to sea. They were able to tell but little as to the bays along the coastline, which they described as very rugged and precipitous. Five or six little streams ran, they knew, down from the mountains. They thought the most likely places for corsairs to rendezvous would be in a deep indentation north of Cape Bellavista, or behind Cape Comino. If not at these places, they might meet in the great bay at whose entrance stands Tavolara Island, and that beyond, there were several deep inlets on the northeastern coast of the Island. Gervaise had a consultation with Ralph.

"The first thing is to find out where these corsairs have their meeting place, Ralph; and this must be done without their catching sight of the galley or of the prizes, which some of them would be sure to recognise."

Ralph nodded.

"It is a difficult question, Gervaise. Of course, if we had a boat speedy enough to row away from the corsairs it would be easy enough; but with wind and oars they go so fast that no boat could escape them."

"That is quite certain, Ralph; and therefore, if it is done by a boat, it must be by one so small and insignificant that they would pay but little attention to it if they caught sight of it. My idea is that we should take our own little boat, which is a fast one, paint it black, to give it the appearance of a fisherman's boat, and hire a couple of good rowers from the village. This, with one knight dressed as a fisherman, should go ahead of us, and explore every inlet where ships could be sheltered. We would follow ten miles behind. When we get near the places where the natives think the fleet is likely to be, the boat must go on at night, while we anchor. In that way they ought to be able to discover the corsairs, while themselves unseen, and to gain some idea of their numbers and the position in which they are anchored, and bring us back news."

"Shall I go myself, Gervaise?"

"I could not spare you, Ralph. The risk of capture does not seem to me to be great, but there certainly is a risk, and I dare not part with you. It had better be an Italian, because there will doubtless be an opportunity of landing at villages and questioning the inhabitants, therefore we will send Fosco. If there are some eight or ten corsairs gathered in any of these bays the news is sure to travel along the shore, and we may get some tidings in that way. The first thing is to send off to the village again to fetch two young fishermen; they must be active fellows, strong, and possessed of some courage. I will ask da Vinci to go himself and select them. While he is away we will paint our boat black, and make ready for her to start at once; the sooner she is off the better."

The Italian knight at once undertook the mission, and started for the shore. Fosco, who had been chosen principally because he was light of frame, as well as very shrewd and intelligent, was then called up, and his mission explained to him. He was delighted at having been selected. Gervaise took him down to the cabin, and they consulted the maps with which the galley was furnished.

"You will row on to Muravera; it is some twenty miles from here. You see, the village lies at the mouth of a river. As soon as you arrive there, you will land and find out whether there is any report of Moorish pirates having been seen along the coast. We shall be there this evening, and you will come on board and report. Next day you will get to Lunasei, which is about five miles on this side of Cape Bellavista, and they will certainly know there if the pirates are lying behind the cape. If they are so, you will row back to meet us; if they are not, you will remain there until we come up in the evening. Remember that, should you on either day be seen and chased, and you find they are overtaking you, you will make for the shore, land, and conceal yourselves. We shall keep along near the coast, and as we pass you can come down to the water's edge and signal to us to take you off. Now you had better disguise yourself, so as to be in readiness to start as soon as da Vinci comes off with the men. You will only need to take a small stock of provisions, as each night you can replenish them here."

An hour later da Vinci came off with two stalwart young fishermen. The little boat had already been painted, and it was lowered at once; Fosco stepped into it, and started.

Two hours later the prizes got up sail, and, accompanied by the galley, coasted quietly along the shore, arriving, late in the afternoon, at Muravera. Fosco at once came on board.

"There is no news here beyond that which we gained this morning, Sir Gervaise," he said. "Strange ships have certainly been seen sailing north, but they did not approach the coast."

A similar report was given at Lunasei; there were certainly no corsairs lying behind Cape Bellavista, or news would assuredly have reached the village. At Orosei, next day, the report was the same; there were no strange ships at Cape Comino. They had been warned overnight that the coast beyond the cape was so precipitous, that there would be no villages at which to make inquiries, and arranged with Fosco that the ships should anchor north of the cape, and that he should go on at once to inspect the next bay. If he found ships there, he was to return at once; if not, he was, at daybreak, to land at one of the villages in the bay, and to make inquiries.

No news was brought in by him during the night.

"It is evident the pirates are not in the bay, Gervaise," Ralph said, as they came on deck at daybreak.

"Yes; and I am glad of it. It is a large bay, and if the Genoese send half a dozen galleys, some of the pirates might still escape, while the next bays are deeper and narrower, and it would be more easy to entrap them all. I have all along thought it most probable that they would rendezvous there. The maps show no villages for many miles round, and they might lie there for weeks without so much as a shepherd getting sight of them from the cliffs. Moreover, it is the nearest point for cutting off ships coming down between Corsica and the mainland, and they can, besides, snap up those proceeding from the south to Marseilles, as these, for the most part, pass between Sardinia and Corsica."

At eight o'clock the boat was seen coming round the point.

"Any news, Fosco?" Gervaise asked, as it approached the galley.

"None, Sir Gervaise. They have heard nothing of pirates, nor seen anything of them."

Exclamations of disappointment broke from the knights.

"That makes it all the more likely," Gervaise said, "that they are lying in one of the inlets to the north. You see, lower down they kept comparatively close to the shore, being careless who might notice them; but as they approached their rendezvous, they would be more careful, and might either pass along at night, or keep far out. If they had not been anxious to conceal their near presence, they would have been likely to put into this bay in search of plunder and captives; for Tempe, one of the largest of the Sardinian towns, lies but a short distance away, and there must be a considerable amount of traffic."

"There are four or five small craft lying there," Fosco, who had by this time stepped on board, put in, "and a considerable number of fishing boats. When I came upon the ships in the dark, I thought at first that I had lighted on the pirates, but on letting the boat drift closely by them I soon saw they were not corsair galleys."

"Shall we get up anchor and go into the bay?" Ralph asked.

"It were safer not to do so, Ralph. Possibly one of the craft lying there might be presently captured by them, and they might learn from her crew of the presence of a galley of the Order there. Therefore I think it best to remain where we are till nightfall, and then to proceed and anchor on the north side of the Island of Madalena, if we can find a sheltered cove where we could not be seen either from the land or by passing ships."

During the day there was a good deal of discussion among the knights as to whether the corsairs might not already have sailed away. It was evident that if all their ships had arrived, there would be no motive for delay. Three ships they knew would never join them, and others might have been detained, from some cause or another. There could be no doubt that the pirates had already ample force for capturing as many merchant vessels as they might come across. But it might be intended to carry out some more daring project-to sack and burn towns along the coast, carry off the leading people for ransom, and fill the vessels with slaves-the attack being made simultaneously on several unprotected towns. A vast amount of plunder could thus be reaped, together with captives of even greater money value. Were this their plan, they would doubtless delay until all those who had promised to join in the expedition had arrived. The balance of opinion, then, was that the corsairs were still in hiding.

By daybreak next morning they were moored in a sheltered little bay to the north of Madalena, the galley lying inside the prizes, so as to be concealed as much as possible from view of any craft that might happen to pass the mouth of the bay. Fosco started as soon as darkness fell in the evening, and returned early in the morning.

"They are there," he shouted, as he neared the galley, "hidden in a deep inlet that runs into one of the narrow bays."

"How many are there of them?"

"Seventeen or eighteen, I could not say which. They are all moored side by side."

By this time Fosco's boat had reached the galley.

"You have done well indeed," Gervaise said, as the young knight ascended to the poop. "Now give us a full account of what you have seen."

"As you know, Sir Gervaise, the bay opposite this island splits up into two, running a long way inland, like the fangs of a great tooth. I had, of course, no difficulty in finding the entrance to the bay itself, as it is but a short distance across the strait. I steered first for the left hand shore, and kept close along under the shadow of the cliffs, which, in many cases, rise almost straight out from the water. We rowed very quietly, fearing to run against a rock; for although it was light enough to see across the water, and to make out any craft that might be anchored there, it was very dark along the foot of the cliffs. There was no need for haste, as I knew I had plenty of time to explore both arms of the bay, and to be back here before day began to break.

"We rowed up to the end of the inlet, and then, having assured ourselves that it was empty, came down the other side, and turned up the western arm. We had got some distance along when I fancied I heard voices, and so let the boat drift along, only dipping the oars in the water occasionally. I could make out no signs whatever of the corsairs, when suddenly we came upon a break in the cliffs. It was only some fifty yards across, and here a creek came in at right angles to the shore. I could have given a shout of pleasure as I looked up it, for there a score of lights were burning above a dark mass, and we could hear the sound of talking and laughter. It was but a glimpse I caught, for the men at once backed water, and we were soon round the corner again.

"Up till then the fishermen had been ready enough to go where I wanted, but the sight of that clump of galleys regularly scared them, and they wanted to row straight away; but of course I pointed out to them that they had taken pay to do this thing, and that they had to do it. They said that if caught they would be either killed or made slaves of, and I could not contradict them, but said that, in the first place, as I was ready to run the risk, there was no reason why they shouldn't do so, and in the second, there was no chance whatever of their being taken, as, if discovered, we should get so long a start that we could either escape them altogether or run the boat ashore at some point where the trees came down to the water's edge, carry the boat up and hide it, and then move up into the hills until the corsairs had gone.

"We waited there three or four hours, looking round the point occasionally. At the end of that time all was quiet. Two or three of the lanterns still burned, but there was no sign of life or movement on their decks. After waiting another half hour to ensure the crews being asleep, we rowed quietly up the creek, keeping within an oar's length of the rocks. There was not much to see; the galleys lay two abreast, and as there was no space between them, I supposed the whole were lashed together. There were eight of them on the side we went along, but I think there were only seven on the other side. As I thought it did not much matter whether there were fifteen or sixteen, and as the men were in a state of horrible fright, we turned and went back again, and I own I felt very glad myself when we got round the point without an alarm being given. We came quietly out, and it was fortunate we did so, for we had not gone a quarter of a mile when we heard the sound of oars, and, lying silently under the cliff, we saw two large galleys row past us."

"It is a strong force, Gervaise," Ralph said, as they paced up and down the poop together. "Probably in each of those galleys are eighty or a hundred men, in addition to the rowers. It is evident that unless Genoa sends us help we shall not be able to interfere with their plans."

"I don't know, Ralph. I think we may injure them sorely, though we might not be able to defeat them altogether. I want you tonight to take one of the prizes, and row round to the bay we passed, and there to buy three coasting vessels and six or eight fishing boats. Get as much pitch, oil, and other combustibles, as you can purchase in the villages on the shore. If you can engage a score of fishermen to man them, all the better. My idea is that if Caretto returns with news that the Genoese have no galleys ready for sea, we must do what we can to injure these corsairs. If we smear these craft you are going to fetch with pitch and oil, and fill the holds with combustibles, and so turn them into fire ships, we may at least do the pirates a tremendous lot of harm. When we get to the mouth of this inlet, we could have the fire ships rowed in by three or four men in each, they having a boat behind in which to escape as soon as the boats are lighted. The sight of a dozen craft coming down on them in flames would cause a terrific panic, for, moored closely together, as they are, if one took fire there would be little chance of the others escaping. Of course, we should add to the confusion by opening a fire with all our guns, and could hope to capture some at least of them as they tried to make their way out."

"It is a grand idea, Gervaise; a splendid idea! It would be a terrific blow to the Moors, and would make the sea safe from them for a long time."

"When you buy the other things, Ralph, get a quantity of black cloth-it matters not how coarse, or of what material; and also some white. As soon as you come back with it, all hands shall set to work to make the stuff up into mantles of the Order, with the white cross. We will put these on to the Christians in the prizes, and the Moors will suppose that they are attacked by four of the galleys of the Order. If you can get some more arms and some iron headpieces, all the better."

"I will do what I can, Gervaise; the arms will certainly be wanted, for those we found on the decks were sufficient only to arm half the Christians. As to the steel caps, that will not matter so much, as in the darkness and confusion the sight of the mantles will be quite enough to convince the corsairs that we are all knights of the Order. By the way, Gervaise, we have not yet looked into the holds of the prizes."

"That is so, Ralph; we knew, of course, that as the ships had but just started we should find nothing in them save the cargo of that unfortunate craft they captured."

On searching they found, as they had expected, that the cargo of the captured ship had been of no great value. It consisted of wine, olive oil, and grain. These were all useful, for the number of mouths to be fed was considerable, and heavy inroads had already been made on the stores of the galley. The rowers of the four vessels were at once set to work to crush the grain between flat stones brought from the shore, and an ample supply of coarse flour for their use for at least a fortnight was obtained before sunset.

As soon as darkness fell, Ralph and two of the French knights started in one of the prizes. Late on the following afternoon a sail was seen coming from the north, and before the sun set they were able to make her out to be the craft in which Caretto had sailed. The anchor of the galley was at once got up, and she rowed out to meet the boat and conduct her into the little bay. It was almost dark when they came within hailing distance.

"What news do you bring, Sir Fabricius?"

"Bad news, I regret to say. I do not think that Genoa will be able to send out any galleys for at least a fortnight. There have been civil dissensions, and fighting between rival factions, and in consequence her ships are all dismantled and laid up. Crews will have to be collected for them, repairs executed, and officers chosen; a fortnight will be the earliest time in which they can be here. Pisa has no war galleys, and unless the Pope sends some out directly he gets the news, the corsairs will have it their own way. Have you discovered them?"

"Yes; they lie but a few miles from here. There were fifteen or sixteen of them two days ago, and two others joined them that night. You have lost no time indeed. We had scarce begun to expect you, Sir Fabricius," he added, as the knight and his two comrades stepped on board.

"I have done my best," the knight said angrily. "But I am in a rage with my ill success. All I have accomplished is that no merchant vessels will put to sea at present. At Ostia they would only send off a message to Rome, to ask for orders. At Pisa the authorities at first treated my story as a fiction, and, I believe, took me for an impostor; but on the news spreading, some knights came forward and recognised me. Then we had a meeting of the council. All talked, wrangled, and protested. They said that it was absurd to suppose that they could, at a moment's notice, fit out ships to cope with a fleet of corsairs; and their sole idea was to man the forts, and to repel an attack. However, mounted messengers were sent off at once, up and down the coast, to give warning to the inhabitants of the towns to put themselves into a posture of defence, and to the villagers to fly with their wives and families into the interior as soon as they saw galleys of doubtful appearance approaching. I was there but four hours, and then started for Genoa."

"There was almost a panic there too, as the members of the council were mostly merchants, and were filled with dismay for the safety of their ships and goods at sea. Of course, there was no thought that the corsairs, however strong, would venture an attack upon Genoa itself. I told them that you had captured three of the corsairs with a single galley, and that if they could send you ten others you would probably be able to make head against the pirates; but, as I have told you, Genoa is at peace with all the world; her war galleys are laid up, and most of them would need repair and recaulking before they would be fit to send to sea. Although they maintained that no more than a week should elapse before they would be ready to sail I am right sure that it will be double that time before they are fitted out.

"Of course, in Genoa I was well known, though my family estates lie near Mantua, and my acquaintances flocked round me and urged me to stay until the galleys were ready for sea. This I would not hear of, and, six hours after my arrival, started again. We made the voyage to Corsica at a good speed, but since then we have had the oars constantly out to help the sails. The men have well earned their pay, I can assure you. It is enough to make one mad with rage to think that these pirates will be able to harry the coast of Italy at their pleasure; for there can be little chance that they will abide quiet much longer at this rendezvous."

"It is annoying, indeed," Gervaise agreed; and a murmur of disappointment ran round the assembled knights. "However, we have the consolation that we have done all we could, and I am sure that we shall do so in the future."

Gervaise had charged Ralph to say nothing about the object of his mission, and the general supposition was that he had sailed to endeavour to purchase some bullocks, as the supply of meat was nearly exhausted. Ralph himself had let drop a few words to this effect, and had indeed been charged by Gervaise to bring off a few oxen if they could be obtained without loss of time. Gervaise was on deck at midnight, and soon afterwards the beat of oars was heard. It was a still night, and one of the knights on watch remarked to him, "It seems to me, Sir Gervaise, that the sound is a confused one, and that there must be several vessels rowing. Shall I call up our companions? It may be that it is the pirate fleet coming out."

"You need not do that," Gervaise replied. "I am expecting Sir Ralph to bring back with him some fishing boats, for which I think I can find a use. We should have heard before this if the corsairs had been putting out. Fosco is in his boat watching the mouth of the inlet, and would have started with the news had there been any stir on board their galleys."

It was a quarter of an hour before a number of dark objects entered the little bay. As soon as they did so, they ceased rowing, and the splashes of the anchors as they fell into the water were heard. Then came the sound of a boat's oars, and Ralph was soon alongside.

"I see that you have succeeded, Ralph."

"There is no fear of failing when one is ready to pay the full value of what one wants to get. I have bought three coasters and eight fishing boats, and have a sufficient store of pitch and oil, with plenty of straw and faggots. There was no difficulty in getting men to come with me. As soon as they heard that a fleet of eighteen Moorish galleys was in the next bay, they were ready enough to aid in any plan for their destruction, for they knew well enough that some of them would be sure to make raids all along the coast, sacking and burning, and carrying off men, women, and children, as slaves. I said I only wanted two men for each craft, but so many were willing to come that I have some thirty more than the number I asked for, and we can divide these among us. They are strong, active looking fellows."

"We will keep them here then, Ralph. You see, there are one-and-twenty of our knights in the three prizes, and as we lost two in the capture, and four others are not fit to put on armour, we have but six-and-twenty, and the addition will be very welcome. What are they armed with?"

"They have bows and arrows, and long pikes and axes."

"Good. Have you managed to collect any more arms?"

"Yes. The people are all charcoal burners and woodmen in winter, and I was therefore able to get together some thirty or forty axes and hatchets, which will be ample, with the arms we took from the Moors, to equip the ninety Christians."

"I think we can depend upon these for fighting, Ralph."

"I don't think there is any doubt about that. A few of them are pretty well worn out with labour and suffering, but all have gained strength and spirits greatly in the past week, and you may be sure that they will fight to the death rather than run the risk of another turn in the galleys."

"And have you got the stuff to make the mantles?"

"Yes. There was plenty of the coarse black cloth which they wear in summer-in winter, of course, they are clad in sheepskins; and I have sufficient white cotton cloth to make the crosses."

"We have only one thing to wish for now, Ralph, and that is, that the corsairs may not take it into their heads to sail tomorrow. Fosco will bring me news at daybreak, and we will at once send another boat off to watch the mouth of the bay when he leaves it. If they sail, we cannot venture to attack them as long as they keep together, the odds are far too heavy, and our only plan will be to follow them at a distance, when we can just keep their upper sails in sight, and then to attack any detachment that may separate from the main body."

"I hope it will not come to that, Gervaise. It would be hard indeed, when you have devised such a splendid plan, and we have got everything ready to carry it out, if they were to give us the slip. Do the others know anything about it yet?"

"No. I thought it better to keep silence till tomorrow. No doubt some of the galley slaves understand enough of one or other of our languages to gather what is on foot. Besides, their late captives might, in their satisfaction at the thought of revenge, say enough to them to let them know that an attack on their fleet was intended, and one of them might, in some way, free himself from his irons and swim ashore. We know there is a small fishing village across the island, and there would be no difficulty in stealing a boat and making off with the news. I do not say that the risk is great; still, it were better not to throw away even a chance. The knights have all turned in in a very gloomy mood, for Caretto has returned with news that there is no hope of assistance from Genoa for a fortnight, and it seemed, therefore, that all our pains had been thrown away. And now we may as well turn in until daylight."

Chapter XV
A Splendid Exploit

Gervaise was up again at dawn. He was amused at the wonder of the knights, as they came up one by one, at the sight of the little fleet anchored outside them. As soon as it was fairly daylight, he sent off to the three prizes to request all the knights to come on board the galley. When all were assembled there he said, "You are all aware, comrades, that Sir Fabricius Caretto has brought news that the galleys at Genoa are all laid up, and that it will be a fortnight before they can put to sea. Long before that, the corsairs will assuredly be ravaging all the villages and small towns along the coast of Italy, unless we can prevent their doing so. It would be simple madness to try to attack them at sea; of that I feel sure you are all conscious. It would be only throwing away our lives and our galley."

There was a murmur of assent among the knights. They were ready for any encounter in which there was a chance, however faint, of success; but all saw that for a single galley to attack one of the largest corsair fleets that had ever set out, would be nothing short of insanity. Their leader's words, however, seemed to show that he had some plan in his mind by which he hoped to strike a blow at the enemy, and all listened eagerly for what was coming.

"We have heard from our comrade Fosco that their ships lie moored in two lines, side by side in a narrow inlet. He has returned this morning with the news that they are still there. He thinks that three or four more have arrived during the last two days, and it is probable they are waiting for the three we captured to join them. Tonight it is my intention to attack them, but not by rowing in and boarding them, for that would be hopeless. Yesterday Sir Ralph Harcourt went, as you are aware, to fetch provisions. But this was a part only of the object of his trip. He has, as you see, brought back eleven craft with him; these, I may tell you, are laden with combustibles-pitch, oil, straw, and faggots. They will be rowed and towed to the inlet tonight, set on fire, and launched against the pirates."

An enthusiastic cheer broke from the knights. They saw at once that, lying as the corsairs were, side by side, the destruction of many of them was certain.

"He has also brought fishermen," Gervaise went on, "two or three of whom will go in each fire ship, having a boat towing behind, in which they will escape as soon as the craft are alongside the galleys. The galley and the three prizes will take their post at the mouth of the inlet. The fire of our guns will add to the confusion among the pirates, and we shall endeavour to fall upon any galleys that may extricate themselves from the mass, and try to make their escape. Sir Ralph has brought back materials for making ninety mantles of the Order, for the Christians on board the three prizes, and thirty fishermen to bring the crew of our galley up to its full strength. The light of the flames will suffice to show the pirates that, as they will believe, four vessels, manned by knights of the Order, are barring the entrance. Many will, we may calculate, jump overboard and swim ashore rather than face us, and we shall be able, at any rate, to capture three or four of their craft, for, as they come out, one by one, we can all close round them; and with nearly fifty knights, ninety released captives, burning for vengeance, and some fifty or sixty fishermen, for those from the fire ships will, of course, join us-we shall make short work of them, and may even hope to entirely destroy their fleet."

Again a joyous shout rose from the knights. This would indeed be an exploit that all might be proud to share in, and, breaking the ranks in which they had stood while Gervaise addressed them, they crowded round him with exclamations of enthusiasm and devotion.

"Now," he said, as soon as silence was a little restored, "the knights of the langues on board the prizes will send at once to the coaster on the left of the other two. Sir Ralph will go there now, and supply each with materials for making the mantles for the Christians; he has brought thread, and fish bone needles. You will see that the stuff is cut up into suitable lengths, and handed over to your crews, and that each man makes up his mantle. There can be but little sewing required for these sleeveless gowns, nor need it be carefully done. The great thing is that the white crosses shall be conspicuous. As soon as you have set them to work, you will examine the state of the arms, see how many more are needed to complete the list, and then send off to Sir Ralph, who will furnish as many as are required: the fishermen have brought their own weapons. See that the slaves are all well fed today, and, before evening, inspect well their fetters, so that you may be free from all anxiety as to an attempt by them to escape during the conflict.

"The rest of you will go on board these native craft, and see that the combustibles are fairly distributed among them, the wood and straw soaked with pitch and oil, as also the sails and ropes, and that the decks are well coated; this is a most important duty. Get some torches made also, so that there shall be two on board each craft; these are to be lighted the last thing before we get to the point, and will be thrown down into the straw and faggots in the hold, by the fishermen when they get close to the corsairs. All this can be prepared before our morning meal, and when you assemble here I hope to receive your reports that everything is in readiness. One of the other coasters has some bullocks on board. Sir Ralph will send one to each of the prizes, and one to us. They had better be killed and cut up at once, in order that the crews may have two good meals today of fresh meat. See that the galley slaves have their share."

No time was lost in carrying out the orders. Ralph, as soon as the cloth, arms, and meat were distributed, went round in a boat to see that the combustibles were properly laid for firing, and everything done to insure that the flames should spread rapidly. The Sards shared in the work, and rations and wine were distributed to them; and when the knights sat down to their meal on board the galley, they were able to report that everything was in perfect readiness, and that the work of sewing the mantles was making good progress.

The day passed slowly to the young knights, all of whom were burning with excitement at the thought of the coming fray. The released Christians were no less exultant at the prospect of taking vengeance for the sufferings they had so long endured, and the scene on board all four ships was most animated.

After talking it over with Ralph, Gervaise told off three more of the knights to each of the prizes, so that there should be ten on board each. This reduced the strength on board the galley to seventeen; but as they would have the assistance of a strong band of Sards they considered this to be ample, under the circumstances. It was arranged that the galley, with one of the prizes, should close with the first corsair that came out, and that the other two prizes should attack the second. After capturing these, they were to assist each other as circumstances might dictate. Gervaise strongly impressed upon the knights in command of each prize that they were not, single handed, to attack a corsair unless one of their consorts was near, and free to give assistance.

"We must run no risk of a reverse," he said. "We are certain of destroying many of their vessels and of breaking up their fleet, and it is far better that a few should escape than that we should run the risk of losing ten of our number, to say nothing of those we have rescued from captivity. In the excitement of the fight this order must be strictly borne in mind. Our victory must be marred by no misfortune brought on by headstrong rashness. The corsairs are bound to be very strongly manned, and ten knights, even aided by such assistance as they may get from the Christians, might find themselves altogether over matched against a crowd of desperate men."

As soon as it was dusk the anchors were drawn up, and the fleet got under way. They proceeded but slowly, for the wind was light, and the fishing boats moved heavily through the water. There was, however, no occasion for speed, for Gervaise did not wish to commence the attack until past midnight. The guns had all been loaded before starting, and a pile of ammunition was placed near each. Presently the wind nearly died out, and the galley and prizes then took the coasters and fishing craft in tow. It was nearly one o'clock when they got within half a mile of the inlet. The tow ropes were then thrown off, the fishermen got out sweeps, and the galley led the way, the fire ships followed in a body, and the three prizes brought up the rear. The oars had all been muffled, and slowly they made their way, until Fosco, who was standing next to Gervaise on board the galley, said that the point just ahead marked the entrance to the inlet. They then stopped rowing until the fire ships were all close up.

These were, as had previously been arranged, in two lines. Five fishing boats, each manned by four men and having its small boat in tow behind it, formed the first line; the three coasters, each with six men at the oars, and the three other fishing boats, formed the second. The torches were now lighted. Ralph took his place in the centre boat of the first line; Gervaise went on board one of the coasters, and the order was given to the men to row. What wind there was was favourable, blowing from the northwest, and therefore right into the inlet. Scarcely had the first boats reached the entrance when a shout was heard.

"Row, men, your hardest now!" Ralph shouted; the Sards bent to their oars, and the five boats advanced rapidly towards the corsairs. As they did so, a babel of shouts and cries rose from the dark mass of ships, which swelled into a tumult of alarm as on Ralph's order, "Throw your torches into the straw!" a flash of flame leapt up from each boat. Five more strokes, and they were alongside the two outside ships. As they crashed heavily into them, the men leapt from their seats and sprang over into the small boats, threw off the painters, and rowed astern, opening on either hand to allow the second line of fire ships to pass. These, by Gervaise's directions, divided, and three bore along on either side of the corsairs, and then ran in among them, throwing grapnels to fasten the fire ships alongside. Then, as the flames sprang up from the holds, the crews betook themselves to their boats, and rowed out of the inlet.

By the time they reached the galley and prizes, the eleven fire ships were a mass of flame, which was spreading to the corsairs. Lying packed together as these were, the confusion was terrible. Numbers of men endeavoured to push off the fire ships, but it was too late; others tried to extricate their galleys from the mass, throwing off the hawsers, and striving with hand and oar to push their vessels out of the line. As soon as the boats were alongside the galley, the guns of the four vessels opened fire with grape into the crowded ships, now lit up by the flames as clearly as at noontide, while the battle cry of the Order sounded high above the din.

"Nothing can save the ships near this end of the line," Ralph said, "but some of those behind may make their way out between the others and the rocks. I can see that some of them there are lowering their yards and sails to prevent their catching fire as they pass."

The knights distributed among the guns worked them incessantly, directing their fire chiefly against the outside ships, so as to hinder the crews in their endeavours to arrest the progress of the flames; but they were soon able to fire impartially into the mass. As the heat of the flames drove the pirates back, scores of men leapt overboard, and made for the shore. Presently, two or three ships were seen making their way along the narrow line of water on either side of the flaming group in front. As the first advanced, the galley and one of the prizes rowed a short distance forward to meet it. Its deck was crowded with men, among whom a discharge of the cannon from both ships created terrible slaughter.

A moment afterwards they closed with it, one on either side, and the knights, the released captives, and the Sards, sprang down on to its deck. The fight lasted but a minute. Appalled by the disaster that had befallen them, by the terrible effect of the broadsides, poured in at a few yards' distance, and by the sight of so many of the dreaded warriors of the Cross, some of the corsairs threw down their arms and flung themselves on the deck or into the hold, crying for quarter; those who resisted fell either under the swords of the knights, the vengeful axes of the late captives, or the pikes of the Sards; but the great bulk, leaping from the bow or stern, swam ashore.

"Back to your ships!" Gervaise shouted, the moment resistance ceased. "Leave her floating here; she will help to block the way."

Six vessels alone managed to make their escape from the blazing mass of ships, and all of these were captured almost as easily as the first had been. As soon as it seemed that all the remainder were involved in the flames, boats were lowered and sent on board the prizes to take possession. Save for the wounded on the decks, they were entirely deserted by their crews, as those who had run below, as soon as they found that their captors had left the vessels, dropped into the water, and made their way, either by swimming or with the assistance of oars, to the shore. There remained only the slaves, chained to their benches. A few of these had been killed by the broadsides; but the guns had been aimed at the poops and forecastles, where the corsairs were clustered together, and consequently the number of galley slaves who had fallen was comparatively small.

In none of the galleys was the proportion of Christians anything like so large as that in the three prizes first taken, the greater portion being men of inland tribes who had been captured in warfare, or malefactors who, instead of being executed, had been sold to the corsairs. Nevertheless, in the six galleys some seventy Christians were found, and at once freed. It was terrible to think that in the galleys that had been destroyed a large number of Christians must have perished in the flames, and Gervaise expressed bitter regret that he had not considered that his attack by fire ships must necessarily involve the loss of so many Christian lives.

"It can't be helped," Ralph said, as Gervaise poured out his feelings to him. "To very many of them death must have been welcome, and if we had not attacked them as we did, and they had sailed for Italy, hundreds, if not thousands, of Christians would have been killed, and as many more carried away into captivity; so, you see, the balance is all in favour of the course we adopted."

Gervaise admitted this, but nevertheless his regret at the fate of so many unfortunate captives quite overpowered for the time his satisfaction at the complete success that had been achieved. The victory had been almost a bloodless one on the part of the assailants. A few of the knights had received wounds. Two among the Christian crews had been killed, and four Sards; while two score had received wounds more or less serious, as, unlike the knights, they had no defensive armour. While waiting for daylight to appear, all their wounds were dressed and bandaged by the knights.

In the morning the captured galleys were towed out, and anchored a short distance away, and then Gervaise rowed up to the head of the inlet, followed by the other three ships. They found that eleven of the corsairs had been burnt, and to their satisfaction, they discovered four uninjured galleys lying there, deserted, save by the slaves.

Seeing the fate of their comrades who had first issued out, the commanders had, instead of trying to escape, rowed quietly to the head of the inlet, the movement being covered by the flame and smoke, and had there landed, having laden themselves with stores for their support on shore. This was a great satisfaction to the knights, for not only did it swell the list of prizes, but it reduced by over thirty the number of Christian slaves who had perished in the flames. Taking the galleys in tow, they rowed out of the inlet, whose banks were strewn with half charred timbers, oars, and relics of the fight.

As soon as they had anchored by the side of their first prizes, a council was held on board the Santa Barbara. It was clearly impossible to take thirteen prizes to Rhodes, for there would be but three or four knights to each, and were they to fall in with but one Moorish pirate, they might suffer great disaster, while, should they meet with a storm, they would fare badly indeed, as they could not depend upon the rescued Christians for the management of the sails and oars in heavy weather. At the same time, all were most anxious that the prizes should be carried to Rhodes. Never, save as the result of some great battle, had such a fleet of captured galleys been brought in, and the knights were prepared to endure all dangers rather than part with one of them. Finally, after much discussion, it was determined that they should make for Genoa. From thence the rescued captives would be able to find their way to their homes. The great majority were Italians and Spaniards; the former could proceed by land or sea to their respective homes, while the Spaniards would have no long time to wait before a vessel of their own nationality entered the port, even if one were not lying there when they arrived. Moreover, in any case it would be necessary to despatch a vessel to Genoa, in order that it might be known that the danger was averted, and that there was no longer any necessity for getting the galleys ready for sea.

The chief ostensible reason, however, for going to Genoa was that there would be no difficulty in engaging as many sailors as might be necessary to take the prizes to Rhodes. Underlying all the arguments was another reason which Ralph laughingly stated.

"It is all very well to bring forward one argument after another, but not one of you has the courage to say what I am sure all of you have at the bottom of your hearts. You know very well that you want to go to Genoa to enjoy a triumph. The Rhodians are all very well, but there are very many more fair faces at Genoa. Fie, Sir Knights! Such a spirit is little in accordance with the vows of the Order. Are we not bound to humility? And here you are all longing for the plaudits of the nobles and ladies of Genoa!"

Some of the young knights laughed, others coloured hotly.

"They need not be ashamed of the feeling," Caretto said. "Is it not the ardent desire of all true knights to do gallant deeds, and do they not value above all things the guerdon of applause from the fair eyes of ladies. Your comrades have performed the gallant deeds, and well deserve the reward. Now, Sir Gervaise, if not for this reason, at any rate for the others that have been brought forward, I suppose we are all agreed that we sail for Genoa. For our part we are heartily glad that such is your decision. We, and the young knights of our langue, have many friends there, and in their name I am sure I can promise you a reception as hearty and sincere as that which we shall ourselves receive."

It was settled that the rescued captives should be divided equally among the thirteen prizes, and that three knights should go in each. The Moorish captives were also divided equally among them, to aid with the sails, and to row a few oars, in case of a dead calm setting in. The commands were distributed according to seniority, the three rescued Italian knights remaining on board the Santa Barbara with Gervaise.

The Sards were anxious to return to their villages, in order to carry the news that several hundreds of Moorish pirates had landed.

"We shall have great trouble with them," one of the young fishermen, who spoke a little Italian, said to Gervaise. "There are always a great number of swine, and herds of goats, up among the forests on the hills. We must send up and drive in as many of these as possible, and of course we shall send messengers to Tempe; but it will need a very large force to combat these pirates, who will be able to come down and plunder and destroy, and then retire to the hills, whence it will be hard to dislodge them."

"I am sorry indeed that such trouble should have been caused to you," Gervaise replied; "but I am afraid that I can give you no assistance."

"We shall hunt them down in time," the Sard said confidently.

"There are many villages scattered about Tempe, and what with us fishermen, and the woodmen and charcoal burners, we shall soon get a strong body together. Besides, we know the mountains, and they do not."

"I should say that you had best avoid a pitched battle with them, but keep on harassing them by night and day, cutting off all who separate themselves from the main body, until at last they are completely worn out."

"We shall deal with them, Sir Knight. We are all hunters, for there are wild boars and stags in the forest, and wolves too, and wild sheep on the higher mountains. Every man among us can use his bow skillfully, and wield pike and hatchet. The hunt will not be unprofitable, either, for we can get a good price for all we take alive, to work in the mines."

An hour later one of the galleys started with the Sards for their villages in the bay of Tempe. After landing them, she was to rejoin the rest of the fleet at their former anchorage at Madalena. By nightfall all were gathered there, and the next morning they set out for Genoa. The wind was light; but in their anxiety to return home as soon as possible the released captives all volunteered to take their former places on the benches, and the vessels were kept going at a fair rate of speed. Two days' rowing took them to Bastia, where their approach created unbounded excitement until the banner of the Order was seen floating from the stern of the Santa Barbara, while smaller flags, that had been hastily manufactured, flew from the mastheads of the thirteen prizes. Even then the inhabitants feared to put out, believing that the flags were but a ruse, and numbers of them fled at once, with their families and valuables, to the mountains. It was not until a boat was lowered, and Ralph, accompanied by three or four other knights, rowed ashore, that the panic was allayed.

As soon as it was understood that the galley of the knights had not only captured the thirteen corsairs, but had destroyed eleven others, and had thus annihilated a fleet that was intended to prey upon the commerce of Italy, and ravage the western coast, the alarm was succeeded by the wildest enthusiasm. By the time Ralph had obtained the fresh meat and stores he came ashore to purchase, the greater part of the population were gathered on the shore, and a flotilla of boats put out with him, filled with picturesquely dressed men and women. Some carried flags, others green boughs, while the ladies had bouquets and baskets of fruit. The galley was the first attraction, and, mounting her sides, the ladies presented their offerings of fruit, while the men cheered, and waved their hats; many musicians came out in the boats, and these played on bagpipes and three-reeded flutes a succession of airs peculiar to the island.

Gervaise received his visitors on the poop. These were at first altogether incredulous when told that it was the lad before them who had commanded the galley, had performed such a remarkable feat, and had freed them from a terrible danger. The youth of the knights of the Order no less surprised them, and had not Gervaise assured them that it was altogether contrary to the rules of the Order for a knight to allow himself to be embraced, many of the ladies would have taken this form of showing their enthusiasm and gratitude. The next morning the fleet started for Genoa. The wind was much stronger than it had been on the previous day, and it was therefore unnecessary for the oars to be put out, except, indeed, on board the galley. There, at nightfall, the Christians relieved the slaves for some hours at their benches, and the next morning the circle of hills round Genoa, with the city nestling at their feet on the water's edge, and climbing for some distance up their slopes, was in view. Caretto at once suggested that it would be well to signal to the fleet to lie to.

"If we do not do so," he said, "they will assuredly think that it is the corsair fleet advancing to attack and burn the vessels in port, and you may be saluted as you approach by a shower of cannonballs. If you will permit me, Sir Gervaise, I will go forward in one of the prizes and explain matters, and will return here in a short time."

"Thank you, Sir Fabricius. As such mischance as you mention might indeed very well occur, we will lower sail and lie here until you return."

While Caretto was away, the knights and crews breakfasted, and the former put on their armour and gayest attire, in readiness for the landing. Gervaise, although with much inward vexation, considered it necessary to do the same.

"I do wish," he said to Ralph, who was smiling at his rueful face, "that you could for today take my place, and let me pass as lieutenant."

"I should not mind at all, Gervaise. But you must put up with the disagreeables as well as the advantages of being commander, and must submit to be honoured and feted here, as well as getting no end of credit at Rhodes. You will have the satisfaction of well deserving it, for I am sure the plan of attacking them with fire ships would never have occurred to any one else, and if it had not been for that, we should have had the mortification of seeing them sail off without being able to move a finger to interfere with them."

"If one were fighting for fame and honour, all that would be true enough; but members of an Order, whose sole object is to defend Christendom from the Moslems, should strive only to do their duty, and care nothing for such things as honour and glory."

"Human nature is human nature, and I don't see any reason why one should despise honour and glory when they come to one in the course of duty. I fancy you will think so too, Gervaise, in course of time. I am quite sure that among the fifty knights, there is not one who does not feel well content that he has not only done his duty to the Order, but has gained a share in the credit and honour that will certainly be given to all who have taken a part in so crushing a defeat of the corsairs. As for myself, I do not for a moment pretend that I am not sensible of the fact that, as second in command of the galley, my chances of obtaining promotion in the Order are very greatly improved."

It was nearly two hours before Caretto returned.

"It was well indeed that I went in," he said to Gervaise, "for I found the city in an uproar. The alarm bells of the churches were calling all citizens to arms, and troops were being hurried down to the forts and batteries. Rumour had of course exaggerated the strength of the fleet, and half the population believed that the safety of the city itself was menaced by the approach of a mighty squadron. As soon as my news was bruited abroad, and they learned that the fleet consisted solely of prizes captured from the Moors by a galley of the Order, alarm quickly changed into delight, the sharp, angry clang of the bells was succeeded by peals of gladness, and the joy of the citizens at being relieved from the cloud of anxiety that had hung over the city since my last visit, was unbounded. I went at once to the council chamber, where I found many of the leading citizens already assembled, having been summoned in hot haste as soon as our approach was made out. At first they were almost incredulous when I told them that every ship of the pirate fleet had been either destroyed or captured, and that the fleet in the offing consisted entirely of your galley and the thirteen corsairs she had captured. As soon as they really grasped the fact, they sent off messengers to the churches to order the joy bells to be rung, and to the dockyard to arrest all work upon the galleys. Then I had to give them a short account of the surprise and destruction of the corsair fleet, and finally they begged me to ask you to delay your entry to the port for a couple of hours, in order that they might have time to prepare a suitable reception for you."

"I suppose there is no help for it," Gervaise said. "Is there anything that we ought to do?"

"I should decorate the galley with all the flags on board: should set every one to work to make great flags with the cross of the Order to hoist to the masthead of the prizes, instead of the little things that are now flying; and under them we will hoist the flags of the corsairs, among which are those of Tripoli, Tunis, and Algiers. I do not know that there is aught else we can do."

Chapter XVI
Festivities

At last the fleet, headed by the galley, to which all the knights had returned, rowed towards the port. A gun flashed out from the fort at its entrance, and at once those from all the other batteries responded; bells pealed out again, and a confused roar of cheering broke from the crowds occupying every spot from which a view of the harbour could be obtained. The ships in the port were all decked with flags, and the front windows and balconies of every house were hung with tapestries and bright curtains. As soon as the galley entered the port, a state barge, flying the flag of the Republic, advanced to meet her from the wharf. As she approached, Ralph gave orders for the oars to be laid in, and the barge was soon alongside. The knights were already ranged along the poop, and, accompanied by Ralph and Caretto, Gervaise moved to the gangway to receive the visitors. At their head was Battista Fragoso, the doge, in his robe of state, and following him were a body of the highest nobles of Genoa, all brilliant in gala costume.

"This, my lord duke," Caretto said, "is Sir Gervaise Tresham, a knight commander of our Order, and the commander of this, their galley. He has before, as you may well believe from his appointment to so honourable a post, highly distinguished himself, but what he has before accomplished is far surpassed by the brilliant action that he has now achieved. He has won a victory that not only reflects the highest honour upon the Order, but is an inestimable service to Italy, and has freed her from a corsair fleet that would have been a scourge to her, both at sea and to the towns and villages along the coast. Not only has he, with the brave knights under his orders, annihilated the corsair fleet, burning eleven of their galleys, and capturing thirteen others, but he has restored to freedom no less than two hundred Christian captives, among them the cavaliers Giacomo da Vinci, Pietro Forzi, and myself."

"In the name of the Republic, Sir Gervaise Tresham, and I may say in that of all Italy, I thank you most heartily for the splendid service that you have rendered us. It would have seemed to me well nigh incredible that a single galley, even if commanded and manned by the most famous knights of your great Order, should have accomplished so extraordinary a feat. Still more strange is it that it should have been performed by so young a knight, with a crew composed, as Sir Fabricius Caretto has told us, of knights chosen from among the youngest of the Order."

"You give far more credit to us, your Highness, than we deserve," Gervaise replied. "Three of the ships were indeed captured in fair fight, but we caught the rest asleep and massed together as to be incapable of successful resistance, and they fell easy victims to the fire ships we launched against them. Any credit that is due to me is shared equally by my subcommander here, Sir Ralph Harcourt, and indeed by every knight of my company."

"This, doubtless, may be so, Sir Gervaise," the doge said, with a slight smile, "but it is to the head that plans, rather than to the hand that strikes, that such success as you have achieved is due; and the credit of this night attack is, as the cavalier Caretto tells me, wholly yours, for until you issued your final orders it seemed to him, and to the two good knights his companions, that there was naught to do but to remain in port and watch this corsair fleet sail away to carry out its work of destruction."

By this time they had reached the poop of the galley. Gervaise now called forward the knights one by one, and presented them to the doge, who expressed to them all the gratitude felt by himself and the whole of the citizens of Genoa for the service they had rendered to the Republic. This ceremony being over, the knights broke up their ranks and conversed for a few minutes with those who had come on board with the doge. The latter then took his place in the barge with his companions, inviting Gervaise and Ralph to accompany him. As the barge left the side of the galley, which followed closely behind her, the guns again thundered out their welcome, and a roar of greeting rose from the inhabitants. On landing, the party waited until the knights had joined them, and then proceeded up the street to the ducal palace, amidst enthusiastic cheering from the crowd that lined the road, occupied the windows and balconies, and even scrambled on the housetops, the ladies waving their handkerchiefs and scarves.

At the palace were assembled all the municipal authorities, and the congratulations given on board were here repeated. After this there was a great banquet, at which Gervaise was placed on the right hand of the doge, who, at the conclusion of the feast, called upon the assembled guests to drink to the health of the knights of St. John, who had saved the commerce and seacoast of Italy from the greatest danger that had menaced them since the days when the Northern rovers had desolated the shores of the Mediterranean. The toast was drunk with enthusiasm, and Gervaise then replied with a few words of thanks for the honour done to himself and his comrades.

The party then left the banqueting hall for the great reception rooms, where the wives and daughters of all the nobles and principal citizens of Genoa were assembled. Most of the young knights, belonging as they did to noble families, and accustomed from childhood to courtly ceremonies and festivities, were quite at home here. Caretto, his two companions, and their six Italian comrades, speedily introduced them, and each was soon surrounded by a group of ladies, anxious to hear from his lips the details of the exploits of the galley.

"But how is it that you are all so young, Sir Ralph?" one of the ladies, to whom Harcourt had been introduced as the second in command, asked him, when he had finished his account of the capture of the galleys. "We heard from those who met you on landing, that all your comrades were young, but we were filled with surprise when you entered the room, for many of them are but lads."

"You may say that all of us are but lads, Countess. I am the oldest of the party, and am but little over twenty-two, but few of the others are over nineteen; they are all professed knights of the Order, who, as you doubtless know, come out to Rhodes when only sixteen. Some, of course, do not join until later, but I think that all here entered at the earliest age permitted, and almost all had served in two or three voyages in the galleys before they were appointed to the Santa Barbara. The reason why so young a crew was chosen was that our commander was also young. He had done such exceptional service to the Order that he was appointed to the command of a galley, and he has, as all will allow, well justified the choice. It was because it was deemed inexpedient to place knights many years his senior under his command, and partly, perhaps, to encourage the younger knights, by giving them an exceptional opportunity of distinguishing themselves, that the crew was chosen entirely from their ranks. I was selected as second in command because Gervaise and I had been special friends when we came out from England in the same ship, and had before fought side by side against the Moslems."

"I see that you wear gilded spurs, Sir Ralph," another lady said; "you must therefore be a dubbed knight?"

"Yes; I had the good fortune to be knighted by D'Aubusson himself, at the same time that Sir Gervaise was also so honoured. It was for an affair with the Turkish pirates. It was Gervaise who really won the honour, for I had no share in the affair, save that of doing my best in the fight."

"And who could do more?" the countess queried.

"Gervaise could do more, Countess, as was shown in that attack on the corsairs by means of fire ships. He has a head to plan, and, in the case I speak of, a happy thought of his not only saved the lives of ourselves and Sir John Boswell, but, indirectly, was the means of preventing two of our galleys being captured by the corsairs."

"Which is Sir Gervaise?" one of the ladies asked.

Ralph smiled.

"Look round the hall, signoras, and see if any of you can pick him out from the rest of us."

The ladies looked round the hall.

"There are only about twenty here; the rest are in the other rooms. Do not set us to work guessing, if he is not in sight, Sir Ralph."

"Oh yes, he is in sight. Now do each of you fix on the one you think most accords with your ideas of what a knight, brave in action and wise and prudent in council, would be like."

The six ladies each fixed on one of the young knights.

"You are all wrong," said Ralph.

"How can we choose?" the countess said laughingly, "when none of them resemble our ideal hero? Most of them are pleasant and courtly looking youths, but as yet there is scarce a vestige of hair on their faces, and one could not fancy any of them as the destroyer of the fleet of corsairs."

"Do you see the one speaking to the elderly lady in the recess?"

"Yes; she is the wife of Fragoso. You do not mean to say that that lad is the commander of the galley? Why, he looks the youngest of you all."

"He is between seventeen and eighteen, and there are several others who are no older. Yes, that is Sir Gervaise, Knight Commander of the Order of St. John."

"But how can he possibly have served his time as a professed knight?"

"He was one of the grand master's pages, and his time in that service counted just as it would have done had he entered as a professed knight; and at fifteen, therefore, he stood in the same position as those three or four years older than himself. He speaks Turkish as well as our own tongue, and, as I told you, we received the accolade at the hands of the grand master, a year and a half ago. He is now a knight commander, and will assuredly one day occupy one of the highest posts in the Order."

"You do not speak as if you were jealous, Sir Ralph; and yet methinks it cannot be pleasant for you all to have one younger than yourselves placed at your head."

"I do not think there is one of us who so feels," Ralph said earnestly. "In the first place, he has performed excellent service; in the next place, even those who did not know him before, have felt, since we started, that he is a born leader. Then, too, we regard with pride one who has brought credit upon the younger members of the Order. Moreover, we all owe our posts in the galley to the fact that he was chosen for its command. It is a difficult position for him to fill, but he has managed so that, while all obey his orders as cheerfully and willingly as if he were a veteran, when off duty we regard him as one of ourselves."

"You are a staunch friend, Sir Ralph."

"I am a staunch friend of Sir Gervaise, Countess, for the more I know of him the more I care for him. He well deserves the promotion and honour that have fallen to his share."

"Will you bring him across here to us, Sir Ralph? I want to talk to this hero of yours, and I am sure that my daughter is longing to be introduced to him."

Ralph waited until Gervaise was disengaged, and then brought him across, and, after introducing him, moved away at once, leaving Gervaise to be interrogated by the ladies.

"You must be accustomed to festivities, Sir Gervaise, for we have just heard that you were one of the grand master's pages?"

"I am accustomed to them, signora; but that is not at all the same thing as liking them."

The reply was given so earnestly that all the ladies smiled.

"Your taste is quite exceptional. Do you mean to say that you would rather be on board your galley than here?"

"It would not be polite," Gervaise said, with a laugh, "if I were to say that I would infinitely rather be on board; but indeed I have not, like most of my comrades, been brought up in court or castle. Until the day I joined the Order, we led the lives of exiles. My father belonged to the defeated party in England, and, save for a few months when the cause to which he was attached was triumphant, we lived quietly on the estates he had recovered, our life being one of care and anxiety. So, you see, I had no training in gaiety and pleasure. At Rhodes there are state receptions and religious pageants, but a meeting such as this, is, of course, impossible in a convent; and since I was eleven years old I think I have only once spoken to a woman. So you can well understand, signora, that I feel awkward in speech, and I pray you to make allowance for my ignorance of the language of courtesy, such as would naturally be expected in a knight, even though belonging to a religious Order."

"There is naught to make allowance for," the countess said gently. "Women can appreciate simple truth, and are not, as men seem to think, always yearning for compliments. Those who are most proficient in turning phrases are not often among those foremost in battle, or wisest in council, and I can tell you that we women value deeds far higher than words. Sir Fabricius

Caretto is a cousin of mine, and has this afternoon been speaking so highly of you to me and my young daughter here, that I am glad indeed to make your acquaintance. How long do you intend to stay in Genoa?"

"No longer than it will take me to engage men to carry the prizes to Rhodes. I am afraid that sounds rude," he broke off, as he noticed a smile on the faces of the ladies.

"Not rude," said the countess; "though most knights would have put it differently, and said that their duty compelled them to leave as soon as the prizes could be manned. But it comes to the same thing. Of course, you will remain the guest of the doge as long as you are here; otherwise, it would have given us the greatest pleasure to have entertained you. My cousin is, of course, staying with us, and you see we all feel a very deep obligation to you. He has been so long a slave among the Moors, that we had almost come to hope death had freed him from his fetters; so you may imagine our pleasure when he arrived here so suddenly ten days ago. We were expecting that he would remain with us for some time, but he says that he must first go back to Rhodes, after which he will ask for leave, and return here. We have a banquet tomorrow evening to celebrate his return, and earnestly hoped that you would be present, but, since you say that you do not care for such gaieties, we shall, if you prefer it, be glad if you will come to join us at our family meal at twelve."

"Thank you, countess, I should very greatly prefer it, and it will give me real pleasure to come."

"Your friend, Sir Ralph Harcourt, has been telling us how you have destroyed the corsair fleet that has been so alarming us. He, too, is an Englishman, though he speaks Italian well."

"Yes, he speaks it a great deal better than I do," Gervaise said. "He is a dear friend of mine, and it is, indeed, chiefly owing to his support and influence that I have been able to manage so pleasantly and well in the command of a body of young knights, most of whom are my seniors."

"He tells us that you speak Turkish?"

"Yes; I thought that it would be very useful, and spent nearly a year in acquiring it, the bailiff of my langue being kind enough to relieve me of all other duties. I was fortunate enough to find in one of the servants of the auberge a well educated and widely informed Turk, who was a very pleasant companion, as well as an excellent instructor, and I learnt much from him besides his language. The knowledge of Turkish has already proved to me most useful, and was indeed the means by which I obtained both my commandery and my appointment as captain of the galley."

"Perhaps you will tell us the story tomorrow; that is, if it is too long to tell us now?"

"It is indeed much too long; but if it will interest you I shall be glad to recount it tomorrow."

The next day Gervaise went to the palace of the Countess Da Forli. She was a widow with no children, except Claudia, the young daughter who had accompanied her to the fete the evening before. Caretto, and four or five relations of the family, were the only guests beside himself. It was a quiet and sociable meal, and served with less ceremony than usual, as the countess wished to place Gervaise as much as possible at his ease. During the meal but little was said about the affair with the pirates, Caretto telling them some of his experiences as a captive.

"It is well, Claudia," he said, laughing, "that you did not see me at the time I was rescued, for I was such a scarecrow that you would never have been able to regard me with due and proper respect afterwards. I was so thin that my bones almost came through my skin."

"You are thin enough now, cousin," the girl said.

"I have gained so much weight during the last ten days that I begin to fear that I shall, ere long, get too fat to buckle on my armour. But, bad as the thinness was, it was nothing to the dirt. Moreover, I was coming near to losing my voice. There was nothing for us to talk about in our misery, and often days passed without a word being exchanged between Da Vinci, Forzi, and myself. Do you know I felt almost more thankful for the bath and perfumes than I did for my liberty. I was able at once to enjoy the comfort of the one, while it was some time before I could really assure myself that my slavery was over, and that I was a free man again."

"And now, Sir Gervaise," the countess said, when the meal was over, "it is your turn. Claudia is longing to hear your story, and to know how you came to be in command of a galley."

"And I am almost as anxious," Caretto said. "I did not like to ask the question on board the galley, and have been looking forward to learning it when I got to Rhodes. I did, indeed, ask the two knights who accompanied me on my mission here, but they would only tell me that every one knew you had performed some very great service to the Order, and that it concerned some intended rising among the slaves, the details being known to only a few, who had been, they understood, told that it was not to be repeated."

"It was a very simple matter," Gervaise said, "and although the grand master and council were pleased to take a very favourable view of it, it was, in fact, a question of luck, just as was the surprise of the corsairs. There is really no secret about it-at least, except in Rhodes: there it was thought best not to speak of it, because the fact that the attempt among the slaves was almost successful, might, if generally known, encourage others to try to escape, and perhaps with greater success. I told you last night, Countess, that I had only once before in the last six or seven years spoken to a woman, and it was on that occasion that the adventure, so far as I was concerned, had its commencement."

He then, beginning at his visit with Ralph Harcourt to the Greek merchant and his family on the roof of the house, recounted the suspicions he had entertained, the manner in which they were confirmed, and the method by which he had discovered the plot for the rising. He was interrupted several times when he attempted to abbreviate the story, or to omit some of the details, and there were exclamations of surprise at his proposal to personate a Turkish prisoner, and to share the lot of the slaves in their prison, and on the benches of the galley.

"I had no idea, Sir Gervaise," Caretto said, when he had concluded, "that you too had been a galley slave, and I understand now the care you showed to render the lot of the rowers as easy as possible. It was a splendid scheme, and well carried out. Indeed, I no longer wonder that you were appointed to the command of a galley, and received a rich commandery in England at the hands of the grand master himself. What think you, Countess; did I speak too highly in his favour?"

"Not one jot, cousin. Why, Sir Gervaise, it seems to me that you have been born two centuries too late, and that you should have been a knight errant, instead of being sworn to obey orders, and bound to celibacy. Do you wear no lady's favour in your helm? I know that not a few of your Order do so."

"As I have said, Countess, I know no ladies who would bestow favours upon me; in the second place, I am but eighteen, and it would be ridiculous for me to think of such matters; lastly, it seems to me that, being vowed to the Order, I can desire no other mistress."

Claudia, who had listened with rapt attention to the story, whispered in her mother's ear. The latter smiled.

"It seems to me, Sir Gervaise," she went on, "that after what you have done for Italy there are many fair maidens who would feel it an honour that their colours should be borne by one who has shown himself so valiant a knight. You see, a gage of this kind does not necessarily mean that there is any deep feeling between the knight who bears it and the lady who bestows it; it shows only that she, on her part, feels it an honour that her gage should be worn by a distinguished knight, and, on his part, that he considers it as somewhat more than a compliment, and wears it as a proof of regard on the part of one whose good opinion at least he values. It is true that among secular knights it may mean even more than this, but it ought not to mean more among knights of an Order like yours, pledged to devote their lives to a lofty and holy aim. My daughter Claudia whispers to me that she would deem it an honour indeed if you would wear her token, accepting it in the spirit in which I have spoken. She is fourteen now, and, as you know, a maid of fourteen here is as old as one of sixteen or seventeen in your country."

Gervaise turned to the girl, who was standing by her mother's chair, looking earnestly at him. He had noticed her the evening before; she had asked no questions, but had listened so intently that he had felt almost embarrassed. Claudia's was a very bright face, and yet marked by firmness and strength. He turned his eyes again to the countess.

"I never thought of wearing a woman's favour," he said; "but if your daughter will bestow one upon me, I shall be proud to wear it, and trust that I may carry it unstained. I shall feel honoured indeed that one so fair, and, as I am sure by her face, so deserving of all the devotion that a knight of our Order can give, has thought me worthy of being one of those on whom she could bestow so high a favour, with the confidence that it would be ever borne with credit and honour."

"What shall I give him, mother?" Claudia asked the countess, without a shadow of the embarrassment with which Gervaise had spoken.

"Not a kerchief, Claudia. In the rough work of the knights, it could not be kept without spot or stain. Moreover, if I judge Sir Gervaise rightly, methinks he would prefer some token that he could wear without exciting attention and remark from his comrades. Go, fetch him any of your jewels you may think fit."

"Then I will give him this," the girl said; and unfastening a thin gold chain she wore round her neck, she pulled up a heart shaped ornament, in pink coral set in gold and pearls.

Her mother uttered a low exclamation of dissent.

"I know, mother; it was your last gift, and I prize it far beyond anything I have; therefore, it is all the more fit to be my token." Then she turned to Gervaise, and went on, without the slightest tremor in her voice, or accession of colour in her cheeks. "Sir Gervaise Tresham, I bestow upon you this my favour, and shall deem it an honour indeed to know that it is borne by one so brave and worthy. You said that you would be glad to be one of those who bore my favours. You will be more than that, for I vow to you that while you live no other knight shall wear a favour of mine."

"Claudia!" her mother said disapprovingly.

"I know what I am saying, mother. I have often wondered why maidens should so carelessly bestow their favours upon every knight who begged for them, and have said to myself that when my time came I would grant it but once, and only then to one whom I deemed worthy of it in all ways-one in whose loyalty and honour I could trust implicitly, and who would regard it as something sacred, deeming it an honour to wear it, as being the pledge of my trust and esteem. Kneel, Sir Gervaise, while I fasten this round your neck."

Gervaise took out the small brooch, that fastened the collar of his silken doublet, and then knelt on one knee. The girl fastened the clasp round his neck, and as he rose he hid the heart beneath the doublet, and fastened the collar.

"Lady Claudia," he said earnestly, "I accept your favour in the spirit in which you bestow it. So long as I live I shall prize and value it beyond any honour I may gain, and as I feel it next to my heart, it will ever recall to me that you gave it me as a pledge of your esteem and trust, and I will strive to the utmost so to bear myself that I may be worthy of the gift."

None of the others spoke while the little ceremony was being performed. Caretto glanced at the countess with an amused smile, but the latter looked grave, and somewhat vexed. However, she made an effort to dispel the cloud on her face, and, when Gervaise ceased speaking, said, "This has been a somewhat more serious business than I intended, Sir Gervaise. But do not think that I regret in any way the course it has taken; 'tis well for a maiden on the threshold of womanhood that she should place before herself a lofty ideal, and that she should entertain a warm feeling of friendship for one worthy of it. So also it is good for a young knight to know that he has the trust and confidence of a pure and innocent maiden; such a knowledge will aid him to be in all ways true to the vows he has taken, and to remember always that he is bound to be not only a valiant knight of his Order, but a sincere soldier of the Cross."

Then she went on more lightly. "Have you heard, Sir Gervaise, that there is a question of making you a noble of Genoa?"

"No, indeed," Gervaise replied, in great surprise; "such an idea never entered into my thoughts."

"Nevertheless, I know that it was spoken of last night, and although it has not yet been finally settled, and will not be until the council meet this afternoon, I should not tell you if I did not think that it was as good as agreed upon; and I am pleased to be the first to whisper to you that it is intended to bestow upon you an honour that is jealously guarded and seldom granted, even to crowned heads, unless as a token of gratitude for some signal service done to the Republic."

"I should feel most honoured and most grateful, Countess, for so extraordinary a favour, did I feel that I had done any extraordinary action to merit it. There can be no doubt that the destruction of the corsairs has saved Genoa and all the maritime towns from immense loss by damage to their trade, and by the raids that would have been made at various points on the coast. But I cannot see that the mere fact that we have destroyed their fleet merits any marked honour. They were caught in a trap, and half of them burned, and this might have been done equally as well by the Sardinian fishermen, unarmed, and without our aid. As to the fighting, it was of small account. The first three craft we captured offered a much stouter resistance, and we lost two of our number; but in the other affair no knight was killed, or even seriously wounded, and believe me, Countess, I feel absolutely ashamed at the fuss that is made over it. It seems to me that I am a sort of impostor, obtaining credit under false pretences."

"No man is a fair judge of his own actions, Sir Gervaise," Caretto said. "A man may believe himself a Solon, or a Roland; others may consider him as a fool, or an empty braggart; and it must be taken that the general opinion of the public is the judgment from which there is no appeal. It is not the mob of Genoa only who regard the services that you have rendered as extraordinary, but it is the opinion of the councillors and authorities of the Republic, and of those who, like myself, have borne our share in warfare, that not only is the service great, but that it is due to the singular ability with which you, in command of only a single galley, have wholly destroyed or captured the fleet that threatened our commerce. As our councillors, therefore, all competent judges, are unanimous in their opinion that you have deserved the highest honours that Genoa can bestow upon you, it is useless for you to set up your own opinion to the contrary. Take the good things that fall to you, Sir Gervaise, and be thankful. It is seldom that men obtain more honours than they deserve, while it very often happens that they deserve far more than they obtain. Fortune has doubtless some share in every man's career; but when it is not once, but several times, that a knight gains special credit for deeds he has performed, we may be sure that fortune has less to do with the matter than his personal merits. Three times have you earned special credit; upon the first occasion, the grand master-no mean judge of conduct and character-deemed you worthy of secular knighthood, an honour which has not, in my memory, been bestowed at Rhodes upon any young knight; on the second, you were promoted to the command of a galley, though never before has such a command been given to any, save knights of long experience; and now, for the third time, the councillors of one of the greatest of Italian cities are about to do you honour. It is good to be modest, Sir Gervaise, and it is better to underestimate than to overrate one's own merits, but it is not well to carry the feeling to an extreme. I am quite sure that in your case your disclaimer is wholly sincere and unaffected; but take my advice, accept the honours the world may pay you as not undeserved, determining only in your mind that if you deem them excessive, you will at least do all in your power to show that they are not ill bestowed. You will not, I trust, take my counsel amiss."

"On the contrary, Sir Fabricius," Gervaise said warmly. "I am really but a boy yet, though by good fortune pushed strangely forward, and I am glad indeed to receive council from a knight of vastly greater experience than myself and, in future, however much I may be conscious in my own mind that anything I have done is greatly overrated, I will at least abstain from protest. And now, Countess, I must pray you to excuse me. I know that Sir Ralph Harcourt is, before this, down at the dockyard waiting my coming to engage sailors."

"You will come tomorrow at the same time, I hope, Sir Gervaise. As Claudia's sworn knight we have now a claim upon you, and for the short time that you remain here you must regard this as your home, although you must necessarily remain the guest of the doge."

"He is a fine young fellow, indeed," Caretto said, after Gervaise had left. "There is no affectation about his modesty, and he really considers that this success he has gained is solely a stroke of good fortune. Of course, I have been asking many questions about him of the young knights of his own langue, Harcourt among them. They tell me that he is always in earnest in everything he undertakes. He is without a rival among the younger knights of the convent in his skill in arms, and for strength and activity in all exercises; he seems to care nothing for the ordinary amusements in which they join at Rhodes, and for nine months was scarcely ever seen by those in the auberge, save when they gathered for meals, so continuously did he work to acquire a perfect command of Turkish. How thoroughly he succeeded is evident from the fact that he was able to live among the galley slaves without exciting any suspicions in their minds that he was other than he pretended to be, a Syrian captive. That he is brave goes without saying, though perhaps no braver than the majority of his companions. The extraordinary thing about him is that although, as he himself says, little more than a boy, he has the coolness to plan, and the head to carry out, schemes that would do credit to the most experienced captain. He is already a credit to the Order, and, should he live, will assuredly rise to the highest offices in it, and may even die its grand master. In the stormy times that are coming on, there will be ample opportunities for him still further to distinguish himself, and to fulfil the singular promise of his youth. That he possesses great tact, as well as other qualities, is shown by the enthusiasm with which his companions regard him. In no case, among those to whom I have spoken, have I discerned the smallest jealousy of him. The tact that is needed to stand thus among fifty young knights, almost all his seniors in age, will assuredly enable him later on to command the confidence and affection of older men."

When the other guests had left, and Caretto only remained, the countess turned to Claudia. "You went too far, Claudia. I was willing enough, when you asked me, that you should bestow a favour upon him. Most young knights wear such a favour, which may be a sign of devotion, but which far more frequently is a piece of gallantry. In the case of a knight hospitaller it can only be the latter; it is in his case merely a sign that he has so distinguished himself that some maiden feels a pride that her gift should be carried into battle by him, and, on his part, that he too is proud of the gift so bestowed by one whose goodwill he prizes. In that way I was willing that you should grant him your favour. But the manner in which you gave it was far more serious than the occasion warranted, and your promise to grant no similar favour to another as long as he lived, surprised, and, I may almost say, shocked me. You are, according to our custom here, considered almost a woman, and had not Sir Gervaise belonged to a religious Order, and were he of a presuming disposition, he might well have gathered a meaning from your words far beyond what you intended, and have even entertained a presumptuous hope that you were not indifferent to his merits. In the present case, of course, no harm is done; still, methinks that it would be far better had the words been unspoken. Your cousin here will, I am sure, agree with me."

Caretto did not speak, but stood playing with his moustache, waiting for Claudia's reply. The girl had stood with downcast eyes while her mother was speaking.

"I only expressed what I felt, mother," she said, after a pause, "and I do not think that Sir Gervaise Tresham is likely to misunderstand me. It seems to me that never among those whom I have met have I seen one so worthy. No praises can be higher than those with which my cousin has spoken of him. He has rescued him, whom we dearly love, from slavery; he has saved Genoa from great disaster, and many towns and villages from plunder and ruin. I do indeed feel proud that such a knight should wear my gage, and, were there no other reason, I should be unwilling that, so long as he carried it, another should possess a similar one from me. I am sure that Sir Gervaise will have felt that this was the meaning of my words; I wished him to see that it was not a favour lightly given by a girl who might, a few weeks hence, bestow a similar one upon another, but was a gage seriously given of the honour in which I held him."

"Very well said, Claudia," Caretto broke in, before the countess could reply. "I warrant me the young knight will not misunderstand your gift, and that he will prize it highly and carry it nobly. He is not one of those who will boast of a favour and display it all times, and, except perhaps to his friend Sir Ralph Harcourt, I will wager he never tells a soul who was its donor."

When Claudia shortly afterwards left the room, he said to the countess, "Excuse me for breaking in, Agatha, but I felt that it was much better to agree with her, and not to make overmuch of the matter; she is just of an age to make some one a hero, and she could hardly have chosen a better subject for her worship. In the first place, he is a knight of St. John; in the second, he is going away in a few days, perhaps tomorrow, and may never cross her path again. The thought of him will prevent her fancy from straying for a time, and keep her heart whole until you decide on a suitor for her hand."

"Nevertheless, I would rather that it had not been so. Claudia is not given to change, and this may last long enough to cause trouble when I bring forward the suitor you speak of."

"Well, in any case it might be worse," Caretto said philosophically. And then, with a smile in answer to her look of inquiry, "Knights of the Order have, ere now, obtained release from their vows."

"Fabricius!" the countess exclaimed, in a shocked voice.

"Yes, I know, Agatha, that the child is one of the richest heiresses in Italy, but for that very reason it needs not that her husband should have wide possessions. In all other respects you could wish for no better. He will assuredly be a famous knight; he is the sort of man to make her perfectly happy; and, lastly, you know I cannot forget that I owe my liberation from slavery to him. At any rate, Agatha, as I said before, he may never cross her path again, and you may, a year or two hence, find her perfectly amenable to your wishes."

Chapter XVII
Captured

Upon the following day the doge requested Gervaise to accompany him to a meeting of the council. Upon entering the grand hall he found not only the members of the council assembled in their robes of office, but a large gathering of the nobles and principal citizens of Genoa, together with the knights of the galley whom, under Ralph Harcourt's orders, Gervaise found, to his surprise, drawn up in order across the Hall. Here, in the name of the Republic, Battista Fragoso announced to him that, by the unanimous decision of the council, he had been elected a noble of Genoa; an honour, he added, on only one or two previous occasions in the history of the Republic bestowed upon any but of princely rank, but which he had nobly earned by the great service he had rendered to the State. His name was then inscribed in the book containing the names and titles of the nobles of Genoa. Next, Battista Fragoso presented him with a superb suit of Milanese armour, as his own personal gift, and then with a casket of very valuable jewels, as the gift of the city of Genoa. Each presentation was accompanied by the plaudits of the assembly, and by the no less warm acclamations of the knights. Ralph was then called forward, and presented with a suit of armour but little inferior to that given to Gervaise, and each knight received a heavy gold chain of the finest workmanship of Genoa.

Two days later the preparations for departure were complete, and a sufficient number of men were engaged to man the prizes. This charge, also, Genoa took upon itself, and put on board much stronger crews than Gervaise deemed necessary for the navigation of the ships. The weather was fine and the wind favourable, and a quick passage was made to Rhodes. When the harbour was in sight, the ships were ordered to proceed in single file, the galley leading the way with a huge banner of the Order floating from her stern, and smaller flags on staffs at each side. It was not until they passed by the two forts guarding the entrance that the flags fluttering at the mastheads of the prizes afforded to those on shore an intimation of the event that had taken place, and even then none supposed that this fleet of prizes had been taken by the one galley that headed them.

As the Santa Barbara slowly rowed up the harbour, the State barge of the grand master put off to meet it, and D'Aubusson, with a party of knights, soon stepped on board.

"Welcome back, Sir Gervaise! although I little expected to see you return so soon. What is the meaning of this procession that follows you? By their rig and appearance they are Moors, but how they come to be thus sailing in your wake is a mystery to us all."

"They are Moors, your Excellency; they form part of an expedition fitted out by the corsairs of Algiers, Tripoli, Tunis, and other piratical strongholds, for the purpose of destroying the commerce and ravaging the coasts of Western Italy. Fortunately, we fell in with a ship that had been plundered by three of them on their way north, and learned from the dying captain, who was the only one of her crew left with life on board, the direction they were taking, and something of the nature of the expedition. We pursued the three galleys, came up with them, had the good fortune to capture them, and then had the delight of finding among their rowers the noble knights, Fabricius Caretto, Giacomo Da Vinci, and Pietro Forzi."

The grand master, and the knights with him, uttered an exclamation of joy, and, as the three knights named stepped forward, embraced them with the liveliest pleasure.

"My dear Caretto," the grand master exclaimed, "it is almost a resurrection, for we have all long mourned you as dead; and your return to us at the present time is indeed fortunate; for upon whose judgment and aid could I better rely than those of my old comrade in arms?" Then, turning to Gervaise, he went on: "It was a daring and brilliant exploit indeed, Sir Gervaise, and in due time honour shall be paid to you and your brave companions, to whom and to you I now tender the thanks of the Order. But tell me the rest briefly, for I would fain hear from these noble knights and old friends the story of what has befallen them."

"My tale is a very brief one, your Highness. The Cavalier Caretto sailed at once in a swift craft from the south of Sardinia, to carry warnings to the cities on the coast of Italy of the danger that threatened them, and in order that some war galleys might be despatched by Genoa to meet the corsair fleet. During his absence we discovered the little inlet in which the pirates lay hidden, waiting doubtless the arrival of the three ships we had captured, to commence operations. On the return of the knight with the news that it would be at least a fortnight before Genoa could fit out any galleys, and fearing that the pirates might at any moment put to sea, we procured some small Sardinian craft, and fitted them as fire ships; with the captives we had rescued, and some Sard fishermen, we manned the three prizes, distributing the knights between them, and at night launched the fire ships against the corsairs, whose ships were crowded together. Eleven of them were burnt; six we captured as they endeavoured to make their way out, and took possession of four others whose crews had run them ashore and deserted them. None escaped."

Exclamations of astonishment and almost of incredulity broke from the knights.

"And is it possible, Sir Gervaise, that these thirteen vessels that follow you are all prizes captured by your galley alone?"

"It is, as I have the honour to tell your Highness. But their capture, except in the case of the first three, was due almost solely to good fortune and to the position in which we found them, almost incapable of defence."

"What think you, knights and comrades?" the grand master said to his companions. "There were some of you who deemed it rash to entrust a galley to so young a commander and so youthful a crew. What say you now? Never in the annals of the Order has such a sight been witnessed as that of thirteen prizes being brought in by a single galley, to say naught of eleven others destroyed. Caretto, you and your comrades must have had some share in this marvellous victory."

"By no means," the Italian replied; "beyond having the honour of aiding to carry out the orders of Sir Gervaise Tresham, the commander of the galley. The plan was wholly of his own devising, its execution solely due to his arrangement of the details, and that without the slightest suggestion on the part of myself or my comrades. I will presently narrate to you the whole story; it will come better from my lips than from those of Sir Gervaise, whose disposition is to wholly underestimate the merit of the action he has performed. But I must also bear testimony, not only to the bravery displayed by Sir Gervaise, Sir Ralph Harcourt, his lieutenant, and every one of the knights his crew, but to the admirable discipline, order, and good fellowship on board the galley, which would have done credit to the most experienced commander and to the most veteran knights of the Order."

The grand master paused a moment, and then said in a loud voice, "Sir Gervaise Tresham, Sir Ralph Harcourt, and knights of the seven langues of the Order-As yet I can hardly appreciate the full extent of the service that you have rendered. I thanked you but now for the capture of three corsairs; but what can I say when I learn that you have destroyed or taken a whole fleet? I invite you all to a banquet that I shall hold tonight, where the Cavalier Caretto will relate to us all the details of this marvellous exploit."

Within a few minutes after the return of the grand master and his party ashore, the flags of the Order were run up to the flagstaffs of every fort and bastion: the bells of the churches chimed out a triumphant peal, and a salute was fired from the guns of the three water forts, while along the wall facing the port, the townspeople waved numberless gay flags as a welcome to the galley. Most of the knights went ashore at once, but Gervaise, under the excuse that he wished to see that everything was in order before landing, remained on board until it was time to go to the banquet, being sure that by that time the knights would have fully told the story at their respective auberges, and that there would be no more questions to answer. The banquet differed but little from that at Genoa, and Gervaise was heartily glad when it was over.

The next day the grand master sent for him.

"If I judge rightly, Sir Gervaise, the thing that will best please you at present, is an order to put to sea again at once, to conclude the usual period of service of the galley."

"It is indeed," Gervaise replied earnestly. "But I should be glad, sir, if you will allow that the time should begin to count afresh from our present start. We have really had but a short period of service, for we wasted a week at Genoa, and ten days on our journey back here, so that we have had really no more than a month's active service."

"Yes, if you count only by time," D'Aubusson said, with a smile. "Reckoning by results, you have done a good five years' cruise. However, so small a request can certainly be granted. The places of the two knights who were killed, and of four others whose wounds are reported to me as being too severe for them to be fit for service for some time, shall be filled up at once from the langues to which each belonged. You will cruise among the Western islands, whence complaints have reached us of a corsair who has been plundering and burning. Sometimes he is heard of as far north as Negropont, at others he is off the south of the Morea; then, again, we hear of him among the Cyclades. We have been unwilling to despatch another galley, for there is ample employment for every one here. After the blow you have struck on the Moorish corsairs, they are likely to be quiet for a little. You had best, therefore, try for a time if you cannot come across this pirate. You must let me know how much you paid for the vessels you used as fire ships, and to the Sards; this is an expense chargeable to the general service. I may tell you that to me it is due that no recognition of your exploits, such as that which Genoa bestowed upon you, will be made. At the council this morning it was urged that some signal mark of honour should be granted; but I interposed, saying that you had already received exceptional promotion, and that it would not be for your good, or that of the Order, for so young a knight to be raised to an official position of a character usually held by seniors, and that I was perfectly sure you would prefer remaining in command of your galley to any promotion whatever that would retain you on the Island."

"Indeed I should, your Highness. I wish to gain experience and to do service to the Order, and so far from pleasing me, promotion would trouble and distress me, and, could it have been done, I would most gladly have sent home the prizes, instead of going to Genoa, and would myself have continued the cruise."

"So the Cavalier Caretto told me," the grand master replied. "Very well, then. In three days you shall set out again. The admiral tells me that never before has a galley returned with the slaves in such good health and condition, and that unquestionably your plan of erecting an awning to shelter them from the midday heat and the night dews has had a most beneficial effect on their health; he has recommended its general adoption."

Three days later the Santa Barbara again left port, and was soon upon her station. For some weeks she cruised backwards and forwards along the coast and among the islands. They often heard of the pirate ship, but all their efforts to find her were unavailing.

One evening there were signs of a change of weather, and by morning it was blowing a furious gale from the north; in spite of the efforts of the rowers, the galley narrowly escaped being driven ashore; but she at last gained the shelter of an island, and anchored under its lee, the slaves being utterly worn out by continuous exertion. As soon as the gale abated they again put to sea, and, after proceeding for some miles, saw a ship cast up on shore. Some people could be made out on board of her, and a white flag was raised.

"She must have been driven ashore during the gale," Gervaise said. "We will row in to within a quarter of a mile of her and see what we can do for them."

As soon as the anchor was dropped a boat was lowered.

"I will go myself, Ralph, for I shall be glad to set my foot on shore again. There must be people on the island; I wonder none of them have come to the aid of those poor fellows. I suppose the villages are on the other side of the island, and they have not yet heard of the wreck."

Gervaise asked three of the knights to accompany him, and the boat, rowed by galley slaves, was soon on its way. All were glad at the change afforded to the monotony of their life on board, and at the prospect of a scamper on shore.

There were but five or six men to be seen on the deck of the wreck, and these had, as the boat approached, come down to the rocks as if to meet those who came to their aid; but as the knights leapt out, they threw themselves suddenly upon them with knives and scimitars that had hitherto been concealed beneath their garments, while at the same moment a crowd of men appeared on the deck of the ship, and, leaping down, ran forward with drawn swords. Two of the knights fell dead before they had time to draw their weapons. The third shook off his two assailants, and for a minute kept them both at bay; but others, rushing up, cut him down.

Gervaise had received a slight wound before he realised what was happening. He snatched his dagger from its sheath, and struck down one assailant; but ere he could raise it to strike again, another leapt on to his back, and clung there until the rest rushed up, when he shouted, "Take him alive! take him alive!" and, throwing down their weapons, half a dozen of the pirates flung themselves upon Gervaise, and strove to pull him to the ground, until at last, in spite of his desperate resistance, they succeeded in doing so. His armour was hastily stripped off, his hands and feet bound, and then at the orders of the pirate who had leapt on his back, and who was evidently the captain, half a dozen men lifted him on to their shoulders. As they did so four guns from the galley flashed out, and the balls flew overhead. The pirates, who had already begun to quarrel over the armour and arms of the fallen knights, at once took to their heels, followed by the galley slaves from the boat.

"Make haste," the captain said to the men carrying Gervaise.

"They are lowering their boats; we must be under way before they come up."

In a minute or two Gervaise was set down on his feet, the cords round his legs were cut, and he was made to hurry along with his captors. In a short time an inlet was reached, and here Gervaise saw, to his mortification, the pirate craft for which the Santa Barbara had in vain been searching. As soon as the party were all on board, the ropes by which she was moored to two trees were thrown off; the great sails hoisted, and she sailed boldly out. Although the gale had entirely abated, there was still a brisk wind blowing, and it was evident to the captain of the corsair that under such circumstances he could outsail the galley that had long been searching for him; when, therefore, the Santa Barbara came in sight, just as he and his crew had finished stripping the wreck of its contents, the idea had occurred to him to attempt to entice some of the knights to land.

As soon as the vessel was under way he abused his followers hotly for not having obeyed his orders to capture the knights without bloodshed; but they pleaded that it was as much as they had been able to do to capture Gervaise in that way, and that they could never have overcome the four together, before the boats would have had time to come from the ship.

Gervaise had been told to sit down with his back to a mast and in this position he could, when the vessel heeled over to the breeze, obtain a view of the sea. It was with a feeling of bitter mortification and rage that he saw the galley lying but half a mile away, as the corsair issued from the inlet. A moment later he heard a gun fired, and saw the signal hoisted to recall the boats.

"If the wind had been favourable," the captain said to his mate, "we would have borne down upon her, and could have reached and captured her before the boats got back, for you may be sure that they have landed almost all their men. However, we can't get there against the wind, and we will now say goodbye to them."

Gervaise knew well that at the pace they were running through the water the galley would have no chance whatever of overtaking her, and that, ere the knights came on board again, she would be already two or three miles away. A point of land soon concealed the galley from view, and when he caught sight of her, as she rounded the point, she was but a speck in the distance.

They passed several islands in the course of the day, changing their direction to a right angle to that which they had at first pursued, as soon as they were hidden from the sight of the galley by an intervening island. As night came on they anchored in a little bay on the coast of the Morea. The sails being furled, the sailors made a division of the booty they had captured on the island, and of the portable property found on board the wreck. A gourd full of water was placed to Gervaise's lips by one of the men of a kinder disposition than the rest. He drank it thankfully, for he was parched with thirst excited by the pain caused by the tightness with which he had been bound.

He slept where he sat. All night four men remained on guard, although from what he heard they had no fear whatever of being overtaken. In the morning his arms were unbound, and they stripped off his tunic and shirt. They had evidently respect for his strength, for before loosing his arms they tightly fastened his ankles together. The removal of his shirt exposed Claudia's gift to view.

"Take that from him and give it to me," the captain said. As the two men approached, Gervaise seized one in each hand, dashed them against each other, and hurled them on the deck. But the exertion upset his equilibrium, and after making a vain effort to recover it, he fell heavily across them. The captain stooped over him, and, before he could recover himself, snatched the chain from his neck.

"You are a stout fellow," he said, laughing, "and will make a fine slave. What have you got here that you are ready to risk your life for?" He looked at the little chain and its pendant with an air of disappointment. "'Tis worth but little," he said, showing it to his mate. "I would not give five ducats for it in the market. It must be a charm, or a knight would never carry it about with him and prize it so highly. It may be to things like this the Christians owe their luck."

"It has not brought him luck this time," the mate observed with a laugh.

"Even a charm cannot always bring good luck, but at any rate I will try it;" and he put it round his neck just as Gervaise had worn it. The latter was now unbound, and permitted to move about the deck. The strength he had shown in the struggle on shore, and the manner in which he had hurled, bound as he was, two of their comrades to the deck, had won for him the respect of his captors, and he was therefore allowed privileges not granted to the seamen of the vessel that had had the ill fortune to be cast on shore so close to the spot where the corsair was hiding. These had been seized, driven to the ship, and having been stripped of the greater portion of their clothes, shut down in the hold.

Although angry that but one out of the four who landed had been captured, the captain was in a good humour at having tricked his redoubtable foes, and was disposed to treat Gervaise with more consideration than was generally given to captives. The latter had not spoken a word of Turkish from the time he was captured, and had shaken his head when first addressed in that language. No suspicion was therefore entertained that he had any knowledge of it, and the Turks conversed freely before him.

"Where think you we had better sell him?" the mate asked the captain, when Gervaise was leaning against the bulwark watching the land, a short quarter of a mile away. "He ought to fetch a good ransom."

"Ay, but who would get it? You know how it was with one that Ibrahim took two years ago. First there were months of delay, then, when the ransom was settled, the pasha took four-fifths of it for himself, and Ibrahim got far less than he would have done had he sold him as a slave. The pashas here, and the sultans of the Moors, are all alike; if they once meddle in an affair they take all the profit, and think they do well by giving you a tithe of it. There are plenty of wealthy Moors who are ready to pay well for a Christian slave, especially when he is a good looking young fellow such as this. He will fetch as much as all those eight sailors below. They are only worth their labour, while this youngster will command a fancy price. I know a dozen rich Moors in Tripoli or Tunis who would be glad to have him; and we agreed that we would run down to the African coast for awhile, for that galley has been altogether too busy of late for our comfort, and will be all the more active after this little affair; besides, people in these islands have got so scared that one can't get within ten miles of any of them now without seeing their signal smokes rising on the hills, and finding, when they land, the villages deserted and stripped of everything worth carrying away."

This news was a disappointment to Gervaise. He had calculated that he would be sold at one of the Levant ports, and had thought that with his knowledge of Turkish he should have no great difficulty in escaping from any master into whose hands he might fall, and taking his chance of either seizing a fishing boat, or of making his way in a trading ship to some district where the population was a mixed one, and where trade was winked at between the merchants there, and those at some of the Greek towns. To escape from Tunis or Tripoli would be far more difficult; there, too, he would be beyond the reach of the good offices of Suleiman Ali, who would, he was sure, have done all in his power to bring about his release. Of one thing he was determined: he would not return to Rhodes without making every possible effort to recover Claudia's gage, as he considered it absolutely incumbent on him as a knight to guard, as something sacred, a gift so bestowed. The fancy of the corsair to retain the jewel as a charm he regarded as a piece of the greatest good fortune. Had it been thrown among the common spoil, he would never have known to which of the crew it had fallen at the division, still less have traced what became of it afterwards; whereas now, for some time, at any rate, it was likely to remain in the captain's possession.

Had it not been for that, he would have attempted to escape at the first opportunity, and such an opportunity could not fail to present itself ere long, for he had but to manage to possess himself of Moslem garments to be able to move about unquestioned in any Turkish town. When it became dark he was shut up in the hold, which was, he found, crowded with captives, as, in addition to the crew of the wreck, between forty and fifty Greeks, for the most part boys and young girls, had been carried off from the villages plundered. It was pitch dark below, although the scuttle had been left open in order to allow a certain amount of air to reach the captives; Gervaise, therefore, felt his way about cautiously, and lay down as soon as he found a clear space. Save an occasional moan or curse, and the panting of those suffering from the heat and closeness of the crowded hold, all was still. The majority of the captives had been some time in their floating prison, and their first poignant grief had settled down into a dull and despairing acceptance of their fate; the sailors, newly captured, had for hours raved and cursed, but, worn out by their struggle with the elements, and their rage and grief, they had now fallen asleep.

It was long before Gervaise dozed off. He was furious with himself for having fallen into the trap; if he had, as he said to himself, lain off the beach in the boat, and questioned the supposed shipwrecked sailors, their inability to reply to him would have at once put him on his guard; as it was, he had walked into the snare as carelessly and confidently as a child might have done. Even more than his own captivity, he regretted the death of his three comrades, which he attributed to his own want of care. The next morning he was again allowed on deck. The vessel was under way, and her head was pointing south. To his surprise some of the crew gave him a friendly greeting; he was unable to understand a manner so at variance with their hatred to the Christians, until one of them said to him in a mixture of Greek and Italian, "We have heard from our countrymen who were in the boat with you, that they received much kindness at your hands, and that of all the Christians they had served under, you were the kindest master. Therefore, it is but right now Allah has decreed that you in turn should be a slave to the true believers, that you should receive the same mercy you gave to Moslems when they were in your power."

The captain came up as the man was speaking. He talked for a time to the sailor, who then turned again to Gervaise. "The captain says that he is told you were the commander of that galley; he has questioned the eight men separately, and they all tell the same story: and yet he cannot understand how so young a man should command a galley manned by warriors famous for their deeds of arms, even among us who are their foes."

"This galley was an exception," Gervaise replied; "the knights on board were all young, as they could be better spared than those more experienced, at a time when your sultan is known to be preparing for an attack on Rhodes."

The captain was silent for a minute when this was interpreted to him; he had at the time noticed and wondered at the youth of the four knights, and the explanation seemed to him a reasonable one.

"I wish I had known it," he said after a pause; "for had I done so, I would have fought and captured her yesterday; I have half a mind to go back and seek her now."

He called up one of the ex slaves who was a native of Tripoli, and who had now taken his place as a member of the crew, and asked him a number of questions. Gervaise felt uncomfortable while the man was answering. Fortunately, his rowers had agreed to say nothing whatever of the destruction of the corsair fleet, of which no word had as yet reached the pirates, deeming that, in their anger at the news, the pirates might turn upon them for the part that they had, however involuntarily, borne in it.

As soon as he perceived that the captain entertained the idea of returning to engage the galley, the man felt that if he were to avoid a return into captivity he must deter him from taking such a step. He therefore, in answer to his questions as to the strength of the crew of the galley and the fighting powers of the knights, reported the capture of the three vessels. The captain listened almost incredulously to his statement, and, calling up another two of the men, questioned them also as to the occurrence. Having heard them, he turned away and paced the deck, in evident anger; however, he gave no instructions for a change of course, and, to the great satisfaction of the eight rescued slaves, the vessel continued her course southward.

As they neared the African coast, Gervaise kept an eager lookout, in hopes that Visconti's galley might appear in sight. The captain's temper had not recovered from the effect of the news of the capture of three Moorish vessels by the galley commanded by Gervaise, and the latter, seeing the mood he was in, kept forward so as to avoid coming in contact with him. He had early taken the opportunity of saying to one of the released galley slaves, "I pray you, if you have any feeling of kindness towards me for the efforts I made to alleviate your condition, say no word of my knowledge of Turkish, and ask the others also to remain silent on this point."

The man had nodded, and the request was observed by them all.

The captain's irritation showed itself in his treatment of the other captives. These were brought up every day from the hold, and kept on deck until dark, as the price they would fetch in the slave market in Tripoli would depend greatly upon their health and appearance; but when the captain came near them he several times struck them brutally, if they happened to be in his way. Gervaise had the greatest difficulty in restraining his indignation, and, indeed, only did so because he felt that his interference would but make things worse for them. When at last the ship cast anchor off Tripoli, the captain ordered the boats to be lowered. As he walked towards the gangway, he happened to push against one of the captives, a Greek girl of some ten years of age. With an angry exclamation he struck her to the deck. Gervaise sprang forward.

"You brute!" he exclaimed in English. "I have a good mind to throw you overboard, and will do so the next time you strike one of these children without cause."

Infuriated by Gervaise's interference and threatening attitude, the corsair drew his long knife; but before he could strike, Gervaise caught his wrist; the knife fell from his hand, and Gervaise kicked it through the open gangway into the sea. The captain shouted to his men to seize the Christian, but the young knight's blood was up now. The first man who came at him he seized by the sash round his waist, and threw overboard; the two next he stretched on the deck with blows from his clenched fist. Some of the others now drew their weapons, but the captain shouted to them to sheath them.

"Fools!" he yelled. "Is it not enough that your cowardice has already cost us the lives of three knights, whose capture would have brought us a big sum? Throw him down and bind him. What! are fifty of you afraid of one unarmed man? No wonder these Christians capture our ships, if this is the mettle of our crews!"

Goaded by his words, the men made a general rush upon Gervaise, and, in spite of his desperate efforts, threw him on to the deck and bound him; then the captain, seizing a heavy stick in his left hand, his right being still powerless, showered blows upon him until Gervaise almost lost consciousness. "Throw some water over the dog," the corsair said, as he threw down the stick, panting with his exertions; and then, without waiting to see if his order was obeyed, he took his place in the boat, and was rowed ashore.

As soon as he had left, three or four of the ex galley slaves carried Gervaise into the shade of the sail. The sailors, several of whom bore signs of the late struggle, looked on sullenly, but offered no opposition when the men took off the ropes and raised him into a sitting posture against the mast. He had not entirely lost consciousness, and was now fast recovering himself.

"Is there anything we can do for you?" one of the men asked in Italian.

"No I shall soon be all right again, although I am bruised all over, and shall be stiff for a day or two. You had best leave me now, or you will incur the enmity of these fellows."

Gervaise was indeed bruised from his neck to his heels. Even in his passion the pirate had avoided striking him on the head, as a disfiguring mark on the face would diminish his value. Sitting there, he congratulated himself that he had been beaten with a stick and not with a whip; a stick is a weapon, and he did not feel the same sense of dishonour that he would have experienced had he been beaten with a whip. That such might be his lot in slavery he recognised. The backs of Caretto and his two companions were seamed with the marks inflicted by the gang master's whip, and he could scarce hope to escape the same treatment; but at present he hardly felt a slave. There was another reflection that to some extent mitigated the pain of his bruises; the pirate captain held his treasured gage, and it was his fixed determination to recover it. The man had at first in a rough way treated him fairly, and had allowed him more liberty than the other captives, and he would have felt reluctant to take extreme measure against him to recover the gage. Now he was not only free from any sense of obligation, but had a heavy score to settle with him.

After a time he got up and walked stiffly and painfully up and down the deck, knowing that this was the best plan to prevent the limbs from stiffening. The corsair did not return until night set in; he was accompanied by an Arab, whose dress and appearance showed that he was a person of importance. The other slaves had all been sent below, but Gervaise still remained on deck, as the mate had not cared to risk another conflict by giving him orders in the absence of the captain. As the pirate stepped on deck he ordered some torches to be brought.

"This is the Christian I spoke of," he said to the Arab, pointing to Gervaise, who was leaning carelessly against the bulwark.

"He is, as you see, capable of hard work of any kind; his strength is prodigious, for it took ten of my best men to bind him this morning."

"Why did you wish to bind him?" the Arab asked coldly; "you told me that although so strong he was of a quiet disposition, and would make a good household slave."

"I struck a slave girl who stood in my way," the captain said, "and he came at me so suddenly that I had to call upon the men to bind him. He threw one of them overboard, and with his naked hands knocked down two others; and, as I have told you, it took all the efforts of eight or ten more before they could overcome him."

The Arab took a torch from one of the sailors, walked across to Gervaise, who was naked from the waist upwards, his upper garments having been torn into shreds in the struggle, and examined him closely.

"And then you beat him," he said, turning to the captain.

"Certainly I beat him. Do you think that a slave is to mutiny on board my ship, and escape unpunished?"

The Arab, without replying, again inspected Gervaise.

"You ask a large sum for him," he said.

"I should ask twice as much," the captain replied, "if it were not for the regulation that one slave from each cargo brought in belongs to the sultan, and his officers would as a matter of course choose this fellow, for the others are merely such as are sold in the market every day. This man is one of the accursed Order of Rhodes, and would fetch a ransom many times greater than the sum I ask for him, only I have not the time to wait for months until the affair could be arranged."

"And, moreover, Hassan," the Arab said grimly, "it has doubtless not escaped you that as the Sultan of Turkey is fitting out an expedition to destroy the community of Rhodes, the chance of their ransoming their comrade is a very slight one."

"Threatened men live long," the captain said. "The sultan has been talking of attacking them for years, and something has always happened to prevent his carrying out his intention. It may be the same again."

"I will take him," the Arab said shortly. "Here is a purse with the sum you named; count it, and see that it is right." As he stood apart while the pirate counted out the money, the eight released slaves came up in a body, and one of them, bowing low before the merchant, said,

"My lord, we have long been slaves of the Christian knights at Rhodes, and have worked in their galleys. We were rescued the other day when this knight was taken prisoner. Our life has been a hard one. We have borne toil, and hardship, and blows, the heat of the sun by day, and the damp by night, but we would humbly represent to you that since we were placed in the galley commanded by this knight our lot has been made bearable by his humanity and kindness. He erected an awning to shade us from the sun's rays, and to shelter us from the night dews. He provided good food for us. He saw that we were not worked beyond our strength, and he forbade us being struck, unless for good cause. Therefore, my lord, now that misfortune has fallen upon him, we venture to represent to you the kindness with which he has treated us, in the hope that it may please you to show him such mercy as he showed to us."

"You have done well," the Arab said, "and your words shall not be forgotten. When you land tomorrow, inquire for the house of Isaac Ben Ibyn. You are doubtless penniless, and I may be able to obtain employment for those of you who may stop at Tripoli, and to assist those who desire to take passage to their homes elsewhere. We are commanded to be grateful to those who befriend us, and as you have shown yourselves to be so, it is right that I, an humble servant of the Great One, should in His name reward you."

Motioning to Gervaise to follow him, the Arab stepped into his boat. Gervaise turned to the men, and said in Italian, "Thanks, my friends, you have well discharged any debt that you may think you owe me. Will you tell that villain" —and he pointed to the captain threateningly —"I warn him that some day I will kill him like a dog!" Then, turning, he stepped into the bow of the boat, and the two men who rowed it at once pushed off.

Chapter XVIII
A Kind Master

When the boat reached the shore the Arab handed a long bernouse to Gervaise, signed to him to pull the hood well over his head, and then led the way through the streets until he stopped at a large house, standing in a quiet quarter of the town. He struck on the door with his hand, and it was at once opened by a black slave.

"Call Muley," the Arab said.

The slave hurried away, and returned in a minute with a man somewhat past middle age, and dressed in a style that indicated that he was a trusted servant.

"Muley," his master said, "I have bought this Christian who has been brought in by Hassan the corsair. He is one of the knights who are the terrors of our coasts, but is, from what I hear, of a kind and humane disposition. I am told that he was a commander of one of their galleys, and though I should not have believed it had I only Hassan's word, I have heard from others that it was so. My wife has long desired to have a Christian slave, and as Allah has blessed my efforts it was but right that I should gratify her, though in truth I do not know what work I shall set him to do at present. Let him first have a bath, and see that he is clad decently, then let him have a good meal. I doubt if he has had one since he was captured. He has been sorely beaten by the corsair, and from no fault of his own, but only because he opposed the man's brutality to a child slave. If any of his wounds need ointment, see that he has it. When all is ready, bring him to the door of my apartments, in order that I may show to my wife that I have gratified her whim."

Then he motioned to Gervaise to follow Muley, who was the head of his household. Gervaise resisted the impulse to thank his new master, and followed in silence.

He was first taken to a bathroom, furnished with an abundance of hot and cold water. Muley uttered an exclamation as, on Gervaise throwing off his bernouse, he saw that his flesh was a mass of bruises. After filling the bath with hot water, he motioned to Gervaise to get in, and lie there until he returned. It was some time before he came back, bringing a pot of ointment and some bandages. It was only on the body that the wounds needed dressing, for here the blows had fallen on the naked skin. When he had dressed them, Muley went out and returned with some Turkish garments, consisting of a pair of baggy trousers of yellow cotton, a white shirt of the same material, and a sleeveless jacket of blue cloth embroidered with yellow trimming; a pair of yellow slippers completed the costume. Muley now took him into another room, where he set before him a dish of rice with a meat gravy, a large piece of bread, and a wooden spoon.

Gervaise ate the food with a deep feeling of thankfulness for the fate that had thrown him into such good hands. Then, after taking a long draught of water, he rose to his feet and followed Muley into the entrance hall. The latter stopped at a door on the opposite side, knocked at it, and then motioned to Gervaise to take off his slippers. The door was opened by the Arab himself.

"Enter," he said courteously, and led Gervaise into an apartment where a lady and two girls were sitting on a divan. They were slightly veiled; but, as Gervaise afterwards learnt, Ben Ibyn was not a Moor, but a Berber, a people who do not keep their women in close confinement as do the Moors, but allow them to go abroad freely without being entirely muffled up.

"Khadja," the merchant said, "this is the Christian slave I purchased today. You have for a long time desired one, but not until now have I found one who would, I thought, satisfy your expectations. What think you of him?"

"He is a noble looking youth truly, Isaac, with his fair, wavy hair, his grey eyes, and white skin; truly, all my neighbours will envy me such a possession. I have often seen Christian slaves before, but they have always been broken down and dejected looking creatures; this one bears himself like a warrior rather than a slave."

"He is a warrior; he is one of those terrible knights of Rhodes whose very name is a terror to the Turks, and whose galleys are feared even by our boldest corsairs. He must be of approved valour, for he was commander of one of these galleys."

The girls looked with amazement at Gervaise. They had often heard tales of the capture of ships that had sailed from Tripoli, by the galleys of the Christian knights, and had pictured those fierce warriors as of almost supernatural strength and valour. That this youth, whose upper lip was but shaded with a slight moustache, should be one of them, struck them as being almost incredible.

"He does not look ferocious, father," one of them said. "He looks pleasant and good tempered, as if he could injure no one."

"And yet this morning, daughter, he braved, unarmed, the anger of Hassan the corsair, on the deck of his own ship; and when the pirate called upon his men to seize him he threw one overboard, struck two more on to the deck, and it needed eight men to overpower him."

"I hope he won't get angry with us!" the younger girl exclaimed. Gervaise could not suppress a laugh, and then, turning to the merchant, said in Turkish, "I must ask your pardon for having concealed from you my knowledge of your tongue. I kept the secret from all on board the corsair, and meant to have done the same here, deeming that if none knew that I spoke the language it would greatly aid me should I ever see an opportunity of making my escape; but, Ben Ibyn, you have behaved so kindly to me that I feel it would not be honourable to keep it a secret from you, and to allow you and the ladies to talk freely before me, thinking that I was altogether ignorant of what you were saying."

"You have acted well and honourably," Ben Ibyn said, putting a hand on his shoulder kindly. "We have heard much of the character of the Order, and that though valiant in battle, your knights are courteous and chivalrous, deeming a deceitful action to be unworthy of them, and binding themselves by their vows to succour the distressed and to be pitiful to the weak. We have heard that our wounded are tended by them in your hospitals with as much care as men of their own race and religion, and that in many things the knights were to be admired even by those who were their foes. I see now that these reports were true, and that although, as you say, it might be of advantage to you that none should know you speak Arabic, yet it is from a spirit of honourable courtesy you have now told us that you do so.

"I did not tell you, wife," he went on, turning to her, "that the reason why he bearded Hassan today was because the corsair brutally struck a little female captive; thus, you see, he, at the risk of his life, and when himself a captive, carried out his vows to protect the defenceless. And now, wife, there is one thing you must know. For some time, at any rate, you must abandon the idea of exciting the envy of your friends by exhibiting your Christian captive to them. As you are aware, the sultan has the choice of any one slave he may select from each batch brought in, and assuredly he would choose this one, did it come to his ears, or to the ears of one of his officers, that a Christian knight had been landed. For this reason Hassan sold him to me for a less sum than he would otherwise have demanded, and we must for some time keep his presence here a secret. My idea is that he shall remain indoors until we move next week into our country house, where he will be comparatively free from observation."

"Certainly, Isaac. I would not on any account that he should be handed over to the sultan, for he would either be put into the galleys or have to labour in the streets."

"I will tell Muley to order the other slaves to say nothing outside of the fresh arrival, so for the present there is no fear of its being talked about in the town. Hassan will, for his own sake, keep silent on the matter. I have not yet asked your name," he went on, turning to Gervaise.

"My name is Gervaise Tresham; but it will be easier for you to call me by my first name only."

"Then, Gervaise, it were well that you retired to rest at once, for I am sure that you sorely need it." He touched a bell on the table, and told Muley, when he appeared, to conduct Gervaise to the place where he was to sleep, which was, he had already ordered, apart from the quarters of the other slaves.

"The young fellow is a mass of bruises," Ben Ibyn said to his wife, when the door closed behind Gervaise. "Hassan beat him so savagely, after they had overpowered and bound him, that he well nigh killed him."

An exclamation of indignation burst from the wife and daughters.

"Muley has seen to his wounds," he went on, "and he will doubtless be cured in a few days. And now, wife, that your wish is gratified, and I have purchased a Christian slave for you, may I ask what you are going to do with him?"

"I am sure I do not know," she said in a tone of perplexity. "I had thought of having him to hand round coffee when my friends call, and perhaps to work in the garden, but I did not think that he would be anything like this."

"That is no reason why he should not do so," Ben Ibyn said. "These Christians, I hear, treat their women as if they were superior beings, and feel it no dishonour to wait upon them; I think you cannot do better than carry out your plan. It is certain there is no sort of work that he would prefer to it; therefore, let it be understood that he is to be your own personal attendant, and that when you have no occasion for his services, he will work in the garden. Only do not for the present let any of your friends see him; they would spread the news like wildfire, and in a week every soul in the town would know that you had a good looking Christian slave, and the sultan's officer would be sending for me to ask how I obtained him. We must put a turban on him. Any one who caught a glimpse of that hair of his, however far distant, would know that he was a Frank."

"We might stain his face and hands with walnut juice," Khadja said, "he would pass as a Nubian. Some of them are tall and strong."

"A very good thought, wife; it would be an excellent disguise. So shall it be." He touched the bell again. "Tell Muley I would speak with him. Muley," he went on, when the steward appeared, "have you said aught to any of the servants touching the Christian?"

"No, my lord; you gave me no instructions about it, and I thought it better to wait until the morning, when I could ask you."

"You did well. We have determined to stain his skin, and at present he will pass as a Nubian. This will avoid all questions and talk."

"But, my lord, they will wonder that he cannot speak their tongue."

"He must pass among them as a mute; but indeed he speaks Arabic as well as we do, Muley."

The man uttered an exclamation of surprise.

"He had intended to conceal his knowledge," Ben Ibyn went on, "which would have been politic; but when he found that my intentions were kind, he told us that he knew our tongue, and now revealed his knowledge, as he thought it would be dishonourable to listen to our talk, leaving us under the impression that he could not understand us."

"Truly these Christians are strange men," Muley said. "This youth, who has not yet grown the hair on his face, is nevertheless commander of a war galley. He is ready to risk his life on behalf of a slave, and can strike down men with his unarmed hand; he is as gentle in his manner as a woman; and now it seems he can talk Arabic, and although it was in his power to keep this secret he tells it rather than overhear words that are not meant for his ear. Truly they are strange people, the Franks. I will prepare some stain in the morning, my lord, and complete his disguise before any of the others see him."

The next morning Muley told Gervaise that his master thought that it would be safer and more convenient for him to pass as a dumb Nubian slave. Gervaise thought the plan an excellent one; and he was soon transformed, Muley shaving that part of the hair that would have shown below the turban, and then staining him a deep brownish black, from the waist upwards, together with his feet and his legs up to his knee, and darkening his eyebrows, eyelashes, and moustache.

"Save that your lips lack the thickness, and your nose is straighter than those of Nubians, no one would doubt but that you were one of that race; and this is of little consequence, as many of them are of mixed blood, and, though retaining their dark colour, have features that in their outline resemble those of the Arabs. Now I will take you to Ben Ibyn, so that he may judge whether any further change is required before the servants and slaves see you."

"That is excellent," the merchant said, when he had carefully inspected Gervaise, "I should pass you myself without recognizing you. Now you can take him into the servants' quarters, Muley, and tell them that he is a new slave whom I have purchased, and that henceforth it will be his duty to wait upon my wife, to whom I have presented him as her special attendant, and that he will accompany her and my daughters when they go abroad to make their purchases or visit their friends. Give some reason, if you can think of one, why you have bestowed him in a chamber separate from the rest."

Gervaise at once took up his new duties, and an hour later, carrying a basket, followed them into the town. It was strange to him thus to be walking among the fanatical Moors, who, had they known the damage that he had inflicted upon their galleys, would have torn him in pieces. None gave him, however, more than a passing look. Nubian slaves were no uncommon sight in the town, and in wealthy Moorish families were commonly employed in places of trust, and especially as attendants in the harems. The ladies were now as closely veiled as the Moorish women, it being only in the house that they followed the Berber customs. Gervaise had learnt from Muley that Ben Ibyn was one of the richest merchants in Tripoli, trading direct with Egypt, Syria, and Constantinople, besides carrying on a large trade with the Berber tribes in the interior. He returned to the house with his basket full of provisions, and having handed these over to the cook, he went to the private apartments, as Khadja had requested him to do. Here she and her daughters asked him innumerable questions as to his country and its customs, and then about Rhodes and the Order to which he belonged. Their surprise was great when they heard that the knights were bound to celibacy.

"But why should they not marry if they like? Why should they not have wives, children, and homes like other people?" Khadja asked.

"It is that they may devote their whole lives to their work. Their home is the convent at Rhodes, or at one of the commanderies scattered over Europe, where they take charge of the estates of the Order."

"But why should they not marry then, Gervaise? At Rhodes there might be danger for women and children, but when they return to Europe to take charge of the estates, surely they would do their duty no worse for having wives?"

Gervaise smiled.

"I did not make the rules of the Order, lady, but I have thought myself that although, so long as they are doing military work at the convent, it is well that they should not marry, yet there is no good reason why, when established in commanderies at home, they should not, like other knights and nobles, marry if it so pleases them."

In the evening the merchant returned from his stores, which were situated down by the port. Soon after he came in he sent for Gervaise. "There is a question I had intended to ask you last night," he said, "but it escaped me. More than two months since there sailed from this port and others many vessels-not the ships of the State, but corsairs. In all, more than twenty ships started, with the intention of making a great raid upon the coast of Italy. No word has since been received of them, and their friends here are becoming very uneasy, the more so as we hear that neither at Tunis nor Algiers has any news been received. Have you heard at Rhodes of a Moorish fleet having been ravaging the coast of Italy?"

"Have you any friends on board the ships that sailed from here, or any interest in the venture, Ben Ibyn?"

The merchant shook his head. "We Berbers," he said, "are not like the Moors, and have but little to do with the sea, save by the way of trade. For myself, I regret that these corsair ships are constantly putting out. Were it not for them and their doings we might trade with the ports of France, of Spain, and Italy, and be on good terms with all. There is no reason why, because our faiths are different, we should be constantly fighting. It is true that the Turks threaten Europe, and are even now preparing to capture Rhodes; but this is no question of religion. The Turks are warlike and ambitious; they have conquered Syria, and war with Egypt and Persia; but the Moorish states are small, they have no thought of conquest, and might live peaceably with Europe were it not for the hatred excited against them by the corsairs."

"In that case I can tell you the truth. Thirteen of those ships were taken into Rhodes as prizes; the other eleven were burnt. Not one of the fleet escaped."

Exclamations of surprise broke from Ben Ibyn, his wife, and daughters.

"I am astonished, indeed," the merchant said. "It was reported here that the Genoese galleys were all laid up, and it was thought that they would be able to sweep the seas without opposition, and to bring home vast spoil and many captives, both from the ships they took and from many of the villages and small towns of the coast. How came such a misfortune to happen to them? It will create consternation here when it is known, for although it was not a state enterprise, the sultan himself and almost all the rich Moors embarked money in the fitting out of the ships, and were to have shares in the spoil taken. How happened it that so strong a fleet was all taken or destroyed, without even one vessel being able to get away to carry home the news of the disaster?"

"Fortune was against them," Gervaise said. "Three ships on their way up were captured by a galley of our Order, and her commander having obtained news of the whereabouts of the spot where the corsairs were to rendezvous, found them all lying together in a small inlet, and launched against them a number of fishing boats fitted out as fire ships. The corsairs, packed closely together, were unable to avoid them, and, as I told you, eleven of their ships were burnt, four were run ashore to avoid the flames, while six, trying to make their way out, were captured by the galley, aided by the three prizes that were taken and which the knights had caused to be manned by Sards."

"The ways of Allah the All Seeing are wonderful," the merchant said. "It was indeed a marvellous feat for one galley thus to destroy a great fleet."

"It was the result of good fortune rather than skill and valour," Gervaise said.

"Nay, nay; let praise be given where it is due. It was a marvellous feat; and although there is good or bad fortune in every event, such a deed could not have been performed, and would not even have been thought of, save by a great commander. Who was the knight who thus with one galley alone destroyed a strongly manned fleet, from which great things had been looked for?"

Gervaise hesitated. "It was a young knight," he said, "of but little standing in the Order, and whose name is entirely unknown outside its ranks."

"By this time it must be well known," Ben Ibyn said; "and it will soon be known throughout Christendom, and will be dreaded by every Moor. What was it?"

Gervaise again hesitated.

"I would not have told you the story at all, Ben Ibyn, had I supposed you would have cared to inquire into the matter. Of course, I will tell you the name if you insist upon it, but I would much rather you did not ask."

"But why?" the merchant asked, in surprise. "If I hear it not from you, I shall assuredly hear it ere long from others, for it will be brought by traders who are in communication with Italy. I cannot understand why you should thus hesitate about telling me the name of this commander. When known it will doubtless be cursed by thousands of Moorish wives and mothers; but we Berbers are another race. None of our friends or kindred were on board the fleet; and we traders have rather reason to rejoice, for, in the first place, so severe a lesson will keep the corsairs in their ports for a long time; and in the second, had the fleet succeeded according to general expectation, so great a store of European goods would have been brought home that the market would have been glutted, and the goods in our storehouses would have lost all their value. What reason, then, can you possibly have in refusing to tell me the name of the commander who has won for himself such credit and glory?"

Gervaise saw that Ben Ibyn was seriously annoyed at what he deemed his unaccountable obstinacy.

"I will tell you, Ben Ibyn, rather than excite your displeasure, though I would much have preferred not to do so, for you speak so much more highly of the affair than it merits. I had myself the honour of being in command of that galley."

The ladies broke into exclamations of surprise, while the merchant regarded him with grave displeasure.

"I had thought you truthful," he said; "but this passes all belief. Dost tell me that a beardless youth could with one galley overcome a great fleet, commanded by the most noted captains on our coast?"

"I thought that you would not believe me," Gervaise said quietly; "and, therefore, would have much preferred to keep silence, knowing that I had no means of supporting my claim. That was not the only reason; the other was, that already a great deal too much has been said about an affair in which, as I have told you, I owed everything to good fortune, and am heartily sick of receiving what I consider altogether undue praise. Ah!" he exclaimed suddenly, "the thought has just occurred to me of a way by which you can obtain confirmation of my story; and, as I value your good opinion and would not be regarded as a boaster and a liar, I entreat you to take it. I heard you tell the eight men who were rowers in my boat when I was captured, to call upon you today, that you might do something for them."

"They came this morning to my store," the merchant said. "They told me their wishes. I promised them that I would make inquiry about ships sailing East; and they are to come to me again tomorrow."

"Then, sir, I beseech you to suffer me to go down with you to your stores and meet them there. The galley of which I was in command at the time I was captured is the same as that in which a few weeks before I fought the corsairs, and these eight men were with me at that time. I begged them for my sake to maintain an absolute silence as to that affair, and I have no doubt that they have done so, for in the fury the news would excite, they might fall victims to the first outburst, though, of course, wholly innocent of any share in the misfortune. Did you question them without my being present, they might still keep silent, fearing to injure me. But if, before you begin to do so, I tell them that they can speak the truth with reference to me, they will, I am sure, confirm my story, incredible as it may now appear to you."

"That is a fair offer," the merchant said gravely, "and I accept it, for it may be that I have been too hasty, and I trust it may prove so. I would rather find myself to be in fault than that the esteem with which you have inspired me should prove to be misplaced. We will speak no further on the subject now. I have not yet asked you how it is that you come to speak our language so well."

Gervaise related how he had studied with Suleiman Ali, and had escorted him to Syria and received his ransom.

"I had hoped," he said, "that the corsair would have taken me to Syria, for there I could have communicated with Suleiman, who would, I am sure, have given me such shelter and aid as he was able, in the event of my making my escape from slavery and finding myself unable to leave by sea."

The next day Gervaise went with Ben Ibyn to his stores. The eight men arrived shortly afterwards, and the merchant, in the presence of Gervaise, questioned them as to whether they knew anything of a misfortune that was said to have befallen some ships that had sailed for the coast of Italy. The men, surprised at the question, glanced at Gervaise, who said, "Tell Ben Ibyn the truth; it will do neither you nor me any harm, and will be mentioned by him to no one else."

Accordingly the story was told. Ben Ibyn listened gravely.

"It was the will of Allah," he said, when it was concluded. "I have wronged you, Gervaise, but your tale seemed too marvellous to be true.

"Do not speak of this to others;" he went on to the eight men. "Now as to yourselves. For the four of you who desire to return to Syria I have taken passage in a trader that sails tomorrow and will touch at Joppa and Acre. Here is money to provide yourselves with garments and to carry you to your homes. For you," he said to two who were natives of the town, "I can myself find employment here, and if your conduct is good, you will have no reason to regret taking service with me. The two of you who desire to go to Smyrna I will give passage there in a ship which will sail next week; in the meantime, here is money for your present wants."

Two days later the merchant's family moved to his house two miles outside the town, and here Gervaise remained for six months. His life was not an unpleasant one; he was treated with great kindness by the merchant and his wife, his duties were but slight, and he had no more labour to perform in the garden than he cared to do. Nevertheless, he felt that he would rather have fallen into the hands of a less kind master, for it seemed to him that it would be an act almost of treachery to escape from those who treated him as a friend; moreover, at the country house he was not in a position to frame any plans for escape, had he decided upon attempting it, nor could he have found out when Hassan made one of his occasional visits to the port.

One evening the merchant returned from the town accompanied by one of the sultan's officers and four soldiers. Ben Ibyn was evidently much depressed and disturbed; he told Muley as he entered, to fetch Gervaise. When the latter, in obedience to the order, came in from the garden, the officer said in Italian, "It having come to the ears of the sultan my master that the merchant Ben Ibyn has ventured, contrary to the law, to purchase a Christian slave brought secretly into the town, he has declared the slave to be forfeited and I am commanded to take him at once to the slaves' quarter."

"I am at the sultan's orders," Gervaise said, bowing his head. "My master has been a kind one, and I am grateful to him for his treatment of me."

Gervaise, although taken aback by this sudden change in his fortunes, was not so cast down as he might otherwise have been; he would now be free to carry out any plan for escape that he might devise, and by his being addressed in Italian it was evident to him that his knowledge of Turkish was unsuspected. When among the other slaves he had always maintained his character of a mute; and it was only when alone in his master's family that he had spoken at all. He had no doubt that his betrayal was due to one of the gardeners, who had several times shown him signs of ill will, being doubtless jealous of the immunity he enjoyed from hard labour, and who must, he thought, have crept up and overheard some conversation; but in that case it was singular that the fact of his knowledge of Turkish had not been mentioned. Gervaise afterwards learned that Ben Ibyn had been fined a heavy sum for his breach of the regulations.

He was now placed between the soldiers, and marched down to the town, without being allowed to exchange a word with the merchant. On his arrival there he was taken to the slaves' quarter; here his clothes were stripped from him, and he was given in their place a ragged shirt and trousers, and then turned into a room where some fifty slaves were lying. Of these about half were Europeans, the rest malefactors who had been condemned to labour.

The appearance of all was miserable in the extreme; they were clothed in rags, and the faces of the Europeans had a dull, hopeless look that told alike of their misery and of their despair of any escape from it. They looked up listlessly as he entered, and then an Italian said, "Cospetto, comrade; but I know not whether your place is with us, or with the Moslems across there. As far as colour goes I should put you down as a Nubian; but your hair is of a hue that consorts but badly with that of your flesh."

"I am an Englishman," Gervaise replied; "but I have been passing under a disguise which has unfortunately been detected, so you see here I am."

The mystery explained, his questioner had no further interest in the matter, and Gervaise, picking out a vacant place on the stone floor, sat down and looked round him. The room, although large, was roughly built, and had doubtless been erected with a view to its present purpose. There were only a few windows; and these were small, strongly barred, and twelve feet above the floor.

"Not easy to get out of them," Gervaise said to himself "at least, not easy without aid; and with these Moslems here it is clear that nothing can be done."

They were roused at daybreak next morning, and were taken out to their work under the guard of six armed Moors, two overseers, provided with long whips, accompanied them. The work consisted of cleaning the streets and working on the roads, and at times of carrying stones for the use of the masons employed in building an addition to the palace of the sultan. This was the work to which the gang was set that morning, and it was not long before the vigour with which Gervaise worked, and the strength he displayed in moving the heavy stones, attracted the attention of the overseers and of the head of the masons.

"That is a rare good fellow you have got there, that black with the curious hair," the latter said. "What is the man? I never saw one like him."

"He is a Christian," one of the overseers said. "He was smuggled into the town and sold to Ben Ibyn the Berber, who, to conceal the matter, dyed him black; but it got to the ears of the sultan, and he had him taken from the Berber, and brought here; I have no doubt the merchant has been squeezed rarely."

"Well, that is a good fellow to work," the other said. "He has just moved a stone, single handed, that it would have taken half a dozen of the others to lift. I wish you would put him regularly on this job; any one will do to sweep the streets; but a fellow like that will be of real use here, especially when the wall rises a bit higher."

"It makes no difference to me," the overseer said. "I will give orders when I go down that he shall be always sent up with whichever gang comes here."

The head mason, who was the chief official of the work, soon saw that Gervaise not only possessed strength, but knowledge of the manner in which the work should be done. Accustomed as he had been to direct the slaves at work on the fortifications at Rhodes, he had learned the best methods of moving massive stones, and setting them in the places that they were to occupy. At the end of the day the head mason told one of the slaves who spoke Italian to inquire of Gervaise whether he had ever been employed on such work before. Gervaise replied that he had been engaged in the construction of large buildings.

"I thought so," the officer said to the overseer; "the way he uses his lever shows that he knows what he is doing. Most of the slaves are worth nothing; but I can see that this fellow will prove a treasure to us."

Gervaise returned to the prison well satisfied with his day's work. The labour, hard though it was, was an absolute pleasure to him. There was, moreover, nothing degrading in it, and while the overseers had plied their whips freely on the backs of many of his companions, he had not only escaped, but had, he felt, succeeded in pleasing his masters. The next morning when the gangs were drawn up in the yard before starting for work, he was surprised at being ordered to leave the one to which he belonged and to fall in with another, and was greatly pleased when he found that this took its way to the spot at which they were at work on the previous day.

At the end of the week, when the work of the day was finished, the head mason came down to the prison and spoke to the governor; a few minutes afterwards Gervaise was called out. The governor was standing in the courtyard with an interpreter.

"This officer tells me that you are skilled in masonry," the governor said, "and has desired that you shall be appointed overseer of the gang whose duty it is to move the stones, saying he is sure that with half the slaves now employed you would get as much work done as at present. Have you anything to say?"

"I thank you, my lord, and this officer," Gervaise replied. "I will do my best; but I would submit to you that it would be better if I could have the same slaves always with me, instead of their being changed every day; I could then instruct them in their work. I would also submit that it were well to pick men with some strength for this labour, for many are so weak that they are well nigh useless in the moving of heavy weights; and lastly, I would humbly submit to you that if men are to do good work they must be fed. This work is as heavy as that in the galleys, and the men there employed receive extra rations to strengthen them; and I could assuredly obtain far better results if the gang employed upon this labour were to receive a somewhat larger supply of food."

"The fellow speaks boldly," the governor said to the head mason, when the reply was translated.

"There is reason in what he says, my lord. Many of the slaves, though fit for the light labour of cleaning the streets, are of very little use to us, and even the whip of the drivers cannot get more than a momentary effort from them. If you can save twenty-five men's labour for other work, it will pay to give more food to the other twenty-five. I should let this man pick out his gang. He has worked in turn with all of them, and must know what each can do; besides, it is necessary that he should have men who can understand his orders."

Gervaise accordingly was allowed to pick out his gang; and he chose those whom he had observed to be the strongest and most handy at the work.

"You will be responsible," the governor said to him, "for the masons being supplied with stone, and if you fail you will be punished and put to other labour."

So far from there being any falling off in the work, the head mason found that, even though the walls began to rise and the labour of transporting the stones into their positions became greater, the masons were never kept standing. The men, finding their position improved, both in the matter of food and in the immunity they enjoyed from blows, worked cheerfully and well. Gervaise did not content himself with giving orders, but worked at the heaviest jobs, and, little by little, introduced many of the appliances used by the skilled masons of Rhodes in transporting and lifting heavy stones. Gradually his own position improved: he was treated as an overseer, and was permitted to sleep under an arcade that ran along one side of the yard, instead of being confined in the close and stifling cell. His dye had long since worn off.

One day as he was going up with his gang under charge of the usual guards to the building, he saw Hassan, who grinned maliciously.

"Ah, ah, Christian dog!" he said; "you threatened me, and I have not forgotten it. The last time I was here I made it known to an officer of the sultan that Ben Ibyn had a Christian slave who had been smuggled in; and here you are. I hope you like the change. Look, I have still got your amulet, and it has brought me better luck than it did you. I have been fortunate ever since, and no money could buy it from me."

He had been walking close to Gervaise as he spoke, and one of the guards pushed him roughly aside.

Time passed on. One day on his return from work a well dressed Moor met him as the gang broke up in the courtyard.

"I have permission to speak to you," he said to Gervaise, and drew him aside. "Know, O Christian, that I have received a letter from Suleiman Ali, of Syria. He tells me that he has heard from Ben Ibyn, the Berber, that you are a slave, and has asked me to inquire of the sultan the price that he will take for your ransom, expressing his willingness to pay whatever may be demanded, and charging me to defray the sum and to make arrangements by which you may return to Europe. This I am willing to do, knowing Suleiman Ali by report as a wealthy man and an honourable one. I saw the sultan yesterday. He told me that I should have an answer this morning as to the ransom that he would take. When I went to him again today, he said that he had learnt from the governor of the prison and from the head mason that you were almost beyond price, that you had been raised to the position of superintendent of the slaves employed in the building of his palace, and that you were a man of such skill that he would not part with you at any price until the work was finished. After that he would sell you; but he named a price threefold that at which the very best white slave in Tripoli would be valued. However, from the way in which Suleiman Ali wrote, I doubt not that he would pay it, great as it is, for he speaks of you in terms of affection, and I would pay the money could you be released at once. As it is, however, I shall write to him, and there will be ample time for an answer to be received from him before the building is finished."

"Truly I am deeply thankful to my good friend, Suleiman Ali; but for reasons of my own I am not desirous of being ransomed at present, especially at such a cost, which I should feel bound in honour to repay to him; therefore, I pray you to write to him, saying that while I thank him from my heart for his kindness, I am not able to avail myself of it. In the first place, I am well treated here, and my position is not an unpleasant one; secondly, the sum required for ransom is altogether preposterous; thirdly, I am not without hopes that I may some day find other means of freeing myself without so great a sacrifice; and lastly, that I have a reason which I cannot mention, why, at present, I would not quit Tripoli, even were I free tomorrow. You can tell him that this is the reason which, most of all, weighs with me. Do not, however, I pray you, let the sultan know that I have refused to be ransomed, for he might think I was meditating an escape, and would order extra precautions to be taken to prevent my doing so. Will you also see Ben Ibyn, and thank him from me for having written to Suleiman Ali on my behalf?"

Chapter XIX
Escape

Gradually a greater amount of liberty was given to Gervaise. Escape from Tripoli was deemed impossible, especially as he was supposed to be entirely ignorant of Arabic. He was, indeed, scarcely regarded now as a slave by the head mason, and instead of being clad in rags was dressed like other overseers. He was no longer obliged to walk with the gang to and from the palace, and was at last granted permission to go into the town for an hour or two after his work was over, instead of returning direct to the prison. The first time this permission was given to him he placed himself on the road by which Ben Ibyn would leave the town, choosing a quiet spot where the meeting would not be observed. Gervaise had for some time taken to staining his face, hands, and legs with walnut juice, beginning with a weak solution, and very gradually increasing the strength until he had reached a shade approximating to that of the lighter coloured portion of the population. The head mason had on one occasion noticed it, and said, "The sun is darkening your skin, Gervaise, until you might verily pass as a Moor."

Gervaise detected an expression of doubt in the tone the officer had spoken to the interpreter, and replied at once, "It is not altogether the sun. Since I have obtained permission to come to my work alone, I have taken to slightly darkening my skin, in order to go to and fro unmolested, and free from the insults that the boys and beggars hurl at Christians."

The master mason nodded approvingly when the answer was translated to him.

"It is a wise step," he said; "for truly the hatred of Christians is very strong among the lower classes, especially since it became known that the galleys that sailed from here nearly two years ago were, with all the fleet from which so much was expected, utterly destroyed. It is well, then, that you should pass unnoticed, for were there a tumult in the street you might lose your life, and I should lose the best labour overseer I have ever had."

Thus, then, as Gervaise walked through the streets on the first occasion of obtaining his liberty, he attracted no attention whatever. When he saw Ben Ibyn approaching he stepped out to meet him. The merchant looked in his face, but for a moment failed to recognise him, then he exclaimed suddenly, "It is Gervaise! Ah, my son, I am indeed rejoiced to see you. We have spoken of you so often at home, and sorely did my wife and daughters grieve when you were torn from us. I did not dare to send any message to you, for the sultan pretended great anger against me, and used the opportunity to squeeze me hardly; but I have frequently made inquiries about you, and was glad indeed to find that even in prison you received promotion; had it been otherwise—had I found that you were in misery—I would have endeavoured, whatever the risk, to aid you to escape."

"I have indeed nothing to complain of, and was sorry to learn that you had suffered on my account. Have you ever learned how it came about that I was denounced?"

"No, indeed; I would have given much to know, and assuredly the dog, whoever he was, should have been made to suffer."

"It was Hassan. The villain met me when I was with the gang, and boasted that it was he who had sent me there. He had told the news to some official, who had, of course, repeated it to the sultan; doubtless he concealed his own share in the matter, otherwise he too would, next time he returned here, have had to pay for his part in it."

"I will make him pay more heavily than the sultan would," Ben Ibyn said sternly; "I will speak to my friends among the merchants, and henceforth no Berber will buy aught from him; and we have hitherto been his best customers. But let us not waste our time in speaking of this wretch. How comes it that you are walking freely in the streets of Tripoli? I can see that your face is stained, although you are no longer a Nubian."

Gervaise told him how it was that he was free to walk in the city after his work was done.

"I shall now," he went on, "be able to carry out any plan of escape that may occur to me; but before I leave, as I shall certainly do ere long, I mean to settle my score with Hassan, and I pray you to send one of the men who were with me in the galley, and whom you took into your employment, directly you hear that his ship is in harbour. Do not give him either a note or a message: bid him simply place himself in the road between the prison gate and the palace, and look fixedly at me as I pass. I shall know it is a signal that Hassan is in the port."

"Can I aid you in your flight? I will willingly do so."

"All that I shall need is the garb of a peasant," Gervaise said. "I might buy one unnoticed; but, in the first place, I have no money, and in the second, when it is known that I have escaped, the trader might recall the fact that one of the slave overseers had purchased a suit of him."

"The dress of an Arab would be the best," the merchant said. "That I will procure and hold in readiness for you. On the day when I send you word that Hassan is here, I will see that the gate of my garden is unbarred at night, and will place the garments down just behind it. You mean, I suppose, to travel by land?"

"I shall do so for some distance. Were I to steal a boat from the port, it would be missed in the morning, and I be overtaken. I shall therefore go along the coast for some distance and get a boat at one of the villages, choosing my time when there is a brisk wind, and when I may be able to get well beyond any risk of being overtaken. Now, Ben Ibyn, I will leave you; it were better that we should not meet again, lest some suspicion might fall upon you of having aided in my escape. I cannot thank you too much for all your past kindness, and shall ever bear a grateful remembrance of yourself and your family."

"Perhaps it were better so," Ben Ibyn said; "for if the Moors can find any excuse for plundering us, they do so. Have you heard the news that the Sultan of Turkey's expedition for the capture of Rhodes is all but complete, and will assuredly sail before many weeks have passed?"

"I have not heard it," Gervaise replied; "and trust that I may be in time to bear my share in the defence. However, the blow has been so often threatened that it may be some time before it falls."

"May Allah bless you, my son, and take you safely back to your friends! Be assured that you shall have notice as soon as I know that Hassan has returned, and you shall have the bundle with all that is needful, behind my gate."

Another two months passed. Gervaise looked in vain for Ben Ibyn's messenger as he went to and from the palace, and chafed terribly at the delay, when, for aught he knew, the Turkish fleet might already have brought Mahomet's army to Rhodes. At last, as he came back from work, he saw with intense satisfaction one of the men, whose face he recognised, leaning carelessly against the wall. The man gave no sign of recognition, but looked at him earnestly for a minute, and then sauntered off up the street. Gervaise went up into the town as usual, walked about until it became quite dark, and then went to the gate that led into the merchant's garden. He found that it was unfastened, and, opening it, he went in and closed it behind him. As he did so he started, for a voice close by said,

"Master, it is I, the messenger whom you saw two hours since. Ben Ibyn bade me say that he thought you might require some service, and, knowing that I could be trusted, bade me wait for you here. He thought that you might possibly need a messenger to Hassan."

"The very thing," Gervaise exclaimed. "I have been puzzling myself in vain as to how I could get speech with him in some quiet place; but with your assistance that will be easy; but first let me put on this disguise."

This was easily effected, even in the dark. A loose flowing robe of white cotton, girt in at the waist, a long bernouse with hood to cover the head, a sash with a dagger, and a scimitar, completed the disguise.

"Here is a pouch," the man said, "with money for your journey, and a long sword, which he says you can hang at your back beneath your bernouse."

Gervaise gave an exclamation of pleasure. By its length and weight he was sure that the weapon must have been the property of a Christian knight.

"Shall I carry the message this evening?" the man asked. "It is early still, and it were best that you should not linger in the city, where there is sure to be a strict search for you in the morning."

"But perhaps he may recognise your face?"

"It is blackened, my lord, and I am dressed as you were when with Ben Ibyn."

"Let us settle our plans, then, before we sally out from here; we could not find a safer place for talking. What message, think you, would be the most likely to tempt Hassan to come ashore? You do not know what spoil he has brought?"

"No; besides, if a merchant wanted to buy he would go on board to inspect Hassan's wares. We must have something to sell. It must be something tempting, and something that must be disposed of secretly. I might tell him that my employer-and I would mention some merchant whose name would carry weight with him-has received from the interior a large consignment of slaves, among whom are three or four girls, who would fetch high prices in Egypt, and as he believes they have been captured from a tribe within the limits of the sultan's territory, he is anxious to get rid of them, and will either dispose of them all cheaply in a lot, or will hand them over to him to take to Egypt to sell, giving him a large commission for carrying them there and disposing of them."

"I do not like tempting even an enemy by stories that are untrue," Gervaise said doubtfully.

"I have no scruples that way," the man said, with a laugh; "and it is I who shall tell the story, and not you."

Gervaise shook his head.

"Could you not say that you came from one who owes him a heavy debt and desires to pay him?"

"I do not think that would bring him ashore. Hassan doubtless trades for ready money, and must be well aware that no one here can be greatly in his debt. No, my lord; leave the matter in my hands. I will think of some story before I go on board that will fetch him ashore. But first we must settle where I am to bring him; there are some deserted spots near the wall on the east side of the town."

"I know where you mean," Gervaise agreed; "let us go in that direction at once, for the sooner you are off the better."

In half an hour a spot was fixed on, near some huts that had fallen into ruin. Here Gervaise seated himself on a sand heap, while the man hurried away. The moon had just risen, it being but three days since it was at its full. The night was quiet; sounds of music, laughter, and occasional shouts came faintly from the town. Seated where he was, Gervaise could see the port and the ships lying there. Half an hour later he saw a boat row off to one of them, which he had already singled out, from its size and general appearance, as being that of Hassan; ten minutes later he saw it returning. At that distance separate figures could not be made out, but it seemed to him that it loomed larger than before, and he thought that certainly one, if not more, persons, were returning with his messenger. Presently he heard men approaching; then Hassan's voice came distinctly to his ears.

"How much farther are you going to take me? Remember, I warned you that unless I found that my journey repaid me, it would be bad for you."

"It is but a few yards farther, my lord. There is my master the sheik of the Beni Kalis awaiting you."

Gervaise rose to his feet as Hassan and two of his crew came up.

"Now," the former said roughly, "where have you bestowed these captives you want to sell me?"

"Will you please to follow me into this courtyard?" Gervaise said. He had, while waiting, reconnoitred the neighbourhood, and found an enclosure with the walls still perfect, and had determined to bring Hassan there, in order to prevent him from taking to flight. Hassan entered it unsuspectingly, followed by his two men. Gervaise fell back a little, so as to place himself between them and the entrance. Then he threw back the hood of his bernouse.

"Do you recognise me, Hassan?" he said sternly. "I am the captive whom you beat almost to death. I told you that some day I would kill you; but even now I am willing to forgive you and to allow you to depart in peace, if you will restore the amulet you took from me."

The corsair gave a howl of rage.

"Christian dog!" he exclaimed. "You thought to lead me into a trap, but you have fallen into one yourself. You reckoned that I should come alone; but I suspected there was something hidden behind the story of that black, and so brought two of my crew with me. Upon him, men! Cut him down!" So saying, he drew his scimitar, and sprang furiously upon Gervaise. The latter stepped back into the centre of the gateway, so as to prevent the men, who had also drawn their swords, passing to attack him from behind. He had undone the clasp of his bernouse, and allowed it to fall to the ground as he addressed Hassan, and his long sword flashed in the moonlight as the corsair sprang forward.

Hassan was a good swordsman, and his ferocious bravery had rendered him one of the most dreaded of the Moorish rovers. Inferior in strength to Gervaise, he was as active as a cat, and he leapt back with the spring of a panther, avoiding the sweeping blow with which Gervaise had hoped to finish the conflict at once; the latter found himself therefore engaged in a desperate fight with his three assailants. So furiously did they attack him that, foot by foot, he was forced to give ground. As he stepped through the gateway one of the pirates sprang past him, but as he did so, a figure leapt out from beyond the wall, and plunged a dagger into his back, while at the same moment, by cutting down another pirate, Gervaise rid himself of one of his assailants in front; but as he did so, he himself received a severe wound on the left shoulder from Hassan, who, before he could again raise his weapon, sprang upon him, and tried to hurl him to the ground.

Gervaise's superior weight saved him from falling, though he staggered back some paces; then his heel caught against a stone, and he fell, dragging Hassan to the ground with him. Tightly clasped in each other's arms, they rolled over and over. Gervaise succeeded at last in getting the upper hand, but as he did so Hassan twisted his right arm free, snatched the dagger from Gervaise's girdle, and struck furiously at him. Gervaise, who had half risen to his knees, was unable to avoid the blow, but threw himself forward, his weight partly pinning the corsair's shoulders to the ground, and the blow passed behind him, inflicting but a slight wound in the back; then, with his right hand, which was now free, he grasped Hassan by the throat with a grip of iron. The pirate struggled convulsively for a moment, then his left hand released his grasp of his opponent's wrist. A minute later Gervaise rose to his feet: the pirate was dead.

Gervaise stooped and raised the fallen man's head from the ground, felt for the chain, pulled up Claudia's gage, and placed it round his own neck; then he turned to his guide.

"I have to thank you for my life," he said, holding out his hand to him. "It would have gone hard with me if that fellow had attacked me from behind. I had not bargained for three of them."

"I could not help it, my lord. It was not until Hassan had stepped down into the boat that I knew he was going to take any one with him; then he suddenly told two of his men to take their places by him, saying to me, as he did so, 'I know not whether this message is a snare; but mind, if I see any signs of treachery, your life at any rate will pay the forfeit.' I knew not what to do, and indeed could do nothing; but, knowing my lord's valour, I thought that, even against these odds, you might conquer with such poor aid as I could give you."

"It was not poor aid at all," Gervaise said heartily. "Greatly am I indebted to you, and sorry indeed am I, that I am unable to reward you now for the great service that you have rendered me."

"Do not trouble about that, my lord. I am greatly mistaken if I do not find in the sashes of these three villains sufficient to repay me amply for my share in this evening's work. And now, my lord, I pray you to linger not a moment. The gates of the town shut at ten o'clock, and it cannot be long from that hour now. But first, I pray you, let me bind up your shoulder; your garment is soaked with blood."

"Fortunately my bernouse will hide that; but it were certainly best to staunch the blood before I start, for it would be hard for me to get at the wound myself."

The man took one of the sashes of the corsairs, tore it into strips, and bandaged the wound; then with another he made a sling for the arm. As he took off the sashes a leather bag dropped from each, and there was a chink of metal. He placed them in his girdle, saying, "I shall have time to count them when I get back."

Gervaise sheathed his sword, and put on the bernouse, pulling the hood well over his head; then, with a few more words of thanks, started for the gate, leaving the man to search Hassan's girdle.

The gate was a quarter of a mile distant. Gervaise passed through with the usual Arabic salutation to the sentry, and with difficulty repressed a shout of exultation as he left Tripoli behind him.

Following the coast road he walked till daylight; then he left it and lay down among the sand hills for five or six hours. He calculated that no pursuit would be begun until midday. His absence was not likely to be noticed until the gangs began work in the morning, when an alarm would be given. The sentries at the gates on the previous evening would be questioned, and when it was found that no one answering to his description had passed out before these were closed, there would be a rigid search throughout the city and port. The vessels would all be examined, and the boatmen questioned as to whether any craft was missing. Not until the search proved absolutely fruitless would it be seriously suspected that he had, either by passing through the gates in disguise, or by scaling the walls, made for the interior. None knew that he could speak Arabic, and it would be so hopeless an undertaking for any one unacquainted with the language to traverse the country without being detected, that the Moors would be slow to believe that he had embarked upon such adventure. However, when all search for him in the town and in the vessels in the port proved fruitless, doubtless mounted men would be despatched in all directions; some would take the coast roads, while others would ride into the interior to warn the head men of the villages to be on the lookout for an escaped slave.

After a sleep of five hours, Gervaise pursued his journey. He had walked for eight hours, and calculated that he must be fully thirty miles from Tripoli, and that not until evening would searchers overtake him. After walking four miles he came to a large village. There he purchased a bag of dates, sat down on a stone bench by the roadside to eat them, and entered into conversation with two or three Moors who sauntered up. To these he represented that he belonged to a party of his tribe who had encamped for the day at a short distance from the village in order to rest their horses before riding into Tripoli, whither they were proceeding to exchange skins of animals taken in the chase, and some young horses, for cotton clothes, knives, and other articles of barter with the tribes beyond them.

After quenching his thirst at a well in front of the mosque, he retraced his steps until beyond the village, then struck out into the country, made a detour, came down into the road again, and continued his journey eastward. He walked until nightfall, and then again lay down.

He was now fully fifty miles from Tripoli, and hoped that he was beyond the point to which horsemen from that town would think of pursuing their search. It was likely that they would not have gone beyond the village at which he had halted on the previous day; for when they learned from the inhabitants that no stranger, save an Arab, had entered it, they would content themselves with warning the head man to be on the watch for any stranger unable to speak their tongue, and would not consider it necessary to push their steps farther.

For four days Gervaise continued his journey. At each village through which he passed he added to his stock of dates, until he had as many as he could carry under his bernouse without attracting observation. He also purchased a large water bottle, which he slung round his neck.

All this time the sea lay to his left like a sheet of glass, and he knew that until a change of weather occurred, it was useless for him to attempt to escape by boat. On the fifth day there were signs of a change. He saw a dark line far out at sea; it came across the water rapidly, and presently a gentle breeze began to blow from the northwest; it gradually increased in strength, and when, in the afternoon, he stopped at a village, the waves were breaking upon the shore.

After repeating his usual story, he sauntered down to the water's edge. There were several boats hauled up, and a hundred yards out two or three larger craft were lying at anchor. He entered into conversation with some of the fishermen, and his questions as to the boats led them to believe him altogether ignorant of the sea. The craft were, they told him, used sometimes for fishing, but they often made voyages to towns along the coast with dates and other produce. Each boat carried a single short mast, to the top of which was attached a long tapering spar, on which the sail was furled.

Gervaise knew that these small feluccas were generally fast sailors and fair sea boats, and resolved to seize one of them, trusting that when once the sail was shaken out he would be able to manage it single handed. Accustomed to boats, he picked out that which he thought would be the fastest, and then walked away for half a mile, and lay down to sleep until the village was silent for the night. He had with him some oaten cakes he had bought there, a string of fish he had purchased from the boatmen, and with these and the dates he thought he could manage for four or five days at least. As to water, he could only hope that he should find a supply on board the boat. When he judged it to be about ten o'clock he went down to the shore again, took off his clothes and made them into a bundle; then, wading out into the water to within fifty yards of the felucca, swam off to it, towing the bundle behind him.

He had no difficulty in climbing on board, and after dressing himself in the clothes he had worn at Tripoli, and had kept on underneath the Arab attire, he pulled the head rope until the craft was nearly over the anchor. He then loosened the line that brailed up the sail, got the stone that served as an anchor on board, hauled the sheet aft, and took his place at the tiller. The wind had dropped a good deal with the sun, but there was still sufficient air to send the light craft fast through the water. He steered out for a time, and then, when he thought himself a good mile from the shore, headed east. By the appearance of the water as it glanced past, he thought that he must be making from five to six miles an hour, and when the sun rose at five o'clock, believed that he was nearly forty miles on his way. He now fastened the tiller with a rope and proceeded to overhaul the craft.

It was decked over forward only, and he crept into the cabin, which was little more than three feet high. The first thing his eye lit on was a bulky object hanging against the side, and covered with a thick black blanket of Arab manufacture. Lifting this, he saw, as he expected, that the object beneath it was a large waterskin well filled; the blanket had evidently been placed over it to keep it cool when the sun streamed down on the deck above it. There was also a large bag of dates, and another of flat cakes, and he guessed that these had all been put on board the evening before, in readiness for a start in the morning. This relieved him of his chief anxiety, for he had been unable to think of any plan for replenishing his supply, or to concoct a likely tale that, were he obliged to go on shore, would account for his being alone in a craft of that size.

The wind increased again after sunrise, and being unable to reef the sail single handed he managed partially to brail it up. All day the craft flew along with the wind on the quarter, making six or seven miles an hour; and he felt that by morning he would be well beyond pursuit. On the run he passed several craft engaged in fishing, but these gave him no uneasiness. He had in the morning, with some old sails he found, constructed three rough imitations of human figures, one with the Arab dress and another with the bernouse, and had placed them against the bulwarks, so that at a short distance it would appear that there were three men on board. Feeling confident that the deception would not be noticed, he kept his course without swerving, and passed some of the fishing boats within hailing distance, waving his hand and shouting the usual Arab salutation to their crews.

During the day he contented himself with eating some dates and an oatmeal cake or two; but at sunset he added to this two or three fish that he had split open and hung up to dry in the sun and wind. There was charcoal on board, and a flat stone served as a hearth in the bottom of the boat, but he had no means of lighting a fire, for this the fishermen would have brought off when they came on board in the morning. After he had finished his meal and taken his place again at the tiller he altered his course. Hitherto he had been steering to the south of east, following the line of coast, but he now saw before him the projecting promontory of Cape Mezurata, which marks the western entrance of the great Gulf of Sydra; and he now directed his course two points north of east, so as to strike the opposite promontory, known as Grenna, more than a hundred miles away. The wind fell much lighter, and he shook out the sail to its full extent. All night he kept at his post, but finding the wind perfectly steady he lashed the tiller so as to keep the boat's head in the direction in which he was steering, and dozed for some hours, waking up occasionally to assure himself that she was keeping her course.

At sunrise he indulged in a wash in sea water, and felt freshened and revived. He now kept a sharp lookout for distant sails, for he was out of the ordinary course a coaster would take, and would have attracted the attention of any corsair coming out from the land; the sea, however, remained clear of ships. All day the felucca made rapid progress, for although the wind freshened, Gervaise did not lessen sail as before, being now accustomed to the boat and confident of her powers. As soon as the wind died away again after sunset, he lay down for a good sleep, feeling this was an absolute necessity, and knowing that before morning he should be obliged to keep a sharp lookout for land. He slept longer than he had intended, for the day was breaking when he opened his eyes. He sprang to his feet, and saw the land stretching ahead of him at a distance, as he thought, of some fifteen miles, and at once put the helm down and bore more to the north.

He judged, from what he had heard on the coast, that he must be nearly off Cape Tejones, behind which lies the town of Bengasi, and was confirmed in the belief on finding half an hour later that the coast, which had run nearly north and south, trended sharply away to the northeast. All day long he kept about the same distance from the land, and at night, instead of keeping on his course, brailed up the sail entirely, and allowed the vessel to drift, as he knew that before morning he should lose the coast if he continued as he was going. He slept without moving until daylight, and then saw, to his satisfaction, by means of landmarks he had noticed the evening before, that the boat had drifted but a few miles during the night. As the day went on, he saw that the coastline was now east and west, and felt that he must be off the most northerly point of the promontory; he accordingly laid his course to the northeast, which would take him close to Cape Saloman, the most easterly point of Crete, and from two hundred and fifty to three hundred miles distant.

For twenty-four hours he sailed quietly on, the wind dropping lighter and lighter; then it suddenly died out altogether; for some hours there was not a breath to stir the surface of the water, and the heat was stifling. Gervaise slept for some time; when he awoke the same stillness reigned, but there was a change in the appearance of the sky; its brightness was dulled by a faint mist, while, although the sea was of a glassy smoothness, there was an imperceptible swell that caused the felucca to sway uneasily. Gervaise had sufficient experience of the Levant to know that these signs were ominous of a change, and he at once set to work to prepare for it. Although he saw that it would be difficult for him unaided to hoist the long spar back into its place, he decided to lower it. This was not difficult, as its weight brought it down on to the deck as soon as he slackened the halliards; he unhooked it from the block, and then lashed the sail securely to it. When he had done this he looked round. A bank of dark clouds lay across the horizon to the northwest, and in a short time he could see that this was rising rapidly.

Before taking down the spar and sail, he had deliberated as to whether it would be better to run before the coming gale or to lie to, and had decided on the latter alternative, as, were it to continue to blow long, he might be driven on to the Egyptian coast. Moreover, the felucca's bow was much higher out of water than the stern, and he thought that she would ride over the waves with greater safety than she would did they sweep down upon her stern.

He had heard that the Greeks, when caught in a sudden gale in small boats, often lashed the oars together, threw them overboard with a rope attached, and rode to them safely through a sea that would otherwise have overwhelmed them. After much consideration as to what had best be done, he took the anchor rope, which was some sixty yards in length, fastened one end to each end of the spar, and then lashed the middle of the rope to the bow of the felucca; then, using an oar as a lever, he with great labour managed to launch the spar over the bow, with the sail still attached to it.

When he had completed this, he looked round at the state of the weather. The clouds had risen so fast that their edge was nearly overhead, spanning the sky like a great arch. Ahead of him it seemed almost as black as night. He had not been out in many of the gales that at times sweep the eastern waters of the Mediterranean with terrible violence, but had seen enough of them to know that it was no ordinary one that he was about to encounter. He looked over the bow; the spar at present was lying in contact with the stem. With an oar he pushed it across so as to be at right angles with the craft, and then, there being nothing else to do, sat down and waited for the storm to burst. In a short time he heard a dull moaning sound, a puff of wind struck the boat, but in a few seconds died out; it was sufficient to give the light craft stern way, and she drifted backwards, the rope tightening, until the spar lay across her bows, and some twenty yards away.

The dull moaning had grown louder; and now ahead of him he saw a white line. It approached with extraordinary rapidity. Knowing the fury with which it would burst upon him, he leapt down, and stood at the entrance to the cabin, with his head just above the deck. With a deafening roar the wind struck the boat, which staggered as if she had on her full course struck on a rock, while a shower of spray flew over her. Half blinded and deafened, Gervaise crawled into the cabin, closed the door, and lay down there; whatever happened, there was nothing he could do. He was soon conscious that the spar and sail were doing their work, for the boat still lay head to wind. The noise overhead and around was deafening; above the howl of the wind could be heard the creaking of the timbers, and the boat seemed to shiver as each fresh gust struck her.

In half an hour he looked out again. There was, as yet, but little sea; the force of the wind seemed to flatten the water, and the instant a wave lifted its head it was cut off as if by a knife, and carried away in spray. The boat herself was moving rapidly through the water, dragging the spar behind her, and Gervaise almost trembled at the thought of the speed at which she would have flown along had it not been for the restraint of the floating anchor. Gradually the sea got up, but the light craft rode easily over it, and Gervaise, after commending his safety to God, lay down, and was soon fast asleep. In spite of the motion of the vessel, he slept soundly for many hours. When he awoke he opened the cabin door and looked out. A tremendous sea was running, but he thought the wind, although so strong that he could scarce lift his head above the shelter of the bulwark, was less violent than it had been when it first broke upon him. He saw to his satisfaction that the felucca breasted the waves lightly, and that although enveloped in spray she took no green water over the bows.

The spar and sail acted not only as a floating anchor, but as a breakwater, and the white crested waves, which came on as if they would break upon the boat, seemed robbed of half their violence by the obstruction to their course, and passed under the felucca without breaking. For forty-eight hours the gale continued; at the end of that time it ceased almost as suddenly as it had begun. The sun shone brightly out, the clouds cleared entirely away. It was some hours before the sea went down sufficiently for Gervaise to attempt to get the spar on deck again. It was a heavy task, taxing his strength to the utmost, but after a deal of labour it was got on board, and then raised to its position at the masthead; the sail was shaken out, and the felucca again put on her course.

Chapter XX
Beleaguered

One morning towards the end of May, 1480, Sir John Boswell was standing with some other knights on St. Stephen's Hill, near the city, having hurried up as soon as a column of smoke from a bonfire lighted by the lookout there, gave the news that the Turkish fleet was at last in sight. A similar warning had been given a month previously, but the fleet had sailed past the island, being bound for Phineka, which was the rendezvous where Mahomet's great armament was to assemble. There could be but little doubt that the long expected storm was this time about to burst. The fleet now seen approaching numbered a hundred and sixty large ships, besides a great number of small craft, conveying a force variously estimated at from seventy to a hundred thousand men.

"'Tis a mighty fleet," Sir John said; "and the worst of it is that we know there are more to follow; still, I doubt not we shall send them back defeated. Our defences are all complete; our recent peace with Egypt has enabled us to fill up our magazines with provisions of all kinds; the inhabitants of the Island have had ample warning to move into the town, carrying with them everything of value; so the Turks will obtain but little plunder, and will be able to gather no means of subsistence on the island, as every animal has been driven within the walls, and even the unripe corn has been reaped and brought in. However long the siege lasts, we need be in no fear of being reduced to sore straits for food. Look over there. There is a small craft under sail, and it comes not from the direction of Phineka. See! one of the Turkish galleys has separated from the rest and is making off in that direction. It may be that the little craft contains one or two of our comrades who are late in coming to join us."

"It may well be so, Sir John, for they have been straggling in by twos and threes for the last month."

"I will get the grand master's leave to put out in one of the galleys," Sir John said, "for, by the way they are bearing, the Turks will cut the little craft off before she can gain the port."

He hurried to D'Aubusson, who was standing a short distance apart from the others, gazing at the Turkish fleet. A minute later he was running down the hill to the town, accompanied by three or four other knights; they made direct for the outer port, where two galleys were lying in readiness, leapt on board one of them, which already contained its quota of knights, and at once rowed out of the port. Just as they did so the Turkish galley fired a gun.

"I fear we shall be too late," Sir John said; "the Turk is gaining fast on the other craft, whatever she may be. There goes another gun. Row your hardest!" he shouted down to the slaves.

The Turkish ship did not fire again; the wind was light, and they were going two feet through the water to every one sailed by the other craft. The galley from Rhodes was still half a mile away when the Turk was close to the boat that was trying to escape. Sir John and the knights chafed as they saw they would be too late.

"I can't make out why the boat did not use her oars," the former said. "Of course, she could not have kept away from the galley, but if she had rowed it would have made some difference, and we might have been nearly up."

"I can only see one man on board of her, Sir John," one of the younger knights said; and two or three others murmured that they were of the same opinion.

"The others must be lying down; she cannot have less than from fifteen to twenty men. The Turk is close alongside. They still hold on. There! She has gone about and escaped the attempt to run her down. Now she is heading for us again! Brave fellows! brave fellows!" Sir John exclaimed, while a cheer broke from those around him; "but they have done for themselves. They must have seen us coming out, and if they had surrendered might have hoped to have been retaken. Their chance of getting quarter was truly not great, for expecting-as the Turks do-to carry off both us and all the inhabitants of the Island, a dozen fishermen would have seemed to them scarcely worth keeping. However, by holding on they have thrown away any chance they may have had. The Turks are alongside; they are leaping down into the little craft. Ah! Two more galleys have just left their fleet, and are heading here."

"See, Sir John," one of the knights exclaimed, "there is a single man standing in the bow of that craft: he is facing the Moors alone. See how they crowd there; you can see the weapons flashing in the sun. They have to press past the mast to get at him, and as yet he seems to hold them all at bay."

"He has chosen his post well, D'Urville. The number of his assailants prevents the archers on the Turkish craft using their bows. Fire those bow guns!" he shouted to the knights forward: "Take steady aim at the galley. It will distract their attention."

"Nobly done indeed!" one of the other knights shouted. "I have seen him strike down four of the Turks."

"Row, men, row! 'Tis useless!" Sir John muttered, as he clenched the hilt of his sword. "Useless! A Roland could not long maintain so unequal a fight."

A groan broke from those around him as suddenly the dark mass of the assailants made a forward move, and the single figure was lost to sight. It was but for an instant; a moment later the crowd separated, and a man was seen to spring overboard.

"They will riddle him with their spears when he comes up; we shall have nothing to do but to avenge him. To your stations, comrades! It is our turn now, and we have no time to lose, for the other two Turks will be up in twenty minutes, and I had orders not to fight if it could be avoided: but we must take this fellow."

Five minutes later the galley ran alongside the Turk, to which those who had captured the boat had already hastily returned. The ships discharged their guns into each other, and then, as the galley ran alongside, the knights tried to leap on board of her. They were opposed by a dense mass of Turks, for in addition to her usual crew the Moslem was crowded with troops. For three or four minutes the knights tried, but in vain, to get a footing on board; then Sir John shouted to them to forbear, and gave orders to the rowers at once to push off. A cloud of arrows swept across the poop as they did so; but for the most part these fell harmless from the armour of the knights. For a time the cannon on both sides continued to fire, but as the Christians increased their distance it gradually ceased.

They had gone but a hundred yards from the Turk when a head appeared over the stern railing of the poop, and a figure swung itself on to the deck. The man was attired in Turkish garments, but his head was bare, and the exclamation, "A Christian!" broke from the knights.

The man strode up to Sir John Boswell.

"You used to say you would make matters even with me some day, Sir John, and you have more than kept your word."

Sir John fell back a pace in astonishment, and then with a shout, "By St. George, it is Tresham!" threw his arms round Gervaise's neck, while the knights thronged round with exclamations of satisfaction.

"And it was you whom we saw keep the Turks at bay for three good minutes single handed," Sir John said, holding Gervaise at arm's length to gaze into his face. "Truly it seemed well nigh impossible that any one who was like to be on that craft could have performed so doughty a deed. And how did you escape?"

"It was simple enough," Gervaise replied. "As soon as I dived I turned and swam along under the boat and came up by the stern, and then held on by the rudder, sheltered from their sight. I saw that the galley would be up in five minutes, and had no fear of their wasting time to look for me. Directly you came alongside her I dived again, and rose under your stern. I did not think that you would be able to take her, for all their craft are crowded with troops; so I contented myself with holding on until you were out of reach of their arrows, and then I climbed up."

"I am delighted to see you again, Gervaise. I was feeling very sore at the moment, and I know the others felt the same, at being obliged to sheer off without making a capture; but the grand master's orders were strict. We noted your craft pursued by the Turks, and I asked leave to take out a galley to cut her off. He said, 'Take one, Sir John, but do not adventure an attack against the Turk unless she is likely to fall an easy prize to you. Her capture would be of little benefit to us, and would be dearly purchased at the cost of a knight's life. Therefore, as soon as we engaged her, and I found that she was full of troops and could not be captured without heavy loss, and that two of her consorts might arrive before we accomplished it, it was plainly my duty to abandon the attempt, although, you may guess, it went sorely against the grain to give the order, especially as I knew that a host would be looking on from St. Stephen's Hill. However, your rescue more than makes up for our failure; and thankful indeed am I that I made the suggestion that we should put out to save that little craft, though I thought it contained but a few fishermen or some coasting sailors, who had, in ignorance that the Turks were at hand, tried to enter Rhodes. One of those looking on with me did, indeed, suggest that she might have on board a knight or two coming to join us, but I did not give the matter a second thought."

"And how go things, Sir John? And how are old friends?"

"Ralph Harcourt and, I think, all your comrades in the Santa Barbara, except the three who fell by your side when you were captured, are well, and at present on the Island, as, for the last two years, none have been allowed to depart. As to other matters, they go not so well as one could wish. The commanderies have not responded to our call for aid as they should have done. For this, however, they are not altogether to blame, for we have been so often threatened with attack, and have so frequently applied for aid in money or men, that they must have begun to doubt whether the danger was really imminent. In other respects we are well prepared. We have obtained large stores of provisions from Egypt, and shall have no ground for uneasiness on that score. The defences have been greatly strengthened, and no one fears that we shall not be able to beat off an attack. We have destroyed the principal buildings outside the walls, though it would have been better could we have gone much further in this direction. And now let us have your adventures and escape."

"'Tis a long story, Sir John, and I must pray you to let me defer it for a time. In the first place, I have two or three wounds that I shall be glad to have bandaged."

"Why did you not say so at once?" Sir John exclaimed. "In those dark clothes, soaked with water as they are, I did not see the bloodstains; but I ought to have looked for them, for surely no one could have gone through that fight-altogether unprotected with armour too-without being wounded. Come below, and we will attend to them."

"Also order me some wine and food, Sir John; I have touched nothing save water for twenty-four hours, and before that fasted somewhat strictly."

By the time Gervaise's wounds, which were not severe, had been bandaged, and he had eaten a hasty meal, the galley was alongside the mole, between the two harbours.

He was provided with some clothes, and went with Sir John straight to the English auberge, where the knight insisted that he should at once lie down.

"I will report your return to D'Aubusson, and will tell him it is by my orders that you are resting. Your wounds are not very deep, but you must have lost a good deal of blood, and were you to exert yourself now, and be pestered with questions, it would probably bring on an attack of fever. There is nothing to do at present, for it must be some days before they can land and bring up their guns."

Gervaise obeyed the orders not unwillingly, for he felt that he was really weak, and was greatly worn out by want of sleep. Sir John Kendall, at Boswell's request, issued orders that he was on no account whatever to be disturbed, and that no one was to enter his room unless he sounded the bell placed by the bedside. Gervaise indeed, falling off to sleep a few minutes after he had lain down, did not awake until the following morning. Having no idea that he had slept more than two or three hours, he sounded the bell in order to inquire whether Ralph had returned to the auberge. He was surprised to find his friend had just risen, and that he himself had been asleep some eighteen hours!

A few minutes later Ralph hurried into the room.

"Thank God that you are back again, Gervaise!" he said, as he grasped the hand of his friend. "I did not return until late in the evening, having been at work with a large body of slaves at the fortifications; and you may guess what joy I felt at the news. You are changed a good deal."

"I don't suppose you will think so at the end of a day or two, Ralph. I lost a good deal of blood yesterday, and have been on short rations; but I shall very soon pick up again."

"They will bring you some broth and wine directly, Gervaise. Early as it is, the grand master has already sent down to inquire as to your health."

"I will reply in person as soon as I have had a meal and dressed."

"And I suppose we must all wait to hear what you have been doing until you return, Gervaise?"

"I suppose so, Ralph. Of course it is a long story; but I must tell you at once that there is nothing very exciting in it, and that it differed little from that of others who have been prisoners among the Moors, save that I was strangely fortunate, and suffered no hardships whatever. And now I want to ask you about clothes. Have my things been sold, or are they still in the store?"

"No; the question was raised but a short time since. It was mooted, by the way, by that old enemy of yours, Robert Rivers, who returned here some three months ago with a batch of knights from the English commanderies. Sir John Boswell answered him roundly, I can tell you, and said that they should be kept, were it for another fifty years, for that he would wager his life that you would sooner or later make your escape."

"I am sorry that fellow has returned, Ralph. Has he got a commandery yet?"

"No; I believe that Sir John Kendall sent home so bad a report of him, that even the great influence of his family has not sufficed to obtain his appointment, and that he has been merely the assistant at one of the smaller manors. Sir John Boswell told me in confidence that he understood that Rivers did not at first volunteer to come out in response to the appeal of the grand master, but that the grand prior informed him that unless he took this opportunity of retrieving his character, he might give up all hope of ever obtaining advancement. Ah, here is your breakfast."

An hour later Gervaise presented himself at the palace, clothed in the suit of armour that had been given to him by Genoa. Although he was engaged with several members of the council at the time, the grand master ordered him to be at once admitted as soon as he heard that he was in attendance.

"Welcome back, Sir Gervaise Tresham," he said warmly, as he entered. "We all rejoice greatly at your return, and I consider it a happy omen for the success of our defence that so brave and distinguished a knight should at the last moment have arrived to take a share in it."

The others present all shook Gervaise cordially by the hand, and congratulated him on his return.

"You must dine with me this evening," D'Aubusson went on, "and tell us the story of your captivity and escape. At present, as you may suppose, we have too many matters on hand to spare time for aught that is not pressing and important. You will need a few days' rest before you are fit for active service, and by that time we will settle as to what post will best suit you."

Twice that day had Gervaise to recount his adventures, the first time to Sir John Kendall and the knights of his auberge, the second to the grand master. Most of the leading members of the Order were assembled at the palace, and, among others, he was introduced to the Viscount de Monteuil, the elder brother of D'Aubusson, one of the most famous leaders of the day. He had brought with him a considerable body of retainers, and, although not a member of the Order, had offered his services in defence of the town. The council had gratefully accepted the offer, and had unanimously named him Commander of the Forces. Many other knights and soldiers had come from different parts of Europe, animated alike by the desire to aid in the defence of Christendom against the advance of the Moslems, and to gain credit and honour by taking part in a siege that was sure to be a desperate one.

"My brother has already spoken of you to me, Sir Gervaise," the viscount said, when the young knight was presented to him; "although indeed there was no occasion for him to do so, since the name of the knight who two years ago saved the commerce of Italy from ruin, and with a single galley destroyed or captured a great fleet of over twenty Barbary pirates, and thus for a time put a stop to the depredations of the infidels, is known throughout Europe. By the way, I am the bearer of a message to you. I took ship at Genoa on my way hither, and stayed two or three days there while she was being got ready for sea. Knowing that I was bound hither, a certain very beautiful young lady of noble family, to whom I had the honour of being introduced, prayed me that if you should by any chance have escaped from captivity-and she said that she was convinced that you would, when you heard that Rhodes was threatened, assuredly endeavour to escape and to come hither to take a share in the defence —I was to tell you that she trusted you still bore her gage, and that she, on her part, had held fast to the promise she made you."

"I still have her gage, Viscount; for though I was for a long time deprived of it, I succeeded in regaining it when I made my escape," Gervaise said quietly; and De Monteuil at once turned the conversation to another topic.

Gervaise found that no attempt was to be made to take the offensive against the Turks, and that they were to be permitted to advance against the city without interference. Many of the more fiery spirits among the knights chafed at this prohibition. The records of the past showed that armies as large as that of Mahomet had suffered defeat at the hands of bodies of knights no stronger than that gathered for the defence of Rhodes. D'Aubusson, however, knew that between the undisciplined hordes that gathered in countless numbers to oppose the crusaders, and the troops of Mahomet, well trained in warfare, who had borne his standard victoriously in numerous battles, there was but little comparison. They were commanded, too, by Paleologus, a general of great capacity. Under such circumstances, although victory might be possible, the chances of defeat would be far greater, and while victory could be only won at a great sacrifice of life, defeat would mean annihilation to the garrison, and the loss of the city upon whose fortifications such an enormous amount of money and labour had been expended.

On the other hand, he felt perfectly confident that the city could be successfully defended, and that at a cost of life far less than would be attained by a victory in the open field, while the blow that would be inflicted upon the prestige and power of the enemy, by being ignominiously compelled to retire to their ships, after the failure of all their attacks, would be as great as if their army had been defeated in the field. Therefore the grand master, with the full assent of his leaders, turned a deaf ear to the entreaties of the younger knights, that they might be allowed to make a sortie. He calmly waited behind the formidable defences he had for the past ten years been occupied in perfecting, in anticipation of the assault of the Moslem host.

Accordingly, after disembarking at their leisure, the Turkish army moved forward, and took their post upon St. Stephen's Hill. From this eminence they commanded a full view of the town, the hills sloping gently down to the foot of the walls. In later times the first care of a general commanding the defence would have been to construct formidable works upon this commanding position. But the cannon of that period were so cumbrous and slowly worked, and so inaccurate in their aim, that the advantage of occupying a position that would prevent an enemy from firing down into a town was considered to be more than counterbalanced by the weakening of the garrison by the abstraction of the force required to man the detached work, and by the risk of their being surrounded and cut off without the garrison of the town being able to aid them.

That the defence of St. Stephen's Hill was considered unnecessary for the safety of Rhodes is shown by the fact that no attempt had been made to fortify it when, forty years later, the Moslems again besieged the city.

There was no shadow of apprehension felt by the garrison of Rhodes as the great array of their foes was seen moving on to the hill, and preparing to pitch its camp. On the summit was the great tent of the pasha; round this were the marquees of the other commanders, while the encampments of the troops stretched far away along the upper slopes of the hill.

Previous to the despatch of the expedition, the sultan had made preparations for aiding his arms by treachery. The agent he had sent to propose a temporary truce had, during his stay on the Island, made himself thoroughly acquainted with the outline of the works. A very accurate plan of them had also been obtained from an inhabitant of Rhodes, who had abandoned Christianity and taken service with the Turks.

In addition to this he had arranged with a renegade German, known as Maitre Georges, a man of very great ability as an artilleryman and engineer, to desert to the city, and there do all in his power to assist the besiegers, both by affording them information and by giving bad advice to the besieged. On the day after Paleologus, who was himself a renegade Greek, had established his camp, he sent in a herald to summon the city to surrender, at the same time making lavish promises that the lives and property of the native population should be respected, and that they should be allowed to continue to reside there, to enjoy the full exercise of their religion and of all other rights they possessed. The pasha had no real hope that the knights would obey the summons, but he thought that he might excite a spirit of disaffection among the townspeople that would, when the crisis came, greatly hamper the efforts of the defenders.

The Rhodians, however, were well satisfied with the rule of the Order. The knights, although belonging to the Catholic Church, had allowed the natives of the Island, who were of the Greek faith, perfect freedom in the exercise of their religion, and their rule, generally, had been fair and just. The wealth and prosperity of the Island had increased enormously since their establishment there, and the population had no inclination whatever to change their rule for that of the Turks. The summons to surrender being refused, the enemy made a reconnaissance towards the walls.

D'Aubusson had no longer any reason for checking the ardour of the knights, and a strong body of horsemen, under the command of De Monteuil, sallied out and drove the Turks back to their camp.

Maitre Georges, who was acting as the military adviser of the pasha, saw at once that the weakest point of the defence was Fort St. Nicholas, at the extremity of the mole along the neck of land dividing the outer from the inner port. At a short distance away, on the opposite side of the port, stood the church of St. Anthony, and in the gardens of the church a battery was at once erected. The garden was but three hundred yards from St. Nicholas, and the danger that would arise from the construction of the battery was at once perceived, and an incessant fire opened upon it from the guns on the wall round the grand master's palace. Numbers of the workmen were killed, but the erection of the battery was pushed on night and day, and ere long three of the immense cannon that had been brought from Constantinople,—where sixteen of them had been cast under the direction of Maitre Georges-were placed in position. These cannon were eighteen feet in length, and carried stone balls of some twenty-six inches in diameter.

Before these were ready to open fire, Gervaise had entirely regained his health and strength. The grand master, being unwilling to appoint him to a separate command over the heads of knights many years his senior, had attached him to his person in the capacity of what would now be called an aide-de-camp.

"I know, Gervaise, that I can rely upon your coolness and discretion. I cannot be everywhere myself, and I want you to act as my eyes in places where I cannot be. I know that the knights, so far as bravery and devotion are concerned, will each and every one do his best, and will die at their posts before yielding a foot; but while fighting like paladins they will think of naught else, and, however hardly pressed, will omit to send to me for reinforcements. Nay, even did they think of it, they probably would not send, deeming that to do so would be derogatory, and might be taken as an act of cowardice. Now, it is this service that I shall specially look for from you. When a post is attacked, I shall, when my presence is required elsewhere, send you to represent me. I do not, of course, wish you to interfere in any way in the conduct of the defence, in which you will take such share as you can; but you are specially to observe how matters go, and if you see that the knights are pressed and in sore need of assistance to enable them to hold the post, you will at once bring the news to me, and I will hurry there with reinforcements."

No post could have been more in accordance with the desire of Gervaise, for the portion of the wall defended by the English langue was far removed from the point selected by the Turks for their first attack, the sea front being defended half by the langue of Italy, and half by that of Castile. Fort St. Nicholas was under the command of the Cavalier Caretto, and as soon as the Turkish battery was completed, Gervaise went down there with an order from the grand master that he was for the present to consider himself as forming part of the garrison. This was pleasant for both Caretto and himself, for the Italian knight had conceived a strong friendship for the young Englishman, and had rejoiced greatly at his return from captivity, but had been so much occupied with his duty of placing the castle in all respects in a state of defence, that he had had no opportunity for a private conversation with him since his return to Rhodes.

Gervaise, on his part, was no less pleased. Caretto had shown so much tact after his release from the Moors, and had so willingly aided him in any capacity allotted to him, without in the slightest degree interposing his council unasked, that Gervaise had come to like him greatly, even before their arrival at Genoa. Circumstances there had brought them closely together, and their friendship had been cemented during their voyage to Rhodes. Caretto had gone back to Italy, where he had a commandery, a few days after Gervaise had sailed on his last voyage, and had only returned to Rhodes three months before Gervaise escaped from captivity.

"This is turning the tables," Caretto said, with a laugh, when Gervaise presented the grand master's order. "I was under your command last time, and now it seems that you are to be under mine. I suppose you applied to come here, in order to have a fresh opportunity of distinguishing yourself. I heard that you had been placed on D'Aubusson's own staff."

"Yes, and am on it still; and it is by his orders and not by my own solicitation that I am here. I will tell you what my duties are. The grand master knows the commanders of posts have their hands so full that they will have no time for sending complete reports to him, and he considers, moreover, that they might, in some cases, however pressed, hesitate to ask for aid until too late for reinforcements to be brought up. My duty will be to let the grand master know how matters are going, and to send to him at once if it seems to me that help is needed. I should, of course, always send for reinforcements, at the request of a commander; but it is only in the event of his being too busy in the heat of the fray to think of aught but resisting an attack, that I should exercise my own judgment in the matter."

Caretto nodded.

"It is a good thought of D'Aubusson's. When one is in the thick of a fight in a breach, with the Moslems swarming round, it does not occur to one to draw out of the fray to send off messages. For myself, I shall be glad indeed to have that matter off my mind, though it is not every one I should care to trust with such a responsibility. Some might send off for aid when it was not needed, others might delay so long that help might come too late; but with one so cool headed as yourself I should not fear any contingency. And now, as I am not busy at present, let us have a comfortable talk as to what has happened since we met last. I was at the banquet at the grand master's on the night when you related your adventures. You had certainly much to tell, but it seems to me for some reason or other you cut short certain details, and I could not see why, as there seemed no prospect of escape open to you, you did not accept the offer of Suleiman Ali to ransom you."

"I saw no chance of escape at the moment, but I did not doubt that I could get away from the town whenever I chose, although it was not clear how I should proceed afterwards. It was for this opportunity I was waiting, and I felt sure that, with my knowledge of the language, it would come sooner or later. In the next place, my captors had fixed an exorbitant sum for my ransom, and I did not wish to impose upon the generosity of Suleiman. There was another reason—a private one."

"You don't mean to say that you had fallen in love with a Moorish damsel, Sir Gervaise?" Caretto laughed.

"For shame, Cavalier! As if a Christian knight would care for a Moslem maiden, even were she as fair as the houris of their creed!"

"Christian knights have done so before now," Caretto laughed, greatly amused at the young knight's indignation, "and doubtless will do so again. Well, I suppose I must not ask what the private matter was, though it must have been something grave indeed to lead you, a slave, to reject the offer of freedom. I know that when I was rowing in their galleys, no matter of private business that I can conceive would have stood in my way for a single moment, had a chance of freedom presented itself."

"It was a matter of honour," Gervaise said gravely, "and one of which I should speak to no one else; but as you were present at the time, there can, I think, be no harm in doing so. At the time that I was captured, I was stripped of everything that I had upon me, and, of course, with the rest, of the gage which the Lady Claudia had given me, and which hung round my neck where she had placed it. It was taken possession of by the captain of the pirates, who, seeing that it bore no Christian emblem, looked upon it as a sort of amulet. I understood what he was saying, but, as I was desirous that my knowledge of Turkish should not be suspected, I said nothing. I was very glad that he so regarded it, for had he taken it to be an ordinary trinket, he might have parted with it, and I should never have been able to obtain a clue as to the person to whom he sold it. As it was, he put it round his neck, with the remark that it might bring him better luck than had befallen me. He told me jeeringly months afterwards that it had done so, and that he would never part with it. Given me as it was, I felt that my honour was concerned in its recovery, and that, should I ever meet Lady Claudia again, I should feel disgraced indeed, if, when she asked whether I still bore her gage, I had to confess that it was lost."

"But lost from no fault of your own," Caretto put in.

"The losing was not indeed from any fault of my own, and had the pirate thrown it into the sea I should have held myself free from disgrace; but as it was still in existence, and I knew its possessor, I was bound in honour to recover it. At the time Suleiman Ali's messenger arrived the corsair was away, and there was no saying when his ship would return; therefore, I decided at once not to accept the offer of freedom. Had it not been for that, I own that I should have done so, for I knew that I could repay Suleiman from the revenues of my commandery, which would have accumulated in my absence; but if I had had to wait ten years longer to regain the gage, I felt that I was in honour bound to do so. It was, in fact, some six months before the corsair put into that port again. The moment he did so I carried out the plans I had long before determined upon. I obtained a disguise from Ben Ibyn, and by a ruse succeeded in inducing the pirate to meet me outside the town, believing that I was an Arab chief who wished to dispose of some valuable slave girls he had brought in. I had with me one of my old galley slaves, who had been taken into Ben Ibyn's employment; and when the pirate came up with two of his crew, and furiously attacked me as soon as I threw off my disguise, it would have gone hard with me had he not stood by me, and killed one of them who was about to attack me in the rear. I slew the other and Hassan, and the gage is in its place again."

Chapter XXI
The Fort Of St. Nicholas

"Well, you have proved indeed," Caretto said, when Gervaise finished his story, "that you are worthy of the bestowal of a gage by a fair damsel. I do not think that many knights, however true they might be to the donor, would have suffered months of slavery in order to regain a token, lost by no fault or carelessness of their own; and no lady could have blamed or held them in any way dishonoured by the loss."

"I had a message by the Viscount De Monteuil from Lady Claudia the other day, saying that she trusted I had kept her gage. I can assure you that the six months of slavery were cheaply purchased by the pleasure I felt that I still possessed it; and I was glad, too, to learn that I had not been forgotten by her."

"Of that you may well assure yourself, Tresham; my commandery is not far from Genoa, and I was frequently with her, but never without her drawing me aside and asking me if I had heard any news of you, and talking over with me the chances there might be of your escape. I can tell you that there are not a few young nobles of Genoa who would give much to be allowed as you are to carry her gage, or wear her colours. You should see her now; you would scarce know her again, so altered and improved is she; there is no fairer face in all Italy."

"I hope some day to meet her again," Gervaise replied; "although I own to knowing it were better that I should not do so. Until she gave me her gage I had scarcely noticed her. I have, as you know, no experience of women, and had so much on my mind at the time, what with the fuss they were making about us, and the question of getting the prizes here, that in truth I paid but slight attention to the fair faces of the dames of Genoa. But the gracious and earnest way in which, though scarce more than a child, she gave me her gage, and vowed that no other knight should possess one so long as I lived, struck me so greatly that I own I gave the matter much more thought than was right or becoming in one of our Order. The incident was much more gratifying to me than all the honour paid me by the Republic, and during the long months of my captivity it has recurred to me so frequently that I have in vain endeavoured to chase it from my thoughts, as sinful thus to allow myself constantly to think of any woman. Do not mistake me, Sir Fabricius. I am speaking to you as to a confessor, and just as I have kept her amulet hidden from all, so is the thought of her a secret I would not part with for my life. I do not for a moment deceive myself with the thought that, beyond the fact that her gift has made her feel an interest in me and my fate, she has any sentiment in the matter: probably, indeed, she looks back upon the gift as a foolish act of girlish enthusiasm that led her into making a promise that she now cannot but find unpleasantly binding; for it is but natural that among the young nobles of her own rank and country there must be some whom she would see with pleasure wearing her colours."

Caretto looked at him with some amusement.

"Were you not bound by your vows as a knight of the Order, how would you feel in the matter?"

"I should feel worse," Gervaise said, without hesitation. "I have oftentimes thought that over, and I see that it is good for me I am so bound. It does not decrease my chances, for, as I know, there are no chances; but it renders it more easy for me to know that it is so."

"But why should you say that you have no chances, Tresham?"

"Because it is easy to see that it is so. I am, save for my commandery and prospects in the Order, a penniless young knight, without home or estate, without even a place in my country, and that country not hers. I know that it is not only sinful, but mad, for me to think so frequently of her, but at least I am not mad enough to think that I can either win the heart or aspire to the hand of one who is, you say, so beautiful, and who is, moreover, as I know, the heiress to wide estates."

"'There was a squire of low degree, Loved the king's daughter of Hungarie,'" Caretto sang, with a laugh. "You are not of low degree, but of noble family, Gervaise. You are not a squire, but a knight, and already a very distinguished one; nor is the young lady, though she be a rich heiress, a king's daughter."

"At any rate, the squire was not vowed to celibacy. No, no, Sir Fabricius, it is a dream, and a pleasant one; but I know perfectly well that it is but a dream, and one that will do me no harm so long as I ever bear in mind that it is so. Many a knight of the Order before me has borne a lady's gage, and carried it valiantly in many a fight, and has been no less true to his vows for doing so."

"Upon the contrary, he has been all the better a knight, Gervaise; it is always good for a knight, whether he belongs to the Order or not, to prize one woman above all others, and to try to make himself worthy of his ideal. As to the vow of celibacy, you know that ere now knights have been absolved from their vows, and methinks that, after the service you have rendered to Italy by ridding the sea of those corsairs, his Holiness would make no difficulty in granting any request that you might make him in that or any other direction. I don't know whether you are aware that, after you sailed from here, letters came from Rome as well as from Pisa, Florence, and Naples, expressive of the gratitude felt for the services that you had rendered, and of their admiration for the splendid exploit that you had performed."

"No; the grand master has had his hands so full of other matters that doubtless an affair so old escaped his memory. Indeed, he may have forgotten that I sailed before the letters arrived."

"Do not forget to jog his memory on the subject, for I can tell you that the letters did not come alone, but were each accompanied by presents worthy of the service you rendered. But as to the vows?"

"As to the vows, I feel as I said just now, that I would not free myself of them if I could, for, being bound by them, I can the more easily and pleasantly enjoy my dream. Besides, what should I do if I left the Order without home, country, or means, and with naught to do but to sell my sword to some warlike monarch? Besides, Caretto, I love the Order, and deem it the highest privilege to fight against the Moslems, and to uphold the banner of the Cross."

"As to that, you could, like De Monteuil and many other knights here, always come out to aid the Order in time of need. As to the vows, I am not foolish enough to suppose that you would ask to be relieved from them, until you had assured yourself that Claudia was also desirous that you should be free."

"It is absurd," Gervaise said, almost impatiently. "Do not let us talk any more about it, Caretto, or it will end by turning my head and making me presumptuous enough to imagine that the Lady Claudia, who only saw me for three or four days, and that while she was still but a girl, has been thinking of me seriously since."

"I do not know Claudia's thoughts," Caretto remarked drily, "but I do know that last year she refused to listen to at least a score of excellent offers for her hand, including one from a son of the doge himself, and that without any reasonable cause assigned by her, to the great wonderment of all, seeing that she does not appear to have any leaning whatever towards a life in a nunnery. At any rate, if at some future time you should pluck up heart of grace to tell her you love her, and she refuses you, you will at least have the consolation of knowing that you are not the only one, by a long way, whose suit has been rejected. And now as to our affairs here. Methinks that tomorrow that battery will open fire upon us. It seems completed."

"Yes, I think they are nearly ready," Gervaise said, turning his mind resolutely from the subject they had been discussing. "From the palace wall I saw, before I came down here, large numbers of men rolling huge stones down towards the church. Our guns were firing steadily; but could they load them ten times as fast as they do, they would hardly be able to stop the work, so numerous are those engaged upon it."

"Yes we shall soon learn something of the quality of their artillery. The tower is strong enough to resist ordinary guns, but it will soon crumble under the blows of such enormous missiles. Never have I seen or heard in Europe of cannon of such size; but indeed, in this matter the Turks are far ahead of us, and have, ever since cannon were first cast, made them of much larger size than we in Europe have done. However, there is one comfort; they may destroy this fort, but they have still to cross the water, and this under the fire of the guns on the palace walls; when they once land, their great battery must cease firing, and we shall be able to meet them on equal terms in the breach. Fight as hard as they may, I think we can hold our own, especially as reinforcements can come down to us more quickly than they can be brought across the water."

The next morning, at daybreak, the deep boom of a gun announced to the city that the great battering cannon had begun their work. In the fort the sleeping knights sprang to their feet at the concussion that seemed to shake it to its centre. They would have rushed to the walls, but Caretto at once issued orders that no one should show himself on the battlements unless under special orders.

"There is nothing whatever to be done until the Turks have breached the wall, and are ready to advance to attack us. Every sword will be needed when that hour comes, and each man owes it to the Order to run no useless risk, until the hour when he is required to do his share of the fighting."

The time required to reload the great cannon was considerable, but at regular intervals they hurled their heavy missiles against the wall, the distance being so short that every ball struck it. After some twenty shots had been fired, Caretto, accompanied by Gervaise, went out by a small gate on the eastern side of the tower, and made their way round by the foot of the wall to see what effect the shots had produced on the solid masonry.

Caretto shook his head.

"It is as I feared," he said. "No stones ever quarried by man could long resist such tremendous blows. In some places, you see, the stones are starred and cracked, in others the shock seems to have pulverised the spot where it struck; but, worse, still, the whole face of the wall is shaken. There are cracks between the stones, and some of these are partly bulged out and partly driven in. It may take some time before a breach is effected, but sooner or later the wall will surely be demolished."

"I will go up and make my report to the grand master."

"Do so, Gervaise. I almost wonder that he has not himself come down to see how the wall is resisting."

Gervaise, on reaching the palace, heard that D'Aubusson was at present engaged in examining no less a person than Maitre Georges, the right hand of Paleologus, who had soon after daybreak presented himself before the wall on the other side of the town, declaring that he had left the Turkish service, and craving to be admitted. News had been sent at once to D'Aubusson, who despatched two of the senior knights, with orders to admit him and receive him with all honour. This had been done, and the grand master, with some of his council, were now closeted with the newcomer. Several of the knights were gathered in the courtyard, discussing the event. There was no question that if the renegade came in good faith, his defection would be a serious blow to the assailants, and that his well known skill and experience would greatly benefit the defenders.

"For my part," Sir John Boswell, who formed one of the detachment which the English langue, as well as all the others, contributed to form the garrison of the palace said, "I would have hung the fellow up by the neck over the gateway, and he should never have set foot within the walls. Think you that a man who has denied his faith and taken service with his enemies is to be trusted, whatever oaths he may take?"

"You must remember, Boswell," another said, "that hitherto Georges has not fought against Christians, but has served Mahomet in his wars with other infidels. I am not saying a word in defence of his having become a renegade; yet even a renegade may have some sort of heart, and now that he has been called upon to fight against Christians he may well have repented of his faults, and determined to sacrifice his position and prospects rather than aid in the attack on the city."

"We shall see. As for me, I regard a renegade as the most contemptible of wretches, and have no belief that they have either a heart or conscience."

When Maitre Georges came out from the palace, laughing and talking with the two knights who had entered with him, it was evident that he was well pleased with his reception by the grand master, who had assigned to him a suite of apartments in the guest house. In reality, however, D'Aubusson had no doubt that his object was a treacherous one, and that, like Demetrius, who had come under the pretence of bringing about a truce, his object was to find out the weak points and to supply the Turks with information. Georges had, in his conversation with him, laid great stress on the strength of the Turkish army, the excellent quality of the troops, and the enormous battering train that had been prepared. But every word he spoke but added to the grand master's suspicions; for if the man considered that the capture of the city was morally certain, it would be simply throwing away his life to enter it as a deserter.

The grand master was, however, too politic to betray any doubt of Georges' sincerity. Were he treated as a traitor, Paleologus might find another agent to do the work. It was, therefore, better to feign a belief in his story, to obtain all the information possible from him, and at the same time to prevent his gaining any knowledge of affairs that would be of the slightest use to the Turks. Instructions were therefore given to the two knights that, while Georges was to be treated with all courtesy, he was to be strictly watched, though in such a manner that he should be in ignorance of it, and that, whenever he turned his steps in the direction of those parts of the defences where fresh works had been recently added and preparations made of which it was desirable the Turks should be kept in ignorance, he was to be met, as if by accident, by one of the knights told off for the purpose, and his steps diverted in another direction.

Georges soon made himself popular among many of the knights, who had no suspicions of his real character. He was a man of exceptional figure, tall, strong, splendidly proportioned, with a handsome face and gallant bearing. He was extremely well informed on all subjects, had travelled widely, had seen many adventures, was full of anecdote, and among the younger knights, therefore, he was soon regarded as a charming companion. His very popularity among them aided D'Aubusson's plans, as Georges was generally the centre of a group of listeners, and so had but few opportunities of getting away quietly to obtain the information he sought. Gervaise delivered his report to the grand master.

"I am free now," D'Aubusson said, "and will accompany you to St. Nicholas. I have been detained by the coming of this man Georges. He is a clever knave, and, I doubt not, has come as a spy. However, I have taken measures that he shall learn nothing that can harm us. No lives have been lost at the tower, I hope?"

"No, sir; Caretto has forbidden any to show themselves on the walls."

"He has done well. This is no time for rash exposure, and where there is naught to be gained, it is a grave fault to run risks."

On arriving at the end of the mole, D'Aubusson, accompanied by Caretto, made an investigation of the effect of the Turks' fire.

"'Tis worse than I expected," he said. "When we laid out our fortifications the thought that such guns as these would be used against them never entered our minds. Against ordinary artillery the walls would stand a long battering; but it is clear that we shall have to depend more upon our swords than upon our walls for our defence. Fortunately, although the Turks have indeed chosen the spot where our walls are most open to the assaults of their battery, they have to cross the water to attack the breach when it is made, and will have to fight under heavy disadvantage."

"Tresham was last night saying to me, that it seemed to him it would not be a difficult matter for one who spoke Turkish well, to issue at night on the other side of the town, and to make his way round to the battery, disguised of course as a Turkish soldier, and then, mixing with the artillery men, to drive a spike into one of the touch holes. He said that he would gladly volunteer for the task."

D'Aubusson shook his head decidedly. "It would be too dangerous; and even were a spike driven in, the Turks would have no great difficulty in extracting it, for the tubes are so big that a man might crawl in and drive the spike up from the inside. Moreover, could one or more of the guns be disabled permanently, others would be brought down and set in their place, so that nothing would be gained but a very short delay, which would be of no advantage to us, and certainly would in no way justify the risking of the life of so distinguished a young knight."

The bombardment of St. Nicholas continued for some days. A breach was fast forming in the wall, and a slope composed of the fallen rubbish extended from the front of the breach to the water's edge. The grand master was frequently on the spot, and as this was at present the sole object of attack, the garrison was strengthened by as many knights as could be sheltered within its walls. At night the shattered masonry that had fallen inside was carried out, and with it a new work thrown up across the mole, to strengthen the defence on that side, should the enemy land between the town and the fort. Small batteries were planted wherever they could sweep the approaches to the breach, and planks studded with nails were sunk in the shallow water of the harbour, to impede the progress of those who might attempt to swim or wade across. For the time, therefore, the functions of Gervaise were in abeyance, and he laboured with the rest of the garrison at the defences.

At daybreak on the 9th of June, a great number of vessels and boats, crowded with soldiers, bore down on St. Nicholas. As they approached, every gun on the fortifications that could be brought to bear upon them opened fire; but in a dense mass they advanced. Some made their way to the rocks and landed the soldiers there; others got alongside the mole; but the majority grounded in the shallow water of the harbour, and the troops, leaping out, waded to the foot of the breach. On its crest D'Aubusson himself had taken up his station. Beside him stood Caretto, and around them the most distinguished knights of the Order. With wild shouts the Turks rushed up the breach, and swarmed thickly up the ruined masonry until, at its summit, they encountered the steel clad line of the defenders. For hours the terrible struggle continued. As fast as the head of the Turkish column broke and melted away against the obstacle they tried in vain to penetrate, fresh reinforcements took the place of those who had fallen, and in point of valour and devotion the Moslem showed himself a worthy antagonist of the Christian. It was not only at the breach that the conflict raged. At other points the Turks, well provided with ladders, fixed them against the walls, and desperately strove to obtain a footing there. From the breach clouds of dust rose from under the feet of the combatants, mingling with the smoke of the cannon on the ramparts, the fort, and Turkish ships, and at times entirely hid from the sight of the anxious spectators on the walls of the town and fortress, and of the still more numerous throng of Turks on St. Stephen's Hill, the terrible struggle that continued without a moment's intermission.

The combatants now fought in comparative silence. The knights, exhausted and worn out by their long efforts beneath the blazing sun, still showed an unbroken front; but it was only occasionally that the battle cry of the Order rose in the air, as a fresh body of assailants climbed up the corpse strewn breach. The yell of the Moslems rose less frequently; they sacrificed their lives as freely and devotedly as those who led the first onset had done; but as the hours wore on, the assurance of victory died out, and a doubt as to whether it was possible to break through the line of their terrible foes gained ground. D'Aubusson himself, although, in spite of the remonstrances of the knights, always in the thickest of the fray, was yet ever watchful, and quickly perceived where the defenders were hotly pressed, and where support was most needed. Gervaise fought by his side, so that, when necessary, he could carry his orders to a little body of knights, drawn up in reserve, and despatch them to any point where aid was needed. The cannon still continued their fire on both sides. A fragment of one of the stone balls from a basilisk struck off D'Aubusson's helmet. He selected another from among the fallen knights, and resumed his place in the line. Still the contest showed no signs of terminating. The Turkish galleys ever brought up reinforcements, while the defenders grew fewer, and more exhausted. During a momentary pause, while a fresh body of Turks were landing, Gervaise said to the grand master,

"If you will give me leave, sir, I will go out at the watergate, swim up the inner harbour, and in a very short time turn a few of the craft lying there into fire ships, and tow them out with a couple of galleys. At any rate, we can fire all these craft that have grounded, and create a panic among the others."

"Well thought of, Gervaise! I will write an order on one of my tablets. Do you take my place for a minute." Withdrawing behind the line, the grand master sat down on a fragment of stone, and, drawing a tablet from a pouch in his girdle, he wrote on it, "In all things carry out the instructions of Sir Gervaise Tresham: he is acting by my orders and authority, and has full power in all respects."

He handed the slip of parchment to Gervaise, who hurried to the water gate in the inner harbour, threw off his helmet and armour, issued out at the gate, and plunged into the sea. He swam out some distance, in order to avoid the missiles of the Turks, who were trying to scale the wall from the mole, and then directed his course to St. Michael's, which guarded the inner entrance to the fort. He had fastened the parchment in his hair, and as some of the garrison of the tower, noticing his approach, came down to assist him, he handed it to them and was at once taken to the commander of St. Michael, answering as he went the anxious questions as to how matters stood at the breach.

"Aid is sorely needed. The Turks have gained no foot of ground as yet, but many of the knights are killed and most of the others utterly exhausted with heat and labour. Unless aid reaches them speedily, the tower, with all its defenders, will be lost."

The instant the commander knew what was required, he bade six of the knights embark with Gervaise in a boat moored behind the tower, and row up the harbour to the spot where the shipping was all massed together, protected by the high ground of the fortress from the Turkish fire. Gervaise waved his hand, as he neared the end of the harbour, to the officer on the walls, and while the six knights who were with him ran off to tell the master of the galleys to prepare two of them to leave the port instantly, Gervaise explained to the officer in charge of the wall at that point the plan that he was charged to carry out, and asked for twenty knights to assist him.

"It will leave us very weak along here," the officer said. "Then let me have ten, and send for another ten from other parts of the wall. Here is the grand master's order, giving me full power and authority, and it is all important that no single moment shall be wasted."

"You shall have twenty of mine," the officer said, "and I will draw ten from the langue next to us to fill their places."

In a few minutes the quay was a scene of bustle and activity. Gervaise picked out ten of the smallest vessels; the knights went among the other ships, seized all goods and stores that would be useful as combustibles, and compelled the crews to carry them on board the craft chosen as fire ships. Then barrels were broken open, old sails and faggots saturated with oil and pitch, and in little more than a quarter of an hour after his arrival, Gervaise had the satisfaction of seeing that the ten boats were all filled with combustibles, and ready to be set on fire. He now called for volunteers from the sailors, and a number of them at once came forward, including many of the captains. He placed one of these in command of each fire ship, and gave him four of the sailors.

"The galleys will tow you out," he said, "and take you close to the enemy's ships. We shall range you five abreast, and when I give the word, the one at the end of the line will steer for the nearest Turk, and, with oars and poles, get alongside. The captain will then light the train of powder in the hold, throw the torch among the straw, and see that, if possible, the men fasten her to the Turk; but if this cannot be done, it is not essential, for in the confusion the enemy will not be able to get out of the way of the fire ship as it drives down against her. At the last moment you will take to your boats and row back here. We will protect you from the assaults of any of the Turkish ships."

Having made sure that all the captains understood the orders, Gervaise took command of one of the galleys, the senior knight going on board the other. The ten fire ships were now poled out until five were ranged abreast behind each craft; Gervaise requested the commander of the other galley to lie off the point of St. Nicholas until he had got rid of his five fire ships, then to advance and launch his craft against the Turks. The smoke of the guns lay so heavy on the water, and the combatants were so intent upon the struggle at the breach, that Gervaise steered his galley into the midst of the Turkish vessels laden with troops ready to disembark, without attracting any notice; then, standing upon the taffrail, he signalled to the two outside boats to throw off their ropes and make for the Turkish ship nearest to them. This they did, and it was not until a sheet of flame rose alongside, that the enemy awoke to the sense of danger.

The other three fire ships were almost immediately cast off. Two of them were equally successful, but the Turks managed to thrust off the third. She drifted, however, through the shipping, and presently brought up alongside one of the vessels fast aground. With but ten knights, Gervaise could not attack one of the larger vessels, crowded with troops; but there were many fishing boats that had been pressed into the service, and against one of these Gervaise ordered the men to steer the galley. A shout to the rowers made them redouble their efforts. A yell of dismay arose from the Turkish troops as they saw the galley bearing down upon them, and frantic efforts were made to row out of her way. These were in vain, for her sharp prow struck them amidships, cutting the boat almost in two, and she sank like a stone, the galley, without a pause, making for another boat.

Looking back, Gervaise saw that his consort was already in the midst of the Turks, among whom the wildest confusion prevailed, each ship trying to extricate herself from the mass, upon which the batteries of the fortress now concentrated their efforts. Two fresh columns of flame had already shot up, and satisfied that all was going well, Gervaise continued his attack upon the smaller craft, six of whom were overtaken and sunk. Three or four of the larger vessels endeavoured to lay themselves alongside the galley, but her speed was so superior to theirs that she easily evaded the attempts, and, sweeping round, rejoined the other galley which had just issued from among the Turks, who were already in full retreat. The defenders of St. Nicholas, reanimated by the sight of the discomfiture of the Turkish fleet, with a loud shout rushed down from the spot which they had held for so many hours, drove their assailants before them, and flung themselves upon the crowd assembled at the foot of the breach.

These had already suffered terribly from the fire of the batteries. Again and again they had striven to storm the mound of rubbish, and had each time been repulsed, with the loss of their bravest leaders. Seeing themselves abandoned by the ships, a panic seized them, and as the knights rushed down upon them they relinquished all thoughts of resistance, and dashed into the shallow water. Many were drowned in the attempt to swim across the deep channel in the middle, some succeeded, while others made their escape in the boats in which they had been brought ashore from the ships.

The struggle was over. The two galleys made for the breach, and the knights leapt out as soon as the boats grounded, and, wading ashore, joined the group that had so long and gallantly sustained the unequal fight. Fatigue, exhaustion, and wounds, were forgotten in the triumph of the moment, and they crowded round the grand master and Caretto, to whose joint exertions the success of the defence was so largely due.

"Do not thank me, comrades," D'Aubusson said. "No man has today fought better than the rest. Every knight has shown himself worthy of the fame of our Order. The meed of praise for our success is first due to Sir Gervaise Tresham. At the moment when I began to doubt whether we could much longer withstand the swarms of fresh foes who continued to pour against us, while we were overcome by heat and labour, Sir Gervaise, who had throughout been fighting at my side, offered to swim into the port, to fit out a dozen of the merchant craft there as fire ships, and to tow them round into the midst of the Turkish vessels behind the two galleys that were lying ready for service. I remembered how he had before destroyed the corsair fleet at Sardinia with fire ships, and the proposal seemed to me as an inspiration sent from Heaven, at this moment of our great peril. I wrote him an order, giving him full authority to act in my name, and in a time that seemed to me incredibly short I saw him round the point with the fire ships in tow. You saw, as well as I did, how completely the plan was carried out. Ten or twelve of the Turkish ships are a mass of flames, and besides these I noted that the galley ran down and destroyed several smaller craft filled with soldiers. The panic in the ships spread to the troops on shore, and rendered the last part of our task an easy one. I say it from my heart that I consider it is to Sir Gervaise Tresham that we owe our success, and that, had it not been for his happy thought, the sun would have gone down on our dead bodies lying on the summit of the breach, and on the Turkish flag waving over the fort of St. Nicholas."

Until now none of the defenders of the breach had known how what seemed to them an almost miraculous change in the fortune of the fight had come about, and they thronged round Gervaise, shaking his hand, and many of them warmly embracing him, according to the custom of the time.

"It was but natural that the idea should occur to me," he said, "having before successfully encountered them with fire ships; and as all on shore, and especially these knights, aided me with all their power, it took but a brief time to get the boats in readiness for burning. Much credit, too, is due to the merchant captains and sailors who volunteered to take charge of the fire ships and to manoeuvre them alongside the Turks."

The grand master and the knights who had borne the brunt of the battle now retired along the mole to the town, bearing with them their most seriously wounded comrades, and assisting those whose wounds were less severe. The twenty knights who had manned the two galleys remained in the fort. Caretto continued in command, as, although he had suffered several wounds, he refused to relinquish his post. Gervaise, who had, —thanks partly to his skill with his weapons, but still more to the temper of the splendid suit of armour presented to him by Genoa, —escaped without a scratch, volunteered to remain with him until next morning, his principal motive for making the request being his desire to escape from further congratulations and praise for the success of his plan. After Caretto's wounds had been dressed by the knights, and he and Gervaise had partaken of some food and wine, which they greatly needed, Caretto was persuaded to lie down for a time, the knights promising to bring him word at once if they perceived any movement whatever on the part of the enemy. Gervaise remained with him, feeling, now the excitement was over, that he sorely needed rest after his exertions in the full heat of the summer sun.

"It has been a great day, Gervaise," Caretto said, "and I only hope that when again I go into battle with the infidel, I shall have you at hand to come forward at the critical moment with some master stroke to secure victory. Claudia will be pleased indeed when she hears how the knight who bears her gage has again distinguished himself. She will look on the gay and idle young fops of Genoa with greater disdain than ever. Now you need not say anything in protest, the more so as I feel grievously weak, and disposed for sleep."

Chapter XXII
The Struggle At The Breach

Two hours later Caretto and Gervaise were roused by the arrival of a hundred knights in place of the previous garrison; these bore the news that the pasha had sent in a flag of truce to ask for an armistice until sundown, to enable him to carry off for burial the bodies of those who had fallen in the attack. The request had been willingly granted; but D'Aubusson had at the same time thought it well to send down a strong reinforcement to the garrison to prevent any attempt at treachery on the part of the Turks.

"I have seldom heard pleasanter news," Caretto said; "for just as I fell asleep I was wondering how we were to rid ourselves of the corpses of the infidels. By tomorrow the place would have become unbearable; and though, living, the Turks could not turn us out of the tower, they would when dead speedily have rid the place of us."

In half an hour a number of Moslem vessels were seen approaching. Caretto did not wish the Turks to imagine that he doubted their good faith, and while directing the main body of knights to remain in concealment near the breach, he placed two on sentry duty on the crest of the ruins, and, with four other knights and Gervaise, went down in complete armour to salute the officer in command of the burying party, as he landed from the boats. The ships anchored a short distance out, and a number of boats rowed from them to the shore. As the Turkish officer landed, Caretto saluted him, and said in Arabic,

"I give you courteous greeting, Sir. When the cannon cease to sound and swords are sheathed, there is no longer animosity between brave men; and no braver than those whose bodies lie stretched there, breathed the air of heaven. If, sir, I and the knights with me do not uncover our heads, it is from no want of respect for the dead, but solely because we dare not stand bareheaded under the fierce rays of the sun."

The Turk answered with equal courtesy, complimenting the knights on their defence.

"Had I not seen it with my own eyes," he said, "I should have deemed it altogether impossible that so small a number of men could thus for hours have withstood the attacks of some of the best of the sultan's troops. Tales have come down to us from our fathers of the marvellous prowess of the knights of your Order, and how at Smyrna, at Acre, and elsewhere, they performed such feats of valour that their name is still used by Turkish mothers as a bugbear to frighten their children. But the stories have always seemed to me incredible; now I perceive they were true, and that the present members of the Order in no way fall short of the valour of their predecessors."

The knights remained with the Turkish commander and some of his officers while the work of collecting and carrying away the dead was performed, the conversation on their side being supported by Caretto and Gervaise. No less than seven hundred bodies were carried down to the boats, besides a great many wounded by the artillery fire. None were, however, found breathing among the great pile of dead at the upper part of the breach, for the axes and double handed swords of the knights had, in most of the cases, cleft through turban and skull.

"This represents but part of our loss," the Turkish commander said sadly, as the last party came down with their burdens to the boats. "At least as many more must have perished in the sea, either in their endeavours to escape when all was lost, in the destruction of their vessels by fire, by the shot from your batteries, or by being run down by your galleys. Ah, Sir Knight, if it had not been for the appearance of your fire ships, methinks the matter might have ended differently."

"In that I altogether agree with you," Caretto said. "We were indeed, well nigh spent, and must have soon succumbed had it not been that the fire ships arrived to our rescue. You have a fair right to claim that the victory would have remained in your hands, had not those craft gone out and snatched it from you."

Then, with salutes on both sides, the Turks took their places in the boats, and the knights returned to the fort. As soon as darkness came on, a large body of slaves were marched down from the town, and, under the direction of the knights, laboured all night at the mound, removing great quantities of the fallen stones and rubbish in a line halfway up it, and piling them above so as to form a scarp across the mound that would need ladders to ascend. Another party worked at the top of the mound, and there built up a wall eight feet high. The work was completed by daylight, and the knights felt that they were now in a position to resist another attack, should Paleologus again send his troops to the assault.

The night had passed quietly. There was a sound of stir and movement in the Turkish battery, but nothing that would excite the suspicion of a large body of troops being in motion. When it became light it was seen that the Turkish ships had sailed away to their previous anchorage on the other side of the Island, and although at considerable intervals the great cannon hurled their missiles against the fort, it was evident that, for the time at least, the attack was not to be pressed at that point. A fresh body of slaves, however, came down from the town to relieve those who had been all night at work, and the repair of the defences was continued, and with greater neatness and method than had been possible in the darkness.

At eight o'clock the bells of St. John's Church gave notice that a solemn service of thanksgiving for the repulse of the enemy was about to be held. Notice had been sent down early to the tower; and all the knights who could be spared, without too greatly weakening the garrison, went up to attend it; the service was conducted with all the pomp and ceremony possible, and after it was over a great procession was formed to proceed to the shrine, where a picture of the Virgin held in special reverence by the Order was placed.

As it wound through the streets in splendid array, the grand master and officials in all their robes of state, the knights in full armour and the mantles of the Order, while the inhabitants in gala costume lined the streets, windows, and housetops, the ladies waving scarves and scattering flowers down on the knights, the roar of great cannon on the south side of the city showed that the Turks had commenced the attack in another quarter. Without pausing, the procession continued its way, and it was not until the service in the chapel had been concluded that any steps were taken to ascertain the direction of the attack. As soon as it was over, the knights hastened to the walls. During the night the Turks had transported their great basilisks, with other large pieces of artillery, from the camp to the rising ground on the south side of the city, and had opened fire against the wall covering the Jews' quarter, and at the same time against the tower of St. Mary on the one hand and the Italian tower on the other.

From other commanding spots huge mortars were hurling great fragments of rock and other missiles broadcast into the town. The portion of the wall selected for the attack showed that the Turks had been well informed by their spies of the weak points of the defence. The wall behind which the Jews' quarter lay, was, to all appearance, of thick and solid masonry; but this was really of great age, having formed part of the original defences of the town, before the Order had established itself there. The masonry, therefore, was ill fitted to resist the huge balls hurled against it by the basilisks. The langue of Provence was in charge of this part of the wall, and, leaving them for the present to bear the brunt of the storm, the grand master sent the knights who could be spared, to assist the inhabitants to erect shelters against the storm of missiles falling in the town.

Sheds with sharply sloping roofs, constructed of solid timber, were built against the inner side of the walls, and beneath these numbers of the inhabitants found refuge. The work was performed with great celerity by the inhabitants, aided by the gangs of slaves, and in two or three days the townspeople were all in shelter, either in these sheds, in the vaults of the churches, or in other strongly constructed buildings.

Among the missiles hurled into the town were balls filled with Greek fire, but the houses being entirely built of stone, no conflagrations of importance were caused by them, as a band of knights was organised specially to watch for these bombs, and whenever one of them was seen to fall, they hurried from their lookout to the spot, with a gang of slaves carrying baskets of earth and buckets of water, and quenched the flames before they had made any great headway.

The roar of the bombardment was almost continuous, and was heard at islands distant from Rhodes, telling the inhabitants how the battle between the Christians and the Moslems was raging.

It was not long before the wall in the front of the Jews' quarter began to crumble, and it was soon evident that it must, ere many days, succumb to the storm of missiles hurled against it. D'Aubusson lost no time in making preparations to avert the danger. He ordered all the houses in rear of the wall to be levelled; a deep semicircular ditch was then dug, and behind this a new wall, constructed of the stones and bricks from the houses destroyed, was built, and backed with an earthen rampart of great thickness and solidity.

The work was carried on with extraordinary rapidity. The grand master himself set the example, and, throwing aside his robes and armour, laboured with pick and shovel like the commonest labourer. This excited the people to the highest pitch of enthusiasm, and all classes threw themselves into the task. Knights and slaves, men, women, and children, and even the inmates of the convents and nunneries, aided in the work, and when at last the outer wall fell, and the Turks thought that success was at hand, the pasha saw with astonishment and dismay that entry to the city was still barred by a work as formidable as that which he had destroyed at an enormous expenditure of ammunition. There was now a short breathing time for the besieged; but the depression which the failure of their efforts excited among the Turks, was shortly dispelled by the arrival of a ship, with a despatch from Constantinople, in which the pasha was informed that the sultan himself was about to proceed to Rhodes with a reinforcement of a hundred thousand men, and a fresh park of artillery.

Paleologus had some doubts as to whether the report was true or was merely intended to stimulate him to new efforts for the speedy capture of the place. Knowing well that the grand master was the heart and soul of the defence, and that the failure of the assault was mainly due to his energy and ability, he determined to resort to the weapon so frequently in use in Eastern warfare-that of assassination. To this end he employed two men, one a Dalmatian, the other an Albanian; these presented themselves before the walls as deserters, and as there was no reason for suspecting their tale, they were admitted within the gates, and welcomed as having escaped from enforced service. They soon spread the tale of the speedy coming of the sultan with vast reinforcements, and as the pasha had on the previous day caused salutes to be fired, and other demonstrations to be made, the news was readily credited, and caused the greatest dismay among the defenders.

Some of the knights of the Italian and Spanish langues believed the prospect of a successful defence against so enormous a force was absolutely hopeless, and determined to put pressure upon D'Aubusson to treat for surrender before it became too late. They opened negotiations with an Italian named Filelfo, one of D'Aubusson's secretaries, who undertook to lay their opinion before the grand master. D'Aubusson at once summoned the knights concerned in the matter before him. They found him with several members of the council.

"Sir Knights," he said, "I have heard from my secretary your opinions in the matter of a surrender, and since you are in such terror of the Moslem sultan, you have my full permission to leave the town; and, more than that, I will myself secure your safe departure, which might be imperilled if your comrades or even the inhabitants of the town came to learn that you had advocated surrender; but," he went on, changing his tone from that of sarcasm to sternness, "if you remain with us, see that the word surrender never again passes your lips, and be assured that, should you continue your intrigues, in that direction, you shall meet with the fate you so justly deserve."

Overwhelmed by the grand master's accusation and sternness, the Italian and Spanish knights threw themselves on their knees and implored him to grant them an early opportunity of retrieving their fault by battle with the infidel. Feeling that the lesson had been sufficiently severe, and that henceforth there would be no renewal of intrigues for a surrender, D'Aubusson forgave them, and promised them a place in the van when next the Moslems attacked. The incident was not without its advantage, for the two pretended deserters, believing that Filelfo, who had also fallen under the displeasure of the grand master, would be ready to join in the conspiracy against his life, approached him. Filelfo, who was greatly attached to D'Aubusson, saw by their manner that they wished to engage him in some intrigue, and, feigning great resentment and anger at his disgrace, led them on until they divulged the entire plot for D'Aubusson's assassination, and made brilliant offers to him if he would afford them facilities for carrying it out, producing, in proof of their power to do so, a letter of the pasha, authorising them to make such promises in his name.

Filelfo at once divulged the whole plot to D'Aubusson. The two men were immediately arrested, tried by the council, and sentenced to death. They were not, however, formally executed, for the populace, obtaining news of their treachery, broke in upon their guards, and tore them to pieces. Foiled in his attempt on the life of the grand master, the pasha prepared for a renewal of the attack, and it was not long before the knights on the lookout at the church of St. John perceived that the fort of St. Nicholas was again to be the scene of the attack. It was ere long discovered that a large number of men were busy some distance along the shore in building a long structure, that could only be intended for a floating bridge. Among the sailors who had aided in the attack with the fire ships were several men belonging to an English trader in the port. All who had done so had been handsomely rewarded for their conduct, and five of the Englishmen had afterwards gone to the English auberge and had asked to be enrolled for service against the Turks, as they were weary of remaining on board in idleness when there was work to be done. Their offer had been accepted, and they had, in common with all the sailors in the port, laboured at the construction of the inner wall. When that was completed, Sir John Boswell, under whose special charge they had been placed, said to Gervaise, "I think that I cannot do better than send these men down to St. Nicholas. It is probable that now the Turks see that they can do nothing at the new breach, they may try again there. Sailors are accustomed to night watches, and there are many of our knights who are not used to such work, and can be better trusted to defend a breach than to keep a vigilant watch at night. Will you take these men down to Caretto, and tell him that he can sleep soundly if he has a couple of them on watch? One of them, Roger Jervis, who is the mate of their ship, can speak some Italian, and as he is in command of them, Caretto will find no trouble in making them understand him."

St. Nicholas had now been put into a fair state of defence, as a party had been kept steadily at work there. Gervaise had not been to the tower since the morning after the assault, and saw with satisfaction how much had been done to render it secure. He found that Caretto was fast recovering from his wounds.

"As it seems probable, Sir Fabricius," he said, after the first greetings to the knight, "that the Turks will favour you with another visit, I have brought you five watchdogs. They are countrymen of mine, and were among those who navigated the fire ships the other day. Sir John Boswell has sent them down; they are, of course, accustomed to keep watch at night. One of them is mate of their vessel, and will be in command of them; he speaks a little Italian, and so will understand any orders you may give him. I have been speaking to him as we came down; he will divide his men into two watches, and will himself be on guard all night. Will you assign them some quiet place where they can sleep in the daytime? They can erect a shelter with a piece of sail cloth and a few bits of board, and they will, of course, be furnished with food."

"I shall be very glad to have them, for I am always restless at night, lest those on watch should close their eyes. You see, they have quite made up their minds that this fort will not be attacked again, and so are less inclined to be vigilant than they would be, did they think that an attack was impending."

Now that there was reason to believe that St. Nicholas might again be attacked, Gervaise was frequently there with orders or inquiries from the grand master. A number of vessels in the harbour were fitted up as fire ships, so as to be in readiness when the attack came. He was about to start early one morning when he saw Roger Jervis coming up with a heavy anchor on his shoulder.

"Why, what are you bringing that up here for?" he asked. "Have you been diving; for I see your clothes are dripping with water?"

"Ay, ay, sir, I have been in the water, and that Italian commander told me to come straight up here to tell the grand master all about the story; and right glad am I to have met you, for I should have made but a poor fist of it alone; I don't know more of their lingo than just to talk a few words of it."

"Then you had better tell me the story before I take you in."

"Well, it was like this, Sir Knight: I had Hudson and Jeffreys posted upon the wall, and I thought I would take a turn down on the rocks, for it was a dark night, and you can see much farther when you are by the edge of the water than you can when you are at the masthead. I sat there for an hour, and was thinking that it was about time to go up and turn out the other watch, when I saw something dark upon the water. It wasn't a ship, that was certain, and if it was a boat there wasn't any one in it; but it was too dark to make quite sure what it was. I watched it for a time, though I did not think much of the thing, taking it for a boat that had got adrift, or maybe a barrel from one of the Turkish ships. Presently I made out that it was a good bit nearer than when I first saw it.

"That puzzled me. There is no tide to speak of in these seas, and there was no wind moving about. I could make out now that it was a boat, though a very small one, but certainly there was no one rowing it. It looked a very strange craft, and as I saw by the way it was bearing that it would come ashore about five or six fathoms from where I was sitting, I slid quietly off the rock, put my sword down by me handy for action, and waited. Presently the boat came up alongside the rock, and a fellow stood up from behind the stern. I was glad to see him, for I had begun to think that there was witchcraft in the thing moving along by itself, but I can tell you I was savage with myself for not having guessed there was a man swimming behind and pushing it on.

"He stooped over the boat, and took something heavy out; then he felt about among the rocks under the water, and then laid the thing down there, and seemed to me to be settling it firm. I had half a mind to jump up and let fly at him, but then I thought it would be better to let him finish what he was doing, and go off with the idea that no one had seen him. So I kept hid until he started again. He waded a short way before he had to swim, and I could see that as he went he was paying out a rope over the stern. It was clear enough now what he had been up to: he had been fixing an anchor. What he did it for, or what use it could be to him, I could not say, but it was certain that he would not take all that trouble, with the chance of being knocked on the head, for nothing; so I waited for a bit till he had got out of sight, and over to the other side of the port.

"Then I got up and felt about, and, chancing to get my foot under the rope, went right over into the water. After that you may guess I was not long in finding the anchor. I unknotted the rope from it and carried it ashore; then it struck me that the Turks might take it into their heads to give a pull on it in the morning, and if they did; they would find out that their game, whatever it was, had been found out; so I got hold of a stone of about twenty pound weight, and fastened the rope's end round it. That was enough to prevent the rope getting slack and make them think that it was still fast to the anchor; but, of course, if they pulled hard on it it would come home directly. I went and reported the matter the first thing this morning to the governor. He seemed to think that it was important, and told me to bring the anchor up to the grand master, who would get one of the English knights to find out all about it; for he could not make out much of what I said."

"It is very important," Gervaise said, "and you behaved very wisely in the matter, and have rendered a great service by your discovery. I will take you in at once to the grand master."

Still bearing the anchor, the sailor followed Gervaise into an apartment where D'Aubusson was taking council with some of the senior knights.

"Pardon my interrupting your Highness," Gervaise said; "but the matter is so important that I knew you would listen to it, however occupied you were." And he then repeated the narrative of the sailor's discovery.

"This is indeed of the highest importance," D'Aubusson said, "and the knowledge that it gives us may enable us to defeat an attempt, that might otherwise have proved our ruin. You see, knights, it solves the question that we were just discussing. We agreed that this long floating bridge that they have been constructing, was intended to enable them to cross the outer port and again attack St. Nicholas; and yet it seemed to us that even by night our batteries would be able to keep up such a fire on the boats, towing the head of the bridge across, as to render it well nigh impossible for them to get it over. Now you see what their plan is. With the aid of this rope, the end of which they think is firmly fixed on our side, they mean to haul the bridge across, and that so silently that they hope to be upon us almost before we have time to don our armour. We shall now be fully prepared, and need have no fear of the result."

There could now be little doubt that the attack would be made without loss of time, especially as the Turks believed that they could get their bridge across unseen. The fire ships-which were altogether more formidable than those Gervaise had improvised-were ordered to be made ready for action. This being arranged, the admiral left the council at once, that no time should be lost in getting them in readiness. D'Aubusson then turned to the English sailor.

"You have rendered us a great service indeed by your vigilance, and showed great prudence by allowing the Turk to believe that he had accomplished his mission unsuspected. Had he thought he had been observed, some other plan would have been adopted. For so great a service it is meet that a great reward should be given."

He then took a bag from the hands of one of his secretaries, whom he had sent to fetch it, while they were discussing the matter of the fire ships.

"Here are two hundred golden crowns," he added, handing the bag to the seaman. "With these you can either settle on shore, or can build a stout ship and pursue your calling. Should you do so, call her the St. Nicholas, in remembrance of the gratitude of the Order of St. John for your having saved that fort from the Turks."

Astonished and delighted at the reward, which represented a very large sum in those days, the sailor stammered his thanks, and added, "I hope tonight that if I again have charge of a fire ship, I may be able to do more to prove to your Highness how grateful I am for the gift."

Throughout the day preparations for the defence of St. Nicholas went on unceasingly. Gangs of men, as usual, worked in the breach; but, as it was deemed advisable that there should be no outward show of activity that would lead the Turks to suspect that their design had been discovered, neither reinforcements of men nor munitions were sent along the mole; everything being taken out by boats, which, rowing closely along under the wall, were hidden from the view of the Turks. Barrels of Greek fire and pitch, cauldrons for heating the latter, a store of firewood, great balls of cotton steeped in oil and turpentine, sheaves of darts, spikes on short staves, that were, after darkness fell, to be thrust in among the fallen masonry to form a chevaux-de-frise —these, and all other matters that the ingenuity of the defenders could suggest, were landed at the water gate of the fort, while the garrison was strengthened by the addition of a large number of knights. Stores of ammunition were collected in readiness at all the batteries that commanded the mouth of the outer port, and by sunset D'Aubusson felt that everything that was possible had been done to meet the impending storm.

At midnight the Turkish preparations were complete. The attack by the bridge was to be assisted by a large number of boats and other craft, and many armed galleys were also brought up to destroy or tow away the defenders' fire ships. Paleologus himself was down by the shore directing the preparations. Some of his best troops were placed upon the floating bridge, and, when all was ready, the order was given to pull upon the rope. No sooner, however, did the strain come upon it than there was a jerk, the rope slackened, and it was at once evident that the anchor had been discovered and the well laid plan disconcerted. Paleologus was furious, but, believing that the attack he had arranged would still be irresistible, he ordered a number of boats to take the bridge in tow, while a still larger force was to make a direct attack upon the breach. The movement was to be conducted as silently as possible until it was discovered, and then a dash forward was to be made.

It was two o'clock before the fresh arrangements were completed and the boats put out. They had gone but a short distance when the anxious watchers in St. Nicholas learnt by the dull, confused sound that came across the water, that the attack was, in spite of the failure of the plan to take the bridge silently across, to be persevered in. A cannon was at once fired to give notice to the other batteries to be in readiness, and as soon as the dark mass of boats was made out the guns of the fort opened a destructive fire upon them, and a moment later were seconded by those from the fortress; these, however, were at present being fired almost at random, as the Turkish boats could not be made out at that distance. Now that all need for concealment was at an end, the Turkish war cry rose shrilly in the air, and the boatmen bent to their oars. The great cannon at St. Anthony's Church hurled their tremendous missiles at the tower, seconded by the fire of a number of other pieces that had in the darkness been brought down almost to the water's edge.

As before, the boats swept up to the foot of the breach, the Turks leaped out, and, undismayed by the storm of shot, climbed up to the assault. The short ladders that they had brought with them enabled them to surmount the escarpments so laboriously made, and with loud shouts of "Allah!" they flung themselves upon the defenders on the crest of the breach. Here they were met by a line even more difficult to break through than before. The knights were ranged three deep; those in the front were armed with swords and battleaxes, while those in the other two lines thrust their spears out between the swordsmen, covering them with a hedge of steel points. Others in the rear brought up buckets of blazing pitch and Greek fire, and, advancing through gaps left for the purpose, hurled the buckets down into the struggling mass on the slope. There the fire not only carried death among the assailants, but the lurid flames enabled the batteries to direct their shot with terrible effect upon the breach, the crowded boats at its foot, and the bridge which was, with immense labour, presently got into position.

It was not long before fresh light was thrown upon the scene, as the fire ships, issuing out from the inner harbour, burst into columns of flame, and, towed by boats, came into action. They were convoyed by the two galleys, each with a full complement of knights, and these soon became engaged in a fierce fight with the Turkish vessels that bore down to arrest the course of the fire ships. The scene was indeed a terrible one, the roar of cannon, the shouts of the combatants, the screams of the poor wretches upon whom the terrible Greek fire fell, the clash of arms and the shouts and cries of the Turks as they pressed across the bridge, united in a din that thrilled with horror the spectators, both in the city and on St. Stephen's Hill.

Several of the Turkish galleys, in their efforts to arrest the approach of the fire ships towards the bridge, became themselves involved in the flames; but they were so far successful that when daylight broke the bridge was still intact and the combat at the breach continued to rage with determination and fury on both sides. The Turks there were led by a brave young prince named Ibrahim, a near relative of the sultan, with whom he was a great favourite, and he was ever in the front line of the assailants, his splendid bravery animating the soldiers to continue their efforts. As the daylight broadened out, however, the light enabled the Christian gunners to aim with far greater accuracy than had before been possible, and, concentrating their fire upon the bridge, across which reinforcements continued to press to the support of the assailants, they succeeded in sinking so many of the boats that it was no longer passable.

Next they turned their fire upon the Turkish galleys, four of which they sank. Shortly afterwards, a ball struck the gallant young leader of the Turks, who, although previously several times wounded, had continued to fight in the front line. He fell dead, and his followers, disheartened by his fall and by the destruction of the bridge, at once abandoned their efforts, and rushed down to the foot of the breach. The terrible scene enacted at the repulse of the previous attack was now repeated. The concentrated fire of the guns of the defenders carried destruction into the crowded mass. Some gained the boats that still remained uninjured, and rowed for the opposite shore; the greater number rushed into the water and strove to recross it either by swimming or by the aid of the debris of the shattered boats. Their total loss was greater even than that suffered by them in the first attack, between two and three thousand being either killed or drowned, among them a number of their best officers. The amount of spoil, in the form of rich jewels and costly gold ornaments, found on the bodies of the dead piled on the breach, was very great.

For three days after this terrible repulse the Turks were inactive, the pasha remaining shut up in his tent, refusing to see any one, or to issue orders. At the end of that time he roused himself from his stupor of grief and disappointment, and, abandoning the idea of any further attack upon the point that had cost him so dearly, he ordered the troops to move round and renew the attack upon the wall in front of the Jews' quarter, and commence the construction of a battery on the edge of the great ditch facing the retrenchment behind the breach before effected. The knights of Italy and Spain determined to seize the opportunity of retrieving the disgrace that had fallen upon them. At night they descended into the deep cutting, carrying across their ladders, and, silently mounting the opposite side, rushed with loud shouts into the unfinished battery. The Turks there, taken utterly by surprise, made but a slight resistance; a few were immediately cut down, and the rest fled panic stricken.

The knights at once set the woodwork of the battery on fire, hurled the guns down into the ditch, and then returned triumphantly into the town, the dashing feat completely reinstating them in the good opinion of the grand master and their comrades.

The incident showed the pasha that he must neglect no precautions, and, accordingly, he commenced his works at a distance from the walls, and pushed his approaches regularly forward until he again established a battery on the site of that from which his troops had been so unceremoniously ejected. While forming the approaches, the workmen had been constantly harassed by the fire from the guns on the walls, suffering considerable loss of life; but their numerical superiority was so vast that the loss in no way affected the plans of the pasha.

As soon as the battery was completed, gangs of men, accustomed to mining operations, set to work in its rear to drive sloping passages downwards, opening into the face of the great cutting, and through these vast quantities of earth and stones were poured, so as to afford a passage across it, the depth being largely diminished by the great pile of rubbish that had already fallen from the breached wall. This novel mode of attack was altogether unexpected. The knights had regarded the fosse that had been cut at such an enormous expenditure of labour as forming an altogether impassable obstruction, and were dismayed at seeing the progress made in filling it up. D'Aubusson himself, full of resources as he was, saw that the defence was seriously threatened, unless some plan of meeting this unexpected danger could be devised.

He consulted Maitre Georges; but the latter could make no suggestion; his only advice being the erection of a battery at a spot where it was almost self evident that it could be of no utility whatever. Other circumstances combined to render the suspicions D'Aubusson had entertained of the good faith of the renegade almost a certainty. Georges was seized, tried, and put to torture, and under this owned that he had been sent into the town for the purpose of betraying it; and he was, the same day, hung in the great square. His guilt must always be considered as uncertain. There was no proof against him, save his own confession; and a confession extorted by torture is of no value whatever. There are certainly many good grounds for suspicion, but it is possible that Georges really repented his apostasy, and acted in good faith in deserting the standard of Paleologus. He was undoubtedly a man of altogether exceptional ability and acquirements, and even the knights who have written accounts of the siege do justice to the fascination of his manner and the charm of his conversation.

D'Aubusson now set to work in another direction to counteract the efforts of the Turks. He erected an immense wooden catapult, which threw huge pieces of rock into the midst of the Turkish works, crushing down the wooden screens erected to hide their approaches, breaking in the covered ways, and causing great loss of life among the besiegers. At the same time galleries were driven below the breach, opening into the ditch, where their exits were concealed by masses of rubbish. Through these strong working parties issued out at night, and carried away up the passages the rocks and other materials that the Turks had, during the day, brought, with immense labour, from a distance to the shoot. The materials so carried away were piled up behind the retrenchment, greatly adding to its thickness and strength.

For some days the Turks observed, to their astonishment, that the road they were constructing across the ditch was diminishing instead of increasing in bulk, and at length it became so evident that the garrison were in some way removing the materials, that the pasha determined to deliver the assault before the heap was so far diminished as to become impassable. His former defeats had, however, taught him that success could not be always calculated upon, however good its prospect might appear; and although he had no real hope that the defenders would yield, he sent a formal summons for them to do so. This was refused with disdain, and preparations were at once made for the assault.

The pasha promised to his soldiers the sack of the town and all the booty captured, and so assured were they of success that sacks were made to carry off the plunder. Stakes, on which the knights, when taken prisoners, were to be impaled, were prepared and sharpened, and each soldier carried a coil of rope with which to secure his captive.

Before ordering the assault, the way was prepared for it by a terrible fire from every siege gun of the Turks. This was kept up for twenty-four hours, and so tremendous was the effect that the knights were unable to remain on the ramparts. The Turkish troops moved into position for attack, their movements being covered by the roar of the guns, and soon after sunrise on the 22nd of July the signal was given, and at a number of different points the Turks rushed to the assault. All these attacks, save that on the breach, were merely feints, to distract the attention of the garrison, and to add to the confusion caused by this sudden and unexpected onslaught. The pasha's plans were well designed and carried out; the knights, unable to keep their places on the ramparts under the storm of missiles, had retired to shelter behind the walls. There was no thought of an instant assault, as they considered that this would not be delivered until the new wall behind the breach had been demolished.

Consequently, the rush of the Turks found the defenders altogether unprepared. Swarming across the mass of debris in the ditch, they ascended the breach without opposition, and their scaling ladders were placed against the new wall before the knights could hurry up to its defence. Even before the alarm was given in the town, the Turkish standard was waving on the parapet, and the Moslems were crowding on to the wall in vast numbers. The suddenness of the attack, the complete surprise, the sound of battle at various points around the walls, caused for a time confusion and dismay among the knights charged with the defence of the wall facing the breach. Roused by the uproar, the inhabitants of the town rushed up to their roofs to ascertain what was happening, and their cries of wild terror and alarm at seeing the Turkish banner on the walls added to the confusion. D'Aubusson sprang up from the couch, on which he had thrown himself in full armour, at the first sound of the alarm, and, sending off messages to all the auberges to summon every man to the defence, ran down into the town, followed by a small party of knights.

Rushing through the streets, now filled with half dressed people wild with terror, he reached the foot of the wall, whose summit was crowded with the enemy, and saw in an instant that all was lost unless they could be driven thence without delay. The effect of his presence was instantaneous. The knights, hitherto confused and dismayed, rallied at once, and prepared for the desperate undertaking. The bank on the inside was almost perpendicular, and those charged with its defence had used two or three ladders for ascending to the rampart. These were at once seized and planted against the wall.

The position of the contending parties was now reversed; the Christians were the assailants, the Turks the defenders. D'Aubusson himself was the first to ascend. Covering his head with his shield, he mounted the rampart; but ere he could gain a footing on the top he was severely wounded and hurled backwards. Again he made the attempt, but was again wounded and thrown down. Once more he mounted, and this time made good his footing. A moment later, Gervaise, who had accompanied him from the palace, stood beside him. Animated with the same spirit as his leader, he threw himself recklessly against the Turks, using a short, heavy mace, which in a melee was far more useful than the long sword. Scimitars clashed upon his helmet and armour; but at every blow he struck a Turk fell, and for each foot he gained a knight sprang on to the wall and joined him. Each moment their number increased, and the war cry of the Order rose louder and fiercer above the din. The very number of the Turks told against them. Crowded together as they were they could not use their weapons effectually, and, pressing fiercely upon them, the knights drove them back along the wall on either hand, hurling them down into the street or over the rampart. On so narrow a field of battle the advantage was all on the side of the knights, whose superior height and strength, and the protection afforded by their armour, rendered them almost invincible, nerved as they were with fury at the surprise that had overtaken them, and the knowledge that the fate of the city depended upon their efforts. After a quarter of an hour's desperate conflict the Turks were driven down the partial breach effected in the wall by the last bombardment, and the Christians were again the masters of their ramparts. Paleologus, however, hurried up reinforcements, headed by a band of janissaries, whose valour had decided many an obstinate conflict. Before ordering them to advance, he gave instructions to a company of men of approved valour to devote all their efforts to attacking D'Aubusson himself, whose mantle and rich armour rendered him a conspicuous object among the defenders of the breach. Advancing to the attack, the janissaries burst through the mass of Turks still continuing the conflict, and rushed up the breach. Then the chosen band, separating from the rest, flung themselves upon the grand master, the suddenness and fury of their attack isolating him and Gervaise from the knights around.

Surrounded as he was by foes, already suffering from two severe wounds and shaken by his falls from the ladder, the grand master yet made a valiant defence in front, while Gervaise, hurling his mace into the face of one of his assailants, and drawing his two handed sword, covered him from the attack from behind. D'Aubusson received two more severe wounds, but still fought on. Gervaise, while in the act of cutting down an assailant, heard a shout of triumph from behind, and, looking round, he saw the grand master sinking to the ground from another wound. With a cry of grief and fury Gervaise sprang to him, receiving as he did so several blows on his armour and shield intended for the fallen knight, and, standing across him, showered his blows with such strength and swiftness that the janissaries shrank back before the sweep of the flashing steel. More than one who tried to spring into close quarters fell cleft to the chin, and, ere his assailants could combine for a general rush, a body of knights, who had just beaten off their assailants, fell upon the ranks of the janissaries with a force and fury there was no withstanding, and the chosen troops of the sultan for the first time broke and fled.

Excited almost to madness by the sight of their beloved master stretched bleeding on the ground, the knights dashed down the breach in eager pursuit. This action was decisive of the fate of the struggle. The panic among the janissaries at once spread, and the main body of troops, who had hitherto valiantly striven to regain the advantage snatched from them, now lost heart and fled in confusion. But their escape was barred by the great body of reinforcements pressing forward across the heap of rubbish that formed the breach over the deep ditch. Maddened by fear, the fugitives strove to cut a way through their friends. The whole of the defenders of the breach now fell upon the rear of the struggling mass, hewing them down almost without resistance, while the cannon from the walls and towers kept up an unceasing fire until the last survivors of what had become a massacre, succeeded in gaining their works beyond the ditch, and fled to their camp. From every gateway and postern the knights now poured out, and, gathering together, advanced to the attack of St. Stephen's Hill. They met with but a faint resistance. The greater portion of the disorganised troops had made no pause at their camp, but had continued their headlong flight to the harbour, where their ships were moored, Paleologus himself, heartbroken and despairing at his failure, sharing their flight. The camp, with all its rich booty and the great banner of the pasha, fell into the hands of the victors, who, satisfied with their success, and exhausted by their efforts, made no attempt to follow the flying foe, or to hinder their embarkation; for even now the Turks, enormously outnumbering them as they did, might be driven by despair to a resistance so desperate as once again to turn the tide of victory.

Chapter XXIII
The Reward Of Valour

Gervaise knew nothing at the time of the final result of the battle, for as soon as the knights had burst through the circle of his opponents, he sank insensible on the body of the grand master. When he came to himself, he was lying on a bed in the hospital of the Order. As soon as he moved, Ralph Harcourt, who was, with other knights, occupied in tending the wounded, came to his bedside. "Thank God that you are conscious again, Gervaise! They told me that it was but faintness and loss of blood, and that none of your wounds were likely to prove mortal, and for the last twelve hours they have declared that you were asleep: but you looked so white that I could not but fear you would never wake again."

"How is the grand master?" Gervaise asked eagerly. Ralph shook his head.

"He is wounded sorely, Gervaise, and the leech declares that one at least of his wounds is mortal; still, I cannot bring myself to believe that so great a hero will be taken away in the moment of victory, after having done such marvels for the cause not only of the Order, but of all Christendom."

"Then you beat them back again from the breach?" Gervaise said.

"That was not all. They were in such confusion that we sallied out, captured their camp, with the pasha's banner and an enormous quantity of spoil, and pursued them to their harbour. Then we halted, fearing that they might in their desperation turn upon us, and, terribly weakened as we were by our losses, have again snatched the victory from our grasp. So we let them go on board their ships without interference, and this morning there is not a Turkish sail in sight. The inhabitants are well nigh mad with joy. But elated as we are at our success, our gladness is sorely damped by the state of the grand master, and the loss of so many of our comrades, though, indeed, our langue has suffered less than any of the others, for the brunt of the attacks on St. Nicholas and the breach did not fall upon us, still we lost heavily when at last we hurried up to win back the wall from them."

"Who have fallen?" Gervaise asked.

"Among the principal knights are Thomas Ben, Henry Haler, Thomas Ploniton, John Vaquelin, Adam Tedbond, Henry Batasbi, and Henry Anlui. Marmaduke Lumley is dangerously wounded. Of the younger knights, some fifteen have been killed, and among them your old enemy Rivers. He died a coward's death, the only one, thank God, of all our langue. When the fray was thickest Sir John Boswell marked him crouching behind the parapet. He seized him by the gorget, and hauled him out, but his knees shook so that he could scarcely walk, and would have slunk back when released. Sir John raised his mace to slay him as a disgrace to the Order and our langue, when a ball from one of the Turkish cannon cut him well nigh in half, so that he fell by the hands of the Turks, and not by the sword of one of the Order he had disgraced. Fortunately none, save half a dozen knights of our langue, saw the affair, and you may be sure we shall say nothing about it; and instead of Rivers' name going down to infamy, it will appear in the list of those who died in the defence of Rhodes."

"May God assoil his soul!" Gervaise said earnestly. "'Tis strange that one of gentle blood should have proved a coward. Had he remained at home, and turned courtier, instead of entering the Order, he might have died honoured, without any one ever coming to doubt his courage."

"He would have turned out bad whatever he was," Ralph said contemptuously; "for my part, I never saw a single good quality in him."

Long before Gervaise was out of hospital, the glad tidings that D'Aubusson would recover, in spite of the prognostications of the leech, spread joy through the city, and at about the same time that Gervaise left the hospital the grand master was able to sit up. Two or three days afterwards he sent for Gervaise.

"I owe my life to you, Sir Gervaise," he said, stretching out his thin, white hand to him as he entered. "You stood by me nobly till I fell, for, though unable to stand, I was not unconscious, and saw how you stood above me and kept the swarming Moslems at bay. No knight throughout

799

the siege has rendered such great service as you have done. Since I have been lying unable to move, I have thought of many things; among them, that I had forgotten to give you the letters and presents that came for you after you sailed away. They are in that cabinet; please bring them to me. There," he said, as Gervaise brought a bulky parcel which the grand master opened, "this letter is from the Holy Father himself. That, as you may see from the arms on the seal, is from Florence. The others are from Pisa, Leghorn, and Naples. Rarely, Sir Gervaise, has any potentate or knight earned the thanks of so many great cities. These caskets accompanied them. Sit down and read your letters. They must be copied in our records."

Gervaise first opened the one from the Pope. It was written by his own hand, and expressed his thanks as a temporal sovereign for the great benefit to the commerce of his subjects by the destruction of the corsair fleet, and as the head of the Christian Church for the blow struck at the Moslems. The other three letters were alike in character, expressing the gratitude of the cities for their deliverance from the danger, and of their admiration for the action by which a fleet was destroyed with a single galley. Along with the letter from Pisa was a casket containing a heavy gold chain set with gems. Florence sent a casket containing a document bestowing upon him the freedom of the city, and an order upon the treasury for five thousand ducats that had been voted to him by the grand council of the Republic; while Ferdinand, King of Naples, bestowed on him the grand cross of the Order of St. Michael.

"The armour I had hung up in the armoury, where it has been carefully kept clean. I guessed what it was by the weight of the case when it came, and thought it best to open it, as it might have got spoilt by rust. It is a timely gift, Sir Gervaise, for the siege has played havoc with the suit Genoa gave you; it is sorely battered, dinted, and broken, and, although you can doubtless get it repaired, if I were you I would keep it in its present state as a memorial-and there could be no prouder one-of the part you bore in the siege. I have seen Caretto this morning. He sails for Genoa tomorrow, where he will, I hope, soon recover his strength, for the wounds he received at St. Nicholas have healed but slowly. He said" —and a momentary smile crossed the grand master's face —"that he thought a change might benefit you also, for he was sure that the air here had scarce recovered from the taint of blood. Therefore, here is a paper granting you three months' leave. His commandery is a pleasant one, and well situated on the slopes of the hills; and the fresh air will, doubtless, speedily set you up. I should like nothing better than a stay there myself, but there is much to do to repair the damages caused by the siege, and to place the city in a state of defence should the Turks again lay siege to it; and methinks Mahomet will not sit down quietly under the heavy reverse his troops have met with."

"But I should be glad to stay here to assist in the work, your Highness."

"There are plenty of knights to see to that," D'Aubusson replied, "and it will be long before you are fit for such work. No, I give my orders for you to proceed with Caretto to Genoa-unless, indeed, you would prefer to go to some other locality to recruit your strength."

"I would much rather go with Sir Fabricius, your Highness, than to any place where I have no acquaintances. I have a great esteem and respect for him."

"He is worthy of it; there is no nobler knight in the Order, and, had I fallen, none who could more confidently have been selected to fill my place. He has an equally high opinion of you, and spoke long and earnestly concerning you."

A fortnight later the ship carrying the two knights arrived at Genoa.

"I will go ashore at once, Gervaise," Caretto said. "I know not whether my cousin is in the city or on her estate; if the former, I will stay with her for a day or two before going off to my commandery, and of course you will also be her guest. I hope she will be here, for methinks we shall both need to refit our wardrobes before we are fit to appear in society."

"Certainly I shall," Gervaise agreed; "for, indeed, I find that my gala costume suffered a good deal during my long absence; and, moreover, although I have not increased in height, I have broadened out a good deal since I was here two years ago."

"Yes; you were a youth then, Gervaise, and now you are a man, and one of no ordinary strength and size. The sun of Tripoli, and your labours during the siege, have added some years to your appearance. You are, I think, little over twenty, but you look two or three years older. The change is even greater in your manner than in your appearance; you were then new to command, doubtful as to your own powers, and diffident with those older than yourself. Now for two years you have thought and acted for yourself, and have shown yourself capable of making a mark even among men like the knights of St. John, both in valour and in fitness to command. You saved St. Nicholas, you saved the life of the grand master; and in the order of the day he issued on the morning we left, granting you three months' leave for the recovery of your wounds, he took the opportunity of recording, in the name of the council and himself, their admiration for the services rendered by you during the siege, and his own gratitude for saving his life when he lay helpless and surrounded by the Moslems—a testimony of which any knight of Christendom might well feel proud."

It was three hours before Caretto returned to the ship.

"My cousin is at home, and will be delighted to see you. I am sorry that I have kept you waiting so long, but at present Genoa, and, indeed, all Europe, is agog at the news of the defeat of the Turks, and Italy especially sees clearly enough that, had Rhodes fallen, she would have been the next object of attack by Mahomet; therefore the ladies would not hear of my leaving them until I had told them something at least of the events of the siege, and also how it came about that you were there to share in the defence. I see that you are ready to land; therefore, let us be going at once. Most of the people will be taking their siesta at present, and we shall get through the streets without being mobbed; for I can assure you that the mantle of the Order is just at present in such high favour that I had a hard task to wend my way through the streets to my cousin's house."

On arriving at the palace of the Countess of Forli, Gervaise was surprised at the change that had taken place in the Lady Claudia. From what Caretto had said, he was prepared to find that she had grown out of her girlhood, and had altered much. She had, however, changed even more than he had expected, and had become, he thought, the fairest woman that he had ever seen. The countess greeted him with great cordiality; but Claudia came forward with a timidity that contrasted strangely with the outspoken frankness he remembered in the girl. For a time they all chatted together of the events of the siege, and of his captivity.

"The news that you had been captured threw quite a gloom over us, Sir Gervaise," the countess said. "We at first consoled ourselves with the thought that you would speedily be ransomed; but when months passed by, and we heard that all the efforts of the grand master had failed to discover where you had been taken, I should have lost all hope had it not been that my cousin had returned after an even longer captivity among the Moors. I am glad to hear that you did not suffer so many hardships as he did."

"I am in no way to be pitied, Countess," Gervaise said lightly. "I had a kind master for some months, and was treated as a friend rather than as a slave; afterwards, I had the good fortune to be made the head of the labourers at the buildings in the sultan's palace, and although I certainly worked with them, the labour was not greater than one could perform without distress, and I had naught to complain of as to my condition."

After talking for upwards of an hour, the countess told Caretto that she had several matters on which she needed his counsel, and retired with him to the next room of the suite opening from the apartment in which they had been sitting. For a minute or two the others sat silent, and then Claudia said,

"You have changed much since I saw you last, Sir Gervaise. Then it seemed to me scarcely possible that you could have performed the feat of destroying the corsair fleet; now it is not so difficult to understand."

"I have widened out a bit, Lady Claudia. My moustache is really a moustache, and not a pretence at one; otherwise I don't feel that I have changed. The alteration in yourself is infinitely greater."

"I, too, have filled out," she said, with a smile. "I was a thin girl then-all corners and angles. No, I don' t want any compliments, of which, to tell you the truth, I am heartily sick. And so," she went on in a softer tone, "you have actually brought my gage home! Oh, Sir Gervaise," —and her eyes filled with tears —"my cousin has told me! How could you have been so foolish as to remain voluntarily in captivity, that you might recover the gage a child had given you?"

"Not a child, Lady Claudia. A girl not yet a woman, I admit; yet it was not given in the spirit of a young girl, but in that of an earnest woman. I had taken a vow never to part with it, as you had pledged yourself to bestow no similar favour upon any other knight. I was confident that you would keep your vow; and although in any case, as a true knight, I was bound to preserve your gift, still more so was I bound by the thought of the manner in which you had presented it to me."

"But I could not have blamed you —I should never have dreamt of blaming you," she said earnestly, "for losing it as you did."

"I felt sure, Lady Claudia, that had it been absolutely beyond my power to regain it you would not have blamed me; but it was not beyond my power, and that being so had I been obliged to wait for ten years, instead of two, I would not have come back to you without it. Moreover, you must remember that I prized it beyond all things. I had often scoffed at knights of an order like ours wearing ladies' favours. I had always thought it absurd that we, pledged as we are, should thus declare ourselves admirers of one woman more than another. But this seemed to me a gage of another kind; it was too sacred to be shown or spoken of, and I only mentioned it to Caretto as he cross questioned me as to why I refused the offer of ransom; and should not have done so then, had he not been present when it was bestowed. I regarded it not as a lightly given favour, the result of a passing fancy by one who gave favours freely, but as a pledge of friendship and as a guerdon for what I had done, and therefore, more to be honoured than the gifts of a Republic freed from a passing danger. Had you then been what you are now, I might have been foolish enough to think of it in another light, regardless of the fact that you are a rich heiress of one of the noblest families in Italy, and I a knight with no possessions save my sword."

"Say not so, Sir Gervaise," she said impetuously. "Are you not a knight on whom Genoa and Florence have bestowed their citizenship, whom the Holy Father himself has thanked, who has been honoured by Pisa, and whom Ferdinand of Naples has created a Knight of the Grand Cross of St. Michael, whom the grand master has singled out for praise among all the valiant knights of the Order of St. John, who, as my cousin tells me, saved him and the fort he commanded from capture, and who stood alone over the fallen grand master, surrounded by a crowd of foes. How can you speak of yourself as a simple knight?"

Then she stopped, and sat silent for a minute, while a flush of colour mounted to her cheeks.

"Give me my gage again, Sir Gervaise," she said gently. In silence Gervaise removed it from his neck, wondering greatly what could be her intention. She turned it over and over in her hand.

"Sir Knight," she said, "this was of no great value in my eyes when I bestowed it upon you; it was a gage, and not a gift. Now it is to me of value beyond the richest gem on earth; it is a proof of the faith and loyalty of the knight I most esteem and honour, and so in giving it to you again, I part with it with a pang, for I have far greater reason to prize it than you can have. I gave it you before as a girl, proud that a knight who had gained such honour and applause should wear her favour, and without the thought that the trinket was a heart. I give it to you now as a woman, far prouder than before that you should wear her gage, and not blind to the meaning of the emblem."

Gervaise took her hand as she fastened it round his neck, and kissed it; then, still holding it, he said, "Do you know what you are doing, Claudia? You are raising hopes that I have never been presumptuous enough to cherish."

"I cannot help that," she said softly. "There is assuredly no presumption in the hope."

He paused a moment.

"You would not esteem me," he said, holding both her hands now, "were I false to my vows. I will return to Rhodes tomorrow, and ask the grand master to forward to the Pope and endorse my petition, that I may be released from my vows to the Order. I cannot think that he or the Holy Father will refuse my request. Then, when I am free, I can tell you how I love and honour you, and how, as I have in the past devoted my life to the Order, so I will in the future devote it to your happiness."

The girl bowed her head.

"'Tis right it should be so," she said. "I have waited, feeling in my heart that the vow I had given would bind me for life, and I should be content to wait years longer if needs be. But I am bound by no vows, and can acknowledge that you have long been the lord of my life, and that so long as you wore the heart I had given you, so long would I listen to the wooing of no other."

"I fear that the Countess, your mother —" Gervaise began, but she interrupted him.

"You need not fear," she said. "My mother has long known, and knowing also that I am not given to change, has ceased to importune me to listen to other offers. Her sole objection was that you might never return from captivity. Now that you have come back with added honours, she will not only offer no objection, but will, I am sure, receive you gladly, especially as she knows that my cousin Sir Fabricius, for whom she has the greatest affection, holds you in such high esteem."

Six months later Gervaise again landed at Genoa, after having stayed at Rome for a few days on his way back. D'Aubusson had expressed no surprise at his return to Rhodes, or at the request he made.

"Caretto prepared me for this," he said, smiling, "when he asked me if you might accompany him to Genoa. The Order will be a loser, for you would assuredly have risen to the grand priorage of your langue some day. But we have no right to complain; you have done your duty and more, and I doubt not that should Mahomet again lay siege to Rhodes, we may count on your hastening here to aid us?"

"That assuredly you may, sir. Should danger threaten, my sword will be as much at the service of the Order as if I were still a member of it."

"I by no means disapprove," D'Aubusson went on, "of knights leaving us when they have performed their active service, for in civil life they sometimes have it in their power to render better service to the Order than if passing their lives in the quiet duties of a provincial commandery. It will be so in your case: the lady is a great heiress, and, as the possessor of wide lands, your influence in Northern Italy may be very valuable to us, and in case of need you will, like my brother De Monteuil, be able to bring a gathering of men-at-arms to our aid. Have no fear that the Pope will refuse to you a release from your vows. My recommendation alone would be sufficient; but as, moreover, he is himself under an obligation to you, he will do so without hesitation. Since you have been away, your friend Harcourt has been appointed a commander of a galley, and Sir John Boswell, being incapacitated by the grievous wounds he received during the siege, has accepted a rich commandery in England, and sailed but two days since to take up his charge. By the way, did you reply to those letters expressing your thanks and explaining your long silence?"

"Yes, your Highness, I wrote the same evening you gave them to me."

"That is right. The money voted you by Florence will be useful to you now, and there is still a sum sent by your commandery owing to you by the treasury. I will give you an order for it. However rich an heiress a knight may win, 'tis pleasant for him to have money of his own; not that you will need it greatly, for, among the presents you have received, the jewels are valuable enough for a wedding gift to a princess."

Gervaise was well received at Rome, and the Pope, after reading the grand master's letter, and learning from him his reason for wishing to leave the Order, without hesitation granted him absolution from his vows. A few months later there was a grand wedding at the cathedral of Genoa, the doge and all the nobles of the Republic being present.

Ralph Harcourt and nine other young knights had accompanied Gervaise from Rhodes by the permission, and indeed at the suggestion, of the grand master, who was anxious to show that Gervaise had his full approval and countenance in leaving the Order. Caretto, who had been appointed grand prior of Italy, had brought the knights from all the commanderies in the northern republics to do honour to the occasion, and the whole, in their rich armour and the mantles of the Order, made a distinguishing feature in the scene.

The defeat of the Turks created such enthusiasm throughout Europe that when the grand prior of England laid before the king letters he had received from the grand master and Sir John Kendall, speaking in the highest terms of the various great services Gervaise had rendered to the Order, Edward granted his request that the act of attainder against Sir Thomas Tresham and his descendants should be reversed and the estates restored to Gervaise. The latter made, with his wife, occasional journeys to England, staying a few months on his estates in Kent; and as soon as his second son became old enough, he sent him to England to be educated, and settled the estate upon him. He himself had but few pleasant memories of England; he had spent indeed but a very short time there before he entered the house of the Order in Clerkenwell, and that time had been marked by constant anxiety, and concluded with the loss of his father. The great estates that were now his in Italy demanded his full attention, and, as one of the most powerful nobles of Genoa, he had come to take a prominent part in the affairs of the Republic.

He was not called upon to fulfil his promise to aid in the defence of Rhodes, for the death of Mahomet just at the time when he was preparing a vast expedition against it, freed the Island for a long time from fear of an invasion. From time to time they received visits from Ralph Harcourt, who, after five years longer service at Rhodes, received a commandery in England. He held it a few years only, and then returned to the Island, where he obtained a high official appointment.

In 1489 Sir John Boswell became bailiff of the English langue, and Sir Fabricius Caretto was in 1513 elected grand master of the Order, and held the office eight years, dying in 1521.

When, in 1522, forty-two years after the first siege, Rhodes was again beleaguered, Gervaise, who had, on the death of the countess, become Count of Forli, raised a large body of men-at-arms, and sent them, under the command of his eldest son, to take part in the defence. His third son had, at the age of sixteen, entered the Order, and rose to high rank in it.

The defence, though even more obstinate and desperate than the first, was attended with less success, for after inflicting enormous losses upon the great army, commanded by the Sultan Solyman himself, the town was forced to yield; for although the Grand Master L'Isle Adam, and most of his knights, would have preferred to bury themselves beneath the ruins rather than yield, they were deterred from doing so, by the knowledge that it would have entailed the massacre of the whole of the inhabitants, who had throughout the siege fought valiantly in the defence of the town. Solyman had suffered such enormous losses that he was glad to grant favourable conditions, and the knights sailed away from the city they had held so long and with such honour, and afterwards established themselves in Malta, where they erected another stronghold, which in the end proved an even more valuable bulwark to Christendom than Rhodes had been. There were none who assisted more generously and largely, by gifts of money, in the establishment of the Order at Malta than Gervaise. His wife, while she lived, was as eager to aid in the cause as he was himself, holding that it was to the Order she owed her husband. And of all their wide possessions there were none so valued by them both, as the little coral heart set in pearls that she, as a girl, had given him, and he had so faithfully brought back to her.

Made in the USA
Las Vegas, NV
31 January 2021